# CATHERINE COOKSON

# CATHERINE COOKSON

The Mallen Streak

The Girl

The Gambling Man

The Cinder Path

The Invisible Cord

Heinemann/Octopus

*The Mallen Streak* first published in Great Britain in 1973
by William Heinemann Limited
*The Girl* first published in Great Britain in 1977
by William Heinemann Limited
*The Gambling Man* first published in Great Britain in 1975
by William Heinemann Limited
*The Cinder Path* first published in Great Britain in 1978
by William Heinemann Limited
*The Invisible Cord* first published in Great Britain in 1975
by William Heinemann Limited

This edition first published in Great Britain
in 1980 jointly by

William Heinemann Limited    Martin Secker & Warburg Limited
10 Upper Grosvenor Street      54 Poland Street
London W1        London W1

and
Octopus Books Limited
59 Grosvenor Street
London W1

ISBN 0 905712 43 9

Printed in the United States of America

# CATHERINE COOKSON

## CONTENTS

# CATHERINE COOKSON

## The
# Mallen
# Streak

# Chapter One

## Thomas Mallen

High Banks Hall showed its sparsely-windowed back to beautiful woodland and the town of Allendale in the far distance, whilst its buttressed and emblazoned and many-windowed face looked out over formal gardens on to mountainous land, so austere and wild that even its short summer beauty brought no paeans of praise except from those who had been bred within the rigours of its bosom.

Away to the south lay Nine Banks Peel; to the north was the lovely little West Allen village of Whitfield; but staring the Hall straight in the face were the hills, for most part bare and barren and rising to miniature mountains which, on this day, Tuesday, the twenty-fifth of February, 1851, were thickly crusted with snow, not white, but pale pink, being tinged for the time being by the straining rays of a weak sun.

The Hall was fronted by a terrace bordered by an open balustrade, its parapet festooned with stone balls, and each pillar at the top of the steps which led to the drive was surmounted by a moss-stained naked Cupid.

The doors to the house were double and of black oak studded with large iron nails which gave the impression that it had withstood the attack of a fusillade of bullets. Over the door was a coat of arms composed of three shields, above it a Latin inscription had been cut into the stone which roughly translated read: *Man is compassionate because he gave God a mother.*

At first the inscription appeared to have religious connotations, but when dissected it proved to many to be blasphemous.

Thomas Wigmore Mallen, who built the Hall in 1767, had himself composed the inscription and had explained to those interested the deep significance of the motto, which was that God, in the first place, had been created of man's need, and the need had been brought about by the frightening mystery of both birth and death; more so the latter. And knowing that no man came into the world except through woman, man felt compelled to be compassionate towards the omnipotent image he had created. Therefore, even in pagan times, even before Christ was heard of, man had given to his particular deity a mother; but with this difference: she was always untouched by man, a virgin who could nevertheless give birth.

Thomas Wigmore Mallen was an avowed atheist and the devil took his soul. Everyone knew this when he was found stone dead seated against a tree with not a mark on him, his horse cropping gently by his side.

It was said, among the hills, that the Mallen streak began with Thomas Wigmore Mallen, but then no one hereabouts had known his forbears for he had hailed from away in the Midlands. However, it wasn't long before he had spread his mark around the vicinity of his new house. No matter what colour the hair of a male Mallen the white streak started from the crown and thrust its wiry way down to the left temple.

Strangely, the streak never left its mark on the women of the family, and again not on all the males either. But it was noted that the Mallen men who bore the streak did not usually reach old age, nor did they die in their beds.

Yet the present owner of the Hall, Thomas Richard Mallen, nicknamed Turk by his friends, seemed to be an exception, for he was hale and hearty at fifty-five, and on this day his voice could be heard booming through the length of the house, calling on his guests to get ready and to have sport while it lasted, for in two days' time the hare-hunting season would end.

The guests had not come to the Hall merely to join the hare hunt, most of them had been there for the past three days. They had come originally for the wedding of Thomas's daughter, his only daughter by his second marriage.

More than half the county, they said, had been invited to the wedding, for it wasn't every day that a Northumberland miss married an Italian count, even if a poor one; and Thomas Mallen had gone out of his way to show the foreigner how things were done in England, especially in the north-east of England.

The festivities had gone on for two full days . . . and nights; only an hour ago four carriages had rumbled away, their occupants hardly able to stand on their feet. And this went for the women too. When Thomas Mallen entertained, he entertained. Mallen was a man, everybody said so. Could he not drink three men under the table? And had he not fathered more brats in the countryside than his bull had heifers? Some mothers, it was said, were for ever dyeing their youngsters' hair with tea, but some children, one here and one there, seemed to be proud of the white tuft, and the evidence of this had just now been brought to Thomas by his son, Dick.

Dick Mallen was twenty-three years old and in looks a younger replica of his father, but in character there were divergent traits, for there was no streak of kindness in Dick Mallen. Thomas could forgive and forget, life was too short to bear the inconvenience of malice. Not so Dick Mallen; Dick always repaid the slightest slur with interest, creating an opportunity to get rid of the debt, which might have been only a disdainful look, or a snub. Yet a snub to young Mallen was worse than a blow; it indicated condemnation not only of himself, but also of the house. Both Mallens were laws unto themselves; whosoever dare question that law – and there were many in the county who did, a few openly, but the majority slyly – would be brought to book by the sole male heir to High Banks Hall.

Thomas's two sons by his first marriage had died, the second of them only last year, since when Dick Mallen had gambled more, drunk more, and whored more, three very expensive pastimes, and over the last three days he had excelled himself at all three. Now prancing down the main staircase with very little sway to his gait, for he, too, could hold his drink, he paused and shouted into the throng below, which looked for all the world like a hunt meeting without the horses.

'D'you hear me, Father! He's arrived; your hill nipper's arrived. I glimpsed him from the gallery.' He thrust his arm backwards.

Most of the faces down below were turned upwards, and the ruddy countenance of Thomas Mallen was split wide in a grin, showing a mouthful of blunt teeth with only two gaps to the side, and he cried back at his son, 'Has he now? He's early; the passes are still snowed up. Well! well!' He now turned to the dozen or so men and women about him. 'Do you hear that? My hill nipper has arrived, earlier than ever this year. November when last he came, wasn't it?' He was looking across the hall now at his son who was threading his way towards him.

'Nearer December.' Dick Mallen pulled a face at a friend and dug him in the ribs with his elbow, and the friend, William Lennox, who could claim relationship with another of that name who was Lord of the Bedchamber to Prince Albert, pushed his young host in the shoulder, then flung his head back and laughed aloud.

In his twenty-eight years William Lennox had stayed in all types of country houses but he would swear that he had never stayed in one quite like this where everything was as good as a play. He turned now to a man at his side who was thrusting down a dog from his thigh, and said, 'What do you think of that, eh? He wasn't lying in his boast, his bastards do risk the mountains just to get a peep at him.'

Carl Breton-Weir merely answered with a tight smile, thinking cynically that this house appeared like a factory for the manufacture of bastards of all kinds. If it wasn't that tonight he meant to recuperate with good interest all the money he had purposely lost to his host and his friends, he would leave now. But tomorrow, if all went well, he would go, good and early. And he wouldn't be sorry to see the back of them all; coarse bores, every one of them. They afforded him amusement at first but one quickly tired of this kind of amusement . . . Where were they going now? And these damn dogs all over the place. 'Get down! Get down!' He flung the dog from him.

'She likes you; she likes you, Carl.' Dick Mallen was laughing at him now. 'You must have a smell about you she recognizes.'

At this there were great guffaws from the men and open titters from the four women present. Kate Armstrong, an overweight woman in her late forties, decked, even in her outdoor garb, with jewellery, one piece of which would have kept six of her husband's miners for a year, slapped out at her daughter Fanny, who at twenty-eight was still unmarried and could, they said, tell a joke as good as any man, saying, 'That Dick. That Dick . . . I tell you!'

There was Jane Ferrier, small, fat and as giggly as a girl, which mannerisms sat odd on her forty-three years. Her husband, John, owned a number of glass works in Newcastle, and to see the extent of their wealth you had to visit their home and be blinded by the chandeliers.

Then there was Maggie Headley. She had a name for being careful with the grocery bills, although her husband, Ralph, owned not only a brewery and a candle factory, but a coal mine also.

Among the men present was Headley's son, John, and his close friend, Pat Ferrier, both happy men at the moment, for they had made enough out of their friend and host and his London guests during the last two nights to keep them in pin money for some considerable time.

'Where was he, in the same place?' Thomas was again calling to his son, and Dick Mallen, who was making for the hall door, cried back to him, 'Aye, the same place. I wonder his legs don't give out by the time he reaches there.'

'Seven miles over and seven miles back he has to go; done it since he was that high.' Thomas measured a distance of four feet from the ground. 'An' I can't get near the beggar. And he won't speak, not a word. Skites off; that is after he's had a good look at me.' He gave an exaggerated heave to his chest and preened himself, and his voice now couldn't be heard for the laughter. 'Come on, come on, we'll change our route, we'll go round by the Low Fields.'

The whole party now swarmed out on to the terrace, where, below on the broad drive, three keepers were waiting. Led now by Thomas, they went through the gardens, skirted the lake, crossed in single file the narrow bridge over the stream that led to the River Allen, then bunched together again and, with the exception of the keepers, laughing and shouting to each other, they stumbled over the stretch of valley called the Low Fields, which edged the north boundary of the estate, and so came to a ridge of shale hills.

After rounding the foot of the hills they were brought to an abrupt stop by Thomas, who was standing, his arm outstretched, pointing.

Before them, about twenty yards distant, a zig-zag pathway cutting up the side of a steep hill met up with the lower mountain road which at this time of the year was the only passable road between Alston and Whitfield. At the foot of the mountain and to the right of this pathway was a high peak of rock, accessible to the ordinary climber from one side only, and on top of the rock sat a boy.

From this distance the boy looked to be about twelve years old. His thin body was dressed warmly, not in the rough working-man's style, nor yet was his dress like that of the gentry, but his greatcoat had a collar to it which was turned up about his ears. He wore no cap and his hair, from this distance, looked jet black.

The whole company looked up towards him and he down at them.

'Why don't you rush him?' It was a quiet voice from behind, and Thomas answered as quietly, 'We tried it. He's as fast as the hare itself; he could skid down from that rock quicker than I can say Jack Robinson.'

'Have you never got any nearer to him?'

'Never. But one of these days, one of these days.'

'Where does he come from?'

'Oh, over the mountain, near Carr Shield.'

'Well, you could go and see him when the weather's fine. Haven't you thought of it?'

Thomas Mallen turned round and gazed at the speaker; his blue eyes were bright and laughing as he said, 'Yes, yes, I've thought of it; but then –' he spread one hand wide '– if I were to visit all my streaks I'd have no time for my estate. Now would I?' Both hands were held out in appeal now and as the laughter rang over the mountain and echoed into the next valley the boy suddenly disappeared from view, and they didn't see him make for the pass although they stood for some time scanning the hills before them.

# Chapter Two

It had snowed for two days, thawed a little, then frozen, and the five guests left in the house had skated on the lake. They were Frank Armstrong, his wife Kate and daughter, Fanny, and Dick Mallen's two friends, William Lennox and Carl Breton-Weir.

Thomas Mallen had allowed his two nieces, Barbara and Constance Farrington, to join the company. It had been a great day for the children for they were seldom, if ever, allowed to mingle with the guests. When Thomas was at home alone, which wasn't very often, he had the children brought down in the afternoon to share his dinner, and he would laugh and joke with them and make funny remarks about their governess, Miss Brigmore. The two girls loved their Uncle Thomas; he was the only man in their lives and they had lived under his care for six years now, having been brought to the Hall when Barbara was four and Constance one year old. They were the children of his stepsister who had, against repeated warnings by him, married one Michael Farrington, a man with only one asset, charm. Michael Farrington had deserted his wife when she was carrying his second child but Thomas had known nothing of this until he had received a letter from her telling him that she was near death and begging him to take into his care her two small children. It says much for the man that he immediately made the journey to London and spent two days with her before she died. Then he brought the children from what, to him, were appalling lodgings, back to the Hall.

First, he engaged a nurse for them and then a governess. The nurse had long since gone, but the governess, Miss Brigmore, was still with them, and Barbara was now ten and Constance seven years old.

The children's world consisted of six rooms at the top of the east wing of the house, from which they descended by a back staircase once a day, if the weather was clement, to the world below, accompanied on such journeys by Mary Peel, the nursery attendant. If the coast was clear and Mrs Brydon the housekeeper, or Mr Tweedy the steward, or Mr Dunn the butler, weren't about, Mary would take them through the kitchen and let them stop and have a cheery word with the cook and kitchen staff and receive titbits in the form of rich sticky ginger-fingers, or a hot yeasty cake split and filled with jam and cream, two delicacies which were forbidden by Miss Brigmore, who was a believer in plain fare for children.

The children adored Mary Peel and in a way looked upon her as a mother figure. Of course, they both knew that Mary was very common and of no account; all the staff in the house were of no account, at least those below Brown, who was their Uncle Thomas's valet, and Taylor, who was Uncle Dick's valet. But they were aware that even these two personages did not come any way near Miss Brigmore's station. Their governess, they knew, was someone apart from the rest of the staff. Miss Brigmore had not stated this in words, but her manner left no one in doubt about it.

The girls had never experienced such pleasure as the afternoon spent on the ice. They squealed and laughed and caused great amusement as they fell on their bottoms and clung to the legs of first one escort and then the other. Barbara fell in love with Mr Weir and Constance with Mr Lennox, because both these gentlemen went out of their way to initiate them into the art of skating. Their Uncle Thomas, too, did his share in their coaching; only Uncle Dick did not take his turn with them for he skated constantly with Miss Fanny Armstrong.

On the side of the lake they ate hot chops which they held in a napkin, and their Uncle Thomas let them sip from his pewter tankard. The drink was hot and stinging and they coughed and their eyes watered and everybody laughed. It was a wonderful, glorious day.

They were still under the spell and talking about it at half-past six when Miss Brigmore retired to her room to have her supper. This was the only part of the day, with the exception of their exercise time, or when they were in bed, that they were free of Miss Brigmore's presence; but even now they weren't alone, for Mary Peel sat with them. But Mary didn't count. They could say what they liked in front of Mary; being with Mary was as good as being by themselves. Even when she joined in their conversation, as now, it didn't matter.

'No right to talk about Mr Armstrong in that manner, Miss Barbara,' she said, lifting her eyes from one of their night-dresses, the front of which she was herring-boning.

'Well I don't like him, Mary.'

'What's there to dislike about him? He's a fine man; he owns a mine, a big mine, away . . . away over the hills.'

'How far?'

'Oh, a long way, Miss Constance; a place I've never seen, near the city, they say; beyond the Penny Hills, and that's a mighty long distance.'

'Have you to be rich before you can be good, Mary?'

'Ah! Miss Barbara, fancy asking a question like that: have you to be rich afore you can be good?'

'Well, you said he was a good man.'

'Well, so he is, according to his lights.'

'What lights?'

'Oh, Miss Constance, don't keep asking me questions I can't answer. Sufficient it be he's a lifelong friend of the master's, an' that should be enough for anybody.'

'Is it true that Miss Fanny is going to marry Uncle Dick?'

Mary now turned her head sharply and looked at the thin, dark girl sitting to one side of the round table, her paint brush poised over a piece of canvas, and she asked sharply, 'How did you come to hear that, Miss Barbara?'

'Little pigs have got big ears.' This came from the fair child sitting opposite, and the two girls leant across the table towards each other and giggled.

'Little pigs have got big ears' was a saying constantly on Mary's lips, and now she reprimanded them sternly, saying, 'Aye; well, little pigs have their ears cut off sometimes when they hear too much.'

'But is she, Mary?'

'You know as much about it as me, Miss Barbara.'

'I don't, Mary. You know everything.'

Mary Peel tightened her lips to suppress a smile, then said in mock harshness, 'I know this much, as soon as Miss Brigmore enters that door I'll tell her to smack your backsides.'

Again they were leaning across the table. They knew that Mary didn't like Miss Brigmore and that whenever she could she opposed her; as for Mary giving them away in anything, they would have sooner believed that Miss Brigmore's God was a figment of the imagination, like the ogres in fairy tales.

'When are the Armstrongs going home?' Barbara now asked.

'The morrow, as far as I know.'

'Oh.' Both the children now sat straight up in their chairs, but it was Barbara who said, 'That means that tonight there'll be carry-on and high jinks and divils fagarties.'

Mary Peel rose hastily to her feet and, coming to the table, she looked fearfully from one to the other, saying under her breath, 'If Miss Brigmore hears you comin' out with anythin' like that, you know what'll happen, not only to you, but to me. An' I'm warnin' you, for she'll have me kept downstairs and then you could have anybody up here, Nancy Wright, or Kate Steel.'

'Oh no! no!' They both grabbed at her hands, crying softly, 'We were only teasing, Mary.' Barbara looked up into the round, homely face which to her was both old and young because twenty-seven was a very great age for anyone to be, and she said, 'We like your sayings, Mary, we think they're nice, much better then Miss Brigmore's.'

Mary nodded grimly from one to the other. 'Well, I can tell you this much, Miss Brigmore wouldn't agree with you. And how do you know anyway about the ... about the divils, I mean carry-on?'

'Oh –' they looked at each other and grinned impishly '– we sometimes get up and creep down to the gallery. We hid in the armour box last week. It's a good job it was empty.'

'Oh my God!' The words came as a faint whisper through Mary's fingers, which she was holding tightly over her mouth. Then giving her attention wholly to Barbara, she whispered, 'Look you, Miss Barbara, look, now promise you'll not do it again. Promise? ... In the armour box! How in the name of God did you get the lid up, child?'

'Well, it was very heavy but we managed to get in. But we couldn't get out.'

'You couldn't get out?' Mary had dropped her hand from her mouth and she gaped at them for a moment before she asked under her breath, 'Well, how did you then?'

'We knocked on the lid and called, and Waite opened it.'

'Waite?'

'Yes.' They were both nodding at her.

'What did he say?'

'He just said what you said.'

Mary screwed her brows up trying to recollect what she had said, and when she seemed to be finding some difficulty Constance put in with a smile, 'He said, "Oh my God!" '

Mary sat down suddenly on the third chair at the table and, picking up the corner of her long white apron, she passed it round her face before leaning towards them and again saying, 'Promise me on God's honour you'll not do anything like that again . . . Now come on, promise?'

It was Connie who nodded her promise straightaway, but Barbara remained quiet, and Mary said, 'Aw, Miss Barbara.'

'Well, I cannot promise you, Mary, 'cos I know I'll break my promise. You see, I like watching the ladies and gentlemen at their games.'

Again Mary put her hand across her mouth. Then the sound of a door closing brought her to her feet and all she could say to Barbara was, 'Oh miss! miss!' before the governess entered the room.

Miss Brigmore was of medium height. She would have been termed very pretty if she hadn't looked so prim. Her hair was brown, her eyes were brown, and her mouth was well shaped. She had a good skin and a well-developed figure, in fact her bust was over developed for her height.

Miss Brigmore was thirty years old. She had come from a good middle class family, and up till the age of sixteen had had her own governess. The fact that her governess's wages, together with those of the eight other staff her father kept in his house on the outskirts of York, and the establishment of his mistress in the heart of that city, were being supplemented by the clients of his bank, wasn't made public until Anna Brigmore was almost seventeen.

Her mother did not sustain the shock of her husband's imprisonment but Anna did. When she buried her mother she also buried her father. When she applied for her first post of governess she said she was an orphan; and she actually was an orphan when, at twenty-four, she entered the service of Mr Thomas Mallen of High Banks Hall in the County of Northumberland, there to take charge of his two nieces.

On her first encounter with Thomas Mallen she had not thought, what a gross pompous individual! for her heart had jerked in her breast. She was not aware that most women's hearts jerked in their breasts when Thomas Mallen looked at them. He had a particular way of looking at a woman; through long practice his look would convince them that they were beautiful, and interesting, and above all they were to be desired.

During her six years in the Hall Miss Brigmore had made no friends. She had been brought up to look upon servants as menials, and the fact that she was now earning her own living did not, in her mind, bring her down to their level.

Miss Brigmore now looked at the children's embroidery and her brief comment was, 'You have been idling; go and get ready for bed,' and turning towards Mary Peel she added, 'See to them.' Then she went through the day nursery and so into the schoolroom. Taking from the shelves three books, she sat down at the oblong table and began to prepare the lessons for the following day, but after a moment or two she pushed the books aside and rose to her feet, then went to the window where she stood looking out into the darkness. Yet through the darkness she pictured the lake as she had seen it earlier in the day. She could see them all in pairs, with hands crossed, weaving in and out; she could see the children tumbling about; she could hear the laughter in which she did not join.

She, like the children, preserved a vivid memory of the skating party because the master had looked at her from the ice. He had not only looked

at her, he had laughed at her. But he had never asked her to skate. No one had thought to ask her to skate. And she could skate; at one time she had been an excellent skater ... at one time she had been young. But now she was thirty. Yet the master had looked at her as if she were still young. ...
Slowly she left the window and returned to the table.

It was around eleven o'clock when the first squeals of delight floated faintly up from the far hall to the nursery and brought Barbara sitting upright in bed. Hugging her knees, she strained her ears to listen. What games were they playing to-night? Would Uncle Dick be chasing Miss Fanny along the gallery, and when he caught her would he pull her behind the curtains like she did with Connie when they were playing hide-and-seek with Mary? Or would one of the ladies slide down the banister again? She had actually seen one start at the top but she had been unable to see what happened when she reached the bottom; but she had heard the squeals of laughter. Then there was the time she had seen three gentlemen in their night-shirts carrying someone shoulder high down the main staircase. She hadn't been able to see if it was a lady or a gentleman they were carrying, only that the person's feet and legs were bare up to the knees.

If Mr Armstrong and his family were leaving tomorrow then Uncle Dick and his friends would leave shortly afterwards, and Uncle Thomas, too, would go about his business. From then onwards the house would become quiet again, except for the laughter of the servants, and there would only be Miss Brigmore, with Mary for light relief.

At this moment the future appeared very dull to Barbara. She looked through the dim glow of the nightlight towards the other bed and saw that Connie was fast asleep. Connie had promised Mary not to go down, but she hadn't promised, had she?

Quietly she pushed back the bedclothes and got out of bed; then getting into her slippers and dressing gown she tip-toed quietly to the bedroom door which opened into the day nursery. Having groped her way across the dark room, she now gently turned the handle of the door leading on to the landing.

The landing was lit by one candle standing in a three-branch candelabrum. She peered first one way and then the other and she was tip-toeing gently to the head of the stairs when she heard the little sound. She stopped, and looked back towards the end of the landing to the door opposite where their bedroom door would have been if it had opened onto the landing instead of into the day nursery. The sound could have been a laugh, or a moan, and it had come from Miss Brigmore's bedroom which was next to her sitting room.

There it was again, a soft moaning sound not unlike the sound she herself made when she had toothache and hid her head under the bedclothes. Was Miss Brigmore ill? She did not care for Miss Brigmore but she must remember that the governess was always kind to them when they felt ill, and now she might be in need of assistance; perhaps she required some mixture out of the white bottle in the medicine cupboard, the same as she gave to them when they had stomach trouble.

She turned and tip-toed down the length of the landing until she was opposite Miss Brigmore's door. The sound was louder now but still soft. She noted that Miss Brigmore's door was just the slightest bit ajar. Slowly her hand lifted and she pressed it open, but only wide enough to take the shape of her face and allow her to see into the room.

What she saw caused her to hold her breath for so long that she imagined she had stopped breathing altogether. Miss Brigmore was in her bed; the bed-clothes were rumpled down to her waist, and the top of her body was bare, and lying by her side leaning over her was her Uncle Thomas. He was supporting himself on his elbow and gazing down into Miss Brigmore's face while his hand caressed her breast. She noticed that Miss Brigmore had her eyes closed, but her mouth was open and from it were coming the soft moans that weren't really moans.

As she went to take in a deep gulp of air she became conscious of a movement behind her and she turned quickly to see Connie coming down the landing. With swift silent steps she reached her sister and, grabbing her hand, she dragged her back into the nursery, and there in the dark she turned and closed the door, but softly. Then pushing Connie before her, she went towards the dim light coming from the night nursery.

'What is it?' Connie turned to her. 'I woke up; you weren't in bed. What . . . what is wrong? Is Miss Brigmore sick?'

Barbara shook her head violently before she could say, 'No, no.'

'There was a noise.'

'She . . . she was snoring.'

'Oh.' Constance giggled now. 'Does Miss Brigmore snore? I didn't know. Perhaps Mary doesn't know either. You must tell Mary. Does she do it like the pigs on the farm, like this?'

The snort brought a hasty 'Ssh!' from Barbara, and she pushed Constance forward as she said, 'Get back into bed.'

'Aren't you going down the gallery?'

'No, no, I'm not. Get back into bed.'

'What's the matter, Barbie?'

'Nothing, nothing; just go to bed. Come on.' She pulled her onto the bed, then tucked the clothes round her.

'You're vexed, Barbie.'

'I'm not, I'm not. Go to sleep.'

'Good night, Barbie.'

'Good night.'

She herself now climbed into bed and lay rigid staring up at the rose-coloured patterns on the ceiling created by the red glass vase which held the night light. Her Uncle Thomas doing that to Miss Brigmore and Miss Brigmore not stopping him. It was wicked. Miss Brigmore herself would have said it was wicked. But she had lain quite still with her eyes closed. Suddenly her body bounced on the bed and she turned onto her face and buried it in the pillow. But having blotted out her uncle and Miss Brigmore from her mind, they were now replaced by the ladies' and gentlemen's games she had watched from the gallery and the balcony, and she knew there was a connection between them and the scene she had just witnessed. Her uncle was bad; Miss Brigmore was bad; all the ladies and gentlemen were bad; the only people who weren't bad were Mary Peel, Connie and herself. She wished the ice had cracked today and she had fallen through and been drowned.

# Chapter Three

'Look, boy, what the hell do you want, waking me at this ungodly hour?'
Thomas Mallen heaved himself round in the bed, then pulled his night-cap
from the back of his head down onto his brow as he screwed up his bleary
eyes at the clock. 'Ten minutes to seven. God sakes! What's up with you?'

'I've got to talk with you, Father.' Dick Mallen hoisted himself up on the
side of the four-poster bed and, leaning forward, he said in a tense undertone,
'I'm in a fix. I . . . I need two thousand straight away. It's imperative I have
two thousand straight away.'

'Ah!' Thomas fell back into the billowing soft pillows with a flop and,
raising his arms towards the ceiling, he waved his hands at it as he addressed
it, saying, 'It's imperative he has two thousand straight away.' Then twisting
on to his side he looked at his son with an alert gaze now and said soberly,
'What's come over you? What's happened?'

'I lost.'

'But you're always losing.'

'That isn't true.'

'Well, what I mean is, you've lost before and it wasn't . . . imperative you
had two thousand right away.' He glanced at the clock again. 'Ten to seven
in the morning and demanding two thousand! There's something more
besides this.' He pulled himself upwards, very wide awake now, and stared
at his son. 'Out with it.'

'I made a mistake.'

'You what?'

'I said I made a mistake.'

'You mean you cheated?'

'No, I tell you I . . .'

'You bloody well cheated! Playin' against fellows like Lennox and Weir,
you had the bloody nerve to cheat. You must be mad.'

'I . . . I didn't cheat; there was a slight mistake.'

'Look. Look.' Thomas shook his fist menacingly at him. 'I'm an old bull;
don't try to put the blinkers on me, boy. If you want two thousand
straightaway you cheated. Who's pressing you?'

'Weir.'

'It would be, that bastard! . . . Well, what's the alternative?'

Dick hung his head. 'He'll finish me in town . . . and everywhere else for
that matter.'

'Has he any proof?'

'Lennox'll stand by his word.'

'By God! boy, you do pick your friends. How much do you owe them
altogether?'

'Four, four thousand. But Lennox'll wait.'

'They'll both bloody well wait. Get by and let me up out of this; I'll deal with them.'

'No! No, you won't.' Dick had his hands on his father's shoulders now, pressing him back. 'See me through this and I'll promise it'll be the last. Honest to God, I promise.'

'I've heard that before. Take your hands off me.' There was a threat in the tone, and when his son quickly withdrew his hold Thomas slowly sat up and, thrusting his feet over the side of the high bed, he sat for a moment and held his face in his hand pressing one cheek in with his thumb and the other with his fingers before he said soberly, 'And now I'm going to tell you something. I've kept it from you for some time, didn't want to spoil your fun and wanted Bessie settled, but I, too, am in it up to the neck. At this present moment I couldn't raise four hundred let alone four thousand.'

The father and son stared at each other. It was Thomas who eventually broke the silence. Nodding slowly, he said, 'I've been banking on you fixing it up with Fanny. That settled, I gathered Frank would see me through, but not otherwise. I know she's a bit long in the tooth, but it won't be the first time a man's married a woman five years older than himself. I haven't pressed you, I thought I could see how things were going on their own. You asked her to stay on. . . .'

Dick's voice, almost like a groan, cut him off. 'Aye, I did, but for God's sake! not because I wanted to marry her, she's been laid more times than an old sow.'

Ignoring the scornful vehemence of his son's tone Thomas said quietly, 'That might be, but beggars can't be choosers. She's your only hope, and not only yours but mine an' all. I'm going to tell you something else, boy, and listen carefully, very carefully, for it means more to you in a way than it does to me, an' it's just this. If you don't marry her it'll be the end of the House.' He now lifted his hand and moved it slowly backwards and forwards in a wide sweep. 'Everything, every damned thing.'

There was a long pause. Then, his voice a mere whisper, Dick said, 'You can't mean it . . . everything?' His face was screwed up against the incredibility of the statement.

'That's what I said, everything. I've survived on borrowed money for the past ten years. It's only by keeping up appearances that I've swum this far. Let them think you've still got it and they'll give you credit. But now, boy' – he sighed deeply – 'I'm tired of swimming against the tide. Mind you, I never thought I'd confess to that, but there it is.' He now gently patted the great mound of his stomach. 'It's beginning to tell here an' all. I haven't the taste for life I used to have.'

'You don't do so badly.' There was deep bitterness in the remark, and Thomas replied slowly, 'No, I don't do so badly, true, an' I'm not grumbling. I've had a great deal of experience of all kinds of things. But you know, I've learned very little, except one thing, boy, one thing, and that is, everything has to be paid for; sooner or later everything has to be paid for. . . .'

'Oh, for God's sake, shut up! Shut up!' Dick had sprung from the bed now and was holding his hand to his brow. 'Don't you start preaching, you above all people, and at this time. Philosophy coming from you is a joke. It isn't philosophy I want. Don't you understand what they can do to me, those two? I won't dare show my face in any club, can't you see that?'

His arms were now hugging himself. His fists dug into his armpits, like a youth with frozen mitts trying to regain warmth, his body swayed backwards and forwards, and the action so lacking in dignity made Thomas turn his head away from the sight. After a moment he said quietly, 'If I ask Frank for it, will you promise to put the question to Fanny before they leave?'

When there was no answer he rose to his feet, saying, 'Well it's up to you. That's the only way. If I lose everything I'm still not losing as much as you, so think on it.'

When he next looked at his son, Dick was standing with his head drooped on his chest, his hands hanging limp at his sides, and Thomas said, softly, 'They'll be leaving about twelve. When you see me going into the library with Frank you corner Fanny, that's if you haven't done it before. If Weir's as mean as he sounds your best policy is to get it settled as soon as possible. I don't expect there'll be any hesitation on her part, she's past the choosing stage.'

Thomas now watched his son flounce about as a woman might have done and stalk down the length of the long room and out into the corridor. Then he bent his head and his eyes came to rest on his bare stomach visible through his open nightshirt, and as if the sight sickened him he turned his head and spat into the spittoon at the side of the bed.

Thomas did not take Frank Armstrong into the study, nor did Dick at the first opportunity ask Fanny to be his wife. These arrangements were cancelled by the arrival on the drive at ten o'clock that morning of a shabby cab, from which three men slowly descended. Having mounted the steps one after the other, the first of them pulled the handle that was hanging below the boar's head to the side of the great door. When the bell clanged within, the man turned and looked at his two companions, and they all waited.

The door was opened by Ord, the first footman. His gaze flicked haughtily over what he immediately stamped as the lower type of business men, and his voice portraying his feelings he said briefly, 'There is a back door.'

The first man, stepping abruptly forward, almost pushed the footman on to his back with a swift jab of his forearm, and when the three of them had entered the hall they stopped in some slight amazement, looking around them for a moment, before the first man, addressing Ord again, said, 'I wish to see your master.'

'My master is engaged. What is your business?'

'I'll tell that to your master. Now go and tell him that a representative of the Dulwich Bank would like a word with him.'

The Dulwich Bank. The very name seemed to convey trouble, and Ord, his manner no less haughty now but his feelings definitely uncertain, made his stately way towards the morning room where his master was breakfasting. There he motioned to Waite, the second footman who was assisting in carrying the heavy silver dishes from the kitchen, to pause a minute and he whispered in his ear, 'Tell Mr Dunn I want him, it's very important. There's fellas here from the Bank.'

A moment later Dunn appeared outside the morning-room door and he glanced across the hall towards the dark trio; then looking at Ord he said, 'What do they want?'

'The master; they're from the Bank.'

The butler looked at the men again, paused a moment, then turned and with unruffled step went back into the morning room.

It was a full five minutes later when Thomas put in an appearance. His head still maintained its jaunty angle, his shoulders were still back, his stomach still protruding, his step still firm, the only difference about him at this moment was that his colour was not as ruddy as usual, but that could have been put down to a series of late nights.

'Well, gentlemen!' He looked from one to the other of the men.

It was the tallest of them who again spoke. 'Mr Thomas Richard Mallen?'

'At your service.'

'I would like a word with you, in private if I may.'

'Certainly, certainly.'

The politeness seemed to disconcert the three men and they glanced at each other as they followed the portly figure across the magnificently carpeted and furnished hall. Their eyes, like those of weasels, darted around the room into which they followed the master of the house; moving from the row of chandeliers down to the furniture and furnishings.

In the middle of the room Thomas turned and, facing the men now, said, 'Well now, gentlemen, your business?'

His casual manner caused a moment's pause; then the tall man said, with some deference in his tone now, 'I represent the Dulwich Bank, sir. I understand that a representative from there called on you some three months gone when your situation was made clear, since when they have had no further word from you.'

'Oh, that isn't right. I said I would see into the matter.'

'But you haven't done so, sir.'

'Not yet . . . no.'

'Then I'm afraid, sir, it is my duty to hand you this.' Whereupon the man drew a long envelope from the inside pocket of his coat and held it out towards Thomas.

For a matter of seconds Thomas's arm remained by his side; then slowly he lifted it and took the envelope, and he stared down at it before opening it. Then still slowly, he withdrew and unfolded the double official paper. After his eyes had scanned the top of the first page he folded it again and replaced it in the envelope, and walking to the mantelpiece he placed the envelope on the marble shelf before turning to the men again saying, 'Well what now?'

'We take possession, sir.'

'Possession?' There was a crack in the coolness of Thomas's manner.

'That is the procedure, sir. Nothing must be moved, nothing. And it . . . it tells you there –' the man motioned to the envelope on the mantelpiece '– when you'll have to appear afore the Justices. Being a private debtor, of course, you'll not be put to the indignity of going inside, sir, as long as you're covered.'

'Oh, thank you.'

The sarcasm was not lost on the man and his chin nobbled before he said, 'I'm just explainin', sir. Anyway if you'd taken action two years gone when you had the chance. . . .'

'That's enough, my man!' Thomas's whole manner had changed completely. 'Do your business but oblige me by not offering me your advice.'

The man's jaw moved from side to side now and his eyes narrowed and it was some seconds before he spoke again, saying, 'This is Mr Connor, and Mr Byers, they will make an inventory. It will take some days. We will board here, you understand . . . sir?'

Apparently Thomas hadn't understood the full significance of the presence of the three men until now, and he exclaimed stiffly, 'Board here!'

'Yes, sir, board here, until the debts are paid or the equivalent is made in the sale. I thought you'd be aware of the procedure, sir.'

There was a definite note of insolence in the man's voice now, and under other circumstances, and if he'd had a whip in his hand, Thomas would have brought it across the fellow's face. But he was wise enough to realize that for the next few hours he would need this man's co-operation, for he was now in a hell of a fix. It would happen that Kate Armstrong would get a belly pain in the night and was now unfit to travel until the afternoon or perhaps tomorrow.

He looked at the man again and forced a conciliatory note into his voice as he said, 'Yes, I understand. And you will be boarded and well, for as long as there is food . . . and –' he gave a weak laugh '– I should say the stocks are pretty ample. But one thing I would ask of you and that is to delay the taking of your inventory until later in the day when, I hope I'm right in saying, there will be no need for it.'

He turned now to the mantelpiece and took down the envelope again and, opening it, he read for some minutes before he said, 'I understand a sum of thirty thousand would assuage the Bank for the moment. Well, it is more than possible I shall be able to give you a note to this effect before this afternoon. . . . Will you comply, gentlemen?'

The three men looked at one another. It wasn't every day that their business settled them in a house like this where they might remain for two to three weeks. It was just as well to keep on the right side of those who were providing the victuals, and – who knew? – there might be some extra pickings. The place was breaking down with finery: the china and trinkets in those cabinets lining the far wall looked as if they might be worth a mint in themselves. And then there were the pictures in this one room alone. Yet, would all the stuff in the house and the estate itself clear him? They said he was up to the neck and over. He had mortgaged, and re-mortgaged for years past now, and that wasn't counting the money owing the trades folk. Why, they said, only three years ago he had carpeted and curtained the place out afresh. Ten thousand it had cost him. Well, it should have cost him that if he had paid for it. Three thousand the firm had got and that, they understood, was all. The only tradesman who hadn't put in a claim apparently was the coal supplier, but then he got his coal straight from Armstrong's pit. Would it be from Armstrong he was hoping to get the loan? It would have to be some butty who would stump up thirty thousand by this afternoon.

The tall man nodded now before he said, 'Very well, sir. But there's one thing: you'd better tell them, the servants, who we are; we want to be treated with respect, not like dirt, 'cos we have a job to do. An' tell them an' all not to try to lift anything; it's a punishable offence to lift anything, prison it is for lifting anything.'

Thomas's face had regained its colour for temper was now boiling in him, so much so that he was unable to speak. He made a motion with his head; then turning to the bell rope at the side of the fireplace he pulled it twice.

When Ord entered the room Thomas looked at him and swallowed deeply before saying, 'Take these men to the kitchen, see that they are fed. They . . . they are to be treated with courtesy. They will remain there, in those quarters, until this afternoon.'

'Yes, sir.'

Ord looked at the men and the men looked at him, then they all went out.

After staring at the closed door for some seconds, Thomas gazed slowly round the room as if he had found himself in a strange place. What was really happening was that now, on the point of losing his home, he was recognizing its full splendour for the first time. His eyes finally came to rest on the portrait over the mantelpiece. It was not a portrait of his father but of his grandfather, the man who had built this house. It had been painted while he was in the prime of his life; his hair was still black and the streak flowed like molten silver from the crown of his head down to his left temple. The face below it was a good face, and yet they said it was with him the ill luck had started; yet it was with him also that the Mallen fortunes had flourished, because although they could trace their family back to the sixteenth century it was only in the Industrial Revolution that the Mallens had come up from among the ordinary merchants.

Through wool, and various other activities, Wigmore Mallen had amassed a fortune. He'd had four sons and each one he provided with an education that could only be purchased with money. One of them gave him cause for great pride for he was sent to Oxford and became a scholar. But not one of his sons died in his bed, all had violent deaths.

Thomas's own father had been shot while deer-stalking in Scotland. It was an accident they said. No one could tell how the accident had really happened. The shot could have come from any one of the dozen guests out that day, or any one of the keepers. Thomas had often wondered how he himself would die. At times he had been a little afraid but now, having passed the fifty mark and having lived vitally every day of his life since he was sixteen, the final incident that would end his existence no longer troubled him. But what was troubling him at this moment, and greatly, was that the end, when it came, might be so undignified as to take place in drastically reduced circumstances and without causing much concern among those who mattered. Such was his make-up that this thought was foremost in his mind, for being a Mallen he must not only be a man of consequence, but be seen to be such. Even the fact that he had confessed to his son that he was weary of the struggle did not alter the fact that he had no desire to end the struggle in penury.

He laid his head on his arm on the mantelshelf and ground out through clenched teeth, 'Damn and blast everything to hell's flames!' He lifted his head and his eyes focussed on the massive gilt frame of the picture. What would become of them if Frank didn't give a hand? Frank Armstrong he knew to be a close man, a canny man. He had clawed himself up from nothing, and had thrust aside his class on the way. He had kicked many a good man down, pressed faces in the mud, and stood on shoulders here and there, all to get where he was today. Frank, he knew, had a heart as soft as the stones he charged his miners for, should they send any up from the depths in their skips of coal. Oh, he had no illusions about his friend. But there was one crack in Frank's stony heart, and it wasn't made by his wife, but by his daughter. Frank would do anything to get Fanny settled, happily settled. Fanny had flown high and fallen a number of times. Now she had pinned her sights on Dick and her father would be willing to pay a good price to secure for her, if not happiness, then respectability. But would he go as far as thirty thousand now and the same again when the knot was tied? He doubted it. And yet he just might, for he had an eye on this house and would be tempted to go to the limit in order to see his daughter mistress of it.

He straightened up, adjusted his cravat, sniffed loudly, ran his hand over his thick grey hair, then went out of the drawing room in search of Frank Armstrong.


## Chapter Four


By dinner-time everyone in the house, with the exception of the guests, knew that the bums were in. Even the children in the nursery knew the bums were in. They had heard Mary talking to Miss Brigmore in a way they had never heard Mary talk before, nor had they witnessed such reaction from Miss Brigmore, because Miss Brigmore could only repeat, 'Oh no! Oh no!' to everything that Mary said.

Earlier, Barbara had been unable to look at Miss Brigmore, at least not at her face, for her eyes were drawn to her bust, now tightly covered. There were ten buttons on her bodice, all close together like iron locks defending her bosom against attack, but Barbara could see past the locks and through the taffeta bodice to the bare flesh as she had seen it last night.

Miss Brigmore had asked her if she wasn't well and she had just shaken her head; Connie had asked if she wasn't well, and Mary had asked her if she wasn't well. Then of a sudden they had forgotten about her for Mary came rushing up the stairs and did the most unheard-of thing, she took Miss Brigmore by the hand and almost pulled her out of the schoolroom and into the day nursery.

She and Connie had tip-toed to the door and listened. 'It's the bums, miss,' Mary had said, and Miss Brigmore had repeated, 'The bums?'

'Yes, duns. You know, miss, duns, bailiffs. They're in the kitchen, they're stayin' put until s'afternoon; then they'll start tabbing everything in the house. It's the end, it's the end, miss. What's goin' to happen? What about the bairns?'

'Be quiet! Be quiet, Mary.' Miss Brigmore often told Mary to be quiet, but she very rarely used her name; and now when she did it wasn't like a reprimand, because she added, 'Go more slowly; tell me what's happened. Has . . . has the master seen them?'

'Oh yes, miss, yes, miss. An' they're all nearly frantic in the kitchen. It means the end. They'll all get the push, miss. But what about the bairns? An' where'll we all go? They say he owes a fortune, the master, thousands, tens of thousands. All the stuff in the house and the farms won't pay for it, that's what they say. Eeh! and the money that's been spent, like water it's been spent. . . .'

'Be quiet, Mary!'

In the silence that followed the children stood looking at each other, their eyes stretched, their mouths wide, until Mary's voice came to them again, saying, 'Will they be able to take the bairns' cottage, miss?'

'The cottage? Oh no, no. Well, I don't think they can touch that. It was left to the children, together with the legacy. They can't touch that. No, they can't touch that.'

There was another silence before Miss Brigmore asked, 'The master, how does he appear?'

'Putting a face on it they say, miss.'

There was a movement in the next room and Barbara and Constance scrambled to the window seat and sat down. But when no one came in Constance whispered, 'What does it mean, Barbie?'

'I . . . I don't rightly know except we may have to leave here.'

'Will we go and live in our cottage?'

'I . . . I don't know.'

'I'd like to live in our cottage, it's nice.'

Barbara looked out of the window. The view from this side of the house took in the kitchen gardens and the orchards and the big farm. The cottage lay beyond the big farm on the other side of the road, nearly a mile along it, and situated, almost like the Hall, with its front to the moors and hills and its back to a beautiful dale. It had eight rooms, a loft and a little courtyard, which was bordered by a barn, two loose boxes and a number of outhouses, and the whole stood in one acre of land.

The cottage had been the home of Gladys Armorer who had been a second cousin to the children's mother. She had objected strongly to Thomas Mallen being given charge of the children for, as she said, she wouldn't trust him to rear a pig correctly; and she would have fought him for their guardianship had it not been she was crippled with arthritis. Yet up to a year ago when she died she had shown little interest in the children themselves, never remembering their birthdays, and only twice inviting them to take tea with her.

So it came as something of a surprise when she left to them her house and her small fortune, in trust, a hundred pounds a year to be allotted to each during their lifetime, with further stipulations which took into account their marriages, also their deaths.

The house stood today as when Gladys Armorer had left it, plainly but comfortably furnished. Two servants from the Hall were sent down now and again to air and clean it, and a gardener to see to the ground.

Gladys Armorer had not made Thomas Mallen a trustee, for despite his evident wealth she still had no faith in him, but had left the business in the hands of a Newcastle solicitor, which, as things had turned out, was just as well.

'Barbie!' Constance was shaking Barbara's arm now. 'But wouldn't you really like to live in the cottage? I'd love to live there, just you and Mary and Uncle and cook, and . . . and Waite, I like Waite.'

'It's a very small cottage. There are only eight rooms, it would only house three people at the most, well perhaps four.'

'Yes.' Constance nodded her head sagely as if to say, 'You're quite right.'

It was at this point that Miss Brigmore and Mary came into the room. They came in like friends might, and Mary, after looking at the children, lowered her head and bit on her lip and began to cry, then turned hastily about and ran from the room.

Miss Brigmore now went to the table and began moving the books about as if she were dealing out cards. 'Come along children, come along,' she said gently. And they came to the table, and Barbara looked fully at Miss Brigmore for the first time that day and was most surprised to see that she actually had tears in her eyes.

The gallery of the Hall had always caused controversial comment, some saying it was in Italian style, some saying it was after the French. The knowledgeable ones stated it was a hideous mixture of neither. But Thomas always had the last word on the period the gallery represented, saying it was pure pretentious Mallen, for he knew that, even among his best friends, not only the gallery, but the whole Hall was considered too pretentious by far.

The gallery was the place Dick Mallen chose in which to propose marriage to Fanny Armstrong. However distasteful the union with her might appear to him, and the thought of it brought his stomach muscles tensing, he knew that life was a game that had to be played, and with a certain amount of panache, and he needed all the help he could get at the moment, so he picked on the romantic atmosphere prevalent in the gallery.

He opened the arched doorway into the long green and gold room and, bowing slightly, waited for her to pass; then together they walked slowly down the broad strip of red carpet that was laid on the mosaic floor.

There were six windows along each side of the gallery and each had at its base a deep cushioned window seat wide enough to seat two comfortably. The walls between the windows were papered or rather clothed with an embossed green velvet covering, and each afforded room for two large gilt-framed pictures placed one above the other. In the centre of the gallery ceiling was a great star, and from it gold rays extended in all directions.

It was in the middle of the gallery that Fanny Armstrong stopped, and after looking to where two servants were entering by the far door, she turned her small green eyes to the side where another was in the act of opening or closing a window and she said, 'Is anything amiss?'

'Amiss? What do you mean?'

'I seem to detect an uneasiness in the house . . . in the servants. When I came out of my room a short while ago two maids had their heads together and they scurried away on sight of me as if in alarm.'

He swallowed deeply before he said, 'You're imagining things.'

'I may be' – she was walking on again – 'but I also have a keen perception for the unusual, for the out of pattern, and when servants step out of pattern . . . well! Servants are barometers you know!' She smiled coyly at him now, but he didn't look at her, he was looking ahead as he said, 'Fanny, I would like to ask you something.'

'You would? Well, I'm listening.' Again the coy glance.

He still kept his eyes from her face as he went on, 'What I have to ask you needs a time and a place. This is the place I had chosen, but the time, because of the' – he paused now and smiled weakly at her as he repeated her words – 'scurry of the servants is inappropriate. Do you think you could brave the weather with me?'

Her coyness was replaced now by an amused, cynical look which made him uneasy. He knew well enough that once married to her life would become a battle of wills; for underneath her skittish exterior was a woman who would have her own way, and if thwarted all hell would be let loose.

'Why so ceremonious all of a sudden?' She was looking him full in the face. 'If I could follow the dogs and your father through slush and mud for hours then I can risk the slightly inclement weather of today, don't you think?' She made a slight moue with her lips.

'Good! We'll go to the summer-house then.' With well-simulated eagerness he caught hold of her hand and drew it through his arm. 'We'll go down the back way; I'll get you a cloak from the gun room.' There was a conspiratorial note in his voice now.

Like two children in step they ran through the door that a servant held open for them; then across a landing towards a green-baized door, and so into a passage where to the right the stairs led up to the nursery and to the left down to the gun room.

The gun room was at the end of a long wide passage, from which doors led to the housekeeper's sitting room and the upper staff dining room, the servants' hall, the butler's pantry; also the door to the cellars, and, at the extreme end, the door to the kitchen.

At the foot of the stairs a maid was kneeling on the flagstone passage with a wooden bucket by her side, and the expanse of stone from wall to wall in front of her was covered in soapy suds.

It was as Dick held out his hand to Fanny, with exaggerated courtesy, in order to assist her to jump prettily over the wet flags while she, with skirts slightly raised, was coyly desisting, that the voice from the butler's pantry came clearly into the corridor, saying, 'I'm sorry for the master, but not for that young skit. Now he'll likely have to do some graft and know what it is to earn his livin', but he won't have the guts for that. By! it's made me stomach sick these last few days to see the carry-on here, the Delavals of Seaton Sluice were nothin' to it. It was them he was trying to ape with his practical jokes, and show off afore his London friends. The Delavals might have been mad with their pranks but at bottom they were class, not a get-up like him.'

The girl had risen from her knees, her face showing her fear, but when furtively she made to go towards the open door Dick Mallen's hand gripped her arm fiercely and held her back. Fanny was still standing at the far side of the soapy patch and he had apparently forgotten her presence for the moment, for his infuriated gaze was fixed on the open door a little to the side of him. The voice coming from there was saying now, 'Those three in the kitchens, bums or bailiffs, call them what you like, they won't wait any longer than s'afternoon, an' they must have had their palms well greased to wait that long. But the old man thinks that by then the young upstart'll have popped the question, 'cos old Armstrong won't stump up any other way. And oh, by God! I hope he gets her. By God! I do, I hope he does, for she'll sort his canister for him, will Miss Fanny Armstrong, if I know anything. Mr Brown tells me that the old man had to kick his arse this morning to get him up to scratch, 'cos he played up like hell. She was all right for a roll in the feather tick, but marriage no. Still, beggars can't be choosers, not when the bums are in, and it means the end of Master Big Head Dick if she doesn't . . .'

When Waite was dragged by the collar of his tight-necked, braided uniform coat and flung against the wall of the corridor he was dazed for a moment, but only for a moment, because the next thing he knew was that he was struggling with the young master, and fighting as if for his life.

When he again hit the wall it was Ord's arm this time that had thrust him there, and he slumped for a moment until he heard Dick Mallen yell at him, 'Out! Out! you swine. Do you hear? Out! You're dismissed. If you're not out of the grounds within half an hour . . .'

Waite pulled himself upright from the wall, but he didn't slink away under the fury of the young master as many another servant would have done, for there was in him a stubbornness born of a long line of protesting peasants. His grandparents and great-grandparents had originally worked on the land, but his father had been forced into the pit at the age of seven and when his first child was born he had stated bitterly and firmly, 'This is one who won't have chains atween his legs an' be pulling a bogie when he's seven. My God! no, I'll see to that.' And he had seen to it, for he had put the boy into service.

Harry Waite had started first as a stable lad but soon, the ambitions of his father prompting him, he had turned his eyes towards the house, for promotion was quicker there and the work was easier and you weren't out in all weathers. He had been in two situations before coming to the Hall five years ago, and since then he had married and his wife had given him two children and was on the point of being delivered of a third.

This morning the fortunes of the house had worried him almost as much as it was worrying his master. Positions were difficult to get, particularly if you had to house a wife and three children; but being turned off because of the fortunes of the house was one thing, being thrown out without a reference was entirely another, and something to be fought against. And now the resilience of his father, and his father's father, against injustice came spurting up in protest, and he dared to face the young upstart, as he thought of him, and say in no deferential terms, 'Oh no, I don't; I don't go out of here by your orders, sir, 'cos I wasn't bonded by you; if anybody's tellin' me to go it'll be the master, not you.'

Even Ord was aghast; as for Mr Dunn, who had just come through the green-baized door and was staring with an incredulous expression at the scene, he was too overcome by the enormity of what he was witnessing to utter a word. Then, his training coming to the fore, he regained his composure and was about to step forward when he was startled by the young master leaping past him and almost overbalancing him as he rushed towards the gun room door.

His intention was so plain to everyone that pandemonium, or something near to it, took place, for now Dunn and Ord almost leapt on Waite and dragged him along the passage and into the kitchen, there to be confronted by the startled staff and three sombre-faced men.

As the butler, releasing Waite, pushed him forward, hissing, 'Get yourself away out, man,' Fanny Armstrong's voice came from the corridor, crying, 'No! no!' Then the kitchen door burst open again and Dick Mallen stood there with a long-barrelled gun in his hand. Lifting it to his shoulder, he pointed it to where Waite, who was actually on his way to the far door, had stopped and turned, scarcely believing that the young master could mean to shoot him, yet at the same time knowing that he would.

'Ten seconds . . . I give you ten seconds!'

Whether it was that Waite couldn't quite take in the situation as real, or that his innate stubbornness was preventing him from obeying the command, he did not turn towards the door and run; not even when the kitchen maids screamed and huddled into a corner with the cook, while Dunn and Ord protested loudly, 'Master Dick! Master Dick!' but keeping their distance the while.

The three bailiffs too stood where they were; that is, until Dick Mallen, narrowing his eyes, looked along the barrel of the gun. Then the one who had done the talking so far said in a voice that held authority, 'Put that gun down, sir, or else you'll do somebody an injury.'

Dick Mallen's eyes flickered for a moment from the gun to the bailiff, and now his hatred of him and all his breed came over in his words as he growled, 'Mind it isn't you.'

When the bailiff sprang forward and gripped the gun there was a moment's struggle in which no one interfered. Then, as Dick Mallen had thrust Waite against the wall only a few minutes previously, now he found himself pushed backwards against the long dresser with the gun across his chest. The indignity was not to be borne. Lifting his knee up he thrust it into the bailiff's belly, then rotating the gun, he brought the butt across the side of the man's head. The bailiff heeled over and hit the stone floor with a dull thud.

There followed a moment of concerted stunned silence, then the women's screams not only filled the kitchen but vibrated through the house.

Only one woman hadn't screamed. Fanny Armstrong had just gasped before turning and fleeing along the corridor, through the green-baized door into the hall, calling, 'Father! Father! Father! Father!'

Like the rest of the household, Frank Armstrong was making his way into the hall, Thomas by his side. They had both been in the library, where Thomas had tactfully touched on the subject of a substantial loan, and Frank Armstrong after humming and ha-ing had then come into the open and said, 'Well, it's up to the youngsters, Turk. You know what I want in that direction; if my girl's happy, I'm happy and I'm willin' to pay for it.' It was at the exact moment when Thomas was exhaling one long-drawn breath of relief that the screams rang through the house. Now as he watched Fanny Armstrong throw herself into her father's arms, he cried, 'What is it? what is it?' But he received no answer, until Dunn, bursting through the door into the hall, came to his side; then was unable to get his words out.

'What is it, man? What is it, those women screaming?'

'Sir . . . sir, an . . . an accident.' The imperturbable butler was visibly shaking. 'M . . . Master Dick, the bailiff, he . . . the bailiff, he's injured. Master Dick used his gun on him.'

Thomas glared at the man as if he were about to accuse him of being drunk which he knew he could have done any night after the man's duties were over. Then he bounded across the hall, banging wide the green-baized door, down the corridor and into the kitchen. But he stopped dead just within the doorway. The expression on his face was much the same as had been on his butler's when he had come upon the scene in the corridor not more than five minutes earlier.

Thomas now walked slowly towards the man lying on the floor and looked down at him. His companions had opened his coat, his vest, and his shirt, and one of them had placed his hand on the man's heart, the other was attempting to staunch the blood pouring from the side of his head and face.

'Is . . . is he bad?' Thomas's words were thin and scarcely audible. One of the two men turned a sickly white face up to him and said, 'Seems so, sir; but he's still breathin'.'

Thomas now swept his glance around the kitchen. Everyone, including his son, seemed fixed as in a tableau. The screaming had stopped; the only sounds came from the girls huddled in the corner of the room.

Thomas's gaze turned on his son. Dick was standing by a side table, on which the gun now lay. He had one hand still on the barrel, the other was hanging limply by his side; his face, which had been red with fury, now looked ashen. He gazed at his father, wetted his lips, then muttered low, ''Twas an accident. An accident . . . I was out to frighten that –' he lifted a trembling finger and pointed to where Waite was standing utterly immobile looking like a mummy which had been taken from its long rest. No muscle of his face moved; he was not even blinking.

Thomas now let out a bellow and, turning to the doorway where Frank Armstrong was standing side by side with the butler, he yelled at Dunn, 'Send the coach! Get a doctor, quick! Clear those women out.' He swept his arm towards the corner of the kitchen. 'Get them to bring a door and bring the man upstairs. . . . See to it, Ord. You!' – he was pointing at the cook now – 'Get hot water. Move! Move yourself.'

The kitchen came to life, scurrying, frightened, apprehensive life.

Frank Armstrong now moved slowly forward and stood at Thomas's side and looked down at the man for a moment before slanting his narrowed gaze towards where Dick was standing, his hand still on the gun. Then without a word, he turned and walked out of the kitchen and back into the hall, where Fanny was supporting herself against the balustrade at the bottom of the stairs. Without a word he took her arm and together they went up the stairs and into her room, and there, facing her, he said, 'How did it come about?'

Fanny Armstrong stared at her father. She was not an emotional type of woman, she was not given to tears. Frank Armstrong couldn't remember when he last saw her cry, but now as he watched the tears slowly well into her eyes and fall down her cheeks he put his arm about her and, leading her to a chair, said, 'Tell me.'

And she told him.

She began by saying, 'It was because he heard a servant, the footman, speaking the truth about him,' and, her lips trembling, she ended with deep bitterness, 'The whole house knows he was being forced into asking me and that he hated the very idea of it. You know something? I hope the man dies, and he dies too for what he's done because I hate him. I hate him. I hate him. Oh Father, let us get out of here, now, now.' The next minute her face was buried against his waistcoat and he had to press her tight into him to stifle the sound of her sobbing.

# Chapter Five

There were four people in the house who weren't aware of what had taken place during the last hour. They were Miss Brigmore, Mary Peel and the children.

Miss Brigmore, Mary thought, had turned almost human over the last few hours. She told herself that never in her life had she seen anyone change so quickly, and when Miss Brigmore, taking her aside, told her of what she planned to do that very day, well, she couldn't believe her ears, she just couldn't.

And this is what Miss Brigmore had worked out. She, Mary, was to go down into the drawing room, or the dining room, whichever room she found empty, and unbeknown to anyone she was to pick up small pieces of silver, such as silver napkin rings and a Georgian cruet. One wouldn't be missed as there were three of them on the table most days. Then there was the small Georgian silver tea service that was in the cabinet in the drawing room, there were six pieces and a tray. She was to take large pins and pin anything with handles to her petticoats – did you ever hear anything like it? And Miss Brigmore had even demonstrated how she was to do it. Then, when she had got as much small silver as possible, she was to take from here and there in the display cabinets cameos and snuff boxes. She had really gaped at Miss Brigmore when she had told her the exact positions of the pieces; she herself had been in this house almost three times as long as Miss Brigmore and she couldn't have told what was in the cabinets, let alone just where each piece was placed. When she had got her breath back she had asked, 'But what'll we do with all that stuff? They'll take account of up here an' all.'

'Don't be stupid, Mary,' Miss Brigmore had said, reverting to her usual tone. 'They won't remain long up here.'

'But how will we get them out, an' where will we put them?'

'Mary' – Miss Brigmore's voice had been slow and patient – 'the children will be going to live at the cottage, won't they? I shall most certainly be accompanying them, very likely you too, and I should not be surprised if the master doesn't reside there for a time. . . .'

'The master at the cottage!'

'Yes,' said Miss Brigmore, 'the master at the cottage, Mary. Now these men start taking an inventory the moment they enter a room, they take mental stock of almost everything they see, bailiffs have eyes like lynxes, nothing escapes them, so it would be foolish, very foolish don't you think, if after collecting the articles we were to leave them up here, or that we should leave the collecting until later for that matter?'

'Yes, miss,' Mary had answered.

'So you will take the children for their airing as you do every day, but today I shall accompany you, and we shall carry as many things as possible on our persons. What can't be pinned or sewn on we must insert in our bodices. The children will help. We can fasten their cloaks with cameos. . . . Now, listen carefully. . . .'

Miss Brigmore then told Mary where the articles in question were placed, and she ended, 'Go to the drawing room first and if you find it empty, collect the miniatures and snuff boxes, and should anyone ask you what you are about refer them to me; just tell them to come to the nursery and see Miss Brigmore.'

And Mary did exactly as she was told. She had even enjoyed doing it, getting one over on them bums, who were spoiling everything, finishing the Hall off, an' the master an' all. But eeh! wasn't that Miss Brigmore a surprise? Who would have thought it? She was acting like she was almost human.

Mary made four journeys from the nursery to the ground floor and only one person had asked her what she was about. This was Waite. 'What you up to there, Mary?' he said. 'You can't get away with that. You want to end up along the line?'

'I'm doin' what I'm told, Harry,' she answered tartly. 'You go and see Miss Brigmore.'

'So that's it,' he said.

'That's it,' she answered.

'That one knows what she's about. What's she going to do with them?' said Waite.

'Take them to the cottage for the master.'

'Well, he's likely to need what they'll bring afore he's finished, I suppose. Here, I'll give you a hand,' he said.

But to his proposal she answered, 'No, I know what I'm to get, but you could keep the coast clear outside and if anybody makes for here or the dining room, cough.'

So Miss Brigmore and her charges and Mary Peel went out for a walk before noon. They walked slowly until they were out of sight of the house and then they walked more quickly through the gardens. But their pace was controlled by the weight of their petticoats. They went out through the main gates and along the coach road to the cottage, where, there being no cellar, Miss Brigmore ordered Mary to look in the outhouses for a hammer and chisel. When these were found Miss Brigmore pushed the dining-room carpet back until it touched the stout, claw-footed leg of the table, then using the hammer and chisel as if so doing were an everyday occurrence to her, she prised up the nine-inch floor board.

After thrusting her hand down into the dark depths, she said, 'This'll do nicely; there's a draught of air passing through and the bottom is rough stone. Now Mary, and you, children, hand me the pieces, carefully, one after the other. There is no need to wrap them as they won't rest here long.'

Constance giggled as she passed her pieces to Miss Brigmore. She was finding the business exciting, whereas Barbara on the other hand showed no outward sign of feeling at all.

Although Miss Brigmore had tried to turn the whole episode into a game Barbara knew it had a very serious side. She was overwhelmed by a sense of insecurity and she remembered this feeling from as far back as the time when her Uncle Thomas had first brought her to the Hall.

Miss Brigmore sensed the feeling in her charge, and after she had replaced the floor board and the carpet was rolled back and the house door closed, she took Barbara's hand and said, 'Come, you and I shall race Mary and Constance to the main road.'

Barbara, too, saw that Miss Brigmore had changed, but in spite of this and the new softness in her, she was still seeing her as she had done the previous night lying on the bed moaning, and she knew she was wicked.

It was with a certain sense of triumph that Miss Brigmore finally marshalled her pirate company through the main gates after their second visit to the cottage. The day was closing in, it was bitterly cold and raining, but the weather didn't trouble her. The last time she had been engaged in such a manoeuvre she had failed, at least her mother had, and it was only the timely assistance of a friend that had prevented her mother being taken before the Justices. But this time she had succeeded. At a rough estimate she guessed they had retrieved some thousand pounds' worth of objects, the miniatures being the most valuable. Of course, she admitted to herself, she might have been precipitate in her action for the master had a good friend in Mr Armstrong. Moreover, if the match between Miss Fanny and Master Dick were to be arranged then the problem would be solved, and indeed her action might be frowned upon – or laughed at, which would be harder to bear. But as Mr Brown had confided in her only yesterday, he had his grave doubts concerning Master Dick's intentions. To quote his own words, Master Dick was a bit of an unruly stallion, and he couldn't see Miss Fanny Armstrong breaking him in. In Mr Brown's opinion, apart from her being much too old for him, she wasn't his type; some stallions, for all their temper and show of strength, had tender mouths, and his guess was that Miss Fanny would pull too hard on the bit.

Mr Brown's similes always favoured the stables. She sometimes wondered how he had chosen the profession of valet, seeing his knowledge, and apparently his sympathies, lay so much with the four-footed creatures. Nevertheless she was inclined to take Mr Brown's opinion with some seriousness for he had proved himself to be right on other occasions with regards both to the master and Master Dick.

It was as she was crossing the drive, ushering the children and Mary quickly before her out of the rain, that she had a mental picture of herself explaining her actions to the master, at the opportune moment of course, and the opportune moment, as seen in her mind, brought a warm, exciting glow to her body, for now she could see no end to the opportune moments. If the master's affairs were in order such moments would continue at intervals; if he were forced through circumstances to retire to the cottage they would most certainly continue and more frequently. Whichever way things went she felt that for once she couldn't lose. Her cloistered, nun-like days were over. She had never been cut out for celibate life. Yet her early upbringing had made it impossible for her to find bodily expression with those males who, in the hierarchy of the staff, were classed as fitting mates for a governess; such were valets and house stewards.

She did not guide her charges towards the front door, nor yet round the corner into the courtyard to the back door, but going in the opposite direction she marshalled them round the side of the house and along the whole length of the back terrace until she entered the courtyard from the stable end. Then, opening a narrow door, she pushed the children into the passage, followed them and was in turn followed by Mary.

Mr Tweedy, the steward, Mr Dunn, the butler, and the housekeeper, Mrs Brydon, who had all been in deep conversation, turned startled faces towards her, and such were their expressions that she was brought to a halt and enquired, 'What has happened?'

It was Mrs Brydon who spoke. 'A dreadful thing, a dreadful thing, Miss Brigmore. You wouldn't believe it; none of us can believe it. Master Dick . . . Master Dick attacked one of the bailiffs, the head one. He was going to shoot Waite, I mean Master Dick was, and the bailiff went to stop him. It's all through Waite, he started the trouble. They've sent for the doctor. He's bad the bailiff, very bad. He could go like that, just like that.' She made a soundless snap with her fingers.

It was Mr Dunn who said in a very low voice, 'If he does, Master Dick could swing for it seeing it's a bailiff.'

'Quiet! That is enough.' Miss Brigmore's voice thundered over them, then she turned from them and pushed the gasping children along the passage and up the stairs, leaving Mary behind.

Mary stood and gaped at her superiors, then she muttered, 'Waite? What's happened to him?'

The steward's voice was the voice of authority now, head of the household under the master. 'He is packing his belongings and going this very hour . . . now.'

'But . . . but Daisy; she's on her time, they can't . . .'

'Peel!' Mrs Brydon checked Mary's further protest. 'Enough. It's none of your business. What is your business is to see to the nursery, and get you gone there this instant.'

After a moment's hesitation Mary went, but slowly, not thinking now of the Master or of Master Dick, or even of the bailiff, but of Daisy Waite and her trouble. The bairn could come any day, she was over her time; and look at the weather. She paused at a window on the first landing and looked out. Through the blur of rain she could see the family cottages, as they were called. They were allotted to those of the staff who had children yet were in indoor service. The three houses were attached to the end of the stables. As she stared, the door of the middle cottage opened and a man came out and although she couldn't identify the figure through the rain she knew it was Harry Waite, for he was lifting a box on to a flat hand-cart that stood outside the door.

The hand-cart, which was nothing but a glorified barrow, had caused a great deal of laughter when he had arrived with his belongings on it five years ago. No one had ever heard of a footman coming to take up a position pushing a hand-cart. But he had withstood the laughter, for apparently his father had made the hand-cart for him when he first went into service, with the words 'When you've got enough luggage to cover that, lad, you'll be all right.' And now, thought Mary tearfully, he had more than enough luggage, he had two children and a wife ready for her bed. What would happen to them? Where would they go? She wanted to run out and say good-bye to them because Daisy was her friend. But Mrs Brydon was still in the passage, she could hear her voice.

She went heavily up the remaining stairs shaking her head as she said to herself, 'Eeh! the things that have happened this day; it's like the end of the world, it is that.'

# Chapter Six

The House was quiet. It was like the quiet that follows a hurricane; it was so peaceful that if it wasn't for the debris no one would believe that a storm had recently passed that way.

The quiet hit Thomas with the force of deep resonant sound as he entered the Hall. Dunn had not met him at the outer door as was usual – Dunn hadn't time these days to listen for the carriage and be there to take his hat, coat and stick, for Dunn was now doing the work of a number of men – and so as he came hurrying from the direction of the study and towards Thomas he said, 'I'm sorry, sir.'

Thomas waved his hand. He had helped himself off with his coat, which he now handed to Dunn, saying, 'Has anyone called?'

'Mr Ferrier's man brought a letter, sir; it's in the study.'

Thomas walked quickly across the hall and into the study. The letter was propped against a paper-weight on the only clear space on his desk. He did not take up the slender hoof-handled paper-knife to open it, but inserted his finger under the flap and whipped it across the top.

He stood while reading the letter. It was short; it said: 'Dear Thomas. You know without my saying that I sympathize deeply with you in your trouble, and if it were possible for me to help you to any great extent you know I would do so, but things are at a critical stage in the works at present. As I told you when I saw you last I'm having to close down the factory at Shields. However, if a couple of hundred would be of any use you're very welcome, but I'm sorry I can't rise to a thousand. Drop in any time you feel like it, you'll always be welcome, you know that.' It was signed simply, 'John.'

'You'll always be welcome.' The words came like grit through his teeth. He couldn't believe it. He just couldn't believe it. He crushed the letter in his hand and, putting it on the desk, he beat it flat with his fist. After a moment he sat down in the high-backed leather chair behind the desk and dropped his head on to his chest. Armstrong, Headley, and now Ferrier, men he'd have sworn would have stood by him to the death, for they were his three best friends; moreover they were men on whom he had lavished the best of his house. Why, when John Ferrier's eldest son, Patrick, was married he bought the pair silver plate to the value of more than six hundred pounds; and when their first child was born his christening mug, plate and spoon had cost something, and now here was John, his very good friend, saying he could manage a couple of hundred. It would have been better if he had done what Frank Armstrong had done and ignored his plea altogether. His appeal to Frank had been returned, saying that Mr Armstrong, his wife and daughter had gone to London, and their stay would be indefinite. . . . And

Ralph Headley? He had pushed business his way when he was a struggling nobody, he could almost say he had made him. What was more, for years he had supplemented his income with money he had lost to him in gambling. In his young days he would bet on a fly crawling up the window, and he had done just that, a hundred pounds at a time, and had paid up smiling because it was to Ralph, and Ralph needed a hand.

And because he knew just how much he had helped Ralph he had asked him for the loan of three thousand: enough to cover Dick's bail and to clear the servants' wages and see him over the next few months. But what had Ralph sent? a cheque for three hundred pounds. Margaret's wedding was going to cost him something, he said, and the young devil, George, had been spending money like water. Later on perhaps, when he knew how he stood after the wedding, he'd likely be able to help him further.

The condescension that had emanated from that particular letter, and something more, something that had come over in the refusal of his friends to stand by him in this terrible moment of his life, had hit him like a blow between the eyes and blurred for a time the knowledge that was pressing against his pride and self-esteem. But now that knowledge had forced its way into the open and could be described by one word, dislike. At one time he would have put the term, 'jealousy', to it, but not anymore. He knew now what he had really known for years; he had no friends. These men had really disliked him, as many such had disliked his father before him. He was a Mallen; Turk Mallen his supposed friends called him because his misdeeds had left their mark on the heads of his fly-blows. All men whored, but the results of his whoring had a brand on them. He was Turk Mallen, 'the man with a harem in the hills,' as one wit had said. All right, he had made cuckolds out of many men, but he had never let a friend down, nor taken a liberty with his wife, nor shied a gambling debt, and no child born of him had ever gone hungry; not to his knowledge.

A knock came on the door and Dunn entered bearing a tray.

'I thought you might like something hot, sir.'

'Oh, yes, yes, Dunn.' Thomas looked down into the steaming mug that held hot rum, and he sniffed and gave a wry smile as he said, 'This must be running short by now.'

'I've managed to secure a certain number of bottles, sir.'

'Ah! Well now, that was good thinking.' Again the wry smile. 'They'll be a comfort, in more ways than one.'

'Is there anything more you need, sir?'

Thomas sipped at the rum, then said, 'How many of you are left?'

Dunn moved one lip over the other before he replied, 'Besides Mr Brown and Mr Tweedy, there is Mrs Brydon and, of course, Miss Brigmore and Mary Peel.'

'Six.'

'Yes, six, sir, indoors, but there are two still in the stables. They . . . they will have to remain there until . . .' His voice trailed off.

'Yes, yes, of course. Where is Mr Tweedy now?'

'Visiting the farms, sir. As you ordered, leaving just the bare staff.'

Thomas now looked down at the desk, his eyes sweeping over the mass of papers and bills arrayed there. Then he took another sip from the tankard before looking up at Dunn again and saying, 'You'll be all right, Dunn; I'll

give you a good reference. Just . . . just tell me when you want to go. There
are a number of houses that'll jump at you.'

'There's no hurry, sir, none whatever.'

'Well, you can't live on air, Dunn, no more than any of us. I won't be
able to pay you after this week.'

'I'm fully aware of that, sir. Still, there's no hurry. Mrs Brydon is of the
same opinion; as is Mr Tweedy; and I'm sure you can rely on Mr Brown.'

Thomas now lowered his head. Forty staff he'd employed in the house
and the farms and six were quite willing to stay with him until such times
as they were all turfed out. You could say it was a good percentage. Strange
where one found one's friends. He looked up at Dunn and said, 'Thank
them for me, will you? I'll . . . I'll see them personally later.'

'Yes, sir.'

As Dunn was about to turn away he stopped and said, 'May I enquire
how Master Dick is, sir?'

Thomas stretched his thick neck up out of his collar before saying, 'Putting
as good a face on it as he can, Dunn. I . . . I had hopes of being able to bail
him out but –' he tapped the crumbled letter that was lying to his hand now
and said, 'I'm afraid I haven't succeeded.' Strange how one could talk like
this to one's butler, and in an ordinary tone, without any command or
condescension on the one hand or false hee-hawing on the other, as one was
apt to do with one's friends.

'I'm sorry, sir.'

'So am I, Dunn, so am I. By the way, where are the men?' He did not
call them bailiffs.

'Two are in the library, sir, cataloguing the books, the other is up in the
west wing doing the bedrooms.'

'How much longer are they likely to take do you think?'

'Two days, three at the most I should say, sir.'

Thomas now narrowed his eyes and thought for a moment before he said,
'By the way, cook went three days ago didn't she? Who's doing the cooking
now?'

'Well, sir –' Dunn inclined his head slightly towards him '– Mrs Brydon
and myself are managing quite well, and Miss Brigmore has been of some
assistance. She has seen to the children's meals and to her own and Peel's.'

'Thank you, Dunn.'

'Thank you, sir.'

Alone once more, Thomas sat back in the chair and, stretching one hand,
he pressed his first finger and thumb tightly on to his eyeballs. He had
forgotten about the children because he hadn't seen them for days, she had
kept them out of his way. Funny, he thought of her as she. Why? It was
much too personal a tag to attach to her prim little packet of flesh. Yet she
had thawed. Yes, she had indeed. Anyway, he was glad the children had
her, and that they had a home to go to, and two hundred a year between
them. But could they exist on two hundred a year? Well, they would have
to. What did she get? He opened a drawer to the side of him and took out
a long ledger and, turning the pages, he brought his finger down to the
name. Brigmore . . . Brigmore, Anna, employed as governess from the first
of September, 1844, at a salary of forty-five pounds per annum. He noted
that there was no mention against this of an allowance of beer, tea or sugar.

Forty-five pounds, that would make a big hole in the two hundred. Then there must be someone to do the work. The Peel girl, how much was she getting? He turned back the pages. Mary Peel, bonded, third kitchen maid, two pounds twelve shillings per annum, extra beer, sugar and tea allowed; promoted second kitchen maid at five pounds per annum; promoted nursery maid 1844 at twelve pounds per annum, extra beer, tea and sugar allowed.

Well, that was another twelve pounds. That would hardly leave three pounds a week to feed them all. Could it be done. He doubted it. What could one get for three pounds a week? What could four people get for three pounds a week?

... And what are you going to do?

It was as if someone were asking the question of him and he shook his head slowly from side to side. If it wasn't for Dick he knew what he would do and this very night, for here he was without a penny to his name and no prospect of having one in the future. Even if the estate sold well, and the contents of the house also, he knew it would not give his creditors twenty shillings in the pound.

But damn his creditors, damn them to hell's flames, each and every one of them, for almost without exception they had overcharged him for years. Why, he asked himself now as he stared at the row of sporting prints hanging above the mantelpiece opposite to him, why hadn't he been like others under similar circumstances and made a haul while the going was good? Even Dunn had had the foresight to look to himself and secure some bottles, and he would like to bet that there wasn't a servant in the house but had helped himself to something. But he, what had he done? Well, what had he done? Could he, when the house was in an uproar, when his son had gone to pieces, when the place was swarming with officers of the law, deliberating whether it might be manslaughter or excusable homicide if the man were to die, and seeming to infer that the eventual penalty would be severe because the victim happened to be a law man, could he then have gone round surreptitiously acquiring his own valuables? Yet there was not one of his so-called friends who would believe that he hadn't done so, either before or after the bailiff incident. No one but a fool, they would say, would let bums have it all their own way, and Turk Mallen was no fool. . . . Yet Thomas Mallen, the Thomas Mallen he knew himself to be, was a fool and always had been.

But now it was Dick he must think about; he must get him bailed out of there or by the time the trial came up he would be a gibbering idiot. Thank God it looked as if the man was going to survive, otherwise there would have been no question of bail. As it was, they had made it stiff, a thousand pounds:

He had never expected Dick to break as he had done. He had imagined, up till recently, there was a tough side to him, or had he just hoped there was? His own father used to say, a man can be fearless when cornered by a rutting stag as long as he's on a horse and has a gun to hand. But meet up with the stag when on his feet and empty-handed, and who do you think will run first?

Dick had met the stag in the form of the law and he had neither gun nor horse. As he had looked on him today in that stark, bare room he had felt both pity and scorn for him, aye, yes, and a touch of loathing, because it was he, this son of his, and he alone, who had brought them all to such a pass. But for the false pride that had made him turn on that bloody ingrate of a footman, everything would have been settled between him and Fanny Armstrong and no doubt at this very moment the whole Hall would have been in a frenzy of preparations for the engagement banquet, whereas he would now be lucky to have one course for a meal tonight.

He sat with his head bowed until his thoughts touched on the children again; he must see to them, get them out of this and to the cottage, the atmosphere of the house wasn't good for anyone anymore. Slowly he reached out and rang the bell, thinking as he did so what it would be like to ring a bell and have no one answer it – well, he would soon know, that was certain.

It was some minutes before Dunn made his appearance and then, deferential as ever, he stood just within the door and said, 'Yes, sir?'

'Tell Miss Brigmore I'd like to see her for a moment . . . please.' Again he felt a tightness in his collar and he ran his finger around the edge of it. That was the first time he could ever remember saying please to his butler. Sometimes he had given him a perfunctory thanks, but that was all. Had one to be destitute before becoming aware of good manners? Strange that he should learn something at this time of trial. . . .

When Miss Brigmore knocked on the study door she was immediately bidden to enter. After closing the door quietly behind her, she walked slowly up to the desk and looked at her master. Her look was open and held no trace of embarrassment. She was grateful to him for ending her years of virginity, her years of personal torment. She had never been able to see any virtue in chastity, and had questioned the right of a piece of paper which legalized a natural desire, a desire which, indulged in before the signing of the paper, earned for the female the title of wanton, or whore, while it was considered the natural procedure for a male, even making him into a dashing fellow, a real man, and a character. She had strong secret views on the rights of the individual – the female individual in particular, and it was only the necessity to earn her livelihood that had kept them secret, and herself untouched, this far.

Still she knew that had Thomas Mallen never taken her she would still have cared for him, looked up to him, and feared him a little. Now she no longer looked up to him nor feared him, but she loved him.

'Sit down –' he paused '– Anna.'

'Thank you.' She did not add 'sir'. He had used her Christian name, there was no need now for titles.

'It's about the children. I . . . I don't know whether you are aware –' he knew she was aware all right, every servant in the house was aware of everything appertaining to his business '– but the children jointly own the cottage and have an income of two hundred pounds a year between them. Now –' he paused and ran his tongue round his lips '– if you'll still consent to take charge of them they could afford to pay you your salary, also perhaps Peel's too, though it would not leave much for living. I'm afraid your fare would be rather scanty, as would other amenities, so I . . . I shall not take it amiss if you decide to terminate your agreement.'

Anna Brigmore would have liked to retort at this moment 'Don't be silly!' What she said was, 'I have already arranged to go to the cottage with the children; everything is in order, the rooms are ready . . . yours too.' She paused here, then added, 'sir', for it seemed at this point a title was called for. 'That is, if you wish for a temporary dwelling before you make other arrangements. The house appears small at first, but it is really quite roomy.

I've had the furniture re-arranged and fresh drapes hung; the place is quite comfortable. What is more, I took the liberty of transferring some of your belongings ... objects, of the smaller type, to the cottage. Certain pieces which I think are of some considerable value, and which ...'

'You what?' He had jerked himself forward in his chair and now, with his forearms on the desk, he was leaning towards her and he repeated, 'You what?'

'I arranged for some objects from the cases in the drawing room to be transferred and ... and with the assistance of Mary Peel and the children they are now safely hidden in the cottage.'

'An-na.' A smile was spreading over his face and he shook his head as he looked at the prim figure sitting before him, prim but pretty. He had noticed her prettiness six years ago when he had first met her, and had remarked laughingly to himself, 'This one's chastity belt's secured all right.' It was strange, he thought now, that she should be the first indoor servant he had taken. He had made a rule never to tamper with indoor servants. His father had put him up to this. 'It's always embarrassing,' he had said, 'to see bellies swelling inside the house and you having to deny claim for your own handiwork. Keep your sporting well outside; your own farms if you must, but further afield is always safer.' But there had been something about Miss Anna Brigmore, something that appealed to him; not only had he wanted to end her virginity but he'd had the desire to strip the primness from her and expose the prettiness. Well, he had taken her virginity, but he hadn't managed to strip the primness from her. She was still Miss Brigmore, softer in a way, yes, but nevertheless Miss Brigmore, even when he addressed her as Anna.

But Miss Brigmore had had the sense to do what he should have done or at least have ordered someone to do on the side. He could have said to Brown, 'See that my personal belongings are put in a safe place.' How many sets of gold cuff links and odds and ends had Brown tucked away in his own valise? He wasn't blaming Brown, he wasn't blaming any of them, let them get what they could while the going was good. But Miss Brigmore hadn't thought of herself, she had thought of him, and his future needs. Strange ... strange the quarters from which help came.

'What did you take?' he asked quietly.

'I should imagine about fifty pieces in all.'

'*Fifty pieces!*' He grimaced in disbelief.

'Some I should imagine more valuable than others, such as the pair of Swiss snuff boxes and the Louis XVI enamelled one.'

His eyes crinkled at the corner and he said softly, 'Fifty! and the Louis snuff box among them?'

'Yes.'

'How did you know what to take?'

Her chin moved slightly upwards before she said, 'I read a great deal about such things. What is more, my parents found themselves in a similar situation to yourself when I was sixteen.'

His mouth was open, and his head nodded twice before he said, 'They did?'

'Yes.'

'And ... and you managed to secure some trinkets of your own before ...?'

'No; we weren't successful. The articles were discovered for the simple reason that there were in no way as many pieces to choose from. The result was very trying.'

He nodded again, saying, 'Yes, it would be.' Then going on, he added, 'Yet knowing it could be very trying here too, you transferred fifty pieces to the cottage? How did you do it?'

'I . . . I selected certain things, and ordered Mary Peel to bring them up to the nursery; then I pinned or sewed what could be pinned or sewed to . . . to our undergarments; the other pieces we managed to secrete on our persons.'

In blank silence he stared at her . . . 'You must have done all this before . . . before the accident, and made several journeys, it's some distance to the cottage.'

'Only two journeys, and the children looked upon it as a game. If . . . if you would care to come to the cottage you will be able to judge for yourself as to the value of what is there. I would have informed you sooner but there has not been the opportunity.'

Slowly he rose from the chair and came round the desk and, standing over her, he put out his hand and when she had placed hers in it he pressed it tightly, saying, 'Whatever they're worth, tuppence or ten thousand, Anna, thank you, thank you.'

Her eyes blinked, her mouth pursed; then, her face suddenly relaxing, she smiled up at him softly as she said, 'I only wish I'd had more time.'

Drawing her to her feet he gazed at her for a moment before saying, 'We will go now to the cottage. Bring the children. It will appear as if we are taking a stroll.'

She looked at him as if he were proposing just that, a stroll with him along a country lane. . . .

Half an hour later they walked down the long drive and through the lodge gates, which Thomas opened himself and found it a strange experience for he hadn't realized how heavy they were. They walked briskly for it was a cold, raw day. The sky was lying low and heavy on the hills and promised snow. After a short while Thomas's step slowed considerably for he found he was out of breath, and he lightly chided the children, saying, 'If you want to gallop, you gallop, but let me trot. And the children ran on ahead; but Miss Brigmore suited her step to his.

When at last they reached the gate of the cottage he leaned on it and stood looking at the house before him. It was built of grey granite; it had been built to withstand wind and weather, and no softness had been incorporated into its design. He followed Miss Brigmore up the narrow winding path and watched her insert the key in the lock, then they all went inside.

'Well, well!' Thomas stood in the small hall and looked about him. It wasn't the first time he had been in the cottage but he remembered it as a dull characterless place; now, even this little hall looked different.

There were five doors leading out of the hall and they were all open. He walked towards the first one to the left of him; it led into a sitting room, tiny by the standards of the Hall, being only fifteen by twenty feet in length he imagined. Yet it looked a comfortable room, solidly comfortable, although at a glance he would say there wasn't one piece of furniture of any value in it.

He turned and smiled at Miss Brigmore, and when Constance grabbed his hand and cried, 'Come on and see the dining room, Uncle,' he allowed himself to be tugged into the next room. Here he stood nodding his head as he looked about him, saying, 'Very, very nice, very nice. You should be quite happy here.' He looked down at Constance and then at Barbara. Barbara wasn't smiling. That was the difference in these two little sisters, Constance always appeared happy, whereas you could never tell whether Barbara was happy or not. He said to her now, 'Do you like the cottage, Barbara?'

'Yes, Uncle.'

'You'd like living here?'

She paused for a moment before saying again, 'Yes, Uncle.'

'I'll love living here, Uncle.' Constance was tugging at his hand again, crying now, 'Come and see your study.'

'My . . .?' He did not look at the child but turned and looked towards where Miss Brigmore was walking into the hall, and again he allowed himself to be tugged out of the room and through the third doorway and into a smaller room. He looked at the long narrow table that served as a desk, at the leather chair, the leather couch, and at the end of the room the two glass doors opening out on to a small terrace.

'This is your room, Uncle, your study.'

He turned to face Miss Brigmore, but Miss Brigmore was not in the room. He could see her now ascending the bare oak staircase.

'Come and see your bedroom, Uncle.' As Constance led him towards the stairs she pointed to the other two doors leading from the hall, saying, 'That one is the morning room and that one leads to the kitchen,' and she added to this, 'The kitchen requires a lot of seeing to; the stove smokes.'

He was on the landing now and being tugged towards a second door that led off from it. 'This is your bedroom, Uncle.'

The room was of a fair size, almost as large as the sitting room. It held a four-poster bed, a stout wardrobe and dressing table, but its most significant feature was the unusually large window that gave a view of the foothills and the mountains beyond.

Thomas turned now to where Miss Brigmore was standing in the doorway. Constance was still hanging on to his hand, and the look in his eyes spoke a different language from his words as he said, 'You have transformed the place; I remember it as a very dismal dwelling.'

'There is a toilet room, Uncle, next door too and you won't have to go out in the . . .'

'Constance!'

'Yes, Miss Brigmore.' Constance hung her head knowing that she had touched on a delicate and unmentionable subject.

Miss Brigmore now said hastily as she pushed open another door, 'This is . . . is a spare room for anyone you might wish to stay –' she did not say 'Master Dick' '– and this –' she opened yet another door '– is the children's room.'

'Isn't it pretty, Uncle? and the desk-bed in the corner is for Mary, she doesn't want to sleep in the attic. But isn't it pretty, Uncle?'

'Yes, my dear, it's very pretty.' He patted Constance's head.

Miss Brigmore did not open the fourth door, she merely said, 'That is my room.' Then leading the way down the stairs again, she added, 'If we can dispense with the morning room I would like to turn it into a schoolroom.'

'Do as you wish, Miss Brigmore, do as you wish.' He was nodding down to the back of her head.

In the hall Miss Brigmore looked at Barbara and said, 'Would you like to gather some wood for the fire? It would be nice if we had a fire, wouldn't it? And then we could have a cup of tea.'

'Yes, Miss Brigmore. Come, Connie.' Barbara held out her hand and took Constance's and forced her now to walk out of the room, not run as she was inclined to.

Miss Brigmore looked at Thomas and said quietly, 'They're in here.'

He followed her into the dining room, and watched with amazement as she knelt down and rolled back the carpet and prised up the floor boards with a chisel. When she put her arm down the hole and began handing him articles of silver, cameos, and trinket boxes he did not utter a word, he just kept shaking his head.

At last the collection was arrayed on the top of the sideboard and the round table, and he stood gazing at it in amazement. Picking up a small Chelsea porcelain figure of a mandarin he fingered it gently, almost lovingly; when he looked at her he found he was still unable to speak. This one piece alone would be worth five hundred, if not more, and then there were the snuff boxes; three of them, no, four. He put out his hand and stroked the Louis XVI gold enamelled box, his fingers tracing the minute necklace that graced the slender neck of the lady depicted in the middle of it.

One after the other he handled the pieces: a pair of George I sugar dredgers; a set of three George I casters; and when he came to the chinoiserie tankard he cupped it in both hands, then, as if it were a child he had lost and found again, he held it tight against his waistcoat while he looked at her. And now he asked quietly, 'What can I say to you, Anna?'

She stared back into his eyes but did not answer.

'An hour ago I was a desperate man; now I'm no longer desperate, you have given me new life.'

There was another silence before she asked in a practical manner, 'Will you be able to sell them immediately?'

He looked away from her for a moment, bit on his lower lip as he nodded his head, and said, 'Yes, yes, Anna, I'll be able to sell them immediately. I know of a gentleman in Newcastle who is of great assistance to people like us.'

Her eyes were unblinking as she kept them fixed on him. He had said 'us'.

'Not that he'll give me half what they're worth; but as long as it's enough to get Dick out of that place. . . .'

Miss Brigmore suddenly gasped as she felt herself almost lifted from the ground and pulled into his embrace. He kissed her, his mouth big, warm and soft, covering hers entirely. When at last he let her go she experienced a strange feeling; for the first time in her life she knew what it was to feel like a woman, a mature fulfilled woman. She hadn't experienced this when he came to her room because then he had merely given her his body. Now he had given her something from his heart.

# Chapter Seven

For five weeks now Thomas had been living in the cottage and he had taken his change of circumstances with good grace, hiding the feeling of claustrophobia that the rooms gave him, hiding the feeling of despair when he thought of the future, and hiding the disturbing feeling of disdain whenever he looked at his son, for Dick Mallen had not taken the change with good grace.

To Dick Mallen the cottage appeared merely as an extension of prison. As for thanking the governess for being the means of his temporary liberation, when his father had suggested that he afford Miss Brigmore this courtesy he had looked at him as if he were mad.

Thank the governess for giving them what was theirs! Very likely they had only received half of what she had taken.

Thomas, who up to that moment had kept his temper, had sworn at his son, saying, 'You're an ungrateful sod, Dick, that's what you are, an ungrateful sod.'

After his release Dick Mallen had visited the Hall, but had returned empty-handed. He had been informed, and in no subservient manner, by the bailiff that his strictly personal belongings, which meant his clothes only, had been sent to the cottage; as for the remainder, they had been tabulated against the day of the sale.

He knew that his man Taylor would surely have lined his pockets with cuff links, scarf pins, cravat rings and the like, and he wished he could get his hand on him but the beggar had gone long since, and he couldn't find out if he had become established in another position.

When he thought of the attitudes of their various friends he just couldn't believe it. He could understand Armstrong's reaction but not that of old Headley and Ferrier. Yet he had to admit that Pat Ferrier had turned up trumps. Then, of course, he should, he would have been damn well amazed if he hadn't, for Pat had cleaned him out time and again over the past three years; and after all, what was a few hundred compared to what he had lost to him.

He had said nothing to his father about Pat Ferrier's help. He said little to his father at all these days; the old man, he considered, had gone soft in the head. The way he treated that governess made him sick, for he constantly deferred to her as if she were an equal. One thing he was certain of, her stay would be short once the trial was over. . . . The trial! It was that word that had the power to take the bombast out of him. He was fearing the trial for although the man had recovered they said he was badly scarred; moreover he knew that public opinion would be against him. If only there were some way out. . . .

Thomas too kept thinking, if only there were some way out, but his thoughts did not run along the same channels as his son's. His idea of a way out was to beat the law by engaging one of the finest barristers and to do this he needed money, big money, and all he could call upon was the refund of the bail money and the little that was left over from the sale of Anna's haul, as he came to think of the pieces she had retrieved.

With the exception of two miniatures and a snuff box he had disposed of all the pieces to the certain gentleman in Newcastle. With regard to these three pieces he had private thoughts concerning them, but had decided he would do nothing about them until the sale was over. . . .

It was on Monday the fourteenth of April that the sale of the contents of the ground floor of High Banks Hall began. It was well attended, and the auctioneer was more than pleased with the result at the end of the day.

On Tuesday, the fifteenth, the contents of the first floor were sold; again the result was favourable. On the morning of Wednesday, the sixteenth, the auctioneer dealt with the contents of the nursery floor, the attics and the kitchens. In the afternoon he sold off the contents of the coach-house, the harness rooms, and the servants' quarters. The livestock, such as the coach horses and the four hunters, had been sent to the West Farm, where the sale of all livestock would take place on the Tuesday following Easter Monday.

But it was Thursday, the seventeenth, the day before Good Friday, that was the important day of the sale, for on this day the Hall and the estate, together with its two farms, was put up for auction. The carriages came from County Durham, Cumberland, Westmorland and Yorkshire. There were gathered in the library quite a number of men bearing names that spelt money. Then there were those others who held themselves apart. These men had names that didn't only spell money but distinction of class. Yet at the end of the day the Hall had gone neither to a self-made man nor yet to one of title.

The Bank had put a reserve price on the estate and no bidder had touched anywhere near it. The auctioneer had at one time become impatient and as he looked at the men he would have liked, very much, to say, 'Gentlemen, I know why you hesitate, as on such occasions of distraint on property, beggars can't be choosers, you're thinking. But you are mistaken in this case. The Bank wants its money and it means to have it, and is prepared to wait. Oh, I know you gentlemen of old, you think if the estate doesn't go today you will tomorrow put in an offer and we will gladly take it. Oh, I know you of old, Gentlemen.'

What he did say was, 'Gentlemen, this is a very fine estate and I've no need to remind you what it contains, you have it all there in your catalogues; five hundred acres of land containing two productive farms, and then this house, this beautiful and, I will add, grand house. You could not build this house for sixty thousand today, and Gentlemen, what are you offering? Twenty thousand below the asking price. We're wasting each other's time, gentlemen. I'll ask you again: what am I bid over the last bidder of thirty thousand? . . . Well now, well, come, come, Gentlemen. . . . No? Then, I'm afraid that today's business is at an end, Gentlemen.' . . .

Thomas Mallen took the news with a deep sigh, but Dick stormed and ranted until his father turned on him angrily, saying, 'Stop it! stop it! Anyway, what good would it do you if they had bid twenty thousand over the asking price?'

'None. I'm well aware of that, none, but it riles me to think they're harping over a few bloody thousand. Pat tells me the Hamiltons were there from Edinburgh; also the Rosses from Glasgow; they're weighed down with it but both as mean as skilly bowls . . . And God Almighty, how you can sit there and take it calmly! . . .'

'Blast you to hell's flames, boy. Stop your stupid ranting, and don't say again I'm taking it calmly. Let me tell you this, I'm neither taking the loss of my house calmly, nor yet the way my son has conducted himself in this predicament. And I will say it, although I told myself I never would, but for your trying to play the injured master we wouldn't be in this position today. You're weak gutted, underneath all your bombast, boy, you're weak gutted. Only the thought of penury prodded you, but too late as it turned out, to ask Fanny Armstrong, whereas if you'd had any spunk you'd have clinched the matter a year gone, for you were up to your neck then. . . .'

The altercation had taken place in the study on Thursday evening, and Thomas's roar had easily penetrated into the children's bedroom above, where Anna was putting them to bed.

'Uncle's vexed,' said Constance; 'perhaps he didn't like his supper, I didn't like it much. We don't have nice meals now, do we, Miss Brigmore?'

'You have good plain food, that is all you require. Now lie down and go to sleep and no more talking. Good night.'

'Good night, Miss Brigmore.'

Anna turned and looked down at Barbara; then she put her hand out and pulled the sheets over the child's shoulder. 'Good night, Barbara,' she said softly.

'Good night, Miss Brigmore.'

Anna looked down for a moment longer on the child. There was something on her mind; she had changed of late, perhaps she was missing the house. She had never been gay like Constance, she was of a more serious turn of mind, but lately there had been an extra restraint in her manner. She must give her more attention; one was apt to talk more to Constance because Constance was more responsive. Yes, she must pay her more attention.

She left the night light burning and, lifting up the lamp, went out and into her own room, and there, taking the coverlet from the bed, she put it around her and sat down in a chair.

Things had not turned out as she had imagined they would. There had been no cosy nights sitting before the fire in the drawing room, Thomas Mallen on one side of the hearth, herself on the other, she doing her embroidery, he reading; or she had seen them talking; or again laughing down on the children playing on the hearth rug before the fire.

The hour that held the picture would always be the hour between six and seven o'clock in the evening. It was an hour that in most cases was lost in those preceding it and those following it, an hour before dinner or supper according to the household; or yet again the hour after the main meal of the day as in some poorer establishments; the hour before children retired, the hour when the day was not yet ended, and the night not yet begun.

But she had never visualized herself sitting huddled in a bed cover in a cold room during any part of that hour. Yet that is what had happened night after night. However, she made use of this time to collect her thoughts, trying to see the outcome of this terrible business. One outcome that didn't please her at all was the possibility that Master Dick might be found guiltless at his trial, for this would mean that he would take up his abode here permanently, until such time when he should perhaps find something better. She had asked herself if she could put up with such a situation, for Master Dick's manner to her was most uncivil. But she never answered this question because she knew that as long as Thomas Mallen needed her she would stay, and she had the firm conviction inside herself that she was the one person he would need most from now on.

Life could be so pleasant here, so happy, so homely. The children would thrive better here than they had at the Hall. They had lived as much in the open air these past weeks as they had done indoors and it hadn't troubled them, much the reverse. And the food, as Constance had so recently complained, was very plain, which in a way was all to the good of one's health. It had already shown to good effect on the master, for he had laughingly said his breeches were slack. Also he walked without coughing so much. But no doubt this had been aided by his drinking less wine.

It was strange, she thought, how wine was considered a natural necessity in the lives of some people. The master had had two visitors over the past weeks who had brought him a case of wine; one was the young Mr Ferrier, the other was Mr Cardbridge. The Cardbridges came from Hexham. They weren't monied people, more poor upper class, she would say, and Mr Cardbridge was merely an acquaintance of the master, but she knew that his visit had given the master pleasure solely because he had brought with him a case of wine. In her estimation the money that the wine had cost would have been much more acceptable; but that, of course, was out of the question. The master would have taken a small gift of money as an insult, but the equivalent in wine he had accepted with outstretched hands.

The question of values, she considered, would make a very interesting topic of conversation one of these nights when she conversed with him; if she were able to converse with him, for this would only come about if Master Dick got his deserts, and she prayed he would. . . .

After supper Thomas went to bed with a glass of hot rum and sugar. He had courteously excused himself to her, saying his head was aching, but she knew that it wasn't his head that was troubling him but his temper. During supper his face had retained a purple hue. He had not spoken to her, nor had Master Dick, but then Master Dick never addressed himself to her at the table, or anywhere else unless it was to give an order.

She was relieved when Master Dick too retired early to bed. While Mary washed the dishes and tidied the kitchen, she herself put the dining room to rights and laid the breakfast for the following morning. She also put the covers straight in the sitting room, adjusted the rugs and damped down the fire.

She was still in the sitting room when Mary opened the door and said, 'I'm away up then, Miss Brigmore.'

'Very well, Mary. Good night.'

'Good night, Miss Brigmore.'

As Mary went to close the door she stopped and added, 'Is it me or is it getting colder?'

'I think it's getting colder, Mary.'

'You know I had the feeling the night I could smell snow.'

'I shouldn't be surprised, Mary.'

'Nor me. I remember me mam tellin' me that one Easter they were snowed up right to the window sill; they didn't roll any of their paste eggs down the hill that year.'

Anna smiled slightly before she said, 'Put another blanket on.'

'I will. Yes, I will, miss. I was froze last night. Will I put one out for you an' all?'

'Yes, yes, you could do, thank you. Good night.'

'Good night, miss.'

When Mary had closed the door Anna looked down at the fire. The top of it was black where she had covered it with the slack coal, but in between the bars it still showed red. Slowly she lowered herself down on to the rug and, her feet half tucked under her, she sat staring at the glow. Mary had said would she put another blanket on her bed. Another blanket wouldn't warm her; once you had been warmed by a man there was no substitute.

This was a cold house. It was still an old maid's house. Strangely, up till a few weeks ago this title could have been applied to herself but she no longer considered she qualified for it. Given a chance she could make this house warm, happy and warm. She could act as a salve to Thomas Mallen's wounds. She could fill his latter years with contentment. If never given a child herself, and oh, how she longed for a child of her own, she could find satisfaction playing mother to the children and turning them into young ladies; and who knew, some friend might present them at Court, as Miss Bessie had been, and they would make good matches. Yet under the present circumstances it was all too much like a fairy tale, something from Mr Hans Christian Andersen or the Grimm Brothers.

She leant sideways and supported herself on her elbow and drooped her head on to her hand. Still staring at the red bars she felt her body relaxing. She knew that she was in a most un-Miss Brigmore pose; she hadn't sat on a rug like this since she was a very young girl, because since she was a very young girl she hadn't known what it was to have a fire in her room – part of a governess's training was austerity and fresh air.

When her elbow became cramped she put her forearm on the floor and laid her head on it. What did it matter? Everyone in the house was asleep. If she wasn't careful she'd fall asleep here herself, it was so warm, so comfortable, even although the floor was hard. Should she lie on the couch? She could pull it up to the fire and sleep here all night, no one would know; and she was usually up as early as Mary in the mornings.

She didn't know how long she had been asleep, but being a light sleeper the opening of the door had roused her. She lay still, blinking towards the faint glow between the bars which told her that her dozing hadn't been a matter of minutes but an hour or more.

She felt the pressure of the footsteps on the carpet rather than heard their tread. The person who had entered the room was either the master or Master Dick. Her mind told her that if she were discovered she must pretend to be asleep, it would be most embarrassing to explain her position to either of them; especially as she realized she was lying flat on her back.

When a light spread over the ceiling her eyes opened wide; then turning her head to the side, she saw a pair of booted feet walking on the other side of the couch towards the davenport in the corner of the room near the window. She did not hear the lid of the davenport being lifted, but she did hear the slight squeak of a drawer being opened and something scraping against the wood. The feet now came down the room again; they didn't pause, but went straight to the door.

She counted up to sixty before she moved; then rising, she silently groped her way up the room to the davenport. And now she lifted the lid and opened the drawer. It was empty; the Louis miniatures and the snuff box were gone. She stood for a moment, a hand gripping her throat. If she were to call out instantly she could raise the master. Master Dick would have a horse and carriage waiting, but it would likely be some distance away and he would have to get to it. There was still time to stop him.

Of all the pieces she had brought from the house she knew that Thomas Mallen treasured most the three articles he had placed in that drawer. He hadn't locked them away, or hidden them underneath the floor boards again, there was no need; if the bailiffs had suspected anything was missing they would have searched the cottage long before this. The three pieces, she knew, would have brought another thousand pounds, enough to ease his way of living for a year or two until he became quite used to the change; enough to get him a case of wine now and again, a few choice cigars and some delicacies for high days and holidays. She had seen those three pieces as an insurance against his despair.

But she did not shout and raise the house; instead, she groped her way back to the couch and, sitting on it, she stared at the dim embers as she thought, this is the answer to my prayers. By the time Thomas gets up tomorrow morning – in this moment she thought of him quite naturally as Thomas – his son will be miles away, and by the time the authorities find he is missing he will no doubt be across some water, either to France or to Norway.

To get to France he would have to ride the length of the country southwards; on the other hand he would have no distance to go in order to catch a boat to Norway. And yet the sea-ways to Norway might still be too rough and dangerous. Anyway, whichever way he had chosen, and he must have had it well planned and had help, he was gone, and at last now there would come the time when she would sit on one side of this fire and Thomas on the other. And better still, she would be warm at nights.

If he had raved and shouted she knew that in time he would recover from the blow, but on the discovery that his son had gone, and that the miniatures and snuff box had gone with him, he did not even raise his voice.

He had been cheery at breakfast. 'Good Friday, Anna,' he said, 'And a sprinkling of snow.' He always addressed her as Anna when they were alone together. 'I remember one year when they had to dig a pathway up the drive on an Easter Monday for the carriages.'

'Really!' she said, as she wondered if it was the same time as Mary's mother had been snowed up to the window sill.

'You look tired,' he said.

'I am not at all,' she replied.

'You are,' he said; 'it's all too much, teaching, housekeeping and playing housemaid, butler and nursemaid to a doddery old man.'

When she did not deny any of this jocular remark, and in particular did not contradict his last statement, he stopped eating and asked quietly, 'What is the matter? Something is wrong with you. It's odd, but I'm more aware of your feelings than of anyone else's whom I can remember. Sit down and stop fidgeting,' he commanded her now.

She now sat down opposite to him at the table, and her hands folded in her lap, her back very straight, she looked at him as she said, 'Master Dick has gone.'

He did not say 'What!' He made no comment at all. All he did was sit back in his chair, jerk his chin upwards, and wipe the grease from it with a napkin.

After he had placed the napkin on the table he asked quietly, 'When?'

'Last night.'

'Why . . . why didn't you let me know?'

'Because –' now her lids veiled her eyes for a moment and she directed her gaze towards the table as she replied, 'You couldn't have stopped him; he must have had a horse or carriage waiting.'

'What time was this?'

'I . . . I don't know, not rightly. I . . . I had been asleep, I was awakened. I heard a movement on the stairs. I thought it was Mary going down because of something connected with the children. Then I saw him leave stealthily. He had a valise with him.'

How easily one lied, but she could not admit to the fact that she had seen his son stealing from him and had done nothing about it. He might have understood the reason for her silence because he was very much a man of the world, and of the flesh; but at the same time he might have considered the price he was being called upon to pay for their companionship together as much too costly.

At least this is what she thought until, rising from the chair, he walked slowly out of the room. It was some seconds before she followed him into the sitting room. He was standing at the davenport. The drawer was open and he was staring down into it, and when he turned and looked at her she felt the urge to run to him and fling her arms about him. But all she did was to walk sedately up to him and say, 'I'm sorry. So very sorry.'

'I too am sorry, very sorry.'

He suddenly sat down on a chair near the window and she knew a moment of anguish as she thought he was going to weep; his head was bowed, his lips were trembling. She watched him pass a hand over his face, drawing the loose skin downwards, then nip the jowl below his left cheek until the surrounding skin was drained of its blood.

It was a full minute before he looked up at her, and then his voice had a croaking, throaty sound as he said, 'I'm sorry for many things at this moment but mostly for the loss of the miniatures. I had the idea that one day, in the near future, I would hand them to you as a token of my thanks for all you have done for me and mine during this very trying time. The snuff box I intended to keep for myself, merely as a matter of pride. But now, well now –' He spread his hands outwards and in this moment he looked old, helpless and beaten.

He had meant her to have the miniatures! Really, really. The kindness of him, the thoughtfulness of him! He was a self-indulgent man, she knew this only too well; he was flamboyant, bombastic, and few people had a good word for him. Even his friends had proved to be his worst critics in this time of trial, yet there was another side to him. This she had sensed right from their first meeting. A few others knew of this side too. Dunn, she suspected, had been one of them, and Brown, his valet. Yet she wasn't sure about Brown. Brown should have stayed with him, put up with the inconveniences; he could have slept on a makeshift bed in the loft. She'd had it in her mind to contrive something like this when he had informed her that he had a new position. She had been vexed and disappointed with him, but her common sense had told her it would be one less to feed – and anyway, how would he have been paid? Her mind was galloping about irrelevant items. She felt upset, so upset.

'Don't cry, don't cry.' He took her hand and gently drew her towards his side.

After a time he said, 'Another scandal to be faced. They won't believe that I was ignorant of this, will they?'

She shook her head.

'. . . Was . . . was there anything in his room, a letter?'

'No; I . . . I searched.'

He now released her hand and running his fingers through his grey hair he muttered thickly, 'God Almighty!' It did not, as usual, sound like blasphemy but more like a prayer. Then looking up at her he asked, 'How am I going to get through these coming weeks?'

For answer she moved closer to him and, holding his head in her hands, she brought it to her breast and pressed it there, and she said, 'You'll come through them, and then you'll forget them. I'll . . . I'll see to it that you forget them.'


# Chapter Eight

It was a Wednesday, June the eighteenth, the day on which the Battle of Waterloo had been fought thirty-six years earlier. Constance had got the date wrong in her exercise that morning and Miss Brigmore had chastised her firmly. But then Constance thought she understood the reason for Miss Brigmore's harshness; she was always short-tempered when Uncle was out of sorts, and he had been out of sorts for some days now. That was the term Mary used. Miss Brigmore's term was lackadaisical. So, between out of sorts and lackadaisical, Constance reasoned it meant that Uncle Thomas couldn't be bothered to take his daily walk any longer. Uncle Thomas sat in the study for hours by himself, and now even his glass of wine at dinner didn't cheer him up. Of course, she supposed, one glass of wine wasn't very much for a man like Uncle Thomas because his big stomach was made to hold so much more.

The wine from the house was finished long ago, and when Mary and Miss Brigmore went into the town for the shopping they only brought one bottle back with them. She had asked Mary why they didn't bring Uncle Thomas more wine and Mary said it was because they couldn't carry any more. Constance knew this was not the right answer, the right answer was they didn't want to spend money on the wine. And this seemed rather mean, especially as she and Barbara had two hundred pounds every year to spend. She had put this to Barbara and to her surprise Barbara had snapped at her, saying, 'Don't be so silly, two hundred pounds is nothing to keep a household on. We're very poor, very, very poor. We are lucky we eat as we do. If it wasn't for Miss Brigmore's management we wouldn't fare so well.'

Constance accepted the rebuff. She supposed she was stupid. She supposed the reason for her stupidity was because she was three years younger than Barbara. When she was Barbara's age she supposed she'd be very wise, but already she was finding that as one grew older one became more puzzled by people. She was puzzled by Barbara's attitude to Miss Brigmore, for sometimes Barbara's manner towards Miss Brigmore wasn't courteous, yet she always spoke well of her behind her back. And then there was that odd time when she found Barbara crying and Miss Brigmore kneeling on the floor in front of her holding her hands and talking rapidly. Since then she had noticed that Barbara had defended Miss Brigmore on a number of occasions, as about the wine.

She was walking by Barbara's side now along the road towards the old house, as she thought of the Hall. Miss Brigmore was walking behind her with Mary. They were all carrying baskets. She turned impulsively and asked, 'May we run, Miss Brigmore?' and Miss Brigmore said, 'Yes, you may. But don't go out of sight for there might be a carriage on the road. If you should meet one on a corner, jump straight into the ditch.'

Before Miss Brigmore had finished speaking Constance had grabbed Barbara's hand and they were running along the road until, hot and panting, they stopped within sight of the iron gates of the Hall.

The Hall still remained unsold. No one as yet had come forward with a suitable offer. The Bank had kept on a skeleton staff to see the crops on the farms and the fruit and vegetables in the Hall gardens and greenhouse.

Twice a week, for some time now, Miss Brigmore had taken her party through the gardens and there, Grayson, who had been head gardener, filled their baskets with vegetables and fruit in season. Over the past two weeks she and Mary, between them, had made over forty pounds of strawberry preserve. There was an ample supply of spring onions and new carrots in the cottage stable and they had a barrel ready in the washhouse in which to salt the beans.

As Miss Brigmore remarked to Mary, Grayson was being very co-operative, and she calculated that by the time the potatoes were up they'd have enought fruit and vegetables stored to last them the entire winter, by which time they'd have their own plot of land under cultivation. This was if she could induce some boy from the village to till the ground. In the long nights ahead a boy could do three hours of an evening and earn threepence, and there was many a one would be glad of it. . . . But the village was three miles away.

There was no need to go near the house. When they entered the gates, they could turn to the right and cut through the shrubbery, along the cypress drive, skirt the lake and the rose walk and so come to the domestic gardens; but the children always wanted to see the house. It was strange, she thought, that they saw more of the lower rooms now than they had ever done when they lived in the house. Their favourite game was to run along the terrace peering through one window after another, and today was no exception.

She followed them at some distance, having left Mary sitting on the house steps. Mary was having trouble with her right leg, her veins were enlarged and very painful. Barbara called to her now, saying, 'Look, Miss Brigmore, there's more soot in the dining room, it's spilled over on to the floor boards.'

'Yes, indeed there is, Barbara.' She stood looking over the child's head, her face close to the glass. 'The climbing boys didn't do their work thoroughly there; all the chimneys were cleaned at the beginning of the year following the big Christmas fires; of course it could be the damp. There must be big pockets of soot in the bends which the boys couldn't get at, and these have come away with the damp. Some boys are not so particular as others.' She gave this information as if it were a lesson, and it was a lesson; everything she said to them, except at very rare moments, was in the form of a lesson.

'Let's go round to the stables!' Constance was running to the end of the terrace. She had reached the corner when she stopped and exclaimed loudly, 'Oh!' then she turned her head in the direction of Barbara and Miss Brigmore, while at the same time thrusting her arm out and pointing her finger.

Barbara reached her first, but she did not make any exclamation, she just stared in the direction that Constance was pointing. Nor did Miss Brigmore make any exclamation when she reached the corner and looked at the boy standing not three yards from them.

The boy seemed vaguely familiar yet she knew she hadn't seen him before, at least not closely. Then, her gaze moving from his dark black-lashed eyes to his tousled black hair, she saw the disordered fair streak, and then she recognized him. This was the boy who came over the hills and stood on the rock to view the house. She had caught a glimpse of him once when out walking, a matter of two years ago. He had looked very small then but now he looked tall, over five feet she would say.

'Who are you, boy?'

The boy did not answer but looked at the little girl.

'Are you from the farm?'

Miss Brigmore shook Constance gently by the shoulder saying, 'Be quiet.' Then, looking at the boy she said, 'You know you are on private ground.'

'Whose?' The voice was thick, the word was thick with the Northumbrian burr, and had a demand about it; whatever home he was from, he wasn't, Miss Brigmore decided, in servitude there. She would have said by the tilt of his head and the look in his eyes that he was of an arrogant nature, as arrogant as a Mallen, or as the Mallens had once been. She gave to her own tone a like arrogance as she answered, 'This estate is the property of Mr Thomas Mallen.'

'Until it's sold . . . You are the gov'ness, aren't you?'

'Yes, I am the governess.'

'And your name is Brigmore. You see, I know.'

'I hope your knowledge affords you some comfort.'

She saw that he was slightly nonplussed by her answer and she took advantage of it, saying, 'Now tell me what you're doing here?'

'Walking round . . . lookin' . . . It's a mess isn't it? It'll soon go to rack an' ruin; all ill-gotten gains return to rack an' ruin.'    '

'You are a very rude boy. This house was not ill-gotten, it was Uncle Thomas's. . . .'

'Barbara.' Miss Brigmore now put her hand on Barbara's arm and patted it three times, not in addition to the reprimand that her tone might have implied but rather as an indication that she was agreeing with her statement.

The boy was staring at Barbara now and she at him, and after a moment he said, 'You live in the cottage at the foot of the tor, and he lives there an' all now . . . Mallen.'

'Mr Mallen, boy.'

The eyes, like black marbles, flashed towards her and the tone again was aggressive as he said, 'There's some must mister him but not me.'

'You really are very rude.' Constance's face had slid into a smile as she endorsed Barbara's words, and when the boy's attention came on her again she asked playfully, 'How old are you?'

'Thirteen.'

'Oh, you are very old. I'm only seven and Barbara –' she nodded now towards her sister '– she's ten. What do you do, do you work?'

Miss Brigmore was for sternly checking Constance but Constance had asked a question, the answer to which would likely give her the boy's background, and so she remained silent while the boy, looking down at Constance, said, 'Aye, of course I work. All men should work; if you want to eat you should work.'

'What do you work at?'

'I farm; me da has a farm.'

'Oh.'

'And it's a fine farm, better'n any on here.' He flung his arms sidewards and the gesture took in the whole estate.

'Come along.' Miss Brigmore now ushered the girls forward and, looking over her shoulder at the boy, said, 'And you get about your business and don't let me catch you here again.'

'I'll come when I think fit.'

Her back stiffened but she did not turn round.

'What a strange boy. He was very rude but . . . but he was nice, wasn't he?'

Barbara turned her head quickly in Constance's direction, saying, 'Don't be silly; how can you be rude and nice at the same time? He was just rude, very uncouth, wasn't he, Miss Brigmore?'

Miss Brigmore didn't look at either of the girls as she replied to the first part of the question. 'Yes, he was very rude. But now let us forget about him and get to the gardens.'

It was an hour later when the children, carrying baskets of strawberries, and Miss Brigmore and Mary Peel the heavier vegetables, were making their way to the lodge gates that they heard the voice calling, 'Matthew! Matthew!'

'It's that boy again.' Constance's eyes were wide, her face bright with expectation, and Mary Peel said, 'And another along of him by the sound of it. He didn't go when you told him then.' She cast a glance towards Miss Brigmore, then added, 'He wants his face skelped; afore you know it he'll have the place cleared. I've heard of him afore, as ready with his fists as he is with his tongue, I hear. Thinks he's as good as the next. Huh!'

They walked on until they came onto the drive, and there a short distance along it, stood the boy, his two hands to his mouth, calling again 'Matthew! You, Matthew!'

They all turned as one now, slightly startled by the sound of running feet approaching along the path they had just left, and the next minute there came towards them another boy. His hair was very fair, his face pale; he was shorter and younger than the boy on the drive who, ignoring the four of them completely, addressed him by demanding, 'Where d'you think you've been? Didn't you hear me callin'? By lad! you'll do that once too often, you will.'

The fair-haired boy too, ignoring the presence of the others and the fact that he was trespassing, answered as if they were alone together. 'I was sittin' by the river,' he said. 'It's lovely down there, man; you should have come. There was a tree hangin' over and I could see the fish in the shade. . . .'

'Shut up!' The dark boy now turned to the group who were staring at him, and by way of explanation said, 'This is me brother . . . I mean me . . .'

Miss Brigmore interrupted him, saying, 'I told you some time ago to leave the grounds, didn't I?'

'Aye, you did, an' I gave you your answer, didn't I?'

Extraordinary boy, really extraordinary. Miss Brigmore was lost for words. There was something in him that – she wouldn't say frightened her, rather annoyed her. The next minute she started as if she had been stung by the younger boy addressing the girls in the most casual and undeferential manner. 'Hello,' he said; 'it's lovely here, isn't it?'

Both Barbara and Constance had their mouths open to reply when she shut them with, 'Come along immediately.'

As they moved away the fair boy ran before them and tugged at the iron gate, but he could open it only sufficiently for them to pass through in single file.

'Thank you.' The words coming from Miss Brigmore were a dismissal, and the boy stood still until he was pushed forward by his brother. Then they followed within a few yards of the party until the most surprising thing happened. The dark boy was suddenly at Miss Brigmore's side and, grabbing her basket, said, 'Here, let's take it.' And she let him take it while staring at him the while.

'Matthew, take t'other.' He was nodding towards Mary Peel now. Mary smiled at the fair boy as he took the basket from her, and said, 'Ta. Thanks, lad, thanks.'

Miss Brigmore, now turning to Constance and putting out her hand, said, 'Let me have yours, Constance; it's too heavy for you.' Whereupon she was checked by the voice coming at her roughly now, stating, 'She's big enough to carry it hersel'. Let her be.'

'You are a funny boy.' Constance had her head back, her mouth wide with laughter, and Miss Brigmore was too perturbed at this moment to check her, even when she went on, 'Would you like a strawberry? You can, we have plenty.'

When she held out the basket towards him he shook his head, saying roughly, 'We grow bigger'n that, and them's been left wet, they'll mould if you cook 'em no matter how much sugar you put with 'em.'

Miss Brigmore was indeed nonplussed. What were things coming to? The boy had no sense of place or class. She was all for fraternizing within limits, the boundaries of which were educational, and this boy, although he undoubt-

edly had good stock in him as his white quiff signified, still remained a
rough farm boy, and the quicker he was made aware of his position the
better. So now she turned her head and said sharply, 'We do not wish to
discuss the merits or demerits of strawberries, so if you will kindly give me
my basket you can get on your way.'

The boy stared at her, his black eyes looking deep into hers; then he
almost caused her to choke when he said, 'We are all goin' the same road,
so get along; the lasses don't mind.'

The girls were staring at her, Mary Peel was staring at her; only by a
struggle could she take the basket from him, and then she doubted if she
would gain anything but ridicule by such an effort. Her chin high, she said,
'Are you aware that these young ladies are Mr Mallen's nieces?'

'Aye, I know that; who doesn't?'

Really! Really! What could one say to such a person. It was evident that
he took pride in his bastardy and because of it considered himself an equal
of everyone. It was a good thing, she thought wryly, that all the master's
dubious offspring weren't of like character and determination or else the
Hall would have been invaded before now. And she thought too it was
strange that the boy, being as he was, should have kept his distance all these
years, viewing the house only from the rock. Not until the house and its
master had fallen had he put in an appearance, and then to gloat apparently.
Well, there was one thing she must see to, and right away, he must on no
account come in contact with his . . . with Thomas, for his manner would
undoubtedly enrage him to the extent of giving him palpitations; and so
when they rounded the next corner she would be most firm and would
relieve him and his brother of the baskets and take the path across the fells
to the cottage. It would be much longer this way but it would be a means
of parting company with this troublesome boy.

But Miss Brigmore's plan was shattered and her mind set in a turmoil
when, rounding the bend, she saw coming towards them none other than
Thomas himself.

It was to her Thomas spoke when still some distance away, saying 'I
needed to stretch my legs, the house is as lonely as a lighthouse when you
are gone. Well now, what have we here?' He had stopped before them, but
was now looking past them to the two boys, and as Miss Brigmore watched
him she saw his lower jaw slowly drop. The boy was staring back at him,
his dark eyes half shaded by his lids, which gave a deeper concentration to
his gaze.

She felt herself gabbling, 'We . . . we met these children on the road; they
were kind enough to help us with the baskets. I'll, I'll take them now. . . .'
She thrust her hand out but it did not reach the boy, for Thomas's voice
checked it, saying, 'It's all right, it's all right.' He gently flapped his hand
in her direction but didn't take his eyes from the boy's face. Then, addressing
him quietly, he said, 'You've come down off your rock at last then?'

The boy made no answer, but his eyes, holding an indefinable look,
continued to pierce the heavy jowled countenance before him.

'What is your name?'

Still the boy made no answer until the younger one nudged him with his
elbow while saying to Thomas, 'They call him Donald, and I'm . . .'

'I'm big enough to speak for mesel'.' The younger boy was thrust angrily
aside, and he would have toppled had not the hand that thrust him grabbed

at him and brought him up straight again. The boy kept tight hold of the younger one now while he spoke from deep in his throat with a man's voice, 'I'm known as Donald Radlet, I'm from Wolfbur Farm an' this –' he jerked the arm in his hand '– is me brother . . . half-brother, Matthew.' There was a pause before he ended, 'An' you are Thomas Mallen.'

There was a suspicion of a smile around Thomas's lips as he answered, 'True, boy, true, I am Thomas Mallen. But tell me, why have you taken this long to introduce yourself?'

''Cos I do things in me own time.'

Thomas now stared at the lad long and hard, and his eyes had a steely glint to them. Then, as if considering the matter, he said, 'Yes, I suppose you would. I suppose you would.' Again he was silent, until on a somewhat lighter note he added, 'Well, don't let us stand here talking like hill farmers meeting in the market, let us go. . . .'

'Don't say nowt against hill farmers, they're the best uns. We're hill farmers.'

Thomas's head jerked to the side, his jaws were tight. Six months earlier he would have taken his hand and skelped the mouth that dared to speak to him in that tone, but now, after a pause, he adroitly pressed the gaping children and Miss Brigmore and Mary Peel before him, and he walked in front of the two boys for quite some way before he said, 'You've got to be a good farmer to make a hill farm pay.'

'We are good farmers.'

'I'm glad to hear it.'

'Our cattle are good an' all.'

'You have cattle on a hill farm?'

'Of course we have cattle. Anyway some; we have three flat meadows. We bought two of your stock a while gone an' they were poor things; your byre man should've been shot. Their udders were sick, full of garget; the shorthorn was half dry, only two teats workin'; an' if t'other ever gets in calf she'll be lucky. Doubt if she'll weather a service; the look of the bull'll scare her. We were done. . . .'

'I'm surprised, and you so knowledgeable. You must have got the rakings, and very cheap at that. . . .'

Miss Brigmore did not hear the boy's answer; she was hurrying the girls forward now. Such talk. Teats and calving, and bulls. And she failed to understand Thomas's attitude towards the boy. He had shown no sign of palpitation at the unexpected meeting. The boy's aggressiveness seemed almost to amuse him; could it be possible he was seeing him as his son, because when all was said and done that's what he was, his son. She cast a quick backward glance. Thomas was now walking alongside the boys; he seemed amused, and more alert than she had seen him for weeks. A thought entering her mind, she asked herself would she object to anything that would give him an interest in life? She was fully aware that she herself could only fill his needs in one way; or perhaps two; she saw to his comfort during the day as well as at night. But a man had to have something else, particularly a man of Thomas Mallen's stamp. Would this boy supply it? She again glanced over her shoulder, at the same time pushing the girls further forward out of earshot. Catching her glance, Thomas made a motion with his head towards her and it was as if he were confirming her thoughts.

Thomas had guessed what his Miss Brigmore, as he playfully called her in the night, was thinking and he was wondering at this very moment if this young, raw, vibrant, brusque individual who bore his mark on his head might not be the answer to a prayer that he hadn't known he was praying, for he was certainly no praying man.

There had, during these past weeks, been a deep void in him, a loneliness, that even Anna hadn't been able to fill. It wasn't, he knew, so much the loss of his home and worldly goods and a way of living, or even the loss of his son; it was the way in which he had lost him, that had left on him the taint of cowardice and shame. He doubted he would ever see Dick again. And this thought brought him no great sorrow but what did sear him, even now, was the knowledge that he had no real friends.

When the hunt for Dick was at its height no one had come near him, at least no friend, but he had had enough company of officials. It wasn't until the newspapers announced that Dick Mallen must by now be well away over the sea – in what direction wasn't stated, for it wasn't known – that Pat Ferrier had paid him a call and told him that Dick was in France. A mutual friend had taken him there on his private boat. But Pat Ferrier had brought no letter from Dick, no word of regret. Nothing. The irony of it struck Thomas when he thought that even his son could produce two good friends at least, while he himself went barren of all but Anna.

He glanced towards the boy walking by his side. There was a resemblance between them, a definite resemblance, and not only in the streak. He could see himself again as a young boy; perhaps his hair had not been so black, or his eyes so dark, and definitely his manner had not been so arrogant, although his upbringing could have warranted it, for the proverbial silver spoon had certainly been in his mouth all his days. Yet here was this lad, brought up on a farm, and whether good, bad or indifferent, it was still a farm, assuming the manner one might expect from someone of breeding and authority.

When the boy turned his dark, fierce gaze on him he was put at a disadvantage, until, aiming to make casual conversation, he said, 'How large is your father's farm?'

'A hundred and twenty acres, and he's not me father. I call him Da; but he's his father.' He jerked his thumb towards the smaller boy while his gaze rested on Thomas's face. And neither of them spoke during the further twenty steps they took, but the boy's eyes were saying plainly, 'Let's have no more fiddle-faddle, you know the position as well as I do.'

It was Thomas who broke the trance-like stare calling in a voice that was much too loud, 'What are we having for supper, Miss Brigmore?'

Miss Brigmore stopped abruptly, as did the girls and Mary, and stared at him. Then she said, 'Cold soup, ham and salad, and a strawberry pastry.'

'Have we enough for two extra?'

She could not prevent her eyes from widening and her mouth opening and shutting once more before looking towards the boys and saying, 'They will want to get home; they have a long way to walk over the hills. Their people may be wondering.'

'They won't be wonderin'.' The boy's voice had that definite, hard, determined ring to it that seemed to be the very essence of his nature. 'Da allows us half-day a week for roamin'; we can go back anytime so long's we're up at five.'

Miss Brigmore was silenced. She seemed to have to drag her eyes from the boy, and when she looked at Thomas he smiled broadly at her and said, 'Well there, you've got your answer. We have two guests for supper.'

She turned, and they all walked on again. She should be happy that he had found a new interest but that boy disturbed her. He was too strong, too dominant for his age. She had never encountered anyone like him before. Now if it had been the younger one, she could have taken to him, for he was much more likeable, gentler, better mannered. But then he wasn't Thomas Mallen's son.

# Chapter One

## Donald Radlet of Wolfbur Farm

Donald Radlet was born in the winter of 1838 when his eighteen-year-old mother, Jane Radlet, had been married about five months.

Jane Radlet had been born on the West Farm of High Banks Hall. Her father was the byre-man, her mother the dairymaid. From the time Jane was born her mother hardly left her bed until the day she died; the midwife's dirty hands had set up an internal trouble, for which there appeared no cure. Constant evacuation wore her body away, yet she lived on for twenty years.

Jane was the only child of the marriage and she could remember back to when she was three years old, when she first visited the cesspool on her own to empty the bucket. She was about four when she began to soss the dirty sheets, and this she did every day of her life, until she was eighteen years and two months old when she left the farm and went over the hills with Michael Radlet.

On that day Michael Radlet took her past his farm without even stopping to look in, and to the church near Nine Banks, and there he married her, with the gravedigger and the parson's wife for witnesses. She cried all the way back to the farm; she cried on her wedding night because she lay alone; and she had cried at intervals during the following days, because she knew that for the first time in her life she was going to be happy.

Michael Radlet was eighteen years her senior and he was known as a good, God-fearing, hard-working man, and a man who had rightly prospered through his hard work, for his farm, although small, was well stocked, and his land, although on hilly ground, was utilized to the last foot by his cattle. He worked daylight and moonlight for six days a week, but on the Sabbath he did only what was necessary for the animals; the rest of the day he read his Bible, as his father had taught him to do, and he allowed his one helper the day off to visit his people.

He first noticed Jane Collins when he took his only two Ayrshires over the hills to be serviced by the High Banks bull. He could have taken them to Pearson's Farm, which was only three miles away, but Pearson's bull was of poor stock. Jane had been barely sixteen then, and for the next year he pondered whether he should speak to her father in case she should be snapped up. Yet he doubted if her father would allow her to be snapped up because, he understood, she was the only support in his house, where she looked after his sick wife and cooked the meals and generally did the work of an adult woman, and had, so he had heard, done so since she was a child.

But he was quick to note that the long years of labour had not marred her beauty, for her face was round and smooth and her eyes gentle, and her hair a shining brown. Her body was good; her hips wide and her breasts promising high.

It was on the day following the Sunday when he had read and dwelt on the birth of Benjamin that he went over the hills to speak to her father, the words of the good book drifting through his mind: 'And they journeyed from Bethel; and there was but a little way to come to Ephrath: and Rachel travailed, and she had hard labour. And it came to pass, when she was in hard labour, that the midwife said unto her, Fear not; thou shalt have this son also.'

He wanted a son, badly he wanted a son. His first wife had been barren; that was God's will, but Jane Collins would not be barren. He had a feeling about Jane, a strong, urging feeling to hold her, to love her. Some of his love was threaded with pity for her plight, for it was evident she'd had a hard life.

John Collins was about his work in the cow-shed when he confronted him, and when he put the proposal to him he was surprised that the man should bow his head deeply on his chest. It caused him to ask, 'What is it? Is she already spoken?' And John Collins had turned his head away before nodding; then looking him straight in the face he said. 'You have come too late, she's been taken down.'

Taken down! He had not spoken the words aloud but they had yelled at him in his mind. He had come too late, she had been taken down. Well, it was as he thought, she could bear children. But he had imagined they would be his children, the children he needed, the son he needed. He experienced a hurt that went beyond anything he had felt before; even when his wife had died the sense of loss hadn't been so great as now.

His voice was hollow as he asked, 'She is to be married then?'

John Collins shook his head before he raised his eyes and said, 'No, no, she is not to be married.'

There was a silence between them, broken only by the jangle of the cows' chains and their splattering.

'You know the man?'

There was another silence before John Collins, looking into Michael Radlet's eyes, said, 'No.'

As they continued to stare at each other they both knew the answer was a lie, and John Collins knew that Michael Radlet knew it was a lie, and the denial told Michael Radlet immediately who the father of Jane's child was, and why this man couldn't speak the truth. There was only one man around these parts he would keep silent about, and that was his master, the whoring rake, Thomas Mallen. John Collins was handicapped. Should he protest to the Justices that his daughter had been raped, for raped she would have been by that sinning devil, then he would be out of a job with no roof over his head and a wife that needed a bed more than she needed anything else. And where would he get it for her but in the workhouse? He was sorry for the man, he was sorry for the girl; and he was sorry for himself also.

When he had crossed the hills back to his farm the loneliness of the vast spaces entered into him as never before. He had lived among the hills and the mountains all his life, as had his forbears for eight generations before him. Space was in his blood, the space of the fell lands, the space of the ever-rolling hills; the awe-inspiring space viewed from the peaks; the space of the sky reaching into infinity. He had always felt at home in space until that day, and on that day he had walked with his head down across the hills. . . .

It was six weeks later when he crossed the hills again, but with his head up now and his mind firm, one purpose in it: he would take Jane Collins in the condition she was. For five Sundays he had prayed and asked guidance of God and yesterday he had received his answer. The Good Book falling open in his lap, his eyes saw the words, 'For I was an hungered, and ye gave me meat: I was thirsty, and ye gave me drink: I was a stranger, and ye took me in: Naked and ye clothed me: I was sick and ye visited me: I was in prison, and ye came unto me.

'Then shall the righteous answer him, saying, Lord, when saw we thee an hungered, and fed thee? or thirsty, and gave thee drink? When saw we thee a stranger, and took thee in? or naked, and clothed thee?

'Or when saw we thee sick, or in prison, and came unto thee?

'And the King shall answer and say unto them, Verily I say unto you, Inasmuch as ye have done it unto one of the least of these my brethren, ye have done it unto me.'

He had wanted a sign, and he took it as a sign, and so the following day when he reached the West Farm he said to John Collins, 'I will marry her,' and the tears had run down the man's face and he said, 'She's a good girl.'

A week later, when Michael Radlet brought the girl over the hill and to the church, she hadn't looked at him until he put the ring on her finger, and it was from then she had begun to cry. . . .

Jane Radlet had been surrounded by old people all her life. The four men on Mallen's West Farm were old, their families grown up and scattered; her father was old. There were two young men on the East Farm, but they were both spoken for by maids in the house. It was on her journey to the East Farm that she had met the other old man, at least he had seemed old to her for he was in his forties, but he was different.

Her only break in the week was on Sunday afternoon when her father took over the household chores and she went to visit his cousin, who was wife to the shepherd on the East Farm. She did not care for her father's cousin but it was somewhere to go and someone to talk to. Sometimes on the road, too, she met people, who gave her a word. It was on the road she had met the man on horseback. He appeared a very hearty man and he had stopped and talked with her, and told her that she was pretty.

It was impossible for her to believe now that she hadn't recognized the man as the master of the Hall. Yet there was an excuse for her for she had never seen him on his visits to the farm. Their cottage stood alone and well back from the farm buildings, and such was its situation that she needn't go near the farm unless she wanted to take her father a message; yet even so she had told herself that anyone but a fool would have recognized the master because her father had talked of him, and her mother had talked of him. Big, dark, pot-bellied with high eating and drinking, but then he was no worse than the rest of the gentry and much better than some, being generous to his staff at harvest and Christmas.

Came the Sunday they had met, he had got down from his horse and walked with her through the wood, and there he had tied his horse to a tree and had laughingly pulled her down beside him on the sward. At first he just talked and made her laugh; at first she hadn't realized what was happening; when she did she had struggled, but he was a big man, and heavy. When it was over and she sat numbed and dazed with her back against the bole of a tree, he dropped a gold piece down the front of her bodice, and patted her cheek before he left her.

Weeks later, when her mother found enough strength to upbraid her, she had retorted with anger, 'Who was there to tell me? I've seen no one but you an' me da for years except for that hour once a week when I've talked with Cousin Nellie. And what does she talk about? Only the doings of her son in faraway America, and how to grow pot herbs and the like. Who was there to put me wise? Who? I had only me instinct to go by, and it didn't come to me aid, 'cos I judged him to be an old man.'

'Old!' her mother had said. 'And him only mid-forty. You're stupid, girl, men are bulls until they die, be they eighteen or eighty . . . Instinct!'

When her father had told her that she was to be saved from disgrace and that Michael Radlet was going to marry her, her only reaction had been, he's old an' all, besides which he was short and thick-set and with no looks to speak of. She had felt she was merely going from one servitude to another, until she finally reached his farm when he told her in simple words that he would not treat her as his wife until after her child was born. She had looked at him fully for the first time and seen that he was not really old, and moreover, that he was kind; and her crying had increased.

The strange thing about her crying was that she couldn't remember having cried at any time in her life before; and afterwards she realized that the constant flow of tears was a form of relief, relief from her years of servitude. Her whole life seemed to have been spent amid human excrement, washing it from linen, smelling it, emptying it. The smell had permeated the very food she ate. She had left her mother with no regret whatever. Her mother had cried at her going, not so much, she knew, at the loss of her as a daughter, but because now she would be at the mercy of an old crone from the village. She was sorry though to have left her father; she liked her father, for he was of a kindly nature.

So it was that after a few days at Wolfbur Farm she knew that she was going to be happy, that Michael Radlet was a good man and, the most surprising thing, he was going to teach her to read the Bible.

Donald Radlet came into the world protesting loudly, and Jane felt he had never stopped since. As his mother, she should have loved him, but she couldn't; he had been a separate being from the moment he left her womb. She would have said that the boy himself did not know what love was if it wasn't for the protective affection he showed for his half-brother.

He was two years old when Matthew was born, and instead of being jealous, as she thought he might become, of a new baby taking his place, he was, from the very beginning, protective towards the boy, who in colouring and character was the antithesis of himself.

Donald was nine years old when he discovered that Mike Radlet was not his father. It happened on a fair day in Hexham.

They had talked about the fair day for weeks. This day was the highlight of the year; it was the day on which the hirings took place, when farm labourer and maid were bonded into service, and there were such delights as the fair ground, inside which there was every kind of entertainment from the shuggy boats to the boxing booths. Last year they had seen a Chinese lady with stumps for feet, a child whose head was so big it had to be supported in a framework, and a fat woman with a beard down to her breasts, which you could pull – if you had the nerve, for she looked as if she would eat you whole.

As soon as they entered the town Michael let the boys go off on their own for he knew that Donald, although only nine, was to be trusted to look after both himself and Matthew as well.

The boys knew where to contact their parents. The horse and flat cart was stabled in the blacksmith's yard and their mother would be drinking tea with the blacksmith's wife, and while they were exchanging their news their husbands would be out and about in the cattle market and recalling the days of their youth together, for Michael Radlet and the blacksmith were cousins.

But it so happened that the two men and the two women were in the house around three o'clock that day when Matthew came flying in to them, the tears streaming down his face and his words incoherent.

When at last he had quietened down somewhat they understood from his gasping words that Donald had been fighting a boy in the fair ground, and another two boys had also set about him.

When Michael demanded to know why Donald was fighting, Matthew looked up at him through streaming eyes and said, "Cos of you, Da.'

'Me? Why me?' Michael frowned down on his son, and Matthew, after shaking his head from side to side, muttered, 'They said you weren't, they said you weren't his da; they said because of his white streak you weren't his da. But you are, aren't you, Da? You are his da, aren't you?'

Michael looked at Jane, and she bowed her head; the blacksmith and his wife bowed theirs also.

It was as Michael stormed towards the door that Donald entered, and as they all looked at him they voiced a long concerted 'Aw!' His lip was split, one eye was rapidly closing, there was blood running from a cut on the side of his temple. His clothes were torn and begrimed, and his hands, which he held palm outwards and close to his sides, gave evidence that he had been pulled over rough ash ground for the thin rivulets of blood were streaked with the cinder dust.

'Oh! boy. Oh! boy.' Jane put her hand to her face as she approached him, then said pityingly, 'Come, let me clean you up.'

He made no move either towards or away from her but stared at her fixedly, and for the first time she knew what it was to suffer his scorn and his condemnation. She had noticed before that when he was angry or deeply troubled, like the time Matthew took the fever and they thought he would die, there came into the bright blackness of his eyes a glow as if from an inner fire. You couldn't say it was a film of pink or red because his pupils still remained black, but there was this change in their gleaming that gave the impression of a light behind them, a red ominous light.

He looked past her at Michael, and he said, 'I want to go home.'

Without a word Michael went out and harnessed the horse to the cart, and five minutes later they set off. Donald, unrelieved of dirt or blood, did not, as was usual, mount the front seat and sit beside Michael; instead, he clambered up into the back of the cart. His feet stretched out before him, his palms still upturned resting on his thighs, his head not bowed but level, his gaze directed unseeing through the side rails of the cart; thus he sat, and didn't move except when the wheels going into a rut or jolting over a stone jerked his body, until they came to the farm.

There, Michael got down from the cart and went to the back of it and, looking at the boy, to whom he had been father in every way possible, said, 'Go and wash yourself and then we will talk. And you, Matthew –' he waved the younger boy towards his brother '– go with him and handle the pump.'

Slowly Donald let himself down onto the yard, and as slowly walked to the pump.

In the kitchen Michael, putting his hand on Jane's shoulder, said kindly, 'Now don't fret yourself, it had to come. Sooner or later we knew it had to come. Perhaps we've been at fault; we should've told him and not waited for some scallywag to throw it at him.'

'He hates me.'

'Don't talk nonsense, woman.'

'I'm not talkin' nonsense, Michael, I saw it in the look he gave me back there.'

'It's the shock; he'll get over that. You are his mother and he should be grateful for it.'

He smiled at her but she didn't smile back. In some strange way she knew that her days of happiness were past. Just as she had been aware of the time they were beginning for her in this house, now she knew that that time had ended as abruptly as it had begun. . . .

Michael led the way into the parlour, which in itself proved that this was a very exceptional occasion, for the parlour was used only on Sundays and Christmas Day. 'Sit down, boy,' he said.

For the first time the boy disobeyed an order given him by the man he had thought of as his father and, speaking through swollen lips, he said, 'You are not me father then?' He had never used the word father before; father and da meant the same thing, yet now he was, by his very tone, inferring a difference.

Michael swallowed deeply before answering, 'No, I am not your father in that I didn't beget you, but in every other way I am your father. I have brought you up an' I have cared for you. You are to me as me eldest son.'

'But I'm not your son! I'm nobody's son, I'm what they said I am, the fly-blow. The fly-blow of a man called Mallen. One of dozens they said; he's fathered half the county, they said.'

Michael didn't speak for a moment; then he was forced to say, 'I wouldn't know anything about that, an' people always make mountains out of molehills. There's only one thing I do know, an' I want you to know it too, your mother was not at fault; she was but a girl, an innocent, ignorant girl, when she was taken down.'

Ignoring completely the reference to his mother, Donald said now, 'Matthew, he's not me real brother.'

'He's your half-brother.'

'He's your real son; you're his father, not just his da.'

'They both mean the same thing, father an' da.'

'Not any more they don't. Not any more.'

It was as Michael stared at the boy, who was at that time almost as tall as himself, that there came into him a feeling of deep compassion, for he saw the lad was no longer a lad or a boy. True, he had never really been childish, always appearing older than his years, both in his actions and his talk, but now the very look of him had changed. He had the look of an adult man about him; it came over in the expression of his eyes. His eyes had always been his most startling feature. At odd times when some pleasant incident had softened them he had thought them beautiful, but he wondered if he would ever think them beautiful again. He said now, 'Nothing has changed; whether you think of me as your da, or your father, or whatever, I remain the same. Go on now and have your meal, an' be respectful to your mother. And hold your head up wherever you go, for no blame lies on you.'

Donald turned about and walked to the door, but before opening it he stopped and, looking back at Michael, he answered his last statement by saying, 'They called me a bastard.'

When, the following Sunday, Matthew came into the house, his head hanging, and stated, 'Our Donald's gone over the hills an' he wouldn't let me go with him,' Jane closed her eyes and muttered to herself, 'Oh my God!' And Michael laid down the Book and said, 'When was this? How long ago?'

'Just a while back. I thought he was going over to Whitfield Law but he changed his mind and went towards the Peel, and then wouldn't let me come on.'

Jane, bringing out her words between gasps, said, 'He must have started asking. What if he should go . . . I mean right . . . right to the Hall? Oh Michael, Michael, do something, stop him.'

Michael wasn't given to running. If you want to walk a long way you don't run, had always been his maxim, but on this day he ran, thinking as he did so that it had been one of his mistakes not to have brought the boy over these hills before. It was six years since he had been this way himself, for now that both Jane's parents were dead there was no need to take this road. Yet, he thought now that in denying this route to the boy when on his Sunday jaunts he must have eventually raised some suspicion in his mind.

He was blowing like a bellows before he had gone very far. He thought the boy, too, must have run for when he reached the peak and looked down into the next valley there was no sign of him.

Michael had been on the road over an hour when at last he saw him. He stopped and stared. The boy, about a quarter of a mile distant from him, was standing on the summit of the last hill. It was the one that towered over the foothills where they spread out into the valley in which was set High Banks Hall. In the winter and the spring when the trees of the estate were bare you could get a view of the entire Hall and the terraces and sunken gardens from that point, but for the rest of the year only a gable end and the windows of the upper floor were visible.

As if he knew he was being watched Donald had turned about and looked in his direction and then waited while Michael walked slowly towards him. When he came up with the boy he said loudly and sternly, 'You're not to go near that place, do you hear me? Anyway, you'd be thrown out on your backside an' made to look a fool.'

The boy stared at him. His face, still discoloured from the blows he had received in the fight, was tinged a deep red as he answered, 'I'm no fool.'

'I'm glad to hear it. Now come away back home.' . . .

From then on Donald went over the hills every Sunday, and on special holidays, the weather permitting, and no one could do anything about it.

But he went no further than the last hill until one day in 1851 when he heard that Thomas Mallen had gone bust and that Dick Mallen had nearly committed murder. That Sunday he walked along the road and stood outside the gates for the first time; but he did not venture inside until after the auction had taken place. Then he walked round the house peering in the windows, not like the children had done, more in the manner of someone returning to his rightful home after a long absence.

The rooms were almost as he had pictured them in his mind's eye over the years. They were big and high and had coloured ceilings. Some were panelled up to the ceiling, and even in those with only skirting boards the wood was moulded three feet high from the floor. He had run his hand over the great front door, then counted the iron studs; there were ten rows of eight.

He walked through the empty stables and saw fittings that he couldn't believe any man would waste on a place where a horse was stabled. The hooks were of ornamental brass, the harness-horse was covered with leather like doe-skin, and four of the stalls each had a silver plate bearing a horse's name.

When he stood back from the house and looked up at it the most strange sensation filled his breast. It began in some region hitherto unknown to him; he felt it rising upwards and upwards until it reached his throat, and there it stuck and grew to a great hard painful thing that was all set to choke him. Even when he was shaken by a violent fit of coughing it didn't entirely dissolve.

He had visited the house a number of times alone before the day on which he took Matthew with him, the day when he encountered Miss Brigmore and the girls, and later his father.

When they had returned home that night he had not stopped Matthew from pouring out the exciting news that they had been to supper with Mr Mallen.

This news had actually shocked Michael, and it had not only stunned Jane but increased her fear of this son of hers, while she asked herself what he expected to get out of it now, for Thomas Mallen, they said, was utterly destitute, living on the charity of his nieces.

That night, when Michael said to her, 'I suppose it's only natural that he should want to see his father' she shook her head violently and answered, 'Nothing he does is natural, and never has been.' . . .

From that time on Jane lived in fear of the years ahead. There was a dread on her that she couldn't explain. Yet as one season passed into another and the two boys grew from youth into young men and nothing untoward happened, she looked back and felt like many another woman, in saying to herself that she had been foolish in wasting her time worrying about someone over whom she knew she had no control, for she was fully aware that she meant less to her son than did the cattle in the byres. Indeed, she had watched him show affection for them, especially when a cow was in labour. He had lost sleep to make sure that a cow was delivered of her calf and that both should survive in good fettle; but for herself, she felt that if she were to drop down dead at his feet he would show very little concern, except to make sure that she was put away decently. This was one trait that was prominent in him, he was very concerned with doing the right thing, and this in turn warranted that he should be well put on in his dress. His taste in dress, she considered, was about that suitable to a farmer; but then she had gleaned one secret thought of his: he considered himself a cut above the ordinary run of farmer. Inside, she knew he was proud to be Thomas Mallen's son, while at the same time despising her for her part in it.

She also knew that he would never admit to this. His thoughts were locked deep within him. He never spoke his real thoughts, not even to Matthew, and if he cared for anyone it was Matthew. Not until the time came for him to act on any plan he had devised in his mind concerning the farm did he even speak of it to Michael. He rarely if ever informed her of what he was about to do.

So it was on this bright autumn Sunday morning in 1861 when the four of them were seated round the breakfast table in the kitchen, and only a second after Michael had finished the grace, saying, 'We thank you, Lord, for our food which has come to us through your charity, Amen,' that Donald said, 'I'm going straight over this morning.' They all looked at him, and each face registered reserved surprise, for they recognized by the tone of his voice and the fact that he'd altered his routine that he was about to impart something of importance.

'I'm going to ask Constance to marry me . . . it's time,' he said.

Now the reserve slipped from their faces and they gaped at him, in a mixture of amazement, disapproval and even horror. On any other occasion they would have been more wary, for they never showed their true feelings to him. This attitude, which had been born of a desire never to hurt him, had developed in varying degrees in the three of them. He had to be humoured as one might a sick person in order that he would not upset himself with bouts of temper or withdraw into a continued silence. There was a similarity in their attitudes towards him that was strange for they all viewed him in different ways. But now Michael blurted out, 'You can't do that, she's near blood to you.'

'She's not near blood to me.'

'She's Mallen's niece.'

'She's not. Her mother was his step-sister, there's no blood tie atween them at all.'

Still Michael's face was grim now. 'It doesn't seem right.'

'And why not?'

'Don't shout at me, boy. Don't shout at me.'

'I'm not shoutin'. And don't forget, I'm no boy.'

'You'll always be a boy to me.' Michael thrust his chair back and stumped – for his left leg was stiff with rheumatism – from the table into the sitting room where, as usual on a Sunday morning, he would read for half an hour from the Book before attending to his Sunday duties on the farm. And even on this morning he did not depart from his usual pattern.

Now Jane spoke. Quietly she asked, 'Does she know?'

'Know what?' He looked at her coldly.

'That . . .' She was about to say, 'That you want her,' but she changed it to, 'What to expect. I mean, have you given her any inkling?'

'Enough.'

She stared at him for a moment longer as she thought. That girl in this house with him for life, he'll suffocate her. Now she rose from the table and walked slowly across the stone-flagged kitchen and out through the low door that just took her height, and into the dairy. It was cool and restful in the dairy and she could ponder there, and she had much to ponder on this day, she knew.

Donald now looked at Matthew, waiting for him to speak, and as he waited his face took on a softness that slipped into a smile. After a time he asked quietly, 'Surprised?'

Matthew didn't answer, he couldn't as yet. Surprised? He was staggered; shocked, dismayed; yes, that was the word, dismayed, utterly dismayed. Dear, dear God, that this should happen, that it should be Constance he wanted. He had always thought it was Barbara, and he had the idea that Barbara thought along the same lines. Why, whenever they had been over there it wasn't to Constance he had talked but to Barbara, and when he had seen them together he had thought, they're much alike in some ways those two, given to silences. There were depths in both of them that were soundless, and their silences were heavy with brooding, secret brooding, lonely brooding. As his thoughts were apt to do, he had dwelt on their brooding because he knew that their brooding coloured their lives. He knew that each in his way was lonely and craved something. When the craving became intense it showed, in Donald's case at least, in bursts of temper.

It was as recently as last summer that Donald had shown this side of himself when, entering the cottage on their Sunday visit, they had found company there. There were two young men, one called Ferrier, scarcely more than a boy, and the other by the name of Will Headley about his own age, which was twenty then. It wasn't the first time he had encountered these two young men; at different times over the years they had met up. He understood them to be the grandsons of Thomas Mallen's old friends and so it was natural that they should visit him.

On this particular Sunday when they entered the sitting room they were engulfed in a burst of laughter. Constance was laughing gaily; but then Constance always laughed gaily, her beauty of face and figure was enhanced by a joyous soul which contrasted sharply with Barbara's looks and temperament. But on this day Barbara, too, was laughing unrestrainedly, and he thought that it was this that had annoyed Donald, for he scarcely spoke during the whole of their visit; in fact his presence put a damper on the gathering. They had hardly left the cottage on their return journey when he burst out, 'That old witch of a Brigmore is planning to marry them off.'

Matthew did not contradict the statement but it overwhelmed him with sickness. He'd be very sorry for Donald if Barbara did marry Will Headley; but rather that than it should be Constance. He did not take into account the Ferrier boy; he was much too young and, as he gathered from the conversation, his mind was on nothing but this Oxford place to which he was going in the autumn.

Matthew now shook his head slowly from side to side. He was shaking it at himself, at his blindness, at his lack of knowledge of this half-brother of his. He should have known that Donald never did anything the way other men did, for he wasn't like other men, he had a canker inside him that gnawed at him continuously. He had been born and brought up on this farm, but from that day when he was nine years old he had disowned it while at the same time attempting to run it, even of late be master of it.

But there was one thing sure, if he didn't belong here, then he certainly didn't belong over the hills in the house where his real father lived, for always when in the company of Thomas Mallen Donald appeared gauche and out of place, and this caused him to assume an air of condescension, as if it was only out of the goodness of his heart that he visited this old man. The butter, cheese and eggs he took over every week only emphasized this attitude. But Thomas Mallen showed plainly that he liked this son; and Donald's attitude seemed to amuse him. And the girls liked him; they, too, had been amused in those early years by his bombast; and when the bombast had, with time, turned into a cautious reticence they had tried to tease him out of it, at least Constance had.

There was only one person in that household who didn't like him and who showed it, and that was Miss Brigmore, and Donald, on his part, hated her. Years ago Matthew had felt he should hate her too because Donald did, but secretly he had liked her, and whenever he could he drew her into conversation because he learned from her. He knew that Miss Brigmore had things that he wanted, she had knowledge, knowledge to give him the power to talk about things that he understood in his mind but couldn't get off his tongue; things that came into his head when he looked down into water, or watched the afterglow, or when his thoughts deprived him of his much needed sleep and he crept quietly from the pallet bed and knelt at the attic window and raced with the moon across the wild sky – Miss Brigmore had once said it wasn't the moon that raced but the clouds, and he just couldn't take that in for a long time. It was she, he knew, who could have made these things more clear to him, could have brought his feelings glowing into words; but he did not talk with her much because it would have annoyed Donald, and he was, and had always been, secretly afraid of annoying Donald.

But oh dear, dear God! Matthew's thoughts jumped back to the present. Donald had just said he was going to ask Constance to marry him. Constance in this house every day. He wouldn't be able to bear it. He had loved Constance from the moment he saw her offering Donald a strawberry; he knew it had happened at that very moment. He also knew that it was a hopeless love, for he considered her as far above him as the princesses up there in the palace. So much did he consider her out of his reach that he had never even thought of her and marriage in the same breath; what he had thought was, I'll never marry anyone, never. And when he thought this he always added, anyway it wouldn't be fair, not with this cough. They hadn't said he had the consumption, but he'd got the cough all right, and as time went on he became more and more tired, so much so that often he thought that it would be a poor look-out for the farm if Donald weren't as strong as two horses. And Donald delighted in being strong. Give him his due, never had he balked at the extra work. Many a day, aye, many a week he had done the work for both of them, and he had been grateful to him. But now as he stared into the dark face, whose attraction was emphasized with a rare smile, he experienced a moment of intense hate. Then he began to cough, and the cough brought the sweat pouring out of him.

'Don't let me news choke you.' Donald came round the table and thumped him on the back. 'Here, take a spoonful of honey.' He reached out for the jar, but Matthew shook his head and thrust the jar away.

When he had regained his breath, Donald asked him, 'Well now, are you going to say something?' and Matthew, after a deep gulp in his throat, muttered, 'Have ... have you thought that she mightn't fit in here, in the house I mean?'

'The house? What's wrong with the house? It's as good as the one she's in now.'

'But . . . but it's different.'

'How do you mean, different? It's got as many rooms, counting the loft, an' the countryside around is bonnier.'

Matthew again shook his head. What could he say? Could he say, Yes, but it's an old house, and it's a cold bare house because it hasn't got in it the draperies and the knick-knacks, nor yet the furniture that's in the cottage? Yet, of its kind, he knew it was a substantial house, a house that many a farmer's daughter would be glad to be mistress of. But Constance was no farmer's daughter, and although she had been brought up in the cottage she had also been brought up in an atmosphere provided by Miss Brigmore, an atmosphere of refinement and learning, Constance was a lady. They were all ladies over there, in spite of their poverty. Then again, their poverty was relative. He understood that they had two hundred pounds a year between them, and that to him, and thousands like him, was far from poverty. He said now, 'I thought it was Barbara.'

'Barbara! Good God, no! Never Barbara. Barbara's all right, mind, she's got a sensible head on her shoulders, but she's as far removed from Constance as night from day; sometimes I wonder at them being sisters. No, never Barbara.' He walked down the length of the kitchen now and stood looking out of the window and into the yard. A line of ducks were waddling down the central drain on their way to the pond. His eyes ranged from the stables, over the grain store and the barn, to the side wall where the cow byres began, and next to them the dairy. He now pictured Constance in the dairy. She would take it all as fun. She mightn't take to the work as quickly as another brought up on a farm, but that didn't matter. There would be no need for her to do all that much, his mother would do the rough as usual. But Constance would transform the house; transform him, she would bring gaiety into his life. He had never experienced gaiety, only as an observer when he went on his Sunday visit across the hills. Although he rarely allowed himself to laugh he liked laughter, he liked brightness in another, and she was all laughter and brightness. She would rejuvenate the whole atmosphere of this place; she'd bring to it a quality it had never known. It was a sombre house, and he admitted to himself that he was responsible for a great part of the feeling. It all stemmed from something in him he couldn't get rid of. Yet even before the knowledge of his parentage had been kicked into him on that day at the fair he could not recall being any different. But once Constance was here, once he was married, he would feel different.

He thought wryly it was as if he were a female bastard and marriage would give him a name, a legal name. He couldn't explain the feeling even to himself; it was mixed up with his children; he knew that as each one was born his isolation would lessen. What was more he intended to give them the name that should rightly be his. He would call his first son after Matthew because he liked Matthew – he did not use the term love – but following the name Matthew he would add the name Mallen. Matthew Mallen Radlet; and as time went on he could see the Radlet fading away and his children being known as Mallens; and if they bore the streak as he did, all the better.

One thing only troubled him and then but slightly, what would be the old man's reaction to him wanting Constance? He knew that the old man liked him, and he took credit for bringing a certain spice to his life. Without his weekly visits he guessed that Thomas Mallen would, over the years, have been very bored indeed with his existence, for he had grown sluggish in his mind if not in his body; the latter had been kept active, no doubt, by that shrew of an old cow, who not only acted as if she were mistress of the house but to all intents and purposes *was* mistress of the house. He had no doubt whatever about her reactions to his wanting Constance because she would not want to lose Constance, nor the hundred pounds a year that went with her.

He himself wasn't unconscious of the hundred pounds that Constance would bring with her. He could make a lot of improvements on the farm with an extra hundred pounds a year. Oh, quite a lot.

When he turned from the window Matthew was gone, and he pursed his thin lips and pushed aside the feeling of irritation that the empty kitchen aroused in him. But he could excuse Matthew for not being enthusiastic at his news; Matthew was sick, and he'd be more sick before he died. He jerked one shoulder, he didn't want to think about Matthew dying. Anyway, the consumption could linger on for years; if he was well cared for he might live till he was thirty.

He walked smartly out of the room; he must away and get changed. This was one day he'd look his best, his Mallen best.

# Chapter Two

Miss Brigmore set the bowl of porridge, the jug of hot milk and the basin of soft brown sugar at one side of the tray, and a cup and saucer and silver coffee jug at the other, and in the middle of the tray she placed a small covered dish of hot buttered toast. As she lifted up the tray from the kitchen table she looked to where Barbara was attending to her own breakfast, as she always did, and she asked, 'Did she cry in the night, do you know?'

'I didn't hear her.'

'She's taken it much better that I expected.'

'You can't tell; beneath her laughter you don't know what she is thinking; her laughter is often a cover.'

Miss Brigmore raised her eyebrows as she went towards the door which Mary was holding open for her, and she thought to herself that she was better acquainted with what went on inside Constance's head than was her sister. In fact, she was well acquainted with what went on in both their heads. It would have surprised them how much she knew of their inner thoughts.

She went slowly up the narrow stairs on to the landing, turned her back to the bedroom door and pushed it open with her buttocks, then went towards the bed where Thomas Mallen was still sleeping.

'Wake up! wake up!' Her voice had a chirpy note to it. 'Your breakfast is here.'

'What! Oh! Oh yes.' Thomas pulled himself slowly up among the pillows, and when she had placed the tray on his knee he blew out his cheeks and let the air slowly pass through his pursed lips, then said, 'It looks a grand morning.'

'It's fine . . . I think you should take a walk today.'

'Aw, Anna,' He flapped his hand at her. 'You and your walks, you'll walk me to death.'

'You'll find yourself nearer to it if you don't walk.'

He looked towards the window, then said, 'It's Sunday,' and she repeated, 'Yes, it's Sunday.'

They both viewed Sundays with different feelings. He looked forward to Sundays; she hated them for this was the day when that upstart came over the hills and acted like the lord of the manor himself. Talk about putting a beggar on horseback and him riding to hell; if ever he got the chance there was one who would gallop all the way.

She had never liked Donald Radlet from when he was a boy; as he grew into manhood her dislike had at times touched on loathing. She, who could explain everyone else's feeling to herself, couldn't give a rational explanation for her own with regard to Thomas's natural son. It wasn't jealousy; no, because if his son had been Matthew not only would she have liked him but she might also have come to love him. But in Donald she saw only a big-headed, dour, bumptious upstart, who made claims on this house because of his bastardy.

But perhaps, she admitted to herself, there was a touch of jealousy in her feelings towards Donald, because although the matter had never been discussed openly she guessed that Thomas not only liked the man but strangely even felt a pride in him. In a way she could understand this, for not having had a sign or a word from Dick all these years he had come to think of him as dead, and had replaced him in his affections with his fly-blow, because that's all Donald Radlet was, a fly-blow. She did not chastise herself for the common appellation for she considered it a true description. But for the tragedy that had befallen the Hall and its occupants those ten years ago, Donald Radlet would not have been allowed past the outer gates and Thomas, although he might have been amused by the persistency of the boy who viewed the Hall from the top of the crag, would no more have publicly recognized him than he would any of his other numerous illegitimate offspring.

Thomas said now, 'How is Constance?'

'I haven't seen her this morning, but Barbara tells me she passed a good night; at least she didn't hear her crying.'

'She was disappointed.'

'More than a little I think. It was dastardly of him to call as often as he did when all the while he was planning his engagement to another.'

'As many a man before him he was likely astraddle two stools. If things had been as they used to be he would, I'm sure, have chosen Constance, but which man in the position the Headleys are in now could take a young woman with a hundred a year? They are almost where I was ten years ago, an' I should crow. But no; having tasted such bitterness, I wouldn't wish it on anyone.'

'He had no right to pay her attention.'

'He didn't pay her attention as such, he's called here for years.'

'You didn't see what I saw.'

He put his hand out towards her now and caught her arm and, gazing into her face, he said softly, 'No one sees what you see, Anna. Have I ever told you you're a wonderful woman?'

'Eat your breakfast.' Her eyes were blinking rapidly.

'Anna.'

'Yes, what is it?' She stood perfectly still returning his look now.

'I should marry you.'

The start she gave was almost imperceptible. There was a silence between them as their eyes held; then in a matter-of-fact way she said, 'Yes, you should, but you won't.'

'If I had put a child into you I would have.'

'It's a pity you didn't then, isn't it?'

'Yes, indeed it is; but you can't say it wasn't for trying, can you?' His voice had dropped to a low whisper and the corner of his mouth was tucked in. She now smacked at his hand playfully before saying, 'Eat your breakfast, the toast will be cold, the coffee too. And then don't linger, get up; we're going for a brisk walk through the fields.'

'We're doing no such thing.'

She had reached the door and was half through it when she repeated, 'We're going for a brisk walk through the fields.' And as she closed the door she heard him laugh.

She now paused a moment before going across the narrow landing and to the door opposite, and in the pause she thought, Men are cruel. All men are cruel. Thomas was cruel; he would have married her if he had put a child into her, and how she had longed that he should. She needed children. There was a great want in her for children. That the time was almost past for her having any of her own hadn't eased the longing, and she assuaged it at times with the thought that once Barbara and Constance were married there would be children again who would need her care; she would not recognize that marriage might move them out of her orbit.

As for Thomas not giving her a child, she knew that the fault did not lie with him – the proof of this came across the hills every Sunday. But over the past ten years he had not strayed for she had served him better than any wife would have done. In serving him she had sullied her name over the county. Not that that mattered; she cared naught for people's opinion. Or did she? She held her head high now but if she had been Mrs Mallen it would have needed no effort to keep upright.

And now here was her beloved Constance suffering at the hands of another man. Will Headley had courted Constance since she was sixteen; there was no other word for it. Before that, on his visits he had romped with her and teased her, but during the past year his manner had changed; it had been a courting manner. Then yesterday when she was expecting a visit from him, what did she receive? A beautifully worded letter to the effect that he had gone to London where his engagement to Miss Catherine Freeman was to be announced. He had thanked her for the happy days they had spent together and stressed that he would never forget them, or her.

After Constance had read the letter, the bright gaiety that shone from her face, even when in repose, had seeped away. She had looked stricken, but she hadn't cried; she had folded the letter in two and, when about to return it to its envelope, she had paused and said, 'Anna,' for now she called her Anna, 'read that.'

When she had read it she, too, was stricken; but her training helped her to keep calm and say, 'I am very disappointed in Mr Headley.' Then she had taken Constance's hand and looked into her face and said, 'These things happen, they are part of your education, what matters is how you react to them. If you must cry, cry in the night, but put a brave face on during the day. You're only seventeen; the same could happen to you again before you marry.'

At this Constance had turned on her, and in the most unusual tone cried, 'It won't! It won't ever happen to me again.'

She had dismissed the outburst by saying, 'Well, we'll see, we'll see.'

Now she went across the landing and gently opened the door. She did not knock, she entered as a mother might and said, 'Oh, there you are; you're up, dear.'

It was evident that Constance was very much up. She was dressed and putting the last touches to her toilet as she sat before the small dressing table; and she looked through the mirror at Miss Brigmore while she continued to take the comb through the top of her brown hair. She did not, as usual, speak first, remarking on the weather or some other triviality; it was Miss Brigmore who, coming to her side, and smoothing an imaginary crease out of the back of her lace collar, said, 'Did you sleep well, dear?'

Constance stared at Miss Brigmore, still through the mirror, and she addressed her through the mirror as she said, flatly, 'I'm supposed to say, yes, Anna, aren't I? Well, I can't, because I didn't sleep well.' She now swung round and, gripping Miss Brigmore's hands, she whispered, 'Do you think I'll ever marry, Anna?'

'Of course you will, child. Of course you will.' Miss Brigmore released one hand and gently stroked the delicate tinted cheek, but her eyebrows moved up sharply as Constance jerked her head away from the embrace, saying, 'Of course you will, of course you will . . . Of course I won't! Where are the men around here who will come flocking for my hand? Whom do we see? Let us face it, Anna, Will was my only chance.'

'Don't be silly, child.'

'I'm not silly, and don't try to hoodwink me, Anna. And I'm no longer a child. Will led me to believe . . . Oh, you don't know . . . anyway, what does it matter? As you're always saying, these are the things that make life and must be faced up to. But –' her head drooping suddenly, she ended, 'but I don't want to face up to them. I . . . I don't want to end up like Barbara, resigned. I'm . . . I'm not made like Barbara, Anna.' Once again she was gripping Miss Brigmore's hands. 'I want a home of my own, Anna; I want . . . I want to be married. Do you understand that, Anna? I want to be married.'

Miss Brigmore looked down into the soft brown eyes with pity. She was saying she wanted to be married and she was asking did she understand. Oh, she understood only too well; she could write volumes on the bodily torments she had endured, not only during the developing years, but in those years between twenty and thirty. She had even taken to reading the lives of the saints and martyrs in the hope of finding some way to ease her bodily cravings.

When Constance turned away from her, saying helplessly, 'Oh, you really don't understand what I mean,' she gripped her shoulders tightly and twisted her none too gently back towards her, and bending until their faces were level, she hissed at her, 'I understand. Only too well I understand. I've been through it all, only much more than you'll ever realize. Now listen to me. You'll marry; I'll see to it you'll marry. We'll make arrangements to do more visiting. We'll go over to the Browns in Hexham; there's always company coming and going there. And the Harpers in Allendale; they've invited you twice and you've never accepted.'

'Oh, the Harpers.' Constance shook her head. 'They're so vulgar; they talk nothing but horses.'

'They may be vulgar, horsey people are nearly always vulgar, but they keep an open house. We'll be going that way next week; we'll call in.'

Constance shook her head slowly from side to side. 'It all seems so . . . so mercenary, so cheap, con . . . conniving.'

'You have to connive in order to exist. Come on now.' Miss Brigmore straightened her back and again smoothed out the imaginary crease in Constance's lace collar. 'It's a beautiful day, and Sunday, and we're going for our walk. Now come along and put a brave face on things, and who knows, it may all have happened for the best. You know what I've always said, every step we take in life has already been planned for us. We are not free agents in spite of all this talk about free will. Have your breakfast so that Mary can get cleared away and I will get your uncle ready.' She always gave the title of uncle to Thomas when speaking of him to them. 'And don't worry, dear.' Her voice dropping to a muted tone, she now looked lovingly at Constance. 'Everything will work out to your advantage, you'll see, you'll see. Don't my prophecies nearly always come true?' She lifted her chin upwards and looked down her nose in a comical fashion, and Constance smiled weakly as she said, 'Yes, Anna; yes, they do.'

'Well now, believe me when I say everything will work out for the best. Come along.'

She turned briskly about and walked out of the room, leaving the door open, and Constance rose from the dressing table and followed her, thinking with a slight touch of amusement, When Anna speaks it's like the voice of God.

# Chapter Three

It was at eleven o'clock when they were on the point of going for their ritual walk that Donald came up the path and entered the house by the front way, and without knocking. Whereas Miss Brigmore didn't knock when she entered Constance's bedroom because she felt that she had the right of a mother, Donald didn't knock at the cottage door because he felt he had the right of a son.

The girls were standing in the small hallway. Miss Brigmore was coming out of the sitting room buttoning her gloves, and behind her, protesting, as he always did on these occasions, came Thomas. When the front door opened and they saw Donald, they all exclaimed in their different ways, 'Why! we didn't expect you till this afternoon.' That is, all except Miss Brigmore, and she fumbled the last button into the buttonhole of her glove while she thought, What brings him at this time? She turned and looked at Thomas, who made a quick effort to hide his pleasure, which she knew at this time was twofold for he would see Donald Radlet's arrival as the means of getting out of taking exercise.

'Well, well! my boy, what have we? Something untoward happened? Have you closed up the farm . . . or sold it?' Thomas's deep-bellied laugh caused his flesh to shake.

'Neither.' Donald never addressed Thomas with any title, either of sir or mister. 'As to something untoward, well it all depends upon how you look at it.' He turned now and smiled at the two young women, who were smiling at him, and he said to them, 'Are you off for your walk?'

'Yes, yes.' It was Barbara who spoke and Constance who nodded.

'Well, do you mind being delayed for a few minutes?'

They looked back at him and both of them said together, 'No, no,' and Barbara added, 'Of course not.'

Donald now turned to Thomas and in a manner that set Miss Brigmore's teeth grating slightly he said, 'I want to talk to you for a minute . . . all right?'

'Yes, yes, all right, all right.' Thomas was always amused by his natural son's manner, for he thought he knew the true feelings that his bumptiousness and pomposity covered. He had been a little like that himself in his young days when at times he wasn't sure of his footing or was out to show that he was not only as good as the rest, but better. He turned to Miss Brigmore now, saying, 'You and the girls go along, go along; we'll catch up on you.'

Looking Thomas straight in the eyes, Miss Brigmore said, 'We'll wait.' Upon this she turned round and went back into the sitting room, and Constance went with her. Thomas now lumbered along the corridor towards his study, and Donald, after casting a half-amused glance in Barbara's direction where she remained standing looking at him, followed Thomas.

Standing by the sitting-room window, and looking towards Barbara as she entered the room, Constance said, 'I wonder what's brought him at this time, and what he wants with Uncle? Did you notice he was wearing a new suit? He can look very smart when he likes.'

Barbara didn't answer, but sitting down, she folded her hands on her lap. Yes, he could look very smart when he liked; to her he had always looked smart. But what had brought him at this time of the morning and all dressed up, and asking to speak to Uncle privately? What? Her heart suddenly jerked beneath her ribs. That look he had given her before he had gone along the corridor. Could it be possible, could it just be possible? He had always paid her attention; but really not sufficient to warrant any hope that his thoughts were other than brotherly. Yet, had some of her own feelings seeped through her facade and had he recognized them, and this had made him bold, and he was in there now asking for her hand? . . . Oh, if it were only so. She had loved him for years, in spite of what she knew to be his failings. His weekly visits had been the only bright spot in an otherwise drab and formal existence. She had, however, kept her secret locked tight within her; the one person she would have confided in she couldn't, because Anna disliked Donald and always had done. But she didn't care who disliked him, she loved him, and if she became his wife she'd ask nothing more from life. . . .

In the study Thomas sat stiffly in the big leather chair staring at Donald. He had been utterly taken aback by the young fellow's request. Now he could have understood it if he had asked for Barbara's hand, because, over the years, it was to Barbara he had talked, and she to him. Sometimes on a Sunday afternoon after they'd had dinner and he was dozing in his chair they had put him to sleep with their talking, she explaining about books and answering his questions, much as a teacher would do. She was in that way very like Anna. But he didn't want Barbara, it was Constance he was after. Well, well now, this was a strange state of affairs. And he had to ask himself a question: did he want his natural son to marry either of these girls, even if they would have him? Well, why not, why not? He had just said he would own the farm when old Radlet died. Apparently Radlet had told him this . . . He said to him now, 'You say the farm will be yours, have you it in writing?'

'No, but I know for certain it will be.'

'What about his own son?'

'He has the consumption, he won't last for very long.'

'You never know, you never know, creaking doors. Anyway, should Radlet die, Matthew, were he alive, would inherit, and then he in turn could leave the farm to anyone he liked.'

'He wouldn't; he can't run the place, he has no strength. Anyway, I'm not worried about that side of the situation. I'm putting money on the place every year with buildings and stock, and will go on doing so. It's a prosperous farm an' I'm thinking of buying more land an' all.'

The self-assurance silenced Thomas for a time. He was buying more land, he was putting in more stock, putting up more buildings, and hadn't a thing in writing. It was wonderful to have such self-confidence. This son of his knew where he was going, and Constance might do a lot worse, for now that Will Headley had failed her, he couldn't see anyone else in the running, not for the time being at any rate. Most of the young fellows today were on the look-out for wives who would bring with them a good dowry. It was as it had always been, if a man had to choose between his heart and hard cash, the hard cash always won. If it didn't, it was a proven fact in most cases that the heart pact soon led to disaster.

'Have you any objections?'

'Well –' Thomas let his head rest against the back of the chair, and his eyes ranged around the room before he answered. 'I don't know whether I have or not; your request has come as a surprise, and if I'm not mistaken I think it will surprise Constance too.'

'It shouldn't, she knows I like her.'

'Like her! Huh! liking and loving are two different things. Of course she knows you like her, everybody likes her.'

Thomas now got to his feet and walked with heavy tread back and forth from the desk to the door a number of times before he said, 'This'll cause talk you know, because folk don't realize that the girls have no blood connection with me. It'll be said I'm letting my niece marry my son.'

He stopped in his striding and the two stared at each other. It was the first time the relationship had been brought into the open, and the fact caused Donald to rise slowly to his feet. Eye held eye until Thomas, chewing on his lip, swung his heavy body around, saying, 'Well, you have my consent, but knowing you, you'd go ahead with or without it.'

When he looked at Donald over his shoulder he saw that he was smiling, and his own lips spreading slowly apart, he said on a laugh, 'You're a strange fellow, a strange fellow, and I should understand you, if anybody should, I should understand you, shouldn't I? But I don't, and I doubt if anybody ever will.'

'I don't see why not; if they understand you they should understand me.'

'No, boy, no; because you know you don't take after me, not really; you take after my father's youngest brother, Rod. He too went after what he wanted and took no side roads.'

'Did he always get what he wanted?'

'I don't know; I don't know whether he wanted to be drowned at sea or not but he was drowned at sea. I don't know if he got what he wanted, but by all accounts he got what he deserved.'

The smile had left Donald's face as if it had been wiped off and, his voice stiff now, he said, 'I've been handicapped for years, an' I've risen above it. I've worked hard all me life, I've worked like two men, many a time like three; I hope I get what I deserve.'

'I meant no offence, boy, I was merely making a statement. And I say with you, I hope you get what you deserve. But ... but' – Thomas now rolled his head from side to side – 'we're getting very serious and deep all of a sudden; come, we were talking of a proposal of marriage, weren't we?' He poked his head forward. 'That was the idea, wasn't it?'

'Along those lines.' The cold look still remained in Donald's eyes.

'Well then, go ahead, you have my consent; I won't say blessing because' – he now laughed a deep rumbling laugh – 'a blessing from me might have little to recommend it, eh?' He thrust out his heavy arm and dug Donald in the shoulder with his fist, and they were both aware that the blow did not even stagger the thin frame.

Thomas now turned abruptly and went out of the room and made straight for the sitting room. He opened the door and said, 'Anna, spare me a minute will you?' And before she could move or answer he had turned away and gone into the dining room.

When Miss Brigmore entered the dining room she closed the door behind her, then walked slowly towards him. He did not take her hand, nor was there any placating note in his voice when he said, 'I have news for you, news that will surprise you and certainly not please you. He has asked that he may marry Constance.'

As he watched her face screw up until her eyes were almost lost from view, he waved his hand at her and turned from her, and when still she didn't speak he turned towards her again and said, 'Now it's no use, don't create a scene. I have given him my consent and that's that. After all, he is my son, and who has a better right I ask you? And –' his voice and manner arrogant now, he went on, '– they're no blood relations, the girls, you know they're not, there's nothing against it. Except that you don't like him. All right, you don't like him, you've never liked him, but I repeat, he is my son, he is part of me.'

When she suddenly sat down in a chair he went to her, and now he did take her hands and, his voice soft, he said, 'What have you against him really? He's hard working, and as he himself has just said, he's lived under a handicap for years. You don't like his manner, he's full of the great I am. Well, in his position I likely would have been the same; I would have had to put on a front. In a way he's to be admired, not scorned.'

'You can't let it happen, Thomas, you can't.'

'Well I have, I have.' He was standing up now, his voice arrogant once again. 'And that's that. It's up to her now, and nobody's going to force her. Oh no, nobody's going to force her. It's ten to one she'll laugh at him an' that'll be the end of it.'

'It's come at the wrong time.'

'What do you mean?'

'She has been rejected. She may take him as a means of escape.'

'Don't be silly, don't be silly, woman. She had no need to escape. Escape from what?'

'You don't understand.'

'I don't see what there's to understand. She either takes him or she doesn't. If she takes him I'll be happy for her.'

'And I will be sad to my dying day.'

'What?'

'I said, and I shall be sad to my dying day.'

'Why, Anna, why?'

'It would be no use trying to explain to you, only time can do that.'

She rose from the chair and went out and towards the sitting room. The door was open and she stood on the threshold and, ignoring Constance and Donald, she looked at Barbara and said, 'Will you come with me for a moment, Barbara.'

'What is it, Anna?' Barbara came hurrying from the room.

'Let us go for our walk.'

They were at the front door now and Barbara turned and looked across the hall and said, 'But . . . but the others.'

'We will go alone this morning.'

'Are you ill?'

'I am not ill, but I am not well.'

They had gone down the path and reached the garden gate before Miss Brigmore said, 'He has come this morning to ask Constance to be his wife, and your uncle has consented.'

She had taken three steps into the road before she stopped and looked back to where Barbara was clutching the top of the gate-post, and for a moment she thought that the stricken expression on her face had been brought about by the shock of the news, but when Barbara put her hand tightly across her mouth and closed her eys in order to suppress the tears that were attempting to gush from them she clutched at her, whispering, 'Oh no, no! Oh my dear, my dear . . . you didn't expect him . . . not you? You're so sensible, if only you could see through him; he cares for nobody but himself, he's a ruthless creature. Oh not you, not you, Barbara.'

When she was pushed aside she made no complaint, but walked slowly after the hurrying figure. And she had thought she knew what went on in both their minds.

From the sitting-room window Constance saw Barbara going down the road with Miss Brigmore following, and she turned to Donald saying, 'They've gone, what's the matter? Where's Uncle?' She was making for the door when Donald said, 'He's in his study. Don't go for a minute, I've got something I want to say to you.'

'Oh.' She turned and looked towards him, her face straight.

He had noticed that she wasn't her merry self this morning, it was as if she'd had a quarrel with someone, but with whom he couldn't imagine, for they all adored her and she them. Even that stiff-necked old cow held her in affection.

He went past her now and closed the door. Then having walked slowly towards her again, he stood in front of her, his back very straight, his head held high, and he said, 'Your uncle has given me permission to speak to you.'

She had asked, 'What? what about?' before the meaning of the phrase struck her, and then she wanted to laugh; long, loud, and hysterically she wanted to laugh. For months she had been imagining how she would respond to Will Headley when he came from the study and said, 'Your uncle has given me permission to speak to you.' Those words could only have one meaning, and here was Donald saying them to her. It was funny, very, very funny; Donald was saying 'Your uncle has given me permission to speak to you;' he would next say, 'Will you be my wife, Constance?' But she was wrong, at least in the form of the proposal, for he did not make it as a request but as a statement. 'I want to marry you,' he said.

'Marry? Marry me? You . . . you want to marry me?'

'That's what I said.' His face was straight now.

She was laughing at him; he couldn't bear to be laughed at. 'Is there anything funny about it?'

'No, no.' She closed her eyes and bowed her head and she wagged it as she murmured, 'No, no, Donald, there's nothing funny about it, only –' she was looking at him again '– I'm . . . I'm surprised, amazed. Why . . . why you can't really be serious?'

'Why not? why shouldn't I be serious?'

'Well –' she put her fingers to her lips now and patted them. 'Well, what I mean is . . . oh!' As Miss Brigmore had done a few minutes earlier, she sat down abruptly on a chair, but her manner was quite unlike that of Miss Brigmore's, for she was laughing again. 'Well, for one thing I would never make a farmer's wife, I'd be useless at milking and making butter and such, I wouldn't know how.'

'You could learn if you wanted to; but there would be no necessity for you to make butter and such.' He did not say his mother saw to that but added, 'That's already seen to. You'd be asked to do nothing you didn't want to do.'

Of a sudden she stopped laughing, she even stopped smiling, and she looked down at her hands which were now joined tightly on her lap. Yesterday the man she loved and had thought one day to marry had written her a letter, which by its very charm had seared the delicate vulnerable feelings of her first love as if she had been held over the blacksmith's fire, and definitely the letter had forged her whole conception of life into a different pattern.

'Well!'

She rose to her feet, her arms thrust out now to each side of her as if pushing away invisible objects, and, her body swaying slightly, she walked from him to the farthest corner of the room, saying, 'I . . . I can't take it in, Donald. Why . . . why you've never given any sign. You've always talked to Barbara more than to me. Why should you want me?' She now turned swiftly and, all animation gone from her body, she stood still, her arms hanging by her sides, staring at him.

He didn't move from where he was, nor did he speak for a time, his words seemed wedged in his throat, and when finally he uttered them they came like an echo from deep within him. 'I love you,' he said.

There was a long pause before either of them moved. During it she looked at him as if she had never seen him before. He was a man, a good-looking, stern-faced young man; he was thin and tall, with jet-black hair that had a white streak running down the side of it; his eyes were dark, bluey-black; he was her uncle's natural son, and because of this he had an opinion of himself. She did not blame him for that; he was hard working and had gained the title of respectability even with the stigma that lay on him. She had heard her uncle say that his judgment was respected in the cattle markets and that men did not speak lightly of him. He would, she felt, make someone a good husband – would he make her a good husband? He had said he loved her. She didn't love him, she had never thought about him in that connection; she liked him, she was amused by him. Oh yes, he amused her. His austere and bumptious manner had always amused her; she had teased him because of it. But love; could she ever grow to love anyone again? She looked him over from head to foot. He was very presentable; in a way he was much more presentable than Will Headley. Change their stations and what would have been her reactions then?

She said, 'But I don't love you, Donald I . . . I've never thought of you in that way.'

'That will come, I'll see it comes.' He moved towards her now and he reached out and took her hand. 'Give me the chance and I'll see that it comes. You will love me, I know you will.'

She gave a small laugh as she said, 'You are as you ever were, so confident, Donald; nothing can shake your confidence in yourself and your ability, can it?'

'I know my own value.'

'And you think you can make me love you?'

'I don't think, I know I can. It may sound like bragging, and I suppose it is when I say I could have married five times over these last few years, and that's not heightening or lessening the number; five times over I say, and to one the daughter of a man who has nearly enough cash stacked away here and there to buy the Hall. I'd just to lift me finger, but no, I knew who I wanted, there was only one for me, and that was you.'

'Oh Donald!' She didn't know now whether she wanted to laugh at his cock sureness, or to cry at his devotion.

When he lifted her hand and rubbed it against his cheek she detected a new softness in him and she said haltingly, 'Will . . . will you give me time, time to think it over?'

'All the time in the world . . . a year.'

'But you said all the time in the . . .'

'I know, but a year is all the time in the world that I'm going to give you. At the end of a year we'll be married, you'll see.' When he put his arms about her she remained still and stiff and something recoiled in her while she thought, Is this in the plan for me? and her mind gabbled rapidly, No, no. Yet when his mouth touched hers she did not resist him, she even experienced a shiver of excitement as she felt the strength of him and smelt the strange odour that emanated from the mixture of soap, rough tweed, and the farm smell that she always associated with him. He was a man, and he wanted her – and Will Headley didn't.

# Chapter One

## Constance

There were periods during the following year when Miss Brigmore's feelings towards Constance's suitor softened and she was forced, even if grudgingly, to show her admiration for him. These were the times when although the hills and mountains were impassable with snow, he would appear as usual for his Sunday visit; that he accompanied these feats with an element of bravado was visible to all, but that he accomplished them at all she was forced to admit was due not only to his physical strength but also to his sheer tenacity.

Of course there were other times when he had to admit defeat. On these Sundays – once there had been three in succession – she had observed Constance's reactions closely. The first Sunday she had taken as a matter of course and even shown some relief, but when he hadn't appeared on the second and third Sundays, she had shown concern, and when the day came that he finally arrived she had greeted him warmly.

Constance had been three times over the hills to the farm. Her first visit had not turned out to be a complete success. Its failure had nothing to do with the farm or its inhabitants; she had spoken highly of his parents and their reception of her, stating only that the farmhouse seemed a little bare after the cluttered homeliness of the cottage. What had actually spoilt the visit for her was the storm; she had a horror of storms. Thunder and lightning terrified her. Since she was child she had always sought the darkest corner during a storm, and its approach always made her nervy and apprehensive. On this occasion she was actually sick and had to delay her return until quite late in the evening; and Donald, although he couldn't understand her fear, had been concerned for her.

Constance could not herself pinpoint the time when she had specifically said to Donald that she would marry him, but the date had been fixed within six months of the particular Sunday when he amazed her with his declaration of love.

As the weeks passed her reactions had varied from excitement to fear bred of doubt. But the latter she always tried to laugh off, even as she laughed at the man who was the cause of it. The questions 'What is there to fear from Donald?' and 'And if I don't marry him who then?' would nearly always dispel the fear.

For the past two days the weather had been sultry owing to the unusual heat that had continued daily for over a week now, and Constance had been on edge as she often was with an impending storm. Added to this, Miss

Brigmore did not discount the nerves that frequently attended marriage preparations, not that the preparations for this wedding were anything elaborate, but nevertheless there were the usual things to be seen to, such as the clothes she would take with her, the linen, and what was more important and what had been causing a great deal of discussion, the amount of money she would retain.

At first Constance had insisted that she transfer her hundred pounds a year income to Barbara; for, as she stated plainly, were the house deprived of it they would find great difficulty in managing. What was more, she had insisted that Donald would confirm her opinion on the matter.

But Donald hadn't confirmed her opinion; when the question was put to him he had remained silent for a time before saying, 'It's a good thing for everyone to have a little money of their own, it makes them sort of independent.'

Thomas had wholeheartedly endorsed this, while at the same time Miss Brigmore knew that he was only too well aware that the household strings were already pulled as tight as it was possible for them to be without actual discomfort. She, herself, had taken no salary from the day they had come to the cottage in order that he might have the little luxuries of cigars and wine that made life more bearable for him. As for Mary, she was on a mere pittance; it was only her devotion to the girls that had made her suffer it all these years.

The question of the money had not, as yet, been resolved. Constance had said only that morning she would have none of it. She had got into a tantrum, which was unusual for her, and said that unless she could do as she pleased with her allowance she wouldn't marry at all. She had made quite a scene in front not only of Donald but of Matthew too.

It wasn't often that Matthew came to visit them now. He hadn't been more than half a dozen times during the past year. Matthew always aroused a feeling of sorrow in Miss Brigmore. Why was it, she asked herself, that a person with such a nice nature as Matthew's should suffer such a crippling disease, while Donald, with his arrogance, be given enough health for two men?

Matthew's speech and manner had always pleased her, and she had thought secretly that if the half-brothers could have exchanged places she would have welcomed the match without reservation.

She looked at the young man now sitting opposite her. They had the room to themselves. Thomas had retired to the study for his after-dinner nap; Barbara was in the garden reading. Barbara read a lot these days, but now she didn't discuss what she read. Instead, she had become very withdrawn over the past year. Deep in her heart she was sorry for Barbara; and here again she wished that the roles could be changed, for she would have been less unhappy about the situation if Barbara had been marrying Donald, because there was a firm adultness in Barbara that was, as yet, lacking in her sister. Yet she felt that perhaps she was not quite right in this surmise, for Constance too had changed during the past year; only at intervals now did her gay girlish self appear; for most of the time she wore a thoughtful expression.

She brought her whole attention to Matthew as she said, 'I have not had time to ask you yet, but how have you been feeling of late? We haven't seen you for such a long time.'

'Oh, about as usual, Miss Brigmore, thank you. No worse, no better.' He shrugged his thin shoulders. 'I'll be quite content if I continue like this. And I could' – he now nodded at her as he smiled – 'if we had this weather through the winter.'

'Yes, indeed,' she laughed with him, 'if we had this weather through the winter. It really has been remarkably warm of late, too warm some days I would have said. Yet in another month or so we shall have forgotten about it, and be shivering once again.'

He said now, 'It's very cold this side in the winter, I think we're more fortunate over our side.'

'I'm sure you are. And Constance tells me it's very pleasant in your valley.'

'You must come over and see it. Don ... Father is going to get a horse and trap or some such, he's going into Hexham for the sales next Friday. My mother suggested, as we were using the horses we come over by the waggon today, but Donald would have none of it.' He now pulled a face at her and they both exchanged smiles. 'Besides the fact it would have to be cleaned up for the journey, it's a bit big and lumbering and has no style about it whatever.'

There was a slight mocking note to his last words, and Miss Brigmore brought her lips together tightly while her eyes smiled back at him with a knowing smile.

There followed a companionable silence between them now, as if each were waiting for the other to speak, and Miss Brigmore wanted to speak, she wanted to ask him so many questions: How did his mother and father view the alliance, particularly his mother? How did Donald act in his own home? Did he still keep up his authoritative manner amidst his own people? Was he kind? Of course he had shown kindness for years in bringing the commodities of the farm on his Sunday visits. But that wasn't the kindness she meant. There appeared no softness in him, no gentleness. A man could appear arrogant and bumptious in public, she knew only too well, but in private he could become a different creature. It was strange but she couldn't imagine Donald becoming a different creature in private. But there was only one person who would ever know if he changed character, and that was Constance. She had often wondered how he acted towards her when they were alone for his manner in public gave off the impression that he already possessed her. She turned her gaze towards the window from where she knew, if she rose, she'd be able to see them going towards the curve in the road, taking the same walk they did every Sunday, because Donald liked that walk, for at the end of it were the gates of the Hall. . . .

It would have surprised Miss Brigmore at this moment if she could have overheard the conversation between the two people who were deep in her thoughts, for the subject was the same as that in her own mind, kindness.

Walking with a slow, almost prim step, Constance was saying, 'He appears to have such a kindly nature.'

'He has.'

'You're very fond of him.'

'Aye, I'm very fond of him. There's nobody I like better except –' he turned his head towards her and paused before he said, 'you. If I were speaking the truth there are only two people I care about in the world, the rest could sink, burn or blow up for me.'

His words brought no change in her attitude, but she asked, 'What about Uncle?'

'Oh.' He nodded his head once or twice, then repeated, 'Uncle? Funny, but I can't explain what I think about him. Pride, hate, grudging admiration, loathing, oh, I could put a name to all the vices and very few of the virtues that go to make up my feelings with regard to him.'

She had paused for a moment in her walking and stared at him as she said, 'But I thought you liked him?'

'I do, an' I don't. I don't and I do.' His head wagged from side to side with each word. 'Aw, don't let's talk about – Uncle, for I wouldn't be able to speak the truth about my feelings for him if I tried, 'cos I don't know them myself. There's only two things I'm sure of, as I've told you, and the main one is I love you.' His voice dropped to a mere whisper as he stopped and turned towards her. 'I love you so much that I'm afraid at times, and that's proved to me the strength of my feelings, for fear and me have been strangers up till now. Now, every time I leave you I fear something'll happen to you. But once I have you safe over the hills, it'll be different. I'll know peace, an' I'll be whole. You know, that's something I've never really felt – whole; but once we're married you'll make me whole – won't you? . . . Aw Constance, Constance.'

Her lips fell slightly apart and she looked at him in something of surprise, for in this moment she was seeing him as never before, and she felt stirring in her an emotion she hadn't experienced before. It wasn't love – or was it? She couldn't tell, for it had no connection with the feeling she had felt towards Will Headley. Was it pity? But how could she pity him, he was the last person one could pity; if he were dressed in rags and begging on the road he would not evoke pity. And yet, when she came to consider it, she could not give to this feeling any other name. She realized that he had allowed her to see beneath the surface of his arrogance wherein she had glimpsed a depth of loneliness. She herself had no understanding of loneliness, never once having been lonely. There came into her mind the fact that she had never been alone in her life except in the privacy of the water closet; sleeping or waking there had always been someone, Barbara, Anna, Mary, or her uncle.

When his arms went about her and pulled her fiercely to him she gasped and whispered, 'We're on the main road.'

'What of that! Have we ever met anyone on the main road at this time on a Sunday?'

His mouth was on hers, hard, searching. After a moment her stiff body relaxed against him and her lips answered his.

When he released her he stood gazing down into her face; then he cupped her chin in his hand as he said, 'A fortnight today we will have been married for twenty-four hours.'

She gave a nervous laugh, drew herself from his embrace and walked on, and he walked close beside her now, his bent arm pressing hers tight against his side.

A fortnight today at this time they would have been married for twenty-four hours.

A fortnight ago she had all but decided to tell him she could not go through with the marriage, and then she had asked herself if she did that, what would life hold for her, what prospects had she of marrying if she refused this opportunity? She could see herself ending up, not only like Barbara, but like Anna, and she couldn't bear the thought. She wanted a husband and a home of her own and children, lots of children. She had read in a Ladies' Journal only recently an article that explained that the bearing of children, and the doing of good works within one's ability and the contents of one's pocket, brought to women great compensation, and contributed towards a better and longer-lasting happiness than did the early experience of so-called love marriages, wherein the young bride saw life through rosy-tinted glasses.

There was another thing that was worrying her, she did not know whether she would like living in the farmhouse; it wasn't that she disliked his mother and father, nor that they disliked her, but there was a restraint in their manner towards her. They acted more like servants might be expected to do and this made her uneasy. The one comforting thought was that Matthew would be there. She got on well with Matthew, she liked Matthew, she had always liked him, he seemed to belong to another world altogether from that which had bred Donald. He was more refined, gentle. She had never teased Matthew as she had teased Donald, which was strange when she came to think of it; perhaps because Matthew had talked little and had been rather shy. He was still shy.

They had walked in silence for some time, and she didn't like long silences; she always felt bound to break silences, and now she reverted to their previous topic and said, 'I thought Matthew was looking very well today.'

'He's well enough considering, an' if he sticks to the horse and doesn't walk too much he'll be better. If I don't keep me eye on him he's off up the hills with a book; he'll be blind afore he dies, I've told him that. Had things been different from what they are with him he would have made a good school teacher; he's learned, you know.' He had turned his head towards her and there was a note of pride in his voice as if he were speaking of a son, and she nodded and said, 'Yes, yes; I think he is.'

'Think!' he repeated. 'Be sure of it; he never goes into Hexham or Allendale but he borrows a book. That reminds me. I've got to go to the sales next Friday an' that's when you were coming over to meet Uncle and Aunt, so Matthew'll come for you early on. He'll bring Ned along; Ned's back's as broad as an ingle-nook, and you couldn't fall off him if you tried.'

She laughed now as she said, 'I could, even without trying, you know I'm no horsewoman. It isn't that I dislike horses, I just can't ride them. Now Barbara, she sits a horse as good as any man. I always think it's a pity we weren't able to keep one; she would have loved it.'

He said abruptly, 'Barbara's grown sullen.'

'You think so?'

'I know it. It's because she doesn't want to lose you. And that's under-standable.' He was nodding at her. 'They all don't want to lose you, but their loss is my gain.' He pressed her arm tighter into his side. Then, his voice unusually soft, he said, 'You know, I determined years ago to get everything I set me heart on, and I set me heart on you from the beginning. But even so there were days and nights, long nights when I doubted me own ability, an' now it's come about, well' – he gazed sideways at her and, his voice just above a whisper, he said, 'Have you any idea how I feel about you, Constance?' Without waiting for an answer he made a small motion with his head and went on, 'No, you never could have, for I can't explain the sense of . . . what is the word?' Again he made a motion with his head. 'Elation, aye, that's it, the sense of elation I feel every time I look at you.'

'Oh Donald! don't, don't; you make me feel embarrassed, as if I were someone of importance.'

'You are. Look at me.' He jerked her arm and when, half-smiling, she looked at him, he said 'You are, you are someone of great importance. Get that into your head. There's nobody more important than you, and there's only one thing I regret.'

When he paused she asked, 'And what's that?'

And now he pointed along the road towards the iron gates. 'Them,' he said.

'Them?'

'Aye, them. If I could perform a miracle I'd have them opened as we get near. The lodge-keeper would hold them wide, and we'd go up the drive sitting in a carriage behind prancing horses, an' the lackeys would run down the steps and open the house door. They'd put a footstool out for you, and they'd bow their heads to me, and the head lackey would say, "I hope you had a pleasant journey, sir?" And we'd go through that hall and up the staircase and into our apartments – not rooms mind, apartments, an' I'd see you take off your hat and cloak; I'd see you change into a fine gown; then down the stairs we'd go together and into the dining room an' . . .'

They had reached the gates now and she gripped the rusty iron railings, and leaning her head against them she laughed until her body shook, and when she turned to look at him her face was wet with her laughter; but his was straight and stiff and he said, 'You think it funny?'

'Yes, yes, Donald, I do, for it would take a miracle, wouldn't it?'

He stared at her for a long moment before saying, 'If I had been brought up in that house as I should have been, as his son, we would be there the day, I know it, I feel it inside.'

'Don't be silly.' Her voice held an imperious note. 'You were a boy then only thirteen; you could no more have made a miracle then than you could now; the miracle that was needed then was the sum of thirty thousand pounds, I understand, and that would only have acted as a stopgap.' Her own face was straight now, and what she said next was a statement rather than a question, 'You have always hated the fact, haven't you, that you weren't recognized as his son.'

When she saw his chin go into hard nodules and his cheek-bones press out against the skin she said hastily, 'Oh I'm sorry, Donald, I . . . I didn't mean it in a nasty way. I'm sure you with your forethought and tenacity would have tried to do something, I'm sure you would, even as young as you were. Believe me – ' she put out her hand and touched his ' – I wasn't intending to hurt you in any way. You do believe me?'

He drew in a deep breath, then let it out slowly before answering, 'Aye . . . aye, I believe you. And what you say is true.' He turned from her, and now he gripped the iron bars and looked through them and up the weed covered drive and into the dark tunnel where the trees were now meeting overhead, and he said, 'It's a blasted shame.' He turned his head and glanced at her. 'I don't mean about me, but about the place. Why didn't they stay, they paid enough for it? Only three years in it and then they cleared out and didn't leave even one man to see to the grounds.'

She, too, was looking up the drive as she said, 'This part of the country accepts or rejects as it pleases. They were from Hampshire, this was another world to them; what was more they were new to money and thought it could buy anything. If they had been disliked I think they could have understood it, but not being ignored. Uncle was disliked. Oh yes.' She nodded at him. 'He was hated by many people; but he was someone they couldn't ignore – not even now.' She chuckled, and he smiled as he muttered, 'No, I'll give him that, you can't ignore him.'

Once again she was looking up the drive and her voice had a sad note to it as she said, 'They'll never get the gardens back in order; it took two years before, but now the place has been deserted for almost four years. The house must be mouldering. This lock always annoys me.' She now rattled the chain attached to the huge lock. 'And that glass they had put all along the top of the walls.' She looked first to the right and then to the left of her. 'It seems an act of spite to me. And when I think of all that fruit going rotten inside. Oh, I feel like knocking a hole in the wall, I do.' She nodded at him, her face straight, but when he said playfully, 'I'll do it for you if you like. Wait till I go and get a pick,' and pretended to dash away, she laughed again.

They turned from the gate, walked a little way along the road, then mounted the fells to take the roundabout way back to the cottage, and when with an impulsive movement she slipped her hand through his arm he gripped it tightly; then swiftly he caught her under the armpits and lifted her into the air and swung her round as if she were a child; and when at last he stopped whirling her and put her feet on the ground she leant against him gasping and laughing and he pressed her to him as he looked away over her head towards the high mountains, and the feeling that he termed elation rose in him and burst from him and formed itself into a galloping creature, and he saw it clear the peaks one after the other until it reached the farm.

# Chapter Two

They were all standing in the roadway outside the gate seeing her off, Matthew at the head of the two horses. Mary was giggling, saying, 'I don't blame you, Miss Constance; you wouldn't get me up on that, not for a thousand pounds you wouldn't.'

'If I offered you one gold sovereign you wouldn't only be on it, but you'd jump over it this minute, woman.'

It spoke plainly for the change in the social pattern that Thomas could joke with his one and only servant and Mary answer, 'Oh, Master. Master, I'd as soon jump over the moon, I would so, as get on that animal. I don't envy you, Miss Constance, I don't that, I ... '

'Be quiet, Mary!' At times Miss Brigmore's manner reverted to that of the Miss Brigmore that Mary remembered from years back, and on these occasions she obeyed her without murmur.

Miss Brigmore now stepped towards Constance where she was standing near the big flat-backed horse and she said, 'You have nothing to fear, he'll just amble.'

'He won't gallop?' Constance divided the question by a look between Miss Brigmore and Matthew, and Matthew, smiling, said, 'His galloping days are over, long since.'

'It's so close; you don't think there'll be a storm?'

Constance was now looking at Barbara who, her face unsmiling but her expression pleasant and her voice consoling, said, 'No, I'm sure there'll be no storm, it's passed over. Look – ' she turned and pointed ' – it's passing to the south of us. By the time you get on to the hills the sun will be out.'

The two sisters looked at each other. It was a long probing look as if each had the desire to fall into the other's arms.

'It'll be tomorrow you'll get there if you don't make a start; hoist her up, Matthew, and get going.'

Matthew bent down, cupped his hands and Constance put her foot on them; the next moment she was sitting in the saddle. Then without a word Matthew mounted the brown mare, and after inclining his head towards those on the road he said, 'Get up there!' and the two horses moved off simultaneously.

No one called any farewell greetings, but when Constance turned her head and looked back at them Miss Brigmore raised her hand in a final salute.

It was almost ten minutes later, after they had left the road and were beginning to mount upwards, that Matthew spoke. Looking towards her, he said, 'You all right?'

'Yes, Matthew, yes. He's . . . he's quite comfortable really.'

'Yes, he's a steady old boy, reliable.'

They exchanged glances and smiled.

A few more minutes elapsed before she said, 'It's looking dark over there; you don't think we'll ride into the storm do you, Matthew?'

Matthew did not answer immediately because he was thinking that that was exactly what they were likely to do. Barbara's statement that the storm was passing south was quite wrong; it was coming from the south-west if he knew anything, and it would likely hit them long before they reached home. He said, 'Don't worry; if it does come we'll take shelter. There's the old house on the peak, you remember it?'

'That derelict place?'

'Yes, it's derelict, but it's been a haven to many in a storm these past years, and even before that when the Rutledges lived there.'

'I can't imagine why anyone would want to live in such an isolated spot.'

'Needs must in most cases; they had their sheep and a few galloways; and some people want to be alone.'

'Yes, I suppose so.' She nodded towards him. His face looked grave, serious. On each of the few occasions she had met him over the past year his expression had been the same; grave, serious. At one time, even in spite of his shyness, he had appeared jolly. When he smiled she thought he looked beautiful, in a delicate sort of way. She had wondered often of late whether he was displeased at the prospect of her coming to live on the farm. If that was the case it would be a great pity for she had imagined him lightening the evenings in the long winter ahead. She had visualized them conversing about books, as he did with Anna. She knew she wouldn't be able to converse with Donald about books; she had remarked to Anna recently it was a pity that Donald wasn't a reader, and Anna had replied tersely that she had to face up to the fact that her husband-to-be was a doer rather than a dreamer. That was a very good definition of Donald, a doer rather than a dreamer. Matthew here was the opposite, he was a dreamer rather than a doer, but it was his health she supposed that made the latter impossible. She felt a deep pity for Matthew and a tenderness towards him. She had realized of late that she had been somewhat hurt by his restrained attitude towards her.

The path was getting steeper. The land on one side of them fell sharply away to a valley bottom before rising again, but more gradually, to form distant peaks. On the other side of them it spread upwards in a curving sweep to form what, from this distance, looked like a plateau.

Matthew, glancing towards this height, calculated that before they covered the mile that would bring them to the top, and within a few minutes' ride of the old house, the storm would break. Even as he stared upwards the first deep roll of thunder vibrated over the hills, bringing a startled exclamation from Constance, and he came closer to her side, saying, 'It's all right. If it comes this way we'll take shelter.'

She was gripping the reins tightly; her face had gone pale. She looked at him and murmured hesitantly, 'I'm . . . I'm sorry but . . . but I'm really afraid of storms. I've tried to overcome the feeling but I can't. It . . . it seems so childish. . . .'

'Not a bit, not a bit. There are plenty of men who are afraid of storms an' all.'

'Really?'

'Aw aye, yes. I know . . . I know two.'

'Men?'

'Yes, men. There's a fellow who lives over by Slaggyford, a farmer he is.'

'And he's afraid of storms?'

'Yes; dives for the cow byre every time the sky darkens.' He hoped she never repeated this to Donald for he would laugh his head off.

'Is . . . is he a grown man?'

'Yes, he's a good age. But it's got nothing to do with age. There's a young boy in the market. I see him at times, that's when there's not a storm about, for he makes for shelter when there's the first sign of thunder, mostly under a cart. So you're not the only one, you see.'

She smiled at him, and he smiled back while he congratulated himself on his ability to tell the tale.

'Get up there! Get up there!' He urged the horses forward, but Ned, having maintained one pace for many years now, refused to alter it; and the coming of a storm didn't make him uneasy, he had weathered too many. But the younger horse was uneasy. She tossed her head and neighed, and Matthew tried to calm her, saying, 'Steady now, steady,' while at the same time thinking whimsically it was no good lying to a horse.

As the first flash of lightning streaked the sky above them Constance bowed her head and smothered a scream, and Matthew, bringing his horse close to hers again, put out his hand and caught her arm, saying, 'It's all right now, it's all right. Look, we're nearly at the top; another five minutes and we'll be in shelter.'

She lifted her head and looked at him and gasped, 'Can . . . can you make it hurry, the horse?'

'No, I'm afraid he'll go his own gait, come flood, storm or tempest. But don't worry, don't worry, everything'll be all right; just sit tight.'

'It's getting dark.'

Yes, it was getting dark; the valley to the left of them was blotted out; the sky in front seemed to be resting on the hills. Her face appeared whiter in the dimness, there were beads of perspiration round her mouth. He looked at her mouth and shivered. Then moving his horse forward, he gripped Ned's rein and yelled, 'Come on! Come on, Ned! Get up with you! Get up!'

The quickening of the horse's stride was not perceivable, but he kept urging her.

When the next roll of thunder came he was startled himself for he thought for a moment that Constance had fallen from the horse. He moved back to her side where she was doubled almost in two, her face resting against the horse's mane, and he leant towards her and put his hand on her shoulder and smoothed her, saying, 'There now, there now, it's passed. Look, it's passed.'

As he spoke, the first big drops of rain descended on them and before they had moved a hundred yards they were enveloped in a downpour, so heavy that his body too was now doubled against it.

It was more by instinct than sight that he left the road at the spot where the derelict house stood. Dismounting, he made his way round to her side and, her body still bent, she fell into his arms and he guided her at a run into the dark, dank shelter. Then leaving her to support herself against the wall, he said, 'I won't be a minute, not a minute; I'll just put them under cover,' and dashing out, he led the horses into a ramshackle lean-to that had once served as a stable, where he tied them before running back to the house.

Groping his way towards her, he found that her body was no longer bent; she was standing with her back pressed tight against the wall, her hands cupping her face, and he said to her, 'Come over here, there's a bench and rough table of sorts. The road travellers use this place as a shelter; there might be some dry wood, we'll make a fire.'

When he had seated her on the form she clutched at his arm and muttered through chattering teeth, 'You're soaked. You . . . you shouldn't be soaked.' Anna had told her that people with the consumption should never get their feet wet, in fact should never be out in the rain; people with consumption should, if they could afford it, go and live in a different climate. 'Take your coat off,' she said; 'it may not have got through.'

He made a small laughing sound at her solicitude, and it held some relief with the knowledge that she had for the moment got over her fear of the storm.

'I'm all right, don't worry about me,' he said. 'You're like a wet rabbit yourself.' He pointed to her hat, where the brim was drooping down each side of her face, and he added, 'A very wet rabbit, its ears in the doldrums.'

When she lifted her hands and took her hat off he said, 'I would take off your coat an' all.'

'No,' she said as she shivered, 'I'm cold.'

He turned from her and made his way through the dimness to the far corner of the room where there was a rough open fireplace, and from there he called, 'We're in luck, there's dry wood here, quite a bit, and kindling. You'll be warm in no time.'

'Have you any matches?'

'No; but if I know anything the roadsters will have left a flint around somewhere; they look out for each other, the roadsters do. That is, the regular ones.'

There was a long pause, and then his voice came again, on an excited note now, 'What did I tell you! In this niche, a box with a flint in it. Here we go.'

As Constance watched the sparks flying from the flint her agitation eased; they would soon have a fire and their clothes would dry. She wished she could stop shivering. Why did storms petrify her? She had tried, oh, she had tried to overcome her fear, but it was hopeless, she seemed to lose control the moment she heard thunder.

'There you are; look, it's alight. Come over here and get your coat dried.'

She rose from the form and was making her way towards the flickering light of the tinder when an earsplitting burst of thunder appeared to explode over the house. When its rumblings died away she was huddled on the floor to the side of the fire, her face buried hard against Matthew's shoulder; his arms were about her holding her close. When at last the only sound they could hear was the hard pinging of the rain on the slate roof and an occasional hiss as it came down the chimney and hit the burning wood, they still remained close pressed together.

The wood was well alight and sending the flames leaping upwards before she raised her head and looked into his face and whispered, 'I'm ... I'm sorry, Matthew.'

He made no answer, he was half kneeling, half sitting, as she was. Their positions were awkward and cramped but neither of them seemed to notice it. She did not withdraw from his hold but she stared into his eyes and could not help but recognize the look they held, and read there the reasons for the change in him these past months.

As she watched the firelight passing shadows over his corn-coloured hair she had the greatest desire to run her fingers through it, bury her face in it, and she told herself she was a fool, a fool of a girl, not to have recognized what was in his heart, and, what was more terrifying still, in her own. She had known she held a certain special feeling for Matthew; even when she was in love with Will Headley she had still retained this feeling for Matthew, but she had looked upon it as sympathy and compassion for his ill health. And perhaps that is how it had begun; but what it had nurtured was something much deeper.

When he whispered, 'Oh, Constance! Constance!' she answered simply, 'Matthew! Oh, Matthew!'

Still with their arms about each other they slid into a sitting position now, and again they gazed at each other in silence while the fire blazed merrily to its height.

After a period he asked softly, 'Didn't you know how I felt about you?'

She shook her head. 'No; not ... not until this moment.'

'And you, Constance, you, what do you feel for me? Look at me, please ... please. Tell me.'

He had to bend his head towards her to hear what she was saying above the noise of the rain which had increased in force. 'I ... I don't know, Matthew, I really don't know. It, it can't be true, I feel it's unreal. Can one suddenly know in a moment? Things ... things like this have to grow.'

'It's been growing for years.'

She was looking at him again. 'But you never gave any sign; why?'

'How could I? And I shouldn't now, no, not at this late stage, when I'm getting ready for my grave.'

'Oh don't, don't!' She put her hand over her mouth now and her head drooped deeply on to her chest.

'Oh, don't worry, dear; don't worry. I shouldn't have said that. It sounded as if I'm sorry for meself, but nevertheless it's a fact that's got to be faced. But . . . but I'm not sorry you know how I feel; no, I'm not sorry.'

'You . . . you could live for years and years.'

He shook his head slowly. 'Not years and years; another winter like last and . . . '

'No, no.' She was holding his hands now. 'Don't say that.'

'But Constance' – he shook his head at her – 'it's the truth. Yet you know something? I feel happier at this moment than I've ever done in me life before. I've died a number of deaths already, thinking of you marrying Donald. But now it doesn't seem to matter so much, and . . . and I don't feel I'm betraying him by . . . by telling you how I feel. When you're married. . . . '

'I could never marry Donald now.'

'What! Oh!' He was kneeling in front of her now, gripping her hands. 'Oh, but you must, you must. You're his life; there's no one in the world for him but you. I know him, I know him inside out. He's a strange fellow, possessive, pig-headed, and big-headed, but his feelin's are as deep as a drawn well, and all his feelin's are for you.'

As she stared up at him a flash of lightning illuminated the bizarre room and once again she flung herself against him and the impact overbalanced him. When there came the sound as if a thunderbolt had been thrown in through the open doorway she almost buried herself in him, and before the last peal of thunder had died away the inevitable was beginning.

On the bare floor they lay, the fire crackling to the side of them, the rain beating on the tiles and blowing through the paneless windows and the open doorway, and strangely it was he who protested, but silently, yelling at himself, 'No, no!' He could never commit this outrage against Donald. Even while his hands moved over her submissive body his mind begged him to stop before it was too late.

But it was too late, and when the lightning once again lit up the room, her crying out was not against it alone but against the ecstasy and the pain that was rending her body.

When it was over he rolled away from her for a moment and hid his face in his hands and groaned, and she lay inert, her eyes closed, her heaving breath stilled like someone who had died in her sleep.

When of a sudden she drew the breath back into her body again he turned swiftly to her and, enfolding her in his arms, cried, 'Oh Constance! Constance, me darling; me darling, me darling.'

She made no move now to put her arms about him, not even when the thunder broke over the house again did she press herself against him; she was spent and her body was no longer her own; she was in it, but not of it. A short while ago she had been a young girl, a prospective bride who was terrified of storms, now she was no longer a young girl, so different was she that she could listen to the thunder unmoved.

It was as if Matthew had read her thoughts, for now he was looking down into her face and talking rapidly, saying, 'I'm sorry. Oh God above, I'm sorry, Constance. Try to forget it, will you? Try to forget it. If Donald knew he would kill me. Oh aye, he would.' He was nodding his head at her as if refuting her denial of this. 'He would slit my throat like he does a pig's. God! if only it wasn't Donald. I don't want to hurt Donald, I wouldn't hurt him for the world.'

Gently she pressed him away from her, and as if she had performed the function a dozen times before she adjusted her clothes, her manner almost prim; then she said, 'I could never marry Donald now, but . . . but I could marry you, Matthew. And . . . and I could look after you. You . . . you could take your share of the farm and we could go away perhaps to a new climate.'

For answer he sat back on his hunkers and covered his face with his hands. When he looked at her again he said slowly, 'I . . . I could claim no share of the farm, I have put nothing into it. What me father would give me would be of his generosity. But then, then again, were I to leave an' take you with me, Donald would leave an' all. I know this; I know it in me heart, he wouldn't be able to stand a second disgrace, a second rejection. You see, that's what he's been suffering from all his life, being rejected. He was a bastard, and all bastards know rejection. Strangely, I know how he feels, and should I take you away the second rejection would hit him worse than the first, he wouldn't be able to bear it. And what's more, it would mean the end of the farm, for me father's a sick man; you've seen yourself he's crippled with rheumatism, he depends on Donald for everything. Donald runs the farm, he is the farm.'

Slowly she rose to her feet, dusting down the back of her skirt as she did so. Then as slowly she walked towards the form and, sitting on it, she put her joined hands on the table and bowed her head over them. And when he came and sat opposite to her and gripped her hands between his she looked at him and asked, 'Could you bear to see me married to Donald?'

He gulped in his throat twice before answering, 'I'll have to, won't I? There's nothing else for it. But now it won't be so bad, for I have part of you that I'll hold tight to until my last breath. Nothing seems to matter now, although I know it shouldn't have happened. It's my fault . . . my fault . . . '

As she looked now at his bowed head, she knew that she was seeing not only a sick man but a weak one; he was as weak as Donald was strong. Yet the blame for what had happened was not only his. She knew in her heart that if blame, as such, was to be apportioned then more than half of it should be put to her credit, for without her mute consent he would have got no further than kissing her. Even if he had forced himself upon her she could have resisted him, for in physical strength she was the stronger; but she hadn't resisted him.

Did she love him? She stared into his flushed face, into the soft tender gaze of his eyes. She didn't know now, she thought she had before . . . before that had happened, but now she felt empty, quite empty of all physical feeling. When she returned to normal, would she know then? Only one thing she was sure of at this moment, and that was she couldn't marry Donald. Nor could she go to the farm now. It would be impossible to look Donald in the face with Matthew there.

She turned her head slowly towards the doorway. The rain was easing now; the thunder was still rumbling, but in the distance. She looked back at Matthew and said, 'I'll return home.'

'No, no' – his tone held fear – 'you can't do that; he's . . . he's expecting you. If you're not there when he gets back tonight he'll be over first light in the morning.'

'Well, that's tomorrow. It'll . . . it'll give me time to think. But Matthew, can't you see, I couldn't possibly meet him today and, and spend the night at the farm. I couldn't. I couldn't.'

'Oh Constance.' He was gripping her forearms now, his voice trembling as he gabbled, 'Let things be as they were. What's happened atween us, let it be like a dream, a beautiful dream. If things were different I'd run off with you this minute; but as I can't support you I won't live on you, so it's no use you bringin' up your hundred a year. Anyway we both know you'd be a widow in no time.'

'Oh Matthew! Matthew!' She screwed up her face. 'Don't keep saying that.'

'I must 'cos you've got to believe it's the truth. If it wasn't I wouldn't be sittin' here persuading you to go ahead and marry Donald.'

They were both quiet now, their heads bowed, until he began to mumble as if talking to himself, 'I feel I've done the dirty on him though, and it isn't right, for he's treated me well over the years; another one in his place, a half-brother with no claim on me father, would have taken it out on me, especially one as strong in body and mind as he is. And . . . and there's another thing. I'm goin' to feel very bad about this later on, but it'll be nothing compared with my feelings if you turn from him. Do you know something, Constance? Look at me. Look at me.' He shook her arms, and when she looked at him he said, 'He's much more in need of you than I am, and God knows I need you, but his need goes deeper than mine.'

She stared at him. He was making excuses. He was a weakling in more ways than one. She turned her gaze towards the fire. The bright glow had dimmed, the thin sticks had dropped to ash leaving red stumps supporting each other. Gradually like one awakening from a dream, she looked about the room. She could see it as a whole now, for the light was lifting outside. It was a filthy place. She noticed now that there was a smell of excrement coming from some part of it. She looked down at the floor. It was criss-crossed with filth, dried mud, pieces of straw and broken sticks. . . . Yet she had lain down there and given herself to a man. How could she! *How could she!* What had come over her? Had her terror of the storm deprived her of her wits? No, no. She had given herself to Matthew because she'd wanted to; with or without a storm she had been ready to give herself to someone. Then why hadn't she waited for just one more week. She had acted like a wanton, a street woman, giving way to the impulses inside her without thought of the consequences.

It was the thought of the consequences that brought her to her feet, and she gasped, 'I must, I mean I can't go on with you, I must go back. You . . . you can tell him that I was very frightened – and I was, I was, that is the truth – and you had to turn back. . . . I must return home, I must, I must.'

'Constance.' He had come to her side now. His hands outstretched appealingly, he said, 'Please, please.' But she shook her head and turned away from him and went towards the door, saying loudly, 'It's no use, I won't go on. I can walk back; it will be downhill all the way. That's it, I'll walk back.'

'Don't be silly.' He caught her hand, and held her still as he stared hopelessly at her. Then saying gently, 'Come on,' he led her outside.

The rain had become a mere drizzle. He brought the horses from their shelter and helped her up on to Ned's back, and there were no more words between them. . . .

They were going down the last slope and were in sight of the cottage when she drew her horse to a standstill and, looking at him, she said, quietly, 'Don't come any further, Matthew. I know your clothes should be dried and you need some refreshment but I couldn't bear to give them my explanation in front of you, as . . . as I'll have to lie, you understand? I'm . . . I'm sorry.'

He nodded at her, then got down from his horse and helped her to the ground. His hands still under her armpits, he gazed at her and asked softly, 'Can I kiss you once more?'

She said to him neither yes nor nay, and she did not respond when his lips touched hers gently; but when he looked at her again her eyes were full of tears and he said brokenly. 'Aw, Constance, Constance. Aw God! if only – ' Then turning round abruptly, he grabbed at the horses' reins, turned them about, hoisted himself up in Daisy's saddle, and tugging at her he muttered, 'Get up there! get up!' and Daisy and her companion moved off, their steps slow, steady and unruffled.

She stood on the rough road for a moment watching him, then she swung about and ran. Her skirts held above her ankles, her coat billowing, she ran until she arrived breathless on the road leading to the cottage, and not until she had reached the gate did she pause; and then, gripping it in both hands, she leant over it.

It was like this that Miss Brigmore saw her from the bedroom window. With a smothered exclamation she hurried out of the room, down the stairs, and so out onto the pathway, saying as she met her, 'Why! Constance, my dear, my dear; what has happened?'

During the journey Constance had rehearsed what she was going to say. 'I just couldn't go on, the storm was terrifying. I made Matthew bring me back some of the way. He was very wet, so I wouldn't let him come any further than the boar rock.' But she said none of this, she just flung herself against Miss Brigmore, crying, 'Anna. Oh! Anna.'

'Ssh! Ssh! What is it? Something's happened?'

They were now in the hall and Miss Brigmore looked about her. Thomas was in his study reading or dozing, Barbara was in the outhouse with Mary pickling onions and red cabbage.

Sensing that something more than ordinary was afoot, Miss Brigmore said again, 'Ssh! Ssh! Now come upstairs. Come.' Soft-footed, she led the way hurriedly up the narrow stairs, and when they were in the bedroom she closed the door and, untying the strings of Constance's hat, she asked, 'What is it? what has happened? Oh my goodness!' She looked down at her skirt. 'Look at the condition of you; your dress is filthy, and your cloak too. Constance.' She backed from her just the slightest, her, brow furrowed; then said sharply, 'Come, get those things off and into a clean dress. Come now, stop crying and change, and then tell me.'

A few minutes later, when she'd buttoned the dress up the back, she turned Constance about and sat her down, and sitting opposite to her she took her hands and said firmly, 'Now.'

It was an order, but Constance couldn't obey it. How could one say to the person who had been teacher, and then friend, since one could remember anything, how could one say, 'I have given myself to a man. The act took place on the filthy floor of a derelict house. So much for all your training . . . Miss Brigmore.'

'Something's happened to you, what is it? Tell me.' Miss Brigmore had leant forward now and was shaking Constance by the shoulders. Then as a thought came into her mind, she suddenly straightened her body, sat back in her chair, and clasping her hands tightly against her breast, murmured, 'You . . . were attacked?'

'No, no.'

Miss Brigmore heaved a short sigh, then demanded, 'Then what?'

' . . . I can't marry Donald, Anna.'

'You can't marry Donald, what do you mean?'

'Some . . . something's happened.'

Again Miss Brigmore joined her hands and pressed them to her breast. 'Then you were attacked . . . ?'

'No, I wasn't attacked. . . . But Matthew, he, he loves me. It was in the storm. We were sheltering in that old house. Something happened, happened to us both. He . . . he isn't to blame.' Her head drooped now on to her breast, and then she repeated in a whisper, 'He isn't to blame.'

'Oh my God!'

Not only the words but how they were expressed brought Constance's head up. She had never heard Miss Brigmore speak in such a way; it was as a mother might, fearful for her daughter's chastity; it was too much. She flung herself forward onto her knees and buried her face in Miss Brigmore's lap.

It was a second before Miss Brigmore laid her hands on Constance's head. The consequences of the situation were looming before her, racing towards her. She was demanding that her mind think clearly but all her mind kept saying was, She must have gone insane, she must have gone insane. And with Matthew of all people!

She said it aloud, 'You must have been insane, girl, and with Matthew of all people! He . . . Donald will kill him when he knows.'

'He . . . he needn't know. He'll never know.' Constance had lifted her tear-drenched face upwards. 'I can't marry him.'

Miss Brigmore stared down at her for a long moment, and then she repeated, 'You can't marry him? Are you going to marry Matthew then?'

'No, no. Matthew. . . . ' She couldn't say ' Matthew won't marry me;' what she said was, 'Matthew can't marry me; he wants to but he can't. He's a sick man as you know, and . . . and as you said, Donald would kill him if he knew, and I believe that.' She nodded her head now. 'He's capable of killing him even though he loves him.'

Once more Miss Brigmore took hold of Constance's shoulders; and now she was hissing at her. 'And you say you are not going to marry Donald? What of the consequences of your act today then? What if you have a child?'

For the second time that day the breath became stilled in Constance's body, and when her lips did fall apart it was to emit it in a thin whisper as she asked the question, 'It could happen after just . . . just that once?'

'Yes, yes, of course, girl, after just that once.' Miss Brigmore's voice was still a hiss.

They stared at each other in wide-eyed silence as if watching the consequence taking on actual shape.

It was Miss Brigmore who broke the silence, her voice weighed with sorrow now as she said, 'This morning if you had said you weren't going to marry Donald I would literally have jumped for joy, but now I'm forced to say you must marry him, and I also must add, thank God that the ceremony is but a week ahead . . . Oh dear! Oh dear!' She put her hand to her brow now and closed her eyes and groaned. 'Constance! Constance! what possessed you? What in the name of God possessed you?'

For answer Constance turned her head slowly towards her shoulder and gazed out of the window, and when she saw that the sun was shining now she almost said, 'It was the weather, you could put it down to the weather.' And in a way that was true because if she had not been afraid of the storm and had not taken shelter in the derelict house it certainly, certainly would never have happened. Who made the weather, God? Well, if He did He had certainly laid it as a trap for her.

She now looked towards Miss Brigmore where she was bustling about the bed, turning down the counterpane, adjusting the pillows; and when she said, 'Get your clothes off,' Constance did not say, 'But I've just changed,' but she did say, 'Why?'

'You're going to bed. Your uncle and Barbara must be given a reason for your return, and they will accept the fact that you're upset by the storm. Moreover, you must be in bed when . . . when he comes, as come he will. This will save you having to talk at length with him.'

Without a murmur she began to undress.

When at last she was in bed, Miss Brigmore said, 'Don't sit up on your pillows like that, lie down, and say little or nothing to anyone except that the storm made you ill, that you just couldn't go on, and Matthew had to bring you back . . . Oh, and it's fortunate in a way that Pat Ferrier is calling this afternoon with a friend. Your uncle received a letter just after you left; he is going back to college at the weekend. His presence will divert Barbara's attention from you, for whatever you do you must not tell her about this. Barbara could never look lightly upon such a matter, she'd be shocked.'

She was tucking the sheet under Constance's chin when Constance, staring wide-eyed up at her, asked in a whisper, 'Are you shocked, Anna?'

In response Miss Brigmore sat down quickly on the side of the bed and, enfolding the girl in her arms, murmured, 'No, child, no; for I did the same myself, didn't I? There's only one difference between us, you have the chance to cover up your mistake, and in this way you are lucky, very lucky. You can have your cake and eat it. It falls to too few of us to have our cake and eat it.'

# Chapter Three

It was over. The wedding party had been driven to the church in Donald's new acquisition; it wasn't a trap but what he called a brake, a sturdy, square vehicle on two large wheels. It seated three people at each side and another beside the driver. It looked more suited to utility than pleasure for the seats were plain unpadded wood and the back rests afforded little comfort, being but two low iron rails. Donald had explained that it wasn't exactly what he wanted, but it was the only one going at the sale and it would do in the meantime.

He had driven over the hills alone. He should have been accompanied by Matthew as his best man, but Matthew, unfortunately, as he explained, had had a bad bout of coughing last night and had shown blood for the first time. It was understood without saying that neither his mother nor his step-father would attend the wedding.

It had been anything but a merry wedding party. The only one who had shown any sign of gaiety was Thomas, and, as he commented to himself, it was getting harder going as the day wore on. What was the matter with everybody? He said this to Miss Brigmore immediately on their return. They were alone in his room. He was loosening his cravat to give himself more air, and he exclaimed impatiently, 'Wedding! I've seen happier people at a funeral. Look,' he turned to her, 'is there something going on that I should know of? I've had a feeling on me these past days. She wanted to marry him, didn't she?'

'Yes, yes, she wanted to marry him.'

'Well then, why does she look as she does? In that church it could have been a funeral and she a lily on the coffin, I've never seen her looking so pale . . . And Barbara, I can't get over Barbara, not a word out of her these days. As for you . . . now Anna,' he came towards her wagging his finger, 'I know when something's amiss in your head, so come on,' his voice dropped to a whisper, 'tell me. Is there something I should know?'

She stared at him for a moment while her nostrils twitched and her lips moved one over the other in an agitated fashion, and then she said, 'If there was something you should know, do you think I could keep it from you. It's your imagination. It's Constance's wedding day; wedding days I'm told are a strain. Though of course I wouldn't know anything about that.'

'Aw An-na, An-na, that's hitting below the belt. Tell me' – he took her chin in his hand – 'do you mind so very much, for if you did . . .'

'If I did, you would still do nothing about it so it's well that I don't mind, isn't it?'

'You're a wonderful woman.'

'I'm a fool of a woman.' There was a deep sadness in the depths of her eyes as she smiled at him. Then taking his hand, she said, 'Come, we must join them now, and please me by being your entertaining self.'

At the wedding breakfast Thomas did his best to please her but as much for his own sake as for hers, for he was susceptible to atmosphere. He could never tolerate company where there was a feeling of strain. If he found it impossible to lighten it, he parted with it at the earliest opportunity. He would have liked nothing better now than to retire to his study, but as that was impossible he spread his congeniality as wide as possible, extending it to the meal and to Mary. When she almost tripped as she was carrying a dish to the table he cried at her, 'You're drunk, woman! Couldn't you wait?'

As Mary placed the dish in front of him she spluttered, 'Oh, Master, the things you say. I've never even had a drop yet; I've not even had a chance to drink Miss Constance's health.' She smiled at Constance and Constance smiled back at her, a white, thin smile.

No one seemed to notice that Mary had excluded the bridegroom. Although she would have said she had nothing against him, and she would have gone further and said there were things about him that she admired, the way he had got on for instance, and the way he presented himself; but she would have also said that in her opinion he wasn't the man for Miss Constance. Miss Constance should have married a gentleman, and although Donald Radlet was the master's son he was in her opinion far from being a gentleman. But anyway, it was done, and there she was, poor lamb, looking as white as a bleached sheet. Yet she supposed that was nothing to go by, most girls looked white on their wedding day. Now that was funny; Miss Constance had never wanted to be married in white. Months ago she had made up her mind to be married in yellow, and she had bought the material, yellow taffeta with a mauve sprig on it, and together she and Miss Barbara and Miss Brigmore had made it; and they had made a good job of it because she looked lovely, really lovely.

Barbara, too, thought that Constance looked lovely, and she knew in this moment that the soreness in her heart was concerned not only with the loss of Donald, because, as she had told herself, how could you lose something you had never had, but with the real loss of Constance herself, for she hadn't been separated from Constance since the very day she was born. In those early days she had cared for her like a little mother, and in this moment the pain of losing her was obliterating every other feeling. She could see the winter days ahead; for her the inside of the house would be as barren as the outside. There would still be Anna and her uncle, but she must face it, they had each other. Even Mary; Mary had someone she went to see on her day off once a fortnight; they lived over near Catton. She said it was an old aunt of hers but she also mentioned that the aunt had a nephew. She had never said how old the nephew was, but it was noted by all of them that Mary always came back from Auntie's very bright-eyed and somewhat gay. For years past Mary's Auntie had been a private joke between Constance and herself. Well, whoever he was, Mary had someone. They all had someone, except herself. And in another few years she'd be twenty-five. Then she would be old, and being plain, past the attractive stage, unless it was to some old man who needed nursing.

But even an old man who needed nursing would be better than reading her life away in this isolated spot where a visit from an outsider was a red-letter day. And she knew now that even the red-letter days would be few and far between once Constance was gone; not even young Ferrier would come any more.

Barbara was startled as a hand gripped her knee tightly and she turned her head to look into Miss Brigmore's eyes. Miss Brigmore was smiling and her eyes were telling her what to do. Miss Brigmore's eyes were very expressive. She remembered the time when she had first realized that Miss Brigmore was two people; it was on the day she had told her she thought she was wicked. She had dared to tell her what she had seen, and Miss Brigmore had knelt before her and held her hands and she had talked as if she were speaking to an adult. Strangely, she had understood all Miss Brigmore had said, and when she had finished she had realized that servants, even governesses, had few privileges compared with people such as herself; and in her old, young mind she had come to the conclusion that Miss Brigmore was someone she should be sorry for. Now, Miss Brigmore – dear, dear Anna – was someone whom she envied.

The meal was almost at an end. When it was over Constance would change her dress and leave immediately. Would she be able to talk to her before she left? She had become very distant this past week, almost as reticent as she herself was; reticence was part of her own nature but it never had had any place in Constance's character. Constance was open, uninhibited, but these past few days she had scarcely opened her lips. This attitude had caused a secret hope to rise in her that perhaps Constance was going to change her mind and not marry Donald. Yet at the same time she was well aware that if this should happen it would avail her nothing because to Donald Radlet she was merely someone who read books and newspapers which gave her a knowledge of everyday matters, on which he could draw for his own information without taking the trouble or time to garner it himself.

Cynically she thought that he had used her as a form of abbreviated news-sheet, and she could imagine him repeating the information he had gathered on his sundry visits to his associates or at the cattle shows, or in the market. She imagined him throwing off bits of world news with an authoritative air, which gave him the name for being a knowledgeable fellow. Oh, in spite of her feelings regarding him she knew him, indeed she thought she knew him better than Constance ever would.

She looked at him now and found that he was surveying her. There was a smile on his lips, a possessive, quiet, controlled smile. He looked so sure of himself, proud, as he should be for he had gained a prize in Constance; much more so than if he had married her, for she had nothing but her brains to recommend her. . . .

Donald, looking back at Barbara, thought, She really hates the idea of me having Constance. She feels as bad in a way about it as that crab across there. He turned his set smile on Miss Brigmore and let it rest there. Well, he had beaten her, well and truly he had beaten her, and she knew it. When he entered the door this morning there had been a look on her face he had never seen before; it was there still. He took it to mean defeat.

He now turned his gaze on the man who was his father and wondered how he really felt about it all. He was the only merry one present; except Mary of course. He didn't seem to mind Constance going. But then you could never tell with the old man really; behind that boisterous laugh and his joking tongue there was a keen awareness, a cunningness that was the shield of his class and which covered his real feelings. Well, let them all react as they might; he had won Constance, she was his. In one hour or less they'd be setting out over the hills. She was his wife, she was his for life. At last he had something of his own! And he would love her as a woman had never been loved before. And each year she'd give him a child, sons first, daughters later. He'd bring the colour back to her cheeks, conquer her fear of storms. By God! yes, he meant to do that after what Matthew had told him about the effect the weather had on her. He wasn't going to allow her to be fear-ridden for the rest of her life; he'd conquer her fear or he'd know the reason why.

They were drinking to them now. There they stood, the old man, and – her, and Barbara. As he gazed at them he quietly groped under the table-cloth for Constance's hand and when he found it he squeezed it tightly; but she did not turn and look at him, for she was looking up at the three beloved faces that were gazing down on her. And they were beloved faces, each and every one of them was beloved. She had never imagined that leaving them would be such a wrench. She knew that she loved them all, but in different ways. She felt like flinging herself forward and embracing them all at once and crying to them, 'Don't let me go. Don't let me go.' She could not believe that she was now a married woman, that the short ceremony in the bare and quiet church had given her over to Donald for life. Yet she recalled that the moment the ceremony was finished she had known a surge of relief, for now should a child be born through her madness there would be no disgrace. No life isolated in this cottage and burdened with the stigma of an unwanted child. No, the short ceremony had made her safe – but at what a price.

Donald did not stand and respond to the toast, he knew nothing of such ceremony, but he drank deeply, one, two, three glasses of wine, and all to his wife, while she still sipped at her first glass.

When Constance left the table and went upstairs both Miss Brigmore and Barbara accompanied her. Miss Brigmore did not want to leave the two sisters alone, so that there could be no private, tear-filled farewell between them. Constance's luggage was already packed, she had only to change her dress. This was quickly done, and when she was arrayed in a brown corded costume and wearing a biscuit-coloured straw hat, she stood for a moment and looked around the room. Then her eyes came to rest, first on Miss Brigmore and then on Barbara, and the next moment they were all enfolded together. But only for a moment, for Miss Brigmore, her voice breaking as she turned hastily away, said as she picked up the pair of gloves from the dressing table, 'No more now; what's done's done; it's over. Come, come.' She turned again and, spreading her arms wide, ushered them like two children through the door, and when they were on the landing she called, 'Mary! Mary! Come and help with the luggage.'

But instead of Mary appearing on the stairs it was Donald who bounded up to them, saying, 'You leave that to me. What is there? Where are they?' Miss Brigmore, pointing back into the room, said, 'There are three cases and four packages.'

'Three cases and four packages.' He imitated her voice, then let out a deep laugh and, going into the room, he picked up two cases in one hand and tucked a bulky package under his other arm before picking up the third case and, as Mary entered the room, he cried at her, 'I've left three for you.' Then in very much the manner that Thomas might have used, he poked his

head forward and uttered in a stage whisper, 'How would you like to come
over the hills and work for me, eh?'

'Go on with you. Go on with you.' She laughed shrilly. 'You're a funny
fellow you are; you're taking enough away when you're takin' Miss Constance. Go on, get off and don't let the master hear you sayin' you want me
an' all; they're losing enough the day, they are that.'

Mimicking her now, he said, 'And you've had more than a drop the day,
Mary, you have that. You like your duckie, don't you?'

He was at the top of the stairs now, she behind him, and she giggled as
she said, 'Eeh! the things you say. Go on with you.' He wasn't so bad after
all, she thought to herself, she liked him she did; yes, she did.

The women were outside now; only Thomas was in the hall. He was no
longer smiling, his expression was sad and there was a tightness to his jaws,
and when Mary, still laughing, said, 'He's a funny fellow this, Master,' he
admonished her as the master of the Hall might have done at one time,
saying, 'Be quiet, woman;' and she became quiet, subdued. Not until she
had put the packages among the others in the back of the brake and
Constance had come towards her and, putting her arms about her, had kissed
her did she speak again; and then her words came out on a flood of tears and
she cried, 'Oh Miss Constance! Miss Constance!' and putting her white
apron to her face she turned about and ran back into the house.

When Constance stood in the circle of Thomas's arms and felt his big
body quiver with emotion, it was too much, and she leant against him and
cried, 'Uncle! Dear Uncle!' and Thomas, his own cheeks wet, looked over
her head to where his son was standing near the horse, waiting, and he said,
'There now, there now. Go on, over the hills with you.' Then he took her
face in his hands and added, 'Don't forget us, my dear. Come and see us
often, eh?'

She nodded at him helplessly. The next moment she was lifted bodily in
Donald's arms and placed in the seat at the front of the brake, and not until
he had taken his seat beside her and picked up the reins did she lift her head
and look at them again. They were standing close together gazing up at her,
and she spoke to them as if they were one, saying, 'Good-bye, good-bye' and
they all nodded their heads at her, but not one of them spoke.

Before the brake rounded the bend in the road she turned right round in
her seat and waved to them, and now they waved back.

As soon as they were out of sight, Donald gathered the reins into one
hand, thrust out his other arm and pulled her to his side with a jerk that
caught at her breath and made her gasp, and his eyes covering her with
their dark gleaming light, he muttered thickly, 'At last, at long last,' and the
words brought home to her more than anything else the depths and the
fierceness of his passion for her; and if it had aroused only fear in her there
might have been some hope for him, but not when it also created revulsion.

# Chapter Four

They greeted her kindly, most warmly. Both Michael and Jane came from the house into the yard as the brake drew up. It was as if they had been waiting together.

'Well, here we are then,' said Michael with a smile, and when Donald had lifted her to the ground Jane held out her two hands and Constance took them gladly. But when Jane said, 'Welcome home, my dear,' all Constance could reply, and in a stiffly polite tone, was, 'Thank you.'

Although the day was warm they had lit a fire in the sitting room. The horsehair suite had been lightened with crotchet arm and head rests, a large new, hand-done proggy mat lay the length of the long stone fireplace, and the round table in the centre of the room was set for tea. On the snowy cloth lay the tea-set that had not been out of the cabinet since Matthew was christened, and the rest of the table was covered with a variety of home-baked cakes and plates of cold ham and beef, and pickles.

'Would you like to go upstairs or would you have a cup of tea first?' Jane's voice was warm, even comforting.

'I should love a cup of tea, please.' And not only one, she thought, but two, three, four, anything to delay going upstairs and being alone with him. It was no use telling herself that she had to be alone with him for the rest of her days; all she could think of at the moment was, she wanted a little breathing space.

She watched Jane bustle from the room to the kitchen back and forth several times, while Michael sat in the high-backed armchair opposite to her and nodded at her at intervals. At last he endeavoured to open a conversation.

'You've got it over then?' He still nodded at her.

'Yes, thank you.'

'How did it go?'

At this she glanced at Donald, where he was standing with his back to the fire; and he answered for her. On a laugh, he said, 'Well, it's done, signed, sealed, and I've put me brand on her.' He leant sideways and lifted up her hand showing to Michael the ring on her finger.

'I'm sorry that Matthew couldn't get along.' Michael was still nodding.

'Yes.' She swallowed, then said again, 'Yes,' before forcing herself to ask, 'Is he any better?'

'Better than he was yesterday, but still rather poorly. We're thinkin' of sending for a doctor come Monday. He won't hear of it, as usual, can't stand doctors; but I'll have me way if he's no better come Monday.'

Jane said now, 'Will you sit up, my dear?' and Constance came to the table, and the four of them sat down. One after the other they handed her the plates, and in order not to seem impolite and ungrateful to this kind little woman she forced herself to eat, and as she ate she thought, Thank God I shall like her. That at least is one good thing. And the father too; they're good people. And she prayed, 'Please God, take this feeling that I have against Donald from me; let me at least like him, don't let me hurt him, for . . . for he means well, and he cares for me.'

That was the trouble, he cared too much for her. She had not realized to the full extent the intensity of his passion; before, it had been somewhat veiled, but during the journey over the hills he had expressed his feelings, not only in words, but in looks, and touch.

She now tried to delude herself into thinking that once tonight was over the fire in him would be damped a little; his intensity would relax, and they would fall into a pattern like other married couples. But what other married couples? Whom did she know who was married? She had come in contact with no young married couples, all she knew about marriage was what she had read, and most of the stories ended up with the couple getting married and living happily ever after. Those that didn't were tragedies, where the husband took a mistress or the wife took a lover. Her husband would never take a mistress, she felt sure of this. Although he was a Mallen in part, he wasn't made like that. In an odd way he was much too proper. But she had already had a lover.

She glanced at Donald. He was sitting straight; he looked arrogant, utterly pleased with himself. He turned and looked her full in the face and jerked his chin upwards at her, and the action expressed more than any words the confidence he had in himself; and rightly, for was she not his wife and sitting, to all intents and purposes, at his table. The air of possession that emanated from him was frightening and she recalled, on a deep wave of sickness, Matthew's words, 'He would slit my throat like he does a pig's.'

It was about a quarter past seven when Jane lit the lamps. Constance stood by the table and watched her fitting on the coloured glass shades, the plain white one for the kitchen and a blue one, patterned with gold spots, for the sitting room. She remarked that the blue one was pretty and Jane replied, 'Aye, it belonged to the father's' – she always referred to her husband as the father – 'it belonged to the father's grandmother and the globe hasn't got a crack in it. I get scared out of me wits every time I light it.'

Jane turned her head to the side and smiled at the girl who was to share her home, and she was surprised that her presence was creating in her a feeling of shy happiness. She told herself that if the girl settled it would be like having a daughter in the house, and somebody to talk to. That is if Donald wasn't about. But of course it all depended on her settling, and at the moment she looked as if she could take flight. She couldn't explain to herself the look on the girl's face; she didn't want to put the word fear to it because she couldn't see what she had to fear; she had taken Donald with her eyes open, she'd had time to think about it, and then gone through with it, so she couldn't see that it was Donald who was making her uneasy. But uneasy she was. And there was another strange thing. When they rose from the table she hadn't gone with Donald but had followed her round the house asking questions about this and that, saying she wanted to be of assistance. Only a minute ago she had smiled at her kindly and said, 'There's plenty of time. Now don't worry, I'll find all the work you feel inclined to do; you never can be idle on a farm you know.' And now here she was wanting to help with the lamps.

She had seen immediately the difference the girl's presence was going to make to Donald; he was like a dog with two tails, she had never seen him so amenable. He had spoken to her as he had never done before, had even made a request of her. He had come into the larder and, standing at her side, had said, 'If she wants to learn the dairy show her, will you, but don't press her. I don't want her to do anything she doesn't want to do.' And she had turned and looked at him. His expression had been soft, and for the first time in his life he looked really happy, and she had answered, 'I'll tell her anything she wants to know.'

He had nodded, and stared at her silently for a moment before turning away, and leaving her standing with her hands pressed flat on the cold marble slab and thinking, it's going to work out all right after all. This is what he needs, a wife such as this one, someone he can be proud of and show off, someone he could have married if he'd had his birthright. And at that moment she had understood a lot about her son she had never understood before.

When she carried the lamp in both hands held well in front of her into the sitting room she did not speak until she had placed it on the table, and then, standing back from it, she looked at Constance and said, 'You'll find life here strange at first because we mostly work to the light, up with the dawn, to bed with the dusk, or pretty near it. At the end of a long day we're ready for our beds, especially in the winter, 'cos that's the warmest place, bed. Of course when I say that' – she now nodded her head and smiled broadly at Constance – 'I'm forgettin' about our Matthew. He'd burn oil to the dawn readin' his books. But not Donald.' She put out her hand now and indicated that Constance should sit on the couch, and as she sat down opposite to her she finished, 'Donald works very hard, very hard indeed. Since the father's had rheumatics it's been extra heavy for him. And there are times, as now, when Matthew can't do anything at all.'

Constance stared back through the lamplight into the round, homely face of this ordinary woman who in a way was on a par with Mary, but who nevertheless was her mother-in-law, and all she could do was nod. She knew already that she liked this woman. She also knew that she was going to need her in the days ahead. What she had the urge to do now was to sit close to her and hold her hands, cling to her hands. She thought too that her liking was returned. Yet what would this woman do if she knew that her new daughter-in-law had lain with one son before marrying the other? Just as Matthew had said of Donald, she would want to slit her throat. That terrible phrase was recurring in her mind more and more.

When she spoke again her question must have appeared as if she were anxious for Donald's return, for what she said was, 'Does it take long . . . I mean the last round at night?'

Jane smiled quietly as she said, 'Well, it all depends. You see the cattle are still out, and he goes round the fields. Then sometimes the hens won't take to their roost. There's a couple in particular go clucking round in the dark; they're deranged, an' one of these mornings they'll wake up and find themselves inside the fox and that'll give them a gliff.'

She laughed, a soft gay laugh, and was herself surprised to hear it; then in a more sober tone she went on, 'Of course, in the lambing time he can be up all hours that God sends; an' then with the calfing an' all. He's very careful of the animals, very careful.' She nodded at Constance, her expression quite serious now, then added, 'He's well thought of as a farmer, oh very well thought of. They take his word for lots of things roundabout.'

All Constance could say to this was 'Yes.' . . .

An hour later Jane thought to herself that she had never talked so much at one go in her life. Michael was no talker; Matthew was always in his books; and when you got a word out of Donald it was usually a comment on the animals, or a definite statement of what he was about to do. She had talked as she had done because the girl was nervous; she was all eyes. She looked a child, too young to be married, yet she was the same age as herself when she was married. She recalled her own first night in this house, her fear of having to go to bed with Michael, and then her overwhelming feeling of happiness when she realized the goodness in the man she had married. But there was a great difference between Michael and Donald, and there was a greater difference between herself at that age and this girl; yet it was the first night of marriage and she was in a strange house, and they were all comparative strangers to her. She must be filled with a great unease.

She leant forward now and said gently, 'Would you like to go upstairs and see to your things and such? You must be tired; it's been a trying day for you.'

Before she had finished speaking Constance was on her feet, saying, 'Yes, I would, thank you. Thank you very much.'

'I'll light your lamp, it's up there already. I'll take the kitchen one to see us up the stairs. I'd better not take that one.' She smiled and nodded towards the blue-shaded light, and Constance said, 'No, no, of course not.'

Constance had been in the bedroom earlier. She had opened one case and hung some of her things in the old dutch wardrobe that stood against one white wall, but she had not attempted to unpack the rest of the luggage. All she had wanted to do was to get away from the sight of the high bed covered by the patchwork quilt. Jane had pointed out to her that she had spent the winter making the quilt, and she had duly admired it; she had also thanked her for decorating the room, which decoration consisted of lime-washing in between the black beams that strutted the walls at uneven angles and those that supported the low ceiling in three massive beetle-pierced lengths, and which gleamed dully where the linseed oil that Jane had applied so generously to them had failed to soak in.

Setting the lamp down on the round oak table to the side of the bed, Jane now turned to Constance and, her hands folded in front of her waist, she said, 'There you are then, dear. I'll leave you now and wish you good night.' But she didn't move immediately, she stood staring at Constance and Constance at her; then, as if motivated by the same thought, they moved towards each other and their hands held and their cheeks touched. Then muttering something like, 'May your life be good. God bless you, dear,' Jane hurried from the room. And Constance was alone.

She looked about the room as she had done earlier in the day, and now, although she was still filled with panic, she knew she could run no farther; she had come up against a rock face as it were, and from now on she'd have to steel herself and climb.

The room was cold, there was a dankness about it. She knelt by one of the cases on the floor and, having opened it, she took out a warm nightdress, a dressing gown and a pair of slippers from where Anna had placed them to be ready to her hand. As she laid them on the bed she hesitated whether to wash her face and hands now or to wait until she was undressed; deciding she'd be less cold doing it now, she went to the corner washhand stand at the far side of the room. The basin was set in a hole in the middle of the stand; the jug in the basin was full to the top with water – and icy cold; the towel she dried on was clean and white but rough; but all these were minor inconveniences and would, she thought, have been endured with something of amusement if only the man with whom she was to share that bed behind her was anyone but Donald. If only it had been Matthew, even a sick Matthew, she would have been happy; or at least she wouldn't have been filled with fear as she was at this moment. But let her get this one night over and she would cope. Oh yes, just let her get this one night over and she would cope.

As she was about to undress she looked at the picture that was hanging above the bed. It was one of three religious prints that Jane had hung in the room; it showed colourful even in the lamplight, the picture itself was a travesty created by an artist who had undoubtedly taken liberties with the book of Esther, for not only did it show King Ahasuerus seated in his marble-pillared palace surrounded by his seven chamberlains, with Vashti, the wife he had put away, standing at a distance from him but it also showed Esther, whom he had taken to be his Queen, seated to his side, and at her feet seven maidens, undoubtedly virgins all.

Quickly now she began to unbutton her dress. Having stepped out of it, she folded it lengthwise and laid it over the back of a chair, as of habit; then she undid the strings of her first waist petticoat and stepped out of that; and she did the same with her under petticoat. It was as she stood in her bloomers, soft, lawn, lace-trimmed bloomers, a new innovation created by an American lady – the daring pattern of which she had copied from a ladies' journal – that the door opened. She did not turn her head to look towards it, but with one swift movement she gathered up her two petticoats and holding them against her neck she dropped down on to the edge of the bed and drew up her knees under their trailing cover.

Slowly and with a look of amusement on his face, Donald came towards her and, standing above her, he shook his head as he put out his hand and gently but firmly made to relieve her of her undergarments. When she resisted he closed his eyes for a moment, then said softly and as if reasoning with a child, 'Constance. Constance, you remember what happened today?' He now stretched his face at her in amused enquiry. 'Eh? You were married, remember? . . . Look' – he now caught her hand and, holding the wedding ring between his finger and thumb, he shook it vigorously – 'you were married . . . we were married. Come.' With a twist of his body he was sitting beside her, one arm about her, the other forcing her joined hands down over her chest.

When her protesting hands touched her lap he released them, and his fingers now moved upwards to the buttons lying between her breasts. As if she had been stung she sprang away from him and, grabbing up her nightdress, pulled it over her head, and now, half shielded by the foot of the bed and with rapid contortions, she undressed under it as she had done as a child when she shared her room with Barbara.

Miss Brigmore had early on introduced them to this pattern, reciting a little poem that went: 'Modesty becomes maidens making ready for the night.' And when alone, they had mimicked her but altered the words to: 'Modesty becomes maidens who are little mealy-mouthed mites.'

Still seated on the bed, Donald surveyed her. He was no longer smiling, no longer amused. From a deep recess in his mind a thought was oozing, like the matter from a sappurating sore. As it gained force it brought him up from the bed, and the action seemed to stem its flow; but he was still aware of it as he gripped her by the shoulders and said from low in his throat, 'Constance you are me wife, you're no longer in the cottage with them, you've started on a different sort of life. And you're not a child, so stop acting like one.'

When he thrust her from him she fell backwards and leant against the brass rail at the foot of the bed. Her eyes were wide, her mouth open. She watched him for a moment as he turned from her and walked across the room and pulled open the top drawer of the chest; then like the child he had denied she was, she scrambled up the side of the bed, tore back the clothes and climbed in.

When she next looked at him he was undressed down to his trousers. At this point she closed her eyes. She did not open them again until she felt him moving by the side of the bed; and what she saw would, under happier circumstances, have made her laugh, for he was dressed in a night-shirt that barely reached his knees. It wasn't the first time she had seen a man dressed in a night-shirt, she had often glimpsed her uncle on his journeys back and forth to the water closet in the early morning. But then her uncle's night-shirt reached his ankles. But Donald's night-shirt exposed his lower limbs and she saw that they were hairy, as also was his chest that she glimpsed through the open shirt; and for a reason she couldn't explain she became more fearful.

Her body stiff, she waited for him to put out the lamp; but when he clambered into the bed the lamp was still burning. Now, leaning on his elbow, he was hanging over her, looking down into her face, saying nothing, just staring at her; and as she stared back at him she saw his whole countenance alter. There came over it the softness that she had glimpsed now and again, and her thoughts, racing madly, gabbled at her. It might have been all right if that storm hadn't overtaken them. Yes, yes, it might. If only she could forget what had happened in the storm, put it out of her mind, at least for to-night. But she couldn't because Matthew was there, somewhere across the landing, coughing – and knowing, and thinking.

He still did not speak when he drew her into his arms and held her body close to his. But he did not bring his face close to hers; he kept his head well back from her and peered at her, and his whisper bore out the expression in his eyes: 'I just want to look at you,' he said; 'look and look. I've dreamt of this moment for years. Do you understand that, Constance?'

As the muscles of his arms suddenly contracted her body jerked against his, yet remained stiff. For the moment he seemed unaware of it, lost in the wonder of his own emotions and not a little blinded by his own achievement. But when his mouth dropped to hers and there was no response from her lips he brought his head up again, and now he asked, almost as a plea, 'What is it? What is it, Constance? Don't be afraid, please. Don't be afraid, I love you. I told you I love you, and I'll love you as no one has ever been loved afore. I need to love you, and I need you to love me. Do you understand that?'

' . . . Say something.' Again her body jerked within his hold.

When she did not speak, the softness seeped from his face and he said thickly, 'That damned old cow has filled your head with bloody nonsense about marriage, hasn't she?'

At this she managed to gulp and mutter, 'No, no.'

'Then what is it?'

If she had replied, 'I'm afraid, Donald; it's all so strange, everything,' he undoubtedly would have thought he understood and might even have given himself another explanation for what he was to discover within the next few minutes; but she could not put on an act for him, she was not subtle enough, sly enough, and she was aware of this.

'*No, no! not yet, please, please, not yet.*' Her voice was strangled in her throat, his mouth was eating her. His hands seemed to have multiplied like the snakes on Medusa's head and were attacking her body from all angles . . .

It was a full three minutes after she ceased to struggle that he raised himself from her. In part she had known the man Donald Radlet five minutes earlier, but she knew nothing of the man who was gazing down at her now. The face that she was staring into had about it a stricken look; then like wind-driven clouds that changed the face of the sky, the expression turned into one of wild black ferocity. She held her breath and tried to press her body deeper into the feather tick in order to ward off the violence threatened by his expression, but to her relief and surprise his body moved away from hers until there was a foot of space between them, and he was sitting upright, half turned from her, but with his eyes still on her.

As if obeying a warning voice within himself, Donald moved still further towards the edge of the bed, but continued to look at her. And as he looked he knew that the pus from the secret sore in his mind was flooding his brain, and that if he didn't control it he would put out his hands and throttle the thing he loved, and wanted to go on loving. But now there was a question about that for he knew that he had been duped; he, Donald Radlet, who was no man's fool, who was as smart as they came, who allowed no one to take the rise out of him without paying for it, who knew, who had always known, that if you followed the principle of wanting a thing badly enough you would surely get it, had been made a monkey out of.

This then was the reason for her attitude. He could see it all plainly now; it was as clear as the white light that occasionally covered the hills, the light that took your gaze away into infinity. Her manner this past week, her being afraid to face him a week gone. She had taken to her bed when he had dashed over the hills to find out what the trouble was.

It was as he was leaving the cottage that he had met the Ferrier boy, because that's all he was, a smooth-chinned, weak-kneed boy. But he was just going back to Oxford he'd said, and it was doubtful if that old cow would have left him alone in the bedroom with Constance for a moment. But if not he, then who else?

There was that family in Allendale, with the two sons. Both were a deal older than her, but what did that matter? Yes, what did that matter? Look at the old man for example. Yet it must have been a month since she had visited Allendale and what had taken place had taken place within the last fortnight.

He looked into her face, beautiful, even angelic looking . . . but fear-filled. Had he made a mistake? Hell's flames, no! he had made no mistake. He was no amateur coming to bed for the first time; he had been but fifteen when he took his first woman. And that was the correct term, took her; she hadn't taken him, although she had been long at the game. She had laughed at him, and liked him, and every market day in Hexham he had managed to slip up the alley. She had supplied him until he was eighteen.

One particular time when he went up the alley the door was opened by a young girl. Bella had died the previous week she said, but would he like to come in. Her name was Nancy; she was fourteen and she was the one and only virgin he'd ever had. But if he'd never had that experience he would have known that she, lying there, his wife, on this the first night of their marriage was no virgin.

His pride was under his feet, his head was dragged down, his arrogance was broken, his self-esteem was as something he had never heard of for his mind was utterly deprived of it. He was no longer a Mallen flaunting his streak, finding pride in his bastardy, and through it feeling he had the right to confer condescension on even those who considered themselves his superiors – he was nothing. He was now as he had been that day in the market place when the Scolley brothers had laughed at him and called him a bastard. Yet he was not even as he had been on that day, he was less, much less, for on that day he had become aware that there was high blood in him, gentleman's blood. On that day he found out that he was the son of a man who owned a grand Hall over the hills, a man of property and substance; and on that day he had sworn that he would grow so big in all ways that nobody would dare turn a disdainful look in his direction without paying for it, and that whatever he desired from life he would get. . . .

And he had got it. She was lying there, and she was no better than any whore.

She smothered a scream as he pounced on her, his hands round her throat, his nose almost touching hers, his words like grit spitting into her face. 'Who was it? tell me! Who was it?'

When her body became limp under his hands he released the pressure of his thumbs; but now he had her by the shoulders, lifting her bodily upwards, and in a whispered hiss he demanded, 'Tell me! else I'll throttle it out of you.'

When she moved her head from side to side and gasped he shook her like a dog shaking a rat, and when the tears spurted from her eyes and a cry escaped her lips he turned his head quickly and looked towards the door before thrusting her back into the mattress.

He remained still, listening. Then satisfying himself that if her cry had carried beyond the room they would likely take it as the result of a marriage bed caper, he moved up to her again. And now leaning over her, his hands one on each side of her, he said slowly, 'You've been with somebody, haven't you?'

Her hands were holding her throat as she shook her head; then she stammered, 'N . . . n . . . no.'

'You're lying. You can't hoodwink me, not on this anyway. Who was he?

I'll not keep askin' you, I'll shake it out of you. I'll beat it out of you. Do you hear, my dear Constance? I'll beat it out of you. Who was it?'

'I tell you, I tell you . . . nobody.'

He screwed up his eyes until they became mere slits, then repeated, 'Nobody? nobody you say? Then why didn't you come over as you intended last week? It must have taken some storm to have put you to bed.'

'It . . . it was . . . it was the storm.'

'You're lying.'

'I'm not.'

As she gazed into his face she realized that not only would she have to lie, but lie convincingly, for she knew that this man was capable, as Matthew had predicted, of slitting her throat as he did the pigs'.

Like an actress taking her cue she obeyed the inner voice in her and, hoisting herself away from him, she tried to assume indignation, and in no small tone she cried at him, 'You are mad. I don't know what you mean, what you suspect, and . . . and I won't stay with you to be treated in such a manner, I'll go home. . . .'

Immediately she knew she had overdone her part for he turned on her now, growling low, 'You what! you what!' His lean face was purple with his anger; the fact that she could even voice such a thing showed him a new aspect of his humiliation, a public aspect, something to be avoided at all costs, especially in his case, for were she even to attempt to go back over the hills he could never outlive the humiliation. But being who he was he knew that he would never allow it to get that far, and he told her so. In a thick whisper now, leaning towards her but not touching her, he said, 'You'll go home, as you call it, when they carry you over in a box to the cemetery but not afore, not if I know it.'

When she closed her eyes and the tears washed down her face his teeth ground into his lip, and he bowed his head for a moment and, in real agony now, he groaned, 'Oh Constance! Constance! why? why? How could you do it?'

'I didn't, I didn't. I tell you you must be mad. I don't know what you're talking about.'

He was looking at her as he said, 'Well, if you don't know what I'm talking about why do you say you didn't?'

Her head wagged on her shoulders in a desperate fashion now as she muttered, 'Because you are suggesting that I . . . I . . .'

She suddenly turned from him and rolled onto her face and pressed it into the pillow to stifle the sound of her sobbing, and he straightened his back and turned from the bed. Having crossed the room to where his clothes lay, he slowly got back into them, all except his shoes, and these he carried in his hand.

Without a backward glance towards the bed, he went to the door and, gripping it firmly so that it shouldn't creak he opened it and closed it after him. Cautiously he crossed the landing and went down the stairs. There was no light; he didn't need one, he knew every inch of this house. Unbolting the back door, he went into the yard.

He looked up at the sky for a moment. It was high and star-studded; the air was sharp with frost, there would be rime on the walls in the morning. He crossed the yard and went through a door next to the cow byres and into the warm steamy atmosphere that came from the boiler where the pig mash was simmering. The room was part harness room, part store-room. He pulled down a bundle of hay and brought it near to the boiler and, sitting on it, he dropped his head into his hands and for the first time in his life Donald Radlet cried.

Towards morning he must have dozed; but he became wide awake at the sound of the cockerel giving answer to the faint echo coming from another of his breed across the valley. He rose from the hay on which he had been lying and dusted himself down, then went out into the yard. He did not look up into the sky to see the light lifting, for his attention was caught by the gleam of the lamp coming from the kitchen. His mother must be up but it was early for her.

When he entered the kitchen and Matthew, a teapot in his hand, swung round from the fireplace, he stopped and stared at him before saying, 'Why are you up?'

Steadying the teapot in both hands, Matthew went to the table and placed the teapot on it before he muttered, 'I . . . I needed a drink; I . . . I had the shivers.'

Donald was standing at the other side of the table now and he said, 'Why didn't you knock for Mam?'

When Matthew gave no answer but reached out and drew a mug towards him Donald's eyes focused on his hand which was trembling; then they lifted to his face. His skin had not the usual transparent glow about it this morning except for the two high spots of red on his cheekbones; it looked yellow, as if it had taken the tint from his hair. His gaze was held by the odd expression in his eyes; it was a startled expression holding fear. Well, he would be fearful, wouldn't he? When a man knew he was going to die it would make him fearful.

'How . . . how is Constance?'

'Look out, you're spilling the tea all over the place. Here! give it to me . . . She's all right, tired, exciting day yesterday.' He actually forced his lips into a smile; it was the first effort in the pattern he had worked out for himself last night. He would act before the others as if everything were normal, and he would see that she did the same. By God! he would. One thing he wouldn't tolerate and that was pity; even from those in this house who were near to him, for he knew that, being human, they could not help but think, And how are the mighty fallen! His da had a saying: If the eagle dies in the air it still has to fall to earth. Well, he had been an eagle and last night a vital part of him had died and he had fallen to the earth; but no one would know of his fall.

'Here, here! hold on a minute.' He could not get round the table quickly enough to save Matthew from falling backwards. When he reached him he was lying on the floor, his face now no longer yellow but deathly white.

'Matthew! Matthew!' He raised his head, then put his hand on his heart; it was still beating and quite rapidly. Bending now, he picked the inert figure from the floor as if it were a child and carried it upstairs, and as he passed the first door on the landing he put out his foot and kicked it as he yelled, 'Matthew's bad, get up.'

He was lifting his foot again to thrust it out towards Matthew's bedroom door when he saw Constance standing in the open doorway of their bedroom. Her face looked almost as white as the one hanging over his arm, and he cried at her, 'Come and make yourself useful.' It was his second move in the new game and it seemed to have an immediate effect on her for she sprang from the doorway to his side and as he made his way towards the bed she muttered, 'What . . . what have you done? What have you done?'

He didn't answer until he had laid Matthew down and was taking off his shoes, then he looked at her from the side and said, 'What do you mean, what have I done?' His eyes followed hers to Matthew's face where the lips and chin were now covered with blood, and he thought he saw the reason for her question.

'It's his lungs, he's fainted.' Then his voice harsh, he growled at her under his breath, 'And don't you do the same, 'cos you'll witness more than a spot of blood afore you're finished.'

The words were like a threat, yet they steadied her for she, too, had actually been on the point of fainting, and for much the same reason that had tumbled Matthew into unconsciousness, relief.

# Chapter One

## Barbara

November and December 1862 had been cruel months. Miss Brigmore had caught a severe cold through sitting on the carrier's cart exposed to a biting wind as it travelled the hills between the cottage and the farm.

The newly married couple had visited the cottage only once, and then she'd hardly been able to have a word alone with Constance for that man had hovered over them like a hawk. But during the short conversation she had gauged enough to gather that life was bearable during the day-time but that at night it became a special kind of purgatory, because Donald was aware of her lapse; he had seemingly been aware of it from the first night of their marriage. Constance had stared at her while waiting for a clearer explanation of this, and she might have been able to satisfy her except that they had been interrupted by Donald.

Repeatedly since that visit Miss Brigmore had blamed herself for having neglected a very important part of the girls' education, yet at the same time excusing herself: should she under any circumstances have had to explain to them that they were virgins but once?

It was when the weather was about to break and there had been no further visit from the farm, that Thomas said, 'You know, I've got a feeling that everything isn't right across there; why doesn't he come like he used to? Hail, rain or snow didn't stop him this time last year, except when the roads were absolutely impassable, and they'll soon be like that again. If it wouldn't be the means of embarrassing both myself and those people across there' – he was referring now to Jane and Michael – 'I would order a carriage and go over, I would indeed.'

He had looked at her as he finished and then had stood waiting for her response, which she knew should have been, 'And where do you think the money is coming from to provide you with a carriage?' But what she said was, 'I will go across myself; the carrier's cart will be running for a while yet.'

So, on a day when six layers of clothes were no protection against the icy wind she crossed over the mountains to the farm, and there, at the sight of her dear Constance, she had wanted to cover her face with her hands and weep. Three months of marriage had put almost twice as many years on her. There was no spark of joy left in her; in fact the mother, who was, Miss Brigmore thought, about her own age, was much more lively than the young wife. Only one consolation did she bring back with her across the hills. The mother was kind to Constance; she evidently had a liking for her, and was glad to have her at the farm. What little she saw of the father, too, she liked. He had welcomed her quite warmly. But she had found it almost impossible to look at, much less sympathize with, Matthew where he sat huddled in blankets to the side of the roaring fire. Indeed, when their eyes had met she knew that there was no secret between them.

What she had found strange too, was that Constance no longer wanted to be alone with her. She had not suggested taking her to her room, and when Jane had said, 'Wouldn't you like to take Miss Brigmore round the farm? Go on, wrap up well, it will do you good to get some air,' she had answered, 'Can you spare the time to come too, you can explain things better than me?' And she had turned her head in Miss Brigmore's direction but had not looked at her directly as she ended, 'I'm new to all this, you understand?'

In fact the whole being that Constance now presented to her was new to Miss Brigmore; the old Constance might never have existed, her spirit had been crushed. This wasn't altogether unexpected; for she had imagined it might happen. Nevertheless she had thought it would take a number of years to come about; yet Donald had accomplished the change in the course of a few weeks.

When she had at last returned to the cottage she was cold to the very core of her being, even her mind seemed numbed, and she had not hidden all the truth from them when they asked how she had found Constance. 'She's changed,' she had said.

'Changed?' Thomas had demanded. 'Changed, what do you mean?'

'She's much more quiet, sort of subdued.'

'Connie subdued? I'll never believe that, I'll have to see it first. When is she coming over?'

'I . . . I don't think she'll be over yet awhile; she's been having a rather distressing time with sickness and such.'

'Oh. Oh.' Thomas had risen from his chair, his head bobbing. He had turned and looked at her and said, 'I don't mind telling you I miss her, I miss her chatter. Do you know something?' He had poked his head forward. 'I realize I've hardly laughed since she left. Funny now that, isn't it? Barbara's different, too quiet. You could always get a laugh out of Constance.'

'No, no, it isn't funny,' she had replied evenly. 'As you say, Barbara is sedate, and I cannot claim that any part of my nature tends towards provoking hilarity either.'

At this he put his head back and let out a bellow of a laugh before saying, 'I take it all back. I take it all back because there are times, my dear Anna, when you appear very, very funny.'

'Thank you.'

'Aw' – he flapped his hand at her as he turned away – 'you can't put me in my place, mentally or otherwise. Go on with you.' And he flapped his hand again as he went out, still chuckling.

Barbara had asked, 'How did you find her?' and she had answered again, 'Very changed.'

'She's not happy?'

She had stared at Barbara. Would it make her happy to know that her sister was unhappy, human nature being what it was? She didn't know.

Barbara now said, 'She's not settling?' and to this she answered, 'Yes, she's settling. But regarding happiness, no, I'd be telling a lie if I said she was happy.'

'Then why did she marry him?' The words were brought out with deep bitterness, and Miss Brigmore answered, 'There was a reason, a special reason. She had changed her mind and wasn't going to marry him. Yes' – she nodded at Barbara's surprised look – 'and something happened and she was forced to marry him.'

Barbara's thin face had crinkled into deep lines of disgust as she whispered, 'She had misbehaved?'

'Yes.' Miss Brigmore nodded her head. She had decided during these last few minutes to tell Barbara the truth. Whether she would sympathize or even understand she didn't know but she felt compelled to tell her the real reason why her sister had married Donald Radlet, and so she repeated 'Yes, she had misbehaved . . . but not with Donald.'

'Not with . . . ?' Barbara's mouth had fallen into an amazed gape.

'It happened in the storm when Matthew was taking her to the farm. You know how fearful she becomes in a storm. They took shelter in a deserted house on top of the hills. He comforted her and that was that. He told her that he had loved her as long as Donald had and she realized in that moment that she loved him too. From what little she told me I gather that she begged him to marry her but for obvious reasons he couldn't, or wouldn't. I think the main reason was he was afraid of Donald and what might happen to him if the truth were ever known.'

Barbara stood with her two hands pressed tightly over the lower part of her face; and after a time she whispered, 'And Donald, he . . . he doesn't know?'

'Yes and no. He knows that she did not come to him as a wife should but . . . but he doesn't know who was responsible.'

'Oh dear Lord! dear Lord!' Still holding her face, Barbara had paced the floor; and then much to Miss Brigmore's surprise she said with deep feeling, 'Poor Connie! poor Connie!' And she had endorsed it, saying, 'Yes, indeed Barbara, poor Connie.'

When, the day following her visit to the farm, Miss Brigmore had developed a cold she had treated it as an ordinary snifter – Mary's term for streaming eyes and a red nose – but on the third day when she went into a fever there was great concern in the house; and the following week when the cold developed into pneumonia and the doctor rode six miles from the town every day for four days a pall of fear descended on them all. What, Thomas had asked himself, would he do with his life if he lost Anna?

And what, Barbara had asked herself, would become of her if she lost Anna? She'd be left here with Uncle and Mary, Uncle who only thought of his stomach and – that unmentionable thing – and Mary, who had appeared to her as a wonderful person during her childhood, but whom she now saw as a faithful but very ordinary, even ignorant, woman. What she needed above everything now was mental companionship, so she went on her knees nightly, or whenever she gave herself time to rest, and beseeched God to spare Anna.

And Mary too – as she rushed between the cooking and the cleaning and the washing and the ironing, and lugging the coal upstairs to see that the room was kept at an even temperature twenty-four hours of the day – had also asked what would she do if anything happened to the Miss? There had been a time when she hadn't liked Miss Brigmore, when she hadn't a good word in her mouth for her; but that was many years ago. But since they had all come to live in this house she had come to look upon her not merely as a woman of spirit, but as a sort of miracle worker. If anything went wrong Miss Brigmore would put it right; moreover she had a way of spreading out the money so that it seemed to go twice as far as it would have done in anyone else's hands; and she never went for her now as she had done in those far-off days back in the nursery. Mind you, aye, she wasn't lavish with her praises, but you always knew when she was pleased. 'You've done very well, Mary,' she would say. 'I don't think you've made a better pie than that, Mary,' she would say. 'Put your feet up, Mary, and rest that leg,' she would say. The only times she showed any displeasure was when she was foolish enough to take more than three glasses of her Aunt Sarah's brew on her days off, for when she came back she couldn't stop her tongue from wagging, or herself from giggling. The girls used to laugh at her, and with her; but not Miss Brigmore. And a telling off would always come the next morning.

She often brought a bottle back with her. At one time, she kept it in her room, but she had more sense now. Now she left it in a rabbit hole beyond the hedge – you couldn't see the hole from this side, and all she had to do was to go on to her knees, put her hand through the privet and pull the bottle out. She generally waited until it was dark and they'd all gone to bed, and then just before she locked up she'd slip down the garden and have a little nip. It was a great comfort, her Aunt Sarah's bottle, on cold nights.

Once, when she had taken more than the three nips and Miss Brigmore had gone for her, she had nearly turned on her and said, 'Well, I haven't got the master to keep me warm, have I!' Eeh! she was glad she hadn't let that slip out, she would never have forgiven herself. And she knew that if it would be any help to Miss Brigmore at this moment she would promise her she would never touch a drop again as long as she lived. But all she could do was to ask God to see to it.

And God saw to it, but He took His time. Miss Brigmore survived the pneumonia but it left her with an infection that the doctor could put no name to, but which, he said, could be cured with time. The infection took the form of making Miss Brigmore unable to assimilate her food. Within half-an-hour of eating a meal her bowel would evacuate it. Patience, said the doctor, patience. He had seen cases like this before. It might take two, or four, or six months, but it could be cured.

Up to date, Miss Brigmore had suffered the infection for four months. She was not confined wholly to bed but she was still unable to do anything other than sit in a chair by the side of the window, near enough to it to see the road, but far away enough from it to avoid a draught. . . .

It was now a March day in 1863, the sky high and clear blue. The snow had gone for the present, except from the hilltops. If you gave your imagination licence you could see spring not very far ahead. At least, this is what Barbara was saying as she bustled about the room. 'In a fortnight's time,' she said, 'three weeks at the most, we'll see the bulbs out, and the rowans too . . . and with the carrier's cart tomorrow we should have a letter from Constance. I must write one tonight and have it ready for him. Do you think you can do a note to her, Anna?'

'Yes, yes, of course I'll write a note.' Miss Brigmore's tone was absent-minded. 'By the way, who is that person talking to your uncle on the road?'

Barbara came to the window and, looking over the garden, she said, 'Oh, I understand her name is Moorhead, a Mrs Moorhead. Mary refers to her as that Aggie Moorhead. She comes from somewhere near Studdon; she's working daily at the Hall doing the rough, I understand. Mary tells me they have engaged half-a-dozen such to get the place to rights before the staff arrive; but as she says, and I agree with her, it'll take six months not six weeks, and that's the time they have allowed them to clean the place down.'

'Why is your uncle talking to her?'

Barbara gave a little hunch to one shoulder as she turned from the window, saying, 'I don't suppose Uncle's talking to her, she's talking to him; to quote Mary again, she's got a loose lip.' She smiled now at Miss Brigmore, but Miss Brigmore was still looking in the direction of the road and she said, 'Your uncle's laughing.'

Barbara had been about to turn away, but she stopped and looked down at Miss Brigmore. Anna was jealous of Uncle. Well, well! It was strange, she thought, that a person could maintain jealousy into middle years. What was she now? Forty-two? No; forty-three? forty-four? Anna never talked about her age, but nevertheless she was a settled woman. She sighed heavily within herself. She wished she was over forty, for then she, too, would be settled, and she was sure that by then she'd be past all feelings of jealousy and discontent – and desire. She glanced out of the window again. The Moorhead person was walking away. She was passing the lower gate and she saw that she had a jaunty walk or, what would be more expressive, a common walk; her buttocks swayed from one side to the other. As Mary had suggested, she was a very common person, low even in the working class stratum. . . .

Down on the road Thomas was thinking much the same thing. She had a lilt to her walk, that piece; she swung her hips like a cow did its udders. And she was a little cow all right; if ever he had met one, there she went.

He had spoken to her on several occasions during the past few weeks. In fact it was she who had told him that his former home had been sold at last. After being confined to the house for days during the rough weather he had been taking the air on the road – he liked to walk on the level, he was past bobbing about on the rough fell land – and on one particular day it was she who had stopped, and smiled at him as she said, 'You're Mr Mallen, aren't you? Your old house's been sold again then.' And he had raised his brows at her and pursed his lips as he said, 'Has it indeed! Has it?'

'He's a man from Manchester way they say has took it.'

'Manchester? Oh, well, if he comes from there he won't stay long here.'

'They say he was born this way, at least his grandparents were. Bensham they called them. He's payin' well, shillin' a day an' your grub.'

She had jerked her head at him. But her familiarity had not annoyed him, he was long past taking offence at not being given his due, because, as he so often asked himself, what, after all, was his due these days? And so with a laugh he had said, 'You are lucky then.'

'Aye,' she replied. 'Aye, I'm always lucky. Never wanted, me. Live and let live I say, an' live it well as long as you've got it 'cos you're a long time dead.'

'You've got the correct philosophy.'

'Eh?'

'You're quite right, you're a long time dead.'

'That's what I said.' She had looked at him with round, bright, unblinking eyes, and her lips had slowly fallen apart showing her strong white teeth, and as they, in turn, widened he had watched her tongue wobbling in her mouth. Then she gave a laugh as her head went back and in a slow movement she turned from him, saying, 'Ta-rah, then, mister.'

He hadn't answered for a moment, but had watched her take four steps before saying, 'Good-bye.'

And she had turned her head over her shoulder and cried at him 'An' to you.'

He had walked on down the road smiling to himself. There went a character. 'And to you,' she had said. It appertained to no part of the farewell that had passed between them, but it had sounded amusing, and meaningful. 'And to you,' she had said. She was no chicken, but what vitality. God! how he wished he were younger. No, no – he shook his head at himself – those days were gone; that past was dead and long since buried. All he wanted now was to end the time left to him quietly, with Anna herself once again. Yes, that was the important thing, Anna to be herself once again.

When he allowed himself to dwell on his past he owned that Anna was the only woman in his life who had satisfied all his needs together, for she played the roles of mistress, wife and mother to him . . . aye, and teacher, for over the past twelve years he had learned much from her, and so realized he owed her much. And at these times he asked himself why he hadn't married her. There was nothing standing in the way.

Deep within himself he knew the answer; he had been afraid that the band of marriage would change her and he would lose the mistress and mother, and there would remain only the wife and teacher. He'd had experience of this state with his two previous wives, for they had been wives and nothing more; not that he had wanted anything more from his first marriage. It was in his second marriage that he had realized he needed something more than a bed partner, because a bed partner could be picked up any time of the night or day. Love, he had learned of recent years, had little to do with the needs of the body, yet the needs of the body were such that they couldn't be put aside. In his own case he had never been able to ignore them. He considered that celibates must be a different species of man, for man, as he understood him, was born with a hunger running through his veins from the moment he felt the breast in his mouth. Here he was in his sixty-eighth year and that hunger was still on him, and of late it had become an irritation because Anna had not been strong enough to feed it. It was months since he had taken her, and it looked as though it might be as many again before she was able to come to his bed.

Of a sudden life had become full of irritations. He didn't like to admit to himself that he missed the weekly visits of his natural son, although he could admit openly that he missed the company of Constance. Yet he had never said this in Barbara's hearing, knowing that it would hurt her because Barbara was a good girl, a good woman. But she had never been a girl in the sense that Constance had been a girl. Still, she was good and kind, and Anna owed her life to her care during these past weeks.

There was another irritation he had to suffer, and this came through

Mary. Mary was a pest. He had known for a long time that the wine she drank when on her visits to her aunt was no wine at all but came from some hidden still, and although he had hinted at first, then asked her openly but on the quiet, to bring him a bottle, she had steadfastly refused. 'Eeh! no,' she had said. 'What would Miss say?' Miss would have her head. He had wanted to say, 'I'll have your head if you don't obey me,' but the days were past when he could take such a line with his one servant, for he knew that he was in her debt, and had been for years.

There was something else he had discovered about Mary that had heightened his irritation towards her. She didn't come back from her aunt's empty-handed. Coming down to the study one night not so long ago to replenish his pipe, he saw the lamp was still burning in the kitchen, and, looking in, there she was, sitting in the rocking chair before the fire, her skirts well above her knees, warming her legs. Her head was lolling and she was dozing. To the side of her on the table was an empty glass. As he had lifted it from the table and smelt it she had woken up, crying, 'Eeh Master! Eeh Master!' And he had nodded at her slowly as he repeated, 'Eeh Master! Eeh Master! Come on, where's the bottle? where've you got it hidden? Go and fetch it.'

She had stammered and spluttered, 'Eeh! no, Master, I wouldn't. And I haven't got none hidden. I wouldn't dare bring any into the house, not a bottle I wouldn't, the Miss would be upset. I had the sniffles, I just had a drop.'

'You've got a bottle somewhere, Mary,' he said slowly. 'Come on now, where is it?'

Mary had looked at him for a moment and what she saw was a big, fat old man, with heavy jowls and a completely white head of hair, but with eyes that were still young and showing a vitality that only death would quench. With innate understanding she recognized what it must be costing this one-time proud man to beg for a drink, for since Miss Brigmore had been ill there had been no hard stuff brought from the town; every spare penny was needed for extra coal to keep the house warm and a few delicacies to tempt the invalid's appetite. And all this had to be done on an income that had been cut by a quarter since Miss Constance had got married. And so she said, as if speaking to one of her own kind, 'Well, sit you down there. Now mind, don't move, I'll be back in a minute.'

It was five minutes before she returned, and she brought him half a tumblerful of the stuff, that was all, no more, and so raw and strong it was that it seemed to rip his throat open as it went down. But it put him to sleep and gave him an easy night's rest.

And that's all she would ever give him, half a tumblerful now and again. He would go down on odd nights hoping to find her in the kitchen warming her legs, but she was crafty now, for the others would hardly retire before she went up to the attic.

And so he got into the habit of watching her whenever possible, trying to find out where she had the stuff hidden. He knew it wasn't in the house, and he had searched the outbuildings from floor to ceiling. He had an idea it was somewhere in the barn. He poked among the potatoes, the onions, the carrots and such-like in the pretence of tidying up; he poked around looking for a hole in the top of the turnip pit. There were times when his body was aching from so many needs that he pleaded with her, 'Come on, Mary, come on, just a drop.' And she would say, and truthfully, 'Master, it's all gone. Honest to God it's all gone, and there's another four days afore me leave.'

Yes, indeed, Mary was an irritation.

But over the past four weeks he had found a little diversion from the daily monotony, because when the weather was fine he'd had an exchange of words with the woman, Moorhead. That she was a trollop of the first water simply amused him; he never thought he'd have the opportunity of chatting with any of her kind ever again. Such a woman had a particular kind of dialogue, stilted, double-edged, and suggestive. He knew that this piece and himself had one thing in common, the needs of the body, and in her case she wasn't particular about who satisfied her.

When years ago he'd been able to pick and choose he would doubtless have passed her over, but now he wasn't able to pick and choose she appeared in a way as a gift from the gods, the mountain gods, in whose fortress he was being forced to end his days. He would not allow himself to think that his thoughts were in any way disloyal to Anna. Anna was a being apart, Anna was a woman who held his life in her hands, who nourished him in all ways; at least she had up till her illness. In any case Anna had a key to his thoughts; she would have understood, for she had known what kind of man he was from the beginning; had he been made in any other but the Mallen pattern he would never have gone up to her room in the first place and, of course, she understood this.

So gradually, over the past weeks he had enjoyed the exchanges with the Moorhead woman, knowing exactly what they were leading to. All he needed now was a time and place. His body was too heavy to allow him to walk far; the length of the road before it bent towards the hills one way and turned towards the Hall the other was the limit of his daily exercise, so a hollow on the fells was out of the question. The only place with cover that would suit his purpose was either the stable or the barn, and both were risky; yet not so much once darkness had fallen, for neither Barbara nor Mary ventured out often in the dark, except when Mary was after her bottle. But wherever the bottle was it was certainly not in the stable or the barn, of that he had made certain.

As he now watched the buttocks wobbling away into the distance he felt his blood infusing new life into him. By God! get her on the floor and he would take some of the wobble out of her. And he could at any time from now on. She had indicated as much by the simple action of heaving up her breasts with her forearm while she looked at him with a look that did not need to be interpreted in words.

He turned about and, squaring his shoulders, walked back up the road to the house, and he did not find it incongruous that he should immediately go upstairs to Anna.

'Ah! ah! there you are.' He almost bustled into the room. 'It's a wonderful day; pity we couldn't have got you out.'

'Did you enjoy your walk?'

'Yes and no. You know I don't like walking, but the air's good, sharp; cleans you as it goes down.'

'The woman you were talking to, who is she?'

He turned his head sharply and looked at her. 'Oh. Oh, her. You saw us? Oh, she's one of the sluts that are cleaning out the Hall; right pigsty she says it is.'

'But I understood the new people are due in shortly.'

'Yes, yes, they are. Well' – he now nodded towards her, saying slowly, 'A right pigsty she said it was when she first went there.' He walked to the window and looked out, and there was a silence between them for a moment until he said, 'Funny, you know, Anna, but it doesn't hurt me to know that someone is going to live there again; in fact I think I'm rather pleased. It was sad to see it dropping into decay. It's the kind of house that needs people. Some houses don't, they seem to have a self-sufficiency built into them from the beginning, but High Banks never had that quality; it was a mongrel of a house, crossed by periods and giving allegiance to none, so it needed people by way of comfort.'

'You sound quite poetical, Thomas.'

He turned to her, his face bright. 'Poetical? I sound poetical? Oh, that's good coming from the teacher.' He bent over her and put his lips to her brow, then ran his forefinger through her hair, following its line behind her ears.

As she looked up at him she caught hold of his hand and pressed it against her cheek and murmured softly, 'I'll soon be myself again, have patience.'

He was now sitting in front of her, having dragged a chair quickly forward. 'Patience? Have patience? What do you mean? I've never been impatient with you.'

'I know, my dear, I know.' She bowed her head. 'But you need comfort and I'm unable to give it to you.'

'Nonsense! nonsense!' He thrust the chair back now and was on his feet again, his tone stern, even angry sounding. 'What's put such ideas into your head? You give me everything I need. Haven't I told you' – he was now bending over her – 'haven't I told you that you are the only person I've really cared for in the whole of my life? God above! woman, if I've told it to you once I've told it to you a thousand times over the past years. Comfort.' His voice suddenly softened to a whisper, 'Oh, Anna, you're all the comfort I want, all the comfort I need.'

When again she brought his hand to her cheek he said in a hearty manner now, 'Another week; give yourself another week and you'll be coming down those stairs dressed in your best finery and I will have a carriage at the door and we shall drive into Hexham. Now, now, no protests.' He waved his hand before his face. 'And don't ask where the money's coming from. I've already thought up an idea that will pay for the trip. We'll take those three first editions in with us. If Barbara is right they'll be worth, twenty, thirty pounds . . . who knows, more. Anyway, I'm positive they'll cover our jaunt. Now what do you say?'

'I say that will be a wonderful treat, Thomas, I should like that. And it was very thoughtful of you to think up the means whereby you could carry it out.'

He stood looking at her, his head on one side, a gentle smile on his face; and then very quietly, he said, 'You know something, Anna. You are two entirely different people; Miss Brigmore who talks like a book during the day, and Anna, the lovable woman of the night; but I love you both . . . Good, good, you're blushing. Go on blushing, you look pretty when you blush.' He wagged his finger as he stepped back from her; then turning away, he went out of the room laughing.

Thomas fully intended to carry out his suggestion of taking his Anna for an outing, as also he fully intended to give the Moorhead woman a time when she could come to the barn or stable.

The following day the carrier cart brought a letter from Constance which afforded him the opportunity of bringing at least one plan to fruition.

## Chapter Two

Barbara sat next to the driver of the carrier's cart, this being the most comfortable seat. Ben Taggert had been most solicitous for her comfort; he had not only tucked a rug around her legs but had asked Mary to bring another shawl that would go over her bonnet and round her shoulders, for, as he said, you couldn't go by the weather at the foot of the hills; up there on the peaks it didn't ask any questions, it just cut you in two.

And Ben Taggert's words were proved right, for as they mounted higher her breath came out of her mouth like smoke from a chimney and mingled with the steam rising from the bodies of the horses.

When they reached the edge of the plateau Ben Taggert pointed his whip, saying, 'That always amazes me, miss, that yonder; from Lands End to John o' Groats you'll never see anything like it, nor, from what travellers tell me, in any other part of the world either. Bonnier, they'll say, prettier, but not grander. There's majesty there. Don't you think that, miss? Majesty, that's the word. Of course there's higher ones than them hills, I admit, but it's the way they're set. And that bowl down there. One fellow I brought across here described it like this. "God," he said, "must have looked at it and thought He'd made it a little bit too rough, craggy like. And so He took His hand and smoothed out the hollow." And it was a mighty hand that did it for it's a mighty hollow. It was a good description, don't you think, miss?'

'Very, very good, Mr Taggert. It's a very impressive sight; but I must admit I find it rather awe inspiring. And I shouldn't like to walk these hills alone, there's a great feeling of loneliness here.'

'Aye, there is, miss, I'll admit that. But many do, you know. Oh aye, I see them every day. Look yonder, there's one of them.' He pointed now to the derelict house where a man was standing in the doorway, his body misshapen by his odd assortment of clothes. 'That's one of 'em.'

'What-cher there. Fine day it is.' The man's voice came to them, each word separate, sharp-edged as if it had been filed in its passage through the air.

'Aye, it's a lovely day, Charlie. But look out, it won't last; weather's changin', I saw the signs this mornin'.'

'That right?'

'Aye, that's right, Charlie.'

Ben Taggert had not slowed the horses, the cart was still rumbling on. The man and house passed out of Barbara's vision but the memory it evoked did not leave her for some time. That was the place where it had happened.

And the child that had been born last week, was it the result of that escapade or was it Donald's child? Would Constance know? She doubted it. Not until the child grew up and showed some resemblance to its male parent would the answer be given.

The letter they had received yesterday from Constance had informed them that her child had come prematurely; it had been born at three o'clock on Saturday morning. She thought that this was the result of the shock she had received when she discovered Mr Radlet dead in the kitchen. She had come down in the night to make herself a comforting drink and she'd found him lying on the floor. The day after he was buried the child was born, a boy. She had ended her letter by saying, 'I am longing to see you, all of you, or any one of you.'

It was the 'any one of you' that was the telling phrase and had made Miss Brigmore insist that Barbara go over the hills at the first opportunity.

She saw the farm when they were quite a distance from it; it was lying in the valley and she looked down on it. It looked like any other farm, the solid stone house, the numerous outbuildings, the walled fields surrounding it, some level over quite an area but others sloping upwards to the hills beyond.

As Ben Taggert helped her down on to the road she said to him, 'What time will you be returning?' and he replied, 'Well, I'm usually at this spot around three, but I could be a bit later the day as I've got a number of messages to do an' things to pick up. In any case it'll be well afore four o'clock 'cos I like to get clear of the hills afore dusk sets in, and home afore dark. Anyhow, miss, I'll give you a "hello", and I won't go back without you, never fear.'

'Thank you, Mr Taggert.'

'You're welcome, miss.'

She took the valise from him, then turned away and walked over the rough ground to where a gateless aperture in a grey stone wall led into the farmyard. She walked slowly, looking from right to left. There was no one about. The front door to the house was away to the side; she made for the door that she guessed was most used and would lead into the kitchen. As she approached, it opened and Jane Radlet gaped at her. Then, a smile stretching her sad-looking face, she said, 'Well! well! I don't need to ask who you are, you're Barbara, aren't you?'

'Yes; and you Mrs Radlet?'

'Yes. Come in, come in. Oh, she'll be pleased to see you. She's just gone back up the stairs this minute.'

Barbara stopped herself in the act of speaking. Constance gone back up the stairs? Constance up from her bed when the child was only seven days old? She asked hastily now, 'Is she all right?'

'Yes, yes. Weakly a bit you know, but that's to be understood; but she's all right, an' the bairn's fine. That's what she went up for, to bring him down. She'll be here in a minute. Give me your hat and coat; I'm sure you could do with a drink, it's sharp outside.'

As Barbara unpinned her bonnet and handed it to Jane she thought, What a nice woman; so thoughtful yet she must still be feeling her own sorrow.

She offered her condolences, saying, 'I was deeply sorry to hear of your loss, Mrs Radlet.'

'Thank you. Thank you. An' it was a loss, for he was a good man. But as he would have said himself, God giveth and God taketh away.' She paused before adding softly, 'I miss him.'

'I'm sure you do.'

They looked at each other for a moment; then Jane, turning abruptly away, began to bustle, saying, 'Come, sit down here, sit down by the fire.' She touched the back of the high wooden chair, and Barbara sat down. Then again they looked at each other without speaking, until Jane repeated, 'Oh, she will be pleased to see you,' and added, 'If I'd known you were comin' I would've had the fire on in the parlour.' Then looking towards the door she said, 'Where is she? Where is she? I'll go an' call her.' She nodded, smiling at Barbara, then bustled across the room and out through a door at the far end.

Barbara looked about her. Everything her eye touched on was clean and shining, showing that it had either been scoured or polished; but like the outside of the house there was a bleakness about the room. It wasn't only that the floor was made entirely of stone slabs and was sparsely covered with two clippy mats, one which lay in front of the hearth, the other placed by the side of the long wooden table that took up most of the space in the middle of the room, or that the walls were lime-washed; it was something to do with the lack of colour. The curtains on the windows flanking the door were of white Nottingham lace, and the chairs were devoid of pads or cushions; the whole room seemed dominated by a big black stove. Her eyes were brought sharply from it and towards the door as it was thrust open, and there stood Constance.

They met at the top of the table and fell into each other's arms and they held tightly, not speaking, the while Constance's body shook with her inner sobbing

They drew apart as Jane, rocking the child gently in her arms, said, 'Here he is then. Here he is,' and Barbara turned and looked down at the swathed bundle. She stared at it for almost a minute without speaking. The child was different from what she had expected. It looked all fair; it had an unusual amount of hair on its head for such a young baby, and it was fair hair. The eyes were blue, but then she understood most babies' eyes were blue to begin with, and a baby's hair often changed colour.

'He takes after his mother, he's going to be as fair as her.'

Barbara felt a little quiver inside her and she brought her eyes from the child and looked at her sister. Could it be the child was of a different fairness from Constance, a golden corn fairness such as the fairness of Matthew which would become evident later?

'How is Anna, and Uncle?'

'Oh, she's improving daily but she's still somewhat weak. But you know Anna' – she smiled – 'she's made up her mind to get well, so she'll get well.'

'And Uncle?'

'Oh, Uncle is still Uncle. He's had a new lease of life lately, he appears quite frisky. He's even taking exercise on his own, without being browbeaten.'

'I don't believe it.'

'Well, it has to be seen to be believed, I admit.' They both gave a little laugh together then looked towards Jane, where she was placing the child in a basket cradle, set in an alcove to the side of the fireplace, and saying as she did so, 'You must be famished, coming all this way and the wind so raw.

The kettle's on the boil; I'll make you a cup of tea first and then get you a meal.'

'Oh, that's very kind of you, but a cup of tea is all I need. I'm not at all hungry, I could wait until you have your meal. Please don't put yourself out.'

'Well, you can have a griddle to put you over. But sit down, sit down and make yourself at home.' Again she motioned to a chair, and again Barbara sat down, with Constance now close to her, and like two lovers they held hands and looked at each other while Jane bustled back and forth between the table and the stove. Their silence must have told on her for she broke it by saying on a high note, 'Shall I go and tell Donald?'

'No, no.' The quick reply brought her to a standstill and she looked at Constance, adding, 'It'll be no bother, he's up on the top field doing the wall.'

'No, no, thank you, Mam. I'll . . . we'll, we'll take a walk up there, won't we?' She turned and glanced at Barbara. 'You'd like to see round the farm, wouldn't you?'

'Yes, indeed I would.'

'That's what we'll do then, Mam. When Barbara's had her drink I'll show her round, and then we'll walk to the top field.'

'Shall I call Matthew down then?'

'I . . . I wouldn't bother. He . . . he was very tired yesterday and. . . .' Her voice trailed away as the door opened and Matthew entered.

Matthew stood looking across the kitchen to where Barbara was sitting, her head turned towards him, and the high spots of colour on his cheek-bones spread outwards and up on to his brow. When he came slowly across the room Barbara rose to meet him and endeavoured not to give evidence of the shock his changed appearance had on her. He had always been thin but now his body looked devoid of flesh; he had always been pale but now his skin looked transparent; his eyes had always been large but now they seemed to fill the entire bone sockets and had sunk back into his head and appeared as dark in colour as Donald's.

She was the first to speak. 'Hello, Matthew,' she said. She did not add, 'How are you?'

He did not repeat her greeting but in a throaty voice said, 'This is a surprise.'

'Yes, yes; I thought I would like to come over and see the . . . the baby.' She motioned her head towards the cradle, and he turned and looked in the same direction and it was a moment before he said. 'Yes, yes.' Then he sat down on a chair near the side of the table although she was still standing; he did not now, as he had been wont to do, show his manners to be those above Donald's and his own class in general, but then, of course, she thought, he was a very sick man.

'Would you like a cup of tea, Matthew?' His mother spoke to him in a gentle voice, her body bent towards him as if she were coaxing a child, and he looked at her for a moment without answering, he looked at her as if he wasn't seeing her, and then on a quick intake of breath, he said, 'Yes, yes, I'd like a cup.'

Jane poured out the tea for them all; she handed round the griddles, but only Barbara accepted one, and this out of courtesy; and it was between herself and Jane that the conversation ranged, and mostly about the weather.

'We're not finished with it yet,' Jane said, nodding her head sagely, 'not by a long chalk; there'll be another big fall you'll see. And the wind's come up in the last hour, it's a wonder you weren't cut in two comin' over the top.'

'It was very keen.'

'Yes, I should say it was. It's years since I was up there in the winter, an' I have no desire to go, it's breezy enough in the summer. You going out now?' She turned to where Constance had risen from the chair, and Constance replied, 'I'm . . . I'm just going to get my cloak.'

'Perhaps your sister might like to go upstairs with you, she might like to see the house, would you?'

It was evident to Barbara that this kindly woman was very proud of her house. It was all a matter of values she thought; but then, the other rooms might show some comfort. She said quite brightly, 'Yes, yes, I would; I'm very interested in old houses.'

'There now, there now. Then take her up with you, Constance.'

The sisters looked at each other for a moment before going out of the room together like children obeying a bidding.

The hall they went into was dark, having only one small window next to the door. The oak staircase mounted steeply from opposite the door, and Constance took hold of Barbara's hand and guided her up it and on to the landing. Here it was lighter, being illuminated by a long window at the far end. She noted that there was no article of furniture on the landing, not even a table on which to place a lamp. Then Constance was opening a door, and she was in her bedroom.

She had often imagined Constance's bedroom and in the early days the thought of it had been bitter to her mind. Now that she was in it the last shreds of jealousy she had felt towards Constance seeped from her, for here, and reflected deeply, she saw the same starkness as in the kitchen, and part of her mind was wondering why it should be so because Constance had an artistic sense; it was she who had gone a long way towards making the rooms in the cottage not only comfortable but pretty.

Alone together now, they did not throw themselves into each other's arms once more but stood somewhat apart, each gazing at the other, waiting.

It was Barbara who spoke first. When Constance lowered her head and extended her hands towards her she gripped them, saying, 'What is it? you don't look well. What possessed you to get up so early? Shouldn't you be in bed for some days yet?'

Constance now drew Barbara to a wooden seat that was placed beneath the window and they sat down before she answered, 'One is not pampered on this side of the hills. A cow walks about immediately after calving, so what's the difference between us?'

Barbara was startled, not only by the bitterness in Constance's voice but by the context of her reply. She moved nearer to her and, putting her arms about her, she asked gently, 'Aren't you happy?'

'Oh Barbie!' Constance was now pressing herself tightly against her, her hands clutching at her as if she were drowning, and Barbara whispered, in concern, 'What is it, what is it? Oh my dear, tell me, what is it? Tell me.'

And Constance might have told her if at that moment a voice had not risen from the yard calling loudly to a dog, saying, 'Leave it, Prince. Leave it. Here! Here, I tell you.' It caused her to raise her head and look sharply towards the window. Then withdrawing herself from Barbara's hold, she got to her feet and began smoothing down her hair, then the front of her bodice, then the folds of her skirt over her slender hips; finally, she brought her hands to her waist where her fingers plucked at each other as she said, 'We'd . . . we'd better go down, that's him – I mean Donald. He must have finished in the top field. It'll save us walking and . . . and you've seen the room.' She now flung one arm wide, then stopped abruptly and turned and faced Barbara again and, her voice dropping low in her throat, she repeated, 'You've seen the room. She . . . I mean Mam, she thinks it's nice, and it is to her. She's . . . she's very good to me; I don't know what I would have done without her.'

Constance was at the door, the latch in her hand, but Barbara, after standing up, hadn't moved from the window seat. She said now in a whisper, 'You're not happy, what is it?'

Constance bit on her lip, swallowed deeply, and her chin gave a nervous jerk before she said, 'Is anyone happy? Do you know of anyone who is really happy?'

'We were happy at one time.'

'At one time, yes.' Constance now nodded slowly. 'The only trouble is we never recognize real happiness when we have it.'

'But . . . but Donald, Donald loves you.' She found it surprising that it didn't pain her to say this aloud, and when she saw Constance close her eyes tightly she said again, 'What is it?' and now she moved swiftly towards her. But before she reached her Constance had opened the door; then they were on the landing, then going down the stairs, silent again.

Donald was in the kitchen when they entered and he greeted her heartily as if he were pleased to see her. 'Well, well! Look what the wind's blown in,' he said, coming towards her with hand outstretched. 'What's brought you to this neck of the woods, eh, on a day like this with the wind enough to stiffen you?'

'Oh, I wanted to see the baby and find out how Constance was.'

'Oh!' The exclamation was high. 'You knew about the baby then?' He turned and glanced in Constance's direction, and Barbara noticed that she didn't look at him and say, 'Yes, I wrote,' so it was left to her to explain, and she did as casually as possible, saying, 'Yes, Constance sent me a note. And oh, by the way' – she turned to Constance now who was at the table laying it for a meal – 'I brought some things for the baby. Not knowing if it were going to be a boy or a girl we knitted white.' She went towards the valise where it lay just as she had left it by the side of the chair and, opening it, she drew out first a white shawl, then a variety of socks, bonnets and coats.

'Oh!' Jane exclaimed delightedly as she fingered the shawl. 'Oh, it's beautiful and so soft. This was knitted with fine wool; indeed it was. And look at the wee boots. Aw! did you ever see anything so dainty, did you now, Constance?'

'No, they are lovely. Thank you, thank you, Barbara. And thank Anna for me too. What a lot of work it must have taken.'

'It was a pleasure.' Their eyes held for a moment longer; then Jane put in, 'Well, you came with a full bag an' you'll go with a full bag. You must take some butter, an' cheese, and eggs back with you.'

'Thank you. . . .'

During the next hour Barbara noticed a number of things. Matthew never uttered a word, Constance only spoke when necessary, and Jane never stopped chattering. But it was a nervous chattering. Her face sad, she kept up a constant conversation as if with herself.

When they sat down to the meal no one sat at the head of the table. Donald sat to the side with Constance opposite him; Jane sat at the bottom of the table with Matthew to her left; but although the chair at the top was empty Barbara had no doubt who was master of this house. Not only had Donald been served first but Jane ministered to him with a deference that she might have extended towards her husband, except that this deference held a nervous quality.

Barbara wondered how the farm had been divided. There would surely have been a will; she must ask Constance.

The food itself was rather tasteless. It was a stew that had been well stewed and, surprisingly, without herbs. But that didn't trouble her; what did was the atmosphere at the table. To say it was strained was not adequate, tense would have been a better description.

One other thing she noticed. Although Donald brought a smile to his face now and again it never touched his eyes. When she had loved him – she noted with relief that she was using the past tense with regard to her affection towards him – she had never seen him look as he did now. His eyes were like pieces of slaty coal, their blackness was a dull blackness. She wondered now how she had allowed herself to become so attached to him. Perhaps because he had flattered her by appealing to her mind. Yes, that was it. Pride, pride.

Before the meal was over she was thinking, I could not have endured this any more than Connie is doing. Poor Connie. Poor, poor Connie.

Rising from the table, Jane said, 'I'll light a fire in the parlour.' She did not look towards Donald as she spoke yet it was as if it were a question directed towards him, a question that required an answer, an answer giving permission, and when the answer was not forthcoming immediately Barbara put in quickly, 'Please don't trouble on my account; Mr Taggert will be here with the cart around three he told me, and it is near two o'clock now.'

'Oh well then, well then.' Jane nodded at her, then bustled around the table gathering up the dishes.

It was at this point that Constance went to the cradle and lifted up the baby and was moving towards the kitchen door leading into the hall when she was stopped by Donald saying, 'Where you going?'

Constance turned slowly and for the first time since coming into the room she looked straight at him, and her voice had a note of defiance in it as she answered, 'I am going to feed the child.'

'There's plenty of room here, isn't there?' He jerked his head in the direction of the empty chairs bordering the fireplace.

Their eyes held, the silence in the kitchen emphasized the sound of the wind buffeting the house, and as Constance turned about and walked out of the room Jane exclaimed loudly, 'Do you hear that? It's gettin' worse.'

Ignoring his mother's remark, Donald looked now at Barbara and said on a thin laugh, 'You can carry modesty too far; what's more natural than feedin' a bairn, I've told her.'

Matthew seemed to have risen clumsily from the table for his chair toppled backwards and hit the stone floor, but as he went to right it Donald was there before him and, swinging it up with one hand, he stood it on its feet, saying on another thin laugh, 'You want to take more water with it, lad.'

Matthew now looked up under his lids at Barbara; then in a voice as tight as the smile on his face he said, 'I'll say good-bye. I'm glad to have seen you. Give my regards to Miss Brigmore, will you, and to your uncle?'

'I will, Matthew, I will.' She held out her hand, and he took it. It felt like a piece of damp dough in her grasp and she was glad to relinquish it.

Donald was now standing with his back to the fire, his coat tails divided, letting the heat fan his buttocks. She often saw her Uncle Thomas stand like that. It was the stance of the master of the house, and it was as if Donald were acting out his part for her. After a moment he asked, 'How are things across there?'

'Oh, very well. Mary and I have re-decorated the sitting room for when Anna comes downstairs. We've had a boy come all last summer in the evenings to do the garden; it's in very good shape. We had two cartloads of wood brought, and he has sawn it up. We're all prepared for an extended cold spell, should it come.'

Her answer did not seem to please him, he made no reply to it; and when there came the sound of a bucket being tumbled across the yard by the wind he made it an excuse to take his leave, saying, 'Well, somebody's got to work round here, so I'll say good-bye to you.'

'Good-bye, Donald.' She nodded politely towards him, then added, 'Will you be bringing Constance across soon? Uncle would like to see the child.'

He had his back to her, walking towards the kitchen door as he said, 'I doubt it; she's afraid of storms, as you know.'

'But the fine weather's coming, there are periods when there won't be any sign of a storm.' She had risen to her feet.

'She's also afraid of the heights. Didn't you know?' At the door he turned and looked towards her.

'The heights?'

'Yes, the heights; terrified of heights, she tells me. Apparently there are lots of things about her you didn't know if you didn't know that.'

As she stared at him across the dim kitchen she thought, He's cruel.

'Good-bye, Barbara.'

She didn't answer, and he went out, having to pull the door closed behind him against the force of the wind.

When she sat down, Jane began to chatter again. She chattered about the cattle, the butter-making, the cheese-making; she referred to her husband as if he were still alive; and every now and again she looked towards the window and said, 'Eeh! that wind.'

It was almost twenty minutes later when Constance returned. Putting the baby once again into the cradle, she smiled at Barbara before saying to Jane, 'What will I do, the dishes, or go in the dairy?'

'You'll do neither, my dear, just you sit here with your sister and have a nice talk, you don't see each other that often. Now sit yourself down.'

Constance sat down at the opposite side of the fireplace to where Barbara was sitting, and they looked towards Jane, who was now standing over the shallow brown stone sink which was full of dishes; then they looked at each other again, and their eyes said, 'What shall we talk about?'

For the next half-hour they talked small talk. Barbara learned that the child was to be named Michael, after his step-grandfather. Constance learned that the Hall had been sold again, and that it was being cleaned up by a small regiment of workers, one of whom was named Aggie Moorhead, a very forward piece who wasn't above stopping Uncle and chatting with him.

By three o'clock Barbara was ready and waiting to hear Ben Taggert's call, and when a quarter of an hour had passed she said anxiously, 'I wonder if he's gone on? Perhaps we didn't hear him call because of the wind.'

'Oh, no.' Jane shook her head. 'Ben would come over an' knock you up. Ben would never go on without a passenger once he had made arrangements. Oh no, that's not Ben. . . . Listen, do you hear? There he is.'

Barbara strained her ears and heard a faint, 'Hello there, Hello there.'

Jane now grabbed up the valise and went out and for a moment Barbara and Constance were alone again. As they had done on first meeting they enfolded each other tightly, and once again Barbara felt her sister's body tremble and she heard her murmur as if in agony of mind, 'Oh Barbie! Barbie!'

Hand in hand now they went out, their bodies bent against the wind, and when they reached the road Jane had already handed Ben Taggert the valise and he had put it in the back of the cart where there was an assortment of bundles and boxes and a bird in a cage.

'If you would like it better I could push them all aside' – Ben nodded to the back of the cart – 'you'd be more sheltered there.'

'Oh, I'll be all right riding with you, Mr Taggert.'

'It's going to be rough, miss, the higher we get, you know that. Still, if you change your mind we can always stop. Come on then.'

Quickly now Barbara turned again to Constance and, taking her face between her hands, she stared at her for a moment before kissing her on the lips; then she shook Jane by the hand and thanked her once more for the dairy produce she had put into the valise, and also for her hospitality.

Sitting high up in the front of the cart she looked down on Constance's upturned face. With an impulsive movement she reached down holding out her hand, and when her sister's hand gripped hers she felt such pain in her heart as she never thought to experience again. It was a more intense pain than she had known a year ago, a different pain, it could have been a pain of farewell. She made herself smile, but it was a smile weighed with sadness, it was as if she knew she would never smile again.

The return journey was eventful with moments that created terror in her, such as the one when the wind seemed to lift the whole cart and the animals from the road and to tip them into a shallow hollow to the side of the rising hill. That they all landed the right way up seemed nothing short of a miracle to her. What had happened was that the horses and cart were blown to the side and left contact with the ground in going over the shallow ditch.

Once on the road again, Barbara, still shaking from her experience, realized that perhaps she was lucky to be able to feel the trembling of her body at all, for if they had been blown the other way then surely they would have rolled down the steeply wooded hillside to the valley below. The snow posts that were spaced at intervals along this stretch of the road and threaded by a wire would not have prevented them from being hurled over the edge to be bounded from one tree trunk to another until they reached the bottom.

Another time she found herself clinging to Mr Taggert's arm. It was most embarrassing, at least to her. She saw his head nodding in assurance, and knew that he was yelling something at her, but she could not distinguish anything he was saying, for his words were carried away on the wind.

When, for a few minutes, there was a lull, he shouted at her, 'I've known some trips but this one'll take a beatin'. Give me snow any time. But don't you worry, don't you worry, miss, Jake'n Fred'll make it; they're as sure-footed as mountain goats.' It was a pity, she thought, that she hadn't his faith in Jake and Fred.

If anything, the storm increased in violence as they descended to lower ground, and it was almost as dark as night when finally Ben Taggert helped her down from the cart and handed her the valise. She thanked him warmly and said she would never forget the journey and he laughed at her and said, 'You must try it in a blizzard, miss; that's what you must do, try it in a blizzard. Go on now, get yersel' inside quick. Good night to you.'

Her reply was lost to him. The cart moved past her, and holding down the shawl that covered her bonnet with one hand and carrying the valise in the other, she fought her way to the gate. But when she went to push it open she found it was held fast. In peering forward she realized that the obstacle holding it closed was a branch of the rowan tree that had stood in the front garden for years. The whole tree had been blown down.

Her body bent, she made her way to the lower gate which led into the yard. The noise of the wind was beating on her eardrums with a force almost equal to that on the heights; in fact, the wind seemed to have increased in fury, which she would have thought impossible a short while ago.

When some object rattled across the path in front of her she fell forward and would have gone on her face had not the end of the wall of the outbuilding saved her. She stood leaning against it for a moment, thankful that she had it as a guide for it was like black night now. She decided to keep near the wall and to skirt the yard until she reached the kitchen door, for if she crossed the yard her feet would likely be whipped from beneath her.

On this side of the yard facing the house was the wood-shed, stables, and lastly the barn. There was a narrow passage between the corner of the barn and the wall of the wash-house which led into the vegetable garden. The wash-house itself was connected to the scullery and larder, which were single-storey buildings, and going off at right angles from the end of these was the house proper.

She had groped her way as far as the barn when her passage was stopped abruptly by two hands grabbing her, and after the first moment of shock she sighed with relief and leant against the bulky figure of her Uncle Thomas. He held her close, protectingly, he held her so close that she dropped the valise onto the ground.

Protecting her further, he pulled her inside the barn, where the noise seemed intensified for the old timbers were rattling like castanets. She went to shout to him, 'Isn't it dreadful?' but he hugged her with a compulsive movement and her breath was taken from her body by a force even stronger than the wind. What was the matter with Uncle? Was he having convulsions? Was he ill? And why . . . why was he out in the storm? It was madness for him to be out, for anyone to be out on a night like this, unless they were compelled.

'Oh, Uncle! Uncle!' She heard herself screaming, but only in her head for her breath had been knocked out of her again as she was borne backwards.

What was happening? what was the matter? It . . . it was her uncle? Of course it was her uncle. She knew by the size of his body it was her uncle. She knew by the odour of him it was her uncle. That particular odour of tobacco and rough tweed and stale wine, a not unpleasant odour and definitely peculiar to him, for no other of her acquaintances smelt like this. But he also smelt strongly of spirits – *Oh my god! My God! She must be going insane, it couldn't be.* She began to fight him, to struggle madly, and it appeared to her that of a sudden the wind had transported her into a lunatic asylum because her uncle was also struggling with her, tearing at her undergarments, actually tearing them from her. *No! No! No! Oh Jesus, Lord of all the earth, what was happening to her.* The weight on her body – She couldn't breathe – She could struggle no longer – She had gone mad, for this thing could not be happening to her. She made one more effort. She dug her nails deep into the flesh of his neck, she couldn't get near his face for it was covering hers.

At the moment her body was shot through with torture, and her mind, standing apart as it were from her, told her that this was death, the death of decency, of self-respect, of love of family life – of life itself.

When the pressure on her body was released she lay still in what seemed comparative silence for the storm seemed to have held its breath for a moment. Then as it released another blast she let out an ear-splitting scream; then another; then another; on and on and no hand came over her mouth to check her; not until a lantern swung above her did she stop. Her eyes wide, she stared up into the light. She could not see the face above it, or who else was present; not until the lamp swung to the side did she see the grey dishevelled bulk of her Uncle Thomas. His body seemed to fill the barn. He looked like a deranged giant. Then the lantern swinging again, she saw the figure of a woman running through the light and towards the open door; then she heard Mary screaming. 'God Almighty!' was what she was screaming. She screamed it a number of times.

Then Mary, dropping onto her knees, lifted Barbara's stiff head and shoulders from the ground and, cradling her, she repeated her cry, 'Oh, God Almighty! Oh, God Almighty!' After a moment, her voice breaking with her sobbing, she cried, 'Come on, get up out of this, me bairn. Get up out of this. Come on, come on.' And Barbara got up and allowed herself to be led from the barn and into the house. . . .

Thomas watched them go. He was leaning against a beam to the side of the door. The lantern was still on the ground. He looked towards it. His eyes stretched wide, his mouth agape, he seemed to see himself reflected in it, an obese, dirty old man, a filthy old man. He was so repulsive in his own sight that his stomach revolted and he turned his head to the side and retched, bringing up the entire meal he had eaten only an hour before at the same table as Anna.

Anna! Anna! Anna! . . . Barbara! Oh, Christ Almighty!

His mind now went completely blank for a moment and shut off from his consciousness the act he had perpetrated. When it moved again it pulled him from the support of the beam and turned him about and he staggered from the barn out into the wind.

When he reached the kitchen door the blast almost drove him through it. There was no one in the room; he crossed it, holding on first to the table and to the chairs for support; then he was in the hall, and in the lamplight he saw Anna coming down the stairs. She stopped and he stopped; they looked at each other for a long moment and the misery their eyes exchanged was untranslatable.

When he could no longer face the pain in her eyes he bowed his head and stumbled towards his study. Once inside he locked the door. Going to the wall above the fireplace he took down his gun and, placing it on the desk with the barrel pointing towards the chair, he released the safety catch; then sitting himself in the chair he leant forward, and as he did so the handle of the door was gently turned. He did not look towards it but put his finger on the trigger and pulled.

# Chapter One

## Matthew

The scandal surrounding Thomas Mallen's death would, the self-righteous in the countryside said, not die down for many a year, seeing he had left living proof of it in a young woman whom he had brought up like a daughter.

It was Aggie Moorhead who had made it impossible to put any version but the true one on Thomas's death. She had looked upon the mix-up between his niece and herself as the best joke in the world, until the girl had begun to scream. Then, when the news spread that old Mallen had shot himself the story made her the centre of attraction, not only locally but with those men who came from the newspapers.

And the newspapers didn't just deal with the incident either; they delved into Thomas Mallen's whole past and it made quite exciting reading. Even though he had been living in retirement for the past twelve years, being a Mallen, he hadn't lived alone but had taken for his mistress the governess of his two nieces, and what made things more interesting still, they stated that one of his nieces had married his natural son.

Yet even with all this, the nine-days' wonder might have died a natural death if the gardener boy hadn't observed the rising globe of Miss Barbara's stomach, and this on the first occasion he had caught sight of her in five months. This latter fact did not appear in the papers but the hill telegraph was as efficient in spreading it around the countryside.

This particular piece of news came to Donald's ears in the market place and he couldn't get back quickly enough to the farm to throw it at Constance.

It was three months since he had allowed her over the hills, and then he had escorted her himself as on the former occasion when that old cow of a Brigmore had sent him the news that Mallen was dead. He hadn't found out how he died until he had entered the cottage. He hadn't seen Barbara at all, not then, and not since.

And now he had learned that she had her belly full of the old man. The Mallen image died hard. By God! it did. And that lot in the market laughing up their sleeve at him. By Christ! he'd let them see who they were laughing at afore he was finished. He'd show them. He'd get land, and more land; he'd drag the respect out of them, then spit in their eyes.

And there was another thing he'd tell his lady wife when he got in: she was bringing that fifty pounds a year over the hills; there wasn't the old man to keep now, and he could do with another fifty a year. Yes, by God! he could. She had stood out against him on this, openly defied him in fact.

She was getting brave over certain things, but she'd better be careful. He hadn't lifted his hand to her yet but there was plenty of time for it.

Sometimes he thought he could have forgiven her the other business if she had been good to him, shown a little affection, but what she had shown him from that very first night couldn't be given any other name but scorn; at times it even overrode her fear of him. Inside her, she looked down her nose at him, and the farm and the house. She got on with his mother because she saw it as policy to keep on the right side of her. And yet that wasn't all there was to it. He suspected, and had for some time now, that there was something between them, a sort of understanding. Whatever it was, the relationship irritated him, for if there was anybody she should look down upon it was his mother who, in her turn, had been a slut. But as they said, birds of a feather, no matter from what class, recognized each other. She even turned her nose up at Matthew; she hardly opened her mouth to Matthew.

Matthew'd had a new lease of life these past few months. Perhaps it was due to the unusually dry warm weather. Nevertheless his time was fast running out for he was no thicker than two laths, and though his cough had eased a bit, the blood came more often. His manner too had changed in the last year or so. He supposed it was his illness, for he could get hardly a word out of him nowadays. There was a sullenness about him; perhaps because he knew that death was galloping on him; it wasn't good for a man to see death before it actually came.

He flapped the reins briskly and put the horse into a trot. The cart bumped over the rough road and the dust rose in clouds about him.

When he came to the junction of two roads he took the left-hand one. This would mean a longer run to the farm, but it might save an axle; on the outward journey he'd had to take the cart through a new subsidence in the road and this had strained it. He'd made a note in his mind to bring a load of stone and fill in the hole.

The road he was on now was a prettier one, it wound its way through woodland and shady lanes, and the open ground was moulded into small hills where the sheep grazed, a burn ran down the valley and there was a rocky outcrop over which the water tumbled so that you could fairly give it the name of a waterfall.

He rarely came by this road, he hadn't time for scenery. All the scenery that interested him was within the stone walls of his farm. . . . And it was *his* farm.

Michael had left no will. By law the place was Matthew's, but by right of work it was his, and let anyone try to say it wasn't. It had never been a bad farm, but it was he who had made a good one into a better one, and from now on he meant to turn it into a rich farm . . . and a rich man's farm.

He passed by the side of a small copse that threw the path into shadow and when he emerged he blinked into the sun for a moment, then screwed up his gaze to take in two figures sitting some distance away in the shade of a mound. With a soft word of command and a tug on the reins he drew the horse to a halt, and his eyes narrowed to slits as he peered into the distance.

If he failed to recognize the couple the sound that now came to his ears would have identified at least one of them. Not once since they were married had he heard Constance laugh, and the reason for hearing her laugh now was that the child's hands were pulling at her nose. He had seen the child doing this before, but it certainly hadn't brought any laughter from her. He had caught her smiling at it, but this would be when he happened on her unawares.

Then he witnessed something that caused a pain to rip through him, as if his body had been licked by a fierce flame. She had passed the child to Matthew and Matthew was holding him up in the air above his head and shaking him from side to side; then lowering him down, he folded him against his chest and rocked him backwards and forwards, as only a mother, or a father might do.

What he next saw was Constance hitching herself forward and smoothing the child's hair back while Matthew still held it. What he was looking at was the cameo of a family.

He was numb. The pain seared all the nerves in his body. It now passed the bearing point, and for a moment he felt nothing; there followed a blessed period of time when all emotion was dead in him.

But the numbness melted, the space filled, and now there swept into him and over him with the force of a mighty wave a feeling of such hatred that if they had been within arm's length of him at that moment he would have murdered them both.

It was a gentle neigh from the horse that caused them to turn their heads in his direction, but they could not see either him or the cart. In the shadow of the trees he watched them remain still for a moment peering towards the road; then there was a quick exchange of words before they got to their feet, she carrying the child now, and they went down the field and made for the gate that led into the extreme corner of the farmland.

Not until they were out of sight did he lead the horse forward, and then he took it from the road and tied the bridle to a tree, after which he walked a short distance and lay down in some long grass. There, at full length, he stared unblinking into the soil while he tore up handfuls of grasses and snapped them into small pieces. After a while, as if his body had suddenly been dropped from a height, he slumped into the earth and with his hand under his mouth he bit on the pad of his thumb until the blood came. . . .

Fifteen minutes later when he entered the house, the baby was in the pen outside the dairy and Jane was in the kitchen, her arms in a bowl of flour. She looked at him as if in surprise, saying, 'You're back early.'

'Where's Matthew?'

'Matthew! Oh, he's in bed. You know he always goes to bed in the afternoon.' She dusted the flour from her hands and turned her back on him and went towards the oven.

He had the urge to pick up the heavy rolling pin from the table and batter her on the head with it. She knew, she knew. They must all have been laughing up their sleeves at him all this time, the three of them. Why? Why hadn't he twigged anything before? He was seeing things now as plainly as a blind man who had been given his sight. That day Matthew had gone over the hills for her and the storm was supposed to have frightened her and he had taken her back; it had happened then. But Matthew had changed towards him long before that. And he could pinpoint the date. It was from the Sunday morning, in this very room, when he had told them he was going to ask her to marry him. God above! Christ Almighty! Why had he been so blind?

The answer was simple. He had trusted Matthew, because he had loved

Matthew. Matthew was the only other person in the world besides her he had loved, and they had both fooled him, right up to this very day they had fooled him. If God Himself had come and told him before he had seen them together he wouldn't have believed it, because they never spoke to each other. . . . Not when he was about. . . . No, that was it, not when he was about.

And his mother, that old bitch there. No wonder they were all thick. He could murder the three of them. He could take a knife and go from one to the other and slit their throats. But where would that get him? The gallows. No, there'd be no gallows for him, he had paid enough for being who he was; but by God! somebody was going to pay for this. He would play them at their own game. Christ! how he would play them. The cat and the mouse wouldn't be in it. He would make them think he knew, then make them think he didn't. He'd give them such hell on earth they'd wish they were dead, all of them. Well, one of them soon would be, but he'd make a vow this minute he wouldn't let him go until he had told him that he hadn't been so bloody clever after all. He'd see he tasted hell afore he died; he'd play him like a tiddler on a pin; he'd play them all like tiddlers on a pin, and he'd begin right now.

As if answering an order, he turned and stamped out of the kitchen, across the yard and into the dairy. She was standing at the far end with her back to him, and even at this moment the sight of her slender form made him ache. She had half turned as the door opened and then turned away again, and he came up behind her and stood close and did not speak until, pressing herself against the stone slab, she slid away from him before turning to face him, her face stiff as always when she confronted him.

'It's a grand day,' he said. 'You should be out in the sunshine with the child.'

She continued to stare at him before she answered quietly, 'You have allotted me duties; you would doubtless have something to say if I didn't carry them out.'

'Yes, yes, doubtless I would.' He nodded his head at her; then went on in a casual tone, 'I heard a bit of news in the market, caused some belly laughs it did. That's funny, belly laughs. Barbara is five months' gone. The old man worked well up to the last. What do you say?'

He watched the colour drain from her cheeks, her mouth opened and shut in a fish-like gape; then he turned from her and was near the door of the dairy before he looked towards her again and added, 'By the way, I was talkin' to a young doctor in the market, I was tellin' him I had a son and about my half-brother being a consumptive. I said there was none of the disease on my side, not that I knew of, and could it be caught like, and he said, aye, it was better not to let the child come in contact with anybody who has the disease, so if I was you I'd break it to Matthew, eh? You can do it better than me, put it more gently like.'

He watched her for a moment as she leaned back against the slab for support; then he went out well satisfied with the result of his new tactics. He would get something out of this, something that would be more satisfying than sticking a knife in their necks. Although one of these days, when he had her on his own, he mightn't be able to prevent himself from doing just that.

# Chapter Two

When Mary opened the door and saw a small, neatly dressed man standing there and, beyond him, on the road a hired cab with the driver slapping his arms about himself as he stamped his feet, she thought, Another of them. What's this one after now? And that is what she said to him, 'What are you after now?' She did not add, 'There's nothing new happened for you to put in your papers.'

'Is this Mr Mallen's home, I mean the late Mr Mallen?'

'Yes, it is; you know quite well it is.'

The small man raised his eyebrows slightly before saying, 'I should like to speak with your mistress.'

'She's not seein' nobody, neither of them.'

There was a slight look of bewilderment on the man's face and he didn't speak for a moment, but surveyed Mary; then he said quietly, 'My name is Stevens, I am Chief Clerk to Maser, Boulter & Pierce, Solicitors, of Newcastle. I have some business I would like to discuss with your mistress. Please give her this.' He held out a square of card, and she took it, glanced at it, then back at him before saying in a more moderate tone, 'Well, come in then.'

In the hall she hesitated whether to leave him standing there or to show him into the breakfast room, the room that had once been the schoolroom. She decided to leave him standing there. Then giving him a look as much as to say, don't you move, she went towards a door, tapped on it, then opened it immediately.

In the room she tiptoed almost at a run across it and, coming to Miss Brigmore, where she was sitting by the fire unpicking the skirt of the last of Barbara's dresses in order to make it fit her during the late months, she whispered, 'There's a man here – not a gentleman, yet he's not one of them – he's from a solicitor's. Look.' She thrust the card at Miss Brigmore and noticed that she hesitated before taking it. She had been like that ever since ... the business, hesitant about any contact with those outside. Well, she was like that herself; she hadn't got over the shock yet and her conscience still worried her, especially at night. She still wondered if it all would have happened if the master hadn't found her hidey-hole. He must have drunk a whole bottle, for that very night she had found it empty. Nothing worse could have happened if he had drunk the two bottles, but being the man he was he had taken only one and left her the other. Oh, the master, the poor, poor master. She was still sorry for him, she couldn't help but be sorry for him. And she was sorry for herself an' all because the business had put her off the stuff and there was no comfort anywhere, no, not anywhere, for this house that had once been merry and full of laughter, in spite of having to stretch every farthing to its utmost, was now as quiet as a cemetery.

'Show him in, Mary.'

Miss Brigmore slowly rolled up the dress and laid it in the corner of the couch and she was rising as slowly to her feet when the man entered.

From his manner and appearance she, too, knew that he wasn't 'one of them'. She looked at the card and said, 'Will you take a seat, Mr Stevens?'

'Thank you, ma'am.' He motioned with a gentle movement of his hand that she should be seated first.

When they were seated facing each other she said, 'It's a very raw day;' and he answered, 'Yes, it is indeed, ma'am.' Then coughing twice, he went on, 'I won't intrude on your time more than is necessary. My firm is wishful to trace the next-of-kin of the late Mr Thomas Mallen and thought perhaps coming directly to his home would be the surest way of getting in touch with his relatives.'

'For what purpose?' Her back was straight, her voice was almost that of the old Miss Brigmore, and he, sensing her distrust, was quick to put her mind at ease, saying, 'Oh it would be something to their advantage, I should explain. Mr Mallen had a son, Richard, that is so?'

'Yes.'

'Well, apparently Mr Richard Mallen has sojourned in France for some years, but under an assumed name. This was the difficulty the French lawyers encountered when dealing with his estate. They eventually gleaned that he had left this country under troubled circumstances, and so their enquiries were slow and cautious, but recently they contacted us through a French associate we have in Paris, and asked us to ascertain the whereabouts of Monsieur le Brett's relatives.' Mr Stevens again coughed twice before continuing, 'We became acquainted with the fact that Mr Thomas Mallen had died intestate, unfortunately only a fortnight after his son's death.'

Miss Brigmore now said, 'He has two nieces, one is married and one still lives here.'

'No close relatives? He was married twice I understand.'

'Yes, his two sons by his first wife died. He has a daughter, she's in Italy.'

'Ah, a daughter in Italy. May I ask if you have her address?'

'Yes, yes, I have her address.'

Yes, she had Bessie's address. She had written to her telling her briefly of the tragedy, and what had she received in return, a letter full of bitterness. They had scarcely got over the '51 affair. Did she know that it had even got into the Italian papers? Alfo was angry, his people were angry, she had barely lived down the disgrace of her father being turned out of his home for debts, and her brother almost killing a man of the law, and now this – well, they said there was a curse on the Mallens. . . .

There was indeed a curse on the Mallens, and all connected with them. If the last Mallen had married her, if Thomas had married her this man would not be searching for his nearest relative at this moment. She asked quietly, 'Did he leave a large fortune?'

'No, when the beneficiary eventually receives it, it will amount to about two thousand five hundred pounds, somewhere in that region. There has been a great deal of expense incurred – you can understand. . . .'

No muscle of her face moved; not a considerable fortune, two thousand five hundred pounds! And they were now reduced to living on a hundred pounds a year. Their menu had been frugal for a long time, for she had seen to it that Thomas always had the pick of what was to be had, and when she became ill Barbara had continued along the same lines. . . . Poor Barbara, poor Barbara. She dared not think too much of Barbara's plight or her whole being would disintegrate in pity.

She thought in justifiable bitterness now that if anyone had earned Dick Mallen's legacy it was herself. Her cheating of the bailiffs had not only helped to get him out of prison but had likely afforded him the basis, through the selling of the snuff box and cameos, of some nefarious business. But there, that was life, and life was bitter, like alum on the tongue, and she couldn't see time washing it away.

She rose saying, 'I will get you the address,' then she added, courteously, 'Can I offer you some refreshment?' As she watched his head move to the side and a thin smile appear on his face she added hastily, 'A cup of tea maybe?'

The smile slid away, his head shook. 'It's very kind of you,' he said, 'but I shan't trouble you; I had breakfast late and my dinner is awaiting me at the hotel, as also is the cab man.' He smiled again, and she went out of the room to see Mary scurrying towards the kitchen door.

In the study she took Bessie's letter from the desk drawer, copied the name and address onto a pice of paper. Then, going back into the sitting room, she handed it to Mr Stevens.

'Thank you, ma'am; I'm much obliged.' He looked down at the address written on the paper. Then, his eyebrows jerking upwards, he repeated, 'Countess. Well, well! I don't suppose two thousand five hundred will mean much to her.'

He walked past her now as she held the front door open, and he doffed his hat and bowed to her, and he noted she did not close the door until he had entered the cab.

The door closed, she did not return to the sitting room but went into the study, and Mary coming into the hall and hearing the study door click shut stopped for a moment, looked towards it, then returned to the kitchen. That was one room she never barged into. When Miss went in there she wasn't to be disturbed. It had become a sort of unwritten law. She sat down by the kitchen table and, laying her hands on it, she joined them tightly together, and, bending her head over them, she shook it from side to side. Two thousand five hundred pounds going to that Miss Bessie, and her an upstart if ever there was one, never written to her father for years. Eeh! things weren't right.

She started visibly when the kitchen door opened and Barbara entered. She was wearing a long coat and had a shawl over her head.

Rising quickly, Mary went towards her, saying, 'Eeh! Miss Barbara, you'll get your death, I thought you were never coming back. Here, come and get warm.' She drew her towards the fire, pulling off her gloves as she did so; then taking the shawl from her head as if she were undressing a child she pressed her into a chair and, kneeling beside her, began to chafe her hands, talking all the while. 'You're froze. Aw, you're froze, lass; you'll do yourself an injury, an' – she stopped herself from adding 'the one you're carrying' and went on, 'You can't walk quick enough to keep yourself warm. You shouldn't go out, not on a day like this; wait till the sun comes out.'

'Who was that, Mary?'

'Oh. Oh, you saw him. Well, you won't believe it, you won't believe it even when I tell you. It was the solicitor's man. He came to find the nearest kin to . . . to the master.' She never said 'your uncle' as she used to do, in fact no one spoke of the master to her in any way; but now, having mentioned his name, she gabbled on, 'Master Dick, you know, well, well he's died and left some money and it goes to the next-of-kin. An' you know who the next-of-kin is? Miss Bessie. You wouldn't believe it, two thousand five hundred pounds. Imagine two thousand five hundred pounds an' going to Miss Bessie. Eeh! if anybody should have that it should be her, meanin' no offence, Miss Barbara, you know that don't you, but the way she's worked, what she's done. . . .'

'And still doing.'

'Aye, and still doing.' Mary now smiled into Barbara's face. It was the first time she had heard her make a remark off her own bat so to speak since 'that business'. She rarely spoke unless to say yes or no; she moved around most of the time like someone hypnotised. She remembered seeing a man hypnotise a girl at the fair some years ago and the girl's mother went hysterical 'cos the man couldn't get the girl to come back to herself and stop doin' daft things and there was nearly a riot. Miss Barbara put her in mind of that girl, only she didn't do daft things, except to walk; she walked in all weathers, storms held no fear for her. Since that night of the great storm when 'that business' happened there had only to be the sign of a storm and out she went.

She rubbed the thin white hands vigorously between her own now, saying again, 'You shouldn't do it, you're froze to the marrow. Look; an' your skirt's all mud. Go upstairs and change your frock. Go on, that's a good lass.'

When Barbara rose from the chair she pushed her gently towards the door, then across the hall and up the first three stairs.

Once in her room, Barbara didn't immediately change her dress, but walked slowly to the window and stood looking out. It was late October. The day was bleak, the hills looked cold and lonely as if they had never felt the warmth of the sun or borne the tread of a human foot; the wind that was blowing was a straight wind, bending the long grass and the dead flowers in the garden all one way; the garden was no longer neat and tidy, for the boy came no more, not since Constance had been forced to deprive them of the second fifty pounds a year. She thought, as she often thought, that they had been cursed, that both of them had been cursed; the tragedy of the Mallens had fallen on them. But they weren't Mallens; there was no Mallen blood in them. He who touches pitch is defiled; perhaps that was the reason. It was like contracting a disease. She and Constance had been in close contact with the Mallens all their lives and they had caught the disease. Her stomach was full of it. She looked down at the mound pushing out her dress below the waistband. The disease was growing in her and she loathed it, hated, hated and loathed it. Given the choice she would have accepted leprosy.

She heaved a deep sigh. All life was a disease and she was tired of it. She would have made an end of it months ago if it hadn't been for Anna. She could not add to Anna's sorrow, she loved Anna, she was the only one left to love. Anna had given unselfishly all her life and what had she got? Nothing. Yet she knew that Anna would refute this. And now this latest injustice, two thousand five hundred pounds going to Bessie. Bessie was just a vague memory to her: a round laughing face and a white train which she and Constance held; it was connected with the memory of people saying,

'Isn't she pretty, isn't she pretty?' But they weren't referring to the bride but to Constance. Poor Connie! Connie, who was now virtually a prisoner on that farm.

Again she asked herself why this should happen to them. Three people who had done no harm to anyone. Her mind checked her at this point. Constance had done harm to Donald before she married him, and she also harmed him by marrying him; but nevertheless she did not deserve the treatment being allotted her. She had not seen Constance since her visit to the farm, but every now and again she had a letter from her, smuggled to the carrier no doubt, for in each letter were the same words 'Please write to me, Barbie, but don't refer to anything I have said.'

She had only once replied to the letters, and that was as recently as a fortnight ago when Constance had desperately beseeched a word from her. The letter was short and terse and held nothing personal, except to hope that she and the baby were well. Her own plight was bad but she considered that her sister's was worse.

She turned from the window and took off her dress and, standing with it in her hand, she said to herself, But what of Anna's plight should anything happen to me when the child is born?

It was the next morning at the breakfast table that Barbara said suddenly, 'Do you think we could afford to ask our solicitor to visit us out here?'

'Our solicitor? . . . why? Why do you want a solicitor, Barbara?'

Barbara lowered her head, rested the spoon against the side of her porridge bowl, then said slowly, 'Should anything happen to me, I . . . I want you to be provided for.'

'Oh, my dear, my dear.' Miss Brigmore rose from her seat and came round the table and put her arms around Barbara and, pressing her head against her breast, whispered, 'Oh child, my dear child, don't think about such things, please, please, for what would I do without you?'

'One must think about such things. If they had been thought of before, you would be two thousand five hundred pounds richer at this moment.'

Miss Brigmore made no answer to this for she was surprised that Barbara had for the moment forgotten her own tragic condition and was concerned for her. It was the first time in seven months that she had made voluntary conversation. And she was right in what she said, if Thomas had thought of her. . . . Oh, she must not start that again. She had wrestled for most of the night with the bitterness in her, not against Thomas, she could never feel bitter against Thomas, but against the quirk of fate that would now further enrich the comfortably off Italian countess by two thousand five hundred pounds, for although the count had been classed as a poor man, his poverty was comparative. Patting Barbara's head now, she said softly, 'We will talk no more about it; nothing is going to happen to you, my dear.'

Barbara withdrew herself from Miss Brigmore's arms and, looking up at her, she said, 'I don't want to go into the town but if I'm forced to I shall.'

'But . . . but Barbara, my dear, the money is in trust, Constance and you only receive the interest. It is something that couldn't be transferred. If . . . if what you say did happen, and God forbid, unless you left . . . issue, the money would go back into the estate.'

'I . . . I don't think so. I've been looking into *Everyman's Own Lawyer*, and there's such a thing as a Deed of Gift. Anyway, this is what I want to find out, and make it legal, that if and when I die my allotment and share in the house will pass to you.' She paused here and, staring fixedly into Miss Brigmore's eyes, she ended, 'Whether I have issue or not.'

'But Barbara dear, you're . . . you're not going to die, you're so young and . . .' Her voice trailed away before she added, 'healthy,' for that would have been, if not a falsehood, a grave exaggeration.

'I shall write to Mr Hawkins to-day.'

Miss Brigmore sighed a deep sigh, went around the table and sat down. She was not thinking of what Barbara's gesture might mean to her in the long run, but of the fact that they could not really afford the ruinous fees the solicitor would ask for coming all this way from Newcastle. If it had been from Allendale or Hexham it would have been expensive enough, but all the way from Newcastle. . . . She wondered what they could do without in order to meet this further expense. . . .

When half an hour later she saw Barbara going down the garden path towards the gate at the bottom which led on to the fells, she opened the windows in the study and called, 'Barbara! Barbara dear! don't go too far, please, please.'

She knew Barbara had heard her although she didn't turn round. She looked up at the sky. It was high and blue and the sun was shining. It was much warmer than yesterday, in fact it was a nice day, an enjoyable Indian summer day. Not that the weather had any effect on her now, except that she worried about the extended cold days when they used more wood and coal than they could afford.

She closed the windows and sat down in the leather chair behind the desk. It did not pain her to sit in this chair, the chair in which Thomas had paid the price for his crime, the crime he had in all ignorance committed, for she knew he would have suffered crucifixion rather than knowingly perpetrate such a sin against Barbara, whom he had loved as a daughter.

She leant her head back against the top of the chair. She was feeling tired, weary, but strangely she was no longer enduring the physical weakness that had plagued her for so long following the pneumonia. Perhaps it was the shock of that night, and the call made on her inner resources, but since she had heard the gun shot she had ceased to be an invalid; necessity had made her strong enough to cope with the terrible circumstances.

'*Miss! Miss! Miss! Come quickly.*'

As she pulled the door open she ran into Mary.

'Oh miss! miss. . . .'

'What is it?'

'Miss Barbara, she's, she's in the kitchen with pains.'

'But she's just gone out.'

'No, she's back; like a ghost she is an' doubled up. . . . Oh! Miss! . . .

When she burst into the kitchen Barbara was sitting by the table, gripping its edge; her eyes were tight closed and she was gasping for breath.

'You have pains?'

She nodded, then muttered, 'Something . . . something seized me. I turned back, and then a moment ago it came again.'

Miss Brigmore now turned to Mary, saying sharply, 'Get an oven shelf, two, she's freezing, and more blankets. . . . Come along, dear, come along.' She put her arm around Barbara's shoulders and eased her to her feet. 'We must get you to bed.' . . .

After putting Barbara to bed with a blanket-covered oven shelf at her feet and one to her side she and Mary had a quick consultation in the kitchen. 'It would be safer to get the doctor,' Mary said. 'It might just be a flash in the pan but on the other hand it mightn't.'

Miss Brigmore did not think it was a flash in the pan. She agreed with Mary that it would be wise to get the doctor; but the carrier had passed and how were they going to get a message to him?

'I could run down to Jim Pollitt's,' said Mary. 'He generally drops in for his dinner around one o'clock. He might be takin' the sheep over that way or going to the farm, an' Mr Stanhope might let him run in for he's not a kick in the backside from Allendale.'

Miss Brigmore did not check Mary for her coarse saying for she knew it was only when she was anxious that she made such slips of the tongue in her presence. She said, 'Get into your coat; wrap up well, for the sun's gone in and there's a mist falling. How long do you think it will take you to get there . . . I mean to Mr Pollitt's?'

'I could do it in half-an-hour if I cut through the bottom of the Hall grounds, an' I will. An' if they catch me I'll explain; they can't hang me.'

As she talked she was winding a long woollen scarf around her head and neck. A few minutes later Miss Brigmore, opening the door for her, said, 'Tell them how urgent it is, Mary,' and Mary nodded at her and answered, 'Yes, miss, I'll do that, never you fear.' . . .

It was two hours later when Mary returned. She had come back much slower than she had gone for the mist had come down thick. After taking off her things she went upstairs and before she reached Miss Barbara's door she heard her groaning.

The doctor arrived when the dusk was falling into dark, and he confirmed what all three knew; the child was struggling to be born.

It struggled for the next ten hours, and when at last it thrust itself into the world it seemed to have little life in it, hardly enough to make it cry.

As Mary took the child from the doctor then hurried out, Miss Brigmore held Barbara's two hands close to her breast and whispered in a choked voice, 'It's all right, my dear, it's all right.' But how, she asked herself, could she say it was all right? Half the time words were stupid, language was stupid for it did not convey what the mind was saying and at this moment her mind was saying that no one should have to suffer as this poor girl had done in order to give birth. For what seemed an eternity she had sweated with her and her own stomach had heaved in sympathy; but even so she had not experienced the excruciating pain of the convulsions, although she would gladly have suffered them for her had it been possible.

The tears were spilling down her face as she murmured, 'It's all over, dear, it's all over.' But even as she spoke she experienced a new terror as she realized that for Barbara it was all over, for she was letting go of life.

Barbara had lifted her hand towards her and her lips were mouthing the name 'Anna, Anna' but without sound; then on a deep sigh her head fell to the side.

'*Oh no! No! Barbara, Barbara my love, Barbara.*'

Miss Brigmore's cry brought the doctor from the foot of the bed. He took hold of Barbara's shoulders as if to shake her while saying, 'No, no! Everything's all right. Come along now, come along now.'

There was a long silence in the room before he gently laid her back on the pillow. Then straightening his back, he looked across the bed at Miss Brigmore and shook his head as if in perplexity as he said, 'It was all right. Everything was quite normal. The child is small but . . . but everything was all right.'

Miss Brigmore brought her agonized gaze from his and looked down on her beloved Barbara, Barbara who had been like her own daughter. Of the two girls, it was Barbara who had needed her most although she would never admit it; she herself had had to make all the advances. And now she was dead, as she had planned. If anyone had arranged her death she had. She had walked herself to death, she had starved herself to death, but more than anything she had willed herself to death. 'Oh Barbara. Oh, my dearest, my dearest.' She fell on her knees and buried her head to the side of the limp body.

A few moments later the doctor raised her up, saying gently, 'Go and see if the child is all right.'

When she shook her bowed head he insisted, 'Go now, and send Mary to me.'

As if she were walking in a dream she went out of the room and down the stairs.

In the kitchen Mary was kneeling on the mat, a bowl of water at her side. She was wrapping the child in a blanket and she didn't look at Miss Brigmore but said, on a light note, 'It's small but bonny.' She placed the child on a pillow in a clothes basket in front of the fire, then turning her head to the side, she looked up at Miss Brigmore and slowly her mouth fell into a gape. She sat back on her heels and shook her head, and when she saw Miss Brigmore drop down into a chair and bury her face in her hands she exclaimed softly, 'In the name of God, no. Aw no, not Miss Barbara now. Aw no.'

When, rocking herself, Mary began to wail, Miss Brigmore got to her feet and, putting her hands on her shoulders, she drew her upwards, and then she held her in her arms, an unprecedented gesture, and Mary clung to her, crying, 'Oh Miss Barbie! oh poor Miss Barbie!'

After a time Miss Brigmore pressed her gently away and in choked tones said, 'Go up. Go up, Mary, will you, the doctor needs you.'

Rubbing her face with her apron, while the tears still poured from her eyes, Mary asked helplessly, 'What'll we do? what'll we do miss? what'll we do without them?' and Miss Brigmore answered, 'I don't know, I don't know, Mary.'

A moment later she knelt down by the wash basket and looked on the child, the child that was the outcome of lust and terror, Thomas's child; Thomas's son or Thomas's daughter, she hadn't up till this moment thought about its sex. As if loath to touch it she took the end of the blanket in her finger and thumb and slowly unfolded it.

It was a girl child.

# Chapter Three

It was towards the end of November, the dreary month, but as if to give the lie to the defaming tag the morning was bright; there was no wind and the earth sparkled with a thick rime of frost.

But the morning had no pleasing effect on Constance, she was numbed to the bone. She felt as if she were standing on the edge of a precipice trying to work up the courage to jump, and she knew she would jump if something didn't happen soon to alter the situation.

Last week when they had returned from burying Barbara she had almost gone mad with grief, and at one moment had almost screamed at him, 'It's Matthew's! Do you hear? It's Matthew's? Do what you like. Do you hear? Do what you like!' Such an outburst would have taken the implement of torture out of his hands, but it was his mother who had prevented her. As if she knew what was in her mind she had said, 'Be patient, lass, be patient, it can't go on for ever;' and she had looked at her and said, 'It can, it can;' and Jane had shaken her head and answered, 'God's ways are strange, they are slow but they're sure.' And in that moment she knew that Jane was not only afraid of her son, but she hated him as much as she herself did, and the bond between them was strengthened.

The dairy door opened, and now Jane's voice came to her softly, saying, 'Come on, lass, there's a drink ready, and he's bawling his head off.'

Constance left what she was doing, rubbed her hands on a coarse towel hanging on a nail in the wall, and went towards Jane who was holding the door open for her. Then on the threshold they both stopped at the sight of Donald crossing the yard with a man and boy by his side.

They themselves crossed the yard and met up with the men at the kitchen door. Donald went in first, but the man and boy stood aside until they entered; then followed and stood just inside the room.

'Give them a drink of tea.' Donald jerked his head towards the pair as if they were beggars; but they were dressed decently if poorly, and didn't look like beggars.

When Jane had poured out two mugs of tea, she motioned the man and boy to sit down on the form, then asked, 'Would you like a bite?' and the man said, 'Thank you, Missis, we would that; we've been walking since shortly after five. The others are outside.'

'My! my!' she nodded at him. 'Where you from?'

'Near Haydon Bridge, ma'am.'

'Haydon Bridge? My! that's a way. You must have found the hills cold this mornin'.'

'Aye, an' slippery underfoot; the rime's thick up there.'

'It would be, it would be.'

'Who told you I wanted a man?' Donald was standing with his back to the fire in his master attitude, and the man answered, 'Mr Tyler who I worked for, at least did, afore he was bought out. He said he heard in the market you were goin' to set somebody on.'

'Aye, I was; but one man, not two of you and a family. You say you've got a family?'

'Only two, I mean a wife and a daughter; we lost the others. But Jim here, he's fourteen gone and can hold his own with any man. And the girl, she's thirteen, an' she's been the last four years in the farm kitchen an' the dairy. She's very handy, me wife an' all.'

'Huh? I daresay, but I'm not asking for your family. Anyway, I've got no cottage to offer you; the only place habitable, and then not much so, are two rooms above the stables.'

'We'd make do with anything.' There was a deep anxiety in the man's voice. 'As long as it's a shelter we'd make do. And you wouldn't lose by it, sir. I'll promise you you wouldn't lose by it. We'd give you more than your money's worth.'

'What are you asking?'

'Well, well' – the man shook his head – 'it'll be up to you sir. But I can tell you we wouldn't press as long as we had a habitation.'

'Aye, yes.' Donald walked from the fire towards the table and, lifting up a mug, he took a long drink of the hot tea before he said, 'Habitations are necessary in the winter. How long were you at Tyler's?'

'Over ten years, sir.'

'Always been in farming?'

'No . . . no.' The man's voice was hesitant now and he said on a weak smile, 'I was a footman at one time in the Hall, High Banks Hall, over the hills.' He now jerked his head to the side and looked at the young woman sitting at the table. She had spilled her mug of tea and the liquid was running between the plates. She did not seem to notice this but she stared at him and he at her. He knew who she was. But that was by hearsay, for he would never have recognized her from the child he remembered, and should she remember him that might be the end of his chances.

'What's your name?'

He brought his eyes back to the master of the house and said slowly, 'Waite, sir. Harry Waite.'

Waite . . . Waite. The name sounded like a bell in Donald's mind awakening the memories of twelve years ago. Hadn't Waite been the man who had started all the hubbub? the man Dick Mallen wanted to shoot? He glanced from him to Constance and at the sight of her face a mirthless laugh rose in him. He had the power to engage a footman, the footman who at one time had waited on her. Well, well! the irony of it. All round, it was going to be a very exceptional day. He had a surprise for her but this bit was added interest.

'Drink up and I'll show you those rooms. If you're as handy as you say you are you should be able to make them habitable.'

Before he had reached the kitchen door the man and boy were on their feet, and the man, nodding first to Jane, and then to Constance, and awkwardly muttering his thanks, followed him.

Waite. The footman who had lifted the lid of the armour box and got them out. The man who had tapped her on the bottom, had tapped them both on the bottom, saying, 'By! you're a couple of scamps.' The nice footman, as she had thought of him, but also the man who was the cause of her sitting in this kitchen at this moment. Without him having expressed his opinion of his young master it was doubtful if anything that had happened since would have taken place; but for that meek-looking man they might all still be in the Hall, Uncle Thomas, Barbara, herself. . . . Yet how could she blame the man. As Anna so often said, lives were cut to a pattern, all one did was sew them up. The man looked desperate for work and shelter for his family, and he would get it. Oh yes. She had seen the look in Donald's eyes; he thought that by engaging him he would be cutting another sinew of her pride.

The child began to cry and she picked it up and started to feed it. The clock ticked the minutes away. Jane bustled about the kitchen washing up the mugs, sweeping up the hearth, doing a lot of necessary and unnecessary things, and neither of them spoke.

When the door leading from the hall opened and Matthew entered they both looked towards him. He coughed all the way across the room, short, sharp coughs. When he reached Constance's side she did not raise her head and look at him but went on feeding the child as she said below her breath, 'He's engaging a new man, with . . . with a family. He was Waite, the second footman at the Hall.'

Matthew looked from the top of her head across the table to his mother, and she nodded silently at him.

His coughing became harsher. Sitting down slowly by the side of the table, he said in a low husky tone, 'Well, he was going to hire a man anyway; but where will he put a family?'

'In the rooms above the stables.' It was his mother who spoke.

'They're not fit.'

'The man's desperate.'

'There's no place for a fire or anything else.'

'They'll likely cook in the store-room. . . .'

'In the boiler with the pig meat!'

Whatever response his mother would have made to this was cut off by the door opening and Donald entering, alone now. He did not walk towards the fire and stand with his back to it as was usual when he had anything special to say, but standing just within the doorway and looking at his mother, he said, 'You'd better set the dinner for one more, there'll be a visitor.'

'The man and . . . and boy?'

'No; what would I be doing with the man and boy at our table . . . Miss Brigmore.'

In one swift movement Constance returned the child to the crib and was on her feet.

'Why?' The word was so laden with apprehension that he laughed before saying, 'Because she's bringing the child across.'

'Bringing the child here?'

They all moved a step forward, and it brought them into a rough line facing him. His eyes swept over them as he said, 'Aye, bringing the child here. Where should it be but with its nearest relations; and we are that, aren't we?' He was looking directly at Constance. 'You're its only relation; apart from meself, that is, because what hasn't appeared to strike any of you afore apparently' – he now nodded first at his mother and then at Matthew

– 'is that the child is as much me half-sister as you, Matthew, are me half-brother, and so, therefore, I want her under my care.'

Constance's words seemed to spray from her twitching mouth as she spluttered, 'What . . . what do you mean? What are you doing? What's going to happen to Anna and Mary? There's the house.'

'I've been into all that.' His voice was calm. 'I saw the solicitor at the beginning of the week. Barbara's share of the property and her income naturally fall to the child, and as the child's coming here we would have no further use for the cottage. I have ordered it to be put up for sale.'

'*No!*' She moved towards him until she was within touching distance of him. 'No, you won't! You won't do this. You're a fiend, that's what you are, a fiend. You're mad. I won't allow it; I have some say, some rights.'

He looked down into her face. The hatred in his eyes rising from deep in their black unfathomable depths struck her like a physical force yet it wasn't so frightening as his voice when he said quietly, 'You have no rights; you are me wife, what is yours is mine and' – he paused – 'what is mine is me own.'

Seconds passed and no words came; as was usual he had frozen them within her. It was Matthew, after a fit of coughing, who said, 'But Anna, she worked for Mallen for years and brought them up.'

Donald took his eyes from Constance and looked at Matthew. He looked at him for a long moment before he said, 'She was paid for her services.'

'She was never paid, you know that, she . . . she's worked for years . . . without pay. . . .' He was coughing again.

'There are more ways than one of receiving payment. *She was a whore.*'

His calmness had dropped from him like a cloak; every word was a bark; his face was contorted with passion. 'And she wasn't the only one, was she? You're all whores, every one of you.' His arm swung before him with such force that had Constance been a few inches nearer it would have felled her to the ground. Then he turned and stamped from the kitchen.

They all stood still for a full minute, then they looked at each other and their eyes said, He's come into the open, what now?

It was eleven o'clock when Miss Brigmore got off the cart and walked into the farmyard, but she had no child in her arms.

Constance met her at the gate and they enfolded each other in a close embrace, and when Constance muttered, 'Oh! Anna, what can I say?' Miss Brigmore answered, 'I didn't bring her; I've . . . I've come to appeal to him. I'll go on my knees to him, anything as long as he doesn't take her from me. She's all I have; there's no other purpose in my life, nothing to live for.' Constance said again in an agonized tone, 'Oh! Anna;' then added, 'I'm helpless.'

As they crossed the yard still clinging to each other, Miss Brigmore murmured, 'I couldn't believe it when I got his letter; he had given no indication of it when I last saw him. I thought, well, naturally I thought I would stay in the cottage with Mary and bring up the child. I . . . I never dreamed for one moment' – she paused and came to a halt and, turning her face to Constance, said, 'Yes, I did dream. I have been in terror for months now in case he should do something to force you to persuade Barbara to fall in with his plans and sell the house, because . . . because, Constance, it is a plan. It is a plan of vengeance. His letter was so cold, so ruthless, it was as if he had been waiting all these years to do this to me. In between the lines I could read that he blames me for everything that has happened.'

Constance could say nothing to this for she knew it was true. He had a hate of Anna that was beyond all reason. He had always disliked her, in the first place because she had not liked him, but the main reason was because she had been close to Uncle Thomas.

'Is . . . is he in the house?'

Constance shook her head. 'No, no, he's out walking *his* land. He walks it every morning. Legally he doesn't own a foot of it but no one would dare to resist his claim to it, he is the farm. He works it, or has done up till now, almost by himself, but now he has engaged a man and his family. You will never guess who that man is.'

'Who?'

'Waite, the footman.'

'Waite! the footman?'

'Yes.'

'And he has engaged him?'

'Yes. Oh, I don't mind the man being engaged; strangely I remember him as a very kindly man. It's the reason he did it. He has no compassion for the man or his plight. He has a family and needed a home for them. Tyler's farm, where he worked, has been sold and the new owner has his own men. Anyway, the man heard that there might be an opening here. It . . . it was the first I knew of it, or, or Mam either. But then' – she shook her head – 'he's determined to expand. He has bought another fifty acres. Most of the dairy produce is sold now. We have an allowance in the house, so much and no more. Oh! Anna, Anna' – she shook her head – 'life is unbearable. Why did I do this? Why?'

Miss Brigmore now drooped her head as she said, 'You didn't do it; you wouldn't have done it, I forced you. On this at least I accept the guilt. You wouldn't have married him if I hadn't pressed you. But any shame you might have had to bear would have been better than your present state.'

'Oh, you mustn't blame yourself, Anna; you did what you thought was best for me. There's one culprit in this business and that is myself. When I look back and see myself distressed at the thought of not being married before I was twenty I think I must have been insane. . . . But come inside, you're cold, and you look ill.'

They had just entered the kitchen, and Miss Brigmore, after greeting Jane, was turning to Matthew where he sat crouched over the fire when the sound of hurrying, almost running steps across the cobbled yard froze them all.

Constance, turning to see Donald coming over the threshold, his face red and sweating, knew that he must have run at high speed from the far fields where he would have seen the carrier pass. The cart was well before its time this morning, the fine weather doubtless having set the pace.

No one spoke for a moment. Then, the colour in Donald's face deepening to a purple hue, he demanded of Miss Brigmore, 'Where is it?'

'I . . . I didn't bring her. I wanted to talk to you.'

'You can talk till you're black in the face, and it'll be useless. What I said in that letter holds; as I've told you already I have the law behind me.'

'I . . . I know you have.' The placating sound of her own voice made Miss Brigmore sick at herself, but she continued in it as she said, 'You . . . you

are quite within your rights to want Constance to bring up the baby, but
. . . but I have come to beg of you to be lenient and to leave her with me.
You know I'll do all in my power to educate her and. . . .'

'Aye and teach her to lie and cheat and whore.'

Miss Brigmore put her hand to her throat and her body swayed slightly
before she said, 'You do me a terrible injustice.'

'I do you no injustice; they took their pattern from you. Well, now you've
come without her so there's nothing for it but for me to go back and fetch
her.'

'You'll not, you'll not do this, I'll never let you.'

He moved slowly about until he was facing Constance and asked, quietly
now, 'How are you going to stop me? You haven't a leg to stand on and you
know it, so what I say to you now is, get yourself ready because you'll be
carrying your niece back with you.'

'I won't! I shan't, and I'll fight you. Do you hear? I'll fight you.'

Still gazing at her, his lip curled in scorn as he said, 'Don't be stupid.'

He had turned from her and had put his foot over the step before his
mother's voice stopped him. 'Don't do this, Donald,' she said.

He glared at her, his eyes narrowing; and then, his voice low, he said,
'I'll advise you to keep out of it.'

'I've kept out of it long enough. When you're talking about legal rights
you forget that Matthew was my husband's only son.'

Donald didn't speak for some seconds, and then he said, slowly, 'I forget
nothing. To all intents and purposes I am Michael Radlet's eldest son; it's
only hearsay that this' – he tugged at the white tuft of hair to the left side
of his brow – 'makes me a Mallen, and it would be hard to prove in law.
There are a number round about with white streaks; it wouldn't be possible
they are all the result of frolics in the wood.' Their eyes held for some
seconds before he finished, 'You're wasting your breath if you think you're
going to achieve anything by that. Now' – he cast his glance over them all
– 'as far as I'm concerned the talkin's finished. In ten minutes' time I'll have
the brake in the yard, an' you' – he nodded towards Constance – 'be ready.'

The kitchen was weighed in a silence like that which follows an announce-
ment of the plague. The three women stood where they were, and Matthew
sat where he was, all immobile, until the child in the cradle gurgled; then
Matthew turned his head and looked towards it. He kept his eyes on it for
some minutes before pulling himself up from the chair, and the almost
imperceivable motion of his head he made towards Constance told her that
he wanted to speak to her.

As if awakening from a dream she looked first at Miss Brigmore, then at
Jane, then back to Miss Brigmore again before, bowing her head deeply on
to her chest, she went out of the kitchen and into the hall.

Matthew was waiting for her just outside the door. He put out his hand
and drew her to the far end of the hall and into a clothes closet that was near
the front door, and there in the dimness he held her face as he said softly,
'Listen now; listen, dear. You . . . you are not to go over there. You must
make on you have taken bad, you must faint or something, and I'll . . . I'll
go with. . .' He pressed his hand tightly over his mouth as he began to cough,
and Constance whispered desperately, 'But . . . but you couldn't stand the
journey, Matthew; it'll be dark before you get back, and the cold will set in
and. . . .'

'Don't, don't worry about that, just listen to me. Listen to me, dear. Pay attention, don't cry. Now listen. I want you to go into the front room and lie on the couch; just say you feel bad. . . .'

'But . . . but he won't believe me. And he'll never take you . . . And why . . . why do you want to go with him?'

'It doesn't matter why, only do what I ask.'

She shook her head slowly. 'He won't take you, he'll bring her himself.'

'He can't, there's only a chain to the back of the brake and a basket could slip through.'

'Oh, Matthew, don't be silly, you know him, he'll think of some way. He'll tie it on. But why, why? what are you going to do if you go?'

'Listen to me, dearest, please. Now you and I know that I've had much longer time than was due to me. I might go the night, I might go in the mornin', but one thing's certain, I won't get through this winter. It was a miracle I got through the last. Now listen, listen. Look at me. We haven't much time.' He stared at her in silence for a moment, then whispered, 'Aw Constance, I love you. Aw, how I love you. It's this that has kept me alive, but now I'm suffering the torments of hell 'cos I know I'll be leaving you here alone to suffer him. 'Cos Mother's no match for him, no more than I am meself. He's turned into a devil, and to think that I once loved him, and he me. I know I wronged him but . . . but . . . Oh! my love, my love, I would wrong him again for you.' He touched her face with his fingers and his voice was scarcely audible as he said, 'I've . . . I've never kissed you but that once.'

Slowly his face moved towards hers and his lips touched her brow and her eyelids, then traced her cheek, but before they reached her mouth a fit of coughing seized him and he turned his head away and held a piece of white linen to his lips, then screwed it up tightly before he looked at her again.

The tears were raining down her face and when she went to speak he put his finger on her lips and muttered, 'No questions, nothing, no more; as he said, the time for talking's past. Come on, my dear; just do what I ask, go and lie down on the sofa.'

'No, Matthew, no.'

'Please, please, do this for me, make me happy Constance, make me happy. Let me think there's been some meaning in me being alive. . . .'

'Oh, Matthew, Matthew, what are you going . . .?'

He had opened the door and drawn her into the hall again, and now pressing her towards the sitting room he said quickly, 'Don't speak to him when he comes in, not a word, be prostrate.' He bent quickly forward and kissed her on the mouth, then whispering, 'Good-bye, my love.' He opened the door and pressed her inside, then closed it quickly as she went to protest. The next minute he was in the kitchen and, with a briskness in his voice that his mother hadn't heard for years, he said, 'Constance has fainted, she's lying down in the sitting room.' Then, putting his two hands out one towards Miss Brigmore and the other towards his mother as they made to move towards the far door, he said, 'Leave her alone, please. . . . Leave her alone. I'm . . . I'm going over with Donald.'

'You? you're not!'

'I am. It's a nice day an' the drive will do me good.' As he stared into his mother's eyes, she put her hand to her mouth and whispered, 'What, what have you in mind, boy? what are you . . .?'

'Nothing, nothing, Mother; I'm just going over in Constance's place to bring the baby back.' He turned now and looked at Miss Brigmore. She was staring at him, her eyes wide and questioning, and he smiled weakly at her and nodded reassuringly before saying, 'Don't worry.'

'No! Matthew, no!' Jane pulled him round to her. 'There's nothin' you can do, nothin'. What chance have you against him, or ever had for that matter? Things have got to take their course.'

'Be quiet.'

The door opened and Donald entered. He stood for a moment looking at them, and then he said, 'Where is she?'

It was Jane who answered, 'She's had a turn, she's lying down.'

'Huh!' His laugh was pitying. 'She's had a turn, she's lying down is she?' He stalked across the room and they heard him going up the stairs, taking them two at a time; then his steps running down again and the sitting-room door opening. In a few minutes he was back in the kitchen. Walking slowly to the middle of the room he looked from one to the other and said, 'Well, whatever you've planned it won't work. I'll bring it back if I've got to nail the basket to the cart or lay her in a bundle under my feet.'

'There won't be any need for that, I'll come along of you.' Matthew's voice was quiet, tired sounding; it was like someone saying, Anything for peace.

Donald turned his head sharply and looked at him. He looked at him for a full minute before he smiled grimly and said, 'Well, that mightn't be a bad idea after all. We could stay overnight and I'll load the brake up with the bits and pieces I want to bring across.' He had turned his gaze on Miss Brigmore, and she closed her eyes against the look in his; then swinging round he went outside.

Jane now ran into the hall and returned with a heavy coat, scarf and cap, and as she helped Matthew into them she kept whispering, 'What is it? Tell me, what is it? what are you up to?'

When he stood muffled up to the eyes he looked into her face and said gently, 'Nothing, Mother, nothing; what could I be up to? Now I ask you, what could I be up to? You go and see to Constance, she needs you. Good-bye.' All he did now was to touch her shoulder with his fingers. Then he turned to Miss Brigmore and, addressing her as he always had done, he said, 'Come on, Miss Brigmore, come along.'

'Can't . . . can't I see Constance just for a moment?'

He went close to her now before he spoke. 'It would be better if you didn't. You'll see her again. Don't worry, you'll see her again.'

She shook her head before letting it fall forward, and like someone in whom all hope had died she went out of the kitchen, without a word to Jane, and across the yard to the brake.

Donald was standing to the side of it. He did not speak to her but pointed into the back of it, and it was left to Matthew to help her up.

Slowly she covered her ankles with her skirts and sat, for once in her life, without any signs of dignity while the cart rumbled out of the yard and began the journey over the hills.

As they drove higher Matthew's coughing became harsher, but only once did Donald turn his head and glance at him and noted there was more blood than usual staining the piece of linen. It would be odd, he thought, if he died on this journey. He wanted him to die, and yet he didn't want him to die. There were still grains of love left in him that at times would cry out and ask, Why had he to do it to me? I could have suffered it from anybody else in the world except him. But such times were few and far between and his hate soon stamped on the grains.

They were nearing the narrow curve in the road where the guard or snow posts stuck up from the edge above the steep partly wooded hillside. It was the place where Barbara had experienced the terrifying fierceness of the gale as it lifted the carrier's cart over the ditch. The line of posts curved upwards for some forty yards and it was at the beginning of them that Matthew, putting his hand tightly over his mouth, muttered, 'I'm . . . I'm going to be sick.'

Donald made no comment but kept on driving.

A few seconds later he repeated, 'I'm, I'm going to be sick, stop, stop a minute. I'll . . . I'll have to get down.' His body was bent almost double now.

The horse had taken a dozen more steps before Donald brought it to a halt, and Matthew, the piece of linen held tightly across his mouth, got awkwardly down from the cart and hurried to the edge of the road, and there, gripping one of the posts, he leaned against the wire and heaved.

Miss Brigmore watched him for a moment from the side of the cart and as she slid along the seat with the intention of getting down, Donald's voice checked her, saying, 'Stay where you are.' Then he called to Matthew, 'Come on, come on.' But Matthew heaved again and bent further over the wire. After a short while he slowly turned around and, leaning against the post, he gasped, 'I'm . . . I'm bad.'

Donald looked down at him. There was blood running from the corner of his mouth, his head was on his chest. He hooked the reins to the iron framework, then jumped down from the cart and went towards him, and as he did so he slipped slightly on the frosted rime of the road, which as yet the sun hadn't touched. When he reached Matthew's side he said sharply, 'Get into the back and lie down.'

'I . . . I can't.' Matthew turned from him and again leant over the wire and heaved.

Donald, bending forward now, looked down. There was a sheer drop below them before the trees branched out. He said harshly, 'Come back from there, you'll be over in a minute.' It was at this moment that Matthew turned and with a swiftness and strength it was impossible to imagine in his weak state he threw both his arms around Donald's shoulders and pulled him forward. Almost too late Donald realized his intention, and now he tore at the arms as if trying to free himself from a wild cat while they both seemed to hang suspended in mid-air against the wire. Donald's side was pressed tight against it; he had one foot still on the top of the bank, the other was wedged sideways against the slope. With a desperate effort he thrust out one hand to grab the post, and as he did so he heard the Brigmore woman scream. Then Matthew's body was jerked from him and he was free, but still leaning outwards at an extreme angle over the drop. As he went to heave himself upwards his foot on top of the bank slipped on the frost-rimmed grass verge, and the weight of his body drew him between the wire and the top of the bank, and with a heart-chilling cry of protest he went hurtling through the air. When he hit the ground he rolled helplessly downwards, stotting like a child's ball from one tree trunk to another. . . .

They lay on the bank where they had fallen, Miss Brigmore, spread-eagled, one hand still gripping a spoke of the cart wheel, the other clutching the bottom of Matthew's overcoat.

When, getting to her knees, she pulled him away from the edge of the drop and turned him over she thought he was already dead, for the parts of his face that weren't covered in blood were ashen.

'Oh, Matthew! Matthew!' She lifted his head from the ground, and he opened his eyes and looked at her. Then his lips moving slowly, he said, 'You should have let me go.'

She pressed his head to her and rocked him for a moment, then murmured, 'Try to stand. Try to stand.' Half dragging him, half carrying him, she got him to the back of the brake and pulled him up, and he lay on the floor in a huddled heap.

Before she got up into the driver's seat to take the reins she walked a few tentative steps towards the edge of the road and looked downwards. Far, far below a dark object was lying, but it could have been a tree stump, anything. If it was Donald he might still be alive.

She urged the horse upwards to where the road widened and, having turned it about, she drove back to the farm.

It was five hours later when the men lifted Donald from the flat cart and carried him into the farm kitchen, where they laid him on the wooden settle to the side of the fireplace.

Miss Brigmore, Constance and Jane stood together near the dresser; one might have thought they had their arms around each other, so close were their bodies.

Matthew was lying back in the wooden chair near the kitchen table. If his eyes had not been wide open and moving he too could have been taken for dead, such was the look and colour of his skin.

The four of them watched the men as they straightened their backs after laying Donald down but no one of them spoke, or moved.

It was Willy Nesbitt from Allendale, a man who had been on many winter rescue expeditions, who broke the silence. Looking at Constance, he said, 'He's fought hard; don't know how he's done it, Missis. He's smashed up pretty bad; he should have been dead twice over, but he's fought to keep alive. I thought he was gone two or three times, but even now there's still breath in him.'

The man's eyes seemed to draw Constance from the protection of Miss Brigmore and Jane, and like a sleepwalker she went around the end of the table, past Matthew, and to the settle, and there she stood looking down on Donald. He looked twisted, all of him looked twisted. His face was bruised and shapelessly swollen, all that is except his eyes, and these were open.

His eyes had always been dark, black when he gave way to emotion, but now they were like pieces of jet on which a red light was playing, and the feeling that emanated from them struck her with a force that was almost physical, for she fell back from it. She even flung out her arm as if to protect herself; and then she cried out as it beat on her and bore her down. When she fainted away the room became alive with movement.

She recovered lying on the mat in front of the fire, Miss Brigmore was kneeling by her side. Donald was no longer on the couch; under Jane's direction the men had carried him into the front parlour.

Miss Brigmore, stroking the damp hair back from Constance's brow, whispered, 'It's all right, my dear, it's all right, he's gone.'

Constance's breast was heaving as if she had raced up a hill. She did not need to be told he was gone, she knew, for with his last look he had tried to take her with him. The strength of his mind, the intensity of his hate, the futility of his life had all been in that last look and he had kept himself alive to level it on her. If ever a man had wished death on another he had, and as she had slipped into the black depths she thought he had succeeded.

When she went to rise Miss Brigmore helped her to her feet, saying, 'Sit quiet for a while, sit quiet.'

Matthew was still in the same position in the chair. It seemed that he hadn't moved and when she looked towards him and whimpered, 'Oh Matthew! Matthew!' he answered through blood-stained lips and in a voice that had a thin, flatness about it, 'It's all right, it's all over.'

Constance leaned her head against the high back of the chair and closed her eyes. It might be over, but it wasn't all right, and it might never be all right. Matthew had killed Donald; as surely as if he had stuck a knife between his ribs he had killed him but the guilt was hers. She had known, as had his mother, when he set out in the cart to go over the hills that it wasn't in order to bring Barbara's child back, but to put an end to Donald. . . . Yet there had had to be an end, it had to come in some way for she could not have stood this way of life much longer. Donald had not been a sane man; his jealousy had turned his brain. . . . But there again, was she not to blame for that? Oh God! God! At this moment she wouldn't have minded if he had taken her with him for then she would not have had to face the prospect of living with this feeling of guilt.

She opened her eyes to look at Anna who was again stroking her brow. But here was something she could be thankful for: Anna's future, however long or short it might last, was secure, and Barbara's child would not be brought up in hatred. And that was another thing, neither would her own. She took in a deep breath. Some good could come out of this deed other than her own release. She'd have to think along these lines.

Matthew now moved in his chair and muttered, 'Get my mother,' and as Constance went to rise Miss Brigmore said, 'I'll go, sit quiet.'

Constance sat quiet and she and Matthew looked at each other, until Matthew closed his eyes to shut out the pain that the sight of her always brought to him. . . .

Miss Brigmore went from the kitchen and into the sitting room where the new woman Daisy Waite was helping Jane to lay out the body of her son.

Donald was lying on the table, the stairs having been too narrow for the men to carry him up. The two women had undressed him down to his long pants and vest, and Daisy Waite was unbuttoning the pants that were stained red around the hips, while she cried as she talked. 'God Almighty! To end like this. Did you ever see anything like it? Aw, the poor man, the poor man. An' no matter what, let everybody have their due, it was him who gave us shelter when nobody else would. And to come to this. Aw, dear God. Where's the sense in anything?'

Miss Brigmore turned her gaze away from the now partly naked body for she too felt on the point of fainting. She touched Jane on the shoulder and said softly, 'Matthew needs you.'

Jane nodded but did not turn and follow her or look at her, but she kept her gaze fixed on the face of her son. He was gone, he was dead, they were rid of him, they were all rid of him, they were free and she was glad. Then why was there this pain in her? She had never wanted him. When she was carrying him she had never wanted him, and when he was born she had never wanted him for she had seen him as something that had been thrust on her – into her, and since the day he had first breathed he had brought strife with him. He in his turn had never liked her, had even hated her. Yet she was feeling an overwhelming pity for him, as if she had sustained the loss of a loved one. She couldn't understand it. If it had been Matthew she could have. And she would be feeling like this again soon, for Matthew wouldn't be long in going now.

What would happen to Matthew when he died? Would he be brought before the Judgment? His father had instilled the Good Book into her, so she must believe in the Judgment, but surely the dear God would take everything into account. But she didn't know, she didn't know, He was a fearsome God at times. Her poor Matthew! her poor Matthew! And Donald? At this moment she could say, if not 'My poor Donald', at least 'Poor Donald', for he had never been hers nor she his, but yes, she could say, 'Poor Donald.'

She turned her dry eyes on Daisy Waite and said, 'I'll be back in a minute.'

'Don't worry, Missis, don't worry, I can manage. He isn't the first, and he won't be the last I've put ready for a journey.'

Miss Brigmore took Jane's arm and led her from the room, but they did not go immediately into the kitchen. In the dim hallway they instinctively turned and looked at each other, and the look was deep. Neither of them said a word but their hands gripped tight for a moment before they moved on again into the kitchen.

When Jane stood beside Matthew's chair and he said, 'I want to go to bed, Mother,' she replied, 'Come away then, lad.' And tenderly she helped him to his feet and with her arm around him led him from the room.

Constance had not moved, and now Miss Brigmore went to her and, bending over her, said softly, 'Try to think no more of it, what's done is done. It . . . it had to be this way, you couldn't have gone on, something would have happened, perhaps something more terrible.'

'But . . . but what will happen to Matthew?'

'Nothing will happen to Matthew. I've told you, I mean to explain it all as I saw it, and nothing will happen to Matthew.'

'Oh! Anna.' Constance jerked to her feet, her hands gripping her neck. She seemed to be on the point of choking, until the tears, rushing from her eyes and nose, relieved the pressure. Miss Brigmore put her arms tightly about her and they both swayed as if they were drunk.

When the paroxysm passed, Miss Brigmore, her own face showing her distress, murmured, 'There, there, my dear. You must forget it, all the past, all of it, all of it. Just . . . just thank God that you've been saved and you're still young and, and beautiful. There's a life before you yet, you'll see. There's a life before you yet.' And to this Constance made a deep dissenting sound.

At the inquest a week later Miss Brigmore explained to the Coroner exactly what had happened. Mr Matthew Radlet, who had the disease of consumption, had been in distress, and because he was feeling sick had got down and stood at the side of the road. His brother, Donald, had gone to his assistance. She could not explain how it had happened because she was sitting in the back of the cart at the time, but she surmised he must have slipped on the frost-rimed verge; the frost had been very heavy the night before; all she knew was Mr Matthew Radlet had made an effort to grab his brother, but without success.

It was an awful tragedy, everyone said so, for Donald Radlet was the most up and coming farmer in the district. They said this aloud, but among themselves in the drawing rooms, the parlours, and the select ends of the inns they reminded each other that, after all, he was a Mallen and did anyone know of any Mallen who had died in his bed?

# Aftermath

It was the end of the harvest supper. The barn had never witnessed such gaiety for it was the first time such a function had been held there. Michael Radlet had not countenanced harvest suppers nor had his father before him, nor, of course, had Donald Radlet, and they would all have stood amazed, not believing their eyes at the changes that had taken place during three short years. In Donald's case, he would surely have experienced chagrin that his farm, as he had always considered it, was now being managed by a woman, a young woman, his wife in fact.

Matthew Radlet had survived his half-brother by only six weeks, and his going had drawn Jane and Constance even closer together. Their guilt, their remorse and their relief were mingled and shared.

For months after Matthew's going they had lived a cheerless, guilt-ridden existence, until one day Jane, as if throwing off a mental illness, had stood in the kitchen and actually cried aloud, 'Look, girl, let us put an end to this. If we're going to live in misery then it's a pity he ever went the way he did. That's how I'm seeing it now, and you must see it the same way. Oh yes, more so than me, you must see it like that, for you are young, and healthy. And you have a child to bring up, and he should be brought up amid cheerfulness, not the gloom that's been hanging over us these months past.'

It was from that time that, as Daisy Waite expressed it, the missis and the young mistress came out of their sorrow.

It would not have been considered unusual had Constance left the running of the entire farm to Harry Waite. Harry was quite knowledgeable on farming matters, and more, more than willing to do all in his power to assist her, as were his wife, son and daughter; but no, from the day Jane lifted the curtain of guilt, as it were, from their shoulders, there had risen in her a determination to manage the farm herself.

And so she went to market, driven by Harry Waite, and stood by his side as he bargained in both the buying and the selling. She said little or nothing on these first visits but kept her head held high and her gaze straight, and her look defied the neighbouring farmers to laugh at her, at least in public. That in the inns it was a different matter she had no doubt, for on one occasion Harry Waite drove her home having only the sight of one eye, the other being closed and fast discolouring, besides which his knuckles were bleeding. She did not ask him if he had been drinking, for Harry Waite, she had discovered, was a moderate man; his main concern in life being the welfare of his family and, since being in her service, protecting her.

His loyalty had been well repaid, for two months ago he moved his family into the three-roomed cottage she'd had built for them in a small enclosure about a hundred yards from the farmhouse proper.

Harry Waite's son, Jim, who was now seventeen was, among other things, a shepherd on the farm, and his daughter, Lily, now sixteen, divided her time between the dairy and the house.

The house had changed beyond all recognition, for the horsehair suite no longer adorned the sitting room, nor was there linoleum on the floor, but a new chesterfield suite now stood on a patterned carpet, and there was never a day in the winter but a fire was lit in this room. Jane no longer sat in front of the kitchen fire warming her feet and knees before going up into the freezing bedroom, but she and Constance usually ended the day sitting side by side on the couch, slippers on their feet, and a hot drink to their hands. On extremely cold nights there was the welcome glow of a fire in their bedrooms, an extravagant innovation this, and there was always a fire, except on days that were really warm, in the room that was now called the nursery.

So in the late summer of 1866 when Constance did her books and found that the profit for the year was well up on the previous one, and this in spite of having to engage extra labour for the threshing and the hay making, which crops were the first results from the land that Donald had so proudly acquired, she decided, with a little glow of excitement, to give a harvest supper. She would bring Anna, Mary, and the child over; they would enjoy it. Then besides the Waite family there would be the Twiggs, the father, mother, and three children – they had been very helpful. Then there were Bob and Peter Armstrong, two brothers who had a farm in the next valley. They had been most kind from the beginning, going as far as to come over and offer her advice; and it hadn't stopped there, for their help had also been practical. She liked the Armstrongs, Bob in particular, he had a merry twinkle in his eye.

The supper had not been lavish as some harvest suppers tended to be. She had provided plenty of wholesome food, and a certain amount to drink; and no one had overstepped the mark in this direction, except perhaps Mary. Two glasses of ale always led to three with Mary, and three to four, and then she became very merry; but she had caused a great deal of laughter tonight and she had got everyone dancing. Constance herself had danced for the first time in years. It had been strange feeling a man's arms around her once again. At first she had felt stiff, resisting both touch and movement in such close proximity; then Bob's merriment, and young Jim's fiddle playing, seemed to melt the aloof encasement within which she had remained for the last three years, and she had ended the dance with her head back and laughing as she used to do years ago when life had spread out before her like a never-ending series of bright paintings.

But now the visitors had gone. Peter Armstrong, shaking her hand as if he would never let it go, had told her in fuddled tones that she was – a grand lass, which had caused great hilarity. Bob had not taken her hand, he had just stood before her and had said simply, 'We'll have to have a night like this again, but not wait till next harvest supper, eh?'

In reply she had said formally, 'I'm so glad you enjoyed it,' and his eyes had laughed at her, but in a kindly way.

And now she and Anna were seated before the fire, to use Mary's term, taking five minutes off, and they were alone, for Jane always tactfully gave place to Miss Brigmore during her visits.

Turning her head from where it rested on the back of the couch, Constance looked at Miss Brigmore and asked quietly, 'Did you enjoy it, Anna?'

'Enormously, enormously, my dear. Now I can understand why there's so much fuss made about them. And to think that years ago when I used to hear of the excitement surrounding them on the Hall farms I used to turn my nose up.'

Constance looked towards the fire again as she said softly, 'We turned our noses up at so many things in those days, didn't we? Life is strange; you've always said that it's a pattern that is already cut. I wonder what shape mine's going to take from now on?'

'A good shape I should think, dear.'

'I'd like it to remain exactly as it is now; I'd like to keep everything and everybody static, Michael for ever small, Jane happy and content, and all the Waites so loyal and good, and myself at rest.'

'You are too young to be at rest, you'll marry again.'

'No, Anna, no.' Constance's voice, although low, held a definite ring.

They were both looking straight ahead into the fire when Miss Brigmore said, 'I like that Mr Armstrong, the younger one; I should say he's an honest man and he has a great sense of humour.'

Constance did not move as she replied, 'I like him too, Anna. He is as you say an honest man, and his company is enjoyable . . . but that's as far as it will go; I wouldn't risk a repeat of what I've been through.'

'Well, time will tell. You are so young yet and life, in spite of the pattern being already cut' – she slanted her eyes towards Constance – 'no doubt has some surprises in store for you . . . as it's had for me. Now who would have thought that I'd ever sit in the Hall schoolroom again! In your wildest stretch of imagination, would you have said that was in my pattern?'

'No.' Constance shook her head as she laughed, then added, 'And you know, I still don't like the idea of you being there. I've always considered you belonged to Barbara and me exclusively, I mean with regards to education. But it would appear that he was determined to have you in the end, and his motto seemed to be: If at first you don't succeed.'

Miss Brigmore laughed gently and nodded towards the fire. 'Indeed, indeed, that is his motto, which he applies to everything, I should say. He's a strange man, Mr Bensham; you dislike him, yet at the same time you admire him, except that is when he's speaking to his wife, for he not only considers her a numskull but tells her to her face she is one, using that very word. Poor Mrs Bensham. Yet it's odd but I find no need to pity her, she's a woman who can hold her own in her own way. As I told you she's such a common type, it's almost impossible to imagine her in the Hall as one of the staff, let alone its mistress, yet it's very strange you know' – she turned her head now and looked at Constance – 'the staff don't seem to take advantage of her. She bustles, shouts, fumbles her way through each day, but there at the end of it she sits in the drawing room quietly knitting. I think she must do this every evening after dinner; and he, when he is at home, sits there too, smoking and reading his newspaper. . . .'

'Smoking in the drawing room?'

'Yes, smoking in the drawing room, and not cigars but a long, smelly old pipe.'

'Have you been to dinner? You didn't tell me.'

'Well, there hasn't been much time. But yes, I went to dinner to discuss the new arrangement. And you know, Constance' – Miss Brigmore's voice had a touch of sadness in it now – 'it was the first time I had sat down to dinner in the dining room of the Hall. It was a strange experience; I felt most odd.'

'Oh, Anna, it is unfair when you think of it, isn't it?'

'No, no.' Her tone became airy. 'Yet it did strike me as peculiar at the time. It was a very good meal, by the way, and well served. The butler had not the dignity of Dunn of course; apparently at one time he had worked in Mr Bensham's mill and ill-health had prevented him from continuing, which doesn't speak well for the conditions there, yet such is the make-up of our Mr Bensham that he took him into his house service when they were in Manchester. Mrs Bensham addresses him as . . . 'Arry as she does her husband. Oh, I shouldn't make fun of them, because they have been, and are still, very good to me.'

'It is to their own advantage.'

'Perhaps, but to mine also because I am using them for my advantage, or at least for little Barbara's. I was adamant at first against going every day; I said I had my ward to see to and couldn't possibly think of leaving her except in the mornings for three hours as the arrangement stood, and then it was he who said, as I hoped he would, "Bring her with you, woman, bring her with you".'

'Does he call you woman?' Constance was laughing.

'Yes, very often. The only time he gave me my title was when he came to see me, and then that was only after he had said, "You're harder to get at, woman, than the Queen herself. I've written you three times. What is it you want, more money? A pound for six mornings a week, you'll not get an offer like that again." It was then I said, "My name is Miss Brigmore. Won't you sit down?" and for the first and only time he gave me my title, "Aye, well, Miss Brigmore," he said; "now let's be sensible. I hear you're a good teacher an' I want you to teach my young 'uns. Three of them I have; a boy of seven, another six and a girl coming five. Three so-called governesses the missus's had for them in a year, an' what've they learned, nowt. The boys will be going off to school in a year or so, private like, but I don't want them to go with nothing in their heads, you understand?" '

Miss Brigmore now stopped her mimicking and leant her head against Constance, and as they laughed together she recalled, but only to herself, how Mr Bensham had ended that introduction by saying, 'I've heard all kinds of things about you but it makes no matter to me; I've always said, a man's reference is in his hands or his head. They say you're a good teacher, and ladylike at bottom, and that's what I want, someone ladylike.'

Strangely she had not taken offence at the man. He was a common man who had made money – there were many such these days – but she saw it was to his credit that he was wanting to educate his children above his own standards. Moreover, as he said, a pound a week for morning work was a very good offer indeed. She now knew security in so far as she owned half the cottage, Constance having transferred to her her own share by deed of gift together with fifty pounds a year, and this with the child's income of a hundred pounds enabled them to live better than they had done since she had left the Hall. Even so this new addition to her income would be a means of carrying out the vague plans that had been formulating in her mind with regard to Barbara's future.

A young lady's education could not be accomplished without money. She regretted that there was no musical instrument in the cottage; Barbara must have music lessons. Then there were languages; she herself unfortunately had only French to her credit. Moreover, a young lady needed dancing lessons if she was to fit into any civilized society; added to this, riding lessons were necessary; and there were so many, many more things her child – as she secretly thought of Barbara's offspring – would need before she could take her rightful place in society, and this she was determined she should do. God sparing her, she would see to it that Thomas's daughter was educated to fit into the life that was rightly hers.

She was recalled to the present when Constance, chuckling, said, 'So you cornered him.'

'Just that, just that.'

'Does he know that she isn't yet three?'

'Yes; he's seen her.'

'And when do you start to take her?'

'She's already been there. I took her along on Thursday and I must say that the first meeting didn't augur well for the future.' Miss Brigmore pursed her mouth and her eyes twinkled as she added, 'Barbara ended her visit by attacking the daughter of the house.'

'No! . . . What happened?'

'Well, she had never seen so many toys in her life before. She has three dolls you know, Betsy and Golly and Fluffy, but the nursery at the Hall is now stacked with toys and dolls of all shapes and sizes. Barbara became fascinated by a Dutch doll. It was neither big, nor small, nor outstanding, it was just a Dutch doll, but apparently it was Katie's favourite. She went to take it from Barbara, but Barbara refused to let it go. When Miss Katie forcibly took possession of her own Barbara gave way to one of her tempers, and oh dear, before we knew what had happened she had slapped Katie and pushed her onto her back, and Katie yelled as she is apt to do when she can't get her own way. Then . . .' Miss Brigmore now stopped and bit on her lip and, her expression serious, she looked at Constance before adding, 'Something strange happened. There had been no surnames used between the children, just Christian names: "This is Barbara, Katie," and "Katie, this is Barbara." But when I lifted Katie to her feet she ran from the room crying, "Ma! Ma! the Mallen girl has hit me. The Mallen girl has hit me, Ma".'

They looked at each other in silence now; then Constance said quietly, 'You never told them her name's Farrington?'

'There was no need, the occasion hadn't arisen when I was required to give her full name, but it proved one thing to me, she's known already as a Mallen. Mrs Bensham must have spoken of her in front of Katie as the "Mallen child", and Mrs Bensham would have heard it from someone else. I think it's going to be difficult to get people to realize that her name is Farrington, and it's going to be awkward as she grows older. It'll have to be explained to her.'

Constance sighed now and, pulling herself to the edge of the couch, she dropped on to her knees and, having taken up a shovel, scooped from a scuttle some small coal and sprinkled it into the dying embers; then she patted it down before saying, 'There's a lot of things that'll have to be explained to her. But in the meantime, let her be happy . . . And she will be happy' – she turned and nodded her head – 'because she'll have her own way or die in the attempt. Look how she dominates Michael already, and he's willing to let her. Oh' – she put out her hand and covered Miss Brigmore's – 'she'll be all right. She has you, so she'll be all right. Come, let's go up; we'll look in on them before we go to bed.'

A few minutes later they stood in the nursery between the cot and the bed. The candle glowed softly in its red glass bowl, showing to one side the boy lying on his back, his fair hair curling over his brow and around his ears; the bed-clothes were under his chin, and his body was lying straight; he looked in deep relaxed sleep. But on the other side the small girl lay curled up into a ball; her forearms were crossed above her head and her black straight hair half covered her face; the bed-clothes were rumpled down to her waist; she looked as if she were pulling herself up out of some dream depth.

As Miss Brigmore gently brought the clothes up around the small shoulders she thought that, even in sleep, the children looked poles apart. They were full cousins yet showed no apparent blood link in either looks or character.

The two women turned and tiptoed quietly from the room, and on the landing they kissed each other good night.

Constance went into the bedroom which now held no resemblance to the one she had shared with Donald, and Miss Brigmore went into the room that had been Matthew's.

Strangely, their thoughts were running along the same channel now, for they were both thinking they would be glad when tomorrow came, Constance so that she could fall back into the daily routine when she and Jane would be alone together and the older woman would become her relaxed and motherly self again. Anna's intellectual presence always put something of a damper on Jane, indeed her whole outlook was foreign to the farm atmosphere. It was lovely to have her for a short time but it was, and Constance hated to admit this, a relief when she went.

She did not probe this feeling too far for it seemed to be linked up with the day of Donald's death and Matthew's act. Would Matthew have taken the step he did if Anna hadn't come to the farm begging to keep the child? If? If? If?

But there was another reason why she·was always glad when Anna departed. It concerned little Barbara, for the child, as young as she was, dominated Michael and in a way that annoyed her. The little girl had an attraction that was unusual, to say the least, in one so young. Yet she herself had never been able to take to the child, and this seemed strange because she had loved her mother dearly. Anyway, she told herself, she'd be glad when tomorrow came.

Miss Brigmore too thought she'd be glad when tomorrow came for then she'd be home where she was mistress, really mistress now, and in the cottage she would have the child all to herself.

It was very nice visiting the farm but the atmosphere was – well, how could she put it, a little raw. And Constance was changing, changing all the time. She noticed it on each visit. She wouldn't be surprised if Constance did marry that Mr Armstrong, and it wouldn't be a case now of marrying beneath her for, of late, she had become very farm-minded. She wasn't being disloyal to Constance, oh no, no, she loved her, and would always love her, she was just facing facts.

Almost the last thing Miss Brigmore told herself before dropping off to sleep was, I go to the Hall on Monday. It was exciting being back at the Hall. There were moments when in the schoolroom she thought she had never left it. Already she had a status in the house, and it would grow; oh yes, it would grow, for she was needed there. She had sensed this from the beginning. Mr Bensham needed her. 'What's the best way to tackle an invitation like that?' he had said to her on one occasion as he handed her a gilt-edged card; and then on another, 'Who do you think's best for running a house, a housekeeper or a steward?' Yes, Mr Bensham needed her.

And Mrs Bensham needed her. 'Do you think this is too flashy-like to go to tea in? What happened in the old days when you lived here and they gave parties? How did they go about it, were they flashy-like or selectish?' Yes, Mrs Bensham needed her very badly.

And Katie needed her. Oh yes, Katie needed her to discipline and train her, and in the coming years to stand as a buffer between the young lady she would become and the parents she would undoubtedly look down on, as was usual in such situations.

And the boys needed her, but their need would only be for a short time. Her influence on them would be felt mostly during their holidays; yet they were very important in the future she was mapping out.

As the necessity for her presence at the Hall grew with the years so would Barbara's future become more and more assured, for 'the Mallen girl' would always have one asset the young Benshams lacked, breeding; but they, in their turn, would have one thing the Mallen girl lacked, money.

Who knew, who knew but Thomas would reign in the Hall once again – through his daughter.

Happy, she went to sleep, forgetting as she did so the adage she so often quoted that the pattern of life was already cut.

# CATHERINE COOKSON

## The
# Girl

# The Girl

### Author's Note

I must express my thanks to Mrs M. J. Wescott for passing on to me her grandfather's treasured book on Allendale and Whitfield which was written by George Dickinson Junior and published in 1884. Her grandfather was Doctor Arnison who, like his own father, practised in Allendale for many years. This little book has afforded me a wealth of information and inspired the idea for *The Girl*.

I have taken the liberty of using the name Arnison for the doctor in the story, but other names are fictitious, as are the personal events and the village of Elmholm.

## Chapter One

### The Girl 1850

From the hills in the early dawn,
Small, thin, mist-wreathed, she came upon him;
Hair sodden to the brow,
Eyes like agates,
Lips apart, tongue flicking at words frozen in her head.
Gliding to his feet,
She caught his hand and said,
'Come help me, mister, or she'll be dead.'

They had taken two days to cover the twenty-three miles from Newcastle to Hexham, keeping mostly to the grass verges or the fields that bordered the side of the road in case they should be knocked down by the coaches or the dray carts or, as was more likely, the travellers on horseback who came upon you quicker and without the warning of the coaches or the drays. As for herself, Hannah could have scooted from the road with the agility of a deer, but not her mother, for she, even before they left Newcastle, had been trailing her feet.

This morning they had risen from the stinking straw in a field barn before the sun was up and for the first four miles of their journey they had shivered. The can of boiling water begged from a cottager into which, at her mother's bidding, Hannah had put a handful of raw oatmeal, had helped to thaw them out. But now, having reached Hexham at three o'clock in the afternoon, they were hot, sweating, hungry and thirsty.

Hannah Boyle was quite used to large towns, she had been born in the packed bustling melée of Newcastle riverside, and whenever her mother had visitors and so would push her outside to play she had gone up into the city by herself and looked at the big buildings, and some of them were so big and so grand that they outdid in her imagination the stories told her by one or other of her mother's sailor friends who had seen wondrous places across the sea.

But this town was different. Although she was weary, she gazed about her with interest because she liked what she was seeing. The market square she dubbed in her mind a canny little place, and the shops bonny, and the streets tidy.

But her mother speaking brought her from her scrutiny. 'Here, take this,' she said, and, handing her two pennies, added, 'Go . . . go over to that baker shop across there an' . . . an' see what you get most for it.'

'Yes, Ma . . . You'll be all right?'

'Aye, I'll be all right. Go on.'

As the child ran across the square Nancy Boyle leaned back against the wall that supported an archway, and she muttered to herself what might have sounded to an outsider like a prayer: 'Christ!' she said, 'let me make it.'

When, of a sudden, she began to cough she brought a rag from her pocket and held it to her mouth; then presently spat into it, clenched the rag in her hand, returned it to her pocket, and once again rested against the wall; all the while her breathing coming in painful gasps.

As she now watched her eight-year-old daughter making her way towards her dodging between a trap, a gentleman on horseback, and a dray cart, she endeavoured to hold her breath, and when the child reached her side she gazed down at her for a moment before she could say, 'I've . . . I've a good mind to skelp your lug for you. I've told you about dodgin' atween carts, haven't I?'

'I'm all right, Ma.'

'One of these days . . . you won't be all right when . . . when you're cut in half . . . What did you get?'

'I asked her for stale bread an' look' – she opened the bag – 'there's some cobs, six or more, two with sugar on, an' a big tea-cake. She was nice, the woman . . . Will we eat them here?'

'No, no. . . . Oh, all right, take one, then let's find a horse trough an' get a drink.'

As they walked from the square, Hannah, her mouth full of the last of the bun, asked, 'How far is it now, Ma, to this place?'

'Some miles I think from what the woman at the cottage said.'

'How many?'

'How do I know? Why the hell do you keep askin' such questions! Aw, I'm sorry. I'm sorry.' The woman now shook her dirt-streaked face from side to side, and the child said quickly, 'It's all right. It's all right, Ma.' Then, as if her last question had not caused her mother to repulse her, she asked, 'Will the man . . . will he be nice, Ma?'

'He'd better be.' The words were scarcely audible.

They were walking down a street now with fine shops on either side and when they came opposite an inn where two dray-men were unloading barrels into a cellar, the woman stopped and enquired of one of the men, 'Could you tell me how far Elmholm is from here?'

The man straightened his back, looked her up and down, and then at the child by her side, before replying, 'Elmholm? 'Tis some way beyond Allendale.'

'Well, how far is that?'

'Oh, all of nine miles I'd say. But Elmholm's a bit further on, another couple of miles. But you might cut it short by going over the hills.'

'Which way's that?'

'Well now, go along the road there for about four miles until you come to a little hamlet by the river, follow it along on the flat till you see the hills, then you've got a steep bit of a climb, but the hills 'll bring you down into Elmholm quicker than going Allendale way. There's plenty of tracks to follow an' once you get up there you'll see the hamlets below. You can't miss Elmholm, it's a tidy size.'

'Ta, thanks.' She nodded at the man, and the man nodded at her; then he watched them walking away, the skirts of both the mother and the daughter trailing the dust on the paving flags. He watched them until they had passed the end of the street and when his mate called to him, 'Hie-up! there,' he turned to him saying, 'Asking the way to Elmholm, she was; I wouldn't like to waste a bet on her makin' it. No, I wouldn't that.' . . .

How long it took them to walk the four miles and for how long they walked by the river they had no idea, but they were resting yet again when the drover came upon them. 'Elmholm?' he said. 'Oh well now, you're on the right track but it's time you left the river and took to the hills. Take that sheep track' – he pointed – 'an' start climbing.'

It was close on five o'clock before they reached the summit of what had appeared to them the last hill because they'd had to take so many rests; and now once again they were sitting down, and the child, standing before her mother, said anxiously as she pointed towards the valley, 'Should I run on, Ma, and see if there's any place we could shelter, an' then I'll come back for you?'

'You . . . you stay where you are; I'll . . . I'll be all right in a minute. He said it was just beyond those hills. After this big one.'

'But you're dead beat, Ma.'

'Don't worry.' There was an unusually gentle note in the woman's voice as she put out her hand and gripped her daughter's arm. 'I've been worse than this'n I've survived. Only the good die young, they say' – she made an attempt at smiling – 'so that leaves me out, don't it?'

Hannah didn't smile back at her mother, and her face was straight as she now reached out with both her arms, saying, 'Come on then, Ma, get on your feet an' . . . an' hang on to me 'cos those hills there look steep.'

The hills were steep. Nancy Boyle crawled on her hands and knees to the top of what again appeared to be the last of them, then she lay face downwards; and now she didn't attempt to bring the handkerchief to her mouth as the blood ran from it.

When she sat up Hannah wiped her mother's face with what looked like a ragged petticoat, which she had taken from out of the bundle she was carrying; then she said, 'Lie still, Ma, 'cos we're nearly there. I can see houses and it'll be easier going now . . . What's the name of the man, Ma?'

Nancy Boyle didn't answer, but she dragged herself to a sitting position, then hitched herself slowly to the side until her back was resting against a butt of rock.

'I can't go on for a while,' she said; 'we'll have to stay put until I get me breath.'

'Ay, Ma. Yes, Ma. An' look; eat this bun with the sugar on. Sugar's good for you.'

The woman took the proffered bun and broke a piece off it, which she put into her mouth and chewed on slowly; and when she had finished the bun and half the tea-cake, Hannah, who had hungrily consumed two dry cobs, said brightly, 'You'll feel better now, Ma, with something in you.'

'Aye . . . aye, I'll feel better soon, but I must sit for a bit.'

And they sat for a bit. But it was a long bit, and all the while Hannah sat gazing at her mother. The fact that she was spitting blood did not alarm her unduly, her mother seemed to have always spat blood, well, for a long time, but what was alarming her now was the deepening pallor of her mother's skin and the way her eyes seemed to be sinking into the back of her head.

She shivered and looked up into the sky. The twilight was beginning, and although it would stretch out it would be dark within the next hour or so. They'd have to get down to those houses because she could see no place to shelter them here. It was a wild place; everywhere she looked appeared desolate and wild. Funnily wild, was how she put it to herself. The sky was so high, not like it was in Newcastle just above the roof tops. And there was too much space; everywhere was filled with space. She didn't like it, she wanted to be closed in, hugged around by walls.

She got on to her knees and knelt by her mother's side, saying softly, 'Can you make it now, Ma?'

'What?' It was as if the woman were being dragged up out of a deep sleep, for she blinked her eyelids, looked about her, then said, 'Oh aye. Oh aye.'

They were only half-way down the first hill when they had to go on to their hands and knees and descend for some distance crabwise, and when they reached a kind of ledge that was pitted with boulders and bare of vegetation the woman once again sat her back against a rock, and after a while, her words coming singly on each gasp, she said, 'How ... much ... further ... does it look?'

Hannah turned her head from side to side, taking in the scene. Hills and hills. Nothing but hills. Those directly in front of her rolling down into a valley appearing a slaty grey; others, a dull green; and those to each side of her were spreading away into that everlasting distance where they finally met the sky.

She was filled with a feeling a panic as in a bad dream. She felt she was alone and that there was no escaping from this place.

Swinging around, she gazed down at her mother; then dropping to her side, she caught at her hand and, gripping it tightly, brought it to her chest and held it there.

'What is it? What's the matter?' Nancy Boyle was roused from her lethargy. 'What did you see? ... What did you see down there?'

'Nothing, Ma, nothing.'

'What d'you mean, nothing?'

'Well, the village must be there, I saw it from the top, but it's still some way down yet.'

'Well ... it ... won't get any shorter ... if ... if we stay here. Give me a hand up.'

Hannah helped her mother to her feet and once again they were stumbling and slipping down the steep side of the hill.

After what appeared to them both as a never-ending space of time they eventually reached the last slope. But bordering this slope was a strip of woodland, and in the now fading light the shadows within it appeared jet black, and it was Hannah now who stopped and said, 'Have we got to go through there, Ma?'

'Well ... it's either that or go round it, an' I can't see us doin' that, 'cos ... 'cos I'm dead beat.'

It was the mother now who held out her hand to the child, saying, 'Come on; it didn't seem that wide from up there, we'll soon be through it.'

But once in the wood with no path to follow, the woman led the way aimlessly between the trees, whose entwined branches, although leafless, shut out the last glimmer of the fading daylight, and she was unaware that instead of walking across the belt of woodland she was traversing its length.

'My God!'

'What is it, Ma?' Hannah was clinging tightly to her mother's arm now.

'Nowt. Nowt.'

They were now groping their way from tree to tree and Hannah whispered, 'Are we lost, Ma?'

When her mother didn't answer, she shivered and pressed close to her side; then peering about her, her mouth fell open before she cried excitedly, 'It's a place, Ma, look!'

Letting go of her mother's arm, she stumbled towards a wooden erection, which turned out to be a three-sided roughly made shelter, its purpose apparently to keep sacks and tools dry from the worst of the weather.

'Look, Ma; we could stay here till the mornin'. There's sacks here an' all. ... An' look, feel, they're dry.'

'Dear God! Dear God!' Nancy Boyle shook her head as she stumbled into the shelter, then bent almost double as a fit of coughing seized her.

'Lie down, Ma. Look, I'll put these three sacks on top of each other and it won't be so hard for your hips.'

'No ... the ground's dry ... lie down aside me here an' we'll put them over us. Is there any bread left?'

'Aye, two buns, Ma.'

'Well, we'd better have them but let's get bedded down first. Then ... then eat slowly an' it'll last longer. It fills you more when you eat slowly.'

Lying close together, the sacks over them, they munched slowly on the buns, but hardly had they swallowed the last mouthful when they both fell into exhausted sleep.

It was the mist that woke her. It was as if the hut was filled with a grey light. The child sat up and coughed. Where was she? What had happened? What was this stuff all about her? When her teeth began to chatter and her whole body shivered she realized it was simply mist, just like the sea fret that used to come off the river and fill their room. She blinked her eyes. The light was breaking; it was daytime again. They could get up and go on now and perhaps find some cottager who would give them a can of hot water. Oh, she was thirsty. She wasn't hungry any more, she was just thirsty, and cold, so cold.

Turning on to her side, she shook her mother, saying, 'Ma! Ma! it's mornin'.' Three times she shook her before her voice rose to a high cry and she yelled, 'D'you hear me, Ma? Ma! wake up. Wake up!'

When her mother groaned she almost fell over her in relief, and she spoke quietly now as she said, 'Ma! it's mornin', we can go on.'

'Hann ... nah!'

'Yes, Ma?'

'I can't go on. Go an' ... an' fetch ... somebody.'

'But ... but, Ma, where? Where will I fetch them from?'

'That ... that village. ... Go on.'

When Hannah stumbled to her feet, her limbs were so stiff she almost fell over. She couldn't see her mother's face now because of the mist and she whimpered, 'But ... but I won't be able to see, Ma.'

'Go on.'

As she stepped from the shelter into the wood she bit tight on her lip, and she stood, not knowing in which direction to move. Then of a sudden the mist in front of her swirled away and there in the distance, not more than ten yards away, was the open hillside.

Picking up her skirts now in both hands, she ran with stumbling gait towards the light, and as she came out of the wood she saw immediately in front of her, across a sloping hillside, a house, a quaint looking house.

As she made to run towards it, it was blocked from her sight by another swirl of mist, but she knew where it was now, and in leaps and bounds she ran through the wet curtain and didn't stop until her feet left the grass and she knew she was walking on paving slabs.

The stamping of horses' hooves and the voice of a man brought her to a stop, but only momentarily, and then she was walking towards where the sounds were coming from.

As she came out of the mist she saw at the end of a long paved yard, which flanked the quaint house, a young man. He was standing amidst a number of horses, tying one to the other, and he stopped in his work and his mouth fell open, while his head poked forward as he peered at the minute figure approaching him.

The young man didn't move or speak until the slight form came near him and put its hand on his arm; then he drew in a long breath, wetted his full lips with his tongue, blinked and said, 'God Almighty! who are you?'

'I'm Hannah Boyle. Come, come help me, mister, or she'll be dead . . . me ma.'

'Your ma?' He bent his back now until his face was level with hers and he asked quietly, 'Where's your ma?'

'In the wood back yonder' – she thumbed over her shoulder – 'in a hut. We got lost last night; we slept in the hut.'

'An' she's bad?'

'Sorely.'

He straightened up, rubbed his hand tightly across his unshaven chin; then taking the rope he was still holding in his hand, he moved towards the stone wall that bounded the yard and, slipping the rope through a ring in the wall, he said, 'Wait there, the lot of yous;' then turning to the Galloway pony that was already saddled, he spoke to it as if to a human, saying, 'Keep an eye on them, Raker, no tricks,' and without further ado strode across the yard, Hannah now hurrying by his side.

'Where you hail from?'

'Newcastle.'

'Newcastle? That's a distance. What's brought you this far? Looking for work?'

'No.'

He glanced down at her. 'What then?'

'I . . . I don't know.'

He paused in his step and screwed up his face as he looked down at her. 'You don't know?' he said, and moved his head first one way then the other as if to get a better view of her. She didn't look an idiot.

They had almost reached the wood before he spoke again. And now he asked, 'What's your ma sick with?'

'The consumption.' She made this statement as another might say 'a slight cold'.

He had stopped dead now. The consumption. You could pick that up. Aw well, he didn't pick things up, so why worry. But what was he going to do with her? Consumptives died. He looked at the child by his side and walked hurriedly on again.

When he reached the hut and bent over the woman lying under the sacks he endorsed in his mind what he had thought a moment earlier. Aye, they died. And if he knew anything it wouldn't be long afore this one kicked the bucket.

'Hello, missis.' He talked loudly as if speaking to a deaf person.

'I'm sick.'

'Aye, I can see that. Can you stand?'

'Aye . . . aye . . . I . . . don't know.'

'Well have a try.' He bent down and put his arm under her shoulders while at the same time turning his head to the side. He wasn't superstitious, and he had a theory that if you had to get the smit you got the smit, but at the same time he didn't believe in going out and looking for trouble, and breathing consumptive breath was one way of doing it.

'That's better . . . it's only a little way down to the house . . . Where you makin' for?'

'The village of . . . of Elmholm.'

'Oh, aye; well, you haven't very far to go now. . . . You know somebody there?'

He was more than half carrying her and he waited for the answer, but when none came he paused in his stride and said, 'I said, do you know somebody there?'

'Aye.'

'Well, I know everybody in the village an' for miles around, happen I could bring them up to you.'

When again she didn't answer he turned his head and stared at her, and as if becoming aware of his critical scrutiny she said something that brought his dark eyebrows meeting above his long nose. 'I want to see their house first,' she said.

'Well, what's their name?'

There was a long pause before she answered, 'Thornton,' and then she added, 'I think.'

To this he made no response but stumbled on. Thornton, she had said . . . I think. Well now what would the likes of her want with Matthew Thornton? It was well known that he had come from ordinary stock, but not so ordinary as he would have relations the likes of the one he was lugging at the moment. And what would his lady wife say to having guests such as these two sprung on her? Oh! God in heaven! she'd have such a fainting fit she would never recover. Oh, if only he could be there to see it. Thornton, she had said . . . I think. . . . Queer what the tide and the mist washed up.

'That's it, just a little further, we're almost there.'

They were now crossing the yard and he added, 'You'll have to bed down on straw for you'll never make the ladder up above.'

Hannah now followed her mother and the young man through a double doorway into what looked and smelt like a stable. Two sides of the large room was taken up with horse boxes, and against the third wall were stacked bales of hay and full sacks, and on nails above these hung a conglomeration of horse equipment. Near the far end of the room a ladder went up almost vertically to a trap door above.

Hannah now watched the man lower her mother on to some loose straw on a long wooden platform raised about a foot from the uneven stone floor, then pull two brown blankets from off a partition and put them over her before bending down and asking, 'Is that better, missis?'

When Nancy Boyle made a small movement with her head, he said, 'I've got to be on me way, I've got to deliver a bunch of horses.' He nodded at her now. 'I'm a horse dealer you see, but ... but you stay there until you get your legs again. I'll go up above' – her jerked his head towards the ladder – 'and bring the old 'un down. He's me grandfather, he'll see to you. He'll make you some crowdy. He's as deaf as a stone but he's still all there up top.' He tapped his brow. 'Nearly ninety he is.' He nodded again as he backed from her and made towards the ladder.

Hannah now climbed on to the platform and knelt beside her mother and smiled widely at her as she whispered, 'You'll be all right now, Ma. He's nice, kind, isn't he? Will ... will the other man be like him?'

'No.'

'Oh!' ...

'What the hell! you should be on your way. What d'you say? Sick? Where?'

Hannah looked upwards at the two men coming down the ladder, the young one sliding from rung to rung as if his feet were greased, but the older one placing each foot firmly on the rungs and gripping the sides of the ladder as he made his slow descent.

Then he was standing gaping at them, and as Hannah stared at him she nearly laughed as she thought, He looks like a sailor, a funny old sailor.

The old man's head was completely bald except for two tufts of white hair sticking out from behind his ears, but what his head lacked in hair his face made up for, for it was almost covered with a thick white stubble. He had once been a very tall man but even now that he was stooped he still retained the appearance of great height.

When he stood by the side of the platform and looked down first on Hannah, and then on the woman, he appeared fearsome, and he sounded so as he cried in a high thick voice, 'Nice bloody kettle of fish this! What's wrong with you, woman?'

When he was pulled around he stared at his grandson as he watched him mouthing words and gesticulating. Then he said, 'The consumption?' His head jerked and he gazed down once more at the figure on the straw before emitting the syllable 'Huh!' and turning and striding out of the stable and into the yard. But from there his voice came clearly to Hannah as he shouted at his grandson, 'What if she snuffs it?'

And the answer, not so loud but still audible, came, saying, 'Don't you worry about that. You won't have to bury her, she's got relations in the village ... Thorntons.'

'What d'you say?'

'I said Thorntons.'

'Her! That pair related to Thorntons! Bloody joke that is.'

'Aye, so thought I; but that's who she's makin' for.'

'Thorntons. Huh!' And this was followed by a deep chuckle.

'I'm off then.'

Hannah started and looked up at the young man who was now standing by the shallow platform. She hadn't heard him come in.

'I won't be back till late s'afternoon. Stay as long as you want . . . till she manages to get on her legs.'

'Ta.'

'Eat plenty crowdy; the old 'un 'll fix it for you.'

'Ta,' she said again.

He stared at her for a long moment, smiled and turned away, and she looked after him until he disappeared through the double doors. Then once again she gazed down on her mother.

Her face was no longer grey but a pink colour; she must be feeling warmer because she was sweating. She wished she felt warm, she was still shivering; and she felt so tired as if she hadn't been to sleep all night.

'Here! get that into you.'

She started then blinked while she held her hands out towards the bowl of steaming porridge. She must have dozed off.

'Can she feed hersel?'

'I'll . . . I'll help her.'

'She wants propping up. Get her on her elbows and I'll push a sack under her.' He now went to the wall, and taking from it a sack of grain, he pulled it on to the platform, then tipped it on to its side so that it fell just below the sick woman's shoulders; then he bawled, 'You drink tea?'

'Yes, please.' Hannah nodded at him, and he stared at her for a moment before saying, 'Aye, you would; you'd be a fool to turn your nose up at tea . . . Doubt if you've ever tasted it.'

He turned away and walked down the length of the room and through an open aperture at the far end, but before disappearing through it he bawled, 'Come and fetch it when you've finished that.'

Alternately now, Hannah spooned the porridge first into her mother's mouth, then into her own – the old man had only put the one spoon into the bowl – but before the bowl was half empty, Nancy pushed it away from her, saying, 'You finish it up.'

'You feel better, Ma.'

'Aye. Aye.'

'Would you like a drink of tea? The old man said we can have some.'

Nancy seemed to consider, then shook her head slowly, saying, 'I'm goin' to sleep; I'll be better after a sleep.'

'Yes, Ma.'

Hannah now almost gulped up the remainder of the porridge. Then rising from the straw, she made her way down the stable and through the aperture; and there she saw the old man sitting near an open kitchen range, which reminded her of the one in the communal bakehouse in Newcastle, only this one wasn't so big. There was a great heat coming from the range, but the old man was sitting quite close to it. He was chewing on a thick slice of bread and pig's fat, and when he opened his mouth she saw he had three teeth in the bottom and one in the top.

'Want some tea?'

'Yes, please.'

'How is she?'

'She's asleep.'

He had turned from her as he spoke and now he turned again to her and bawled, 'I said, how is she?'

'She's asleep.' She mouthed the words, then remembering what the young man had done she rested her head on her hand and closed her eyes, and he said quietly now, 'Best thing. Best thing in the world, sleep. How old are you?'

'Eight.'

'What?'

She could count up to ten on her fingers so she demonstrated, and he repeated 'Oh, eight;' then smiled at her, and she smiled back, and as she drank the tea he had poured out for her he went on munching the bread and lard.

Once when he turned and looked at her she was staring round the room. It was like a kitchen, she thought, in that there was a battered delf rack against the wall with a lot of odd pieces of crockery on it, and on the floor in the corner was a frying pan and two kale pots; and along one wall was an old settle with a horse-hair pad on it. She could see the horsehair sticking out in several places. And there was a wooden kitchen table and three straight-backed chairs. But mixed up with everything were straps of leather, and horse traces, horse brasses, and horseshoes. The horseshoes were hanging on nails driven in between the large stones that made up the walls. She had never seen such big stones. The houses in Newcastle were made of bricks, but all along the way here she had seen houses made of stones, but never as big as the stones in this one.

He startled her now by shouting, 'Do you like it, me Pele house, me Pele tower?'

She nodded at him.

'Fine house.'

She nodded again.

'Stood up to wind and weather, women and wars.' He now put his head back and laughed; and when he looked at her again she smiled at him, and after a moment his face became serious and he bent towards her and, his voice a little quieter now, he said, 'I was born here, bred here, brought three wives here; reared two sons but they're gone now, dead, the bloody mine; and what have I left? Ned, only Ned. He's a good lad, Ned.' He bent further towards her now. 'He's like me, chip off the old block, goes his own way, owns no master, nobody'll bond him, no by God! Me, I was the same. But my lads, well they were funny, took after their mothers, no spunk. And the lead got them. I told them it would, but no, they wanted to make money, quick money. And who were they making it for? Bloody old Beaumont. Stick to horse dealing I said. As long as there's mines they'll want mules and Galloways, but no, they had to go smelting. Poison, that's what lead is, poison. Do you know that? Poison.'

He now sat back in his chair, reached for the big brown teapot from off the top of the stove, poured himself out a steaming mug of the boiled black tea, took a long drink of the scalding liquid, smacked his lips, then once again bent towards her, where she sat wide-eyed staring at him, and said, 'Biggest horse dealer hereabouts in the country me da was; sold the Galloways by the dozen to the mines. They used to bring all the ore out on saddleback at one time; then what did they go and do? Build bloody roads inside an' out an' use carts. Not so many Galloways needed then; but still enough.' He now stretched out a grubby hand and patted her knee and, his face wide with laughter, he said, 'Cart no bloody good without a horse to pull it, is it?'

She shook her head, smiled and said, 'No, no,' and was about to add her quota to the conversation by saying, 'The horses in Newcastle are three times the size of yours, with big, bushy feet, especially the ones that pull the beer drays;' but she decided very quickly in her mind that she wouldn't be able to imitate horses with bushy feet, so she continued to smile and gaze at him while he went on talking.

'D'you know, I could turn over more money in a day when I was young than both my lads could pick up in a month in the mine. A pound a month each they got down on the nail, the rest was kept for the pays. You don't believe me? It's as true as I'm sittin' here. Subsistence money they called it, and begod! they subsisted poorly on it. Anybody that goes into a lead mine is a bloody fool, their soul's not their own. Look what happened last year when they went on strike. Eighteen weeks they were out, then what? Sacked, over a hundred of them sacked, and more than half of them lost their homes, the very roof over their heads. And what's going to happen to them? They're sailing away to America come next month. That's for you and your mines. The only ones who make anything out of the mines are the owners an' their agents. And Thornton's one of them. . . . Why you goin' down to Thornton's?' On the last question his voice had dropped almost to a normal tone.

'I don't know.' When she shook her head as she answered he understood what she was saying and repeated, 'You don't know?'

'No.'

'Huh! . . . Huh!' He gave two short laughs. 'Well hinny, Ned says you walked all the way from Newcastle with your ma and you tell me you don't know why you've done it? Well, all I can say is you're either a stupid little bugger or a clever little bugger an' from the looks of you I don't think you're stupid, so' – he nodded at her – 'keep your own counsel, I don't blame you, keep your own counsel. But if you're goin' down there' – he now thumbed towards the opening – 'an' to the Thorntons, why it won't be long afore you know what you're after, an' the village an' all.'

# Chapter Two

The village of Elmholm was about two and half miles south of Allendale. It consisted of forty-five houses. These included the two short rows of miners' cottages, which were situated behind the houses on the right hand side of the village green if you were journeying from Allendale towards Sinderhope. They had been built some fifty years previously to house the overflow of miners then employed in the lead mines and smelting mills. They were low two-roomed stone dwellings with mud floors, except where flagstones had been laid down; and at first the sanitary habits of their occupants had been similar to those which prevailed in the town of Allendale itself; their middens had been in front of their front doors, to the disdain of the artisans in the village who kept their middens at the back of their houses, or better still at the bottom of their gardens. But time had wrought change so that now not only were all middens to be found behind the cottages but for most of the year the villagers all lived peaceably together, except on days such as fair days, or the Friday after the pays. This was the day on which the miners received their accumulated pay. Then the rowdiest among them fought, cracked each other's heads, and beat up their women. The return to normal wouldn't take place until work started again.

The village proper was shaped like a pear, the road from Allendale entering it between Ralph Buckman's blacksmith's shop and Will Rickson's house and builder's yard before dividing to pass round both sides of the green, joining up again to leave the village where, like the stalk of the pear, it narrowed between the wall of the churchyard and Elmholm House.

The cottages and houses making up the village were of various designs and sizes. Ted Loam's was a two-storied dwelling, the ground floor of which he used as a butcher's shop.

Two others that stood apart belonged to Walter Bynge the stonemason and Thomas Wheatley the grain chandler who, although his main business was in Allendale Town, used his ground floor, too, for the sale of flour and pulses in times of necessity.

But most of the inhabitants were either farm labourers or drovers who, however respectable they were during the week, would invariably, like the miners, become mortallious on fair days, at weddings, christenings, funerals, and occasionally on a Saturday night.

There were, of course, the Methodist Chapel and the inn, which seemed to be of equal attraction to the villagers if one could go by the numbers directing their footsteps towards the one place or the other.

But across the road from the cemetery wall were the low iron gates leading to the short drive fronting Elmholm House, which was Matthew Thornton's home.

It could be said that everyone in the village liked Matthew Thornton in some degree but no one in the village could be said to like his wife in any degree. It was common knowledge that Matthew Thornton had come up in the world and this he never denied. Nor did he deny that his people had kept a small huxter shop in Haydon Bridge, and that he owed what education he had to an old retired schoolmaster who came to live near his home and who had taken him under his wing. The schoolmaster had not only taught him to read, write and reckon, but had instilled into him a bit of the Latin language as well. It was the latter that in a way made him feel different, but as he had told himself from the beginning it could be of no help to a man who was going in for engineering. Anyway, as most of the old 'uns repeatedly stated when discussing the family in the inn of an evening, she, that madam, his missis, must have been captivated by the results of his education, which had given him not only a fine speaking voice but a singing one as well, for, as they said, they had to be fair, she was from different stock, being the daughter of a solicitor in Newcastle. And moreover, as everybody knew, from the parrot in the pub to Frank Pearson's pig, wasn't she related to the Beaumonts through her cousin Marion, and wasn't her cousin Marion's husband half cousin to old Beaumont himself. Dig deep enough down and you reach Adam and Eve, they said.

The male habitués of the inn found a lot to laugh at in Mrs Thornton's claim to the gentry, as did the church and chapel frequenters of the village – but not so their wives, for without exception Mrs Anne Thornton's unspoken claim to being the first lady of the community was to say the least aggravating.

Anne Thornton was a tall woman, her fair hair and pale skin emphasizing the clearness of her round blue eyes. Her nose was small, her lips full, almost overfull but well shaped. She had neither bust nor hips to speak of, but what she lacked in these parts of her anatomy she rectified by means of padding. Furthermore, she was a good housekeeper, and a good mother to her four children; as to being a good wife, only Matthew Thornton could have given an answer to that question.

Had her two servants been asked their opinion of her, Bella Monkton who acted as cook-general, and Tessie Skipton who was housemaid, hand-maiden, and nursemaid rolled into one, would have looked at each other, pressed their lips together, but said nothing in reply. Bella Monkton, at forty, knew she was a lost woman as far as marriage was concerned, and since positions were hard to get unless you had a mind to bond yourself, she would have thought it expedient to keep her opinion of her mistress to herself.

As for Tessie Skipton, Tessie at eleven years old knew from experience that any place was preferable to the workhouse whence she had been delivered by Mr Thornton four years ago, and for whom she stated daily she would work her fingers to the bone. But it wasn't for him she was called upon to work her fingers to the bone but for the missis. And what did she think of her? She wasn't saying. Only to Bella could she express her opinion, and then it would be whispered in the privacy of the attic, which they shared, each with a straw pallet on the floor.

They got on well, did Bella Monkton and Tessie Skipton. Each found in the other a substitute; the one a daughter, the other a mother, and their association helped to run the house smoothly because between them they carried out the work of four servants.

The only other servant was Dandy Smollett, who also had come from the workhouse. He was fourteen years old and his duties were to see to the garden and attend to the needs of the horse, with which he slept in the stable.

John Thornton, the elder son, was aged twelve. He was already tall; but although he took after his mother in looks, he did not as yet appear to have inherited her character.

The elder girl, Margaret, definitely took after her father in looks. She had a squarish face, light brown hair, grey eyes, and a wide mouth. But she was a highly sensitive child and was given to crying over animals of all kinds.

Robert, aged ten, also took after his father in looks and was already much taller than Margaret. He was of an adventurous spirit and had a strong stubborn personality; qualities, he understood, he had inherited from his grandfather Thornton.

Beatrice, the youngest child and commonly called Betsy, was an exact replica of her mother, in face, in form, and in character, and being but nine years old her pettiness was attributed to her being the baby of the family and, therefore, having been spoilt.

At the moment all the children were at home, John being on holiday from his boarding school in Hexham, and Margaret and Robert on holiday from the day school in Allendale; Betsy did not yet attend school, being considered too delicate, but this didn't mean that she had no lessons. Each day, for an hour in the morning and an hour and a half in the afternoon, her mother read to her from the Bible, taught her the three Rs, how to embroider, and how to perform on the spinet.

And it was at the spinet that Anne Thornton was now seated, with John, Margaret and Betsy around her. Her hands were on the keys, her eyes directed towards the music, but she remained perfectly still; her lids did not blink, nor did her fingers move as she called sharply, 'Robert!'

The children by her side fidgeted. Margaret nudged John, who grinned back at her, while Betsy rose on tiptoe in her soft house-shoes and, looking sidewards, craned her neck to its fullest extent as she looked towards the sitting-room window; and then her voice a squeak, she cried, 'He's gone out, Mama; he's going down the path.'

Anne Thornton rose from the round swivelling piano stool in such a flurry that her wide skirt slapped at her younger daughter, almost overbalancing her; then she was at the window rapping on it sharply. The next moment she had pushed the window up and again she was calling, 'Robert!' and the tone was a command.

The boy turned and stared at his mother for a moment; then he tossed his head and swung his shoulders from side to side before reluctantly returning up the path and into the house.

As he crossed the long narrow hall towards the sitting-room door his mother was waiting for him, but before she had time to chastise him he said, 'We're on holiday, Mama; it's a lovely day, I want to go to the hills.'

'What you want and what you must do, Robert, are two different things! I've told you before, and if you disobey me once again I shall speak to your father about you.'

This threat seemed not to make a very strong impression on the boy who, pushing his hands into his breeches pockets, his head thrust forward and throwing one foot reluctantly before the other, crossed the sitting-room towards his brother and sisters who were all surreptitiously eyeing him.

Anne Thornton had just seated herself on the stool once more, arranged her skirts and lifted her hands to the keys when again she was forced into stillness by the voice of her troublesome son exclaiming, 'Oh, not that one! *"How Oft Has the Banshee Cried"*. It calls it a dirge, and it is a dirge.'

There was heavy evidence of the struggle for patience in his mother's voice as she replied, again without moving either her hands or her head, 'This is one of Mr Thomas Moore's finest songs. What's more, it's the only one in the book that is arranged for four voices and I want you to get it perfect to surprise your father.'

'It will.'

There was a splutter from John now and a titter from Margaret; then the sounds dying away, the children looked past their mother as she sat still, straight and silent, towards the music on the stand.

There was a long pause before Anne Thornton said, 'I'll sing the verse and you each know where to come in, in the chorus. You first Margaret, then you, Robert, and you, John.' And now she turned her head and looked full at her second son as she said, 'And remember, all of you, this song is to be sung as it says here' – she pointed – 'slow and with solemnity.'

She now turned to the piano and in a thin, but not unpleasant soprano, she began to sing:

> 'How oft has the Banshee cried,
> How oft has death un-tied
> Bright links that Glory wove,
> Sweet bonds en-twin'd by love!'

At this point she lifted her hand and slapped at the air and Margaret brought in her voice, singing:

> 'Peace to each man-ly soul that sleep-eth;
> Rest to each faithful eye that weepeth;
> Long may the fair and brave
> Sigh o'er their eye that weep-eth,
> Long may the fair and brave,
> Sigh o'er the he-ro's grave.'

Here their mother again slapped at the air as the signal for John and Robert to come in.

On the voices went, rising and falling in the dirge, to the final words to be sung in unison: 'Sigh o'er the hero's grave.'

Margaret piped hers; John gave full alto strength to his; even Betsy squeaked: 'Hero's grave;' but Robert, determined to bury the hero deep, sang: 'Hero's gra . . . a . . . ave.'

It was too much for the children; it was too much for their mother. As John, Margaret and Betsy tried to contain their laughter their mother's hands crashed down on the keys with such force that it checked the sound abruptly as if it had been smothered. Swinging about, she caught her troublesome son by the ear, marched him out of the sitting-room, across the hall to the foot of the staircase, and there, shaking his ear until he sought refuge for the side of his head deep in his shoulder, she cried at him, 'Go to your room! I shall have your father deal with you when he comes in.'

As she thrust him forward he fell against the first step; then putting his hands to his burning ear, he slowly mounted upstairs, but stopped just before he reached the landing and turned as his mother cried to him, 'I shall see that he forbids you to go to Mr Beaumont's celebrations.'

The boy's lips trembled and it looked for a moment as if he might be about to burst into tears; but he jerked his chin upwards, turned his back on his mother, and ran across the landing to his bedroom.

Mrs Thornton now turned and looked towards the sitting-room door where the other three children were standing, and going towards them and in controlled tones, she addressed Margaret, saying, 'Bring *The Young Lady's Manual*, Margaret.' Then looking at her son, she asked, 'What were you thinking of doing, John?'

'Nothing, Mama.' He couldn't very well have said, 'Take a walk over the hills, Mama,' but that is what he would have liked to say.

'Well then, come into the conservatory with us. Margaret has been reading about metals from *The Young Lady's Manual.* Her father will be delighted to know that she takes an interest in ores and such.'

She turned now saying, 'Oh, there you are, my dear,' and held out her hand to take the book from her daughter.

As they crossed the hall in the direction of the conservatory she opened it lovingly and read aloud:

'*A Young Lady's Book; A Manual of Elegant Recreations, Exercises and Pursuits.*'

Smiling, she glanced from one to the other, saying, 'Every time I read that I can recall the wonderful pleasure I experienced when my dear mama presented me with this book on my fourteenth birthday.'

The two girls, one on each side trotting beside her rustling skirts, looked up at her, but made no comment. Betsy did not say, 'Tell us about the party you had on your fourteenth birthday, Mama,' because she had heard the tale so many times it had ceased to be exciting, while Margaret wondered why fairy tales never bored you whereas tales about grown-ups did.

When they were all seated amid the potted ferns in the conservatory Margaret began stumbling her way through the discourse on metals. Slowly and in a flat tone, she read words that conveyed no sense to her:

'Is it not singular, that the ores should sometimes be so totally unlike the Metals? Many earthy minerals we see frequently almost in their natural state; but few persons are acquainted with the ores of the Metals most commonly in use, or reflect on the many processes which are necessary to produce from them such articles as we call, from habit, the most simple conven . . . conveniences. What can be less like Copper than those beautiful green specimens, exhibiting con . . . concentric shells of a delicate radiate structure? or that fine light blue one, surpassing the richest velvet, in its soft and silky appearance? The latter is hy . . . drate of Copper; – that is copper combined with water; the green ones . . .'

At this point the laboured soliloquy was happily interrupted by the conservatory door being opened without first being knocked upon, or even having the door knob rattled, and Tessie rushing in most unceremoniously and exclaiming in an awed whisper, 'Missis! Ned Ridley be at the front door with two people.'

'Ned Ridley at the front door?'

'Aye, missis, with two people.'

Anne Thornton had now risen to her feet and, moving slowly towards Tessie, she bent over her as she asked, 'What do you mean, two people? Explain yourself, girl.'

'Well, missis, like tramps they are . . . worse, mucky, a woman and a child.'

Anne Thornton drew herself up, joined her hands at her waist and said, 'Tell them all to go to the back door, and ask cook to ask them what their business is.'

'Aye, missis.'

'John, sit down.'

The boy had gone to the end of the conservatory from where, if he craned his neck hard enough, he could glimpse the steps outside the front door.

When the boy was again seated his mother resumed her own seat but she didn't tell her daughter to continue with her reading; instead, she sat, in fact they all sat, waiting for Tessie's return. And Tessie came back so quickly that no one of them could imagine she had been so far as the front door, but she gave evidence that she had by saying immediately, and in an awed tone now, 'He won't budge, missis, Ned . . . Ned Ridley. He says the people have come to see the master.'

Anne Thornton rose slowly to her feet and in a characteristic fashion she put her fingertips first under one padded breast, then under the other, adjusted the buckle of the belt at the front of her gown, patted the white lace collar at her neck and finally, after tapping the back of her starched and gofered linen cap, she marched out of the conservatory, across the hall and to the front door.

Tessie, who had closed the door in the face of the visitors, pulled it open again and, hanging on to it, thrust her head round and stared at her mistress.

As Anne Thornton surveyed the three people standing on the step her expression was at its stiffest. She could not conceive what these other two dirty individuals wanted, but that Ned Ridley should dare to come to her front door incensed her; that he should dare to come to her house at all was an outrage. Her past failure to redeem Ned the young boy from his wild ways had been humiliating, but nothing compared to the derision she had suffered when she failed lamentably with Ned the young man. The memory of their last meeting rankled deeply within her. She had gone over the hills the Christmas before last taking John and Robert with her and proffered a gift to him and his disreputable old grandfather, and they had both laughed at her.

'What do you want for this, missis?' the old man had said to her as he unwrapped the piece of bellypork. ''Tis a poor inducement,' he had added, 'to get us on to our knees. Why Methodist's wife brought us a standing pie, and even that couldn't get us through the chapel door.'

But the final insult had come from the boy as he escorted them with mock courtesy to the break in the wall that acted as a gate when, bending towards her, a wicked grin on his face, he had whispered, 'Now if you had thought of bringing him a bottle of the hard stuff, ma'am, you would have got him to come down and sing on your step; but not hymns exactly.' . . . Oh, those Ridleys!

'What do you want?'

'Good-day, ma'am.' The young fellow doffed his cap with a sweeping movement, then held it against his jacket with both hands as he said, 'I just directed these two folk, they came out of the mist this mornin'. They slept in the open all night, they did, on their way to see you.'

There was a look of utter amazement on Anne Thornton's face as she looked from the woman to the girl, then back to the woman, and now she demanded, 'Why do you wish to see me?'

The woman gave two short, sharp coughs, swallowed, then answered, ''Tisn't you, but your man I want to see.'

'My . . . my husband isn't at home. And please tell me what you consider is your business with him.'

Again the woman coughed, but longer this time. When finally she raised her head she looked into the clear, piercing blue eyes and replied, ''Tis my business and his.'

For a moment Anne Thornton seemed lost for words, until she looked into the straight and presumably solemn countenance of Ned Ridley, which solemnity was denied by the laughter in his eyes, and to him she said, 'Whatever these people want with my husband I'm sure they'll be able to manage without your help, so will you kindly take your leave. And . . . and remember in future there is a back door.'

'Oh yes, ma'am, yes, ma'am, I'll remember in future.' Ned thrust his cap on to his head, backed two steps away, then, looking at the woman and child, said, 'Good luck, missis; good luck, whatever you're after.'

Anne Thornton watched him march down the pathway, swing open the iron gate, turn sharply about and close it, then in a mocking gesture give her a salute by touching the peak of his cap.

Oh, that creature! If anyone in this world could upset her it was that boy. Since she had first made his acquaintance, seeing him as a small boy with his bare behind sticking out of his torn knickerbockers, he had annoyed and irritated her; and further meetings had simply resulted in anger and disgust being added to her emotions concerning him.

'I want to see your man.'

Her eyes seemed to jump in their sockets from the departing figure of Ned Ridley on to the woman standing below her; and now she demanded again, 'What business have you with my husband?'

'That's my affair.'

'Who are you?'

'Me name's Nancy Boyle, and this is me daughter, Hannah.' The woman now put her fingertips lightly on to the child's shoulder.

Anne Thornton stared at the child before she said, 'If you are begging it isn't my husband you want to see, it's me. There are alms given to the needy at the church. . . .'

'Tisn't no alms I want, missis; 'tis your man I want to see.'

'My husband is at work, you can tell me what business you have with him.'

The woman stared up into the stiff, pale face for a long moment before saying quietly, 'You'll know soon enough; I'll bide me time until he comes in. . . . Come!' She turned the child about and pushed her towards the gate.

Anne Thornton watched them from the doorstep. Her eyes narrowed, her lips slightly apart, she pondered in some alarm the connection between this dirty creature and her husband. Surely she was no relation to him? She knew only too well that he had come from ordinary folk. Hadn't she been trying to live the fact down for years? But still, as lowly as his people were they would surely have scorned any connection with that person and her child.

What could she want with Matthew? She turned and looked at the brass-faced grandfather clock, and as she did so the mechanism made a grating sound, which was followed by the slow striking of the hour.

Four o'clock. It would be another two hours before he arrived home. What if that creature went and sat on the seat on the village green and someone got into conversation with her and she should say she was sitting there waiting for Matthew Thornton! . . . Dear, dear! She should have kept her in the yard. Where had she gone!

In agitation, she turned now and, lifting the front of her skirts, ran across the hall past Tessie, whose face and gaping mouth were expressing utter amazement at seeing her mistress run. And Tessie's mouth sagged even further as she witnessed the speed with which Anne Thornton covered the stairs, and from the number of footsteps she counted across the landing she gauged her mistress had gone into the boys' room, and she thought she knew why.

Robert, too, was amazed at the speed with which his mother crossed the bedroom, and he was almost pushed off the deep window-sill as she bent forward and leant her face against the pane.

From the window she had an unobstructed view of the road leading to the centre of the village but all she could see on the road were the two Bynge girls, Alice and Mary, chatting to Bill Buckman, and indulging in unseemly laughter, too, if the way their heads were wagging was anything to go by. Where was their mother in all this? Everyone knew that Bill Buckman had a wife in Hexham; and it was rumoured he might have a mistress there as well. . . . Oh! why was she bothering about such things? Where were those two creatures?

'Who are you looking for, Mama?' The boy's voice held no resentment at the fact that he was undergoing punishment.

'No one. No one.'

'Is it the persons who were at the front door?'

She turned sharply and looked down at her son. Of course he would have seen them come up the path.

'They didn't go through the village, Mama, they went the other way.' He pointed. 'Over by the cemetery wall and up the hill. Look' – he now jumped on to the sill – 'there they are on the knoll.'

His mother followed his pointing finger; and yes, there they were, the woman sitting on the knoll, the child standing by her side.

The small hill to the side of the cemetery wall looked down on to the road along which her husband would come riding from the mine. Did the creature know that? It was possible that Ned Ridley could have informed her. What did she want?

*What did she want?*

She now addressed her son, saying, 'Keep watching those persons, Robert, and should they leave the hill call down to me quickly. You understand?'

'Yes, Mama. . . . Why do they want to see Papa, Mama?'

She stopped abruptly on her way to the door but didn't turn round as she answered, 'I don't know.'

That boy, he must have opened the window and overheard the conversation. But then, so had Tessie, and that meant that Bella would already know, and what Bella knew the village would shortly know.

Oh! what was this about? If only it was six o'clock.

Matthew Thornton, about to mount his horse before leaving the mine top, looked across the ordered chaos to where Joe Robson, an experienced miner, was demonstrating to his son, Peter, the best way to go about buddling. The art lay in the manoeuvring of the rake back and forth over small ore, or smiddum, on the large flagstone which was encased on three sides by a wooden frame and over which flowed a strong current of water.

After watching them for a moment Matthew got astride his horse while shaking his head at himself. Young Peter, although fourteen and sturdy, wasn't strong enough as yet for buddling, but because Joe had asked that the boy be given a try he had complied, for Joe was a good man and, unlike most of his mates, a sober one. Four of his sons were already in the mine engaged in one capacity or another. Two of them, Archie and Hal, both as yet under seventeen years of age, worked on the knockstones on which they crushed the mixed stones by means of buckers, and his youngest son, although only twelve, acted as a hand sieve boy, so once a month on money week when they received their subsistence, Joe picked up more than most men in this particular mine. He wished there were more like Joe.

All in all, the past week had proved very good. Mr Byers was very pleased with the results, and being a fair and upright agent, he always showed the men his pleasure. Now if that Mr Sopwith over at Allenheads was as forthright as Mr Byers, Allenheads wouldn't have known that disastrous strike last year.

The bouse they had brought up today was rich, a good twenty per cent of ore in it. It wasn't every day that happened.

He rode round the perimeter of the reservoir and along by the slime pits, then cut across the hill to the cart track, and from there to the road, wide enough here to allow a horse and rider to pass a string of ponies without having to mount the bank.

He was both hungry and dirty and he had a longing to be home and seated at the head of his table looking down on the four bright faces of his children. He was so glad John was home. He'd take him to the mine tomorrow . . . that's if Anne didn't kick up. Well let her, let her; the boy would follow his own bent in the end whether it was law, as she wanted, or lead, as he himself wanted.

He drew his horse to a walk as he rounded the foot of a hill and saw ahead of him the well-known figure of Ned Ridley riding one pony and leading two others, and he was still some yards behind when he called to him cheerfully, saying, 'Hello there, Ned; off to the cobbler's again, are you?'

'Oh aye; aye, Mr Thornton.' Ned twisted round in the saddle. 'As you say, off to the cobbler's again. . . . You don't know anything harder than iron that would serve as shoes, do you?'

'No, I don't Ned.' Matthew laughed. 'But I could enquire over at the smelting shops for you.'

'Aye, you could.'

They both laughed together as they rode on.

'How's your grandfather?' asked Matthew after a while. 'I haven't seen him down in the town on market days for some time now.'

'No, he's gettin' lazy in his old age. I told him I'd kick him in the backside from here to Haydon if he doesn't come and see me knock hell out of Bull Tiffit on Saturday.'

'Oh yes . . . yes, you're boxing Tiffit again. It was a draw last time.'

'It won't be this; we'll sweat it out on our knees if necessary.'

Matthew looked at the profile of the young fellow sitting straight and jaunty on the pony and he said quietly, 'It's a daft game after all, Ned; you could be spoilt for life.'

'In what way?'

'All ways. Bull Tiffit is a nasty piece of work and I should say he's heavier than you by a couple of stone.'

'That's to me benefit, Mr Thornton. I'm like a lintie on me feet to his scooped-back dray horse.'

'Why don't you put some of your strength into making regular money and go up to the mine?'

'Aw, Mr Thornton.' Ned jerked his chin upwards and laughed. 'You're jokin' again. I've always told you you wouldn't get me into your mine. I'll supply you with cuddies, mules or Galloways, even a broken-down racer if you want it, but that's as near as you'll get me to your mine. Not, mind you, that I wouldn't be pleased to work for you; if I had to have a master I wouldn't look further than yourself, an' it's the truth I'm speakin'.'

'Thanks, Ned, thanks; that's a compliment for my character I'll cherish.' Again they looked at each other and laughed, and now they were within sight of the house and the cemetery, and to the side of it the knoll, and when a few minutes later they passed below it Ned glanced upwards, and he saw the woman and the girl standing looking down on them. Turning his head sharply, he looked at his companion, but Mr Thornton hadn't even glanced in the direction of the knoll, but was looking towards his own gate, and when they came abreast of it he said cheerfully, 'Good-bye, Ned, it's been pleasant meeting you.'

'An' you, Mr Thornton . . . an' you.'

Dandy Smollett was waiting in the yard to take the horse and Matthew spoke sharply to him, saying, 'No skimping with the rubbing down tonight mind, Dandy,' and the boy, touching his forelock, replied hastily, 'No, master. No, master.'

As was his habit, he now entered his house by the kitchen, and sitting on the wooden stool just inside the door he unstrapped the buckles of his gaiters, unlaced his boots and took the pair of slippers Tessie handed to him, saying as he looked at them, 'It's about time I had a new pair, don't you think?'

Another night, had he made this remark Tessie would have giggled and said, 'Eeh! master, there's nowt wrong with them;' but tonight she took no such liberty, only stared at him until he said, 'Lost your tongue, Tessie?'

'No, master.'

'The cat died?' He was standing up now, taking off his dusty jacket.

When she again made no comment he looked to where Bella was stooped over the oven taking from it a large dripping tin in which was a sizzling joint of lamb, and when she walked to the middle of the room and put it on the table within an arm's length of him, he sniffed and said, 'Oh, I've been waiting for that all day, Bella.'

'Well, 'tis ready, master, when you are.'

He stared at her for a moment. There was no smile on her face, something was wrong. What had the two of them been up to? Likely they had annoyed Anne and had suffered for it. Ah well, he had better go and find out what it was all about.

He went up the kitchen, pulled open the heavy oaken door and entered the hall and saw his wife waiting for him. He knew by the way she stood that she was impatient for his coming, and a thought crossed his mind that he could wish there were certain and proper times when she would be impatient for his coming.

'Come into the sitting-room for a moment.'

'I haven't washed yet.' Had she forgotten her rule that he must always change his coat and boots in the kitchen and perform his ablutions in the closet adjoining the morning-room?

'Leave it, leave it; I must talk to you.'

As he walked slowly past the foot of the stairs his glance was brought sharply upwards by the appearance of his son Robert, his arms spread between the top stanchion of the banister and the wall. He was calling, 'Ma-ma! Ma-ma! they are coming down.'

It seemed to Matthew that his son's remark, not understandable to himself, had yet a full meaning for his wife, for now her step tripped almost to the point of a run towards the sitting-room, and with his face screwed up in some perplexity he followed her. She closed the door behind him and, facing him, demanded, 'Have you any relatives in Haydon Bridge that you haven't told me of?'

'Relatives in Haydon Bridge? You know I haven't.'

'What about Hexham?'

'There's no one in Hexham belonging to me. What's this?'

'Well then, there's some need for explanation here. Two hours gone a dirty creature came to the front door, accompanied by a child. That pest, Ned Ridley, brought them.' She drew in a short, sharp breath. 'The woman wouldn't tell me her business, she said it was with you. You're sure you have no relatives?'

'You know I haven't. The last one was my grannie, and she died in Newcastle these nine years back.'

She now let out a long, slow breath, turned from him, walked up the room until she came to the couch and, gripping the back of it, said, 'For some reason personal to herself this woman wants to see you. There . . . there, listen!' She swung round and pointed towards the door. 'That'll be her again. She's been sitting up on the knoll waiting for you.'

'Sitting on the knoll waiting for me? Well, we'll soon get this cleared up.' He now tugged at each shirt-sleeve, pulling the cuffs half-way up his forearms; then loosening his string neckerchief, he pulled it off and threw it aside as he marched out of the room and across the hall towards the front door.

Anne Thornton was by his side when he opened the door, and now she didn't look at the woman and child standing on the step, but she looked at her husband. She watched his eyes first narrow, then stretch wide, while at the same time his jaw dropped, leaving his mouth in a gape.

' 'Tis me, Matthew, Nancy Boyle. Remember?'

Yes. Yes, he remembered; and the memory struck him dumb. The woman before him, dirty and dishevelled as she was, was Nancy Boyle all right. But not the woman he had once known. And why in the name of God had she to turn up here. God Almighty! How was he going to explain her? How was he going to explain her to Anne? Oh, he'd never be able to explain her to Anne. Never! Never, in this world.

As he stood dumbfounded he could already feel his home life toppling about his ears, and he knew in this moment that from now until the day he died, he would suffer in one way or another because this woman for some reason, as yet known only to herself, had come walking out of the past.

He had uttered no word and had given no open sign of recognition, but his hand went out involuntarily towards the woman when, overtaken by a fit of coughing, she bent her body from the waist as she spat into a piece of rag, which was red and brown in parts.

'Come in.'

'Matthew!' His very name held a reprimand, and he turned on his wife, whispering fiercely, 'Well! what shall I do? Have her explain her business on the doorstep?'

When the woman and the child stepped into the hall he said abruptly, 'Come this way,' and he was about to lead them towards the sitting-room when again his wife called him by name. 'Matthew ... please!' she said; 'not in the sitting-room.'

'Where then?' His voice was almost a bark.

'The ... the morning-room.'

It was she who now marched forward and led the way, and when they were all in the morning-room with the door closed Matthew pulled a straight-backed wooden chair from under the round table and without looking at the woman said, 'Sit down.'

Nancy Boyle took the seat, then leant back and looked up at the man she hadn't seen for almost nine years and who seemed to have grown taller and broader and more handsome, and she thought it strange that out of her own anguish she could in this moment spare a tinge of pity for him, until he said stiffly, 'What can I do for you?' Then the pity fled and she answered gruffly, 'Just one thing you can do for me, you can look after your own, she's yours!' And with this she thrust the child towards him.

Matthew's response was to step back as quickly as if he were being confronted with a double-headed cobra.

Although he heard Anne gasp and knew that she was holding her face in her hands he did not look towards her but stared dazedly down on the child, who in her turn was staring up at him, and all the while her mother was talking, short disjointed sentences broken by her breathing as if she were under the influence of drink. 'Newton,' she was saying, 'doesn't sound all that different from Thornton. ... I went to the Temperance Hotel. ... Remember the Temperance Hotel? The old faggot said nobody there ... never had nobody there the name of Newton. Of course the old bitch wouldn't have let on if she had known you by your right name ... 'cos she knew what I was after ... with me belly full. ... Funny how I found you. Saw you goin' into that office in Grey Street. Fine office with doorman, so I said to him, "Was that Mr Matthew Newton went in there?" No; you were Mr Matthew Thornton, he said, and you had to do with lead mines ... them were the offices. I waited an' waited but you didn't come out ... Didn't know there was another door. You see, 'cos I knew me time was runnin' out I said to meself, find him; who better to see to her than her father? And so I worked at it from there.'

The crash brought him out of the nightmare and he saw the chair that Anne had been holding on to fall sideways on to the floor and her body waver as if she were about to faint. But when he put his arm around her she did not slump against him, in fact the contact seemed to revive her for she thrust his hand from her and staggered to another chair.

'She's had a shock; 'tis natural, I suppose.'

He turned and looked at the woman again, this time as if he could kill her; then went towards her and bent down until his face was level with hers, staring into the sunken eyes as he whispered hoarsely, 'You have no proof; there were others.'

'Aye.' Her voice came flat and calm as she replied, 'Afore and after; but she's yours. I told you when you last came, an' that made you skedaddle, didn't it?'

He closed his eyes tightly, straightened his back, turned towards the fireplace and, gripping the marble mantelpiece, laid his head on the edge of it and ground his teeth.

In the name of God why had this to happen to him! He had a vivid mental picture of the consequences spreading in all directions away down the years. The village would be agog; the men in the mines. It would be the high spot of market day in Allendale Town, it might even jeopardize his chance of becoming chief agent at the mine. Yet all these outside reactions didn't seem to matter. What did matter, what was hurting him with an indescribable pain was that his home life, as he had known it, would be no more.

He'd had the love and adoration of his four children, and although he hadn't been at the receiving end of the former from his wife for many years now, and she'd never showered the latter on him, nevertheless she had loved him. That it was in a narrow, pious, pinching way, he had no doubt; still she had been, and still was an excellent housekeeper and an excellent mother. Yet if the truth could be sifted through the events of their married life it was she who should face the blame for his present predicament, for from the time Betsy was born she had feigned a weakness which she said prevented her from carrying out her duties as a wife. When the child was six months old, and her own vigour belied any weakness, she openly stated that in future her duty to him would be at intervals compatible with her cycle; which had meant that his body could crave satisfaction for weeks at a stretch without relief.

It was about this time that Mr Byers had given him the pleasant duty of carrying some samples of ore to Mr Beaumont's chief agent, and this in turn led to him making four visits to Newcastle within the following months, sometimes having to wait for results. The visits could cover two to three days, during which he put up at the Temperance Hotel.

On his very first stay in the city he had come across Nancy Boyle by the mere fact of pulling her from the road just in time to save her from being knocked over by an open coach being driven by a drunken young buck to the delight of his accompanying friends.

Nancy, he saw at once, was pretty, and common; but on further acquaintance he found that she was also of a warm nature and very obliging.

When she had first taken him to her room, an attic at the top of a boarding-house behind the warehouses on the riverfront, he found it poor in the extreme but clean, and as she had explained straightaway it suited her because she was scarcely in it, having to work twelve to fourteen hours a day in the basement of a milliner's in the city. He had not enquired into her past life, nor had she probed into his. But he had taken the precaution of giving her a false name, because after all he was a married man with a family, and a churchman into the bargain, and he was well aware that it was due as much to the latter as it was to his wife's efforts that he held the position he did in the lead mine, because Mr Byers, the agent, was a very strong churchman, and a man who loved to hear good singing, especially good hymn singing.

He recalled now the feeling of panic he experienced when he had last met her when, pointing to her stomach, she said bluntly, 'I'm in trouble, you've done it on me. What about it?' And he could even now hear himself repeating his promises that everything would be all right.

But what had he done? He had skittered back to the Temperance Hotel, taken up his bag, and left. He had spent that night at an inn on the other side of the town; the following day, after concluding his business, he had ridden for home as if the devil were after him.

And now standing behind him was the outcome of that episode. . . . Be sure your sins will find you out.

Although he raised his voice in praise to God each Sunday, he had more so of late been privately questioning the whole fabric of the established church, but what he never questioned was the truth that came out of the Old Book. Time and again its truths seemed to have been shown him. Be sure your sins will find you out.

He raised his head slowly when the woman's voice said, 'Well, I'll be on me way. I've done what I came to do; me job's done; she's yours to see to now.'

He turned towards her, but she was looking at the child and the child at her, and he watched the little girl throw her arms about her mother's waist, crying in a raucous tone, 'Aw, Ma! Ma! where you goin'? I'm not stayin' here. Ma! Ma! I want to come with you.'

'Listen. Listen, that's the gentleman I've told you about.' She pointed towards Matthew. 'He'll take care of you 'cos he's your da. Now you be a good lass an' do as you're told an' some day I'll come an' see you. Aye, I'll come an' see you.' She was smiling weakly now, and when the child again clung to her she looked towards the lady of the house, who was now sitting like a ramrod, her face as white as lint, her eyes straining from her head, and she said to her, 'She's a good bairn, she'll give you no trouble.'

On this she pushed her daughter from her, turned and walked slowly out of the room and into the hall, where she saw four children. They all stared at her, their mouths slightly apart, their eyes round as if with wonder. She paused for a moment in front of them and said, 'You . . . you've got a new sister. Be kind to her;' then she went to the front door where Tessie was standing, the latch in her hand and, if it were possible, her mouth and her eyes wider than those of the children.

Tessie stood for a moment watching the woman going down the path before she quickly closed the door and turned to where her young masters and mistresses were now all staring towards the morning-room from where the raised voices of their parents were coming.

Margaret looked at John and John at her; then quickly their glances parted. Their parents never quarrelled. Her mother scarcely ever raised her voice. Sometimes, if she woke up late at night, she had heard rumblings from her parents' bedroom, but she imagined they were just discussing the events of the day. But now, her mama was almost screaming.

Anne Thornton wasn't almost screaming, she was screaming; and what she was screaming was, 'She's not staying here! Do you hear me? She's not staying here!'

'Be quiet, woman!' Matthew's voice answered her scream with a bawl, and Anne became quiet for a moment as she stared in amazement at this man who wasn't showing an atom of remorse. This vile tragedy had not brought him to his knees, there was no repentance in either his voice or his manner, and he was daring to speak to her, shout at her as he would at some creature like that one who had just departed.

'She's here and she stays. For good or bad she stays.' He turned and glanced at the child whose face, now streaked with tears, looked almost as white as her mother's had done.

'Never! I will not have her in my home; you can put her in the House.'

Matthew became still as he stared at her, his shoulders slumped. Then his head wagged slowly and, his voice quiet now but holding more authority than his bawl had done, he said, 'Put her in the workhouse? No! No! Never!'

Anne Thornton turned about and glared at the child. Then she did an unprecedented thing. For a moment it brought her down to the ordinary level of the people among whom she lived, for she flung her arms around herself as in an effort to comfort the shocked and distressed being inside and rocked herself deeply backwards and forwards. She only needed to utter a wail and she would have been like one of the Irish miners' wives mourning the death of her man or her child.

As Matthew looked at her he understood in a measure what this had done to her, and it aroused his pity and tempered his manner and brought from him softly a plea. 'Anne' – he went towards her – 'I did wrong and I'm sorry, but if you'll only forgive me and face up to it we'll weather this together.'

'Weather this together!' She had stopped her rocking motion but her hands still hugged her waist and she glared at him and repeated, 'Weather this together! How dare you! You are vile, filthy, you are not fit to . . . to –' She pressed her lips tightly together in an effort to stop her tears flowing, and then she ended, gabbling, 'And . . . and the church. Think of the church.'

'Damn the church! And damn you for that matter, because if there's anybody to blame for her' – he now thrust his hand back at the silent fear-filled face of the child – 'it's you! If you had acted as a wife should, I wouldn't have had any need to look further.'

'You would blame me for your vileness?'

'Yes. If there's any sin, as you call it, connected with this business it stems from you . . . Aw, God!'

They stood confronting each other like combatants who would know no peace until one or the other was slain. And then she did slay him, for now she brought out through her teeth, 'Well! Well then! if I have been wanting in my duty before I shall be doubly wanting in the future for I shall never let you lay a hand on me in my life again.'

Time seemed to stand still as they stared at each other.

'We'll see about that.' The words came sieved through his lips. 'But when you're making such a promise I'd remind you to think of the Scargill household. Yes, yes.' He nodded slowly at her now as he saw her face blanch ever further. 'His wife, I understand, presented him with a similar proposition and what did he do? He brought three young lasses into the Hall as servants. One of them is still there, and his wife is long since dead. What one man can do another can imitate.'

Again he felt his pity rising for her when she put her hands to her throat and audibly gulped at her spittle, but he knew that it would be fruitless to show it, and so what he said was, 'It is understood that this child stays, and I'm giving you the opportunity to see to her well-being. If you don't I shall take it into my own hands. And you know what that means, your authority as the mistress of the house will be undermined. You have a choice.'

He could almost see her weighing up the consequences of his words. He watched her turn slowly now and look at the child. Then her back seeming to stiffen even more, she turned about and went swiftly from the room.

In the hall, the children were standing in a group at the bottom of the stairs, and the little maid was standing near the kitchen door. It was to her that Anne Thornton beckoned, but when Tessie stood before her, she had to open her mouth wide twice before she was able to give her the order 'Take the girl,' she said motioning her head slowly backwards, 'into the washhouse and see that she bathes. Miss Margaret will bring you some fitting clothes. Burn those she has on now.'

'Yes, ma'am.' Tessie dipped her knee, then looking towards the child who was standing near the master at the morning-room door, she held out her hand, saying, 'Come on. Come on,' and Hannah, seeming to recognize one of her own kind, went forward and took the proffered hand.

They were walking across the hall past the children when there came a sharp rap on the front door. Tessie paused and looked towards it, then turning her head over her shoulder, her glance asked her mistress if she should open it. But it was her master who said abruptly, 'Go on with your business, Tessie, I'll see to it.'

When he opened the door there stood Maudie, the parson's maid, and without any preliminaries she gabbled at him, 'The Reverend, he says will you come on quick 'cos she's dying, the woman. She mentioned you.'

Matthew drew in a long shuddering breath, paused for a moment while he looked sideways towards Anne, then fully round to where his four children were staring wide-eyed at him, and lastly at Tessie and the child she was still holding by the hand. And Hannah, quickly taking in the gist of what the maid had said, pulled herself from Tessie and, running towards the door, cried, 'I want me ma! I want me ma!'

Matthew catching hold of her thrust her back towards Tessie, saying, 'Do what your mistress ordered, bathe her.' Then going out, he banged the door closed behind him and hurried down the pathway.

The Reverend Stanley Crewe was a small, thin man. He was no preacher, no real advocate for his calling, and he was tolerated rather than loved by his parishioners, but he was sincere and kind. He was kneeling now by the side of the woman lying on the grass verge that bordered the drive to the vicarage and he looked up at Matthew and shook his head as he said quietly, 'I'm afraid she's gone, poor soul. I . . . I sent for you, Matthew, because she mentioned your name and . . . and something about her daughter whom she left with you. I couldn't understand this. I . . . I thought she was rambling until she gave me this.' He now picked up from the grass at his side a long thumb-marked envelope and held it up for Matthew to see, saying, 'She said she wanted me to keep it until the day her daughter married, as it says on the envelope, see.' He now nodded his head. 'It's written in a very good hand.'

Matthew bent forward and read: ' "Concerning Hannah Boyle. This letter is to be put into the care of a minister of God, or some legal person, and to be given to the above-named on the day that she weds." '

'It is sealed too.' The minister turned the letter over and showed the large blob of red sealing wax. 'She seemed very concerned about the letter.' He now nodded down towards the still figure on the grass. 'She said something about it having been written by . . . the penny lawyer.'

Matthew straightened his back. Written by the penny lawyer? These were clerks with a little knowledge of law, who wrote letters for the poor. He looked down at the letter again. Why hadn't she left it with him? But need he ask? People like Nancy knew all about temptation, and would he have been strong enough not to open it? No, it would likely have been one of the first things he did, even if afterwards he didn't destroy it but sealed it again. No, Nancy, poor Nancy had been wise in her own way. But why was he thinking poor Nancy? He should be cursing her. And part of him was, for she had come into his life like a charge of explosive, and with the same devastating effect. He still couldn't visualize the extent of the consequences of her appearance; and not only her appearance, for that after all had been short, but what she had saddled him with . . . the child.

Why had he accepted the fact without thorough probing and questioning that the child was his? Why?

Because the memory of his running away from her that night like a scalded cat had always remained at the back of his mind.

'I'll have to get in touch with the House.'

'What!' He brought his attention fully to the parson now.

'She'll have to be buried.'

'Oh yes, yes, of course. But . . . but I'll see to it.'

'You?' The parson's eyebrows moved slightly up and then he gave a short, self-conscious laugh as he said, 'Well, if you knew her. Is she any relation, Matthew?'

Matthew looked down on the still body and the white face that strangely now was recognizable as the Nancy he once knew and he said slowly. 'You could say so. In a way you could say so.'


# Chapter Three


For days the village had been agog, and the town of Allendale too. But why, some of the dalesmen said, couldn't the Thornton affair have been brought into the open at another time when there was no excitement about, for it had almost overshadowed the great event of 11 April, the day on which young Master Beaumont came into his own. By! that was a day and a half wasn't it; something to be remembered for years ahead. Two hundred workmen from the Allen Smelt Mills following the Allendale Town band to the King's Head, there to feast and drink. They even set off a cannon in the young master's honour, and illuminated the whole town at night, so showing up to even greater beauty the decorations of flowers and evergreens. And this wasn't to mention the bonfires that had blazed on the surrounding hills. In each of the dales the miners and smelters had dined and rejoiced in their own particular way: eight hundred and seventy in East Allendale, five hundred odd in West Allendale. And what about Weardale? Over a thousand there. Nigh on three thousand altogether, including the youngsters, enjoyed Mr Beaumont's hospitality on that day.

And when the cups had been drained many times and the laughter and joking was mounting high, what subject caused the men to splutter into their mugs and the women to cover their mouths with their hands? Why, the affair up at the Thornton house. Not that anything was actually said in front of Matthew himself because Matthew was respected and liked. In fact, the newcomer into Elmholm House had put a feather into his cap. No, it was his wife that the laughter was against, that madam who looked down her nose at honest working people and who almost strained the muscles in her arms grabbing at the fringe of the gentry.

At the same time however, they all agreed they had to hand it to her for sheer bare-faced audacity for endeavouring to palm the youngster off as Matthew's niece. Matthew's niece indeed! Would a man like Matthew Thornton have let his sister die on the road? Moreover, it was known that the only sister he had was far away in Australia. Who did Madam Thornton think she was hoodwinking?

Anyway, the top and the bottom of it was the woman who died in the vicarage drive had once been a young lass whom Matthew had taken down, and when she knew her end was near and there was no one to look after her bairn, what did she do? She made a bee-line for him. It was as simple as that.

Yes, that part was simple, but the life that the bairn was being made to lead wasn't so simple. Young Tessie said that she was made to eat in the kitchen, and she had a bed of sorts up in the back garret; it was all right in the summer up there but it was as cold as charity in the winter. And the child was a canny bairn, Tessie said; her name was Hannah but the mistress always called her *The Girl*.

It would be interesting to see how things worked out, the villagers said. By! yes, it would that.

Hannah had been living her new life for three weeks. At times it seemed that she had always lived here, and she would have liked living here if it hadn't been for two things. First, she missed her ma; and secondly, she didn't like the missis, she was afraid of her. Every time the missis looked at her she thought she was going to hit her. She thought she could like the mister but he didn't speak to her much although he, too, looked at her. But it was in a different way from the missis. And she wholeheartedly liked the children, that is all except Betsy. Betsy was a spiteful bitch. She was like Annie Nesbit who had lived in the room opposite them in Newcastle and who used to stuff black beetles into the keyhole, and they used to crunch when her ma turned the key.

She liked Tessie and Bella; oh aye, she did, they were nice to her, kind. She looked at Bella now standing at the table, her thick arms pounding the dough in a great earthenware dish as she talked to Tessie who was greasing tins at the other end of the table. They were talking about her. They always talked about her. She didn't mind, in fact she liked it. It made her feel. . . . She couldn't explain to herself how it made her feel, except to think that she wasn't lost.

'Damn shame!' Bella pounded the dough with her fist. 'She's tret like scum. Why, if she tret me like that I'd walk out, begod! I would.' She now leant over the dish towards Tessie and, her voice a whisper, she said, 'You said she told them they hadn't got to speak to her?'

'Aye, she did, Bella, unless it was absolutely necessary. That's exactly what she said, absolutely necessary. An' Miss Margaret spoke up, she said something I couldn't catch. An' Master Robert did an' all. But she shouted at them. Eeh!' Tessie now started to giggle. 'Do you mind when she used to lecture me for raisin' me voice? Eeh lad! sometimes now her voice sounds like a candy-man's trumpet.'

They both turned now and looked at Hannah, and she, smiling back at them, said 'I like peelin' taties. Me ma and me used to peel them all day at an inn. Me ma said if they'd been kept together they would have filled a ship's hold, but as quick as we did them they come an' took 'em away.' She laughed again, and Tessie laughed with her. But not Bella; Bella shook her head sadly and said, "Tis true the sayin', one half doesn't know how the other half lives. I can remember the time meself when I was so hungry I could eat a man with the smallpox.' Then she continued pounding the dough with increased vigour as if in thankfulness for her privileged lot.

It was as she lifted the dough with a great plop on to the floured board that the kitchen door opened and the mistress entered. She was dressed for outdoors in a pink-sprigged linen gown and a short light fawn alpaca coat, the back of it sticking out like a fan over the bunched skirt of the dress. On her head she wore a small straw bonnet, the front decorated with a number of blue velvet bows. Altogether she looked a lady, a well-dressed lady.

She stood pulling on her short grey silk gloves as she spoke to Bella, saying, 'I am going into the town, I am taking Miss Betsy to see Doctor Arnison; her teeth are troubling her.'

'Yes, ma'am.' Bella dipped her knee just the slightest.

'You have the orders for dinner?'

'Yes, ma'am.' Again she dipped her knee.

'I have left your weekly allowance of tea on the dining-room side table. See that you make it last this time, and I forbid you to use the leaves from the house pot, it is nothing but gluttony.'

'. . . Yes ma'am.'

She directed her attention towards the fastening of the last button on her glove as she said, 'You will see that *The Girl* does not leave the house.'

'. . . Yes, ma'am.'

Anne Thornton had not looked once in Hannah's direction. She turned about now and, her skirt and petticoats rustling like crumpled parchment, walked with erect carriage out of the kitchen.

Bella gave one final thump to the dough as she exclaimed '*The Girl!* Even the cat's got a name. An' don't use the tea leaves again. Huh! Anyway, what she lets come out of the dining-room pot is so like water bewitched an' tea bedamned you can see through it, an' I hope they pull all that 'un's teeth out . . . little madam that she is.'

The children stood in the hall, surrounding Betsy who was on the point of tears as she whimpered, 'He'll hurt me. He'll put big pinchers in like the picture in the nursery book.'

'Don't be silly!' Robert pushed her none too gently on the shoulder. 'They don't use pinchers any more, they strap you down on to a table and Ralphy

Buckman comes with his blacksmith's hammer and goes bang! bang! bang!'
He demonstrated, flinging his joined hands from one side to the other.

It was as Betsy let out a shrill cry that her mother entered the hall
demanding, 'What is it? Stop that noise, Betsy! What is the matter?'

'Rob ... Robert says they are going to knock it out with a hammer
and. ...'

Anne Thornton now put a protective arm around her youngest child as
she looked at Robert and said, 'You're a cruel boy. I've warned you about
frightening your sister before, haven't I? Now when your father comes. ...'

She stopped abruptly, and the three elder children stared at her. For years
now it had been her usual procedure when they were naughty to threaten
them with dire reprimands to come from their father, which frightened them
not at all; but during the past weeks she hadn't mentioned their father's
name once to them. And so after a pause, during which she moved her lips
tightly over one another, she finished, 'You will be dealt with.'

She pushed the still clinging Betsy from her, saying sharply, 'Stop
snivelling! Dry your face and straighten your bonnet.' Then looking down
at the child's feet, she said, 'Your shoes haven't been polished.'

'Tessie said she had done them, Mama.'

Anne Thornton now clicked her tongue and gave a small jerk to her head;
then looking at the other children, she said, 'Behave until I return. You,
John, better continue with your studies as you're returning to school
tomorrow, and you don't want to be unprepared. ... And you, Margaret,
will read the chapter in the *Young Lady's Book* on escrutoire. Your hand-
writing leaves a lot to be desired.' She smiled thinly at her daughter now as
she added, 'Remember the heading:

> For careless scrawls ye boast of no pretence;
> Fair Russell wrote, as well as spoke, with sense.

'And you, Robert.' She now drew in a long breath. 'If I remember rightly
you were discussing with your father some time ago the work of Mr Forster,
the book he wrote on "Strata". You will read the part that deals solely with
the lead mines, and I will hear you when I return. And' – she now stabbed
her finger at him – 'don't for a moment think you'll be able to hoodwink me
because I have informed myself to some lengths on that particular part.
... Come, Betsy.' She pushed her daughter before her, went through the
door that John was holding wide for her, then out on to the garden path;
and the three children stood and watched her until she had passed through
the gate and disappeared behind the hedge.

After slowly closing the door, John turned and looked at the other two,
but as he was about to speak Robert checked him with, 'It's all right for
you, you're going to school tomorrow.'

John made no reply but he lifted his head as if the prospects were pleasing,
and when Margaret said 'Escrutoire!' in a voice that was deep with disdain,
he laughed and repeated 'Escrutoire.'

'Tell you what.' Robert leant towards him. 'Let's go and see Hannah.'

Both John and Margaret exchanged glances before Margaret, her voice
now a whisper, said 'She didn't say that we couldn't see her, only that we
hadn't to converse with her unless it was absolutely necessary.'

As they all turned towards the kitchen John pulled them to a stop saying, now, 'Hadn't we better see if they are on their way?'

'Yes, yes, you're right.' Robert dived towards the stairs now, the other two following him, and without ceremony they burst into his bedroom and dashed to the window.

It was John who jumped up on the sill. Then after peering over the village and remaining quiet for a moment, he said, 'Yes, yes, there they are, they are passing Rickson's yard. Good, come on.' He jumped off the sill, and once more they were dashing, down the stairs this time and across the hall. But at the kitchen door they stopped and grinned at each other; then Margaret opening the door, they filed decorously into the kitchen and walked towards the table.

Bella had finished making the bread, and Tessie had just arranged the loaf tins along the fender and covered them with a warm cloth. She turned her bright face towards them exclaiming, 'Oh! hello, Miss Margaret.'

'Hello, Tessie.'

It was as if they hadn't met for a week, but each party knew what the other was about; that is all except Hannah who had stopped peeling the potatoes and was now looking towards the children, who had moved towards the end of the table and were within an arm's length of her.

It was Robert who spoke to her first. His face was straight and his words expressed a feeling that had been troubling him for days. 'You all right?' he asked.

'Oh aye, I'm all right.'

It was Margaret now who asked, 'Is it hard work peeling potatoes?'

'No, no.' Hannah shook her head. 'I like doin' taties. Don't I, Tessie?'

Tessie now joined the group. Except for her dress and voice she could perhaps have been taken for their sister; and she said, 'That's what she says, miss. An' she says she used to peel them all day long where she lived in the big city in Newcastle. Didn't you?'

'Aye.' Hannah nodded brightly. 'But once I didn't get nowt cos I took too much skin off . . . only some stew.' Her eyes were now fixed on John. He was almost a head taller than the rest, and his hair looked all gold. She was faintly reminded of someone she had seen who looked like him, bonny, beautiful. As she stared at him the memory became clearer in her mind. It was in that church she had crept into where the singing was going on. There was a picture in a window and the sun was coming through it. . . . He was bonny was the big one called John. She liked looking at bonny people. Her ma used to say she too was bonny. She missed her ma. She would like to go every day over the road to the corner of the cemetery where her ma was buried, but she could only look towards it on a Sunday when she followed the family to church. She didn't like church; she always wanted to fall asleep, and there was a funny smell in there, musty, like the wet cellar below the house in Newcastle.

'Tell us what you did in Newcastle. Did you go to school?' Margaret was bending down towards her now so that their faces were on a level, and Hannah smiled into the kindly eyes and said, 'School? No, no, I never went to school. But I can count, I can count up to ten. Look' – Hannah now lifted up her dirty wet hands and one after another she bent her fingers and thumbs, and when she had finished Margaret slowly straightened up and cast a glance at Robert and then at John.

Staring down into Hannah's upturned face, John was telling himself that she had beautiful eyes. He had never seen anyone with eyes like hers; they held your attention, you wanted to keep looking at them. He had experienced this feeling since first seeing her; he had thought then it was because she was so curiously dirty and ragged, but now he knew it was her eyes that made him want to keep looking at her.

John's fascinated gaze was brought abruptly from Hannah's face by a proposition Bella was making to them. 'Wouldn't you like to take the little 'un up into the nursery for a while?' she was saying.

They all turned and stared at her; then again they were looking at each other.

'It'll take the mistress all of two hours to walk there and back into the town, an' then God knows how long she'll be at Doctor Arnison's. She might even have to wait; he could be out, way over the hills or any place, bein' him.'

'Let's!' The exclamation was from Robert. Swinging round, he grabbed Hannah's hand and pulled her upwards, and as he did so Tessie cried, 'Eeh! Master Robert, wait a tick; let's get the muck off her hands, she'll make you all clarty.'

As Tessie wiped Hannah's hands on a rough towel they laughed at each other as if sharing a joke; then Tessie pushed her towards Margaret, and, she now taking Hannah's hand, they all ran out of the kitchen, leaving Bella and Tessie gaping at each other, their faces full of glee.

Sweeping the table with a wet dish-cloth, Bella cried in no small voice, 'Eeh! that's done me as good as a rise in pay. It isn't often you can get one over on the missis, is it, lass?' and to this Tessie replied, 'No, you're right, Bella, 'tisn't often you can get one over on the missis. No, by gum!'

Hannah had never felt so happy in her life, nor had she laughed so much. John had lifted her on to the rocking horse in the nursery and they had all rocked her backwards and forwards so vigorously that she nearly fell off, which had made them all laugh. Then Margaret had let her nurse her dolls, and Robert actually let her wind up a model of a crane he had made to which a basket was attached; but the most exciting thing of all that happened to her was when John showed her how to close one eye and look through a glass, and there see colours the like of which she had never before imagined.

But all the fun stopped abruptly when Margaret, happening to look at the painted wooden clock on the nursery wall, put her hand to her mouth and exclaimed, 'Look at the time! And I've done no reading.'

The three stared at each other, then at Hannah, and it was John who spoke to her now, saying quietly, 'You'd better go, Hannah, we've got work to do before Mama comes back.'

'Oh aye, all right.' She backed from them.

'We'll play another time.'

She nodded at Margaret now, still backing.

'I'll take you up into the hills one day.'

She turned her gaze on Robert and again she said, 'Oh aye. Oh aye.'

She turned and opened the door, but as she made to go she looked back at them again and said, 'Ta,' and they glanced quickly at each other and laughed; then in a chorus they answered her, each replying, 'Ta!'

She did a little skip now out on to the landing, and pulling the door closed behind her, she stood for a moment listening to their laughter, her face widening into an even broader smile. Then she walked down the narrow stairs and across the landing in the direction of the main staircase. To reach it she had to pass a number of doors, and one being partly open, she slowed her step and moved towards it; then paused a moment before pushing it open a little further.

By! it was a bonny room. There was a bed with a pretty pink cover on it, and the window to the side was framed in lace curtains with frills to them. She could see part of a dressing-table with coloured boxes on it and shiny things. Oh, it was a bonny room.

Gently now she pressed the door still further open, then stood with her hand on the white china knob as she gazed in amazement about her. It was a bedroom, but there were chairs in it and a couch, and pictures on the walls. She had already earlier glimpsed the children's rooms, but they were nothing like this. Their beds were wooden, this bed was made of brass, shining, golden brass.

On tiptoe now, she went into the room and pushed the door behind her, and in the middle of it she turned a slow circle. Eeh! if her ma had had a room like this she wouldn't have had the cough, would she? And look at all those bonny boxes on the dressing-table. She walked forward and lowered herself on to the seat that was shaped like a cradle without sides, and her hand went out and very gingerly she picked up a blue enamelled box and, raising the lid, stared at the brooches lying on the pink velvet pad. Fancy having all those brooches! One, two, three . . . she counted up to eight.

The next box she picked up held three rings; one with white stones in it, the others red ones. She liked the red ones, they were warm and shiny.

Then there was the box with the beads, strings and strings of beads.

Eeh! she'd love a string of those beads, the blue ones. She'd seen her ma nick beads and things off the shop counters. Hankies too, lace hankies. Oh, her ma had been good at nicking lace hankies. Her ma said that the shop had so many they never missed them, but they had run once when the shopman had tried to grab her ma. By! they had run that time.

There were such a lot of trinkets here she was sure nobody would ever miss one or two bits. She started at the beginning again and opened the box with the brooches in and, having selected one, she put it in the pocket of her frock; then the rings. She liked the red one. She tried in on her finger. It was much too big but her finger would grow. She placed that in her pocket also. And the beads. She would like a string of beads. She would just take one strong. . . . Oh! She hadn't noticed that. She moved the strings of beads and disclosed a gold chain with a heart-shaped locket on the end. Aw now, that was pretty, wasn't it? The prettiest of the lot. And the locket had a stone in the middle of it. Oh, she would like that. Oh yes, she would. But she'd better not wear these things, not yet at any rate, she'd better hide them like her ma used to do. Her ma had made a hole in the bed tick where she used to stuff the things, the little things, in among the feathers. . . . Eeh! that locket was bonny. She lifted the chain and tried to get it over her head, but it wasn't big enough. Then she laughed to herself. Of course, there was a catch on it. She had only to open the catch.

She had to fiddle about quite a while before she could undo the clasp on the locket, but eventually she had it opened. Then she put the chain around her neck and in order to fasten the clasp she brought it to the front, slanting her eyes down to it. But she never got as far as closing it, for she heard a great gasp behind her, and she spun round on the seat to see, standing in the doorway, the missis.

. . . Anne Thornton had had a trying morning. The walk to Allendale Town had been hot and dusty; Betsy had been fractious; and Doctor Arnison had kept her waiting an interminable time. He had even seen to Miss Cisson before her, and yet they had both entered his waiting room together. He had even still further delayed her to attend to a farm labourer who had stupidly thrust a pitchfork through his foot. But these indignities had been small compared to the looks that had been levelled on her by the locals of the town. Even Mr Hunting, the grocer, who had always been most deferential towards her, even he'd had a smirk on his face when he served her. In fact, for one awful moment she had thought that he was going to detail his assistant to see to her needs.

Then there was the village. Oh, the village. She would never forget what she had suffered at their hands on the day of Mr Beaumont's celebration. Even those who in the past had dipped their knees to her looked her full in the face and walked straight past her. And it had been the same this morning. And all this had come about through a man's sensuality.

She hated Matthew; deep, deep in her heart she hated him, and she would never forgive him for the disgrace he had brought upon her. And what was adding to the injustice of it all was that he himself wasn't suffering for his wrongdoing; in fact he was being hailed more loudly than before. And she wasn't imagining this. 'How goes it, Mr Thornton?' they cried across the street to him. 'Fine day, Mr Thornton.' 'Hope I see you well, Mr Thornton.' There was one time during the evening of the festivities when she was so enraged that she had become fearful, for she imagined herself actually striking out at them, felling them right and left with her clenched fists. She had seen them lying in heaps dead and dying from her blows. The image had caused the sweat to pour from her.

. . . And now here was the cause of all her distress daring to enter her bedroom and finger her jewellery.

'Get off that seat, girl!'

Hannah sidled to her feet and, trembling, watched the woman advance towards her. As the locket and chain was being grabbed from her hand the chain seared her palm, then when the hand caught her full across the face she fell sidewards on to the floor, and as she fell the ring and the brooch tumbled from the pocket of her dress almost to Anne Thornton's feet.

'You thief! You horrible dirty little thief!' She stooped and grabbed up the brooch and the ring and stared at them for a moment; then she looked down on the child.

Hannah wasn't crying. Her mother had boxed her ears so often that she considered such a blow not worth worrying about, but although she wasn't crying she was afraid, very much afraid because her mother, after boxing her ears, would usually pull her towards her and hold her tightly, but this woman's face was frightening. She sidled herself back on her hip thinking to escape under the bed, but the hands came down and grabbed her.

'John! Margaret!'

As she called out the children's names she shook Hannah viciously; then pulling her towards the open door she called again, 'John! Margaret!'

A moment later the four children appeared on the landing and gazed at their mother in amazement where she stood just within her bedroom holding Hannah by the shoulders.

'Bring me the whip from the rack, John.'

'Mama!'

'You heard what I said, bring me the whip.'

The boy looked from his mother to the petrified face of the small girl and he shook his head twice before saying, 'You mustn't, Mama. You mustn't.'

'Do as I say, boy!'

'No, Mama, you mustn't.'

'Margaret!'

Margaret's answer to her mother's command was to back silently towards the far wall, there to stand with her palms pressed tightly against it.

Their mother now looked at Robert, and the children could almost see her dismissing him from her mind: If John or Margaret wouldn't obey such an order Robert never would.

'Betsy! go into the hall, stand on a chair and bring the ornamental horsewhip to me.'

Betsy stared at her mother for a moment, glanced towards her two brothers; then whimpering, she turned about and ran down the stairs.

In the interval it took for Betsy to return with the whip Anne Thornton explained to her children, between sharp gasps of breath, the reason for her actions. 'She was stealing, she had my ring and brooch in her pocket, and she was about to take the locket, my mother's locket that holds a lock of my father's hair. She's wicked and she must be punished. I will not tolerate a thief in this house.'

'Papa would not do this.'

She turned her blazing gaze on to Robert now.

'Wouldn't he? He has used the whip on you and John before today.'

'Only once.' Robert's lips were trembling. 'And . . . and because we did something bad. We let the dog loose among the sheep and . . . and he had to shoot it; it . . . it was bad.'

As Betsy scrambled across the landing now, her arm extended and holding a short-handled whip in her hand, John protested again, 'Don't do this, Mama. Please don't do this,' and of a sudden Hannah's voice was added to his and she cried, 'No, no! don't you whip me, missis. I'll . . . I'll not do it again. Don't you whip me.'

It was as if the child's voice inflamed Anne Thornton's anger to madness for, now grabbing the whip from Betsy and swinging Hannah from her feet, she went back into the bedroom, thrusting the door closed with her buttocks, and there she held the child at arm's length while she brought the whip around her feet. But Hannah being agile jumped and the whip's end merely curled round her long skirt, the tip of it only flicking her ankles. But such was the stinging feeling that it incensed her, and now she began to fight, in her turn kicking at Anne Thornton's legs and lurching and clawing at the hand that held the whip.

She was still struggling wildly when she was lifted bodily and thrown on to the bed; then she felt she was being smothered when her dress and petticoats were pulled over her head and her face pressed into the feathered tick.

She had no stockings on, nor did she wear long frilled knickers like Betsy did, or a little habit shirt; all she was wearing were two long petticoats and her dress and pinafore, so when the whip contacted her small bare body she screamed and bounced as if she were on a hot griddle.

Each time Anne Thornton brought the whip down she was striking at a particular villager: Ralph Buckman's two sons, Bill and Stan, who had dared to laugh in her face when she passed the smithy; that little devil of a woman, Daisy Loam, the butcher's wife, who had dared to say to her last week, "What will I be sending you up the day, missis, you'll want a bit extra with one more mouth to feed?" And then Miss Cisson, who that very morning in the doctor's waiting room had dared to ask her if she would be wanting anything cut down for the new little miss; there were miners and their wives who now had the effrontery to approach her without first being bidden; and Susanna Crewe, who was supposed to be her friend, but who aimed to be more pious than her parson husband, daring to suggest to her certain passages in the Bible dealing with forgiveness ... And then there was *him, him, him.*

She might easily have flayed the child to death but for John and Robert coming into the room and grabbing hold of her arms.

The boys' faces were chalk white as they stared from their mother to the small, now merely whimpering, partly naked body on the bed, the back showing a mass of criss-cross weals, some oozing little spots of blood. Then a slight thud brought their attention back to their mother again. She had dropped down on to the dressing-table stool, and after a moment she bent her head forward and buried her face into her hands. But when John, now going towards the open door and saying softly to Margaret, who was still standing against the wall, 'Go down and tell Bella to come and see to Mama,' Anne Thornton pulled herself up from the seat and, her hands massaging her throat as if to force the words out, said, 'No, no! I'm all right. Stay where you are.'

Margaret stayed where she was, but she turned and looked towards the stairhead where both Bella and Tessie were standing. They had heard what their mistress had said and so they came no further; but they continued to stand there until they saw Master John come out of the room carrying Hannah in his arms, with Robert supporting her feet. They watched them stumble along the landing and into their own room and Miss Margaret and Miss Betsy scamper after them; then they heard the mistress's door close.

Silently they looked at each other for a moment before turning and going slowly down the stairs. It wasn't until they were in the kitchen that Bella said, 'Bairns have to be whipped, granted, but there's a difference atween whippin' and flayin'. Anyway, what had she done to be so treated? Wait till the master comes in, I bet there'll be hell to pay. He won't stand for her being flayed, not if I know anything about him.'

# Chapter Four

Anne Thornton had made up her mind what course she must follow. She must be the first to tell Matthew what had happened and why it had happened. She had washed herself down to her waist in cold water, she had changed her dress and done her hair; she had made herself go into the kitchen and see that the dinner was under way. One thing she hadn't done was face her children.

She had seen Robert in the back garden. He seemed to be looking for something. He must have gone down the back staircase for she hadn't heard him cross the landing. At one point she had heard them all upstairs in the nursery, their footsteps crossing and recrossing the floor.

Now aiming to keep her own steps firm, she left the sitting-room, crossed the hall, went down the garden path and on to the main road. Here she turned away from the village, walking by the hawthorn hedge that bordered their land, and when she reached the end of it she stood waiting.

Within five minutes Matthew made his appearance and the amazement showed on his face when he saw her standing in the roadway, and before he reached her he called out, 'Something wrong? Something happened?'

Dismounting quickly from his horse, he led it forward towards her, asking again, 'What is it?'

'I . . . I have something to tell you.'

'Don't beat about the bush, woman, has something happened to the children?'

'No, nothing has happened . . . my children.'

She watched his face stiffen. 'What have you done to the child?' His words were slow and deep.

'That . . . that is what I have come to tell you. I had been to Doctor Arnison's and on my return I found her in my room. She was stealing my jewellery. I thrashed her.'

'You thrashed her?'

He let out a long breath, there was even the suspicion of a smile on his face. For a moment he had thought she was going to say she had killed the child, because he knew that her hate of the poor waif went deep. This, of course, in a way was understandable; he had hoped that the child's natural charm, and time, would erase the feeling.

'Is that all?'

She swallowed deeply. 'Yes, that's all,' she said.

He moved slowly forward now, walking the horse as he said, 'Well, her background must have been pretty rough, and I don't suppose she looks upon stealing as a crime.' He turned and looked at her. 'Wasn't she just playing with the things?'

'She had them in her pocket, a ring, a brooch and . . . and my mother's locket.'

Oh. Oh, her mother's locket. She laid as much stock on that as on the crown jewels. If the child had to steal something it was a pity it had to be that. 'Well, I don't suppose it'll be the first thrashing she's had and it won't be the last, she's got to be made to learn the difference between right and wrong. What were you doing at Doctor Arnison's?' He smiled as he asked the question. It seemed as if they were getting back on to the old footing. Perhaps in chastising the child she had also chastised herself for her attitude these last few weeks.

'Betsy's had toothache, quite a lot of late. I . . . I felt it had to be seen to.'

'Oh yes; yes, of course, she was crying last night. Did he take it out?'

'No; he said it wasn't bad. He said there was nothing wrong with it. I don't think he knows much about teeth.'

'Don't you? Oh well, it's my opinion that he's forgotten more than most doctors know.'

They were going up the drive now, but opposite the front door they parted company, she going into the house and Matthew continuing towards the yard where Dandy Smollett was waiting for the horse. There was no grin on the boy's face, and when in silence he led the horse away, Matthew looked after him for a moment before entering the kitchen.

As usual, Bella and Tessie were preparing the dinner. Bella was pounding potatoes in the iron pan with a wooden pestle and her 'Good evening, master' had, he thought, a strange inflexion to it.

'Good evening, Bella,' he answered. 'Everything all right?'

'It depends on what one calls all right, master; what's right to some folk is wrong to others.'

After giving her a keen glance he sat down and changed his shoes, took off his coat, then left the kitchen, making note that Tessie hadn't opened her mouth.

He washed himself, then went to the dining-room. As he entered he heard his wife saying to Tessie, who was placing the vegetable dishes on the table, 'Did you do as you were bid and tell the children?'

'I did, ma'am, I told them twice.'

'What's all this about?' He looked from Tessie's departing figure to his wife, and he watched her neck swell and her lips move over each before she said, 'They did not hold with my chastising *The Girl*.'

He stared at her, his face blank now, then turned abruptly and went out. He took the stairs two at a time and when he reached the landing he called 'John! Robert!' then went up the attic stairs and thrust open the nursery door, and there in a close group confronting him were John, Margaret, and Robert, but Betsy was running towards him, crying, 'Papa! Papa! they wouldn't let me come.'

'What's all this about?' He unloosened Betsy's clinging hands and moved towards the others, and again he said, 'Come, tell me what this is about.' Although he was looking at John it was Robert who answered. 'She, Mama, she whipped Hannah.'

Matthew now saw the tears spurt from his younger son's eyes and the words came choked from his mouth as he gasped, 'She . . . she used the fancy trap whip on her and . . . and she was all weals and bleeding and kept screaming.' Now his voice became so choked that he drooped his head and put his hand over his mouth.

Margaret, too, was crying. Only John was dry-eyed and it was to him that Matthew said, 'Where is she?'

'I . . . I . . . we . . . we don't know, Papa.'

'What do you mean, you don't know?'

It was evident that John, too, was almost in tears, and Matthew shouted at him, 'Tell me what you mean, you don't know.'

'Well, after . . . after we had carried her from the room into . . . into our bedroom, we washed her back, and Margaret' – he pointed blindly towards his sister – 'she . . . she rubbed her with butter, and . . . and it eased her and we left her lying quiet. We . . . we thought she was asleep and . . . and we came up here and . . . and we talked about it because . . . because it was dreadful, Papa. And when we went downstairs again she was gone.'

'Gone?'

'Yes, Papa. We went in the garden, and all about, but we couldn't find her.'

Matthew now put his hand to his head. She had met him on the road and said she had thrashed the child and he had imagined that by thrashing she had meant spanking. He had pictured her bending the child across her knee, baring her bottom and whacking it. But then he should have known she wouldn't have brought the child in contact with her own body. She had never as much as put a finger near her since the day she had come into the house, and so when she had said she had thrashed the child she had meant just that. She had thrashed her with a horsewhip and in such a way that she had shocked her own children. Was the woman going mad? Yet on the road she had appeared calm enough, calm and contained. But where was the child?

He looked at the children now and said, 'Margaret, take Betsy downstairs to the dining-room. John and Robert, you come with me.' He turned and made for the door, but stopped and asked, 'What time was this, when you last saw her?'

'About . . . about three hours ago, Papa.'

Three hours! She could be anywhere, on the moors or fells by now, and if she were left out all night in that state she could be dead by morning because the nights still held frosts. In any case, even a summer's dawn was chilling to the bones in these heights.

There was no sign of his wife as he and the boys passed through the hall, and outside the front door he directed them. 'You, John, search round by the vegetable garden and the greenhouse, and you, Robert, make your way down to the stream. I'll go behind the house to the woodland. If you find her, whistle; if you don't, come back here.'

In less than fifteen minutes when he returned to the drive the boys were waiting for him and he didn't waste any time in questioning them, but said, 'We'll go on the fells; she'd likely go down the back staircase and out of the side door. You both go behind the village in the direction of the town; keep within hailing distance of each other. I'll go by way of the churchyard. Yes, yes' – he nodded to himself – 'she might just have gone that way. But whatever distance you go be sure you're back here before the twilight sets in. Understood?'

'Yes, Papa.'

'Yes, Papa.'

'Off you go then.'

Both boys now turned about and ran round the side of the house while he himself strode down the drive, across the road, and into the churchyard, and wending his way between the headstones he came to the mound that as yet bore no stone. But there was no sight of the child lying on top of it. Jumping the wall, he now made for the hills.

Once out of earshot of the village he began to call, softly at first, 'Hannah! Hannah!' for there were boulders and small gullies behind or in which she could be hiding.

When he was standing atop of a hill he saw, far across the valley, Ned Ridley leading a string of horses up the steep rise which led to the Pele house, and as he watched him disappear from view behind the tall erection a thought came to him and he put his hand to his chin and slowly rubbed it. That was the only other house she knew; Ned and his old grandfather were the only other people she knew; but could she possibly have made for there? He began his descent at a run, and when finally he came within hailing distance of the house he saw Ned Ridley come round the back of it and stand waiting, as if he were expecting him.

His running came to a stop a few yards from Ned, and he was too short of breath to speak for a moment or even to answer Ned when he said, 'Are you looking for somebody?'

'Yes. Yes, Ned, I am.'

'I thought you might be.'

He stared into the stiff face of the young fellow as he said, 'I just got in. I thought it was you I made out over there on the hills an' I wondered why, until a few minutes ago. You know, Mr Thornton, there's two kinds of folk I hate, them as lay mantraps, and women what take whips to flay bairns.'

As they stared at each other their jaws reacted in the same way, tensing the muscles of their cheeks.

'Perhaps you'd like to come in and see what your lady wife has done, eh?'

Another time Matthew's retort would have been, 'Don't you dare speak to me in that manner, boy!' but now all he could do was to stare at Ned, then follow him around the side of the house past the steep stone steps that led to a door in the first floor and into the stable-room.

It was dim inside and the lantern was already lit. Ned pointed towards where it hung from a hook in the stone wall, its diffused light shining down on Hannah and the old man seated by her side.

At the sight of Matthew, old man Ridley pulled himself to his feet and walked towards him as if he were about to take him on in a fight and, his voice high and cracked, he cried, 'Your bloody wife should be hung, mister. If I had her here I'd show her what flayin' was. I'd curl that whip around her belly.' He pointed to a long horsewhip that was lying against a stall. 'She must be a bloody maniac. Come and have a look at this.'

Matthew walked slowly forward until he was standing against the edge of the shallow platform on which the child now lay on a bed of hay. Her eyes were open and she stared at him, not moving until, dropping on to his hunkers his hand went out towards her, and then she shrank from him, and the movement must have caused her pain because her face twisted and she winced.

''Tis all right, hinny, 'tis all right.' The old man was pulling the horse blanket from off her now, saying as he did so, 'I took her clothes off 'cos they were stickin' to parts of her skin. Turn over, hinny. Gently now, gently.' As he helped her to turn he unwound the cotton sheet in which she was swathed. And then Matthew saw her back and legs. From above her little waist down to her heels was a mass of blue weals; some had bled quite a bit judging by the blood on the sheet and the dry clots on the skin. A wave of sickness overwhelmed him, not only at the sight of the little flayed body, but because his wife had inflicted this on a child, a small defenceless child.

'What do you think of that?'

He raised his eyes and looked at Ned but said nothing. What could he say? And what was adding to his present agony of mind was the fact that the child had become afraid of him.

'Hannah!' He bent his face down close to hers. 'Listen to me, dear. Listen to me. I'm sorry. Do you understand! I'm so very, very sorry this has happened to you. It will never happen again.'

He did not turn his head when a deep 'Huh!' came from behind him but went on, 'I shall see that it will never happen to you again. Nor shall anyone ever raise their hand to you again. Do you understand?'

Hannah gulped in her throat, wiped a piece of hay from her cheek and whispered, 'She did it with a whip.'

He closed his eyes tightly for a moment, bit hard on his lip, then looking at her again, he said, 'I'm going to take you home.'

'No, no!' She shrank away from him. 'I want to stay here. I like it here; I want to stay here.'

'You can't stay here, Hannah. And I promise you, listen to me.' He now put his hand on her brow and stroked her hair back. 'I promise you, dear, that your life will be different from now on, nobody will harm you again as long as I live. Do you understand?'

'I shouldn't think about movin' her the night.'

He glanced up at Ned.

'You can feel her head.' Ned nodded down to her. 'If I'm any judge she's in a fever.'

When he again put his hand on Hannah's head he realized that she was indeed very hot and might even be in a fever. It would do no harm to leave her here for the night. He again bent his face close to her and said, 'I'll come back for you in the morning, Hannah, when you're feeling better. But remember, nobody will ever hit you again. Everything is going to be different from now on. That's a promise.'

Gently he stroked her cheek; then rising to his feet, he left her to the ministrations of the old man, who was once again covering her up; and walking to the door of the stable-room he gazed out into the fast approaching night, and his heart was sick inside him.

'We don't blame you.'

He turned and looked at Ned and said harshly, 'Well, you should, for she came into the world through me.'

'Aw, there speaks the churchman, Mr Thornton, but if every man carried the blame for what he drops on the way there'd be few in these hills walking head high. Things like that happen, 'tis nature, and who's to deny nature when it comes at you. Not me for one, so I blame no man for fathering a bairn, not me.'

Matthew turned his head fully and looked at the young fellow. He had heard tales of Ned's exploits, but had taken most of them with a pinch of salt. People made mountains out of molehills and fathoms out of tiddler ponds, yet he had no doubt but that there was a grain of truth in the stories, and the irony of it was a fellow like Ned would get off scot-free with his escapades while he himself, who had slipped up but once, had it brought right home to his hearth, and the consequence of it lay flayed on the hay behind him.

Well, now he knew what he had to do, what in justice he must do. He had never been a violent man, but now he felt violent. He hadn't believed in retribution but now he knew he was going to act as God and deal out retribution. It was as if he had been planning for weeks what he must do this night and what he must do tomorrow. But to begin with he must ask Ned for his silence.

'I want to ask you something, Ned.'

'Aye, fire ahead, Mr Thornton.'

'Do you think you can keep a closed mouth about what's happened to the child?'

'Keep a closed mouth, me? Well, I've never found it too hard to keep a closed mouth about most things, but why should I keep a closed mouth about this?'

'Because I ask you as a great favour to me.'

'But what about t'others, there's bound to be talk from Bella and Tessie, not to mention young Dandy. They must know what went on for she must have squealed like a stuck pig.'

'I'll deal with those in turn, as I'll deal with the one who flayed her.'

Their eyes as they gazed at each other were deep and dark, then Ned said, 'Very well, if it's like that you've got me word I'll say nowt.'

'And your grandfather?' Matthew jerked his head backwards.

'Oh, he'll say nowt an' all if I tell him not to, but he'll do it more readily when he knows you're gonna deal out fair punishment. Aye, he'll do it more readily then.'

'Thank you, Ned. I'll be back in the morning for her.'

'Aye, well, I'll be here; I'm not due over at Allenheads till noon.'

Saying no more, Matthew turned abruptly away and walked from the yard down the hill towards the village and his home.

It was almost dark when he reached the house, but the boys were still waiting for him at the gate. He checked their enquiries by saying, 'I've found her, she's up at the Pele house with Ned Ridley, She'll stay there until morning.'

'Is she all right, Papa?'

He looked at Robert for a moment before answering, 'She will be. She will be.' Then turning to John, he asked, 'Have you had your supper?'

'No, Papa.'

'Then I want you to go indoors now and have something to eat, but don't take long over it. Then you must both go to your room . . . And listen to me.' He looked from one to the other. 'No matter what you hear you must not leave your room, you understand?'

When they didn't answer he said again, 'I said to you, no matter what you hear you must not leave your room. And you will tell the girls this from me too. Do you understand me?'

'Yes . . . yes, Papa.'

'Yes, Papa.'

They nodded at him.

'Go along then.' He watched them go up the drive and into the house; but he remained where he was for quite some time before he, too, approached the house.

He did not enter by the front door but went round the side and so into the kitchen.

Bella was sitting at one side of the fire, Tessie at the other, and Dandy Smollett in between them, and they all rose quickly to their feet as he entered.

It was Bella who asked, 'Did you find her, sir?'

'Yes, yes, I found her, Bella. Sit down.' With a wave of his hand he motioned them all to their seats. And now looking from one to the other, he asked, 'Have you been out into the village since this afternoon?'

They all shook their heads, and again it was Bella who spoke. 'No; no one's left the house, sir' she said.

'Has anyone called?'

'No, no, only the coalman, and that was this mornin'; groceries don't come till the morrow.'

'So you have told no one what transpired this afternoon?'

There was a pause before Bella said, 'No, sir, nobody, nobody.'

'Well then' – again he passed his glance over them – 'I want your promise that you will never mention what happened this afternoon, or what might happen tonight . . . to anyone. If I find that the business of my house becomes common knowledge in the village then, Bella, I shall dismiss you; and you, too, Tessie. As for you, Dandy, you will go back to the House.'

'No, sir, not me, I wouldn't let on. No, sir, not me. I wouldn't do anything that would take me back to the House, sir.'

'Well and good. As for you, Bella, and you, Tessie, I think I can even speak for you, can't I?'

'Oh yes, sir.' Bella nodded her head slowly, and Tessie followed suit, saying, 'Oh aye. Aye, sir, I wouldn't open me mouth.'

'Good, good. Now what I want you to do is this. I want you all to go to your beds and remain there until tomorrow morning at the usual time for getting up. No matter what you hear, don't come out of your rooms. You understand that?'

They all stared up at him, their mouths slightly agape, their eyes wide, their faces awe-filled, and again it was Bella who answered, but her voice was merely a whisper as she said, 'Aye, sir, we'll stay in our rooms, if that's what you want.'

'That's what I want. Now if you're finished for the night I would get away. Good-night. Good-night to you all.'

'Good-night, sir.' Their voices were merely whispers that followed him from the room.

He now went into the dining-room where the boys were sitting eating some cold pie and he said to them briskly, 'Take what you want upstairs.'

'Yes, Papa. Yes, Papa.' They scrambled to their feet, dragged pieces of pie from the central plate on the table and a square each of cheese from the board, then hurried out of the room, their heads down as if they were escaping after having stolen the food.

He remained in the dining-room until he heard their footsteps above him crossing the landing, then he went out and towards the sitting-room door. This he flung open but didn't enter the room until he saw that it was empty. Walking towards the fireplace, he noticed that the cushions had been arranged in a symmetrical line along the back of the couch, their corners all pointing directly upwards, and also that the fire had been banked down and a guard placed around it, which all spoke of her having retired for the night. Well, that's what he wanted her to have done, retired for the night; in a way it would simplify things.

What time was it? Half past nine o'clock. He would wait a short while.

He was about to lower himself down on the couch when the arrangement of the cushions brought his bent back to a halt. She did not like the room disarranged once she had settled it for the night. Blast the room, and her, to hell's flames! He took his hand and swiped the four cushions into a jumbled heap in the corner of the couch, then fell back with a plop on to the horsehair seat. It seemed in this moment that all his life he had been following a routine, a routine that had an army discipline about it. During the first months of his marriage her housewifery had pleased him; in fact, amongst other things he had looked upon it as one of her accomplishments. But it had begun to irritate him before the first child arrived, although after the arrival of John he had bowed to it again, for he knew only too well that children could disrupt the household. In any case he had had to admit to himself then that he did like his meals on time, and he did like peace in the evenings to work on his mining papers, which work was an absolute necessity if he ever intended to rise to the position of head mining agent.

But here, thirteen years later, he was still as far away from that position as he had been when he first read *Forster's Strata*. He knew it wasn't even likely now he'd ever reach Mr Sopwith's position, or even that of the under agents, William and John Curry at Allenheads. But in this moment he asked himself what did that matter, the only thing that mattered was what he intended to do in the next half-hour, what must be done within the next half-hour, for after that his rage might wane, although this he doubted because it would be a long while before he looked on her face and didn't see it over-patterned by the child's back.

He sat staring into the dull glow of the fire until the clock in the hall chimed ten; then he rose to his feet, walked firmly to the door, went into the hall and took from the rack the riding whip, picked up the lamp from the side table, then went up the stairs.

Placing the lamp on a bracket on the landing wall he turned the wick down, then opened the bedroom door and entered the room.

Her light was turned low. She was lying well down in the bed, her head on the pillow; but she wasn't asleep for her eyes swivelled towards him as he approached the bedside. He saw that, as usual, she had been reading a passage from the good book before settling down, it lay open where she had left it. He picked it up with one hand and screwed up his eyes. She had been reading David's psalm of thanksgiving.

His eyes scanned the page. There were ticks against various numbers but none against Verse 20 which read: 'The Lord rewarded me according to my righteousness; according to the cleanness of my hands hath he recompensed me.'

He looked down on her now where she had risen on her elbow, her eyes not on the book in his left hand but on the whip in his right hand, and his next words brought her sitting bolt upright in the bed for he read to her from the book: 'according to the cleanness of my hands hath he recompensed me.' And with a backward sweep of his hand he threw the book across the room and, his voice a growl, he demanded, 'Did you read that before or after you flayed the child?'

She was sitting with her back pressed tight against the brass rails of the bed now and her voice had a tremor to it as she replied, 'She stole; I told you I chastised her.'

'Huh! chastised her! When you said you thrashed her I thought you had aired her backside and given it to her with your hand, but no, no, you used this.' He flicked the whip and the thong swished an inch from her face causing her to gasp aloud.

'Yes, that made you jump, didn't it? It didn't even touch you but it made you jump, so what do you think that child felt like when you whipped her almost to death. Aye, almost to death, because if she hadn't gone up to the Ridleys and been attended by the old man she'd have run on to the fells, and the night would have finished her. And then what do you think would have happened when they found out, eh? You would have been for it; it would have been your neck. And I would have seen you go without raising me hand. Do you hear?'

His face was close to hers now and his lips shrank back from his teeth as if he were looking on something repulsive, and his voice indicated as much as he said, 'You know what you are, you're a cruel, vindictive bitch of a woman. You're nothing, do you hear? nor ever have been anything else but a bloody upstart. You've been the laughing-stock of the village and the town for years, and it's never got through to you because you imagined you were somebody, somebody different from the common herd. Well, there are women in that village down there, did they get wind of what you've done to that child, they'd spit on you. They'd pelt you with horse muck, they'd rub your nose in it.'

'How . . . how dare you sp . . . speak to me in such a fashion. . . .'

'Shut up! And never use those words to me again. How dare I? I'll speak to you any way I like! Now you know what I'm going to do, I'm going to speak to you in your own language, but before I start I'm going to tell you something else because by the time I've finished with you you won't be able to take it in, not clearly. Well, now listen. Tomorrow morning I'm going to give you some rules whereby you and I are going to live together in this house, and you'll obey them or you'll go, the choice will be yours. Now!'

With a quick movement of his hand he ripped the bedclothes right down to the foot of the bed and before she could leap from it he brought the whip around her bare calves; then as she cried out and wreathed on the bed her night-gown exposed her lower thighs and when the whip stung them she let out an ear-piercing scream. Now, his hand on her shoulder, he swung her around as if she had been a sack of coal, and holding her down by the neck, he pulled up her night-dress until it exposed her buttocks and lower back and then he brought the whip down on her for perhaps ten times, and each time it contacted her skin she screamed.

When at last he stood back from her she lay sobbing and moaning, her hands grabbing handfuls of the feather tick. He stood taking in long slow breaths of air, and when he exhaled his stomach seemed to sink in, dragging his shoulders forward. He had to make an effort to turn away from the bed, and when at last he did, his step was slow and heavy.

Out on the landing, he closed his eyes tightly before making for the stairs.

He replaced the whip in the rack before going into the little study adjoining the dining-room. Here he opened a cupboard below the book rack, and from it he took a tray on which stood a bottle half full of whisky, and putting the tray on the desk, he poured out a full glass of the liquor. After drinking deep from it he sat down at the desk and drooped his head forward on to his folded arms.

The following morning, before sending Dandy Smollett on the horse to the mine to tell Mr Byers that he would be a little late, he caught hold of his leg and, looking up at him, said, 'You remember what we talked about last night, Dandy?' and the boy remarked, 'Aye, master.'

'Good; then go on your way.'

This done, he went into the kitchen where Bella and Tessie looked at him silently, but their eyes speaking volumes, and to Tessie he said, 'Make the bed up in the spare room, Tessie; I'll be using that for the time being. Then I want you to take the pallet from the little room and put it in the boxroom next to it. I'll see about getting a single bed as soon as possible. That room is to be for my daughter . . . Hannah. You understand?' He looked from her to Bella, and they both nodded their heads, and together they said, 'Yes, master.'

'One thing more.' He was now addressing Bella. 'She won't be helping you in the kitchen here again.'

There was a pause as he and Bella stared at each other. Then with native boldness, Bella answered, 'As I see it that's how it should be, master.'

'Then we both see it the same way, Bella. I'll be bringing her down from Ridley's shortly, she might need some attention. I'd be grateful if you'd see to her.'

'I'll do all I can for her, master; and Tessie here an' all, we like the bairn.'

'Thank you.' He nodded from one to the other, then went out, with Bella calling after him, 'Won't you have no breakfast, master?' and he answered, 'Not until I get back.'

The mist was still thick as he mounted the fell, and although the path led upwards, the higher he went the more dense the mist became; and when it seemed to seep through to his skin and made him shiver he thought again of what would have happened to the child if she had been left out all night, and in her condition.

When he pushed open the door of the stable-room both Ned Ridley and his grandfather turned from the platform and looked towards him, and from the looks on their faces he thought for a moment that the child must have died.

'She's in a fever.' Ned had risen to his feet. 'She's had a bad night.'

Matthew bent over the hay and looked down on Hannah. She was awake and he said to her softly, 'How are you feeling, my dear?'

'I'm sore, mister.'

'You'll feel better tomorrow.'

'I'm sweatin'.'

He put his hand on her head and when it came away wet he looked across at Ned, but it was the old man who said, 'She's full of the fever; you cannot take her down there like this.'

Matthew bit on his lip for a moment, thinking, then said, 'Will I bring the doctor up?'

'What's he say?' The old man turned to Ned, and Ned mouthing loudly as he gesticulated, cried at him, 'He says will he fetch the doctor?'

Old Ridley now turned his head sharply and confronted Matthew again, saying, 'Doctor! What could he do I haven't done? Cured more complaints than he's ever heard of, me. I've given her a dose of ipecacuanha, that'll clear her bowels, cool her down. An' she's had a few drops of laudanum an' all.'

'Laudanum?' Matthew's eyebrows moved upwards, and as much from his expression as from the mouthing of the word the old man gauged Matthew's questioning and repeated, 'Aye, laudanum. She wanted somethin' to settle her nerves after that lot. But you're not takin' her down there the day unless you want to polish her off altogether.'

Matthew now turned and looked at Ned and he said quietly, 'It's very good of you both to take the trouble.'

'Oh, trouble!' Ned shrugged his shoulders. 'We do it for dogs, horses, an' strays; an' I think you could number her in the last lot.'

'She's no stray, Ned.'

'No? Well, you could have hoodwinked me, Mr Thornton. Aye, you could have that, you could have hoodwinked me, 'cos mind I'm only repeatin' what I've heard, but strays have always got to work for their livin', earn their bite so to speak. Of course, as I've said, you can only go by what you hear. But if one only goes by half of it I would say that in her case she's worked for her keep.'

Ned's eyes had never left Matthew's face. Nor had Matthew's lids blinked once. Under other circumstances such bold talk would have made him want to lash out at the fellow, at least with his tongue for he could never hope to beat him with his fists, not Ned Ridley; but he had learned over the years that young Ned could be stung by the tongue and it carried more effect than a blow. Yet on this occasion he did not retaliate in the only way left open to him; instead, his voice slow, his tone steady, he said, 'She is my daughter and in future she'll be known as such.'

'I'm glad to hear it, Mr Thornton. Aye, I am that. But, of course, you're speakin' for yourself; do you think you'll get others to act in the same way to her?'

There was a long moment before Matthew replied, 'Yes, others will act in the same way towards her or else they'll have to answer to me.'

Ned said nothing to this, and Matthew turned and looked at Hannah again. The old man was wiping the sweat from her brow with a cold wet rag, and he bent down to her and, taking her chin gently in his hand, he brought her face to the side until she was looking at him, and quietly and firmly he said, 'I'll be back later to take you home, either tonight, or tomorrow, depending on how you feel. I've got a room ready for you, it's next to mine. You'll be sleeping near me, you understand?'

She made the slightest movement with her head; her eyes, unblinking, stared up into his.

'Everything from now on is going to be different, you are going to be happy. Yes, yes' – he stroked her cheek gently – 'you're going to be happy.'

Straightening up, he turned and walked from the platform and Ned went with him as far as the door, where they stood silently side by side looking out into the morning.

The mist was still thick and shrouding everything. There was a blanket on all the sounds outside, yet behind him there was clatter and snufflings and warm activity. He hadn't noticed before that all the stalls were full. There must be eight to ten horses in there; perhaps there hadn't been a time since this place was built that there had never been horses stabled on the ground floor.

He glanced now towards the sharp-featured, tousled dark-haired, thick-shouldered youth at his side. Young Ned looked the spit of his father, and his bone formation was recognizable in his grandfather's face. The Ridleys had a name going right back for centuries, and not one to be proud of, for only in latter years had they become established as bona fide horse-dealers. One of them during the last century had definitely been hanged for horse stealing, two had been transported, and old Ridley himself back there had done time, being lucky to get off lightly with a stretch. It was only the fact that now and again he had picked up a good horse for Lord Buckly that had saved his neck.

All the Ridley men had been characters: outspoken, independent men, but a hard drinking, hard fighting, quarrelsome breed, especially on fair and festival days. . . . Yet who but they would have looked after the child back there without going down to the village and spreading the news of what had happened to her. And in the present circumstances it was doubly commendable that Ned should keep quiet about this affair, for he knew well enough that the young fellow had no liking or even respect for Anne, for she looked upon him as scum and never failed to hide her opinion of him when they met.

'I'm takin' two ponies into Hexham the day.' Ned jerked his head backwards. 'It's a private deal so it may be close on evenin' afore I get back, but she'll be all right with the old 'un, never fear. He's brought me through fever more than once. He's good at that kind of thing and he knows herbs an' such.'

'I'll pop over at dinner-time.'

'Aye, you could do that if it will ease your mind, but as I said she'll be all right with him. An' he loves wee 'uns.'

Matthew stepped from the doorway into the mist, then turned and said briefly, 'Thanks.'

As briefly Ned answered, 'You're welcome,' and on this they parted. . . .

The mist had lifted by the time he reached the house. There was a pink glow over the yard. He looked towards the stable. Dandy had not returned. As he went towards the kitchen the door opened and Tessie, looking towards him, said, 'Oh, master, you're wet.'

'The mist's thick on the hills.'

'''Tis very wettin'.'

'You're breakfast's all ready for you in the dining-room, master.'

He turned to Bella, saying, 'Thanks,' then asked, 'Are the children astir yet?'

'No, I haven't heard them, master.'

He did not put the same question about their mistress, and now without changing his boots or taking off his coat he walked up the kitchen, out into the hall, and from there into the dining-room; and the new procedure was not lost on either Bella or Tessie.

It was Tessie who, with her finger patting her lips, said in awe-filled tones, 'Did you see that, Bella? Did you see that? He never took off his coat or boots.'

In the dining-room Matthew waited until Tessie brought the porridge in; then he sat down at the table and ladled himself out four spoonfuls from the bowl she was holding. As this was only a third of what he usually took she said, 'Is that all you'll be needin' master?' and he answered, 'Yes, Tessie, I haven't much appetite this morning. Have you mashed the tea?'

'No, master; the mistress hasn't been down to unlock the caddy.'

'Here.' He took a key from a ring he brought from his pocket, saying, 'I think that'll fit it. And tell Bella to make it doubly strong.'

'Aye, master, aye. Oh, yes, aye.' She scurried out, amazed at the turn of events. . . .

It was as he was finishing the third cup of tea that the door opened and the children entered. John came in first, then Margaret pushing Beatrice before her; Robert came last and closed the door behind him; then they approached the table but they did not speak.

Putting down his cup, Matthew looked at them and said quietly, 'Good-morning, children.'

In a chorus they answered, 'Good-morning, Papa.'

'You return to school today, John?'

'Yes, Papa.'

'And you, Robert?'

'Yes, Papa.'

'Well, I want to talk to you. I'm . . . I'm glad I have this opportunity before you go. First of all I want you to know that there are going to be changes in the house.' He stared at them and they stared at him. 'What those changes are going to be I shall tell you in a little while after –' He now took up a napkin from the table and rubbed it hard across his lips before he ended, 'I have presented them to your mama, but this much I will say now. Hannah is my daughter, therefore she is your half-sister, and in future you will treat her as you would each other. Now' – he rose from the table – 'I want you to get your breakfast and remain in the room until I come back, for then I shall be able to tell you of the changes I referred to.'

Not one of them spoke, and he rose from the table, cast a glance over them that touched on a weak smile, then went from the room and up the stairs.

He expected the bedroom door to be locked but it wasn't. He expected her to be lying on the bed face downwards but she wasn't.

She was sitting propped up with pillows, and it was evident that she had been out of bed because the blinds were drawn. The sight of her face caused a momentary pang for it had a bleached, stark look; that she had been weeping profusely was evident from her swollen eyelids, but her expression was as he had expected it. He did not advance towards the bed but stood in the middle of the room and for a moment he found difficulty in speaking. Then when he did, his words came out so formally that he imagined for a moment he could be reading from a legal document. 'I have come to inform you, Anne, that there are to be changes in the household; from now on the child will be recognized as my daughter. I've already given instructions that she will have a room to herself on this floor. She will also eat at the table with us and will no longer do any menial work.' He paused for a moment as he saw her endeavour to move her body further up the bed. At the same time her mouth opened to speak, and he said, 'Wait! I haven't finished. With regard to the children, I have decided to send Margaret and Betsy to the private school in Hexham. Hannah will go with them. They will go as weekly boarders, and you shall have the company of them at week-ends, all . . . or none.'

Again her mouth opened.

'As for Robert, he will join John this . . .'

'You can't do this. You won't do this!' Her voice sounded strange; her thin high-faluting twang had disappeared; her words had a grating, ordinary tone about them.

'I thought you would have welcomed the idea. You have always stressed that the teaching responsibilities took up so much of your time that you couldn't practise your own accomplishments, your piano playing, your embroidery and such important things.' There was a sneer in his voice as he ended, 'Things you called the niceties of life.'

'You! You won't do this. Do you hear?' She had brought her back up from the cushions, and the movement had evidently caused her pain because she winced and gulped in her throat before she went on, 'I'll take action against you. I'll go to Mr Beaumont, I'll see him personally. You . . . you only got the position through my influence. I'll . . . I'll have it taken away from you. I will! I will!'

'You're welcome to try. Oh yes, you're welcome to try. See Mr Beaumont by all means, and I, too, shall see him. I'll take Hannah with me, and I'll show him her back and legs. The lash marks are so deep she'll carry their shadows until the day she dies. Do; go to Mr Beaumont; but by doing so you'll undo the good work I've already done on your behalf, for I've sworn the three in the kitchen to silence; I have also done the same with Ned Ridley and his grandfather.'

She was resting on one elbow, and now her other hand came up and covered her mouth. He nodded at her, saying, 'Yes, the Ridleys. You remember I told you last night that but for them you might not have got off with just a whipping. And it's true, only too true.'

'Well—' He now lifted the heavy lever watch from his waistcoat pocket and looked at it; then replacing it, he said, 'I think that's all I've got to say. Oh, except one more thing, perhaps the most vital. For years now you have done your duty as a wife only under protest and, as you may remember, at long intervals apart, and I bore with you because I enjoyed my family life and wanted peace. I can tell you with truth that I haven't had another woman since I took Nancy Boyle but now all that will be changed. As you said, you could not in the future bear me to touch you; nor would I for that matter be able to touch you, so I intend at the first opportunity to satisfy my needs elsewhere. I only think it fair to tell you this. But you will still, of course, be mistress of this house and nothing on the surface will apparently have changed, so your face will be saved in the village, and in the town.'

'You're a fiend, a wicked fiend. You won't do this to me, you can't.'

'What is the alternative? Will you allow me in the bed with you tonight?' He now took two quick steps towards her and the lightness of his tone changed to a deep growl as he bent forward and demanded, 'Will you? All right, I'll give you an option. I'll come to you tonight and every night when I need you and I don't go for my pleasures elsewhere. What do you say?'

She looked up at him. She was still leaning on her elbow. Her breathing was coming in short gasps and it seemed that she was unable to speak. But then she did, and what she said was, 'I hope God strikes you down dead.'

He remained in his bent position while they glared at each other; then he swung round and almost at a run went out of the room, across the landing and into the room where he had slept last night and, banging the door behind him, he turned his face towards it and, lifting his joined hands above his head, pressed them tightly against the wood.

As he stood thus it wasn't of Hannah he thought, nor of the future and the liberty he had afforded himself in it, but he thought of last night, and like a spectator he saw himself wielding the whip across her bare flesh and hearing her scream with each downward drive of his arm, and he knew that in flaying her he was merely giving vent to an urge that had lain just below the surface of his mind for years. The fact that Hannah had broken the skin was incidental. He would have done it some time or other, he would have had to, to express his dislike of her, because that is what his feelings towards her consisted of, and had done, he knew, for years past now, dislike, not love or hate, merely dislike. Even whilst loving her he disliked her.

# BOOK TWO

## Chapter One

### The Girl Growing Up 1858

Matthew stepped on to the bare boards that felt cold to his feet, and reached for his linings; and as he pulled them on he looked at the woman lying in the bed.

His rising had turned the bedclothes back off her, and she lay on her side naked to the middle of her thighs, and she scratched one gently as she answered a question of his, saying, 'Why should I lie to you, 'tis but a small matter? They didn't kiss or nothin', but 'twas the way they looked at each other, with their hands joined.'

'When was this?'

'Oh, 'twas in the summer.'

'Had you seen them before, I mean together up on the hills here?'

'Aye, when you come to speak of it, aye.'

'With the others or just alone?'

'Just alone, together, walkin' like, laughin'. But why worry your head? They know what they are; being related nothing can come of it. Still –' She turned on to her back, stretched her hands above her head and gripped the brass rails of the bed as she went on, 'What am I talkin' about, there's Peg Docherty who lives on the bottoms, she had one by her father an' two by her brother, so they say. Well, they were by somebody 'cos her man was at sea. Folks always look for him comin' back to see which one he'll half murder this time.'

'Be quiet, Sally.'

The tone of his voice brought her head round sharply and the laughter seeped from her face as she said, 'I didn't tell you it to disturb you, Matthew, but I wondered if you knew like.'

When he didn't answer but went on buttoning his waistcoat she got quickly from the bed and pulled on her petticoats and skirt and lastly her bodice; but by the time she was dressed he had his top coat on and his hat in his hand, and when she came to him and stood before him he said, as always, 'Thanks, Sally,' and she, as always, shook her head from side to side, saying ''Tis nothing. 'Tis nothing.'

Time and again he had thought how odd it was that their partings always followed the same pattern. 'Thanks, Sally ... 'Tis nothing. 'Tis nothing.'

When his hand went to his pocket she put hers out and touched his arm, saying, 'No, not this time. Anyway, I'm hard-pressed to find where to hide it; his eyes are all over the place. And what's the use of it to me if I can't spend it? The only one who enjoys it is me sister. An' by! she does, she looks forward to me goin',' she said laughing.

'You never know, it might come in handy some day; you should keep some by you.'

'Well, if that day comes an' I'm ever in need I hope you'll be there.'

'I'll be there, Sally.'

She now put her hand up and touched his cheek and, leaning her body against him, she said, 'Do I make you happy, Matthew?'

'Happier than I've ever been in my life, Sally.'

'Well, I've got God to thank for that anyway.' She now drew her body away from him and said softly, 'It could be another fortnight afore he's off again, but you'll be able to tell by the stones. I'll see to them.'

He now pinched her cheek gently, kissed her as gently, nodded at her, then, turning up the collar of his coat, he crossed the small room of the cottage, went through a stone-flagged scullery and out into the dark night.

His horse was tethered in the shelter of some bushes, and he untied him but did not mount him; instead, he led him on to a narrow path that slowly wound its way uphill, then down again. He did not tread warily for he had come to know the path well in the dark, and not until ten minutes later when he approached the coach road did he stop and light the lantern hanging from the pommel, then mount the horse and ride down on to the road.

The night was bitingly cold; there was a smell of snow in the air. The horse's breath floated up like a grey mist through the flickering light. It neighed loudly, telling him that it was both cold and hungry, but instead of spurring it forward into a trot, he kept it at a walking pace; he had a lot to think about before he entered the house. John and Hannah. No! No! the lad couldn't be so mad. Yet he was in the hot years of his youth, and a girl like Hannah was enough to stir any man's blood, let alone when it was flooding the loins for the first time. He must talk to him. But how? What could he say? Well, he could start by talking about Miss Pansy Everton. He had ridden with her at the shoot, and they had followed the dogs at the hare coursing. True, she wasn't the type he would have chosen for his son had he any say in it, but as a daughter-in-law she would certainly please Anne, for although she was of farming stock it was wealthy stock, and unlike most farmers' daughters she hadn't been made during her early days to help out on the farm, but had been sent to school, the same one as Margaret and Hannah had attended. Moreover, being an only child she would likely come into everything when her parents went, and he couldn't but admit that Mulberry Farm was a good inheritance and situated in a beautiful part Riding Mill way. No, John could do much worse financially than marry Miss Pansy Everton, and if all that Sally had implied was true the quicker it came about the better. But the question still remained, how was he going to approach the lad?

The horse neighed again and he himself shivered, and as he did so he felt the soft caress of the first snowflakes falling on his face.

Well, well, he wasn't surprised, it was the middle of November. The country signs had been prophesying a hard winter; some folks were saying it would be a repeat of '53. There had since been no snowstorm such as that winter had provided, yet while it had caused the death of a young stonemason up on Kilhope Head who was caught out on it, it had been the means of providing himself with body solace over the past five years.

One bitter night he was returning from the mine when he heard a cry for help coming from the direction of the river. It had been thawing for days and the river was running freely, but on this particular day it had begun to freeze again. Before he reached the river bank he had guessed what had happened. Someone had foolishly tried to cross by the stepping stones instead of walking further up and taking the bridge, and they had undoubtedly slipped into the river. And the accident must have only just happened for after a short while in that water no one would be able to shout as this one was doing.

In the early winter twilight he saw that the victim was a young woman lying half in and out of the water, she was clutching at one of the stepping stones.

Cautiously, he made his way towards her and, taking her hands, jerked her upwards; and when they were on the bank her teeth were chattering so much that she couldn't even thank him. 'Where are you bound for?' he had asked her.

And still unable to speak she had pointed in the direction of Sinderhope, then after a moment had stammered, 'L . . . Lode Cottage, Sinderhope way.'

Sinderhope was a good two miles further on whichever way she walked, and he had been through the village time and again but couldn't remember having seen her.

'Is it far from the village?' he had asked her, and she had nodded, then said, 'A distance.'

'Come on.' He had taken her by the arm and led her at a run across the field to where the horse was impatiently stamping on the road, and hoisting her up into the front of the saddle, he mounted and put the horse into a quick trot, shouting to her, 'You'll have to tell me the road for it's getting dark.'

She told him the road, and when they arrived at the cottage, seemingly in the midst of nowhere, she was so stiff with the cold she couldn't help herself down from the horse, and he lifted her to the ground, then led her towards the door, where she bent down and took a heavy iron key from under the stone in which was set a boot scraper. Inside, he saw that the place was small, but clean and comfortable. From the shape of the house outside he guessed that all it consisted of were the two rooms downstairs and an attic under the apex of the roof. Seeing that the fire was banked down, he took a pair of bellows from the stone wall and blew the ash into flames; then he turned to her and saw that she was shivering as if with ague, so much so that she couldn't unfasten the loop of her coat.

As his hands pushed hers aside and undid the buttons he asked, 'Your husband, where is he? Is he a mine worker?'

She shook her head, then stammered, 'Dr . . . dr . . . drover. He's . . . away to . . . to the market, Newcastle.'

'Newcastle?' He nodded at her. 'That's some way off, Newcastle.' And when she nodded back at him, he said, 'You'd better get to bed, I think.'

This time she made no attempt to answer him but, her eyes closing, she slumped to the floor.

What he did next was to hurry to the other room, pull the patchwork quilt and a brown blanket from the bed, then proceed to take her wet things from her. She was wearing a rough serge skirt, a striped blouse, two woollen petticoats and a print one; under the blouse she wore a habit shirt, and under that a cotton chemise, but no pantalets. Her black stockings were held up by the simple procedure of twisting the top into a knot then looping it under the rolled down top of the stocking.

She recovered from her faint as he was taking off her chemise, but her hands made no protest, she just lay looking at him as he rolled her first in the blanket and then in the quilt, and when he had finished he stared down at her for a moment before saying, 'That feel better?'

'Aye, yes.' Her voice was low and conveyed a pleasing sound to his ears, as had the sight of her body to his senses.

He had thrown off his own outer coat, and now he went to it and taking from the back pocket a flask of whisky, the carrying of which being a habit he had acquired over the past two years, he lifted a mug from a wall rack to the side of the fireplace, poured a measure of the whisky into it, then tilting the big iron kettle standing pressed against the low black hob, he filled the mug to the brim. And now, bending over her, he put his hand under her head and raised it, saying, 'Drink this.'

And without murmur she drank it.

Having poured himself a measure and heated this too, he squatted down by her side, and as he sipped at it he asked, 'What's your name?'

'Sally Warrington,' she replied.

'I haven't seen you about before, not in the market or anywhere.'

And to this she had explained, 'I seldom go down that way. Bill brings back our needs.'

'What time will he be home?'

'He won't be comin' the night,' she said; 'perhaps the morrow towards evening.'

'Oh.' After that they had continued to look at each other.

'How old are you?' he had next asked her, and she replied, 'Coming twenty-eight.'

'No children?' He had glanced about him, and at this she had shaken her head.

'Been long married?'

'Since sixteen.'

'Since sixteen,' he had repeated. She didn't look much more than sixteen lying there and her body still plump and firm. He'd had a few women over the past three years but they were women who had been used frequently for the same purpose, as he himself used them. They were the dregs of the back streets of Hexham.

He was forty years old and there was great unrest in him; he had known of late an understanding of those men who packed up and went, just went. There one minute, gone the next, men who walked out of the house in the morning and were never seen again.

He had risen to his feet as he said, 'I'd better be on my way; you'll be all right then?'

She hadn't answered, only stared up at him.

'You're not afraid to be alone?'

'No.' She had moved her head slightly. 'I'm used to it. I'm alone most of the time. He goes all over the county drovin'. He brings them down from Scotland one time, the cattle, or takes them up another, or into Hexham or Newcastle, anywhere where there's a good market. There's a number of them, drovers, they like being together, 'tis company.'

'Don't you get lonely?'

'Aye. Aye, I get lonely.'

She shivered again, and he said quickly, 'I'll bring another hap,' and when he tucked it round her his face hung over hers and he asked softly, 'You'd like me to stay a while?' and she answered simply, "Twould please me if it would you.'

That's how it had begun; and for five years now she had pleased him and he her, and no one knew.

Way back there on the road was a broken gate. It lay drunkenly against the gap in the broad stone walls. On top of the stone wall to the right of the gate were some loose stones. The manner in which these were placed told him whether it was safe for him to turn off further down the road or if it were better that he ride on.

It had all been easy because Anne could no longer question his comings or goings; she had no authority over him any more; she was, in a way, like an unpaid housekeeper carrying out her duties for which she received board and lodgings, and two gowns and two bonnets a year, besides free transport to Hexham whenever she wished to do special shopping. That she spoke to him civilly in company was, he knew, simply because she couldn't bear the real situation between them to be made public either in the village or in the town. Yet he felt in this direction she was deluding herself, for the fact that they had occupied separate rooms for years must have seeped out of the house.

Bella, Tessie, and Dandy, as loyal as they were, wouldn't have been human had they not talked about the situation in the house, particularly when the children were home from school, for then Hannah was allowed to roam free without let or hindrance, while the others came under their mother's strict surveillance with regard to holiday duties of reading and improving their accomplishments.

But now John was twenty and a promising engineer, and Robert, eighteen, had for the past year been working in the mine offices over at Allenheads; they could no longer be treated as schoolboys. Nor could Margaret, a young woman of nineteen, be tied to the house under the pretext of improving herself.

Margaret was of an independent nature and was definitely showing it at the present time by stating openly that she wanted to marry a bank clerk in Hexham. Well, everyone knew what bank clerks earned, hardly enough to keep body and soul together, but as her father he had spoken openly to her saying that if this young man would come and state his case honestly he would give the matter his attention.

Then there was Beatrice. Beatrice, Matthew was afraid, was the least loved of his children, at least by him, for she was too like her mother; in thought, word and deed they were almost a pair. But she, too, had left school last year. And now there remained only Hannah.

In the ordinary course of events Hannah would have left school at the end of the Easter term, but there was no ordinary course of events where Hannah was concerned, and the thought of what she might have to endure, being in the house all day with Anne, had made him arrange that she should stay on for a further year. He understood she was very expert on the pianoforte, and had a good singing voice, but strangely he had never heard her sing in the house, and only once had he seen her perform on the piano.

Anne's treatment of Hannah had to be witnessed to be believed. They could be in the same room together but Anne could act as if the girl weren't there; she appeared as insubstantial as vapour to Anne. He had never known her address Hannah openly; when she was forced to speak of her it would always be to a third party, when she would allude to her as *The Girl*. 'Tell *The Girl*,' she would say to Tessie, 'she must be ready at such-and-such a time.' 'Tell *The Girl*,' she would say to Margaret, 'she is not to chatter while walking behind me.'

'You are not to go on to the hills with *The Girl*,' she had said countless times to Robert, and that strange determined boy had sometimes just stared at her, and at others replied, 'Very well, Mama,' then had run out of the house and caught up with Hannah as she rambled over the fells.

Only once had he seen her lose control. This was when she pushed John to the door and cried at him, '*That Girl* has gone out. Go and tell her she is forbidden to go near the Ridleys'.'

How anyone could sustain hate at the pitch his wife had done all these years he was at a loss to understand, especially against someone as warm-hearted as young Hannah, for she was so grateful for the slightest kindness, so outpouring in her gratitude. As Bella had once said to him, 'She's the kind that would give you the clothes off her back if she thought it would help you.' But he had wondered if she would give the clothes off her back to the woman who had ignored her from the day she had laid the whip across her. What did Hannah think of Anne? He didn't know, but as generous as her nature was, it wasn't possible that she could harbour anything but loathing for the missis, as she still referred to her. And, strangely, she referred to him, too, in the same form; she never addressed him as any other but 'Mister'. But she could induce more feeling, more love into that one word than any of his children could with their 'Dear Papa's'.

What was he to do with Hannah? Well – he turned the horse into the gateway and up the drive – one thing he couldn't do with her, and that was to let her go on thinking there could be anything but brotherly affection between her and John. It was sheer madness on both their parts, more so on his, he being the elder by four years.

There were three horses attached to the household now, and when Matthew entered the yard the neighing from the boxes told him that both John and Robert had already returned home.

A few minutes later he entered the house, as usual through the kitchen, and after changing his boots and coat and washing his hands – he had soon taken up the old routine again, because as he put it to himself, he liked to eat clean – he went straight to the dining-room where the family were already assembled, and he greeted them as one, saying, 'Hello, I'm a bit late.'

'Are you very cold, Papa?'

He turned to his tall plain daughter and answered her homely smile with 'Frozen inside and out,' and he chaffed his hands and walked to the blazing fire. He had not openly addressed Anne, nor she him, but after a moment when he said, 'We'll be seated then,' he took his place at the head of the table, she at the foot, while John and Robert went to one side and Margaret and Betsy the other.

Betsy, like her mother, had little to say during meals, in fact she didn't utter a word during this one, yet her eyes darted from one speaker to the other as if she were about to contradict them, or at least answer them, but she refrained.

'I'll have to take Prince in to be shoed tomorrow, Papa.'

'It's no time since he was down there.'

'I know, but he's a kicker. I'm sure he likes to see the sparks flying off the stones.'

'You should get Mr Buckman to shoe him himself. Those boys pay no attention to their work.'

'Oh, Mama!' Robert jerked his head disdainfully. 'They've been at it since they could toddle; if they can't shoe a horse now they never will.'

'No one can do their work properly when they're half drunk.'

'May I have some more potato, Mama?' John handed his plate to his mother and she helped him; and as he took it from her, again he looked at his father and said, 'I shouldn't wonder we'll have snow before the morning.'

'We've got it now; it started as I came along.'

'I hope we have it at Christmas and it stays hard enough for sleighing.' Margaret smiled across the table at her brother. 'You remember last year on the knoll when I shot the ditch and scooted across the road?'

As the boys laughed Anne said, 'All very exciting, but you don't think that you could break your bones and be crippled for life.'

'Aw, nonsense!' Robert waved his hand. 'With drifts eight feet high on all sides?'

Matthew bowed his head over his plate and paid attention to his eating. If Anne and he had been living like real man and wife he would immediately have chastised Robert, saying, 'Don't speak to your mother in that manner, boy,' but he had left the bringing up of the children to her, and how they treated her he felt was the result of her training, or lack of it. Robert was a rebel, and had been difficult to manage since he was a child, and it had always been evident that there was no love lost between him and his mother.

John's approach to her was different. John was pliable, he did everything to keep the peace. His asking for another helping of potatoes a moment ago was an example of it. Margaret on the other hand had a bit of both Robert and John in her make-up. She wanted peace but not at any price. Margaret would make a stand for what she believed in.

Betsy, on the other hand, was her mother pure and simple. That phrase, he had always considered, was never applicable in the way it was used, and never was it less applicable when applying it to his wife, for Anne was neither pure nor simple, but her impurity was mental rather than physical.

The meal over, he rose from the table, saying, 'I'd like a word with you, John.'

'Yes, Papa.'

That was another thing. He would much rather have been called father, papa coming from the lips of the tall, blond young man seemed misplaced. But very likely he was the only one who thought so, for they were all so used to the title he didn't imagine they gave it a second thought.

In his study, he sat behind his desk, and John sat in the chair opposite him, and they exchanged glances of silent appraisal until Matthew said, 'You're twenty. My! my! I can't believe it, it makes me feel an old man.'

'Well, you don't look it, Papa; you carry your age very well.'

The reply which was meant to be reassuring caused Matthew to lower his head and grin to himself and John added quickly, 'What I meant to say was . . .'

'I know what you meant to say, John, but there's no use turning one's back on the fact. I am forty-five this year and once you reach this age it's only a jump to fifty, then a step to sixty, then a stumble to seventy.'

'Oh, Papa!'

'It's true . . . it's true, boy, life takes on a gallop once you've reached forty. I suppose it thinks, "Well, you've done your job, you've married, raised a family, what do you want time for now?" And that brings me to a point, raising a family I mean.' He wetted his lips, leant his forearms on the desk, bent his body slightly forward and asked quietly, 'Have you got marriage on your mind, John?'

'Marriage, Papa?'

Matthew watched the colour flooding over his son's fair skin; it even seemed to light a flame in his hair, or was that a trick of the lamplight?

'That's what I said. You've heard of it?' He pulled a face at his son.

'Yes, yes, I've heard of it.' John now rubbed the knuckles of one hand against the palm of the other, then said slowly, 'I . . . I haven't given it much thought.'

'No? What about Miss Pansy Everton? You've been seeing quite a bit of her over the past year, haven't you?'

'We've met occasionally.'

'Do you like her?'

'Oh yes, yes I like her, she's a very nice girl.'

'. . . But.'

'What? . . . What did you say, Papa?'

'I said but . . . but you hadn't any thought of marriage in your mind when you went courting her?'

'Courting her, Papa! I . . . I never went . . .'

'John. John, you know, and I know, that when a young man goes out of his way to see the same young woman a number of times running, that is a form of courting. And if you want my opinion you could do very much worse than court Miss Pansy Everton. Of course it's up to you in the end. I just thought I'd mention it to see which way the wind was blowing, and to know if one of the family was going to please their mother in their marriage choice, because by the look of it Margaret won't. And I think we all know that Robert will go his own road whether he chooses a barmaid or a baron's daughter. And that only leaves Betsy and Hannah. Betsy, I think, will follow her mother's choice . . . whereas Hannah. Well!' – he moved his head slowly – 'I myself will have to look out for Hannah. And I have somebody in mind. He's in quite a good position in the legal world. A bit older than her, but I think that's a good thing.'

Matthew felt a wave of pity sweep over him as he looked at his son. His fair skin had become a pasty white now. The grey eyes had darkened, the well shaped lips, more suitable to a woman than a man he had often thought, were dry and were moving over each other as if in search of moisture. He forced himself to say now, 'You don't look very pleased at your sister's prospect. I should have thought you would be happy for her to make such a good match.'

'You . . . you must be referring to Mr Walters, Papa. I . . . I don't see it as a good match. He is double her age. Moreover, he has been married before. His wife has but recently died.'

'I'm aware of all that, John, but allow me to know what is best in this case for Hannah. I've got no need to tell you what her life would be like if she has to spend it in this house, now have I? The situation should need no explanation. So, for her own happiness the quicker she is married the better, and I won't rest until I see her settled. Anyway, the intention of this little chat was to tell you that I would welcome Miss Everton as a daughter-in-law, and I think you'd be very wise to go ahead before someone else recognizes her value, because she's a very attractive girl.'

John made no reply, he just stared at his father for a moment, then without a word of leave-taking he rose, opened the door and went hastily from the room.

Matthew inserted his finger into his high collar and eased it from his neck. Sally was right after all. My God! what a situation? Well, there was one thing now he must see to, and quickly, and that was to get one or other of them married, and the sooner the better.

John at present was his best bet. That supposition about Arthur Walters had been nothing more than wishful thinking based on the few times that the solicitor had met Hannah. The last time was in the summer in the square at Hexham. He and John had been waiting in the trap for Hannah to come out of the haberdasher's, into which shop she and Margaret had gone to buy the ribbons and odds and ends that women buy in haberdashers'. While they waited Walters had passed and stopped for a moment, and as they talked the girls had come out of the shop and he had noted that Arthur Walters's eyes had dwelt on Hannah in warm appraisal.

But then most men looked at Hannah with warm appraisal, so why had his mind selected Walters? Because, he told himself now, Walters would be a very good match for Hannah. He was a fine-set-up young man; and hadn't he asked after Hannah only last week again, and this was another time when John had been present.

Anyway, if it wasn't Walters, it must be somebody and soon. If not, there was going to be trouble, and such trouble that would overshadow all that had gone before. He should, he told himself now, be thankful for one thing. Since Margaret had left school Hannah had only come home at holiday time, so the affair, if affair it was between John and her, couldn't have made all that progress.

Hannah's staying at school was the result of Anne's covert suggestion, and he had complied with it, not because he wanted to please his wife in any way, but because it saved him that weekly trip to Hexham in all weathers to bring her home.

# Chapter Two

'Good-bye, Miss Barrington.'
'Good-bye, Miss Rowntree.'
'Good-bye, Miss Emily.'
'Good-bye, my dear.'
'Good-bye, Hannah.'
'Good-bye, child.'

Miss Emily Barrington reached into the coach and tucked the rug around Hannah's knees, saying, 'Keep warm, and give our love to Margaret and all the family.'

'I will, Miss Emily, I will. A happy Christmas.'

A shout from the driver caused Miss Emily Barrington to step quickly back and allow the inn boy to lift up the step and close the door. Then the coach was off, and Hannah lay back smiling. She smiled at the other five occupants and they smiled at her; then she closed her eyes.

Wasn't it good of them, the two Miss Barringtons and Miss Rowntree, to come and see her off. If it weren't for one thing she could wish she were spending Christmas with them. Oh yes, she would love that, as she had loved every day she had been in their school. She knew that they marvelled at her love of school and her willingness to learn, even though there were some things she couldn't take in, such as higher arithmetic, or the rudiments of biology; nor was she outstanding in French; but she had made up for these deficiencies in embroidery and the pianoforte, and last year she had made great strides under Miss Emily in household management.

Yet not one of her dear teachers guessed that her love for their school had grown out of relief at not having to live continuously in her father's house. Not that she disliked her father. Oh no, far from it. She thought he was a wonderful man. And she thought of him as 'Father' even while she addressed him as 'Mister'. It was the missis, his wife, she couldn't bear to live with, the woman who had never uttered a word to her in years and would have paid more attention to a ghost.

It was during the last two years that she had ceased to fear her, and now very often at times she had to pray that the loss of her fear hadn't been replaced by hate, for only as recently as the summer holidays she had, on one occasion, experienced the awful desire to rush at the woman, grab her by the arms, and yell into her face, 'I didn't ask to come into your home! I was brought here. And after all he is my father, and I am his daughter and have the right to be treated as a human being.' Yet she knew that if she had been brave enough to carry out her desire, even if she had knocked her down, she would have risen to her feet, straightened her gown, looked through her and walked away without uttering a word.

How could anyone be so cruel? She could have forgiven her the whipping, but not the silence of years. What would happen when in the spring she left the school for good? The thought of having to spend her life under the shadow of that woman was creating nightmares in her sleep. The only escape would be marriage. But she would never marry. No; never, never. There was a great door locking that escape.

Oh, John! John!

When had she first known that she loved him and he her? In the spring when they had walked over the fells together? This time last year when she had slid down the bank into some bushes and he pulled her out and she had lain against him laughing, until his arms had tightened about her and she had looked up into his eyes, and he down into hers? No, no, long before that. She had known for years that she loved him. Even as a child her first thought when coming home at the week-ends had always been, I shall see John.

Not that she wasn't fond of Robert. Oh, she liked Robert very much . . . and Robert was always so good to her. He stood up for her even more than John did. John had never openly stood up for her, never openly defied his mother; but then John was possessed of a gentle nature that hated to hurt anyone, even his mother, although she felt he couldn't help but see her as a wicked woman.

What was going to happen between her and John? She didn't know, she only felt that it he didn't kiss her soon she would die. She dreamed of being kissed by him. That day by the hayrick, he had nearly kissed her, but a woman had appeared on the hill and spoilt it all. But if this snow were to lay and they could go off somewhere together on the sledge, then he might. Yes, he might.

She opened her eyes and looked out of the breath-smeared window. The coach had left the town but from its slow progress she guessed that the horses were finding the going very heavy.

And so must have thought the rest of the passengers, for now they were discussing the possibility of it ever reaching Haltwhistle. A more pessimistic traveller even wanted a bet they'd get no further than Haydon Bridge.

And this particular traveller proved to be right. The coach was over half an hour late when eventually they reached Haydon Bridge, and the carrier cart, which usually met it and took the by-road past Langley and over the crossroads up to Catton and so to Allendale, was not to be seen; likely buried in a drift in some ditch was the verdict. But another opinion was that they'd all be better off in the inn while they waited to see what was to transpire.

The inn parlour was packed, and Hannah sat on the wooden settle near the window, her valise at her feet. When one of the coach travellers offered to bring her a hot toddy she refused politely, saying, 'No, thank you; I had a hot drink just before we left. Thank you all the same.'

That was the strange thing about her education, and Miss Barrington had spoken to her openly of it, she still retained colloquial terms in her form of speech. On this occasion Miss Barrington would have said, 'You thanked them once, my dear, there was no need to repeat it by adding thank you all the same.'

It was half an hour later when the coachman came in and said he would take a chance and hope they would reach Bardon Mill, but should they all end up in the river not to blame him.

Warmed inside and out the travellers took their leave, all wishing Hannah a happy Christmas and a quick journey home.

When another fifteen minutes had passed and Hannah was beginning to feel the cold seeping through her brown caped coat, she wished she had accepted the proffered warm drink. She could, she told herself, go to the bar counter, but what would she ask for? Perhaps the innkeeper would advise her.

She placed her valise on the seat behind her, then threaded her way through the throng standing between her and the counter. Once there, she waited until she could attract the barman's attention, and when she had done so she leant slightly towards him and said in a voice little above a whisper, 'Could you recommend a hot drink, please?'

'A hot drink, miss? Well, yes, yes. What would you like?'

'I'll . . . I'll leave it to you.'

'Oh then' – he smiled broadly – 'I'll make up something that will warm the cockles of your heart.'

'Thank you. . . . Oh!' The last was a gasp as she was pulled round as a voice said, 'In the name of God! what you up to here?'

'Oh, hello Ned. Oh, I am pleased to see you.' Her smile was wide. 'I'm ordering a drink.'

'A drink? What you doing here?' There was no smile on his face.

'Well, I've just told you, Ned.' She was laughing at him now. 'I've ordered a hot drink.'

Ned looked from her to the barman, and the barman nodded at him, then pointed to the glass that was half full of hot water, and at this Ned said, 'Go canny.'

'Yes. Aye, aye, Ned.'

'Tell me, what you doing here?'

'Well, I came by coach from school and I'm waiting for the carrier cart.'

'Well, you'll have a long wait.'

'Why?' Her face became straight.

'It went into a ditch last night and broke the axle; not only that, it crippled the horse.'

'Oh dear! How shall I get to the town?'

'You won't, not by carrier, not the day.'

'Oh, but I must get home, Ned, I must, they'll be worrying.'

'Well, if there's no carrier cart running they'll know the reason why you can't get back. On the other hand, I can get you home all right if you can sit a horse.'

'Oh yes, yes, I can sit a horse. You know I can.'

'Half one.'

'Half one? What do you mean, Ned?'

'I've only got The Raker with me this trip; you'll be up afront of me.'

'Oh.' She bit on her lip, then laughed as she said, 'Well if the horse can bear it I can.'

'There you are, miss, get that down you.' She turned and thanked the barman, but when she sipped at the hot toddy she screwed up her face, swallowed deeply, then coughed and spluttered a little. The barman laughed, then looked at Ned as he said, ''Twasn't strong, Ned. 'Twasn't strong, honest.'

'I'll take your word for it.' Ned stared at the man for a moment, then added, 'But give me a strong one, straight, a double.'

'Aye, Ned.'

When the barman had pushed the double whisky towards him, Ned lifted it up, took hold of Hannah's arm and guided her towards a seat; but before sitting down she pointed, saying, 'I was sitting over there where my valise is.'

He now pushed her forward through the customers towards the settle, and as they sat down he said, 'Daft thing to do, leave your luggage to take care of itself.' Then after a pause he asked, 'Do you like it?'

'It's very warming.'

'It should be; that's what keeps sailors going at sea.'

'Really! Oh!' – she went to spring up – 'I forgot to pay the innkeeper for it.'

'Sit yourself down, that'll be seen to. . . . Are you hungry?'

'Yes, come to think of it, Ned, I am a bit.'

'Would you like a pie? Hot or cold?'

'Oh, a hot one, please.'

She watched him going towards the counter again and noticed that some men even made way for him, in fact all seemed to acknowledge him in one way or another, and she thought what a blessing it was she had come upon him.

It was very odd, when she considered, how Ned seemed to turn up at times when she most needed him. Nor was it the first time this thought had entered her head. The morning that she came upon him in the mist was as clear today as it was when it happened, in fact clearer, for then she hadn't been able to see his face distinctly. Was it all of eight and a half years ago? . . . And then again at the time of the thrashing. And there had been other times since then. The day she fell into the quagmire, when she could have drowned because Margaret hadn't the strength to pull her out. Ned had been making his way home, on foot this time, and rolling from side to side. He had been very drunk, but drunk or not he had come right to the end of the bog and almost slipped in himself, yet he had got her out. And he had taken both her and Margaret back to the Pele house where he had taken off her clothes and wrapped her in a blanket and sent Margaret running home to ask Bella, on the quiet, for a clean change.

She had liked his grandfather too. She was so sorry when he died last year. In the holidays she had gone up to the house to tell Ned so, and he had been abrupt with her, almost growling that he didn't want to talk about him. And she knew then that he was missing the old man very much, for now he had to live alone. All he had were his two dogs and the horses. But the horses came and went.

Years ago the missis had forbidden John, Margaret and Robert to go near the Pele house or to speak to Ned Ridley. She had no need to forbid Betsy for Betsy turned her nose up at the smell of the stable-room. But the order hadn't included herself, and so over the years she had spent quite a lot of time talking with Ned Ridley. She liked him, she liked him very much, although according to Betsy he was a very bad man: he not only boxed and ran cockfights, and had bouts of heavy drinking, but did other unmentionable things that could not be spoken of, things indicated only by deep obeisance of the head. Well, be what he may, she liked him; and she was more than pleased to be sitting with him at this minute.

She watched him now coming towards her. His thick black hair seemed to bounce on his head as he walked, and his deep brown eyes looked bright and merry. He had grown heavier during the past eight years, so that now at twenty-six a little of his litheness had gone. Although he was still slim-waisted and had no paunch he wasn't looked upon as the bare-knuckled battling boy he had been at eighteen. Yet she had heard Robert say that he was boxing better, he was more steady, that now he weighed things up and didn't barge in blindly. Robert liked going to boxing matches, John didn't.

There had been talk of Ned getting married last year to a girl in Sinderhope; then for some reason the wedding was called off. Apparently it had been Ned's fault because the girl's two brothers had waylaid him one night, and although he had beaten them off and left them both bloody, he had not got off scot-free, and it was some months before he could box again.

She could imagine him being very attractive to the girls, for apart from his prowess as a boxer he had a certain appeal about him. She couldn't put a name to it. It wasn't that he was handsome, though he was good looking in a sort of rough way. It was something in his eyes, she supposed, the way they would look at one, sometimes laughing, sometimes scornful, sometimes kind. . . . She was glad she had met him today.

It was after they had eaten the warm pies and Ned had finished his second double whisky, and had followed this with a whole pint of ale, that he grinned at her and said, 'Well, what about it, me ladyship? If we want to reach the castle before dark we must away to our mounts.'

She choked on the last mouthful of the pie and he, getting to his feet, said, 'Go on, go on, that's it, choke yourself.' And with this he thumped her on the back, which caused her to laugh all the more.

As they left the inn the innkeeper himself called after them, 'Bye, Ned. Take it slowly.'

'Aye, Sandy. Aye, I'll let her go her own gait.'

Out in the yard, he strapped Hannah's valise to the saddle; then putting his arms under her oxters, he cried, 'Hie-up there!' and with a great lift swung her on to the horse. The next minute he was seated behind her. His arms about her, he pulled on the reins, and the animal turned and walked out of the yard and on to the snow-packed road.

'It's a good job she's got a broad back. You all right?'

'Yes, Ned.'

'Like it?'

'Yes, yes, I do.'

'Good. Get up there, Raker.' He flapped the reins, and the horse quickened its stride but didn't trot. And so they went along at this pace, saying nothing for quite some way until Ned said abruptly, 'You'll be leaving that school next year, won't you?'

'Yes, Ned, in the spring.'

'What you gona do?'

'I . . . I don't know, Ned.'

There was another pause before he said, 'You'll likely get married.'

'Oh.' She gave a small laugh. 'I don't think so.'

'You don't think so? What you talkin' about? Of course you'll get married, a girl like you.'

When she made no reply to this he roughly demanded, 'What's up with you, don't you ever think about gettin' married? 'Tis natural, especially with someone who's got what you've got. . . . You know you're bonny, don't you?'

'It's nice of you to say so, Ned.' Her voice was low, her tone subdued.

'Aw, don't come coy, 'tisn't like you. You damn well know you're more than bonny, you're beautiful. You're the beautifulest thing in these hills, you know that. You know it fine well.'

'Aw no, I don't, Ned.' She bristled slightly within his hold.

'Well, if you don't, you damn well should do. Haven't you got a mirror in that house, or in the school? And anyway, good looking or not, the best thing you could do would be to marry. What's gona happen to you when the rest go? You lookin' forward to being left with her?'

'No, Ned, no, I'm not.'

'I should damn well say not. There should be a law against people like her, they should be put down, drowned when young, like kittens in a pail. The very sight of that woman makes me bile rise. You know what?'

'No, Ned.'

'I'll tell you somethin', 'cos she won't.' He laughed now. 'I always spit when I pass her. I do it on purpose, I just spit into the gutter. I hawk deep in me throat an' I spit.'

'Oh! Ned, you shouldn't.'

'Why shouldn't I? She's a bad woman that, Hannah, bad. An' dangerous. You know she's got a funny smell comes off her? I know about smells an' women. I think the devil must smell like she does.'

Again she said, 'Oh! Ned.'

He went on now as if talking to himself. 'It maddens me when I consider that the likes of she look down on me, it does. She used to put it round even when I was a lad that I was bad. If she hadn't been so badly liked people would've believed her. You don't believe that I'm a bad man, do you, Hannah?' He now bent his head down to hers, and when the smell of the spirits from his breath wafted over her she wasn't offended by it, but she laughed gently and said, 'You a bad man? Of course not, Ned. To me you're a fine man. Always have been.'

'Of course I'm a fine man.' He was yelling now as if to an audience, and when of a sudden he burst into song she leant her head back against him and shook with laughter, while he sang:

'I am what I am,
Look at me do,
For I am, believe it or not,
I am you.
Neither good nor bad,
Nor middling to best,
We are, you and me,
Like all the rest.'

And now he yelled even louder, 'All join in the chorus!' Then he was singing again:

'God help you,
God help me,
God help us all;
We were all quite decent
Afore the fall.'


When he finished they rocked together with laughter until they nearly slipped from the saddle.

Her face wet, she cried at him, 'Oh! Ned, you are funny.'

'Now I'm funny.'

'Yes, you are; you're the funniest man I know. And' – she turned her face half towards him – 'the nicest.'

Their gaze linked and held, hers open, frank with gratitude in its depths, his a mixture of hardness and sadness with desperate frustration in its depths.

'Sit straight,' he said, 'or you'll be out of the saddle.'

'Oh, I'm sorry, Ned.'

As the journey passed, she began to wonder if she had said anything to offend him because all his jollity seemed to disappear, and when she spoke to him he merely grunted.

When at last they reached the gate and he had lifted her down and unstrapped the valise she looked into his face and said quietly, 'Thank you, Ned. Every now and again in my life I find I have got to say "Thank you, Ned".'

When he made no comment but stood staring at her, she asked quietly, 'Have I said something to offend you?'

'Offend me?' His voice was high. 'Now what could you say to offend me? Perhaps you haven't noticed, I'm half tight.'

'Oh.' She laughed now, then said, 'No, I hadn't noticed; perhaps because I was the same; that was a very strong drink.'

'Aye, it was that; but it would have been stronger if I hadn't come in at the time.'

'You think so?'

'Sure of it.' He grinned at her.

'Well, that bears out what I say, Ned, you always turn up at the right time in my life.'

'Aye well.' He turned from her and gathered the reins in his hand as he said, 'I hope you noticed I brought you home the back way so to speak, for wouldn't the old wives' tongues have wagged to see you mounted afore me, and me three sheets in the wind, eh? An' you'd better not let madam know either or she'll have you cleansed as if you had the plague.' He stared at her for a moment before he added, 'I hope you have a good Christmas.'

'And you too, Ned. But perhaps I'll see you before then. We'll be on the hills sledging if the snow holds.'

'Aye, you might, you might that.' He mounted the horse, turned it about, then touched his forehead with his index finger by way of salute and rode off.

She watched him for a moment as he made the horse mount the slippery bank that led to the road that ran along by the cemetery wall, and she had a strong desire to shout after him, 'I'll come up to see you on Christmas Day,' because on Christmas Day he'd be alone and no one should be alone on Christmas Day. But she didn't shout after him, she turned in at the gate and went quickly up the snow-packed drive, and with each crunching step her heart began to race the faster, because within a matter of minutes now she'd look into John's face, and he would take her hand and the pressure of his fingers would tell her what his own heart was feeling.

## Chapter Three

'What is wrong, Margaret?'

Both Hannah and Margaret were looking down at the icy path as they picked their way towards the village square, and Margaret after a moment, only answered half of Hannah's question when she replied, 'It's Mama; she's forbidden me to even mention Mr Hathaway, but I've told her that if I don't marry him I shan't marry anyone. He came all the way here yesterday and Mama wouldn't see him. He couldn't go on to the mine to see Papa because he had to get back, he had only a day's leave and the transport is so uncertain.'

'Is that why you walked all the way into Allendale yesterday? I was upset because she wouldn't let me accompany you. Oh! Margaret.' She caught hold of Margaret's arm. 'Why didn't you tell me?'

'What good would it have done? And Mama forbade me to speak of it, and I couldn't have a word with Papa last evening because he was so late in coming home.'

'Everyone seems at sixes and sevens.'

'Yes, they do, don't they?'

They exchanged glances.

'Margaret.'

'Yes, Hannah?'

'John. Is . . . is he not very well?'

'In health, yes, but perhaps you didn't know.' Now Margaret's voice dropped to a muttered whisper and she seemed to give all her attention to where she was placing her feet as she went on, 'There's talk of him marrying Miss Everton. You remember Miss Everton, you must remember her, she was at school, but in a higher class. She is, I think, twenty-one now, but you saw her at the hill race in the summer?'

Hannah made no reply. She, too, was paying attention to where she was placing her feet, and Margaret went on, 'She's a very nice girl although high-spirited. Anyway, Mama is all for it, and Papa, too, I understand. Robert says that Papa is very much for it. Oh! be careful.' She put out her hand and clutched at Hannah's cloak. 'It's so terribly slippery. Are you all right?'

There was a long pause before Hannah replied, 'Yes; it's . . . it's the ice.'

'You are very fond of John, aren't you, Hannah?'

Again there was a pause before Hannah said, 'Yes, Margaret, I'm very fond of John.'

'Well, that's as it should be, he is your brother; at least your half-brother, you are of the same father.'

Their glances furtive now as if shame were being revealed between them, they turned from each other and neither of them spoke again until they reached their destination, which was Fred Loam's butcher's shop.

They scraped the caked ice from the insteps of their boots before mounting the two steps into the room with its sawdust-strewn floor, on which stood a small counter and a butcher's block.

Fred Loam, who had inherited the business at his father's death two years ago, stood behind the block. He was of medium height but looked taller because of his breadth. His shoulders were broad, almost making his back appear humped, and his hands, too, were large, and like the beef he was cutting, his face was of a ruddy hue, but its expression was pleasant. He was a pleasant young man altogether.

There was only one other customer in the shop and after Fred finished serving her he turned to the girls, saying brightly, 'Oh, there you are, and 'tis pleased I am to see you both. By! Hannah, aye, I can hardly believe it; you're grown nigh on a foot since the last time I saw you.'

'Well, not quite a foot, Fred, perhaps three inches.'

'Aw well, a foot or three inches, you grow bonnier.'

When Hannah lowered her glance and made no reply Fred turned to Margaret and, adopting now a polite business attitude, he asked, 'And what can I do for you this mornin', Miss Margaret?'

The distinction that Margaret was being addressed as 'Miss' and that the prefix had been omitted in Hannah's case was not remarkable, it had always been this way. Mrs Anne Thornton had always spoken of her family as Master John and Master Robert, Miss Margaret and Miss Betsy, but it was a well-known fact that she in no way acknowledged Matthew Thornton's bastard, so the villagers did not take it upon themselves to elevate the child to the same standard as her half-sisters. When small, they had called her Young Hannah, now she was simply addressed by her christian name.

Margaret answered the young butcher saying, 'Mother would like a chine of beef and a leg of pork, please.'

'Will that be all? She's not having a fowl?'

'We had one sent.'

'Oh!'

It was evident to Margaret that the news didn't please Mr Fred Loam and she added quickly, 'It was a gift from my mother's cousin.'

'Oh, a gift was it? Oh, well then, I hope it turns out to be tender. But as they say, don't look a gift horse in the mouth.' He laughed at Margaret, then turned his attention to Hannah again, saying, 'You won't be goin' back to school after this then, I suppose?'

'Yes, until Easter.'

'By! they'll have you so learned that you won't look the side we're on shortly.'

'Oh, I don't think that 'll ever happen, Fred.' She made herself smile at him and add, 'As you yourself would say, there's more brains in a sheep's head than in mine.'

'That I wouldn't. That I wouldn't.' He sounded indignant. 'Not when talkin' of you, I wouldn't. By! no. But the next thing we'll know' – he leant towards her now – 'you'll be gettin' wed, eh? Anyone in your eye?'

Hannah was saved from answering by the shop door opening at the same time as Margaret said, 'Thank you, Fred. We must be getting along.'

'Happy Christmas to you both.'

'Happy Christmas, Fred,' they both answered, and as they reached the door, he called, 'There's the big New Year's dance comin' off in the town, will we be seein' you there?'

'I . . . I don't think so, Fred.'

''Twill be a gay affair, country folk droppin' in. It won't be one of your club feasts; although I hold nowt against them if you want a blow out for nowt once a year. . . . It'll be a proper do.'

'I'm sure it will. Good-bye.' As Margaret went to close the door, his voice so loud now as though he were on the other side of the square from them, he cried, 'What about you, Hannah? I'd like to bet your feet can trip the light fantastic.'

Margaret gave Hannah no time to answer for she pulled the door closed so sharply that they could hear the bell still jangling when they were someway down the street.

'He takes too much on himself does Fred Loam.'

Hannah cast a glance towards Margaret. For a moment she had sounded just like her mother, and she answered quietly, 'He means no harm.'

'I don't know, his manner is much too free towards you. Pity his mother hadn't kept him in hand in the same way that she did his father, and everyone else for that matter who comes across her path.'

Hannah made no reply to this, although she thought it was good to know that Fred stood up to his mother. Mrs Loam was a little vixen. She wasn't five foot high but she had been known to bray her big husband around the upstairs rooms with a stick the morning after a drinking bout. Her antics had caused much secret laughter from time to time in the village, usually around the festive season, for she apparently had her own way of dealing with her husband when he came home the worse for drink. She would undress him, put him to bed, then withhold his clothes the next morning until she had lathered into him. But no villager had yet been brave enough to laugh in her face, for she could use her tongue as well as her hands. In a way Hannah felt sorry for Fred, as she had done for his father, for his father had always had a kind word for her, and even as a child he had told her how bonny she was.

'I'll be glad to leave the village.'

'What did you say, Margaret?'

'You are scatter-brained this morning, Hannah. I said, I shall be glad to leave the village.'

'I thought you loved the hills and all the country around.'

'I do, but the hills don't make the village; it is the people that make the village and they are so narrow in their outlook. They think and act differently altogether from those who inhabit the larger towns. They cling to their old customs. Look at what happens on hiring days in Allendale, with those travelling auctioneers, and the maids openly strolling about the town waiting to be picked by the young men. It's almost feudal. And they still have the fiddlers in the inns and dancing well into the night. Oh, and so many customs that could be well done without.'

'But I thought you liked dancing, Margaret.' Hannah was showing open astonishment at Margaret's attitude, which up to now she had considered so liberal.

'I do; but there is dancing and dancing and modes of conduct here that are so different from those in the town. You must have realized that yourself. Hexham is a different world. Don't you think so?'

'Yes, I suppose so; but only because of the buildings, I . . . I didn't find the people all that different. There are good and bad, nice and nasty, there too. You remember Miss Ormaston. She was a horrible creature. She was cruel to some of the girls and they were so afraid of her they daren't say anything. Then there was Brown, you remember Brown, the gardener who beat his wife so much he was taken to the Port House to answer a charge. I think people are the same all over, Margaret, some good, some bad, but most of them middling. As for customs, I like the old customs. . . .'

'Well! Huh!' Margaret gave a gentle laugh now and, her manner reverting to its usual pleasantness, she said, 'We are spouting wisdom this morning, aren't we? But I suppose you're right. It's only that . . . well –' Her voice dropped to a mutter as she ended, 'my heart's in the town. He's so different from anyone I've ever met. I suppose that's why I want to be there, I long to be there, and I view everything there in a different light.'

'I'm sorry, Margaret.'

Hannah now linked her arm in Margaret's, then said wistfully, 'Remember Miss Barrington? At the beginning of every term she would start her English lesson with, "Never think in clichés"; but I think some clichés are very true and apply to life, such as: The path of true love never runs smoothly.'

'Yes, you're quite right.' Margaret nodded at her and smiled. 'One thing I must say in truth, Hannah, and that is, when I do leave home for the town I shall miss you very much.'

'And I you, Margaret, because –' She paused and her lids shaded her eyes as she said, 'Above all you have been a comfort to me since I came into your home.'

It was the first time that Hannah had alluded to herself and her position in the family and now the words 'your home' embodied all her feelings with regard to the years she had spent in Elmholm House, for it had never been her home.

Silently Margaret gripped at the gloved fingers that were lying on her arm and together they went up the drive and into the house.

Christmas came and went without a great deal of jollity, and the New Year too was much the same. During the holidays they had spent a number of evenings playing card games but although on such occasions Anne Thornton was generally out of the room, the atmosphere between all of them was strained. Hannah hadn't had one minute alone with John, and as the time drew near for her return to school she had to face up to the fact that he was deliberately avoiding her.

It was the fourth day of the New Year. The men had all returned to work. Margaret was sitting at the writing table in the sitting-room penning a letter, while Betsy and her mother sat on a couch opposite the fire stitching at embroidery.

Hannah never went into the sitting-room when the missis and Betsy were there if she could help it.

Today she had been in the kitchen talking to Bella and Tessie for a long while. She liked talking to them, she felt at home in the kitchen. But she couldn't stay there for ever, so now she was sitting huddled up under the quilt in her room, and the cold was adding to her feeling of misery.

There was still a lot of daylight left that had to be filled and the sun was shining. She didn't want to read. She could wrap up and go out for a walk. Yes, that's what she would do. And perhaps she could call in the Pele house and see Ned. She had promised to go over during the holidays but she hadn't as yet done so, for she hadn't wanted to move away from the presence of John, not even for a moment.

She had no need to tell anyone she was going for a walk, she had come and gone on her own for years, and so, having put on a woollen jacket over her dress and a cape over that, she donned her close fitting bonnet and picked up the new fur muff the mister had bought her at Christmas, and went quietly down the back stairs, along the passage and out into the yard.

She gave Dandy Smollett a greeting as she passed the stables and he called after her, 'Nice to see the sun, Miss Hannah,' to which she answered, 'Yes, Dandy.' Then she went out through the gates, crossed the road and climbed the stile by the cemetery wall, then dropped into snow that almost reached her knees.

It was evident that no one had been this way for days for the path was almost obliterated, she was able to pick it out only by the lower level of snow on it compared with that on the banks.

As she struggled on she told herself that she had been stupid to come this way, she should have taken the main road for there the wind had cleared most of the snow into drifts leaving great patches of bare ground, still very slippery in parts but much easier to get over than the drifts.

When she reached higher ground she dusted the snow from her skirts and cloak and stood for a moment looking about her. The hills all around were bathed in a pale pink light that merged here and there into rose and mauve, which in turn faded away into lilac, to fall behind the horizon of the far hills in a soft downy grey.

The world was beautiful. She wished she were happy enough to enjoy it. What was to become of her? She was beginning to be worried more and more about her future. If only she were clever like Margaret and could teach. Yet she had no desire to inform. She could be a nursemaid. Yes, she supposed she could be a nursemaid. Yet she had no experience of little children, she herself having been the youngest in the household.

She walked on, slithering at times and once sliding on to her buttocks, where she sat for a moment laughing before getting up and going on again. Then there was Ned's house before her seeming to be rearing up out of the snow-covered hill on which it was perched.

She liked Ned's house, especially the rooms upstairs. These were full of curious things, all having been made by Ned's father, or his grandfather, or his great-grandfather: chairs, tables, cupboards, delf rack, pipe rack, even a wooden bed. Oh, the wooden bed was a fine piece of work. Instead of knobs at each corner it had birds carved from the wood. And everything was kept so clean. She was always astonished by the cleanliness of the upstairs rooms compared with the jumble in the kitchen behind the stable room, and the mass of oddments that littered the corners and hung from the walls of the stable-room itself.

She entered the gateless gap between the walls, crossed the yard, then knocked on the big oak door; but as she did so her eyes travelled to the lock. The chain was through the loop and fastened to the lock itself.

She knew a keen sense of disappointment and an emptiness as if she had suddenly been deserted by everybody in the world. She went round the side of the house and up the slope towards the narrow belt of woodland, the sight of which always brought back the distant memory into the present, and she could see herself again, running shivering through the mist towards the house and the figure of the man with the horses.

She skirted the woodland, and went walking towards the far hills, but when she came to the foot of them, she didn't attempt to climb them for in parts they were shining like sheets of silver, which meant ice, so she turned to the left and kept to the level ground which she knew would lead her to the road.

It was about half an hour later as she walked along the top of the bank, and again in deep snow, looking for an easy access down to the road that she saw the horseman coming out of the distance, and her heart gave a sudden jerk, then began to race.

John had seen and recognized her too, from a distance, and when he came level with her, where she was standing still and straight above him on the bank, he drew the horse to a stop and looked at her for a moment before asking, 'What you doing out here?'

'Just taking a walk. I . . . I was looking for a place to get down.'

He said nothing more but dismounted: then leaving the horse he looked to right and left before pointing and saying, 'I think there's a place along there.' And he walked back along the road while she walked along the top of the bank, and when they came to the dip in the bank he stood on what would have been the grass verge and held out his hands towards her.

Leaning forward, she gripped them, and when he said 'Jump!' she jumped, and he caught her, and as he had done once before he held her close, but not for as long as he had done on that other occasion. Then they were standing apart gazing at each other.

'You have been avoiding me, John.'

'No, I haven't. I haven't.' He shook his head quickly.

'Yes, you have. Don't bother to deny it.'

He now drooped his head deep on his chest and she watched his jaw bones moving in and out before he said, 'It's got to be this way, Hannah.'

'Yes, yes, I know, but . . . but you needn't have avoided me.'

'I thought it was best.'

'You . . . you are going to be married?'

His head slowly came up and he looked at her, his eyes full of sadness as he said, 'I suppose so.'

'Miss Everton?'

He made an almost imperceivable movement with his hands which he was holding gripped in front of him. It was as if he were attempting to unlock them.

'I . . . I hope you'll be very happy, John.'

'Oh, Hannah!' There were almost tears in his eyes now. 'If only things had been different, we . . . we could have come together. Yes, yes, we would. I would have run off with you, taken you away from the house and mother, taken you away to the ends of the earth.'

It sounded all very fanciful but it acted like a great warm poultice on her heart. She put out her hand to him and he clutched at it; then she said softly, 'I'm . . . I'm glad you told me, John, for I, too, would have gone with you to the ends of the earth, or followed you there. But as it is it can't be.'

'No' – he shook his head – 'it can't be, Hannah. But we have one comfort, we'll both have something to remember until the day we die. I shall never forget you, Hannah.'

'Nor me you, John.'

He let go her hand, took in a deep breath, and stepped back from her, saying, 'I . . . I must be on my way.'

'Where are you going?' Her voice was a cracked tearful whisper now, and he said, 'Back to the mine. I've been over to Allenheads with a message for Mr Sopwith. Good-bye, my dear Hannah.'

'Good-bye, John.' Their eyes held for a moment longer; then he turned abruptly and hurried back to where the horse was chaffing at its bit and pawing the ground with impatience. She stood where she was until he had ridden out of sight; then, the tears raining down her face, her head bent, she walked the two miles home at a snail's pace, and with every step she took she repeated and savoured every word he had said, because she felt she must imprint them on her memory for they would have to last her a lifetime.

That same evening Matthew arranged that he should be alone with his wife, as he did at times when there was something he was to demand of her that would brook no opposition and he had no wish to belittle her further before the family. He had sent Tessie with a message to ask her mistress to join him in the dining-room. He was standing when she entered and he did not ask her to be seated but came to the point straightaway. 'I would like you to know,' he said, 'that I intend to take Margaret and Hannah to a ball in Hexham, which is to be held a week on Friday. John and Miss Everton will likely attend too. I am hoping Margaret's suitor will be there so that I can take stock of him. It will also afford me the opportunity of ascertaining the correct nature of Mr Arthur Walter's feelings towards Hannah. As you know he is a solicitor of good standing in his early thirties; he lost his wife last year; I feel it is his aim to replace her as soon as possible.'

Anne Thornton stared at this man whom she hated with an intensity that was second only to the feeling that she had for *The Girl*, and now he was telling her he proposed to arrange a marriage for his bastard with a solicitor while his own daughter must be satisfied with a poor bank clerk, because all bank clerks were poor and would always remain so.

The unfairness of the situation, the injustice of it, was past understanding. There were times when she didn't think she could bear living under the same roof with this man for one minute longer, yet she calmed herself at such moments telling herself that her day would come. If God was just her day would come, and deep inside herself she believed firmly that it would. God in His justice and His mercy would not let the wicked conquer.

For eight years now she had lived under the pressure of a great insult; a personal indignity. Her husband, the man who should have protected her from jibes and ridicule, had exposed her to these things, not only from the villagers but from the townsfolk. No doubt they relished each new amour of his, for that he had carried out his threat to satisfy his lust elsewhere she had not the slightest doubt; but no one had as yet dared to hint to her who the recipients were.

When abroad, she held her head high and spoke only when it was necessary to give orders to shopkeepers. There were times she felt so lonely that she became desperate. She had only one friend in the world, and she was the parson's wife, Susanna Crewe. Not all her children even were true to her. Betsy yes; Betsy was the only one who really loved her. And John, yes; John esteemed her. But Robert and Margaret, no. About their affections she had never misled herself; they were too like their father to appreciate her. This being so, she should not in Margaret's case have worried about her choice of a suitor, and she wouldn't have, except that he was placing *That Girl* above his legal flesh and blood.

'They should have new gowns. It's short notice, but I suppose they could get something ready-made in Hexham?'

'And the money, where is the money coming from?' Her voice was thin and cold, her lips hardly moving as she spoke, the words coming like pressed steel from between her teeth. 'You informed me last month that the house expenditure must be cut.'

'I'm aware of that; and I was right to inform you when I saw an order for French preserves from the dairy shop in Hexham.'

'It was to be a gift at Christmas for Miss Everton, I told you.'

'Well, and as I told you, you could get something more substantial than a box of foreign sugared fruits for sixteen shillings. I understood you were making embroidery as a Christmas gift for her.'

Her full lips began to tremble as her face became suffused with a dark passion. Then turning her head slightly to the side, but with her eyes still riveted on him, she said, 'I can't stand much more of this treatment; I'm warning you.'

'Warning me? What of?'

'You will pay for your cruelty to me.'

'Cruelty? That's a strange accusation coming from your mouth, you to accuse someone else of an emotion that you are past mistress of!'

'You are responsible for any cruelty I have perpetrated.'

'No, no, Anne. No, no; I haven't got that on my conscience. I can pinpoint your acts of cruelty since the first year we were together, and towards me. Sadistic, I think, is the correct term for your attitude. Yes, sadistic. Remember the darning needle you drove into me hand . . . by accident? Why did you need to have a darning needle on the bedside table? Oh, I know it had dropped from your work basket, but even so why did you need to use it on me? I lost a lot of blood that night; it went through a vein. Look' – he extended his hand – 'see, it left that little spot. If ever my conscience pricks me for what I've done to you, I just need to lift my hand and look at that.'

She was actually talking through partially clenched teeth as she cried low at him, 'What chance had a woman to retain a vestige of dignity when dealing with a man like you? An animal would have had more control.'

'Oh my God!' He lowered his head and, swinging it from side to side, he laughed mirthlessly, saying as he did so, 'It's no good! It's no good! Oh, I wish to God you had married some men that I know of. Oh, I do, I do.' He was staring at her now, the smile still on his face. 'Still, you married me. Looking back, I didn't pick you, you picked me. As you once said, to make something out of me; and let's give credit where it's due, you did; you got me to buy this fine house; you got me to work from dawn on Monday morning till sunset on Saturday night. Oh yes, you made something out of me. And now' – the smile slid from his face – 'you are enjoying the results of your efforts. Well' – he turned from her now – 'I see no further need for discussion. I've told you of my plans, and don't attempt to interfere with them because it will be fruitless.'

After he had gone, closing the door none too gently behind him, she stood for a moment with her eyes closed, and her hands joined together in the hollow of her neck pressed so tightly on the bow of her bodice that the button behind it dug into her flesh, until she felt she was almost choking; and as she stood thus she prayed again, 'Oh God, act justly and let me see my day with him.'

# Chapter Four

None of Matthew's plans worked out as he had hoped. John and Miss Everton had not attended the ball, Miss Everton having already accepted an invitation for them both for that particular evening. Then Robert had only been induced to attend under pressure, because Robert didn't like dancing. But these were minor irritations; what were of a graver nature were, first, Margaret's suitor had not put in an appearance, and secondly his plan to ensure Hannah's future was doomed at the outset, for the first person they should see at the ball was Mr Arthur Walters, and he was accompanied by a young lady whom he introduced proudly as his fiancée.

If it had been at all possible Matthew would have bundled them all back into the hired coach that was to take them to their hotel for the night, but the coach would not return until half-past eleven. So for most of the evening he had to sit it out, for he himself was no dancer. He danced only with Margaret who had no names on her card and had to depend upon him and Robert, one being as club-footed as the other. But to Margaret it didn't much matter who partnered her, for her misery was deep.

Hannah on the other hand had five names on her card, which was exceedingly good seeing that most of the men were escorting their own partners.

As Matthew watched her being whirled around the ballroom, he thought she was by far the best-looking young woman in the room. And what was strange to him was, she did look a young woman; not yet seventeen she looked all of nineteen. He felt proud of her; guiltily he felt more proud of her than he did of Margaret. And that shouldn't be.

He had no doubt but that his wife was wallowing in satisfaction over the failure of his plans. Although he had said nothing to her – nor, he was sure, had Margaret – her divining sense was such that she would have known immediately that all had not gone right on the evening. . . .

As the weeks wore on, Matthew became troubled about many things. He was troubled about John, about Margaret, about Hannah. Oh aye, about Hannah.

Then there was the ever increasing worry about money. Three horses in the stable now to be fed and shod. It was true that both John and Robert subscribed towards their maintenance, but it made little difference to the overall expense. As children grew into adults they naturally ate more, and their clothes cost more. Then their school fees over the years had been a drain.

The way things stood at present there was a possibility he might have to take out a mortgage on the house. Of course it was no disgrace, but he had always prided himself on keeping clear of debt of any kind.

He needed comfort. He hoped the stones were in the right direction when he passed them this morning so that he could go over to Sally's tonight. It was only a week since he had last seen her, but oh, he needed her more than once a week, if only to lie against her and be soothed. . . .

As he rode out on this March morning the dawn was just lifting and the whole landscape as far as he could see was painted in silver. There had been a slight sprinkling of snow during the night and it had frozen, and now as the light became stronger the shimmering whiteness hurt his eyes, while at the same time he thought, The whole world looks pure, unsullied, as if it had just been born.

Along the road he passed several small groups of miners and all hailed him cheerfully.

'Grand morning, Mr Thornton.'

'Yes, Joe, grand, really grand.' Joe Robson was a good man, a God-fearing man, not in a chapel or a church sense, but in the right sense, commonsense and loyalty. Yet the eldest of his six children was along the line at the present moment doing six months for beating up a policeman in Hexham.

He came upon another group trudging along, the vapour from their nostrils sailing before them like a cloud. 'Mornin', Mr Thornton. Snifter, ain't it?'

'Yes, Bill, 'tis a snifter all right, but bonny.'

'You can keep your bonniness, Mr Thornton, an' send me home to me fire an' me bed.'

As Matthew laughed at Jack Heslop's remark, Bill Nicholson cried at his mate, 'You don't want your fire in your bed, man, you want your wife.' The joined laughter rang over the hills and followed Matthew along the road, and he repeated to himself, 'You don't want your fire in your bed, man, you want your wife.'

As the bend in the road brought him in sight of the broken gate where the stones lay, he saw two of his workmen walking away from the wall and up the hill. He recognized one as Frank Pearman, the other at first he could not distinguish, until the man turned round and looked down the hill towards him, when he saw that it was Tom Shields. He shook his head slightly to himself. They were a pair those two, prank players, like young lads. Only yesterday he had to pull them up. They were working on the new inlet and the richness of it had gone to their heads.

A few weeks ago, as was usual when breaking new ground, the men had formed their partnerships; some of four, some six, some eight, but these two stuck together, deciding as always to go it by themselves.

They had all agreed on the price per bing, and the veins they had struck weren't too bad at all, with more than ten per cent ore after the vein stone, soils and spars had been taken out of the bouse. As things went it was really very good for from the old veins they had been getting only five per cent ore. But these two, Tom Shields and Frank Pearman had started gabbing about who got the lion's share. Although in the main they were jokers, they could be agitators, and agitators today were fools with short memories. They should think back to '49 and the results of that strike. But there'd always be men like Shields and Pearman, half clowns, half knaves. . . . But why were they taking that road? Of course, it would cut off nearly a mile on an ordinary day, but to get over those hills this morning it would be two steps forward and one step back. Had they got a still some way over there? He wouldn't be surprised at anything those two would get up to.

He came opposite the stones and he smiled softly as he saw the direction in which they were pointing. Good Sally. Dear Sally. Comforting Sally. She must have been down early this morning in the dark or late last night.

The day seemed long and tiresome. John, getting his practice in on a surveying job with the head agent and chief engineer from Allenheads, had stopped on his way past and had a hurried word with him, beginning abruptly with, 'I don't seem to be able to talk to you in the house, Papa, so I'd better tell you that Pansy has consented to marry me and we shall announce our engagement at Eastertime.

'Good. Good.' He had put out his hand and gripped his son's arm. 'I'm happy for you; she'll make you a good wife. What do her parents say?'

'They seemed pleased.'

'Well, they should' – he had smiled broadly now – 'they're getting a fine handsome fellow for a son-in-law and one who is going to rise in the world, if I know anything.'

John had smiled, not unpleased with his father's flattery, then said, 'I must be off,' but as he turned away Matthew had asked quietly, 'Does your mother know?'

'I mean to tell her tonight.'

'She'll be pleased.'

They had looked straight at each other before John, his face solemn, moved his head once, saying, 'Yes, I think she will.'

Whilst standing looking after his son until he should disappear from view, Matthew had thought that once engaged John would soon go, for it wouldn't be a three to five year engagement with her. And Margaret too could go at any time, out of compassion for her suitor if not out of love, his daughter being consumed with both. Apparently the young man hadn't turned up at the ball simply because he couldn't afford the dress for such an occasion. Shortly after the miserable night she had received a letter that should have reached her before she was due to leave for Hexham, explaining his reason for not attending her. He seemed forthright if nothing else, this poor bank clerk.

Then Hannah would follow. Somebody was bound soon to snatch Hannah up; the only question that troubled his mind was, who?

All this pointed to the prospect of him being left in the house with only Betsy and her. And what of the day when even Betsy would be persuaded to leave her? What would happen then? He had not taken Robert into account, for he wouldn't be a bit surprised if one morning there was a note from Robert saying he had gone to sea, or joined an expedition of some kind or another.

As he rode away from the mine in the gathering dusk, calling out good-nights here and there, he thought how wonderful it would be, how easy and how uncomplicated life would be if he were going home to Sally, even to that little cottage where the fire was always bright and the kitchen table scrubbed white, and the stone floor kept so clean that, as she so often said herself, you could eat your meat off it.

Before reaching the stone wall he had turned up a bridle path and into the hills. He always made sure before leaving the road that there was no one coming towards him or following on behind.

As he neared the cottage he always experienced a stir of excitement in his stomach. Tonight it was intensified by the lamplight shining from the window.

He put the horse into the lean-to shelter that was supported by a stone wall, unrolled a blanket from the saddle and put it over him, patted him twice on the rump, then went towards the light.

Lifting the latch of the door he went in calling softly, 'Sally!' Then again 'Sally!'

Then he saw her. She was standing near the open doorway leading into the little bedroom; her fingers were spread across her mouth, and as she stared at him and muttered, 'Oh my God!' she was pushed aside and a man came into the room. He was of medium height, but heavily built. His hair was cut short and stood up from his scalp as if each strand were a piece of wire. And his moustache looked as stiff. After staring at Matthew he turned and looked at his wife; then walking slowly towards Matthew he said, 'Aye, aye! And what can I do for you, mister?'

'I . . . I was just passing. My . . . my wife asked me to call in and see if . . . if Mrs Warrington –' He inclined towards Sally as he swallowed a dobble of spittle, then went on, 'If . . . if she could come and give her a hand.' Some part of his mind was registering amazement at the ease with which he was adapting to the situation, until the man spoke again.

'Give her a hand? Your wife sent you to come and ask me wife to give her a hand?' The man stared at Matthew through narrowed lids and, his lower jaw thrust out now, he said, 'You come into my bloody house without a knock or by your leave, you call my wife Sally as if 'twasn't the first time, an' as far as I know, mister, me wife's never been out helpin' anyone, top, middlin' or low. I married a woman who would be here when I got back, not one to be a skivvy, so now' – his voice rose to a bawl – 'who the bloody hell do you think you're hoodwinkin'? What's been goin' on here?' He jerked his head and glanced back at Sally, where she was standing with her two hands gripping the front of her blouse. Then his voice almost reaching an hysterical scream, he cried, 'Bugger me eyes! I see it all now. Aye, aye! I see it all now. You bitch you! You've had little to give me 'cos you were empty. By God! I'll murder you for this, I will.'

As Matthew was about to speak, Sally, pulling herself together, yelled in her turn at her husband, crying, 'What you on about Bill Warrington, with your mucky mind? The truth is Mr Thornton saved me from drowning once. I didn't tell you 'cos you wouldn't have been interested. And over the years he's looked in once or twice, that's all. An' you speak to him like that.'

The man now stared at her, not knowing whether to believe her or not, and she went on, 'You should be ashamed of yourself. We have few callers here, God knows, and when anybody comes you insult them. An' a man like Mr Thornton an' all?' She now turned to Matthew and said, 'I'm sorry, Mr Thornton. Go on your way now, an' don't look us up again, not after this reception.'

Looking at her, and picking up the signal from her sad, frightened gaze, Matthew said, 'Yes, I'll be on my way. I am sorry I intruded. Good-bye, Sally.'

In the emotion of the moment she forgot her little bit of play acting and, her voice low now, she said, 'Good-bye, Matthew.'

As the door closed behind Matthew, Bill Warrington turned on her. He didn't yell now but he seemed to blow the words through the straggled hairs of his moustache, saying, 'Matthew! Good-bye, Matthew! You loose, lying bitch! . . . Come to ask you to go and help his wife? I know what he come to ask you for. I was right.'

Before she could speak or protest in any way, his fists shot out, first his right and then his left, full into her face.

He did not even stoop over her when she fell but, picking up the poker from the fireplace, he went to the door and, pulling it open, he ran out into the night and towards where he could hear the jingle of harness and the snorting of the horse.

The first time Matthew regained consciousness he thought he was dead and had dropped into the bowels of hell, except that hell, as he understood it, was a place of warmth, and wherever he was there was certainly no warmth, for his body was so numb he could scarcely feel it; in fact, at first he thought that his head had been separated from his body. He had no idea where he was and that the sound of horses' hooves on the ground somewhere above him were part of the shivering nightmare.

The second time he came to himself he opened his eyes and saw the stars shining brightly in the black sky. And now he put his hands out and groped about him; but when he went to raise his body the agony in his head was so intense that he fell back and lay still

He had to make a number of efforts before he was finally able to turn on to his hands and knees, and when by clutching at the earth to the side of him he was able to stand swaying on his feet, he could make out the road level with his chin. He had been lying in a ditch.

He did not know how long he stood supporting himself and staring blankly at the frozen black earth before his eyes, but it was some time before he could gather enough strength to pull himself up on to the road. But once there he found that without support he was unable to stand.

On his hands and knees again, he peered about him. He guessed he was on the coach road, but on which part of it and how far from home he was he had no idea; nor did he know which direction he should take to get there. It was as he knelt thus that the sound of horses' hooves came to him again, and when he went to shout 'Help!' and there merely issued from his throat a croak, he experienced a sharp shivering fear.

He seemed to be in a direct line with the oncoming animal and he raised one hand as if to protect himself, and again he attempted to shout, but the effort was too much for him and he fell on to his side.

Then it seemed to him that in the next minute he was being hoisted to his feet, and he heard Robert's voice and that of Fred Loam exclaiming over him, Robert saying, 'Papa! Papa! Oh! thank God,' and Fred using stronger language, his voice loud, as he cried, 'What a bloody mess! He's been done over. Hold the lamp up, Mr Robert. This is the second do of late. There was that one down near Catton last week, but there they took the horse, 'cos that's what they were after. . . . He can't sit; we'll just have to put him over the saddle.' . . .

When Matthew next came to himself he was warm, in fact hot, sweating. He did not open his eyes immediately but lay feeling safe, knowing that he was in bed, but also aware that his head ached with such intensity that he felt he couldn't bear it and begged to drop off into unconsciousness again.

'Papa, are you awake?'

With an effort he lifted his lids and peered at Margaret.

'How are you feeling, Papa?'

He made no reply but moved one dry lip over the other, and when he felt the spout of the feeding cup he sucked at it. Then after a moment he asked faintly, 'Time? What time is it?'

'Eleven o'clock . . . in the morning. Oh, Papa – ' she bent over him, tears running down her face – 'I'm so glad . . . that . . . that you are home. Oh, lie still, don't move.' She put her hand on his shoulder. 'Doctor Arnison will be in shortly again.' She sat down now by the side of the bed and held his hand. 'We were so worried when Bob came galloping back on his own; everyone was worried, all the villagers. The men went out . . . and the miners too, they think so highly of you, Papa.' Her tears choked her voice, and he patted her fingers gently; then after a moment he asked, 'Where . . . where did they find me?'

'On the main road, near the creek. You must have been lying in the ditch because John and Mr Wheatley had been along that way twice earlier in the night.'

'In the night?'

'Yes' – she nodded at him – 'it was on two o'clock this morning when they came across you.'

Two o'clock. His mind was working slowly. How long had he been lying in the ditch? She said it was near the creek, but why was he lying in the ditch near the creek?

Slowly a picture began to form in his mind, and he saw Sally standing in the doorway with the man behind her. But he had left the cottage unharmed? The picture became clearer. He had his foot in the stirrup when he felt the man behind him; he hadn't time to turn. He could remember nothing after that except the sound of the horses' hooves and the sudden fear that he was going to be trampled on.

But why was he at home, Bill Warrington? Sally had never made a mistake in all the years they had been together. She had timed her husband's comings and goings accurately, and he had read her signs accurately. The sign yesterday morning had said all was clear. Behind his closed lids he saw the wall again and the arrangement of the stones. Then another picture was interposed on the wall and he saw the figures of the two miners climbing the hill, the slippery hill, the road that would take them much longer to get to the mine than would their usual route. Who were they, those two? His mind began to grope throught the muzziness of his thoughts. He knew them, he had been thinking about them as he watched them disappear. Yes. Yes, of course, Shields and Pearman, the jokers, the vindictive jokers. Did they realize what they were doing? Had they thought of what the consequences might be? Did they imagine for a moment that Bill Warrington would touch his forelock and say, 'Carry on, sir. Take your pleasure.' Why did people act so? Why? Why? Damn silly question; need he ask? They were getting their own back because he had warned them about their agitating. And another thing, they must have known about him and Sally. Good God! and he'd thought he'd been so clever all these years.

His head was buzzing; he was very hot; his body seemed on fire and his head twice, three times its size, so big that he imagined it was spreading over the pillows. . . .

His next lucid thought was, just wait till he got back, he would sort those two out. By God! he would, if it was the last thing he did.

I could have died. I could have died. I could have died. Why did he keep saying that? He was very hot, and so thirsty, and his head ached.

I could have died. I could have died. I could have died. The lamp was lit, it was night time. Where had the day gone?

'Am I dying, John?'

'No, Papa, no, of course not. You've caught a chill.'

Day and night seemed all mixed up. It was no sooner daylight than they lit the lamp again. But his head no longer ached; he just felt very hot and his throat was sore and it was difficult to breathe. But he was glad that his head was better, for that pain had been dreadful.

'Do you think I'll pull round, Robert?'

'Yes, yes, of course, you will, Papa. Of course. You must pull round, Papa. Oh, you must.'

'Hello, Hannah.'

. . . 'Hello, mister.'

'Now, now, Hannah, don't . . . don't cry.'

'All right, I won't if you promise not to talk.'

'Doesn't . . . doesn't matter, Hannah, if I talk or not, makes no difference now. What time is it?'

'Three o'clock.'

'In the morning?'

'Yes, in the morning.'

'Where is everyone?'

'John and Margaret have just gone downstairs to make a drink. Robert is resting in my room.' She nodded towards the communicating door.

'My . . . my wife?'

' . . . The missis is resting in her room. She . . . she is very tired.'

'Very tired. Very tired . . . Hannah.'

'Yes, mister?'

'Hannah, say father. . . . '

. . . 'Father.'

'Now, now dear, don't . . . don't cry. You know something? I'm . . . I'm feeling much better, stronger.'

She couldn't speak for a moment; then her voice almost of a like croak to his, she said, 'Oh . . . oh, that's wonderful.'

'Will . . . will you do something for me, Hannah?'

'Yes, mister . . . father, anything, anything.'

He made a movement as if to turn on his side but the effort seemed too much and he lay gasping for a moment before going on, 'Will . . . will you take a message to a woman, a friend of mine? She is called Sally, Sally Warrington. She lives in Lode Cottage. You know . . . that way . . . between the creek . . . and the mine. . . . In . . . in the bottom of the wardrobe' – he lifted his hand slightly from the coverlet in the direction of the big Dutch cupboard taking up almost one wall of the room – 'under . . . underneath the end board you'll . . . you'll find a bag. Twenty . . . twenty sovereigns . . . in it. I want you to take them . . . to her. It . . . it might help her . . . to get away, and . . .'

A bout of coughing racked his chest and cut off his words, but lifting his hand now well up above the coverlet he stabbed his finger towards the wardrobe again, and Hannah went hastily to it, opened the door, thrust the hanging clothes to one side, then stooping down, she groped at the boards. But they all seemed nailed fast until her fingers slipped over the edge of the last one. Pulling the single board away from its resting place, she bent sidewards and felt underneath it until her fingers came in contact with a small leather bag.

But at the bedside once more, she extended her hand holding the bag towards him, and he nodded at her, saying very slowly now, 'Hide it until . . . you . . . you find an opportunity to go over. Tell her I . . . I thought of her. You'll . . . you'll do this for me, Hannah?'

'Yes, yes, of course. Anything, anything.'

'She was a good friend to me . . . you understand what I mean?'

She stared down at him for a moment before she nodded slowly. Yes, she understood what he meant. The woman had been the kind of friend to him that her mother had once been. She didn't blame him. No, no, not at all, she didn't blame him. Having a wife such as the missis, he would have to find comfort of some sort.

When she heard the sound of footsteps on the stairs she slipped the bag down the front of her bodice and if fell between her breasts.

When John and Margaret entered the room she moved aside, and John, after looking at his father for a moment, turned swiftly to Margaret and whispered, 'Go and bring Mama.'

As Margaret hurried from the room Hannah went to the other side of the bed, and bending over Matthew, she gathered his limp hand between both her own and, bringing it to her face, she rubbed it gently against her cheek. She could not see him because her face was awash, nor could he see her because he had closed his eyes; but he was still breathing.

She was standing well back near the dressing table when Anne Thornton entered the room followed by Margaret and Robert. She did not wait to see the parting between the husband and wife but went quickly out and into her own room.

The mister was dying. Her father was dying. The man who had wrecked his marriage, and even his family life, by harbouring her was dying. She owed him a debt that she could never repay. For years now she had wanted to repay it in love but she'd had to restrain herself, not only because of his wife but because of his younger daughter. The others would have understood and accepted the affection she had longed to show.

She lit the candle on the small table, then sat down on the edge of the bed. She supposed she should pray but she couldn't, she could find no words with which to communicate her sorrow with the God who ruled life and death.

She sat for a long while perfectly still, how long she didn't know, she only knew that she was aware of the moment of his passing, and she turned now and fell on to the bed and smothered her weeping in the pillow.

It was some long time later when she pulled herself upright and, staring before her, whispered to herself, 'Oh! Mister. Mister. What will happen to me now, now you are gone?'

# Chapter One

## The Girl Married 1859

'Mama.'

'Yes, dear?'

'I saw her talking to Fred Loam again; they were standing openly in the square. That must be the third time this week.'

Anne Thornton slowly lowered the small embroidery frame on to her black-draped knees and after sticking the needle in the canvas she raised her hands, which were partly encased in hand-done fine black-thread mittens, and laying them one on top of the other on her chest she sat silently looking at her daughter.

They were both encased in black from head to foot. Betsy's black cap was a replica of her mother's, the mittens also; only her dress was slightly different.

Anne Thornton's voice was low as she asked now, 'Did you bring up with Margaret the subject of what transpired at the ball?'

'Yes, I did, Mama, but you know Margaret, she accused me bitterly of talking of balls, and Papa so recently gone.'

Anne Thornton turned her head slowly and looked through the gloom of the room towards the window where the blind was still half drawn, and the fingers of one hand began to tap the other rhythmically. She knew that things had not gone according to her husband's plan on the night of the ball. But she didn't know whether his disappointment was because Margaret's suitor had failed to materialize – this was all she could get out of Robert – or Mr Walter's interest in *The Girl* had for some reason flagged. What was troubling her though was the possibility that the solicitor, hearing of her husband's death, might turn up on the doorstep and ask for the hand of that creature. They might have been meeting during her last term at school; how was she to know!

That her husband's flyblow should ever attain the position of a solicitor's wife in the town of Hexham, while her own daughter might, if she herself did not put a stop to it, become the wife of a mere clerk was unthinkable. The idea wasn't to be borne.

She rose abruptly to her feet now, upsetting the frame, and when it fell to the floor Betsy stooped quickly and picked it up. Then they were standing face to face.

'I want you to go down to the shop and . . . and say to Mr Loam that I wish to see him. Should he enquire why, say it is a private matter.'

'Yes, Mama.' Betsy's face was bright.

'Go at once; you'll likely catch him before he goes off to Allendale for a killing, it being Monday.'

'Yes, Mama.'

Anne Thornton watched her daughter almost scurrying from the room. She knew that Betsy would be as glad to see the back of *The Girl* as she was. But glad was an inadequate word to express her feelings, for she didn't want to see the back of *The Girl* altogether, she wanted to be in a place of observation from where she could witness her humiliation, and what she had in mind now would go a long way towards bringing this about.

Fred Loam, she considered, was an ignorant, gormless young man, and his wife, whoever she should be, wouldn't have only him to deal with but his mother also. . . . Oh, his mother! If ever there was a vixen in this world it was Mrs Loam; and she had it in her heart to pity anyone doomed to become her daughter-in-law . . . that is with the exception of one person.

She had a mental picture of the enjoyment she would derive from observing the suffering of *The Girl* under the domination of that coarse, loud-mouthed little tartar, not to mention what she would endure, literally, under Fred Loam's hands.

How she hated that girl, for it was she who had ruined her life, it was she who had bred in her a devastating hate for her husband; and hate him she had, right until the end when, with his eyes open, he had looked at her as he drew his last breath. She hoped, she prayed, that his Maker was dealing justly with him at this moment. That being so, she could see him being made to suffer for a long, long time, as she had suffered for years. Dear, dear Lord, and how she had suffered lying in that room alone, deprived of the companionship that a wife should expect from a husband; companionship that had nothing to do with the demands of the body.

She imagined now that before *The Girl* had come on the scene a strong mental and spiritual companionship had existed between them. She told herself from time to time that they might have had slight differences of opinion now and again about certain things, but that was all; otherwise all had been harmony for those first thirteen years of her marriage.

But now he was gone, and if she had hated him in life she hated him more now, for he had left them penniless. He had left no will, at least none that could be found. Anyway, he had nothing to leave except the house, and by rights that should have gone to John; but John in his generosity had said he would pass it on to her legally, for when he was married he would live in his wife's home, as least for a time. The farmhouse was large and his future in-laws had shown a preference for him to live with them.

So she had the house; but how was she to keep it up? Last week she had heard from Mr Beaumont to the effect that he was allowing her a pension of a guinea a week; which she considered a very mean gesture. How was she to exist once John and Robert had left home? She wished it was Robert who was marrying, then she could have been sure of John saying, 'Don't worry, Mother, I will support you;' but not so Robert. She and Robert had never seen eye to eye; in fact, there was a dislike in her for him, and she was sure he reciprocated the feeling.

But first things first; she must get that *Girl* out of this house. If it wasn't for the outcry that would have been raised against her by her sons and Margaret she would have turned her into the street on the day of the funeral.

Her feelings now drove her from the room and into the kitchen. She still put no check on *The Girl's* movements but she wanted to know where she was, and when she returned from one of her rambles she usually entered the house by way of the kitchen.

The kitchen was empty except for Bella, and she passed her without a word, which wasn't at all unusual, went through into the yard and towards the stable as if she were looking for Dandy. Then as she was about to enter the kitchen again, she saw Betsy hurrying towards the front door.

Betsy, catching sight of her mother, came into the yard and as they met, she whispered excitedly, 'I just caught him going out. He's coming, Mama; he should be here any minute.'

Anne Thornton gave two small coughs, looked back towards the kitchen door, then walked on to the drive, saying softly, 'Wait on the step for him, then bring him straight into the sitting-room.'

'Yes, Mama.'

It seemed that she had hardly composed herself in a chair with her back to the light, arranged her skirts, and taken up her embroidery frame, before the sitting-room door opened and Betsy entered, saying in a stage whisper, 'Mr Loam to see you, Mama.'

'Come in, Fred.'

'Good-day to you, ma'am.'

'Good-day, Fred.'

He was standing awkwardly in the middle of the room, his cap in his hand, and she did not ask him to be seated but, adding another stitch to the embroidery, she kept her eyes on it as she said, 'May I ask you a personal question, Fred?'

'A personal question, Ma'am? Ask me what you likes an' I'll answer.'

'Have you ever thought of getting married?'

His silence brought her head up to see him gaping at her, and when she realized how he had taken her question she felt inclined to spring up, crying, 'How dare you! To think I should suggest such a thing to you of all people, you must be mad!' Instead, she said stiffly and quickly, 'I wondered if you had any idea in that direction concerning my' – how could she describe *The Girl?* She found the word that was non-committal 'my ward?'

'You . . . you mean Hannah, missis?'

She saw his shoulders sink downwards as he spoke.

'Yes.'

'You mean thoughts of marryin' her?'

'Yes.'

'Aye, begod! Well – ' He was now turning his cap around rapidly between his hands while his head swung from one side to the other and the beam on his face seemed to spread down into his thick neck; then his head becoming still, he looked at her and asked, 'You'd allow it?'

'Yes, I would allow it.'

'My! Well! . . . Well, if I've got your go-ahead. Eeh! mind, I'll tell you this, missis. I've thought about it, an' not once or twice either, but I never dreamed. Well, I thought you'd have other ideas for her. Even as things stood an' you didn't care a . . . ' He broke off abruptly and his head drooped once more, to be brought up with startling suddenness as she said, 'You have my permission to marry her as soon as you think fit. You need not consider any disrespect to her father. There are to be changes made in the house and her marriage will be the first of them.'

'Have you spoken to her? Does she know?'

She looked directly at him as she replied, 'She will do what she is told and be grateful.'

His face was solemn now as he said, 'Well, all I can say is thanks, missis, an' I only hope she sees it like you said.'

'Good-day, Fred. I shall leave the rest to you.'

'Thanks, ma'am.' He stood a moment longer before turning about and walking straight and steadily from the room.

## *Chapter Two*

It was a lovely day, a day for walking. The sun was bright but not warm; there was a pale mauve light resting on all the hilltops, but when you looked up into the sky your eyes were lost in a never-ending whiteness through which you could see right to where the stars were.

Twice within the past three weeks she had set out intending to deliver the mister's last message to the woman in the cottage. The first time, she took the wrong road and wandered about for hours and only just managed to get home before dark. The second time, she was caught in a hail-storm. But today, she was on the right road.

Yesterday she asked Ned where the cottage lay, and after describing just where she must leave the main road in order to reach it, he had asked, 'Why do *you* want to go to Sally Warrington's?' And she had been evasive, saying, 'No reason.' Then under his stare she had muttered, 'I . . . I have a message for her. You . . . you won't say anything, will you, Ned?' and his reply had been characteristic; 'Say anything? What's it got to do with me?'

And now she could see the cottage, and there was a woman outside, a bucket in her hand; and she had seen her, too, and was waiting for her coming.

Hannah stopped by the gate in the wall, and the woman stood beyond it, and they looked at each other.

'Are you Mrs Warrington?'

'Aye, yes, I am.'

'May I have a word with you?'

Hannah noticed that the woman seemed to weigh up in her mind whether or not to reply; and then she said abruptly, 'Come in.'

Hannah followed her into the cottage, and when the woman pointed to a seat and herself took one opposite, she tried not to look at her face, for it was so discoloured. Not only were there purple hues around the eyes but the top lip showed a scar where a cut had been, and one side of her face looked bigger than the other.

'What did you want to say to me?'

'I have a message for you from . . . from my father.'

It was the first time she had said those words aloud and she gave a little shiver as if she had received a cold douche.

The woman's head was bent and she didn't speak for some time; then, her voice scarcely above a whisper, she said, 'What did he say?'

'He . . . he said I had to give you this.' She now opened her cloak, put her hand down the front of her bodice, and brought out the small leather bag, which she handed to the woman.

Sally looked at it for a long moment before taking it, saying, 'What is it?'

'It's . . . it's money. He thought you would need it. It . . . it might help you to get away, he said.'

'Oh my God!' Sally dropped the bag into her lap, then covered her distorted face with her hands, and when she began to cry the sound filled the room and her choked words spilt from her bruised lips. ' 'Twas my fault. 'Twas my fault. But he should swing. He should, he should. 'Twas murder, but who's to prove it. He was far away in Hexham next morning. He's got those who'll swear to it. But he did this 'fore he left. Twice he went at me.' As she touched her streaming face gently with her fingers Hannah rose from the chair and went towards her and, putting her arm around the woman's shoulders, she said, 'Don't. Please don't cry like that.' Yet she herself was crying now unrestrainedly, as she had not cried since the time Matthew had died.

By way of comfort she said quietly, 'He . . . he cared for you; he had great concern for you. There are twenty sovereigns in the bag. It . . . I think it was all he had of ready money. He did not leave any.'

Sally gulped in her throat, then muttered, 'He left no money?'

'No, only what was due to him in his wage. But he . . . he wanted you to have this; he seemed anxious that you should get away.'

'Oh. An' God, how right he was! Oh, lass, the thought's never left me head but to get away, nobody knows, but I had nothin'. Your father was always generous, but at times I wouldn't take it 'cos I was feared he, me husband, would find it. So when I went into Newcastle twice a year at the hirings an' then the cattle-shows I . . . I went to me sister Lizzie's an' give her what I'd got 'cos she's got a big family and is hard pushed. She would have taken me in now but I wouldn't go empty-handed. But now, oh this, this!' She hugged the bag to her; then, shaking her head, she said, 'He was a good man, a wonderful man, an' I'll say it without shame, I loved him, I did.' She stood up now and gently wiped her face, then said, 'Can I get you a cup of something, soup or milk?'

'No thanks; I'll . . . I'll be on my way. May I ask if you'll be going to your sister's now?'

'Aye, lass, I'll go.' Sally's voice was deep now and held a strong note of bitterness. 'Aye, I'll go. An' you know somethin'? I'll go this very day 'cos he's away over the border and won't be back for two days. Once there, I can lose meself in the city. Me sister Lizzie 'll fix it. And I've got enough now to pay me way till I get work. I can be away afore dark for I've got little belonging to me except what I stand up in an' a change of shift and a frock an' coat. The lot wouldn't make a decent bundle. Aye, lass, I'll go this day. An' thank you, thank you for comin' and bringin' me his message.' She shook her head at this point, saying, 'I've got one regret, an' that is I couldn't have been with him at the end, for I can say this to you, she'd be no comfort to him, not from what I've heard. But afore you go' – she put out her hand – 'tell me what you gona do with yourself?'

'I wish I knew. I would like to get some sort of situation but I'm not qualified for anything. I'm . . . I'm not like Margaret, that's my half-sister, she's very clever. My accomplishments are more homely, so to speak.' She smiled wanly.

'Well, lass, to my mind they'll stand you in better stead than all your fancy learnin'. But never fear, you'll marry, you're so bonny. You'll be grabbed up afore you know where you are. I only hope you get a good man, a kind one, like your da was. Good-bye, lass.' She held out her hand, and Hannah took it, then turned quickly away.

Out on the hills again, Hannah made her way slowly down towards the main road. She could understand the mister liking that woman, she was nice, kindly, and before her face was scarred she must have appeared bonny. She was glad she would be going away. As she said, she could lose herself in the city. She recalled the city. She had lost herself many times there, having strayed only a short way from the waterfront. She'd love to go back to Newcastle just to walk through its streets again. If only she knew someone there like the woman did, someone to go to who'd shelter her.

There was a fear rising in her as to what would really become of her. The woman had said she'd be married, she'd be snapped up, but she didn't want to be snapped up, she didn't want to be married. There was only one man who filled the picture of her husband, and because she couldn't have him she told herself with girlish vehemence that she would never marry anyone.

But the question remained, what was she to do? because even if she wanted to, she doubted whether she'd be allowed to live in the house much longer. There was something brewing, an undercurrent; she could feel it.

She was descending the hill above the road when she caught sight of Ned, and her heart lifted. She picked up her skirts and ran down to the wall, then on to the road, where he had drawn his lead pony to a stop.

Looking down at her, he said, 'Well, been for one of your strolls?'

'Yes, Ned.'

He looked away over her head now towards the hills and said in an offhand tone, 'To Lode Cottage?'

'Yes, to Lode Cottage.'

'What would you be doin' there if it's not impidence to ask?'

She stared up at him, then said quietly, 'I was taking a message.'

'Oh aye.' He nodded at her; then again he said, 'Oh aye, it all fits in.'

'What does?'

'Well, there's a rumour goin' about that your da wasn't set on by any mad Scot from across the border, or hill highwayman, or horse thief; but 'tis only a rumour.'

She blinked at him, then asked, 'Where are you off to now?'

'Oh, a long trip this time down into Westmoreland, a house atween Hilton and Coupland, a private deal.' He grinned now. 'I like private deals, they generally do you well. Kip for the night with plenty to eat and drink.'

'Will you be away long?'

'Oh, it all depends if I pick up another lot of them on the way back.' He nodded towards the four ponies behind him. 'You never know where a blister might light in this business; you don't always get them on the seat of your pants.' He smacked his buttock with the flat of his hand.

She made no reply to his joke, but, her face straight, she looked up at him and only just stopped herself from saying, 'Hurry back' because that would have been silly; yet somehow when she knew he was in the Pele house she never felt entirely friendless, it was like having a big brother up there to run to.

His tone sounded flat now as he asked, 'How's things back there?'

'Oh – ' She swallowed, then said, 'About . . . about the same.'

'What are you thinkin' of doing?'

She shook her head and looked down towards her feet before she replied, 'I don't know, Ned, I wish I did, I'm all at sea.'

'Can you swim?'

Her head jerked up. 'What? . . . What do you mean, can I swim?'

'Just what I said, can you swim?'

'No.'

'Well, if you're all at sea and you can't swim you won't survive long will you?' The corners of his mouth were turned upwards, but there was no answering smile on her face and her voice was matchingly stiff when she said, 'I don't find it funny, Ned.'

She started visibly when, suddenly bending low down towards her until he was almost out of the saddle, he growled at her, 'Then you should do something about it. People who can't swim clutch at straws, whereas if they opened their bloody eyes wide enough and stretched out their arms, they would see a plank to their hand. You're not a bairn any longer, you're a young woman. And you know something? You're as dangerous as damp dynamite in a mine. . . . You are. You are that. An' if you don't open your eyes and see what's under your nose one of these days you'll sink, an' *Ned* won't be there to haul you out. . . . Get up there! Get up! Damn you, get up!'

She stood with her mouth open watching the string of ponies trotting down the road and listening to him bawling at the top of his voice 'Put a move on! Pick your feet up, damn you! Get on with you!'

What had she done? Why had he turned on her like that? Saying that she was as dangerous as dynamite in a mine. She looked about her as if the hills would give her an answer. Ned and she had always been good friends, he had been like a relative to her. Why had he turned on her like that? All that talk about swimming and sinking and grabbing at straws. She could understand now why some people didn't like him if he went for them like that. After all, she had done nothing to upset him. She remembered him being rude to her once before, practically ordering her out of the Pele house. It was around the time when he was going to marry, then didn't. Perhaps he was having trouble in that way again. But that was no reason why he should turn on her like that. Yet men didn't need a reason to be rude. Robert was very rude at times, John never. Oh! John. John.

John hardly spoke to her these days, and when he looked at her it was in a shamefaced way.

She turned now and walked briskly along the road in the direction of the place she still thought of as home.

It was the following morning. Betsy went to Hannah with a message to say that she was to take an order to the butcher's and she had to go alone and immediately.

As she took the slip of paper from Betsy's hand, Hannah looked at her but said nothing. She liked Betsy as little as Betsy liked her. Going into the hall, she collected her bonnet and short coat from the cloakroom, then went out upon her errand.

When she entered the butcher's shop there were no customers present, and Fred turned from the block, chopper in hand, and, his face spreading into a broad grin, he said, 'Why! hello.'

'Hello, Fred. I . . . I've brought the order.'

'Oh aye.' He took the paper from her, then going to a door at the side of the shop, he pulled it open and, looking up the steep stairs which led from it, he called, 'Ma! Ma! will you come down here a minute?'

During the time that Fred waited for his mother to descend the stairs he kept his eyes on Hannah, grinning all the while; then when Mrs Loam came into the shop he said, 'She's come,' and inclining his head towards Hannah he said, 'Take over for a minute, will you?'

The tight-bodiced, tight-lipped little woman looked squarely at Hannah, then walked to the counter where she turned and said, 'Well, get upstairs if you're goin'.'

Hannah looked behind her wondering for a moment if Mrs Loam was speaking to someone else; then pointing to herself, she asked, 'You mean me, Mrs Loam?'

'Well, I'm not talkin' to meself, lass.'

'Come upstairs a minute, Hannah, will you?' Fred's voice was low and persuasive now, and Hannah, looking at him enquiringly, asked simply, 'Why?'

'Didn't she say anything to you?' Fred now moved towards her. 'The missis?'

'What about?'

'Aw, God in heaven!' As his head wagged frantically his mother cried harshly, 'Either tell her here or tell her upstairs, but get it over.'

'Come along of me a minute, Hannah.' The young fellow now held out his hand towards her, but Hannah didn't take it, yet she walked past him and for the first time mounted the stairs to the rooms above the shop.

She stood for a moment gazing about her at the cold, stiff orderliness of what was evidently a kitchen-cum-sitting-room, then she started as she felt her hand gripped in Fred's two beefy ones and, his face close to her, heard him saying, 'Don't you know? Didn't she tell you?'

'Tell me what?' Hannah went to withdraw her hand, but he held on to it.

'Well –' He straightened his shoulders now, took a small step back from her while still retaining hold of her hand, and ended, 'She gave me leave to court you.'

'*She what!*' She almost jumped from his hold. 'You! to court me?'

'Aye, that's what I said, court you.' His face was straight now. 'An' it shouldn't come as so much of a surprise to you. I've talked to you a lot lately an' you haven't offsided me; pleased you seemed like to stop an' chat.'

'Only . . . only because you helped to find Father. I . . . I was grateful.'

'Aye well, I didn't take it just like that. Anyroad, she says it's all right an' you're not spoken elsewhere, an' me ma's agreeable an' all, so everything's plain sailin'.'

'Oh no, it isn't. No, it isn't.' She was backing from him now towards the door. 'You are under a misapprehension. I . . . I cannot marry you.'

'Why not?' His bulky body became stiff now, his manner aggressive, and again he demanded, 'Why not? Not good enough you think? Let me tell you I've got more put by than most in this village, I'm a warm man, an' me wife 'll want for nowt.'

Hannah took a deep breath, then closed her eyes for a moment before lowering her head and saying, 'Oh, Fred, I'm sorry. I'm . . . I'm sure you're very worthy, and . . . and I thank you for the compliment you have paid me.' And now she smiled weakly. 'It's the first proposal I've ever received and . . . and I do thank you. But I'm sorry, Fred.'

'Are you going to tell her that?'

'Yes, yes, I am.' Her reply was made in firm tones.

'Well, I wouldn't like to be there when you say your piece, 'cos let me tell you, Hannah, she means to get rid of you, an' if it isn't to me it'll be to somebody else. An' although I say it meself, you could look further an' fare worse. Aye, you could that.'

'I know that, Fred. I do, I know thåt.'

'You don't dislike me, do you?'

'Oh no, Fred, I don't dislike you.'

'Well then, why not let's give it a try? Look' – he stepped towards her – 'think on it. Go on back and think on it. I'll wait till the morrow and then I'll take your yes or nay for final. But . . . but afore you go I'll tell you this, Hannah. I care for you and I'd be a good husband to you if you're a good wife to me. Of course I know there's me ma, and she's hard to stomach at times, but I know how to handle her and I'll see she doesn't interfere. What do you say? Leave it till the morrow mornin'?'

She moved her head in denial; then, her only wish being to escape, she said, 'All right then, Fred, we'll . . . we'll leave it till tomorrow morning.'

'That's a good lass.' As he made to come nearer she turned and, opening the door, went on to the small stairhead and ran down the dark stairs so quickly that she almost fell down the last three steps.

There were still no customers in the shop and Mrs Loam stopped her sanding of the block and, resting both hands on the long scrubbing brush, turned her head and demanded, 'Well?'

Hannah gave her no answer, she merely paused a moment, looked at the little woman, then ran out of the shop.

Minutes later she was in the sitting-room actually shouting at the stiff figure who had risen from the couch and was now standing with her back to her. 'You can't do this! You can't make me marry him! You have no hold over me. You can't make me do anything. Do you hear?'

When Anne Thornton turned about and walked slowly down the room towards the door, Hannah stepped aside expecting that the woman would at last confront her and speak to her openly, but she watched in amazement the figure sweep past her, pull open the door and go out.

Hannah now stumbled up the room. She had a hand under each oxter and her body was bent forward as if in pain, and she groaned to herself, 'She's wicked. She's wicked. She can't do this. I'll leave the house, I'll go away.' . . . But where? . . . Ned. She'd go and tell Ned. Ned would advise her, tell her what to do, tell her what rights she had, because this was her father's house; although he was dead she was still his daughter.

It was only as she made for the door once more that she realized that Ned would now be far away on his journey over the hills. But there was Margaret. She would tell Margaret. Margaret was sensible, much older than her years; Margaret would know what she should do. Margaret had gone into Allendale earlier; she would go and meet her.

She was in the hall on the way to the door when Betsy came from the office towards her and, standing in front of her, she said calmly, 'Mama says that if you don't comply and accept Mr Loam's offer, then you must leave the house immediately as she cannot afford to support you any longer.'

Hannah's answer to this was to bend forward, clench her teeth for a moment, then say slowly, 'You horrible, horrible creature you! You spiteful, mean individual! I don't know what is going to happen to me, but this I do know, you'll end your days just like her' – she thrust out her arm and pointed towards the study door – 'lonely, alone, hated.' On this she turned and rushed out on to the drive; then on to the road and through the village; and her passing caused heads to turn, not only to see her running, with both hands holding up the front of her skirt, but also because she had no covering at all on her head, neither lace nor starched cap, shawl, hat, nor bonnet. To some of the older residents it appeared as if they were seeing her running naked through their village.

She was approaching Allendale when she met up with Margaret and she fell upon her, gasping and crying, 'Oh, Margaret! Margaret!'

'What is it? What's the matter? What is it, dear? Come and sit down.'

Margaret led her to a broken stone wall at the side of the road and, pressing her down on to it, she sat by her side and, taking her hands, she asked again, 'What's happened?'

'She's . . . she's arranged I should marry Fred, Fred Loam. Oh, Margaret! Margaret.'

'Oh no!'

'Yes, yes, Margaret. It's cruel, isn't it? It's cruel.'

When Margaret gave her no answer, Hannah insisted, 'It is. Don't you think it is? It is.'

'Yes, yes. It's cruel, and she intends it to be cruel. Oh, I know Mama, she intends it to be cruel. But, Hannah, Hannah my dear, it . . . it might turn out to be your salvation.'

'What do you mean, Margaret, my salvation? To marry a man like Fred Loam?'

'Oh, I know he is far beneath you, and is really of low intelligence and without education, but . . .'

'Oh, I don't mean that. It's got nothing to do with education as I see it, it's . . . it's just Fred himself, what he looks like, how he talks, how he acts.'

'Well, that's what I'm meaning. These things are all part of a man's education.'

Hannah now swung her head as she said flatly, 'Education! There's Ned Ridley, he's had no education but he's got more brains than most people in the village put together.'

'Yes, well, Ned's a bit of an exception. He's highly intelligent and he could have made something of himself if he had cared, I'm sure of that. But . . . but we have a point here, Hannah.' She now caught hold of her arm. 'You could likely make something of Fred.'

'Oh no! No! . . . Look, Margaret, in my desperation I thought of something as I came to meet you. If I could get back to school, Miss Barrington would help me. I'm sure she would.'

When Margaret slowly lowered her eyes and bit on her lip Hannah muttered, 'No, you think not?' Then Margaret, her eyes still cast down, said, 'There is something I must tell you, Hannah, I'm leaving home tomorrow morning, I . . . I meant to leave you a letter. I'm going back to school.' She now raised her eyes and looked straight at Hannah. 'They're going to give me my board and room in exchange for looking after the smaller children and helping generally. But . . . but what I didn't know about the Barringtons, in fact no one knew about them, is that they are very poor and they just manage to exist. Miss Emily told me privately that during the holidays when there's no income they live very meagrely, and they spend their time renovating all the linen and the household goods. They even dismiss the gardener during those weeks and do the work themselves, so you see I . . . I couldn't ask them to take you, it would be an imposition. I . . . I couldn't do it, Hannah.'

Hannah slid quietly off the wall but she didn't move away from it, she stood with her buttocks pressed against it and her hands gripping the jagged stone edge. After a moment she asked quietly, 'Are you going to be married?'

'Yes, as soon as Mr Hathaway can find an apartment suitable to his income.'

'Does anyone know? John or Robert?'

'No, no; only Miss Pearce in the town, you know who keeps the sweetshop. She's in sympathy with me, and what I didn't know until recently she is a distant relative of Miss Rowntree. For the past three weeks, ever since Father died, I've been taking a few of my belongings, and putting extra clothes on my person and leaving them with her. Tomorrow morning I shall be gone before Mama is about; I'm catching the first carrier cart into Hexham.'

'What will you do if . . . if your mother should come after you?'

Margaret gave a small mirthless laugh, saying, 'Oh, Mama won't come after me, Mama cares for only one of her family, and that's Betsy; perhaps a little for John. But in John's case I think it is more pride than love.'

Margaret now lowered herself to her feet and she, too, stood with her back to the wall, but she didn't grip it; instead, she threw one arm wide as she exclaimed, 'I'll be glad to see the last of this; hills, hills, hills, wherever you go you are hemmed in by hills, some of them tortured by the mines, other desecrated by residue and muck. Having been born here, I should love the place, I suppose, and there's no getting away from it it is beautiful in parts if you like harsh grandeur, but it holds little appeal for me. I prefer people, even in the narrow confines of the city, but you' – she turned now and looked at Hannah – 'you love the hills, don't you?'

'What? Oh yes, I suppose so.' Hannah's answer was flat. 'They were some place to escape to from the house, I felt free when I walked them.' Now she turned and looked at Margaret as she ended, 'Have you any idea what my life has been like in your home, Margaret?'

'Yes, Hannah, to a small extent; but not being you yourself, I couldn't experience your hurt to the full.'

'I hate your mother, do you know that?'

'Yes, I know that.'

'At one time I was only afraid of her, and the thought of hating her was like an assumption, something forbidden me. Even up to a year ago I hid this feeling from myself, but now I want to shout it, bawl it into her face. There have been times of late when I've wanted to strike her, as if by doing so I could make her address me, speak to me openly. To her I'm a thing, *The Girl*. She's never called me anything but *The Girl*. As if I weren't there, as if she were speaking of someone who was dead. Oh, I do hate her, Margaret. I do, I do!'

'Then that is all the more reason why you should get away from her. There are likely other men who would offer you marriage but at present only Fred has come forward, and if you don't comply she might be as good as her word and turn you out, and no one could stop her. Robert might try; but I'm sorry to say as much as you care for John, Hannah, I doubt if he would oppose her. What you haven't recognized yet in John is that he is weak.'

Margaret turned away as she said this, adding, 'Come! and walked slowly up the road. Then after a moment she said, 'That's why he is attracted to Miss Everton because she is a strong character. . . . And he is very attracted to her, Hannah.' She now turned her head and nodded at Hannah. 'You must face up to this fact and not mourn in your heart for something you imagine you have lost.'

They walked on in silence for some way now as if they were enjoying a stroll in the April sunshine.

Presently Margaret said, 'It is strange that in the main women are always stronger than men, yet they have to be subordinate to them. They cannot claim any of the man's rights, they are chattels; and yet in most cases happy to be chattels. I suppose love helps. In my own case I know I am of a stronger character than Mr Hathaway, yet I will become subordinate to him. You see, I have asked myself would I rather be like Miss Barrington, Miss Emily and Miss Rowntree? I don't think so. . . .'

'I would!'

The vehemence with which Hannah made this statement startled Margaret. 'Oh, don't shake your head like that, Margaret. I would change places with any one of them at this moment. I don't want to marry . . . I don't want to marry anyone, and I mean it. I know within a little what marriage means. Miss Emily made it clear to me in her going-away talk. She likely said the same to you. There is a personal element that can be highly distasteful, and before marriage, she said, you've got to ask yourself whether you could submit to it. Well, I don't feel I can; not with Fred Loam, or anyone else for that matter.'

'Then what do you intend to do?' Margaret had stopped and they were facing each other. 'You could never live on your own in a town, you would be eaten up. A girl who looks like you, whether you wanted to or not, you would fall prey to men and end up like your mother. There! I've said it. I'm sorry but it's true. Please don't be hurt.' She put out her hand and gripped Hannah's arm. 'And let me say this; Miss Emily is a maiden lady and maiden ladies don't know all that much about the intimacies of marriage. How can they? And look about you and see the men and women who are happily joined together with a family around them. I am sure there is nothing to be afraid of. It . . . well, what Miss Emily never emphasized was that it's all a part of nature . . . Accept Fred's offer, Hannah. At least you'd be safe and well housed and cared for if you marry him. But if you don't, then I don't dare to think what will happen to you, because let me say this finally, such are my mother's feelings towards you that she will brave any opposition that might arise against her in the village, she'll even put forward a statement that will make her actions appear justified, and the statement will be that you are trying to seduce your half-brother, because let me tell you I am sure she is aware to some extent of your feelings for John. . . . Marry Fred, Hannah, if only to save the name that you have held respectable so far, marry him.'

## *Chapter Three*

They said in the village that they had never known a marriage happen so soon after the asking, unless it was where the bride wanted to bamboozle the months of the calendar in an effort to shorten her pregnancy.

Some said that couldn't be so in this case; but others said, time would tell, if not, why the rush?

Well, said the wise ones, didn't everybody know the feeling that had existed in that house since young Hannah was dumped on them years ago? And now that the master was gone that stiffnecked martinet had everything her own way, and it was evident she wanted to get rid of the lass.

But why pang her off on to Fred Loam? for all were agreed that Fred was no catch for a lass who looked like Hannah, and educated into the bargain. And then there was Fred's mother. Oh aye, there was Fred's mother.

Fred's mother now stood in the front pew, and to her side stood her sister and two distant relatives, while behind her, filling four rows, were neighbours and the tradesmen of the village.

On the other side of the aisle were Mrs Anne Thornton and her daughter Beatrice, and behind them Bella and Tessie and Dandy Smollett; but the rest of the pews were empty. Although it was high summer the church felt cold and smelt of damp. It smelt of damp at any time but the rain over the past four days seemed to have seeped through the thick stone walls until now even the pews felt wet.

The Reverend Stanley Crewe's muttering voice had seemed to those present to skip over the service, but to Hannah each of his words appeared to be long-drawn-out, weighty, pressing her down, while at the same time sounding unreal.

'I pronounce that they be Man and Wife together.'

Hannah, already half turned towards Fred, stood rigid, but he, with a grin on his face, bent towards her and planted a wet kiss to the side of her lips. Her reaction to it was as if she had been stung for she started and turned about, there to see Robert, who'd had the unenviable task of giving her away, looking at her with a sort of warning glance, and she drew in a deep breath and gasped as if she had just checked herself from flight.

Only last night Robert had said to her he thought the whole thing was a crying shame, and if it wasn't for the situation of their birth he would, more than gladly he had emphasized, marry her himself.

She had cried over Robert's concern, yet she hadn't cried when John, standing in the hall, the least private place in the house, had wished her happiness and said he hoped she understood that it would be impossible for him to attend the ceremony as since his father's decease he was working over at the old mine, and she had made herself reply, while looking at him straight in the eyes, that she understood perfectly. And strangely she did. But what she understood more than anything else was that Margaret was right; John, although big and handsome and manly looking, was a weak man. Yet weak or not, she told herself that she would gladly give up her entire life if she could be compensated with just a day of his love.

She was in the vestry now signing the register and she was about to write Hannah Thornton when the Reverend Crewe's voice said gently, 'Write your own name, Hannah.'

She glanced at him for a moment, then wrote Boyle.

There was talk all around her, there was even laughter, when a voice above the rest cried, 'You're gona be drowned on your weddin' night, Fred, I can see you havin' to swim to bed.' The laughter became louder.

She felt dizzy, faint. She looked for a moment into the eyes of her new mother-in-law. They were unsmiling, coldly pale blue, like the colour of the marbles the boys played with in the lanes. Some of these though were warmed with pink stripes, but there was no glint of warmth in the eyes of the undersized little woman.

Then she looked at the woman standing far back, the woman who should have been a mother to her, and her eyes were smiling now, gleaming as if with triumph.

She heard The Reverend Crewe say, 'I would like to speak to you, Hannah, for a moment in private, and Fred too. Come this way.'

Fred had his arm around her waist, and she submitted to it, for there was nothing she could do about it. They were following the parson into a small room that led off the vestry. It too smelt musty. Two of the walls were lined with racks holding boxes and books. All the books were thick tomes.

She was married, she was no longer Hannah Boyle or Hannah Thornton, she was Mrs Loam . . . Loam, it was of the soil; she wished she were under it, right under the soil at this moment, dead, without breath, without feeling, without fear. Oh yes, without fear, for there was a great fear on her now, and it was centred around Fred's big red hands.

She watched the minister take a key and unlock the door of a wall cabinet and from its shelf lift out an envelope. Then as he moved towards her holding the envelope in both hands he smiled his weak, watery but kindly smile, as he said, 'This is for you, Hannah. It was put into my care by your mother on the day she unfortunately died. It was her request that it should be given to you on your wedding-day. I kept it until after the ceremony because I felt it would afford you both pleasure and comfort on this particular day.'

Her lips slightly apart she gazed at the minister for a moment before extending her hand, then she took the long envelope and looked at it and her lips moved as she read the words to herself: 'Concerning Hannah Boyle.

This letter is to be put into the care of a minister of God, or some legal person, and to be given to the above-named on the day she weds.'

She glanced now at Fred who was gazing at her with a look on his face that showed definite pride of possession.

'Aren't you going to open it, my dear?' The minister was now handing her a paper knife which she took from him and slowly slit open the envelope. Then taking out the long sheet of paper that was doubled in three and had inside it a yellowed printed form, she looked from one to the other before she began to read.

I, Harold Penhurst Wright, solicitor's clerk, do pen this last will of Nancy Boyle in her own words as she so dictates them to me.

Dated this Seventh day of February in the year 1850.

I know that I'm not long for the top so want to do what is best for my child. If she is left alone here she will go to the bad and be used in a whore shop, as young as she is, or put in the House. One or t'other is bad. I was at my wits' end when I saw Mr Matthew Thornton in the city. Hadn't seen him since that time I told him I was carrying a bairn. I thought it no harm if he believed it his'n cos I was hard put to live but he went off that night and I never clapped eyes on him again until last week in the city. 'Twas then I made it my business to find out who he really was and where he abided. So what I mean to do is to go to him and put her in his charge, but at the same time I would like her to know that she isn't a bastard for she was got by the man I married, who went to sea and didn't come back, but I didn't know he wasn't coming back at the time, I just thought he was on his two-year trip.

I want my daughter to have this letter on her weddin' day along with her birth certificate so as her husband can't cast it up to her she's from the wrong side of the blanket. I hope she marries a decent man and is happy.

Signed by Mrs Nancy Boyle with her cross.

The seventh day of February 1850.

'*No! No! No!*'

She was waving the letter first at the minister and then at Fred; then almost pushing it into the minister's face, she cried, 'You should have given it to me this morning. I should have had it this morning. I shouldn't have been married then. It says . . . it says he wasn't my father, the mister, Mr Thornton. He wasn't! He wasn't! . . .'

She was tossing her head now from side to side, and when Fred caught hold of her arm in a rough grip crying, 'Stop your yelling! What's the matter with you? What does it say?'

She tore herself from him and again she waved the letter in his face; and now she said distinctly and slowly while thrusting her face towards his, 'I am not Mr Thornton's daughter. That's what it says, I had a proper father, I mean this' – she was now holding up the birth certificate – 'and I would never have married you had I known. I wouldn't! I wouldn't!'

'Hannah! Hannah! hush, you are married. Hush! you mustn't say that.'

The little minister was almost knocked on to his back. It was only Fred's outstretched arm that caught him, and even he staggered back against the bookcase as Hannah rushed for the door, pulled it open, and sped on to the grass between the gravestones, and away past the laughing crowd who were taking shelter in the church porch.

Before she reached the cemetery wall the thin white dress she wore was clinging to her like a bit of wet paper. She had worn a hood and cloak on the short journey from the house to the church, but had left the cloak at the back of the church before going up the aisle on Robert's arm.

When she clambered over the wall her leather shoes sank into mud and she almost fell on her face as she pulled them out one after the other. When her feet found hard ground again she tore like the wind in the direction of the hills and the short cut to the mine.

She had only one thought in her mind, and she was possessed by it, she must see John, she must tell him. It didn't make any difference now, she knew, but she must tell him. It hadn't been wrong, she knew in her heart it hadn't been wrong to love him. And they could have been married. They could. They could.

The wind was driving the rain in slanting sheets across the hills and it also brought to her the distant sound of voices and running feet. They were coming after her. Well, they didn't know where she was going; no one would think of her going to the mine. They might think she would go to Ned's. She would never go to Ned's again. He had passed her twice of late and never looked the side she was on. The first time she had gone to speak to him he had turned his head away and spat into the road, just as he said he did when he passed the missis. . . . The missis, that fiend of a woman, the missis. Had she known about this? No, no, she couldn't have; she would have turned out sooner had she realized that her husband had been made use of, that all her suffering had been caused through a lie. And that the woman had suffered was true. Oh yes, she had suffered. It was because she had been aware of this, even as a child, that she hadn't allowed herself to hate the woman, until recently.

She had a stitch in her side; she must stop. Where was she? She stood bent double gasping; her hair had come loose from its pins and strands of it were straggling over her face. She pushed it from her eyes and peered this way and that way through the rain. She was at the end of the old by-road that wound among the web hills. No one used this way very much now since the new road had been made. It was tortuous in dry weather, it was a real danger in wet; there were potholes that would take you up to the waist in water. But what did it matter, it cut the distance to the mine by almost a mile. Another half-hour at the most and she'd be there.

She had been cold a short while back but now she was warm. Even though she was wet to the skin she was warm. She must look a dreadful sight, but again what did it matter? John would understand. . . . But if he wasn't at the mine?

He was bound to be at the mine, he said he'd be there, that's why he couldn't come to the wedding.

On the top of a hill she paused for breath again. To one side of her the land fell away in rain-swept layers like floating landlocked islands. The hills themselves seemed to be moving, rising and falling in waves of black and silver mist.

She must be nearing the mine now. Stumbling and gasping, she made her way up a slope to the top of a hill, and there before her on the other side she saw it, the mine, as she had never seen it before. Perhaps it was because she was seeing it through the rain but it appeared as if a number of small huts had been thrown haphazardly at the hill, and there had stuck. On the level area were expanses of slaty water, but all the hill below right down to the valley was covered with dead matter; the whole place looked dead as if it had been laid bare by a plague.

Was this how Margaret saw the hills?

What was the matter with her? What did it matter if the mines destroyed all the hills? What matter how they looked; it was how John would look when he knew.

There were men pushing wooden bogies coming out of the hole in the hillside. They appeared like gnomes popping up out of the earth; they had hessian sacks over their heads, the points sticking upwards yet dropping at the top like fools' caps. There were young boys shovelling muck; there were men riddling stones. They all stopped what they were doing and gaped at her, and one of them, his mouth wide open, licked the rain from his lips before calling to her, 'What 'tis, miss?'

He came towards her. 'You lost or summat?'

'Mr Thornton. I . . . I want to see Mr Thornton, Mr John Thornton.'

'Oh aye, aye.' The man wiped the rain from his eyes. 'Oh, I see who you are now. But by! lass, you're in a state. And wet to the skin. Where's your cloak?'

'I want to see Mr Thornton.'

'All right, lass, all right. Ower yonder, that place there.' He pointed to a long, low shed-like structure with a door in the middle and two windows on each side, and she turned from him without even a thank you and ran, wending her way between obstacles of stacks, of props, and bogies, and mounds of earth, unaware of the men here and there straightening their backs, wiping the rain from their eyes and peering at her, then looking at each other.

She did not knock on the door but thrust it wide open, and the sight of her startled the three men around the table. Two were sitting at it and one was bending over it. They had been examining drawings on a large sheet of stiff paper and now they stared at her open-mouthed as if they were seeing an apparition; there was still evidence that her gown was white but it was bespattered with mud and clinging to her body here and there as tight as skin, and her hair had fallen about her making her appear like someone wild.

'Hannah! in the name of God what's . . . what's the matter with you?'

'Oh John! John!' She came towards him, but there was the distance of the table between them and the presence of the other two men, and it was to one of these John looked and said, 'I'm . . . I'm sorry, sir. This . . . this is my sister, my . . . my . . .'

'No, no, I'm not!'

'*What!* . . . What's the matter with you? I thought. . . .'

The two men rose from the table, the elder of them saying, 'We'll go; you deal with your family matter, John. It's all right. It's all right.' He raised his hand to silence something that John was about to say, then he stared at Hannah for a moment before taking up his hard hat from a nail on the wall and a coat that was hanging near by it, and he donned them both and went out followed by the other man who wore neither hat nor overcoat.

'Have you gone mad, Hannah? What do you mean by coming here? I . . . I thought you were being ma . . .'

'I know, I know I shouldn't have come, but . . . but I had to tell you. John –' She came slowly round the table, hanging on to the edge for support, until she was standing close to him and she looked into his face now as she said between gasps, 'We . . . we are not related. They . . . I mean the Reverend Crewe, he . . . he gave me a letter. It was to say that your father . . . your father hadn't fathered me. It's all in the letter here.' She put her hand down the front of her dress and pulled out the sodden envelope and proffered it to him. But he did not take it, he even shrank from her, saying now, 'It's no good, Hannah, I'm . . . I'm promised. It's all arranged. You should have married Fred, it would have been the best thing . . . I'm sorry, I'm sorry.'

She stared at him blankly for some seconds, then she closed her eyes tightly and blinked. It was as if she were rousing herself from a deep sleep. It was right what Margaret had said, he was a weak man, but she had told herself that, weak or not, she would have given her life for one day of love from him. But now she knew that even if she had come to him last month and told him what she had just told him, he wouldn't have given her that day of love.

'I am married, I was married before I saw the letter.'

She watched his whole face change, the furrow smooth out from between his brows, his cheeks drop, his lips fall together; her words, she thought, had acted on him like a hot iron over wet linen; she felt she could smell his relief.

Slowly she dragged her eyes from his face and walked towards the door, and when he said softly, 'Hannah,' she looked at him over her shoulder and said, 'I thought I would just come and tell you.'

She was outside now. The rain was coming straight down, it was like a weight on her head. She passed between the obstacles once more; she passed by the men pushing the bogies now towards the mouth of the mine; and the man who had spoken to her before stopped and called, 'You see him, miss?'

And she stopped and answered, 'Yes, thank you.'

When she found she was actually smiling at the man she thought, I'm going mad; people don't smile under these circumstances. I must be going mad. . . .

Before she had left the precincts of the mine she was running again, but she wasn't taking the same road back, for she had turned in the opposite direction from that by which she had come.

After a while she stopped running and just walked steadily but aimlessly forward. She had no idea where she was going, nor did she care. Vaguely, she knew that if she stayed out in the wet long enough, perhaps all night, she'd get pneumonia and die, as the mister had done. It was odd to think he wasn't her father. In a way now she was sorry. What would have happened had he lived and found out? He wouldn't have held it against her. Oh no, not he. Why couldn't John have taken after his father? John. John. The relief on his face when she said she was married, she would feel the pain of that for evermore.

Married! She was married! There'd be a commotion in the village. Fred would be searching for her. Married? One didn't feel any different being married, at least not yet. It was what happened in bed that made the difference. Miss Emily had suggested that a woman could never be the same after that experience. Until that conversation with Miss Emily she had actually thought that babies came by kissing. It was something to do with the tongue in your mouth, that's why it had been very wrong to allow a man to kiss you, except on the cheek, until you were actually married. She had been shocked and very worried the day she had seen Dandy kissing Tessie on the mouth. That was about two years ago. She had waited for news of the baby coming and had wondered in her naivety if the missis would attend her or the midwife be brought in from Allendale Town.

Yesterday, she had been a girl, today she felt a woman, and yet so far she was married in name only. And that's how it would remain for she'd never go back down there to Fred Loam's house. Never! Never!

What time was it? She was married at two o'clock. It would have taken her almost an hour to get to the mine; and how long had she been walking since then? She didn't know. An hour? Two hours? Would she reach some sort of habitation before dark? She didn't know where she was; the rain was coming down even heavier now, and she couldn't see the outline of the hills. Well, what did it matter? But she was cold, she was shivering. She must lie down in some place and rest. But where? If she sat down here she might never get up again, she could die. Well, isn't that what she wanted? No, no; she only wanted to get away from the village and everyone in it, away from Fred.

When some time later the belt of trees loomed up before her, it was as if nine years had rolled back and she was leading her mother into the darkness of the wood.

She stopped and leant against the bole of a tree. She must have walked for hours in a huge circle, and she was now within a few minutes' walk of the Pele house and Ned. She would go to Ned. . . . But wait; Ned wouldn't speak to her. But she needn't go to the house, she needn't see him. There was the shippon at the end of the yard. It was full of old bits of machinery, the overspill from the horse room; if she could get in there she could hide and rest till morning.

She went slowly through the wood now, her steps dragging. She made sure there was no one in the yard before she entered it and keeping close to the wooden wall of the shippon she made for the door, pushed it open, then went in.

. . . 'What the hell have we here?' The voice was thick and guttural.

She was staring at Ned who was holding a lantern above his head while his other arm supported a number of pieces of old harness.

'What the hell do you want? Now look here! Get the blazes out of it.'

He came lunging towards her, almost tripping over the debris on the floor, and when he stood within an arm's length from her the lantern showing up his face told her he was drunk.

The light also revealed to his befuddled mind the terrible state she was in, and his head swaying on his shoulders, he looked her up and down. Twice he went to speak but closed his mouth again before, his tone a little quieter but still a growl, he said, 'They're lookin' for you. They've been round here twice. You know that?'

She didn't speak, she simply stared at him.

'God! look at you.' He took a step back from her now and for a moment she thought he was going to fall backwards, the lantern with him; but she did not start or put out her hand to stay him for it was as much as she could do to support herself now against the wooden door to stop herself from sliding down to the ground.

'Why the bloody hell do you come to me, eh! You're trouble. You know that? That's what you are, trouble. Ever since I first clapped eyes on you you've brought me trouble. An' you know what? He now stepped towards her again. 'You're a bloody ungrateful sod.'

Still she didn't speak or move. He, too, became silent; but then barking at her again, he yelled, 'Ger out of here an' into the house!' and lunging forward again, he gripped her by the shoulder, swung her round, pushed her out of the door and into the yard and, staggering, followed her into the stable-room.

The familiar smell, the warmth, the jumbled comfort, the clanking of the ponies in the stalls, the whole atmosphere was too much and, dropping down on to the platform where she had lain once before and where he and the old man had attended her, she bent her body double and sobbed aloud.

And all the while he stood over her yelling at her. 'Bloody cryin' 'll do you some good now; you were married, they said, and skedaddled. By God! if I was him I'd murder you when I caught you, if you did that to me. . . . He's a bloody numskull, we all know that, but no man deserves to be deserted at the altar. 'Tis the woman who's deserted at the altar. . . . Stop that bloody cryin' an' tell me' – he gripped her by the shoulder and pulled her upright – 'why make for me, eh? Come on, tell me, why make for me? You overlooked me, didn't you? You were in a tight corner but it wasn't so bloody tight as you were goin' to stoop an' take Ned Ridley.'

She was gasping; her mouth was open, her eyes wide as she stared at him.

'You've tormented me since you were a bairn, you know that? From you come into that yard' – he threw his arm back and pointed towards the door and nearly fell sideways as he did so – 'all those years gone, from that very mornin' you had me under your thumb. You know what I did? I wrote a bloody piece of poetry about you comin' at me that morning. That's something you didn't know, I write bits of poetry, boxes upstairs, full of 'em. I write 'em and forget 'em. But not that bit, no. Like the bloody fool I am, I used to say it to myself when I saw you.' He stopped and they stared at each other, she gasping as if fighting for air, and he, his hands on his knees, his face level with hers, swaying slightly.

'Ah, to hell! What's the use.' He turned from her now, saying, 'You want a drink an' something hot inside you, and some dry togs on you, or it's a bloody corpse the groom 'll be pickin' up.'

She watched him go towards the back kitchen. She heard the clanging of the kettle and the rattle of the tin mugs, and as she listened a voice was speaking in her head. The tone was incredulous and almost touching on laughter. She could have married Ned. Ned had wanted her. All this time Ned had wanted her. That's why he wouldn't speak to her when he came back and heard she was going to marry Fred Loam. Why hadn't he said? But if he had, would it have made any difference? She had loved John. . . . Somewhere in her mind she recognized she had thought, had loved, not did love.

'Drink that.' He pushed the mug between her trembling hands; then moving some distance from her, he slumped down on to a bale of hay and for a moment he dropped his head into his hands and shook it. Then looking at her again, he said slowly, 'Of all the times I could have taken you an' didn't. The times you've been in here an' tempted me silly. She's only sixteen I said. Then a few months ago what did I say to meself? She's seventeen now, so what about it? No, no, I said; hold your hand, man, an' there'll come a day when she'll turn to you. That bitch of a witch down there 'll do summat to her an' she'll run. An' when he died I said to meself, Now show your hand, I said, do the thing properly. Go down to that bitch an' say, 'I could buy and sell you where money's concerned.' An' I could.' He was nodding widely at her now. 'There's money stacked round here that would make your eyebrows rise. Me great-great-grandad didn't swing for nowt, he left his token behind a brick in the wall.' He threw out his arm again in a dramatic gesture. 'Then me great-granda died and he left his token an' all. Then the old 'un died recently, and by! what was his token? If I'd the old bugger here this minute I'd token him, I would that! Me father, he left nowt, miners never leave nowt, so I could say to her, "Missis, I could buy you out of house an' home," or "I could build on to that place up there an' make it into a small mansion for her," but I didn't get the chance, did I? You up and bloody well took a gormless nowt like Fred, an' him having a mother like he has. My God! you'll go through it with her. An' you know what I say? I say, serve you damn well right 'cos you haven't got the sense you were born with.'

He now dragged himself to his feet; then his voice flat, he went on, 'Aw well, it's finished, I've learned me lesson. It's the only bloody fool thing I've done in me life, but never again. An' to think I didn't get married 'cos of you. Huh!' He threw his head back now and laughed so loud that he startled the animals; then ended, 'Well, they'll be on their rounds again shortly to pick you up. That's if you don't drop down dead afore that ... Stop shivering.' He turned from her now. 'You want something to put round you, a sack. No, a shawl. I'll get you a shawl; but mind' – he stabbed his finger towards her – 'I want it back – 'twas me mother's.'

She watched him now pulling himself slowly up the ladder to the room above, and the minute he disappeared through the trap-door she dropped the mug on to the platform as she struggled to her feet; then she ran to the door and out into the rain again.

They could come but they wouldn't find her; she wouldn't be able to stand the humiliation of being dragged down into the village by a man who would now be beside himself with anger.

She was in the middle of the belt of trees when she heard Ned calling her name. 'Hannah! Hannah! Don't be a bloody fool. Hannah! come back I say.' His voice coming through the rain-drenched trees sounded as if he were calling through a long tunnel.

It wasn't until she emerged into the open again that she realized the rain had stopped. She didn't attempt to take the hill path this time knowing that she would slip and slide and that Ned would soon catch up with her because he could run like a hare, at least when he was sober.

Away to the left the land sloped to the valley and fields, and away beyond was the beginning of the Buckly Estate. If she could get into there she could lose herself.

When she reached the valley bottom she was gasping for breath and she paused and turned; and there he was bounding drunkenly down the hillside. She ran on again but more slowly now as if she, too, were drunk.

The grassland in the valley gave way to ploughed fields, and the soil stuck to her shoes. Ned wasn't far behind her now and intermittently his voice came at her, just calling her name, 'Hannah! Hannah!'

There was the wood ahead. Once in there he'd have a job to find her, and anyway she doubted if he would follow her because Lord Buckly came down hard on trespassers, at least his keepers did. But they wouldn't hurt a woman, so she told herself, because she wouldn't be after the young pheasants.

The stone wall was only about four feet high and her mind registered surprise that its top wasn't fortified in any way with glass chippings or spiked wire, and as she rolled over it Ned's voice came from just yards behind her and his tone was different now and held the sound of a gasping plea. 'For God's sake, Hannah, stop! Stop! Not in there. Not there, you bloody fool you. . . .'

She was about ten paces beyond the wall when his next words, screaming high above her head, brought her to a freezing standstill. 'It's trapped! Mantrapped. For God's sake listen to me!'

She was standing stiffly but swaying from one side to the other listening now, and she turned her heads towards where he was leaning over the wall gasping, and she watched him slowly raise his hand upwards as he said, 'Don't move, just don't move, they could be anywhere, the place is ringed, just keep still.'

As she stared at him through the fading light she wondered if this was his kind of a trap, that he was just saying this to get hold of her, but the expression on his face and the fact that he seemed to have sobered up told her that it was no ruse on his part. She watched him climb over the wall, then keep his eyes on the ground as he came towards her. The grass was long and tangled in the open belt of land between the wall and the wood proper. She watched him coming near, planting each foot carefully but still swaying a little.

When he was within an arm's length of her he stopped and, pointing ahead of her, said, 'You . . . you would never have got in. Look! it's all wired. But this is where they catch 'em, the fools who try. He's a dirty bugger, Buckly, he takes payment in limb for his birds, an' even for a rabbit. . . . Give me your hand.'

As she held out her hand to him, he muttered thickly, 'By God! you want to consider yersel lucky.'

As she stepped towards him he let out a fearful oath; then pointing to the ground within a yard of her, he growled, 'Look at that! That'll tell you just how lucky.'

She looked in the direction of his pointing finger but couldn't make out anything except a patch of tangled grass.

He now led her slowly back to the wall; then pushing her roughly against it, he said, 'Now you stay put. Don't you dare move. I'm gona make sure that that one catches neither fox, hare, nor some poor bugger's leg.'

She stood now gripping the front of her sodden dress in both hands as she watched him pick up a broken branch, cautiously walk back towards the clump of grass, and when he lifted up the stick it was as if he were about to attack a wild beast.

It all seemed to come about from the force he put into the blow, for as he brought the stick down on the trap his feet left the ground and he stumbled forward; then as the unearthly scream re-echoed through the trees she screwed up her eyes tight and covered her face with her hands. But the next moment she was running towards him where he was lying on his side, his legs now thrashing the ground, his left arm extended, its hand spread and running red with blood.

'Oh Ned! Ned! Ned! Ned!' She was tugging fruitlessly at the iron teeth that was clamping the side of his hand.

He was on his knees now, his body contorted, his face turned into that of a gargoyle. When she saw what he was aiming to do, she got her two hands on one side of the trap while his was on the other, and when the teeth came apart his mangled hand fell away and he rolled on to his side and tucked his hand under his oxter while the toes of his boots beat into the earth.

She was kneeling beside him holding him as she moaned and cried, 'Oh Ned! Ned! I'm sorry. Oh, what have I done? Oh Ned! Ned! Come on, get up; you must get home.'

As if he were obeying her he stumbled to his feet. His hand still held tightly under his oxter, he staggered to the wall and rolled over it; then, his body almost double, his chin tucked tightly into his chest, he started the journey home.

When he swayed and she thought he would fall she put both arms about him and held him; otherwise, she held on to his right arm. But not once did he speak to her, nor did he utter any sound at all now.

Twice on the journey he stopped and dropped on to his knees to rest, but he didn't take his hand from his oxter. . . .

It was dark when they reached the yard and, once inside the stable-room, he spoke for the first time. Looking towards the lantern that was still burning he muttered, 'Fetch it,' then he went on into the kitchen.

Quickly, carrying the light, she followed him. Then she watched him go to a bucket of water that was standing near the wall and, kneeling before it, slowly ease his hand from his oxter and plunge it into the bucket.

When he lifted it out again and she saw his two fingers dangling as if by threads she felt she was about to faint away.

He stared at his hand for a moment before plunging it back again and muttering, 'A sheet. Get a sheet.'

She looked about her wildly, 'Where? Where?'

'Upstairs, in the drawer. Take . . . take the lantern.'

She didn't know how she got up the steep stairs to the room above, and half-way up she trod on the front of her dress and only in time saved herself from falling to the ground, lantern and all.

In the room, she pulled open three drawers before finding the sheets. They were flannelette. She pulled two out and hurried down the ladder again, and when she entered the kitchen she found him now sitting with his back to the wall, his feet straight out but his hand still in the bucket.

'Tear it into strips.'

It was tough material and wouldn't rip like linen and when he screamed at her 'Cut it! Take a knife,' it almost fell from her cold trembling hands.

When she had at last torn off two strips he said, his tone quiet again, 'Fold one up and make it into a pad.'

After she had done this, he signalled to her to put it on the floor by the side of the bucket, then swiftly he lifted up his hand and placed it on the pad of sheeting; then putting the mangled fingers into place he folded the sheeting over them before saying to her, 'Now wrap it up as tight as you can,' but before she even had time to begin the bandaging the pad was soaked red.

When at last the bandaging was done he said to her, 'Tear the rest up; I'll likely need them afore the night's out.'

'Will . . . will I fetch Doctor Arnison?'

'No, there's not much use now; I'll go down to him in the mornin'.'

'Oh, Ned. Oh, I'm sorry, I am. . . .'

'Shut up!'

'I just want to say . . .'

'Shut up, will you! Do you hear! Shut up! else I'll kill you.'

She stared down at him. His face was white, a dirty pasty white, but his eyes were burning, blazing black in his head.

When he pulled himself up from the floor he went to the rack where the crockery was kept, and picking up a bottle that was still a quarter full of whisky, he filled a tin mug almost to the brim with it. He held it in his hand for a moment as he looked at her and said, 'I'm going to kip down on the straw, I'll leave you to fend for yourself,' and with that he walked past her where she was standing at the open doorway to the stable and she watched him walk down its almost dim length to where the hay was stacked. She saw him lower himself on to the bales, drink deep from the cup, then lie back.

She stood thus looking in his direction for almost five minutes before she turned and, sitting down by the wooden table, she lowered her head on to her folded arms and groaned to herself, 'Dear Lord! Dear Lord! what have I done this day?'

It was in the middle of the night when she heard him groaning. She had lit another two lanterns before wrapping herself in the horse blankets and lying on the platform further along the wall from where the bales of straw were. She realized that she must have fallen asleep and that the night had turned very cold because even in here with the thick walls keeping in the body heat from the horses she was shivering; yet there was sweat between her breasts and on her brow.

Half dazed, she got up and staggered towards him and, kneeling by his side, she said softly, 'Can I get you anything, Ned? A drink?'

When he didn't answer she realized that he was asleep, and so she went back to the platform and lay down again. But it was some long time before she fell into a doze because she was so cold.

She was dragged from a deep nightmarish sleep by someone gripping her shoulder and calling her name, and she sat bolt upright and stared blinking through the morning light at Ned.

'Get up, will you?'

'Oh, Ned!' She was on her feet, her hands out supporting him, even while she found it difficult to stand herself. 'You're ill. Look, lie down, lie down here.' She turned him about and he dropped on to the platform. Then she gave a small gasp as she looked at his arm. The sleeve was rolled up and his forearm looked scarlet and twice its normal size.

He blinked at her, wetted his lips and said slowly, 'I . . . I can't go down; can . . . can you get somebody?'

'Yes, yes, Ned; I'll . . . I'll go to the town, I'll get Doctor Arnison.'

'Get me . . . a drink first . . . will you? Tea . . . anything.'

'Yes, Ned.' But as she went to hurry away her legs almost gave way beneath her. She was acting like someone drunk. What was the matter with her?

She blew up the banked-down fire with the bellows, put the kettle on, and when it boiled she mashed the tea; then she poured out a mug full, put in three spoonfuls of sugar and took it to him. It was scalding but he drank it almost at once, then lay back.

She went into the kitchen again, and as she poured herself out a mug of tea she told herself that she felt ill; that she didn't know how she was going to get to the town, it was all of three miles away, that's if she gave the village a wide berth, and she must give the village a wide berth. But she must go; his hand was infected, his arm was infected. It was dreadful, a dreadful thing to happen to him, and she was to blame. She wished she was dead. . . . Oh! how she wished she was dead.

She pulled herself to her feet, went into the stable-room and, going to Ned, bent over him and said, 'I'm away then, Ned, I'll be as quick as I can.' This time she did manage to stop herself from adding yet again, 'I'm sorry, Ned. I'm sorry.'

He merely nodded at her, then turned his head away; and she went out into the morning light, into the clear bright sunlight, and for the first time since she had woken she looked down at herself. She was filthy. She put her hands to her hair. It was hanging about her shoulders in matted strands; she must look like a wild woman. But what did it matter? The only think that mattered at the moment was getting the doctor for Ned.

She was only half-way across the hills to Allendale Town when she told herself that she couldn't go any further. Her head was spinning, she was feeling ill.

When she reached a bridle path she sat on the grass verge and held her head in her hands. Perhaps if she rested for a while she'd be able to go on.

When the voice above her said, 'Eeh! Eeh! it's you. By! you're not half in a mess. . . . They're lookin' for you. The whole village's been out lookin' for you,' she raised her head and saw a young boy standing above her. It was Peter Wheatley.

'Pe-ter! Pe-ter!' She was finding now it was painful to speak. 'Pe-ter! I must . . . get Doctor Arnison. Ned is ill, Ned Ridley. He . . . he got caught in a trap. Will . . . will you go to the town and fetch him? The doctor . . . the doctor.'

'The doctor's not in the town, he's along there, away at the bottom of the road there.' The boy pointed. 'Mrs Thompson's had a bairn.'

'Thompson's? The cottage? Oh.' She pulled herself to her feet. 'Oh thanks. . . . Thanks, Pe-ter.'

She was some yards away from the cottage when she saw the doctor come out of the door and walk towards his horse, and she called 'Doc-tor! Oh Doc-tor! Doc-tor! don't go.'

Doctor Arnison turned slowly about and looked towards the bedraggled creature that was stumbling towards him, and when she came abreast of him he muttered under his breath, 'My God! child, what's happened to you?'

She was hanging on to him now. 'Doctor, you must come, it's Ned, Ned Ridley. The trap's taken off his fingers.'

'What! Ned, Ned Ridley?'

'Yes, yes, doctor, Ned Ridley. He got his hand caught in a trap, a mantrap.'

The doctor now put his hand on her head and said quietly, 'You're very hot, child. Where have you been all night? You know there's a hue and cry out for you? Now about Ned. Are you imagining this . . .?'

'No, no, doctor. Come.' She tried to pull him. 'Ned, he . . . he saved me. I nearly walked into the trap, and he slipped and it took his fingers off.'

'Oh no! No!'

'Yes, yes, doctor.'

'Get up.' He went to help her up on to the horse and she shook her head, saying, 'Not through the village. Oh no, doctor, no . . . not yet. I'll go back over the hills.'

'You've got to go through the village some time, Hannah, you've got to go back. From what I hear you are now a married woman.'

'Later, doctor, later I . . . I must go back to Ned now. Please, please.'

'Very well.'

He watched her stumble away. He didn't know what was really wrong with Ned Ridley and he wouldn't until he saw him, but he knew what was wrong with her. She was in a high fever. He shouldn't have let her go over there alone, yet he could imagine her reception whenever she were to join the Loam household, and she wasn't in any fit state to be badgered. Well anyway, he'd be at the Pele house before she was, that was sure.

He mounted his horse and set it off at a trot. . . .

On her journey back Hannah had to rest four times before she reached the yard again; and when she saw the doctor's horse already there she stood leaning against the wall and her head drooped on to her chest; then after a moment she crossed the yard and went into the stable-room.

The doctor turned from bending over Ned and said abruptly, 'Good; come and hold the lantern.'

Reluctantly it seemed, she went towards him; it was as if she had to drag her legs after her. She took the lantern from the doctor and as she held it breast high she looked down on Ned, but he was looking at the doctor, and his lips scarcely moving, was muttering, 'What do you mean about the arm, not takin' it off?'

'No, not if I can help it . . . and if you're lucky. But if that inflammation goes any further, well –' He paused then added, 'First things first. I'll have to get them off and tidy you up.' He made a short stab with his forefinger towards the hand lying on the bloodstained bandages. 'Got any spirits about?'

'Aye.'

'Well, you'd better take a long swig of it, Ned, for I'll have to take the top of your middle one off an' all.'

There was a moment's stillness in the stable, broken only by the neighing of one of the horses, and this seemed to convey something to Ned because, closing his eyes, he muttered thickly, 'They've never had their feed.'

'Aw well, they don't die by losing one meal. Don't worry about them, let's get you tidied up. Where's the whisky?'

'Kitchen . . . cupboard.'

The doctor now turned to Hannah and said quietly, 'Do you think you can fetch it?'

She made no answer but put down the lantern and went towards the kitchen. There were two bottles of whisky in the cupboard. She took out one, looked at it for a moment, then pulling out the cork, she poured about half an inch into a tin mug, which she raised to her lips and swallowed the contents in one gulp as she had seen Ned do. The next minute she was bending over the table coughing and spluttering and clutching at her chest; but when the spasm was over she straightened up and told herself she felt better, warm in fact all the way down to her waist.

When she reached the doctor's side again he glanced at her and, his lips set in a tight smile, he said knowingly, 'You should never gulp at that stuff. Give it here.' He took the bottle from her; then more than half filled a tin mug she held out towards him, and when he handed the mug to Ned he said, 'No need to tell you the best way to get it down you, is there, Ned?'

Ned made no reply but, rising on his elbow, he gulped at the contents and when he handed the mug back the doctor, in an aside to Hannah, said quietly, 'Fill it again; he's going to need it.'

It was as she went to do his bidding that the stable-room door was thrust open and Fred Loam stalked in; but he stopped in the middle of the room and stared at the three people on the low platform.

It was the doctor who spoke first and then quite casually, 'Glad to see you, Fred; I'm going to need help here.'

'Glad to see me, be damned! What's all this about? You!' He was advancing on Hannah now when the doctor took the short step down from the platform and, thrusting out his hand, grabbed Fred by the shoulder, saying sternly, 'Whatever your differences they can be settled later; if I don't see to Ned right away it'll be his arm I'll be taking off next. Now I want you to give me a hand.'

Fred turned his gaze slowly from the doctor and glared at Hannah, where she was standing now, her back pressed tight against the stone wall at the far side of the platform, and she in turn looked at him.

He was as dishevelled as she was, and he looked wild, half crazy. She stopped herself from whimpering, 'I'm sorry;' the time was past for saying such futile words, and sorry wouldn't cover what she had done, both to him and to Ned.

It was her mother to blame. Yes! Yes! it was. She was now shouting in her head at her mother: 'You should have kept your mouth shut. I'd have rather been the mister's flyblow. Yes, I would, I would.'

It must be the whisky, she thought, that was burning up her body, for even the tangled strands of her hair seemed to be giving off heat, for they lay hot against her face and she pushed them back from each side of her cheeks as she watched Fred standing by Ned's side now looking down at the hand and saying, 'How did he get that?'

The doctor made a small movement with his head, then said, 'Trap, he got it in a trap. Hannah, bring me a bowl of boiling water, and Fred, bring my bag nearer.'

As they went to do the doctor's bidding they had to pass each other, and when Fred glared at her and his lips squared away from his teeth she turned her head away as if warding off a blow.

The doctor rummaged in his bag for a moment; then taking out an implement that looked like a miniature three-sided poker with a wooden handle, he handed it to Fred, saying below his breath, 'Go and stick that in the fire. When it's red bring it back quick; the joints are dirty I'll have to cauterize them.'

Fred looked at the small instrument in his hand for a moment, then turned and went into the kitchen.

Again Hannah and he had to pass each other and when he came abreast of her he caught her by the shoulder and, bringing his face down to hers, he growled, 'You've made a bloody laughing stock of me, haven't you? But by God! you'll pay for it. I promise you that, I'm not to be laughed at. An' where've you been all night? In here with him?'

'Leave go of me.' She took her two hands and thrust them against his chest and he let go of her, but he remained standing a pace away. 'Leave go of you, you say! You forget who you are. You forget what happened yesterday. You married me, do you remember? You married me. God! I could kill you this minute. I could take a knife and slit you up.'

When she closed her eyes and her hands fell flat on the table and she bent over them, he stared at her for a moment and, his voice changed and quiet now, he said brokenly, 'You shouldn't have done this to me, Hannah, you shouldn't.' Then he went to the fire and thrust the implement with such force between the bars that his fingers were singed and he had to pull the instrument back to save the handle catching alight. . . .

They were all on the platform again. The two mangled fingers and the top of Ned's middle finger were lying on strips of blood-soaked sheets to the side of her. Ned had just finished drinking another half mug of whisky and his face looked like parchment spotted here and there with dark stubble. The doctor, taking the implement from Fred's hand, said, sharply now, 'Hold him down by the shoulders.'

She watched Fred's great hands gripping Ned's shoulders. When the doctor put the hot instrument to the raw stumps of the fingers it was the smell of burning flesh that made her stomach heave, but it was Ned's piercing scream which seemed to lift her bodily up, then throw her down to the floor, that blotted everything out for the next three days. . . .

'Go down,' said the doctor to Fred, 'and bring Mother Fletcher up from the village; he can't be left alone for the next few days. And it'll be touch and go whether or not I shall have to move up further; it all depends on the singeing; if it does the trick.'

'What about her?' Fred pointed to where Hannah was lying insensible on the straw, and the doctor replied, 'Well, as soon as you're back we'll take her down. She's another one that'll need attention for the next few days, or perhaps weeks.'

'Why?' The word was an abrupt demand.

'Because Fred, if my diagnosis is right your wife's got a fever on her, but as yet I can't tell what kind. Once she's in bed and I can examine her then I'll know more.'

'A fever?' There was actual fear on Fred's face. Fever could mean cholera, and there had been an outbreak of that along the Tyne.

'Oh, don't get worried, it could just be an ordinary fever caused by exposure, and by the look of her she's certainly been through some exposure.'

'It's her own bloody fault.'

'Yes, perhaps it is, Fred. But that's your business, for you to sort out; mine is. . . .'

'Aye, take it from me, doctor, an' I will sort it out an' all.'

'No doubt you will, Fred, no doubt you will, but now go on, get down and bring Mother Fletcher, because I can't stay here all day, I've got a full list.

Ah, and your cart to take Hannah down. Go on now.'

It was an hour later when they lifted Hannah into the cart. She had
regained consciousness but was gabbling incoherently most of the time, and
of his two patients the doctor was more concerned about her at the present
moment than he was about Ned. Ned was a tough type; even if later he
should have to take his arm off to the elbow, he would survive, but this girl
was a different piece of humanity, and although her physical condition was
causing him some worry, her mental state was of even more concern to him.
     He had only a garbled idea of what had happened since the wedding
ceremony. The village gossip had quickly spread to the town and everybody
in that small but widespread community had known about it before the light
failed. Some of the townsmen had even joined in the hunt for her, looking
upon it, he thought, as a bit of a lark, helping a man to hunt his bride on
his wedding-day. . . .
     It was as if the whole village had had word of their coming for there
wasn't a door that was closed, except perhaps that of her one-time house,
thought the doctor; and that was hidden from view anyway behind trees.
     When he pulled his horse to a stop outside the butcher's shop and Fred,
having jumped from his seat was walking towards the door, the doctor cried
at him, 'Carry her in, man! She's in no fit state to walk.'
     He watched Fred cast a furtive and angry glance up and down the street
and across the green before coming back to the cart where he grabbed at
Hannah's inert body and, as he would have carried a dead sheep, pig, or
young bullock, he threw her over his shoulder and stamped into the shop,
the doctor following him.
     'So you've found her?' Mrs Loam, her small body bristling, turned to the
doctor and cried, 'Nice how-do-you-do. If I had my way she wouldn't get
in the door.'
     'If you'd had your way, Daisy, half the population of the village and the
town, even, would be under the sod. Out of me way.' He almost pushed her
aside and followed Fred with his burden up the stairs, through the kitchen
and into a small bedroom, most of which was taken up with an iron and
brass bed, and when Fred dropped Hannah's limp body unceremoniously
on to it, he cried at him, 'Careful! Steady on, man. Have I to keep reminding
you, she's a sick woman?'
     'You've to keep remindin' me of nowt, doctor, not even the fact that I've
been made a bloody monkey out of. How would you feel in my place?'
     'I don't know, never having been in such a situation, although I think I
would tell myself, the better face I put on the matter the less the neighbours
would have to laugh about. And now send your mother in here, she'll be
more use than you at this time.'
     A minute later, Daisy Loam came marching into the room. Her hands on
her hips, her small face grim, her chin thrust out, she faced the doctor saying,
'If you think that I'm gona nurse that 'un, doctor, you're mistaken.'
     'Daisy' – the doctor now bent down to her – 'you and I have known each
other for a long time, and we've both got our faults. Mine is meanness I'm
told, because I demand my fee on the spot, and in cash instead of eggs,
chickens, or a bit of pork, although at times I've been known to make
exceptions. Your fault, Daisy, is that your mouth is too big for your body.'
His voice had risen on the last words until it was almost a shout, and he

ended, 'Always has been and likely always will be. They won't need to dig a grave for you when you die, they can just double you up and stick you in your mouth. . . . Now get at that side of the bed and help get those clothes off her.'

Like two combatants, they stared at each other. Then, her lips parting from their tight compressed line, she wagged her head as she said, 'You don't frighten me none. I'm tellin' you for nowt I'm not havin' her here; she's not respectable.'

'Whether you keep her here or not will be yours and your son's business. If you decide to send her back to where she came from, well and good; if you decide to send her into the workhouse hospital, well and good; but before either of those things happens I've got to get her clothes off, examine her, and make her ready, as it were, for wherever she's going. And' – his face was close to hers again – 'it might be into her coffin, Daisy. Now that would satisfy you, wouldn't it?'

The little woman turned her head slowly now and looked at the bed and the doctor's last words did seem to satisfy her because without further ado she started to undress Hannah. It would be a better description to say that she started to tear the mud-and-blood-stained clothing from her. . . .

It was about twenty minutes later when the doctor went into the kitchen and, looking from the son to the mother, then back to the son again, he said, 'She's very ill and she's got little resistance; the next twenty-four hours or so will be the most crucial. She could die, but if she doesn't I'd better warn you she'll need nursing for some weeks ahead. So Daisy' – he now turned his full attention to Mrs Loam – 'I'd see about getting her a place in the workhouse hospital, eh?'

'What d'you mean, workhouse hospital?' Fred was looking from one to the other.

'Well' – the doctor turned to Fred now – 'your mother tells me she's not having her here, so you can't just leave her in the street, and I doubt whether she'd be given admittance in the house along the road, so it's nothing but the House hospital.'

'The House hospital!' Fred was looking at his mother. 'Aye, I think you would an' all, you would send her there. Well, let me tell you, whatever she's done, she's done it to me an' I'll be the one who says if she goes or stays.'

'Talkin' big all of a sudden, aren't you?'

The doctor picked up his bag, and as he passed between them he moved one hand as if his action were meant to separate them, then said, 'I'll be along later in the day. In the meantime give her all the drink she can take, water, tea, anything.'

As no one went to open the stairhead door for him or follow him down the stairs he said loudly, 'It's all right, it's all right, I can see myself out.'

Not until the shop door clanged closed did Daisy Loam turn on her son. Taking her fist she banged it on the bare kitchen table as she cried at him, 'Blasted fool! that's what you are, a laughing stock. The whole countryside's afire. You won't be able to lift your head in the town, and on Hexham Fair day . . . well, the town crier 'll be chantin' it. He was right, the doctor, she should go into the House.'

'Shut up!'

'Don't you tell me to shut up.' She came at him, her forearm raised. 'I'm warnin' you I wouldn't stand any old lip from your father, so I'm not standin' it from you.'

'Listen, Ma.' He now bent down towards her. 'As I see it now, my father was a bloody fool, a soft-headed, frightened, bloody fool. Now this is my house, my shop, my business; all he asked was that I take care of you, an' I'll do that, but I'm goin' to run me own life. . . . Don't you bloody well dare!'

She had picked up a long wooden rolling-pin from the table and had raised it above her head, but his voice stayed her hand, and, his face now almost purple, he went on, 'As true as I'm standin' here, I'll fell you to the floor if that as much as flicks me.'

The rolling-pin was lowered. She stepped back from him, her lower lip thrust out so much that it exposed where it joined the gums, and her face twisted into a sneer as she cried, 'God! to think I should live to see the day. I could spit on you. That anything that came out of me should turn so bloody soft, an' for that 'un in there' – her arm bent at the elbow, she thrust her thumb out stiffly towards the bedroom door – 'after all you know about her, after all the whole countryside knows about her. What for did she run from the church after she read that?' She was now stubbing her finger towards the crumpled rain-smeared paper lying on the table. 'She'd heard that she was no relation to them. Well, why didn't she turn to the second one, Robert, and declare her news? Why did she have to run hell for leather over the hills to the mine, to the big, fair-headed ninny? The men that were on shift there had their own ideas why, an' they didn't keep it to themselves, did they? Came through the rain like a wild woman in her bride's frock, mud up to the waist, hair streaming. Some said she looked like a witch. And then she goes gasping into the cabin and shouts at him, "We're not related." Pat Sculley was outside and heard the lot. Then apparently getting no satisfaction from that quarter, what did she do? She runs to Ned Ridley; an' she runs to the right bloke, doesn't she? for if ever there was a whoremaster he's one; he's been at it more times than Barney's bull. And tell me this, where did she spend the night? In the Pele house, if all is to be believed. And do you think they would lie with a bale of straw atween them?'

'Be quiet! D'you hear? Be quiet! You've said enough. But let me tell you this, no matter what you've got right you've got the last bit wrong.'

'Wrong, have I?'

'Aye, because some time yesterday Ned Ridley got his hand caught in a trap an' I've just this mornin' helped to take his fingers off.'

She remained silent for a moment, her body straightened from its aggressive position, and she blinked her eyes, then said, 'His hand in a trap?'

'That's what I said, his hand in a trap. An' he's lost three fingers and half the hand, and he's likely to lose the rest of it up to the elbow.'

As she turned away now and went towards the fire, he went on, 'From the little bit the doctor told me, an' what he got out of her, Ned saved her from goin' headlong into the trap itself.'

'To my mind he should have let her go.' She threw a steely glance at him over her shoulder. 'However bad he is, he's of more use in the world than she is. But what's a man with only one hand?'

'By! Ma, you're a bitter pill. And I'll tell you something now when the truth is on the table. 'Tisn't the day or yesterday I've thought it. An' another thing, you've taken me for a softy all these years, an' for peace's sake I've let you wear the trousers, but no more. When I pull them on each day from now on it'll be as the man of the house.'

'God Almighty! God Almighty! the new order.' She was looking into the fire and her head bobbed forward with each word, and he repeated, 'Aye, God Almighty! God Almighty! the new order. An' the first part of it is this, I'll see to her meself, and you see to the shop.'

She turned on him now like a little fury, screaming, 'Why don't you also tell me if I don't like it I know what I can do?'

His face running sweat, his thick lips pushed outwards, he answered her in kind. 'You've said it, so let it stick. She's me wife, an' she's going to be given her place by you and everybody else, or they'll know the reason why.'

When he stalked from her out of the room and banged the door behind him she gazed at it for a moment; then her head back, she let out a high, shrilling laugh and, looking up towards the low ceiling, she asked, as if of God, 'Did you ever see one of those great big turnips, an' when you opened it up there was nowt inside, all boast, full of wind an' watter? That's my son, wind an' watter.'

Fred, standing at the side of the bed looking down on Hannah thrashing from side to side, heard his mother's words, and he bowed his head against them.

He had stood up to her, but could he keep it up? His father hadn't been able to and he had been a strong man; he had bartered his strength for peace. . . . And he, too, liked peace.

# Chapter One

## The Woman

It was July. The world was bright outside; the hills were blue, green, purple and black and the sky was like a white veil trailing over them.

She had been able to get up out of bed now for three days and to sit by the small square bedroom window. Her chair was low and the sill shut from her gaze the back earth yard, with the dry midden at the bottom and the ditch beyond, in which the residue from the village flowed into the river.

How long had she been in this room? Four and a half weeks if she counted the days, but four and a half lifetimes if she went by the change within her, for not only had her body lost its flesh but her mind had lost something too. Never again would she feel young, never again would she count her age in years, never again would she think as a girl thinks.

At times she was devastated at the change that had taken place in her being, but at others she recognized the inevitableness of it. She had caused so much havoc in one day that had it not wrought a change in her, then she would have questioned whether or not she was human.

She could have accepted her change of environment and quickly adapted to it, but for two things: Fred's mother and Fred's hands.

Fred's mother was an inhuman woman. Apparently she herself wasn't the only one who thought so, for the two villagers who had kindly called to see her had expressed their opinion of Mrs Loam in whispered but emphatic terms. Mrs Wheatley, the chandler's wife, and Mrs Buckman, the blacksmith's wife, had both looked in on her, and she had not underestimated the courage it took for them to brave Mrs Loam, nor the significance of their visit. She liked to think it showed that no matter what she had done she wasn't being condemned by the entire village. Yet at the same time she wondered if they weren't merely taking advantage of the situation to get a sly dig at Mrs Daisy Loam.

'You stick to your guns, lass,' the blacksmith's wife had said.

'Stand up to her or she'll wipe her feet on you,' the chandler's wife had said.

Stick to your guns . . . stand up to her, it was easier said than done. If only she felt stronger. Doctor Arnison said it would be another month before she felt herself again, and only yesterday she had asked the doctor to tell Fred just that. And he must have done so, for Fred came in and stood by the window here and, looking out of it while speaking to her, he had said, 'She won't stand for you bein' in here much longer; she says she wants help, it's her back.' He had turned and looked down at her and in a form of appeal had added, 'If you could make the push, just to get about the kitchen an' do odd jobs for a start, it would pacify her.'

As she looked up at him she had experienced a feeling of pity for him, and all of a sudden the thought came to her that if they were on their own something good might evolve from this union; that was until he pulled a chair to her side, sat down, then, slipping his hand under the blanket, caressed her thigh.

It was strange but when she thought of him she seemed to divorce him from his hands, those big, red, wandering hands that seemed to have a separate life apart from him, how he spoke, how he acted. If they strayed beyond her own hands their touch made her whole body recoil . . .

That was yesterday; and from something he had said then she had dreaded today. And today was here, and Fred was here, coming into the room to sit beside her again and put his hands on her.

'Grand day outside.'

'Yes; yes, it looks lovely. I . . . I wish I was able to walk over the hills.' As she made this remark she had a vivid picture of the Pele house and the mangled fingers lying on the bloody sheet. No one had mentioned Ned to her since she had been better, not even the doctor; and every day she meant to bring up the subject, but she felt she couldn't.

'Oh well, it won't be long now, you'll soon be on your feet and trotting about. I . . . I told her' – he thumbed down towards the floor and the shop – 'that, come the end of the week, you'd be lendin' a hand.'

Sticking his foot out, he deftly hooked it around the supporting rails of the wooden chair and dragged it towards him and sat down by her side.

She hadn't put the blanket round her today, not because she felt too warm, for even with the sun hot outside she still felt the cold; but she had left it off in the hope that its absence might deter his hand from straying; and for a moment it seemed to be having the desired effect . . . But only for a moment, for, resting his elbows on his knees and clasping his hands between them he leant forward and, seeming to address them, he said, 'I'm cramped to bits on that couch out there; I think the time's come for me stretchin' me legs so I'll turn into bed the night.'

When he turned his head and looked at her she swallowed deeply, then gave a little gasp, and he brought himself fully round to her now and whispered fiercely, 'I've been patient, you can't say I haven't. 'Tisn't everybody that would have waited as long as me. And she's scorned me she has. Me life's been hell on earth lately with one thing an' another, but that most of all. Now you can't say I pushed you; an' don't look at me like that. You're me wife, and there's a time for everything. Anyway' – he got abruptly to his feet – 'I can't wait no longer and that's the top and bottom of it, so I'll be in the night.' He nodded abruptly at her, then went out.

She leant her head back against the rail of the wooden chair. A time for everything. She turned her eyes towards the window in the direction of where the Pele house lay and a voice rang through her head, crying, 'Oh Ned, why weren't you there when I needed you?' But it came back at her, asking now, 'Would you have known why you needed him?' She shook her head from side to side. No, perhaps she didn't know then, but she knew now; oh yes, she knew now why she had needed Ned Ridley, why she'd always needed him, as he had apparently needed her, because now her mind was a woman's mind and tonight her body would be turned into a woman's body.

Why were lives planned in such a way? Why were people made in such a way that the thought of one particular being touching you could fill you with revulsion and terror even though he was not bad, not evil.

Life was a strange, complicated thing; she had a strong almost compelling urge to be rid of it.

## Chapter Two

'Now! mistress.' Mrs Loam weighed the term with scornful ridicule and she repeated it, 'Now! mistress, you've had nigh on three weeks fairy-footin' it around the house, washin' a cup here, dustin' a vase there. Well, the time has come when you've got to earn your title, because I'm not able to carry on both top an' bottom, so in future I'll lay out your duties for you – I wouldn't sit down if I were you 'cos you'll only have to get on your feet again in a minute.'

'I'll sit down when I wish, Mrs Loam.'

'Will you, begod! Well now, let me tell you, lass.' The little woman altered her tone from one of mockery to that of threat as she poked her sharp ferret face towards Hannah and went on, 'I can make your life bearable, but only just, or I can make it sheer hell on earth. Now get that into your head straightaway. An' listen to this an' all. Me son could do without you; if you had been lost for ever on those fells, he would have got by as if he had never known you; but me, I'm a horse of another colour, he can't do without me 'cos I've forgot more about butcherin' than he'll learn in his lifetime. He's a dunderhead, he can hardly give a customer the right change for a florin, do you know that? He had the chance like any other village lad, he went to Allendale Town School for nigh on three years, but did he take anything in? Nowt, only air. I run this business . . . *me*! As I did in his father's time. Who went to the market then and still goes to pick the beasts? *me*. If he went on his own they could pang a sack filled with straw on him and he'd buy it for a heifer; but me, they don't pass skin and bones on to me. Monday 'tis the only time he does any butcherin' because then he does the killin'; but any damned fool with a hammer can kill a beast as long as there's a couple to hold it. So now, mistress, you see the position. If there were to be a toss-up atween us, he'd let you go, he'd have to, so we'll start by allottin' out the work, eh?'

Gripping hold of the edge of the table, Hannah drew herself to her feet. She was trembling inwardly, her stomach seemed to be loose within its casing, but she saw to it that her hands did not give her away; and now, looking steadily back and down on her mother-in-law, she said quietly but firmly, 'I shall do my share, but don't think you can intimidate me, Mrs Loam, because you can't, for if I care to put my mind to it I'll learn about the butchering business. Yes, and go into the market too.' Her voice was gathering strength and she nodded her head down at the little woman as she went on, 'And I'm sure people would welcome me and help me, and Fred too. You make your son out to be almost an idiot; well let me tell you something, Mrs Loam, if he were a complete idiot, drooling at the mouth, he'd still be a better person than you.'

'You brazened young bugger you! Who do you think you're talkin' to?' Mrs Loam's fist shot out.

'You! Mrs Loam, you! And don't you dare push me again.' Hannah had staggered back as the little woman dug her in the shoulder. 'Let that be the first and last time because should you lift your hand to me again, I'll strike you back . . . with . . . with the first thing I can lay my hands on.'

Dear Lord! Dear Lord! what had she sunk to. Fancy her saying that, that she would strike this woman, this old woman, because she was fifty if she was a day. She had a mental picture of her teachers who had coached her in courtesy. Then as if they were indeed present she wiped them away with an imaginary sweep of her arm. What had education to do with the situation she was in? Was she not merely reacting as her inborn nature prompted her? And if she wished to survive and escape this woman's domination she would have to let that nature have rein; that nature that had been bred of two ordinary common people in the roughest quarter of the city of Newcastle.

She now made herself walk away from the table and towards the bedroom; but before she had closed the door behind her the little woman's voice battered on her eardrums, crying, 'All right, me girl! You're the mistress now but listen to what this mistress has been doin' for years past, but not any more. Monday you wash, bedding, clothes, slaughter cloths, aprons, the lot; Tuesday you scrub out downstairs every bit of wood in the shop, includin' the floor, that's after you sweep up the old sawdust; Wednesday you bake, and you make a batch of pies, an' in between times you've done your ironin' an' your cooking; Thursday you prepare for the week-end's cleaning, you do your brasses and the steel fire-irons and the bedrooms. Are you listenin'?' She was now yelling through the door. 'Friday you finish in here, then you go down in the yard and clear up the entrails that's gone stinkin' and you finish up doin' the netty; pleasant job that, emptying the buckets; Saturday if you're still on your feet you help in the shop. An' that, me girl, is an easy week.' Her voice as she finished rose to the pitch of a scream.

Hannah was now standing at the window, her hands pressed hard across her mouth, and her eyes were tightly closed as she cried inside, 'I won't be able to stand it, I won't, I won't, I'll break.' For a moment she had the mental picture of herself running through the village back up to the house and flinging herself at Anne Thornton's feet and begging to be taken in.

She opened her eyes and looked downwards. There were women in their backyards on each side of the railed space and they were mouthing words to each other across it.

The whole village would know that Mrs Loam was 'giving it' to her. She turned from the window and sat down on the edge of the bed. There was silence in the house now, and as she sat there arose in her a strength born of defiance, and she nodded her head to her thinking. Margaret had learned to work with her hands, do rough work with her hands; little Tessie had done rough work with her hands all her life, as had Bella. All the women in the village did their own housework, washed, baked, cleaned. Was she herself stupid? Couldn't she learn? She was gaining strength every day; all she needed now to accomplish such menial tasks was strength of will and the determination to show that little vixen out there that the accomplishment she was so proud of could be attained by anyone who had even the mental capacity attributed to her son. There was only one snag, she had never done any washing or baking before. Yet she had watched both Bella and Tessie performing the household chores countless times, so what she must do was to try and remember the processes by which they achieved clean clothes and new bread.

If she had been able to spend another year in the house she likely would have learned how to cook, because after Margaret left school Bella instructed her in the making of special dishes.

Margaret. She was hurt by Margaret's indifference towards her. She had thought she might come and visit her when she was ill, just once, but all she had done was send her two short notes; the first one said she was so sorry to hear of her illness, she herself was very busy at the school; the second note said she was glad to hear she was recovering, she was still very busy at the school. There was no mention of Mr Hathaway or her forthcoming marriage.

Then there was Robert. He had been to see her only once, but even on that occasion he appeared ill at ease and had seemed glad to go.

And John. John was soon to be married . . . Did this fact hurt her? Strangely, not at all, which showed how changed she had become, in fact now she was amazed at the person she had once been, the person who had felt she would die without John's love, or at least go to her grave a maiden lady. How young she had been, and silly.

It seemed to her at the present time that not only had the missis thrown her off, but the entire family too; yet she had got on so well with all the others; except Betsy of course. Even Bella and Tessie had drifted away from her. They both had a half-day's leave a month; she would have thought that one or other would have popped in to see how she fared.

Well, it would appear that she had to stand on her own feet now and if she wished to survive in this house she had best follow the advice that Miss Emily doled out at the beginning of every term to new and old pupils alike: 'There is no time like the present to tackle the difficult task.' So she must go down now, right now, to the wash-house, light the fire and initiate herself into the disagreeable task of learning to do a day's washing . . .

She had the pleasure a moment later of seeing her mother-in-law's countenance stretched in surprise when she marched into the kitchen, took up the tinder box from the mantelshelf, some dry sticks from the pan hob to the side of the fireplace, and an old newspaper from a rack in the corner.

Whipping a rough hessian apron from a nail on the door, she laid it on the fender and placed the other articles on it. Then she rolled up her sleeves, gathered up the hessian apron and without casting a glance at the now silent staring little woman, she pulled open the stairhead door and went down the stairs, her back stiff with the knowledge that whatever reaction her first day's work might bring, the attempt at it had silenced her mother-in-law, at least temporarily.

Her back ached, her arms ached, her legs ached, in fact there wasn't a part of her that didn't ache. She had asked herself a number of times this day how little Tessie managed to get through a mountain of washing, and not only get through it but sing as she worked.

She sat at the table now, scarcely able to eat the meal of stewed mutton and solid dumplings that her mother-in-law had thrust before her. She had noted earlier on in the day that when the little woman was doling out her duties she had said nothing about cooking the daily meals, because as she had already found out, Mrs Loam was a glutton where food was concerned, and she would attend to at least the needs of her stomach if to nothing else.

Fred sat opposite her shovelling the food into his mouth as if he had not eaten for a week, and in between his chewing he jerked his head at her, grinned, and for the third time since sitting down at the table he congratulated her in his own way on her efforts. 'By! I can't get over it, you gettin' your hand in with a whole day's wash, eh! By! that's somethin', that is for a start.'

'God Almighty!' Mrs Loam's spoon clattered into her bowl. 'Why don't you pin a medal on her? Every woman in the village washes on a Monday, come hail, sleet or snow, an' I never heard of their men gapin' and yappin' like open-mouthed cods . . .'

'Now, Ma, shut it! an' give honour where it's due . . .'

'Oh my God!' The little woman raised her hands and her eyes to the ceiling; then getting up abruptly from a half-finished meal, she cried, 'This's too much for me, I'm away to me bed.'

When her bedroom door banged closed, Fred leant across the table and, grinning widely at Hannah, whispered, 'Once we're out of the way she'll be back in here stuffin' her kite. Oh, I know her of old.'

Hannah made no comment whatever, she was too weary and too tired even to eat. But before she could go to bed there would be the crocks to wash up, and the great basket of linen that she still had to sort, fold and roll up for ironing on the morrow . . . But even when she went to bed her work wouldn't be finished. Oh no!

No! She shook her head at the mental picture. If he touched her tonight she would scream, she would claw at him, she would fight him . . . She looked at him. No she wouldn't, she wouldn't have the strength. She would have to do what she had tried to do other nights, lie passive and let it pass over her as if it were all happening to someone else, for she had discovered that this side of marriage wasn't only physical but mental too. If for instance you couldn't obliterate it from your mind altogether you could in the dark imagine it was happening with someone else . . .

While she washed up the dirty crocks, and scraped the soot from the encrusted bottom of the stew pan, then saw to the linen, Fred sat by the fire, his stockinged feet on the fender, a clay pipe in his mouth, and he talked. He talked about getting the horse shod and a new hub on the cart wheel. He talked reminiscently of his father telling of the great times they had at the Corn Suppers – he pronounced it 'kern' – which were now dying out as the farmers were using their land more for grazing. 'End of harvest they'd go on till the dawn,' he said, 'eating, dancing, dressin' up or dressin' down.' He laughed. 'I was at a couple when I was but a youngster – By! lad, the things that they got up to. Dad never got to one after he married. She had religion bad then.' He jerked his head towards the bedroom door and, his voice low, he added, ''Tis bad enough now but then it was served up with the mornin' crowdy and the supper an' all, seven days a week. Oh, she's better now. You won't believe it, but she is.'

Hannah said nothing, she said nothing until he began to talk in detail about the big strong beast he had killed that morning. 'By God! hefty he was. Took three of them to hold him while I hammered at him . . .'

Quickly turning from the table, Hannah cried below her breath, 'Please! I don't want to hear about that,' and he laughed now and said, 'Aye, well, I don't suppose you would, havin' a weak stomach like. But it's got to be done nevertheless.' Then after a pause he went on, 'I heard somethin' in the town about up there.'

Although she had her back to him and she didn't see him jerking his head in the direction of the house at the end of the village, she knew to whom he was referring. 'He's to be married come September. Big do an' all I hear. Our Master John's tryin' to ape young Mr Wentworth Beaumont. But I'd say he'll have a job. By! he will that 'cos that was a day to remember. You were at school then.' He turned his head towards her. 'Funny that, only two years gone an' you were at school. By! but I never forget that day an' the stuff we sold here. What the others must have made at Hexham, Bywell, and in Weardale, God only knows, 'cos there was some meat chewed up in Allendale that day, I can tell you. All the miners had a field day . . . an' his tenants an' all. The bands playin' and the balls at night. The town was illuminated. As to what happened up at Bywell Hall, lordy! they say that was a do . . .

'Course, about the jollifications at Allenheads, that was a pity that was, but more of a pity for John Sanderson and Isaac Short 'cos they were suffocated by smoke at the mine that very day. Just near the mouth an' all. An' all through some daft buggers throwing their candle ends into a heap afore they left off work. Anyway, the food didn't go wastin', the poor around there got a bellyful. So I've got to laugh to meself when I think of Mr John Thornton tryin' to cap that lot, and him not one penny to rub against the other. In any case it's her father who's standin' the racket; he's always liked to play big, has Farmer Everton. Gentleman farmer he calls hissel'; his wife's even worse.'

He twisted round in the chair now, 'I bet you what you like you're not invited, 'cos you know why?' He waited for her to make some comment, but when she didn't, he went on, 'Well, 'tis plain isn't it, you're married to me, an' they couldn't ask one without t'other, now could they? . . . Bloody snots the lot of them!'

There was silence in the kitchen for a while: then of a sudden he took his feet from the fender, knocked out the doddle from his pipe on the grate and, standing up, he looked at the fire, saying, 'No use banking it down 'cos she'll be out.' Then turning towards Hannah where she was bending over the table slowly folding a sheet, he touched her arm, saying abruptly, 'Leave that and come on.'

She remained in the bent position for a moment while the muscles of her stomach tensed; then putting the sheet on the top of the pile of linen, she lifted it from the table and placed it in the basket before, her feet dragging, she followed him into the bedroom.

# Chapter Three

It was the third Friday in September and the day of the cattle show and sheep fair, the Tup Fair, over near Allenheads corn mill. Both Fred and his mother had gone to the fair; as Mrs Loam had said, she had never missed a fair since as far back as you could remember and she wasn't missing the one today, and her son was going to take her . . . or else.

Mrs Loam had been amazed that Fred himself should have wavered about going just because that upstart bitch of a wife of his had said she didn't wish to go. Apparently she didn't like the sight of cattle being pushed about. And she had married a butcher! Dear God! it was laughable.

And now Hannah had the house to herself and it felt strange. Neither of them had need to enquire what she would do with herself in their absence because there was still plenty to be done. Fair or no fair, it was still Friday and there was the kitchen to finish cleaning. Moreover, as always, they opened the shop on a Saturday morning bright and early, and there was fresh sawdust to be put on the floor; and the back yard had to be scraped over and the midden cleaned.

She walked into the bedroom and to the window and looked over the yard, over the middens and the ditch, away to the hills, the clean hills, the hills she hadn't trodden since the day she had stumbled across them back to the Pele house. She had no memory of being brought back over them to this house.

She had now been married over three months, and for almost two months of that time she had been ill; for the remainder she had been learning what hard work was; and she hadn't been, as Bella would have said, across the doors since, except to go through the backyard to the lavatory.

Last week her mother-in-law had demanded to know which church or chapel she was going to attend on a Sunday: Was she for going back to that 'un at the top of the road? or was she going to pray to God in a proper manner? Which meant, Hannah took it, was she going to attend the Primitive Methodist Chapel?

She could smile to herself when she remembered how she turned on her mother-in-law, crying, 'Neither the Primitive Methodist, nor the Wesleyan Methodist, nor the Church of England, nor the House of Friends.' And she felt she could give herself credit for her stand, for she knew that had been a very bold attitude to take because in the village, as well as in Allendale, you had to belong to one or the other, that is if you were a woman. Men could be indifferent; men attended the religious ceremonies only if it pleased them, and if they didn't it wasn't held against them. But should their wives and children not attend, then the families were known as godless . . . Moreover, an entire lack of religious choice was very bad for business, if you happened to be in business.

As she stared into the distance she felt her heart beat quicker. She had not been ordered to stay in the house but she knew that even if she had been she would not have obeyed, for of a sudden the hills were calling, the hard rock, heather-padded, rainbow-hued hills.

She went quickly now to the cupboard in which she hung her clothes and having taken down a brown corded dress she held it at arm's length for a moment before tearing off the bibbed coarse apron that almost enveloped her and her stained blouse and skirt. Within a matter of minutes she was ready for outside with a cloak over her dress and her bonnet on.

The shop door was bolted on the inside but the back door was never bolted, nor was the low gate at the bottom of the yard. She went through it, past the midden, jumped the smelling ditch, crossed the piece of open grassland, skirted the tangle of bramble bushes that ran like a hedge for some distance, and within a few minutes she was at the foot of the first rise.

She didn't stop or look back until she reached the top and there she stood drawing in great gulps of air and gazing about her. She had turned her back on the village and a little way in front of her the land sloped into a shallow valley before rising again to another hill; but away to the left it fell into gentle shallows that spread out into fields. Walking on again she went down the slope but now she veered to the right where the ground rose less steeply and the hills were drawn out.

When she next stopped it was to look at the steep rise on which the Pele house stood; and now without hesitation she made straight for it, not hiding the fact from herself any longer that this was the main reason why she had wished to get out of doors.

She had wanted fresh air, she had wanted to feel the wide barrenness of the hills and the contradictory close enfolding comfort of them; but more than anything else she wanted to speak to Ned, to look at his hand, to find out how he was managing, to see him and to hear him.

She saw him as she was nearing the wall, and he must have seen her, for she watched him stop abruptly in the yard near the door to the Pele, stare towards her for a moment, then turn swiftly and walk back around the side of the house.

Her step slowed, then stopped. He didn't want to see her. But she must speak to him, she must, just this once.

As she passed the stable-room there was no sound of the chink, chatter and stamping of the ponies, which meant that he had completed a sale and hadn't started on gathering another bunch. But if that was the case why hadn't he gone to the fair? There would be ponies there.

She walked around the side of the house, but he wasn't there; then she saw him on the hillside bending over and scraping at something.

Walking very slowly now she approached him, then stopped when she was about three yards from him.

'Hello, Ned.'

'What? Oh!' He jerked his head as if in surprise. ''Tis you.' He stared at her for a moment, then again bent his back and went on raking at the earth.

'How are you?'

'Me? Never better. How's yourself?'

She made no answer to this but took another two steps towards him. He was holding the rake in his right hand, while with what was left of his other hand he was pushing pieces of stone here and there over the ground.

He didn't stop what he was doing, he didn't straighten his back, he didn't speak. The silence spread round them and even covered the sound of the metal rake tearing at the ground.

'What are you looking for?'

'Looking for?' He screwed his head round and cast his glance up at her. 'Gold, lead gold; I'm gona open a mine here.'

Her eyes widened, her lips parted, and she said incredulously, 'A mine? A lead mine?'

'Aye, why not?' He straightened up now and stared at her.

'No . . . no reason, except . . .'

'Except what?'

'I . . . I always thought it took a lot of money to open a mine.'

'Who says I haven't a lot of money?'

She recalled his bragging about the savings behind the stones in the Pele house.

'And what you haven't got there's always somebody ready to lend it to you if you've got the right security. And this is the right security. It's a hill; there's water handy' – he pointed down to the stream – 'an' I bet there's veins under here as rich as any hereabouts. You only want to drive an adit into it an' we'll soon see. But anyway I don't need to see, I don't need an adit. I've found plenty of shoad ore on this hill afore now, and it's the real stuff, not float ore. Look.' He picked up a piece of stone that looked as if it had been bleached and he said, 'That's it, that's where the money lies. I've found pieces of that from the size of peas to pigs' bladders.' He was talking rapidly now, the colour on his face deepening as he went on, 'And there's not only lead in it' – he kicked the ground with the toe of his boot – 'but silver. Aye, silver. Old Beaumont sent a cake weighing over twelve thousand ounces to that exhibition in London in fifty-one, worth over three thousand pounds it was, the one cake. What one can do another can, you've got to start somewhere. An' if I want to open up a mine here I'll open up a mine and no bloody combine of Beaumont's and his lackeys, like Sopwith and the rest, will stop me.' He took the rake now and flung it from him, and she watched it circling in the air before it fell somewhere up the hill, then slide down again. 'And what the hell do you want comin' here for anyway? Think I've been free from trouble long enough and 'twas time you brought me some more?'

Her face twitched. She bit on her lip, her head drooped, then she turned about and walked from him; but when he bawled at her, 'That's it! walk away. You bring trouble wherever you go, but do you stand to face the consequences? Not you.'

. . . 'Hello there.' They both turned and looked in the same direction. To the side of them, from the path leading round the belt of trees, a woman was approaching. Even from the distance she looked big, and to Hannah she seemed to grow larger as she approached. She had a basket on her arm and a shawl over her head and clogs on her feet.

'Hello there,' she said again. 'Nice day.' She stopped and looked from one to the other, and now Ned spoke to her, saying, 'Hello, Nell, how is it?'

'Oh pretty fair, pretty fair. I brought you a bite. I was at me bakin', an' I thought, I know who'd like a pie.'

'You thought right, Nell.' He had moved towards her and Hannah stood looking at them both. They looked of a like age, or perhaps the woman could be a little older than him, in her early thirties. Her body was straight and sturdy looking, her face big-boned but pleasant. They were talking together now as if she weren't there.

'I thought you might be at the fair, Ned.'

'Aw no, Nell, I've other fish to fry. An' I can get drunk without goin' to the fair.' They laughed together. 'Come in and have a sup tea.'

'Aye, I will, Ned, I will.'

They walked on now past her; then as if Ned had suddenly remembered her, he said, 'There'll be enough for another cup if you want one.'

She moved her head slowly and said, 'No thank you.'

'Please yourself. That's the best way, Nell, isn't it? Please yourself an' then you won't die in the pet.'

'You're right there, Ned; you're right there.'

'Why weren't you at the fair yourself, Nell?'

'Oh, 'cos I'm more partial to small company, Ned.' Their voices faded away.

As she watched them round the corner of the house she had the wild urge to run again as she had done that night in the rain, but the feeling passed as quickly as it had come.

She did not look back towards the stable-room as she went through the yard but she was aware that the doors were closed, and with their closing she knew she had to relinquish something, something she'd never had, something she should have had. But now it was gone, shut in behind the doors of the stable-room. From now on she must face up to the fact that she was a married woman, who washed and scrubbed and baked; she was an ordinary village wife who must forget that she had once played the piano, read books, liked poetry, painted a little, and sang.

She walked down the hillside, up and across the other hills, over the ditch, past the midden and into the house once more. She'd had all the fresh air she needed and she felt she never wanted to walk the hills again.

# Chapter Four

She had been married a year and her mother-in-law's new taunt now was that she must be barren because, as she said, give her son his due he was as full-bloodied as any bull he had ever slaughtered, but by the looks of things he had landed himself with a heifer and, work as he might, he wouldn't be able to change her into a cow.

Hannah let the old woman talk. Over the past months she had found silence to be her best weapon; in fact there were times when she felt she had lost the art of talking except in monosyllables, because when Fred talked he only needed a listener; his conversation ranged between the condition of the beasts he slaughtered, the rise or fall in price of meat, and the gossip that he heard in the market.

She had not even had the pleasure of bidding the time of day with the customers for he would not let her serve in the shop; not that she wanted to, because she hated handling the great slabs of wet meat, hated the sight of the blood, the smell of it, the sticky feel of it on her fingers.

Looking back over the year she couldn't believe that she had been but twelve months in this house, for it seemed she had passed her whole existence here. Yet there had been other times when she felt that it was but yesterday she had found herself in these dull rooms, and that if she didn't escape she would go mad. When this feeling came upon her she fostered it because it seemed to bring her alive again, wrench her out of the dullness of each day, the sameness of each day. It had the power to wipe out her apathy. Whenever she felt like this she would tell herself she must break her self-made rule, the only one she had stuck to, and accompany her husband and mother-in-law to the market.

And then something happened that brought her up out of the depths. Tessie came into the shop.

It was a Saturday morning. She was carrying a bucket of slops down the stairs, and such was the situation of the rooms that the staircase door led into a corner of the shop, and the door leading into the back shop was next to it, and so when she made this journey on the days when the shop was open she would for a brief moment see the customers, and this morning she saw Tessie; and Tessie, looking towards her, cried impulsively, 'Oh! hello, miss, I mean missis.' And with this she turned her face in apology towards Fred and leaning over the counter, whispered, 'Could I have a word with her, Fred, do you think?'

'Why, aye, I won't charge your missis for it. Go on.' He nodded, and she went hastily into the back shop; and there both she and Hannah stood looking at each other.

'It's a long time since I've seen you, Tessie.' Hannah found it difficult to speak.

'Aye, it is, miss.' Tessie now walked towards the far door, drawing Hannah with her, and there, straining her face upwards, she whispered, 'I've been tryin' to get a word with you for ages.' She glanced back towards the shop. 'You know she threatened us, Bella and me, that if we spoke to you we'd get the push? She seems mad at times, she seems beside herself.' She didn't add, 'She's never got over your wedding-day when she found out you'd really no claim on the master,' but went on, 'For weeks past now I've been comin' down with an order, ever since Miss Betsy caught cold, an' I haven't clapped eyes on you.' She reached up and placed her lips now against Hannah's ear. 'I've got a message for you.'

'A message?'

'Aye, 'tis from Ned Ridley.'

The colour swept up over Hannah's face, while at the same time she screwed up her cheeks questioningly, then whispered back, 'Ned?'

'Aye; I met him on my half-day. 'Twas a market day in the town an' we got crackin', an' he said if ever I saw you I was to ask you to go up.'

'Me?' Hannah now pointed to herself, then whispered, 'Go up, to the Pele house?'

Tessie was nodding. 'Aye, that's what he said. An' I had to keep me mouth shut. Well, I did, I didn't even tell Bella, 'cos Bella's tongue wags itself loose at times, an' I thought the way you're placed . . . well, you know what I mean.'

Hannah nodded dumbly; then they both started as Fred appeared in the doorway. There was laughter on his face but there was a question in his voice as he said, 'Tellin' secrets?'

'No, no, Fred . . . well' – Tessie tossed her head and laughed now – 'it'll soon be no secret that Mr Robert's done a bunk.'

'Mr Robert done a bunk?' Fred now moved slowly forward, wiping his hands on his apron. 'Well, well! When did this happen?'

'Oh.' Her head was bobbing up and down. 'Eeh! well, I'm not supposed to know or say anythin', but three days ago he went off like that.' She snapped her fingers. 'Left her a note . . . the missis, sayin' he was going to the Americas, somethin' about his da's cousin. From what I could gather that went on atween the missis and Miss Betsy, Master Robert had been writing to his aunt who was married to a man on a farm. Anyway, off he went, telling them in the letter not to worry, and that he couldn't stick the mine.'

'Well, well! Master Robert gone off. There'll soon be nobody there for you to look after, Tessie. Then what'll you do?'

'I'll still have a pair of hands on me, Fred.'

'Eeh! you're a cocky monkey, that's what you are Tessie Skipton. Come on, your meat's ready.' He half turned, then looked back at them and said, 'Have you had your fill of gossip atween you?'

'Aye, yes.' Tessie came towards him. 'I just wanted to tell miss, I mean missis, that bit about Master Robert, an' the latest about Miss Margaret not getting married after all. By! the missis was cock-a-hoop about that.' Tessie turned and nodded towards Hannah. 'All the bits in the Bible came out for days: As ye sow so shall ye reap, and what happens to them who don't honour their father an' mother. Oh, we got it morn, noon, an' night.'

She laughed now, and Fred with her, and Hannah, picking up the pail of slops again, went out into the yard and towards the ditch. Margaret not married; what had happened? Poor Margaret; she had been so sure of the man, so willing to give up everything for him . . . And Robert going off like that to America. As Fred said, they were nearly all gone. Of course there was John, but John was living far over the hills.

But these events weren't what Tessie had come to tell her . . . Ned wanted to see her. Why? Why? She raised her head and looked away over the ditch, over the field, and over the rise, but she felt no great impulse to rush in the direction of the Pele house because she was asking herself again, why? Did he want to put her in the picture, to tell her that he was marrying that woman, that big woman called Nell; the woman who baked for him, and had said openly and meaningfully that she preferred the company of two to a crowd?

She turned about and not looking where she was going she trod in some mire and, her face wrinkling in deep distaste, she wiped the mess from her clog on to a clump of grass; then walking along the bank to where a rivulet of clean water ran out of a gravel bank into the stream, she took off the clog and washed it, then rinsed her bucket in the stream before going further up the bank and laying it on the gravel bottom until it was half full of water, which would go towards filling the wash-house pot for Monday's task.

As she entered the shop Fred was standing idly looking out of the window and he turned to her and said, 'They're cutting down up there all right; one-and-six-worth, that's all she got. I've seen them spend as much as ten shillings a week when he was alive. It's hardly worth while keeping open; it's only the bloody miners who come in regular, an' then they can't pay up until the end of the month, an' some of them not then, an' they're grumbling like hell at havin' to pay fourpence ha'penny a pound. I'm almost paying that for it meself.'

He shook his head, then banged the chopper into the block before saying now and with bitterness, 'I could always be sure of the Bynges and Ricksons havin' a collop three times a week, but there was Mrs Rickson and Flora Bynge in Allendale Town, and Mrs Wheatley an' all, all buyin' there. They were shamefaced when they saw me. I'm all right to be made use of in the winter when they can't get out of their bloody doors for snow, but in the summer they jaunt into the town. Well, I'll . . . I'll remember, I'll remember.' He nodded at her. 'And there's that lot along there' – he motioned his head towards the other end of the village – 'joining together to have a mart at Christmas. Hope the next one they have one of 'em gets felled to the ground instead of the beast.'

She closed her eyes for a moment against the picture that the mart conjured up. It was a custom towards Christmas-time for a number of people to join together and buy a fat beast; then the men, who would be mostly drunk, killed the animal by a slow process; some would hold the animal's head whilst another attempted to strike the beast. Should he miss, as happened often, he had to pay a forfeit in the form of more liquor. The animals could die slowly and in agony. Finally the meat was carved up and dried for winter use and the money that was obtained for 'skelping the hide', which meant stripping it of tallow before selling the skin, was also spent in drink.

She turned from him and went up the stairs. They were barbarians, all of them, cruel barbarians; not only the poor, but the rich. Mantraps, deer stalking, rabbit coursing, cock fighting, bull baiting . . . and bull killing, men holding an animal while another beat it to death. The world was a cruel place.

On the Saturday night Mrs Loam reminded her son once again that he was driving her to the chapel at Allenheads on the morrow, where a minister on a circuit was stopping to preach; and to this Fred replied, 'You don't let me forget. Every day this week you've been on about it. You rattle on as much as your loom.' He nodded towards her where she was sitting in the corner of the kitchen weaving a narrow strip of cloth on a small loom.

'But you still haven't washed the cart down,' she said.

'I'll wash it down all it's gona get in the mornin',' he replied. 'And it's a useless task, as I see it, 'cos it'll be as bloody again within a few hours . . .'

In bed that night Fred whispered. 'Why won't you come along of us the morrow? and she answered, 'You know why; I think you'll agree that I have enough of your mother's company as it is.'

It said something for Fred's even temper and his understanding of his mother, and his wife also, that he didn't press the point; nor did he in any way rebuke her for her plain speaking, but what he did say was, 'Well, what will you do with yourself, it being Sunday?'

'I may go for a walk.'

'Over the hills?'

'Yes, over the hills.'

'Ah well' – there had come a solemn note into his voice now – 'you want to be careful, as I see it those hills spell trouble for you.'

And there he let the matter rest; and, pulling her into his arms, he went about the business of claiming the rights of a husband.

The sky was low; it seemed as if the hills all about were trying to pierce it and that soon one of them would break its skin and let a deluge fall. The air was heavy; it swelled her lungs and pressed hard against her ribs as she breathed it in.

She pulled off her bonnet that seemed to weigh on her head and opened her cloak and wafted the bodice of her cotton frock back and forward from her breasts to give herself air. She was hot yet shivering, but the shivering was inside, in her chest, causing a sickly feeling. Suppose he were away, he would have no knowledge of her coming; and if he wasn't in, she would get drenched before she got back. But what did that matter, really?

As a streak of lightning flashed across the hills and the peals of distant thunder vibrated about her, she started to run, and when she had climbed the slope and reached the wall of the yard she had to stop for a moment to get her breath.

She stood now looking across to the doors. They were shut, and there was no sign of life about. But she was only half-way across the yard when she saw that the big lock was hanging on its chain to the side.

She was about to open the door without knocking when she thought better of it. What if that woman were there; being a day of rest people took walks on Sundays. She tapped once; then twice; and when there was no answer she pushed the door slowly open and went inside.

Owing to its size and the small windows the room always looked dim, but now because of the lowering sky outside it was as if she had walked into the night, and she had to stand some minutes before she could accustom herself to the darkness.

She heard the champing of the ponies in their stalls. Moving slowly forward, she came abreast of the platform to the right of her, and there on the straw he was lying, stretched out, sound asleep.

Softly now she walked towards him and stood looking down at him. He was flat on his back, his hands on his stomach. The first finger on his right hand was linked between the remaining finger and thumb of his left, and the stump of the middle finger stuck up just above the knuckles of his right hand. For the rest there was a zigzag scar running up to the bone of his wrist, and the back of the hand looked twisted, as if it had been tortured.

When another flash of lightning illuminated the room and was immediately followed by a deafening clap of thunder, the ponies neighed and stamped and Ned opened his eyes. His lids opening slowly, he looked up towards the cobwebbed beams for a moment, but the next second he was sitting bolt upright, his feet over the edge of the platform, gaping at her.

'It . . . it was the thunder that . . . that woke you, that . . . that . . .' It was as if she were saying, 'Don't blame me.'

He wetted his lips, blinked, rubbed his hand tight round his chin, but said nothing.

'I . . . I saw Tessie yesterday. She . . . she gave me a message.'

'What?'

She had noticed before that he always said 'What?' even when he had heard aright; but she repeated, 'Tessie. Tessie gave me a message; she said you wanted to see me.'

Again he was staring at her in silence, and again he rubbed his hand tightly over his skin; then getting to his feet, he walked away from her towards the middle of the room, saying, 'Aye, aye. Yes I did. But 'twas some time ago I saw her.'

Another clap of thunder caused her to hunch her shoulders up against it and she watched him go towards the line of stalls, saying, 'It's all right. It's all right. Calm yourselves.' Then he turned towards her and spoke across the room, his voice loud, 'They don't like storms, makes them uneasy . . . Do you want a drop of something, a cup of tea?'

'Yes, yes, please.'

Slowly she followed him into the back kitchen, and she was quick to note that everything looked tidy and so thought she detected a woman's hand here.

'Sit yourself down.' He motioned towards a chair. 'And we'd better have some lights on the subject or we'll have to put our fingers in our eyes and make starlights.' He gave an embarrassed laugh, but she said nothing.

She sat by the table now and watched him light the lamp, then thrust the big black kettle into the heart of the fire, after which he took the teapot from the delf rack, spooned into it four spoonfuls of tea, which told her that it would be so strong she wouldn't be able to drink it. Then with one of his quick jerky movements he swung a chair round and was sitting opposite her; and they stared at each other for a moment or so before he said, 'Well, how are things with you?'

She did not answer his question, but through the lantern light she stared him straight in the face and said, 'Why did you want to see me?'

'Oh that.' He was now rubbing the side of his face with the finger and thumb of his left hand. 'Well, 'twas . . . Oh' – he shook his head vigorously – 'you always get me off on the wrong foot. An' that time you came upon me on the hillside, there you were goin', marching off leaving me high and dry. You have a habit of doing that, walkin' off. And I wanted to tell you it was all right, you needn't worry. I mean about this' – he now wagged his hand by the wrist in front of her – ''cos 'tis funny, I've learned a lot through this, it's been like an education to me, proved the things you can do without. That's true you know, you can learn to do without most things. Well mind, if it had been the thumb' – he wagged his thumb – 'I don't know how I would have felt then, because that's the most important part of the hand. Did you know that?'

She stared at him wide-eyed without blinking.

'Well.' He brought his hand down on to his knee and left it resting there and, looking down at it now, he went on more quietly. 'That's it then, I just wanted you to know you needn't worry about me, 'cos from what I hear you've got enough on your plate. God!' – he shook his head now – 'that you should have ended up like that, under a she-devil out of hell such as Daisy Loam. And to think she might have been my mother.' He gave a short laugh. 'She was after my dad years ago. By! if ever there was a bastard of a woman she's one. An' Fred. Well, he's gormless; but there's no badness in him, not like her, at least I shouldn't say so. But you'd be the best judge of that.' He was looking at her sideways now.

Her eyes were still wide, still unblinking; she couldn't speak, not to utter one word. There was a great swelling inside her, it was rising upwards like a river in flood; she watched it mounting, knowing that in a moment it would drown her.

When it burst from her she let out a cry and fell forward over the table while her two hands, doubled into fists, beat the top of her head.

When his arms went about her and pulled her round and upwards to be pressed tightly against him, she still moaned, she still wailed, she still cried.

'There! There! Hannah. Hannah. It's all right. It's all right. Aw! for Christ's sake don't, don't make that noise, Hannah.'

He was holding her from him now, shaking her by the shoulders, until, gasping and choking, the wailing subsided even while her tears still flowed.

When after a moment she fell against him, he gripped her so tightly that she could have cried out with the pain of it.

'Oh God! Oh God! Hannah, don't blame yourself. You're not to blame, you're not.' He was talking into her hair now. 'I should have told you; even before you were married I could have gone down and told you and given you a choice; him or me, I could have said; but I was too bloody stubborn, too bloody hurt. I blamed you for not knowing, not guessing. And what were you? A bit of a lass, brought up mostly in that school with the old she-women, like nuns. What did you know?

'Hannah!' He held her from him now and, pressing her down into a chair, he dropped on to his hunkers before her and, holding her hands in his, he said quietly. 'You know what I'm saying to you, don't you? I love you. I love you, Hannah. I always have. An' I guess that's how it will go on. I've lived no saint's life, no good denyin' it, I've got a name. Well, you know that, don't you? But that isn't love, that isn't the thing that burns you up, gets atween you and your wits, makes you walk when you should be sleepin', and so damned tired that you sleep when you should be working. . . . How do you feel about me, Hannah?'

'Oh, Ned! Ned!' she drew one hand from his and touched his cheek. 'I . . . I didn't know what it was all about, I . . . I only knew that I've always needed you. I . . . I thought I loved John, and then . . . then when she said I had to marry Fred I came rushing up to you. And you were away. And then when I tried to speak to you, you . . . you wouldn't have any of me.'

He bowed his head, saying, 'I know, I played the big fellow, an' by God! haven't I suffered for it since.' Then looking at her again, he said, 'You care for me? Really care for me, I mean, not as a child or a young lass? . . . Well, you know what I mean.'

'Yes, Ned, yes, I know what you mean.' Her face was moving slowly towards him as she spoke, and when her lips touched his mouth he became totally still for a moment; then once again she was whipped up from the chair and into his arms, and he was kissing her in a way that she had never been kissed before, not even by Fred at the height of his rough passion. But this, this was a different kissing because she was responding to it, as she had never imagined herself responding to anyone in her life. She was holding him as tightly as he was holding her, she was sinking into him, becoming lost in him, her senses were reeling; then she was back on the chair again where he had pushed her, and now he was standing above her laughing, as she had seen him laugh years ago, yet with a difference, because now there was joy in his laughter and, his voice thick, he said, 'Do you want that tea?'

She stared back at him speechless, then watched him hurrying away from the kitchen, and when she heard the bolt being pushed into the main door she turned her head to the side and bit tight on her lip for a moment in an effort to stop the trembling of her body.

He was standing at the kitchen door now, his hand extended towards her, and she rose swiftly and placed hers in it; then he was leading her up the steps and into the room above. Still holding tight to her hand he drew her across it and into the bedroom and there, holding her at arm's length, he looked at her through the dim light and said softly, 'You're sure?'

'Oh yes, Ned. Oh yes, I'm sure.'

His hands now went to the collar of her dress and slowly he unloosened the top button, and the next, and the next, and she remained still all the while staring at him.

Finally he lifted her up in his arms and laid her on the bed, and she lay and watched him as he undressed. His movements were still slow, even leisurely, and when he lay down beside her he took her face between his hands and, his words so emotionally weighed that he seemed to growl them out, he said, 'The times I've dreamed of this. Way back even before I first saw you, I dreamed of someone like you lying beside me like this. It's sad to think that I've lost part of that dream, through my own fault. Mind, I'm not blamin' you. No, no.' He moved his head slowly. 'But a fellow such as Fred could never have meant anything to you, stirred you, loved you. . . . Did he?'

She closed her eyes and whispered, 'No, Ned, no. I've wanted to die. Then I learned to think of you and that helped.'

'You did? You thought of me when you were with him?'

'Yes, Ned.'

'Aw, Hannah! Hannah!'

He rose on his elbow and bent over her, but now it seemed as if a different man still was kissing her, for now his loving was gentle, slow, and her body seemed to expand with it until her happiness filled the room and spilled over on to the hills, and rose high into the air and sang like a chorus of larks.

Neither of them was aware of the time when the storm passed, but eventually the brightness of the room brought his gaze from her, and he laughed aloud as he said, 'The sun's out.'

'Oh yes, yes!' She turned on her back and looked towards the window. He was looking down on her again as he said, 'Could you do with that cup of tea now?'

'Oh Ned! Ned!' She cupped his lean cheek.

'You happy, Hannah?' The question was quiet.

'Happy!' She moved her eyes from one side of the room to the other. 'I only know I've never felt like this in my life and never expected to feel like it. I don't care what happens to me now.'

'What do you mean, you don't care what happens to you now?'

'Just that. I could die and be happy.'

'Don't talk so soft.' He rolled off the bed, stood up, pulled on his small clothes, then his trousers, and lastly his shirt; and when he had tucked it in his trousers he stood tightening his belt as he looked towards her and said,

'We're going on from here, Hannah. I don't know how yet, but this is only
the beginning for us. Understand?'

She stared at him for a moment. Then pulling the patchwork quilt over
her, she sat up, saying quietly, 'It's . . . it's going to be difficult, Ned. If they
once saw me coming up here. . . .'

'To hell with them!'

Now he was bending over her and grinning at her as he asked, 'She goes
to chapel on a Sunday I suppose, every Sunday?'

'Yes.'

'Aye. Well, what does he do?'

'Goes to bed in the afternoon.'

'And you?' The grin slid from his face.

'No. Never.'

'Well, you could take a walk, couldn't you?'

'Yes, yes, I could take a walk.' She smiled quietly.

'Then we'll take it one bit at a time, eh? Come on, get up out of that.' He
took her hand and pulled her across the bed, and when she went to grab at
her things, he said, 'Hold on; I took them off, and I'll put them on; an' from
now on.'

'Oh Ned! Ned!' She was in his arms again, and he was kissing her eyes,
her nose, her ears and in this moment she realized that his love-making was
the outcome of practice but that it didn't matter because she was special. She
knew that, she believed that. If she were ever to believe anything in her life
again she believed that.

When finally they went into the other room, he said, 'Stay here; I'll bring
the tea up,' and she sat down in the wooden rocking chair to the side of the
fireplace. There was no fire in this grate but she could imagine what it
would be like of a winter evening with the flames roaring up the wide grate
and a pan of broth on the hearth, and the table there set with a white cloth
and those wooden bowls for their supper.

She looked at the set of wooden bowls on top of the oak rack. There were
six of them, three large and three small. Like the rest of the furniture, they
looked hand-made. She gazed about the room, so different from the one she
had left an hour ago . . . two hours ago . . . three hours ago. What time was
it? Close on six o'clock she would say. She must be soon getting back.

As she sat she noticed again that everything here, too, was tidy as had
been the kitchen downstairs, and this fact brought a little niggling fear into
her. That woman. Did she come here and tidy up for him? And not only
tidy up for him?

She was standing by the dresser fingering the bowls when he came into
the room carrying a tin tray on which was the brown earthenware teapot,
a jug of milk, a bowl of sugar, and two mugs, and she lifted the largest bowl
and turned it in her hand as she said, 'Everything looks neat and tidy; have
you someone come in?'

She heard him put the tray down on the table, and when he didn't answer
she swung round and looked at him. His face was straight but his eyes were
laughing at her. 'Aye,' he said; 'Nell Dickinson. You met her. Twice a week
she comes over. She lives over on The Bottoms,' He jerked his head in the
direction of the window and the belt of woodland.

'Oh.' She turned and put the bowl back in its place.

'Aye; fine lass, Nell. . . . How much sugar?'

'Oh, just one spoonful, please.'

He poured out the tea, then said, 'Aye well, aren't you going to come and get it.'

She turned from the delf rack, saying, 'You have some nice pieces of china.'

He let her sit down, then he pushed the mug towards her and, bringing his face close to hers until their noses were almost touching, he said, 'She's got a husband, as big and strong as two bulls. He taught me all I know about boxing. He married her when she was fifteen; he's given her eleven bairns; she lost four at one go with the cholera; and she took me to school, that is when she could get me there; and I've never had her to bed, at least not yet.' As he nodded his nose flicked hers and he ended, 'But mind, she's of good heart, there's not a kinder, and if she thought I needed someone very badly that way I'm sure she would have obliged. Oh aye, I'm sure of it.'

She had her arms about his neck; they were laughing loudly together; and once again he was on his hunkers before her and now, his mouth wide, his eyes twinkling, he said, 'You're jealous.'

'No, no; I just wondered.' She was shaking her head.

'That for a tale.' He gently slapped her cheek. 'Own up and shame the devil, you're jealous. What would you have done if it had been as you were thinking?'

Her face became serious now and her voice equally so as she said, 'Very hurt, but . . . but I wouldn't have blamed you, knowing of your need. And I would have wished that I could have been in her place because' – she paused – 'I love you so, Ned. I love you so.'

'Aw . . . aw, don't; don't, my dear one, don't cry.'

'I'm not. I'm not.'

'Come on, drink this tea. Funny, a day like this, a day to celebrate, and I haven't a drop of hard in the house. Do you know something?' He had dropped from his hunkers on to his knees now, and he put his arms around her waist and laid his head between her small breasts as he said, 'This is the happiest day of me life.'

# Chapter Five

During the following months a number of events happened which dominated the talk in the dale.

There was the band contest, an event never to be forgotten. The contestants were from Allendale Town, Acomb, Catton, Carrshield, Langley and Nenthead. Allendale Town, Acomb and Catton took first, second and third prizes in that order; the other bands didn't see eye to eye with this decision and they showed their displeasure by setting about the judge, a Mr Boosey, a well-known composer and adjudicator from London. So violent were they in their attitude towards him that the poor man had to be spirited away to

Haydon Bridge and then to the nearest railway station. This fiasco created laughter, arguments and disgust according to the place where it came under discussion.

Then there was the weather, always a thing to be taken into consideration, especially by the farmers. It was such a dry summer that corn and hay crops were light and the grub got into the turnips and almost destroyed the whole crop.

Then the weather, still remaining contrary, produced one of the hardest and longest winters anyone could remember. The pity of it was that animals died by the score, mostly the sheep, and it was said that the entire flocks would have been wiped out had it not been for the importation of large quantities of hay from Holland.

The winter seemed long to everyone, but most of all to Hannah. There were weeks on end when she never saw Ned. Even when the snow was packed down hard and it would have been possible to walk she couldn't get out, for if her mother-in-law was house-bound, then so was she.

She had made arrangements with Ned that should it be possible he would walk the ridge of the first hill in the direction of Allendale Town around noon on a Sunday just to let her know that all was well with him. Obviously, they would not signal to each other but she would see him plainly against the skyline, and he might see the darkened form of her against the window-pane.

During the summer and autumn she had been hard put at times to suppress her inward happiness. One day, thinking her mother-in-law was out in the yard and Fred in the back shop, she began to sing quietly to herself, only for her voice to be cut off by the little woman standing behind her demanding, 'An' what have you got to sing about may I ask?'

She had been whitening the hearth and she remained for a moment on her hands and knees before swinging round, the wet cloth in her hand, and crying in no small voice, 'Nothing that you have given me. But I'll sing in spite of you. Do you hear? Because nothing you do or say has any effect on me any more. So when you're going blue in the face with temper it would be to your benefit if you remembered you can't hurt me, only yourself.'

'You cheeky young bugger, you!'

At this Hannah rose to her feet and, bending over the old woman, hissed at her, 'And you bitter vicious old one!'

When she saw the little woman scurrying from the room down the stairs she stood with her back to the table and, her chin drooping on her chest, she chuckled to herself.

Then Fred appeared in the doorway, saying, 'What's up now? She . . . she says you insulted her.'

Hannah threw back her head and let out a high laugh, crying, 'She said that? Well, if she thinks I've insulted her then I've achieved something. And you can tell her that from now on I'll go on insulting her.'

'What's come over you lately?' he demanded. ''Twas a time when you didn't open your mouth.'

'I've grown up since then.' She bent and picked up the wet whitening cloth from the hearth, adding, 'And I'm not standing for her bullying me any more; and you can go down and tell her if she shouts an order to me when I'm passing through the shop again I'll shout back at her, and let the neighbours see she's not getting it all her own way. And that'll please them, because she's hated. Do you know that, Fred? Your mother is hated, almost as much, in fact more than Mrs Thornton is; it's a shame to waste two houses between them.'

He stood staring at her slightly bewildered. This wasn't the refined, educated miss he had married; she was reacting in the same way as any lass in the village would have done. There was a time when he had wished she would stand up for herself a bit more and answer his mother back, but now she was overdoing it. Of course, he wasn't entirely displeased that she was tackling the old girl, he wished he himself had done it years ago; but it was too late now for him to start.

But he wasn't quite happy about the change in Hannah's attitude. Up till now it had been a source of pride to him that he had married someone from the Thornton house, even if as it turned out she was no connection with them, because she had been educated as a lady, but the way she was acting lately was far from ladylike. He turned from her, saying, 'I'd go steady; she won't stand for too much.'

And then she almost choked with laughter inside as she called after him, 'All right, if she won't stand for too much she can sit down while I'm giving her three much.'

It was an old silly saying of Bella's and she had to turn quickly about and make her way to the bedroom because the expression of amazement on her husband's face had almost made her burst again into loud, even raucous laughter this time.

In the bedroom with her back to the door and her hand over her mouth, she breathed deeply as she said to herself, 'Really! fancy me reacting like that. But oh! thank God I can. Thank God I can.'

She went to the window and, leaning her hands on the sill, looked out over the hills towards the Pele house. The joy she had experienced over the past Sundays was, she felt, intoxicating her. A moment ago in the kitchen she had acted like someone slightly drunk; and she was drunk, deeply, deeply drunk with love of the man over there, and he with her. Oh yes, he with her. She knew now what it felt like to be worshipped. The thought was blasphemous but she didn't care, she was worshipped . . . in a rough, natural way she was worshipped.

At their very last meeting he had said, 'What are we going to do? We can't go on like this, not even seeing each other once some weeks.' And she had answered, as if the matter was quite simple, 'I'll leave him, I'll come up. Just say the word, Ned.'

He had shaken his head slowly at her as he replied, 'No, no; your life wouldn't be worth living. We'd have to go away, we'd have to sell the place and start up elsewhere.'

'But you wouldn't want to sell the Pele, you love it.' And to this he had answered, 'I love you more.'

Then before they knew it the winter had come upon them, the winter that became an eternity, snow, sleet, blizzards, packed ice; days, weeks, shut in these three rooms with the two of them. The evenings spent with her mother-in-law madly treadling the loom, Fred snoring by the fireside, and herself patching, turning sheets, ends to middle, darning socks, or on some nights silently sitting at one end of the frame while Mrs Loam sat at the other making hooky mats. Sticking the hook through the taut hessian, pulling the rag up into the required loop, on and on and on, row after row after row;

and as she progged she would recall how Tessie and Bella had made similar mats for the kitchen, and she had looked upon it as their recreation. Recreation! At the end of the evening her fingertips were so sore that sometimes she imagined that they would burst.

But now it was a Friday towards the end of February and a thaw had set in, though there were still flurries of snow showers that could at any time turn to blizzards. If the thaw continued, by Sunday the roads would be passable, even if ankle or knee-deep in parts with sludge.

She knew that her mother-in-law was as anxious to leave the house as she was, and so she prayed that she would go to chapel on Sunday evening and that Fred would follow a custom he had taken up some months ago, to his mother's disgust, that of spending the evenings in the local inn, and not always staying in the local one, but sometimes going as far afield as Allendale Town, or in the opposite direction to an inn on the road close to Allenheads. When he went to either of these it would be by the cart, and once or twice of late it was only the knowledgeable horse that had got him home.

Strangely, Hannah didn't mind Fred getting drunk, the drunker the better, for then he made no demands on her, all he did was chatter and talk until he fell into a snoring sleep.

Of course, Mrs Loam laid the blame on Hannah for her son taking to drink. Before his marriage, she insisted her son had been a sober, God-fearing individual. Whenever she put this version to customers they would listen with grave shakes of the head, then go out and laugh themselves silly.

The thaw lasted, but it was late on the Sunday afternoon before Hannah was able to fly over the hills. The twilight had set in and she knew she'd have to make her way back in the dark, she hadn't brought a lantern, but what did it matter? She was panting when she reached the door of the Pele house. Pushing it open, she hurried into the horse room, then stopped abruptly when the sound of voices came to her from the kitchen. As she moved slowly across the room Ned appeared in the doorway. For a moment he looked startled and, turning his head, said, 'Won't be a minute, Peter,' before coming towards her and grasping her hand and whispering, 'I thought you couldn't get.'

'Who have you got here?' She was staring into his eyes.

'A couple of bodgers.'

She screwed up her face, and he explained in a whisper, 'Bodgers, drovers you know.'

'Oh, yes, yes.'

'They just looked in; they're about to go.'

'Will I . . . will I slip into the barn?'

He was about to answer when two men appeared in the kitchen doorway, one of them saying, 'Well, Ned, we're for the road again'.

'Oh yes. Aye.' Ned turned and looked at the approaching figures, but they were looking past him towards the young woman with the mass of chestnut hair which was uncovered for she had thrown her hood back on her shoulders. They stared hard at her, and as they passed her they acknowledged her with a jerk of their chins; her head already half bowed, she returned their salute with the slightest of nods.

'Well, we'll be seeing you, then, Ned?'

'Aye, aye, Arty. An' I'll think on what you said. It sounds as if it could be profitable.'

'Oh, it'll be profitable all right. Of course' – the man now laughed – 'you'll have to keep awake to beat the Welshman, but trust you, Ned, you weren't born yesterday.'

'Nor the day afore,' added the other man, and at this Ned laughed and said, 'Well, 'tis one fact that I was born on one day and a second fact that I'll die on another day, and that's about the only thing a man can be sure of in this life.'

'Aye, aye; or how to break a horse in. You're sure of that, Ned, nobody surer. So long, so long.'

'So long, Peter. So long, Arty.' He closed the door behind them, but waited a moment before placing the bar quietly across it. Then he was standing in front of her again, swearing now. 'Damn and blast them to hell's flames! Never seen them for months and they would look in the day. But what does it matter, what does it matter. . . . Hello, love.'

She didn't answer, but fell into his arms, then lost herself for a moment as his lips found hers.

They were in the kitchen now, she sitting in a chair by the side of the roaring fire, he in his favourite position on his hunkers at her knees, and when he asked quietly, 'How goes it?' she answered, 'Unbearable at times. And it's been so long. Oh Ned!' She cupped her face in her hands. 'What are we going to do? I can't bear the thought of going on like this for ever.'

'Well, you needn't, it's up to you. We'll up and go just like that.' He snapped his fingers.

'But . . . but this is your home. I wouldn't mind what the villagers said, what the town said, what anybody said, I'd come up and . . .'

He put his hand out now and his fingers pressed gently on her lips as he spoke. 'You don't know what you're talking about. It'd be all right for a couple of weeks, a couple of months, then it would get you down. I've seen it happen. I've seen it come about in this very house.'

She shook her head and lifted his hand from her lips and said, 'Here?'

'Aye, here. After me ma died, me da got thick with a woman, she was from the next village, an' she'd had a life of it with her man. He was a miner and never sober; he'd beg, borrow or steal to get his drink, and so she left him and come here. But she also left behind her a fifteen-year-old son and a fourteen-year-old daughter, and when she dared to go into Allendale Town one market-day her own son picked up a stone and threw it at her. And that seemed to act like a signal. They tried to put her in the stocks; the stocks were still there then. I can see it plainly although I was only about six at the time. I can see me da fighting them off, and in the scuffle the pen that used to house the stray cattle an' sheep was broken down and the animals scattered like mad. The overseers came out and things quietened down, but she hardly ever put her nose outside these doors again until the day she died. And that wasn't long after.'

Still on his hunkers, he turned from her, took up the poker and stirred the fire; then went on, 'She was supposed to get caught in the swollen river when she was crossing by the stones, just below here, but me da knew what she had done because it was the first time she had gone further than the yard since that day in the market. So you see, Hannah' – he turned to her again – 'I know what I'm talkin' about. And although that took place twenty-two years back folks haven't altered; they don't alter in these parts. Do you know, some of 'em, at least half of them in that village down there, have never been as far as Allenheads in their life. And there's others, believe it or not, who've not been into Hexham, ten miles away; you could walk to either place there and back on a fine day. No' – he shook his head slowly – 'no, Hannah, when you come to me for good, it won't be in this house. But don't worry, it'll be sooner than you think. Those two that have just gone, they've put me on to a good thing. You know I collect me ponies from here and there but they're getting hard to come by, for the farmers are nipping them up and think they have priority in supplying the mines. But Peter, Peter Turnbull, the tall fellow, he's just come back from Gearstones, driven a big herd back from there. He said they walked on their bones they were so lean, poor beggars, but he brought them for the Batemans' farm. There's plenty of good pasture down there and come Christmas he says Bateman will make a packet on them, but that apart, what he told me is that the Welshman brings ponies as far as there, and a fine, sturdy wild lot they are, and they go cheap because not only have they to be broken in but to be herded to the place where they're going to be broken in, and it isn't everyone who can handle a string of mettlesome ponies like meself, I'm pleased to say.' He grinned at her. 'So a couple of trips down there and a little bit of hard work this end and come the end of the summer I should be well set; added to what I've got here.'

He now dug her gently in the waist with his fist as he said, 'Do you remember one particular night when I bragged about all the money that was stacked away here? Well, like all braggarts I stretched it a bit. But mind, there should have been a nice little pile, but the old 'un had gone through it. On what, God only knows. You see it was a kind of unwritten law that the bag behind the bricks belonged to the eldest till he went, and it wasn't anybody's business to nosey into what was there, an' I, like a damn fool, felt that the old 'un had been adding his bit to the pile. I remember me da saying that all told there should be nigh on a hundred, an' that was in his time. Anyway, when I rolled the stones away, like they did in the Bible, what did I find? Well, like them, nowt behind two of them – they'd all had their own hidey holes you see – and about thirty pounds in the last one. An' that was the lot.'

'Thirty pounds.' She shook her head slowly. 'Well, that seems quite a bit of money.'

'Aw, lass' – he patted her knee – 'not when you're starting from scratch. But the house. Now if I could sell this, it would bring nigh on a hundred because there's two and a half acres of signed and sealed land around it.'

'Wouldn't it be worth more than that if it was mining land, as you said?'

'Aw, Hannah' – he hung his head deeply on his chest now – 'you mean all that spouting I did the day you found me raking?' He raised his eyes to her and, his expression sheepish, he muttered, 'I was raking for flints, arrow-heads as they call them. There's lots to be found hereabouts, but if you come across good ones in good shape there are men who are interested in them an' will buy them off you. But mind' – he now wagged his finger at her – 'it could just be possible that someone like Beaumont would buy this house and the land, and that's exactly what they'd do, they'd open a mine here. . . . Oh yes, aye, they would. But as for yours truly starting one, well, as you so wisely remarked that day, it takes a lot of money to dig out a lead mine.'

'Hannah.' He rose and pulled her to her feet and, his face quite straight now, he said, 'If you take me on for good it'll be as a horse-dealer, because

that's all I can do. At one time I had another string to me bow, I could box.
... Now, now, now' – he held up his hand in warning – 'if this hadn't
happened' – he wagged the finger and thumb at her – 'me boxing days
would still have been over. It's a young man's sport. Bare knuckles are not
enough, you want fleet feet and the stamina of a horse. But ... but you
know something, love? We're wasting time. Come on.'

As he pulled her up to him he whispered, 'The bed's warm. You know
something else? I always stick the oven shelf in every Sunday dinner-time
after I've cooked me meat, hoping ... hoping.'

Their heads drooped together for a moment, then they went out and up
the ladder to the rooms above.


# Chapter Six


In April she suspected she was pregnant, but she wasn't sure for her cycle
had always been erratic – and painful. Moreover, she had no one with whom
she could discuss her condition.

The weather had gone mad again and continued in much the same fashion
until the middle of May, and for most of the month Mrs Loam had been
house-bound with a chest cold. But when Hannah began to feel sick on
rising she knew she was carrying a child.

She had managed to keep her condition to herself by making for the closet
first thing in the morning; that was until a certain Monday morning in the
wash-house when the news was broken to her husband, but not by her.

She had risen at six o'clock and lit the fire under the wash-house pot and
had a boiling of coarse sheets rinsed and mangled when a wave of nausea
attacked her. She had thought she was over this stage for she hadn't felt sick
for some time. But now as she stood leaning on the splash board of the
wooden mangle a voice to the side of her said, 'Well, you've managed it at
last, have you? What you tryin' to hide, are you ashamed of it? But this I'll
say, you've taken your time over it.'

She stared at the old woman while her stomach heaved.

'Why haven't you told him? He's got a right to know, hasn't he?'

'I'll ... I'll tell him when I think fit.'

'Oh you will, madam, will you? By God!' – the little woman shook her
head – 'I've never met anybody like you in me life afore. You're not human.
Here he's been waitin' for this to happen for two years now, and when it
does you keep it to yersel. An' I'd like to bet if I hadn't caught you spewing
you wouldn't have mentioned a word of it until your belly gave you away.'

When Mrs Loam turned about and left the wash-house, Hannah gripped
the splash board and closed her eyes, and as she lowered her head deeply
on to her chest she swore to herself that no matter what happened she
wouldn't be here when the child was born. . . .

'Is it true then?'

She turned and looked at Fred. His big red face was aglow. He looked
so pleased with himself that for a moment she felt pity for him.

'Why didn't you let on?' He was standing close to her now. 'Eeh! you're
a funny lass. But by! I'm glad. God, I thought it would never happen. I was
beginnin' to worry; I thought perhaps I was no use.' He pressed his lips
together and grinned while he wagged his head from side to side at an absurd
notion; then he kicked out at the poss tub, took hold of the poss stick and
banged it twice up and down on to the wet clothes, saying as he did so,
'They were beginnin' to chaff me down at the pub. Well now, I've let them
see, haven't I?' He turned his head towards her and stared at her for a
moment before asking, 'Why don't you say something? Aren't you glad?'

She could look him fully in the face as she answered, 'Yes, I'm glad.'

'Well then' – again his head was wagging – 'we go on from here, don't
we?' . . .

But that night he found to his amazement that they didn't go on from
there, for when he went to put his arms about her she actually sprang out
of bed and through the darkness she hissed at him, 'I won't be touched, do
you hear me? I won't be touched again until . . . until it's born?'

'What d'you mean . . . you won't be touched?'

She knew he was sitting up in the bed.

'Just what I said.'

'Why' – there was utter bewilderment in his tone – ''tis better for the
bairn to have it, every fool knows that, helps feed it, it does, makes it healthy
an' keeps it from catching things. An' if by what you say you're well gone
so you've been touched.'

'Well, I won't be any more. And . . . and if you insist I'll lie in the
kitchen.'

'God Almighty! there's months to go. Now look here, Hannah, I'm havin'
none o' this. What do you take me for, a bloody mug?'

When his hand came on her she actually cried out and he let go of her
as quickly as he had caught her, saying, 'Shut up for Christ's sake! You'll
have her in here in a minute.'

'Well, leave me alone. It's been night after night, night after night, I can't
bear any more. Now . . . now you should be satisfied I'm . . . I'm carrying
a child.'

There was silence in the darkness now, it was as if he was pondering her
last remark.

When she heard him getting back into the bed she waited, her body stiff
but shivering with the cold; then he spoke. 'Aye well, we'll see about this.
Get back into bed.'

She still waited a moment before she moved; then when she finally lay
down it was on the edge of the bed with her back to him and she let the
bedclothes fall around her so that she wouldn't come in contact with him.

On the following Sunday she almost thought she would go mad when her
mother-in-law was unable to go to chapel because of another stomach upset,
and how she got through the following week she didn't know. When Sunday
came round again she had to warn herself not to get agitated in case she
should give herself away and one or other of them would suspect something.

When at last Mrs Loam, still muttering implications of what would
eventually happen to her for not turning to God, left the house, and Fred,

surly now, made for the inn, she could hardly make herself wait the required minutes before she flew out of the back door. At least she was flying inside, for she always made herself saunter until she was out of sight of the village.

The twilight was deepening when she reached the Pele house. But tonight Ned had no visitors and he was waiting for her outside the wall.

After their first embrace in the stable-room he muttered into her hair, 'Where've you been all these years?' Then pressing her from him, he asked, 'Did you pass John and Annie Beckett on your way over?' and she shook her head, saying, 'You mean from next door? No, no; I didn't see them.'

'They must have turned down towards the cemetery then, I felt sure you'd run into them if you were on your way.'

'I could have,' she laughed, 'because I had my head down and I was running most of the time. But' – her face straightened – 'why do you ask?'

'Aw, nothing, nothing; only this is the third time I've seen them pass the wall there in the last month. The first time I thought it was just a Sunday jaunt, now I'm not so sure . . . Does she speak to you?'

'Hardly ever. She nods at me sometimes when I'm down at the midden emptying the slops.'

'My God!' He ground his teeth now. 'When I hear that I feel like a bull looking at a red rag. Down at the midden emptying the slops. Why the hell can't he do that? How does he pass his time anyway? He rarely kills more than one beast a week; a few sheep perhaps, an' a pig or two. But what's that?'

'Never mind; come in here.' It was she now who was leading him by the hand into the kitchen, and when she was standing in front of him and he was unloosening the neck of her cloak she said, 'I have something to tell you, Ned Ridley. Oh' – she shook her head – 'I don't know how I haven't shouted it across the hills. I nearly died when I couldn't get across last Sunday.'

'Just as well you didn't, I was away; but come on, Hannah Boyle.' He had never called her by her married name. 'Don't keep me in suspense.'

'Guess what?'

He screwed up his face and looked up towards the ceiling as he said, 'Dame Thornton has come down and begged you to go back home.'

'Huh! that'll be the day I'll never live to see. And it's odd you know, but I've never seen her once since I left the house . . . the church that day. But be serious, look at me.'

He looked at her and said, 'Well?'

She waited for a number of seconds before she said slowly, and with emphasis on one word, 'I'm going to have . . . *your* child.'

For almost a minute he stared at her. His expression did not alter; then he said briefly, 'Mine?'

'Yes, yours.'

She watched now as his lips spread wide and his teeth clamped together; and then with his eyes closed tightly his arms shot out and about her and they swayed as one, and their laughter joined for a moment. Then he was holding her by the shoulders and looking into her face, his expression once more blank as he asked her, 'How can you be sure?'

'I am. I can. The time, in February, and . . . oh' – she shook her head and turned it from him – 'and other things that I can't explain. I only know, Ned, it's yours, ours.'

'February? February? My God! then you're well on. Why didn't you say?'

'I . . . I wasn't sure. To tell the truth, I didn't know much about it. I . . . oh, I can't explain.'

'Aw, Hannah! Hannah!' He took her face in his hands and moved it gently from side to side. Then drawing her to a chair, he knelt by her, and he said now, 'Well, that puts the lid on it. I'll have to get cracking; I will that. It's a good job I've something in the offing. You know what I told you about the Welsh ponies? Well, I've been over to Gearstones; it's a trek and a half. Peter Turnbull and Arty Heslop, you know the two fellows you met in here, they were droving sheep back and so I went along with them, so I would know the way meself. And it's a good job I did for I'd never been along that trek afore. Anyway, I saw the fella and he's promised me a string, and another if I want them afore the bad weather sets in. Between trips I should have me hands full at breaking them in, at least manageable in a way, for by the sound of it some of them are imps of Satan. But also, by the sound of it, I should have a nice little packet at the end of the job. And I'll tell you something else I'm doing, I'm going over into Hexham the morrow to a property dealer there to ask him to come out here and tell me what I'll get for this.'

She sat looking at him, her throat too full to speak, and he said softly, 'Come on, love, don't cry; it's not a time for cryin', it's a time for celebratin', for a drink. And you know something?' He stood up. 'I haven't a drop of hard in the house. Can you imagine it? This happening too often now, me without a drop of hard in the house. Anyway, we'll have a sup tea, strong enough to stand up by itself.'

'I'll make it.'

'You'll do no such thing.' He turned and swept up a number of loose sheets of paper from the table and as he went to put them on the delf rack he looked at them, then said, 'I mapped out me way. Look at that; not bad for somebody who couldn't stand schooling, is it?'

She took the three sheets of paper from him and looked at the contours of the hills and paths he had sketched on them; then glancing up at him, she said, 'You drew all this?'

'Yes, who else?' He tossed his head in mock pride. 'And mind, it's some distance.' He was now bending over her. 'Seventy-five miles or more.'

'Seventy-five miles!' Her tone was awe filled.

'Yes, look there. I go to Allenheads, and on to Wearhead – see that mark, that means I stop there the night; then the next day I make for Langdon Common, and like Peter and Arty did, I'm following the river Tees towards Newbiggin. And there's the mark again. I kip there the second night. The next day – that's over the page, look there – I go over Lunedale and Baldersdale and by God's Bridge, and then if I'm lucky I reach the inn at Tan Hill.'

'Now on this page' – he had taken the third piece of paper from her – 'I go down to Stonesdale Moor and on to Thwaite, through Buttertubs Pass on to Hawes. And you see there's the mark again, I stop for the night. I could at a pinch, that is if I gallop, go up Widdale Beck and right to Gearstones, but that's another seven to eight miles, so I'll likely stop as I've said at Hawes. Now what do you think about that for a journey?'

'Tremendous! And you're going to bring the ponies back all that way?'

'Well, I'm not just going for the walk, love.'

They laughed together now; then he said soberly, 'It's a real bonny trek, some wonderful scenes from the hills and the valleys, but oh, lonely mind. Oh aye, I used to think there was no lonelier place in the world than that stretch between Whitfield and Alston, but some of the places on that route are lonelier still.'

At the mention of Alston, she asked quietly, 'Couldn't you buy as good bargains at the Alston Horse Fair?'

'No; there's too many at the same game round here, too many farmers with side-lines. Gearstones is a bit too far for them to trek, although there's nothin' to stop them paying a drover to do the work for 'em, as some of the bigger farmers do with their cattle. But sooner them than me 'cos I wouldn't trust any drover as far as I could toss him.'

He turned swiftly to her again and, bending, he kissed her on the lips before saying, 'I'll be back afore you've known I've gone. I hate to cause you worry but at the same time I like to know you're worrying over me.'

She put her arms around his neck as she asked, 'Where will we go when we leave here?'

'Any place in the world, but I've got a fancy to see the countryside that lies beyond London. That's where we'll go, beyond London.'

She knew the geography of the land much better than Ned did, but at this moment the country beyond London appeared to her further away than America where Robert had gone, further away than Australia that was right below her feet at the other side of the world. It was another planet and no one would find them there. They would start life anew; she'd be Mrs Ridley, and her child would be called Ridley, and that would be his rightful name.

# Chapter Seven

The child was heavy in her when Ned made his second trip to Gearstones. He had been gone almost three weeks now. She hadn't worried so much on the second Sunday when she found the Pele house door still barred, but on the third Sunday when she had to take shelter in the shippon doorway she felt sick with worry.

It had rained almost all the time he had been away. Last summer had been known as one of the driest in memory, this, one of the wettest. The crops were soggy and the corn impossible to dry. The roads were like quagmires, the air continually chill, and the houses damp.

Although she felt better in herself, her spirits were at a low ebb. She was now nearing her eighth month of carrying the child. Her duties in the house were no lighter; her mother-in-law frequently informing her that she herself had had to work up till the last minute, scrubbing, washing, and baking, and there had been no one to pamper her. But yesterday she had dared to turn on her and retaliate by saying that if what she had to do came under the heading of being pampered, then she wasn't likely ever to experience cruelty. Whereupon Mrs Loam had almost screamed at her, 'Cruelty! What do you think you're doin' to my lad? He's told me of your capers. You should be horsewhipped. You know what I'm gona do? I'm gona bring the minister to you, an' if he doesn't shame you into doin' your duty nobody will. You know something? I can sympathize with her at the far end of the village now, by! I can that. What she must have had to put up with from you! It's a wonder she didn't throw you out years ago.'

As Hannah now stood in the shippon doorway she wondered just how much longer she could put up with the repeat of yesterday. Women, she thought, were much more cruel than men; men could be brutal, physically brutal, but women seemed to have the knack of torturing you mentally. Mrs Thornton had never spoken to her directly in her life, and that had been a special kind of torture, whereas her mother-in-law never stopped talking at her, and that was another kind of torture; she didn't know which was the worse; perhaps the silence was more unbearable than the talking because with the latter you could always answer back.

It was getting dark, it was no use waiting. She drew in a long breath, then let it slowly out and murmured to herself, Oh Ned. Ned.

She now walked from the shelter of the doorway and across the yard, out through the opening in the stone walls and on to the hillside again. As she turned her head against the driving rain she saw a dim figure in the distance and stopped for a moment, hope rising in her. But then the figure was lost to her as it moved away in the opposite direction. Anyway, if it had been Ned he would have bounded towards her.

She slipped quietly into the back shop, took off her cloak, shook it vigorously to get the wet off it, saw that her clogs were clean by wiping them with some rags – her fine leather shoes were worn out – then as she went up the stairs she wiped her face and the front of her hair with her handkerchief.

It was when she opened the stairhead door that she came to a stiff halt for there, standing in the middle of the kitchen, was Mrs Loam.

'Well, well! so you've got back then?'

'I . . . I went for a walk.' She went past her now towards the bedroom.

'In the rain?'

'In the rain.'

As she went to hang her cape in the cupboard she heard the pounding on the stairs, and the sound made her heart jump and her body tremble with a new kind of fear. It was as if she already knew what was about to happen. In a way she had been expecting it; and suddenly she was sorry for Fred for he wasn't really to blame for what had happened; they were both victims. To someone else he would have been a good husband. He would have been so to her if she had been able to love him; and perhaps without his mother that might have come about . . . No! She glanced towards the bed, and the memory of the nights that seemed to stretch back into eternity echoed loudly, No! No! Never!

Shaking from head to foot, she turned about and went to face what was coming.

When she re-entered the kitchen he was standing near the table. His face had lost every hue of its ruddy complexion and looked livid. He kept his eyes fastened tight on her while he spoke to his mother. 'You were right then, Ma. An' to think I nearly knocked Arty Heslop's teeth down his bloody neck. . . . That's what they've been sniggerin' at for weeks. "Have a pint, Fred. How's your wife, Fred? . . . Hear you're goin' to be a dada, Fred. Well, better late than never. . . . Reckon you managed it on your own, Fred?" . . .

'By God! do you know what I could do to you?' He was advancing on her. 'I could pull your entrails out, you dirty little whorin' bastard you!'

As his hand came up she heard her mother-in-law cry, 'Them next door knew about it all the time. Soon as we were out of the house she skitted across, Sunday after Sunday. . . . Shameless bitch!'

When the flat of his hand landed full across the side of her face her feet left the floor and she seemed to remain horizontal for a moment before falling by the side of the steel fender.

If he had struck her with his doubled fist it would surely have killed her, because his hand that wielded the hammer on the beasts was like an iron club in itself.

'Oh my God! you've done for her.' Daisy Loam straightened the prostrate form out; then, her fear-filled face turned up to her son, she said again, 'You've done for her, and the bairn.'

He stood above them trembling, his face working as if with ague; and now he started to mutter like someone demented: 'She asked for it. They won't do anythin' to me, she asked for it. Unfaithful wife, that's what she was. I'll tell them. . . .'

'Shut up! Bring that dish of water.' She thrust her arm out towards the side table.

Even when he brought the water and handed it down to her he was still muttering, 'They can't do anything to me. She fell, that's what happened, she fell.'

'Don't be so bloody gormless, her face 'll be black and blue in any case by mornin', and Arnison's only got to see that, then he'll have your neck. He's never had any time for either of us.'

After having splashed handfuls of water on to Hannah's face with no response, she cried, 'Get her up out of this!'

When he had lifted Hannah up and carried her into the bedroom and laid her on the bed, he turned to his mother, and like a child now said, 'Do somethin', can't you?'

Pushing him aside she did something. She laid her ear to Hannah's breast, then stood up, and her small frame seemed to expand with relief, then as she let the air out of her body she muttered, 'She's breathin'.'

They stood looking at each other for a moment. But then, the colour rushing back into his face, he shouted at her, 'You're to blame for this, you've driven her to it. An' you've always been at me to belt her.' But before he could get any further she interrupted his tirade with equal fury, crying, 'Get out of me sight, you great soft lout! It's a pity you hadn't finished her off; you might have died like a man at the end of a rope then.' Whereupon, his whole body jangling as if on strings, he went towards the door, spluttering, 'You! You! you're a bitch of a woman. That's what you are, Ma, a bitch of a woman, an' if anything happens me bairn. . . .'

'Whose bairn?'

'What?' He turned in the doorway, and she repeated slowly 'Whose bairn? That's what I said, whose bairn?'

# Chapter Eight

She was three days in bed. One side of her face was swollen to almost twice its size and from her brow to her chin the skin was a purplish blue; added to this, she had a pain in her side where it had struck the end of the fender. She ate nothing for two days but she drank the cups of tea her mother-in-law brought in and silently placed on the little table beside the bed.

Mrs Loam had spoken to her only once, and that was when she had first come round. It was then she had said, 'You've got nobody to blame but yourself, you've asked for it.'

For the three days she had been in bed she hadn't seen Fred – he must have slept on the couch in the kitchen – but when at last she got up he was waiting for her.

It was as if he had never moved from the spot where she had last seen him standing, and he repeated almost word for word what his mother had said. His head wagging, he muttered, 'You asked for it, you can't say you didn't. You've only yourself to blame. Anyway, I'll say to you now, I'm willin' to let bygones be bygones if you'll tell me you'll not go up there any more.'

She stared at him, her eyes unblinking, her lips set tight.

'Well?'

She didn't speak.

'I've asked you a civil question an' I want a civil answer.'

Still she didn't speak, and, his head wagging even more widely now, he blustered, 'Well, if that's your attitude 'tis all right with me, but . . . but I'll see to it you take no more trips alone, by God! I will, if I've got to chain you up.' . . .

And in the days that followed Hannah felt that that's what he had done, chained her up, because never for a moment was she alone.

Then there came the Allendale Town market-day when she was forced to accompany him to the town.

It should happen that Mrs Loam was troubled with a loose bowel that made her so weak she had taken to her bed, and she had said to her son, 'I can't see to her, you'll have to take her along of you.' So that is what he did. Sitting beside him on the high seat of the wooden cart, she went into Allendale.

The journey wasn't made in complete silence for every now and again Fred would make a remark such as, 'Nice bloody state of affairs.' 'Might as well be married to a deaf-and-dumb mute.' 'Don't think you can carry on like this 'cos I won't put up with it, making a bloody fool out of me, that's what you're doin', a laughing stock. Well, the next one that laughs at me he'll go home without any bloody teeth, an' I'm tellin' you.'

Though the market square seemed to be full of people, it wasn't, as many remarked, so full as in other years. A newfangled railway was having an effect; people were now carrying their wares far and wide. Things were changing. Why, forty years ago there were a thousand people living in the town and now there was less than half that number. Yet the King's Head and the Golden Lion, the Temperance Hotel and the six inns still did a roaring trade on days such as these. Better, some of the hard cases laughed, than the Wesleyan and Primitive Methodist chapels did on a Sunday, not forgetting the Quakers.

But the town was too full for Fred; he couldn't see everybody at once, and he was on the look out for one particular man, yet at the same time hoping he didn't come across him, for Ned Ridley might have only one and a half hands but he would still know how to use them; he hadn't been a boxer for nothing. Not that he himself couldn't hold his own. No, by God! no, as anybody who had seen him fell a beast knew. And on this thought he pushed his shoulders back and thrust out his chest and looked about him; then put his hand quickly to his stomach.

Now what was he going to do? He had caught his mother's damn trouble. He had gone just before he came out, and now he'd have to go through one of the pubs and into the back. Since they had been stopped using the open middens it meant that a man had almost to pay for going to the netty.

'Hannah.'

He turned quickly to see the speaker standing in the middle of the pathway.

'Oh, Margaret. Oh, Margaret. Oh, it is good to see you.'

'And you. And you.'

They were clasping hands tightly.

'What are you doing here, visiting?'

Margaret shook her head. 'No; I've been to say good-bye to John. . . .'

Before Hannah could enquire further Fred was speaking. 'Look,' he said; 'I've got to go over there.' He pointed to the inn. 'I won't be more than five or ten minutes.' He stared at her. 'Not more mind. You can go in there till I come back.' He pointed to the hotel behind them. 'You can get some tea up in the general room, or something.' He now turned to Margaret and added, 'You stay along of her, won't you, Miss Margaret?'

Margaret looked questioningly at Fred, then said, 'Yes, yes, of course, Fred.' But Fred had already turned and almost at a run was making his way through the crowd towards the low-fronted inn across the square, and now she turned to Hannah, saying, 'Shall we go into the coffee room?'

'I . . . I haven't any money, Margaret.'

'Oh, well, I have enough.'

They said no more until they were seated side by side on the wooden settle in the corner of the large room, and after Margaret had given an order for coffee and had added, 'No thank you, nothing else,' she looked hard at Hannah before saying, 'You've had a fall?'

'Yes, I had a fall, Margaret.'

As their gaze held Margaret muttered, 'Oh, I'm sorry, Hannah,' and to this Hannah replied, 'Well, I suppose some would say he was within his rights. You see I've . . . I've been seeing Ned.'

'Ned? You mean Ned Ridley?'

'Yes, Ned Ridley.'

Margaret now shook her head slightly before going on, 'You mean you've been seeing him for . . .?'

'Yes, Margaret, for other purposes than friendship. You see I found out too late that I loved Ned; it's he I should have married. I think I would have if he had been there at the time your mother made other arrangements for me.'

'Oh, Hannah!' Margaret's hand came across the table and clasped Hannah's wrist; then slowly and sadly she said, 'What a mess she's made of our lives! More so in your case; in mine, I had a choice, but it was the wrong choice.'

'What happened?'

'Oh.' Margaret now brought her two hands together; her fingers touching, she made as if to clap them. 'I thought he was attracted to me, but apparently it was my supposed position. He saw me as the daughter of a man who could afford to send me to a private school, and so, therefore, there must be money in the family. And, of course, the house was another proof that we were, if not wealthy, then very comfortably off, and that my father would surely do something for his eldest daughter's husband. At least that's how I reasoned it out. There was no other explanation for his polite note and his scampering from the town.'

'Oh, I'm so sorry, Margaret.'

When Margaret made no answer but continued to sip her coffee, Hannah asked, 'What are you doing now?'

'The same as I did when I first went back to the school; but just as then I still receive no wage. I think sometimes I might as well be in a convent; at least there I would be given a free habit.' She smiled wryly, and with a touch of bitterness she added, 'It's . . . it's disquietening to say the least, how people can change towards you when they know you are dependent on them.'

'You mean Miss Barrington?'

'Yes, and Miss Rowntree. Miss Emily tries to remain the same, but she finds it difficult for she has to do the housekeeping. You see I must eat, and also the room I occupy is depriving them of another pupil; as you remember, the house wasn't large.'

Hannah found her throat so full that she couldn't make any comment. She had considered her own life hard, and even unbearable, but at the back of it she had the love of Ned; apparently Margaret had no one.

'It's all right. It's all right.' Margaret was holding her hand again. 'I'm on the look-out for a situation as a governess.' She gave a slight laugh now. 'I went to an agency two months ago thinking they would jump at me. Dear, dear!' She shook her head. 'I never realized there were so many emancipated young women looking for employment. The agent's book was full of young ladies offering themselves as governesses and companions, even as lady-housekeepers. But something is bound to come along soon. Anyway, let me tell you about John.'

'Oh yes . . . John. You said you had come to say good-bye to him?'

'Yes; he and Pansy are leaving on Monday for America; they are joining Robert.'

'No!'

'Yes.' Margaret's head moved deeply up and down. 'Now would you believe that?'

'But why?'

'Oh, for many reasons, but mainly because, I think, Mrs Everton is a replica of Mama; she still treats her daughter as if she were a child and not a married woman, and Pansy is a very high-spirited girl. Moreover, I think Mr Everton found John rather slow. He considered he must have very little initiative or he would have risen higher in the mining industry. Moreover, John was expected to help on the farm . . . in a gentlemanly way of course.' She pulled a face now at Hannah. 'But at every spare moment. Anyway, apparently Robert sent glowing reports of his life on this cattle ranch and I understand him to have said if a man is willing to work and a woman willing to help there are fortunes to be made; whether that be true or not, John grasped at it as a chance to get away, and Pansy backed him, and so they leave on Monday. John wrote and asked me to come for a few days and, to be truthful, I was glad of the invitation, but after only three days in the house I was equally glad to take my leave. . . . It's odd' – she shook her head sadly now – 'I shan't miss John like I did Robert. Robert was the only one I really cared for. And you, of course; and you Hannah. Yes, I cared for you. And I miss you. Oh, don't cry, dear, don't cry.' But even as she appealed to Hannah there were tears in her own voice. 'I . . . I suppose,' she said now, 'you know that Mama has sold the house?'

Hannah's eyes widened as she shook her head.

'Oh, yes. Yes; and I understand they'll be moving any time now. They've taken a little place in Corbridge, very small by what John says, but Mama will be near her cousin. She is to act as companion to her. She lost her husband lately, I mean Mama's cousin did.' She gave a short laugh now as she added, 'I don't envy Mama her new position; Aunty Riverdale, as we called her, was a martinet at the best of times. I've only met her on three occasions. She never visited us, our station was much too lowly.' Again she pulled a face.

'Tessie and Bella and . . . and Dandy, what are they going to do?'

'Oh, Dandy went a long time ago; and she was able to keep Bella and Tessie on only because of Aunty Riverdale. Now they will likely come to the hirings here' – she motioned her hand towards the window and the town square – 'and be bonded to someone, a farmhouse likely . . . I hope they don't get separated. Bella looks upon Tessie as a daughter and Tessie sees Bella as her mother, they've been so long together. The trouble is Bella is getting on in years and won't be everybody's choice. It's a sad state of affairs. I'm glad to say Dandy found work on a farm.' She again sipped from her cup, then said, 'You haven't drunk your coffee, Hannah.'

'Oh! Oh no.' Hannah took two sips from the now almost cold liquid, then said, 'Will you write to me, Margaret?'

'Yes, yes, of course.'

'I . . . I don't mean just now and again but . . . but every week?'

'Yes; yes, I will. In future I'll write to you every week. I promise.'

'I . . . I want to know what's happening to you.'

'I'll let you know, dear, don't worry. Anyway, I don't want you to be concerned over me, you have enough to contend with by all accounts, and I feel guilty at times about my share in it.'

They stared at each other hard for a moment, then simultaneously rose and went from the room.

Fred was outside waiting and, looking at Margaret, he said abruptly, 'If you're going by carrier into Hexham you'd better look slippy, he's ready.'

'Oh!' Margaret looked quickly across the square, then said, 'Oh yes, yes.

Well, good-bye, dear.' She bent forward and kissed Hannah on the cheek, and Hannah held her tightly for a moment, then watched her hurrying towards the carrier cart, the hem of her serge skirt dusting the ground. She looked shabby, lost somehow, and no longer a girl, not even a young woman.

'Let's get a move on.'

She turned and went with him, not by his side but by choice a step behind him, yet to those who saw them together it appeared that Fred Loam couldn't after all be all wind and watter for he had mastered his wife – as was evident by her face – and so much so that he had put her in her place and made her tail behind him.

They were about half-way home, just rounding the bend where the burn ran below a steep bank to the left side of them. Hannah had her head down. She was lost in thoughts of Margaret and John and Robert and herself and what had happened to them all in the past two years, when out of the bushes at the near side of the road a man stepped, grabbed the horse's bridle rein, and pulled the animal to a stop.

When Hannah saw who the intruder was, her heart seemed to stop within her breast. She put her hand over her mouth, and when the long stick came up towards her, its end like a shepherd's crook, and with an expert twist flicked her hood from her head she looked down into Ned's face and whimpered, 'No! no! don't. Please, please Ned, go away.'

'What the hell do you think you're up to?'

Ned looked at the blustering countenance on the far side of Hannah, then said quietly, 'I heard you had marked her. Get down!' At this he walked round the back of the cart and to the other side, and Fred, who had made no move as yet, now yelled at him, 'Aye, I'll get down, and you'll be sorry for it.'

'No, no, please!' When Hannah grabbed with both hands at Fred's arm, he thrust her back with such force that he almost toppled her from the cart; and then he was facing Ned, in the stance of a boxer.

Ned was standing apparently at ease with his arms hanging by his sides and his voice sounded quite ordinary as he said, 'Before I give it you, I want you to know she's mine, an' she always has been, and she'll continue to be.'

It seemed that even before he finished the last word his right fist shot out and into Fred's stomach, and as the blow brought Fred bending forward he caught another blow under the chin, this time from the half hand, and although the second blow hadn't the force of the first it was still enough to bring Fred momentarily to his knees.

Ned looked down at Fred for a moment, dusted the palms of his hands together as if knocking dirt off them, then, turning his back on Fred he went to the cart and, swinging his arm up to the seat he said, 'Come on, get down out of that, you're going home.'

It was at the moment that she put her hand out towards him that she also let out a shrill cry, for Fred, his animal stamina coming to the fore, had risen drunkenly to his feet, and Ned, although warned by Hannah's cry, turned swiftly but too late; and then it was he who was doubled up and in agony as the toe of Fred's heavy boot caught him full in the groin. Perhaps it was the sight of Ned writhing on the ground that turned Fred into a madman for the moment, because now he started to kick him all over his body and was only brought to a shuddering stop when Hannah threw herself on top of Ned, for the next blow from his foot would have contacted her.

Like an enraged giant he stood over them, his face crimson, the sweat running down it dripping from his chin, his saliva running from his mouth in long driblets. Then uttering unintelligible sounds, he bent over them and swung her upwards by one shoulder, before using his foot again to thrust the prostrate form off the road and down the bank towards the stream.

She struggled and screamed at him, 'No! No! he'll die. You devil you! He'll die; you can't leave him there. I'll see you hang. Yes I will! I will! . . . Oh, don't leave him there. Oh!'

She was blinded now with her crying and weak from her struggling when, gripping her with both hands, he growled, 'Get . . . up . . . there! An' you'll not live to see me hang. By God! I'll swear on that. No, you'll not live to see me hang.'

Gripping the reins in one hand, he held on to her with the other; then yelling at the horse, he drove it forward, almost at a gallop.

Having no stable of their own, he rented space for the horse and cart from Ralph Buckman, the blacksmith, and it was his usual procedure, except when there was a dead beast in the cart, to drive straight to the stables behind the smithy, see to the horse, then carry his purchases home; or, if his mother was with him, send her on ahead. But today, as when he was carrying a beast, he drove the cart around the back lane that was thick with glar; then, pulling Hannah from the seat, he thrust her up the yard, through the back shop and to the foot of the stairs, and there he yelled, 'Ma!'

After calling three times and receiving no response he pushed Hannah before him up the stairs and towards his mother's bedroom.

When he thrust her door open she was leaning on her elbow in bed and, her voice weak for her, she said, 'What's up with you? I'm bad; I've never been off the pot since you left.'

'Sick or no sick, keep your eye on her, and she'll tell you what's up. Anyway, I've put her fancy man out of action for a bit. I'm away to see to the horse.'

He was about to close the door when he thrust his head in again and, looking at his mother, said fiercely, 'Whatever you have, you've given it to me.'

When the door banged closed, Mrs Loam lay back on her pillows in the big box bed and gasped, 'What 've you caused now, girl? Trouble is your shadow. . . . Oh my God!' She now turned on her side, her body almost doubled, and Hannah, swaying on her feet, stood watching her, not moving either towards her or away from her. She herself was feeling sick and ill, her mind was in a turmoil, her only clear thought was she must get help for Ned. If he lay there in the stream he could be dead by morning; if he wasn't already gone.

'Get me a drink, girl. Get me a drink. . . . Don't stand there! Do you hear? Get me a drink.'

As if in a nightmare, Hannah turned slowly about, went into the kitchen and to the pail that stood on a side table under the window and there ladled a tin mug full of water, then took it into the bedroom and handed it to her mother-in-law.

When Mrs Loam had drunk the water she lay back and, her head tossing from side to side on the pillow, she muttered, 'He'll have to get me the doctor. I should have had him a week gone when it first started. I've caught a fever, I know I have.'

As Hannah turned towards the door, Mrs Loam cried, 'Don't go, girl. Don't go, I need you. The pot's full; empty it.' Then in her next gasping breath, she said, 'No, no, don't. Wait till he comes back. He's mad, I can see that, never seen him like that afore. Oh you! the things you bring on folk, girl.'

Hannah sat slowly down on the wooden chair near the door. She was being called *Girl* again. She had been knocked into a woman, but it was strange, those who hated her never allowed her to lose her youth, it was always *The Girl* or merely *Girl*. At times she forgot she had a name, except when she was with Ned.

Ned. Ned. She must get to Ned, or get someone to go to him. Who? The doctor? Yes, the doctor. Her brain began to work. Mrs Tyler across the green, her baby was due. Ma Fletcher had gone over this morning, she had seen her; that meant it was near; and although Ma Fletcher would bring the baby, the doctor would look in once. Had he been today?

She heard herself speaking across the room to the hated woman on the bed. 'Mrs Tyler's baby's due; the doctor may be calling on her.'

It seemed a long moment before Mrs Loam answered her. Then she said, 'You've said something useful at last.'

After that there was silence between them until Fred entered the room; then without giving him the chance to speak, his mother cried, 'Go across the way to Tyler's; she's due, the doctor mayn't have been yet. If not, tell them to tell him to come across. I'm poorly. Oh, I'm poorly.'

'An' you're not the only one.' Then as he turned to go, she cried after him, 'She can't sit in here all day an' I want the pot emptied.'

'Well, that'll have to wait till I get back; I'm lockin' the doors. An' you' – he stabbed his finger down at Hannah – 'if you don't want murder done an' you know what's good for you, you'll stay put.'

Silently she looked back at him, staring him out; then, his head wagging like that of a bull about to charge, he turned on his heel and went out.

The shop door banged and she rose from the chair, went out of the room, across the kitchen and into her own bedroom. There she took off her cloak and, sitting on the edge of the bed, her hands gripped tightly on her bulging stomach, she rocked herself as she planned what she would do if the doctor didn't call tonight. She'd open her mother-in-law's bedroom window that faced the square and scream out to anybody who was passing to go to the burn bend because Ned Ridley was lying there, perhaps dead; and somebody would go, if only out of curiosity.

What the result of her action would be she didn't care, she had gone through so much of late that of a sudden she wished for an end to it all. And if Ned died, as well he could, well, the sooner she went the better.

Doctor Arnison came at seven o'clock. When he examined Mrs Loam he found her stomach tender to pressure and rose-coloured spots on her abdomen, chest, and back; but it was her stools that confirmed his diagnosis. Mrs Loam had typhoid fever and she must have had it for a week or more.

The doctor coming out of the bedroom, put his black bag on the table, looked straight at Fred, who was standing with his back to the fire, and said abruptly, 'How's your bowels, are you costive or the other way?'

'Costive? No, I wish to God I was, doctor; I've nearly been run off me legs this last few days, just like her.'

'Well, I'm sorry to hear that. How you feeling otherwise?'

'Bit hot at times, headaches, a bit off me food an' all; but then I've had plenty to knock me off me food, doctor.' He now glanced towards Hannah where she was standing at the far side of the table.

'Well, Fred, I'm sorry to hear this because I'm afraid you're in for what your mother's got.'

'And what's that?'

There was a long pause before the doctor said, 'Typhoid. Typhoid fever.'

Hannah now looked from the doctor to Fred and she saw his high colour slowly seep from his face, and from the blustering figure of a man he seemed to change almost instantly into a frightened boy.

'Ty . . . typhoid? God! how . . . how did we get that? Is it about? I've never been further than the town. Never heard nobody's got it.'

'Well, it isn't a thing that people notify the crier about, not in the beginning at any rate. But I've had three cases already this week, and for your information, Fred, I'll tell you don't have to go any further than that.' He now turned and pointed to the bucket standing on the table.

'The watter?'

'Aye, the water. . . . Where do you get it from?'

'She draws it mostly.' He now jerked his head towards Hannah, then demanded, 'Where did you get it from?'

Hannah looked at the doctor as she said quietly, 'I always put the bucket under the ripple that comes out of the bank, never into the stream.'

'Well, the ripple is usually clean, but it's the water or the milk.'

'Milk?' Fred's face was screwed up now.

'Yes, milk. It's been discovered of late that that's how you catch typhoid. Dirty water and milk. The water is polluted, the cows drink the water, you drink the milk. There you have it. In future' – he now looked at Hannah – 'boil every drop of water you bring into the house. The same with the milk.' He pulled at his beard as he said musingly, 'It's a pity about the milk, I like milk.'

'God! what's going to happen to us?'

'Nothing much if you take care. Go to bed and stay there. I'll call in tomorrow. In the meantime I promise you you won't feel hungry. Sip the boiled water or the boiled milk, keep warm and quiet and you'll get through it.'

Fred stared at the doctor as he went past him towards the door. For the moment he seemed to be bereft of speech, until Hannah said, 'I'll see you out, doctor.' Then coming to life, and his fear damped down for a moment, Fred said, 'No, you won't! Oh no, you won't! I'll see the doctor out.'

'Doctor!' The note in Hannah's voice brought the doctor around to her and he said quietly, 'Yes? What is it, Hannah? You're all right?'

'I haven't got the fever, doctor, but I'm in great fear.' She now cast a hard glance towards Fred, then rushed on, 'I'm in fear for Ned, Ned Ridley. He's lying down by the burn bend, at least he was at four o'clock this afternoon. He may be still there for the grass is high near the water and you could pass by without seeing him. . . .'

The doctor now turned from her and looked at Fred, saying slowly, 'You and Ned had a fight.'

'That's about it, doctor. He set on me, stopped the horse, and when I got down he set on me.'

'He . . . he just hit you with his hands.' Hannah was bending towards him now, her chin thrust out. 'But you kicked him. You not only kicked him to the ground but you kicked and kicked and kicked him when he was lying there. Like a madman you were. And when he was lifeless you kicked him over the edge.' Her voice and her whole body trembling, she now turned to the doctor, crying, 'If he's dead, doctor, he's been murdered.'

The doctor's face was very straight as he looked from one to the other; then his gaze resting on Fred, he said, 'Well, I hope for your sake, Fred, that he's not dead, because if he is it would be senseless getting over the fever.' And on this he turned, saying, 'I can let myself out.'

They were left alone in the kitchen staring at each other, and Fred put his hand to his neck cloth and pulled it loose, then loosened the top button of his striped shirt before saying, 'You want to see me dead, don't you? Well, let me tell you I won't go alone. You can rely on that. I won't go alone because this I swear on, he'll never get you, you're me wife an' me wife you'll stay.'

He went to move across the room towards his mother's bedroom but, with his hand going quickly to his stomach, he turned and ran down the stairs. . . .

Typhoid fever. People died with typhoid fever. Well, an old woman like his mother might die but he wouldn't, he was too strong. He bragged about having a constitution like a horse and that constitution would see him through. But once they were both in bed, too sick to move, they'd be unable to stop her leaving. And if anything fatal happened to Ned, nothing would stop her from flying from this house. She wouldn't let either pity or compassion turn her, she would get away. Where she would go to she didn't know, and it wouldn't matter, but she'd go . . . run . . . fly. She had to put her hand over her mouth to stop herself from screaming.

The doctor came the next morning and, finding Fred standing stoically in the shop, he said to him, 'All right, if you want to die, you stay there. And as for selling that meat that you're cutting up, I can't allow that. The very fact that you've handled it could contaminate the whole village.

'What am I to do with it then?'

'Burn it. Bury it. But what you've got to do with yourself is get upstairs and into bed. . . . Man, don't be so stupid!' He pushed him towards the stairway. 'You're dropping on your feet.'

'How long will I have to stay in bed?'

'That depends on you, and how quickly you let yourself get over it.'

Up in the kitchen Fred turned to the doctor while he pointed backwards towards Hannah washing up crocks at the side table, and said bitterly, 'If I take to me bed, she'll walk out.'

'No, she won't; she's your wife and she's not inhuman, even if you are, so go on, get in there and get your things off, and let me have a look at you.'

Fred now almost staggered towards the bedroom door, and when it closed behind him Hannah turned swiftly from the table and, coming to the doctor, she whispered, 'Have . . . have you any news of Ned?'

'No.' He shook his head. 'I went down to the burn bend straightaway. There was no sign of him there. I even went back to the Pele house. That was all locked up. I then enquired in the town thinking he might have staggered back there. But don't worry' – he put his hand on her arm – 'someone must have picked him up. I'll enquire on my rounds.'

As she drooped her head forward on to her chest, he said, 'Now look, Hannah, you've got enough to worry about here; they're two very sick people.'

She was looking at him again and, her voice slow and bitter, she said, 'I don't care how sick they are, doctor, I don't care if they die.'

'Hannah!' He sounded shocked.

'I mean it, doctor. You don't know what I've gone through these past two years, no one does. That woman is a fiend.'

'Well –' He turned and opened his bag and made a sound like a small laugh before he said, 'I was well aware of that long before you, Hannah; but now you must show your Christian spirit. That's what the good book tells us we must do.' He cast a quizzical glance at her. 'But I'm going to tell you something in confidence.' He pushed his head close to hers. 'I myself find it very hard to follow it at times' – his head jerked upwards now – 'we must make the effort, we must try, especially at times like this. Now, do your best, Hannah. Whatever you decide to do afterwards, when they're on their feet again, is up to you. But the first thing you must do now is to stick a notice on the door saying shop closed. Anyway, I don't suppose there'll be many customers come near here for some time; the fever scares them as bad as the cholera.'

As he went towards the bedroom, he said, 'Let everything slide except what is necessary, and you'll have your work cut out doing that. See the pots are emptied often and rinse your hands afterwards. Yes, see to that. Don't let any of the stools get on your hands because that way you can catch it. I mean it might infect your food, or the milk, or anything. Oh yes, and the milk and water. It's important that every drop be boiled. Now don't forget.' ...

As if she could forget. All day long she went silently between the two rooms, her face stiff. She emptied their chambers, she placed glasses of boiled water to their hands on the bedside tables and she even swabbed their sweating faces with cold water, while her whole body recoiled whenever she touched them.

She was exhausted long before the twilight set in and as she took the last pail of the day and emptied it into the stream the stench made her want to vomit; the smell inside the house was unbearable but there seemed to be no getting away from it outside either.

No one had been near her all day. The village seemed quiet, it was as if everyone had deserted it; and there had been no banging on the shop door, the reason for the notice being now well known.

During the last twenty-four hours the child seemed to have grown inside her, so heavy had her body become.

When she re-entered the back shop, the sight of the great collops of meat turned her stomach and she had to turn and run quickly into the yard and there, standing with her hand against the house wall, she retched.

After a few moments she straightened up and wiped her mouth. She couldn't go on, it was too much to expect of any human being, she just couldn't go on.

As she was going throught the back shop again she was startled out of her weariness by a sharp rapping on the shop door, and when she opened it there stood the doctor.

She had hardly closed the door when she muttered, 'You . . . you've found him?'

'Yes, yes; I've found him. Now it's all right. It's all right. Come and sit down.' He looked round for a chair but there were none in the shop; and so he pushed her through into the back place, and she sat down on the box set against the wall. He looked round the room, saw another box, pulled it swiftly towards him, then sitting down opposite her, he said, 'You look exhausted, but if it's any comfort I can tell you you're not the only one; this thing's spreading.'

She was staring at him as she said quietly, 'Ned?'

'He's at the Dickinsons'. They live quite some way out on The Bottoms.'

'He's . . . he's all right?'

He paused a moment before he answered, 'No, no; I'm afraid he's not all right, he's far from all right.'

She went to rise from the box. 'He's not going to . . .?' She couldn't bring herself to say the word, and as he pressed her down again, he said, 'Now don't get hysterical. I don't know whether he's going to die or not, but if he doesn't it's because of two things: his strong constitution and Nell Dickinson.' He shook his head slowly. 'It's a long time since I've seen a man so badly handled, and as you so rightly said if he had been left out all night he certainly would have been found dead. It should happen that young Dickinson saw the whole thing. He was along in the brushwood hiding. He didn't say why he was hiding, and I didn't enquire because he's second to none at poaching, and that's taking account of his father Big Dick an' all. Anyway, the lad tells me he ran hell for leather over the hills and brought his mother and one of the other lads, and Nell Dickinson sent the lad post haste into the town to find his father; it being Friday and the day of the pays she knew exactly which inn he'd be drinking at. To cut a long story short, between them they carried Ned back over the hills to the house, and I'm telling you, Hannah, that must have taken some doing for it was all of two miles and no easy going, and although they're a big couple, Ned is no light weight. Anyway, the next thing they did was to send word for me and I got the message when I arrived home late last night. It just said would I call round at the Dickinsons', so I put them on my list for today. What with all the calls I didn't get there until late afternoon. I tell you, Hannah, I was shocked at the sight of Ned. And I must also tell you something else. It doesn't matter whether he lives or dies, the matter won't rest there, for Big Dick was so incensed he goes off into the town this morning and brings the constable. So it's now turned into a case, and the constable would have been here before now confronting Fred with what he's done but for the fact that it's known the two of them' – he jerked his head towards the ceiling – 'are down with the fever. But come he will, and that's certain. And if anything should happen to Ned, well, it's going to be a poor look-out for Fred. Even if he survives, Fred could go along the line because if there was ever a case explained by the term "assault and battery" Ned is it.'

They were peering at each other in the dimness and the doctor, now putting his head on one side, said, 'It's strange, Hannah, how you seem to court disaster wherever you go. . . . Unwittingly you seem to breed trouble wherever your feet tread. No, no' – he put his hand on her knee – 'don't

take it to yourself I'm not meaning it as a criticism, just trying to work out
why beauty must always pay the price of beauty. 'Tis no fault of yours, my
dear, you're just fated. From time to time there's women put into the world
like you who have the power to drive men crazy. 'Tisn't only how you look.'
He shrugged now, his hands going out wide. 'I don't know what it is. The
gods must laugh anyway when they dole it out.' He sighed, then ended, 'I
don't know where it's all going to end, my dear.'

She swallowed deeply, pressed her lips together, blinked the tears back
from her eyes and said soberly, 'I do, doctor. When Ned gets better . . . and
he must get better, we're going away. We had it all planned. He was to
bring the second string of horses over from Yorkshire and then we'd have
enough money to start somewhere else, even if he didn't sell the house.'

He nodded at her as he rose from the box, saying quietly now, 'Well,
who's to blame you? Who's to blame you? But in the meantime' – he put
out his hand and touched her shoulder – 'do what you can for those two.
They don't deserve it, neither of them, yet I must say if we all got our
deserts many of us would be lying naked on the fells.' He smiled wearily
now as he ended, 'I'll look in on them, then make for home; I've had a long,
hard day.'

'I'm sorry, doctor.'

'Well then, we're both sorry for each other, and we're both very tired, so
after I'm gone get yourself bedded down. By the way' – he turned in the
doorway – 'talking about bedding. The sheets you take off the bed you'll put
straight into the pot and boil, won't you?'

She nodded slowly before she answered, 'Yes, doctor, yes.'

Alone in the room, she joined her hands together, then turned and pressed
them against the rough stone wall, and leaning her brow on them she prayed,
'Oh God, I'm sorry I bring trouble on people. I don't mean to, you know
that, you know that. And don't punish me by taking Ned. Keep him safe,
that's all I ask. That's all I'll ever ask, just keep him safe.'

## Chapter Nine

Hannah felt that her mind had ceased to function. For fourteen days now
she had worked like a machine. She carried slops down the stairs, brought
water up, boiled it, carried it into the bedrooms, took more slops down the
stairs, brought more water up. In between times she changed the sheets on
the beds. This she found to be the worst task of all because she had to touch
their bodies. She'd take the linen downstairs, put it into the boiling wash
pot, which she kept going day and night, rinse, and mangle the bedding,
nightshirts, and nightgowns, dry them if it were possible outside, then hang
them round the kitchen to air. Some days this process had to be gone through
twice.

But for the fact that the doctor brought her daily news of Ned she would, she knew, going by the dictates of her body, have given up; she would not, however, have walked out, she was too weary for that now. She would have just lain down on the pallet of clean straw she had placed on top of the horsehair sofa and let sleep and the desire for death have their way. But there was Ned, there was still Ned, and he was recovering; at least the doctor said they could count him out of danger now, but it would be some time before he'd be on his feet.

It was on Wednesday, the twelfth day, that she noticed a change in Fred. Whereas she knew that all along he had been aware of her and her ministrations, now he began to be mentally confused and to take her for his mother or his Aunt Connie. She had met his Aunt Connie only three times. She lived on the far side of Allendale Town and ran a wayside inn. She was Mrs Loam's sister, but appeared totally unlike her in temperament, being big-made and jolly.

Besides going into delirium, he had bled twice during the day from the nose and had brought himself up in bed groaning and holding his stomach as if he were experiencing intense pain.

Once he called out, she was in Mrs Loam's room, and that lady asked querulously, 'What's up with him?'

'He seems in pain.'

'Well, I'm in pain an' all; he's not the only one. But what's he yelling like that for?'

'I think his fever has increased.'

'Well, his constitution should be able to fight any fever. And he's young; his years should battle for him. . . . Give me a drink, girl, I'm parched.'

When Hannah, who was at the window, didn't answer, Mrs Loam groaned at her, 'Do you hear me, girl? Stop your stargazing and get me a drink.'

'I will in a minute.' The tone of Hannah's voice silenced the woman and she stared from the bed in amazement as Hannah, thrusting up the window, shouted, 'Bella! Tessie! stop a minute. Stop a minute! I want a word with you.' When she thrust the window down, Mrs Loam brought herself up from her pillow and demanded, 'What you at now? I told you to give me a drink.'

Hannah almost thrust the glass into her hand, saying, 'There you are then.'

'Where you going? Who are you callin'? Was that Bella Monkton and young Tessie? What do you want with them?'

As if injected with new life, Hannah ran down the stairs. She knew what she wanted with Bella and Tessie. Pulling open the shop door, she looked at them where they were standing below the step in their outdoor clothes, each with a bundle on one arm and a bass bag held in the other hand.

'You're going to the market?'

'Aye, Miss Hannah, we're going to the hirings. An' I'm not sorry to leave there I can tell you that; she's mean to the core she is. There they are coming down the street in the trap now' – she jerked her head to the right – "and never offered us a lift.'

Hannah looked to her right, and yes, there was the trap coming down the road, the missis driving, with Betsy at her side.

She turned her gaze back to Bella and Tessie and she asked quietly, 'Would you be frightened to come in?'

'No, not me, Miss Hannah. Some folks are afraid of the death they'll never die, but as I said to Tessie here only last night, it's one thing you don't do twice, you die but once and after that the judgement.'

'And you, Tessie?' Hannah was looking at Tessie, and Tessie gave a little grin and she replied, 'Where Bella goes I go.'

'Come in then.' Her voice was eager, but as she pushed the door backwards and thrust out her other arm as if gathering them to her she stopped; in fact they all stopped and turned and looked towards the trap that was passing them on the roadway, for both Anne Thornton and her daughter were looking towards them, at least they were looking at Hannah; and Hannah stared back over the distance to the woman whose bane she had been, and who in turn had been hers. Then with a welcoming gesture her arms seemed to encircle both Bella and Tessie and she drew them over the step and banged the door. Then turning to them, she said, 'That will give her something to think about, won't it?'

'Oh aye,' Tessie laughed, 'it certainly will, miss. It certainly will.'

'You know they've both got the fever?' Hannah thrust her hand backwards.

'Aye, we know that.' Bella nodded towards her.

'Well, I must tell you it's the bad kind, and it's getting worse with him, but I'm at my wit's end, I can't cope for much longer on my own.' She put her hand on the raised dome of her stomach that was pushing out the apron from below her breasts. 'I'm weary both inside and out. It's the washing and the running up and down stairs. Do you think you could stay for a few days? You'll miss the Allendale hirings but there'll be one next week-end in Hexham, and . . . and I'll see you get paid.'

Bella remained silent for a moment, then she looked at Tessie as she said, 'Well, speaking for meself I'm willin' enough, but it's Tessie here.'

'Well, I'm willin' an' all. Don't worry about me, I'm not afraid of the death I'll never die.'

'Oh, thank you. Thank you both.' She put her arms out and her hands held each of them on the shoulders; and Tessie now laughed and said, 'Eeh! isn't it funny how things turn out? I never did think I'd be workin' for you, miss, but I'm right glad I am, I am that. 'Twill be like a holiday.'

'Oh.' The word was a groan and Hannah drooped her head forward slowly as she said, 'Oh, Tessie, it'll be no holiday.'

'Well' – Tessie's voice was still bright – 'it all depends how you look at things. You think things are bad till you meet something worse. Anyway, tell us what we've got to do, an' then we'll see.'

'Well, it's mostly washing, and emptying slops. And then there's the meat outside; it's gone rotten and it has to be buried or burned. And the whole place' – she wrinkled her nose – 'it needs a scrub down. All that and a thousand and one other things.'

'Where will we put our bits an' pieces?' Bella's tone was brisk.

'Well now' – Hannah looked about her – 'you could clear the back shop out and leave your things in there. And as for sleeping, well, you haven't much choice. I sleep on a straw pallet on the sofa; you can make similar ones and sleep upstairs or down here. It'll be warmer upstairs. But then I'll leave it to you.'

'First things first then, we'll clear this place up.' As Bella bustled into the back shop Hannah said on the lightest note that had been in her voice for weeks, 'I'll make you a pot of tea.' And on this she went heavily upstairs.

As soon as she got up to the kitchen she was greeted by Mrs Loam's voice calling, 'Girl! Girl!'

Standing at the bedroom door she looked across the room and said flatly, 'Yes?'

'What you up to? You bring those two in?'

'Yes, I've brought them in, and they're going to stay in and help me.'

'They're what!'

'You heard what I said.'

A bout of harsh coughing almost choked the woman and she gasped, 'You . . . you brought them into my . . . my house?'

'It's either I have help or I walk out; you can take your choice.'

'By God! I'll deal with you when I'm better. Oh, by God! I will. See if I don't.'

'And me with you.'

As another fit of coughing attacked Mrs Loam, Hannah turned away and went about the business of making a pot of tea.

During the doctor's visit that afternoon he became greatly disturbed not only by the change in Fred but also by Hannah's condition.

Coming into the kitchen where she was waiting for him, he said, 'This is serious, he's a very ill man. He's the last person I would have imagined would have succumbed like this. Now if it had been the old one' – he nodded towards the other door – 'I wouldn't have been a bit surprised. But Fred, with a constitution like he has!'

'What has happened?'

'Oh, a number of complications have set in. I . . . I think he is bleeding from the bowel. There's a perforation there. The fact that he's in pain and that he has been vomiting bears this out. Yet I would have imagined his stamina would have weathered this. But I'm afraid, very much afraid, it's going to result in peritonitis.'

'What is that?' Her voice was low, tired sounding.

'Oh, it is difficult to explain in a few words but it can lead to death.'

She remained still and checked herself from the blasphemy of thinking God was answering her prayers. Then of a sudden she was made to imagine that He was indeed chastising her for she was brought double by a grinding pain in her stomach.

'Hannah. Hannah. Oh! don't start that; not at this time.'

'Oh! Oh! Doctor.' The sweat was running off her as she gasped, 'It's too early isn' it?'

'If we're sticking to the book, yes; but with the first it can come early or late. Is this the first pain you've had?'

'Yes. Yes, like this. Yet I haven't felt well for some days, but I put it down to the work and . . . and worry. . . . Ned. I . . . I wanted to ask you. . . . How is he?' Her words were brought out between gasps.

'Oh, going along slowly.' He did not look at her as he spoke but attended to his bag and added, 'I'm not worried about Ned at the moment.'

'What is actually . . . wrong with him, doctor? Tell me, please.'

'Well now, if you were to ask me what isn't wrong with him I'd be able to answer that more simply. He's had bad concussion; he was bruised from head to foot; his groin was split open.'

'Split open!' She mouthed the words twice before they made any sound.

'Yes, split open. He had to be stitched in various parts, but he's standing up to it.' He turned and bent towards her now and whispered, 'I shouldn't be carrying messages because I in no way represent a messenger of the gods, and after all you are still a married woman, but I'll tell you this, he was sufficiently himself yesterday to ask after you.'

She took a long breath, then said, 'Thank you, doctor. . . . Oh!' Her mouth opened wide; she groaned, and again she was bending forward and holding herself, tightly now.

'Goodness! Goodness me! This is bad. You're for it, my girl. Bella! Bella!' His voice rang through the house as he held her. 'Talk about God working in a mysterious way; if those two hadn't come your way we'd be in a nice pickle at this moment, for I don't see any of the neighbours rushing about. It's funny how people will generally dash forward for most things, even dive into the ice cold river to save a dog, yet with typhoid or cholera they flee from the very name of it. As Bella just said to me, you've only got to die once. Good woman, Bella, very good woman. . . . Ah, there you are, Bella . . . see what we've got here, somebody struggling to be born, while back there –' He shook his head. 'You and Tessie are going to have a night of it, I'm afraid.'

'It won't be the first time, doctor. . . . Come on, my dear, come on.'

As Bella led Hannah towards the couch the doctor said, 'I've got to go, I've had an urgent call from the Burn farm, but I'll look in on my way back.'

'Thank you . . . doctor. Thank you for, for everything.'

'That's all right, Hannah . . . keep pressing, and who knows he may arrive before me.' . . .

When he had gone Bella said, 'There now, we'll get your clothes off and make you comfortable . . . at least as comfortable as it's possible on a horsehair sofa.'

'Oh! Bella.' Hannah grasped Bella's hand. 'What . . . what would I have done if you, you hadn't come?'

'Well, I did. God seems to know what He's about, at least sometimes, an' we're told He makes the back to bear the burden, and tempers the wind to the shorn lamb.'

Hannah gave birth to a son at two o'clock the following morning. Bella delivered it as if she had been performing the function at regular intervals all her life. When Hannah gave one final heave and an agonized gasp, Bella brought the child forth, and she didn't need to hold it by the legs or slap it to make it breathe for it gave evidence of vital life almost immediately, and within seconds of its cry, another cry came from Mrs Loam's room demanding to know what it was.

'What is it? What is it?'

'Let her wait.' Bella turned towards Tessie. 'The old vixen. Here, take him, till I see to Miss Hannah.'

'Oh, he's bonny. Oh, he is. He's bonny, Miss Hannah, he is.' Tessie leant towards the couch where Hannah lay in complete exhaustion and when she made no response, Bella said, 'Don't bother her; let me see to her; you wash him an' keep him warm. Listen to that old devil. Listen to her.' She turned her head towards the door. 'Go on, tell her or else we'll have her in here in a minute. . . . Lay him in the clothes basket there afore the fire. . . . Oh, my God! Listen to her. If I go in I'll give her a mouthful.' . . .

When Tessie entered Mrs Loam's room the old woman was sitting on the edge of her bed, and when, her croak coming from high in her head, she demanded, 'Well, what is it? You heard me calling, didn't you, you young scut!' Tessie compressed her lips tightly for a moment, then came out with the old senseless rhyme about birth: 'A goat on a hayrick an' a three-legged poss stick, if you want to know.'

'You! You!' It looked and sounded as if Mrs Loam was about to choke.

'It's a lad.' And on this abrupt information, Tessie went out closing the door none too gently after her, muttering as she did so, 'Wicked old witch!'

It was an hour later when Bella laid the baby in Hannah's arms, saying, 'He's a fine lump of a lad.'

Hannah turned her face slowly on the pillow and looked at the child. She was concerned not about the size of him but how he looked. Did he look like Fred, or Ned? He looked like neither. He hadn't Fred's square face, or Ned's long one; his face looked oval, heart-shaped like hers. If he didn't change too much as babies often did, he would grow to look like her. All the time she was carrying she had been sure it was Ned's child in her; now perhaps she'd never know; well, not until his character began to form.

Hannah started, as did Bella, when Mrs Loam's bedroom door was pulled open and, looking like the witch Tessie had called her, she came staggering across the room, supporting herself by gripping the backs of the chairs until she reached the head of the couch, and there, bending over it, she glared down on Hannah and the child.

'Tis not like him, not a feature. 'Tis not like him.'

'Go back to bed, Mrs Loam.' Bella had hold of her arm now, and the old woman turned to her. 'You've got eyes. 'Tisn't like him. You can see for yourself.'

'The child's like his mother.'

'Bah! jiggery-pokery! Like his mother!'

'Go on back to bed.'

Mrs Loam now put her hands to her stomach, drew in two sharp breaths, then turned about and stumbled back towards her room. But before she reached it the main bedroom door opened and Tessie came out carrying a bucket of slops.

'How is he?' Mrs Loam stood gripping the stanchion of her door now.

'I'd say he was right bad, that's what I'd say. An' he's smellin' like a poke of devils.'

Whatever retort Mrs Loam was about to make she thought better of it, and with her remaining strength she stumbled back into the room. But her weakness didn't prevent her from banging the door behind her.

Doctor Arnison was very pleased with Hannah, and he was equally pleased with Bella. 'You did a fine job, Bella, I couldn't have done better myself. Afterbirth, the lot. Glad you had the sense to keep it for me. She's a good midwife, isn't she, Hannah?'

'She's wonderful. They both are.' Hannah smiled weakly from one to the other where they stood behind the doctor. 'And they must be so tired, they've had hardly any sleep.'

'Well, they'll have to take it in turns, because there's going to be a lot of work before them.' He nodded from one to the other. 'There's a very sick man in there.'

When the doctor jerked his head backwards Hannah lowered her gaze. She was weary in body and mind, she was feeling strangely apart from everything around her. At one point during the early hours of this morning she had thought she wouldn't mind if she were to die; neither her need of Ned, nor the child's need of her, seemed to have the power to hold her to life; and certainly not the need of the man who was her husband, the very sick man.

'I wish we could move you to some place more comfortable, Hannah.'

'Oh, that's all right, doctor. I'll . . . I'll be up in a day or two.'

'Oh no, you won't. You'll stay there for a week or more.'

She didn't say 'We'll see;' she didn't want to talk, not even at this moment to ask after Ned.

A groan coming from the main bedroom caused the doctor to turn and look towards the door before, picking up his black oblong, bulbous bag, he said to no one in particular, 'I'll be along later in the day.'

True to his word, Doctor Arnison came back that same evening and then on each of the next three days he called twice, because as he said, it was touch and go with Fred.

On the third day of Fred's delirium his mother staggered from her room and into his; then returning almost immediately into the kitchen she cried at Hannah who was propped up in the couch, 'He's dying. God Almighty! he's dying. Do you know that, girl? He's dying.'

Hannah made no reply, she just stared dully back at her mother-in-law; then watched her turn to Tessie and cry, 'Bring me a paper an' pen, girl. Paper an' pen, quick! Off that shelf there!'

Tessie did as she was bid, and when she held out the pen and paper Mrs Loam grabbed at it, then slapped it on to the table and, her hand shaking visibly, she scrawled something on the paper. Then turning to Bella and Tessie she asked, 'Can you write your names?'

They both looked at her without speaking, and so she demanded, 'Tell me! can you write your names?'

'We make our crosses.' Bella's reply was muttered.

'Well, come on in here and make your crosses.'

As she went to move from the table, Bella and Tessie spoke almost simultaneously, 'No. No.'

'What!'

'We're not making our crosses on that' – Bella pointed to the piece of paper in Mrs Loam's hand – ' 'cos I know what it is, I know what you're up to.'

The look that the old woman passed over them would, if it had been possible, have struck them dead; and now turning on Hannah, she ground out through her almost closed lips, 'I'll see it burnt down afore you get it. And what's more, I'll have the bringing up of him.' She now pointed to where the child lay in the basket before the fire. And visibly swaying now she made for her son's bedroom. And there, bending over Fred, she cried, 'I'm here! I'm here, lad! Listen to me.'

'Ma. Ma.'

'Listen to me, Fred. Listen to me. Take this pen in your hand. . . .' The
pen was suddenly knocked flying as the great arm began to thrash up and
down on the quilt. Then his body became still for a moment, and he gasped
and passed his swollen tongue round his swollen lips as he turned and looked
at her in recognition, croaking now, 'Ma. Ma.'

'Fred, listen!'

'Ma . . . I'm bad . . . Ma.'

'Yes, lad, I know, I know. But do this for me, will you? Do this for your
ma. Sign your name on this paper here. I'll hold your hand. 'Tis about the
house. . . .'

' 'Tis done. 'Tis done . . . Got to get the meat . . . cut up.' The paper and
pen were again knocked out of her hand and fell at the foot of the bed.

Mrs Loam picked the paper up and, her head moving from side to side,
he gazed down at the words she had written there: I leave everything I have
to me mother. Then she turned one long look at her son before stumbling
from the room and into the kitchen again. But she stopped at her own
bedroom door and, supporting herself against it, she cried at Hannah,
'Whatever happens to him, I'll live, if it's only to see me day with you. I've
said it afore an' I'll say it again, I'll see me day with you, me girl. By God!
I will; I'll see you on the street beggin' your bread.'

All three watched the figure in the long calico nightdress stumble the few
steps into her room, and when her door was closed, Tessie whispered, 'She
is . . . she is like a witch, a wicked witch!'

But what Bella said was, 'Can she do you out of the house an' all that if
he dies, Miss Hannah?'

Hannah stared back at Bella before replying, 'She'll try, Bella. I can't see
how she'll do it but she'll try.' And it was in this moment that there returned
to her the urge to live, if only to beat that dreadful old woman.

# Chapter Ten

On the fifth day Hannah got up from the couch, and two days later Fred
died. He died at four o'clock on the Sunday morning. He was unconscious
to the end; and when the breath left his body his face slowly changed and
Hannah, looking down on him, saw for a moment the young fellow who
was always pleasant to her when, as a schoolgirl, she went into the shop.
But she felt no remorse, only a great, great intense relief, as if she herself
had died and her body and mind were floating free in a new atmosphere,
a new world.

Bella and Tessie laid him out, and when Bella said, 'Shall we tell her?'
Hannah replied, 'No; don't waken her, we'll wait till daylight. But go now,
both of you, and get some rest for you look worn out.'

When reluctantly she entered her mother-in-law's room at seven o'clock that morning, she did not go near her bed; seeing she was awake she stood just within the doorway and said quietly, 'He's gone.'

The answer she received amazed her, for Mrs Loam, looking steadily back at her, said, 'I could have told you that. He's been gone these last two days. So now once they've laid him away you'll be free to go, won't you? An' those two with you.'

'Perhaps I will and perhaps I won't.'

'What do you mean by that?'

'Just what I say. I was his wife, I have rights.'

'What rights have you?' Mrs Loam pulled herself up in the bed. 'You've got no rights in this house. You try an' claim them an' you'll see what'll happen to you.'

'You forget I have a son.'

'Huh! that! Whose son, eh? Wait till I open me mouth, you won't have a leg to stand on.'

To this Hannah made no reply, she merely turned about and went out of the room.

Doctor Arnison said the normal period for the body to lie coffined in the house before burial must be waived; in this case the matter must be dealt with as soon as possible; and so on the third day after he had died Fred was buried, and it was said the grave-digger had a job to dig the grave, so frozen was the ground.

The following to the funeral was small. There was Ralph Buckman the blacksmith; Will Rickson the joiner; Walter Bynge the stonemason; Thomas Wheatley the grain chandler; backed by a few of the older male inhabitants of the village and three business men from Allendale Town . . . and the doctor.

Breaking with tradition, no one came back to the house of the deceased to indulge in a gargantuan meal except the doctor, and he didn't come to eat. Standing in the back shop facing Hannah, he said, 'Well, now it's all over, Hannah, what are you going to do?'

'I don't know, doctor; I need some advice. How do I stand as regards what was his, the property, money from the business and such?'

'Oh' – the doctor let out a long breath – 'I'm not in the legal profession but I think, as the law stands, if the child hadn't been born before Fred died then you and the old 'un would have shared the estate, or something like that. As it is now, I don't think she comes into the picture, unless there's a will.'

'I don't think he left a will. She . . . she tried to force him to sign a paper that she had written one day last week but he was too ill to comply. She still thinks though that she can claim everything.'

'Well then, if that's the case she's a stubborn old fool. Of course she always has been. Anyway, she should have the sense to know that when a man takes a wife it misplaces his mother, at least in part.'

'Do . . . do you think I should see a solicitor, Doctor?'

'Yes. Yes, I do. Have you got Fred's papers, business papers and things?'

'No; they're in a box in her room.'

'Well, I should just walk in and take them. Then go and see Mr Ransome in Allendale . . . you know, he has an office just off the square, he'll advise you as to what your rights are. As far as I can judge from my experience, there shouldn't be any hitch. That being so' – he smiled at her now – 'the tables will be turned, she'll be relying on your charity. Oh, and Dame Loam won't like that a bit, will she?'

'No, doctor, she won't.' Hannah didn't return the doctor's smile, but she said, 'Thank you very much, not only for your advice but for everything you have done for me. . . . Will you be seeing Ned soon?'

'I'll be going that way tomorrow, that's if the snow doesn't start again and the road is passable, for it lies deep down on the bottoms.'

'Does . . . does he know about Fred?'

'Yes, he knows.'

'What . . . what did he say?'

'Well, since you ask, he quoted God's ways, which was unusual, at least coming from Ned because he's no churchman. What he said was, God doesn't take side tracks over the mountain when He's got a miracle to perform. His translation might be a bit free but his meaning was plain. Of course' – he smiled wryly now – ''tisn't everybody who would look upon Fred's death as a miracle. Yet for you and Ned it must appear so. As for me, well, from where I stand I view it as a most unexpected happening, because with a constitution like his I would have bet my last shilling he would have battled through; at the same time I would have gambled a hundred to one against his mother surviving. Yet she will survive. . . . But where she survives, well, that seems to be up to you, Hannah, doesn't it?'

'There is one thing I can assure you of, doctor, and you can gamble on it too, and you'll win, and that is she won't survive alongside me.'

'No? Well, that's something you'll have to work out for yourself.'

'And I'll do that, doctor.'

'Good-bye, Hannah.'

'Good-bye, doctor. Doctor.'

'Yes, Hannah?' He turned from the door.

'Do . . . do you think I could go across and see Ned if . . . if the weather holds?'

'No, no, I definitely don't. That's one thing you shouldn't think of doing, Hannah, because in his present low state he could pick up anything.' His heavy eyebrows strained upwards towards his receding hairline as he went on, 'Who knows but you could be a carrier; carriers never seem to catch the disease themselves but they spread it. I'm not saying you are, but you've been here in the thick of it, and in a very low state of health yourself, and you haven't picked it up. No, no; don't expose him to that risk. Have patience a little longer; you'll see enough of each other likely before you're finished.' He went out muttering something that sounded like 'if nothing else happens.'

Mrs Loam's recovery was slow; it seemed as if she was making the most of Tessie's ministrations, as rough as they were. When either Bella or Tessie was in the room she would always remain tight-lipped, but some days later, following the funeral, she spoke to them both, and what she said was, 'If you two think you're gona be paid you've got a surprise comin' to you.'

'Is that so?' put in Tessie quickly. 'Well, I'm gona tell you something. We won't be the only ones.'

'What do you mean by that?'

'Just what I said. Miss Hannah's gone into the solicitor's and it'll be up to him to decide who runs things from now on.'

'*Me box. Me box.*'

Mrs Loam was sitting upright in the bed now looking towards the corner of the room, where on a small table had stood a wooden box, its top inlaid with mother-of-pearl. In it her husband had kept the deeds of the house, their marriage certificate, the baptism certificate of their son, together with his savings bank book. Now the box was no longer there.

The piercing scream the little woman let out of her almost lifted both Bella and Tessie from the ground, and Tessie, putting her hands over her ears, shouted back, 'Stop that!'

'She's a thief! She's a thief!'

Taking the woman by the shoulders, Bella pushed her none too gently back into the pillows and, bending over her, she said, 'She's no thief; she's left your marriage lines and your son's birth certificate there, the rest she's taken into the solicitor. If he's not holding any kind of a will then she says, and rightly, that the place and all in it is hers . . . and the child's.'

'And' – put in Tessie now – 'the money that's in the bank an' all; so if I was you, Mrs Loam, I'd keep a civil tongue in me head . . . to all concerned, that is.'

Both Bella and Tessie glanced at each other apprehensively as they watched the woman on the bed gasping for breath, for they thought she was about to choke.

'Have a drink of water.' Tessie was now holding the glass out to Mrs Loam. But she made no movement to take it, and Tessie, putting it back on the table, said, 'Well, please yersel.'

They were both about to leave the room when there came the sound of pebbles being thrown against the window-pane, and again they looked at each other in surprise; then hurrying to the window, Bella pushed it open and looked out and down into the large face of a large woman.

'Do you want something?'

The woman in the street below now called up, 'Just to know how she's farin'.'

'Oh, she's getting on nicely, I would say.'

'Tell her I won't come in; 'twouldn't be wise.'

'I'll tell her. What's your name?'

'I'm her sister Connie.'

'Oh, her sister?'

'Connie! Connie!' Now Mrs Loam was sitting up in bed again and, waving her hand towards Bella, she cried, 'Tell her to come up. I want her, I want to see her.'

'She says will you come up, she wants to see you?'

'No, no. As I said, 'twouldn't be wise, but tell her as soon as she's over it to come along to me an' we'll settle what's to be done about the business and such like, you know.'

'I'll tell her.' Bella closed the window and looked towards the bed, then said, 'Well, you heard that, didn't you? She says as soon as you're well you've got to go over to her, and you can arrange about the business and such like.'

Mrs Loam swallowed deeply, then brought out slowly, 'When I get out of this bed God help you two, I'm tellin' you.'

'You're still sure of yersel.' Tessie's head was wagging at her now. 'I wouldn't count me chickens afore they're hatched, if I was you.'

It again appeared to Bella that Mrs Loam was about to have a seizure so she pushed Tessie before her out of the room, and as she did so Mrs Loam's croak followed them, spluttering, 'An' God'll strike her down dead. Blasphemy . . . going across the doors afore she's churched!'

In the kitchen, Bella whispered, 'If Miss Hannah can get the better of that one, then she'll be able to tackle anybody. But she's right about one thing . . . she did go out afore she was churched, an' she's church, not chapel.'

They stared at each other. Then Tessie said, 'Aw, what matter. It's the solicitor man that matters; it'll all depend on what he says.'

'Yes. Aye,' Bella repeated; 'aye, it'll all depend on what he says.' . . .

About this time the solicitor man was treating Hannah with great courtesy. On his desk before him he had the documents she had brought with her, and he moved them here and there with his forefinger as if he were playing cards as he said. 'It would seem, Mrs Loam, by what you tell me with regard to your mother-in-law trying to get your husband to put his name to a paper that there was no will made. It's very odd about wills.' He now put his elbows on the arms of the chair and joined his fingertips together. 'Men have to be persuaded to make wills. They have the idea that once they sign their name to a will it is as it were the signature to their death sentence; the smaller the business the greater their reluctance to sign it away, because that is what they feel they are doing, signing it away. If a man has children, then he knows that without a will his wife will inherit a third of the estate, and the children the rest; and should his own mother be alive he would expect them to look after her. But to get some of them to put in writing just how they wish their mother to be taken care of is considered to be nothing less than an insult to their integrity, and that of their offspring. And so, in this case as there appears to be no will then the law will say that your son and you are the rightful inheritors, he will come into two-thirds and you one-third, and it will be up to you what provision you make for your mother-in-law out of the whole. It will be merely a matter of your charity.' He paused here, then added, 'I did not do business for either Mr Loam Senior or Junior, but from what you have told me your husband inherited everything from his father, so things should be plain sailing as to your claim, and naturally that of your son; and I would be pleased to act for you in this matter, if you so wish.'

'I'd be very grateful if you would, Mr Ransome. . . . How . . . how long do you think it would take to settle?'

'Oh' – he shook his head – 'the law is slow in these cases of probate, yet there is no one to contest your claim, as I see it.'

'I . . . I think my mother-in-law might.'

'How can she' – he brought his head forward, his chin thrust out – 'if there is no written word to the effect that she is in any way a beneficiary? You, as I see it, have a double claim. You are not only the deceased's wife, but you are the mother of his child. . . . There is one thing that puzzles me though, it is the bank book. It states here that the amount is four hundred and thirty-five pounds, but the last entry was made in June 1856. Now your husband's business was small compared with some butchery businesses, but in some years there was deposited in the bank' – he tapped the book on the table – 'as much as sixty pounds; but nothing since June 1856, which makes me think that there must be money stored somewhere else. There was no other place in the house where deeds or bank books could be kept?'

'No; only in the box as I explained. It was always kept in my mother-in-law's bedroom, and it was always locked; but recently when cleaning the room I happened to find where she kept the key.'

Again the solicitor put his elbows on the arms of the chair, and now his fingertips drummed against each other and his face moved slowly into a smile while his lips remained tightly closed, until he said in low amused tones, 'I think I can give a good guess where the money is, that is the profits since '56. Does your mother-in-law lie on a box bed?'

'Yes; yes, she does.' Hannah's eyes stretched wide now. 'Of course. Of course, that's why she would never let me turn the bed tick.'

'It happens all the time, Mrs Loam. A man suddenly decides that the bank or outsiders know too much about his business; if they think he's got money someone might want to borrow from him. He cannot believe that bankers or solicitors can keep secrets, in fact must keep secrets, as well as doctors or priests. So they put around they've had a bad year, and the profits go into the box bed or behind a brick in the wall.'

As he continued to smile at her, she thought of Ned and the loose bricks in the Pele house.

'Can you get access to the bed?'

'Pardon?' She blinked and he repeated, 'Is it possible for you to strip the bed and find out if there's any money hidden there?'

'Not at present; she's convalescing from the fever.'

'Could she be moved?'

'Yes, yes, in a day or so, I suppose she could.' She returned his smile and nodded, adding, 'Yes, she could be moved, with a little persuasion, that is.'

'Well then, you must use a little persuasion. And I'll be interested to know your findings. In the meantime, I shall get in touch with the bank and you will likely have to come in to town again in a day or two for the account to be transferred to your name. You'll then be able to meet such debts as are outstanding, such as the funeral expenses. . . . And then, of course, you must live. Now do you want to take the deeds of the house back with you or leave them with me?'

'I'd prefer to leave them with you; and also the bank book, if I may.'

'Certainly, certainly, Mrs Loam.'

When she rose to her feet he rose too.

'Good-bye, Mr Ransome, and thank you.'

'Good-bye, Mrs Loam, It's been a pleasure meeting you.'

He preceded her through the outer office and opened the door for her himself while his clerk, who had risen to his feet, stood to the side. Again she inclined her head towards him, then went out into the square, conscious that through the clear upper half of the window both men were watching her progress.

She wasn't wearing her cloak today but a thick grey Melton cloth long-coated costume with a fur collar. It was the last outfit the mister had bought her and she had not worn it since she was married.

The last time she had walked across this square she had kept her head down in order to cover her bruised face; now she held it high and she made her step jaunty although she was feeling far from jaunty inside. Not only was she still feeling weak, but also the stench of body excrement remained in her nostrils and so strong was it she felt it would be years before she was rid of it.

What would have happened, she asked herself now, if she hadn't looked out of the window and seen Bella and Tessie that day? She'd likely be dead herself. She would never forget them, and she would repay them a thousandfold for what they had done for her. Oh yes, she had plans for Bella and Tessie . . . and Margaret.

Yes, she could now send the letter off to Margaret. She had hesitated to do so until her position had been confirmed by the solicitor. It was still early in the day and it would catch the mail van and be in Hexham by this evening and Margaret would receive it at the latest by tomorrow morning; then perhaps by the following day she would be with her. It would be wonderful to be all together again, Margaret, Bella, Tessie. . . . Strange how things were turning out. . . . Very strange.

As Hannah waited for the carrier cart she was the subject of covert glances from the people who passed back and forth across the square, for she was a figure of interest. Was she not the cause of hell being let loose between Ned Ridley and Fred Loam? Now one was dead and the other in such a state it was said he'd be lucky if he ever got over it. And many of them, as they glanced at her, remembered back to the story of her being dumped on the Thornton household by a woman of the Newcastle streets who claimed that Matthew Thornton was her father. And it had been the cause of misery in that household, and all for nothing because hadn't she found out on her wedding-day that she had no claim on Matthew Thornton. And what had she done then? Run helter-skelter to the mine to the young fellow who was supposed to be her half-brother, she had, and her not married an hour gone to Fred Loam. Then from him on to Ned Ridley. Aye, and what happened then? To save her from the man-trap he loses half his hand. But if all tales were true he had already lost more than half his heart to her, and that was saying something for Ned Ridley whose heart had been spread around the hills since he was a chip of a lad. But they were saying that it was because of her he hadn't married Lena Wright.

Then after all that caffuffle what does she go and do but take secret trips up to the Pele house; and as is often the case the whole village knew about it, except the man most concerned; and when he does, what happens? He swipes her one. Well, who's to blame him? No man is going to stand being made a monkey out of. Then big Dickinson's lad finds Ned battered almost to a pulp and big Dickinson goes and gets the polis. Now that was surprising, wasn't it? Big Dick going for the polis and the polis hoping to catch him out for years! 'Twas a laugh, that one. Then them all waiting for Fred to get over the fever so they can lock him up; and what does he do? He goes and kicks the bucket.

Who says, they asked of one another, that nothing happens in the country?

And there she was standing now as straight as a die, and after just giving birth an' all. And when you took a good dekko at her you could see what all the trouble was about, for there was no doubt she had grown into a fine lump of a woman, a beautiful woman. And she had something about her. What, they couldn't exactly put a name to: something to do with her eyes, or her hair? Now that alone could fetch a man.

Not that her looks would have any effect on her mother-in-law. By God! no. There was a little vixen if ever there was one. Indomitable she was, harder to get through than the Roman Wall. It would be something to look forward to seeing how the young matron intended to stand up to her.

Hannah was not completely oblivious of the trend that the conversation would take that evening in the inns and hotels of the small town, but it didn't disturb her. There was a disdain in her for most of them and it showed in the tilt of her chin. Not even Mrs Thornton could have called her *The Girl* any more.

Apart from the doctor, Mr and Mrs Wheatley and Mr and Mrs Buckman and their sons Bill and Stan, hardly anyone else had given her a pleasant word during the last two years, and the way she felt now she could do without their good opinion.

When she returned to the house Bella had a meal ready for her, and although she wasn't at all hungry she ate it because Bella would have been upset if she hadn't, and as she sat at the table Mrs Loam's voice came at her from the bedroom every now and again, crying loudly first of all, 'You're back then!'

Then: 'You daren't show your face in here.'

'Where's me box?'

'I'll have the polis on you, you thieving skit you!'

'You'll go out neck and crop, an' them two along of you as soon as I'm on me feet proper. By God! you will.'

As she sopped up the last of the gravy with a piece of new bread, Hannah looked from Bella to Tessie, who sat one on each side of her, and said quietly, 'I'd better get it over.'

And on this she rose and went into the bedroom, and her tone even, she said, 'You wanted to see me?'

'Wanted to see you! You thievin' bitch! I tell you I'll have the polis on you, I'll take you to court.'

'No, you won't take me to court. And if you continue to be uncivil I'll take you to court . . . for abuse.' She now walked nearer to the bed and continued, 'I've been to see a solicitor; I've put the whole case before him. He says that my son and myself are the rightful owners of this house, all it contains, and the money in the bank.' She refrained from adding, 'And what lies under you.'

'You can't!' Mrs Loam was now sitting upright in the bed, her hands opening and shutting over handfuls of quilt. 'They won't allow it. I won't allow it. It's mine. All this.' She now flung one arm wide over her head. 'I've worked for it all me life.'

'Your husband worked for it, Mrs Loam; and you led him, as everyone knows, a hell of a life. Your husband left you nothing, he left it all to his son. I married your son. Now he has gone. What was his is mine and his son's. The solicitor tells me that how you fare in the future relies entirely on my discretion.' As she talked there was part of her feeling gratitude for the education she had received for otherwise she would not have been able to state her case in this fashion. And she continued to talk in the same manner: 'And if you are amenable then I may see my way clear to making some provision for you; but I must inform you straightaway, Mrs Loam, it won't be in this house. Your sister seems a very pleasant woman, and has some concern for you, because I should imagine she has not suffered at your hands, so I would suggest that you take up your abode with her. What sum

I shall provide you with I have yet to consider but I shall discuss it with my solicitor. So as soon as you're fit to travel, arrangements will be made to take you wherever you wish to go.' . . .

She stopped abruptly because she really thought that her mother-in-law was about to have a fit. She was now lying back on the pillows, her whole face working while her two thumbs and forefingers continuously plucked at the counterpane as if she were stripping a fowl. Her mouth opening and shutting like a fish landed on a bank, she lay glaring at Hannah. Then after some time, her voice cracking in her throat, she said, 'You can't do this to me.'

'I can, Mrs Loam, and I shall. During the time I have been in this house you have treated me inhumanly; never one civil word, let alone a kind word, have you given me. You have tormented me on every possible occasion. If I were to put you out in the street nobody would blame me, but I won't do that, I shall see that you are provided for by giving you a sum of money on the condition that you leave this house quietly. If you don't agree to this then I shall make no allowance for you whatever; but I shall still insist that you leave this house, and if you end up in the Workhouse then it will be no one's fault but your own. I'll leave you now to consider my proposition.'

She was trembling and feeling a little sick herself as she turned from the woman, and when she entered the kitchen she had to sit down hastily, and Bella, bending over her, said, 'You're upset. You're bound to be. But you've told her, an' you were right. That woman would drive a saint mad. She's getting me down, miss, I'll tell you that, she's getting me down; how you've stuck her all this time God in heaven only knows. The missis, she was bad enough, but she was a different kettle of fish altogether to that 'un in there. She's a demon she is, a demon. Don't worry yourself about her; but the quicker she's gone the better.'

It was odd, Hannah thought, but all her life she had been subjected to demons of women.

It was four days later when Margaret arrived. Her face bright, her eyes wide, she stood in the shop and embraced Hannah, murmuring, 'Oh, Hannah! Hannah! When I got your letter I . . . I couldn't believe it. It . . . it renewed my faith in God. For weeks, months, I have prayed that something like this would happen, yet never believing that it would eventually come about. Your . . . your idea is marvellous.' She looked around the shop; then nodded and said, 'Yes, yes; I can see it all.'

'Oh! Tessie.' She was now holding out her hands to Tessie, and Tessie was exclaiming, 'Eeh! Miss Margaret. Oh! Miss Margaret. Isn't it lovely to see you! Bella! Bella!' She simply bawled out the name, and Bella came stumbling down the stairs; and now she too was exclaiming, but slowly and in a tearful voice: 'Aye, Miss Margaret, I never believed I'd live to see the day we'd all be together again. I mean we lot that mattered most to each other.'

'Oh! Bella, I'm so happy to see you. I was just saying to Hannah, God has answered my prayers. And it's strange how He answers prayers. But' – she turned to Hannah again, adding softly, 'you had to suffer very much before all this could come about. . . . How is the baby?'

'Oh, he's fine. You'll see him in a minute.'

'He's the spit of her, Miss Margaret.' Tessie poked her head forward, and Margaret, the tears in her eyes, looked again at Hannah, and Hannah said hastily, 'It's all over, it's all past, there's just the days ahead, the future. Come on, give me your things.'

As Hannah took Margaret's handbag from her, Tessie relieved her of her coat and hat, while Bella lifted up the bass hamper, shaking her head over it and saying, 'Miss Margaret, fancy you havin' to travel the country with a bass hamper.' Then turning to Hannah, she asked, 'Where am I to put her things, Miss Hannah?'

'Well' – Hannah looked at Margaret – 'that's a problem at present, it's something we'll have to sort out. But come in here, Margaret. This was the back shop, you remember, where the meat used to be hung, but Bella and Tessie have scrubbed it from ceiling to floor. And look, they've unblocked the old fireplace. It was the original kitchen I suppose, and I'm sure there's a good oven behind that wall. Anyway, we'll see.' She turned quickly to Tessie, now saying, 'Make some coffee Tessie and bring down the scones Bella baked this morning.' . . .

Ten minutes later they were all seated round what had once been the butcher's block, drinking the coffee and eating scones and listening to Hannah talking.

'What gave me the idea,' Hannah said with excitement in her voice, 'was when I remembered back to the summer and the people passing the house on their way to the hills, women wearing quite short skirts and wielding walking sticks. One day I counted all of eight women, four pairs, and two more accompanied by men. These stopped at the inn door. The men went in but the ladies had to stay outside, and it was then I thought what they needed was a cup of tea or coffee, not ale. Once I did see a lady standing outside Mrs Robson's drinking a mug of water. Well, it was recalling that memory that set me thinking again.'

She glanced from one bright face to the other. 'I thought, this was a butcher's shop, why not make it into a bakery shop, a cake shop. Bella used to excel at cakes.' When she nodded towards Bella, Bella flapped her hand at her. 'And there's nobody waits on people better than Tessie. And so I thought, added to the cake shop could be a little rest room, with say three or four tables and the requisite number of chairs. The villagers mightn't take to it at first, I mean buying fancy bread and cakes, but I'm sure they'll come to it in time. You remember, Margaret, the little shop near the market place in Hexham?'

'Oh yes, yes. Some days you couldn't get near the door; people coming to the market always took cakes back home with them.'

'Well, in a much lesser way it could be the same here. But it doesn't matter so much about making a big trade, just as long as it supported the three of you.'

'Just the three of us?' Margaret stared hard at Hannah now, her face straight, and Hannah said, 'Yes, just the three of you, because as soon as Ned comes for me I am leaving to go and live at the Pele.'

'Oh. . . . And you're willing to let us stay here and . . . and work a business?'

'More than that, Margaret, more than that; but I'll have to talk it over with the solicitor. What I can tell you now is, so far there's four hundred and thirty-five pounds in the bank, and a third of it will be mine. When all the bills are paid I should come into well over a hundred pounds. There may be more to add to it, I don't know yet but I have worked it out like this. If the bank will advance me my money until the estate is settled by law I'll leave you twenty-five shillings a week for the time being: fifteen shillings to cover your food; five shillings for your personal needs, Margaret; three shillings for you, Bella, and two shillings for you, Tessie. Will that be satisfactory to you?' She was looking at Bella and Tessie now, and Bella said, 'Oh! miss. Satisfactory! Why I'd be willin' to work for nowt but me grub and a good home. Oh! miss.'

'Me an' all, Miss Hannah.' Tessie swallowed deeply.

Margaret said nothing, but she bowed her head and Hannah went on rapidly now, 'Once I have the assurance from the solicitor I'm going to contact both Mr Rickson and Mr Bynge. I'll get Mr Bynge to take that wall down' – she pointed towards the fireplace – 'and if there isn't an oven in there he'll install one. Then I'm going to get Mr Rickson to put up a partition to form another corridor from the shop to the back yard and have installed there a water closet, a real water closet with a pipe running from it to the ditch. It'll make this' – she spread her arms wide – 'a little narrower but there'll be a separate door to enter the corridor next to that one there.' She pointed. 'And upstairs, you, Bella and Tessie, will have what is my room and Miss Margaret the front room. And we'll have some new pieces of furniture, comfortable pieces for the kitchen upstairs which will be turned into a sitting-room.'

'Now, I don't know what this will all cost' – she looked around them – 'but I should imagine that the alterations will run to nigh on thirty pounds. Oh, of course' – she laughed gently now – 'there will be a new shop counter and the tables to buy, and wooden shelves for display in the window. Oh yes, it will be all of thirty pounds. But as long as eventually you take in as much as will pay and feed you, then all will be well. Even if you don't there'll still be enough money for some time to keep things going; but I'm sure, I'm positive it will be a success. . . . Oh, Margaret, please don't, don't cry.'

'Aw, Miss Margaret, aw, don't.' They were all standing round Margaret now for she had lowered her head on to her arms and was sobbing bitterly.

After a few moments Hannah silently shooed Bella and Tessie away; then with Margaret to herself, she looked at her and said with a little hesitation, 'You . . . you won't be ashamed to go into business like this?'

'Oh' – Margaret now jerked her whole body upwards and, putting her hand to her brow, she said, 'Hannah! Hannah! Ashamed? After my drudgery and humiliation at the school it's like having an honour bestowed on one. That was something I didn't tell you. Whenever I met some of our late friends in the town, or they came with their parents to visit their younger sisters, they would nearly all ignore the fact that we had once been bosom companions. I think that was the hardest cross to bear. . . . Oh! Hannah. Ashamed of going into business? You really, really don't know, nor ever will know what you have given me, what you are doing for me; and never, never will I be able to repay you. I shall try. Oh I shall try, but I can't see myself ever being able to do anything for you that will compare with your kindness to me. And while we're on the subject, Hannah, I must tell you that you've weighed heavily on my conscience. You see I blame myself for being the cause of your suffering over the past two years, because it was I who persuaded you to go ahead and marry Fred. The only thing I can say in my defence is that I really thought he'd be kind to you, and that his mother must surely come to love you. Oh, I've. . . .'

'Now, now!' Hannah took her hand. 'Look at it this way, Margaret. If you hadn't persuaded me we wouldn't be here together now. But as for Fred being kind to me, give him his due, if I could have loved him in the smallest degree he would have been kind, but my open dislike of him brought out the worst in him. I can see now that he had some good qualities which under other circumstances I might have fostered. As for his mother' – she shook her head widely now – 'his mother is a woman so insensitive that to compare her with an animal I would consider an insult to the animal. But come, see for yourself. You remember one side of Mrs Loam, well, during the next few days you will definitely see and hear another.'

A further addition to the family seemed to stun Mrs Loam, and contrary to Hannah's warning Margaret found the present Mrs Loam much quieter than the one she remembered behind the counter in the butcher's shop; that was until the day Hannah gave the order that the patient must become convalescent and sit up for an hour in the kitchen while Bella and Tessie thoroughly cleaned the room.

Mrs Loam didn't object to sitting up but she wished to stay in her room. 'They can work round me,' she said.

'No, they can't,' Hannah said and, looking fully at Mrs Loam, went on quietly, 'I wish you to sit in the kitchen for a while. If you don't feel strong enough to manage it Bella and Tessie will carry you out.'

After a long silence during which the old woman glared with open ferocity at Hannah, she walked slowly and unaided into the kitchen. As soon as she was seated comfortably before the fire, Hannah, with a movement of her head indicated to Bella and Tessie that they were to begin their task.

During this time Margaret had been making a pot of tea which she placed on a tray, together with a plate of small fancy cakes, and, setting it on a side table to Mrs Loam's hand, she drew up a chair opposite her and, much to the amazement of Mrs Loam, began to dispense tea and cakes as if she were at an afternoon's party. And she bemused her because she talked all the while about the baby and how well it looked, and how like Hannah it was; and wasn't she, Mrs Loam, lucky to have Hannah to look after her during her awful illness. She talked so sweetly and so fast that Mrs Loam didn't notice Hannah go into the bedroom.

Once in the room Hannah tiptoed quickly towards the bed which Bella and Tessie had stripped down to the base, and, Tessie, looking at Hannah, whispered, 'There's nothing hidden under here, miss.'

'Wait.' Hannah inserted her fingers into the small opening between the end of the box bed and the base and, lifting it up, held it for a moment as she turned her head slowly and looked from one to the other; then swiftly she lifted out from the bottom of the box a number of small bags, six in all. Five were full and tied at the top with string, the sixth was open and lay flat in her hand. Quickly now, she lifted her skirt and transferred the bags to the pocket of her petticoat. Lastly she bent again and swished her hand as far up underneath the bed boards as it would go but she found nothing further.

Nodding at Bella and Tessie, whose faces both showed their glee, she signalled to them to remake the bed; then, having straightened her back, she

walked quietly from the room and into the kitchen, to be met by a hard
enquiring stare from Mrs Loam, and a question from Margaret: 'Would
you like a cup of tea, Hannah?'

'No, thanks, Margaret; I've got a touch of indigestion. It's Bella's good
cooking I think' She paused to let this sink in before adding, 'I don't want
to give Matthew wind.'

'Matthew! Who said he's going to be called Matthew?'

'I did.'

Before the old woman could retort, Hannah had turned away and gone
down the stairs.

Hurrying through the back shop and into the wash-house, she knelt down
by the side of the wash-house pot where she removed a loose stone from
near the bottom of the wall; then taking the bags from her petticoat, she
thrust them one by one down into the cavity, and replaced the stone.

Many of the stones of the wash-house walls were loose; she had tested a
number of them yesterday at the time she was pondering on what she would
do with the money, should she find it, until she had time to take it into
Allendale and the solicitor's.

Standing up, she now dusted her hands whilst nodding down to the stones
and saying, 'And so much for you, Mrs Loam. May your heart stand the
shock of the discovery you're about to make.' Then of a sudden, her mood
changing, she sat heavily down on the upturned rinsing tub and whispered
to herself, 'Oh! Ned. Ned.'

She'd had a strange feeling about Ned for some days now, and she had
put it down to weakness. Yet it seemed that something other than his illness
was keeping them apart. It was more than six weeks since she had seen him
being kicked into the stream and it seemed like six years. She must see him
soon; it was becoming more imperative that she see him soon. Doctor Arnison
appeared reluctant to talk about him. 'All in good time,' was the only answer
he gave her when she asked how long it would be before she was able to go
to him. She was sure the doctor was keeping something from her.

It was as if her thinking had conjured up the doctor for when she returned
through the back shop Tessie was letting him in the front door.

'Oh, there you are, Hannah,' he said. 'How are you feeling?'

'Oh, quite well, doctor. Quite well.'

'Good. Good. And how is the patient?'

'Oh, I think I'll leave you to be the judge of that.'

The doctor laughed, then went before her up the stairs.

As soon as he entered the kitchen and saw Mrs Loam, he exclaimed,
'Good! Good! I'm glad to see you on your feet.' And at this Mrs Loam got
to her feet and went into her room.

As he followed her, Doctor Arnison looked towards Margaret and said,
'Nice to see you settled, Margaret. Nice to see you settled,' and she replied
briefly as she smiled at him, 'Thank you, Doctor.'

In the bedroom, Doctor Arnison let out a long breath before he commented,
'Ah well, now you'll soon be making for your sister's. . . .'

'Who said anything about me goin' to me sister's?'

'Oh, I've been given to understand that you agreed to that proposal.'

He watched her sitting champing on her lip before she ground out, 'I've
been swindled, robbed.'

'Well, if you think that then you must go and see your solicitor, but if he takes the matter up it'll cost you something. Whether you win or lose it'll cost you something. And to win you've got to have proof, and proof, in this case, as I understand it, means being able to produce a will entirely in your favour. But if you lose, again as I understand it, you won't have much choice about where you'll live, will you, because I don't suppose even your sister will welcome you empty-handed? People don't, you know.' He let out another long breath. 'I think if you're wise you'll accept your daughter-in-law's proposal.'

'And what does she propose?'

'Well, what she tells me she proposes to give you is to my mind a very generous offer under the circumstances.' He turned his head now and cast a hard sidelong glance on to her. 'You know, many in her position would see you further before giving you a penny. Anyway, as I understand it, when the matter has gone through probate she proposes to give you a hundred pounds. And she can, I understand, do this because she'll be trustee for her son until he comes of age.'

'A hundred pounds! It won't keep me for life, will it?'

'I don't see why not. You'll shortly be able enough to take up light work. You could buy yourself a little cottage, grow your own vegetables, keep your own hens, and still have a good bit over. You can do a lot with a hundred pounds.'

'This is my house.'

He didn't answer until he reached towards the door, and then he said, 'Not any more it isn't, Daisy. That's what you've got to face up to, not any more it isn't.' And then he went out.

Hannah was waiting for him at the foot of the stairs, and he patted her on the shoulder and smiled as he said, 'I don't think you'll have any trouble with her; I know her, she's ready to go. And I think she was quite bowled over by the offer of the hundred pounds. It was a generous gesture. And you did right, for you won't have her on your conscience.'

'Thank you, doctor.'

As he went towards the shop door he looked about him and, his face moving into an appreciative smile, he nodded back at her and said, 'It's a very good idea of yours; I can see it working. It needs something like this in the village. . . . And it's nice to see Margaret back. Strange how things have turned out for that family, strange, very strange. Well, let's hope all is peace from now on. Good-bye then. Good-bye.'

'Good-bye, doctor. And thank you so much.'

Margaret and Hannah were lying side by side in bed, and the wash-basket holding the baby was on the floor to the side of the bed. Bella was on the sofa and Tessie on a straw tick in front of the fireplace but out of range of sparks; and they were all asleep, or dropping off to sleep, when the scream brought them bolt upright.

Margaret reached the kitchen first. Hannah didn't hurry, for she knew what had happened and knew what to expect, and as she came out of the bedroom Mrs Loam's door was pulled open and the enraged woman stood for a moment gripping the front of her calico nightgown in both hands as if she were to tear it from her body; then the gown seemed to swell as she opened her mouth wide, drew in a long breath and screamed, 'You thieving bugger you! You've taken me money.'

'Your money?' Hannah stepped in front of Margaret and Bella and Tessie who were now standing together in the middle of the room, and advancing towards Mrs Loam and endeavouring to keep her own voice low, she said, 'I wasn't aware you had any money, Mrs Loam. You accused me only a day or two ago of turning you out penniless.'

'Th . . . that money ba . . . back in there' – she was now thrusting her arm in the direction of the bed – 'that was my hard-earned savin's of years.'

'No, Mrs Loam. Going on the solicitor's reckoning, I should say the forty pounds in each bag was the profit for each of the last five years. Since your husband died there has been no money put into the bank, and no one but a fool would be convinced that this business has been run without a profit.'

Mrs Loam now clutched at the stanchion of the door with two hands. It was evident she was under great emotional strain, and Hannah said, 'I'd advise you to go back to bed, Mrs Loam, and we'll discuss the matter further in the morning, but before . . . before you leave for your sister's.'

The look Mrs Loam levelled at Hannah should have at least paralysed her with fear, if not killed her outright, and now she ground out through clenched teeth, 'You'll come to a bad end. I'll pray every night of me life to God that He'll give you your just deserts and bring you to a tortured end.'

There was a concerted gasp from behind her, and although Hannah knew the words were merely the mouthings of a bitter, cruel natured woman, she nevertheless shuddered. But she didn't take her eyes from those of her mother-in-law, and she didn't move until the woman had turned about and banged the door after her with such force that the house shuddered; then she moved slowly round and looked at the others.

Margaret, coming towards her, took her by the arm, saying softly, 'Come. Come away; it'll be all over by this time tomorrow.'

Hannah returned to bed but not to sleep. After Margaret, holding her gently, had said, 'Think nothing of it, go to sleep now. She's a wicked woman! you did the right thing;' she lay still until Margaret, under the impression that she had fallen asleep, released her hold and turned away on to her side. But the dawn was showing its light through the small window before she finally closed her eyes, and then not before she had given the child its feed from her swollen breast.

Her mother-in-law's curse was lying heavily on her, filling her with dread, recalling the doctor's words, 'Unwittingly you seem to breed trouble wherever your feet tread.' . . . Was she fated? Was there something about her that always led to tragedy? Would she in the end be the cause of bringing final tragedy to Ned? Through her he had lost half his hand, through her he had almost lost his life, and she had yet to find out exactly what scars Fred's boots had left on him. Was she bad? Was there some deep badness in her inherited from her mother?

*No! No!* The protest against this self-accusation was loud in her head. She had never wished people ill, not even the missis, and God knew she'd had every cause to pray that something bad would befall that woman. But she hadn't. And she hadn't up to the last wished any evil on her husband, although she had grown to hate him. . . . Had she on his mother? Perhaps, for she'd wished her dead, but now all she wished was to put distance between them. . . .

When she finally awoke the weak rays of sun were lying across the counterpane. She could hear a murmured conversation from the kitchen.

She lay for a moment recalling the incident of last night, then told herself she must get up and face the day and the last battle with that woman. But when she went to rise, her head swam and she fell back on the pillow. She felt sick. What was wrong with her? She put up her hands to her head. She wasn't going to have the fever? . . . No. No. It was the long night lying thinking of that woman and her curses. She couldn't face her. She couldn't.

She called out, 'Margaret! Margaret!'

A moment later Margaret was standing by her side saying, 'What is it, dear?'

'I don't feel well, Margaret, I have a headache, and I feel sick.'

'It's all the worry. You stay in bed this morning. You need rest anyway. It's a wonder you've stood up to it this long with what you've been through.' She tucked the clothes around her.

'Margaret. I . . . I want her to go today.'

'Yes, I know you do, dear. Leave it to me. I've been thinking about it. I'll make the arrangements. She certainly can't go by carrier cart so I thought of sending Tessie down and asking Mr Buckman if he would allow Bill or Stan to bring your cart and drive her over to her sister's.'

'Yes, yes, Margaret, that's a good idea. And' – she put her hand out – 'tell her . . . tell her that when she gets settled in a cottage of her own – ' She drew in a deep breath and paused before she went on, 'Tell her she can have her own bed and bedding and some cutlery, and the easy chair and the small table from the kitchen, and a mat or two, and . . . and her ornaments and any trinkets she wants. Tell her . . . tell her that.'

Margaret now squeezed her hand and smiled as she said, 'Yes, I will, dear; I'll tell her.'

'And . . . and Margaret, tell her to go to Mr Ransome, the solicitor in Allendale and . . . and he'll give her the sum of money I promised as soon as it's possible. She'll have to sign for it there. If . . . if I was giving it to her in sovereigns there would be no proof but that I had turned her out penniless. But anyway the money must be put in the care of the bank first.'

'Yes, I'll tell her. Now don't worry, just lie still. Would you like some breakfast?'

'No, thanks, dear. A cup of tea perhaps.' . . .

Hannah lay all morning listening to the bustle in the kitchen and every now and again the deep ominous tones of her mother-in-law's voice. It was strange, she thought, that a woman so small should have such a deep, booming voice.

It was towards noon when the commotion in the kitchen seemed to intensify, and Hannah actually jumped in the bed when there came three loud bangs on the bedroom door and Mrs Loam's voice followed, crying, 'You'll regret this day, me girl. I'll turn the whole countryside against you; you won't be able to lift up your head in the town. An' I'll curse you till the day I die.'

'Mrs. Loam! Mrs Loam! please. Come, the cart is waiting.'

The voices died away. She lay taut on the bed listening to the footsteps going down the stairs, then the shop door opening.

She didn't hear the door close for some time and in the interval she seemed to hold her breath; then when finally she heard the distant click she sank back into the bed. She was sweating profusely. It was over. It was over.

Dear God, could she believe it. That woman had gone . . . that creature had gone.

She now turned her head slowly to the side and her tears swamped her face and rained into the pillow. . . .

She was in bed for a week. Doctor Arnison said it was reaction and all she needed was rest and care.

And she was getting the latter in abundance for Margaret seemed to take pleasure in fussing over her. She had just tucked the clothes about her and had straightened the top sheet over the quilt; and now, sprinkling some eau-de-cologne on to a lawn handkerchief, she pressed it into the cuff of Hannah's nightgown as she said, 'We've had three callers already today asking how you are. And Mrs Ramsey left a jar of pickles.'

'Mrs Ramsey?' Hannah's eyes opened wide. 'You mean the Mrs Ramsey from the other end of the street?'

'Yes, yes, that Mrs Ramsey.'

'And one of the Nicholson boys from the pit cottages called and left a cabbage.' Margaret laughed outright here. 'He was very funny. He said his ma had told his da to cut the biggest in the plot, and he said his ma sent a message to say she wished you well. Then Mrs Buckman called and left a pie. She wanted to come up and see you but I said you weren't quite well enough yet, but in a day or two you'd be very pleased to have a visit from her.'

'She wanted to come up and see me?' Hannah's eyes stretched wide.

'Yes, yes, she did. Of course, the gift of the pie didn't please Bella because she considers Mrs Buckman a very poor cook.'

Her mother-in-law had prophesied that she would turn the village and the whole countryside against her. Well, the curse didn't seem to be working, it was comforting in a way, but only in a way, a small way. . . .

It was about two o'clock in the afternoon when she heard the knocking on the front door, and then the sound of voices below in the shop followed by the tread of heavy feet on the stairs. It wasn't the doctor, he had called earlier. Margaret was bringing someone up.

When the bedroom door opened Margaret stood there, her face smiling gently as she said, 'Here's a visitor for you, Hannah.'

She raised her head from the pillows and waited. The visitor seemed a long time putting in an appearance; then, walking with the aid of a stick, there came through the doorway a man she hardly recognized.

'N . . . ed!' The name was drawn in a thin whisper through her lips as she pulled herself into a sitting position and stared up into the face now hanging over her. It was his face, Ned's face, but not as she had ever seen it before. She found her mind playing strange tricks with her. It was working out his age. He was twenty-nine years old, at least he should be, but the face that was looking at her seemed to be that of a man twice that age because there was no flesh left on it, the cheeks looked hollow, the skin drawn tight over the bones was pale, almost like that of a woman's. Ned's skin had been brown and ruddy, hard looking, like hide.

'Well, have you nothin' to say to me?'

She closed her eyes tightly, gulped in her throat, drooped her head for a moment, then took a deep breath. It was Ned's voice; that hadn't changed. This was Ned . . . *Ned*. She thrust up her arms and when she flung them round his neck he stumbled and had to support himself on the bed as he said, 'Now hie up! Hie up! You want me in there with you?'

When Margaret pushed a chair behind him, he turned and, groping for it, sat down and, looking up at Margaret, he said, 'Thanks.'

'Would you like a cup of tea, Ned?'

'That would be very nice, very nice, thanks.'

When the door closed on Margaret they looked at each other; then, their hands linked tightly, they continued to stare until Ned said, 'I . . . I didn't know till this mornin' you were bad. He kept saying you were all right . . . Doctor Arnison. An' not to worry, you'd be along to see me shortly now that the fever scare was over. I . . . I wondered what was keeping you. . . . Where is he?'

'Other side of the bed.' She pointed; and now he rose stiffly to his feet and went round the foot of the bed, and there, bending over the basket, he stared down on the child for some time before slanting his eyes in Hannah's direction saying, 'Can't see any resemblance to me in him.'

'It's inside; outside I'm told he takes after his mother.'

'That's good enough for me.'

Again he looked down on the child before turning away and coming back to her side again.

'Oh Ned! Ned!' She hitched herself nearer the edge of the bed and him. Again her arms went up; and now his went around her, and he held her tightly but didn't kiss her.

After a moment he pulled away, straightened up, and said thickly, 'I've been kept well informed of all you've been up to.'

'Doctor Arnison?' ,

'Aye. But he only told me what he thought was good for me. The real news I got through Big Dick. He tells me that there were some wanted to hang flags out for you the way you've handled the old girl. Funny, isn't it, that you've had to have dealings with the two most hated women in the district. You know something?' He bent towards her. 'Daisy Loam was really feared by half the villagers, and not a few in the town either. Some were afraid of her tongue, others thought she had an evil eye an' that nothing could down her. But . . . but apparently – ' He moved his head slowly and there was the old grin on his taut features as he ended, 'They hadn't reckoned with Hannah Boyle.'

She didn't answer the smile on his face but said sadly, 'I could never had downed her, Ned. It was just the simple fact that Fred left no will, and that the child was born before he died, otherwise I doubt if I'd be here this minute.'

'Well, in that case you would have been some place else, wouldn't you?'

He had been smiling, but now his whole expression changed and he was silent for a moment before he said, 'We've got to talk, Hannah. That's what I've come about really. Things have changed all round. By! they have that. And, well, you're a woman of property now and not short of a bob or two, and as I understand it with ideas an' all of what you're going to turn this place into. Now me.' He spread his good hand wide. 'Well, to put it plainly, Hannah, I'm not the man I was. His boots didn't only kick the daylights out of me, they kicked something else. What it is, well, I don't know, I can't put a name to it, but it's as if he's dampened down the fires in me an' all.'

'Oh! Ned. Ned.' She was gripping his hands and pulling him to her breast.

'No, no; listen to me, Hannah. Listen me out.' He pressed her from him. 'It'll be some time afore I can sit a horse again. Sitting a horse is me business, so as I see it, although I'll likely get along on me own, I cannot see meself providing for a wife an' family for some time to come an' . . . an' – ' He held up his hand quickly now and, his voice harsh, he went on, 'Hear me out, I say.' Then after a pause he went on, 'There's one thing I don't feel inclined to do, an' that's live on Fred Loam's earnin's. You, yourself, you've got a right to them; as I see it you've worked for them, suffered for them; but in my case, well, it's different. If I have a wife an' bairns I want to support them.'

'Ned. Ned, listen to me.' She was shaking his hand. 'I don't want the money, the house, or anything in it, all I want is you. All I want is to be near you, to live in the Pele house. Oh yes, to live in the Pele house. That is my home, the Pele house. The only time I ever felt at home as a child was in that house. And another thing, Ned. You'll grow well and strong again; it'll be impossible not to, being you. But you know something? If you had come in that door without arms or legs, well, to me you'd still be a better man, a bigger man, than any I've ever met in my life.'

She looked at his bowed head. Even his black hair had lost its lustre. She bent forward and buried her face in it. Then their arms were again entwined. And now their lips were close, clinging hungrily. But after a moment he pulled himself away from her, twisted round in the chair and, turning his head still further from her, he bowed it.

She had never thought in her life to see Ned cry. She could well imagine him being deeply moved, sad, and if his sadness should be caused through injustice then it would show in anger. But she had never imagined him being reduced to tears. She reached out and brought him gently around to her again; and now she soothed him, saying, 'Don't. Don't, my dear, don't. Oh, dearest Ned, don't be upset.' . . . Strange, she hadn't used that term to him before. She had told him she loved him, but she had never used such an endearment on him. Now she poured endearments over him, murmuring and stroking his hair, and he remained still in her arms until the sound of laughter coming from the kitchen brought him upwards, and after rubbing his face with his red handkerchief he blew his nose and muttered, 'You see, you see what the great Ned, the big fella Ridley has been reduced to? Bubbling.'

Softly now she said, 'I'll . . . I'll be with you in a day or two.'

'No, no.' He shook his head. 'There's . . . there's a lot of talking to be done.' He paused now as he glanced sideways at her, and again making reference to the child, he said, 'And you've got to look after him.'

'I'll look after both of you.'

'Well, we'll see later on.'

'Don't talk like that, Ned. Look, if you keep on so you'll make me believe in that woman's curses. Do you know she cursed me before she left and said she would pray each day for me to be brought low? Oh, and much more.'

'Well, you can laugh at that.'

'I hope I can, Ned, I hope I can. But it will depend upon you in the end. In the end it will all depend upon you.'

He took out his watch now and said, 'I'll have to be on me way. Dick said half an hour. He dropped me off at the end of the village; he was taking a load of wood to Paterson's.'

'Oh, won't you stay and have a meal? Oh' – she put her hands out towards him, her disappointment showing in her face and voice – 'I'm sure they're getting something ready.'

'Another time, Hannah, another time.' He pulled himself to his feet, and now he seemed to back from her, and she leaned further forward in the bed, beseeching, 'Don't go like this, Ned, please. You'll leave me distraught. Come here.'

He now leant over and, taking her face gently in one hand, he kissed her on the lips; then picking up his stick that was leaning against the bed, he turned away.

'Ned! Ned, wait.' There was anguish in her plea. 'Are you still with the Dickinsons? I must know.'

He half turned towards her but didn't look at her as he replied quietly, 'No, I'm back in the house and managing fine. Nell has seen to everything for me.' And on this he went slowly from the room.

When the door closed on him she fell back in the bed and covered her face with her hands and whimpered through her fingers, 'Oh Ned! Ned! I've lost you. I've lost you. What is the matter with me? There is a curse on me. There must be. They're right. They're right.'

The next minute she was sitting bolt upright in the bed. No! no! She wouldn't let this happen, not this thing that was a matter of life and death to her, because without Ned she really wouldn't want to go on living, she would finish it and take the child with her. And Mrs Loam would have triumphed.

'Margaret! Margaret!' She found herself yelling at the top of her voice.

'Yes, dear? What is it?'

'Close the door.'

Margaret closed the door and came hastily to the bed.

'Sit down.'

Margaret sat down and listened wide-eyed and open-mouthed as Hannah gabbled at her, 'He won't have me; he's pushing me off because . . . because I've got the house and Fred's money. He won't live on Fred's money, and he thinks he'll never be well enough to earn enough to keep us. Margaret – ' She wagged her head frantically now and gathered spittle into her mouth, then almost choked on her words as she went on, 'Margaret, I don't give a damn about the money, the house, anything, all I want is to be near Ned. Do you understand? Do you understand?'

'Yes, dear, yes, dear; but please don't get so excited.'

'Excited! Margaret. I'm going after him, today . . . now!'

'Oh, my dear. . . . No! no! That would be madness.'

'Madness or not I'm going. . . . Listen. Go now, right now, and tell Tessie to go down to Mr Buckman's again and ask him if he'll do me the service of letting Stan or Bill take me and the child up to the Pele house.'

'Hannah . . . Hannah, you mustn't get so excited.'

'I'm not excited, Margaret. I know what I'm doing, it's now or never. This is important to me. It means life to me. Yes, just that, because if I don't have Ned I'll want nothing from life, and it won't be worth going on with. I've gone through too much to let this chance of happiness slide through my fingers for the matter of pride. Will you tell Tessie, or shall I call her?'

Margaret rose from the bed, went out and gave the order to Tessie; then coming back, she resumed her seat and Hannah, now taking hold of her hand, said, 'This is what I'm going to do, Margaret. Now listen carefully and don't interrupt. I'm going straight up to the Pele house and I'm going to stay there, but when I'm gone I want you to go to the Reverend Crewe and ask him if he will call on us at his convenience with regard to putting up the banns. Don't look like that, Margaret. I know Fred's hardly cold, but that doesn't matter to me. I know there'll be talk, but that doesn't matter to me either; nothing matters, only that I shall be legally married to Ned, that I know he'll be mine and I his. Now for another important part, and don't say a word. Now I'm telling you, don't say one word while I'm speaking. I'm going into Allendale to the solicitor's as soon as possible and I'm going to transfer what money is coming to me to you.' She now shook Margaret's hands that were jerking between her palms and she repeated, 'What money is coming to me . . . to you, and it won't be all that much if they don't take the hundred pounds that I promised to that she devil out of Matthew's inheritance. But there will be a condition. I shall ask you to make a will that should you die, which God prevent you don't until you are a very, very old woman, but should it happen, then the monies and what has been made out of the business shall revert to me or my husband, or children. It's funny.' She shook her head now from side to side. 'It's as if I'd been planning this in my mind for weeks, it's all so very clear. Anyway, it will all be stated in writing – done legally. Oh, and also provision for Bella and Tessie in their old age. But we'll have to go into all this with Mr Ransome. I'm just giving you a rough idea. . . . Open your eyes, Margaret, and look at me.'

Margaret opened her eyes and said quietly, 'I cannot accept this amazing offer, Hannah; it will be quite impossible for me to accept it.'

'If you love me and want my happiness you'll do as I ask.'

'I can't, because it's too much. And you may live to be sorry for your generosity. Ned feels like this now but he'll change, and when he's stronger he'll see sense.'

'Not Ned. No; I know Ned, he's all men rolled into one in that he must be master; when it comes to his pride being touched, the pride of the breadwinner to support a wife and family, he must be master. No, I know Ned.'

'What can I say?'

'Nothing, only do as I ask. You are my friend, my very, very dear friend, my sister . . . yes, my sister. No one else could do this for me but you.'

'But . . . but there must be some provision made for you, a safeguard, like a share in the business or something. I couldn't take it wholesalely.'

'Well, we'll go into that, dear, only let me be able to go up there and say that I'm passing it on to you.'

'And he will call you a fool.'

'Not him. Oh, not him, Margaret. He'll look at me steadily; he'll take me in his arms and he'll say, "Hannah. Hannah Boyle." '

'Help me now to get dressed, then pack up a couple of bundles for me, and the child. Some warm clothing and night attire; we'll see to the rest later.'

'Will . . . will the place be aired?'

'Yes, yes; Mrs Dickinson's seen to everything. He's back there living on his own.' . . .

It was just half an hour later when Hannah went back into the bedroom and closed the door behind her. She wanted, she told herself, to look round this room for the last time, this room that had represented nights of purgatory and hell to her; this room that had witnessed her entry into womanhood, a slow painful awakening, that had flung romance away as a thing of dreams and brought her face to face with the realities of life.

She looked towards the side table whereon lay her mother-in-law's Bible. She had forgotten to take that with her. At one stage of Fred's illness she had brought it in and read a passage from it and left it there.

That a woman so vicious could imagine that God was on her side would always remain a great puzzle to her. She walked towards the table now and picked up the book. It fell open at a page wherein lay a piece of folded newspaper, one of the hundreds of squares that she herself had cut for Fred's use after using the chamber. She lifted the paper out with her finger and thumb as if it were already soiled. Then she noticed something different about it; it had writing scrawled across it, but it was almost illegible against the close black print. She put her head to one side and narrowed her eyes as she endeavoured to read the writing. Then going to the window, she held it at an angle to enable her to make out the pencilled words, and after a few moments this is what she read:

> I'm feeling very bad. If I am to go I want me mother to have everything. And it's up to her what she does for the other one.
>
> > Fred Loam.

Hannah turned her eyes from the scrawled writing, and looked out of the window, and not until she drew a sharp breath into her lungs did she realize that her mouth was wide open. Like a stone now she sat down on the edge of the bed. This was a will, but there were no witnesses to it. Would it stand up in court? Maybe. And if it did it would make the way plain for her, she could go to Ned without any fuss. She'd be penniless, thrown out on to the world because Mrs Loam would not of her charity give her a hundred pounds. Nor would she support the child. Oh no, not Mrs Loam unless it was under her care. . . .

But then what would happen to Margaret, Bella, and Tessie? That woman would throw them out on to the street and praise the Lord while she was doing it. Bella and Tessie would be bonded again and used as drudges for a pittance. . . . And Margaret. What would become of Margaret? Her lot would be even worse than theirs; the mere fact of her being refined would make her suffering more intense.

She turned her head in the direction of the chatter coming from the kitchen. They were all so happy together; they were a family.

The door opened and Margaret said, 'Well, dear?'

She stared at Margaret, not speaking, and Margaret came towards her, saying, 'What is it? What's wrong?'

'Oh. Oh' – she shook her head and blinked – 'nothing. Nothing. I . . . I was just looking at that.' She pointed towards the Bible on the table. 'Mrs Loam forgot to take it with her; she'll likely want it when she comes for the things.'

'Well, she'll certainly have it, my dear, and I hope it will do her some good. What is that?' She pointed to the piece of paper Hannah was holding, and Hannah, screwing the square tightly up into her fist, said, 'Oh, nothing, nothing; only one of the hundreds of squares I had to cut up.' She walked swiftly from the room and into the kitchen and, standing before the fire, she hesitated a moment before stretching her hand out and dropping the paper into the flames; then turning towards the three faces looking at her, she held out her arms, and they all came into them and entwined her in their embraces.

Her laughter was a little hysterical as she said, 'You'd think I was going miles away. I'll be down here every day. Don't you forget that, Bella. I'll be down for my buns and I want plenty of currants in them.'

'There's the cart.'

Bella and Tessie, picking up the bundles and Margaret's bass hamper, ran on ahead down the stairs, while Hannah and Margaret stood looking at each other for a moment before Margaret picked up the basket with the child in it, and Hannah said quietly, 'Don't worry if I'm not down for a day or two. But if you shouldn't see me for three or four days bring me up some nice things to eat.'

'Oh! my dear.'

'Now, now, stop it, Margaret.'

Hannah turned from her and went down the stairs, through the shop and into the street, and there Stan Buckman looked at her from under his brows, touched his cap and said, 'Nice to see you out again, missis.'

She paused a moment and smiled at him. He hadn't called her Mrs Loam or Hannah, but he had given her the title of missis, and so she said, 'Thank you, Stan. It's nice to be out.'

He now almost lifted her up into the front seat of the cart, tucked an old rug round her, then took the basket from Margaret and put it on the floor at Hannah's feet before taking his place behind the horse and shouting, 'Gee up there!'

As the horse trotted off, Hannah turned and waved to the three standing by the door.

But they weren't the only ones standing by their doors. It was as if the word had gone round the village that *she* was off some place; and they knew this some place, for not a couple of hours ago hadn't Ned Ridley been to visit her? Well, well! some people were laws unto themselves. And when all was said and done it really was indecent for she was hardly out of childbed, and her man hardly cold.

Those who thought along these lines didn't wave to her, they just stared, but a few others called a greeting from their doors.

And towards these she inclined her head, but gave them no reply.

Twenty minutes later the cart went through the opening in the wall and drew up opposite the open door of the stable-room, and when Stan had lifted her to the ground and handed down to her the basket, she said, 'Just drop the bundles to the side of the door, Stan.'

After Stan had done this, she put down the basket again and from her purse brought out a half sovereign and said, 'I would like you and Bill and your father to have a drink on me in return for your kindness to the horse.' She smiled as she nodded towards the animal, and Stan looked at the golden piece in his hand for a moment; then, a broad grin on his face, he said, 'And we'll do that certainly. Aye, we will, missis. And what's more' – he leant towards her – 'we'll drink to your future. And may it be bright for a change.'

'I'm sure it will, Stan. Thank you.'

'Good-bye, missis. Be seein' you down yonder.'

'Good-bye, Stan.'

She watched the horse turn the cart around and go towards the opening before she picked up the basket again and went through the door.

She knew that Ned must have heard the cart but he had made no effort to come out. He was standing just in front of the opening to the kitchen. It was as if nothing had happened. She was a young girl of fourteen, fifteen, sixteen, seventeen, coming into the Pele house to see Ned Ridley, and he was always either coming down the ladder or coming out of the kitchen, except, of course, when he was tight and lying on the platform sleeping it off.

He made no move towards her and she walked over the stone floor, but stopped a few arm lengths from him and, laying down the basket once again but on a bale of straw now, she said quietly, 'Well! here I am. I haven't any money and my possessions are outside the door. I've given all that Fred left to Margaret. We're going into the solicitor's in a day or two to have it signed and sealed. She's agreed, so what do you say?'

She watched his face lengthen, she saw his jaw drop, she saw it snap closed and his lips press tight together; then his head hung down for a moment deep on his breast before he walked towards her. And his head was still down when his arms went about her and, his voice thick, his words choked, he muttered, 'Oh Hannah! Hannah Boyle!'

He was kissing her, kissing her as he had done on that particular day when they came together for the first time; he was kissing her as if he were drawing strength from her body; he was kissing her as if he never meant to stop; and although she was feeling faint and weak on her legs she didn't beg him to stop. This was Ned Ridley, alive and vital still behind his scarred body, so vital was his love for her that it was like a smelting mill that would reduce to ashes her mother-in-law's curses and evil wishes for her, and at the same time dredge the dross and the dirt from their lives and leave only the worthwhile lead and a sprinkling of silver.

He sealed her happiness when, pushing her bonnet back, his lips went into her hair and he muttered, 'Oh! Woman. Woman. There's not another like you in the wide world.'

Woman, he had called her. *The Girl* was gone, buried in the past. She never wanted to hear that name again. She was a woman for better for worse. Whatever the future might bring she could face it as a woman, Ned Ridley's woman.

# CATHERINE COOKSON

# The
# Gambling
# Man

# The Gambling Man

## THE CONNORS

Paddy Connor *a steelworker*
Ruth Connor *his wife*
Rory Connor *their elder son, a rent collector*
Jimmy Connor *their younger son, apprenticed to a boat builder*
Nellie Burke *their only daughter, married to Charlie Burke*
Lizzie O'Dowd *Paddy Connor's half-cousin*

## THE WAGGETTS

Bill Waggett *a widowed docker*
Janie Waggett *his daughter, a nursemaid and engaged to marry Rory Connor*
Gran Waggett *his mother*

## THE LEARYS

Collum Leary *a coal miner*
Kathleen Leary *his wife*
*Nine surviving children of whom three have emigrated to America*

John George Armstrong *Rory's friend and fellow rent collector*

Septimus Kean *a property owner*
Charlotte Kean *his only daughter*

# Chapter One

### 1875 Rory Connor

Tyne Dock was deserted. It was Sunday and the hour when the long dusk was ending and the night beginning. Moreover, it was bitterly cold and the first flat flakes of snow were falling at spaced intervals, dropping to rest in their white purity on the greasy, coal-dust, spit-smeared flags.

The five arches leading from the dock gates towards the Jarrow Road showed streaks of dull green water running down from their domes. Beneath the arches the silence and desolation of the docks was intensified; they, too, seemed to be resting, drawing breath as it were, before taking again the weight of the wagons which, with the dawn, would rumble over four of them from the coal staithes that lay beyond the brick wall linking them together. Beyond the fifth arch the road divided, one section mounting to Simonside, the other leading to Jarrow.

The road to Jarrow was a grim road, a desolate road, and a stretch of it bordered the slakes at East Jarrow, the great open stretch of mud which in turn bordered the river Tyne.

There was nothing grim about the road to Simonside, for as soon as you mounted the bank Tyne Dock and East Jarrow were forgotten, and you were in the country. Up and up the hill you went and there to the left, lying back in their well-tended gardens, were large houses; past the farm, and now you were among green fields and open land as far as the eye could see. Of course, if you looked back you would glimpse the masts of the ships lying all along the river, but looking ahead even in the falling twilight you knew this was a pleasant place, a place different from Tyne Dock, or East Jarrow, or Jarrow itself; this was the country. The road, like any country road, was rough, and the farther you walked along it the narrower it became until finally petering out into a mere cart track running between fields.

Strangers were always surprised when, walking along this track, they came upon the cottages. There were three cottages, but they were approached by a single gate leading from the track and bordered on each side by an untidy tangled hedge of hawthorn and bramble.

The cottages lay in a slight hollow about twenty feet from the gate, and half this distance was covered by a brick path which then divided into three uneven parts, each leading to a cottage door. The cottages were numbered 1, 2 and 3 but were always called No. 1 The Cottages, No. 2 The Cottages, and No. 3 The Cottages.

In No. 1 lived the Waggetts, in No. 2 The Connors, and in No. 3 the Learys. But, as this was Sunday, all the Waggett family and three of the

Learys were in the Connors' cottage, and they were playing cards.

'In the name of God, did you ever see the likes! He's won again. How much is it I owe you this time?'

'Twelve and fourpence.'

'Twelve an' fourpence! Will you have it now or will you wait till ye get it?'

'I'll wait till I get it.'

'Ta, you've got a kind heart. Although you're a rent man you've got a kind heart. I'll say that for you, Rory.'

'Ah, shut up Bill. Are you goin' to have another game?'

'No, begod! I'm not. I've only half a dozen monkey nuts left, an' Janie there loves monkey nuts. Don't you, lass?'

Bill Waggett turned round from the table and looked towards his only daughter, who was sitting with the women who were gathered to one side of the fire cutting clippings for a mat, and Janie laughed back at him, saying, 'Aw, let him have the monkey nuts; 'cos if you don't, he'll have your shirt.' She now exchanged a deep knowing look with Rory Connor, who had half turned from the table, and when he said, 'Do you want me to come there and skelp your lug?' she tossed her head and cried back at him, 'Try it on, lad. Try it on.' And all those about the fire laughed as if she had said something extremely witty.

Her grannie laughed, her wrinkled lips drawn back from her toothless gums, her mouth wide and her tongue flicking in and out with the action of the aged; she laughed as she said, 'That's it. That's it. Start the way you mean to go on. Married sixty-five years me afore he went; never lifted a hand to me; didn't get the chance.' The cavity of her mouth became wider.

Ruth Connor laughed, but hers was a quiet, subdued sound that seemed to suit her small, thin body and her pointed face and black hair combed back from the middle parting over each side of her head.

Her daughter, Nellie, laughed. Nellie had been married for three years and her name now was Mrs Burke. Nellie, like her mother, was small and thin but her hair was fair. The word puny would describe her whole appearance.

And Lizzie O'Dowd laughed. Lizzie O'Dowd was of the Connor family. She was Paddy Connor's half-cousin. She was now forty-one years old but had lived with them since she had come over from Ireland at the age of seventeen. Lizzie's laugh was big, deep and hearty; her body was fat, her hair brown and thick; her eyes brown and round. Lizzie O'Dowd looked entirely different from the rest of the women seated near the fire, particularly the last, who was Kathleen Leary from No. 3 The Cottages. Kathleen's laugh had a weary sound. Perhaps it was because after bearing sixteen children her body was tired. It was no consolation that seven were dead and the eldest three in America for she still had six at home and the youngest was but two years old.

It was now Paddy Connor, Rory's father, who said, 'You were talkin' of another game, lad. Well then, come on, get on with it.'

Paddy was a steelworker in Palmer's shipyard in Jarrow. For the past fifteen years he had worked in the blast furnaces, and every inch of skin on his face was red, a dull red, like overcooked beetroot. He had three children, Rory being the eldest was twenty-three.

Rory was taller than his father. He was thickset with a head that inclined to be square. He did not take after either his mother or his father in looks for his hair was a dark brown and his skin, although thick of texture, was fresh looking. His eyes, too, were brown but of a much deeper tone than his hair. His lips were not full as might have been expected to go with the shape of his face but were thin and wide. Even in his shirt sleeves he looked smart, and cleaner than the rest of the men seated around the table.

Jimmy, the younger son, had fair hair that sprang like fine silk from double crowns on his head. His face had the young look of a boy of fourteen yet he was nineteen years old. His skin was as fair as his hair and his grey eyes seemed over-big for his face. His body looked straight and well formed, until he stood up, and then you saw that his legs were badly bowed, so much so that he was known as Bandy Connor.

Paddy's third child was Nellie, Mrs Burke, who was next in age to Rory.

Bill Waggett from No. 1 The Cottages, the son of Gran Waggett and the father of Janie, worked in the docks. He was fifty years old but could have been taken for sixty. His wife had died six years before, bearing her seventh child. Janie was the only one they had managed to rear and he adored her.

Bill's love for her had been such that he did not demand that she stay at home to keep house for him when his wife died but had let her go into service as a nursemaid, even though this meant that once again he would be treated as a young nipper by his mother who was then in her seventy-ninth year. But he, like all those in the cottages, gave her respect if only for the fact that now at eighty-five she still did a full day's work.

Collum Leary was a miner. He was now forty-eight but had been down the pit since he was seven years old. His initiation had been to sit twelve hours a day in total blackness. At eight he had graduated to crawling on his hands and knees with a chain between his legs, which was attached to a bogie load of coal, while his blood brother pushed it from behind. He could not remember his mother, only his father who had come from Ireland when he himself was a boy. The nearest Collum had ever got to Ireland was the Irish quarter in Jarrow and as he himself said, who would bother crossing the seas when almost every man-jack of them were on your doorstep?

Collum at forty-eight was a wizened, prematurely aged man who carried the trade-mark of his following on his skin, for his face and body were scarred as with pocks by blue marks left by the imprint of the coal. But Collum was happy. He went to confession once a twelve-month, and now and again he would follow it by Communion, and he did his duty by God as the priest dictated and saw to it that his wife gave birth every year, at least almost every year. Those years in which she failed to become pregnant were the time he took Communion.

'How's the shipbuilding goin', Jimmy?' Collum Leary now poked his head forward across the table.

'Oh, grand, fine, Mr Leary.'

'When are you goin' to build your own boat?'

'That'll be the day, but I will sometime.' Jimmy nodded now. Then catching Rory's eye, he smiled widely. 'I said I will, an' I will, won't I, Rory?' The boy appealed to his older brother as to one in authority.

Rory, shuffling the cards, glanced sideways at Jimmy and there was a softness in his expression that wasn't usual except when perhaps he looked at Janie.

'You'll soon be out of your time, won't you, Jimmy?'

Jimmy now turned towards Bill Waggett, answering, 'Aye, beginnin' of the year, Mr Waggett. And that's what I'm feared of. They turn you out, you know, once your time's up.'

'Aw, they won't turn you out.' Bill Waggett pursed his lips. 'You hear things around the docks you know; there's more things come up on the tide than rotten cabbages. I hear tell you're the best 'prentice Baker's ever had in his yard; a natural they say you are, Jimmy; mould a bit of wood with your hands, they say.'

'Aw, go on with you.' Jimmy turned his head to the side, his lips pressed tight but his whole face failing to suppress his pleasure at the compliment. Then looking at Bill Waggett again and his expression changing, he said, 'But I'll tell you somethin', I wouldn't be able to finish me time if old Baker saw what I was doin' at this minute.'

'You mean havin' a game?' Rory had stopped shuffling the pack and Jimmy nodded at him, saying, 'Aye. Well, you know what some of them's like. But now there's a notice come out. Didn't I tell you?'

'No, you didn't. A notice? What kind of a notice?'

'Well it says that anybody that's found playin' cards on a Sunday'll lose their jobs, an' if you know about somebody having a game an' don't let on, why then you'll lose your job an' all.'

Rory slapped his hand of cards on to the table. 'Is that a fact?'

'Aye, Rory.'

'My God!' Rory now looked round at the rest of the men, and they stared back at him without speaking until his father said, 'You don't know you're born, lad.' There was a slight touch of resentment in the tone and the look they exchanged had no friendliness in it. Then Paddy, nodding towards Bill Waggett, said, 'What did you tell me the other day about when you worked in the soda works, Bill?'

'Oh that. Well' – Bill brought his eyes to rest on Rory – 'couldn't breathe there. If you were a few minutes late you were fined, and if it was a quarter of an hour, like it might be in winter when you couldn't fight your way through the snow, why man, they stopped a quarter day's pay. And if you dared to talk about your work outside you were fined ten bob the first time, then given the push if it happened twice. That's a fact. It is, it is. An' you might be sayin' nowt of any account. And if anybody covered up for you when you were late . . . oh my God! they were in for it. You know what? They had to pay the fine, the same fine as you paid. You were treated like a lot of bairns: back-chat the foreman and it was half a dollar fine. My God! I had to get out of there. You see, Rory, as your da says, you don't know you're born being a rent collector. Your da did something for you lettin' you learn to read. By! aye, he did. It's somethin' when you can earn your livin' without dirtyin' your hands.'

Rory was flicking the cards over the flowered oilcloth that covered the wooden table. His head was lowered and his lids were lowered, the expression in his eyes was hidden, but his lips were set straight.

Jimmy, as always sensing his brother's mood, turned to Collum Leary and said, 'It's a pity our Rory isn't in America along with your Michael and James and on one of them boats that ply the river, like Michael said, where they can gamble in the open.'

'Aye, it is that, Jimmy,' Collum laughed at him. 'He'd make his fortune.'

He turned and pushed Rory in the shoulder with his doubled fist, adding, 'Why don't you go to America, Rory, now why don't you?'

'I just might, I just might.' Rory was now fanning out the cards in his hand. 'It would suit me that, down to the ground it would. A gamblin' boat. ...'

'Gamblin', cards, fortunes made in America, that's all you hear.' With the exception of Rory the men turned and looked towards Lizzie O'Dowd, where she had risen from her chair, and she nodded at them, continuing, 'Nobody is ever satisfied. Take what God sends an' be thankful.' Then her tone changing, she laughed as she added, 'He's gona send you cold brisket this minute. Who wants pickled onions with it?'

There were gabbled answers and laughter from the table and when she turned away and walked down the room past the chiffonier, past the dess-bed that stood in an alcove, and into the scullery, Janie, too, turned and followed her into the cluttered cramped space and closed the door after her.

Hunching her shoulders upwards against the cold, Janie picked up a knife and began cutting thick slices off a large crusty loaf. She had almost finished cutting the bread before she spoke. Her head still bent, she said quietly, 'Don't worry, Lizzie, he won't go to America.'

'Aw, I know that, lass, I know that. It's me temper gets the better of me.' She turned from hacking lumps of meat from the brisket bone and, looking full at Janie, she said, 'It's funny, isn't it, it's funny, but you understand, lass, don't you?'

'Aye, I understand, Lizzie. Aw, don't worry, he understands an' all.'

'I wish I could think so.'

'He does, he does.'

Lizzie now put the knife down on the table and, bringing one plump hand up, she pressed it tightly across her chin as she remarked, 'I'm not a bad woman, Janie, I never was.'

'Aw, Lizzie, Lizzie.' Janie, her arms outstretched now, put them around the fat warm body of Lizzie O'Dowd, whom she had known and loved since she was a child; even before her own mother had died she had loved Lizzie O'Dowd as if she were a second mother, or perhaps she had placed her first, she was never quite certain in her own mind; and now, their cheeks pressed close for a moment, she whispered, 'It'll all come right. It'll all come right in the end, you'll see.'

'Aye, yes. Yes, you're right, lass.' Lizzie turned her head away as she roughly swept the tears from her cheeks with the side of her finger. Then picking up the knife again and her head bowed once more, she muttered, 'I think the world of Ruth an' I always have. She's the best of women. ... Life isn't easy, Janie.'

'I know it isn't, Lizzie. And Ruth's fond of you, you know she is. She couldn't do without you. None of us could do without you.'

'Ah, lass.' Lizzie was smiling now, a denigrating smile. 'Everybody can be done without.' She gave a short laugh. 'Have a walk around the cemetery the next time you're out.'

'Aw, Lizzie –' Janie was leaning against her shoulder now laughing – 'you're the limit. You know, every time I feel down I think of you.'

'Huh, that's a left-handed compliment if ever I heard one: When you're down you think of me. You can't get much lower than down, can you?'

'You!' Janie now pushed her. 'You know what I mean. Look, is that enough bread?'

'That! It wouldn't fill a holey tooth; you'd better start on another loaf. . . . How is that nice family of yours?'

'Oh, lovely as always, lovely, Eeh! you know I often wonder what would have become of me, I mean what kind of job I would've got in the end. I'd likely have landed up in some factory, like most others, if I hadn't had that bit of luck. Life's so different there, the furniture, the food, everything. The way they talk, the master and mistress, I mean. Do you understand, Lizzie? You know I'm not bein' an upstart but I like bein' there. Mind you, that's not to say I don't like comin' home; I love coming home, even when I know me grannie is goin' to choke me with words and her bloomin' old sayin's. Eeh! the things that she remembers.' They were laughing again. Then she ended, 'But there's different kinds of life . . . I mean livin', Lizzie. You know what I mean?'

'Aye, lass, I know what you mean, although I've never lived any other kind of life but this and I don't want to, not for meself I don't, but for you and . . . and others. Yes, yes, I know what you mean.' She now placed portions of the meat on the slices of dry bread which she then stacked on a plate. Patting the last one, she exclaimed, 'Well now, let's go and feed the five thousand an' find out if it?s tea they want or if they're goin' to get the cans on.'

In the kitchen once more, Lizzie slapped down the heaped plate of meat and bread in the middle of the table, saying, 'Is it tea or are you gettin' the cans on?'

The men glanced furtively from one to the other, their eyes asking a question. Then Paddy and Bill turned simultaneously and looked towards the women, and as usual it was Lizzie who answered them, crying loudly now, 'There's none of us goin' trapesing down there the night an' it fit to cut the lugs off you. If you want your beer there's the cans.' She thrust out her thick arm and pointed towards four assorted cans, their lids dangling by pieces of string from the handles.

The men made no answer but still continued to look towards the women, and then Ruth spoke. Quietly and in levelled tones, she said, 'It's Sunday.'

The men sighed and turned back to the table again, and Bill Waggett muttered under his breath, 'An' that's that then. Bloody Sunday. You know' – he glanced up from the cards and, catching Jimmy's attention, he nodded at him, saying softly, 'I hate Sundays. I always have hated Sundays ever since I was a lad 'cos she kept me going harder on a Sunday than when I was at work.' He had inclined his head backwards towards the fire-place and had hardly finished speaking when his mother, her dewlap chin wobbling, cried across the room, 'Lazy bugger! you always were. Wouldn't even kick when you were born; slid out like a dead fly on hot fat.'

As the roars of laughter filled the kitchen Bill Waggett turned towards his mother and yelled, 'That's a fine thing to say; you should be ashamed of yersel'.' He now looked towards Ruth as if apologizing, but she was being forced to smile, and Ruth rarely smiled or laughed at ribaldry.

'Remember the day he was born?' Old Mrs Waggett had got their attention now. 'Me mother an' me grannie pulled him out, an' I remember me grannie's very words. "Like a Saturday night rabbit he is," she said. You know' – she turned towards Janie – 'when the last of the rabbits are left in the market, all weary skin an' bone? "You'll never rear him," she said; "he'll go along with the other five." But I never had no luck, he didn't.'

She now glanced in impish affection towards her son, where he was sitting, his head bowed, moving it slowly from side to side. The movement had a despairing finality about it. His mother had started and it would take some kind of an event to stop her, especially when as now she had the ears of everyone in the room. He could never understand why people liked listening to her.

'And it was me own mother who looked at him lying across her hands an' said, "I don't think you need worry about the press gang ever chasin' him, Nancy." An' you know somethin'? The press gang nearly got me dad once. Around seventeen ninety it was. I'm not sure of the year, one, two or three, but I do know that all the lads of the Tyne, the sailors like, put their heads together; they were havin' no more of it. They ran the press gang out of the town, North Shields that is, not this side. Then in come the regiment. Barricaded the town, they did, an' forced the lads on board the ships. But me dad managed to get over to this side of the water; he said himself he never knew how.'

'He walked on it.'

There were loud guffaws of laughter now and Gran cried back at her son, 'Aye, an' he could have done that an' all, for at one time you could walk across the river. Oh aye, they once made a bridge with boats, me mother said, and laid planks over 'em, and a whole regiment passed over. The river's changed.' She nodded from one to the other. 'You know, me grannie once told me they caught so much salmon on the Tyne that it was sold at a farthin' a pound. It was, it was. Can you believe that? A farthin' a pound!'

'Yes, yes, Gran.' All except her son were nodding at her.

'And I don't need to go as far back as me grannie's or even me mother's time to remember the great shoals of fish that were caught in these waters. An' there were nowt but keels and sailin' ships takin' the coal away then. None of your Palmer's iron boats. What did you say, our Bill?' She frowned towards her son. ' "Oh my God!" that's what you said. Well, I'm glad you think of Him as yours.'

She joined in the titter that now went round the room. Then nodding her head from one to the other, she went on. 'Talkin' of coal. I can remember as far back as when Simon Temple opened his pit at Jarrow. I was only eight at the time but by! I remember that do. The militia was marching, the bands playing, an' when he got to Shields market the lads pulled the horses from his carriage and drew him themselves. His sons were with him and his old dad. They pulled them all the way to the Don Bridge, where the gentlemen of Jarrow met him. And that was the day they laid the stone for the school for the bairns of his workmen. By! I remember it as if it was yesterday. Simon Temple.' She shook her head and lapsed for a moment into the memory of one of the rare days of jollification in her childhood.

In the pause that followed Collum Leary put in, 'Simon Temple. Aye, an' all the bloody coal owners. Grand lads, grand fellows, great gentlemen. Oh aye, especially when they're shedding crocodile tears over the dead. Ninety-nine men and lads lost in the Fellon pit and over twenty at Harrington. . . .'

'That was a long time ago, Collum.' Grannie Waggett thrust her chin out at the small man who had usurped her position of storyteller and he turned on her, no longer jocular as he cried, 'Don't be daft, Gran. It's happenin' almost every month in one pit or t'other. Don't be daft, woman.'

'Leave be. Leave be.' It was the first time Kathleen Leary had spoken and her husband looked at her as he repeated, 'Leave be, leave be, you say. Bloody coal owners!'

The mood of the kitchen had changed as it nearly always did when the subject of work was brought up, whether it was Paddy Connor talking of the steel works or Bill Waggett of the conditions in the docks, or Collum Leary of the soul destroying work in the mines; and nearly always it was on a Sunday when the atmosphere would become charged with bitterness because nearly always on a Sunday Grannie Waggett was present.

'Come on, Gran.' Janie had taken hold of her grandmother's arm.

'What! What you after? Leave me be.'

'It's time we were goin' in.' Janie nodded towards the wall. 'An' I'll soon be making for the road.'

Grannie Waggett stared up into Janie's face for a moment. Then her head nodding, she said, 'Aye, aye, lass; I forgot you'll soon be making for the road. Well –' She pulled herself up out of the chair saying now, 'Where's me shawl?'

Janie brought the big black shawl from where it had been draped over the head of a three-seated wooden saddle standing against the far wall pressed between a battered chest of drawers and a surprisingly fine Dutch wardrobe.

The old woman now nodded, first to Ruth, then to Nellie, then to Lizzie, and finally to Kathleen Leary, and to each she said, 'So long,' and each answered her kindly, saying, 'So long, Gran,' and as she made for the door with Janie behind her, Lizzie called to her, 'Put the oven shelf in the bed, you'll need it the night.'

'I will, I will. Oh my God! look at that,' she cried, as she opened the door. 'It's comin' down thicker than ever.' She turned her head and looked into the room again. 'We're in for it, another window-sill winter. I can smell it.'

Janie had taken an old coat from the back of the door and as she hugged it around her she glanced back towards the table and Rory, and when she said, 'Half an hour?' he smiled and nodded at her.

'Go on, Gran, go on; you'll blow them all out.' Janie went to press her grandmother on to the outer step, but the old lady resisted firmly, saying, 'Stop a minute. Stop a minute. Look, there's somebody coming in at the gate.'

Janie went to her side and peered into the darkness. Then again looking back into the room, she cried, 'It's John George.'

Rising slowly from the table and coming towards the door, Rory said, 'He wasn't coming the night; he mustn't have been able to see her.'

'Hello, John George.'

'Hello there, Janie.' John George Armstrong stood scraping his boots on the iron ring attached to the wall as he added, 'Hello there, Gran.'

And Gran's reply was, 'Well, come on in if you're comin' an' let us out, else I'll be frozen stiffer than a corpse.'

Janie now pressed her grannie none too gently over the step and as she passed John George she said, 'See you later, John George.'

'Aye, see you later, Janie,' he replied before entering the kitchen and closing the door behind him and replying to a barrage of greetings.

Having hung his coat and hard hat on the back of the door he took his place at the table, and Rory asked briefly, 'What went wrong?'

'Oh, the usual. . . . You playing cards?' The obvious statement was a polite way of telling the company that he didn't wish to discuss the reason for his unexpected presence among them tonight, and they accepted this.

'Want to come in?'

'What do you think?'

As John George and Rory exchanged a tight smile Bill Waggett said, 'You'd better tighten your belt, lad, an' hang on to your trousers 'cos he's in form the night. Cleared me out of monkey nuts.'

'No!'

'Oh aye. We were sayin' he should go to America and make his fortune on one of them boats.'

'He needn't go as far as that, Mr Waggett, there's plenty of games goin' on in Shields and across the water, and they tell me that fortunes are made up in Newcastle.'

'Gamblin'! That's all anybody hears in this house, gamblin'. Do you want a mug of tea?' Lizzie was bending over John George, and he turned his long thin face up to her and smiled at her kindly as he answered, 'It would be grand, Lizzie.'

'Have you had anything to eat?'

'I've had me tea.'

'When was that?'

'Oh. Oh, not so long ago.'

'Have you a corner for a bite?'

'I've always got a corner for a bite, Lizzie.' Again he smiled kindly at her, and she pushed him roughly, saying, 'Death warmed up, that's what you look like. Good food's lost on you. Where does it go? You haven't a pick on your bones.'

'Thoroughbreds are always lean, Lizzie.'

As she turned and walked away towards the scullery she said, 'They should have put a brick on yer head when you were young to make you grow sideways instead of up.'

The game proceeded with its usual banter until the door opened again and Janie entered, fully dressed now for the road in a long brown cloth coat to which was attached a shoulder cape of the same material. It was an elegant coat and like all the clothes she now wore had been passed on to her from her mistress. Her hat, a brown velour, with a small flat brim, was perched high on the top of her head, and its colour merged with the shining coils of her hair. The hat was held in place by two velvet ribbons coming from beneath the brim and tied under her chin. She had fine woollen gloves on her hands. The only articles of her apparel which did not point to taste were her boots. These were heavy-looking and buttoned at the side. It was very unfortunate, Jane considered, that her feet should be two sizes bigger than her mistress's, yet she always comforted herself with the thought that her skirt and coat covered most parts of her boots and there was ever only the toes showing, except when she was crossing the muddy roads and the wheels of the carts and carriages were spraying clarts all over the place.

'Eeh! by! you look bonny.' Lizzie came towards her, but before reaching her she turned to Rory, who was rising from the table, saying, 'You going to keep her waiting all night? Get a move on.'

The quick jerk of Rory's head, the flash of his eyes and the further straightening of his lips caused Janie to say quickly, 'There's plenty of time, there's plenty of time. I've got a full hour afore I'm due in. Look, it's only eight o'clock.'

'It'll take you all that to walk from here to Westoe an' the streets covered.'

'No, it won't, Lizzie. When I get goin' George Wilson, the Newcastle walker, or me grannie's fusiliers aren't in it.' She now swung her arms and did a standing march and ended, 'Grenadier Waggett, the woman walker from Wallsend!' Then stopping abruptly amid the laughter, she looked to where John George was taking his coat from the back of the door, and she asked flatly 'You're not comin' surely? You haven't been here five minutes.'

'I've got to get back, Janie, me Uncle Willy's not too good.'

'Was he ever?'

The aside came from Lizzie and as Ruth went to admonish her with a quick shake of her head Rory turned on her a look that could only be described as rage, for it was contorting his features. He did not shout at her, but his low tone conveyed his feelings more than if he had bawled as he said, 'Will you hold your tongue, woman, an' mind your own business for once!'

Strangely Lizzie did not turn on him, but she looked at him levelly for a moment and countered his anger with almost a placid expression as she said, 'I've spent me life mindin' me own business, lad, an' me own business is to take care of those I'm concerned for, and I'm concerned for John George there. That uncle and aunt of his live off him. And what I'm sayin' now I've said afore to his face, haven't I, John George?'

'You have that, Lizzie. And I like you mindin' me business, it's a comforter.'

'There you are.' She nodded towards Rory, who now had his back to her as he made his way down the long narrow room towards the ladder at the end that led into the loft, which place was Jimmy's and his bedroom and had been since they were children, one end of it at one time having been curtained off to accommodate Nellie.

With no further words, Lizzie now went into the scullery, and Janie began saying her good-byes. When she came to Nellie she bent over her and said below her breath, 'You all right, Nellie?'

'Aye. Aye, Janie, I'm all right.'

Janie stared down into the peaked face; she knew Nellie wasn't all right, she had never been all right since she married. Nellie's marriage frightened her. Charlie Burke had courted Nellie for four years and was never off the doorstep, and Sunday after Sunday they had laughed and larked on like bairns in this very room. But not any more, not since she had been married but a few months. It was something to do with – the bedroom. Neither her grannie nor Lizzie had spoken to her about it and, of course, it went without saying that Ruth wouldn't mention any such thing. But from little bits that she had overheard between Lizzie and her grannie she knew Nellie's trouble lay in – the bedroom, and the fact that she had not fallen with a bairn and her all of three years married. Charlie Burke rarely came up to the house any more on a Sunday. Of course he had an excuse; he worked on the coal boats and so could be called out at any time to take a load up the river.

Janie now went into the kitchen to say good-bye to Lizzie.

Lizzie was standing with her hands holding the rim of the tin dish that rested on a little table under the window, which sloped to the side as if following the line of the roof.

'I'm off then Lizzie.'

Without turning and her voice thick and holding a slight tremor, Lizzie said in answer, 'He's a bloody upstart. Do you know that, Janie? He's a bloody snot. I'm sorry to say this, lass, but he is.'

'He's not; you know he's not, Lizzie.' She shook her head at the older woman. 'An' you're as much to blame as he is. Now yes you are.' She bent sideways and wagged her finger into the fat face, and Lizzie, her eyes blinking rapidly, put out her hand and touched the cream skin that glowed with health and youth and said, 'Lass, you're too good for him. And it isn't the day or yesterday I've said it, now is it? He's damned lucky.'

'So am I, Lizzie.'

'Aw, lass.' Lizzie smiled wryly. 'You'd say thank you if you were dished up with a meat puddin' made of lights, you would that.'

'Well, and why not? And it wouldn't be the first time I've eaten lights.'

They pushed against each other with their hands; then Janie said, 'Remember that starving Christmas? How old was I? Ten, eleven? No work, strikes, trouble. Eeh! we had lights all right then. Me grannie cooked them seven different ways every week.' She paused and they looked at each other. 'Bye-bye, Lizzie.'

Spontaneously now Janie put her arms around Lizzie and kissed her, and Lizzie hugged her to herself. It was an unusual demonstration of affection. People didn't go kissing and clarting on in public, it wasn't proper; everybody knew that, even among engaged couples kissing and clarting on was kept for the dark country lanes, or if you were from the town, and common, a back lane or shop doorway; the only proper place for kissing and clarting on was a front room, if you had one; if not, well then you had to wait for the bedroom, as every respectable person knew. She was going to wait for the bedroom, by aye she was that, even although she wasn't all that taken with what she understood happened in the bedroom.

She now disengaged herself and went hurriedly from the scullery, leaving Lizzie once more gripping each side of the tin dish.

Rory and John George were already dressed for outdoors and waiting for her, Rory, although not short by any means, being all of five foot ten, looked small against John George's lean six foot.

John George wore a black overcoat that had definitely not been made for him. Although the length was correct, being well below his knees, the shoulders were too broad, and the sleeves too short, his hands and arms hanging so far out of them that they drew attention to their thin nakedness. There was a distinct crack above the toecap of one of his well-polished boots and a patch in a similar place on the other. His hard hat was well brushed but had a slight greeny tinge to it. His whole appearance gave the impression of clean seediness, yet his position as rent collector in the firm of Septimus Kean was superior to that of Rory, for whereas Rory had only worked for Mr Kean for four years John George had been with him for eight. Now, at twenty-two years of age and a year younger than Rory, he showed none of the other's comparative opulence for Rory wore a dark grey overcoat over a blue suit, and he had a collar to his shirt, and he did not wear his scarf like a muffler but overlapping on his chest like a business gentleman would have worn it. And although he wore a cap – he only wore his hard hat for business – it wasn't like a working man's cap, perhaps it was only the angle at which he wore it that made it appear different.

Looking at him as always with a feeling of pride welling in her, Janie thought, He can get himself up as good as the master.

'Well then, off you go.' Ruth seemed to come to the fore for the first time. She escorted them all to the door and there she patted Janie on the back, saying, 'Until next Sunday then, lass?'

'Yes, Mrs Connor, until next Sunday. You'll give a look in on her?' She nodded towards the next cottage and Ruth said, 'Of course, of course. Don't worry about her. You know' – she smiled faintly – 'I think she'll still be here when we're all pushing the daisies up.'

'I shouldn't wonder.' Janie went out laughing, calling over her shoulder, 'Ta-rah. Ta-rah everybody. Ta-rah.'

Out in the black darkness they had difficulty in picking their way in single file down the narrow rutted lane. When they reached the broader road they stopped for a moment and Rory, kicking the snow aside with his foot, said, 'By! it's thick. If it goes on like this we'll have a happy day the morrow, eh?'

'I'd rather have it than rain,' John George replied; 'at least it's dry for a time. It's the wet that gets me down, day after day, day after day.'

'Here, hang on.' Rory now pulled Janie close to him and linked her arm in his. 'It's comin' down thicker than ever. Can't even see a light in the docks. We'll find ourselves in the ditch if we're not careful.'

Stumbling on, her side now pressed close to Rory's, Janie began to giggle; then turning her head, she cried, 'Where are you, John George?'

'I'm here.' The voice came from behind them and she answered, 'Give me your hand. Come on.'

As she put her hand out gropingly and felt John George grip it, Rory said, 'Let him fend for himself, he's big enough. You keep your feet, else I'm tellin' you we'll be in the ditch.'

It took them all of twenty minutes before they reached Tyne Dock, and there, taking shelter under the last arch, they stopped and drew their breath, and Janie, looking towards a street lamp opposite the dock gates, said, 'Isn't it nice to see a light?'

'And you can just see it and that's all. Come on, we'd better be goin'. It's no use standin', we soon won't be able to get through.'

As Rory went to pull Janie forward she checked him, saying, 'Look, wait a minute. It's daft, you know, you walkin' all the way to Westoe, you've only got to tramp all the way back. It isn't so bad in the town 'cos there's the lights, but from the bottom of the bank up to our place . . . well, we've just had some, haven't we? An' if it keeps on, as you say it'll get worse underfoot, so what's the sense of trapesing all the way there with me when John George's place is only five minutes away?'

'She's right, Rory. It's daft to tramp down all the way to Westoe for it'll be another couple of hours afore you get back. And then with it coming down like this. Well, as Janie says . . .'

Rory peered from one to the other before he answered, 'Imagine the reception I'd get if I told them back there I'd left you at the arches. They'd wipe the kitchen with me.'

'But you're not leavin' me at the arches; John George'll see me right to the door. Look.' She turned and pushed John George away, saying, 'Go on, walk on a bit, I'll catch up with you in a minute at the Dock gates.'

When John George walked swiftly from the shelter of the arch Rory called, 'Hold your hand a minute . . .'

'Now just you look here.' Janie pulled at the lapels of his coat. 'Don't be such a fathead; I'd rather know you were safely back home in the dry than have you see me to the door.'

'But I won't see you for another week.'

'That didn't seem to bother you all afternoon, 'cos you've done nowt but play cards.'

'Well, what can you do back there? I ask you, what can you do? There's no place to talk and I couldn't ask you out in the freezing cold or they'd've been at me. And I wanted to talk to you, seriously like 'cos it's . . . it's time we thought about doin' something. Don't you think it is?'

She kept her head on the level, her eyes looking into his as she replied, 'If you want a straight answer, Mr Connor, aye, I do.'

'Aw, Janie!' He pulled her roughly to him and pressed his mouth on hers and when she overbalanced and her back touched the curved wall of the arch she pulled herself from him, saying, 'Eeh! me coat, it'll get all muck.'

'Blast your coat!'

Her voice soft now, she said, 'Aye, blast me coat,' then she put her mouth to his again and they stood, their arms gripped tight around each other, their faces merged.

When again she withdrew herself from him he was trembling and he gulped in his throat before saying, 'Think about it this week, will you?'

'It's you that's got to do the thinking, Rory. We've got to get a place an' furniture 'cos there's one thing I can tell you sure, I'm not livin' in with me dad and grannie. I'm not startin' that way up in the loft. I want a house that I can make nice with things an' that . . .'

'As if I would ask you. What do you take me for?'

'I'm only tellin' you, I want a decent place . . .'

'I'm with you there all the way. I'm not for one room an' a shakydown either, I can tell you that . . . I've got something in me napper.'

'Gamblin'?'

'Well, aye. And don't say it like that; I haven't done too badly out of it, have I now? But what I'm after is to get set on in a good school . . . A big school. And there's plenty about. But you've got to be in the know.'

'What! be in the know afore you can get into a gamblin' school?' Her voice was scornful. 'Why, you've been up at Boldon Colliery where they have schools . . .'

'Aye in the back yards an' in the wash-houses. I know all about Boldon Colliery and the games there, but they're tin pot compared to what I'm after. The places I mean are where you start with a pound, not with a penny hoping to win a tanner. Oh, aye, I know, there's times when there's been ten pounds in a kitty, but them times are few and far between I'm telling you. No, what I'm after is getting set on in a real school, but it's difficult because of the polis, they're always on the look out – it's a tricky business even for the back-laners. That's funny,' he laughed, 'a tricky business, but it is. Remember what Jimmy said the night about notices in the works? They try everything to catch you out: spies, plain-clothes bobbies, touts. It's odd, you know; they don't run you in for drinking, but you touch a card or flick a coin and you're for it . . . Anyway, as I said, I've got something in me napper, and if it works out . . .'

'Be careful, Rory. I . . . I get worried about your gamin'. Even years ago when you used to play chucks and always won, I used to wonder how you did it. And it used to worry me; I mean 'cos you always won.'

'I don't always win now.'

'You do pretty often, even if it's only me da's monkey nuts.'

They both made small audible sounds, then moved aside to let a couple of men pass. And now she said, 'I'll have to be goin', John George'll get soaking wet . . . Eeh! I always feel sorry for John George.'

'Your pity's wasted, he's too soft to clag holes with, I'm always telling him. It's right what she said' – he jerked his head – 'those two old leeches suck him dry. He gets two shillings a week more than me and yet look at him, you'd think he got his togs from Paddy's market. And he might as well for he picks them up from the second-hand stalls. And this lass he's after . . . he would pick on a ranter, wouldn't he?'

'Well, he's not a Catholic.'

'No, I know he's not. He's not anything in that line, but he goes and takes up with one from the narrowest end of the Non-conformists, Baptist-cum-Methodist-cum . . .'

'What's she like?'

'I don't know.'

'Doesn't he talk about her at all?'

'Oh, he never stops talkin' about her. By the sound of it she should be a nun.'

'Oh Rory!'

'She should, she's so bloomin' good by all his accounts. She's been unpaid housekeeper to a sick mother, her dad, two sisters and a brother since she was ten. And now she's twenty, and she daresn't move across the door for fear of her old man. He even escorts his other two lasses to work. They're in a chemist's shop and he's there when it closes to fetch them home.'

'What is he?'

'He's got a little tailor's business, so I understand. But look, forget about John George for a minute. Come here.' Once again they were close, and when finally they parted he said, 'Remember what I said. Think on it and we'll settle it next Sunday, eh?'

'Yes, Rory.' Her voice was soft. 'I'm ready anytime you are, I've been ready for a long time. Oh, a long time . . . I want a home of me own . . .'

He took her face gently between his hands and as gently kissed her, and she, after staring at him for a moment, turned swiftly and ran from under the arch and over the snow-covered flags until she came to John George, who was standing pressed tight against the dock wall. She did not speak to him and together they turned and hurried on, past a line of bars arrayed on the opposite side of the road, and so into Eldon Street.

Her throat was full. It was strange but she always wanted to cry when Rory was tender with her. Generally, there was a fierceness about his love-making that frightened her at times, it was when he was tender that she loved him best.

'Daft of him wanting to come all this way.'

'Yes, it was, John George.'

'Of course I was just thinking that if I hadn't have come along he would have taken you all the way, and that, after all, was what he wanted. I'm blind about some things some times.'

She was kind enough to say, 'Not you, John George,' for she had thought it a bit short-sighted of him to accompany them in the first place, and she added, 'Don't worry. And you know what? We're goin' to settle something next Sunday.'

'You are? Oh, I'm glad, Janie. I'm glad. I've thought for a long time he should have a place of his own 'cos he doesn't seem quite happy back there. And yet I can't understand it for they're a good family, all of them, and I like nothing better than being among them.'

'Oh! What makes you think that? What makes you think he's not happy at home, John George?'

'Well, he's surly like at times. And I get vexed inside when I hear the way he speaks to Lizzie 'cos she's a nice body, isn't she . . . Lizzie? I like her . . . motherly, comfortable. Yet . . . yet at times he treats her like dirt. And I can't understand it, 'cos he's not like that outside, I mean when he's collecting; he's civility's own self, and all the women like him. You know that, don't you? All the women like him, 'cos he's got a way with him. But the way he speaks to Lizzie . . .'

Janie paused in her walk and, putting her hand on John George's arm, she drew him to a stop. Then flicking the falling snow away from her eyes, she asked quietly, 'Don't you know why he goes on at Lizzie like that?'

'No.'

'He's never told you?'

'No.'

'You mean he's never told you an' you've been workin' with him and coming up to the house for . . . how many years?'

'Four and over.'

'Eeh! I can't believe it. I thought you knew.'

'Knew what?'

'Well, that . . . that Lizzie, she's . . . she's his mother.'

'*Lizzie?*' He bent his long length down to her. 'Lizzie Rory's mother? No! How does that come about? I don't believe it.'

'It's true. It's true. Come on, don't let us stand here, we'll be soaked.'

'What . . . what about Mrs Connor? I mean . . . his mother . . . I mean.'

'It's all very simple, John George, when you know the ins and outs of it. You see they were married, Mr and Mrs Connor for six years an' there was no sign of any bairn. Then Mr Connor gets a letter from Ireland from a half-cousin he had never seen. Her name was Lizzie O'Dowd. Her ma and da had died – as far as I can gather from starvation. It was one of those times when the taties went bad, you know, and this lass was left with nobody, and she asked if she could come over here and would he find her a job. Everybody seemed to be comin' to England, particularly to Jarrow. They were leaving Ireland in boatloads. So what does Mr Connor do but say come right over. By the way, she had got the priest to write 'cos she couldn't write a scribe and Mr Connor went to a fellow in Jarrow who made a sort of livin' at writing letters an' sent her the answer. It was this by the way, Mr Connor having to go an' get this letter written, that later made him see to it that Rory could read and write. Anyway, Lizzie O'Dowd arrives at the cottage. She's seventeen an' bonny, although you mightn't think it by the look of her now. But I'm goin' by what me grannie told me. And what's more she was full of life and gay like. Anyway, the long and the short of it is that she and Mr Connor . . . Well, I don't need to tell you any

more, do I? And so Rory came about. But this is the funny part about it.
Almost a year later Ruth had her first bairn. That was Nellie. And then she
had another. That was Jimmy. Would you believe it? After nothing for
seven years! Eeh! it was odd. And, of course, we were all brought up as one
family. You could say the three families in the row were all dragged up
together.'

As she laughed John George said solemnly, 'You surprise me, Janie. It's
quite a gliff.'

'But you don't think any the worse of Lizzie, do you?

'Me think any the worse of . . .? Don't be daft. Of course I don't. But at
the same time I'm back where I started for I understand less now than I did
afore, Rory speaking to her like that and her his mother.'

'But he didn't always know that she was his mother. It was funny that.'
She was silent for a moment, before going on, 'There was us, all the squad
of the Learys, me da, me ma, and me grannie. Well, you know me grannie,
her tongue would clip clouts. But nobody, not one of us, ever hinted to him
that Mrs Connor wasn't his mother, it never struck us. I think we sort of
thought that he knew, that somebody must have told him earlier on. But
nobody had; not until six years ago when he was seventeen and it was Lizzie
herself who let the cat out of the bag. You know, Lizzie is one of those
women who can't carry drink. Give her a couple of gins and she's away;
she'll argue with her own fingernails after a couple of gins. And it was on
a New Year's Eve, and you know what it's like on a New Year's Eve. She
got as full as a gun an' started bubbling, and Rory, who up till that time had
been very fond of her, even close to her, when she hadn't got a drink on her,
'cos this is another funny thing about him, he can't stand women in drink.
Well, I don't remember much about it 'cos I was only a lass at the time, but
as I recall, we were all in the Connors' kitchen. It was around three o'clock
in the morning and I was nearly asleep when I hear Lizzie blurting out,
'Don't speak to me like that, you young . . .!' She called him a name. And
then she yelled, 'I'm your mother! Her there, Ruth there, never had it in her
to give breath to a deaf mute till I went an' had you.' And that was that.
From then on he never has been able to stand her. An' the pity of it is she
loves him. He went missing for a week after that. Then he turned up one
night half starved, frozen, and in the end he had the pneumonia. He had
been sleeping rough, and in January mind. It's a wonder it didn't kill him.
Now do you begin to understand?'

'I'm flabbergasted, Janie. To think that I've known him all this time and
he's never let on. And we talk you know, we do; I thought we knew
everything there was to know about each other. Me, I tell him everything.'
The tall length drooped forward. His head bent against the driving snow,
he muttered now, 'I'm that fond of Rory, Janie, 'cos, well, he's all I'd like
to be and never will.'

'You're all right as you are, John George; I wouldn't have you changed.'
Her voice was loud and strong in his defence.

'You wouldn't, Janie?' The question was almost eager, and she answered,
'No, I wouldn't, John George, because your heart's in the right place. An'
that's something to be proud of.'

They walked on some way in silence now before she said quietly, 'I hope
you don't mind me askin', but the lass you're gone on, why don't you bring
her up to the kitchen?'

He didn't answer immediately but took her arm and led her across the road and up the street towards the beginning of Westoe and the select section of the town, where the big houses were bordered by their white railings and the roads were broad enough to take two carriages passing, and he said now, 'I wish I could, oh I wish I could 'cos she's nice, Janie, and bonny. Not as bonny as you, but she's bonny. And she's had a life of it. Aye, one hell of a life. And still has. Her da's got religion on the brain I think. Her mother's bedridden, and, you know, they spend Sunday praying round her bed, taking turns. The only time she's allowed out is on a Saturday afternoon when she's sent to Gateshead to visit an aunt who's dying and who seems to have a bit of money. Her da wants to make sure of who she's leaving it to and as he can't go up himself and the other two lasses are in jobs – there was a brother, Leonard, but he ran off to sea, and good luck to him I say – Anyway, Maggie is allowed to go to Gateshead on a Saturday afternoon. That's how I met her first, on one of me Saturday train jaunts.'

'You go on a train to Gateshead every Saturday? I didn't know that. Eeh! on a train . . .'

'Well' – he laughed self-consciously – 'not every Saturday, only when funds allow. And then not to Gateshead, but Newcastle. I take the train up half-way, say to Pelaw, and walk the rest. I love Newcastle. Aw, lad, if I had the money I'd live there; I wouldn't mind rent collecting around Newcastle.'

'Aren't there any slums up there then?'

'Oh aye, Janie, plenty. But I don't look at the slums, it's the buildings I look at. There's some beautiful places, Janie. Haven't you ever been to Newcastle?'

'No, I've been across the water to North Shields and Cullercoats, and once I went as far as Felling on this side, but no, I've never been to either Gateshead or Newcastle.'

'Rory should take you up, he should take you to a theatre.'

'There's a good theatre here, I mean in Shields.'

'Oh aye, it's all right, but it isn't like Newcastle.'

'They get the same turns, only a little later.'

'Oh, I'm not thinkin' about the turns, nothing like that, it's the buildings you know. I suppose it was a wrong thing to say that he should take you to a theatre, but I think he should take you up to Newcastle to see the lovely places there, the streets and buildings.'

'I never knew you liked that kind of thing, John Geroge?'

'Oh aye, an' have ever since I was a lad. It was me da who started it. On holiday week-ends we'd walk up there. Me mother never came, she couldn't stand the distance and she wasn't interested in buildings. It was because of me da's interest in buildings and such that I was taught to read and write. He was standing looking up at a lovely front door once. They're called Regency. It was off Westgate Hill; it was a bonny piece of work with a lovely fanlight and the windows above had iron balconies to them when a man came alongside of us and started crackin'. And it turned out he worked in an architect's office and he seemed over the moon when he knew me da was interested in masonry and such and was leading me along the same lines. That was the first time I heard the name Grainger mentioned. He was the great builder of Newcastle. And John Dobson, he used to design for Grainger and others. I'd heard of the Grainger Market, and had been

through it, but you don't think of who built these places. And then there's
Grey Street. Eeh! there's a street for you. The best time to see it is on a
Sunday when there's no carts or carriages packing it out and few people
about. By! it's a sight. As me da once said, that's what one man's imagination
could do for a town.'

Janie now blew at the snow that was dusting her lips and turned her
head towards him and blinked as she said, 'You're a surprise packet you
are, John George. Do you ever talk to Rory about it?'

'Aye, sometimes. But Rory's not really interested in Newcastle or buildings
and such.'

'No, no, he's not.' Janie's voice held a dull note now as she added, 'Cards,
that's Rory's interest, cards. Eeh! he seems to think of nothing else.'

'He thinks of you.'

'Aye, he does, I must admit.' She was smiling at him through the falling
snow and she added now, 'You've got me interested in Newcastle. I'll tell
him . . . I'll tell him he's got to take me up.'

'Do that, Janie. Aye, do that. Tell him you want to see Jesmond. By!
Jesmond's bonny. And the houses on the way . . . Eeh! lad, you see nothing
like them here.'

'I think I'd like to see the bridges. I heard me da say there's some fine
bridges. Funny me never ever havin' seen Newcastle and it only seven miles
off. And there's me grannie. She worked there at one time, she was in service
at a place overlooking the river. She used to keep talking about the boats
laden down with coal going up to London. It was funny, she never liked
Newcastle. She still speaks of the people there as if they were foreigners;
she's always sayin' they kept the South Shields men down, wouldn't let them
have their own shipping rights or nothing until a few years back. It's funny
when you come to think of it, John George, we know more about the people
from Ireland, like the Learys and Rory's folks, than we do about them in
Newcastle. I'm beginning to see the sense of some of me grannie's sayings;
she always used to be saying, "You could be closer to a square head from
Sweden than you could to a man with a barrow from Jarrow." '

John George laughed now, saying, 'I've never heard that one afore.'

'Oh, I think it's one of me grannie's make-up ones. You know, half the
things she says I think she makes up. If she had ever been able to read or
write she would have been a story teller. I've said that to her. Oh –' She
sighed now and shook her gloved hands to bring the circulation back into
her fingers as she said, 'We're nearly there.' Then on a little giggle, she
added, 'If the missis was to see you she'd think I was leading a double life
and she'd raise the riot act on me.'

As they stopped before a side gate that was picked out by the light from
a street lamp she looked at John George, now blowing on his hands, and
said with deep concern, 'Oh, you must be frozen stiff, John George. And no
gloves.'

'Gloves!' His voice was high. 'You can see me wearin' gloves, I'd be taken
for a dandy.'

'Don't be silly. You need gloves, especially goin' round in this weather,
scribbling in rent books. At least you want mittens. I'll knit you a pair.'

He stood looking down on her for a long moment before saying, 'Well,
if you knit me a pair of mittens, Janie, I'll wear them.'

'That's a bargain?'

'That's a bargain.'

'Thanks for comin' all this way, John George.'

'It's been my pleasure, Janie.'

'I . . . I hope you see your girl next week.'

'I hope so an' all. I . . . I'd like you to meet her. You'd like her, I know you'd like her, and what's more, well, being you you'd bring her out, 'cos she's quiet. You have that habit, you know, of bringing people out, making people talk. You got me talkin' the night all right about Newcastle.'

Janie stood for a moment blinking up at him and slightly embarrassed and affected by the tenderness of this lanky, kindly young fellow. His simple talking was having the same effect on her as Rory's gentle touch had done. She felt near tears, she had the silly desire to lean forward and kiss him on the cheek just like a sister might. But that was daft, there was no such thing as sisterly kisses. That was another thing her grannie had said and she believed her. There were mothers' kisses and lovers' kisses but no sisterly kisses, not between a man and woman who weren't related anyway . . . Yet the master kissed his sister-in-law, she had seen him. Eeh! what was she standing here for? She said in a rush, 'Good night, John George. And thanks again, I'll see you next Sunday. Ta-rah.'

'Ta-rah, Janie.'

She hurried up the side path, but before opening the kitchen door she glanced back towards the gate and saw the dim outline of his figure silhouetted against the lamplight, and she waved to it; and he waved back; then she went into the house . . .

Mrs Tyler, the cook, turned from her seat before the fire, looked at Janie, then looked at the clock above the mantelpiece before saying, 'You've just made it.'

'There's three minutes to go yet.' Her retort was perky.

She wasn't very fond of Mrs Tyler. She had only been cook in the Buckhams' household for eighteen months but from the first she had acted as if she had grown up with the family. And what was more, Janie knew she was jealous of her own standing with the master and mistress.

The cook never said anything outright to her but she would talk at her through Bessie Rice, the housemaid, making asides such as 'Some people take advantage of good nature, they don't know their place. Don't you ever get like that, Bessie now. In Lady Beckett's household, where I did my trainin', the nursemaid might have her quarters up on the attic floor but below stairs she was considered bottom cellar steps. Of course, a governess was different. They were educated like. Why, in Lady Beckett's the still-room maid sat well above the nursemaid.'

On the occasion when this particular remark was made, Janie had had more than enough of Lady Beckett for one day and so, walking out of the kitchen, she remarked to no one in particular, 'Lady Beckett's backside!'

Of course she should never have said such a thing and she regretted it as soon as she was out of the door, and before she had reached the nursery she knew that the cook was knocking on the parlour door asking to speak to the mistress. Ten minutes later the mistress was up in the nursery looking terribly, terribly hurt as she said, 'Janie, I'm surprised at what the cook has been telling me. You must not use such expressions, because they may become a habit. Now just imagine what would happen if you said something like that in front of the children.' She had gulped and stood speechless before the young woman who had shown her nothing but kindness and when the mistress had gone she had laid her head in her arms on the table and cried her heart out until young Master David had started to cry with her, and then Margaret, and lastly the baby.

She looked back on that day as the most miserable in her life, and yet when she went to bed that night she had had to bury her head in the pillow to smother her laughter. Having earlier decided that feeling as she did she'd get no rest, she had gone downstairs to apologize to the mistress and to tell her that never again would she use such an expression in her house, and that she need not have any fear that the children's minds would ever be sullied by one word that she would utter.

She had reached the main landing when she was stopped by the sound of smothered laughter coming from the mistress's bedroom. The door was ajar and she could hear the master saying, 'Stop it. Stop it, Alicia, I can't hear you . . . what did she say?'

She had become still and stiff within an arm's length of the door as her mistress's voice came to her spluttering with laughter the while she made an effort to repeat slowly: 'She . . . said . . . you . . . can . . . kiss . . . Lady . . . Beckett's . . . backside.'

'She didn't!'

The laughter was joined now, high, spluttering; it was the kind of laughter that one heard in the Connors' kitchen when Lizzie said something funny.

'Well done, Waggett!'

There was more laughter, then the master's voice again saying, 'I can't stand Tyler. You want to get rid of her.'

'Oh, she's a good cook; I can't do that, David. And Janie mustn't be allowed to say things like that. But oh, I don't know how I kept my face straight.'

She had backed slowly towards the stairs, and when she reached the nursery floor her face split into one wide amazed grin; yet her mind was saying indignantly, 'I didn't say that. It's just like cook to stretch things. But eeh! the master, I've never heard him laugh like that afore. Nor the missis. They sounded like a young couple.'

It wasn't until she was in bed that she thought to herself, Well, I suppose they are a young couple. Yet at the same time it was strange to her to realize that people of their class could laugh together, spluttering laughter; for they always acted so very correct in front of other folk, even when the sister came. But then the sister was married to a man who had a cousin with a title, a sir, or a lord, or something, and, of course, she wouldn't expect them to act in any way but refinedly. But, anyway, they had laughed, and the mistress actually repeated what she herself had said, only, of course, with a bit added on by the cook.

And that night she had told herself yet once again that she liked her master and mistress, she did, she did, and she would do anything for them. And as she had recalled their laughter the bubbling had grown inside her, and to stop an hysterical outburst she had turned and pressed her face tightly into the pillow. And her last thought before going to sleep had been, I'll have them roaring in the kitchen next Sunday. And she had.

# Chapter Two

It was the Saturday before Christmas; the sky lay low over the town and the masts of the ships were lost in grey mist.

Rory shivered as he walked up the church bank and entered Jarrow. He passed the row of whitewashed cottages, then went on towards the main thoroughfare of Ellison Street. He hated this walk; he hated Saturday mornings; Saturday mornings meant Pilbey Street and Saltbank Row. Pilbey Street was bad enough but the Row was worse.

He had six calls in Pilbey Street and fifteen in the Row, and as always when he entered the street he steeled himself, put on a grim expression and squared his shoulders, while at the same time thinking, Old Kean and those other landlords he represents should be lynched for daring to ask rent for these places.

For four years now he had collected the rents in these two streets. In the ordinary way he should have collected them on Monday, Tuesday or Wednesday because on these days he came this way collecting, and right on into Hebburn, but you couldn't get a penny out of anybody in Pilbey Street or the Row on any other day but a Saturday morning. And you were lucky if you managed to get anything then; it was only fear of the bums that made them tip up.

He lifted the iron knocker and rapped on the paint-cracked knobless door. There was a noise of children either fighting or playing coming from behind it, and after a few minutes it was opened and three pairs of eyes from three filthy faces peered up at him. All had running noses, all had scabs around their mouths and styes on their eyes. The eldest, about five, said in the voice of an adult, 'Aw, the rent man.' Then scrambling away through the room with the others following him, he shouted, 'The rent man, Ma! 'Tis the rent man, Ma!'

'Tell the bugger I'm not in.'

The woman's voice came clearly to Rory and when the child came back and, looking up at him, said, 'She's not in,' Rory looked down on the child and as if addressing an adult said, 'Tell her the bugger wants the rent, and somethin' off the back, or else it's the bums Monday.'

The child gazed at him for a moment longer before once more scrambling away through the room, and when his thin high voice came back to him, saying, 'He says, the bugger wants the rent,' Rory closed his eyes, bowed his head and pressed his hand over his mouth, knowing that it would be fatal to let a smile appear on his face with the two pairs of eyes surveying him. If he once cracked a smile in this street he'd never get a penny.

It was almost three minutes later when the woman stood before him. She had a black shawl crossed over her sagging breasts, the ends were tucked into a filthy ragged skirt, and in a whining tone and a smile widening her flat face she exclaimed, 'Aw begod! it's you, Mr Connor. Is it the rent you're after? Well now. Well now. You know it's near Christmas it is, and you know what Christmas is for money. Chews it, it does, chews it. An' look at the bairns. There's not a stitch to their arses an' himself been out of work these last three weeks.'

Without seeming to move a muscle of his face Rory said, 'He's in the rolling mills and never lost a day this six months, I've checked. You're ten weeks in arrears not countin' the day. Give me five shillings and I'll say nothing more 'till next week when I want the same and every week after that until you get your book clear. If not, I go to Palmer's and he'll get the push.'

It was an idle threat, yet she half believed him because rent men had power, rent men were rich; rent men were a different species, not really human.

They stared at each other. Then the smile sliding from her face, she turned abruptly from him and went through the room, shouting, 'You Willy! You Willy!' And the eldest child followed her, to return a moment later with two half-crowns and the rent book.

Rory took the money, signed the book, marked it in his own hard-backed pocket ledger, then went on to the next house. Here he pushed open the bottom door and called up the dark well of the staircase, 'Rent!' and after a moment a man's voice came back to him shouting, 'Fetch it up.'

His nose wrinkled in distaste. If he had a penny for every time that worn-out quip had been thrown at him he considered he'd be able to buy a house of his own. After a moment of silence he again shouted, 'Rent, or it's the bums Monday.'

The moleskin-trousered bulky figure appeared on the stairhead and after throwing the rent book and a half-crown down the stairs he yelled, 'You know what you and the bloody bums can do, don't you? then as Rory picked up the money and the book and entered in the amount the man proceeded to elaborate on what he and the bums could do.

Without uttering a word now Rory threw the book on to the bottom stair, looked up at the man still standing on the landing, then turned about and went towards the end of the street.

There was no answer whatever from the next three doors he knocked on, but he had scarcely raised the knocker on the fourth when it was opened and Mrs Fawcett stood there, her rent book in one hand, the half-crown extended in the other, and without any greeting she began, 'You won't get any change out of them lot.' She nodded to one side of her. 'Nor to this one next door.' Her head moved the other way. 'Off to Shields they are, the lot of them, to the market and they won't come back with a penny, not if I know them. Lazy Irish scum. And I'll tell you somethin'.' She leant her peevish face towards him. 'Her, Flaherty, she's got her front room packed with beds, and lettin' them out by the shift; as one lot staggers out another lot drops in. Great Irish navvies with not a drop on their faces from Monday mornin' till Saturda' night, but Sunday, oh, that's different, away to Mass they are, and straight out and into the bars. Disgrace!'

Rory closed her rent book, handed it to her, looked at her straight in the eye, then turned and walked away. He did not bother knocking at the door next to hers for he believed what she had said, they were all away on a spending spree. It was odd, she was the only good payer in the street; she'd always had a clear rent book; but of the lot of them, scum Irish they might be, he preferred any one of them to Mrs Fawcett.

Pilbey Street was bad but Saltbank Row was worse. Here it was the stench that got him. The dry middens at the back of the Row, dry being a mere courtesy title, seeped away under the stone floors of the two-roomed cottages, and the dirt in front of the cottages was always wet to the feet. In winter the stench was bad enough but in summer it was unbearable. Why the Town Corporation did not condemn the place he didn't know. Vested interests he supposed; in any case anything was good enough for the Irish immigrants, and they didn't seem to mind, for as it was well known they had been used to sleeping among the pigs and the chickens in their tiny hovel huts over in Ireland.

Yet there were Irish in the town among Palmer's men whom he had heard were buying their own houses. That had come from old Kean himself, and the old boy didn't like it.

His own father had worked in Palmer's for years, but there was no sign of him being able to buy his own house. Likely because he didn't want to; his father spent as he went, he ate well and drank as much as he could hold almost every day in the week, because his body was so dried up with the heat from the furnaces.

Drinking was one thing he didn't blame his father for, but he did blame him for his carry-on with her ... Lizzie. He supposed it was by way of compensation that he'd had him sent to the penny school but he didn't thank him for that either, for he hadn't attended long enough to take in much beyond reading, writing and reckoning up. When funds were low the last thing to be considered was the penny fee. And he wouldn't go to school without it. Nor would his father have his name put down on the parish list so that he could send him free – not him.

Anyway, his reading and writing had enabled him finally to become a rent collector with a wage of fifteen shillings a week. He was told from all quarters that he was damned lucky to be in such a job. Fifteen shillings for neither bending his back nor soiling his hands. And his employer, more than others, emphasized this statement.

Mr Kean owned about half the cottages in Saltbank Row, and the rent of each was two shillings a week, but when he reached the end of the Row all he had in the back section of his leather bag was twenty-five shillings and sixpence.

It was just turned twelve o'clock when he reached the main street and joined the stream of men pouring out of Palmer's and the various side streets which led to different yards on the river. They were like streams of black lava joining the main flow, faces grey, froth-specked with their sweat. He was carried along in the throng until he reached the church bank again by which time the blackness had dwindled into individual pockets of men.

He reckoned he should be back at the office by one o'clock. He never carried a watch, not on his rounds, because it could be be nicked in the time he blinked an eyelid. A gang of lads supposedly playing Tiggy could rough you up. He had seen it done. But he told himself as he paused for a moment on the Don bridge and looked down at the narrow mud-walled banks of the river that there was no immediate hurry today, for old Kean was off on one of his duty trips to Hexham to see his old father. When this happened the day's takings were locked up until Monday. Saturday's takings didn't amount to very much, not on his part anyway. John George took more, for he did the Tyne Dock area and the better part of Stanhope Road.

He was getting a bit worried about John George. There was something on his mind; he supposed it was that damned ranter's lass he had taken up with. Only last night he had told him to think hard about this business, for being her father's daughter, she might turn out to be a chip off the old block and be 'God-mad' like the rest of them.

The whole of Shields was becoming 'God-mad'; there were chapels springing up all over the place and the more of them there were the greater the outcry against drink and gambling. And them that made the fuss, what were they? Bloody hypocrites half of them. Oh, he knew a thing or two about some of them. That's why he had warned John George.

As he walked on into Tyne Dock he forgot about John George and his troubles for his mind was taken up with the evening's prospects. He had heard tell of a square-head, a Swede who lived down Corstorphine Town way. He was known as Fair Square; he did summer trips there and back to Norway and Sweden, but in the winter he stayed put somewhere along the waterfront and ran a school, so he understood, and not just an ordinary one, a big one, for captains and such. But as little Joe, the tout, had said, they didn't often let foreigners in . . . That was funny that was, a Swede calling an Englishman a foreigner, and in his own town at that. Anyway, little Joe had promised to work him in somewhere.

He felt a stir of excitement in his stomach at the thought of getting set-in in a big school; none of your tanner pitch and tosses or find the lady, but banker with a kitty up to twenty pounds a go. By, that was talking. Twenty pounds a go. Once in there it wouldn't be long afore he could set up house – he and Janie, setting up house. He wanted to get married, he ached for Janie. And that was the right word, ached. At night he would toss and turn until he would have to get up and put the soles of his feet on the ice-cold square of lino that stood between the beds.

He'd see her the morrow. Just to be with her lifted him out of the doldrums; just to look at her pulled at his heart, 'cos she was bonny, beautiful. And he wasn't spending the whole afternoon the morrow playing cards for monkey nuts. Huh! He wondered why he let himself in for it Sunday after Sunday. No, hail, rain or shine they'd go out up the lanes, and he'd settle things in his own way. Aye he would.

'Rory! Rory!'

He turned swiftly and looked up the dock bank to see John George pushing his way through a press of men towards him, and when he came up Rory stared at him saying, 'You're late, aren't you? You're generally done around twelve.'

'I know, but there was an accident back there at the Boldon Lane toll-gate. I helped to sort the carts out. A young lad got crushed. Toll's finished next year they say, an' a good thing an' all.'

'Getting into a throng with money in your bag, you must be mad . . . And where did you get that?'

Rory was now looking John George over from head to foot. 'You knock somebody down?'

Stroking the lapels of a thick brown overcoat that, although a little short, fitted his thin body, John George said, 'I picked it up last Saturday in Newcastle, in the market.'

'What did you give for it?'

'Half a dollar.'

'Well you weren't robbed, it's good material. You should have got yourself some boots while you were on.' He glanced down at the cracked toecaps. 'It's a wonder the old fellow hasn't spotted them and pulled you up. You know what he is for appearances.'

'I'm going to see about a pair the day when I'm up there.'

'You're going to Newcastle again?'

'Aye.' John George now turned his head and smiled at Rory. 'I'm meeting her on the three o'clock train an' I'm going to show her round. Look' – he thrust his hand into the overcoat pocket, then brought out a small box wrapped in tissue paper – 'I bought her this for Christmas. What do you think of it?'

When Rory took the lid off the box and looked at the heart-shaped locket and chain he stared at it for some seconds before turning to John George again and asking quietly, 'What did you give for it?'

'Not . . . not what it's worth, it's second-hand. It's a good one.'

'What did you give for it?'

'Seven and six.'

'Seven and six! Are you mad? How can you afford seven and six? You tell me that your Aunt Meg needs every penny to keep the house goin' and three bob's as much as you can keep back.'

'Well, it's . . . it's true. But . . . but I worked out a system.'

'You worked out a system, you!' Rory screwed up his face. 'You worked out a system! On what? Tell me on what?'

'Aw, not now, man, not now I'll . . . I'll tell you after . . . later on. I wanted to have a word with you about something else . . . You see I'm thinking of moving, trying to get a better job. I could never hope to get Maggie away on the wage I've got and having to see to them at home and . . .'

'Where could you get a better job than what you've got?'

'There's places in Newcastle.'

'Aye, I know there's places in Newcastle, but them chaps don't get even as much as we do. There's no trade unions yelling for us. I'm not satisfied, but I know damn well that if I want more money I won't get it at rent clerking. Look, are you in some kind of fix?'

'No, no.' John George shook his head too vigorously and Rory, eyeing him from the side, shook his head also. They walked on in silence, taking short cuts until they came to the market, then they wound their way between the conglomeration of stalls, turned down a narrow side lane known as Tangard Street, and past what appeared to be the window of an empty shop, except that the bottom half, which was painted black, had written across it: Septimus Kean, Estate Agent, Valuer, and Rent Collector. Next to the window was a heavy door with a brass knob that had never seen polish, and above it a keyhole.

As John George was about to insert his key into the lock the door was pulled open from inside and they were both confronted by Mr Kean himself.

'Oh! . . . Oh! Mr Kean. We thought you were away.'

The small, heavy-jowled man looked at Rory and barked, 'Evidently. Do you know what time it is?' He pulled out a watch, snapped open the case and turned the face towards Rory. 'Ten minutes past one. When the cat's away the mice can play.'

'But we finish at one.' Rory's voice was harsh, the muscles of his neck were standing out and his face was flushed with sudden temper.

'Be careful, Connor, be careful. Mind who you're speaking to. You know what happens to cheeky individuals; there's never an empty place that cannot be filled. I know that you're finished at one, and damned lucky you are to be finished at one, but you should have been back here before one and your book settled, and then you could have been finished at one . . . And what's the matter with you?' He was now glaring at John George. 'You sick or something?'

John George gulped, shook his head, and remained standing where he was on the threshold of the door.

And this caused Mr Kean to yell, 'Well, come in, man! What's come over you? Close the door before we're all blown out. And let me have your books; I want to get away.'

With this, Mr Kean turned about and went through a door into another room. The door was half glass, but it was clear glass, clear in order that the master could look through it at any time and see that his two clerks weren't idling at their desks.

'What is it? What's the matter?' Rory had taken hold of John George's shoulder. 'You look like death, what is it?'

John George gulped twice in his throat before he whispered, 'Lend . . . lend me ten bob.'

'Lend you ten bob?'

'Aye. Look, just for now, I'll have it for you Monday mornin'. Just . . . just lend it me. Aw, Rory, lend it me. For God's sake, lend it me.'

Rory looked towards the glass door and as he put his hand into his pocket, he hissed, 'You were paid last night.'

'Aye, I know, but I'll explain, I'll explain in a minute or two.' The hand he held out was trembling and when Rory put the gold half sovereign on to the palm John George's fingers pressed over it tightly for a moment before swiftly dropping it into the leather bag which he still held in his hand.

*'Come on, come on.'*

They exchanged glances before John George turned away and almost stumbled across the room and into his master's office.

Rory remained gazing at the half open door . . . He was on the fiddle. The damn fool was on the fiddle. It was that lass. God, if he hadn't been here and old Kean had found him ten shillings short!

Mr Kean's voice came bawling out of the room again, saying, 'What's the matter with you, Armstrong? You look as if you're going to throw up.' Then John George's voice, thin and trembling, 'Bit of a chill, sir. Got a cold I think.'

There was a pause, then Mr Kean's observation: 'That coat's new, isn't it? You shouldn't feel cold in that. About time you did smarten yourself up. Bad impression to go around the doors looking like a rag man.' Another pause before his voice again rasped, 'Mrs Arnold, she's paid nothing off the back for four weeks. Why haven't you seen to it?'

'She's been bad. She . . . she took to her bed a few weeks ago. But she says she'll clear it up soon because her girl's got set on across the water at Haggie's . . .the Ropery you know.'

'Yes, I know, I know the Ropery. And I know the type that works there. She'll likely drink her pay before she gets back across the water. She's got others working, hasn't she?'

'Yes. Yes, she's got a lad down the pit. But . . . but he's only a nipper, he's not getting more than tenpence a day. She's . . . she's had hard times since her man went.'

'That's neither my business nor yours, I don't want the family history, I only want the rent and the back rent. Now you see to it. You're getting slack, Armstrong. I've noticed it of late.'

There followed another silence before John George returned to the other office, his face looking bleak, his eyes wide and in their depth a misery that caused Rory to turn away, pick up his bag and go into the other room.

When he had placed the money from the bag on the table, Mr Kean separated each single coin with his forefinger, then after counting them he raised his eyes without lifting his head and said, 'You mean to tell me this is the result of a morning's work?'

'It was Saltbank Row and Pilbey Street.'

'I know damned well it was Saltbank Row and Pilbey Street, it's always Saltbank Row and Pilbey Street on a Saturday, but what I'm saying to you is, do you mean to tell me that's all you got out of them?'

Rory moved one lip over the other before replying, 'It's always the same near Christmas.'

'Look!' The thick neck was thrust forward, then the head went back on the shoulders and Mr Kean directed an enraged stare on to Rory's grim face as he cried, 'One gives me family histories, the other festival dates as excuses. Now look, I'm telling you they're not good enough, neither one nor the other, Christmas or no Christmas. If that sum' – he now dug his finger on to one coin after another – 'if it isn't doubled at the next collection then there'll be a lot of barrows needed to shift their muck. You tell them that from me. And that's final.' Again he stabbed the coins. 'Double that amount or it's the bums for the lot of 'em'

When Rory turned abruptly from the table Mr Kean barked at him, 'Answer me when I'm speaking to you!'

Rory stopped, but it was a few seconds before he turned to face Mr Kean again, and then he said slowly, 'Yes, sir.'

Seconds again passed before Mr Kean said, 'There's going to be changes here, Connor,' and again Rory said, 'Yes, sir.'

'Get yourself out.'

The buttons on Rory's coat strained as he drew in a deep breath before turning round and leaving the room, closing the door after him.

John George was standing by his narrow, high desk. A little colour had returned to his face and he was about to speak when the outer door opened and they both looked towards it and at Miss Charlotte Kean.

Charlotte was Kean's only child but she bore no resemblance to him, being tall, extremely tall for a woman, all of five foot eight and thin with it. Moreover, she had what was commonly called a neb on her. Her nose was large; her mouth, too, was large but in proportion to her face. Her eyes were a greeny grey and her hair was black. She was an ugly young woman yet in some strange way she had just missed being beautiful for each feature taken by itself was good even though, together, one cancelled another out. Her features gave the impression of strength, even of masculinity. It was understood in the office that she knew as much about the business as did her father, yet she rarely came here. Rory hadn't seen her but half a dozen times in four years, and each appearance had given him material for jokes in the kitchen, especially at the Sunday gatherings.

He had from time to time openly teased John George about her. John George had said he felt sorry for her, because a young woman like her had little chance of being married. His words had proved true, for here she was at twenty-eight and still on the shelf.

But there was one thing his master's daughter possessed that he couldn't make game of, in fact it had the power to make him feel ill at ease, and that was her voice. There was no hint of the Tyneside twang about it. This he understood had come about by her being sent away to one of those posh schools when she was no more than ten, from which she hadn't come back to Shields for good until she was turned seventeen.

She gave them no greeting – one didn't greet clerks – but stared at Rory before demanding briefly, 'My father in?'

'Yes, miss.' Rory inclined his head towards the door.

She stood for a moment longer looking from one to the other. Then her eyes resting once more on Rory, she surveyed him from head to toe, as he said bitterly afterwards, 'Like some bloody buyer at a livestock show.' But he wasn't going to be intimidated by any look she could cast over him, and so he returned it. His eyes ranged from her fur-trimmed hat down over her grey velour coat with its brown fur collar, right to her feet encased in narrow-toed brown kid boots. He had noticed her feet before. They were so narrow he wondered how she balanced on them, how she got boots to fit them. But when you had money you could be fitted from top to toe and inside an' all, but he'd like to bet with that face her habit shirts would be made of calico, unbleached at that, no lace camisoles for her. Anyway, she had nothing to push in them.

As she went towards the door he looked at her back. It was like a ramrod, she wasn't like a woman at all. He beckoned to John George, who seemed to be glued to his desk, and as he opened the door he heard her say, 'You'll be late for the ferry, I came with the trap. Come along or you'll never get there.'

The old man always went by ferry up to Newcastle; he didn't like the trains although he had to take one from Newcastle to Hexham. When he went on his usual trips there he generally left early on a Saturday morning. What had stopped him this time? Anyway, whatever had stopped him had also nearly stopped John George's breath.

They were crossing the market again before he said, 'Well now, come on, spit it out.'

'I'll . . . I'll give you it back, I . . . I can give you six bob of it now. I'll get if from home and . . . and the rest on Monday.'

'What were you up to?'

'Aw' – John George wagged his head from side to side – 'I . . . I wanted to give Maggie something and it had to be the day, it's the only time I can see her. I mightn't see her again after the holiday and so, thinkin' he wouldn't be in till Monday, I . . . I took the loan of ten bob out of the . . .'

'You bloody fool!'

'Aye, I know, I know I am.'

'But . . . but how did you expect to put it back by Monday if you haven't got it now?'

'Aw well, man' – again his head was wagging – 'I . . . I usually put me good suit in and me watch and bits of things . . .'

'You usually do? You mean you've done this afore?'

John George nodded his head slowly. 'Aye. Aye, a few times. The times that he goes off at the week-ends and doesn't count up till Monday. I . . . I thought I'd drop down dead when I saw him standing there.'

'You deserve to drop down dead, you bloody fool you. Do you know he could have you up? And he's the one to do it an' all; he'd have you along the line afore you could whistle. You must be up the pole, man.'

'I think I'll go up the pole soon if things don't change.'

'What you want to do is to pull yourself together, get things worked out straight. Leave your Uncle Willy and Aunt Meg, he's able to work, he's nothin' but a scrounger, and take a place on your own.'

'What!' John George turned his face sharply towards him. 'Take the furniture and leave them with three bare rooms or tell him to get out? What you don't understand, Rory, is that there's such a thing as gratitude. I don't forget that they were both good to me mother after me da died, aye, and long afore that; and they helped to nurse him the two years he lay bedridden.'

'Well, they've been damned well paid for it since, if you ask me . . . All right then, say you can't do anything about them, an' you want that lass . . . well then, ask her to marry you and bring her into the house.'

'That's easier said than done. If I took her away her father would likely go straight to old Kean and denounce me.' He now put his hand to his brow, which, in spite of the raw cold, was running with sweat, and muttered, 'But I'll have to do something, and soon, 'cos . . . oh my God! I'm in a right pickle . . . Rory.'

'Aye, I'm still here, what is it?'

'There's something else.'

'Aw.' Rory now closed his eyes and put his hand across his mouth, then grabbed at his hard hat to save it from being whipped by the wind from his head. 'Well, go on.'

'It doesn't matter. Another time, another time; you're not in the mood . . . Look – ' he pointed suddenly – 'Isn't that Jimmy?'

They were passing the road that led to the Mill Dam and the river front. Rory stopped and said, 'Yes that's our Jimmy . . . Jimmy!' he shouted down the lane, and Jimmy who had been walking with his eyes cast down looked upwards, then came dashing up the slope at his wobbling gait.

'Why, fancy seein' you, I mean both of you. An' I was just thinking of you, our Rory.'

'You were? Why? You another one that wants a sub?'

'No, man.' Jimmy laughed. 'But I was thinkin' that when I got home I'd ask you to come down here again. Now wasn't that funny.'

'I can't see much to laugh at in that, not yet anyway.'

'Well, it was something I wanted to show you down on the front.' He nodded towards the river. 'Come on.' He again indicated the river with his head, then added, 'And you an' all, John George.'

'I can't, Jimmy, I'm sorry. I'm . . . I'm on me way home.'

'Aw, all right, John George, I understand, it's your day for Newcastle.' He laughed.

John George didn't laugh with him, but he repeated, 'Aye. Aye, Jimmy, it's me day for Newcastle.' Then nodding at him, he said, 'Be seeing you. So long. And so long, Rory. Aw, I forgot. What about the other, I mean. . . ?'

'Leave it till Monday. And mind, don't do any more damn fool things until then.'

'I'll try not to. But what's done's done. Nevertheless thanks, thanks. You'll have it on Monday. So long.'

'So long.'

'What's up with him?' Jimmy asked as they went down towards the road that bordered the river.

'He's been a damned fool, he's mad.'

'What's he been and gone and done?'

'Nothing . . . I'll tell you some other time. What do you want me down here for?'

'I want to show you something.'

'A boat?'

'Aye, a boat. An' something more than that.'

Rory looked down into the young face. It was always hard for him to believe that Jimmy was nineteen years old, for he still looked upon him as a nipper. He was more than fond of Jimmy, half-brothers though they were; he liked him the best of the bunch.

'Where we going?'

'Just along the front, then down the Cut.'

'There's nothing but warehouses along there.'

'Aye, I know. But past them, past Snowdon's, on a bit, you'll see.'

After some walking they had turned from the road that bordered the warehouse and wharf-strewn river front and were clambering over what looked like a piece of spare ground except that it was dotted here and there with mounds of rusty chains, anchors and the keels and ribs of small decaying boats, when Jimmy, squeezing his way between a narrow aperture in a rough fence made up of oddments of thick black timber, said, 'Through here.'

Rory had some difficulty in squeezing himself between the planks, but when once through he looked about him on to what appeared to be a miniature boatyard. A half-finished skeleton of a small boat was lying aslant some rough stocks and around it lay pieces of wood of all shapes and sizes. A few feet beyond the boat was the beginning of a slipway bordered by a jetty and he walked towards the edge of it and leant over the rail and looked down into the water; then from there he turned and surveyed the building at the far end of the yard.

It wasn't unlike any of the other warehouses cluttering the river bank except that it had three windows in the upper part of it, and they were big windows, one on each side of the door and one fitting into the apex of the roof. There was no name on the front of the structure like there was on the rest of the boatyards and warehouses, and Rory now turned and looked into Jimmy's bright eyes and said, 'Well?'

'It's a little boatyard.'

'I can see that but I wouldn't say it was a prosperous one. You're not going to leave Baker's for here, are you?'

'No, man, no. I'm not going to leave Baker's at all. I wish I could. At the same time I'm terrified of being stood off. No, I just want you to see it.'

'Why?'

'Oh, 'cos . . . it's up for sale.'

'Up for sale?'

'Aye.'

'Well, what's that got to do with us?'

'Nowt . . . nowt, man.'

Rory watched the light slowly fade from Jimmy's face. He watched him turn away and look at the river, then up at the house, and lastly at the boat on the stocks, and he said softly now, 'I know what you're thinkin', but it's like a dream, lad, that's all, it can never come true.'

'I know.'

'Then what did you bring me here for?'

'I just wanted you to see it, just to show you.'

'What good is that going to do you or anybody else?'

'Well, I just wanted to show you that a man could start on almost nowt an' build up. They've done it all along the river. The Pittie Brothers, they started from nowt. A sculler among the three of them, and now they've got the run of the place, or they think they have. But there's always room for another one or two. Some say the keelman's day is over since they've widened the river and the boats can go farther up and pick up their coal straight from the staithes, but as Mr Kilpatrick used to say there's other things to be carted besides coal. Anyway, I'd never aim to be a keelman 'cos it's as tight to get in as a secret society, an' they're a tough lot, by aye! Nor do I want to build keels, with a cabin an' hold, 'cos it takes all of three men to manage a keel. No; but I've got something in me mind's eye; it'd be under thirty foot but with space for timber, packages and such, something I could manage meself or, at a push, just two of us. Mr Kilpatrick used to say he could design . . .'

'Who's Mr Kilpatrick?'

'The old fellow who owned this place.'

'Did you know him?'

'Aye, in a way. I used to pop in in me bait time. He's always given me tips, things that you don't come by only by experience. He used to take the wood from the river' – he pointed to the wood scattered around the boat – 'and when he was finished with it, it was as good as new. He had a way with wood. He said I had an' all.'

'And he's dead?'

'Aye.'

'Who's sellin' it then?'

'His son. Well, he's selling the goodwill.'

'Goodwill!' Rory gave a short laugh. 'What goodwill is there here? The back end of a boat and wood you can pick up from the river.'

'There's a house up there and there's some decent pieces of furniture in it. And then there's his tools. And he's got a bond on the place for the next ten years.'

'You mean it's just rented?'

'Aye.'

'How much is it a week?'

'Three and a tanner.'

'Huh!' the sound was sarcastic. 'They're not asking much, three and a tanner for this!'

'But everything is included. And a permit to ferry stuff up and down the river.'

'And what's the son wanting for it?'

'Thirty-five pounds.'

'*What!*' It was a shout. 'You havin' me on?'

'No, I'm not, that's cheap. There's the boat, and all the wood. And you haven't seen his tools. Then there's the furniture. There's three rooms up there, I've been in them. He used to give me a cup of tea now and again. He lived on his own. They're big rooms. You don't get much of an idea from here.'

'But there's no boat, he must have had a boat.'

'Aye, his son took that.'

'That son knows what he's doing. Has he been pumping you?'

'No. Why no, man, why would he pump me? Only that he knew I used to talk to his old man. He came here once or twice when I was in the yard and when he saw me t'other day he told me. He said – ' Now Jimmy turned away and walked up towards the house, his body seeming to rock more than his bowed legs and Rory called after him, 'Well, go on, finish telling me what he said.'

'It doesn't matter; as you said, it's a dream.' And now he swung round and stabbed his finger towards Rory as he ended. 'But some day, mark my words, I'll make it come true. I don't know how but I will. I'll have a place of me own where I can build a boat an' ply a trade. You'll see. You'll see.'

'All right, all right.' Rory walked towards him now. 'No need to bawl your head off.'

'You bawled first.'

'Well, I had a right.' He now passed Jimmy and walked up and into the end of the slipway, over which the building extended, and looked towards the ladder that was fixed to the wall and ended in a trap-door, and he called back over his shoulder in an amused tone, 'Is this how you get in?'

'No, of course, it isn't,' Jimmy said scornfully; 'there's steps up and a door, you saw them. But – ' And his eyes were bright again as he went on, 'I can show you inside, I know how to get in through the hatch.'

'What we waitin' for, then, if it's going to cost us nothin'? So go on, get up.'

The desire was strong in him to please this brother of his and to keep his dream alive for a little longer. He watched him run up the vertical ladder with the agility of a monkey. He saw him put his flat hand in the middle of the trap-door, jerk it twice to the side, and then push it upwards. He stood at the foot of the ladder and watched him disappear through the hole. Then he was climbing upwards, but with no agility. He wasn't used to crawling up walls he told himself.

When he emerged into the room he straightened up and looked about him but said nothing. Just as Jimmy had said, there were some good pieces of furniture here. He was amazed at the comfort of the room. The whole floor space was covered with rope mats fashioned in intricate patterns. There was a high-barred fireplace with an oven to the side of it and a hook above it for a spit or kettle. A good chest of drawers stood against one wall, and by it a black oak chest with brass bindings. There was a big oval table with a central leg in the middle of the room, and the top had been polished to show the grain. There were three straight-backed wooden chairs and a rocking chair, and all around the walls hung relics from ships: brass compasses, wheels, old charts. He walked slowly towards the door that led into the next room. It was a bedroom. There was a plank bed in one corner but slung between the walls was a hammock. And here was another seaman's chest, not a common seaman's chest but something that a man of captain's rank might have used, and taking up most of the opposite end of the room was a tallboy.

'It's good stuff, isn't it? Look at his tools.' Jimmy heaved up the lid of the chest to show an array of shining tools hung meticulously in order around the sides of the chest.

'Aye, it's good stuff. He was no dock scum was your Mr Kilpatrick. Everything orderly and shipshape.'

'Of course he wasn't dock scum. He was a gentleman . . . well, I mean not gentry, but a gentleman. He had been to sea in his young days, ran off, so he told me. His people were comfortable. They took his son when his wife died, that's why the son doesn't want anything to do with the water front. He's in business, drapery.'

'What's up above?'

'It's a long room, it runs over both of these. It's full of all kinds of things, maps and papers and books and things. He could read. Oh, he was a great reader.'

Rory looked down on Jimmy. He looked at him for a long moment before he was able to say, 'I'm sorry.'

'What've you to be sorry for?' Jimmy had turned away and walked towards the window where he stood looking out on to the river.

'You know what I'm sorry for, I'm sorry you can't have it. If I had the money I'd buy it for you this minute, I would.'

He watched his brother's face slowly turn towards him. The expression was soft again, his tone warm. 'I know you would. That's why I wanted you to see it an' hear you say that, 'cos I know if you had it you would give it me, lend it me.'

Rory went and sat in the rocking chair and began to push himself slowly backwards and forwards. Thirty-five pounds. A few nights of good play somewhere and he could make that. He once made thirteen pounds at one sitting, but had lost it afore he left. But if he were to win again he'd smilingly take his leave. That's if he wasn't playing against sailors, for some of them would cut you up for tuppence.

Suddenly jumping up from the chair, he said, 'Come on.'

'Where?'

'Never mind where. Just come on, let's get out of her.' But before dropping down through the trap-door he looked about him once again as he thought, It'll kill two birds with the one stone. Janie. Janie would love it here, she would be in her element. There was the room up there, that would do Jimmy. He closed his eyes and shook his head. He was getting as barmy as Jimmy . . . But there was nothing like trying.

When they were out of the yard and on the road again he stopped and, looking down at Jimmy, said, 'Now I want you to go straight home. You can say that you saw me, and I was with a fellow. We . . . we were going to see the turns later on. Aye, that's what to say, say we were going to the theatre later on.'

'You're goin' in a game?'

'Aye, if I can find a good one.'

'Aw, Rory.'

'Now, now, don't get bright-eyed, nowt may come of it. But I'll have a try. And if we could put something down to secure it –' he punched Jimmy on the shoulder – 'the fellow might wait, take it in bits like, eh? If he's not short of a bob he could wait, couldn't he? And it isn't everybody that's going to jump at a place like that. But . . . but as I said, don't get too bright-eyed. Just tell them what I told you, and if I shouldn't be back afore they go to bed, tell them . . . well, tell them not to wait up.'

'Aye, Rory, aye, I'll do that. And . . . and you be careful.'

'What have I got to be careful of?'

'You hear things, I mean along the front, about the schools an' things. There are some rough customers about.'

'I'm a bit of one meself.'

'You're all right.'

They looked at each other, the undersized bow-legged boy with the angelic face and his thick-set straight-backed, arrogantly attractive-looking half-brother, and each liked what he saw: Rory, the blind admiration in the boy's face, and Jimmy, the strength, determination and apparent fearlessness in this man he loved above all others.

'Go on with you, go on.' Rory thrust out his hand, and Jimmy turned away. Again he was running, and not until he had disappeared from view into the main thoroughfare did Rory swing about and stride along the waterfront in the direction of the pier. But before he came to the high bank known as the Lawe, on which stood the superior houses with their view of the sea and the North and South piers, and which were occupied by ships' captains and respectable merchants of the town, he turned off and into a street which, from its disreputable appearance, should never have been allowed to lie at the skirt of such a neighbourhood as the Lawe. There were only eight houses in this street and they all had walled back yards and all the doors were locked. It was on the third yard door that he knocked, a sharp knock, rat-tat a-tat, tat-tat, and after some minutes it was furtively opened by a man hardly bigger than a dwarf.

'Hello, Joe.'

'Oh. Oh, it's you, Mr Connor?'

'Aye, Joe. I wanted a word with you.'

'Oh well, Mr Connor, I'm off on a message you see.' He brought his two unusually long and fine-shaped hands in a sweeping movement down the front of his short coat, and Rory, nodding, smiled and said, 'Aye, you've got your best toggery on, must be some special message.'

He had never before seen little Joe dressed like this. He had never imagined he had any other clothes but the greasy little moleskin trousers and the old broadcloth coat he usually wore. Not that he couldn't afford to buy a new suit because he must do pretty well on the side; besides being a bookie's runner, little Joe could be called upon to negotiate odd jobs, very odd jobs, along the waterfront. Last year it was said he almost went along the line when two lasses went missing. They couldn't prove anything against him for he was a wily little beggar. But the case recalled the outcry of a few

years earlier when some lasses were shipped off. Afterwards of course this
line of business had of necessity quietened down for a time, but nature being
what it is a demand for young lasses, especially young white lasses, was
always there, and so was Joe.

He said to him now, 'I want you to get me in some place the night, Joe,
like you promised. But no back-yard dos.'

'Aw, it'll take time, Mr Connor, an' I told you.' He came out into the
lane now and pulled the door closed, and as he walked away Rory suited
his steps to the shorter ones.

'Now you can if you like, Joe. You said . . .'

'I told you, Mr Connor, it takes time that kind of thing. And they're on
to us . . . coppers; they're hot all round the place.'

'You have ways and means, you know you have, Joe. An' I'd make it
worth your while, you know that.'

'Oh, I know that, Mr Connor. You're not tight when it comes to payin''
up. Oh, I know that. And if I could, I would . . . There's Riley's.'

'I don't like that lot, I told you last time.'

'Well, I'll admit it, they're a bit rough.'

'And twisted.'

'Aw well, you see, I don't play meself, Mr Connor, so I wouldn't know.'

'There's other places, Joe.'

'But you've got to be known, Mr Connor, an' . . . an' it's me livelihood
you know.'

'You could do it, Joe.'

And so the conversation went on, flattery pressing against caution; but by
the time they parted caution had won.

'I'm sorry, Mr Connor, but . . . but I'll let you know. I'll take a walk
around your office as soon as I can manage anything for you. That's a
promise; it is.'

Rory nodded, and as he stood and watched the small shambling figure
hurry away and disappear around the bottom of the street he repeated
bitterly, 'That's a promise.' Then he asked himself the question, 'Where's
he off to, rigged out like that?' He wouldn't need to dress up to go round
his usual haunts. He was going some place special?

As if he had been pushed from behind he sprang forward, but when he
came out into the main street he slowed to a walk. Little Joe was well ahead,
but he kept him in sight until he turned into Fowler Street.

There he was impeded in his walking by a number of people who had
stepped hastily up on to the pavement from the road to allow a private coach
and a dray-cart to pass each other. There were angry shouts and strong
language among those who had their clothes bespattered with mud, and as
he didn't want his own mucked up, he kept as near as he could to the wall,
and because of the press he was only just in time to see little Joe turn off
into Ogle Terrace.

Ogle Terrace, apart from Westoe, was in the best end of the town. Who
was he going to see up there? On the small figure hurried until at the top
of Plynlimmon Way he disappeared from view.

Rory, now about to set off at a run towards the end of the terrace, was
impeded for a second time by a party of ladies coming through an iron
gateway and making for a carriage standing at the kerb.

When he eventually reached the top corner of Plynlimmon Way there was no sight of little Joe.

He stood breathing deeply, working things out. Joe wouldn't have had access to a front door, not around here he wouldn't, yet it was into one of these houses he had disappeared. So the place to wait was the back lane.

The back lane was cleaner than many front streets. It was servant territory this, at least two or three maids to a house, hired coaches from the livery stables for the owners and trips abroad in the fashionable months. And little Joe was in one of these houses delivering a message. He was on to something here.

When a back door opened and a man wearing a leather-fronted waistcoat swept some dust into the back lane, he did a brisk walk past the end of the lane and as briskly returned. The man was no longer in sight, all the back gates were closed. He moved up slowly now, past the first one, and the second, then stood between it and the third. It was as he paused that the third door opened and out stepped little Joe.

The small man stood perfectly still and gazed at Rory with a pained expression before he said, 'You shouldn've, Mr Connor. Now you shouldn've. You don't know what you're at.' He cast a glance back to the door he had just closed, then hurried on down the lane. And Rory hurried with him.

They were in the main street before the little man slowed his pace, and then Rory said, 'Well now, Joe, what about it?'

And again Joe said, his tone surly now, 'You don't know what you're at, you don't.'

'I know what I'm at, Joe.' Rory's voice was grim. 'The buggers that live along there are like those in their mansions up Westoe, they run this town; they control the polis, the shippin', they own the breweries, an' have fingers in the glassworks, chemical works . . . Aye, the chemical works on the Jarrow road. There's one in Ogle Terrace who's on the board. You forget I'm a rent collector, Joe. There's no rent collected in this area. No, they're all owned. But I know about them. Who doesn't? By the morrow I'll find out who's in that particular number and that's all I'll need to know because now I know he's on the fiddle. What is it, Joe? Gamin' or girls . . . lasses?'

'Mr Connor, you'd better mind yourself, aye you'd better.' Little Joe's voice held a note of awe now. 'You want to be careful what you say, he's . . .'

'Aye, aye, I've got the message, Joe, he's powerful. Well now, let's sort this thing out, eh? He's one of two things: he's a man who likes a game or he's a man who runs a game. We'll leave the lasses out of it for the time being, eh? Now havin' the kind of mind I have, Joe, I would say he's a man who runs a game, and likely in that house, 'cos if he wanted to go some place else for a game he wouldn't need you as a runner. A man in his position would have a key to open any door, even the ones in Newcastle. And there's some big games there, aren't there, Joe? No pitch an' toss, Joe, it's Twenty-Ones, or Black Jack, whatever name they care to call it; isn't it, Joe?'

He looked down on the little man, and although the twilight was bringing with it an icy blast Joe was sweating. He now said in some agitation, 'Let's get out of this crush.'

'Anything you say, Joe. Where you makin' for now?'

'I've got to go up Mile End Road.'

'Another message?'

'No, no.' The little man now turned on him and, his tone for the first time really nasty, he said, 'An' there's one thing I'm gona tell you. Whatever come of this you'd better not let on 'cos . . . an' I'm not funnin', Mr Connor, with what I'm about to say, but things could happen, aye, things could happen.'

'I've no doubt of it, Joe.'

'Don't be funny, Mr Connor.'

'I'm not being funny, Joe, believe you me. Things are happenin' all the time along the waterfront an' I should imagine in Plynlimmon Way an' all. Now, you know me, Joe, I'm as good as me word. If I've owed you a couple of bob in the past you've got it, haven't you, with a bit tacked on? And I've never had a win on a race but I've seen you all right, haven't I? And I haven't got a loose tongue either. So look, Joe.' He stopped and bent down to the little man. 'All I want from you is to get me set on in a decent school.'

'They go in for big stakes, Mr Connor.' The little fellow's voice was quiet again.

'That's what I want, Joe.'

'But you haven't got that kind of ready. You couldn't start in some of them under ten quid, an' that's so much hen grit.'

'You say some of them, there must be a few who start on less. I'll come to t'others later on. Aye, Joe, the big ones, I'll come to them later on, but in the meantime . . .'

The little man blinked, gnawed at his lip, looked down to the cobbles on which they were standing, as if considering. Then his eyes narrowing, he squinted up into Rory's face, saying conspiratorially, 'There's one in Corstorphine Town I might manage; it's not all that cop but they can rise to five quid a night.'

'It'll do to start with, Joe.'

'An' you'll say nowt about?' He jerked his head backwards.

'No, Joe, I'll say nowt about . . .' Now Rory imitated Joe's gesture, then added, 'Until you take me in there.'

'That'll be the day, Mr Connor.'

'Aye, that'll be the day, Joe. An' it mightn't be far ahead.'

'You worry me, Mr Connor.'

'I won't get you into any trouble, Joe, don't you worry.' Rory's tone was kindly now.

'Oh, it isn't that that worries me, it's what'll happen to you, if you take a wrong step. You don't know this game, Mr Connor.'

'I can play cards, Joe.'

'Aye, I've heard tell you can. But there's rules, Mr Connor, rules.'

'I'll stick to the rules, Joe.'

'But what if you come up against those who don't stick to them, Mr Connor?'

'I'll deal with them when I come to them, Joe. Now this place in Corstorphine Town.'

'What time is it now?' Joe looked up into the darkening sky, then stated, 'On four I should say.'

'Aye, on four, Joe.'

'Well on seven, meet me at the dock gates.'

'Seven, Joe, at the dock gates. I'll be there. And thanks.' He bent down to him. 'You won't regret it. I'll see to you, you won't regret it.'

Once again Rory watched the little man hurry away, his feet, like those of a child, almost tripping over each other. Then almost on the point of a run himself he made for home.

When he entered the kitchen Jimmy stared at him, exclaiming almost on a stutter, 'I told them –' he indicated both his mother and Lizzie with a wave of his hand – 'I told them you met a fellow an' you were going to . . . to see the turns.'

'So I am, but it was so bloomin' cold walkin' around waiting, he's gone home for his tea. I was going to ask him up but thought the better of it. But I wouldn't mind something.' He looked towards Ruth. 'I'm froze inside and out. I'm meeting him at seven again.'

'Aw –' Jimmy smiled broadly now – 'you're meeting him at seven? And you're going to see the turns?'

'Aye, we're going to see the turns.'

As Lizzie, walking into the scullery, repeated as if to herself, 'Going to see the turns,' Rory cast a hard glance towards her. She knew what turns he was going to see; you couldn't hoodwink her, blast her. But Ruth believed him. She came to him now, smiling and saying, 'Give me your coat and come to the fire; I'll have something on the table for you in a minute or so.'

He grinned at Ruth. He liked her, aye, you could say he loved her. Why couldn't she have been his mother? Blast the other one. And blast his da. They were a couple of whoring nowts. Aw, what did it matter? He had got his foot in, and Jimmy would get his yard, and he and Janie would be married and they would live in that house overlooking the water. And Jimmy would build up a business and he would help him. Aye, with every spare minute he had he'd help him. He knew nowt about boats but he'd learn, he was quick to learn anything, and he'd have his game and he'd have Janie. Aye, he'd have Janie.

It did not occur to him that he had placed her after the game.


# Chapter Three


All the while she kept looking from one to the other of them, but they remained smilingly silent. Then she burst out, 'But the money! You've got the money to buy this?' Flinging both arms wide as with joy she gazed about the long room.

'Well –' Rory pursed his lips – 'enough, enough to put down as a deposit.'

'He didn't get in till six this mornin'.' Jimmy was nodding up at her, and she turned to Rory and said, 'Gamin'?'

'Yes. Yes, Miss Waggett, that's what they call it, gamin'.'

'And you won?'

'I wouldn't be here showing you this else.'

'How much?'

'Aw well' – he looked away to the side – 'almost eleven pounds at the beginning, but' – he gnawed on his lip for a moment – 'I couldn't manage to get away then, I had to stay on and play. But I was six up anyway when I left.'

'Six pounds?'

'Aye, six pounds.'

'And this place is costin' thirty-five?'

'Aye. But five pounds'll act as a starter. Jimmy's goin' to get the address of the son and I'll write to him the morrow.'

There was silence between them for a moment until Rory, looking at Janie's profile, said, 'What is it?'

'The waterfront, it's . . . it's mostly scum down here.'

'Not this end.'

She turned to Jimmy, 'No?'

'No, they're respectable businesses. You know, woodyards, repair shops, an' things like that. An' there's very few live above the shops. There's nobody on yon side of us, an' just that bit of rough land on the other. Eeh!' he laughed, 'I'm sayin' us, as if we had it already . . .'

'What do you think?' Rory was gazing at her.

'Eeh!' She walked the length of the room, put her hand out and touched the chest of drawers, then the brass hinges on the oak chest, then the table, and lastly the rocking chair, and her eyes bright, she looked from one to the other and said, 'Eeh! it's amazing. You would never think from the outside it could be like this 'cos it looks ramshackle. But it's lovely, homely.'

'Look in t'other room.'

She went into the bedroom, then laughed and said, 'That'll come down for a start.'

She was pointing to the hammock, and Rory answered teasingly, 'No. Why, no. Our Jimmy's going to swing in that and we'll lie underneath.'

'Aw you!' Jimmy pushed at the air with his flat hand, then said, 'I'll be upstairs, I'll make that grand. Come on, come on up and have a look. Can you manage the ladder?'

Janie managed the ladder, and then she was standing under the sloping roof looking from one end of the attic to the other and she exclaimed again, 'Eeh! my! did you ever see so many bits of paper and maps and books and things? There's more books here than there are in the master's cases in his study.'

'Aye.' Jimmy now walked up and down the room as if he were already in possession of the place, saying, 'By the time I get this lot sorted out I'll be able to read all right.'

'Talkin' of reading.' Janie turned to Rory. 'The mistress is having a teacher come in for the children, sort of part time daily governess. She said I could sit in with them. What do you think of that?'

'You won't be sittin' in with them long enough to learn the alphabet. And anyway, I'll teach you all you want to know once I get you here, an' you won't have any spare time for reading.'

'Rory!' She glanced in mock indignation from him to Jimmy, and Jimmy, his head slightly bowed and his lids lowered, made for the ladder, muttering, 'I'm goin' to see if there's any wood drifted up.'

Alone together, they looked at each other; then with a swift movement he pulled her into his arms and kissed her. He kissed her long and hard and, her eyes closed tightly, she responded to him, that was until his hand slid to her buttocks, and then with an effort she slowly but firmly withdrew from him, and they stood, their faces red and hot, staring at each other.

'I want you, Janie.' His voice was thick.

Her eyes were closed again and her head was nodding in small jerks and her fingers were moving round her lips wiping the moisture from them as she muttered softly through them, 'I know, I know, but ... but not until ... no, no, not until. I'd ... I'd be frightened.'

'There's nothing to be frightened of. You know me, you're the only one for me, always have been, an' ever will be. There's nothing to be frightened ...'

'I know, I know, Rory, but I can't, I daren't.' She was flapping both hands at him now. 'There's me da, an' me grannie, and all the others.'

He was making to hold her again. 'Nothing'll happen, just once.'

'Aw –' she now actually laughed in his face – 'me grannie's always told me, she fell the first night. An' you can, you can ... Eeh!' She now pressed her fingers tightly across her mouth. 'I shouldn't be talkin' like this. You shouldn't make me talk like this. It isn't proper, we're ... we're not married.'

'Don't be daft, we're as good as married. I tell you there's only you, there's only ...'

'No, Rory, no, not until it's done.' She thrust his hands away. 'I mean proper like in the church, signed and sealed. No, no, I'm sorry. I love you, oh, I do love you, Rory, I've loved you all me life. I've never even thought of another lad an' I'm twenty. I can't tell you how I love you, it eats me up, but even so I want to start proper like so you won't be able to throw anythin' back at me after.'

'What you talking about?' He had her by the shoulders now actually shaking her. 'Me throw anything back at you? Actually thinking I'd do a thing like that?'

'You're a man and they all do. Me grannie ...'

'Blast your grannie! Blast her to hell's flames! She's old. Things were different in her day.'

'Not that. That wasn't any different. Never will be. It's the only thing a woman's really looked down on for. Even if you were to steal you wouldn't have a stamp put on you like you would have if ... if you had a bairn.'

'You won't have ...'

'Rory, no. I tell you no. We've waited this long, what's a few more months?'

'I could be dead, you could be dead.'

'We'll have to take a chance on that.'

'You know, Janie, you're hard; there's a hard streak in you, always has been about some things ...'

'I'm not.' Her voice was trembling. 'I'm not hard.'

'Yes you are. ...'

'I'm not. I'm not.'

'All right, all right. Aw, don't cry. I'm sorry, I am. Don't cry.'

'I'm not hard.'

'No, you're not, you're lovely ... It's all right. Look, it's all right; I just want to hold you.'

When his arms went about her she jerked herself from his hold once more and going to the window, stood stiffly looking down on to the river, and he stood as stiffly watching her. Only his jaw moved as his teeth ground against each other.

She drew in a deep breath now and, her head turning from one side to the other, she looked up and down the river. As far as her eyes could see both to the right and to the left the banks were lined with craft, ships of all types and sizes, from little scullers, wherries and tugs to great funnelled boats, and here and there a masted ship, its lines standing out separate and graceful from the great iron hulks alongside.

Rory now came slowly to the window and, putting his arm around her shoulders and his manner softened, he said, 'Look. Look along there. You see that boat with a figurehead on it – there's a fine lass for you ... Look at her bust, I bet that's one of Thomas Anderson's pieces, and I'll bet he enjoyed makin' it.'

'Rory!'

He hugged her to him now and laughed, then said, 'There's the ferry boat right along there going off to Newcastle ... one of the pleasure trips likely. Think on that, eh? We could take a trip up to Newcastle on a Sunday, and in the week there'll always be somethin' for you to look at. The river's alive during the week.'

She turned her head towards him now and said, 'You said the rent's three and six?'

'Aye.'

'You won't get anything from Jimmy, not until he gets set-in.'

'I know, I know that. But we'll manage. I'll still be workin'. I'll keep on until we really do get set-in and make a business of it. I mightn't be able to build a boat but I'll be able to steer one, and I can shovel coal and hump bales with the rest of them. I didn't always scribble in a rent book you know; I did me stint in the Jarrow chemical works, and in the bottle works afore that.'

'I know, I know, but I was just thinkin'. Something the mistress said.'

'What did she say?'

'Well –' she turned from him and walked down the length of the room – 'she doesn't want me to leave, I know that, she said as much.' She swung round again. 'Do you know she even said to me face that she'd miss me. Fancy her sayin' that.'

'Of course she'll miss you, anybody would.' He came close to her again and held her face between his hands. 'I'd miss you. If I ever lost you I'd miss you. God, how I'd miss you! Oh, Janie.'

'Don't ... not for minute. Listen.' She pushed his hands from under her oxters now and said, 'Would you demand I be at home all day?'

'I don't know about demand, but I'd want you at home all day. Aye, of course I would. Who's to do the cooking and the washing and the like? What are you gettin' at?'

'Well, it was something the mistress said. She said she had been thinking about raising me wage ...'

'Ah, that was just a feeler. Now look, she's not going to put you off, is she?'

'No, no, she's not. She knows I'm goin' to be married. Oh, she knows that, but what she said was, if ... if I could come for a while, daily like, until the children got a bit bigger and used to somebody else, because well, as she said, they were fond of me, the bairns. And she would arrange for Bessie to have my room and sleep next to them at night and I needn't be there until eight in the morning, and I could leave at half-six after I got them to bed.'

He swung away from her, his arms raised above his head, his hands flapping towards the low roof, and he flapped them until he reached the end of the room and turned about and once more was standing in front of her. And then, thrusting his head forward, he said, 'Look, you're going to be married, you're going to start married life the way we mean to go on. You'll be me wife, an' I just don't want you from half-past six or seven at night till eight in the morning, I want you here all the time. I want you here when I come in at dinner-time an' at tea-time.'

'She'll give me three shillings a week. It's not to be sneezed at, it would nearly pay the rent.'

'Look. Look, we'll manage. A few more games like last night, even if nothing bigger, and I can spit in the eye of old Kean . . . and your master and mistress.'

'Don't talk like that!' She was indignant now. 'Spittin' in their eye! They've been good to me, better than anybody in me life. I've been lucky. Why, I must be the best-treated servant in this town, or in any other. She's kept me in clothes. And don't forget –' she was now wagging her head at him – 'when things were rough a few years ago with their damned strikes and such, she gave me a loaded basket every week-end. And your own belly would have been empty many a time if I hadn't have brought it. Meat, flour, sugar . . .'

'All right, all right; have you got to be grateful for a little kindness all your life? Anyway, it was nothing to them. The only time that kind of charity has any meaning is when the giver has to do without themselves. She likely throws as much in the midden every week.'

'We haven't got a midden, as you call it.'

'You know what I mean.'

Both their voices were lowering now and in a broken tone she replied, 'No, I don't know what you mean. There's things about you I don't understand, never have.'

He didn't move towards her but turned his head on his shoulder and looked sideways at her for some seconds before saying, 'You said you loved me.'

'Aye, aye, I did, but you can love somebody and not understand them. I might as well tell you I don't understand how you're always taken up so much with cards. It's a mania with you, and I shouldn't be surprised that when we're married you'll be like the rest of them; the others go out every night to the pubs but you'll go out to your gamin'.'

'I'll only go gamin' when I want money to get you things.'

'That'll be your excuse, you'll go gamin' because you can't stop gamin', it's like something in your blood. Even as far back as when we went gathering rose hips you wanted to bet on how many you could hold in your fist.'

They were staring at each other now, and he said, 'You don't want to come here then?'

'Aw yes, yes. Aw Rory.' She went swiftly towards him and leant against him. Then after a moment she muttered, 'I want to be where you are, but

... but at the same time I feel I owe them something. You don't see them as I do. But ... but don't worry, I'll tell her.'

He looked at her softly now as he said, 'It wouldn't work. And anyway I want me wife to meself, I don't want her to be like the scum, gutting fish, or going tatie pickin' to make ends meet. I want to take care of you, I want a home of me own, with bairns and me wife at the fireside.'

She nodded at him, saying, 'You're right, Rory, you're right,' while at the same time the disconcerting mental picture of Kathleen Leary flashed across the screen of her mind. Mrs Leary had borne sixteen children and she was worn out, tired and worn out, and she knew that Rory was the kind of man who'd give her sixteen children if he could. Well, that was life, wasn't it? Yes, but she wasn't sure if she was going to like that kind of life. She drew herself gently from him now and made for the trap door, saying, 'I'll have to get started on some sewing, I haven't got all that much in me chest.'

As he took her hand to help her down on to the first step she looked up at him and said, 'The mistress is goin' to give me me bed linen. I didn't tell you, did I?'

'No.'

'Well, she is. And that'll be something, won't it?'

'Aye, that'll be something.'

As he looked down into her face he stopped himself from adding, 'She can keep her bloody bed linen, I'll make enough afore long to smother you in bed linen.'

# Chapter Four

Rory didn't make enough money in a very short time to smother Janie in bed linen. By the third week of the New Year he had managed to acquire only a further eight pounds and this after four Saturday nights' sittings. And the reason wasn't because of his bad play or ill luck, it was because he was playing against fiddlers, cheats, a small gang who worked together and stood by each other like the close-knit members of a family.

Well, he was finished with the Corstorphine Town lot, and he had told little Joe either he got him into a good school or he himself would do a little investigating into No. 3 Plynlimmon Way. He could have told him he had already done some investigating and that the occupier, a Mr Nickle, was a shipowner. Even if not in an ostentatious way, nevertheless he was big enough to be a member of the shipowners' association, known as the Coal Trade Committee, which had its club and meeting room in a house on the Lawe. Moreover, he was understood to have shares in a number of businesses in the town, including those which dealt not only with the victualling of ships with bread and beef but also in ships' chandlery. And then there was the tallow factory, and many other smaller businesses. In his favour it could be said that he subscribed generously to such causes as distressed seamen

and their families. And at times there were many of these; the bars along
the waterfront were not always full, nor the long dance rooms attached to
them in which the sailors jigged with the women they picked up.

Mr Nickle had also been a strong advocate for better sewerage, especially
since the outbreak of cholera in '66, and the smallpox outbreak in 1870. He
had helped, too, to bring about the new Scavenging Department under the
Borough Engineer. Before this the removal of the filth of the town had been
left to contractors.

Oh, Mr Nickle was a good man, Rory wasn't saying a thing against him,
but Mr Nickle had a failing which was looked at askance by the temperance
societies and the respectable members of the community.

And although Rory himself thought none the less of Mr Nickle, for if the
crowned heads could gamble . . . and it was well known that Bertie, the
Prince of Wales, was a lad at the game, why not Mr Nickle, and why not
Rory Connor, or any working man for that matter? But it was the same
injustice here, one law for the rich, another for the poor. Yet these sentiments
did not deter him from harassing, or even threatening little Joe, nor did
little Joe see any injustice in Mr Connor's treatment of him. He had a
rough-hewn philosophy: there were gents of all grades, there were the high
gents, middle gents, and the lower gents. Mr Connor was of the lower gents,
but his money was as good as anybody else's and often he was more generous
than the middle gents. The real toffs were open handed, and the waterfront
gamblers were free with their money when they had it, but the middle gents
were mean, and although Mr Nickle was prominent in the town and lived
in one of the best ends he was, to little Joe, a middle gent, in the upper
bracket of that section maybe, but still a middle gent. But he was a man who
had power, as had those who worked for him, and they could be nasty at
times.

Little Joe was worried for Mr Connor, but apparently Mr Connor wasn't
worried for himself. In a way Joe admired a fellow like Mr Connor; he
admired his pluck because it was something he hadn't much of himself.

So it was that little Joe spoke to Mr Nickle's man. Mr Nickle's man was
a kind of valet-cum-butler-cum-doorman, and his wife was Mr Nickle's
housekeeper, and his two daughters were Mr Nickle's parlour-maid and
housemaid respectively. Altogether it was another close-knit family. There
was no Mrs Nickle, she had died some years previously.

Little Joe did not lie about Mr Connor's position, that is not exactly.
What he said was, he was a gent in the property business. Also, that he
played a good hand and was very discreet. He had known him for some
years and had set him on in schools along the waterfront, and he had added
that, as he understood that two of Mr Nickle's friends had passed away
recently, he had stressed the word friends, he wondered if Mr Nickle was
looking for a little new blood. One thing he told Mr Nickle's man he could
assure his master of, and that was Mr Connor was no sponger.

Mr Nickle's man said he would see what could be done. What he meant
was he would look into Mr Connor's mode of business. He did.

When next little Joe met Rory all he could say was, 'I've got you set-in
for a game in a place in Ocean Road, just near the Workhouse.'

'Do you think you'll make it the night, Rory?' Jimmy asked under his
breath as he stood near the door watching Rory pull on his overcoat.

'I'll have a damned good try, I can't say better. It's a new place; I'll have to see how the land lies, won't I?'

'You'll find yourself lying under the land if you're not careful.'

Rory turned his dark gaze on to Lizzie where she sat at one side of a long mat frame jabbing a steel progger into the stretched hessian. He watched her thrust in a clipping of rag, pull it tightly down from underneath with her left hand, then jab the progger in again before he said, 'You'd put the kibosh on God, you would.'

Ruth looked up from where she was sitting at the other side of the frame. In the lamplight her face appeared delicate and sad, and she shook her head at him, it was a gentle movement, before she said, 'Just take care of yourself that's all.'

'I've always had to, haven't I?'

'Aw, there speaks the big fellow who brought himself up. Suckled yourself from your own breast you did.'

Rory now grabbed his hard hat which Jimmy was holding towards him, then wrenching open the door, he went out.

It was a fine night. The air was sharp, the black sky was high and star-filled. He could even make out the gate because of their brightness, and also with the help of the light from the Learys' window. They never drew their blinds, the Learys.

He picked his way carefully down the narrow lane so that he shouldn't splash his boots. He had also taken the precaution of bringing a piece of rag with him in order to wipe them before he should enter this new place because the houses in King Street and down Ocean Road were mostly decent places.

The rage that Lizzie always managed to evoke in him had subsided by the time he reached Leam Lane and entered the docks. And he decided that if there was a cab about he'd take a lift. But then it wasn't very likely there'd be one around the docks, unless it was an empty one coming back from some place.

He didn't find a cab, so he had to walk all the way down to Ocean Road, a good couple of miles.

Although the streets were full of people and the roads still packed with traffic, but mostly flat carts, drays and barrows now, he kept to the main thoroughfare because the bairns seemed to go mad on a Saturday night up the side streets, and in some parts lower down in the town one of their Saturday night games was to see which of them could knock your hat off with a handful of clarts. The devil's own imps some of them were. Once he would have laughed at their antics, but not since the time he'd had a dead kitten slapped across his face.

The market place was like a beehive; the stalls illuminated with naphtha flares held every description of food, household goods, and clothing; the latter mostly second, third and fourth hand. The smells were mixed and pungent, and mostly strong, especially those emanating from the fish and meat stalls.

In King Street the gas lamps were ablaze. People stood under them in groups, while others gazed into the shop windows. Saturday night was a popular night for window-gazing and there was no hurry to buy even if you wanted to; the supplies never ran out and most of the shops were open until ten o'clock, some later.

He stopped within a few yards of his destination. He had come down here last night to make sure of the number. It was a corner house, not all that prosperous looking but not seedy. He stooped and rubbed his boots vigorously with the rag, then threw it into the gutter, after which he straightened his coat, tilted his hard hat slightly to the side, pulled at the false starched cuffs that were pinned to the ends of his blue-striped flannelette shirt sleeves, then, following little Joe's directions, he went round the corner, down some area steps, and knocked on the door.

He was surprised when it was opened by a maid, a maid of all work by the look of her, but nevertheless a maid.

'Aye?' She peered up at him in the fluttering light from a naked gas jet attached to a bracket sticking out from the wall opposite the door, and in answer he said what Joe had told him to say. 'Me name's Connor. Little Joe sent me.'

'Oh aye. Come in.'

He followed her into a room which by its appearance was a kitchen and, after closing the door, she said, 'Stay a minute'; then left him. A few minutes later she returned, accompanied by a man. He was a middle-aged half-caste, an Arab one, he surmised. It was his hair and his nostrils which indicated his origin. He looked Rory up and down, then said in a thick Geordie accent that was at variance with his appearance, 'Little Joe said you wanted a set-in. That right?'

'That's right.'

'You've got the ready?'

'Enough.'

'Show us.'

Rory stared back into the dull eyes; then slowly he lifted up the tail of his coat, put his hand in his inside pocket and brought out a handful of coins, among which were a number of sovereigns and half-sovereigns. Without speaking he thrust his hand almost into the other man's chest.

The man looked down on it, nodded and said briefly 'Aye.' Then turning about, he said, 'Come on.'

As they passed from the kitchen into the narrow passage the man said over his shoulder, 'You'll be expected to stand your turn with the cans. Little Joe tell you?'

Little Joe hadn't told him but he said, 'I'll stand me turn.'

The man now led the way into another room, and Rory saw at once that it was used as a storage place for some commodity that was packed in wooden boxes. A number of such were arrayed along one wall. The only window in the place was boarded up. There was an old-fashioned stove at one side of the room packed high with blazing coals, and the room was lit by two bracket gas lamps. There were six men in the room besides Rory's companion and himself; four of them were in a game at the table, the other two were looking on. The players didn't look up but the two spectators turned towards Rory and the half-caste with a jerk of his head said, 'This's who I was tellin' you about. Connor –' he turned to Rory – 'What's your first name?'

'Rory.'

'What!'

'Ror-ry.'

'Funny name. Haven't heard that afore.'

The two spectators at the table nodded towards Rory and he nodded back at them. Then the man with arm outstretched named the players one after the other for Rory's benefit.

Rory didn't take much heed to the names until the word Pittie was repeated twice. Dan Pittie and Sam Pittie. The two brothers almost simultaneously glanced up at him, nodded, then turned their attention to the game again.

Rory, standing awkwardly to the side of the fireplace, looked from one to the other of the men, then brought his attention back to the two Pitties. They looked like twins. They were bullet-headed men, heavy-shouldered but short. These must be the fellows, together with a third one, whom Jimmy said had started the keel business from nothing. They looked a tough pair, different from their partners at the table, who didn't look river-front types; the elder of the two could have been Mr Kean; he wasn't unlike him, and was dressed in much the same fashion.

Well, he had certainly moved up one from Corstorphine Town, because, for a start, they were playing Twenty-Ones, but as yet he didn't know whether he liked the promotion or not; he certainly didn't like the half-caste. But he wasn't here to like or dislike any of them, he was here to double the money in his pocket and then see that he got safely outside with it. On the last thought he looked from the half-caste to the Pittie brothers again and thought it would take him to keep his wits about him. Aye . . . aye, it would that.

# Chapter Five

'You're tellin' me she's in the family way?'

'Don't put it like that, man.'

'How do you expect me to put it? You bloody fool you, how did you manage it? Where? On the ferry or in the train? . . . All right, all right.' He thrust John George's raised arm aside. 'But I mean just what I say, for you've seen her for an hour or so a week, so you've told me, when you've taken her around Newcastle making a tour of ancient buildings. From the Central Station into Jesmond Dene, there doesn't seem to be one you've missed, so that's why I asked you . . . Aw, man . . .'

They were standing on a piece of open land. A building was being erected to one side of it while at the other old houses were being knocked down. There was a thin drizzle of rain falling, the whole scene was dismal and it matched John George's dejected appearance. His thin shoulders were hunched, his head hung down, his gaze was directed towards the leather bag in his hand but without seeing it. He mumbled now, 'It's all right. Don't worry, I'll manage. I'm sorry I asked you; you'll want everything you can lay hands on to get the yard, I know.'

'It isn't that. You can have the two pounds, but what good's that going to do you in this fix, I ask you. It's a drop in the ocean and what'll happen when she tells her folks?'

John George raised his eyes and looked up into the grey sky. 'God! . . . I just don't know. He'll be for murdering her. He's an awful man from what I can gather. I want to get her out of there afore he finds out.'

'How far is she?'

'Over . . . over three months.'

'Well, it won't be long then will it afore he twigs something?'

Rory shook his head, then put his hand into his back pocket, pulled out a small bag and extracted from it two sovereigns, and as he did so his teeth ground tightly together. This was putting him in a fix, he'd had just five pounds left to make a start the night, and it could be a big night, now he was left with only three.

He hadn't won anything that first Saturday night down in the cellar but he hadn't lost either, he had broken even. And the following week he had just managed to clear three pounds ten; the week after he was nine pounds up at one o'clock in the morning, but by the time he left it had been reduced to four pounds, and even then they hadn't liked it. No, none of them had liked it, the Pittie brothers least of all.

Last week when he had cleared six he said he was calling it a day and, aiming to be jocular, had added, and a night. It was the elder of the Pittie brothers who had looked at him and said, 'No, not yet, lad.' But he had risen to his feet, gathered his winnings up and stared back at the other man as he replied, grimly, 'Aye, right now, lad. Nobody's going to tell me when I come or go. I'll be along next week and you can have your own back then, but I'm off now.'

There had followed an odd silence in the room, it was a kind of rustling silence as one man after the other at the table moved in his seat. 'So long,' he had said, and not until he was up the steps and into the street did he breathe freely. For a moment he had thought they were going to do him. He had decided then that that was the last time he would go there.

Three times this week he had tried to find little Joe but with no success. He was keeping out of his way apparently, so there was nothing for it if he wanted a game but to show up in the cellar again the night.

He never went with less than five pounds on him and he'd had a job to scrape that up today because during the week he had, by putting twelve pounds ten down, cleared half the cost of the boat yard, and signed an agreement that the other seventeen pounds ten was to be paid within six weeks, and he knew, his luck holding out and as long as he didn't get into a crooked game, he would clear that. One thing about them in the cellar, they played a straight game. Anyway, they had so far.

But if he went in with only three and lost that in a run, well then, the sparks would fly. He'd have to put his thinking cap on. Oh, this bloody fool of a fellow.

As he handed the two sovereigns to John George and received his muttered thanks he asked himself where he could lay his hands on a couple of quid. It was no good asking any of them back in the house. His dad usually blew half his wages before he got home; by the time he had cleared the slate for the drinks he had run up during the week Ruth was lucky if there was ten shillings left on the mantelpiece for her. There was Janie; she had a bit saved but he doubted if it would be as much as two pounds. Anyway, he wouldn't be able to see her until the morrow and that would be too late. Oh, he'd like to take his hand and knock some damn sense into John George Armstrong.

They were walking on now, cutting through the side streets towards the market and the office, and they didn't exchange a word. When they reached the office door they cast a glance at each other out of habit as if to say, Now for it once again, but when the door didn't move under Rory's push he shook it, then, looking at John George, said, 'That's funny.'

'Use your key. Aw, here's mine.'

John George pushed the key into the lock and they went into the office and looked about them. The door to the far room was closed but on the front of the first desk was pinned a notice and they both bent down and read it. There was no heading, it just said, 'Been called away, my father has died. Lock up takings. My daughter will collect on Monday.' There was no signature.

They straightened up and looked at each other; then Rory jerked his head as he said, 'Well, this's one blessin' in disguise, for I've had the worst morning in years. He'd have gone through the roof.'

'Funny that,' John George smiled weakly; 'my takings are up the day, over four pounds. About fifteen of them paid something off the back and there wasn't one closed door.'

'That's a record.'

'Aye.' John George now went towards the inner office, saying, 'I hope he hasn't forgot to leave the key for the box.'

Standing behind Mr Kean's desk and, having opened the top drawer on the right-hand side, John George put his hand into the back of it and withdrew a key; then going to an iron box safe that was screwed down on to a bench table in the corner of the room he unlocked it. He now took out the money from his bag, put the sovereigns into piles of five and placed them in a neat row on the top shelf with the smaller change in front of them, and after placing his book to the side of the compartment he stepped back and let Rory put his takings on the bottom shelf.

As John George locked the door he remarked, 'One day he'll get a proper safe.'

'It would be a waste of money, it's never in there long enough for anybody to get at it.'

'It'll lie in there over the week-end, and has done afore.'

'Well, that's his look-out. Come on.'

John George now replaced the key in the back of the drawer; then they both left, locking the outer door behind them.

As they walked together towards Laygate, Rory said stiffly, 'What you going to do about this other business, have you got anything in mind?'

'Aye. Aye, I have. I'm going to ask her the day. I'm going to ask her to just walk out and come to our place. She can stay hidden up there until we can get married in the registry office.'

'Registry office?'

'Aye, registry office. It's just as bindin' as any place else.'

'It isn't the same.'

'Well, it'll have to do for us.'

'Aw, man.' Rory shook his head slowly. 'You let people walk over you; you're so bloomin' soft.'

'I'm as God made me, we can't help being what we are.'

'You can help being a bloody fool, you're not a bairn.'

'Well, what do you expect me to do, leave her?'

'You needn't shout unless you want the whole street to know.'

They walked on in silence until simultaneously they both stopped at the place where their roads divided.

'See you Monday then.' Rory's tone was kindly now and John George, looking at him, said, 'Aye, see you Monday. And thanks Rory. I'll pay you back, I promise I'll pay you back.'

'I'm not afraid of that, you always have.'

'Aw . . . I wish, I wish I was like you, Rory. You're right, I'm too soft to clag holes with, no gumption. I can never say no.'

It was on the tip of Rory's tongue to come back with the retort, 'And neither can your lass apparently.' Janie had said no, and she'd kept both feet on the ground when she said it an' all. But what he said and generously was, 'People like you for what you are. You're a good bloke.' He made a small movement with his fist. 'I'll tell you something. You're better liked than me, especially up in our house. It's John George this, an' John George that.'

'Aw, go on, man, stop pulling me leg. But it's nice of you to say it nevertheless, and as I said –' he patted his pocket – 'I won't forget this.'

'That's all right, man. So long and good luck.'

'So long . . . so long, Rory. And thanks. Thanks again.'

They went their ways, neither dreaming he would never see the other again.

When Rory went into the cellar that same evening he had eight pounds in his pocket.

The Pittie brothers were already at the table, but the two men partnering them were unknown to Rory until he realized that one of them was the third Pittie brother. He was a man almost a head taller than the other two. His nose was flattened and looked boneless. This was the one who was good with his fists, so he had heard, but by the look of him he wasn't all that good for his face looked like a battered pluck. The fourth man looked not much bigger than little Joe and he had a foxy look, but he was well put on. His suit, made of some kind of tweed, looked quite fancy, as did his pearl-buttoned waistcoat. During the course of conversation later in the evening he discovered that he was from across the water in North Shields and was manager of a blacking factory.

Rory kicked his heels for almost an hour before he got set-in at the table, for after the game they spent quite some time drinking beer and eating meat sandwiches. Although he always stood his share in buying the beer he drank little of it and tonight less than usual, for he wanted to keep his wits about him. Some part of him was worried at the presence of the third Pittie brother, it was creating a small niggling fear at the back of his mind.

The big Pittie was dealer. He shuffled the cards in a slow ponderous way until Rory wanted to say, 'Get on with it'; then of a sudden he spoke. 'You aimin' to buy old Kilpatrick's yard I hear?'

Rory was startled, and he must have shown it for the big fellow jerked his chin upwards as he said, 'Oh, you can't keep nowt secret on the waterfront; there's more than scum comes in on the tide . . . Your young 'un works at Baker's, don't he?'

'Aye. Yes, he works at Baker's.'

'What does he expect to do at Kilpatrick's, build a bloody battleship?'

The three brothers now let out a combined bellow and the thin man in the fancy waistcoat laughed with them, although it was evident he didn't know what all this was about.

Rory's lower jaw moved from one side to the other before he said, 'He's going to build scullers and small keel-like boats.'

'Keel-like boats. Huh!' It was the youngest of the Pittie's speaking now. 'Where's he gona put them?'

'Where they belong, on the river.'

'By God! he'll be lucky, you can hardly get a plank atween the boats now. And what's he gona do with the keel-like boats when he gets them on the water, eh?'

'Same as you, work them, or sell them.'

As the three pairs of eyes became fixed on him he told himself to go steady, these fellows meant business, they weren't here the night only for the game. He kept his gaze steady on them as he said, 'Well now, since you know what I have in mind, are we going to play?'

The big fellow returned to his shuffling. Then he dealt. When Rory picked up his cards he thought, Bad start, good finish.

And so it would seem. He lost the first game, won the next two, lost the next one, then won three in a row. By one o'clock in the morning he had a small pile of sovereigns and a larger pile of silver to his hand. Between then and two o'clock the pile went down a little before starting again to increase steadily.

At the end of a game when the man in the fancy waistcoat had no money in front of him he said he must be going. He had, he said, lost enough for one night and what was more he'd have to find somebody to scull him across the river. And at this time of the morning whoever he found would certainly make him stump up, and what he had left, he thought, was just about enough to carry him over.

When Rory, too, also voiced that he must be on his way there were loud, even angry cries from the table.

'Aw, no, no, lad,' said the big fellow. 'Fair's fair. You've taken all our bloody money so give us a chance to get a bit of it back, eh? We've to get across the river an' all.' There was laughter at this, but it was without mirth.

And so another game started, and long before it finished the uneasy sickly feeling in the pit of Rory's stomach had grown into what he hated to admit was actual fear.

Another hour passed and it was towards the end of a game when things were once again going in Rory's favour that the youngest Pittie brother began speaking of Jimmy as if he were continuing the conversation that had centred around him earlier in the play.

'Your young 'un's bandy,' he said. 'Bandy Connor they call him along the front . . . Saw him from the boat t'other day. Drive a horse and cart through his legs you could.' He now punched his brother in the side of the chest and the brother guffawed: 'Aye, his mother must have had him astride a donkey.'

Any reference to the shape of Jimmy's legs had always maddened Rory; he had fought more fights on Jimmy's account than he had on his own. But now, although there was a rage rising in him that for the moment combated his fear, he warned himself to go steady, for they were up to something. They were like three bull terriers out to bait a bull. He was no bull, but they were bull terriers all right.

The stories of their past doings flicked across the surface of his mind and increased his rising apprehension, yet did not subdue his rage, even while the cautionary voice kept saying, 'Careful, careful, let them get on with it. Get yourself outside, let them get on with it.'

When he made no reply to the taunt, one after another, the three brothers laid down their cards and looked at him, and he at them. Then slowly he placed his cards side by side on the table.

The three Pitties and the half-caste stared at his cards and they did not lift their eyes when his hand went out and drew the money from the centre of the table towards him. Not until he pushed his chair back and got to his feet did one of them speak. It was the youngest brother. 'You goin' then?' he said.

'Aye.' Rory moved his head slowly downwards.

'You've had a good night.'

'You all had the same chance.'

'I would argue about that.'

'Would you?'

'I think you had a trick or two up your sleeve.'

'What! Then search me if you've got a mind.'

'Aw, no need for that, I wasn't meanin' the actual cards. But you're a bit of a clever bugger, aren't you?'

'I'm bucked that you think so.' He stood buttoning his coat, and noted that the half-caste was no longer in the room. He picked up his hat from a side table and went towards the door, saying, 'So long then.'

The brothers didn't speak. When he pulled at the door it didn't open. He tugged at it twice before turning and looking back into the room. The three men had risen from the table. He stared at them and now the fear swept over him like a huge wave and his stomach heaved.

'What you standing there for? Can't you get out?'

The big fellow was approaching him, his arms hanging loosely at his sides. But strangely it wasn't the fellow's arms or his face that Rory looked at, but his feet. He hadn't noticed them before. They were enormous feet encased in thick hob-nailed boots. The boots had the dull sheen of tallow on them with which they had likely been greased.

When the arms sprang up and grabbed at his shoulders Rory struck out, right, then left; right, then left, but his blows were the wild desperate punches used in the back lanes or among the lads in a scrap, as often happened in a work's yard.

He remembered hearing the big fellow laugh just before the great fist struck his jaw and seemed to snap his head from his body.

He was on the floor now and he screamed when the boot caught him in the groin. Then he was on his feet again, somebody holding him while another belted into him, the big fellow. They left it all to the big fellow. He was still struggling to hit out but like a child swatting flies when the blow came under his chin, and once more he was on his back. But this time he knew nothing about it. He didn't feel them going through his pockets, nor when the three of them used their feet on him. He was quite unaware of being hoisted across the big fellow's shoulder and being carried past the half-caste who was standing in the doorway now and up the area steps into the dark side street, then through the back alleyways towards the river.

That he didn't reach the river was due to the appearance of two bulky figures coming through a cut between the warehouses. One was a dark-cloaked priest who had been to a ship to give the last rites to a dying sailor. The man accompanying him was the dead man's friend who was seeing the priest safely back into the town. But to the three brothers their shapes indicated two burly sailors or night-watchmen, and both types could do some dirty fighting on their own, so with a heave they threw the limp body among a tangle of river refuse, broken spars, boxes, and decaying fruit and vegetable, and minutes later the priest and the sailor passed within six feet of it and went on their way.

# Chapter Six

They were all in the kitchen, Bill Waggett, Gran and Janie – Janie still had her outdoor things on; Collum Leary and Kathleen and with them now was their son Pat; Paddy Connor, Ruth, Jimmy; and lastly Lizzie; and it was Lizzie who, looking at young Pat Leary said, 'Talk sense, lad. 'Tis three o'clock on Sunday afternoon an' he left the house round six last night. Who would be playin' cards all that time I ask you?'

'It's true, Lizzie. 'Tis true. I've heard of games goin' on for twenty-four hours. They win an' lose, win an' lose.'

'He would never stay all this time; something's happened him.'

Nobody contradicted her now but they all turned and looked at Janie who, with fingers pressed tightly against her lower lip, said, 'You should have gone down and told the polis.'

'What should we tell the polis, lass?' Paddy Connor now asked her quietly. 'That me son was out gamin' last night an' hasn't come back? All right, they'll say, let's find him an' push him along the line. Where was he gamin'? I don't know, says I. Lass –' his voice was still gentle – 'we've thought of everything.'

Grannie Waggett, who was the only one seated, now turned in her chair and, her pale eyes sweeping the company, she said, 'If you want my advice the lot of you, you'll stop frashin'. It's as Pat there says, he's got into a game. He's gamin' mad, always has been. It affects some folks like that, like a poison in their blood. Some blokes take to drink, others to whorin' . . .'

'Gran!'

The old woman flashed a look on Janie. 'Whorin' I said, an' whorin' I mean, an' for my part I'd rather have either of them than one that takes to gamin', 'cos with them you're sure of a roof over your head some time, but not with a gamer for he'd gamble the shift off your back an' you inside it. There was this gentleman who used to come to the house when I was in service in Newcastle. Real gentleman, carriage an' pair, fancy wife, mansion, he had. One day he had everything, next day nowt. I tell you, me girl –' she turned and stabbed her finger towards Janie – 'you want to put your foot down right from the start or get used to livin' in the open, for I tell you, you won't be sure of a roof . . .'

'Be quiet, Ma.'

Grannie Waggett turned on her son. 'Don't you tell me to be quiet.'

'Be quiet all of you, please.' It was Ruth speaking gently. 'What I think should be done is somebody should go down to the Infirmary, the new Infirmary. If anything had happened to him they'd take him there.'

'And make a fool of themselves askin'.'

Ruth now looked at her husband. 'I don't mind lookin' a fool, I'll go.'

'No, Ma.' Jimmy who had not opened his mouth so far went towards the bottom of the ladder now, saying, 'I'll go, I'll change me things an' I'll go.'

As he mounted upwards Collum said, 'It's odd it is that he made no mention of whereabouts he'd be, now isn't it? But then again perhaps it isn't; if he'd got set on in a big school the least said the soonest mended, for you can't be too careful: the polis just need a whisper and it's up their nose it goes like a sniff to a bloodhound.'

Up in the loft Jimmy went straight to a long wooden box and took out his Sunday coat and trousers, but he didn't get into them immediately. For quite some minutes he stood with them gripped tight against his chest, his eyes closed, his lips moving as he muttered to himself, 'Oh dear God! don't let nowt happen our Rory. Please, please, don't let nowt happen him.'

As he came down the ladder again, Janie said, 'I'll go with you.' But he shook his head at her. 'No, no, I'll be better on me own. Well, what I mean is, I can get around the waterfront. If he's not in the hospital I can get around and ask.'

'Be careful.'

He turned to Lizzie and nodded, saying, 'Aye; aye,' and as he went to let himself out, Ruth followed him and, opening the door for him, said quietly. 'Don't stay late, not in the dark, not around there.'

'All right, Ma.' He nodded at her, then went out.

He ran most of the way into Shields and wasn't out of breath. He took no notice of the urchins who shouted after him:

> 'Bow-Legged Billy,
> Bandy-randy,
> One eye up the chimney, the other in the pot,
> Poor little sod, yer ma's given you the lot.'

At one time the rhyme used to hurt him but he was inured to it now. Nothing could hurt him, he told himself, except that something should happen to their Rory. He'd want to peg out himself if anything happened to their Rory. What was more, if it had already happened he would be to blame because if he hadn't yarped on about the boatyard Rory wouldn't have gone gambling . . . But, aye, he would, he would always gamble. But not at this new place, this place he had gone to these past few Saturdays. He hadn't let on where it was. He had asked him, but the laughing answer had been, 'Ask no questions and you'll get no lies . . .'

The porter at the Infirmary said, 'No, lad, nobody with the name of

Connor's been brought in the day. Then they don't bring people in on a Sunday less it's accidents like.'

'Well, I was thinkin' it could've been an accident.'

'Well, there's no Connor here, lad. Neither mister nor missis.'

'Ta . . . thanks.' He didn't know whether he was disappointed or relieved.

He was going down the gravel drive when the porter's voice hailed him, saying, 'Just a minute! There's a fella, but I hope it isn't the one you're lookin' for. There was a bloke brought in round dinner-time, no name on him, nothing. He was found on the waterfront. Not a sailor. His clothes were respectable, what was left of them, but I expect by now he's kicked the bucket.'

Jimmy walked slowly back towards the man, saying as he went, 'What's he like?'

'Oh, lad, his own mother wouldn't be able to recognize him, he's been bashed about worse than anybody I've seen afore.'

'Had he brown hair, thick, wavy . . .?'

'Whatever colour this fellow's hair once was, lad, I couldn't say, but the day it was dark red, caked with blood.'

Jimmy stood looking up at the man, his mouth slightly agape. Then closing it, the words came dredged through his lips as he said, 'Could . . . could I see him, this . . . this fella?'

'Well. Well, I'll ask the sister. Come on back.'

'Sit there a minute,' he said a moment later, pointing to a polished wooden chair standing against the painted brick wall of the lobby.

Jimmy sat down, glad to get off his legs. He was feeling weak, faint, and frightened, very frightened.

The porter came back and beckoned to him. Then with his hand on Jimmy's shoulder, he pointed and said, 'Go down there, lad, to the end of the corridor, turn left, an' you'll see the sister.'

The sister was tall and thin. She put him in mind of John George. He had to put his head back to look up at her. She said to him, 'You're looking for your brother?'

'Aye, miss.'

'How old is he?'

'Twenty-three, comin' up twenty-four next month.'

'There's a young man in there,' she nodded towards the wall. 'He's in a very bad state, he's been badly beaten. But . . . but you may be able to recognize him, if he is your brother.'

She turned away, and Jimmy followed her towards the figure lying on the bed. It was very still. The head was swathed in bandages, the face completely distorted with bruises. He found himself gasping for breath. He had once seen a man taken from the river. He was all blue, bluey black and bloated. He had been dead for days, they said. This man on the bed could be dead an' all. He didn't know if it was their Rory. The sister was whispering something in his ear and he turned and looked dazedly at her. Then he whispered back as he pointed to his thumb. 'He had a wart atween his finger an' thumb towards the front. He'd always had it.'

The sister gently picked up the limp hand from the counterpane and turned it over; then she looked at Jimmy as he stared down at the flat hard wart that Rory had for years picked and scraped at in an effort to rid himself of it.

The sister drew him backwards away from the bed, and when they were in the corridor again she still kept her hand on his shoulder as she endeavoured to soothe him, saying, 'There now. There now.'

The tears were choking him. Although they were flooding down his face they were packing his gullet, he couldn't breathe.

She took him into a room and said, 'Where do you live?'

When he was unable to answer she asked, 'In the town?'

He shook his head.

'Tyne Dock?'

He brought out between gasps, 'Up . . . up Simonside.'

'Oh, that's a long way.'

He dried his face now on his sleeve, then took a clean rag from his pocket and blew his nose. After some minutes he looked up at her and said, 'I'll bring me ma and da,' then added, 'Will he . . .?'

She said kindly, 'I don't know, he's very low. He could see the morning, but then again I don't know.'

He nodded at her, then walked slowly from the room. But in the corridor he turned and looked back at her and said, 'Ta,' and she smiled faintly at him.

He didn't run immediately, he walked from the gates to where the road turned into Westoe and as he looked down it he thought of Janie. Poor Janie. Poor all of them. In their different ways they'd all miss him, miss him like hell. He had been different from them, different from his da and Mr Waggett and Mr Leary, and all the women had looked up to him. He had become something, a rent collector. There were very few people from their walk of life who rose to rent collectors . . . And himself? He stopped in the street. If Rory went then his own life would come to an end. Not even boats would bring him any comfort. The feeling he had for Rory was not just admiration because he had got on in the world, it was love, because he was the only being he'd really be able to love. He had another love, but that was in a secret dream. He'd never have a lass of his own for no lass would look the side he was on; but that hadn't mattered so very much because there'd always be Rory.

As if he were starting a race he sprang forward and ran. He ran until he thought his heart would burst, for it was uphill all the way after he left the docks, and when finally he staggered into the kitchen he dropped on to the floor and held his side against the painful stitch before he could speak to them all hanging over him. And when he did speak it was to Janie he addressed himself.

They walked quickly, almost on the point of a run, all the way back with him into Shields in the dark, Paddy, Ruth, Lizzie and Janie, and for hours they all waited in the little side room. It was against the rules, but the night sister had taken pity on them and brought them in out of the cold.

Janie left the Infirmary around eleven o'clock to slip back to her place, and the look on her face checked the upbraiding from the cook and her master and mistress. The master and mistress were deeply concerned over the incident and gave her leave to visit the hospital first thing in the morning. Fortunately it was not more than five minutes' walk from the house, they said, so she was to go upstairs and rest, as she would need all her strength to face the future.

It was a term that ordinary people used when a man had died and a woman was left to fend for herself and her family with no hope of help but the questionable charity of the Poor House. It was as if Rory were already gone. Well, the family expected he would go before dawn, didn't they? Men in his condition usually went out about three in the morning.

She asked politely if she could go back now because she'd like to be with him when he went.

Her master and mistress held a short conference in the drawing-room and then they gave her their permission.

Rory passed the critical time of 3 a.m. He was still breathing at five o'clock in the morning, but the night sister informed them now that he might remain in a coma for days and that they should go home.

Ruth and Paddy nodded at her in obedience because they both knew that Paddy must get to work; and Ruth said to Janie, 'You must get back an' all, lass. Don't take too much advantage an' they'll let you out again.' And Janie, numb with agony, could only nod to this sound advice. But Lizzie refused to budge. Here she was, she said, and here she'd remain until she knew he was either going or staying. And Jimmy said he'd stay too, until it was time to go to work.

So Ruth and Paddy nodded a silent good-bye to Janie when their ways parted at Westoe and walked without exchanging a word through the dark streets that were already filling with men on their way to the shipyards, the docks, and farther into Jarrow to Palmer's. But when they had passed through the arches and came to where the road divided Paddy said, 'I'd better go straight on up else I'll be late.'

'You've got your good suit on.'

'Bugger me good suit!'

Ruth peered at him through the darkness before she said quietly, 'If he goes things'll be tight, think on that. There'll be less for beer and nowt for clothes. I depended on him.'

'Aw, woman!' He swung away from her now and made for the Simonside road, saying over his shoulder, 'Then stop skittering behind, put a move on. If they dock me half an hour it'll be less on the mantelpiece, so think on.'

Think on, he said. She had thought on for years. She had thought on the pain of life that you managed to work off during the daytime, but which pressed on you in the night and settled around your heart, causing wind, the relief of which brought no ease. She had loved him in the early years, but after Rory was born she hated him. Yet her hate hadn't spread over Lizzie. Strange that, she had always liked Lizzie. Still did. She couldn't imagine life without Lizzie. When Nellie was born a little wonder had entered her life, yet she had actually fought him against the conception. Every time he had tried to touch her she had fought him. Sometimes she conquered because he became weary of the struggle, but at other times after a hard day at the wash tub and baking and cleaning, because she'd had it all to do herself then as Lizzie went out daily doing for the people down the bank, she would surrender from sheer exhaustion. When Jimmy came life ran smoothly for a time. She felt happy she had a son; that he should have rickets didn't matter so much. As he grew his legs would straighten. So she had thought at first. Then came the day when hate rose in her for Paddy again. It was when he tried once more to take Lizzie. She had come in from next door and found them struggling there in the open on the mat and the bairns locked in the scullery. There had been no need for Lizzie to protest 'I want none of him, Ruth, I want none of him,' the scratches on his face bore out her statement.

From then on the dess bed in the kitchen became a battleground. Finally he brought the priest to her; and she was forced to do her duty in the fear of everlasting hell and damnation.

She had never asked herself why Lizzie had stayed with them all these years because where would a single woman go with a bairn? Anyway, it was his responsibility to see that she was taken care of after giving her a child.

And now that child was lying back there battered and on his way to death. What would Lizzie do without him? He had scorned her since the day he learned she was his mother. But it hadn't altered her love for him; the only thing it had done was put an edge to her tongue every time she spoke to him. Funny, but she envied Lizzie. Although she knew she had Rory's affection, she envied her, for she was his mother.


Rory regained consciousness at eight o'clock on the Monday morning. Lizzie was by his side and he looked at her without recognition, and when his lips moved painfully she put her ear down to him and all she could make out was one word, which she repeated a number of times and in an anguished tone. 'Aye. Aye, lad,' she said, 'it is a pity. It is a pity. Indeed it is a pity.'

He would rally, they said, so she must leave the ward but she could come back in the afternoon.

Without protest now she left the hospital. But she didn't go straight home. She found her way to the Catholic church, which she had never been in before; on her yearly visits she patronized the Jarrow one. She waited until the Mass was finished, and then approaching the priest without showing the awe due to his station and infallibility, she told him that her son was dying in the Infirmary and would he see that he got the last rites. The priest asked her where she was from and other particulars. He showed her no sympathy, he didn't like her manner, she was a brusque woman and she did not afford him the reverence that her kind usually bestowed on him, nor did she slip anything into his hand, but she did say that if her son went she would buy a mass for him.

He watched her leave the church without putting a halfpenny in the poor box.

The priest's feelings for Lizzie were amply reciprocated. She told herself she didn't like him, he wasn't a patch on the Jarrow ones. But then she supposed it didn't make much difference who sent you over to the other side as long as there was one of them to see that you were properly prepared for the journey.


It was around half-past one when Lizzie, about to pick up her shawl for the journey back to the hospital, glanced out of the cottage window, then stopped and said, 'Here's John George; he must have heard.'

By the time John George reached the door she had opened it and, looking at his white drawn face, said quietly, 'Come in, lad. Come in.'

He came in. He stood in the middle of the room looking from one to the other; then as he was about to speak Ruth said softly, 'You've heard then, John George?' and he repeated 'Heard?'

'Aye, about Rory.'

'Rory? I . . . I came up to find him.'

'You don't know then?'

He turned to Lizzie. 'Know what, Lizzie? What . . . what's happened him?' He shook his head, then asked again. 'What's happened him?'

'Oh lad!' Lizzie now put her hand to her brow. 'You mean to say you haven't heard? Jimmy was going to tell Mr Kean at break time.'

'Mr Kean?'

'Aye, sit down, lad.' Ruth now put her hand out and pressed John George into a chair, and he looked at her dumbly as he said, 'Mr Kean's not there. Miss Kean, she . . . she came for a while.' He nodded his head slowly now, then asked stiffly, 'Rory. Where is he?'

'He's down in the hospital, John George. He was beaten up, beaten unto death something terrible.'

When John George now slumped forward over the table and dropped his head into his hands both women came close to him and Lizzie murmured, 'Aye, lad, aye, I know how you feel.'

After a while he raised his head and looked from one to the other and said dully, 'He's dead then?'

'No.' Lizzie shook her head from side to side. 'But he's as near to it as makes no matter. It'll be one of God's rare miracles if he ever recovers, an' if he does only He knows what'll be left of him . . . Was Mr Kean asking for him?'

It seemed now that he had difficulty in speaking for he gulped in his throat a number of times before repeating, 'He wasn't there, won't be; won't be back till the night, his father died.'

'Ah, God rest his soul. Aye, you did say he wasn't there. Well, you can tell him when you do see him that it'll be some time afore Rory collects any more rents, that's if ever. It's God's blessin' he hadn't any collection on him when they did him. Whatever they took from him, an' that was every penny, it was his own.'

John George's head was bent again and he now made a groaning sound.

'Will you come in along of me and see him, I'm on me way? It's the Infirmary.'

He rose to his feet, and stared at her, then like someone in a daze, he turned and made for the door.

'Aren't you stayin' for a cup of tea, lad?' It was Ruth speaking now.

He didn't answer her except to make a slight movement with his head, then he went out leaving the door open behind him.

They both stood and watched him go down the path. And when he was out of sight they looked at each other in some amazement, and Lizzie said, 'It's broken him; he thought the world of Rory. It's made him look like death itself.'

'Get your shawl on and go after him.' Ruth pointed to where the shawl was lying across the foot of Lizzie's bed which was inset in the alcove. But Lizzie shook her head, saying, 'He wants no company, something about him said he wants no company.' She moved her head slowly now as she stared back at Ruth. 'God knows, this has hit everyone of us but in some strange way him most of all. It's strange, it is that. Did you see his face, the look on it? It was as if he himself was facing death. Me heart's breakin' at this minute over me own, yet there's room for sorrow in me for the lad. Poor John George.'

# Chapter Seven

Janie sat by the bed and gazed down on the face that she had always thought was the best looking of any lad in the town and she wondered if it would ever go back into shape again. Oh, she hoped it would, for, being Rory, he'd hate to be marked for life. And she couldn't stand the thought either of him being disfigured; but as long as he was alive that's all that really mattered. And he was alive, and fighting to keep alive.

He had opened his eyes once and looked at her and she thought that he had recognized her, but she wasn't sure. His lips were moving continuously but all he kept saying was 'Pity. Pity.' There must be something on his mind that was making him think it was a pity, and she thought too that it was the greatest of pities that he had ever gone gaming because she had no doubt but that he had been followed from wherever he had played, and been robbed, and by somebody in the know; likely one of them he had played against. But as Jimmy said last night, they mustn't breathe a word of it because if it got to Mr Kean's ears that would be the finish of his rent collecting. You couldn't be a gambler and a rent collector . . . And then there was this business of John George.

Eeh! she was glad to the heart that Rory didn't know about that because that would really have been the finish of him. Of all the fools on this earth John George was the biggest. She couldn't really believe it, and if the master hadn't told her himself she wouldn't have, but the master's partner dealt with Mr Kean's business. Odd, but she hadn't known that afore. But still, she asked herself, why should she? Anyway, he had pricked his ears up when he heard that one of Mr Kean's men had swindled him because, as he said, he knew that her intended worked for Mr Kean.

Rory's head moved slightly on the pillow, his eyelids flickered, and she bent over him and said softly, 'Rory, it's Janie. How you feelin', Rory?'

'Pity,' he said. 'Pity.'

The tears welled up in her eyes and rolled down her cheeks and she whispered, 'Oh, Rory, come back from wherever you are.' Then she said softly, 'I've got to go now, I've got to get back, but I'll come again the night. The mistress says I can take an hour off in the afternoon and evening. It's good of her.' She spoke as if he could understand her, then she stood up, whispering softly, 'Bye-bye, dear. Bye-bye.'

Five minutes later she was turning off the main road and into Westoe when she saw the two dark-clothed figures of Ruth and Lizzie approaching. She ran towards them, and immediately they asked together, 'You've been?'

'Aye, yes.'

'Any change?'

She looked at Lizzie and shook her head, then said, 'He opened his eyes but . . . but I don't think he knew me, he just keeps sayin' that word, pity, pity . . . Have . . . have you heard about John George?'

'John George? Was he in?'

'No, Mrs Connor –' she always gave Ruth her full title – he's . . . he's been taken.'

'Taken?' They both screwed up their faces while they looked back at her.

'Yes, for stealin'.'

'John George!' Again they spoke simultaneously.

She nodded her head slowly. 'Five pounds ten, and . . . and he's been at it for some time.'

They were speechless. Their mouths fell into a gape as they listened. 'Mr Kean was away and Miss Kean came early on, earlier than usual to collect the money. She was on her way to some place or other an' she just called in on the off-chance. She had her father's key and she opened the box and . . . and there was five pounds ten short from what was in his book. Apparently he had been doin' a fiddle.'

'No! Not John George.' Ruth was holding the brim of her black straw hat tightly in her fist.

'Yes. Aye, I couldn't believe it either. It made me sick, but the master, he heard it all in the office. The solicitors, you know. He . . . he said he was a stupid fellow. I . . . I put a word in for him I did. I said I'd always found him nice, a really nice fella, and he said, "He's been crafty, Janie. He's admitted to using this trick every time he was sure Mr Kean wasn't goin' to collect the Saturday takings." Apparently he would nip something out then put it back on the Monday mornin' early, but this time he was too late. And then he said nobody but a stupid man would admit to doing this in the past, then try to deny that he had taken five pounds ten. He wanted to say it was only ten shillings, and he had that on him to put back . . . He had just been to the pawn. They found the ticket on him.'

'Oh God Almighty! what'll happen next? Rory and now John George, an' all within three days. It isn't possible. But this accounts for his face, the look on his face when he came up yesterday. Eeh! God above.' Lizzie began rocking herself.

'It's this lass that he's caught on to, Lizzie.' Janie nodded slowly. 'Rory said he was barmy about her. He bought her a locket an' chain at Christmas and he takes her by the ferry or train to Newcastle every week, then round the buildings. He's daft about buildings. I never knew that till he told me one night. Then last week he gave her tea in some place. Yes, he did, he took her out to tea. And not in no cheap café neither, a place off Grey Street. An' Rory said Grey Street's classy.'

'Women can be the ruin of a man in more ways than one.' Lizzie's head was bobbing up and down now. 'But no matter, I'm sorry for him, to the very heart of me I'm sorry for him 'cos I liked John George. He had somethin' about him, a gentleness, not like a man usually has.'

Ruth asked quietly, 'Do you know when he'll be tried, Janie?'

'No, but I mean to find out.'

'Somebody should go down and see him, he's got nobody I understand, only those two old 'un's. And you know, it isn't so much laziness with them –' Ruth turned now and shook her head at Lizzie – 'it isn't, Lizzie, it's the rheumatics. And this'll put the finish to them, it'll be the House for them. Dear, dear Lord!' – Ruth never said God – 'You've got to ask why these things happen.'

The three of them stood looking at each other for a moment. Then Janie said, 'I've got to go now, but I'm gettin' out the night an' all. The mistress said I can have an hour in the afternoon and in the evenin's. She's good, isn't she?'

They nodded at her, and Lizzie agreed. 'Aye, she's unusual in that way. Bye-bye then, lass.'

'Bye-bye.' She nodded from one to the other, then again said, 'Bye-bye,' before running across the road and almost into a horse that was pulling a fruit cart, and as Lizzie watched her she said, 'It only needed her to get herself knocked down and that would have been three of them. Everythin' happens in threes, so I wonder what's next?'

# Chapter Eight

Janie had never before been in a court. She sat on the bench nearest the wall. At the far end of the room, right opposite to her, was the magistrate; in front of him were a number of dark-clothed men. They kept moving from one to the other, they all had papers in their hands. At times they would bend over a table and point to the papers. The last prisoner had got a month for begging, and now they were calling out the name: 'John George Armstrong! John George Armstrong!'

As if emerging out of a cellar John George appeared. The box in which he stood came only to his hips, but the upper part of him seemed to have shrunk, his shoulders were stooped, his head hung forward, his face was the colour of clay. One of the dark-suited men began to talk. Janie only half listened to him, for her eyes were riveted on John George, almost willing him to look at her, to let him know there was someone here who was concerned for him. Poor John George! Oh, poor John George!

. . . 'He did on the twenty-fourth day of January steal from his employer, Septimus Kean, Esquire of Birchingham House, Westoe, the sum of five pounds ten shillings . . .'

The next words were lost to Janie as she watched John George close his eyes and shake his head. It was as if he were saying, 'No, no.' Then the man on the floor was mentioning Miss Kean's name . . . 'She pointed out to the accused the discrepancy between his entries in the ledger and the amount of money in the safe.'

Rory had always said they hadn't a safe, not a proper one. She looked towards Miss Kean. She could only see her profile but she gathered that she was thin and would likely be tall when she stood up. She wore a pill-box hat of green velvet perched on the top of her hair. She looked to have a lot of hair, dark, perhaps it was padded. Even the mistress padded her hair at the back, especially when she was going out to some function.

'The accused argued with her that he was only ten shillings short and he had the amount in his pocket, and he had intended to replace it. He asked her to recount the money. This she did. He then admitted to having helped himself on various previous occasions to small sums but said he always replaced them. He insisted that there was only ten shillings missing. He then tried to persuade her to accept the ten shillings and not mention the matter to her father . . . When taken into custody he said . . .'

Oh John George! Why had he been so daft? Why? It was that girl. If she ever met her she'd give her the length of her tongue, she would that, and when Rory came to himself and heard this he'd go mad, he would that. But it would be some time before they could tell Rory anything.

The magistrate was talking now about trusting employers being taken advantage of, about men like the prisoner being made an example of; about some men being nothing more than sneak thieves and that the respectable citizens of this town had to be protected from them.

'Do you plead guilty or not guilty?'

'I . . . I didn't take five pounds, sir.'

'Answer the question. Do you plead guilty or not guilty?'

'I didn't take five . . .' John George's voice trailed away. There was talk between the magistrate and one of the men on the floor, then Janie's mouth opened wide when the magistrate said, 'I sentence you to a total of twelve months. . . .'

She shot to her feet and actually put her hand up to try to attract John George's attention, but he never raised his head.

A few minutes later she stood by the door of the Court House. The tears were running down her face. Her hour was nearly up and she wanted to call in at the hospital. That's where she was supposed to be. She didn't know what she would have done or said if the master had been in the court, but he wasn't there. Oh, John George! Poor John George!

A policeman came through the door and looked at her. He had seen her in the court room, he had seen her lift her hand to the prisoner. He said, not unkindly, 'He got off lightly. I've known him give three years, especially when they've been at it as long as he has. He always lays it on thick when he's dealin' with men who should know better. He had the responsibility of money you know an' he should have known better. Anyway, what's a year?' He smiled down at her, and she said, 'Would . . . could . . . do you ever allow anybody to see them for a minute?'

'Well now. Aye, yes, it's done.' He stared at her, then said quickly, 'Come on. Come this way. Hurry up; they'll be movin' them in next to no time. There's more than a few for Durham the day and he'll be among them I suppose.'

She followed him at a trot and when he came to an abrupt stop she almost bumped into his back. He opened a door and she glimpsed a number of men, definitely prisoners, for the stamp was on their faces, and three uniformed policemen.

Her guide must have been someone in authority, a sergeant or someone like that, she thought, for he nodded to the officers and said 'Armstrong for a minute, I'll be with him.'

'Armstrong!' one of the policemen bawled, and John George turned about and faced the door. And when the policeman thumbed over his shoulder he walked through it and out into the corridor.

The sergeant now looked at him. Then, nodding towards Janie, said, 'Two minutes, and mind, don't try anything. Understand?' He poked his face towards John George, and John George stared dumbly back at him for a moment before turning to Janie.

'Hello, John George.' It was a silly thing to say but she couldn't think of anything else at the moment.

'Hello, Janie.'

'Oh!' Now as the tears poured from her eyes her tongue became loosened and she gabbled, 'I'm so sorry, John George. Why? Why? We're all sorry. We'll come an' see you, we will. There'll be visitin' times. I'll ask.'

'Janie!' His voice sounded calm, then again he said 'Janie!' and she said, 'Yes, John George?'

'Listen. Will you go and see Maggie? She won't know, at least I don't think so, not until she reads the papers. She's . . . she's going to have a bairn, Janie, she'll need somebody.'

She put her hand tightly across her mouth and her eyes widened and she muttered, 'Oh, John George.'

'Time's up. That's enough.'

'Janie! Janie! listen. Believe me; I never took the five pounds. Ten shillings aye, but never the five pounds. You tell that to Rory, will you? Tell that to Rory.'

'Yes, yes, I will, John George. Yes, I will. Good-bye. Good-bye, John George.'

She watched him going back into the room. She couldn't see the policeman now but she inclined her head towards him and said, 'Ta, thanks.'

He walked with her along the stone passage and to the door, and there he said, 'Don't worry. As I said, what's a year? And you can visit him once a month.' Then bending towards her he said, 'What are you to him? I thought you were his wife, but I hope not after what I heard . . . You his sister?'

'No, only . . . only a friend.'

He nodded at her, then said, 'Well, he won't need any friends for the next twelve months, but he will after.'

'Ta-rah,' she said.

'Ta-rah, lass,' he said, and as she walked away he watched her. He was puzzled by her relationship to the prisoner. Just a friend, she had said.

She walked so slowly from the Court House that she hadn't time to call in at the hospital and when she arrived in the kitchen she was crying so much that the cook called the mistress, and the mistress said, 'Oh, I'm sorry, I'm sorry, Janie,' and she answered her through her tears, 'No, 'tisn't . . . 'tisn't that, he's . . . he's still as he was. It's . . . it's John George. I know I shouldn't have but I went to the court, ma'am, and he got a year.'

Her mistress's manner altered, her face stiffened. 'You're a very silly girl, Janie,' she said. 'The master will be very annoyed with you. Court rooms are no places for women, young women, girls. I, too, am very annoyed with you. I gave you the time off to visit your fiancé. That man's a scamp, a thieving scamp. I'm surprised your fiancé didn't find it out before. . . . What sentence did he get?'

'A year, ma'am.'

'That was nothing really, nothing. If he had been an ordinary labouring man, one could have understood him stealing, but he was in a position of trust, and when such men betray their trust they deserve heavy sentences. Dry your eyes now. Go upstairs and see to the children. I'm very displeased with you, Janie.'

Janie went upstairs and she was immediately surrounded by the children. Why was she crying? Had their mama been cross with her?

She nodded her head while they clung to her and the girls began to cry with her. Yes, their mama had been cross with her, but strangely it wasn't affecting her. Another time she would have been thrown into despair by just a sharp word from her mistress. At this moment she did not even think of Rory, for Rory had turned the corner, they said, and was on the mend, but her thoughts were entirely with John George. His face haunted her. The fact that he had told her that he had got a girl into trouble had shocked her, but what had shocked her even more was his mental condition, for she felt he must be going wrong in the head to admit that he took the ten shillings but not the five pounds. Poor John George! Poor John George! And Rory would go mad when he knew.

# Chapter Nine

A fortnight later they brought Rory home in a cab actually paid for by Miss Kean. Miss Kean had visited the hospital three times. The last time Rory had been propped up in bed and had stared at her and listened silently as she gave him a message from her father.

He was not to worry, his post was there for him when he was ready to return. And what was more, her father was promoting him to Mr Armstrong's place. Her father had taken on a new man, but he was oldish and couldn't cover half the district. Nevertheless he was honest and honest men were hard to come by. Her father had always known that but now it had been proved to him.

Miss Kean had then asked, 'Have you any idea who attacked you?' and all Rory did was to make one small movement with his head. He had stared fixedly at Miss Kean and she had smiled at him and said, 'I hope you enjoy the grapes, Mr Connor, and will soon be well.' Again he had made a small movement with his head. It was then she said, 'When you are ready to return home a cab will be provided.'

His mind was now clear and working normally and it kept telling him there was this thing he had to face up to and it was no use trying to ignore it, or hoping it would slip back into the muzziness that he had lain in during the first days of his recovery when they had kept saying to him, all of them, the nurses, the doctor, Ruth, his dad, her, Janie, all of them, 'Don't worry, take it slowly. Every day you'll improve. It's a miracle. It's a miracle.'

Although after the third day he had stopped saying the word 'Pity' aloud it was still filling the back of his mind. Whenever he closed his eyes he saw the big feet coming towards him; that's all he remembered, the big feet. He couldn't remember where they had hit him first, whether it was on the head or in the groin or in his ribs; they had broken his ribs. For days he had found it difficult to breathe, now it was easier. His body, although black and blue from head to foot, and with abrasions almost too numerous to count, was no longer a torment to him, just a big sore pile of flesh. He did not know what he looked like, only that his face seemed spread as wide as his shoulders.

He didn't see his reflection until he reached home. When they helped him over the step he made straight for the mantelpiece. Although Ruth tried to check him he thrust her gently aside then leant forward and looked at his face in the oblong mottled mirror. His nose was still straight but his eyes looked as if they were lying in pockets of mouldy fat. Almost two inches of his hair had been shaved off close to the scalp above his left ear and a zig-zag scar ran down to just in front of the ear itself.

'Your face'll be all right, don't worry.'

He turned and looked at Ruth but said nothing, and she went on, 'The dess-bed's ready for you, you can't do the ladder yet. We'll sleep upstairs.'

He said slowly now, like an old man might, 'I'll manage the ladder.'

'No,' she said, 'it's all arranged. Don't worry. Now come on, sit yourself down.' She led him towards the high-backed wooden chair, and he found he was glad to sit down, for his legs were giving way beneath him.

He said again, 'I'll make the ladder,' and as he spoke he watched Lizzie go into the scullery. It was as if she could read his mind; he didn't want to lie in the same room with her, although she lay in the box bed behind the curtains. He couldn't help his feelings towards her. He knew that she had been good to him over the past weeks, trudging down every day to the hospital, and he hadn't given her a kind word, not even when he could speak he hadn't given her a kind word. It was odd but he couldn't forgive her for depriving him of the woman he thought to be his mother. But what odds, what odds where he slept; wherever he slept his mind would be with him, and his mind was giving him hell. They thought he wasn't capable of thinking straight yet, and he wasn't going to enlighten them because he would need to have some excuse for his future actions.

Nobody had mentioned John George to him, not one of them had spoken his name, but the fact that he had never been near him spoke for them. Something had happened to him and he had a good idea what it was; in fact, he was certain of what it was. And he also knew that he himself wasn't going to do anything about it. He couldn't. God! he just couldn't.

'Here, drink that up.' Lizzie was handing him a cup of tea, which he took from her hand without looking at her and said, 'Ta.'

'It was good of old Kean,' she said 'to send a cab for you. He can't be as black as he's painted. And his daughter comin' to the hospital. God, but she's plain that one, stylish but plain. Anyway, he must value you.'

'Huh!' Even the jerking of his head was a painful action, which caused him to put his hand on his neck and move his head from side to side, while Lizzie concluded, 'Aye well, you know him better than me, but I would say deeds speak for themselves.'

When Lizzie took his empty cup from him and went to refill it, Ruth, poking the fire, said, 'I'll have to start a bakin',' and she turned and glanced towards him. 'It's good to have you home again, lad. We can get down to normal now.'

He nodded his head and smiled weakly at her but didn't speak. It was odd. Over the past weeks he had longed to be home, away from the cold painted walls and clinical cleanliness of the hospital, but looking about him now, the kitchen, which had always appeared large, for it was made up of two rooms knocked into one, seemed small, cluttered and shabby. He hadn't thought of it before as shabby, he hadn't thought of a lot of things before. He hadn't thought he was cowardly before. Afraid, aye, but not cowardly. But deep in his heart now he knew he was, both cowardly and afraid.

He had always been afraid of enclosed spaces. He supposed that was why he left doors open; and why he had jumped at the collecting job, because he'd be working outside most of the time in the open. He had always been terrified of being shut in. He could take his mind back to the incident that must have created the fear. The Learys lads next door were always full of devilment, and having dragged a coffin-like box they had found floating on the Jarrow slacks all the way down the East Jarrow road and up the Simonside bank, they had to find a use for it before breaking it up for the fire, so the older ones had chased the young ones, and it was himself they had caught, and they had put him in the box and nailed the lid on. At first he had screamed, then become so petrified that his voice had frozen inside him. When they shouted at him from the outside he had been incapable of answering; then, fearful of what they had done, they fumbed in their efforts to wrench the heavy lid off.

When eventually they tipped him from the box he was as stiff as a corpse itself, and not until he had vomited, after the grown-ups had thumped him on the back and rubbed him, did he start to cry. He'd had nightmares for years afterwards, and night after night had walked in his sleep, through the trap door and down the ladder. But having reached the kitchen door that led outside he would always wake up, then scamper back to bed where he would lie shivering until finally cold gave place to heat and he would fall into sweaty sleep.

But since starting collecting, he'd hardly had a nightmare and he hadn't sleep-walked for years. But what now, and in the weeks ahead?

Jimmy came in at half-past six and stood just inside the door and stared towards the dess-bed where Rory was sitting propped up, and he grinned widely and said, 'Aw, lad, it's good to see you home again,' then went slowly towards the bed. 'How you feelin'?'

'Oh, well, you know, a hundred per cent, less ninety.'

'Aye, but you're home and you'll soon be on your feet again. And you know somethin'?' He sat on the edge of the bed. 'I've seen him, Mr Kilpatrick. I told him how things stood, an' you know what he said? He said the rest can be paid so much a month. If you could clear it off in a year he'd be satisfied.'

'He said that?'

'Aye.'

'Oh well –' Rory sighed – 'that's something. Yes –' he nodded at Jimmy – 'that's something. We can go ahead now, can't we?'

'You know, he came to the yard for me 'cos he was down that way on business. And Mr Baker wanted to know what he was about 'cos I had to leave me work for five minutes, and so I told him.' Jimmy pulled a face. 'He wasn't pleased. Well, I knew he wouldn't be. You know what he said? He said he had intended keepin' me on an givin' me a rise . . . That for a tale. He asked what we were givin' for it and when I told him he said we were being done, paying that for the goodwill when it was just a few sticks of furniture and half an old patched sculler. One of the lads told me that he had seen him round there himself lookin', an' what he bet was that the old fellow was after the place for himself. Anyway, we scotched him.' He jerked his head and grinned widely, then added, 'Eeh! man, I'm excited. I never thought, I never thought.' He leant forward and put his hand on Rory's. 'And if it wasn't for what happened you we'd be over the moon, wouldn't we?'

'Aye, well, we can still be over the moon now.'

'Get off the side of that bed with your mucky clothes on!'

'Aw, Lizzie.' Jimmy rose to evade her hand and he laughed at her as he said, 'You're a grousy woman,' and when she made to go for him he ran into the scullery, his body swaying and his laughter touched with glee.

Jimmy was happy, Ruth was happy, and, of course, Lizzie was happy; and Janie would be happy; everybody was happy . . . except himself . . . and John George. John George. God Almighty, John George!

Yes, Janie was happy at the news that they had got the yard, for this meant she could be married any time now. Yet her excitement seemed to have been stirred rather by the fact that she had been granted a full day's leave next Thursday. She sat by the bed gazing at Rory as she gave him the news. He wasn't actually in bed, just lying on the top of it fully dressed. His legs and ribs still ached, and so the bed was left down during the day so that he could rest upon it.

Janie glanced from him to the Sunday company, all assembled as usual, and she hunched her shoulders at them as she said, 'I told a fib, well, only a little one. I told her, the missis, it would need time to clear up the place an' put it to rights an' suggested like if I could have a full day. But you know what I wanted the day for? I thought we'd go up to Durham and –' She clapped her hand over her mouth, then stared at Rory before looking back at the others again and saying, 'Eeh! I forgot.' Again she was looking into Rory's unblinking stare and, taking his hand, she said softly, 'We . . . we didn't tell you, 'cos you were so bad, and you wouldn't have been able to take it in.' She gave him an apologetic look now. 'I mean, with your head bein' knocked about an' that. And we knew that if you had been all right you would have asked for him, you know. Now, Rory, don't be upset.' She gripped his hands tightly. 'John George's been a silly lad. It's all through that lass. You know, you said he was daft. Well, he was, and . . . and he took some money. He meant to put it back. I don't know whether you knew or not but he had been on the fiddle for a long time and so . . . and so he was caught and' – her head drooped to one side as she shook it – 'he was sent along the line. He's in Durh . . . Oh, Rory . . .'

They were all gathered round the bed now looking down on him. The sweat was pouring from him and Lizzie cried at them, 'Get back! the lot of you's an' give him air.' She looked angrily across the bed at Janie. 'You shouldn't have given it him like that.'

'I'm sorry. I know, but . . . well, he had to know some time, Lizzie.'

'He'll be all right. He'll be all right.' Ruth was wiping the sweat from his brow and the bald patch on his head. 'It's just weakness. It's like how he used to be after the nightmares. Go on –' she motioned the men towards the table – 'get on with your game.'

'Bad that,' said Grannie Waggett. 'Bad. Don't like it. Bad sign.'

'Anybody can have sweats, Gran.' Jimmy's voice was small, his tone tentative, and she bent forward from her chair and wagged her bony finger at him, saying, 'Nay, lad, not everybody, women but not men. Bad look out if all men had sweats. Always a sign of summit, a man havin' sweats. I remember me grannie when she worked for those high-ups in Newcastle sayin' how the son got sweats. Young he was an' the heir. Lots of money, lots of money. He started havin' sweats after the night he went out to see Newcastle lit up for the first time. Oil lamps they had. Eighteen and twelve was it, or eleven, or thirteen? I don't know, but he got sweats. Caught a chill he did going from one to the other gazin' at 'em, got the consumption . . .'

'Gran!'

'Aye, Ruth . . . Well, I was just sayin' about me grannie an' the young fellow an' the things she told me. Do you know what the bloody Duke of Northumberland did with a pile of money? Gave it to buildin' a jail or court or summat, an' poor folks . . .'

'Look, come on in home.' Bill Waggett was bending over his mother, tugging at her arm now, and she cried at him, 'Leave be, you big galoot!'

'You're comin' in home, Rory wants a bit of peace an' quiet.'

'Rory likes a bit of crack, an' I've said nowt.'

'Go on, Gran.' Janie was at her side now pleading.

Spluttering and upbraiding, the old woman allowed her son to lead her from the cottage. And this was the signal for the Learys, too, to take their leave, although it was but six o'clock in the evening, and a Sunday, the day of the week they all looked forward to for a game and a bit crack.

The house free from the visitors, as if at a given signal Jimmy went up the ladder into the loft, and his father followed him, while Lizzie and Ruth disappeared into the scullery, leaving Janie alone with Rory.

She had pulled her chair up towards the head of the bed, and, bending towards him, she asked tenderly, 'You feeling better?'

He nodded at her.

'I knew when it came it would be a shock, I'm sorry.'

He made no motion but continued to stare at her.

'I . . . I thought we should go up and see him on Thursday. It'll be the only chance we have, he's allowed visitors once a month . . . All right, all right.'

She watched his head now moving backwards and forwards against the supporting pillows, and when he muttered something she put her face close to his and whispered, 'What do you say?'

'I . . . I can't.'

'We'd take the ferry up to Newcastle an' then the train. It . . . it might do you good, I mean the journey.'

'I can't; don't keep on.'

She looked at him for a moment before she said, 'You don't want to see him?'

'I . . . I can't go there.'

'But why, Rory? He's ... he's your friend. And if you had seen him in the court that day, why ...'

Again he was shaking his head. His eyes, screwed up tightly now, were lost in the discoloured puffed flesh.

She sat back and stared at him in deep sadness. She couldn't understand it. She knew he wasn't himself yet, but that he wouldn't make an effort to go and see John George, and him shut up in that place ... well, she just couldn't understand it.

When he looked at her again and saw the expression on her face, he said through clenched teeth, 'Don't keep on, Janie. I'm sorry but ... but I can't. You know I've always had a horror of them places. You know how I can't stand being shut in, the doors and things. I'd be feared of making a fool of meself. You know?'

The last two words were a plea and although in a small way she understood his fear of being shut in, she thought that he might have tried to overcome it for this once, just to see John George and ease his plight.

She said softly, 'Somebody should go; he's got nobody, nobody in the world.'

He muttered something now and she said, 'What?'

'You go.'

'Me! On me own, all that way? I've never been in a train in me life, and never on the ferry alone, I haven't.'

'Take one of them with you.' He motioned his head towards the scullery. And now she nodded at him and said, 'Aye, yes, I could do that. I'll ask them.' She stared at him a full minute before she rose from the chair and went into the scullery.

Both Lizzie and Ruth turned towards her and waited for her to speak. She looked from one to the other and said, 'He won't, I mean he can't come up to Durham with me to see John George, he doesn't feel up to it ... not yet. If it had been later. But ... but it's early days you know.' She nodded at them, then added, 'Would one of you?'

Ruth looked at her sadly and said, 'I couldn't lass, I couldn't leave the house an' him an' them all to see to. Now Lizzie here –'

'What! me? God Almighty! Ruth, me go to Durham! I've never been as far as Shields Market in ten years. As for going on a train I wouldn't trust me life in one of 'em. And another thing, lass.' Her voice dropped. 'I haven't got the proper clothes for a journey.'

'They're all right, Lizzie, the ones you've got. There's your good shawl. You could put it round your shoulders. An' Ruth would lend you her bonnet, wouldn't you, Ruth?'

'Oh, she could have me bonnet, and me coat an' all, but it wouldn't fit her. But go on, it'll do you good.' She was nodding at Lizzie now. 'You've hardly been across the doors except to the hospital –' she paused but didn't add, 'since you came from over the water' but said 'in years. It's an awful place to have to be goin' to but the journey would be like a holiday for you.'

'I'd like to see John George.' Lizzie's voice was quiet now. 'Poor lad. A fool to himself, always was. He used to slip me a copper on a Sunday even though I knew he hadn't two pennies to rub against one another. And I didn't want to take it, but if I didn't he'd leave it there.' She pointed to the corner of the little window-sill. 'He'd drop it in the tin pot. The Sunday there wasn't tuppence in there I knew that his funds were low indeed. Aye, lass, I'll come along o' you. I'll likely look a sketch an' put you to shame, but if you don't mind, I don't, lass.'

Janie now laughed as she put out her hand towards Lizzie and said, 'I wouldn't mind bein' seen with you in your shift, Lizzie,' and Ruth said, 'Oh! Janie, Janie,' and Lizzie said, 'You're a good lass, Janie. You've got what money can't buy, a heart. Aye, you have that.'

It took some minutes before Janie could speak to John George. It was Lizzie who spoke first. 'Hello there, lad,' she said, and he answered, 'Hello, Lizzie. Oh hello, Lizzie,' in just such a tone as he would have used when holding out his hands towards her. But there was the grid between them.

'Hello, Janie.'

There was a great hard lump in her throat. The tears were blinding her but through them the blurred outline of his haggard features tore at her heart. 'How . . . how are you, John George?'

'Well . . . well, you know, Janie, not too bad, not too bad. Rough with the smooth, Janie, you know. Rough with the smooth. How . . . how is everybody back there?'

'All right. All right, John George. Rory, he . . . he couldn't make it, John George, he's still shaky on his legs after the knockin' about, like they told you. Eeh! he was knocked about, we never thought he'd live. He would have been here else. He'll come later, next time.'

John George made no reply to Janie's mumbled discourse but he looked towards Lizzie and she, nodding at him, added, 'Aye, he'll come along later. He sent his regards.'

'Did he?' He was addressing Janie again.

'Aye.'

'What did he say, Janie?'

'What was that, John George?'

He leant farther towards the grid. 'I said what did Rory say?'

'Oh well.' She sniffed, then wiped her eyes with her handkerchief before mumbling, 'He said to keep your pecker up an' . . . an' everything would work out once you get back.'

'He said that?' He was holding her gaze and she didn't reply immediately, so that when she did say 'Aye,' it carried no conviction to him.

'We've brought you a fadge of new bread an' odds an' ends.' Lizzie now pointed to the parcel and he said, 'Oh, ta, Lizzie. It's kind of you; you're always kind.'

'Ah, lad, talkin' of being kind, that's what's put you here the day, being kind. Aw, lad.'

They both looked at the bent head now; then when it jerked up sharply they were startled by the vehemence of his next words. 'I didn't take five pounds, I didn't! Believe me. Will you believe me?' He was staring now at Janie. 'I did take the ten bob. As I said, I'd done it afore but managed to put it back on the Monday morning, you know after going to the pawn.' He glanced towards Lizzie now as if she would understand the latter bit. Then looking at Janie again, he said, 'Tell him, will you? Say to him, John George said he didn't take the five pounds. Will you, Janie?'

It was some seconds before she answered, 'Aye. Yes, I will. Don't upset yourself, John George. Yes, I will, an' he'll believe you. Rory'll believe you.'

His eyes were staring into hers and his lips moved soundlessly for a moment before he brought out, 'Did you go and see Maggie, Janie?'

Janie, flustered now, said, 'Why, no; I couldn't, John George, 'cos you didn't tell me where she lived.'

Just as he put his doubled fist to his brow and bowed his head a bell rang, and as if he had been progged by something sharp he rose quickly to his feet, then gabbled, 'Horsley Terrace . . . twenty-four. Go, will you Janie?'

'Yes, John George. Yes, John George.' They were both on their feet now. 'Ta, thanks. Thank you both. I'll never forget you. Will you come again? . . . Come again, will you?'

They watched him form into a line with the others before they turned away.

Outside the gates they didn't look at each other or speak, and when Lizzie, after crossing the road, leaned against the wall of a cottage and buried her face in her hands, Janie, crying again, put her arms about her and having turned her from the wall, led her along the street and into the town. And still neither of them spoke.

# Chapter One

## *Miss Kean*

Rory stood before the desk and looked down at Charlotte Kean and said, 'I'm sorry to hear about your father.'

'It's a severe chill, but he'll soon be about again. As I told you, you are to take Armstrong's place and you will naturally receive the same wage as he was getting . . . You don't look fully recovered yourself, Mr Connor. Are you feeling quite well?'

'Yes. Yes, miss, I'm quite all right.'

'I think you had better sit down.' She pointed with an imperious finger towards a chair, and he looked at her in surprise for a moment before taking the seat and muttering, 'Thank you.'

'As I told you, we took on a new man.'

He noticed that she said 'we' as if she, too, were running the business.

'He was the best of those who applied; with so many people out of work in the town you would have thought there would have been a better selection. If it had been for the working-class trades I suppose we would have been swamped.'

He was surprised to know that rent collecting didn't come under the heading of working-class trade, yet on the other hand he knew that if they had been living in the town, in either Tyne Dock or Shields, he wouldn't have been able to hob-nob with neighbours such as the Learys or the Waggetts; the distinction between the white collar and the muffler was sharply defined in the towns.

'My father suggests that you take over the Shields area completely. Mr Taylor can do the Jarrow district, particularly the Saturday morning collection.' She smiled thinly at him now. 'As he says, it's a shame to waste a good man there . . . He has a high opinion of your expertise, Mr Connor.'

Well, this was news to him. Shock upon shock. If things had been different he would have been roaring inside, and later he would have told John George and . . . Like a steel trap a shutter came down on his thinking and he forced himself to say, 'That's very nice to know, miss.'

She was still smiling at him, and as he looked at her he thought, as Lizzie had said, God! but she's plain. It didn't seem fair somehow that a woman looking like her should have been given all the chances. Education, money, the lot. Now if Janie had been to a fine school, and could have afforded to dress like this one did, well, there would've been no one to touch her.

As he stared across the desk at the bowed head and the thin moving hand – she was writing out his district – he commented to himself that everything she had on matched, from her fancy hat that was a dull red colour to the stiff ribboned bow on the neck of her dress. Her green coat was open and showed a woollen dress that took its tone from the hat, but had a row of green buttons down to her waist. He could see the bustle of the dress pushing out the deep pleats of the coat. It took money to dress in colours and style like that. The old man seemingly didn't keep her short of cash.

When she rose to her feet he stood up, and when she came round the desk she said, 'I can leave everything in your hands then, Mr Connor?' She handed him a sheet of paper.

'Yes, miss.'

'I've got to go now. Mr Taylor should be in any moment.' She turned the face of the fob watch that was pinned to the breast of her dress and looked at it. 'It isn't quite nine yet, make yourself known to him. And this evening, and until my father is fully recovered, I would like you to bring the takings to the house. You know where it is?'

'Yes, I know where it is.'

Yes, he knew where it was. He had caught a glimpse of it from the gates. He knew that it had been occupied by Kean's father and his grandfather, but that's all he knew about it, for he had never been asked to call there on any pretext. But what he did know was that all the Keans had been men who had made money and that the present one was a bully. More than once, when he had stood in this office and been spoken to like a dog, he'd had the desire to ram his fist into his employer's podgy face.

'Good morning then, Mr Connor.'

'Good morning, miss.'

He went before her and opened the outer door, then stood for a second watching her walking down the alley towards the street. She carried herself as straight as a soldier; her step was more of a march than a walk, and she swung her arms; she didn't walk at all like women in her position usually did, or should.

He closed the door, then looked around the office and through into the inner room. Then walking slowly into it, he sat in the chair behind the desk, cocked his head to the side and, speaking to an imaginary figure sitting opposite, he said, 'Now, Mr Taylor, I will assign you to the Jarrow district.' Oh yes, he would always speak civilly to subordinates because, after all, he was a subordinate himself once, wasn't he? A mere rent collector. But now. He looked around the office. He was master of all he surveyed.

Huh! This was the time to laugh, if only he had someone to laugh with.

When he heard the outer door open he got quickly to his feet and went round the desk.

He looked at the clean but shabbily dressed figure standing, hat in hand, before him, and he said quietly, 'You, Mr Taylor?'

'Yes, sir.' The old man inclined his head, and Rory, now making a derogatory sound in his throat, said, 'You needn't sir me, Mr Taylor, I'm just like yourself, a roundsman. Me name's Connor. The old man – Mr Kean – is in bed with a cold. His daughter's just been along. She says you're to take my district.'

'Anything you say, Mr Connor. Anything you say.'

God! had he sounded as servile as this when he was confronted by Kean? There should be a law of some kind against bringing men to their knees.

As he stared at the old man it came to him that everything in his life had changed. And it was to go on changing. How, he didn't know, he only knew that things would never again be as they were.

It was half-past five when he made his way from the office to Birchingham House in Westoe, and it was raining, a fine chilling soaking rain.

The house was not in what was usually called the village, nor did it stand among those that had sprung up to run parallel with that part of Shields that lay along the river, nor was it one of a small number that remained aloof in their vast grounds. But it was of that section the social standing of which was determined by its size, the number of servants it supported, and whether its owner hired his carriages.

And Birchingham House had another distinction. Although it stood in only two acres of ground it was situated on the side road that led off the main road to Harton and to two substantial estates, one belonging to a mine owner, the other to a gentleman who was known to own at least six iron ships that plied their trade from the Tyne.

The histories of the houses of the notabilities of the town were known to the nobodies of the town; and the notabilities themselves formed a topic of gossip, not only in the bars that lined the river-front, but also in the superior clubs and societies that flourished in the town.

But the situation of his master's house or of his master himself had not up till this moment impressed Rory with any significance. Kean, to him, had been just a money-grabbing skinflint who owned rows of property, particularly in Jarrow, which should have been pulled down years ago, and streets in Shields that were fast dropping into decay for want of repair. Yet in this respect he admitted Kean was no worse than any of the landlords he represented.

Now, as he neared the house in the dark and saw the front steps leading to it lighted by two bracket lamps, he stopped for a moment and peered at it through the rain. It was big. There were ten windows along the front of it alone. Moreover, it was three-storey. He couldn't quite make out the top one, only that there was a gleam of glass up there. Likely attics. There was a carriage standing on the drive at the foot of the steps and he paused near it to look up at the driver sitting huddled deep in a cloaked coat. The man hadn't noticed him; he seemed to be asleep.

He hesitated. Should he go to the front door or the back door? Damn it all, why not the front! Why not!

He went up the steps and pulled the bell.

The door was answered by a maid. She was wearing a starched apron over a black alpaca dress. The bib of the apron had a wide, stiff frill that continued over the straps of her shoulders. She had a starched cap on her head and the strings from it looked as stiff as the cap itself and were tied under her chin in a bow. She was evidently flustered and said, 'Yes, yes. Who is it?'

'I'm Mr Connor. Miss Kean told me to come. I've brought the takings.'

'Oh! Oh!' She looked from one side to the other, then said, 'Well, you'd better come in.' And she stood aside and let him pass her into the small lobby, then opened another door into a hall, which he noted immediately was as big as the kitchen at home.

'Stay there,' she said, 'an' I'll tell her, that's if she can come, the master's had a turn. They've had to send for the doctor again. He's right bad.' She nodded at him, then made for the stairs that led from the hallway in a half spiral and disappeared from view.

He stood looking around him, frankly amazed at what he saw. To the right of the staircase was a side table with a lamp on it. He noted that it was oil, not gas. Yet they had gas outside. The soft light from it illuminated a large oil painting on the wall showing the head and shoulders of a man; he had a broad, flat face, and the high collar was wedged into the jowls below his chin; he had a white fringe of hair above his ears, the rest of his head was bald; his eyes were round and bright and seemed to be looking with stern condemnation at the visitor. Rory did not need to guess that this was an ancestor of Mr Kean, and also that the lamp was there as a sort of illuminated commemoration to do him honour.

A cabinet stood against the wall at the far side of the stairs. He had never seen the like of it before, not even in a picture. It was glass-fronted and made of yellowish wood picked out in gold; the legs were spindly with fancy cross-bars connecting the four of them. It had two shelves. The top one held figures, some single, some in groups; the lower shelf had glass goblets standing on it. From what he could see at this distance they were etched with paintings.

There were a number of doors going off all round the hall, and the thick red carpet he was standing on reached to the walls on all sides except where one door was deeply inset in an alcove and had a step down to it.

He felt his mouth closing when he heard the rustle of a gown on the stairs and saw Charlotte Kean coming down towards him. Her face wore a worried expression. She said immediately, 'My father has taken a turn for the worse, we are very concerned. Will you come this way?'

Without a word he followed her down the step and through the door that was set in the alcove and found himself in an office, but an office very different from the one in Tangard Street. The room in a way was a pattern of the hall, thick carpet, highly polished desk, the top strewn with papers and ledgers. There were paintings on all the walls except that which was taken up with two long windows over which the curtains had not been drawn.

He watched her turn up the gas light; the mantle, encased in its fancy globe gave out a soft light and set the room in a warm glow.

He couldn't understand the feeling he was experiencing. He didn't know whether it was envy, admiration, or respect, that kind of grudging respect the symbols of wealth evoke. He only knew that the feeling was making him feel all arms and legs.

'Sit down, Mr Connor.'

This was the second time in one day she had invited him to be seated.

He hesitated to take the leather chair that she had proffered; instead, looking down at the bag he had placed on the desk, he opened it for her and took out a number of smaller bags and the two pocket ledgers, which he placed before her, saying, 'I've counted everything, it's in order.'

She glanced up at him, saying, 'Thank you.' Then with her hand she indicated the chair again. And now he sat down and watched her as she emptied each bag and counted the money, then checked it against the books.

In the gaslight and with her expression troubled as it was, she looked different from what she had done in the stark grey light this morning, softer somehow.

The money counted, she returned the books to the bag; then rising, she stood looking at him for a moment before saying, 'I'm sure I can trust you, Mr Connor, to see to things in the office until my father is better. I . . . I may not be able to get along. You see' – she waved her hand over the desk – 'there is so much other business to see to. And he wants me with him all the time.'

'Don't worry about the office, miss, everything will be all right there. And . . . and Mr Taylor seems a steady enough man.'

'Thank you, Mr Connor.'

'I'm sorry about your father.'

'I'm sure you are.'

He stared back into her face. There was that something in her tone. Another time he would have said to himself, Now how does she mean that?

He opened the door to let her pass out into the hall, and there she turned to him and asked, 'Is it still raining?'

'Yes. Yes, it was when I came in.'

'You have a long walk home. Go into the kitchen and they will give you something to drink.'

Crumbs from the rich man's table. Soup kitchens run by lady bountifuls. Clogs for the barefoot. Why was he thinking like this? She only meant to be kind, and he answered as if he thought she was. 'Thank you, miss, but I'd rather get home.'

'But you don't look too well yourself, Mr Connor.'

'I'm all right, miss. Thank you all the same. Good night, miss.'

'Good night, Mr Connor.'

The maid appeared from the shadows and let him out. He walked down the steps and along the curving drive into the road, feeling like some beggar who had been given alms. He felt deflated, insignificant, sort of lost. It was that house.

He walked through the rain all the way back to the beginning of Westoe, down through Laygate and on to Tyne Dock, through the arches and the last long trek up Simonside Bank into the country and the cottage.

Opening the door, he staggered in and dropped into a chair without taking off his sodden coat, and he made no protest when Lizzie tugged his boots from his feet while Ruth loosened his scarf and coat and held him up while she pulled them from him.

He had no need to pretend tonight that he was ill, at least physically, for the first day's work had taken it out of him, and the trail back from Westoe had been the last straw.

When later in the evening Jimmy, by way of comfort, whispered to him, 'When we go to the yard it'll be easier for you, you could cut from the office to the boatyard in five minutes,' he nodded at him while at the same time thinking, not without scorn, The boatyard! With thirty-five pounds he could have got himself a mortgage on a decent house. Slowly it came to him the reason why he had allowed himself to become saddled with the boatyard. It wasn't only because he wanted to kill two birds with one stone: marry Janie and give Jimmy something of his own to live and work for; it was because he wanted to get away from here, from the kitchen; and now from their concern for his mental state, which must be bad, so they thought, when he still wouldn't go and see his best friend, and him in prison.

Only last night when he said good-bye to Janie the rooms over the boatyard had appeared to him like a haven. And later, as he lay awake staring into the blackness listening to Jimmy's untroubled breathing, he had thought, Once we get there, once I'm married, I'll see it all differently. Then like a child and with no semblance of Rory Connor, he had buried his face in the pillow and cried from deep within him, 'I'll make it up to him when he comes out. I'll make him understand. He'll see I could do nothing about it at the time 'cos I was too bad. He'll understand. Being John George, he'll understand. And I'll make it up to him, I will. I will.'

But now, after his visit to Birchingham House, he was seeing the boat house for what it was, a tumbledown riverside shack, and he thought, I must have been mad to pay thirty-five pounds for the goodwill of that. Look where it's landed me. And the gate shut once again on his thinking as an inner voice said, 'Aye; and John George.'

# Chapter Two

They were married on the Saturday after Easter. It was a quiet affair in that they hadn't a big ceilidh. They went by brake to the Catholic church in Jarrow, together with Ruth, Paddy, Lizzie, Jimmy, and Bill Waggett. A great deal of tact and persuasion had to be used on Gran Waggett in order that she should stay behind. Who was going to help Kathleen Leary with the tables? And anyway, Kathleen being who she was needed somebody to direct her, and who better than Gran herself?

Janie's wedding finery was plain but good, for her flounced grey coat had once belonged to her mistress, as had also the blue flowered cotton dresss she wore underneath. Her blue straw hat she had bought herself, and her new brown buttoned boots too.

She was trembling as she knelt at the altar rails, but then the church was icy cold and the priest himself looked blue in the face and weary into the bargain. He mumbled the questions: Wilt thou have this man? Wilt thou have this woman? And they in turn mumbled back.

After they had signed their names and Rory had kissed her in front of them all they left the church and got into the brake again, which was now surrounded by a crowd of screaming children shouting 'Hoy a ha'penny oot! Hoy a ha'penny oot!'

They had come prepared with ha'pennies. Ruth and Lizzie and Jimmy threw them out from both sides of the brake; but they were soon finished and when there were no more forthcoming the shouts that followed them now were, 'Shabby weddin' ... shabby weddin',' and then the concerted chorus of:

Fleas in yer blankets,
No lid on your netty,
To the poor house you're headin',
Shabby weddin', shabby weddin'.


The fathers laughed and Ruth clicked her tongue and Lizzie said, 'If I was out there I'd skite the hunger off them. By God! I would.' But Janie and Rory just smiled, and Jimmy, sitting silently at the top end of the brake, his hands dangling between his knees, looked at them, and part of him was happy, and part of him, a deep hidden part, was aching.

Out of decency Jimmy did not immediately go down to the yard. The young married couple were to have the place to themselves until Monday, and on Monday morning the new pattern of life was to begin, for Janie had had her way and was continuing to go daily to the Buckhams'.

Of course, in the back of her mind she knew that the three shillings had been a great inducement to Rory seeing her side of the matter, for now that he wasn't gaming there was no way to supplement his income, and what was more, as she had pointed out, he would be expected to give a bit of help at home since he was depriving them of both his own and Jimmy's money. So the arrangement was that, until Jimmy got some orders, for his sculler was almost finished, then she would continue to go daily to her place . . .

Having clambered up the steps in the dark and unlocked the door and dropped their bundles and a bass hamper on to the floor, they clung to each other in the darkness, gasping and laughing after the exertion of humping the baggage from where the cart had dropped them at the far end of the road.

'Where's the candle?'

'On the mantelpiece of course.' She was still laughing.

He struck a match and lit the candle, then held it up as he looked towards the table on which the lamp stood.

When the lamp was lit he said, 'Well, there you are now, home sweet home.'

Janie stood and looked about her. 'I'll have to get stuck in here at nights,' she said.

'Well, if you will go working in the day-time, Mrs Connor.' He pulled her to him again and they stood pressed close looking silently now into each other's face. 'Happy?'

She smiled softly, 'Ever so.'

'It's not going to be an easy life.'

'Huh! what do I care about that as long as we're together. Easy life?' She shook her head. 'I'd go fish guttin' if I could help you, an' you know how I hate guttin' fish, even when we used to get them for practically nowt from the quay. Do you remember walkin' all the way down into Shields and getting a huge basketful for threepence?'

'Only because they were on the point of going rotten.'

'Ger-away with you . . . Do you want something to eat?'

'No.'

'You're not hungry?'

'Not for food.'

Her lips pressed tightly together, she closed her eyes and bowed her head.

He now put his hands up to her hair and unpinned her hat and throwing it aside, unbuttoned her coat.

'I'll have to get these bundles unpacked and . . . and tidied up.'

He went on undoing the buttons. 'There's all day the morrow and the next day and the next day and the next, all our life to undo bundles . . .'

'Hie! what're you doin'? That's me good coat. Look, it's on the floor.'

'Leave it on the floor; there's more to follow.'

'Rory! Rory! the bed isn't made up.'

'The bed is made up, I saw to it.'

'Oh Rory! . . . An' I'm cold, I'm cold, I'm cold. I'll have to get me nightie.'

'You're not going to need a nightie.'

'Aw, Rory! . . . Eeh!' She let out a squeal as, dressed only in her knickers and shift, he swung her up into his arms and carried her through into the bedroom and dropped her on to the bed. She lay there just where he had dropped her and in the dim light reflected from the kitchen she watched him throw off his clothes.

When he jumped on to the bed beside her she squealed and said, 'Eeh! the lamp.'

'The lamp can wait.'

They were pressed close, but she was protesting slightly, she didn't want to be rushed. She was a bit afraid of this thing. If she could only make him take it quietly – lead up to it sort of. Her grannie had said it hurt like hell. His lips were moving round her face when she murmured, in a futile effort to stem his ardour, 'Oh Rory, Rory, I'll never be happier than I am at this minute. It's been a wonderful day, hasn't it? . . . They were all so good, an' they enjoyed themselves, didn't they? I bet they'll keep up the jollification all night.' She moaned softly as his hands moved over her; then, her voice trailing weakly away, she ended, 'If-only-John-George-had-been-there . . .'

His hands ceased their groping, his lips became still on her breast and she screamed out now as he actually pushed her from him with such force that her shoulders hit the wall as he yelled at her, 'God Almighty! can't you give him a rest? What've you got to bring him up now for, at this minute? You did it on purpose. *You did!*'

In the silence that followed he listened to her gasping. Then she was in his arms again and he was rocking her. 'Oh lass, I'm sorry, I'm sorry. I didn't mean it. Did I hurt you? I'm sorry, I'm sorry. It was only, well, you know, I've waited so long . . . And, and . . .'

When she didn't answer him, or make any sound, he said softly, 'Janie. Janie. Say something.'

What she said was, 'It's all right. It's all right.'

'I love you. I love you, Janie. Aw, I love you. If I lost you I'd go mad, barmy.'

'It's all right. It's all right, you won't lose me.'

'Will you always love me?'

'Always.'

'You promise?'

'Aye, I promise.'

'I'll never love anybody in me life but you, I couldn't'. Aw, Janie, Janie . . .'

Later in the night when the light was out and he was asleep she lay still in his arms but wide awake. It hadn't been like she had expected, not in any way. Perhaps she wasn't goin' to like that kind of thing after all. Her grannie said some didn't, while others couldn't get enough. Well she'd never be one of those, she was sure of that already. Perhaps it was spoiled for her when he threw her against the wall because she had mentioned John George.

It was most strange how he reacted now whenever John George's name was mentioned. She could understand him not wanting to go to the prison, him having this feeling about being shut in, but she couldn't work out in her own mind why he never spoke of John George. And when the name was mentioned by anybody else he would remain silent. But to act like he had done the night just because . . . Well, she was flabbergasted.

Her grannie, as part of the advice she had given her on marriage last Sunday, had said, 'If he wants any funny business, out of the ordinary like, and some of them do, you never know till the door's closed on you, you have none of it. An' if he raises his hand to you, go for the poker. Always leave it handy. Start the way you mean to go on 'cos with the best of them, butter wouldn't melt in their mouths afore they get you in that room. But once there, it's like Adam and Eve racing around the Garden of Eden every night. An' if you cross your fingers and say skinch, or in other words, hold your horses, lad, I've had enough, they bring the priest to you, an' he reads the riot act. "Supply your man's needs," he says, "or it's Hell fire and brimstone for you." So off you gallop again, even when your belly's hangin' down to your knees.'

She had laughed at her grannie and with her grannie. She had put her arms around the old woman and they had rocked together until the tears had run down their faces, and the last words she had said to her were, 'Don't worry, Gran, nowt like that'll happen to me. It's Rory I'm marrying, and I know Rory. I should do, there's only a thin wall divided us for years.'

But now they hadn't been hours married afore he had tossed her against a wall, and tossed her he had because he had hurt her shoulder and it was still paining. Life was funny . . . odd.

# Chapter Three

Septimus Kean died, and Rory continued to take the day's collections to the house for some four weeks after Mr Kean had been buried, and each time Miss Kean received him in what she called the office. But on this particular Friday night she met him in the hall and said to him, 'Just leave the bag on the office table, Mr Connor, we'll see to that later. By the way, are you in a hurry?'

He was in a hurry, he was in a hurry to get home to Janie, to sit before the fire and put his feet up and talk with Jimmy, and hear if he had managed to get an order, and to find out if any of the Pitties had been about again . . . The Pitties. He'd give his right arm, literally, if he could get his own back on the Pitties. There was a deep acid hate in him for the Pitties. And it would appear they hadn't finished with him for they had been spying about the place. He knew that to get a start on the river Jimmy would have to take the droppings, but if it lay with the Pitties he wouldn't get even the droppings. They were beasts, dangerous beasts. By God he'd give anything to get one over on them.

He answered her, 'Oh no, not at all.'

'There is something I wish to discuss with you. I'm about to have a cup of tea, would you care to join me?'

Old Kean's daughter asking him to join her in a cup of tea! Well! Well! He could scarcely believe his ears. Things were looking up. By lad, they were.

In the hall she said to the maid, 'Take Mr Connor's coat and hat.'

Then he was following her to the end of the hall, and into a long room. There was a big fire blazing in the grate to the right of them. It was a fancy grate with a black iron basket. It had a marble mantelpiece with, at each end, an urn-shaped vase standing on it, and above the mantelpiece was another large oil painting of yet another past Kean.

At first glance the prominent colour of the room seemed to be brown. The couch drawn up before the fire and the two big side chairs were covered with a brown corded material. The furniture was a shining brown. There were three small tables with knick-knacks on them. A piece of furniture that looked like a sideboard but like no sideboard he'd ever seen before had silver candlesticks on it. The velvet curtains hanging at the windows were green with a brown bobble fringe and were supported from a cornice pole as thick as his upper arm.

'Sit down, Mr Connor.' She motioned him towards one of the big chairs and he sat down, then watched her pull a handbell to the side of the fireplace.

When the door opened she turned to the maid, not the same one who had opened the door to him, and said, 'I'll have tea now, Jessie; please bring two cups.'

The girl bent her knee, then went out.

He noticed that although her tone was uppish, as always, she had said 'Please.'

He watched her as she sat back in the corner of the couch. She made a movement with her legs and for a moment he thought that she was actually going to cross them. But what she did was cross her feet, and as she did so her black skirt rode above her ankles and he saw the bones pressing through what must have been silk stockings . . . She certainly looked after herself in the way of dress did this one. She was in mourning but her mourning was silk.

'I will come to the point, Mr Connor. I have a proposition to make to you.'

'A proposition?' His eyes widened slightly.

'I don't know whether you are aware that property dealing was only one of my father's interests.' She did not wait for him to comment on this but went on, 'Among other things, he had interests in a number of growing concerns and, since my grandfather died, other small businesses have come into the family. Do you know the Wrighton Tallow Works?'

'I've heard of them.'

'Well, my grandfather owned the works and naturally they fell to my father, and unfortunately, I say unfortunately, because of the loss of my father they are now my concern . . . How far have you advanced in book-keeping Mr Connor?'

'Advanced?' He blinked at her. 'What . . . what do you rightly mean, miss?'

'What I mean is, have you studied any further than that which is required to tot up rent accounts? Have you thought of your own advancement in this line, such as that of becoming a fully fledged clerk in a bank, or to a solicitor, say?'

'No, miss.' The answer was curt, his tone cold. 'The opportunities didn't provide themselves.' He knew too late that he should have said present, not provide.

'Opportunities are there for the taking, Mr Connor. This town offers great opportunities to those who are willing to take advantage of them. It isn't only the shipyards and the boat builders and such who offer apprenticeships in particular crafts; there are the arts.'

The arts! He narrowed his eyes at her. What was she getting at? Was she having him on, trying to get a bit of amusement out of him? The arts! Why didn't she come to the point?

She came to the point by saying, 'I have in mind that I need a manager, Mr Connor, someone who is capable not only of taking charge of the property side of my affairs but who could assist me in the running of my other businesses. There are places that need to be visited, books to be gone over. Of course I have my accountant and my solicitor but these are there only for the final totalling at the year's end, and for advice should I need it. But there is so much to be seen to in between times and my father used to attend to this side of affairs, for you know, if a warehouse or business is not visited regularly those in charge become slack.' She stared at him without speaking for almost a full minute before saying, 'Would you consider taking on this post if, and when, you became qualified to do so? You would, of course, need a little training.'

His heart was thumping against his ribs causing his breath to catch in his throat. He couldn't take it in. She was proposing that he should be her manager. He was peering at her through the narrow slits of his eyes now, he was puzzled. Why wasn't she advertising for somebody right away if the burden of the businesses was so great on her?

As if she were reading his thoughts she said, 'I have no doubt I could get someone to fill this post almost immediately, but then the person would be strange to me, and . . . and I don't mix easily. What I mean is, I take a long time in getting to know people.'

They were staring at each other through the fading light, and in silence again. It was she who broke it, her voice low now, ordinary sounding, no uppishness to it. 'I . . . I have known you for some time, Mr Connor, and have always thought that you should be capable of much better things than mere rent collecting.'

Before he could answer the door opened and the maid entered pushing a tea trolley.

When the trolley was by the side of the couch she looked at the maid and
said, 'I'll see to it, Jessie. I'll ring when I need you.'

'Yes, miss.' Again the dip of the knee.

'Do you take sugar, Mr Connor?'

'No. No, thank you.'

'That is unusual; men usually like a lot of sugar.'

He watched her pour the weak-looking tea from a small silver teapot and
add milk to it from a matching jug, and when a few minutes later he sipped
at it he thought, My God! dish-water.

'Oh, I'm sorry, I didn't ask what tea you preferred. You see, they're so
used to bringing me China; I'll ring and get some . . .'

'Oh no, please don't. It's nice, it's only different. And' – he grinned now
at her – 'you can understand I'm not used to havin' China tea.'

She actually laughed now, and he noticed that it changed her face and
made her almost pleasant-looking, except that her nose remained just as
sharp. 'I hope it will be a taste you will learn to acquire in the future.'

He doubted it but he nodded at her, smiling in return.

He took the buttered scone she proffered him and found it good, and had
another, and by the time he had eaten a cake that melted in his mouth he
was laughing inside, thinking, By gum! they just want to see me now, all
them in the kitchen. They just want to see me now. And wait till I tell
Janie. My! who would believe it? She had asked if he was willing to learn
to manage her affairs. God! just give him the chance. By lad! he had fallen
on his feet at last. It wouldn't matter now if the boatyard never made a go
of it. But he hoped it would, for Jimmy's sake. He mentioned the boatyard
to her now. It was when she said, 'I mustn't keep you any longer, Mr
Connor, you have a long walk home. But I will leave you to think over my
proposition. Perhaps tomorrow evening you will tell me what you have
decided. If your answer is favourable I can put you in touch with a man
who would teach you book-keeping and the rudiments of management. And
perhaps you could attend night school. But we can discuss that later.'

He rose to his feet saying, 'I'm not more than ten minutes' hard tramp
from my home now; I'm . . . I'm on the waterfront.'

She raised her eyebrows as she repeated, 'The waterfront?'

'Yes.' He squared his shoulders. 'I became interested in a boatyard, a very
small one mind.' He smiled as he nodded at her. 'A pocket handkerchief,
some folks would call it, but nevertheless it's big enough to make a keel and
scullers and such like. There's a house of sorts attached. I . . . I took it for
my brother. He's served his time in boat building, small boats that is, the
same line, scullers, wherries and such, and it's always been his dream to
have a place of his own where he could build. So I heard of this concern.
The man had died, and . . . and it was going reasonable, so I took a chance.'

Her face was stretching into a wide smile, her lips were apart showing
a set of strong white teeth. 'Well, well!' She inclined her head towards him.
'I wasn't wrong, was I? You do have business acumen. Where is this place?'

'Oh, it's yon side of the mill dam. It's so small you wouldn't be able to
see it, not among all the other yards along there. It used to belong to a Mr
Kilpatrick.'

'Kilpatrick?' She shook her head. 'I don't recall hearing the name. But
. . . but I'm very interested in your enterprise. I must come and see it some
time.'

'Yes, yes, do that.'

She walked with him to the door and although the maid was standing ready to open it she herself let him out, saying, 'Good night, Mr Connor. We will reopen this subject tomorrow evening.'

'Yes, as you say, miss. Good night.'

He was walking down the drive . . . no, marching down the drive.

'We will reopen this subject tomorrow evening.'

Indeed, indeed, we will.

Would you believe it?

They said the age of miracles was past.

Would he go to night school?

He'd go to hell and sit on a hot gridiron to please her.

But on the road he slowed his pace and again asked himself why she had picked him. And he gave himself her own answer. She didn't mix and it took her a long time to get to know people. Aye. Aye well, he could understand that. She wasn't the kind that most people would take to. No looks and too smart up top for most men, he supposed, for he had the idea she'd be brainy. And that would apply to her effect on women an' all.

Hip-hip-hooray! He wanted to throw his hat in the air. Things were happening. They were happening all the time. Janie! Here I come . . . A manager!

What wage would he get?

He'd have to leave that to her of course but he'd know the morrow night.

# Chapter Four

Janie left the Buckhams' with the mistress's words racing round in her mind. 'Well, you have a month to think it over, Janie,' she had said. 'It would be wonderful for you and it'll only be for three weeks. And just think, in all your life you might never have the opportunity to go abroad again. And the children would love to have you with them, you know that.'

Yes, Janie knew that, but she also knew that she was being asked to go to keep the children out of the way and let the master and mistress enjoy their holiday in France.

She had said she would talk to her husband about it, but she already knew what his answer would be. He hated the idea of her being out every day and if it wasn't that he had needed her wages he would have put his foot down before now. But with this new development and Miss Kean offering to make him manager, well, she knew that her days at the Buckhams' were numbered; in fact, she could have given in her notice this morning.

There was something else on her mind. She had promised John George she would go and see that lass of his, but with one thing and another she had never had time. But tonight Rory would be late, for even now he'd be in Westoe clinching the matter, and so she told herself why not clear her

conscience and go round and see that girl. She must be all of six months'
gone.

When she reached the end of the road she did not, automatically, turn
right and cut down to the river but went into a jumble of side streets and
towards Horsley Terrace.

They were, she considered, nice houses in the terrace, respectable. It was
number twenty-four; it had three steps up to the front door and an iron
railing cutting off four feet of garden. She went up the steps and rapped on
the door with the knocker. When it was opened she stared at the young
woman in front of her. She wasn't pregnant. 'Could . . . could I speak with
Miss Maggie Ridley please?'

The young woman cast a quick glance over her shoulder, then stepped
towards her, pulling the door half closed behind her.

'She's not here.'

'Oh, I had a message for her.'

The girl's eyes widened. 'A message? Who from?'

'Well, he's . . . he's a friend of hers.'

The young woman stared at her for a moment, then poked her face
forward, hissing, 'Well, if it's the friend I think it is you can tell him that
she's married. Tell him that.'

'Married?'

'That's what I said.'

'Oh well' – Janie was nodding her head now – 'In a way I'm glad to hear
it. I . . . I hope she'll be happy.'

The face looking into hers seemed to crumple and now the whispered
tone was soft and laden with sadness as she said, 'He . . . he was a friend
of, of my father's, he's a widower with a grown-up family.'

In the look they exchanged there was no need to say any more.

Janie now nodded towards the young woman and said, 'Thank you, I'll
. . . I'll tell him,' then turned and went down the steps. Poor John George!
And the poor lass. A dead old man likely. The very thought of it was mucky,
nasty.

Rory hadn't returned when she got in, but Jimmy was there with the
kettle boiling and the table set, and immediately he said, 'Sit down and put
your feet up.'

'I'm not tired.'

'Well, you should be. And will be afore the night's out, I've put the
washing in soak.'

'Thanks, Jimmy. Any news?'

'Aye, Mr Pearson, you know Pearson's Warehouse, I went in and asked
him the day. I said I'd carry anything. He joked at first and said he had
heard they were wantin' a battleship towed from Palmer's. And then he said
there were one or two bits he wanted sending across to Norway.' He laughed,
then went on excitedly, 'But after that he said, "Well, lad I'll see what I can
do for you." He said he believed in passing work around, there was too
many monopolies gettin' a hold in the town. I've got to look in the morrow.'

'Oh Jimmy, that's grand.' She took hold of his hand. 'Eeh! you just want
a start. And when I'm home all day I could give you a hand, I could, I'm
good at lumpin' stuff. And I could learn to steer an' all . . . But I'd better
learn to swim afore that.' She pushed at him and he laughed with her,

saying, 'Aye, but if they had to learn to swim afore they learned to row a boat on this river it would be empty; hardly any sailors swim.'

'Go on!'

'It's a fact.'

'Eeh! well, I'll chance it, I'll steer for you, or hoist the sail, 'cos have you thought you'll need another hand?' At the sound of footsteps she turned her head quickly away from him and towards the door, and she was on her feet when Rory entered the room, and she saw immediately that he was in great high fettle.

'It's settled then?'

'Out of me way, Mrs Connor.' He struck a pose and marched down the room as if he were carrying a swagger stick, and when he reached Jimmy he slapped the top of his own hat, saying, 'Touch yer peak, boy. Touch yer peak.'

Then they were all clinging together laughing, and he swung them round in a circle, shouting:

'Ring a ring o' roses,
Keels, scullers and posies,
Managers, managers,
All fall down.'

'But we're all going up!' He pulled them to a stop and, looking into Janie's laughing face, he added, 'Up! Up! We're going up, lass; nothing's going to stop us. She's for me, why God only knows, but she's the ladder on which we're going to climb. You take that from me. All of us' – he punched Jimmy on the head – 'all of us . . . She's got influence, fingers in all pies, and that includes this river an' all. We're going up, lad.'

Later, when in bed together and closely wrapped against each other, he said to her, 'You haven't seemed as over the moon as I thought you would be. There's something on your mind, isn't there?'

She didn't answer, and when he insisted, 'Come on,' she said, 'There's two things on me mind, Rory, but if I mention them they'll both cause rows, so I'd better not, had I?'

He was quiet for a moment before saying, 'Go on, tell me. I won't go off the deep end, whatever they are . . . I promise, whatever they are.'

It was a long moment before she said, 'Well mind, don't forget what you said.'

He waited, and then her voice a whisper she began, 'The missis, she wants me to go with them to France for a holiday. Of course, it's only to keep the bairns out of the way, I know, but she keeps tellin' me that I won't get the chance again . . .'

'Who says you won't get the chance again? They're not the only ones who can go to France. You're not goin'. You told her you're not going? All right, all right, I'm not going to get me neb up about it, but you did tell her you weren't goin'?'

'I said I didn't think you would hear of it.'

'That's right I won't. And you can also tell her when you're on, that you're putting your notice in . . . Well now, the other thing?' He waited.

'I went the night to take a message to . . . to John George's lass. She's
. . . she's married.'

'Married!'

'Yes, to an old man, a widower with a grown-up family.'

'It's . . . it's the best thing.' She could hardly hear his voice but she was
relieved that he had kept his promise and hadn't gone for her for mentioning
John George or his affairs. And now, a minute later, he was mumbling into
her neck, 'When he comes out I'll set him up. I've . . . I've always meant to
do something for him but now I can, I'll set him up properly in something.'

'Oh, Rory, Rory. Aw, that's . . . that's my Rory. I knew you would. Aw
ta, thanks, lad, thanks. I'll tell the missis the morrow straight out, I'll tell
her me husband's put his foot down and said no France and that I'll have
to be givin' in me notice shortly. Oh, Rory, Rory . . .'

In the middle of the night she was wakened by him crying out. His arms
were flaying about and when she put her hand on his head it came away
wet with sweat and she cried at him, 'Rory! Rory! wake up,' but he continued
to thrash about in the bed, gabbing out words from which she could
distinguish bits of the conversation that they'd had last night. 'I'll make it
up to John George, I will, I will. I always meant to.' Then he began to
shout, ''Twas being shut in, 'twas being shut in.'

When she finally managed to wake him he spluttered, 'What's it? What's-
the-matter?' Then putting his hand to his head, he added, 'I was dreamin'
. . . Was I talking?'

'Just jabbering. It was all the excitement.'

'Aye, yes,' he said, 'all the excitement. By! I'm wringing.'

'Yes, you are. Lie down, right down under the clothes here.' She drew
him towards her and held him closely, soothing him as if he were a child,
until he went to sleep again.

# Chapter Five

On three afternoons and three evenings of each of the next three weeks Rory
visited Mr Dryden, to be coached in the matter of accountancy and business
management.

Mr Dryden had in his early years been in accountancy, and later had
become a solicitor's clerk, and the reports he gave to Miss Kean on the
progress of his pupil were most encouraging. 'He shows great acumen,' he
told her. 'I think you have made a wise choice,' he told her. But he also told
his friends with a smirk that old Kean's daughter had taken on a protégé.
Ha! Ha! they said. Well, she wasn't likely to get a husband, so she had to
resort to a pastime. Yet, as some of them remarked, she ought to have known
her place and picked her pastime from a grade higher than that of rent
collectors, and this one by all accounts wasn't a skin away from a common
labouring man. If it wasn't that the fellow was already married you could

put another version to it, for as had already been demonstrated in one or two instances she was a strong-headed young woman who took little heed of people's opinions. Look what she was like on committees. She had got herself talked about more than once for openly defying the male opinion. Of course, this was due to the type of education she'd been given. She had been sent away, hadn't she? To the south somewhere, hadn't she? That was her mother's doing, So ... well, what could you expect?

Rory was not unaware of Mr Dryden's personal opinion of him. He gauged it in the condescending tone the old man used when speaking to him. But what did it matter, he could put up with that.

He was now receiving the handsome sum of twenty-five shillings a week, with the promise of it being raised when he should finally take over his duties. He'd had glimpses into what these would be during the past few days when he had seen the number of properties in Hexham and Gateshead, and the haberdashery and hatters shops that had been left by Grandfather Kean. All this besides the business old Kean himself had had on the side.

He became more and more amazed when he thought of what his late employer must have been worth. Yet never a night had he missed, winter or summer, coming to the office to pick up the takings, except when he was called away to visit his father. He had never, not to his knowledge, taken a holiday all the time he had been there, and yet he was rolling in money.

He wondered what she would be worth altogether. If she ever married, some man would come in for a packet. But apart from her not being the kind to take a man's fancy he thought she was too independent to think that way. No one, he considered, could be as business-like as her without having the abilities of a man in her make-up ...

It was Saturday morning and he had brought the takings from his two men – he thought of them as his now. She had allowed him to choose the second man himself. This fellow was young and hadn't done any rent collecting before but he had been to school continuously up till he was fourteen, and that was something to start on. Moreover, he was bright and eager and in need of work. He felt he had made a good choice. And he told her so. 'Patterson's doing well,' he said. 'Gettin' round quickly. And so far he's allowed nobody to take advantage of him, you know, soft-soap him.'

'Good.' She smiled at him from across the desk; then she said, 'I would like you to accompany me to Hexham on Monday.'

'Hexham?' He moved his head downwards while keeping his eyes on her. 'Very well.' He sometimes omitted to say miss, but she had never pulled him up for it.

'I think it's time you saw the places you're going to be responsible for.'

'Aye, yes, of course.' He'd have to stop himself saying aye.

'By the way –' she was still smiling at him – 'I should like to come and see your boatyard. I'm very interested in it. I may be of some assistance in supplying freight – in a small way. Would this afternoon be convenient?'

He thought quickly. What was the place like, was it tidy? Was there any washing hanging about? No, Janie had cleared the ironing up last night and scrubbed out last thing.

He nodded at her, saying, 'Yes, that'll be all right with me. Me wife won't be in because she works until four on a Saturday, she's nursemaid at the Buckhams in Westoe, but you'll be welcome to see ... '

'Your . . . wife?' The words came from deep within her chest and were separate as if they were strange and she had never spoken them before.

'Yes. Yes, miss, me wife . . .' His voice trailed off for he was amazed to see the colour flooding up over her face like a great blush.

'I . . . I wasn't aware that you were married, Mr Connor . . . Since when?'

'Well, well –' he moved uneasily in the chair – 'just recently, miss. I didn't like to mention it to you at the time because the date was fixed for shortly after your father's funeral. I couldn't change, it, but it didn't seem proper to . . .'

Her eyes were shaded now as she looked down towards the desk and on to her hands which were lying flat on the blotter, one on each side of the ledger that he had placed before her. Her back was straight, her body looked rigid. She said coolly, 'You should have informed me of your change of situation, Mr Connor.'

'I . . . I didn't think it was of any importance.'

'No importance!' She did not look at him, but now her eyes flicked over the table as if searching for some paper or other. 'A married man cannot give the attention to business that the single man can, for instance, he hasn't the time.'

'Oh, I have all the time . . .'

'Or the interest.' She had raised her eyes to his now. The colour had seeped from her face leaving it moist and grey. 'This alters matters, Mr Connor.' ·

He stared at her, his voice gruff now as he said, 'I don't understand, I can't see why.'

'You can't? Well then, if you can't then I am mistaken in the intelligence I credited you with.'

His back was as straight as hers now, his face grim.

As she held his gaze he thought, No, no, I'd be barmy to think that. I haven't got such a bloody big head on me as that. No! No! Yet it was pretty evident that the fact that he was married had upset her. She was likely one of these people who didn't believe in marriage, there were such about; there was one lived in the end house down the lane. She dressed like a man and it was said that she handled a horse and a boat as well as any man, but she looked half man. This one didn't. Although she had a business head on her shoulders she dressed very much as a woman of fashion might. He couldn't make her out. No, by God! he couldn't.

He said now, 'I can assure you, miss, me being married won't make any difference to my work. I'll give you my time and loyalty . . .'

'But as I have indicated, Mr Connor, only a certain amount of time and an equal amount of your loyalty . . . a married man has responsibilities. We can discuss the matter later. Mr Dryden has been paid in advance for your quarter's tuition, you will continue to go to him. That'll be all at present, Mr Connor. Good day.'

He rose stiffly from the chair. 'Good day . . . miss.'

The maid let him out; she smiled at him broadly. 'Good day, sir,' she said.

He had acquired the title of sir since it was known Miss Kean was sending him for training to be her manager and there was a significant deference in the servants' manners towards him now. She kept six altogether, with the gardener-cum-coachman. He answered her civilly, saying, 'Good day,' but as usual he did not address her by name. His position wasn't such that he felt he could do so yet.

Out on the drive he walked slowly, and at one point he actually stopped and said to himself, No! No! And before he entered the main thoroughfare he again slowed his walk and exclaimed aloud now, 'Don't be a fool!'

He had no false modesty about his personal attraction. He knew that many a back door would have been left open for him if he had just raised an eyebrow or answered a gleam in a hungry woman's eyes. He didn't class himself as particularly handsome but was aware that he had something which was of greater appeal. If he had been asked to define it he would have found it impossible; he only knew that women were aware of him. And he had liked the knowledge, it gave him what he called a lift. But at the same time he knew there was but one woman for him.

But he couldn't get away from the fact that she had done what she had for him because she thought he was single. Now the question was, why? Why?

Yet again he shook his head at himself and said no, no. Why, the woman must be worth a fortune, and although she was as plain as a pikestaff there were men in the town who, he thought, would more than likely overlook such a minor handicap in order to get their hands on what she owned. Doubtless, some were already trying, for twice of late there had been carriages on the drive and he had seen sombre-clothed gentlemen descending towards them as he approached the house. And he recalled now they had looked at him pretty hard.

But coming to know her as he had done over the past weeks, he imagined she would have all her wits about her with regard to such suitors who would be only after the main chance. She was the kind of woman who would do the choosing rather than be chosen, and apart from her face she had a lot on her side to enable her to do the choosing ... *Had she been going to choose him?*

He didn't answer himself this time with, 'No! No!' but walked on, muttering instead, 'God Almighty! it's unbelievable.'

'You're quiet the night. Nothing wrong is there? And what made you go back to the office this afternoon?'

'Oh, I had some work to get through. It's been a heavy week, and I've got that Pittie mob on me mind. Did he say he'd seen them around the day?'

'No. He only stayed in for a few minutes after I got home, I told you. He said he was goin' down to collect some wood he had roped together.'

'But that was this afternoon. It's dark, he should be back by now. I'd better take a walk out and see if he's comin'.'

He looked towards her where she was kneading dough in a brown earthenware dish, then went out and down the steps into the yard. There was a moon riding high, raced by white scudding clouds. He walked to the end of the little jetty and looked along each side of the river where boats large and small were moored. He liked the river at night when it was quiet like this, but he had made up his mind, at least he had done until this morning, that it wouldn't be long before he moved Janie away from this quarter and into a decent house in the town. He had thought Jimmy could stay on here, Jimmy wouldn't mind living on his own, for he was self-sufficient was Jimmy. But now things had changed. This morning's business had blown his schemes away into dust.

He'd had the feeling of late that he was galloping towards some place but he didn't know where. So many strange things had happened over the past months. He wasn't even wearing the same kind of clothes he wore a few weeks ago for she had hinted not only that he should get a new suit but where he should go to buy it. However, he hadn't patronised the shop she suggested; he hadn't, he told himself, enough money as yet for that kind of tailoring. Nevertheless, he had got himself a decent suit, with a high waistcoat and the jacket flared, and the very cut of it had lifted him out of the rent collector's class. But now the rosy future had suddenly died on him. What would she say on Monday? . . . Well, he'd have to wait and see, that's all he could do.

He heard a soft splash and saw the minute figure of Jimmy steering the boat towards the jetty. He bent down and grabbed the rope that Jimmy threw to him, then said, 'You all right? Where you been all day? What's taken you so long?'

'The wood I'd had piled up, it was scattered, some back in the river, all over. I had a job collectin' it again.'

'The Pitties?'

'I shouldn't wonder. I don't think it could be bairns, it would have been too heavy for them.'

'Well, leave it where it is till the mornin', we'll sort it out then.'

When Jimmy had made fast his boat and was standing on the quay he peered at Rory saying, 'What's up? You look as if you'd lost a tanner and found a threepenny bit. Anything wrong?'

'No, no, nothing. How about you?'

'Oh well, they were around early on in the mornin' again, two of them. They moored just opposite and sat lookin' across, just starin'. But I went on with me work, and I stood for a time and stared back. Then they went off.' And he added, 'If they try anything I'll go straight and tell the river polis.'

'It'll likely be too late then. The only thing is be careful and don't be such a bloody fool stayin' out in the dark. They're not likely to try anything in the daylight, but give them a chance in the dark, and you're asking for it.'

All Jimmy replied to this was, 'Aye. By! I'm hungry,' and ran up the steps, and when he opened the door he sniffed loudly and said, 'Ooh! that smells good.'

Janie turned to him from the table, saying, 'Aye well, now you'll have to wait a bit, we've had to wait for you.'

'I'm hungry, woman.'

'Are you ever anything else?' she laughed at him. 'Well, there's some fresh teacakes there, tuck into them.'

As he broke a hot teacake in two, he asked, 'What's for supper?'

'Finny haddy.'

'Good, and hurry up with it.'

She thrust out her arm to clip his ear, but he dodged the blow and went and sat himself on the steel fender with his back to the oven and laughed and chatted as he ate.

Looking at him, Rory knew a sudden spasm of envy as he thought, he was born bowed, but he was born happy. Why can't I be like him? But then the answer to that one was, they had different mothers. He hadn't thought along these lines for some time now; it was odd but it was only when he was faced with trouble that he let his bitterness against Lizzie have rein.

Of a sudden he said to neither of them in particular, 'Will we have to go home the morrow again?'

Both Janie and Jimmy turned a quick glance on him and it was Janie who said, 'Of course we'll have to go home the morrow. We always do, don't we? It's Sunday.'

'That's it, that's what I mean, we always do. Couldn't we do something different, take a trip up the river or something? We've got our own boat.'

'But they'll be expectin' us. It won't be Sunday for them if we don't go up; they'll all be there.'

'Aye, they'll all be there.' His voice trailed away on a sigh and he turned and went into the bedroom while Janie and Jimmy exchanged another look and Jimmy said under his breath, 'Something's wrong. I twigged it right away.'

'You think so?' Janie whispered back.

'Aye, don't you?'

'Well, I did think he was a bit quiet, but when I asked him he said everything was all right.'

'Aye, that's what he says, but there's something up. I'm tellin' you, there's something up.'

When, in the middle of the night, Janie was again woken from her sleep by Rory's voice, not mumbling this time but shouting, she hissed at him, 'Ssh! ssh! Wake up. What is it?'

But he went on, louder now, 'I'll make it up to you, I will . . . I know . . . I know, but I couldn't.'

'Rory! Rory! wake up.'

'Five pounds. I had it, I had it. You're to blame.'

'Rory! do you hear me?' She was trying to shake him.

'Wha'? Wha'?' He half woke and grabbed at her hands, then almost at the same time threw her aside, crying, 'What was the good of two of us doin' time! I'm not goin' in there, so don't keep on. You won't get me in there, not for five pounds, or fifty. Five clarty pounds. Five clarty pounds. If I'd had the chance I'd have put it back, I would. I . . . would . . . ' His voice trailed away and he fell back on the pillows.

Janie sat bolt upright in the bed staring down through the darkness, not on to Rory but towards where her hands were gripping the quilt . . . *That was it then. That was it!* It should have been as clear as daylight from the beginning.

She saw John George's face through the grid saying, 'Tell Rory that, will you? Tell him I didn't take the five pounds.' And what John George was actually saying was, 'Tell him to own up.' She couldn't believe it, yet she knew it was true. He had let John George, his good friend, go to that stinking place alone. It was true he couldn't have done much about it at first, but after he regained consciousness in hospital he must have known. That's why he hadn't asked for John George. It should have been one of the first things he mentioned. 'What's the matter with John George?' he should have said. 'Why hasn't he come to see me?'

No, she couldn't believe it, she couldn't. But she had to. She now turned her head towards the bulk lying beside her and instinctively hitched herself away from it towards the wall. But the next move she made was almost like that of an animal, for she pounced on him and her hands gripping his shoulders, she cried, 'Wake up! Wake up!'

'Wha'? What's-it? What's-up? What's-wrong?'

'Get up. Get up.'

As he pulled himself up in the bed she climbed over him, grabbed the matches from the table and lit the candle, and all the while he was repeating, 'What is it? What's the matter?'

The candle lit, she held it upwards and gazed down into his blinking eyes.

'What's up with you? You gone mad or something?'

'Aye, I've gone mad, flamin' mad; bloody well flamin' mad.'

She sounded like Lizzie and her grannie rolled into one. He pushed the clothes back from the bed but didn't get up, he just peered at her. 'What the hell's up with you, woman?'

'You ask me that! Well, you've just had a nightmare an' you've just cleared up somethin' that's been puzzling me for a long time. *You!* Do you know what I could do to you this minute? I could spit in your eye, Rory Connor. I could spit in your eye.'

He now leant his stiff body back against the wall. He'd had a nightmare, he'd been talking. He was sweating, yet cold, it was always cold on the river at night. With a thrust of his arm he pushed her aside and got out of the bed and pulled his trousers on over his linings, but didn't speak; and neither did she. But when he went towards the door to go into the other room she followed him, holding the candle high, and she watched him grab the matches from the mantelpiece and light the lamp. When it was aflame he turned and looked at her and said quietly, 'Well, now you know.'

'Aye, I know. And how you can stand there and say it like that God alone knows. My God! to think you let John George take the rap for you . . .'

He turned on her. His voice low and angry, he said, 'He didn't take the rap for me, he took it for himself. He'd have been caught out sooner or later; he'd been at it for months.'

'Aye, he might have, but only for a few shillings at a time not five pounds.'

'No, not for a few shillings, a pound and more. I'd warned him.'

'You warned him!' Her voice was full of scorn. 'But you went and did the same, and for no little sum either. It was for your five pounds he got put away for the year, not for the little bit.'

'It wasn't. I tell you it wasn't.

'Oh, shut up! Don't try to stuff me like you've been doin' yourself. That's what you've been tellin' yourself all along, isn't it, to ease your conscience? But your conscience wouldn't be eased, would it? Remember our first night in this place. You nearly knocked me through the wall 'cos I mentioned his name. I should have twigged then.'

'Aye, yes, you should.' His tone was flat now, weary-sounding. 'And if you had, it would have been over and done with, I'd have gone through less.'

'Gone through less! You talkin' about goin' through anything, what about John George?'

'Damn John George!' He was shouting now. 'I tell you he would have gone along the line in any case.'

'You'll keep tellin' yourself that till the day you die, yet you don't believe it because the other night you promised to set him up when he came out. Eeh! –' she now shook her head mockingly at him – 'that was kind of you, wasn't it? And I nearly went on me knees to you for it.'

'Janie –' he came towards her – 'try to understand. You . . . you know how I feel about being locked in, and I was bad at the time. I was bad. God! I nearly died. And that was no make game, I couldn't think clearly not for weeks after.'

As his hand came out towards her she sprang back from it, saying, 'Don't touch me, Rory Connor. Don't touch me, not until you get yourself down to that station and tell them the truth.'

'*What!*' The word carried a high surprised note of utter astonishment. 'You'd have me go along the line now?'

'Aye, I would, and be able to live with you when you come out. It isn't the pinchin' of the five pounds that worries me, an' if nobody had suffered through it I would have said, "Good for you if you can get off with it," but not now, not the way things are; not when that lad's back there. And you know something? When I think of it he could have potched you, he could have said you were the only other one who had a key. He could have said you were a gambling man and would sell your own mother. Oh aye –' she wagged her head now – 'you would sell your real mother for less than five pounds any day in the week, wouldn't you? Poor Lizzie . . .'

The blow that caught her across the mouth sent her staggering, and at the same moment Jimmy came rushing down the ladder. Without a word he went to her where she was leaning against the chest-of-drawers, her back arched, her hand across her mouth, and he put his arm around her waist as he looked towards Rory and said, 'You'll regret that, our Rory. There'll come a day when you'll be sorry for that.'

'You mind your own bloody business. And get out of this.'

'I'll not. I've heard enough to make me as sick as she is. I can't believe it of you, I just can't. And to John George of all people. He'd have laid down his life for you.'

Rory turned from the pair and stumbled to the mantelpiece and, gripping its edge, he stared down into the banked-down fire. That he was more upset by Jimmy's reactions than by Janie's didn't surprise him, for he knew he represented a sort of hero to his brother. He had never done one outstanding thing to deserve it but he had accepted his worship over the years, and found comfort in it, but now Jimmy had turned on him.

God Almighty! why did everything happen to him at once? Her, yesterday, blaming him for being married, now this with Janie; and not only Janie, Jimmy. Yet he knew that if, come daylight, he took himself along to the polis station they'd both be with him every inch of the road. But he couldn't, he knew he couldn't go and tell them the truth. Apart from his fear of imprisonment look what he stood to lose, his job; and not only that but the good name that would help him to get another. Never again would he be allowed to handle money once he had been along the line. And this place would go, Jimmy's yard. Had he thought of that? He swung round now, crying at them, 'All right, if I was to give meself up, what would happen? No more yard for you, Jimmy boy, your dream gone up in smoke. Did you think of that?'

'No, but now you mention it, it wouldn't be the end of me, I could always

get me other job back. And I can always go home again. Don't let that stop
you. Don't you try to use me in that way, our Rory.'

'And her, what's gona happen to her then?' He was speaking of Janie as
if she weren't sitting by the table with her face buried in her hands, and
Jimmy answered, 'She won't be any worse off than she was afore, she's
always got her place.'

'Aw, to hell's flames with the lot of you!' He flung his arm wide as if
sweeping them out of the room. 'What do you know about anything? Own
up and be a good boy and I'll stand by you. You know nowt, the pair of you,
the lot of you, you're ignorant, you can't see beyond your bloody noses.
There's swindlin' going on every day. Respectable men, men looked up to
in this town twisting with every breath. And you'd have me ruin meself for
five pounds.'

'It's not the five . . . '

'Be quiet, Jimmy! Be quiet!' Janie's voice was low. 'You won't get
anywhere with him 'cos he'll keep on about the five pounds, he'll try to
hoodwink you like he's hoodwinked himself. Well –' she rose from the table
– 'I know what I'm gona do.' She walked slowly into the bedroom and they
both gazed after her. When the door banged behind her Jimmy made for
the ladder and without another word mounted it and disappeared through
the trap door.

Rory stared about the empty room for a moment, then turning towards
the mantelshelf again he bowed his head on it and slowly beat his fist against
the rough wall above it.

# Chapter Six

'Why, lass, it's the chance in a lifetime. In a boat cruising? My! my! round
France. My! the master's brother must have plenty of money to own a boat
like that.'

'I think it's his wife who has the money, he married a French lady.'

'And you tell us it's a sort of castle they live in?'

'Yes, that's what the missis says.'

'We'll miss you, lass.' Lizzie sat back on her heels from where she had
been kneeling sweeping the fallen cinders underneath the grate and she
looked hard at Janie as she said, 'I know it's only for three weeks, but what
puzzles me is him lettin' you go at all. Didn't he kick up a shindy?'

Janie turned away and looked towards Ruth where she was coming out
of the scullery carrying plates of thickly cut bread, and she answered, 'Yes,
a bit. But then he's taken up with his new position an' such, and . . . and
often doesn't get in till late.'

'Aye.' Lizzie pulled her bulk upright and bent to her sweeping once again.
'His new position. By! he's fallen on his feet if anybody has. It was a whole
day's blessin' when old Kean died, you could say.'

'You're off first thing in the mornin' then, lass?'

Janie nodded towards Ruth and said, 'Yes, we've got to be in Newcastle by eight o'clock; we're goin' up by carriage.'

'Then all the way to London by train.' Ruth shook her head. 'It's amazing, wonderful; the sights you'll see. It would have been a great pity if you hadn't taken the opportunity; such a thing as this only comes once in a lifetime . . . And you won't stay for a bite to eat?'

'I can't, thanks all the same, there's so much to do, to see to you know. And that reminds me. I needn't ask you, need I, to see to me grannie?'

'Aw, lass –' Ruth pulled a face at her – 'you know that goes without sayin'. At least you should.'

'Aye, I know. And thanks, thanks to both of you.' She cast her glance between them, then looking at Lizzie, who had now risen to her feet, she said, 'Well, I'd better say ta-rah,' and the next moment she was hugging Lizzie, and Lizzie was holding her tight and saying brokenly, 'Now don't cry, there's nowt to cry about, goin' on a holiday . . . Don't. Don't lass.'

'There, there.' She was enfolded in Ruth's arms now and Lizzie was patting her shoulder. Then swiftly pulling herself away from them, she grabbed up her bag from a chair and ran out of the cottage.

It was Ruth who, having closed the door after her, came back to the centre of the room and looking at Lizzie said, 'Well, what do you make of it?'

'What can I make of it? There's somethin' wrong, and has been for weeks past, if you ask me. He's hardly been across the door. And Jimmy, look what he was like the last time he was here, no high-falutin' talk of boats and cargoes and contracts an' such like.'

'Whatever it is, it doesn't lie just atween the both of them, not when Jimmy's concerned in it.'

'No, you're right there.' Lizzie nodded. 'And it couldn't be just marriage rows. Jimmy would take those in his stride, havin' been brought up on them.' She smiled faintly. 'No, whatever it is, it's somethin' big and bad. I'm worried.'

'In a couple of days' time we could take a walk down and tidy up and do a bit of baking and such like. What do you say, Lizzie?'

'That's a sensible idea. Aye, we could do that, and we might winkle out something while we're there.'

'It could be. It could be.'

'Things are changin', Ruth. Folks and places, everything.'

Ruth came to her now and, tapping her arm gently, said, 'Don't worry about him, he'll straighten things out. Whatever trouble there is he'll straighten things out. He's your own son, and being such he's bound to be sensible at bottom.'

'You're a good woman, Ruth, none better.'

They turned sadly away from each other now and went about their respective duties in the kitchen.

Janie had been gone ten days and his world was empty. If she were to appear before him at this minute he would say to her, 'All right, I'll go, I'll go now, as long as I know you'll be here, the old Janie, waiting for me when I come out.' His mind was like a battlefield, he was fighting love and hate, and recrimination and bitterness.

The recrimination was mostly against his employer. He had seen her only twice in the past three weeks. He still took the takings to the house in the evenings but his orders were to leave them in the study and to call for the books the next morning.

During their two meetings there had been no discussion about future plans of any kind. Her manner had been cool and formal, her tone one that he recalled from her visits to the office years ago. It was the tone in which orders were issued and brooked no questions.

But although in one breath he was telling himself that if Janie were here now he would do what she asked, in the next he was asking himself what was going to happen when she did return. After the night of the show-down she had slept up in the loft, and Jimmy had slept on a shaky-down in the kitchen. Would it go on like that until he gave in? He could have asserted his rights as many a man before him had done by well-directed blows, but the fact that he had hit her once was enough; that alone had created a barrier between them. She wasn't the type of girl who would stand knocking about, she had too much spirit, and he was ashamed, deeply ashamed of having struck her. He had acted no better than his father whom, at bottom, he despised.

It was Saturday again. He hated Saturdays, Sundays more so. He hadn't gone up home since she had left, but they had been down here, at least Ruth and she had. They had cleaned up and cooked, and spoken to each other as if they were back in the kitchen. They hadn't asked any questions regarding how he felt about her going away, which pointed more forcibly than words to the fact that they were aware that something was wrong.

Then there was Jimmy. Jimmy was making him wild, sitting for hours at night scratching away with a pencil on bits of paper and never opening his mouth. He had turned on him the other night and cried, 'If anyone's to blame for this business it's you. Who pestered me into buying this bloody ramshackle affair, eh? Who?' and snatching up a miniature wooden ship's wheel from the mantelshelf he had flung it against the far wall, where it had splintered into a dozen pieces, and Jimmy, after looking down on the fragments with a sort of tearful sadness, had gone up the ladder, leaving him to increased misery.

He stood at the window now looking down on to the yard. The sun was glinting on the water; there were boats plying up and down the river; on the slipway Jimmy had set the keel of a new boat in the small stocks and he was working on it now. In the ordinary way he would have been down there helping him, they would have been exchanging jokes about what they would do when they had the monopoly of the river, or grinding their teeth at the Pitties and their tactics.

As he looked down on Jimmy's fair head, he was suddenly brought forward with a jerk, for there, coming round the side of the building, was Ruth and his da and Lizzie. It wasn't the fact that they'd all turned up together to visit him, it was the expression on their faces that was riveting his attention for both Lizzie and Ruth were crying, openly crying as they talked rapidly to Jimmy, and his da was now holding out a paper to Jimmy. He watched Jimmy reading it, shake his head, then put his hand to his brow before turning and looking up at the window. Then they were all looking up at the window.

He didn't step back but started down at them as they remained still, their postures seemingly frozen into a group of statuary. He noticed that Lizzie was wearing her old shawl, and old it was, green in parts. And Ruth too was in a shawl; she nearly always wore a bonnet. And they both still had their aprons on.

He moved from the window and went to the door and, having opened it, looked down the steps at them. They came towards him. It was his father who mounted first, and he said to him, 'What's up?' But Paddy didn't answer, he just walked into the room, followed by Ruth and Lizzie and, lastly, Jimmy.

Rory's gaze travelled from one to the other, then came to rest on Jimmy who was gripping the paper with both hands and staring at him.

He did not repeat his question to Jimmy, but took the paper from him and began to read.

'It is with deep regret that we hear of the terrible tragedy that has overtaken a Shields family on holiday on the coast of France. Mr Charles Buckham, his wife, three children, and their nursemaid Mrs Jane Connor, together with Mr Buckham's brother, are feared lost, after their yacht was caught in a great storm. Mrs Buckham's body and that of one child were washed ashore, together with pieces of wreckage from the boat. There is little hope of any survivors. Two other boats were wrecked at the same time, with a total loss of twenty-six lives. Mr Charles Buckham was a prominent member . . . '

Someone must have brought a chair forward for him to sit on because when next he looked at them they were standing in a half-circle before him and they were all crying, even his da. His own eyes were dry; his whole body was dry, he was being shrivelled up; his mind had stopped working except for a section which oozed pain and ran like a burning acid down into his heart, and there it was etching out her name: Janie. Janie.

'Janie. Janie,' he said the name aloud and turned and saw Lizzie lift up her white apron and fling it over her head, and when she began to moan like a banshee he made no protest because the sound was finding an echo within himself. 'Janie. Janie. Aw, Janie, don't go, Janie. Don't be dead, Janie. Come back to me, Janie. Don't leave me. Don't leave me. I'll see about John George, honest to God I promise, now, right now. Oh, Janie.'

'Give him a drop out of the bottle.'

Paddy put his hand into his inside pocket and drew out a flat flask of whisky and, picking up a cup, he almost half-filled it. Then handing it to Rory, he said, 'Get it down you, lad. Get it down you. You need to be fortified. God knows you need to be fortified.'

When Lizzie suddenly cried, 'Why does God bring disasters like this to us? What have we ever done to Him?' Paddy turned on her, hissing, 'Whist! woman. It's questions like that that bring on disasters.'

Her wailing increased, and she cried, 'It's the third thing. I said there would be three, didn't I? Didn't I? An' I told Andrews the polis when he brought the paper up, didn't I, didn't I?'

'Oh Janie, Janie. Come back, Janie. Just let me look on you once more.' It was sayings like that that brought disaster his da had just said. He was ignorant. They were all ignorant. That's what he had said to Janie, they were all ignorant. And he had compared their talk, their ways, and their dwelling, the dwelling that he had known since birth, with Charlotte Kean and her fine house. Yet their ignorance was a warm ignorance, it was something you didn't have to live up to; pretence fell through it like water through a sieve. Their ignorance was a solid foundation on which he could lean. He was leaning against it now, his head tucked against warm, thick flesh, nor when he realized it was Lizzie's flesh, his mother's flesh, did he push it away. In this moment he needed ignorance, he needed love, he needed warmth, he needed so many things to make up for the loss of Janie.

'Aw, Janie, Janie. I'm sorry, Janie. I'm sorry, Janie.'

# Chapter Seven

Charlotte Kean did not read the paper until late on the Saturday evening. She had returned from Hexham about seven o'clock feeling tired, irritable and lonely. After a meal she had gone into the office with the intention of doing some work on the mass of papers that always awaited her on the desk, but after sitting down she stared in front of her for a moment before closing her eyes and letting her body slump into the depths of the leather chair.

How much longer could she go on like this? She'd asked herself the same question numbers of times over the past weeks. There was a remedy, in fact two. But the cure offered by either Mr Henry Bolton or Mr George Pearson was worse, she imagined, than her present disease. Henry Bolton was forty-eight and a widower. George Pearson would never see fifty again. She wasn't foolish enough to think that either of them had fallen in love with her. She would go as far as to say that they didn't even like her, considering her ways too advanced by half, having heard her opinions from across a committee table. But since the death of both her father and her grandfather they had almost raced each other to the house.

*No. No. Never.*

She rose from the desk. She was a spinster and she'd remain a spinster. The wild fantastic dream she'd had was only that, a wild fantastic dream. She had humiliated herself because of her dream; she had been willing to be publicly humiliated because of her dream.

She went from the office and upstairs to her room, the room that until a few weeks ago had been her father's. It was the largest bedroom in the house and faced the garden and shortly after he died she had it completely redecorated and had made it her own. She knew that the servants had been slightly shocked by such seeming lack of respect for the dead but she didn't care what servants thought, or anyone else for that matter.

It was very odd, she mused, as she slowly took off her day clothes and got into a housegown, a new acquisition and another thing that had shocked the servants, for it wasn't black or brown, or even grey, but a startling pink, and its material was velvet. Yes, it was very odd, but there was no one for whose opinion she cared one jot. And more sadly still, there was no one who cared one jot about what happened to her. She hadn't a close relative left in the world, nor had she a close friend. There were those in the town who would claim her as a friend, more so now, but to her they were no more than acquaintances.

She sat before the mirror and unpinned her hair and the two dark, shining plaits fell down over her shoulders and almost to her waist. As her fingers undid each twist the hair seemed to spring into a life of its own and when, taking a brush, she stroked it from the crown down to its ends it covered her like a cloak.

The brush poised to the side of her face, she stared at herself in the mirror. It was a waste on her; it should have been doled out to some pretty woman and it would have made her beautiful, whereas on her head it only seemed to emphasize the plainness of her features. She leant forward and stared at her reflection. How was it that two eyes, a nose, and a mouth could transform one face into attractiveness while leaving another desolate of any appeal? She was not misshapen in any way, yet look at her. She dressed well, she had a taste for dress, she knew the right things to wear but the impression they afforded stopped at her neck. She had even resorted to the artifice of toilet powder, and in secret had applied rouge to her lips and cheeks with the result that she looked nothing better, she imagined, than a street woman.

She rose and glanced towards the bed. Were she to go to bed now she wouldn't sleep. She couldn't read in bed at all. This was the outcome, she supposed, of being taught to read while sitting in a straight-backed chair. Her father had enforced this rule and the teachers at the school to which her mother had sent her were of a like mind too. When she was young her idea of heaven had been to curl up on the rug before the fire and read a book, but when finally she had returned home from school she had found no pleasure in this form of relaxation.

She decided to go down to the drawing-room and play the piano for a while. This often had the power to soothe her nerves. Then she would take a bath, after which she might get to sleep without thinking.

It was as she was crossing the hall that she noticed the local paper neatly folded, together with a magazine, lying on a salver on the side table. She picked up both and went on into the drawing-room. But before laying them down she glanced at the newspaper's headlines: Shields Family Lost at Sea.

'It is with deep regret that we hear of the terrible tragedy that has overtaken a Shields family on holiday on the coast of France. Mr Charles Buckham, his wife, three children and their nursemaid, Mrs Jane Connor, together with Mr Buckham's brother are feared lost, after their yacht was caught in a great storm. Mrs Buckham's body and that of one child were washed ashore, together with pieces of wreckage from the boat. There is little hope of any survivors . . .'
Mrs Jane Connor, nursemaid.
*Mrs Jane Connor, nursemaid.*

He had said she was nursemaid to the Buckhams. Yes, yes, it was the Buckhams of Westoe. She knew him, Charles Buckham, and she had met his wife a number of times, and . . . and there couldn't be two nursemaids by the name of Jane Connor.

He hadn't said his wife had gone away, but then she hadn't spoken to him for weeks, not since he had startled her by saying he was married.

She was sorry, very sorry . . .

*Was she?*

Of course she was, it was a terrible thing. Could she go to him now and tell him? What time was it? She swung round and looked at the clock on the mantelpiece. Quarter-to-nine. It was still light, yet she didn't know exactly where the place was; but it was on the waterfront and would be dark by the time she got there.

She found herself walking up and down the room. Her stomach was churning with excitement. She said again, 'What a tragedy! A terrible tragedy. And those poor young children.'

She suddenly stopped her pacing and, dropping into a chair, bent her body forward until her breasts were almost touching her knees. She mustn't make herself ridiculous; nothing had altered, things stood as they had done a few minutes earlier.

Slowly she drew herself up and, taking in deep draughts of air, said to herself, 'You can call tomorrow morning. It will be quite in order then for you to go and offer your condolences. He's in your employ and naturally you have his concern at heart. Go and have a bath now and go to bed; you can do nothing until tomorrow.'

She had a bath and she went to bed, but it was almost dawn before she finally fell asleep. And she was still asleep when the maid came in with her early morning tea at eight o'clock.

She hardly gave herself time to drink the tea before she was out of bed dressing, and at nine o'clock she left the house, presumably to go to an early service. She had informed Jessie that she wouldn't need the carriage, it was a fine morning and she preferred to walk.

The only answer Jessie could give to this was 'Yes, miss,' but the expression on her face told Charlotte that she considered that by breaking yet another rule she was letting the prestige of the family down; no one of any importance in this district went to church on foot.

Because the occasion demanded sobriety she had dressed in the black outfit she had worn to her father's funeral and so she wasn't conspicuous as she made her way from the residential quarter of Westoe to the long district lining the waterfront. Yet she did not pass without notice for she was tall and slim and her walk was purposeful as if she knew where she was going. But on this occasion she didn't, at least not precisely.

Having almost reached the Lawe she stopped an old riverside man and asked him if he could direct her to Mr Connor's boatyard.

'Connor's boatyard? Never knew no boatyard by that name along this stretch, ma'am. No Connor's boatyard along here.'

'It's . . . it's a small yard, I understand.'

'Big or small, ma'am, none of that name.'

'Mr Connor has only recently taken the yard over.'

'Small yard, taken it over?' The old man rubbed the stubble on his chin and said, 'Oh aye, now I come to think of it, it's old Barney Kilpatrick's place. Oh aye, I heard tell of a young 'un startin' up there. Takes some grit and guts to start on your own along this stretch. Well now, ma'am, you turn yourself round and go back yonder till you pass a space full of lumber, bits of boats . . . odds and ends. There's a cut at yon side atween a set of palings, the gate into Kilpatrick's place is but a few steps down there.'

'Thank you. Thank you very much.'

'You're welcome, ma'am. You're welcome.'

She walked swiftly back along the potholed road, followed the directions the old man had given her and within a few minutes found herself opposite a wooden gate in a high fence of black sleepers.

The gate opened at a touch and she went through and stood for a moment looking at the ramshackle building before her. There were steps leading up to a door and, having mounted them, she knocked gently and waited. After a short interval she knocked again, harder now, and after knocking a third time she tried the handle and found the door locked.

She descended the steps and looked about her. There was evidence of a small boat being built. She walked into the slipway, then out again and stood looking up at the windows. She could see the place as a boatyard, even though it was very small, but as a residence, never. She gave a slight shudder. Being almost on the river's edge it would be overrun with rats and so damp. And he lived here and had spoken of it with enthusiasm!

Where was he now? Most likely at his parents' house. Of course, that's where he would be. Well, she couldn't go there . . . or could she?

'You mustn't. You mustn't.'

She walked out of the yard, closing the gate behind her, and again she chastised herself, sternly now. 'You mustn't. You mustn't. Please retain some sense of decorum.'

But it was such a long time until tomorrow. Would he come to work? Well, the only thing she could do was to wait and see, and if he didn't put in an appearance, then she would go to his home. It would seem quite in order to do so then.

She walked slowly back through the town. People were making their way to the churches. There were a number of carriages in the market place adjacent to St. Hilda's. She wondered for a moment whether she should go in there, then decided not to. What would she pray for? She mustn't be a hypocrite. She'd always prided herself on being honest, at least to herself. She went to church, but she was no churchwoman. She knew why more than half the congregation attended her own particular church. Their reasons were various, but had nothing to do with God and worship: to see and be seen; to make connections. It was an established fact that it did one no harm in the business world to belong to a congregation, especially if you paid substantially for your pew and had your name inscribed on a silver nameplate.

In her loneliest moments she warned herself against cynicism knowing that if she didn't want to lose those few people who termed themselves her friends she must keep her radical opinions to herself. But oh, she had thought so often how wonderful it would be, how comforting to have someone with whom she could talk plainly. A male. Oh, yes a male, someone like . . .

When had she first thought of him in that way? All her life seemingly. Don't be ridiculous. Well, four and a half years was a lifetime.

Sunday was a long day, and on Monday morning she was awake early and dressed for outdoors by eight o'clock, and by a quarter to nine she was seated behind the desk in the inner office in Tangard Street.

If he were coming to work he would come here to see to the men. If he didn't put in an appearance, well she must see to them, and once they were settled she would go on to Simonside and offer her condolences . . .

He came into the office at ten minutes to nine and she was shocked at the sight of him, and sad, truly sad; yet the same time envious of a woman who, by her going, could pile the years almost overnight on a man.

She rose swiftly from the chair, then came round the desk and stood in front of him, saying, and with sincere feeling, 'I'm so sorry. Now you shouldn't have come, I didn't expect you. You . . . you must go home and stay there as long as you feel it is necessary; there's no hurry, I can see to things . . .'

She watched him wet his lips before saying in a voice so unlike his own in that it was quiet, like that of a sick man bereft of strength, 'I'd . . . I'd much rather be at work, if you don't mind.'

'Well –' she shook her head slowly – 'it's as you wish. But . . . but you don't look well. And . . . and haven't you got . . . ? Well, aren't there things you must see to officially?'

'No.' He shook his head. 'We . . . I went to Saturday. The police said they'd let me know if they heard anything further. Mr . . . Mr Buckham's father has gone over, I'm to see him when he comes back.'

'Oh.' She stared into his face. It was grey, lifeless. She realized as she looked at him that his appeal did not come from his looks at all, as one might imagine, as she herself had imagined years ago, but from the vitality within, from the bumptiousness and the arrogance that was part of his nature. At the moment there was no life either in his face or in his body. But, of course, it was to be understood this was only temporary; he was under shock, he would revive . . . she would see that he revived. The decision he had taken to come straight to work was the best possible thing he could have done.

She said now, 'Then I can leave you?'

'Yes.'

She picked up her bag and gloves from the desk, and turning to him again, she said, 'If you wish you may send Mr Taylor with the collection.'

'Thanks.' He inclined his head towards her.

'Are you staying with your parents?'

'No.' He shook his head. 'I've been with them over the weekend but I'm going back to the boatyard.'

She said with some concern now, 'Do you think it wise for you to be alone at this time?'

'My brother will be with me.'

'Oh.' She stared at him; then again she said, 'I'm deeply sorry.'

He made no reply but turned from her and she had to stop herself from going to him for she imagined he was about to cry, and if she were to see him cry . . . She turned hastily and went out.

Alone now he stood staring down at the desk as if he had never seen it before, as if he were surprised to find it there; then going behind it, he sat down and, drawing a handkerchief from his pocket, wiped it quickly round his face before blowing his nose. He had said he'd be better at work. He'd never be better anywhere, anytime, but being here was better than remaining in the kitchen. He'd go mad if he had to listen to any more talk of Janie. Since Saturday night they had talked about her, wailed about her, cried about her, and he too had cried and wailed, but inside. To them it was as if she were lying in the coffin in the corner of the room. They had drunk their beer and had their tots of whisky as if they were holding a wake. They had sat up all night, the Learys and her da and grannie, and his own father and Ruth and Jimmy . . . and her. Nellie had come and her husband with her. And that had been another thing that had nearly driven him mad. When Nellie announced through her tears that she was pregnant at last, and her, his big slob of a slavering mother, had cried, 'That's God's way. That's God's way, when He shuts one door He opens another.' Another day among them and he would have gone out of his mind.

There was only one good thing that had come out of it, he and Jimmy were back where they were before. Nothing had been said but Jimmy hadn't left his side since Saturday, not even during the night, the longest night of his life. All Saturday night he had sat by his side up in the loft, and last night too, and it was he who had said early this morning, 'Let's get back away home, eh?' It was odd that Jimmy should think of the boatyard as home rather than the place in which he had been brought up. But Janie had made it home.

He thought with shame and guilt of how he had begun to compare it with Charlotte Kean's place. God, he wouldn't swop it for a palace decked with diamonds at this moment if Janie was in it.

Aw Janie. Janie. Oh! God, and they had parted like strangers. The last words he spoke to her were, 'You are hard. I said it afore in this very house and I say it again, there's a hard streak in you.'

She had gazed at him and replied, 'Aye, perhaps you're right.'

Then she was gone, and when the door closed on her he had beaten his fists against his head.

Why the hell was he standing there! Why didn't he go after her and drag her back by the scruff of the neck? He was her husband, wasn't he? He had his rights – was he a man? No other bloody man in the town would have put up with what he had these past two weeks, they would have knocked the daylights out of her. Why was he standing here?

Back in the cottages they referred to him, behind his back, as 'the big fella', and he had come to think of himself, and not without pride as 'a gambling man'. But what in effect was he? He . . . he was nothing more than a nowt who couldn't keep his wife, a nowt who had let a little chit of a lass best him. Had it happened to John George he would have said, 'Well, what do you expect?'

. . . John George!

This morning he had taken up a jug and hurled it almost at the same place at which he had thrown the ship's wheel. It was because of him he was in this pickle.

Janie! Janie! How am I to go on?

There was a knock on the door and Mr Taylor entered and provided him with the answer . . . work. It was either that or the river.

# Chapter One

## The Bargain

In 1877 those who were enlightened by reading newspapers discussed among other things such topics as Disraeli proclaming Queen Victoria Empress of India and seeing to it that she had the adulation of Indian princes and African chiefs. But for the ordinary man and woman in towns such as South Shields, there were other happenings that struck nearer home, very much nearer home.

The sea which provided most of the inhabitants with a livelihood also created havoc and disaster. There was that awful night in December last year when three vessels were wrecked and the sea, still unsatisfied, had engulfed and destroyed another two later in the day, and all under the eyes of horrified townspeople who could only watch helplessly. Even though the Volunteer Life Brigade did heroic work, many lives were lost.

Such tragedies had the power to unite the townspeople, at least for a time. Rich and poor alike mingled in their sorrow until the poor, once again forgetting their place in God's scheme of things, protested against their lot. And how did they protest? They protested through societies called trade unions.

Since the first national union of the Amalgamated Society of Engineers had been founded in 1851, in every town in the country where skilled workers were employed trade unions had sprung up, to the fear and consternation of the middle classes who looked upon them as a network of secret societies, whose sole purpose was to intimidate honest citizens, plot to confiscate their property, cause explosions and mob violence and bring the country to total revolution if they were allowed to get the upper hand.

The County of Durham was a hotbed of such people. They agitated in mines, in steel works, in shipbuilding yards, in factories, and it was even whispered they tried to inveigle young women into their ranks; and not only those, let it be understood, from the common herd, but women of education and property.

Such a one who was suspect in South Shields was Miss Charlotte Kean. She wasn't accused openly of supporting trade unions because then that would be ridiculous, for she not only held shares in some quite big concerns but owned outright a number of small ones. No, they weren't accusing her of giving her sympathy to the quarter that would eventually precipitate her ruin through business, but what they did say was, she pushed her nose into too many cultural activities in the town, activities that had hitherto been inaugurated and worked mainly by gentlemen, such as the Public Library that had been opened four years previously.

This grand building could boast its eight thousand two hundred volumes only because of generous donations from men like the Stephensons, and Mr Williamson, and Mr Moore. What was more, the library had grown out of the Mechanics' Institute and the Working Men's Club, and this joint establishment had its origins in the Literary, Mechanical and Scientific Institution which was one of the earliest mechanics' institutions in the kingdom, having come into being in the November of 1825.

And who had created such places of learning? *Men*, gentlemen of the town, not women, or even ladies. Why the efforts of the gentlemen of the town had made The Working Men's Club and Institution so popular that in 1865 they'd had to seek new premises yet once again, premises large enough to contain now not only a newsroom and library but two classrooms and a conversation and smoking room, besides rooms for bagatelle, chess and draughts, and, progress and modernity being their aim, a large space was set off in the yard for the game of quoits.

For such progress men, and men only, could be given the credit. But now there were people like Charlotte Kean pushing their way into committees and advocating, of all things, that the library should be open seven days a week. Did you ever hear of such a suggestion that the Lord's Day should be so desecrated! She had been quoted as saying, if the wine and gin shops can remain open on a Sunday why not a reading room? One gentleman had been applauded for replying that God's house should be the reading room for a Sunday.

Then there was the matter of education. She would have made a ruling that no fee be charged for schooling and that a poor child should have admission to a high-class teaching establishment merely on his proven intelligence.

Some gentlemen of the town were amused by Miss Kean's attitude and said, Well, at least credit should be given her for having the mentality of a man. However, the majority saw her as a potential danger both to their domestic and business power. To light a fire you needed tinder, and she was the equivalent to a modern matchstick. Look how she was flaunting all female decorum by parading that upstart of a rent collector around the county. Not only had she made him into her manager but she took him everywhere as her personal escort. She was making a name for herself and not one to be proud of. By, if her father had still been alive it would never have happened. He had made a mistake by allowing her to become involved with the business in the first place, because she had developed what was commonly termed a business head. She was remarkable in that way. But they didn't like remarkable women, neither those who were against her nor those who were for her. No, they didn't hold with remarkable women. This was a man's town, a seafaring town; women had their place in it, and they would be honoured as long as they kept their place; but they wanted no remarkable women, at least not the kind who tended to match them in the world of commerce.

Her manager, too, had his reservations about his employer, and the things she got up to. Yet he granted, and not grudgingly, that she *was* a remarkable woman. Odd in some ways, but nevertheless remarkable.

A year had passed since the news of Janie's death and the old saying of time being a greater healer had proved itself true yet once again, for Rory, over the past months, had come up out of despair and settled on a plane of not ordinary but, what was for him, extraordinary living.

Though Janie still remained in his heart as a memory the ache for her was less. Even in the night when he felt the miss of her he no longer experienced the body-searing agony and the longing for her presence.

Two things had helped towards his easement. The first was the combination of Jimmy and the yard, and the second – or should he have placed her first? – was Charlotte Kean.

When, six months ago, he had taken up the position as her manager she had raised his wage – salary she called it now – to three pounds a week. It was incredible. Never in his life had he dreamed of ever being able to earn three pounds a week. To get that much and ten times more by gambling, oh yes, he had dreamed of that, but never as an earned wage. And did he earn it? Was the work he was doing worth three pounds a week, going to the town office in the morning, then around ten o'clock up to the house and the office there, he at one side of the table, she at the other?

'What would you advise in a case like this, Mr Connor?'

The first time she had pushed a letter across the table towards him he had stared at her blankly before reading it. It was from her solicitor advising her that a certain new chemical company was about to float its shares, and suggesting that she would do well to consider buying.

Utterly out of his depths Rory had continued to stare at her, for he sensed in that moment that a great deal depended on how he answered her. And so, holding her gaze, he said, 'I can't advise you for I know nothin' whatever about such matters;' but had then added, 'as yet.'

She hadn't lowered her eyes when she replied, 'Then you must learn . . . that is if you want to learn. Do you, Mr Connor?'

'Yes . . . yes, I want to learn all right.'

'Well, that's settled,' she had said. 'We know now where we stand, don't we?' And then she had smiled at him, after which she had rung the bell, and when Jessie opened the door she had said, 'We'll have some refreshment now, Jessie.'

And that was the pattern he followed on the days he didn't go to Hexham or Gateshead or over the water to Wallsend to cast an eye over her interests, until two months ago, when the pattern had changed and she began to accompany him.

Journeying by train, they would sit side by side in the first-class carriage. He helped her in and out of cabs, he opened doors for her, he obeyed her commands in all ways, except that he would refuse her invitation to stay for a meal after he had delivered the takings of an evening, or when they had returned from one of their supervising trips. The reason he gave was a truthful one, his brother expected him, he was alone.

When he first gave her this reason she looked at him with a sideward glance and asked, 'How old is your brother?'

'Coming up twenty.'

'Twenty! And he needs your protection at nights?'

And he answered flatly and stiffly, 'Yes, he does. Only last week a boat he had started to build was smashed up to bits, and it could be him next.'

'Oh!' She showed interest. 'Did you inform the police?'

'No.'

'Have you any idea who did it, and why?'

'Yes, both; I know who did it, and why. There's a family on the river who run the wherries, three brothers called Pittie . . .'

'Ah! Ah! the Pitties.' She had nodded her head.

'You've heard of them?'

'Yes, yes, I've heard the name before. And I also know of some of their activities.'

'Well, you know what they're like then.'

'Yes, I've a pretty good idea. And –' she had nodded and added, 'I can see the reason why you must be with your brother at night. But you, too, must be careful. What they've done once they can do again.'

His head had jerked in her direction as he asked, 'What do you mean?'

'Well, they could break up another boat.'

'Oh. Oh yes; yes they could.'

So he had stayed at home every night, including Saturdays, up till recently when, the urge rearing once more, he had joined a game, not on the waterfront, nor in the town, but away on the outskirts of Boldon.

It was odd how he had come to be reintroduced to the Boldon house for he had forgotten he had ever played there. He was in the train going to Gateshead when a 'find the lady' trickster took him for a mug. He had followed him into the compartment at Shields, then got on talking with a supposedly complete stranger who boarded the train at Tyne Dock, whom he very convincingly inveigled into 'finding the lady', and, of course, let him win, all the while making a great fuss about his own bad luck, before turning to Rory and saying, 'What about you, sir?' It was then that Rory had turned a scornful glance on the man and replied, 'Don't come it with me. That dodge is as old as me whiskers.'

For a moment he had thought the pair of them were going to set about him. Then the one who had supposedly just won peered at him and said, 'Why I know you, I've played in with you. Didn't you use to go up to Telfords' in Boldon?'

Yes, he had played in the Telfords' wash-house, and in their kitchen, and once up in the roof lying on his belly.

From that meeting the urge had come on him again, not that it had ever really left him. But he had played no games, even for monkey nuts since Janie had gone.

So he had got in touch with the Telfords again and he went to Boldon on a Saturday night, where it could be simply Black Jack or pitch and toss. Sometimes the Telford men went farther afield to a barn for a cock fight, but he himself would always cry off this. He didn't mind a bit of rabbit coursing but he didn't like to see the fowls, especially the bantams, being torn to shreds with steel spurs. To his mind it wasn't sporting.

His winnings rarely went beyond five pounds, but neither did his losses. It didn't matter so much now about the stake as long as he could sit down to a game with men who were serious about it.

But now, at this present time, he was also vitally aware that he was playing in another kind of game, and this game worried him.

He looked back to the particular Saturday morning when, having told her he was married, her reaction had made him jump to conclusions which caused him to chastise himself for being a big-headed fool. But he chastised himself no longer.

He saw the situation he was in now as the biggest gamble of his life. There were two players only at this table and inevitably one would have to show his hand. Well, it wouldn't, it couldn't be him, it could never be him for more reasons than one. *Him* marry Charlotte Kean, a woman years older than himself and looking, as she did, as shapeless as a clothes prop, and with a face as plain as the dock wall! True, she had a nice voice . . . and a mind. Oh aye, she had a mind all right. And she was good company. Yes, of late he had certainly been discovering that. She could talk about all kinds of things, and he had realized that by listening to her he too could learn. She could make a very good friend; yet even so there could be no such thing between him and her for two reasons: on his part, you didn't, in his class, make friends with a woman, oh no, unless you wanted one thing from her: on her part, it wasn't a friend she wanted, it was a man, a husband.

Oh, he knew where things were leading. And he wouldn't hoodwink himself, he was tempted all right. Oh aye, he was both tempted and flattered. At nights he would lie thinking of what it would mean to live in Birchingham House in the select end of Westoe and to be in control of all those properties and businesses, all that money. My God! just to think of it. And he would be in control, wouldn't he? What was the wife's was the husband's surely. And there she was, willing, more than willing, to let him take control, him, Rory Connor, once rent collector from No. 2 The Cottages, Simonside. It was fantastic, unbelievable.

And them up in the kitchen, what would they say if he took this step? Lord! the place wouldn't hold them. No, he was wrong there. It wouldn't affect Ruth. As for her, his mother, after one look at Charlotte Kean she would be more than likely to say, 'My God! everything must be paid for.' She had a way with her tongue of stating plain facts. It would be his da who would brag. Every man in his shop would know, and it would be talked of in every pub in Jarrow from the church bank to the far end of Ellison Street.

But what would Bill Waggett say?

Ah, what the hell did it matter! It wouldn't happen. It couldn't. He couldn't do it. He wouldn't do it. Anyway, he was all right as he was. Jimmy wasn't doing so bad; he'd do better if it wasn't for them blasted Pitties. By, he'd get his own back on them if it was the last thing he did in life. Hardly a day passed but that he didn't think of them, when he would grab at this or that idea to get even with them. And he would, he would. He'd get a lead one day, and by God, when he did, let them look out! . . . He could have a lead now, right away. With money you had power, and it needed power to potch the Pitties. All he had to do was to say, 'Thank you kindly, Miss Kean, I'll be your man,' and he was home, safe home from the stormy sea, with chests full to the top.

But what would he really say? He knew what he'd say. 'I'm sorry, miss, but it wouldn't work.'

And, strangely, he realized that when he should say the latter he would be sorry, for, banter as he would, and did, about her in his mind there was a part of him that was sorry for her, and it had been growing of late. He pitied her lonely state, and he understood it because of the loneliness within himself. But although her kind of loneliness had gone on for years and she was weary of it, she was not yet resigned to it. That was why she had set her sights on him.

But why him? People of her station usually classed the likes of him as muck beneath their feet. And what was more, just think how she'd be talked about if anything should come of it. Lord! any link up with him would set the town on fire.

He was already vaguely aware that sly looks were being cast in their direction. When they were last in Durham to look over some property along the river bank they had gone to an inn to eat. She had chosen it, she said, because she thought he would like it; it was a man's place, oak-trestle tables, hefty beams, meat pudding and ale. And he would have liked it if it hadn't been in Durham . . . the gaol was in Durham.

Well, he had done what he could in that direction. He had tried to make reparation; he had given Jimmy ten pounds and sent him up to visit John George and to ask him if he would come and see him when he came out. But Jimmy had returned with the ten pounds; John George was already out and they couldn't tell him where he had gone. For days afterwards he had expected a visit from him, but John George hadn't come. So he told himself that the business was closed; he had done his best. It was only in his recurring nightmare, when he would relive the awakening to Janie shouting at him, did he realize that his best hadn't been good enough and that John George would be with him like an unhealed wound until the end of his days.

But on that day in the inn in Durham, two Shields' men – gentlemen – had come to their table to speak to Charlotte Kean, and she had introduced him to them. They were a Mr Allington and a Mr Spencer. He knew of both of them. Allington was a solicitor, and Spencer owned a number of small grocery shops. He had started with one about fifteen years ago, and now they had spread into Jarrow and beyond.

After the first acknowledgment, they hadn't addressed him again until they were bidding her good-bye, and then they had merely inclined their heads towards him. Oh, he knew where he stood with the gentlemen of the town. He was an upstart rent man.

Then came the day when Charlotte Kean showed her hand and brought an abrupt end to the game by laying her cards face up on the table.

They had returned from Newcastle where she had been to see, of all things, an iron foundry with a view to taking a part share in it. The journey had been taken against the advice of her solicitor. The Tyneside foundries, he had said, were unable to produce iron as cheaply as they once had done; the railways had killed the iron trade in this part of the country. But she had explained, and to Rory himself, that she could not follow her solicitor's reasoning, for, as she saw it, people would always want iron stoves, kitchen grates, fenders, and railings of all kinds, from those that enclosed parks to small private gates; and then there were bedsteads and safes and such-like. She went on to say she wasn't thinking of competing with Palmer's and making ships but merely of supplying household requisites. What did he think?

He had answered her bluntly, as always, for he had learned that she preferred the truth, at least in most things. 'I think that I agree with Mr Hardy; he knows what he's talking about.'

'And you think I don't?'

'Well, I wouldn't say that you know very much about the iron trade.'

'You are aware that I read a great deal?'

'Yes, I'm aware of that, but as I understand it it takes more than reading to get an insight into such trades; the workings of them go deeper than books.'

'The workings might, but I would leave the workings to managers and men, of course.'

He shrugged his shoulders slightly and smiled as he said, 'Well, I won't say you know best, but what I will say is, you'll do what you want in the long run.'

That he could speak to her in this fashion was evidence of how far they had travelled in their association over the past year. He now rarely used the term miss, and although from time to time she would call him Mr Connor, it was usually done when in the presence of servants; at other times she addressed him without using his name at all.

Whatever her servants thought of the situation they treated their mistress's new manager with respect, even deference, which at one time would have amused him. At one time, too, such subservient attitudes would have given him material for mimicry and a big joke in the kitchen; in fact, his association with Miss Charlotte Kean would have been one big joke. At one time, but not now. Anyway, Sundays were different now. He did not always visit the cottage on a Sunday, he went up only on Jimmy's urging. He did not ask himself why he had turned against the Sunday gatherings, but he knew that the general opinion was he had become too big for his boots. And that could very well be near the truth, for he admitted to himself that the more he saw of the Westoe side of life the less he liked that in which he had been brought up.

He had, on this day, gone through a mental battle which left him thinking he didn't know which end of him was up. It was the anniversary of Janie's death, and there was no fierce ache left in him, and he felt there should be. He should, in some way, have held a sort of memorial service, at least within himself, but what had he done? Gone up to Newcastle, walked blithely by his employer's side as she paraded around a foundry, sat with her at a meal, which she called lunch, at the Royal Exchange Hotel; then had waited like a docile husband while she went shopping in Bainbridge's. He had sauntered with her through the Haymarket, where they had stopped and examined almost every article in the ironmongery store. Then she had said they would go to the Assembly Rooms and he wondered what her object was, until, standing outside, she looked at the building and said almost sadly, 'My mother once danced in there. She often told me about it. It was the highlight of her life; she was taken there by a gentleman – and they danced the whole evening through.'

When she had turned her face towards him he had ended for her, flippantly, 'And they married and lived happy ever after.'

'No, she married my father.'

What could he make of that?

Her last call was at Mawson & Swan's in Grey Street, where she purchased a number of books.

By the time they reached the railway station he likened himself to a donkey, he was so loaded down under parcels, and he thanked God he wasn't likely to come across anyone he knew. When they arrived at Shields she hired a cab, and they drove through the drizzling rain to the house, and into warmth and comfort and elegance.

Elegance was another new word he had of late added to his vocabulary; it was the only word to describe this house, its furniture and the comforts of it.

'Ah, isn't it nice to be home?' She had returned from upstairs, where she had evidently combed her hair and applied some talcum powder to her face for her chin had the same appearance as Ruth's had when she wiped it with a floured hand.

'It's an awful night; you must have something before you go, something to eat that is. Did Mr Taylor bring the takings?'

'Yes; I've checked them, they're all right.'

This was a new departure; he no longer went to the office to collect the rents. Mr Taylor had been promoted and so came each evening to the house.

On the days she did not send him off on tours of inspection he would receive the money from the old man, count it, then check the books, and never did he hand them back to him but he saw himself as he was a year ago, a younger edition of this man. That was the only difference, a younger edition; the old man's insecurity did not make his own position in comparison appear strong, quite the reverse.

Only a week ago he had felt he could play his hand for a good while yet, but today, the anniversary of Janie's death, he had a feeling in his bones that soon all the cards would be laid face up, and as always they would show a winner and a loser; there could never be two winners in any game . . .

Why not?

Oh my God! He'd been through it all before, hadn't he, night after night? He was what he was, that was why not.

Below his outer covering, his jaunty aggressive air, the look that gave nothing away while at the same time suggesting that what it had to hide was of value, behind all this, only he himself knew the frailties of his character. Yet, in this particular case, he wasn't going to be weak enough – or did he mean strong enough? – to cheat at this game and let her be the winner.

And again he told himself he had to stop hoodwinking himself on this point too, because it wasn't really the moral issue that would prevent him from letting her win, but the fact that he didn't think he was up to paying the stake. It was too high. Yet he liked her. Oh aye, it was very odd to admit, but he liked her. He liked being with her; she was good company, except at those times when she made him feel so small that he imagined she could see him crawling around her feet. Once or twice she had done this when he had dared to contradict her on some point with regard to the business. And yet she never took that high hand with him when they were in company. At such times she always deferred to him as a woman might to her husband, or her boss.

She was a funny character; he couldn't get to the bottom of her. He had never known anyone in his life so knowledgeable or so self-possessed. But then, never in his life had he been in contact with women of her class.

'You will stay for something to eat?'

He hesitated, then said, 'Yes. Yes, thank you.'

'Good.' She smiled at him, put her hand to her hair and stroked it upwards and back from her forehead; then she said, 'Don't sit on the edge of that chair as if you were waiting to take off in a race.'

His jaw tightened, his pleasant expression vanished. This was the kind of thing that maddened him.

'Oh! Oh, I'm sorry.'

Now she was sitting forward on the edge of the couch leaning towards him. 'Please don't be annoyed. I have the unfortunate habit of phrasing my requests in the manner of orders.' She made a small deprecating movement with her head. 'I . . . I must try to grow out of it. All I intended to say was, please relax, be comfortable . . . make yourself at home.' The last words ended on a low note.

After a moment he slid slowly back into the chair and smiled ruefully at her.

Settling herself back once again on the couch, she stared at him before saying, still in a low tone, 'I'm going to call you . . . No' – she lifted her hand – 'again my phrasing is wrong. What I mean to say is, may I call you by your Christian name?'

He did not answer but stared at her, unblinking.

She was looking down at her hands now where they were joined on her lap, her fingers making stroking movements between the knuckles. 'You see, I . . . I want to talk to you this evening about . . . about something important, if you can afford me the time after dinner. Which reminds me. Would you mind ringing the bell, please?'

He rose slowly to his feet and pulled the bell by the side of the fireplace, and they didn't speak until the maid appeared; then she said, 'Mr Connor will be staying for dinner, Jessie. How long will it be?'

'Well . . . well, it's ready now, miss, but' – The girl cast a glance in Rory's direction, then added, 'Say five minutes' time, miss?'

'Very well, Jessie, thank you.'

When the door was closed on the maid, she said, 'I have never seen you smoke, do you smoke?'

'Yes. I have a draw at nights.'

'My father never smoked. I like the smell of tobacco. About . . . about your Christian name. What does the R stand for . . . Robert?'

'No, Rory.'

'Roar-y. What is it short for?'

'Nothin' that I know of. I was christened Rory.'

'Roar-y.' She mouthed the word, then said, 'I like it. My name, as you know, is Charlotte. My father once said it was a very suitable name for me.' Her head drooped again. 'He was an unkind man, a nasty man, a mean nasty man.'

He could say nothing to this. He was so amazed at her frankness he just sat staring at her, until she said. 'Would you care to go upstairs and wash?'

He blinked rapidly, swallowed, wetted his lips, and as he drew himself up from the chair answered, 'Yes. Yes, thank you.'

She did not rise from the couch but looked up at him. 'The bathroom is the third door on the right of the landing.'

He inclined his head towards her, walked out of the drawing-room, across the hall and up the stairs. This was the first time he had been upstairs and he guessed it would be the last.

After closing the bathroom door behind him he stood looking about him in amazement. A full length iron bath stood on four ornamental legs. At one end of it were two shining brass taps, at the foot was a shelf and, on it, an array of coloured bottles and fancy boxes. To the left stood a wash basin, and to the left of that again a towel rack on which hung gleaming white towels. In the wall opposite the bath was a door, and when he slowly pushed this open he found he was looking down into a porcelain toilet, not a dry midden as outside the cottage, or a bucket in a lean-to on the waterfront, but something that looked too shiningly clean to be put to the use it was intended for.

A few minutes later as he stood washing his hands, not from any idea of hygiene, but simply because he wanted to see the bowl fill with water, he thought, I'm a blasted fool. That's what I am, a blasted fool. I could use this every day. I could eat downstairs in that dining-room every day. I could sit in that drawing-room, aye, and smoke every day. And I could sleep up here in one of these rooms every . . . He did not finish the sentence but dried his hands, gave one last look around the bathroom, then went downstairs.

The meal was over and once again they were sitting in the drawing-room.

He had hardly opened his mouth from the moment he had entered the dining-room until he left it. Talk about arms and legs; he could have been a wood louse, and he felt sure he had appeared just about as much at home too at that table as one might have done. Nor had it helped matters that she had been quiet an' all. She usually kept the conversation going, even giving herself the answers, and now here they were and the game had come to an end, the cards were face up.

He felt sorry. In so many different ways he felt sorry, but most of all he knew that at this moment he was feeling sorry for her because he could see from her face, and her attitude, that she, too, was in a bit of a spot, and he was wishing, sincerely wishing that it would have been possible for him to help her out of it, when she spoke.

Sitting perfectly still, staring straight ahead as if she were concentrating on the picture of her grandfather above the mantelpiece, she said, 'I . . . I really don't know how to begin, but this thing must be brought into the open. You . . . you are aware of that as much as I am, aren't you? It was some seconds before she turned her head towards him, and now such were his feelings of pity that he couldn't hold her gaze. He looked down on his hands, as she herself had done earlier and, like hers, his fingers rubbed against each other.

She was speaking again, softly now, her voice scarcely above a whisper. 'I am putting you in a very embarrassing situation. I'm aware of that. Even if your feelings were such that you wanted to put a certain question to me, you wouldn't under the circumstances have the courage to do so, but let me tell you one thing immediately. I know that you have no wish to put that question to me. If you agree to what I am going to ask of you, I won't be under the illusion it is through any personal attraction, but that it will be for what my offer can bring to you in the way of advantages.'

His head was up now. 'I don't want advantages that way.'

'Thank you at least for that.' As she made a deep obeisance with her head towards him, he put in quickly, 'Don't get me wrong. What I meant was –' He shook his head, bit hard down on his lip as he found it impossible to explain what he meant, and she said, 'I know what you meant, but . . . but you haven't yet heard my proposition.'

She turned her face away and once again stared at the picture as she went on, 'Suppose I were to ask you to marry me, you would . . . you would, on the face of it I know, refuse, foregoing all the advantages that would go with such a suggestion, but suppose I were to say to you that this would be no ordinary marriage, that I . . . I would expect nothing from you that an ordinary wife would from her husband. You could have your own apartments, all I would ask for is . . . is your companionship, and your presence in this house, of which . . . of which you would be the master.' She again turned her face towards him.

He was sitting bolt upright in the chair now; his eyes were wide and his mouth slightly open. He said under his breath, 'That would be the poor end of the stick for you, wouldn't it?'

'Poor end of the stick?' She gave a short laugh. 'Well, if I would be quite satisfied with the poor end of the stick, shouldn't that be enough for you?'

He shook his head. 'No! No! It wouldn't be right, for as I see it you wouldn't be gettin' any more out of me than you do now. . . . So why not let things be as they are?'

There now came upon them an embarrassed silence, before she said, 'Because I need companionship, male companionship. Not just anyone, someone, an individual, someone whom I consider special, and . . . and I chose you. What is more, I feel I know you, I know you very well. I know that you like this house, you like this way of living, I know that you could learn to appreciate finer things. Not that I dislike the roughness in you; no, it is part of your attraction, your bumptiousness, your arrogance. It is more difficult to be arrogant when you have nothing to be arrogant about than when you have something.'

His face took on its blank look. This was the kind of clever talk that maddened him, and he had no way of hitting back except by using the arrogance she was on about. He said gruffly, 'You seem to think you know a lot about me, everything in fact.'

'No, not everything, but quite a bit. I've always given myself the credit of being able to read character. I know a lot of things about a lot of people, especially in this town, and I know what a good many of them are saying at this very moment – and about us.'

'About us?'

'Oh yes, yes, about us. Don't you know that we're being talked about? Don't you know they're saying –' she now dropped into the local inflexion which patterned the speech of even many of the better-off of the townsfolk – "What d'you think, eh? Kean's daughter and the rent collector. And her five years older than him and as plain as a pikestaff. She's brazen, that's what she is, she's buying him. And, of course, he's willing to be bought. He's no fool, who would turn down that chance? She should be ashamed of herself though, using her money as bait. You can't blame the fellow. And you know, this didn't start the day, or yesterday; they were going at it when his wife was alive"? . . . That's what they're saying.'

His face was burning, the colour suffusing it was almost scarlet.

'Oh, please don't get upset about it; you must have been aware that our association would cause a minor scandal?'

'I wasn't!' His answer was vehement. 'If . . . if I'd thought they'd been saying that I ... I wouldn't have gone on. I ... I was your manager. Anyway, if you knew this, why didn't you put a stop to it? Why did you let it go on?'

'Oh ... huh! Why? Well, to tell you the truth, it made me all the more determined to go on. I don't care a fig for their chatter. What are they after all, the majority of them? Braggarts, strutting little nonentities, men who have clawed their way up over the dead bodies of miners, or of their factory workers. Oh, there are a good many hypocrites in this town. I could reel them off, sanctimonious individuals, leading double lives. You know, you'd think Newcastle was at the other end of the world, and it is for some of them, keeping their second homes ... It is very strange you know but women talk to me, they confide in me; perhaps it's because to them I'm unfeminine. But anyway –' she tossed her head to the side – 'I have no room to speak, at least on the point of clawing one's way up, for what did my father do for anyone except himself? And for that matter what have I done but talk? But this is where you come in. I have thought that with you I might begin to do things for other people. I –' her voice dropped – 'I might become so at peace with myself that I could turn my thoughts on to the needs of others, and there are many in need in this town. And you know that better than I do, because you have been on that side of the wall. You have had to say "Yes, sir", and "No, sir", and of course –' she nodded at him – ' "Yes, miss", and "No, miss", and it's only recently and only through you that I have realized how people such as you, in your position, must feel.'

She now rose from the couch abruptly and, going to the mantelpiece, she put her hands on it and looked down into the fire as she muttered, 'I am not saying this in order to make the future appear more attractive. If ... if closer association with me would be intolerable to you, very well, you have only to say so.'

'And what if I did, what then?' The question was quiet, soft, and her answer equally so. 'I don't know, because ... because I haven't allowed myself to look into the future and face the desolation there.'

As he stared up at her he thought, She's remarkable. By aye, she's a remarkable woman. He had never imagined anyone talking as frankly as she had done; no man would ever have been as honest. He said softly, 'Will you give me time to think it over?'

'*No!*'

The word was barked and it brought him to his feet as if it had been the crack of a gun. He watched her march down the room, then back again towards him. At the head of the couch she stopped, and he saw her fingers dig into the upholstery as she said tersely, 'It must be now, yes or no. I ... I cannot go on in uncertainty. I ... I'm not asking anything from you but to come into this house and stay with me as a ... a friend, a companion. You don't believe it now, but you'll find out there's more lasting happiness stems from friendship than has ever done from love. I know you don't love me, couldn't love me, and never will ... No! No! Don't protest.' She lifted her hand. 'Let us start from the beginning being honest. When you lost your wife I knew that you must have loved her deeply, and that kind of love only happens once, but there are other emotions comparable with love. A man can have them towards a woman and be happy. That can also apply to a woman, although' – She swallowed deeply in her throat here before ending, 'In most cases she needs to love even if she's not loved in return.'

God, he was hot, sweating. What could he say? What could he do? Strangely, he knew what he had the desire to do, and it was scattering to the winds all his previous decisions, for at this moment he wanted to go behind that couch and put his arms about her, comfort her. Just that, comfort her. Nothing else, just comfort her. Then why wasn't he doing it?

He was surprised to hear himself saying in a voice that sounded quite ordinary, 'Come and sit down.' He was holding his hand out to her, and slowly she put hers into it. Then he drew her round the head of the couch and on to its seat, and still with her hand in his he sat beside her, and as he looked at her an excitement rose in him. He seemed to be drawing it from her. Aye yes, that was the other word he wanted for what he felt for her, excitement. It was almost akin to the feeling he got when he was in a good game. He hadn't been aware of it, but that was why he had liked to be in her company, liked to hear her talk; even when she was getting her sly digs in at him, she was exciting.

If she hadn't been so tall and thin and plain what was happening now would likely have happened months ago. But now he realized that her thinking, her voice, her manner, the way she dressed, all the things she did were in a way a compensation for her looks. In fact, they formed a kind of cloak over them because there had been times lately when in her company that he had forgotten how she looked. He hadn't realized this until now. Suddenly he felt at ease with her as he'd never done before. He knew he could talk to her now, aye and comfort her. He bent towards her and said, 'Can I tell you something?'

Her eyes had a moisture in them when she answered, 'I'm eager to hear whatever you have to say, Rory.'

'It's going to be difficult for me to put into words 'cos you see I haven't your gift, your gift of the gab.' He wagged the hand that was within his. 'You know you've got the gift of the gab, don't you? But there's one thing, when you open your mouth something meaningful always comes out. That's the difference between you an' me . . . and the likes of me. But I . . . I want to tell you, I've been learnin' these months past. There's not a day gone by when I've been with you but I haven't learned something from you. It mightn't show, it still hasn't covered up me aggressiveness.' Again he shook her hand. 'And I want to tell you something more. I've liked being with you . . . I mean, I do like being with you. You won't believe this, but well, I . . . I find you sort of exciting. I've never known any other woman like you. Well, I wouldn't, would I, not coming from my quarter? Mind, I must say at this point that Janie was a fine girl and I was happy with her. I've got to say that; you said a minute ago let's be honest. Yet, at the same time, I've got to admit she wasn't excitin'. Lovable aye, but not excitin'. Looking back, I see that Janie had little to teach me, only perhaps thoughtfulness for others; she could get really worked up over other people's problems, you know, and after all, that's no small thing, is it?'

'No, it isn't . . . Rory.'

'Yes?'

'What is the answer you're giving me? I . . . I want to hear it in . . . in definite terms. You are being kind now but I don't know whether it is merely to soothe me. I want to hear you say, "Yes, Charlotte," or "No, Charlotte." '

Their hands were still joined, their knees almost touching, their faces not more than two feet apart, and he knew that if he said no, his life would in some way become empty, barren, and not only because he might no longer have admittance to this house.

' . . . Yes . . . Charlotte.'

He watched her close her eyes. When she opened them they were bright; in any other face they would have been starry.

'It's a bargain.'

'Aye, it's a bargain.'

As he uttered the words he again had a vivid mental picture of the kitchen. He could see his dad, Ruth, her, and Jimmy, all staring at him, all saying, 'What, her, Miss Kean! Never! . . . What about Janie?'

He said suddenly, 'I'm not going to make any excuses about me people; I'm not going to hide them; you'll have to meet them.'

'I'll be pleased to, very pleased to. I've never had any people of my own.'

He said suddenly on a laugh, 'You know something? I'll never make excuses to you, I'll always tell you the truth. That's a promise. It'll likely not always please you . . .'

'It won't.' She was pulling a long face at him now and her laughter was high, slightly out of control as she said, 'It certainly won't if you tell me you are going out gambling every night.'

When his eyes widened and his lips fell apart her laughter increased and she cried with the air of a young teasing girl, which lay awkwardly on her, 'Didn't I tell you I know most things about most people in this town?'

His face straight and his voice flat, he asked, 'How did you know about that?'

'Deduction, and the one word you kept repeating when you were in hospital. When I first saw you, you said again and again, "Pittie. Pittie. Pittie". The second time I visited you you were still saying it.'

'I was?'

'Yes, and you know when a man gets beaten up as you were there's nearly always something behind it. A footpad might have hit you on the head and knocked you senseless, but then I don't think he would have kicked you within an inch of death's door. After thinking about it, I realized you were telling everyone the name of your assailants, but no one seemed to be taking any notice, they thought you were saying, "Isn't it a pity?" when what you were really doing was giving them the name of the men who attacked you, the Pittie brothers. The Pittie brothers are well-known scoundrels, besides being dirty gamblers. They were fined for gambling some short time ago.'

'Huh! Huh!' A smile was spreading over his face, widening his mouth. He now put his head back on his shoulder and laughed until his body shook, and she laughed with him.

His chest was heaving and he was still laughing when he looked into her face again and said, 'I've thought it, but now I'll say it, you're a remarkable woman.'

'Oh, please don't judge my intelligence on the fact that I recognized something that should have been staring everyone in the face, the police into the bargain. Yet at the same time I don't think the police were as stupid as they made out to be, but when they asked you had you seen the assailant or assailants, I was given to understand you said no, you had been attacked while walking down a side street.'

He screwed up his eyes at her now and, his face serious, he asked, 'But . . . but how could you know that I gambled?'

She stared at him for a long moment before saying, and seriously now, 'A short while ago you said you'd always tell me the truth. I understood, of course, that you were referring to the future, but now I'm going to ask you: Is there anything further you want to tell me, anything, about your past say?'

For a moment he wondered if she were referring to his birth. He stared into her eyes, then gulped in his throat as he thought, She can't know about the other business, else I wouldn't be here now.

'Think hard before you answer.'

He felt the colour flooding his face again. They were staring into each other's eyes. His body was sweating; it was as if he were having a nightmare in broad daylight. His voice was a gruff whisper when he said, 'Well, knowin' what you know, or think you know, why am I sitting here now?'

Her voice was equally low as she replied, 'I'll answer that in a moment when you answer my question.'

His gaze riveted on her, he pondered. If she didn't know, if she wasn't referring to John George's business then what he was about to say would likely put the kibosh on her proposal. But if it was that she was hinting at, then indeed, aye, by God! indeed she was a remarkable woman.

He closed his eyes for a moment, lowered his head, and turned it to the side before he muttered, as if he were in the confessional box: 'I took the five pounds that John George did time for. I went back that night and helped meself, but like him I expected to be there first thing on the Monday morning to return it. If . . . if I had been there and you had caught me I would have stood me rap along of him, but by the time I knew what had happened I was sick and weak, and petrified at the thought of prison.' His head still to the side, he jerked his neck out of his collar before going on, 'I . . . I have a fear on me, always have had since I was nailed down in a box as a child. I fear being shut in, I can't stand being behind closed doors of any kind. I . . . I should have come forward, I know, but there it is, I didn't . . . Is that what you want to know?'

There was a long pause and when she made no reply he looked at her again and said 'You knew this all along?'

'No, not from the beginning,' she shook her head slowly. 'But in the court I felt the man was speaking the truth and I recalled his amazement when I mentioned that not ten shillings but five pounds ten was missing. He was so astonished he couldn't speak. But in any case, five pounds ten or ten shillings he had to be brought to book, for, as he admitted, he had been tampering with the books for some long time, and as he also admitted, not only for ten shillings at a time either.'

All this time their hands had been joined and he looked down on them as he asked quietly, 'Why am I here now? Tell me that. Knowing all this about me, why am I here now?'

She now withdrew her hands from his and, rising to her feet, went towards the fire and once again looked at the picture above the mantelpiece. Then she wetted her lips twice and drew in a long breath before she said softly, 'I . . . I happen to care for you . . . This, of course, wipes out all my fine talk about friendship et cetera, but you see –' again she wetted her lips – 'I've loved you since the first time I saw you in my father's office. It was just like that, quickly, the most sudden thing in my life. I remember thinking, that's the kind of man I would like to marry if it were possible. I knew it was a preposterous desire, quite hopeless, utterly hopeless. My father would never never have countenanced it. Strangely, he didn't like you. But then he liked so few people, and if I'd shown the slightest interest in you, even mentioned your name in a kindly fashion, he would have dismissed you.'

She turned and looked at him. 'I'm a fraud, but I really did not intend that you should know this. I ... I was going to acquire you under false pretences. But ... but it makes no difference to the bargain. That can remain as it stands. But –' she laughed self-consciously – 'so much for all my fine platonic talk. You know, Rory, the emotions are not measured in proportion to one's looks: if that were so all the beauties in the world would be passionate lovers, but from what I have gauged from my reading they're often very cold women. My ... my emotions don't match my looks, Rory, but as I said the bargain stands: you give me your friendship and protection as a husband, I will give you what ... well, what I cannot help giving you.'

He rose from the couch and went slowly towards her, and he stared into her face before he said softly, 'There must be a dozen men in this town who'd be only too glad to have married you, and would serve you better than I'll ever be able to.'

'Doubtless, doubtless.' She nodded slowly at him. 'But you see, and here we come to the question of truth again, they would have been marrying me for one thing, my money, and they would likely have been men with whom I couldn't bargain. In their cases I would most assuredly have wished them to have their own apartments, but in their cases they would assuredly not have complied, for let us face the fact that most men's needs do not require the stimulus of love. . .'

Slowly and firmly now he put his arms about her and drew her thin form towards him, and when he felt her taut body relax against him, and her head bury itself in his shoulder, he put his face into the dark coils of her hair and murmured, 'Don't. There, there, don't cry. Please don't cry. I'll ... I'll make you happy, Charlotte. I promise I'll make you happy.'

He didn't know how he was going to do it. The only thing he was sure of in this fantastic moment was that he'd have a damned good try.

# Chapter Two

He stood in the kitchen at the end of the long table, while they, like a combating force, stood at the other end, Ruth, his father, and Lizzie. Jimmy stood to the side towards the middle of the table, his face pale, anxious, his eyes darting between them like a troubled referee.

'Well, you can say something, can't you?' His voice re-echoed through the timbers in the roof.

It was his father who spoke. Quietly he said, 'Janie's hardly cold.'

'Janie's been dead over a year, a year and three weeks to be exact.'

'Huh! Well.' Paddy broke away from the group and walked towards the fireplace and, picking up a clay pipe from the mantelpiece, he bent and tapped it on the hob, knocking out the doddle as he said, 'You're doin' well for yersel, there's that much to be said. Aye, aye. They used to say old Kean could buy Shields, that is the parts Cookson hadn't bought up. Money grabbers, the lot of them! . . .'

'It wasn't the money . . .'

'Well, begod! it couldn't be her face.'

Rory swung round and glared at Lizzie. It looked for a moment as if he would spring down the table and strike her. Their eyes held across the distance before she snapped her gaze from his and, swinging round, went towards the scullery, muttering, 'My God! My God! What next!'

The anger in him blinded him for a moment. Any other family in the town, any other family from here to Newcastle, would, he imagined, have fallen on his neck for making such a match, but not his family, aw no. In their ignorance they thought you must keep loyal to the dead, if not for ever, then for a decent period of years.

His vision clearing, he glared now at Ruth. She was usually the one to see both sides of everything, but she wasn't seeing his side of this, there was a stricken look on her face. He put his hands on the table and leant towards her now as he cried, 'You didn't condemn her da, did you –' he jerked his head back in the direction of the cottage next door – 'when he went off and lived with his woman in Jarrow after Gran died. He couldn't wait. Six weeks, that's all he stayed there alone, six weeks. But you said nothin' about that. And I'm marrying her. Do you hear?' He flashed a glance towards his father's bent head. 'I'm not taking her on the side. And one at a time'll be enough for me.'

There was no sound in the kitchen. Paddy hadn't moved, Ruth hadn't moved, Lizzie hadn't burst into the room from the scullery. He stood breathing deeply. Then looking at Jimmy, he yelled, 'I came here, you know I came here to say that she wanted to meet them. My God! she didn't know what she was askin' . . . Well, it doesn't matter. I know where I stand now; you'll want me afore I'll want you, the lot of you.' And on this he turned round and marched out of the room.

Before the door had crashed closed Lizzie appeared in the kitchen. Paddy turned from the fireplace, and Ruth, putting her hand out towards Jimmy as if she were pushing him, said quickly and in a choked voice, 'Go after him. Stay with him. Tell . . . tell him it'll be all right.'

She was now pressing Jimmy towards the door. 'Tell . . . tell him I understand, and . . . and she'll be welcome. Tell him that, she'll be welcome.'

Jimmy didn't speak but, grabbing up his cap, he pulled it tight down on his head, then ran wobbling down the path and out of the gate, calling, 'Rory! Rory!'

He was at the top of the bank before he caught up with Rory.

'Aw, man, hold your hand a minute. It's . . . it's no use gettin' a paddy. I . . . I told you afore we come it would give them a gliff; it gave me a gliff, not only . . . not because of Janie, but . . .'

'But what?' Rory pulled up so suddenly that Jimmy went on a couple of steps before turning to him and looking up at him and saying fearlessly, 'You want the truth? All right, you'll get it. She's different, older; plain, as Lizzie said, plain an' . . .'

'Aye, go on.' Rory's voice came from deep within his throat.

'Well . . . All right then, I'll say it, I will, I'll say it, she's a different class from you. You'll . . . you'll be like a fish out of water.'

Rory, his voice a tone quieter now, bent over Jimmy and said slowly, 'Did you feel like a fish out of water last night when you met her?'

Jimmy tossed his head, blinked, then turned and walked on, Rory with him now, and after a moment, he answered, 'No, 'cos . . . 'cos I felt she had set out to make me like her. But I won't be livin' with her.' He now turned his head up to Rory. 'That's the difference, I won't have to live her life and meet her kind of people. I won't have to live up to her.'

'And you think I can't?'

Jimmy's head swayed from one side to the other following the motion of his body, and he said, 'Aye, just that.'

'Thanks. Thanks very much.'

'I . . . I didn't mean it nasty, man, no more than they meant to be nasty.'

'Huh! They didn't mean to be nasty? My God! You must have ten skins. You were there, you were there, man, weren't you?'

Jimmy didn't answer for a while, and then he said quietly, 'Me ma says she'll be welcome; you can bring her and she'll be welcome.'

'Like hell I will! Take her up there among that bigoted tribe? Not on your bloody life. Well –' he squared his shoulders and his step quickened and his arms swung wider – 'why should I worry me head, they're the losers, they've potched themselves. I could have put them all on their feet, I could have set them all up, set them up for life.' He cast a hard glance down now on Jimmy and demanded, 'Do you know how much I'll be worth when I marry her? Have you any idea? I'll be a rich man, 'cos she's rollin', and I'll be in control. Just think on that.'

'Aye well, good for you, I hope it keeps fine for you.'

The colloquial saying which was for ever on Lizzie's tongue caused Rory to screw up his eyes tightly for a moment.

I hope it keeps fine for you.

Would he ever do anything right in this world? Would he ever do anything to please anybody? . . . Well, he was pleasing her, wasn't he? He had never seen a woman so openly happy in his life as he had her these past three weeks. Her happiness was embarrassing; aye, and humbling, making him say to himself each night when he left her, I'll repay her in some way, and he would, he would, and to hell with the rest of them. The kitchen had seen him for the last time, he'd go to that registry office whenever she liked and he'd show them, by God! he'd show them. He would let them see if he could live up to her or not.

I hope it keeps fine for you.

And Janie was dead!

# Chapter Three

He let himself in through the front door, but as he opened the door leading from the lobby into the hall Jessie was there to close it for him.

'What a night, sir. Eeh! you are wet.' As she took his hat and thick tweed coat from him he bent towards her and said in a conspiratorial whisper, 'Well, don't shout it out, Jessie, or I'll have to take cough mixture.'

'Oh, sir.' She giggled and shook her head, then said, 'The mistress is upstairs,' and as he nodded at her and went towards the staircase she hissed after him, 'Your boots, sir.'

He looked down at his damp feet, then jerking his chin upwards and biting on his bottom lip like a boy caught in a misdemeanour he sat down on the hall chair and unlaced his boots. He then took his house shoes from her hand and pulled them on, and as he rose he bent towards her again and said in a whisper, 'Between you all I'll end up in a blanket.'

Again she giggled, before turning away towards the kitchen to inform the cook that the master was in. She liked the master, she did; the house had been different altogether since he had come into it. He might have come from the bottom end of nowhere but he didn't act uppish. And what's more, he had made the mistress into a new woman. By! aye, he had that. She had never seen such a change in anybody. Nor had she seen such a change in the house. Everybody was infected; as cook said, they'd all got the smit . . .

On opening the bedroom door he almost pushed her over and he put out his arm swiftly to catch her, saying, 'Why are you standin' behind the door?'

'I wasn't standing behind the door, Mr Connor, I was about to open the door.'

She put her face up to his and he kissed her gently on the lips.

'I didn't hear you come in.'

'Well, you wouldn't.' He shook his head from side to side. 'Jessie carried me from the front door to the foot of the stairs, made me put my slippers on, and told me to be a good boy.'

She shook his arm and smiled at him; then she unloosened his tie as she asked, 'How did things go?'

He now pressed her from him and on to the long padded velvet stool set before the dressing table, and as he stood back from her he took off his coat and tugged the narrow tie from his high collar; then turned and as he walked towards the wardrobe that filled almost one entire wall, he pulled his shirt over his head, saying, 'Very well. Very well. I've enjoyed meself the day.' He looked over his shoulder.

'More so than usual?'

'Oh, much more so than usual.'

He now took from the wardrobe drawer a silk shirt with a wide soft collar, put it on, then divested himself of his trousers and, after selecting another pair from a rack, he stepped into them, while she watched him in silence and with seeming pleasure. Lastly, he donned a matching coat, then returned towards her, saying, 'I met someone I've been hoping to meet for a long time.'

'Lady or gentleman?'

He gave her a twisted smile now before answering, 'Gentleman.'

'Oh –' She placed her hand on her heart now, saying, 'My rage is subsiding, please proceed.'

He gave a small laugh, then sat down beside her on the stool. 'Do you know a man named Nickle?'

'Nickle? I know two men by the name of Nickle, Mr Frank Nickle and Mr John Nickle, but they're not related. Which one did you meet?'

'Oh, I'm not sure. This one lives in Plynlimmon Way.'

'Oh, that's Mr Frank Nickle. Why have you wanted to meet him? I'm sure you would have nothing in common.'

'That's where you're wrong . . . What do you know of him?'

She put her head on one side as if considering, then said, 'I know I don't care much for him, yet I have nothing against him except that I don't think he was kind to his wife. I met her twice. It was shortly after I came back from school, Mother was alive. We went to dinner there once, and she came here. She was a sad woman. I think she was afraid of him. Yes –' she nodded – 'looking back, I think she was afraid of him. I don't think Mother had much time for him either, but they were all members of the same church and . . . What are you laughing at?'

'Oh, there's the bell for dinner. I'll tell you after.'

'You'll tell me now.'

He stared at her for a moment, then said quietly, 'I'll tell you later, Mrs Connor.'

She bit on her lip to stop herself from laughing, bowed her head slightly, then, holding her hand out to him, rose from the seat. When he didn't immediately follow suit she said, 'Would you mind accompanying me down to dinner, Mr Connor?'

'Not at all, Mrs Connor.' He did rise now and gave her his arm, and she laid her head against his for a moment and they went out and down the stairs and into the dining-room like a young couple who were so in love that they couldn't bear to be separated even while going into a meal . . .

They had been married for five months now and Rory had grown so used to this way of life that it was hard at times for him to imagine he had ever lived any other. He was dressed as became a man of means; he ate like a man of means; he was beginning to enter the society of the town as should a man of means, because twice lately they had been asked out to dinner, and only four days ago he had played host to ten guests at this very table.

As day followed day he became more surprised at himself; he had never thought he would have adapted so quickly and so easily. Even Jimmy had said recently, 'It's amazing how you've learned to pass yourself. You'll be hobnobbing with Lord Cole next.'

He had laughed and said, 'I shouldn't be at all surprised at that either, lad,' at the same time knowing that while he might have gained access to certain houses in the town, there were still those whose doors would never be open to the one-time rent man, and among the latter were certain members of her church.

She'd tried to get him to church. He should attend for two reasons, she had laughingly said, in God's cause, and the cause of business. But no, he had put his foot down firmly here. He couldn't be that kind of a hypocrite. He had been brought up a Catholic and although he had never been through a church door for years, except when the banns were called and on the day he was married, he'd been born one and he would die one, he wasn't going to become a turncoat.

He was happy as he had never expected to be happy again in his life. It was a different kind of happiness, a steady, settled sort of happiness; a happiness made up partly of material things, partly of gratitude, and . . . and something else. It wasn't love, but at the same time it came into that category, yet he couldn't put a name to it. But he liked her, he liked her a lot, and he admired her. Strangely, he had ceased to be sorry for her. He couldn't imagine now why he'd ever been sorry for her. And strangely too, he was more at ease in her company than he had ever been with anyone in his own family, apart from Jimmy that was . . . He hadn't always been at ease with Janie. It was funny that, but he hadn't. No, he couldn't put a name to the feeling he had for Charlotte, he only knew that he liked being with her and that this was the life for him. He had fallen on his feet and he meant to see that they carried him firmly into the future . . .

The meal over and in the drawing-room, she sat by his side on the couch and watched him begin the process of filling his pipe – This liberty had even shocked the servants. No gentleman smoked in a drawing-room, but there, the mistress allowed it – and now she said, 'Well, I'm waiting. What have you discovered about Mr Nickle that has filled you with glee?'

'Glee?'

'Yes, glee. It's been oozing out of you since you came in.'

'He's a good churchman, isn't he?'

'Yes, as churchmen go, he's a good churchman.'

'A highly respected member of the community.' He pressed the tobacco down into the wide bowl of his red-wood pipe.

'What is it?' She put her hand out and slapped his knee playfully, and he looked at her steadily for a minute before he said flatly, 'He's a two-faced hypocrite.'

'Oh, is that all? Well, he's not alone in this town, is he?'

'He runs a gaming house.'

Now she was startled. 'Mr Nickle running a gaming house? You're dreaming, Rory.'

'Oh no. Oh no, Charlotte, Rory isn't dreaming,' he mimicked her. 'Rory once tried to get into Mr Nickle's gaming house, but he was politely warned off, then recommended to a house in King Street. And you know what happened to Rory in King Street, don't you?'

'You can't mean it?' Her face was straight and his also, and his tone was deep and bitter when he answered, 'I do. And it's not only gaming he's interested in when he can frighten little Joe . . .'

'Who's little Joe?'

'He's a bookie's runner, you know, one who goes round taking bets. But he's many more things besides, some things that it would be dangerous to look into. Not that he could do much on his own. But those who hire him could, such as our Mr Nickle. You know – ' he now rose and went to the fire and lit a spill and after drawing on his pipe came back towards her, saying, 'You know, I wouldn't have told you. I mean I wouldn't have given him away, only I met him the day across the water in Crawford's. He was doing the same as I was, getting the lay of the land, seeing if the place was worth buying, and he talked loudly to Crawford for my benefit about the stupidity of competing against rope works just farther up the river, such as Haggie's. And all the while he eyed me. Yet he ignored me, completely ignored me. Then Crawford, who's as blunt as an old hammer, said, "Aw well, if that's your opinion of the place you're not interested, are you? So what about you, Mr Connor, you think the same?" "No," I said, "I'm here to talk business." And on that the old fellow turned his back on our Mr Nickle and walked with me into the office, leaving his highness black in the face. And that's why I'm oozing glee, as you call it, 'cos Crawford's askin' much less than we thought. I told him we weren't thinking of rope, but a foundry, at least material from it to make household goods.'

'Good. Good.' She put her hand out towards him, and he held it and went on, 'And later, I saw his highness in the hotel when I was having a meal, and again he cut me dead. Now I could've understood such an attitude from any number of men in this town, and took it, but not from him, not knowin' what I know about him. Because it isn't only gambling, it's lasses.'

'Lasses?'

'Yes, there's quite a number of lasses disappear now and again.'

'Oh no! Rory, he . . . he wouldn't.'

'He would, and he does. Little Joe, the fellow I mentioned, was very much afraid of our Mr Nickle, and a game on the side wouldn't have caused him to sweat so much so that he got washed and cleaned up afore going to his back door. I'd never known little Joe so clean in his life as when I saw him that day, the day I found out about Nickle . . . Look.' He tugged her towards him. 'I've thought of something. Do you think you could invite him here to dinner?'

'Invite him here?'

'That's what I said. Say your husband would very much like to meet him.'

'But after he's cut you, do you think . . .?'

'Aye. Aye, I do. Invite him in a way that he'll think twice about refusing . . . Put that something in your voice . . . You can do it.'

'Blackmail?'

'Aye. Yes, if you like.'

She began to smile slowly, then she nodded at him. 'Yes, I see your point. Yes, I'll invite him. If I'm not mistaken I'll be meeting him next week; he's a member of the Church Council. We'll likely be sitting side by side in the vestry. Yes –' she laughed outright now – 'I'll invite him here, and enjoy it . . . that's if he accepts the invitation.'

'He will, after you've put it over in your own way . . . Huh! it's a funny life.' He leant back in the couch and she twisted her body round and looked fully at him.

'How are you finding it?'

'Finding what?'

'Life, this funny life.'

Taking the pipe from his mouth, he said, 'I'm liking this life fine, Mrs Connor. I never dreamed I'd like it so well.'

'I wish I were beautiful.' Her voice was low, and he pulled her suddenly towards him and encircled her with his arm, saying, 'You've got qualities that beat beauty any day in the week. You're the best-dressed woman in the town, too. Moreover, you've got something up top.'

'Something up top?' Her face was partly smothered against his shoulder. 'I'd willingly be an empty-headed simpering nincompoop if only I ... I looked different.'

Quickly now he thrust her from him and said harshly and with sincerity, 'Well, I can tell you this much, you wouldn't be sitting where you are now, or at least I wouldn't be sitting where I am now, if you were an empty-headed nincompoop.'

'Oh, Rory.' She flung herself against him as any young girl might, and he lay back holding her tightly to him.

Hardly a week passed but he had to reassure her with regard to her looks. It seemed that she was becoming more conscious of her plainness as time went on, and yet strangely, he himself was actually becoming less aware of her lack of beauty as the days passed; there were even times when her whole face took on an attractive quality. Then there was her voice. Her voice was beautiful. He never tired listening to it, even when she was in one of her haughty moods, which were becoming rarer.

She was saying, 'You've never asked what I've been doing all day today?'

'What have you been doing all day today?'

'Nothing. Nothing much. But ... but I have two things to tell you.'

'Two things? Well, get on with them. What are they?'

She pulled herself gently from his arms, saying now, 'Don't be disturbed, but Jimmy came this afternoon. One ... one of the boats has been sunk ...'

He was sitting on the edge of the couch now. 'Why ... why, didn't you tell me this afore?'

She placed her hands on his shoulders, saying, 'Be quiet. Don't get agitated. I've seen to it.'

'Where's Jimmy now?'

'Where he always is, in the boathouse.'

'Look, I'd better go down, he shouldn't be there alone. I'll ...'

'I told you I've seen to it. Mr Richardson is staying there with him.'

'The boat ... what happened to the boat?'

'A plank had been levered from the bottom.'

'And it would have been full. He was transporting for Watson yesterday.'

'Yes, it had on the usual cargo.'

'And it all went to the bottom?'

'They salvaged it. I went back with Jimmy; you hadn't been gone half an hour.'

He pulled himself up from the couch and began to pace back and forth in front of the fire, grinding out between his teeth, 'Those bloody Pitties!' He never apologized for swearing in front of her, nor did she ever reprimand him. 'If they're not stopped they'll do murder. Something's got to be done.' He was standing in front of her, looking down at her now, and she said quietly, 'Something will be done; I've seen to that as well. I ... I called on the Chief Constable. I told him of our suspicions. Of course you cannot accuse anyone unless you have absolute proof, but I knew by the little he said that he was well aware of the Pitties' activities and would be as pleased as us to convict them. And he said something that I found very interesting.

He ended by saying it was difficult of course to catch little fish when they were protected by big fish. What do you make of that?'

He rubbed his hand tightly along his jawbone. 'What do I make of it? Just that it links up with what I was saying earlier: there are some respectable people in this town leading double lives . . . big fish behind little fish.' He narrowed his eyes at her. 'Who would be protectin' the Pitties? Only somebody who wants to use them. And what would they use them for? What's their job? Running freight, anything from contraband whisky, silk, baccy, or men . . .'

'Or maidens? As you were saying earlier.'

He nodded at her. 'Aye, men or maidens, anything.' He bowed his head and shook it for a moment before saying, 'What I'm really frightened of is, if they should go for Jimmy. He's no match for any of them, although he's got plenty of guts. But guts aren't much use against them lot, it's guile you want.'

'If you are so worried about him then you must make him come here to sleep.'

He gave a weak smile and put his hand out and touched her shoulder, saying, 'That's nice of you, kind, but I doubt if he would.'

'Why not? He's got over his shyness of me, he's even, I think, beginning to like me. It gives me hope that your family may well follow suit.'

He turned from her and went towards the mantelpiece. And now he looked up into the face of her great-grandfather, and he thought, That'll be the day. That pig-headed lot. Even Ruth was included in his thoughts now.

Jimmy, acting as a kind of go-between, had arranged that he should take her up one Saturday, and because she also demanded it, but much against the grain, he had complied. And what had happened? Nothing. She had sat there trying to talk her way into their good books, and how had they responded? By staring at her as if she were a curio.

Later, she had remarked, 'I think your mother is a gentle creature.'

His mother. That was one secret he had kept to himself. She knew everything about him but that, and he couldn't bring himself to tell her that the slight, quiet, little woman, with a dignity that was all her own, was not his mother. His mother was the woman he had introduced to her by merely remarking, 'This is Lizzie', and explaining later that she was his father's cousin. Why was it that some things were impossible to admit to? He felt as guilty at being Lizzie's son as if it were he himself who had perpetrated the sin of his conception.

Damn them! Let them get on with it. It was Jimmy he was worried about, and those bloody Pitties were beginning to scare him. Little fish protected by big fish!

He turned to her. 'I'm goin' down,' he said.

'All right.' She rose from the couch. 'I'll go with you.'

'You'll do nothing of the sort. It's coming down whole water now.'

'If you're going down there tonight I'm going with you.'

He closed his eyes for a moment; he knew that tone. 'Well, get your things on.' His voice was almost a growl.

As she was walking towards the door, she said, 'I'll tell Stoddard.'

'No, no.' He came to her side. 'You don't want to get the carriage out at this time of night. And he'll be settled down. I meant to walk.'

'All right, we'll walk.'

'Oh, woman!'

'Oh, man!' She smiled at him and tweaked his nose, then left the room smiling.

Half an hour later they went up the steps and into the boathouse and startled Jimmy and Mr Richardson who were playing cards.

'Oh, hello.' Jimmy slid to his feet; then looking from one to the other, he asked, 'Anything wrong?'

'Not at our end; what about this end? What's this I'm hearin'?'

'Oh that.' Jimmy nodded, then said, 'Well, it's done one thing.' He was looking at Charlotte now. 'The river polis have been past here three times to my knowledge this afternoon. That's . . . that's with you going down there. Hardly seen them afore. That should warn the bug . . . beggars off for a bit.'

'Aye, for a bit.' Rory pulled a chair towards Charlotte. She sat down, and what she said was, 'Have you plenty to eat?'

'Oh aye.' Jimmy smiled at her. 'Lizzie's been down this afternoon an' baked. She feeds me up as if I was carryin' tw . . .' He swallowed and the colour flushed up over his pale face as he amended Lizzie's description of pregnancy, carrying twins for eighteen months, with 'cartin' coals to Newcastle.'

As he looked at Charlotte he saw that her eyes were bright, twinkling. She had twigged what he was about to say. It was funny but he liked her, he liked her better every time he met her. He could see now what had got their Rory. When you got to know her you forgot she was nothing to look at. He had said so to Lizzie this very afternoon when she was on about Rory, but she had come back at him, saying, 'You another one that's got a short memory? I thought you used to think the world of Janie.' Well, yes he had, but Janie was dead. And he had said that to her an' all, but what had she come back again with, that the dead should live on in the memory. She was a hard nut was Lizzie, she didn't give Rory any credit for making life easier for the lot of them. Three pounds every week he sent up there; they had never been so well off in all their lives. New clothes they had, new bedding, and they ate like fighting cocks. If Lizzie kept on, and his ma too didn't really soften towards Charlotte – he wasn't concerned about his da's opinion – he'd give them the length of his tongue one of these days, he'd tell them straight out. 'Well,' he'd say, 'if you think like you do, you shouldn't be takin' his money.' Aye, he would, he'd say that. And what would they say? 'It isn't his money, it's hers' . . . Well, it didn't matter whose it was, they were taking it and showing no gratitude. For himself he was grateful. By lad! he was grateful. Three boats he had, but one without a bottom to it.

He said to her, 'Will you have a cup of tea?'

'No, thank you, Jimmy. We . . . we just came to see that everything was all right.' She smiled from him to Mr Richardson.

Mr Richardson was a burly man in his forties. He had worked in Baker's yard alongside Jimmy but had gladly made the move to here when Rory offered him five shillings a weeek more than he was getting there. He was a married man with a family, so the arrangement of keeping Jimmy company at nights could not be a permanent one.

'We're grateful for you staying, Mr Richardson,' she said.

'Do anything I can, ma'am.'

'Thank you. We won't forget it, Mr Richardson.'

The man nodded and smiled widely. Then she rose to her feet and, looking at Rory, said, 'Well now, are you satisfied?'

Before he could answer she turned her head towards Jimmy, saying, 'The trouble with your brother, Jimmy, is he won't recognize the fact that you are a young man and no longer an apprentice.'

Jimmy laughed back at her, saying, 'Well, we'll have to show him, won't we? You tell him when you see him I'll take him on any day in the week an' knock the stuffin' out of him. You tell him that, will you?'

Rory now thrust out his fist and punched Jimmy gently on the head, saying, 'You've always been a daft lad; you always will be.'

'Daft? Huh! Who's daft comin' down this end in the black dark an' it pouring'. Don't you think you're askin' for trouble yourself, walking along the dockside, an' not alone either?' He nodded towards Charlotte.

'She came along to protect me. Can you imagine anybody tacklin' me when she's there?' He now took hold of Charlotte's arm and led her towards the door as she tut-tutted and cast a reproving glance up at him.

'Keep that door bolted, mind.'

'Aye. Don't you worry.' Jimmy smiled quietly at Rory.

The farewells over, they took the lantern and went down the steps and made their way through the stinging rain on to the road and along the waterfront, and as they hurried through what, even in daytime, was known to be an unsavoury thoroughfare Rory thought. He was right, I was crazy to let her come, and at this time of night.

And so he didn't breathe easily until they emerged into the main street, and there she said to him, 'Now you can relax.'

He did not reply, only heaved a telling sigh as he thought for the countless time, There's no doubt about it, she's remarkable.

His mind more at ease now with regard to Jimmy, he said, 'There were two things you were going to tell me the night. Well, let's have the second one now.'

'No, not now; it will have to wait until we get out of this, the rain is choking me.'

'Serves you right; you would have your own way.'

'Far better have my own way than sit worrying until you returned.'

'You're a fool of a woman. You know that, don't you?'

'Yes, I know that, I've known it now for five months and three days.'

'Oh, Charlotte!' He pressed her arm closer to his side.

She had taken a bath and was now dressed in a pale grey chiffon nightdress with matching negligee. It was night attire which one might have expected to see on a picture postcard such as sailors brought over from foreign countries, like France, on which were painted ladies in flowing robes, their voluptuousness alone signifying their lack of virtue.

He had now become used to seeing her dressed, or undressed, like this. His own night attire not only would have caused the women in the kitchen to throw their aprons over their heads, but would have raised the eyebrow of many a smart gentleman in the town, for his nightshirt was of a pale blue colour, the flannel being so fine as to be almost like cashmere. Moreover, it had cuffs that turned back and were hemmed with fancy braid, as was the deep collar. It, and a dozen more like it, were one of the many presents she had given him. And to hide his embarrassment he had made a great joke the first time he had worn one, but now he never even thought of his nightshirts, even when a fresh one was put out for him every other night.

As he pulled this one over his head he called to her, 'I'm waiting.' 'So am I.'

When her flat reply came back to him he bit on his lip, closed his eyes, tossed his head backwards and laughed silently. She was a star turn really. Who would have thought her like it?

He went from the dressing-room into the bedroom smiling. She wasn't in bed but was sitting on the edge of it, and at this moment she looked ethereal in the soft glow of the lamplight. He had the idea that if he opened the windows the wind that was blowing in gusts around the house would waft her away. He sat down beside her on the bed and, adopting an attitude of patience, he crossed his slippered feet, crossed his arms and stared ahead.

'Are you feeling strong?'

'Strong? In what way?' He turned his head sharply to look at her. 'Oh, in all ways.'

'Look, what is it?' He twisted his body round until he was facing her. 'Stop beating about the bush; what have you got up your sleeve now?'

She gave a little rippling laugh that might have issued from the lips of some dainty creature, then said, 'Nothing up my sleeve. No, decidedly not up my sleeve; I happen to have become pregnant.'

'Preg . . . *pregnant?*'

As his mouth fell into a gape she nodded at him and said, 'Yes, you know, "A woman with child" is how the Bible puts it.'

He drew in a long breath that lifted his shoulders outward. She was pregnant, she was with child, as she had said. Well, well. He had the desire to laugh. He stopped himself. She was going to have a bairn. Charlotte was going to have a bairn. And he had given it to her . . . Well, what was surprising about that? With all that had happened these past months why should he be surprised, for if anyone had worked for a bairn she had? He would never forget the first night in this bed. He had thought to treat her tenderly because right up to the moment they had first stood outside that door there, she had given him the chance to take advantage of the agreement she had first suggested; in fact, she had stood blocking his way into the room as she said, 'I won't hold it against you. Believe me, I won't hold it against you.' And what had he done? He had put his hand behind her and turned the knob. And she had entered with her head down like some shy bride, and he had told himself again that it was as little as he could do to be kind to her, to ease her torment, and make her happy. And he had made her happy. Aye by God! he had made her happy. And himself too. She had been surprising enough as a companion, but as a wife she had enlightened him in ways that he had never thought possible, because she had loved him. Aye, it was she who had done the loving. Up till then he hadn't been aware that he had never been loved. He had loved Janie. A better term for it would be, he had taken Janie. And she had let him, but she had never loved him in the way he was loved now. Perhaps it was his own fault that things had not worked out that way with Janie, it was the business of John George coming between them on that first night. He had known a few other women before Janie. On his first year of rent collecting there had been one in Jarrow – her man went to sea – but what she had wanted was comfort not love. Then another had been no better than she should be, she had given him what she would give anybody at a shilling a go.

No, he had never been loved until Charlotte loved him. It was amazing to him how or from where she had gained her knowledge, for one thing was certain, he was the first man she'd had in her life. Perhaps it was instinctive. Whatever it was, it was comforting. And now, now she was saying . . . 'Huh! . . . Huh! . . . Huh!'

He was holding her tightly to him. They fell backwards on to the bed and he rolled her to and fro, and they laughed together; then, his mouth covering hers, he kissed her long and hard.

When finally he pulled her upright the ribbon had fallen from her hair and it was loose about her shoulders and he took a handful of the black silkiness and rubbed it up and down his cheek.

'You're pleased?'

'Oh! Charlotte, what more can you give me?'

'One every year until I grow fat. I'd love to grow fat.'

'I don't want you fat, I want you just as you are.' And in this moment he was speaking the truth. He now took her face between his hands and watched her thin nostrils quiver. Her eyes were soft and full of love for him, and he said, 'You're the finest woman I've ever known, and ever will know.'

And she said, 'I love you.'

He could not say, 'And me you,' but he took her in his arms and held her tightly.

# Chapter One

## The Resurrection

The foreign-looking young woman handed her ticket to the ticket collector, stared at him for a moment, then passed through the barrier. She was the last of a dozen people to leave the platform and his look followed her. She was a foreigner. He could tell by her dress; she had strange-looking clogs on her feet and a black cloak hung from her shoulders right down to the top of them. She had a contraption on her head that was part hat, part shawl, with a fringe, and strings from it, like pieces of frayed twine, were knotted under her chin. Another odd thing about her was, although her skin was brown her hair was white and frizzy, like that of an old Negro's, yet her face was that of a young woman. She reminded him of a man that used to live near him who had white hair and pink eyes. They said he was an albino. He had been an oddity.

When the young woman reached the main thoroughfare she seemed slightly bemused; the traffic was so thick, and the Saturday evening crowd were pushing and shoving. She stepped into the gutter and the mud went over the top of her clogs. She stared at one face after another as if she had never been in a crowd before, as if she had never seen people before.

She walked on like someone in a daze. She skirted the stalls in the market place and when she heard a boat horn hooting she stopped and looked down the narrow lane that led to the ferry, then she went on again.

She was half-way down the bank that dropped steeply to the river when again she stopped. And now she put her hand inside her cloak and pressed it against her ribs. Then she turned her head upwards and gazed into the fading light.

Two men paused in their walking and looked at her, and she brought her head down and stared back at them. And when they looked at each other in a questioning way she ran swiftly down the bank away from them, her clogs clip-clopping against the cobbles.

On the river-front now, she hurried in a purposeful way along it until she came to where had stood the square of waste land, and here she looked about her in some perplexity, for the ground was now railed in, its railings joining those which surrounded the boatyard. Her steps slowed as she approached the alleyway; the light was almost gone, and when she went to open the gate and found it locked, she rattled it, then knocked on it, waited a moment, and, now almost in a frenzy, took her fist and banged on it.

When there was still no reply she looked up and down the alleyway before hurrying towards the far end where it terminated at the river wall; and now she did what she had done a number of times before when Jimmy had bolted the gate from the inside, she gripped the last post of the fence where it hung out over the river and swung herself round it, and so entered the boatyard.

Now she stood perfectly still looking up towards the house. There was a light in the window of the long room. Again she put her hand inside her cloak and placed it over her ribs, then slowly she went towards the steps and mounted them. She didn't open the door but knocked on it.

She heard the footsteps coming across the wooden floor towards it, but it didn't open. A voice said, 'Who's there?'

She waited a second before answering, 'Open the door, Jimmy.'

There was complete silence all about her now, no movement from inside the room. She said again, 'Open the door, Jimmy, please. Please open the door.'

Again there was no answer. She heard the steps moving away from the door. She turned her head and saw the curtains pulled to the side; she saw the outline of Jimmy's white face pressed against the pane. She held out her hands towards it.

She didn't hear the footsteps return to the door; nor was there any other sound, not even any movement from the river. It seemed to her that she was dead again. Her voice high now, beseeching, she called, 'Jimmy! Jimmy, it's me. Open the door. Please open the door.'

When at last the door opened it seemed it did so of its own accord; it swung wide and there was no one in the opening. She stepped over the threshold and looked along the room to where Jimmy was backing slowly along the side of the table towards its far end, and she stood with the door in her hand and said, almost in a whimper, 'Don't be frightened, Jimmy, I'm ... I'm not a ghost. It's ... it's me, Janie. I ... I've been bad. I ... I wasn't drowned.' She closed the door, then leant her back against it and slowly slid down on to the floor and slumped on to her side.

Jimmy gazed at the crumpled figure but didn't move. He had never been so terrified in all his life, he wanted to run, jump out of the window, get away from it ... her. Yet ... yet it was Janie's voice, and she said she was Janie. That's all he had to go on, for from what he could see of her, her skin was like an Arab's and her hair was white. Janie had been bonny, and her skin was as fair as a peach and her hair brown, lovely brown.

When she moved and spoke again, he started.

'Give me a drink, Jimmy, tea, anything.'

As if mesmerized now, he went to the hob and picked up the teapot that had been stewing there for the past hour, and with a hand that shook he filled a cup, spooned in some sugar, then slowly advanced towards her.

He watched her pulling herself to her feet, and as he stood with the cup in his hand, staring wildly at her, she passed him and went towards a chair, and after a moment she held out her hand and took the cup from him, and although the tea was scalding she gulped at it, then asked, 'Where's Rory?'

The gasp he gave brought her leaning towards him, and she asked softly, 'Nothin' ... nothin's happened him?'

His head moved as if in a shudder and then he spoke for the first time. 'Where've you been?' he said.

'I ... I was washed up there. I don't remember anything about it but they told me ... at least after a long time when the priest came over the hills; he could speak English. The fishing-boat, it found me off Le Palais. I was clinging to this wood and they thought I was dead. I must have been in the water for a long time swept by a current, they said, and . . . and when I came to meself I didn't know who I was. I . . . I never knew who I was till a month ago.'

'Just a month ago?'

'Aye.' She nodded slowly.

He gulped twice before he asked, 'Well, how did you get on? Who did you think you were?'

'Nobody; I just couldn't remember anything except vaguely. I seemed to remember holding a child. I told the priest that, and when he came next, he only came twice a year, he said he had inquired along the coast and he'd heard of nobody who had lost a wife and child. There had been great storms that year and lots of boats had been sunk. He told me to be patient an' me memory'd come back and I'd know who I was. It . . . it was Henri who brought it back.'

'Who's Henry?'

'He was madame's son. They're all fisherfolk, she looked after me. Life was very hard for them all, so very hard, much . . . much harder than here.' She looked slowly around the room. 'I . . . I remember how I used to talk about guttin' fish as being something lowly. I had to learn to gut fish. They all worked so hard from mornin' till night. It was a case of fish or die. You don't know.' She shook her head in wide movements. 'But they were kind and . . . and they were happy.'

Jimmy gulped. His mind was racing. This was Janie. It was Janie all right. Eeh! God, what would happen? Why couldn't she have stayed where she was? What was he saying? He muttered now, 'How did you get your memory back?'

'It was through Henri, he couldn't understand about me not wantin' to learn to swim. The young ones swam, it was their one pleasure, and this day he . . . he came behind me and pushed me off the rock. It . . . it was as I hit the water it all came back. He was sorry, very sorry I mean that it had come back.' She looked down towards the table and up again suddenly. 'Where's Rory? Is he up home?'

Jimmy turned from her. He was shaking his head wildly now. He lifted up the teapot from the hob, put it down again, then, swinging round towards her, he said, 'You've . . . you've been away nearly . . . nearly two years, Janie, things've happened.'

She rose slowly to her feet. 'What things? What kind of things?'

'Well . . . well, this is goin' to be another shock to you. I'm . . . I'm sorry, Janie. It wasn't that he wasn't cut up, he nearly went mad. And . . . and it was likely 'cos he was so lonely he did it, but –' now his voice faded to a mere whisper, and he bowed his head before finishing, 'he got married again.'

She turned her ear slightly towards him as if she hadn't heard aright; then her mouth opened and closed, but she didn't speak. She sat down with a sudden plop, and once more she looked around the room. Then she asked simply, 'Who to?'

Jimmy now put his hand across his mouth. He knew before he said the name that this would be even harder for her to understand.

'*Who to?*' She was shouting now, screaming at him.

If he had had any doubts before that this was Janie they were dispelled.

'Miss . . . Miss Kean.'

'*What!*' She was on her feet coming towards him, and he actually backed from her in fear.

'You're jokin'?'

'No, no, I'm not, Janie. No.' He stopped at the foot of the ladder and she stopped too. With one wild sweep she unhooked the clasp of her cloak and flung it aside, then she tore the bonnet from her head and flung it on to the cloak. And now she walked back to the table, and she leant over it as she cried, '*Money! Money!* He married her for money. He couldn't get it by gamin', but he had to have it some way.'

'No, no, it wasn't like that . . .'

She swung round and was facing him again, and he noted with surprise that her figure was no longer plump, it was almost as flat as Charlotte Kean's had been before her body started to swell with the bairn. Eeh! and that was another thing, the bairn. Oh my God! Where would this end? He said now harshly, 'It's nearly two years, you've got to remember that. He . . . he was her manager, and . . . and she was lonely.'

'Lonely? *Lonely?*' She started to laugh; then thrusting her white head forward, she demanded, 'Where's he now? Living in the big house? Huh! Well, his stay's goin' to be short, isn't it, Jimmy? He can't have two wives, can he?'

'He didn't know, you can't blame him.'

'Can't blame him? Huh! I was the only woman he'd ever wanted in his life, the only one he would ever love until he died. You . . . you know nowt about it. Can't blame him, you say!'

'You should never've gone; it was your own fault, you going on that holiday. I . . . I told him he shouldn't have let you.'

'But he did, he did let me, Jimmy. What he should have done the day I left was come after me and knock hell out of me an' made me stay. But he didn't, did he? He let me go.'

'You know why he let you go. It was because of John George, that business, an' you sticking out and wanting him to go and give himself up. You're as much to blame as he is, Janie, about that. But . . . but he's not to blame for marryin' again, 'cos how was he to know? He waited a year, over a year.'

'That was kind of him. Well now, what are we going to do, Jimmy, eh? You'll have to go and tell him that his wife's come back. That's it . . . just go an' tell him that his wife's come back.'

He stared at her. This was Janie all right, but it was a different Janie; not only was she changed in looks but in her manner, her ways, and as he stared at her he couldn't imagine any disaster great enough to change a woman's appearance as hers had been changed.

She saw his eyes on her hair and she said quietly now, 'I mean it, Jimmy. You'd better go and tell him. And . . . and tell him what to expect, will you?' She put her hand up towards her head. 'I . . . I lost all me hair. I was bald, as bald as any man, and . . . and they rubbed grease in, fish fat, an' . . . an' this is how it grew. And . . . and living out in the open in the sun and the wind I became like them, all brown 'cos of me fair skin likely.'

She sat down suddenly on a chair and, placing her elbows on the table, she lowered her face into her hands.

'Don't cry, Janie, don't cry.' He moved to the other side of the table. And now she looked up at him dry-eyed and said, 'I'm not cryin', Jimmy. That's another thing, I can't cry. I should cry about the children and the master and mistress and how I look, but something stops me . . . Go and fetch him, Jimmy.'

'I . . . I can't, Janie. It would . . .'

'It would what?'

'He'd . . . he'd get a gliff.'

'Well, if he doesn't come to me, I'll have to go to him. He'll get a gliff in any case, and he'd far better meet me here than up home . . . What's the matter? . . . What is it now?'

'Your grannie, Janie, she's. . . .'

'Aw no!' She dropped her head to the side and screwed up her eyes, then after a moment said, 'When?'

'Last year, after . . . shortly after she heard the news.'

'And me da?'

'He . . . he went to Jarrow to live with . . . he took lodgings in Jarrow. There's new people in the house, an old couple. An' the Learys have gone an'll. I never thought they'd ever move but he started work in St Hilda's Colliery, and it's too far for him to trek in the winter. They live down here now in High Shields. It's all changed up there.' He wanted to keep talking in a hopeless effort against what she was going to say next, but she stopped him with a lift of her hand as she leant back in the chair and drew in long draughts of breath, then said, 'I don't think I can stand much more. And I'm so tired; I haven't been to sleep for . . . aw, it seems days . . . Go and fetch him, Jimmy.'

The command was soft, but firm and brooked no argument. He stared at her for a moment longer; then grabbing his coat and cap from the back of the door, he dragged them on and rushed out. But once down in the yard he didn't run; instead, he stood gripping the staunch post that supported the end of the house as he muttered to himself, 'Eeh! my God! What's gona happen?'

# Chapter Two

Charlotte straightened the silk cravat at Rory's neck, dusted an invisible speck from the shoulder of his black suit, and finally ran her fingers lightly over the top of his oiled hair, and then, standing slightly back from him, she said, 'To my mind you're wasted on a gaming table.'

'I'm never wasted on a gaming table.' He pressed his lips together, jerked his chin to the side and winked at her.

Her face becoming serious now, she said, 'Be careful. The more I hear of that man, Nickle, the more perturbed I become.'

'Well, you couldn't ask for a quieter, better mannered or refined gentleman, now could you?'

'No; that makes him all the more sinister. It's really unbelievable when you think of it, but I'm glad that he knows I'm aware of what he is. I wish I had been there when he put his tentative question: "Your wife, of course, knows nothing of our little . . . shall we say excursions into chance?"'

He took up a haughty stance and mimicked, '"Sir, my wife knows everything; she's a remarkable woman." And she is that.' He put out his hand and slapped the raised dome of her stomach, and she laughed and tut-tutted as she in return slapped at his hand. Then her manner becoming serious again, she said, 'Well, there's one thing I can be assured of, he won't try any of his underhand business on you, because if he wants to silence you he'll also have to silence me. Who are you expecting tonight?'

'Who knows! My, my! It gets more surprising. You should have seen the look on Veneer's face when he saw me there, in the Newcastle rooms I mean. I thought he was going to pass out. I nearly did meself an' all. I couldn't believe me eyes. Him, a staunch supporter of the Temperance League! They would burn him at the stake if they knew. Just imagine the ladies of this town who wave the banners for temperance getting wind of what their Mr Veneer's up to . . . And you know something? I'd gather the kindling for them; I never could stand him. I remember your father once sending me on some business to his office. He spoke to me as if I were so much clarts. Sorry, madam.' He pulled a face at her. 'Mud from the gutter.'

She was now standing in front of him holding his face firmly between her hands, and she said with deep pride, 'Well, we've shown them. You've outwitted two of them already in business deals, and that's only a beginning. What's more, you're the most fashionable dressed, best-looking man in the town, or the county for that matter.' She tossed her head.

He didn't preen himself at her praise, but he said, 'I keep sayin' you're a remarkable woman, and you are. Every day that passes I discover something more remarkable about you. The very fact that you raised no protest at my gaming amazes me.'

'What is one evening a week? As long as your failings only embrace cards and wine I'll be content.'

He bent towards her now and kissed her gently on her lips, then said, 'You can rest assured, Mrs Connor, that these shall be the limit of my failings. But now for orders.' His manner changed, his voice took on a sterner note. 'You are not to wait up for me, do you hear? Stoddard will pick me up at twelve, and when I get in I shall expect to find you in bed and fast asleep. If I don't, then there's going to be trouble.'

'What will you do?'

He stared at her for a moment before replying, 'I'll take up the other vice.'

'No, don't say that.' There was no flippancy in her tone now. 'Not even in joke say you'll take up the third vice. That's something I couldn't bear.'

'You silly woman, don't you ever believe anything I say?'

'I want to.'

'Well, what can I say to make you believe it?'

She looked into his eyes. They were smiling kindly at her and she only just prevented herself from blurting out, 'Say that you love me. Oh, say that you love me.'

'Go on.' She pushed him from the room and into the hall. It was she who helped him into his coat and handed him his hat and scarf. Then she stood at the top of the steps and watched him go down them and into the carriage, and she waved to him and he waved back. Then stretching out his legs, he leant his head against the leather upholstery and sighed a deep contented sigh.

They were nearing the gate when the carriage was brought to an abrupt halt and he heard Stoddard shouting, 'Whoa! Whoa, there!' then add, 'Who's you?'

He pulled down the window and looked out, and there in the light of the carriage lamps he saw Jimmy. Quickly opening the door, he called to the driver, 'It's all right, Stoddard,' then to Jimmy, 'Get in. What's up? What's happened?'

As the carriage jerked forward again Jimmy bounced back on the seat, and again Rory demanded, 'What is it? What's happened now? Have they sunk another one?'

'No.' Jimmy shook his head. 'It's nowt to do with the boats.'

'Well, what is it? Something wrong at home?' Rory's inquiry was quiet, and when again Jimmy shook his head, he said almost angrily, 'Well, spit it out, unless you've just come for a chat.'

'I haven't just come for a chat, and . . . and I've been hangin' around for nearly an hour waitin', waitin' to see if you'd come out on your own.'

'Why?' Rory was sitting forward on the seat now. Their knees were touching. He peered into Jimmy's white face, demanding, 'Come on, what-ever it is, tell us.'

'You're going to get a gliff, Rory.'

'A gliff?'

'Aye, you'll . . . you'll never believe it. You'd . . . better brace yourself. It's . . . it's something you won't be able to take in.' When he stopped, Rory said quietly, 'Well, tell us.'

'It's . . . it's Janie.'

Jimmy's voice had been so soft that Rory thought he couldn't possibly have heard aright; Jimmy's words had been distorted, he imagined, by the grinding of the carriage wheels, so he said loudly, 'What did you say?'

'I said, it's Janie.'

'Janie?' A sudden cold sweat swept over his body and his own voice was scarcely audible now when he asked, 'What . . . what about Janie?'

'She's . . . she's back. She's . . . she's not dead, she wasn't drowned . . .'

Rory didn't utter a word, no protest, nothing, but his body fell back and his head once more touched the upholstery, and as if he had been shot into a nightmare again he listened to Jimmy's voice saying, 'I was petrified. It was her voice, but . . . but I wouldn't open the door at first. And then . . . and then when I saw her, I still didn't believe it was her. She's . . . she's changed. Nobody . . . nobody would recognize her. It . . . was the shock. Her hair's gone white, and her skin, her skin's all brown like an Arab's in Corstorphine Town. It's the sun, she said. She's . . . she's been in some place in France miles off the beaten track. She talks about a priest comin' once every six months. She's changed, aye. I knew you'd get a gliff but . . . but I had to come. If . . . if I hadn't she would have turned up herself. Eeh! she's changed. What'll you do, Rory? What'll you do?'

His world was spinning about him. He watched it spiralling upwards and away, taking with it the new way of living and the prestige it had brought to him. Sir, he was called, Master. She had given him everything a woman could possibly give a man, a home, wealth, position, and now a child. He had never been so happy in his life as he had been since he married her; and his feelings for her were growing deeper every day. You couldn't live with a woman like that and receive so much from her and give nothing in return; something had been growing in him, and last night he had almost told her what it was, he had almost put a name to it. He had never thought he would be able to say to another woman, I love you. That kind of thing didn't happen twice, he had told himself. No; and he was right, that kind of thing didn't happen twice. But there were different kinds of love. It was even appearing to him that what he was feeling now would grow into a bigger love, a better love, a fuller love. Charlotte had said there were better marriages based on friendship than on professions of eternal love.

He had once sworn eternal love for Janie, but he knew now that that had been the outcome of a boy's love, the outcome of use, the outcome of growing up together, seeing no one beyond her . . .

*She couldn't be back. She couldn't.* No! No! Life couldn't play him a trick like that. He had gone to the Justice before he married Charlotte and the Justice had told him it was all right to marry again. "Drowned, presumed dead," was what he had said. And she was dead. She had been dead to him for nearly two years now, and he didn't want her resurrected.

God Almighty! What was he saying? What was he thinking? He'd go mad.

'Rory. Rory.' Jimmy was sitting by his side now, shaking his arm, 'Are you all right? I . . . I knew it'd give you a gliff; she . . . she scared me out of me wits. What are you gona do?'

'What?'

'I said what are you gona do?'

He shook his head. What was he going to do?

'She's back in the boathouse; she wants to see you.'

He stared dumbly at Jimmy for a time, then like someone drunk he leant forward and tapped on the roof of the carriage with his silver-mounted walking stick, and lowering the window again, he leant out and said, 'We'll get off here, Stoddard; I . . . I've a little business to attend to.'

A few minutes later Stoddard was opening the carriage door and pulling down the step, and when they alighted he said, 'Twelve o'clock, sir?'

'What? Oh. Oh yes; yes, thank you.'

'Good night, sir.'

'Good . . . Good night, Stoddard.'

He walked away, Jimmy by his side, but when the carriage had disappeared into the darkness he stopped under a street lamp and, peering down at Jimmy, said, 'What, in the name of God, am I going to do in a case like this?'

'I . . . I don't know, Rory.'

They walked on again, automatically taking the direction towards the river and the boatyard, and they didn't stop until they had actually entered the yard, and then Rory, standing still, looked up at the lighted window, then down on Jimmy, before turning about and walking towards the end of the jetty. And there he gripped the rail and leant over it and stared down into the dark, murky water.

Jimmy approached him slowly and stood by his side for a moment before saying, 'You've got to get it over, man.'

Rory now pressed a finger and thumb on his eyeballs as if trying to blot out the nightmare. His whole being was in a state of panic. He knew he should be rushing up those steps back there, bursting open the door and crying, 'Janie! Janie!' but all he wanted to do was to turn and run back through the town and into Westoe and up that private road into his house, *his house*, and cry, 'Charlotte! Charlotte!'

'Come on, man.'

At the touch of Jimmy's hand he turned about and went across the yard and up the steps. Jimmy had been behind him, but it was he who had to come to the fore and opened the door. Then Rory stepped into the room.

The woman was standing by the table. The lamplight was full on her. She was no more like the Janie he remembered than he himself was like Jimmy there. His heart leapt at the thought that it was a trick. Somebody imagined they were on to something and were codding him. They had heard he was in the money. He cast a quick glance in Jimmy's direction as if to say, How could you be taken in? before moving slowly up the room towards the woman. When he was within a yard of her he stopped and the hope that had risen in him flowed away like liquid from a broken cask for they were Janie's eyes he was looking into. They were the only recognizable things about her, her eyes. As Jimmy had said, her skin was like that of an Arab and her hair was the colour of driven snow, and curly, close-cropped, curly.

Janie, in her turn, was looking at him in much the same way, for he was no more the Rory that she had known than she was the Janie he had known. Before her stood a well-dressed gentleman, better dressed in fact than she had ever seen the master, for this man was stylish with it; even his face was different, even his skin was different, smooth, clean-shaven, showing no blue trace of stubble about his chin and cheeks and upper lip.

Her heart hardened further at the sight of him and at the fact that he didn't put out a hand to touch her.

'Janie.'

'Aye, it's me. And you're over the moon to . . . to see me.' There was a break in the last words.

'I thought . . . we all thought . . .'

'Aye, I know what you thought, but . . . but it isn't all that long, it isn't two years. You couldn't wait, could you? But then you're a gamblin' man, you couldn't miss a chance not even on a long shot.'

He bowed his head and covered his eyes with his hand, muttering now, 'What can I say?'

'I don't know, but knowin' you, you'll have some excuse. Anyway, it's paid off, hasn't it? You always said you'd play your cards right one day.' She turned her back on him and walked to the end of the table and sat down.

He now drew his hand down over his face, stretching the skin, and he looked at her sitting staring at him accusingly. Jimmy had said she had changed, and she had, and in all ways. She looked like some peasant woman who had lived in the wilds all her life. The dark skirt she was wearing was similar to that worn by the fishwives, only it looked as if she had never stepped out of it for years. Her blouse was of a coarse striped material and on her feet she had clogs. Why, she had never worn clogs even when she was a child and things were pretty tight. Her boots then, like his own, had been cobbled until they were nothing but patches, but she had never worn clogs.

Aw, poor Janie . . . Poor all of them . . . Poor Charlotte. Oh my God! Charlotte.

'I'm sorry I came back.' Her voice was high now. 'I've upset your nice little life, haven't I? But I am back, and alive, so what you going to do about it? You'll have to tell her, won't you? Your Miss Kean . . . My God! You marryin' her of all people! *Her!* But then you'd do anything to make money, wouldn't you?'

'I didn't marry her for . . .' The words sprang out of his mouth of their own volition and he clenched his teeth and bowed his head, while he was aware that she had risen to her feet again.

Now she was nodding at him, her head swinging like that of a golliwog up and down, up and down, before she said, 'Well, well! This is something to know. You didn't marry her for her money. Huh! You're tellin' me you didn't marry her for her money. So you married her because you wanted her? You wanted *her*, that lanky string of water, her that you used to make fun of?'

'*Shut up!* My God! it's as Jimmy said, you're different, you're changed. And yet not all that. No, not all that. Looking back, you had a hard streak in you; I sensed it years ago. And aye, it's true what I said, I . . . I didn't marry her for her money, but it's also true that I didn't marry her 'cos . . . 'cos I was in love with her.' He swallowed deeply and turned his head to the side and, his voice a mutter now, he said, 'She was lonely. I was lonely. That's . . . that's how it was.'

'And how is it now?'

He couldn't answer because it was wonderful now, or at least it had been.

'You can't say, can you? My God, it's a pity I didn't die. Aye, that's what you're thinkin', isn't it? Eeh! I wouldn't have believed it. I wouldn't, I wouldn't.' She was holding her head in her hands now, her body rocking. Then of a sudden she stopped and glared at him as she said, 'Well, she'll have to be told, won't she? She'll have to be told that you can have only one wife.'

As he stared back at her he was repeating her words, 'I wouldn't have believed it,' for he couldn't believe what he was recognizing at this moment, that it could be possible for a man to change in such a short time as two years and look at a woman he had once loved and say to himself, 'Yes, only one wife, and it's not going to be you, not if I can help it' – What was he thinking? What was he thinking?

He was trapped. Standing before him was his wife, his legal wife, and he'd have to tell Charlotte that his wife had come back and that she herself had no claim to him and the child in her couldn't take his name. He couldn't do it. What was more, he wouldn't do it. He heard his voice saying now, clearly and firmly, 'I can't tell her.'

'You what!'

'I said I can't tell her, she's going to have a ch . . . bairn.' He had almost said child, so much had even his vocabulary changed.

There was complete silence in the room, until Jimmy moved. He had been standing at the side of the fireplace and now his foot jerked and he kicked the brass fender, which caused them both to look towards him. And then she said, 'Well, it's going to be hard on her, isn't it, bringing up a bairn without a father? But then, her way will be smoothed, money's a great compensation. Oh yes, money's a great compensation. You can make things happen when you've got money. I had four sovereigns. The mistress give them to me to buy presents for you all to bring home. I put them in me little bag, an' you know me an' me little bag. Whenever I changed I used to pin it under me skirt, and when they found me there was me little bag still pinned under me skirt. But I didn't know anything about it until I got me memory back. Madame, the old woman I lived with, had taken it, but when I came to meself and wanted to come home and didn't know how, the son put the bag into me hand. He was very honest, the son, and so I travelled in luxury all the way here. First, in the bottom of a cart with pigs; then for miles on foot, sleeping on the floors of mucky inns; then the boat; and lastly, the back end of the train, like a cattle-truck; and –' and now she screamed at him – 'you're no more sorry for me than you would be for a mangy dog lying in the gutter. The only thing you're worried about is that I've come back and your grand life is to be brought to an end. Well, if you don't tell her, I will; I'm not gona be pushed aside, I'm gona have me place.'

'Janie. Janie.' His voice was soft, pleading, and she stopped her ranting and stared at him, her face quivering but her eyes still dry. 'I'll . . . I'll do what I think is right. In . . . in the end I'll do what I think is right. But give me a little time, will you? A few days, time to sort things out, to . . . to get used to –' He gulped in his throat. 'You can have what money you want . . .'

'I don't want your money. Anyway, 'tisn't *your* money, you've never worked for it, it's her money.'

'I do work for it, begod! and hard at that.' His voice was loud now, harsh. 'I work harder now than ever I've done in me life. And now I'm goin' to tell you something, an' it's this. Don't push me; don't drive me too far. This . . . this has come as a surprise. Try to understand that, but remember I'm still Rory Connor and I won't be pushed.' He paused for a moment, then ended, I'll . . . I'll be back the morrow night,' and on this he swung round on his heel and went out.

Jimmy, casting a look at Janie, where she was standing now, her hands hanging limply by her side and her mouth open, turned and followed him. In the yard he saw the dim outline of Rory standing where he himself had stood earlier in the evening against the stanchion post, and he went up to him and put his hand on his arm, and held it for a moment before saying, 'I'm sorry, Rory. I'm sorry to the heart of me, but . . . but you can't blame her.'

'What am I going to do, Jimmy?' The question came out as a groan.

'I don't know, Rory. Honest to God, I don't know. Charlotte'll be in a state. I'm sorry, I mean I'm sorry for Charlotte.'

'I . . . I can't leave her, I can't leave Charlotte. There's her condition and . . . Oh dear God! what am I goin' to do? Look, Jimmy.' He bent down to him. 'Persuade her to stay here out of the way, don't let her go up home. Look, give her this.' He thrust his hand into an inner pocket and, pulling out a chamois leather bag, emptied a number of sovereigns on to Jimmy's palm. 'Make her get some decent clothes; she looks like something that's just been dug up. I could never imagine her letting herself go like that, could you?'

'No. No, Rory. I told you, she's . . . she's changed. She must have gone through it. You'll have to remember that, she must have gone through it.'

'Aye, and now she's going to make us all go through it.'

As he moved across the yard Jimmy went with him, saying, 'Where you makin' for? Where were you going'?'

'To a game.'

'Game? Does Charlotte know?'

Rory stopped again and said quietly, 'Aye, Charlotte knows and she doesn't mind. As long as I'm happy, doing something that makes me happy, she doesn't mind; all she minds is that she'll ever lose me. Funny, isn't it?'

They peered at each other through the darkness. 'Where you goin' now, back home?'

'No, no, I'll . . . I'll have to go on to the game. They're expecting me, and if I didn't turn up something would be said. Anyway, I've got to think. I'm I'm nearly out of me mind.'

Jimmy made no reply to this and Rory, touching him on the shoulder by way of farewell, went up the yard and out of the gate.

He did not go straight to Plynlimmon Way but walked for a good half-hour, and when at last he arrived at the house Frank Nickle greeted him with, 'Well, Connor, we thought you weren't coming, we've been waiting some –' he drew from the pocket of his spotted grey waistcoat a gold lever watch attached to a chain across his chest – 'three quarters of an hour.'

'I . . . I was held up.'

'Are you all right? Are you unwell?'

'Just . . . just a bit off colour.'

'No trouble, I hope?'

'No trouble.'

'Then let us begin.'

Nickle's tone was peremptory, it was putting him back into the servant class as far as he dared allow it. That the man hated him he was well aware, for he knew he was cornered, and had done since the night he came to dinner. But he also knew that he'd have to be careful of him in all ways. However, at this moment Nickle and his nefarious doings seemed of very minor importance.

They went into what was known as the smoking room. It was part office and part what could be considered a gentleman's rest room, being furnished mostly with leather chairs, a desk, and a small square table, besides four single chairs.

The two men present were smoking cigars and they greeted Rory cordially, speaking generally, while Frank Nickle lifted a china centrepiece from the square table, laid it aside, then opened the top of the table which was cut in the shape of an envelope, each piece being covered with green baize. This done, they all took their seats around the table and Nickle, producing the cards from a hidden drawer underneath, the game began . . .

Three hours later Rory rose from the table almost twenty pounds poorer. At one time in the evening he had been thirty pounds to the good.

He left before the others, and at the door Frank Nickle, smiling his thin smile, said, 'You weren't your usual brilliant self tonight, Connor.'

'No, I think I'm in for a cold.'

'That's a pity. Give my regards to your lady wife.' The large pallid face now took on a slight sneer. 'Tell her not to slap her little boy too hard for losing.'

He had the urge to lift his hand and punch the man on the mouth. But wait, he told himself, wait. Give him time, and he would do it, but in another way. He left without further words, went down the pathway through the iron gate and to the road where the carriage was waiting.

Nickle had suggested covertly that it was unwise to come by carriage, servants talked . . . ordinary servants, and to this Rory had replied that Stoddard was no ordinary servant, he was as loyal as Nickle's own. And anyway, wasn't he visiting the house for a 'Gentlemen's Evening'? They were common enough. How could one discuss the finer points of business if it weren't for 'Gentlemen's Evenings'?

When he arrived home Charlotte was in bed, but she wasn't asleep, and when, bending over her, he kissed her she pushed him slightly away from her, but holding him by the shoulders, she said, 'What is it? What's happened?'

'Nothing.'

'Oh, come, come, Rory, you . . . you looked strained. Something happened at Nickle's?'

'No.' He pulled himself from her. 'Only that I lost . . . twenty pounds.'

'Oh!' She lay back on her pillows. 'Hurt pride. Twenty pounds, quite a sum. But still I suppose you must let them have their turn. If you won every time they would say you were cheating.'

'Yes, yes.' When he went into the adjoining room to undress she called to him anxiously, 'There's nothing else wrong, is there? I mean, he didn't say anything, there wasn't any unpleasantness?'

'No, no; he wasn't more unpleasant than usual. He was born unpleasant.'

'Yes, yes, indeed.'

In bed he did not love her but he held her very tightly in his arms and muttered into her hair, 'Oh, Charlotte. Charlotte.'

It was a long time before he went to sleep, but even then she was still awake, although she had pretended to be asleep for some time past. There was something wrong; she could sense it. By now she knew every shade of his mood and expression. Her love for him was so deep that she imagined herself buried inside him.

At four o'clock in the morning she was woken up by his screaming. He was having a nightmare, the first he had had since his marriage.

## Chapter Three

Three days passed before Charlotte tackled him openly and very forcibly. 'What is it?' she said. 'Something is wrong. Now –' she closed her eyes and lifted her hand upwards – 'it's no use you telling me, Rory, that there's nothing amiss. Please give me credit for being capable of using my eyes and my ears if not my other senses. There *is* something wrong, and I must know what it is. Rory, I must know what it is.'

When he didn't answer but turned away and walked down the length of the drawing-room towards the window she said, 'You're going out again tonight; you have been out for the last two nights supposedly to see Jimmy. When I was passing that way today I called in . . .'

'You what!' He swung round and faced her.

She stared at him over the distance before rising to her feet and saying slowly, 'I said I called in to see Jimmy. Why should that startle you? I have done that before, but what puzzled me today, and what's puzzling me now, is that you are both reacting in the same way. I asked him if he was feeling unwell and he said, no. I asked him if there had been any more tampering with the boats, he said, no . . . Rory, come here.'

When he made no move towards her, she went swiftly up the room and, putting her arms about him, she demanded, 'Look at me. Please, look at me,' and when he lifted his head, she said, 'Whatever it is, it cannot be so awful that you can't tell me. And whatever it is, it's leaving its mark on you, you look ill. Come.' She drew him down the room and towards the fire, and when they were seated on the couch she said, softly now, 'Tell me, Rory, please. Whatever it is, please tell me. You said once you would always speak the truth to me. Nothing must stand between us, Rory. Is it that man, John George? Is he blackmailing you? After all I did for him is he . . .?'

'Oh no! No! Oh God, I wish I could say he was, I wish that's all it was, John George. John George wouldn't blackmail anybody, not even to save his life. I know that, don't I? . . . Charlotte –' he now gathered her hands tightly between his own and held them against his breast – 'I've . . . I've wanted to say this to you for some time past, but . . . but I didn't think I could convince you because, to tell you the truth, when . . . when all this first started between you and me, I never thought it would ever be possible, but Charlotte . . . Charlotte, my dear, I . . . I've grown to care for you, love you . . .'

'Oh Ror-y, Ror-y.' She made a slow movement with her head, then pressed her lips tightly together as he went on, 'I want you to know this and believe it, for . . . for what I'm going to tell you now is going to come as a great shock. If it were possible to keep it from you I would, especially now when the last thing in the world I want you to have is worry, or shock, but . . . Aw God! how can I tell you?' When he turned his head to the side she whispered. 'Rory. Rory, please; whatever it is, listen to me, look at me, whatever it is, whatever you've done, it won't alter my feelings for you, not by one little iota.'

He was looking at her again. 'I haven't done anything, Charlotte, not knowingly. It's like this.' He swallowed deeply on a long breath. 'The other night, Saturday, when you sent me out so gaily to the game, Jimmy was waiting at the bottom of the drive. He . . . he had news for me . . .'

He stopped speaking. He couldn't say it but gazed at her, and she didn't say, 'What news?' but remained still, very still as if she knew what was coming.

. . . 'He told me something amazing, staggering. I . . . I couldn't believe it, but . . . but Janie, she had come back . . . *Charlotte! Charlotte!*'

As she lay back against the couch he watched the colour drain from her face until she had the appearance of someone who had just died, and he took her by the shoulders and shook her, crying again, 'Charlotte! Charlotte! it's all right. Listen, listen, it's all right, I won't leave you, I promise I won't leave you. I know she can claim through law that . . . that she's still my wife, but . . . but after seeing her, hearing her . . . I don't know, I don't

know.' He lowered his head, 'She's no more like the woman I married than
...'

Charlotte had made a small groaning sound, and now he gathered her
limp body into his arms and, stroking her hair, he muttered, 'Believe me.
Believe me, Charlotte, I'll never leave you. No matter what happens I'll
never leave you unless . . . unless you want me to . . .'

. . . 'Unless I want you to?' Her voice was scarcely audible. 'How . . . how
can you say such a thing? I'd want you near me even if I knew you were
a murderer, or a madman. Nothing you could do, nothing, nothing would
ever make me want to be separated from you.'

'Oh my dear! My dear!'

They were holding each other tightly now and, her mouth pressed against
his cheek, she was murmuring, 'How . . . how are you going to go about it?
Does . . . does she know?'

He released her and sat slowly back against the couch. 'I'm . . . I'm going
down to tell her tonight.'

'Where is she?'

'In the boathouse.'

'Yes, yes, of course, she would be there. That is why Jimmy was so
concerned. It is strange but . . . but already I seem to have lost a family. I
liked Jimmy, I liked him very much indeed. I . . . I had great plans for him,
a new yard. I had been looking about on my own. It . . . it was to be a
surprise for you, and your . . . your people. I thought they were coming to
accept me, particularly your aunt, for it was she who from the beginning
appeared the most distant. But these past few weeks, in fact only last
Thursday when I met her in the boathouse, she was cooking for Jimmy, and
she made a joke with me, and for the first time she didn't address me as
ma'am . . . and now . . . Oh! Oh, Rory!' She turned and buried her face in
his shoulder, and when her body began to shake with her sobbing his heart
experienced an agony the like of which hitherto he hadn't imagined he was
capable of feeling. It was only the second time he had heard her cry. She
wasn't the weeping type; she was so strong, so self-assured; she was in
command of herself and of him and of everyone else.

As he held her tightly to him he dwelt for a moment on the strangeness
of life and what two years could do to a man's feelings, and he realized that
no man could really trust himself and say that what he was feeling today
he would still feel tomorrow. A few moments ago he had told Charlotte he
loved her and would never leave her; two years ago he had told Janie that
he loved her and she would always and ever be the only one in his life.
What was a man made of when he could change like this? It was past him,
he couldn't understand it. Yet there was one thing at the moment he was
certain of, and that was that he no longer wanted Janie but he did want
Charlotte, and that what he felt for her wasn't mere gratitude but love, a
love that owed nothing to externals but sprang from somewhere deep within
him, a place that up till now he hadn't known existed.

# Chapter Four

Janie had refused to take the money that Rory had left. Not until she was back in her rightful place, she had said, would she take a penny from him.

'But Janie,' Jimmy had pleaded, 'you can't go round looking like that, and . . . and all your clothes . . . well, they were given away, the Learys got them.'

'Why can't I go round like this, Jimmy? This is what I've worn for the last two years, and as I said, when I'm back in me rightful place then I'll take money from him for clothes.'

On that night one of the first things she asked when he had come back into the room was, 'What's happened to John George?'

'Oh,' Jimmy had answered, 'John George's all right. He has a newspaper shop in Newcastle . . . and that lass is with him. When he got out he came back and saw her, and she left the man. Her father went after her and threatened both of them, but she said it was no good she wouldn't go back. They're all right,' he had ended.

She had looked at him hard as she asked, 'How did he come by the paper shop?'

'Well.' Jimmy had brought one foot up on to his knee and massaged his ankle vigorously while he said, 'It was her . . . Charlotte, she saw to it.'

'*She* saw to it? You mean to say, after sendin' him along the line she set him up in a shop?'

'Aye.'

'And he let her?'

'Oh aye, he held no grudge. That's John George, you know. He's too good to be true really, or soft, it's how you take him. But she found out where he was, and she went up to him and talked with him and . . . and well, that was that . . . She's kind, Janie.'

She had looked hard at him as she said, 'I don't know about kind, but one thing's clear, she's wily. She's bought the lot of you. You're for her, aren't you, Jimmy? Hook, line and sinker you're for her. And I'll bet you'll be telling me next that all them in the kitchen are at her feet an' all.'

'Oh no, Janie, oh no. There was hell to pay. They . . . they didn't speak to him for ages.'

Slightly mollified, she held out her hands towards the blaze, then said quietly, 'He doesn't want me now, Jimmy. You can see it; he doesn't want me.'

And Jimmy could make no reply to this by way of comfort . . .

Nor could he the next night after Rory had gone, nor last night, because each time they met they seemed to become further apart. They were like two boxers who hated each other. Even if Rory were to leave Charlotte he couldn't see them ever living together again. He began to wonder why she was insisting on it.

He had just come in from the yard and the sight of her cooking a meal caused him to say, 'Lizzie . . . Lizzie'll be down the morrow; she . . . she comes to bake. What you gona do, Janie?'

'What do you think?' She went on cutting thick slices from a piece of streaky bacon.

'Well, you'll give her a gliff.'

'We've all had gliffs, Jimmy.' Still continuing slicing the bacon, she didn't look up as she said, 'You didn't mention it, but I suppose her ladyship's been supportin' them up there an' all?'

It was some seconds before he answered, 'Rory has, and it's his own money, 'cos as he said he works hard for it. And he does, Janie. He travels about a lot, seein' . . . . seein' to different businesses and things . . . and he studies . . .'

'Studies!' She raised her head and looked at him scornfully. 'Rory Connor studies! What? New tricks in the card game?'

'Don't be so bitter, Janie.'

She flung the knife down so hard on to the table that it bounced off on to the floor, and, leaning towards him, she cried, 'Jimmy, have you any idea how I feel, comin' back here and finding I'm not wanted by nobody? *Nobody.* Oh –' she moved her head slowly from shoulder to shoulder – 'how I wish I'd never got me memory back. Do you know something? I was happy back there. The life was hard, but there were good people, jolly, and they took to me.' She now looked down towards the table. 'There's something else I'll tell you. There was a man there, the son . . . he wanted to marry me. There were few young ones in the village and they had to go miles and miles to reach the next settlement. But . . . but I still had me wedding ring on' – she held out her hand – 'and I said I must be married to somebody. They all worked it out that I'd been with me husband and child and they must have been both drowned 'cos I kept talking about the child afore I came round, so the priest said. He was on one of his visits when I was picked up. It was Miss Victoria. And . . . and then Henri pushed me off the rock and when I came up out of the water I remembered. They were all strange to me. I looked at them an' saw them as I hadn't afore, rough fisherfolk, rougher than anything you see round here, livin' from hand to mouth. They only had two old boats atween the lot of them. It was his, Henri's boat, that picked me up. He' – Her voice trailed away now, as she ended, 'He sort of felt I belonged to him 'cos of that.'

When she raised her eyes again to Jimmy she said softly, 'They all came and saw me off. They walked the five miles with me to where we met the priest and he took me on to the next village in the cart. And you know something? He warned me, that priest. He warned me that things would've changed. And do you know what I said to him, Jimmy? I said to him, "Well I know, Father, of one who won't have changed, me husband . . ."'

It was half an hour later when they'd almost finished the meal that Jimmy, scraping the fat up from his plate with a piece of bread, said tentatively, 'What'll happen, Janie, if . . . if he won't leave her?'

'He's got to leave her. He's got no option, it's the law.'

'Janie –' He chewed on the fat-soaked piece of bread, swallowed it, then said, 'Rory's never cared much for the law. I mean he hasn't bothered about what people think. What if he says, I mean 'cos of the bairn comin', "To hell with the law!" and stays with her, what then?'

'What then? Well, she'll be living in sin won't she? And she's prominent in the town, and the gentry won't stand for that, not in the open they won't. Things can happen on the side, but if it came out in court that he wouldn't take me back, and me his wife, and he went on living with her, why neither of them would dare show their faces. There's things that can be done and things that can't be done, especially in Westoe; it isn't like along the riverfront here. And he'll find that out. Oh aye, he'll find that out.'

It was at this point in the conversation that the door opened and Rory entered. She did not turn and look at him, and he walked slowly towards the fireplace.

Jimmy, rising flustered from the table, said, 'Hello there.'

Rory nodded towards him, but gave him no reply. He had taken off his hat and was holding it in one hand which was hanging by his side; then looking at Janie he said, 'Do you think we could talk quietly?'

'That's up to you.' She did not even glance towards him.

'I've . . . I've made a decision.'

She said nothing, but waited, and he glanced towards Jimmy, whose eyes were tight on him. Before he spoke again he stretched his chin up out of the collar of his overcoat. 'I'm not going to leave her, Janie.'

She made no move in any way, no sign.

'You'll take me to court as is your right, and I'll maintain you, and well too, as is also your right, but . . . but she's carrying my child and I'm not leaving her.'

Now she did turn towards him and, like a wild cat, she spat her words at him. 'You're a swine! Do you know that? You're a rotten, bloody swine, Rory Connor! And, as I said to Jimmy, you do this and you won't be able to lift your head up in this town. Aye, and I'll see you don't, I'll take you to court. By God! I will. It'll be in all the papers; both you an' her'll have to hide yourselves afore they've finished with you. And her money won't save you, not from this disgrace it won't . . .'

As he stared back into her face which was livid with passion, he thought, even if Charlotte were to die at this minute I wouldn't go back to her; I could never live with her again. His thoughts, swirling back over the past, tried to find the man he had been, the man who had loved this woman, the man who had sworn always to love her, but in vain. And so he said, 'Do what you think you have to do; if it'll make you feel any better go the whole hog; but I'd like to remind you that Shields isn't the only town on the planet. The world is wide and when you have money you can settle where you like.' He felt no compunction now at throwing his money at her.

He stared at her a moment longer. She was not recognizable to him; the white hair, the brown skin, even her eyes were no longer Janie's. He pulled on his hat, saying, 'Well, that's that; the rest is up to you,' and, turning, went out; and as he always did on these visits, Jimmy followed him into the yard.

It was a bright evening; the twilight was long in passing. They walked side by side down to the end of the yard and stood against the railing bordering the river. The moored boats were bobbing on the water beneath them. They stood looking down into them, until he asked, 'Do you blame me?'

There was a short pause before Jimmy answered, 'No, not really, Rory, no. But . . . but I'm sorry for her. I can see her side of it an' all.'

'Well, I would expect you to 'cos she has got a side. And I'm sorry for her too. At this moment I'm sorry for us all.'

He looked up and down the river as he said, 'Things were going so fine. I was riding high, I was me own man. Even with Charlotte's money I was me own man, because I knew I was making meself felt in the business.' He looked down at Jimmy. 'You know, as I said, we could go away. I thought of that as I came along. We could move to any place in the country, but somehow I don't want to leave this town. And I know she doesn't. But anyway, no matter where we go we'll see you're all right.'

'Aw . . . aw, don't worry about me, Rory, I'll get through. And you've done more than enough already. By the way, I didn't tell you, 'cos you've got enough on your plate, but those buggers down there must have been up to something last night. I heard somebody in the yard, more than one. I . . . I thought they were comin' under the house, and then a patrol boat came up and stopped – it stops most nights – and I heard nothing after that. I . . . I was a bit scared.'

'Get Richardson to come along and stay with you.'

'Aye, I will, but I think I must look for somebody else, somebody single. You see, he's got a wife and family.'

'You do that. Tell them they'll be well paid.'

Jimmy nodded; then he asked quietly, 'What's going to happen to her . . . Janie? I mean, will she want to go on livin' here? It's awkward. She says she's going up home the night or the morrow. Well, if she does she might decide to stay up there.'

'Home? Huh!' Rory tossed his head back. 'They'll have a field day with this. Our dear Lizzie will come out with all the sayings back to Noah: As ye sow so shall ye reap; Pride goes before a fall; Big heid small hat. Oh, I can hear her.'

'I . . . I don't think so, Rory. You know, I've always meant to say this to you, but you don't see Lizzie as she really is. She's all right is Lizzie, and I've never been able to understand why you still hold it against her. And I look at it this way: after what's happened to you if you don't see her side now you never will.'

'Aye. Aye, I suppose you're right . . . Well, I'll be off. I . . . I won't come back as long as she's here. Come up, will you, whenever you can and let me know how things are going? I'll want to know when I'm to expect the authorities.'

'All right, Rory, I'll let you know. Tell Charlotte I wish her well, and I'm sorry . . .'

'I will; she'll be grateful. So long then.'

'So long, Rory, so long.'

They looked at each other for a moment longer, then Rory turned away and walked slowly out of the yard.

Jimmy waited a while before returning to the house, and it was as he mounted the steps that he heard her crying. When he entered the room he saw her, her face buried in her arms on the table, her body shaking.

He did not go to her but went and sat by the side of the fire and, following his habit, he brought his foot on to his knee again and stroked his ankle vigorously. It would do her good, he told himself, to cry it out. Perhaps it would wash away some of the bitterness in her.

After a moment he slid his foot off his knee and looked down at the triangular shape made by his legs; he had always hated them for from the beginning they had erased any hope of him ever finding a lass of his own; no lass wanted to be seen walking the streets alongside him. He had gone through a lot of body torment, and occasionally he still did, but these feelings he mostly sublimated in his affection for the family and his love for Rory ... Aye, and her sitting behind him there.

But now at this particular moment as he looked down at his legs he was in a way grateful to them, for because of them he would never experience the agony that Rory, Janie and Charlotte were enduring at this minute.

Life was funny, it handed out compensations in very odd ways.

## Chapter Five

'You're sure, darling, quite sure.'

'I'm as sure as I will be of anything in me life.'

'You won't regret it. I'll never let you regret it for one moment.'

'There'll be a hell of a rumpus. As she said, we won't be able to lift our heads up in the town ... Should we leave?'

'No, no, we won't leave ... we won't leave. We married in good faith; she has no children by you, I'm to have your child. We are as it were the victims of circumstance.'

'They won't look at it that way. You know as well as I do what they'll say. He's on to a good thing, that's what they'll say. He's not going to give all that up and go back to rent collectin', or some such.'

'Do you mind very much what they say?'

He thought for a moment before answering, 'Yes, I do, because ... because it won't be true. I'm staying with you now for one reason only, although I can't say I haven't got used to all this –' he spread his arms wide – 'but if I had retained any feeling for her, as it once was, say, this wouldn't have mattered.'

'I know that ... Oh, why had this to happen? We were so happy, so content; there was only one thing missing in my life.'

'One thing?'

'Yes, and then you gave it to me earlier this evening ... You said you loved me.'

'Oh, Charlotte!' He put his hand out and caught hers.

'When do you think she'll take proceedings?'

'Tomorrow likely. The mood I left her in, she'll waste no time. But you know something? In spite of all I know is going to happen, the scandal, the gossip, the papers, the lot: "Woman returns from the dead. Husband, married again, refuses to acknowledge her" – You can see them, can't you,

the headlines? – Well, in spite of it all, the moment I came back, the moment
I stepped through the door and saw you sitting there I had the oddest feeling.
It was strange, very strange. I can't remember feeling anything like it before.
It was a feeling . . . well, I can't put a name to it, a sort of joy! No, no –'
he shook his head – 'I shouldn't say joy . . . Certainty? No, I really can't put
a name to it, but I knew that everything was going to turn out all right. I
thought, in a way it's a good job it's happened; we'll start a new life, you
and me and him – or her.' He placed his hand gently across the mound of
her stomach, and she put her two hands on top of his and as she pressed
them downwards she looked into his face and said, 'I love you, I adore you.
Blasphemy that, isn't it? But to me you are my God.'

He now dropped on to his knees and, burying his face in her lap,
murmured, 'Charlotte, Charlotte, I'll want no other but you ever, believe
me . . .'

When there came the tap on the drawing-room door he turned round
hastily and knelt before the fire and busied himself attending to it as Charlotte
called, 'Come in.'

Jessie closed the door softly behind her, came up the room, and, standing
at the edge of the couch, she said, 'There's . . . there's a man at the door, sir.
He . . . he says he would like to speak to you.'

'A man?' Rory got to his feet thinking, My God she hasn't lost much
time. 'Did he give you his name?'

'No, sir. He just said it was important, and . . . and he must speak with
you. He's a little man, very little, sir.'

A little man, very little. Who did he know who was very little? Only little
Joe.

'Where is he now?'

'I've . . . I've left him in the lobby, sir. He's . . . he's workman type.'

He looked down towards Charlotte. Then went swiftly past Jessie.

When he opened the hall door and looked into the lobby he was looking
down on to little Joe.

'Evenin', Mr Connor.'

'Hello, Joe. What's brought you here?' His voice was stiff.

'Mr Connor, I'd . . . I'd like a word with you.'

'I don't need to be set-on any longer, Joe, you should know that.' His tone
held a slight bitterness.

''Tisn't about that, Mr Connor. I . . . I think you'd better hear me, and
in private like; it's . . . it's important, very, I should say.'

Rory hesitated a moment, then said, 'Come away in.' He opened the door
and let the little fellow pass him. He watched him as his eyes darted around
the hall. Then he led the way to the office. Once there, he seated himself
behind the desk and, motioning to a chair, said, 'Sit yourself down,' and
when Joe was seated he said, 'Well, let's have it.'

'I thought you should know, Mr Connor, but . . . but afore I tell you
anythin' I want you to believe that I wasn't in on the other business when
they done you over. They're a dirty crew an' they've got me where they
want me, the Pitties an' him – Nickle. But . . . but there's some things I
don't stand for, and if they knew I was here the night me life wouldn't be
worth tuppence. But . . . but I thought you should know.'

'Know what?'

'Well.' Joe stretched his feet downwards until his toes touched the carpet;

then he leant forward towards the desk and, gripping it, he said under his breath, 'They're up to something. I just got wind of it a while ago. They're gona get at you through your brother. I've . . . I've seen him. He's not much bigger than me, and he's got his own handicap, and . . . and I didn't think it was fair 'cos of that, so I thought I'd come and tell you, 'cos you always played straight by me, never mean like some of them. And . . . and after that business when you didn't drag me into it, and you could 'ave, oh aye, you could 'ave, I thought to meself, if ever . . .'

'Get on with it, Joe. What are they up to?'

Joe now brought his hands from the table and, joining them together, he pressed them between his knees before he announced, 'They're gona burn you out.'

'*Burn me out?* Here?'

'Oh no, not here; they wouldn't dare come up this way. No, the boatyard and the boathouse. Steve Mackin let it drop. They'd been to him for paraffin.'

'What!' Rory was on his feet and around the desk. 'When?'

'Oh, late on's afternoon. I . . . I was payin' him a bet and he said, "Poor little bastard."' Joe now looked from one side to the other as if to apologize to someone for his language, then went on, 'I said, "Who?" and he said, "Connor. Little bandy Connor. But what can you do against those three buggers?"'

Rory was going towards the door now. 'What time was this?'

'Oh, an hour gone or more. I took a stroll by that way 'cos I thought if I saw him, I mean your brother, I would tip him off to keep clear like, but I saw big Pittie standing at the corner. He was talking to a fellow, just idling like, standing chattin'. But he doesn't live down that end, and so I thought it wasn't fair, Mr Connor, an' so I came . . .'

They were in the hall now and the drawing-room door was opening.

'What is it?'

'I . . . I've got to go down to the boatyard. Nothing, nothing.'

Charlotte came up to him as he was taking his coat from the hall wardrobe and again she asked, 'What is it?' then added, 'Oh, what is it now, Rory?'

'Nothing.' He turned to her, a faint smile on his face. 'This chap here, well –' he thumbed towards Joe – 'he's been kind enough to come and give me a warning. The Pitties mean business; I think they're going to loosen the boats.'

'Don't go.' Her voice was stiff now. 'Don't go, please. Let us go straight to the station; the police will deal with it.'

'Now, now.' He put his hands on her shoulder and turned her about, then led her towards and into the drawing-room. Once inside he closed the door, then whispered to her, 'Now look, it's nothing. All right, all right –' he silenced her – 'I'll get the police. I promise I'll get the police.'

'It's dark; anything could happen; it's dark.'

'Look, nothing's going to happen. Richardson'll be there with him. He's a tough fellow is Richardson. Now look, I've got to go. You stay where you are.'

'No, let me come with you. Please let me . . .'

'*No. No.* Now don't you dare move out of here.' He opened the door and called, 'Jessie!' and when the maid appeared he said, 'See that your mistress doesn't leave the house until I get back. Now, that's an order.'

The girl looked from one to the other, then said, 'Yes, sir. Yes, sir.'

He turned again to Charlotte and, putting his hand out, he cupped her chin and squeezed it before hurrying towards the door, where little Joe was standing.

The little fellow cast a glance back towards Charlotte, touched his forelock and said, 'Evenin', ma'am,' and she replied, 'Good evening,' Then he sidled out quickly after Rory.

They hadn't reached the bottom of the steps before Charlotte's voice came after them, crying, 'Wait for the carriage!'

'I don't need the carriage. Go back inside. Do what you're told.' His voice trailed away as he hurried down the drive.

Once in the lane, he began to run and little Joe kept up with him, but by the time they had reached Westoe village the little fellow was lagging far behind.

Fire. It only needed a can of oil and a match and the whole place would go up like dried hay lit by lightning, and they mightn't be able to get out in time. If Jimmy was up in the loft he could be choked with smoke. There were so many books and papers up there, and all that wood, oiled wood inside and out, and the tarred beams underneath in the covered slipway . . . He'd kill those Pitties; one or all of them he'd kill them. It had to come sooner or later; it was either them or him. If they hurt Jimmy . . . And she was there an' all, Janie. To come back from the dead and then be burned alive. And that's what could happen, if they'd both gone to bed. Those buggers! They were murderers, maniacs.

He was racing down the bank towards the market. Dark-clothed figures stopped and looked after him, then looked ahead to see if he was being chased.

It was as he turned into the Cut that he smelt the smoke, and then he looked up and saw the reflection of the flames. Like a wild horse he tore down to the waterfront and along it. But he was too late. He knew before he reached the crowd that he was too late.

The place was alive with people. He pushed and thrust and yelled to try to get through them. But they were packed tight and all staring upwards towards the flaming mass inside the railings.

Dashing back, he climbed the stout sleepers that he'd had put up to encase the spare land they had bought only a few months earlier. When he dropped on to the other side he saw men dragging a hawser from a river boat, and he ran, scrambling and falling over the debris, yelling, 'Jimmy! Jimmy!'

He grabbed hold of a man's arm. 'Are they out?'

'Who, mate?'

'Me . . . me brother.' He was looking wildly around him. 'And . . . and Janie.'

'There's nobody in there, man. Anyway, look at it, nothin' could live long in that, they'd be choked with the smoke afore now.'

'Jimmy! Jimmy!'

He was hanging over the rail yelling down into the wherries when a woman appeared. She swung round the end post from the passage and he stared into her face, made pink now by the reflection from the fire. 'Janie!' He gripped her arms. 'Where's . . . where's Jimmy?'

'Jimmy? I . . . I left him. I left him here, I've been up home.'

'Oh my God!'

He turned now towards the house and gazed upwards. It looked like a huge torch. Flames were coming out of the two bottom windows but only smoke out of the upper one. As he stared there came the sound of breaking glass. It could have been caused by the heat but instinctively he swung round to Janie, and there flashed between them a knowing glance. Then she put her hand over her mouth as she cried, 'God Almighty, Jimmy!'

He raced towards the steps, but as he attempted to mount them the heat beat him back. To the side of him two men were playing a hose that spurted intermittent water into one of the bottom windows. His hand was gripping the stanchion of the balustrade over which a sack was lying; it was the hessian hood that Jimmy wore when working in the rain. Tearing it from the railing he dashed towards the men and pulling the hose downwards he saturated the sack; then, throwing it over his head, he went up the steps again, and into the house.

Everything that was wood inside was alight. The floor felt like slippery wet mush beneath his feet. Blindly he flew over it and to the ladder. One side of it was already burning but he was up it in a second and had thrust the trap-door open.

The room was full of smoke, but through it he saw the glow of the burning bookcase at the far end. Coughing and choking he dropped flat on the floor and pulled himself towards the window, and there his groping hands touched the limp body, and it wasn't until he went to drag it towards the trap door that he realized that both Jimmy's hands and feet were bound. There was no time to unloosen them. So gripping him under the armpits, he pulled him backwards towards the trap-door, but there he had to pause and stuff the wet hessian into his mouth and squeeze the water down his throat to stop himself from choking.

To descend the ladder he had to get on to his knees, then hoist Jimmy's slight body on to his shoulder. By now he wasn't really conscious of his actions, one followed the other in automatic frenzy. Even the agony of gripping the burning rungs didn't penetrate his mind.

The room now was one inferno of hissing flame and smoke; his coat was alight, as was Jimmy's guernsey. Half-way along the room he felt the floor giving way, and as his feet sank he threw himself and his burden in the direction where he thought the door was. His lungs were bursting, his whole body seemed to be burning as furiously as the room.

One hand groping blindly, he felt for the opening, and found it. The steps were below. He let Jimmy slide to the ground. He was choking. He was choking. Dimly he was aware of yells and screams and at the same time he felt the whole building shudder. That was all he remembered.

He was alive when they raised the burning beam from him, then beat the fire out of his clothes.

When they carried him to where Jimmy was lying covered with coats, Janie stumbled by his side, and when she went to take his blackened hand, his skin came away in her palm.

As if totally unconscious of the turmoil in the yard she knelt between the two men with whom she had been brought up, and she groaned aloud.

Someone went to raise her up but she pushed the hands aside. The voices were floating over her: 'We must get him to the hospital. Get a stretcher, a door, anything.' Then there followed a period of time before a voice said, 'Here, Mrs Connor. He's here, Mrs Connor,' and she lifted her head to see a tall figure dropping on to her knees at the other side of the man who was her husband. She stared at the woman who was putting her arm under Rory's shoulders and crying to him, such words, endearing words that she had never heard said aloud before. 'Oh my darling, my darling, dearest, dearest. Oh Rory, Rory, my love, my love.' Such private words all mixed up with moans.

Janie felt herself lifted aside, almost pushed aside by a policeman. He was directing the lifting of Jimmy on to a stretcher. When they went to take up Rory they had to loosen the woman's hands from him, and she heard the voices again saying, 'We must get him to hospital.' And now the woman's voice, 'No, no, he must go home. Both of them, they must come home. I . . . I have the carriage.'

'They'll never get in a carriage, ma'am.' It was a policeman speaking.

'A cart then, a cart, anything. They must come home.'

There were more voices, more confusion, then a discussion between three uniformed men.

When they carried the two still forms out of the yard Janie followed them. They crossed the waste land to avoid the fire which was now merely a mass of blazing wood to where, on the road stood a flat coal cart that had been commandeered. She watched them putting the two stretchers on to it, and as it moved away she saw the woman walk closely by its side. Then the driver got down from a carriage that was standing by the kerb in the road and ran to her. She watched her shake her head at him, and he went back and mounted the carriage and drove it behind the cart. And Janie followed the carriage.

Even when it turned into the drive and up towards the house she followed it. She stopped only when it moved away to the side, past the cart and towards the stables. She watched the men who had accompanied the cart lifting the stretchers off it. She watched the servants running up and down the steps. Then everyone disappeared into the house, and for a few minutes she was standing alone looking at the lighted windows, until the coachman came racing down the steps, rushed into the yard, turned the carriage and put the horses into a gallop and went past her.

Then again she was alone for a time and she stood staring unblinking at the house. She did not move when the carter and three other men came down the steps and mounted the cart and rode away.

She did not know how long she stood there before she saw the carriage return and the doctor, carrying his leather bag, get out and hurry into the house, but she imagined that it was near on two hours before he came out of the house again.

As he went to get into the carriage she seemed to come out of a trance and, stumbling towards him, asked, 'Please, please. How is he? How are they?'

The doctor looked her up and down, her odd hat, her cloak, her clogs. She looked like a field peasant from the last century, and not a peasant of this country either. He peered at her for a moment before he answered, 'The young man will survive but Mr Connor is very ill, seriously so.' He made an abrupt movement with his head, then stepped up into the carriage, and the driver, after giving her a hard stare, mounted the box, turned the carriage and was about to drive away when a servant came running down the steps, calling, 'Will! Will!' When the coachman pulled the horses up, the servant, gripping the side handle, looked up at him and said quickly, 'The mistress, she says, you're to go straight on after dropping the doctor and . . . and bring the master's people. You know where.'

'Aye. Aye.' The coachman nodded and cracked his whip and the horses once again sped down the drive.

The servant now looked at the woman standing to the side of the balustrade. 'Do you want something?' she asked.

Janie shook her head.

'Did . . . did you come with them?'

Janie nodded once.

The servant now looked her up and down. She had never seen anyone dressed like her, she looked a sketch, like a tramp, except that her face didn't look like that of a tramp for it was young, but she looked odd, foreign, brown skin and white hair sticking out from under that funny hat. She said, 'What do you want then?'

'Just to know how they are.'

The voice, although low and trembling, was reassuring to the servant. She might look foreign but she was definitely from these parts.

'They're bad. The master's very bad and . . . and the mistress is demented. The master's brother, he'll pull through. Come back in the mornin' if you want to hear any more. Do . . . do you know them?'

'Aye.'

'Aw . . . well, come back in the mornin'.'

As the servant went up the steps Janie turned away, but only until she heard the click of the door; then she stopped and took up her position again, staring at the two upper brightly lit windows.

# Chapter Six

Rory lay swathed in white oiled linen. His face was the same tone as the bandages. At five o'clock this morning he had regained consciousness and he had looked into Charlotte's face, and she had murmured, 'My dearest. Oh, my dearest.'

As yet he wasn't conscious of the pain and so had tried to smile at her, but as he did so it was as if the muscles of his face had released a spring, for his body became shot with agony. He closed his eyes and groaned and turned his head to the side, and when he opened his eyes again he imagined he was dreaming, because now he was looking into Lizzie's face. And he could see her more clearly than she could him, for her face was awash with tears. But she was crying silently.

Vaguely he thought, she generally moans like an Irish banshee when she cries . . . then, What's she doing here? He turned his head towards Charlotte again and her face seemed to give him the answer. He was that bad. Yes, he was bad. This pain. He couldn't stand this pain. He'd yell out. Oh God!

God! what had happened to him? The fire. The Pitties! The Pitties. They were murderers. He had always meant to get the Pitties but they had got him and Jimmy . . . Jimmy . . . Jimmy . . .

He said the name a number of times in his head before it reached his lips. '*Jimmy*.'

'He's all right, darling. Jimmy's all right. He's . . . he in the other room, quite close. He's all right. Go to sleep, darling, rest.'

'Char-lotte.'

'Yes, my dear?'

The words were again tumbling about in his mind, jumping over streams of fire, fire that came up from his finger nails into his shoulders and down into his chest. His chest was tight; he could hardly breathe but he wanted to tell her, he wanted to tell her again, make her understand, make her believe, press it deep into her that he loved her. He wanted to leave her comfort . . . What did he mean? Leave her comfort. Was he finished? Had they finally done for him? Was he going out? No. No. He could put up a fight. Aye, aye, like always he could put up a fight, play his hand well. If only the burning would stop. If he could jump in the river, take all his clothes off and jump in the river.

'Char-lotte.'

'Go to sleep, darling. Rest, rest. Go to sleep.'

Yes, he would go to sleep. That's how he would fight it. He would survive; and he'd get the Pitties. Little Joe, he'd make Little Joe speak out . . . and about Nickle. God! Nickle. It was him who was the big fish, aye he was the big fish . . . Aw, God Almighty. Oh! oh, the pain . . . He only needed thirty-five pounds to get the boatyard for Jimmy. If he could get set into a good game he'd make it in two or three goes. He wanted to give Jimmy something to make up for those lousy legs he was stuck with . . . Somebody was scorching him . . . burning him up . . .

'Drink this.'

The liquid sizzled as it hit the fire within him, then like a miracle it gradually dampened it down . . .

'He'll sleep for a while, lass.'

Lizzie took the glass from Charlotte's hand and placed it on a side table and, coming round the bed, she said, 'Come away and rest yourself.'

'No, no; I can't leave him.'

'He doesn't need you now, he needs nobody for the time being. It's when he wakes again and that won't be long, come away.'

Charlotte dragged her eyes from the face on the pillow and looked up into the round crumpled face of the woman she had come to think of as Rory's aunt. Then obediently she rose from the chair and went towards the other room, and Lizzie, following her, said, 'I would change me clothes if I was you and have a wash, then go downstairs and have a bite to eat. If you don't, you'll find yourself lying there along of him, and you won't be much use to him then, will you?'

Charlotte turned and stared at the fat woman. She spoke so much sense in her offhand way. She nodded at her but didn't speak.

Lizzie now closed the door and walked back to the bed and, sitting down, stared at her son, at the son who hadn't given her a kind word for years. As a boy he had liked her and teased her, as a man he had insulted her, scorned her, even hated her but all the while, through all the phases, she had loved him. And now her heart was in ribbons. He was the only thing she had of her own flesh and he was on his way out.

On the day he was born when he had lain on her arm and first grabbed at her breast she had thought, He's strong; he'll hold the reins through life all right. And everything he had done since seemed to have pointed the same way, for he had earned a copper here and there since he was seven. And hadn't he been sent to school? And hadn't he been given full-time work afore he was fourteen? And then to jump from the factory into the high position of a rent man. Moreover he had been the best dressed rent man in the town because he made enough out of his gaming to keep himself well rigged out and still have a shilling or two in his pocket. Then his latest bit of luck, marrying into this house. Who would ever have believed that would have come about? He'd always had the luck of a gambling man.

Aye, but she hadn't to forget that a gambling man's luck went both ways. And she had thought of that at tea-time yesterday when that ghost walked in the door. How she stopped herself from collapsing she'd never know. Only the fact that Ruth was on the verge of it herself had saved her, for to see Janie standing there, the Janie that wasn't Janie, except when she spoke. God in heaven! Never in all her born days had she had such a shock. And nothing that would happen to her in this life or the next would equal it. But a couple of hours later, as she watched Janie go down the path looking like something from another world, she asked God to forgive her for the thoughts that were passing through her mind, for there had been no welcome in her heart for this Janie, whose only aim in life now seemed to be the ruin of the man she had once loved, and whose wife she still was. Aye, that was a fact none of them could get over, whose wife she still was. And that poor soul back there in the room carrying a child. Well, as she had always said, God's ways were strange but if you waited long enough He solved your problems. But dear, dear God, she wished He could have solved this one in some other way than to take her flesh, the only flesh she would ever call her own.

When the door opened behind her she rose to her feet, and going towards Charlotte, she said, 'I'll call Ruth and the young maid, an' I'll come down along of you and put me feet up for a short while.'

Charlotte passed her and walked to the bed, and, bending over it, she laid her lips gently on the white sweat-laden brow, and as she went to mop his face Lizzie took her arm and said, 'Come. No more, not now. And them nurses should be here by daylight.'

Out on the landing, Jessie was sitting on a chair by the side of the door, and Charlotte said to her, 'Sit by the bed, Jessie, please. I'll . . . I'll be back in a few moments.'

'Yes, ma'am.'

The girl disappeared into the room and Charlotte crossed the landing and gently opened the door opposite, and Ruth turned from her vigil beside Jimmy's bed and asked in a whisper, 'How is he?'

'Asleep.' She went to the foot of the bed and, looking at Jimmy, she said softly, 'His hair will grow again, it's only at the back. He's sleeping naturally.' Then she asked, as if begging a favour, 'Would you sit with Rory just in case he should wake? Jessie's there, but . . . but I'd rather –' She waved her had vaguely. 'You could leave the door open in case Jimmy calls.'

Ruth stared up at her for a moment, then looked at Lizzie before she said, 'Aye, yes, of course'. . . .

In the drawing-room, Charlotte sat on the couch, her hands gripped tightly in front of her, and stared at the fire, and when the door opened and Lizzie came from the kitchen carrying a tray of tea and a plate of bread and butter she did not show any surprise.

The time that had passed since nine o'clock last night was filled with so many strange incidents that it seemed to have covered a lifetime, and that this woman should go into her kitchen and make tea seemed a natural thing to do; it was as if she had always done it.

It seemed to Charlotte from the moment she had knelt beside Rory last night that she had lived and died again and again, for each time she thought Rory had drawn his last breath she had gone with him. That he would soon take his final breath one part of her mind accepted, but the other fought hysterically against it, yelling at it, screaming at it: No, no! Fight for him, will him to remain alive. You can't let him go. Tell him that he must not go, he must not leave you; talk to his spirit, get below his mind, grasp his will, infuse your strength into him. He can't. He can't. He must not die . . .

'Here, drink that up and eat this bit of bread.'

'No, thank you. I . . . I couldn't eat.'

'You've got to eat something. If nothin' else you need to keep the wind off your stomach when you're carryin' or you'll know about it.'

'I'm sorry, I couldn't eat. But you . . . please, please help yourself.'

'Me? Aw, I've no need to eat.' Lizzie sighed as she sat down on the edge of a chair. There followed a few moments of silence before Charlotte, wide-eyed, turned to her and said, 'What do you think?'

'Well, lass, where there's life there's hope they say. As long as he's breathin' he's got a chance, but if you want my opinion, it's a slim one. He was always a gamblin' man, but he's on a long shot now.' She put her cup down on a side table and her tightly pressed lips trembled.

Again there was silence until Lizzie said quietly, 'It's not me intention to trouble you at this time, for God knows you've got enough on your plate, but . . . but I think there's somethin' you should know 'cos there's only you can do anything about it . . . Janie. She's been outside all night sittin' in the stables, your coachman says. He doesn't know who she is of course. He told one of your lasses that there was a strange woman there and she wouldn't go, she was one of his relatives he thought.'

Lizzie now watched Charlotte rise to her feet and, her hands clasped tightly in front of her, go towards the fire and stand looking down into it, and she said to her, 'When she walked into the kitchen last night I was for droppin' down dead meself.'

Charlotte's head was moving in small jerks. The woman, the girl, his wife . . . his one-time wife in her stables? She had a vague memory of seeing a black huddled figure kneeling at Rory's side in the yard, then again when they had lifted him on to the cart, and for a moment she had glimpsed it again in the shadows of her drive. What must she do? Would Rory want to see her? He had once loved her . . . She couldn't bear that thought; he was hers, wholly hers. The happiness she had experienced with him in the months past was so deep, so strong, that the essence of it covered all time back to her beginning and would spread over the years to her end, and beyond. And he loved her, he had said it. He had put it into words, not lightly like some unfledged puppy as he had been when he married his childhood playmate, but as a man who didn't admit his feelings lightly. So what place had that girl in their lives? What was more, he had told her he wanted none of her . . .

'If he had been taken to the hospital she would have seen him, she would have claimed the right.'

Charlotte swung round. Her face dark now, she glared at the fat woman, and for a moment she forgot that she knew her as Rory's aunt. She was just a fat woman, a common fat woman, ignorant. What did she know about rights?

'Don't frash yourself, 'cos you know as well as I do the law would say she had a right. They would take no heed that his feelings had changed.' She nodded now at Charlotte. 'Oh, aye, Janie told me he wouldn't go back to her, he had told her so to her face, and that must have been hard to stomach. So havin' the satisfaction that he wanted you, and seemingly not just for what you could give him, it should be in your heart, and it wouldn't do you any harm, to let her have a glimpse of him.'

'I can't.'

Lizzie now got to her feet and heaved a sigh before she said, 'Well, if you can't, you can't, but I'd like to remind you of one thing, or point it out, so to speak. As I see it, you should be holding nothing against her. You've got nothin' to forgive her for except for being alive. She's done nothin' willingly to you. The boot's on the other foot. Oh aye –' she dropped her chin on to her chest – 'it was all done in good faith, legal you might say, but nevertheless it was done. How would you feel this minute if you were in her place? Would you be sitting all night in the stables hoping to catch a glimpse of him afore he went?'

Charlotte sat slowly down on the couch again and, bending her long body forward, she gripped her hands between her knees.

It was some time, almost five minutes later when she whispered, 'Take her up. But . . . but I mustn't see her; I . . . I will stay here for half an hour. That is, if . . . if he doesn't need me.'

She was somewhat surprised when she received no answer. Turning her head to the side, she saw Lizzie walking slowly down the room. She was a strange woman, forthright, domineering, and she had no respect for class . . . of any kind. Yet there was something about her, a comfort.

She lay back on the couch and strained her ears now to the sounds coming from the hall. She heard nothing for some minutes, then the front door being closed and the soft padding of footsteps across the hall towards the stairs brought her upright. She was going up the stairs, that girl, his wife, she was going up to their bedroom, to hers and Rory's bedroom. And she would be thinking she was going to see her husband. *No! No, not her husband*, never any more. Hadn't he told her she could do what she liked but he'd never return to her?

She'd be by his bedside now looking at him, remembering their love, those first days in the boathouse.

*'My wife won't be there, miss, but you're welcome.'*

She was back sitting behind the desk again looking at him as he told her he was married.

She almost sprang to her feet now. She couldn't bear it, she couldn't bear that girl being up there alone with him. She must show herself. She must let her see that she was the one he had chosen to stay with, not someone who was seven years her junior, or young and beautiful, but her, as she was . . . herself.

She was out of the drawing-room and running up the stairs, and she almost burst into the bedroom, then came to a dead stop and stared at the three women standing round the bed, his mother, his aunt and the person in the black cloak who wasn't a beautiful young girl but a strange-looking creature with dark skin and white frizzy hair; she was young admittedly, but she could see no beauty in her, no appeal.

She walked slowly up to that side of the bed by which Ruth stood and she stared across into the eyes of the girl called Janie. The eyes looked sad, weary, yet at the same time defiant.

A movement of Rory's head brought their attention from each other and on to him. He was awake and looking at them.

If there had been any doubt in Rory's mind that he was near his end it was now dispelled. Janie and Charlotte together. Through the fire in his body was now threaded a great feeling of sadness. He wanted to cry at the fact that this was one game he was going to lose. The cards were all face up, and his showed all black . . . dead black. But still he had played his hand, hadn't he? The game had been short but it hadn't been without excitement. No, no, it hadn't. But now it was over . . . almost. He wished the end would get a move on because he couldn't stand this pain much longer without screaming out his agony. Why didn't they give him something, a good dose, that laudanum . . . laudanum . . . laudanum . . .

He was looking into Janie's eyes now. They were as he remembered them in those far-off days before they were married when she was happy, because she had never really been happy after, had she? It was funny, but in a way Janie hadn't been made for marriage. She looked it, she had the body for it, but she hadn't been made for marriage, whereas Charlotte. Ah! Charlotte.

Charlotte's face was close above his. He was looking up into her eyes. Charlotte. Charlotte was remarkable. Charlotte could forgive sins. She was like all the priests rolled into one. There'd been a priest here last night, hadn't there? He couldn't really remember. Well, if there had been he knew who would have brought him . . . A dose . . . Why didn't they give him something?

'Darling.'

It was nice to be called darling . . . Oh God! the pain. Why the hell didn't they give him something? . . . Janie had never called him darling. She had said she loved him, that was all. But there was more to love than that, there was a language. Charlotte knew the language. Charlotte . . . Should he fight the pain, try to stay? He could hardly breathe . . . If only they'd give him something.

He closed his eyes for a second; when he opened them again he was looking at Lizzie. There was something in her face that was in none of the others. What was it? Why had he hated her so? It seemed so stupid now. Why had he blamed her as he had done? If there had been anybody to blame it was his father. Where was his father? He was surrounded by women. Where was his father? Where was Jimmy? They'd said Jimmy was near. Jimmy was all right. And his father? His father had a bad leg; his father had been burnt at the blast furnace . . . He had been burnt . . . *Burnt. Burnt.* He was back in the boathouse gasping, struggling. The floor was giving way. He slid Jimmy from his shoulder. He was getting out, he was getting out ...

'He's asleep again. Leave him be, let him rest.' Lizzie moved from the bed as she spoke, and Ruth followed her, leaving Janie and Charlotte standing one on each side.

Janie looked down on the man whose face was contorted with agony. She did not see him as the virile young man she had married, nor yet as the boy she had grown up with, but she saw him as the stranger, dressed as a gentleman, who had confronted her in the boathouse. Not even when he had looked into her eyes and recognized her a moment ago had she glimpsed the old Rory, but had seen him as someone who had transported himself into another world and made that world fit him – and having won that world, so to speak, and being Rory Connor, he was determined to hang on to his winnings.

She was the first to turn away from the bed. She knew she had looked at the face on the pillow for the last time and she could not, even to herself, describe how she felt.

As Charlotte watched her walking towards the door she was amazed that the turmoil in her mind had disappeared; she was feeling no jealousy against this girl now, no hate. Amazingly she was experiencing a feeling of pity for her. As Lizzie had said, put yourself in her place; she was the one who had been rejected.

She bent over Rory now and, the tears blinding her, she gently wiped the sweat from his face, murmuring all the while, 'Oh my dearest, my dearest.'

When the door opened and Jessie entered she said brokenly 'I ... I won't be a moment. If the master should wake call me immediately,' and Jessie whispered, 'Yes, ma'am,' and took her seat beside the bed once more.

On the landing she stood for a moment drying her face and endeavouring to overcome the choking sensation that was rising from the anguish in her heart, as it cried, 'Oh Rory, what am I to do without you? Oh my darling, how am I to go on now? Don't leave me. Please, please don't leave me.' Yet as she descended the stairs she knew it was a hopeless cry.

In the hall she showed her surprise when she saw Ruth in her cape and tying on her bonnet. Going to her, she murmured, 'You're not leaving? You, you can't ...'

Ruth swallowed deeply before she said, 'Just for ... for a short while; I'm takin' Janie back home. And there's me husband, he's got to be seen to. He can do nothing with his leg as it is. I'll be back later in the mornin'.'

'I'll call the carriage for you then.' There was a stiffness in her tone.

'That would be kind.'

'But why?' Charlotte was now looking at Ruth with a deeply puzzled expression. 'I ... I should have thought you'd have let Lizzie go back and take care of things ... Being his mother, you would have –' she paused as Ruth, nodding at her now, put in quietly, 'Aye, yes, I know what you're thinkin', it's a mother's place to be at her son's side at a time like this. Well, he'll have his mother with him. For you see, lass, I'm not his mother, 'tis Lizzie.'

'What!' The exclamation was soft.

'Yes, 'tis Lizzie who's his mother.'

'But ... but I don't understand. He's never, I mean he's got such a regard for you, I'm ...'

'Aye, it is a bit bewilderin' and it's a long story, but put simply, me husband gave Lizzie a child when she was but seventeen. Rory regarded me as his mother for years and when he found out I wasn't and it was Lizzie who had borne him he turned against her. I'm not surprised that you didn't know. It's something very strange in his nature that he should be ashamed of her, for she's a good woman, and she's suffered at his hands. I shouldn't say it at this stage, but to be fair I must; many another would have turned on him as he did on her, but all she did was give him the length of her tongue. Her heart remained the same towards him always. She's a good woman is Lizzie . . . So there it is, lass, that's the truth of it. Well, I'll be away now, but I'll be back.'

When the door had closed on her Charlotte remained standing. The hall to herself, she looked about it; then in a kind of bewilderment she walked down the step into the office and, sitting behind the desk, she put her forearms on it and patted the leather top gently with her fingers. He had admitted to her the theft of the five pounds; he had told her everything about himself; he had confessed his weaknesses, and boasted of his strength; yet he had kept the matter of his birth to himself as if it were a shameful secret. *Why?* Why couldn't he have told her this? She felt a momentary hurt that he should have kept it from her. She had wondered at times at him calling his mother, Ruth. He had appeared very fond of the gentle-voiced, quiet little woman, even proud of her. And yet of the two women she was the lesser in all ways, body, brain, intelligence. She remembered that Rory had once referred to Lizzie as ignorant, and she had replied that she should imagine her ignorance was merely the lack of opportunity for her mind always seemed lively.

It was strange, she thought in this moment, that he could never have realized that all the best in him stemmed from Lizzie – for now she could see he was a replica of her, in bulk, character, obstinacy, bumptiousness . . . loving. Her capacity for loving was even greater than his, for, having been rejected, she had gone on loving.

There came a knock on the door and when she said, 'Come in,' it opened and Lizzie stood on the threshold.

'I was wondering where you were, I couldn't see you. You mustn't sit by yourself there broodin', it'll do no good. Come on now out of this.'

Like a child obeying a mother, Charlotte rose from the chair and went towards Lizzie. Then standing in front of her, she looked into her eyes and said quietly, 'I've just learned that you're his mother. Oh, Lizzie. Lizzie.'

'Aye.' Lizzie's head was drooping. 'I'm his mother an' he's always hated the fact, but nevertheless, it was something he could do nowt about. I am what I am, and he was all I had of me own flesh and blood an' I clung to him; even when he threw me off I clung to him.'

'Oh, Lizzie, my dear.' When she put her arms around Lizzie, Lizzie held her tightly against her breast, and neither of them was capable of further words, but they cried together.

It was three days later when Rory died. He was unconscious for the last twelve hours and the final faint words he spoke had been to Charlotte. 'If it's a lad, call him after me,' he murmured.

She didn't know how she forced herself to whisper, 'And if it should be a girl?'

He had looked at her for some time before he gasped, 'I'll . . . I'll leave that to you.'

It was odd but she had hoped he would have said, 'Name her Lizzie,' for then it would have told her of his own peace of mind but he said, 'I'll leave it to you.' His very last words were, 'Thank you, my dear . . . for everything.'

Through a thick mist she gazed down on to the face of the man who had brought her to life, who had made her body live, and filled it with new life – his life. She was carrying him inside of her; he wasn't dead; her Rory would never die.

When she fainted across his inert body they thought for a moment that she had gone with him.

## Chapter Seven

Rory's funeral was such that might have been accorded to a prominent member of the town for the sympathy of the town had been directed towards him through the newspaper reports of how he had been fatally injured in saving his brother from the blazing building, and the likelihood that charges, not only of arson, but of murder or manslaughter as well, would soon be made against local men now being questioned by the police.

No breath of scandal. No mention of former wife reappearing.

Other reports gave the names of the town's notable citizens who had attended the funeral. Mr Frank Nickle's name was not on it. Mr Nickle had been called abroad on business.

Two of the Pittie brothers had already been taken into custody. The police were hunting the third. And there were rumours that one of the brothers was implicating others, whose names had not yet been disclosed. Not only the local papers, but those in Newcastle as well carried the story of how there had been attempts to monopolize the river trade, and that Mr Connor's boats had not only been set adrift, but also been sunk when they were full of cargo.

The reports made Jimmy's little boats appear the size of tramp steamers or tea clippers, and himself as a thriving young businessman.

The private carriages had stretched the entire length of the road passing Westoe village and far beyond. The occupants were all male. In fact, the entire cortège was male, with one exception. Mrs Connor was present at her husband's funeral and what made her presence even more embarrassing to the gentlemen mourners was that it was whispered she was someway gone in pregnancy. She wore a black silk coat and a fashionable hat with widow's weeds flowing low down at the back but reaching no farther than her chest at the front. She was a remarkable woman really . . . nothing to look at personally, but sort of remarkable, a kind of law unto herself.

Another thing that was remarkable, but only to the occupants of the kitchen, was that John George had been present at the burial, but had not shown his face to condole with them nor had he spoken with Paddy who had struggled to the cemetery on sticks. All except Jimmy said they couldn't make him out. But then prison changed a man, and likely he was deeply ashamed, and of more than one thing, for was he not now living with another man's wife?

Poor John George, they said. Yet in all their minds was the faint niggling question, Who was the poorer? John George was alive; Rory, the tough gambling man, was dead.

And this was exactly what had passed through Jimmy's mind when he had seen John George standing against the wall of an outbuilding in the cemetery.

It happened that as they left the grave-side he had become separated from Charlotte. He'd had to make way for gentlemen who had ranked themselves on each side of her. He could not see his father, and so he walked on alone, weighed down with the pain in his heart and the sense of utter desolation, and wondering how he was going to live through the endless days ahead.

It was as he crossed an intersecting path that he saw in the distance the unmistakable lanky figure of John George. He was standing alone, head bowed, and his very stance seemed to be portraying his own feelings.

Without hesitating, he went towards him; but not until he was almost in front of him did John George raise his head.

For almost a full minute they looked at each other without speaking. Then it was Jimmy who said, 'I'm glad you came, John George.'

John George swallowed deeply, wet his lips, sniffed, then brought out a handkerchief and rubbed it roughly around his face before mumbling, 'I'm sorry, Jimmy, sorry to the heart.'

'Aye, I knew you'd feel like that, John George. In spite of everything I knew you'd have it in your heart to forgive him.'

'Oh, that.' John George shook his head vigorously, then bowed it again before ending, 'Oh, that was over and done with a long time ago.'

'It's like you to say that, John George. You were always a good chap.'

'No, not good, just weak, Jimmy. And you know, in a funny sort of way I feel responsible for . . .'

'*No!* Don't be silly, John George.' Jimmy cut in. 'Now don't get that into your head. It's me, if anybody, who should shoulder the blame for Rory's going. It's me. If I hadn't wanted the damned boatyard he'd be here the day. Aye, he would.'

'No, no, don't blame yourself, Jimmy. It was just one of those things. Life's made up of them when you think about it, isn't it?' He paused, then asked softly, 'How's she, Miss . . . I mean his wife? How's she taking it?'

'Oh, hard, though she's puttin' a face on it to outsiders. She was more than fond of him you know.'

'Aye. Yes, I guessed that. Yet it came as a surprise when I heard they'd married. But I got a bigger surprise when she sought me out. I couldn't take it in. After all . . . well, you know, doing what I did, and the case and things. I'd imagined she was like her father. You knew about what she did for me, like setting me up?'

'Yes, John George.'

'And you didn't hold it against me for taking it?'

'Why, no, man. Why, no; I was glad; it showed you held no hard feelings.'

'Some wouldn't see it that way. What did they think about it in the kitchen?'

'Oh, they just thought it was kind of her; they don't know the true ins and outs of it, John George.'

Again they stared at each other without speaking. Then John George said, 'Well, they'll never hear it from me, Jimmy. I've never let on to a soul, not even to Maggie.'

'Thanks, John George. You're one in a thousand.'

'No, just soft, I suppose. He used to say I was soft.' He turned and looked over the headstones in the direction of the grave, but there was no rancour in his words. Then looking at Jimmy again, he said, 'It's eased me somewhat, Jimmy, to have a word with you. I hope I'll see you again.'

'Me an' all, John George. Aye, I'd like that. I'll come up sometime, if you don't mind.'

'You'd be more than welcome, Jimmy, more than welcome.'

'Well, I've got to go now, they'll likely be waiting and I'll be holding up the carriages. So long, John George.' Jimmy held out his hand.

John George gripped it. 'So long, Jimmy.'

They now nodded at each other, then simultaneously turned away, John George in the direction of the grave and Jimmy towards the gates, the carriage and Charlotte, and the coming night, which seemed the first he was about to spend without Rory, for up till now his body had lain in the house.

It was as he crossed the intersecting path again that he saw Stoddard hurrying towards him.

'Oh, there you are, sir. The mistress was wondering.'

'I'm sorry. I saw an old friend of . . . of my brother's. I . . . I had to have a word . . .'

'Yes, sir. Of course, sir.'

It was funny to be called sir, he'd never get used to it like Rory had.

They were making their way through small groups of men in order to reach the gates and the carriage beyond when he saw her. Perhaps it was because of the strong contrast in dress that the weirdly garbed figure standing in the shadow of the cypress tree stood out. Both Jimmy and Stoddard looked towards it, and Jimmy almost came to a stop and would once again have diverted had not Stoddard said quietly, 'The mistress is waiting, sir.'

'Oh yes, yes.' Poor Janie. What must she be feeling at this moment? Rory's wife, his real wife after all was said and done, hidden away like a criminal. But she had come; despite the protests she had come. Her presence would surely cause comment.

So thought Stoddard. But then, as he told himself yet again what he had said to the staff last night, it was a lucky family that hadn't someone they were ashamed to own because of their oddities. It happened in the highest society, and certainly in the lowest, and you couldn't blame the master or his folks for not wanting to bring that creature to the fore.

# Chapter Eight

They were gathered in the kitchen. Paddy sitting by the fire with his leg propped up on a chair; Ruth sitting opposite to him, a half-made shirt lying on her lap, her hands resting on top of it; Jimmy sitting by the corner of the table, and Lizzie standing by the table to the side of him, while Janie stood at the end of it facing them all.

She was dressed as she had been since she came back; even, within doors she kept the strange hat on her head. She looked from one to the other as she said, 'You're blamin' me for taking it, aren't you? After the stand I made you think I should have thrown the money back in her face?'

'No, no.' They all said it in different ways, shakes of the head, movements of the hands, mutters, but their protests didn't sound convincing to her, and now, her voice raised, she said, 'You took from her. It was all right for you to take from her, all of you. And what had she done to you? Nowt.'

'Nobody's sayin' you shouldn't 've taken it, Janie. We're just sad like that you still feel this way about things.'

She turned and looked at Jimmy, and her body seemed to slump inside the cloak. She said now flatly, 'How would any of you have felt, I ask you? Look at yourselves. Would you have acted any differently? And don't forget, I could have gone to the polis station, I could have said who I was? I could have blown the whole thing into the open, but I didn't, I kept quiet. I didn't even go and see me da. I kept out of his way even when I saw him at the funeral. And I won't see him now, 'cos he'd open his mouth. It would only be natural. But . . . but when she send for me and . . . and she knew I was going back there, she asked if she could do anything for me and I said aye, yes, she could. I told her, I told her what it was like there. They had nothing or next to nothing. The boats were dropping to bits. It . . . it was she who named the sum. Five hundred, she said, and I didn't say, yes, aye, or nay.'

'You mean she gave you five hundred straightaway like that?' Paddy was peering at her through narrowed lids.

'No, she gave me a paper. I've . . . I've got to go to a French bank. She's puttin' four hundred and fifty pounds in there; she gave me the rest in sovereigns.'

'And after that, lass, you still haven't got a good word in yer belly for her?'

She dropped her eyes from Lizzie's gaze, then said, 'I can't be like you all, fallin' on her neck.'

'Nobody's fell on her neck.'

She turned and looked at Jimmy. 'No, you didn't fall on her neck, Jimmy, just into her arms. You were as bad as Rory. I've got to say it, it's funny what money can do, by aye, it is. I wouldn't 've believed it.'

'Well, you're not turnin' your nose up at it, are you Janie?'

'No, no, I'm not, Jimmy, but as I look at it now I'm only takin' what's due to me, 'cos as things were he would have had to support me. And in the long run it would have cost him more than five hundred pounds 'cos I'm likely to live a long time.'

They all stared at her, Ruth, Lizzie, Paddy and Jimmy. This was the little girl who had grown up next door. This was the young lass, the kindly young lass, who had cared for her grannie, who had been full of high spirits and kindliness. Each in his own way was realizing what life could do to any one of them. Each in his own way knew a moment of understanding, and so it was Ruth who spoke first, saying, 'Well, wherever you go, lass, whatever you do, our good wishes'll go with you. Our memories are long; we'll always remember you.' She did not add 'as you once were.'

'Aye, that goes for me an' all.' Paddy was nodding at her. 'We've had some good times together Janie, and in this very kitchen. I'll think back on 'em, Janie.'

Lizzie's face and voice was soft as she said, 'As you say, you'll live a long time, lass, and you'll marry and have a sturdy family, an' when you do, name some of them after us, eh?'

Janie's head was up, her lips were tight pressed together, her eyes were wide and bright; then as the tears sprang from them, they came around her, patting her, comforting her; even Paddy hobbled from his chair, saying, 'There, lass. There, lass.'

'I've ... I've got to go.'

'Yes, yes, you've got to go.' Ruth dried her eyes and smiled. 'And have a safe journey, lass. It's a long way to go, across the sea to another country. Aren't you feared?'

'No.' Janie shook her head as she blew her nose. 'I know me way, an' I won't have to ride in the cattle trucks.' She smiled weakly, and Lizzie said somewhat tentatively now, 'Why didn't you get yourself a decent rig-out, lass, to go back with?'

'No, Lizzie, no.' Again she shook her head. 'I came like this and that's how I'm goin' back. And ... and you see, they wouldn't understand, not if I went back dressed up. I'll ... I'll be one of them again like this. But at the same time I've seen things, and I know things what they don't, and I'll be able to help ... It's funny, isn't it, how life works out?'

As she looked from one to the other they saw a glimpse of the old Janie, and they smiled tenderly at her.

'Eeh! well, I'll be away. I've got to get the train.'

She backed from them now and, with the exception of Jimmy, they didn't move towards her, not even to come to the door. Jimmy opened the door for her, and with one backward glance at them she went out, and he followed her down the path. At the gate he said, 'Look, wait a minute, I'll go back and get me coat and come down with you to the station.'

'No. No, Jimmy. Thanks all the same. Anyway, you're in no fit state to be about yet, never mind walking to the station.'

He took her hand and they stared at each other. 'Be happy, Janie. Try to forget all that's happened. And ... and another thing I'd like to say, thank you for not letting on to them' – he jerked his head back towards the cottage – 'about, well, you know what, the John George business.'

She stared at him blankly. This was the second time those very words had been said to her within a short space.

Yesterday she had stood in that beautiful room and thought to herself
with still remaining bitterness, I can see why he didn't want to come back,
for who'd want to give up all this for a boathouse, ignoring the fact that it
was the tall black-garbed, sad-looking woman facing her who had been the
magnet that had kept him there. Nor had she softened towards her when,
in open generosity Charlotte had said, 'I understand how you feel for he was
such a wonderful man,' but she had blurted out before she could check
herself, 'You didn't know him long enough to know what he was like . . .
really like.'

'I did know what he was really like.' Charlotte's tone had altered to
tartness.

She had stared hard at the women before retorting, 'I shouldn't say it at
this time, but I doubt it,' and the answer she received was, 'You needn't, for
I knew my husband' – the last word was stressed – 'better than most. I was
aware of all his weaknesses. I knew everything about him before I married
him . . . with the exception of one thing . . .'

'Yes, and I know what that was,' she had said. 'He wouldn't let on about
that.'

It had appeared as if they were fighting.

'Do you?'

'Aye.'

'Well, tell me what you think it was,' said Charlotte.

She had become flustered at this. 'It was his business,' she said. 'It's over,
it's best left alone.' Then she had stood there amazed as she listened to the
woman saying, 'You are referring to the John George Armstrong affair and
Rory taking the five pounds and letting his friend shoulder the blame for the
whole amount, aren't you?'

She had gaped at her, then whispered, 'He told you that?'

'Yes, he did, but I already knew all about it. I had pieced things together
from the events that followed the court case.'

'And you did nothin', I mean to get John George off?'

'He had been stealing for some time. His sentence would have been the
same . . .'

She had stared open-mouthed at the woman, she couldn't understand her.
She was a lady yet such were her feelings for a fellow like Rory that she had
treated as nothing something that she herself had thought of as a crime and
condemned him wholesale for. In fact, so big was it in her eyes that she saw
it now as the cause of all that had happened to her – all the heartache and
the hardship.

She hadn't been able to understand her own feelings at that moment for
strange thoughts had galloped about in her mind. She had made a mistake
somewhere. Had she ever loved Rory? Of course, she had. But not like this
woman had loved him. Perhaps her own mistake lay in that she had liked
too many people, and it had sort of watered down her love; whereas this
woman had concentrated all her feelings in one direction and had gained
Rory's love in return . . . she hadn't bought him. It seemed to be the last
bitter pill she had to swallow.

. . . 'The only thing he kept from me was the fact that Lizzie is his
mother.'

'That?'

'Yes.'

'Well, he always was ashamed of it. Yet I couldn't understand why 'cos Lizzie's all right.'

'Yes, Lizzie's all right.'

She had asked her to sit down after that, and then she had offered her the money. But even when she took it she still couldn't like her, or soften towards her . . .

. . . 'You all right, Janie?'

'Aye, Jimmy.'

'Try to forgive and forget.'

'Aye, I will. It'll take time, but I will, Jimmy. I'll marry. I'll marry Henri. I liked him well enough, but that isn't lovin'. Still, we've got to take what we get, haven't we?'

'You'll be happy enough, Janie.'

'Aye, well, think on me sometimes, Jimmy.'

'There'll never be a time when I won't, Janie.' He leant towards her and they kissed quietly, then, her head bowed, she turned swiftly from him and went through the gate and down the narrow path and became lost from his view in the hedgerows.

For quite some time he stood bent over the gate-post. He had been in love with her since he was a lad. During the time Rory courted her he had lived with a special kind of pain, but when he had lain in the loft above them he had suffered an agony for a time because he had loved them both. Now in a way they were both dead, for the Janie he had loved was no more. She hadn't just disappeared down the road; paradoxically she had died when she had come back to life and showed herself as a strange creature that night in the boathouse. Her resurrection had freed him. Life was odd. Indeed it was. As she had said, it was funny how it worked out.

He knew that a different kind of life lay before him. Charlotte was setting him up in a new boatyard and, what was more, she wanted him to take an interest in business.

Yes, a new kind of life was opening up before him, but whatever it offered it would be empty, for Rory was no longer in it. He ached for Rory, and night following night he cried silently while he wished that God had taken him too . . . or instead. Aye, instead. Why hadn't he died instead, for he wouldn't have been missed like Rory was? He had emptied so many lives by his going. Charlotte's, Janie's, Lizzie's, his ma's, aye and even his da's, all their lives were empty now . . . Yet free from the scandal that his living would have created. It was funny, weird. In a way it was like the outcome of Lizzie's saying, leave it to God and He'll work it out.

He went up the path and into the kitchen that housed the old life.

# Chapter Nine

They were all in the kitchen again, but now they were waiting for the carriage to take them on what had become for all of them, up till now, one of their twice-weekly visits to Birchingham House.

Ruth stood facing Lizzie and Jimmy as, spreading her hands wide, she said, 'Don't worry about me, I'll have me house to meself for once an' –' she nodded towards Paddy – 'I've got your dad to look after.'

'But both of us goin', ma?' Jimmy screwed up his face at her.

'Well, now look at it this way, lad.' Ruth's tone was unusually brisk. 'You're goin' into business, and it's on the waterfront, practically at the end of it. Now, unless you're going to have a carriage and pair for yourself, you can't make that trek twice a day. Now Westoe's on your doorstep so to speak. And there's always the week-ends, you can come home at the week-ends. As for you, Lizzie.' She turned her gaze on Lizzie. 'You know, if you speak the truth, you're breakin' your neck to stay down there; you can't wait for that child to be born.'

'What you talkin' about, woman? Breakin' me neck!' Lizzie jerked her chin upwards.

'I know what I'm talkin' about and you know what I'm talkin' about. And you've lost weight. The flesh is droppin' off you.'

'Huh!' Lizzie put her forearms under her breasts and humped them upwards. That should worry you. You've told me for years I'm too fat. And anyway, what do you think Charlotte will have to say about this?'

'Charlotte will welcome you with open arms, the both of yous, she needs you. Remember the last time we saw her as we went out the door, remember the look on her face? She was lost. She's no family of her own, she needs family.'

'The likes of me?' Lizzie now thumped her chest.

'Yes, the likes of you. Who better? Now stop sayin' one thing and thinkin' another. Go and pack a few odds and ends. And you an' all, Jimmy. Now both of yous, and let me have me own way for once in me own house with me own life. I've never had much say in anything, have I? Now, have I?' She turned and looked towards her husband who was staring at her, and he smiled; then nodding from Lizzie to Jimmy, he said, 'She's right, she's right, she's had the poor end of the stick. Do what she says and let's have peace.'

Stoddard was a little surprised when the two leather-strapped bass hampers were handed to him to be placed on the seat beside him, but then so many surprising things had happened of late that he was taking them in his stride now.

Three-quarters of an hour later, when the carriage drew up on the drive, he helped Mrs O'Dowd, as she was known to the servants, down the steps;

then taking up the hampers, he followed her and the young gentleman up towards his mistress who was waiting at the door. As the greetings were being exchanged he handed the hampers to the maid, and she took them into the hall and set them down, and when Charlotte glanced at them, Lizzie, taking off her coat, said, 'Aye, you might look at them; you're in for a shock.'

A few minutes later, seated in the drawing-room, Lizzie asked softly, 'Well, how you feeling now, lass?' and it was some seconds before Charlotte, clasping and unclasping her hands replied, 'If I'm to speak the truth, Lizzie, desolate, utterly, utterly desolate.' Her voice broke and she swallowed deeply before ending, 'It gets worse, I, I miss him more every day. I was lonely before but, but never like this.'

Lizzie, pulling herself up from the deep chair, went and sat beside her on the couch and, taking her hand, patted it as she said, 'Aye, and . . . and it'll be like this for some time. I know. Oh aye, I know 'cos I've a world of emptiness inside here.' She placed her hand on her ribs. 'But it'll ease, lass; it'll ease; it won't go altogether, it'll change into something else, but it'll ease. We couldn't go on livin' if it didn't. So in the meantime we've put our heads together, haven't we, Jimmy?' She looked towards Jimmy, where he sat rubbing one lip tightly over the other and he nodded, 'And this is what we thought. But mind, it's just up to you, it's up to you to say. But seeing that in a short while Jimmy'll be working on the waterfront, well, as Ruth pointed out, it's a trek and a half right back to the cottage twice a day, and in all weathers. And –' she gave a little smile now – 'she also reminded him that he hadn't got a carriage and pair yet, and that he'd have to shank it, so she wondered if you wouldn't mind puttin' him up here for a while, 'cos . . .'

'Oh, yes, *Oh, yes,* Jimmy.' Charlotte leant eagerly towards him, holding out her hand, and Jimmy grasped it. And now with tears in her voice she said, 'Oh, I'm so grateful. But . . . but your mother?'

'Oh, she's all right.' Jimmy's voice was a little unsteady as he replied. 'She has me da, and I'll be poppin' up there every now and again. She's all right.'

'Oh, thank you. Thank you.' Now Charlotte looked at Lizzie, and Lizzie said, 'An' that's not all, there's me.' She now dug her thumb in between her breasts. 'I've got nothin' to do with meself, I'm sittin' picking me nails half me time, an' I thought, well, if she can put up with me I'll stay until the child comes 'cos I've a mind to be the first to see me grandson, or me granddaughter, or twins, or triplets, whatever comes.'

'Oh, Lizzie! Lizzie!' Charlotte now turned and buried her face in the deep flesh of Lizzie's shoulder, and Lizzie, stroking her hair, muttered, 'There now. There now. Now stop it. It's the worst thing you can do to bubble your eyes out. Grannie Waggett used to say that you should never cry when you're carryin' a child 'cos you're takin' away the water it swims in.' She gave a broken laugh here, then said, 'There now. There now. Come on, dry your eyes. What you want is a cup of tea.' She turned towards Jimmy, saying, 'Pull that bell there, Jimmy, an' ring for tea.' Then with the tears still in her eyes, she laughed as she lifted Charlotte's face towards her, saying, 'Did you ever hear anythin' like it in your life? Me, Lizzie O'Dowd, saying ring for tea. What's the world comin' to, I ask you?'

Charlotte stared back into the face of the mother of her beloved. Two years ago she had been alone, but since then she had experienced love, and such love she knew she would never know again. But on the day she had bargained for Rory's love she had said to him that there were many kinds of love, and it was being proved to her now at this moment.

When Lizzie said to her, 'If you don't watch out I'll take over, I'm made like that. Ring for tea, I said, just as if I was born to it. I tell you!' Charlotte put out her hand and cupped the plump cheek, and what she said now and what she was to say for many years ahead was, 'Oh, Lizzie! Lizzie! My dear Lizzie.'

# CATHERINE COOKSON

# The
# Cinder
# Path

# The Cinder Path

To the one and only
to whom I owe so much

# Chapter One

## Moor Burn Farm

'Bless the food on this table, Lord. Bless my labour that has provided it and give me strength for this day. Amen.'

'Amen. Amen. Amen.'

Before the echo of the last amen faded, Edward MacFell was firmly seated in the big wooden armchair at the top of the table, and during the seconds of silence that followed he screwed his heavy buttocks further into the seat before, with an almost imperceivable motion of his head, giving the three people standing behind their chairs permission to sit, and the elderly woman and young girl on their knees just inside the door of the room permission to rise.

Sitting in silence facing her husband, Mary MacFell wondered, and not for the first time, what would happen if she were suddenly to open her tight-lipped mouth and scream. Yet she knew what would happen; he'd drag her outside and throw her bodily into the horse trough. And if this didn't restore her to his idea of sanity, he'd despatch her to the madhouse and leave her there to rot, whilst he himself would continue here with his daily work as appointed by God.

Her husband and God were on the best of terms; in fact she sometimes thought he handed out orders to God for the day: 'Now today, God, you'll not only clean the byres you will lime wash them; then you will clamp the beet, all of it, mind, and you will do it yourself, don't expect Dawson or Ryton to give you a hand.' He always called people by their surnames, other farmers used Christian names. Over at Brooklands, Hal Chapman always called his men Bob, Ronnie, Jimmy. But not so Edward MacFell. No, if God had a Christian name he would still have addressed Him as God, not Bob, Ronnie, or Jimmy. . . . Jimmy God. That was funny, Jimmy God.

Her mind rarely offered her anything to laugh about for her sense of humour which had never been strong was entirely blunted, but now a strange noise erupted from her throat and brought all eyes on her. Her husband's, which seemed to have no white to them but to be made up entirely of a thick, opaque brown substance that toned with his square weather-beaten face and thick shock of dark hair which showed not a streak of grey for all of his forty-eight years, were fastened hard upon her.

Her son's eyes, clear grey, held that constant tenderness that irritated and annoyed her for it expressed his alienation from his surroundings and those of the immediate household, and this included herself.

She sometimes thought that her husband, in spite of all his sly cleverness and his power, was ignorant and blind because he could not see that there was no part of himself in his son, and that the education of which he was insisting his son have the benefit would, in the end, separate them. He thought to make his son a gentleman farmer, utterly ignoring the fact that the boy, although born and bred on the farm, had no leanings whatsoever towards the land. All he thought about was reading, and tramping the countryside, at times like someone in a daze, or not quite right in the head. Moreover, the boy at sixteen was tall and fair and was as unlike his father in looks as he was in character. Yet she knew that her husband was inordinately proud of his son, almost as proud of him as he was of his farm and his fifty acres of freehold land.

Her daughter Betty's eyes, which were fixed tight on her father, were a replica of his own, the only difference being that the brown of the small irises was clear and there was a rim of white to be seen around their edges. Her nose, too, was the same as his, not only long and thin but swelling to a knob at its end; and her mouth, which as yet at fourteen was a thick-lipped pouted rosebud, would undoubtedly widen into sensuousness and become at variance with her other features.

She was startled into awareness by her husband speaking to Fanny Dimple. 'Stop fumbling, woman! And what have I told you about those hands.'

It shattered, too, the waiting silence at the table. It was not a coarse or loud voice, nor did it have a distinctive Northumbrian burr to it, but it was a voice that always arrested its hearers. Those hearing MacFell speak for the first time, in most cases, were unable to hide their surprise, for it was a cultured voice, melodious, belying his lack of education and being completely at variance with the sturdy roughness of his body and features.

Edward MacFell's eyes now travelled from Fanny Dimple's gnarled work-worn hands to her face where the loose skin was drawn upwards by strands of her grey hair knotted tight on the back of her head and hidden under a white starched cap that had the appearance of a bonnet.

'If you can't keep your nails clean cut them off down to the quick, or I'll do them for you!'

'They're already at the quick, master.'

The knife and fork almost bounced off the table, so fiercely did he bang them down. 'Don't dare answer me back, woman!'

His face consumed with rage, he glared at his servant who had been maid of all work in the house for years, and she, as if she had lost her senses, as those at the table thought she had, glared back at him; then turning away, she lifted two bowls of porridge from a tray that young Maggie Benton was holding, and walked to the end of the table where she placed one bowl before her mistress and the other in front of her young master. Returning to the tray, she lifted the last bowl. This she laid, none too gently this time, in front of the only daughter of the house.

Now making no effort to quieten her withdrawal, she went from the room into the long narrow hall lit by two small windows, one at each side of the front door, through a green-baized door and into the kitchen. *And* it was as she turned to close this door that she gave vent to another bout of defiance. Stretching out her arms, she grabbed the handle and thrust the door violently forward.

An ordinary door would have made a resounding crash, so fiercely had she thrust it, but the green-baized door merely fell into place with a muffled thud.

'Him and his gentry doors!'

The green-baized door was a recent acquisition. When they were pulling down the old manor house her master had gone there precisely to buy the door, and afterwards had personally supervised Fred Ryton and Arnold Dawson as they hung it in place of the scarred oak one.

Fanny now came to the table where Maggie Benton was standing gaping at her, and the small girl took in a deep breath before exclaiming, 'Eeh! Mrs Dimple.'

Maggie knew what had upset Mrs Dimple; it was the cinder path; but to answer the master back, and him after only just saying grace. Eeh! she had never known anything like it. Wait till she got home and told them.

'He's a cruel bugger.' Fanny was leaning across the table, her jaw thrust out towards Maggie.

'Aye. Aye, he is, Mrs Dimple.'

'He thinks he's God Almighty and can scare the daylights out of you with just a look. Well, here's one he can't scare. He's a fornicatin' hypocrite, that's what he is. Him and his mornin' prayers and havin' us kneel! Copyin' the gentry again. I had to kneel with the rest of 'em when I was at Lord Cleverley's; but there was twenty-eight of us inside the house and he was a gentleman, his lordship. But him back there, well, he's a sin unto God and takes others with him. An' *you* know what I mean, Maggie Benton, don't you?'

Maggie turned her eyes away from the thrust-out chin. Her head drooped. Yes, she knew what Mrs Dimple meant; no one was supposed to know but everybody on the farm knew. Except, she thought, Master Charles and the missis. Even so she had her doubts about the missis. She never really knew what the missis was thinking, she was so quiet. There was one, though, she wished didn't know, but she knew that he knew all right. Oh aye, he knew, her da knew, you could see it in his face.

Her poor da. He wasn't long for the top. She'd miss him when he went. But not as much as their Polly would. Their Polly would go mad when he died, 'cos their Polly had looked after him for so long now. She had feelin's had their Polly, and that had been proved again this morning 'cos eeh! look how she had got upset about the cinder path and Ginger Slater.

They all knew that Ginger Slater was for the cinder path at nine o'clock, and that was the cruel part of it, Polly said, the waiting to be thrashed. If the master had done it straight off when he had caught him looking at the picture book again, Polly said, she could have understood it, but to make him wait a whole day with his mind on it, it was like a sentence to be hung, she said.

Of course, being a workhouse lad, Ginger expected to be badly treated, and it wasn't the first time he had been on the cinder path, and all because of books. That was funny because, like everybody else who lived on the farm and in the row, he had had the chance to go in the cart to school. He had gone for a time, but then the master, like all the parents, saw no need for so much schooling; in fact they were all dead against it, especially the parents, for it meant the loss of wages, so with one excuse and another they kept them off most of the time. She herself had got off through a bad chest, but when she was there she had learnt her letters and to read a little bit, but

Ginger, who wasn't daft in any way, had never picked up reading. The teacher had skelped his backside raw, but still he couldn't read. And yet more than any of them, he wanted to. Oh aye, he did that; that's why he went after books; and that's why he was for the cinder path.

The only one who'd had any real schooling was their Polly. Once when their da was a bit better she had gone to school for over a year at one go, but when he collapsed again and Bob the carrier died about the same time that put an end to it, for she couldn't do the five miles each way for half-a-day's learning. And she, too, wanted to learn; like Ginger, she wanted to learn.

As if Fanny had been picking up her thoughts, she said, 'That lad's bright, he wants to learn; but how in the name of God did he get up to the attic and get that story book!'

'He must have scaled the drainpipe.'

'Aye, that's the only way. But why didn't he ask Master Charlie, he'd have sneaked him a book. I would have meself if I'd known he'd wanted one so badly. But why anybody wants to read I don't know, we learn enough bad things by listenin' and lookin' without pickin' them up off a page.'

'It wasn't a bad book, Mrs Dimple, an' it was an old 'un, it had all the weekly *Chatterboxes* in it for 1895. Master Charlie once lent it to our Polly, an' she read it out to us; all about Mr Dickens an' his little Nell. An' there was wonderful pictures in it. One we laughed at was of pigs pulling a plough. In France that was. I told Ginger about it an' how it said pigs is sensible and could be made to count. You know what, Mrs Dimple?' Maggie now bit on her lip, and became thoughtful. 'Perhaps that's why he picked on that book because I told him about pigs bein' clever.'

'Don't be daft, girl. How could he pick on it if he couldn't read, your readin' hasn't given you sense. That's evident.'

'But he'd seen the book, Mrs Dimple, when our Polly gave it back to Master Charlie, an' he would know it 'cos it was big an' in a black cover.'

Fanny stared at Maggie for a moment; then shaking her head impatiently, she said, 'Aw, let's get on. . . . Listen! there's the bell, and he's knockin' hell out of it. He can't wait to stuff himself now in order to give his right arm strength. God blast him! And He will one of these days, I'm tellin' you.' Fanny now stabbed her finger towards Maggie. 'He won't be mocked, not God, he'll get his deserts, him in there.' Her arm now swung in the direction of the green-baized door. 'An' I hope I'm here to see it. I'll dance on his grave, I will that.'

Eeh! the things Mrs Dimple said. Maggie shook her head as she watched the older woman bang the covered dishes on to the tray, saying as she did so, 'They had their breakfast served up on plates at one time but now it's covered dishes to match the green-baized door. Eeh! the things one lives to see. Get goin'!' She lifted the tray and thrust it into Maggie's hand, and her final words sent the girl scurrying towards the door: 'I hope it chokes him.'

# Chapter Two

It was said that there had been a farm at Moor Burn for the past three hundred years but that the house in those bygone days had been little more than a cottage. The land had been farmed from the earliest times by a family named Morley, and for two hundred and fifty years one Morley had succeeded another, and as each prospered so he added his quota to the house.

The last extension had been in 1840, to accommodate the ever growing family of the then present owner; but the fact that this man sired fifteen children and only two survived to reach thirty, and they both girls, tended to turn his mind, and he became convinced there was a curse on the place for his Bible showed that although there had never been more than two Morleys in any generation, the survivors up till then had been male, so he decided to be gone from the place.

It was about this time on a day in 1858 that William MacFell came riding back from the Scottish side of Carter Bar, accompanied by his wife, after having attended her father's funeral. And he was a happy man at that time, at least as happy as his nature would allow – for his wife had come in to a tidy sum of money.

It should so transpire that the trap they had hired almost lost one of its two wheels just after they had passed Kirkwhelpington, and it was Farmer Morley's younger daughter who came upon them and led them over the fields and along the paths to the farm, the freehold farm that was up for sale. It was then that William MacFell decided to become a farmer . . . on his wife's money. When his wife pointed out to him that it would be an utterly different life from working in a gentlemen's hatters, he had replied briefly that that was precisely the reason why he wanted to farm.

Christine MacFell had not protested against her money being used in this fashion; she had given up protesting years ago when she realized that her people had been right from the beginning and that she had lowered herself in marrying the hatter. Her idea of bringing out the real man she imagined to be hidden beneath the taciturn skin had been a failure, a frightening failure, for what had emerged was an individual given to bouts of ferocious temper, and it was this temper he used as a weapon when thwarted in any way.

So the MacFells took up residence at Moor Burn Farm and although you could walk in the district for hours and not see a soul, and the houses were few and far between, William MacFell soon became well known. Those in the big houses scattered around ignored him, he was of less account to them than one of their dogs; the real farmers laughed at him behind his back; the tradesmen served him but with no respect, to them he was a jumped-up nowt. Only the hands he engaged on the farm feared him, for gone was the security they had felt under Farmer Morley, because the present owner would, they knew, should they displease him, turn them out of their cottages on to the road without giving the matter a second thought.

And then there was the cinder path.

The ashes from the fires in the house and from the piggery boiler had been strewn on the yard to sop up the mud in bad weather, and over the years the remainder had formed a sizeable mound behind the cow byres. The byres were almost opposite the kitchen door, and, between them and the barn, was a narrow passage that led out to an open space bordered on two sides by a privet hedge where the cinders were dumped, or at least where they had been dumped, for one of the first things that William MacFell did was to order his men to level the dump. He decided on a path being made from the back of the byres where the ground ran level, to where, thirty yards distant, it sloped down towards the burn, beside which stood the tiny two-roomed dilapidated cottage.

When the mound of cinders was levelled, the path to the burn was only three parts made, but each morning the maid of all work gradually lengthened it by adding to it the huge buckets of cinders taken from the house.

Why, asked the farmhands of each other, did he want a path leading down there? The stone cottage would never be used again; and who wanted to go and look at the burn at that point where it was only a couple of yards wide?

William MacFell didn't give his reasons for taking the path down to the burn, but it soon became evident that he had another use for it, and the first example he gave of this was when he took his eight-year-old son by the collar, threw him on to the cinders, and laid about his back with a birch stick.

That was the beginning.

Jimmy Benton was the next to experience what it was like to be thrown on the cinder path. He was seven years old at the time and scarecrowing on the farm. Jimmy had at an early age developed a taste for raw eggs; he had discovered they would keep him going and would take the gnawing hungry feeling from his stomach.

The morning he stole two eggs from the hen cree William MacFell caught him, and, taking the eggs from him, he had without a word lifted him up bodily by the scruff of the neck and, ignoring the boy's flaying arms and legs . . . and howls, he had thrown him on to the path where the cinders had torn at the palms of his hands and his bare knees. He had thrown one egg after the other on to the back of the boy's head, then kicked him in the buttocks. The action had lifted the child from his hands and knees and sent him sprawling flat out.

The boy's father had been for going and knocking hell out of William MacFell, but the mother reminded him that it was their livelihood, and after all the boy was only scraped on his hands and knees.

With the youngsters on the farm, the cinder path became a fear. The mothers in the cottages no longer threatened the children with the bogey man, but with the cinder path. One thing the farm workers did say in favour of their master, he had no favourites for the path for he treated his own son to an equal share of it.

Such are the quirks of nature that instead of Edward MacFell hating his father, the boy admired him and if he had ever really loved anyone it was his male parent. His mother, to whom one would have expected him to turn, she being of a sympathetic and gentle nature, he almost ignored. Perhaps it was because subconsciously he sensed that she had no love for him, for in character and looks he was the facsimile of her husband.

Edward MacFell was twenty-seven years old when his father had died. William had left no will for the simple reason that he had imagined wills precipitated death, and so according to law Edward was entitled to two-thirds of the estate and his mother to one-third. That almost immediately the legal affairs were settled his mother should take her share and leave the farm to join a cousin in Scotland came as no surprise to him; rather it afforded him a great deal of relief. He was no longer responsible for her; now he could look round for a wife, a wife who was different but, like his mother, someone with a bit of class.

He knew only too well in what esteem his father had been held in the surrounding countryside, and he set out to show them that he himself was different, that he was no ordinary tinpot little farmer, he was as good as they came in the county, and he determined to make the farm an example for others because it contained some of the best pasture land in the county, besides fields that yielded reasonable grains. Even Hal Chapman, over in Brooklands, had had to admit there wasn't another place like it for miles, and he was an authority on land was Chapman.

Edward MacFell was thirty when he married, and like his father before him he, too, aimed high. In his case he went even further than his father for he chose to honour the daughter of a Newcastle surgeon. The surgeon had, the previous year, died, otherwise it was debatable whether he would have countenanced the marriage. But his nineteen-year-old daughter Mary Rye-Davidson was living under the guardianship of an old aunt and uncle, who seemed only too ready to be rid of their frivolous fair-haired, blue-eyed charge, and they congratulated each other on having spent their holiday in Hexham, where their niece had been fortunate enough to meet the sturdy, prosperous farmer.

At what time after the marriage both Edward MacFell and his wife, Mary, realized their joint mistake neither of them could pin-point, but it was well within the first six months.

For MacFell's part, he realized he'd married a scatter-brain, a woman who, if she had been allowed, would have spent her time reading, playing the harpsichord, and titivating herself up with new clothes. Now these things in their place were all right for it proved that she was of the class, but that she had no intention of using her hands to cook or to help in the dairy, and wasn't even capable of managing the house, infuriated him, and for the first time in his life he began to appreciate his mother and her qualities that had gone unrecognized during all the years together.

As for Mary MacFell, she was brought out of a girlish dream to the realization that she had married, not a strong, silent lover, but a man with a fiendish temper, and an egotistical ignorant one into the bargain. During the first month of their marriage she playfully opposed him, but these tactics came to an abrupt end when one day, feeling bored, she dared, without asking his leave, to take the trap and drive into Otterburn. On her return he almost dragged her upstairs. What he did was literally to tear the clothes from her back, then, his face red with passion, to thrust it close to hers as he growled at her, 'You take anything on yourself like that again and begod I'll put you on the cinder path.'

When her first child was born Mary MacFell experienced a secret happiness. At his birth her son looked like her, and as he grew he developed more like her. He took on her tall, thin fairness; the only difference in their features being his eyes, which were round, while hers were oval-shaped, and whereas hers were blue, his were grey.

The contrariness of MacFell's nature made itself evident again as he grew fulsomely proud of the son who showed no resemblance to himself, yet when, two years later, his wife gave him a daughter who, as she grew, became a replica of himself, both inside and out, he had little time for her. And again the oddities of nature came into play, for his small dark daughter adored him, while his son secretly feared and hated him.

And never did Charles MacFell hate his father more than at this moment when his eyelids compressed themselves into a deep blink each time the cane came down hard, not only across Ginger Slater's narrow buttocks, but across the backs of his knees, left bare by his breeches being drawn upwards.

As the blows continued to make the small body bounce on the cinders Charlie was unable to witness any more, but as he went to turn away, run away, he was brought to a stiff standstill by the sight of Polly Benton emerging from the further end of the hedge. Polly had one hand held tightly across her mouth while the fingers of the other convulsively gathered up her print skirt until not only did she expose the top of her boots but also her bare shins.

Charlie stood staring at her; and when her hand dropped from her mouth he became aware that the swishing had stopped. He could also hear the crunching of his father's feet on the path and the moaning of the boy he had left behind him.

As he moved towards her, Polly turned and came towards him, her teeth tightly pressed into her lower lip and her eyes full of tears. When they came abreast neither of them spoke, nor did they move from behind the hedge until the sound of MacFell's voice reached them from the yard; then going quickly on to the path, they bent one on each side of Ginger and pulled him upwards.

'Don't cry, Ginger. Don't cry.'

Ginger's head was deep on his chest and his body was trembling, but once on his feet he tugged his arm away from Charlie's and turned fully towards Polly, and she, putting her arms around him, murmured, 'Come on down to the burn, the water'll cool you.'

Her arm still about him, she led him along the cinder path down the slope, past the cottage that MacFell had had renovated and furnished, supposedly to let to the people who tramped the hills in the summer, and to the bank of the burn.

'Take your knickerbockers off.'

'No, no!' The boy now grabbed at the top of his short trousers.

'Go on, don't be silly. There's three of them back home, I'm used to bare backsides.'

When the boy still kept tight hold of his trousers, she said, 'All right I'll go but Charlie'll stay with you, won't you, Charlie?'

It pointed to a strange relationship that the daughter of the one time cowman could address the master's son in a way other than as young Master

MacFell or Mister Charlie, and that she was the only one connected with the farm, besides his parents and sister, who did address him so.

'Yes, yes, Polly.'

'I . . . I don't want to take 'em off.' Ginger sniffed, then wiped his wet face with the back of his hand. 'I'll . . . I'll just put me legs in.'

'All right, have it your own way. But wait a tick till I take me boots off an' I'll give you a hand down the bank.'

With a speed that characterized all her movements, Polly dropped on to the grass and rapidly unlaced her boots, stood up again, shortened her skirt by turning in the waistband several times, then, her arm around Ginger once more, she helped him down the bank; and when their feet touched the ice-cold water the contact forced her into momentary laughter.

Glancing up the bank at Charlie, she cried, 'It would freeze mutton,' and almost in the same breath she went on, 'Come on, a bit further, Ginger, get it over your knees. And here, let me get the grit off your hands.'

As if she were attending to a child, and not to a boy almost two years her senior, she gently flapped the water over his grit-studded palms, saying as she did so, 'They're not bleedin' much, it's your knees that are the worse. . . . There, is that better? It gets warm after you've been in a minute. Feel better, eh?' She lowered her head and, turning it to the side, looked into his face, and he nodded at her and said, 'Aye, Polly.'

A few minutes later she helped him up the bank, although he now seemed able to walk unaided, and when he sat down on the grass she sat close beside him; then, her round, plump face straight, her wide full lips pressed tight, she stared up at Charlie for a moment before saying, 'You know what I'd like to do? I'd like to take your da and kick him from here to hell along a road all made of cinders.'

Looking down into the angry green eyes, Charlie was prompted to say, 'And I'd like to help you do it,' but all he did was to turn his gaze away towards the burn, until she said, 'I don't blame you; you know I don't, Charlie. . . . Sit down, man.'

As if he, too, were obeying the order from an older person, Charlie, like Ginger, did as she bade him and sat down, and as he watched her dabbing at Ginger's knees with the inside of her print skirt he wished, and in all sincerity, it had been he himself who had suffered the cinder path this morning, just so he could be the recipient of her attentions.

He couldn't remember a time when he hadn't loved Polly Benton. He was three years old when Big Polly first brought her into the kitchen and dumped her in a clothes basket to the side of the fire while she got on with the business of helping Fanny Dimple. He had stood fascinated by big Polly's knee as she bared her equally big breast to the infant. He had grown up with young Polly, close yet separated. At times when the master was absent they had played together openly; when he was present they had continued to play, but secretly; and always in their play she had been the leader and he the willing follower.

When, four years ago, his father had taken it into his head to send him to the boarding school in Newcastle, the only one he had really been sorry to leave was young Polly; he hadn't been sorry to leave his mother, although he loved her and pitied her, but her need of him drained him and he was glad to get away from it. As holidays approached it was only the thought that he would see Polly again that compensated him for the irritations that lay ahead in the house.

'You'd better get back if you don't want another dose.'

They all turned and looked upwards and towards Polly's elder brother, Arthur.

Arthur was fifteen years old. He was stockily built with dark hair and a ruddy complexion. He looked strong, dour, aggressive, and he was all three.

'Get up out of that, our Polly, and stop molly-coddlin' him; he'll get worse than that afore he's finished.'

'Aw, you! our Arthur! you want a taste of it to know what it feels like.'

'I've had me share. But not any more' – his chin jerked upwards defiantly – 'he stops when you can look him in the eye.'

It was as if the latter part of his remark had been addressed to Charlie, who had risen to his feet, and again Charlie would like to have endorsed the sentiment by saying, 'You're right there,' for as yet his father had never flayed anyone over fifteen. Instead, he watched Arthur Benton push the small red-headed boy forward with a thrust of his hand, saying, 'Go on, bring some hay down. If you fall it'll be softer on your arse. An' you' – he now turned to Polly – 'get back to the house. You shouldn't be over here anyway.'

'You mind your own interferences, our Arthur. And don't think you'll order me about 'cos you won't.'

Polly was now pulling on her boots, the laces of which passed through only half the holes, and when she rose to her feet the tops of the boots spread out like wings from her shin bones.

'Pull your skirt down.'

'Shut up! An' you go to the devil. I'll leave it up if I want to leave it up. I'll put it round me neck if I feel so inclined.' As she finished she looked at Charlie and laughed; then with a toss of her head she walked away from them, and they both watched her go, not in the direction by which they had come but along by the burn which would bring her out below the cottages.

'Eeh!' Arthur jerked his head to the side. 'She gets cheekier every day.' And there was definite pride in the remark, which caused Charlie to smile at him and say quietly, 'She's Polly.'

'Aye, you've said somethin' there, she's Polly all right.'

They turned together now and walked across the grass and on to the cinder path, and the exchanges between them were again unusual in that they were as between equals.

'You going for a ride s'afternoon?' asked Arthur.

'Yes, I'm to go over to Chapmans'.' Charlie did not say, 'I'm going over to Chapmans' ' but 'I'm to go over to Chapmans'.'

'Is the boss thinkin' of buying the mare?'

'No, no, it isn't about that; I'm to take an invitation for them to come to supper on Saturday night.'

'O . . .h! O . . . h! It's like that, is it? Supper Saturda' night. You'll have to watch yourself.' He jerked his head towards Charlie, and Charlie, looking at him with a blank countenance, said, 'What do you mean, watch yourself?'

'Why, Miss Victoria.'

'*Miss Victoria!*' Charlie's brows drew together.

'Lor'!' Arthur was grinning. 'If I was lookin' like you at this minute an' somebody said I looked gormless they'd be right. 'Twas as I said, you'd better look out for Miss Victoria. Old Chapman would like nothin' better than to see the lands joined; an' the boss, well, let's face it, the Chapmans are the cream of the milk round here, an' the boss is all for the cream off the milk.'

Charlie brought himself to a sudden stop. He looked at Arthur for a moment; then, his head going back on his shoulders, he let out a laugh. It was a loud laugh, a long rollicking laugh, a sound that was rarely heard around the farm. It even startled Arthur into protest. Casting his glance towards the back of the byres to where the alleyway ran into the yard, he said, 'Stop it, man! What's got into you? There's nowt funny about that. Aw, give over. Stop it!'

Slowly Charlie's laughter subsided, and, taking a handkerchief from his pocket, he wiped each cheekbone; then, his face still lit with laughter, he looked at Arthur and said, 'Victoria . . . she's eighteen,' it was as if he were speaking of someone as old as his mother. 'The things you get into your head, Arthur. Anyway, if I was her age what would a high-stepper like Miss Victoria want with me? I'm tongue-tied when I meet her; it's as if we spoke different languages. She goes to balls in Hexham and Newcastle, she's been to London; she's left school, and I'm still there, and likely to be for years; and what's more, she's mad on horses and hunting and can talk of nothing else. Now if I was bringing up that subject with her I'd put my foot in it right away by saying her tastes are a contradiction for she's supposed to love horses, yet she takes them over fences that could rip their bellies open. Moreover, I don't think she's read anything but a lady's journal in her life. As for reading poetry, she would laugh herself sick if I mentioned it, even young Nellie is better informed than she is.'

'Well, who wouldn't? Poetry isn't for men.'

'Oh, now who's being gormless, Arthur?' Charlie waved his hand before his face as if shooing away a fly. 'It's men who write the poetry.'

'Aw, no, I don't agree with you there, for they're not what you'd call real men, just those fancy half-buggers.'

'Don't be silly. What about Wordsworth? Is he a . . .?'

Charlie couldn't bring himself to repeat Arthur's phrase but substituted the word 'effeminate' which part of his mind told him was hitting Arthur below the belt; he knew Arthur would show no offence at being put down in this way, for he liked to talk, and to get him talking too. And it was odd, but he could talk to Arthur, and Arthur's pet response, 'I don't agree with you,' always pointed to the fact that he was enjoying the talk, having a crack as he called it. He was aware that Arthur was very ignorant and was likely to remain so, for he was too bigoted to learn. Yet he liked Arthur. He liked all the Bentons. Yes, he liked all the Bentons.

Arthur was now saying, 'Wordsworth is different, anybody who lives among the hills is different. I'm talking about the fancy blokes up in Newcastle an' London.'

Charlie blinked rapidly, swallowed, but made no further comment except to repeat to himself, Newcastle and London. They imagined everything bad happened in Newcastle or London and that all the rich people, too, were in these places. They took no account of the vast space all about them which was dotted with manors and huge country houses. To people like Arthur, Newcastle and London were the places where odd people lived and bad things happened; the bad things, the unnatural things that took place among themselves they laid down to nature.

He himself hadn't travelled further than Newcastle but he knew that one day he would break away and see the world, and stop to listen, listen to people talking. He would love to listen to people who could really talk about things besides farming and horses and ... *the other thing*. ... But then the other thing wasn't very often talked about, it was simply done in the hay field, or behind the barn, or in the copse along by the burn. It hadn't happened much lately, but then the harvest was over. It was at its worst, or at its best – it was how you looked at it – when the hands came over from Chapmans to help out, to beat the weather or to clear a harvest. *The other thing* had been troubling him a lot of late and it was always mixed up in his mind with young Polly.

When they reached the alleyway they parted without further words, or even a nod, Arthur going on towards the piggeries and Charlie cutting through into the main yard, there to be met by his father.

'Who was that laughing?'

'Me, Father.'

Edward MacFell's head moved slightly to the side, his eyes narrowing just a fraction. This son of his was sixteen years old and he couldn't recall ever hearing him laugh out loud before.

'It must have been something very funny.'

It was some seconds before Charlie answered. His gaze fluttering away as if searching for something in the yard, he said, 'Oh, 'twas only something silly that Arthur said.'

Edward MacFell waited to know the substance of what Arthur had said but when it wasn't forthcoming he didn't, as one would have expected of a man of his type, bawl, 'Well, out with it! If it was a joke I would like to share it.' What he said was, 'It was bound to be something silly if a Benton said it.' Then stretching out his arm he placed his hand on his son's shoulder and, turning him about, led him towards the end of the yard and on to a flagged terrace that ran along the front of the house, saying as he did so, 'Come and see what I've got in mind.'

Standing on the edge of the terrace, he now lifted his arm and pointed. 'The burn down there where it widens, I've got the idea to dig out a tidy piece to form a small lake; we'd be able to look down on it from the parlour window. ... What do you think of that?'

Charlie looked over the gently sloping piece of grassland that led down to the burn. The idea surprised him. A lake in front of the house. Immediately his mind linked it with the green-baized door and the morning prayers; but he could see no harm in it, so he said pleasantly, 'I think it would be very nice, Father.'

'An addition to the house you think?'

'Yes, oh yes.' He nodded while still looking down towards the fast flowing narrow rivulet of water.

'And I'll have a stone seat built at the top end where one can sit and look right away through the valley.' MacFell nodded to himself now as he saw in his mind the grandeur of a lake and a stone seat.

When his father's arm came round his shoulders Charlie could not suppress a slight shudder and when, with an unusual show of outward affection, he was pressed to his father's side, he had an upsurging feeling of revulsion.

'Come, there's something I want to talk to you about.' MacFell now took his arm abruptly away from his son's shoulder and marched ahead off the terrace into the yard and up to the kitchen door.

After scraping his boots on the iron bar that stuck out from the wall, he went into the kitchen, passing Fanny and Maggie as if he wasn't aware of their presence, through the green-baized door, across the hall in the direction of the stairs, then up a narrow passage and into a small room that was almost filled by a heavy ornate desk and a big leather chair, both placed at an angle to the long narrow window. At the near side of the desk was a smaller chair, and the wall close behind this was almost taken up with a breakfront bookcase. There was no space for any other furniture in the room.

'Sit down.' MacFell pointed to the chair, and slowly Charlie lowered himself into it. This wasn't the first time his father had had him in his office room to talk to him, but never before had he invited him to be seated. Whatever was about to be said must be of some importance.

When it was said, he was visibly startled.

After taking up a pen from the tray in front of him and wiping the nib clean on a handworked square of stained linen, MacFell jerked his head upwards, looked straight at his son and said, 'Have you had a woman yet?'

As Charlie's lips parted, a valve was released in his stomach sending out a great spurt of colour that not only tinted his pale face a deep red, but heated all the pores of his body.

'Well! answer me, boy.' MacFell was smiling now. 'There's nothing to be ashamed of either way. You needn't go into details, just say yes or no.'

'. . . No, Father.' The heat was intensified, the colour deepened.

Once more MacFell wiped the pen nib, giving it his attention as if it were the important issue of the moment; then again jerking his head upwards, he looked at his son and said, 'Well now, something should be done about it, shouldn't it? This thing can be very irritating and frustrating, and if the mind is continually dwelling on it you won't be able to pay attention to your school work, will you? So the quicker you get release from it the better.'

Laying down the pen, MacFell moved his fingers along the stem of it as if he were stroking fur, before he went on, 'It's of no great importance but it has its place in life . . . mostly as an irritant.' On the last words his tone changed and his jaws visibly tightened. With an impatient movement now he threw the pen on to the brass tray, then drawing in a deep breath, he leant against the back of the chair and asked, 'Is there anyone who has taken your fancy roundabouts?'

Charlie gulped in his throat and his words came out on a stutter as he said, 'I . . . I ha . . . I . . . haven't thought about it, Father.'

MacFell gazed at him under his brows for a moment and a slow smile spread over his face before he said softly, 'Well, it's about time you did, isn't it?'

'. . . Yes, Father.'

'I'd go away now and think about it, and you can leave the rest to me.'

Charlie rose from the chair as if he had been progged with a spoke from underneath, but as he almost scurried from the room he was brought to a standstill by his father saying, 'How do you like Victoria? . . . Oh!' MacFell put his head back and chuckled deeply as he added, 'Don't look like that, I wasn't intending you should start on her. No begod! not yet anyway. All I asked you was, do you like her?'

'Yes . . . yes, she's all right.'

'All right! Is that how you see her, just as, all right? She's a handsome girl, lively, and comes from good stock.' The smile now slid from his face and his eyes took on that look that had frightened Charlie as a boy, and still did, because he wasn't able to fathom what it meant.

MacFell's voice was stiff as, pulling a sheet of paper towards him and picking up the pen again, he began to write, saying abruptly, 'You're going over to Brooklands this afternoon but be back here by five, not later.'

Outside the office door Charlie stood for a moment, his hand pressed tightly over his mouth. He was feeling slightly sick. Whom would his father pick for him? Not Maggie, she was but twelve. Lily Dawson? She was fifteen but she was odd and her nose always running. He shuddered. There were Nancy and Annie Ryton, they were twins; but they worked over at Brooklands. That left only Polly. . . . *No! No! never Polly.*

As he crossed the hall his mother came out of the sitting-room and, stopping in front of him, asked, 'What did he want you in there for?'

'He . . . he told me I've got to go over to Brooklands this afternoon.'

'You knew that already. Come, what was he on about?'

'Nothing, nothing.'

'He never takes anyone in there to talk about nothing. Look, boy, tell me what he wanted you to do.'

He stared at her for a moment. What did his father want him to do? Just, he supposed, what he wanted to do himself, what he had wanted to do for a long time, have a woman . . . a girl.

Staring into his mother's thin tight-lipped face, he knew he would have to give her some explanation and so he said, 'He was asking me what I thought of Victoria.'

'Oh! oh!' Her head bobbed. 'He's bringing it into the open now, is he? Now, look, Charlie –' She grabbed his arm and pulled him backwards into the sitting-room and there, closing the door, she whispered at him, 'Don't be bullied into doing anything you don't want to do. Anyway, you're just a bit of a boy yet and she's two years older than you. And that's only in years, for she's old in other ways. She's a fly-by-night if there was ever a one. Now I'm telling you this, Charlie –' she gripped his hands –'he'll push you from this end and Hal Chapman will push her from that end, and they'll join you up without a thought of what your lives together will be, simply because they both want the other's land. And when it's joined they'll spend their time praying for one or other of them to die, and you too, so that they can be lord of all they survey. Oh . . . men! Men!'

As Charlie watched her teeth grinding over each other he released his hands from hers and took hold of her arms, saying softly, 'Don't worry; at least don't worry about Victoria and me. Why, she appears as old as you at times. And what's more' – he smiled wanly – 'she thinks me a numskull; and about some things I suppose I am. But what isn't recognized, Mother, is I have a mind of my own. The few years of education I've had has revealed that much to me and it has shown me I have no taste for land or farming, what I want to do is to travel, to see places, places I've read about. And to meet people. . . .' His voice trailed away and his face took on a dreary softness. *The other thing* was forgotten for the moment, and when his mother put her hand up and touched his cheek he placed his hand over hers and pressed it to his face, only to regret the gesture the next moment when he was engulfed in her embrace.

As she sobbed pitifully he patted her head, whispering the while, 'Ssh! ssh! he'll hear you,' yet knowing that if his father did hear her crying he would not come to her for he had ignored the sound for years.

As he stood trying to comfort her he thought that it was strange he should experience such embarrassment by the outward demonstration of affection from his parents. Perhaps it was because it was so rarely shown, or perhaps he sensed it wasn't the result of love on their part, merely a need that had to be filled.

# Chapter Three

The Bentons' cottage was the third along the row. The two end ones to the left, as you approached them from the burn, were empty. The two at the other end were occupied by the cowman Arnold Dawson and his family, and by the shepherd Fred Ryton and his wife. All the cottages were the same in construction, two rooms and a scullery downstairs and a room under the eaves in which it was possible to stand upright only immediately under the ridge.

Peter, aged ten, Mick, eleven, and Arthur slept in comparative comfort in this room because each had a straw pallet to himself. Flo, aged nine, Maggie, twelve, and Polly had the questionable comfort of sleeping together in the three-quarter size iron bed in the front room, while Jim Benton and big Polly occupied the bed set up in the corner of the kitchen.

This bed was wedged between the wall and the end of the fireplace and if Jim Benton was lying on his side he could reach out and move the pan on the hob to stop it from boiling over, or to bring it to the boil, whichever was necessary. This often happened when they were all out in the fields and big Polly had prepared a scrag end of mutton hash or a rabbit stew for their return. But today young Polly was seeing to the meal and talking as she did so.

'Things aren't fair, Da, they aren't right.' With an impatient twist of her hand which indicated her inner feelings, she pulled the skin of the rabbit's body, tugged it from its legs, then, picking up a small chopper, expertly split the carcass in two before looking towards the bed and adding, 'Why has he to do it on the cinder path? Why not in the barn or in the yard?'

Her father gave her no answer, what he did was to raise himself slightly, cough, spit into a piece of paper, then without his eyes following his hand, drop the paper into a chamber under the bed before lying back on the straw pillows. Why? she asked; why did he do it? His Polly was so young in some ways while being as old as the hills in others, but if she lived long enough she'd find out the reason why Edward MacFell did the things he did. The reason was simple, he loved cruelty, he was in love with cruelty; he'd never loved anything or anyone in his life. Oh aye, he thought he loved his son, but that was simply pride because he wanted to be able to show him off to the county folk. That's why he was stuffin' him with education. Edward MacFell loved no one but himself and found no satisfaction in anything but suffering, making others suffer. What had he said? No, that wasn't quite true. There was one avenue that was providing him with satisfaction, for if it wasn't, why did he keep it up? The thought brought him on to his side and, looking towards Polly, he said, 'Where is she?'

'Taken some washin' down to the burn.' Polly had kept her attention on her work as she answered him but when he asked, 'What time is it?' she turned her head towards the mantelpiece and glanced at the little clock that was held in place by a couple of close-linked Staffordshire figures. 'Ten past eleven.'

Jim coughed again and went through the procedure attached to it. Well, she wouldn't be along the burn bank at this time of day. Or would she? He glanced towards the window. At one time he'd had his bed over there from where he could watch her every move, but it had been too much to bear, and so under the pretext of being cold – and that was no lie for he was always cold – he'd had the bed moved into the corner here from where he kept telling himself that what the eye didn't see the heart didn't grieve over. But then he hadn't taken into account his mind's eye.

He lay now looking at his daughter hurrying between the table and the fireplace, and for the countless time he asked himself the question, 'What would I have done without her all these years?' and the same answer came, 'I'd have gone clean mad likely.' She was bonny was his Polly. And then she had that something, a quality that went beyond bonniness. He couldn't put a name to it only to think that it was like the scent that came from some wild flowers and kept you sniffing at them. He looked at her thick mass of hair tied back into a bushy tail with a piece of faded ribbon. The colour was like that of the heather, the dead heather that swept like waves over the desolate land away towards Ray Fell. Then again, it wasn't as dark as the dead heather, more like the bracken when, the summer over, it bent towards the ground. . . . He'd soon be in the ground, and he'd be glad to go. Oh aye, if it wasn't for her standing there he'd be glad to go. Not that he would miss her 'cos he wouldn't know nowt about anything, he had no belief in the hereafter, but he knew she would miss him.

As he lay looking up at the discoloured ceiling, he wondered how much longer he had left before they carried him down the road, past the farm, over the fields and gentle hills and across the 'new line' road that now ran from Newcastle far away to the North, to Carter Bar and over that mighty mound into Scotland. He wished he'd been able to travel that road just for a few miles. Some said it was a fine road and a boon to the farmers to get their stuff into the markets; but others said it was the beginning of the end, nothing would ever be the same again because of that road.

Anyway, they would have to carry him across the road to get to the cemetery in Kirkwhelpington. He was glad he would lie there for it was a bonny cemetery, perched high on the top of a slice of rock which his father had once described as being cut out by the hand of God Almighty to keep off the heathen Scots from attacking the church and the little village beyond.

He had been christened in the church of Saint Bartholomew, and as a lad on his half-day off a fortnight, he had liked to walk that way. He had only once been more than twenty miles from the farm in his life. That was a day long ago when as a young lad he had gone with the drovers into Newcastle. In his young days they could go all year round and not see a strange soul, but things were different now. In the summer strangers came tramping over the hills with packs on their backs, boots on their feet with soles thicker than clogs, and wearing strange hats, and they sometimes stopped at a cottage door and asked for a drink of water.

Just this summer a young fellow had put his head through the open door there and said quite friendly like, 'Anybody at home?'. Polly had given him a cup of buttermilk, which he hadn't liked very much, and it had made her laugh. She and the young fellow had stood talking for a long while and it had worried him somewhat, because it had brought home to him the fact that his Polly was no longer a little lass. She'd soon be a young woman, fourteen in November, she'd be. She had brought him luck because, before her, they had buried five, but from the time she came there was one each year for the next four years and they all lived. Maggie, Mick, Peter, and Flo, they were all past the danger age now. Flo, the youngest, was nine.

He turned his gaze towards the window. There had been no more bairns since Flo; there had been no more nothing since Flo, for it was at that time that palsy attacked his legs, and as disasters never come singly he took the consumption. He marvelled at times that he had lasted so long, but he wouldn't have if it hadn't been for Polly.

His head jerked and he opened his eyes and stared up into his daughter's face.

'I must have been noddin' off.'

'Aye.' She punched gently at the pillow to the side of his head. 'It does you good to sleep. Would you like a drink?'

'Aye, lass; it does you good to sleep.' He caught hold of her hand now and stared into her eyes as he said, 'I'll soon be takin' a long sleep. You know that, don't you?'

'Aw, Dad, don't. Don't!' She tugged her hand from his and her whole body wriggled in protest. 'Don't talk like that, it upsets me, you could live for years. Looked after proper, you could live for years, an' I'll look after you.'

'All right, all right, don't frash yourself. It's as you say, I could live for years, so it's up to you to keep me goin', eh. . . . There, now, there now, don't start bubblin'. Aw, lass' – he again had hold of her hand – 'there's nobody like you in the wide world. By! some fella's gona get a prize some day.'

'Prize, huh!' She gave a broken laugh now. 'Surprise you mean, when he finds out he's got a quick-tempered bitch on his hands.'

'He'll admire you for your spunk. An' you've got spunk. By! aye!' – he moved her hand up and down as if shaking it – 'you have that. You've got more spunk in your little finger than the other five put together.'

'Oh, our Arthur's got spunk, Da; he'll let nobody tread on him, will our Arthur.'

'Aye.' He released her hand now and his fingers plucked at the patchwork quilt on the bed as he said, 'But there's spunk and spunk, lass. Don't be deceived by those who shout the loudest. It's often the quiet ones who show up the best. It's a funny thing you know, but fear breeds spunk. Aye, it does. I, myself, thought I hadn't much spunk until I was frightened, and then I stood me ground. You're like me' – his eyes lifted to her again – 'you'll always stand your ground. Not' – he nodded at her now smiling – 'that you can be classed as a quiet one, not if me ears tell me aright.'

'Go on with you, our Da! Go on.' She flapped her hands at him, then turned from him, saying, 'If I have any more of your old lip I'll dock your drink.'

As she went to lift the tea caddy from the mantelpiece she was brought abruptly round by the door being thrust open, and she saw Arthur standing there with his arms outspread, one hand gripping the latch and the other on the stanchion of the door. He was gasping as if he had been running. He looked from her to the bed, then back to her again, and on a gasp he said, 'Have . . . have you seen our Mick?'

'No; well, not since he went out this morning. He's . . . he's up in the beet field.' She motioned her hand towards the side wall.

'Oh aye, aye.' His arms dropped to his sides. Then stepping into the room, he asked, 'You makin' tea?'

'Aye, I'm just gona mash it.'

'I'll . . . I'll have a cup.'

'What's wrong?' It was his father speaking.

'Nowt. Nowt.'

'Don't tell me nowt's wrong, you said you were workin' in the bottom fields this mornin', why are you here?'

'I was just passin'.'

'Just passin'!' Jim pulled his useless body upwards in the bed, then said, 'Don't try to stuff me, lad.'

'I'm not tryin' to stuff you, Da. I said I was just passin' and that's what I was doin', just passin', lookin' for our Mick.' Arthur now turned his back on his father and glanced at Polly, where she was standing with the teapot in her hand staring at him, and with a silent grimace and a movement of his eyebrows he indicated he wanted to speak to her; then saying, 'Ah, to the devil!' he went towards the door again and out on to the rough gravel that fronted the cottages.

Thrusting the empty teapot on to the hob, Polly looked towards her father, nodded at him, then hurried from the room and into the open, there to see Arthur standing near the door of the end cottage.

'What is it? What's the matter?' She was close to him whispering as if afraid of being overheard, and he grabbed at her arm, saying, 'I'll tell you what's the matter, come in here,' and pushing the cottage door open he thrust her into the dank room and there, still holding her, he said, 'Brace yourself for the latest.'

'What do you mean? An' leave go of me arm, you're hurtin' me.'

He released his hold on her and she stood rubbing her arm while she looked into his face. His lips were working tightly one over the other; she saw his cheekbones moving under the skin; there were beads of sweat running between his brows and down the centre of his nose; his Adam's apple was working as if he were swallowing – he had a big Adam's apple for a boy.

'You're for the cottage.'

'*What!*'

'I said you're for the cottage. She's down there now, me ma, an' I heard them. I was at the back near the scullery. I'd set a trap in the thicket. He never comes down there in the mornin's, it's always late afternoon, you know it is, but I saw him coming down the cinder path, and her along the burn bank. She must have got a signal. God knows what it is, I wish I did. And then they went inside, and when I heard him raise his voice straightaway I knew . . . aye well!' – he turned his head away – 'I knew they weren't at it, an' that it was something else, so I sneaked up to the scullery window an' I heard me ma keep saying "No! No!" and then she mentioned your name. "Not young Polly!" she said, an' he said "Aye", and she had to send you down atween four and five. . . . I was for goin' in there and rippin' them up. You're not goin'! D'you hear? You're not goin'!' He had hold of her shoulders now shaking her; and she allowed him to do so for some seconds for she was feeling dazed by what she had just heard. But of a sudden she wrenched herself from him and cried at him, 'You've no need to tell me I'm not goin', our Arthur, wild horses won't drag me down there.' She was standing at the far end of the little room now, and he remained where he was, his hands hanging limply by his sides again and his head on his chest, all the aggressiveness seemed to have left his body, and his voice was low and flat as he said, 'That's what me ma said all those years ago when me da could no longer do his stint; but it was either that or the road. It could be the same again, but this time' – his voice took on a stronger, bitter note now – 'it'll be the road we'll take, even if it means pushin' me da on the flat cart.'

'You couldn't take me da from his bed. Anyway, the master wouldn't do that, those roundabout wouldn't stand for it and . . . and he values people's opinion. He . . . he would never turn us out.'

'Well, we'll wait and see, won't we, when you say you're not goin'. But if he doesn't turn us out there's one thing he'll do, he'll make life hell for the lot of us. The cinder path'll be nothin' to it.'

Polly was leaning against the dirty whitewashed wall, her arms folded tightly under her small breasts, and she was shivering inwardly. The master wanted her. He'd . . . he'd had her mother for years, and now he wanted her. Oh no! No! She shook her head in a slow wide sweep. Never! She'd jump in the burn first. But then there were so few places you could drown in the burn unless it was in flood, and she had to think of her da.

'Don't worry; I won't let it happen.' With his arm around her shoulders Arthur pulled her from the wall and led her towards the door. She was in the road again before she said as if coming out of a dream, 'But . . . but what'll I tell our da?'

Arthur gnawed at his lip for a moment, then offered her the solution of his father's one-time weakness by saying, 'Tell him there's a basket of eggs missin' and our Mick an' Flo were gatherin' them first thing, an' the boss is wild.'

She nodded at him, then watched him turn away and walk towards the beet field; but she herself didn't go immediately into the cottage. Again she leant against the wall, and as she did so she saw a figure on horseback riding along the bridle path in the direction of Brooklands Farm, and she knew it was Charlie. Almost instantly she was enveloped in a sweat that clouded her vision and for the first time in her life her feelings touched on ecstasy, and when, some seconds later, her vision cleared she knew that had it been the master's son she had been bidden to meet in the cottage she would have gone gladly.

MacFell had been over to see John Hodgson about a young bull he had for sale. Hodgsons had been tenant farmers of The Manor for generations, yet none had prospered. It was still a poor farm, due mostly to the layout of the land which was fit only for sheep grazing and a few cattle; even so MacFell scorned him for it.

He knew that John Hodgson needed to sell the bull and so he quibbled about the price, and but for the fact that he wanted to be back on his farm before five o'clock, he would have gone on quibbling until he eventually wore Hodgson down. Instead, he told the man that he would leave it for another day and let him think over his offer.

MacFell had no doubt but that Hodgson's curses helped him on his way back over the fields. However, this troubled him not at all, what concerned him at the moment was that his son's needs must be met; then once that was out of the way the boy would apply himself solely to his work, the work of becoming a scholar, an educated man who would be able to converse with the best, be better than the best, the best anyway that lived within the folds of these hills. What were they after all, them in their big houses and their manors, but idle good-for-nothings who had never earned a penny of the money that they were spending, nor yet contributed a stick of furniture to their mighty rooms? Oh, his son would show them. He might not after all decide that he should take over the farm, he could become a barrister, a judge, or even enter Parliament; with education such as he was receiving in the grand school in Newcastle he could go on to a university, and from there he could pick and choose, be whatever he desired, and marry whom he liked, even into the class. Yes, definitely into the class, the top class, from where he could even look down his nose at Chapman's horsy daughter. . . . But what about the land? Well, after all it meant more to Chapman than it did to him. Chapman, for all his style, had no freehold land.

He passed the narrow way that led down to the village of Kirkwhelpington, then a little further on he left the road and mounted the grassy bank and, bringing his horse to a stop for a moment, he glanced at his watch. He had left it late, he must hurry.

When he drove his heels into the horse's side it set off at a gallop and he kept it at its pace for the next three miles until the sweat was running out of the beast. Then when he came to the top of the rise from where, over a rough copse, he could see his farm and its outbuildings lying as if in the palm of a hand, he let the animal drop into a canter before taking the path that ran down through the copse and to the burn.

His intention was not to cross the burn but to remain in the shadow of the trees and watch the Benton chit going to her breaking, if all her mother said was true, and, in his imagination, relish his son's pleasure.

Charlie did not stay long at Brooklands Farm. Mrs Chapman and her husband welcomed him most warmly and said how disappointed Victoria and Nellie would be to have missed him, but Josh Pringle had ridden over from Bellingham way that morning and they had gone back to his place to see a new foal. Mrs Chapman asked after his dear mother, his father, and his sister Betty; then when she received the invitation she said they'd all be delighted to come over on Saturday evening, wouldn't they, Hal?

Hal Chapman endorsed his wife's sentiments; then, his hand on Charlie's shoulder, he once again took him on a tour of his farm, and it was as if he were showing him everything for the first time as he pointed out the value of this horse and that cow, and the fine breed of pigs, and the sheep dotting the hillsides far away.

And so it was with relief that Charlie said his good-byes and made his way hurriedly back home for there were two things he had made up his mind to do.

First, he was going to tell his father that he had no bodily needs that couldn't wait to be satisfied.

When just before setting out for Brooklands his father had told him whom he had chosen to initiate him into manhood, he was so amazed as to be unable to voice any protest. The indecency of it shocked him. That his father could use big Polly and calmly arrange for him to do the same with young Polly was utterly abhorrent to him. In some way, it even sullied the feelings he bore Polly, it ripped from them the secret sweetness of his first love and left it smirched, brought down to the level of 'the other thing' enacted in the hay.

The second thing he must do was to find Polly and ease her mind. How he would go about this he didn't know.

The farm seemed devoid of life; there was no one about the yard except young Peter Benton who, as Charlie unsaddled the horse in the stable, took the saddle from him and with surprising strength and agility for one so young threw it over the saddle stand, then said, 'I can see to him, Mister Charlie,' in reply to which Charlie, smiling at him, said, 'You'll have to stand on something then, Peter.'

'Aye well, I've done it afore an' I like rubbing him down.'

'Where's everybody?'

'Oh, about.' The answer and attitude was that of a man, and for a moment Charlie forgot the weight on his mind and laughed down on the youngster. He was a funny little fellow was young Peter, he'd be a card when he grew up.

Then as if belying this impression, the boy turned a serious face up to Charlie and said, 'What's wrong, Mister Charlie? Is our Arthur in for it? What's he done?'

'Arthur? Done? Nothing that I know of. What makes you ask?'

'He's been goin' around in a tear all day, wouldn't open his mouth. That's not like our Arthur, he's always goin' for me. He was in a while back for a rope and I said what did he want it for, was he thinking of hangin' hissel', an' he clipped me lug, knocked me flyin' he did. Is he in for it, Mister Charlie? What's he done?'

Charlie stared down at the boy before he repeated, 'Nothing that I know of, Peter. Where is he now?'

'He went the copse way.' He thumbed over his shoulder.

'Don't worry' – Charlie grinned now – 'Arthur gets that way, he has fits and starts, you should know that by now.'

'Aye. Aye, Mister Charlie, but . . . but somethin's up, 'cos me ma didn't come in to her dinner an' our Polly was sick in the sink. Is the boss gona do somethin' to us, Mister Charlie?'

Polly sick in the sink. . . . 'The boss. . . . No, no, don't be silly. Whatever it is, it's got nothing to do with your work, you're all splendid workers.' He absentmindedly ruffled the boy's hair; then looking at the horse, he said quietly, 'You'll give her a good rub, won't you?'

'Aye, Mister Charlie, aye, I'll see to her well,' and taking the bridle, the boy tugged the horse forward into its stall, and Charlie went out into the yard and stood looking about him for a moment.

Polly had been sick in the sink. She had heard what she had to do and was terrified at the prospect. And Arthur knew and he was mad about it, and of course he would be, because in his rough way he was fond of his sister, deeply fond. And the mother, she was keeping out of the way, likely unable to face her husband, a poor sick man.

He turned quickly about. He must find Arthur and tell him, and he could tell Polly and put her mind at rest. He went past the cut that led to the cinder path, through the big barn and out of a side door, then across the field to the rise and the copse.

As he entered the piece of woodland he asked himself what Arthur would be wanting with a rope in here for all the dead trees had been taken down last Christmas and hauled up to the sawing bench; he himself had helped and enjoyed doing so.

It was at this point of his thinking that he saw Arthur. He was crouched down behind a stunted holly, growing near the foot of an oak tree. Almost immediately, he heard the approach of a horse from the far end of the copse. It was coming at some speed and although he couldn't see the rider he knew it would be his father.

He remembered afterwards how he had stood rigidly still and wondered what had kept him so, why he hadn't gone straight on down the slope towards Arthur. But no, he had remained stock still until the horse and rider came into view around the curve of the path. The horse was cantering, sending the dried leaves like spray from its hooves. Then he saw his father rise from its back into the air as if he were beginning to fly, except that he was doing so in reverse. His head back, his arms widespread like wings and his legs like a divided tail, he seemed to hover in the air for a moment, then his limbs converging together he fell to the ground, at the same time as the horse's forefeet struck the path and the frightened animal's neighing died away. It was like a scene enacted in the blink of an eyelid.

Dear God! Dear God! Charlie was conscious that his mouth was wide open and that his face muscles were stretched to their fullest extent, but for the life of him he couldn't move from the spot, until he saw Arthur spring up from his hiding place and clutch at the bole of the oak, tearing at something there. It was then he moved. Like a goat leaping down a mountain, he sprang down the hillside and reached the prostrate, huddled form lying amid the leaves just as Arthur stopped in his frantic running, the rope loose in his hand, and stared down at his master.

The two boys now lifted their eyes from the man on the ground and gazed at each other. Then Charlie, dropping onto his knees, went to turn his father from his side on to his back, but no sooner had his hands touched him than they left him again, for as he went to move the body the head lolled drunkenly on to the shoulder.

Again the boys were gazing at each other, Charlie looking upwards, Arthur looking down; and it was Arthur who, on a deep gulp, spluttered, 'God Almighty no! Maim him, break his leg, his arm, aye, that's all I meant, to stop him. You don't know what he was up to. But no, no! Almighty God!

no, not kill him. No! Charlie. No.' He was backing away now, the rope dangling from his hand, his words incoherent. 'Just to stop him goin' to the cottage. Our Polly, she's too young for it, for him anyway.'

Of a sudden he stopped his jabbering and, his head drooping forward, he looked at the rope in his right hand. Then as if already experiencing the consequences of his act his left hand came up sharply and gripped his throat. It was this action that brought Charlie out of the dazed, dream-like feeling that was enveloping him. His father was dead. His father was dead. And Arthur would be hanged for it.

The first fact stirred no emotion whatever in him at the moment, but the second alerted him. He stood up, then looked down at the twisted form for a moment longer before turning back to Arthur, whose face was now drained of every vestige of colour and whose whole body was shaking, and so, taking the rope from his hand he ran with it to the other tree, unloosened the end from it, then quickly looping the rope over his hand and his elbow, as he had seen Fanny Dimple do with the clothes line over the years, he thrust it inside his coat. Grabbing the dazed boy now by the arm, he turned him about and ran him through the copse down towards the burn, then along it until they came to the cottages on the rise.

Panting, they both stopped and their eyes lifted upwards towards the end of the row where big Polly and young Polly were standing facing each other evidently arguing. But as Charlie, still hanging on to Arthur, led him up the slope the mother and daughter turned towards them, and big Polly, moving a few steps away from her daughter, cried, 'What's now? What's up?'

When the two boys reached the pathway, big Polly's hands went out towards her son and, taking him by the shoulder, she looked into his face and her voice was low in her throat as she asked, 'What is it? What's happened you?'

Arthur didn't speak but his head drooped onto his chest, and it was Charlie who said, 'Let's . . . let's go in here.' He pointed to the empty house, and one after the other they went into the dank room. It was noticeable that young Polly hadn't opened her mouth, but all the while her eyes were fixed tight on her brother.

'There . . . there's been an accident.' Charlie's mouth was so dry the words came out gritty as if they'd been dragged over sand.

'An accident? Who?'

Charlie looked at the woman who had caused his mother so much heartache all these years yet who had been as much a victim of his father as his wife had been. Everybody knew why big Polly had to serve the boss; as he had heard Arnold Dawson once laughingly say, 'She paid the rent.'

'My father, he fell from his horse.'

'Fell from his horse!' Big Polly's mouth dropped into a gape, then closed as her son began to gabble, 'I didn't mean it, Ma, I didn't mean it. I just meant to trip 'im. I . . . I thought the rope would catch him round . . . round his chest, but he came at a canter, his head down. I . . . I just wanted to break . . . to break his leg or something to stop him takin' her.' He now jerked his head towards young Polly. Then his mouth agape, he watched his mother gather the front of her blouse into her fist until her breasts looked as if they would burst through the material, and all the while her face seemed to grow larger; her mouth and eyes stretched, her nostrils dilated until it seemed as if the whole face was going to explode in a scream; then

her body slumped like a deflated bladder and she whispered, 'You mean
. . . you killed him . . . he's dead?'

When in the fear-filled silence the only answer her son gave her was the
drooping of his head she sprang on him and, gripping his shoulder, she
shook him like a rat while she screamed now, 'You maniac! You bloody
maniac you! You interferin' numskull! You'll swing, you'll swing! An' for
what? 'Cos he wanted his son broke in. 'Twasn't him. He got what he
wanted from me, you all knew that. Aye by God! an' you've let me know
it an' all over the years.' She stopped her shaking and thrust him against the
wall where he leaned looking at her like a frightened child, all his aggressiveness gone, no vestige of the bumptious youth left.

Big Polly now turned and looked at her daughter. The saliva was dripping
from one corner of her mouth, her tongue lolling in the open gap, and she
gasped as she said, 'It . . . it was for young master there you had to go down,
not the boss. I . . . I didn't tell you 'cos . . . well, oh my God!' She put her
hand to her head and rocked herself back and forward. 'What's come upon
us this day? As if I hadn't had enough all me life. But now murder. Oh my
God!' She turned to Charlie, and as if she were talking about some animal
on the farm she said to him simply, 'He wanted you broken in, and he
picked on Polly here. I . . . I didn't tell her what she had to go down to the
cottage for till the last minute, I . . . I couldn't bring meself to. And now
. . . now –' She put her arms under her flagging breasts and, turning from
him, began to walk round the small room, her pace quickening to almost a
run.

All this time Charlie hadn't once looked at Polly, he had kept his eyes
fixed on her mother. Vaguely now, he realized the torment the woman had
endured all these years at the hands of his father, for no matter in what
capacity anyone was connected with his father they would, in some way,
suffer.

His father had been the source of so much suffering, and now he was
dead. He clamped down on the feeling of intense relief, even joy, that was
straining to escape from some secret cell in his brain and envelop him, and
ordered his mind to dwell on the fact that Arthur had killed him and Arthur
would undoubtedly be hanged for it, that is if something wasn't done, and
soon.

He found himself taking the three steps to bring him face to face with big
Polly and which caused her to stop in her pacing. He had never stood so
close to her for years, and now was recalling the peculiar smell that emanated
from her, it was a mixture of sour milk and sweat. His voice sounded
surprisingly firm, even to himself, as he said, 'It . . . it was an accident.'

'Accident! Huh!'

'It could be looked upon as such . . . he fell from his horse, it . . . it must
have stumbled and . . . and the fall broke his neck.'

Her hand was again gathering up the material of her blouse. 'He broke
his neck?' The words were a whimper.

For answer he nodded his head just once; then putting his hand inside his
coat he handed her the coiled rope, saying, 'There's . . . there's no one knows
the facts except us.' His eyes flicked from one to the other; then on an instant
recalling his conversation with young Peter earlier, he put in hastily, 'There's
. . . there's Peter. It was he who told me that Arthur had taken a rope and
gone down to the copse. I . . . I think it would be wise if you talked to him.'

There was silence in the room; then big Polly said quietly, 'Aye, Master Charlie, aye, I'll talk to him. And God bless you this day.' On this she grabbed at his hand and, bringing it up to her breast, she pressed it there for a moment, still keeping her eyes on him.

He was blushing again, the heat was flushing his body like a hot drink. He looked from big Polly to Arthur who was still leaning against the wall as if he were drunk. Then his gaze flicked to young Polly whose face was expressing stark fear, and without a word he turned and left them.

On the gravel outside he stood for a moment, the latch of the door in his hand, and as he stared down towards the farm he straightened his shoulders and jerked his chin to the side. He felt strange, elated; he had gone into that room a boy and he had come out a man. He had managed a dangerous situation on his own. Big Polly had called him Master Charlie and her tone by itself had given him prestige.

He walked slowly along the row of cottages and down the slope towards the farm, and as he did so he saw the cinder path snaking away from the back of the byres down to the cottage, the cinder path on which his father had that morning flayed Ginger Slater. Well, he would flay no more, and one of the first things he himself would do would be to get rid of that path.

He stopped for a moment. Why wasn't he feeling just the slightest regret at his father's passing? Was he unnatural? Shouldn't he be feeling a little sorrow in spite of everything, for his father had loved him? No. No, his father hadn't loved him, his father had loved no one but himself. What feeling his father had had for him was founded on his desire for power and prestige, and he would have used him to this end. He mustn't feel guilt at his lack of compassion, and he could console himself that he wasn't the only one who would find himself in this state, there was his mother. . . . He must break the news to his mother. . . . What was he talking about? He wasn't to know his father was dead. If the horse made its way back to the stable, which it would likely do, someone would go out looking. Well, it wouldn't be him. No, no, he couldn't bear to look down on that figure for a second time.

Turning abruptly to the left, he now jumped the dry stone wall and made his way in the direction of the far hills. It was nothing for him to go tramping for miles; he wouldn't be missed and when he came back the hubbub would be over. But then again – he drew his step to a halt – he'd have to simulate surprise, a kind of grief, could he do it? His step was slow as he moved on. He had never been any good at acting a part. He had found that out at school. One of his masters had said he was of the stuff that made good audiences.

He had walked some miles before he reached the first hill and when he dropped down on to the dead heather he lay stretched out, his face buried in the crook of his arm. He had the desire to cry. All this had come about because his father had wanted to break him into manhood. But he knew now it would be a long, long time before that happened; and then not with Polly, never with Polly. Dear, dear Polly.

The sprigs of dry heather tickled his nose and as he went to rub it he brushed away the tears that were streaming freely from his eyes. And strangely now, he knew he wasn't crying because he had lost Polly but because his father had been deprived of life in that sudden and horrible way. If he had died in bed it wouldn't have mattered so much, perhaps not at all.

But the way he had gone it had been equivalent to him being slaughtered. He had never been able to tolerate slaughter, that's why he'd never be any good as a farmer.

His crying broke into sobs and some grazing sheep turned in surprise towards the sound. They had heard nothing like it before.

# Chapter Four

The funeral had been well attended. The privileged mourners who had returned for a meal had packed the dining-room, and the atmosphere had taken on the air of a party, helped no doubt by the lavish spread and the spirits with which most of those present kept washing it down. But as each took his farewell of the bereaved woman, his solemnity returned.

When all but the solicitor had gone, Mary MacFell, Charlie, and Betty went with him into the sitting-room. There the solicitor prepared to read the will, and much to Mary MacFell's chagrin he did not address her but looked directly towards Charlie as he said, 'I didn't draw up this will, your father deposited it with me, but it was signed and witnessed in my presence, so although it is brief and simple, everything is in order; and it reads as follows –'

He now took out his handkerchief, blew his nose and returned the handkerchief to his pocket, then began, ' "I, Edward MacFell, being of sound mind, leave entirely to my son Charles MacFell the real estate, which estate includes the farm and freehold land there attached. . . ." '

But he got no further than this for Mary MacFell almost bounced to her feet crying, '*What!* everything to Charlie? It's scandalous. It isn't right, it's . . .'

'Please, Mrs MacFell. Please wait one moment.' The solicitor held up his hand. 'Your husband didn't forget you; his wishes read as follows –' He waited for her to sit down again and then went on:

' "And to my wife, Mary MacFell, I leave one third of the monies in the bank and of that in bonds, and to be the legal guardian. . . ." '

'One third of the money?' Her voice broke in again, high and excited now.

'One third,' the solicitor repeated – ' "and the remainder to my son Charles". And that seems almost to conclude the matter. As I said, it is a very brief statement. I wish all were so simple, but nevertheless it will take some little time for the legalities to be taken care of.' He smiled weakly, then looked at the plain, tight-lipped young daughter who was staring fixedly at him, coughed, and rose to his feet. . . .

Charlie showed the solicitor to the hired cab which was waiting for him, and when he returned to the sitting-room it was to find that his mother was no longer there; but Betty was, and she was pacing the floor in much the same manner as his father had been wont to do. But when Charlie entered the room she stopped and cried at him, 'He never once mentioned me. None of you cared for him like I did, and he's left me nothing. You hated him. Yes you did; I know, I know.' She stretched her small frame upwards and wagged her finger in his face. 'Like her' – she now jerked her head towards the ceiling – 'you hated him; and you were afraid of him. I was never afraid of him. He knew that, yet' – she now shook her head slowly, bit on her lip and started her pacing again – 'not to mention me, not to leave me anything.'

'He knew you'd be taken care of.' He sat slowly down.

Swinging around, she repeated scornfully, 'Taken care of! I can take care of myself. I can see I'll have to. As for you taking care of anybody, you're too weak-kneed, and he couldn't see it. He was obsessed with the idea of making you what he wanted to be himself, a gentleman. Huh!' She pursed her lips as if about to spit. 'Well, you'll have to forget about that now, won't you, and get down to some real work, a man's work, muck work. Oh' – her lower jaw grated from one side to the other – 'if only I was in your shoes.'

'I wish you were.' Charlie had risen to his feet and he stood looking down at her as he repeated with deep bitterness, 'I wish you were.' And on this he turned from her and walked towards the door. But before reaching it he was brought to a standstill with his head jerking backwards and his eyes cast towards the ceiling, for from above there was coming the sound of high laughter. Swinging round he looked at his sister, and she, as startled as he was, gazed back at him; then they both ran from the room, across the hall, up the stairs and into their mother's bedroom.

Mary MacFell was lying in the middle of the bed; her arms were widespread and she was kicking her heels in a childlike fashion on top of the quilt.

'Mother! Mother! stop it.' Charlie had her by the shoulders. But Mary did not cease her laughing. Her mouth wide, the tip of her tongue curled downwards, her laughter rose to a higher pitch.

'Mother! Mother! give over.'

'Get by!' Charlie found himself thrust aside, and now clutching the brass rail of the bedhead he watched his small sturdy sister lift her hand and bring it in a whacking smack across her mother's face.

In hiccuping gasps the laughter died away, and they stood in deep silence for a moment until the creaking of a floor board told them that Fanny had entered the room. But they did not look towards her where she stood at the bottom of the bed staring at her mistress.

Mary, her body perfectly still now, looked from one face to the other, her expression like that of someone awakening from a deep dream. Slowly she hitched herself upwards in the bed, then leaning her head back against the rail, she looked at her daughter and said, 'It would be you who would do that, wouldn't it, Betty? Don't worry' – she made a small motion with her hand – 'I'm not going mad. Oh no, I've no intention of going mad.' She now raised her body upwards and with a quick movement of her legs, which made her daughter spring aside, she brought herself upright on to the side of the bed. And now looking at her son, she said, 'You heard what he said, Charlie, I'm to have one third. I've a right to one third. Do you know what that means to me, a right to something, something of my own, after all this time? No' – she shook her head – 'not even you, you don't understand, you couldn't understand what it means. Well, you'll see in the future because' – she now looked at her daughter again, then repeated the word, 'because

I'm going to spend, spend and spend what is mine. For the first time in years I'm going to handle money. . . . And Betty' – she bent her body forward towards the girl – 'I want you to get this into your head. That licence you took a moment ago will be the one and only time you will take the initiative from now on. As long as I'm mistress of this house, and that's what I am, mistress of this house, you will do what you're told, and by me.'

It was as if she had forgotten the presence of her son and Fanny, and strangely it was as if she were addressing a woman of her own age, not a fourteen-year-old girl, but as Charlie looked at them both he knew that his mother was not seeing a child of fourteen, she was seeing her late husband, for, just as he did himself, she realized that as long as Betty remained in this house his father would not really be dead. He also realized that a great change had come over his mother, she was a different person; he couldn't imagine her as the same woman who was continually weeping, who could go for days without uttering a word, who always walked behind her husband, never at his side; and he didn't know whether he liked the change or not.

The following morning Charlie knew that he didn't like the change in his mother and that unless he himself changed, unless he asserted himself and showed himself now, young as he was, as master, his father in some strange way had died in vain.

He looked at his mother where she stood dressed for the road in her new black clothes. They were expensive looking clothes: the three-quarter length coat was of alpaca, and the full skirt below it was of a fine woollen material with a deep mud fringe showing round the bottom. On her head she had a large black hat with a feather in it; it looked too gay for a mourning hat, in fact, her whole attire looked out of place for mourning. But then she wasn't acting as if she were in mourning. There was a lightness about her, an air of excitement, both in her attitude and in her voice. But the tone of her voice now was threaded with vindictiveness and the content of her words was amazing him. 'I'm giving them notice,' she was saying. 'The lot, out, they're going out, every single Benton; there's going to be a clean sweep here. Oh yes' – she pulled on a black silk glove, stroking each finger down to the knuckle with such force that the stitching gave way in one of the sockets.

Charlie gazed at her in amazement, his eyes narrowed as if to get a different view of her; and now she cried at him, 'Yes! you can look surprised, but that's only the beginning, there's going to be changes here.'

'You can't do this, Mother.'

'I can't? But oh, I can.'

'No! no! you mustn't.'

'Boy!' – she moved a step towards him now – 'do you know what I have suffered at that woman's hands all these years?'

Charlie closed his eyes for a moment, then he looked down towards his feet as he said, 'It wasn't her fault. You know it wasn't her fault.'

'Don't be ridiculous, boy; it takes two to form an alliance like that. She could have said no.'

'And what would have happened then?' His head had jerked up, his words were rushing out, one after the other linked as in a chain. His voice, filling the room, startled her. 'He would have done the same as you're doing now, he would have turned them out; he would have had as much compassion for them as a mad bull. Nobody should know that better than you. You suffered from him all your life, now you're going to act in the same way as he did. Well . . . no, I won't have it. Big Polly's not to blame. And Jim . . . why Jim's on his last legs, you know that and you would talk of putting them out.' He made a swift movement with his hand as if giving someone a back slap. 'Well, you'll not do it, Mother, not as long as I'm here.'

Her body was taut, her face set as if in a mould but her voice had a control about it as she said, 'Do you know who you're talking to?' But his answer nonplussed her as it came back quick and sharp: 'Yes, yes, Mother, I do know whom I'm talking to. And . . . and while we're on the subject, I would remind you –' He faltered now, swallowed deeply in his throat but after a moment went on, 'Whether you like to face it or not, Father left the farm to me. In all respects it . . . it is mine.'

Her gaze was ice cold upon him and he was already beginning to wilt under it, when she said, 'And who, may I ask, is going to run *your* farm for you when you are at school? Who is going to manage the affairs, eh? Tell me that. Mr Big Fellow all of a sudden.'

Up till this present moment he hadn't given the matter a moment's thought, he had taken it for granted he would return to school and finish his education, but in this instant he knew that his schooldays were over, and he heard himself saying so. 'I'm going to manage it myself.'

'You're going to *what*?'

'You heard what I said, Mother. I'm going to manage the farm.'

'Huh! Don't be an idiot, boy. You manage the farm! You don't know the first thing about the farm. You might have been born and bred on the place, but you've shown a distaste for it all your days.'

Perhaps it was the scorn in her voice that gave him the courage to come back, in a voice as loud as her own, 'Perhaps the distaste wasn't so much for the farm as for the man who was running it; but . . . but now I mean to manage my farm, Mother. And I don't want to keep repeating it, but it is my farm, and what I don't know I'll learn. Arnold and Fred will help me. . . .'

'Arnold and Fred!' Her lip curled upwards. 'They were Dawson and Ryton in your father's time.'

'Well, that being the case, Mother, and knowing that you never approved of anything Father did, I should have thought you would have welcomed the men being called by their Christian names. Anyway, I've always known them as Arnold and Fred; and as I said, I'm sure they'll help me in that part of my education which has been lacking.'

'Oh dear God!' She looked upwards. 'Even your phraseology is wrong. They'll laugh at you, boy, they'll take advantage of you. They'd take much more notice of Betty out there than they would of you.'

The gibe triggered off the distressing feeling of embarrassment and this in turn brought the colour flooding up to his face. She was right, they would take more notice of Betty; he wasn't cut out to be a farmer. He had always known that, yet here he was assuming the position of master, and he'd make a laughing-stock of himself. But what else could he have done, for he knew that, even though his presence in the house might deter her from carrying out her threat, the minute he returned to school she would throw the Bentons out.

Strange, but the Bentons were like the hand of fate directing his life.

'Mother, the trap's ready.' Betty appeared in the doorway. She, too, was dressed for the town.

As she slowly drew on her other glove, Mary MacFell looked towards her daughter and said, 'I'm sure you will be pleased to know, Betty, that your brother is going to run the farm. He feels he must be master in word as well as in deed.'

'Run the . . . run the farm? *You!* . . . You're not going back to school then?'

Charlie looked down on his young sister who, like his father, had always possessed the power to intimidate him, but now he stared straight into her small round dark brown eyes as he said, 'No, I'm not going back to school, Betty; as Mother has said I am going to run the farm, and I am going to start this very day . . . now, and I'd like you to keep it in mind, Betty.'

For once Betty had no ready retort. She looked from her brother, whom she had never made any secret of despising, to her mother, whom she disliked intensely, and there was a note of utter disbelief in her voice when she eventually said, 'And you're going to let him?'

Mary MacFell walked across the room until she was facing her daughter, and then she answered her. 'Apparently I've very little option, but what he forgets is that I'm his legal guardian and I could put spokes in his wheel, but however I'm not going to!' Turning her head on her shoulder, she now glared at her son and she spat her words at him as she said. 'But now I'll point out to you, Charlie, that there are more ways of killing a cat than drowning it, and you'll find this out before you're finished. Let your wretched Bentons stay and we'll see . . . we'll see. Come, Betty.' And on this she went from the room and into the hall. She did not, however, turn and go through the kitchen and so to the yard where the trap stood waiting, but she went out of the front door and on to the gravel drive; and there without turning her head she said to Betty, 'Tell them to bring it round'. . . .

A few minutes later Fanny, with Maggie Benton standing behind her, watched from the end of the yard the trap jogging its way down the drive and on to the bridle path, and turning and looking at Maggie, she said, 'God Almighty! would you believe it? I always said I'd dance on his grave when he went but the old sayin's proving truer than ever, 'tis better to work for the devil you know than the devil you don't know! for who would have thought it, the quiet body that she's been all these years turning out to be as snarly as a ferret. The idea! to turn you all out on to the road. My God! she would have done it an' all if it hadn't been for young Charlie. I couldn't believe my ears, I just couldn't, but he stood up to her. Aye, by God! he did that. I never thought he had it in him. Soft, I thought he was, with book-learning. The things you live to see.' Fanny shook her head dolefully, then added, 'Ah well, let's get in and get some work done. But if I know owt we're going to see changes here, lass. I only hope he has the gumption to stick to his guns and stand up for himself as he did back there, otherwise . . . well, God knows.'

When they reached the kitchen door they both self-consciously stood aside to allow Charlie to enter the yard, and he turned to Fanny and asked, 'Where would Fred be this morning, Fanny?'

'Fred? Oh well, I saw him go early on with Bett and Floss, so that means he's bringin' the sheep down into the lower pen – there's some for market next week – so about now he should be up at Top Loam. Do you want him?'

'Yes, yes; I'd like to have a word with him, Fanny.'

'Then off you go, Maggie.' She turned to the girl standing wide-eyed to the side of the kitchen door. 'Take to your legs and tell Fred the master wants him. Just say that! the master wants him.' On this she turned and nodded deeply at Charlie, and her words and her action infused strength into him and he smiled at her and said softly, 'Thanks, Fanny.'

'You're welcome.'

He was about to turn away when she put her hand out and lightly touched his sleeve, saying, 'If there's any way I can be of help you've only got to ask; I'm old in me head as well as in me body.'

He said again, 'Thanks, Fanny.' He did not ask himself how she knew about the present situation, she had ears and was soft-footed for all her years.

In the doorway of the byres he looked at Arnold Dawson, who was brushing the muck through the trough that bordered the line of stalls, and he called to him, saying, 'Would you come to the barn in ten minutes, Arnold? I'd ... I'd like to have a word with you.'

Arnold Dawson leant on the head of his brush for a moment and stared at Charlie, and then he said, 'Yes, aye, yes, Mister Charlie, I'll be there. In ten minutes you say?'

'Yes, Arnold.'

'I'll be there.'

As he crossed the yard towards the barn Ginger Slater came out from the horse-room. The boy stopped and looked at him. His expression was no longer a frightened one, his hangdog air had gone; in fact there was a cockiness about him. But Charlie did not notice the change in the boy, and he said to him, 'Find Arthur and come to the barn, I ... I want to have a word with you.'

Ginger didn't say, 'Yes, master', or 'Yes, Mister Charlie', but he turned away and went through the passage that led to the cinder path. . . .

It was a quarter of an hour later when the two men and the two boys assembled in the barn. They stood in a rough half-cirlce and looked at their mistress's son, for in each of their minds it was the mistress who was the boss now. And Charlie, vitally aware of this, asked himself how he was to begin? The idea born of the unusual outburst of anger his mother had evoked had seemed good, easy. He would talk to the hands, to tell them that he was now master and ask for their help. But here they were standing staring at him, two men older than his father had been, and Arthur and Ginger only a year younger than himself yet years older in experience. He'd have to say something, start somewhere. But how?

'You wanted to have a word with us, Mister Charlie?' Fred Ryton's voice was kindly.

'Yes. Yes, Fred.' Thankfully he turned to the shepherd and, his tongue loosened now, he went on hastily, almost gabbling, 'I ... I just want to say that I'm not returning to school, I ... I intend to work the farm myself, that is' – his eyes swept the four of them now – 'with your help.' He gave a shaky laugh. 'I know I'll need help for ... as I said to you, Fred, during my last holiday, at the calfing, you remember? I said I didn't think I was cut out for a farmer. And you agreed with me then. But now –' He straightened his slumped shoulders, rubbed his hand tightly over his chin on which the bristles were few and far between, then ended, 'Well, I mean to have a shot at it.'

There was what seemed to Charlie an endless silence before the cowman spoke.

'You'll find it different from book-learning, lad.'

Charlie brought his eyes to those of Arnold Dawson and his reply was surprisingly curt now. 'I'm aware of that, Arnold, but my education, what little I've had, won't, I hope, be a drawback to me managing my own affairs.'

They all stared at him blankly now. This wasn't the gangling young lad they all knew, the lad who couldn't bear to see a cow heaving in labour and didn't appreciate that she would be well recompensed with the first lick of her calf; the lad who had been known to release a rabbit from a trap when it was caught only by the foot; the lad who stood mooning on the hills looking into the distance like some loony, or walked out before dawn to see the sun rise, and came back sodden wet with dew, which landed him in bed for a week. At different times over the years they had had cause to think he was a bit funny in the head the things he did, but the young fellow talking to them now didn't sound like someone funny in the head. It could have been his father speaking, that is if ever his father had spoken civilly to a human being.

Arnold and Fred almost spoke together; then Fred, giving way to the older man, waited while Arnold Dawson said his piece. It was short and to the point. 'Speaking for meself,' he said; 'I'll work as I have always done, fair's fair, I'll earn me wage; apart from that if I can help you you've only got to ask, lad.'

'The same goes for me,' Fred Ryton was nodding at him now. 'But all I can say is you can't learn farmin' from books.'

He should have been satisfied with their response but he felt they still saw him as the boy, the master's son who was destined to be a country gentleman. He now turned his eyes towards Arthur, and Arthur gulped in his throat, jerked his head to the side and what he said was, 'You know me.'

Next, he looked at Ginger Slater and the boy's answer surprised them all, for what he said was, 'Well, me, I never had much choice, had I?'

His answer was understandable yet puzzling, because Ginger had never been known to stand up to anybody in all the years he had been on the farm.

The other three were still looking at him when Charlie said, 'Well, that's settled then. We'll go on from here . . . a day at a time.'

'Aye, a day at a time, you can't take it much slower.' This came from Arnold Dawson as he made for the barn doorway, and the rest followed, leaving him standing alone, and feeling alone, more alone than he had ever been in his life. They weren't for him, not really; they didn't want him as boss.

It was odd – he shook his head and gave a small rueful smile – they would sooner have continued to work under his father, who had paid them barely a living wage, and who, had they asked him for a penny rise, would have thrown them out.

He felt tired, weary, sort of sick in the pit of his stomach. He went to lower himself down on to a bale of hay. His back bent, his buttocks almost touching the hay, he stopped and straightening himself abruptly, muttered aloud, 'I'll have to show them, won't I? I'll just have to show them that I'm me father's son, that they're not going to get away with anything, and that they've got to recognize me as master.' Not one of them had given him the title. Well then, he'd have to earn it, wouldn't he? He'd have to be firm, harden himself; if only outwardly, to make himself a replica of his father. The thought indeed of stiffening his fibre, brought his shoulders hunched and his head hanging forward as he walked slowly from the barn. . . .

Yet it was less than an hour later when he knew to his great relief that there would be no need to alter himself for the men's attitude towards him changed completely. Both, within a short time of each other, addressed him as sir, and there was in their manner the acceptance of him as their master. It was Fred Ryton who came to him first, 'Can I have a word with you, sir? It's about the sale over at Bellingham come next week. It would be educational like, in a different sort of way' – he gave a hic of a laugh – 'if you come along of me, showed yoursel' like an' got to know the ropes.'

Charlie smiled at the man as he answered, 'Thank you, Fred; I'd be glad to.' And when Fred put his forefinger to his eyebrow that just showed beneath the peak of his cap it was, Charlie recognized, a definite sign of acceptance.

Arnold Dawson approached him next, saying, 'About Hodgson's bull, sir. I don't know if your father clinched the deal or not, but if it's to your likin' I'd go over along of you when you're ready an' look at the beast. Hodgson's a tight man 'cos he needs the money so he'll take you for every penny he can get out of you.'

'Good. . . . Good enough, Arnold.' He blinked, gulped in his throat, then added, 'I'll try to make it one day this week.' His shoulders were back again, his head up; his manner was matching theirs.

'Right, sir. Right.' Arnold, too, put his finger to his eyebrow.

Then there was Arthur. They came face to face as Arthur was leading a horse across the yard. His approach was different: he stared at him for a moment before muttering, 'It'll take us all to die afore we get out of your debt.'

So that was it. The change in their manner, it was because he had stopped his mother from evicting the Bentons. They had, he surmised, considered he must have guts of some sort to stand up to his mother, whose silence all these years had been formidable in its own way.

He gave no response whatever to Arthur's words, there was no need to: their lives were bound together by the secret they shared.

He walked on now towards the space between the brick walls that formed the entrance to the farm proper thinking as he did so that there was only Ginger who hadn't approached him. But then in a way Ginger didn't matter, his opinion would carry no weight. Yet he had always been sorry for the workhouse boy, and had shown it. There was, he decided, one thing he could do for him now, he could give him books to read. As to his attitude towards himself, well, that was of no account. What did matter was the attitude of the men, and it seemed that they had accepted him wholeheartedly.

Many years later when he was to recall that morning and his summing up of the response of his few workers towards him and of how utterly wrong he had been in his evaluation of Ginger Slater, he was to tell himself he couldn't have known that before noon of that particular day as recognized master of the farm he was to be given evidence of things to come; but even then he wouldn't realize the full consequences of the power that lay in the hands of the undersized ginger-headed lad.

He stood now between the walls and looked over the rough road to where the cows were grazing in the long meadow that sloped towards the burn. What should he do?

What had his father done at this time of the day?

He had walked his land . . . with a walking-stick in his hand.

Well, that's what he would do now, he'd walk his land. Tomorrow he'd have the aid of a walking-stick too, but today he'd just walk. . . .

He set off, his arms swinging in unison with his long thin legs, and his chin was high as he turned his head from one side to the other and looked over the landscape; and as he walked he told himself that this was his farm, his land, and he was master of it. Yet before he had covered half the perimeter his step had slowed, his shoulders were slumped, his chin was in its usual position, and he was asking himself why it was he could love the hills and the countryside so much, yet could not, even mildly, be stirred by the knowledge that he was walking on his own ground.

He stopped and looked away towards the hills and he had the childish desire to take to his heels and run, run to them, over them, then all the way to Carter Bar and into Scotland. No, not into Scotland. He swung round and faced the other way. If he was going to run he'd run to Newcastle and there board a boat that would take him to Norway, Sweden, Denmark, and on to Germany and Poland, on, on, on. . . .

But he couldn't run, he couldn't sail away, for, to use the old phrase, he had burnt his boats. Because of the Bentons he had lost the chance to see the world and, what was more important at the moment, the chance of further education. And further education to him meant literature, reading, travelling, seeing.

Well – he began to walk again – he could still read literature, couldn't he? There was nothing to stop him reading. Only the atmosphere of the house; the farm house wasn't conducive to reading, never had been, there was no restful corner in it.

The sun went in, the sky from being high above the hills seemed now to be settling on them; the mist came from nowhere suddenly. A pale grey curtain, it seemed to rise and fall like a mighty kite. As it enveloped him he shivered and, turning quickly as if he were being pursued, he made his way back to the farm.

It was as he neared the gateway that he caught sight of Polly standing talking to Ginger. He could discern their mist-wreathed faces turned towards him, but before he reached them Ginger Slater had gone through the opening into the yard.

As he came abreast of Polly, he thought that the paleness of her face was caused by the drifting mist, until he saw the look in her eyes. It was the same look that had been there when she had stood speechless in the empty house a little over a week ago.

'Are you all right?'

Polly looked back into his face and, her voice thick as if the very mist were clogging her throat, she said, 'No; no, I'm not, Charlie. Not at this minute I'm not. Do . . . do you know what he's just said?'

'Ginger?'

'Aye, Ginger. He . . . he came on me as I passed, an' he said I've . . . I've got to tell our Arthur to go easy on him. He *knows* . . . he knows, Charlie.'

'Knows what?'

'What Arthur did with the rope.'

'No! *No!* Oh, no!'

'Aye. Aye, he saw it all; you helpin' . . . everything. He said he's not out to cause trouble but our Arthur's got to stop bullyin' him.'

They were standing within a foot of each other; he was looking down at her and she up at him; their breaths were mingling with the mist; then simultaneously, as if both seeking protection, they stepped to the side and close to the wall, and there was no vestige of the young master about him now, for his tone was rather that of a frightened lad as he said, 'Do you think he'll say anything?'

'I don't know.' Her voice was a thin whisper. 'He says he won't. And anyway I can't see what good it'd do him if he did. But you never know with workhouse lads, you don't know where they come from; I mean you've got nothin' to go on when you don't know their mothers or fathers, have you?'

Charlie turned from her and leant his back flat against the wall, and putting his thumb to his mouth be bit hard on his nail. He had been in the habit of biting his nails a lot at one time, but since starting the school in Newcastle the habit had slowly disappeared. More to himself than to her now, he said, 'He could cause trouble, big trouble.'

'Aye . . . aye, he could; we'd . . . we'd better keep on the right side of him.'

'Yes.' He turned and nodded to her; and as she stared up at him she said quietly, 'You shouldn't be in this, you've got yourself mixed up in all ways with us. Now you're up against your mother through us. I . . . I don't know what to say, Charlie, how to thank you.'

He pulled himself from the wall. 'I don't want any thanks.'

Again they were facing each other.

'If . . . if ever I can do anythin' for you, you've only got to ask, Charlie.'

Her eyes were round, mist-filled, and now she gripped his hand and whispered urgently, 'I mean it. You understand? I mean it, anything.'

'Yes, yes, Polly, thank you. Yes, I understand.' He withdrew himself from her hold, then backed two steps away from her. And he was nodding at her again as he said, 'I'll have a word with Arthur; I'll tell him.'

As he went into the yard he knew she hadn't moved away. He also knew what she was offering him by way of thanks. He knew too that he wanted to accept her thanks – Oh yes, he wanted to accept her thanks – but he never would.

*Why? Yes, why?*

The answer came with the picture of his father taking her mother.

It was ten mintues later when he told Arthur of the new situation that had cropped up, and he watched him as he flopped down on an upturned bucket in the pig-room and thumped one fist against the other as he groaned, 'God Almighty! he's got me in the hollow of his hand. If he opens his mouth I'll go along the line . . . or worse; aye, or worse. The bloody hungry-looking workhouse brat that he is!' Then turning his head to the side, he gazed up at Charlie as he ended, 'An' he's got you there an' all. And that ain't fair. No, that ain't fair.'

Looking back at Arthur, he experienced a feeling of revulsion. Arthur had always appeared to him as fearless, rugged, tough; in a way he had hero-worshipped him for these qualities; but now there was an abjectness about him that was distasteful. His saying 'He's got you there an' all; it ain't fair' didn't ring with true concern, it was more of a statement, 'We're all in this together.' He turned abruptly away, saying, 'Don't worry about me; only go lightly on him for your own good.'

Out in the yard, with the mist almost obliterating the house from his view, he walked towards the kitchen door. He had said 'Don't worry about me' as if he weren't troubled by the fact that young Slater knew of his part in the awful event; but deep inside he was more than worried, he was fearful, for in a way he was as much involved as was Arthur. There was such a thing termed accessory after the fact, and for his part in the affair he would be condemned more so than Arthur, for what had he done but shield the person who had killed his father, whereas as a dutiful son he should have brought him to justice.

The mist bathing his face was mingled with sweat now.

When he opened the kitchen door he actually gulped audibly as he saw young Slater sitting by the table, a mug of tea in one hand and a large shive of bread in the other.

As the boy slithered to his feet Fanny put in quickly, 'Just giving him a bite, Mister Charlie, just a bite.'

Charlie looked from the round penetrating gaze of Sidney Slater to Fanny, then to Maggie who was standing behind her, a toasting fork in her hand and on which was stuck a slice of bread, and he knew that how he reacted now with this boy would set the pattern for future time. Fumbling in his breast pocket, he drew out the watch that his father had given him on his sixteenth birthday, and he made himself stare at it for a moment before taking his eyes from it and fixing them on Slater, then saying, 'It's quarter past eleven in the morning, you have your breakfast at eight and your dinner at one, isn't that so?'

The round eyes looking back into his had a slightly puzzled expression, and Slater's voice faltered slightly as he said, 'Aye . . . aye.'

'Aye what?'

There was a pause in which he heard Fanny's intake of breath.

'Aye, sir . . . Mister Charlie.'

'Well, in future you'll stick to your mealtimes. That understood?'

'Aye, Mister Charlie.'

'Good. Well you may finish that.' He waved his hand towards the mug and the bread on the table; then giving a lift of his shoulders he walked away, up the kitchen and through the green-baized door.

It was actually seconds after the door had closed on him that Fanny spoke. She had one cheek cupped in the palm of her hand as she did do. 'I can't believe it,' she said. 'What's come over him? He was as like the one who's gone as ever I've seen, yet this very mornin' he stood up to the missis and saved the Bentons.' She shook her head. 'I can't believe it. I just can't believe it.'

'I can.' Sidney Slater had lifted the latch of the door, and he turned and looked over his shoulder, adding, 'But don't you worry none about me, Mrs Dimple. Don't you worry none about me.'

Fanny moved towards him now, saying, 'Come back, Sidney, and finish your bite.' She motioned towards the table, but he shook his head, saying, 'No, no. Ta all the same. I tell you what though.' He was actually grinning at her now. 'You give it to him, he'll likely need it long afore I will.'

When the door closed on him Fanny turned and stared at Maggie and, her hand again cupping her cheek, she said, 'I can't believe it. I just can't believe it. There's somethin' here I don't understand: Mister Charlie takin' on the guise of his father, an' Sidney there not frightened any more. Did you see the look on that lad's face? It was strange, it was as if he feared neither God nor man any more. You know somethin' Maggie? An' you might think me barmy for sayin' this, but he looked the same as the master used to after he'd lathered one or t'other on the cinder path, like as if he had satisfied something inside himself. 'Twas an unholy look.'

# Chapter One

## Brooklands Farm

'Why you must have your birthday party between Christmas and New Year the Lord only knows.'

'. . . Not forgetting Mother and Father; they should have arranged my coming at a different time, they were very careless about their indulging.'

'Nellie! stop that kind of facetious chatter. If Father were to hear you, he'd skelp your ears for you.'

'Yes, I suppose he would. Yet Mother wouldn't. Strange that, isn't it?'

Nellie Chapman brought her legs up and tucked them under her where she was squatting on the side of the bed, and putting her head on one side, she gazed at her sister who was sitting before the mirror turning the long strands of her hair into a plait, and she said, 'You know you are just like Father, coarse as a pig's back in one way yet finicky refined in another.'

'Don't you dare say I'm as coarse as a pig's back!' Victoria twisted round on the dressing-table stool, her squarish handsome face flushed with irritation, which increased as her sister smiled at her and undauntedly went on, 'Well, you are. You know you are. All you think about is horses. You ride horses, you talk horses, you swear horses. You outdid Father yesterday when you were buggering Phil for not seeing to Laddy right away. It didn't matter about the other two horses, they could sweat themselves to death, but Laddy must be seen to. And your language was such that it even pushed up old Benny's eyebrows.'

'That's a different thing, that's got nothing to do with talk about . . . birth. I mean. . . .' Victoria now twisted the end of the plait into a knot and was about to wind it tightly round the back of her head when her sister said, 'What you mean is cohabiting.'

'Nellie Chapman, get off that bed, and get out of my room! Go on, get out this minute!'

'All right, all right, I'll go. But that's what the books call it, and it proves what I said about you and Father. You know what?' She now leant her plump body towards her tall well-proportioned sister and she said, 'I'm always amazed by this stuffy attitude of yours, I really can't understand it. You're a hypocrite, you know that; even the Bible can speak plainly about it, procreation it calls it. And it's going on around us almost twenty-four hours a day. But here you are on the point of collapse because I mention it. But' – she gave an exaggerated sigh – 'it's as I said, you and Father are fakes because underneath you're worse than big Billy for it, and you know you are. . . .'

As Victoria swung round to the dressing-table, her hand groping for something to throw, Nellie sprang to the door, opened it and, bent almost double, was scrambling on to the landing when a large china powder bowl, parting from its lid, whizzed over her head and struck the wall opposite and shattered into pieces.

'In the name of God! what's this?' Florence Chapman took the last three stairs at a run. Then stopping dead, she gazed from one to the other of her daughters, then at the broken china bowl that had left a trail of pink powder across the red patterned carpet, and now her angry gaze resting on Victoria, she cried, 'Have you gone mad? You could have knocked her out with that.'

'It's a pity I didn't; I won't miss next time if she dares to put a foot in my room.'

The bedroom door banged and Florence turned her attention to her younger daughter. For a moment she kept her teeth together and her lips spread wide from them while her head moved in small nods; then she said, 'And what did you do to bring this about?'

'Nothing; we were just talking.'

'*Talking!*' Florence now rushed forward and, grabbing Nellie by the shoulders, she pushed her along the landing and into the end room, and there she demanded, 'Out with it! It must have been something stronger than usual for her to throw a thing like that at you, for if it had hit you it could have split your head open. Come on now, what did you say?'

'Well, nothing really.' Nellie shrugged, then grimaced before she said, 'She was getting at me about my birthday party tomorrow. It was the same last year. She said she didn't see why I couldn't make it one do with the New Year's Eve party. But that wouldn't be my birthday party, would it?'

'No. I can see your point there; but, come on, that isn't what enraged her. What did you really say to her to upset her like that?'

'Aw.' Nellie walked down the length of the large bedroom towards the window; then resting her knee on the padded window-seat she looked out on to the white snow-covered garden and beyond to where the furrowed fields lay, showing crests of straight black earth like ruled lines on children's primers, and she muttered, 'I said she took after father and they both took after big Billy.'

Florence Chapman's large unlined handsome face remained perfectly blank for a moment; then her eyes seeming to take their direction from her mouth stretched wide, but she spoke no word until, having closed her mouth again and taken in a deep breath through her dilated nostrils, she exclaimed, 'You said what!'

'Aw, Mother!' Nellie turned round and sat down on the window seat. 'Don't look so shocked because you know you're not. And anyway, you know what I say's true. Look how she eggs on Josh Pringle. And she's got Archie Whitaker slobbering. I've seen her and Archie behind . . .'

'Nellie! be quiet! Now you listen to me.' Florence approached her daughter and, sitting down beside her, she wagged her finger in her face as she went on, 'Josh and Archie have merely been friends, and you know it. . . .'

'I don't, Mother, I don't know it' – Nellie's face was straight now, her tone harsh – 'because if I were to get up to some of the things that I've seen her and Archie at and I told you it was all in friendship, by!' – she now turned her head to the side, nodding it as she did so – 'I know what you'd say. . . . Lord! don't I!'

Florence Chapman turned her face away from her daughter for a moment and held her brow in the palm of her hand. What was she to do with this girl, this terror of a daughter, this honest individual . . . this her beloved child, for of her two daughters she had love for only one. It was true what Nellie had said, Victoria was very much like her father, talking one way and acting another. Not that she didn't care for Victoria, she did, as she cared for her husband, but she recognized the faults in both of them. Especially did she recognize those in her husband. But going on the premise that no one was perfect, she had for years condoned all his little sharp practices, and the last thing she would have ever thought of doing was to point out his faults to him. But not so Nellie. Nellie was sackcloth on the skin of both her father and her sister, although strangely that wasn't her intention.

Nellie's intention, she knew, was just to present her idea of things and people as they appeared to her. Ever since she had passed the lisping stage she had gone to great pains to express herself fully on all manner of subjects. Having been placed in the most embarrassing situations by their daughter's frankness when in company she and her husband had learned it was wiser to keep their opinions of their neighbours to themselves, at least until they were in the privacy of their bedroom.

That her daughter had of late learned a little discretion, at least with regard to outsiders, was very small comfort, for hardly a day went past but she irritated her father or infuriated her sister, while at the same time, Florence had to admit guiltily, affording herself not a little amusement. And the funny thing about it all was that Nellie's verbal attacks always held more than a smattering of truth, as in her latest statement that her husband and daughter took after the bull, for, as in her father, so there was raging in Victoria deep physical passion, which could only be really assuaged by marriage. . . . At least she kept hoping so.

She was in a way worried about Victoria. She wished this business between young Charlie MacFell and her could be settled. Her father was bent on it, had been for years, and Victoria herself didn't seem all that averse. But what about Charlie?

He was an odd fellow was Charlie, not like a farmer at all; took after his mother really. . . . Yet no; that woman was a silly bitch if ever there was one, stacking the house with her fancy furniture and dressing like a girl half her age. That place would soon go to rack and ruin if it wasn't for young Betty. She should have been the man, should Betty. Yes, she should have been the man; there was too much of the woman in Charlie. Not that he wasn't manly. In his own fleshless long-boned way he was an attractive young fellow. But gutless. Aye, that was the word, gutless.

Charlie needed someone strong, someone to guide him; and Victoria would be the right one in the right place there. It was a pity he was two years younger than her, it made things a little more difficult. But it was a difficulty that must be overcome if she wanted life with Hal to be bearable.

Her husband had a bee in his bonnet about merging the lands. If the positions of the farm had been altered and most of their land had been freehold, like Moor Burn was, then Hal might have taken a different view of the marriage. Oh yes, he undoubtedly would have.

It was funny how land got hold of men. Her husband, almost twenty years her senior, was turned sixty. In the order of things he hadn't all that time to enjoy the acquisition of more land, yet she knew it wasn't only of himself he was thinking but of his grandchildren. He wanted grandchildren, male grandchildren, in whom he could live on, walk in their steps as it were over the land, following the seasons from spring dawns to the mist-shrouded setting suns of winter. Men like her husband wanted to perpetuate themselves for ever. It was when they saw no prospect of this happening they would tend to make life pretty uncomfortable, to say the least, for those around them.

For herself, she didn't like to live uncomfortably: she enjoyed good food, good wine, she liked a soft bed and a warm house; she liked to dress well, according to her station, and have enough spare cash over from the house-keeping and dairy not to have to beg for coppers. She had a good life, an enjoyable life, and she wanted this to go on, so she turned to her daughter now and, her voice low and harsh, she said, 'That was a nasty crude thing to say; but we'll forget about it and we'll talk of tomorrow and your party. Now you want your party to go off well, don't you, Nellie?'

Nellie stared back at her mother but made no reply, and Florence, straightening her broad shoulders, drew in a deep breath and went on, 'Well, it's going to be up to you, because if you get your father's back up – and Victoria's – this will be your final birthday party. Now I mean that, Nellie. There'll be a lot of people here tomorrow, not only your friends but your father's and mine . . . and Victoria's, and I want us all to enjoy ourselves.'

'As it's my party why can't I have just my friends?'

'Well, one reason that should be evident to you is that your friends have all got to be driven here, and you can't leave their parents or their brothers standing on the doorstep . . . now can you?'

They looked at each other for a moment before Nellie said, 'I suppose Betty won't be able to ride over by herself, Charlie will have to bring her?'

'Yes, Nellie.' Florence's words were weighty now. 'Charlie will be bringing Betty . . . and her mother.'

'Oh, that'll be nice, if not for Charlie, for Dad I mean.'

'Nellie!' Florence now ground her teeth. 'There are times when I could skelp you hard.'

'For speaking the truth, Mother? It's under everybody's nose.'

Nellie now rose sharply from the window-seat and, making for the door, she said,'Poor Charlie; she'll eat him alive. He won't know which horse has kicked him by the time she's finished with him. It's like throwing a Christian to the lions.'

Before she had time to turn the knob of the door her mother had her by the shoulders again and, swinging her about, she hissed at her, 'Nellie Chapman! now I'm warning you, you say one word to spoil things for Victoria tomorrow and I'll never forgive you.'

Nellie gazed back at her mother, sighed a deep sigh and said, 'All right. All right, keep your hair on. But you can't stop me feeling sorry for Charlie.'

On the landing Nellie paused a moment and looked towards Polly Benton who was on her knees sweeping up the powder from the carpet and there passed between them an exchange of glances expressing mutual understanding.

# Chapter Two

The birthday party was going with a swing, it had been going with a swing for the past three hours. The guests had sat down at five o'clock to a high tea and it was well past six before they rose from the table. In the sitting-room they chatted and talked for a time and teased Nellie the while she, as usual, gave back more than she received. Then Florence was persuaded to sit at the piano, and from then the party got under way. They danced the polka; they waltzed; they jigged; there were enough couples to form three sets of lancers, and sufficient of the older ones present to clap and applaud from their seats which had been pushed against the wall in order to clear the floor.

By ten o'clock a deal of wine and spirits had been imbibed and the quantity was beginning to tell on some of the guests, as was evident when the sound of their hoots and laughter reached the kitchen.

Lindy Morton, piling the plates of sandwiches and mince pies on to the tray that Polly was holding, giggled as she said, 'It's like New Year's Eve afore its time in there, isn't it? By! they're goin' at it an' by the look of him the master's nearly blotto, an' the missis isn't far off either. An' your Charlie's knockin' it back an' all.'

'Don't call him my Charlie, Lindy; I've told you that afore.'

'Well, you're always talkin' about him.'

'Not in that way. And if the missis heard you, what do you think she'd say?'

'Aw, she'd just laugh. Well, she would about somebody in your position havin' a shine on someone like Mister Charlie. All right! All right! Look, you'll upset the tray. . . . I'm sorry; I was only havin' you on.'

'Well, don't have me on about that.' Polly bounced her head at her work-mate; then swinging abruptly about she went up the kitchen and, turning her back to the door, thrust at it with her buttocks, then edged herself around it and into the broad passage. Using the same procedure with the door at the far end of the passage, she emerged into the hall and although, while crossing it, she kept her eyes averted from where Miss Betty was sitting on the bottom stair by the side of Mr Robin Wetherby, she did note that they both had their heads down and that their shoulders were shaking with laughter, and she remarked to herself that Miss Betty must have had a drop an' all if she was letting herself go on a laugh.

She ignored a second couple standing against the wall in the passage bordering the side of the staircase. They weren't so close together but their shoulders were resting against the panelling as they gazed at each other and this conveyed to her a sense of intimacy, as close as if they had been in each other's arms.

At first she couldn't make her way into the sitting-room because there was a jig in process. Miss Victoria was doing a kind of highland fling opposite Mr Whitaker. They were twirling and hooting to the beat of the clapping, which was almost drowning the music of the piano.

Her arms were breaking with the weight of the tray, but she moved her head back and forward between the shoulders in front of her to get a better view, and as she stared wide-eyed at the two dancing figures, her thoughts ran along the same lines as Nellie's had done yesterday: She's like a wild horse, she'll trample him to death.

Her eyes left the dancers now and searched the room, as much as she could see of it; and then she saw him in the corner of her vision. She could see only his head and his hands; he was laughing and was clapping as loudly as the rest.

There was a final great whoop of sound; the dancing stopped and the clapping faded away; but she had to repeat a number of times, 'Excuse me. Excuse me, please,' before those in the doorway parted to allow her through to the table that had been cleared at the end of the room.

As she put the full plates on the table and picked up the empty ones, the laughter and voices beat down on her and she said to herself, 'It isn't fair; it's Miss Nellie's birthday party but they're making it more like a rowdy New Year's do.'

This was the third Christmas she had been here, having taken up the post almost immediately after her father had died, but in all the parties they had had she had never seen so much drink flowing as there was tonight; nor so much – she hesitated on the word – jollification. And anyway, it wasn't like a jollification; well, not a jollification people of the Chapmans' standard were known to indulge in, it was more approaching something she imagined one would see in the Wayfarers' Inn on the high road, where the drovers got together after a big market and things went on, so she had heard, that would sizzle your eyebrows.

As she stretched over to retrieve an empty plate, she glanced to where Mrs MacFell was sitting, and she gave a small shake of her head. She got worse as she got older. Dressed to kill. Her frock would have suited someone half her age. They said she was on the look-out for a man. Well, if nothing else, her get-up would make her fall between two stools, for to a young man she would look like mutton dressed up as lamb, while to a farmer who wanted a working wife she'd look like a giddy-headed goat. Mr Chapman said that she had gone back twenty years to when she first came to the farm as a young scatter-brained lass, and that was what she was acting now. Her head was back, her mouth was wide open and her hands were flapping at Farmer Kelly.

As she wended her way out of the room, Polly's eyes again searched for Charlie. She must have a word with him, she must; but the only hope she'd have of waylaying him would be when he went to the men's closet outside. And so from now on she'd keep on the watch because surely they'd want nothing more to eat, not for a while anyway; she'd carried four tray-loads of food in there in the past half hour.

She had heard the boss say that you could drink your fill to overflowing as long as you ate with it, and he was certainly seeing that everybody did that night. The stuff he had hauled up from the cellar was nobody's business; he had even brought up bottles that were twenty years old, the ones he usually bragged about.

She paused for a moment between the doors. It wasn't like a birthday party at all, it was as if he was celebrating something . . . aye, or hoping to celebrate something. She turned about on a gasp as a hand caught her arm.

'Hello there, Polly.'

'Oh!' She now took in a short, sharp breath, smiled, then said again, 'Oh! . . . hello, Charlie.'

'I've been wanting to get a word with you, I've never seen you over the holidays. I wanted to say Happy Christmas.'

'Oh, thanks, thanks, Charlie an' the same to you.'

In the lamplit passage they smiled at each other. Then her face suddenly becoming straight, she whispered rapidly, 'And I . . . I want to have a word with you, Charlie. Can I see you, I mean outside like, for a minute or so? It's important, Charlie. I'll . . . I'll go over to the dairy in . . . in ten minutes or so, an' I'll wait. It's important.'

There was a burst of laughter beyond the passage door, then it was pushed wide and Nellie entered, accompanied by two laughing girls about her own age. She paused a moment to look at Polly disappearing into the kitchen; then laughing, she came towards Charlie, saying, 'There you are, boyo! And what are you up to, eh? What are you up to?' She lifted her hand and tickled him under the chin, and he caught her wrist and, laughing down at her, answered, 'Looking for you.'

'Liar! Isn't he a liar?' She turned to her companions, and they laughed and said, 'Yes, yes, you are, Charlie MacFell, you're a liar.'

Charlie looked from one to the other of the laughing faces. They were flushed, their eyes were bright. He had the desire to kiss one after the other, just in fun, that was all, just in fun. The wine that was making their faces bloom like roses before his eyes was also making him feel gay enough to sip the dew from them, so he told himself. He had drunk more tonight than he had ever done in his life before; he had never known Chapman to be so generous with his cellar.

'What are you all up to in here?' The voice brought them round to face Victoria standing with the door in her hand, and Charlie stared over the heads of the three girls towards her. She looked beautiful. He had thought so when he had first seen her tonight, but she had grown more so as the evening wore on. Oh yes, he had told himself already that he was seeing her through the fumes of hot rum and old brandy, in fact only a short while ago he had warned himself that he wouldn't be able to see her at all if he indulged himself further.

She was standing in front of him now. She was wearing a green velvet dress, her flesh appearing to pour over the low cut neck like rising cream. Her dark hair was piled high on her head, and two strands had come loose in the dancing and were lying one on each of her cheeks.

'Come on, come on, you're going to dance this one with me.'

'Oh, Victoria! you know I'm no dancer.'

'Leave him alone, our Vic, it's my party.' Nellie's voice was a hiss now, and he looked from one to the other; then stretching his arms wide between them, he laughed with the two young girls who were convulsed with what they took to be a comic situation.

'What's on here?' Hal Chapman had joined them in the passage, and Victoria's voice, still holding laughter, said, 'I want Charlie to dance and she's trying to stop him.'

'Don't be silly, Nellie. Behave yourself!'

The slap that brought Nellie's hand from Charlie's arm was almost in the nature of a blow and she winced and sprang back, and stood against the wall and watched her father pushing her sister and Charlie through the door and into the hall.

'Did he hurt you?' One of the girls had remained behind, and Nellie shook her head vigorously, saying, 'No, no. Go on, go on in; I'll be with you in a minute, I'm just going to the toilet.' On this she ran down the corridor, past the door leading into the hall and up the back stairs and into her bedroom.

Three times during the next hour Polly scurried across the icy yard and into the dairy, but Charlie did not come.

'What you keep going out to the netty for, you got diarrhoea?'

'Yes, a bit.' Polly nodded at Lindy.

'What's given it you, you been drainin' the glasses?'

Polly smiled weakly as she answered, 'Aye, a few,' thinking as she did so, I'd be hard put for a drink to drain glasses, I would that.

'Well, you missed a few 'cos I've had a lick at some. Eeh! the stuff that's been swilled in there the night, you could launch a boat on it. The boss must be in a generous mood. It's some party.'

'Aye; but it isn't like a birthday party, it's not as Miss Nellie wanted it, I'm sure of that.'

'No, you're right there; 'tis more like a wake or a weddin'. . . . You off again?'

'Yes.' Polly pressed her hand against her stomach and, grabbing a cape from the back of the door, she put it over her head, and ran out into the yard once more; and as she did so she saw the side door open and a dark figure show up against the snow and make its way unsteadily towards the dairy.

'That you, Charlie?'

'Yes, Polly. S . . . sorry I couldn't get here before. Goin' mad in there.' He laughed.

They were inside the dairy now. The cold seemed more striking than outside, and the clean bareness of the place could be sensed even through the darkness.

'Wait a minute,' Polly whispered now; 'I'll light the candle. It won't be seen if we keep it this end.'

As the flame of the candle flickered upwards, Polly looked into his face. It wasn't the face she knew so well, the face that was deeply etched in her mind burnt there by the trammels of young love. His thoughtful, even sombre, look was replaced by a large inane grin; the grey eyes, whose kindness and concern was usually covered by blinking lids, were half closed as if he were about to fall asleep where he stood.

'Charlie.'

'Yes, Polly.' He had hold of her hand.

'It's Ginger.'

'Ginger? What about him?'

'He . . . he wants me to marry him.'

'What!' For a moment he seemed to sober up completely, his eyes widened, and his lids blinked rapidly. 'Ginger . . . you marry Ginger? You'll not! Wait till I see him. The bloody insolence!'

Funny, it was the first time she had ever heard him use a swear word, but then she hadn't been with him much since they had grown up and she had come over here to work. She took him by the arm and shook him slightly and, reaching her face up to his, she whispered as if they might be overheard, 'There's . . . there's nothing else for it, Charlie, is there?' Her last two words seemed to pierce the fug of his brain and he repeated to himself, 'Is there? Is there?'

'Do . . . do you want to marry him?'

'No. *No!*'

'Well then.' He knew as he said it it was a stupid answer to give her and that was why she was actually shaking him.

'But don't you see, Charlie? If I don't he could . . . he could split.'

He looked down into her face and for a moment he forgot about Sidney Slater as he thought, She's bonny; not beautiful, but bonny, warmly bonny. That's what he wanted, warmth. He had always wanted Polly, the warmth of her. He had continually dreamed of her until recently, when he had realized the stupidity of it. But what was she saying? That Slater! that ginger-headed weasel wanted to marry her! It was strange but he had never imagined that he could really hate anybody, yet as he had watched the undersized skinny lad sprout inches and his shoulders broaden until now at eighteen he was a presentable young fellow, he knew that his mere dislike of the boy had grown into hate, for never once had Slater looked at him over the years but his eyes had said, 'Don't come the master with me; we know who's got the upper hand, don't we?' As for the fellow's effect on Arthur, at times he wouldn't have been surprised if Arthur hadn't tried his hand at a second murder.

He said now, 'Arthur, does Arthur know?'

'Yes.'

'What did he say?'

'Well –' She turned her head away and looked towards a bench on which stood a gleaming row of copper pans, the candlelight bringing out gold from their depths, and her voice was low in her throat as she said, 'When me mother told him, she said he banged his head against the wall, then went out and got drunk.'

Again there was silence between them, and now he stuttered, 'You . . . you're too young to be married.'

'Don't be silly' – her tone was astringent – 'me ma was married at sixteen.'

'Do . . . do you like him?'

Again she turned her head to the side, right on to her shoulders now, and out of the corner of her eyes her gaze rested on the wooden churn, the handle of which had hardened the muscles of her arms since she had come on the farm, and she looked at it for a full minute before saying, 'I don't dislike him; he's . . . he's always been decent towards me, not like he's acted with Arthur . . . an' you. He hates you both.'

'I'm well aware of that. Anyway –' He made an attempt to straighten his shoulders and his lips worked one over the other before he said, 'Leave it to me, I'll see to him. I'll bring it into the open. . . . Should have done it years ago. Who's going to believe him, eh? Who's going to believe him? Think he's mad, that's what they'll think, think he's mad. Don't worry, Polly' – he put his hand on her shoulder and his face hung over hers for a moment – 'you'll not marry him, I'll see to that. Leave it to me, eh? Leave it to me.'

She gazed back into his eyes before she whispered, 'Yes, Charlie. All right, Charlie.'

Their faces were close, their noses almost touching, he felt himself swaying. Once she had offered to pay him for what he had done for them. He would like to take the payment now. Oh aye, he would like to take the payment now, to hold her in his arms, to kiss her, to hug her, to roll with her on the floor . . . to love her. Oh, to love Polly. The old dream was returning. Their noses touched; his arms were moving upwards when she sprang back from him, 'I've . . . I've got to go; I've been comin' back an' forward for the last hour, an' Lindy's been wonderin'.'

He didn't speak. His arms were still extended in front of him as he watched her nip out the candle, then walk through the open door into the whiteness of the yard. There went his love, his buried love. He knew he'd never have Polly. Yet he had said, 'Leave it to me.' What did he mean? Aye, what did he mean? . . .

Polly didn't run across the yard, she walked, her head deep down on her chest until it was brought abruptly up, when a cry bordering on a scream came from her open mouth as she felt her arm being gripped. She was pulled into the side doorway, then into the light of the passage and the sound of merriment.

'What've you been up to?'

It was almost with relief that she looked down into Nellie's face.

'Oh . . . Miss Nellie . . . Miss Nellie . . . I've just been to the dairy.'

'Yes, I know you've just been to the dairy, and I know who's been in the dairy with you. What I'm asking you is what you are up to.'

'Nothin', Miss Nellie, honest, nothin'. Well . . . there's trouble at home' – there was always trouble at home so that was no lie – 'an' I asked Mister Charlie to give me a minute of his time 'cos I wanted him to take a message . . . a message to me mother.'

'And you had to go into the dark dairy to do it?'

'It wasn't dark, Miss Nellie, I lit a candle.'

'Oh, you lit the candle . . . the better to see him with. Well' – Nellie was now stabbing her anger into Polly's chest – 'you know I've always been decent to you, don't you?'

'Aye, Miss Nellie. Oh, aye.'

'Well, I'm going to give you some advice; get Mister Charlie out of your mind.'

'What?'

'You heard what I said. Oh, I haven't been blind all these years, I've seen you watching him every time he comes to the place. I'm not blaming you, mind, I'm not blaming you, but I'm just telling you there's no future in it for you. And you're sensible enough to know that, so why do you carry on?'

Polly's mouth opened and closed, then her hands working agitatedly on her apron smoothed the bands around her waist, then the wide bib before she ran her fingers down the broad side hems as far as her hands could reach, and when she stopped pressing and plucking she said in a tone that definitely held dignity, 'I think you're barking up the wrong tree, Miss Nellie, never such a thought crossed me mind. I . . . I'm . . . well . . . I'm about to give me word to Sidney Slater at the farm.'

There was silence between them for a moment; then in a soft voice now, Nellie said, 'Honest?'

'Yes, honest.'

'Oh well . . . well I'm sorry, but you must admit it looked fishy. And just think Polly, if Mother had caught you or . . . or her ladyship.' She grinned now. 'If you had told her you were going to marry ten Sidney Slaters it wouldn't have convinced her but that you were up to something.'

Again they looked at each other; then with a slight toss of her head Polly turned and walked away, and as she disappeared through the doorway into the kitchen Nellie turned and ran into the yard again, and it was just as she reached the door of the dairy that Charlie came out.

'Ah-ha! Master MacFell, what have you been up to? Come on, come on, I want to know.'

She had him by the arm now leading him across the yard, not in the direction of the house but towards the barn, and as they skipped and staggered on the ice she talked at him, saying, 'Romeo, Casanova, and Benny Blackett the drover, you're all of them rolled into one. Do you know that, Charlie MacFell? Heart breaker, that's what you are.'

She had pushed open the door of the big barn and their joined laughter was smothered by the padding of the bales of hay.

'You're a naughty girl, do you know that?'

'Yes, I know that, Charlie. And you're a daft lad, do you know that?'

He paused before saying solemnly, 'Yes, I know that, Nellie.'

'Well, naughty and daft, let's join forces and enjoy ourselves, eh? Come on . . . here, light the lantern, I've got something to show you.'

'But wait . . . wait' – he pulled at her arm – 'we'd better get back, they'll be missing us.'

'You didn't think that when you took Polly into the dairy, did you?'

'Oh now, now Nellie, wait.'

She was laughing loudly at him as she said, 'I'm not waiting. Here! hold it.' She thrust the lantern into his hand. 'And keep yourself steady else you'll set the place on fire. You're tipsy, you know that?'

'What about you?'

'I'm only half tipsy yet, but the night's young. Come on.'

'Where you going?'

'Up on to the floor,' she said, making for the ladder.

'Now, now, Nellie.'

'Now, now, Charlie.' She turned her head over her shoulder and scoffed at him, 'Come on, be a brave boy, follow little Nellie.'

He followed her, but slowly, having to feel his way up the ladder. She was a caution was Nellie, lovable in a way. You couldn't help liking Nellie, but she was a terror for all that. By! yes. To them back there in the house she had brought some blushes in her time with her tongue. She had a sharp wit, had Nellie, like a rapier, and he had no doubt that she was also cruel at times, but she had never used the sharp edge of her tongue on him. No, funny that, she'd always been kind and sympathetic towards him. He liked Nellie. Oh aye, he liked Nellie. And he loved Polly, and he admired Victoria. . . . Was that all the feeling he had for Victoria? Victoria was beautiful; in a heavy sort of way, but she was beautiful. They wanted him to marry Victoria and he'd be a fool if he didn't because it was someone like Victoria who was needed to cope with his mother, he himself was no match for her.

There were times when she irritated him so much he felt like striking her. And that was strange because he couldn't even watch a beast being goaded without feeling the nail piercing himself. Yet how near he had come to hitting her. Oh yes, he'd had the desire more than once to lift his hand and skelp his mother across the mouth. Nature was a funny thing.

'Look where you're goin', you'll fall over the edge, you fool!'

Nellie grabbed him and pulled him down on to the hay. She had hung the lantern on a nail in the stay post that reached from beneath the floor in the middle of the barn right up to the apex of the roof. They said that piece of wood had been carved out of a single tree three hundred years ago and she didn't disbelieve them. It was still unmarred by beetle rot, strong, sturdy, oozing strength.

She wished she could draw some of the strength from it and inject it into this lovable soft, long individual by her side. She turned from him and began to grope among the straw close under the roof, and when she found what she was looking for she brought it out with a flourish and dangled it before his face, crying, 'One of the best, eighteen ninety. He never dipped that far down tonight, but nevertheless he'll have fits when he sobers up tomorrow an' finds out just how far he did dip down among his precious bottles. . . . An' you know why he did it Charlie? You know why he's made such a splash?'

As she dangled the bottle before his face dull purple and green lights swam before his eyes, and as she widened the arc the lantern light added shots of gold reflected from the straw.

Grabbing at the bottle now, he peered closely at it as he said thickly, 'That's brandy. Oh, Nellie, you shouldn't.'

'Well, oh Charlie, I did. And it's not the first time neither.'

'You don't mean . . . you don't mean you drink the lot?'

'No, no, not the lot, I share it with old Benny. I . . . I get it for him. He loves a drop of good stuff does Benny, and when would he ever be able to afford stuff like that? And I'm telling you this, dear papa wouldn't afford it either if he didn't get it on the cheap. It's all customs fiddled stuff, like Mother's expensive scent . . . and Vic's and mine. Do you know he's got a secret place upstairs for it? Well, he has, he has. So what chance has anybody like old Benny to taste a drop of the real stuff?' She slapped the bottle with her hand. 'Things are badly distributed, don't you think, Charlie?'

'Yes, yes.' He nodded at her. 'Oh yes, Nellie, things are badly distributed, I agree with you. Yes, I agree with you there.' His head was bouncing on his neck as if on wires. But all the same this is real old stuff, priceless really. Couldn't you have taken a younger brand, sort of?'

'Yes" – she sat back on her heels – 'I suppose I could, but I heard somebody coming. It was his nibs himself and Lord! There was only just time to get out, and as I made my escape I took the first thing that came to hand, and it was this.' She laughed now, adding, 'My hands have very good taste; what do you say, Charlie?'

'I say you're a rip, Nellie. That's what you are, a rip, an', an' I think you'd better put it back an' get old Benny a younger bottle.'

'Not on your life! And anyway, there won't be very much left for Benny when we're finished with it.'

'Now, now, Nellie.' As he made to rise from the straw she pushed him back, saying, 'Be brave, Charlie, be brave. For once in your life be brave.'

'Nellie.' His face became straight and his tone took on an offended note. 'That isn't nice, Nellie; you are talking as if I'd sometime acted as a coward. I'm not a coward, Nellie, I'm . . . I'm simply sen . . . sensitive to people's feelings.'

'I know that, Charlie, but everybody doesn't look at it that way. The way they see it is you're short on guts.'

'*Now Nellie.*'

'Stop sayin', now Nellie. Here, drink that.' She handed him a battered tin mug which he pushed away, saying, 'No, I don't think . . .'

'Well, don't think, just drink.'

'Oh, Nellie.' He shook his head over the tin mug; then he put it to his lips, swallowed, screwed his eyes up tightly, turned his face towards his shoulder as if to bury it there, then coughed and spluttered as he said, 'By! you swa . . . swallow the d . . . date all right with this stuff, eighteen ninety . . . eighteen ninety.'

Nellie had just taken a drink from her mug and now she, too, was coughing, and as she thumped her chest she gasped, 'Oh boy! giant's blood.'

'What?'

'I . . . I said it's like giant's blood. Stuff like this's not supposed to be gulped. Sip it. Go on, sip it.' She pushed the mug towards his lips, and he, laughing now, sipped at the brandy again, while she, twisting about, pressed herself closely to his side, then followed suit.

There must have been the equivalent of two double brandies in each of the mugs and when she poured the third draught out for him he made no objection. He was sitting with his back to a bale of straw, his knees up, his wrists dangling between them, the mug held loosely in his hands, and she sat in much the same position, her knees up, the mug held between her hands.

There was a quietness all around them and in them; they were suffused with a great but gentle mellowness; they had no desire to laugh any more, they were content just to sit on this hazy planet and to talk at intervals. They touched on subjects that had no relation to each other such as the day when Big Billy had taken the prize for the best bull at the fair, how well her mother played the piano, and from that to the difference the new road had made. Their remarks on each subject were disjointed, terse, but lucid enough to evoke some sort of reasonable answer. And then she said, 'You know all this is for your benefit to-tonight, Charlie.'

'What . . . what do you say, Nellie?'

'I said, over at the house, the big do, me birthday party, they don't give a damn if I'm seventeen or se . . . seventy, it's all been done to bring you up to . . . to scratch.'

'Scratch?'

'Yes, scratch.'

'What scratch?'

'Oh, don't be so damn dim, Charlie. Vicky, Victoria the great, the she stallion, that's the scratch, *Victoria!*'

'Vic . . . Victoria?'

'Aye, yes, an' you. You were meant to pop the . . . the question the night.'

'No.'

'Fact. Fact.'

''Magination, Nellie.'

''Magination the bull's backside!'

At this they fell against each other hooting. When their laughter eased away they were still sitting but now their arms were about each other, and when they hiccuped loudly together they laughed again.

'She'll swallow you alive, Charlie.'

'Never get the chance.'

'Oo-oh! but she will. It's like when . . . when she gets her legs over a horse, she digs her knees in an' . . . an' the poor old beast goes where she wills; you're her latest poor old beast, Charlie.'

'Oh no! Nellie, not me.'

'Yes, you, Charlie, you're next in line for breakin' in. They've got it arranged 'tween 'em, Father'n her. Not a word spoken, but I know. Oh I know. I know the lot of 'em . . . aw!' She turned on to her hip and laid her face in his neck and now she whispered, 'Tell you somethin', Charlie, tell you somethin'. I'd hate to see you marry her, Charlie; you're too nice for her. You're too nice for me an' all, but me, I wouldn't treat you like she treats you, Charlie. An' you're older'n me, which's as it should be, isn't it? . . . Would you marry me, Charlie?'

He was shaking with laughter inside. It bubbled up to his lips and spilled over as, easing her face from his shoulders, he held it between his hands. And now he pushed out his lips and wagged his head and said, 'Marry you, Nellie? Course I'll marry you. Nothin' better to do come New Year but marry you, Nellie. An' we'll bring our bed up here an' live in the barn happy ever after. Oh! . . . The lantern's gone out.'

'You would, Charlie, you'd marry me?' She groped at him.

'Any . . . day . . . in the week . . . Nellie. Any . . . day . . . day . . . in the week . . . 'cept the month's got an R in it.'

'Oh Charlie!' She had her arms around his neck. 'That's a promise?'

'A promise, Nellie.'

He held her tightly for a moment; then they both overbalanced and fell into the straw. And there they lay for the next hour or more oblivious of the voices calling in the yard; oblivious of the lanterns swinging on the ground floor of the barn; oblivious of everything until she was brought from the comfort of his arms and her drunken sleep by a mighty hand which held her swaying body upright as the voice thundered over her, 'What in hell's flames are you up to now! You slut you! You slut you! God! for two pins I'd thrash . . .'

'Don't! Don't! Leave her alone!'

Charlie staggered to his feet but had to put his hands behind him to support himself from falling again, and with his mind so fogged that he imagined himself to be in some sort of nightmarish dream where all the figures were swaying; he tried to sort out the faces coming and going before him.

His gaze swung from Hal Chapman to Nellie, then from her to where Victoria was climbing on to the platform, and beyond her to where figures were milling about in the straw below, their faces all turned upwards.

'You! you little bitch you!' Victoria made a lunge towards her sister, but her father's arm swinging backwards thrust her aside and she, losing her footing, fell plump on to a bale of hay.

Charlie now had to subdue a strong desire to laugh: it was all so funny.

What were they making the fuss about; it was a party, wasn't it? But what was he doing up here? He must have fallen asleep. Was he still asleep?

The next minute he knew he wasn't asleep as Nellie's voice startled him with its loudness and the content of her words as she screamed and strained towards her sister. 'It's not what you think, you mucky-minded horse-mad harlot you! Yes, harlot you! We didn't do anything, nothing. We don't jump at it like you, we can wait 'cos . . . 'cos we're going to be married, Charlie'n me, we're going to be married. He asked me. You did, didn't you, Charlie?'

He was standing straight now. Marry Nellie? He had asked Nellie to marry him? Nonsense! Oh God! his head was thumping. Somewhere in the dream, right back, he could recall somebody talking about marrying Nellie; but he wasn't going to marry Nellie; he didn't want to marry Nellie.

'Is . . . is this true?' Hal Chapman, his body swaying, thrust his beer-red face gleaming with sweat in front of Charlie's. 'D'you hear me? Is it true?'

'What . . . what's true?'

'You silly bugger!' Hal Chapman now let loose of his younger daughter and, gripping Charlie by the shoulders, shook him, saying, 'You're so bloody drunk you don't know if you asked her to marry you or not, an' likely put a seal on the bargain?'

'Yes, I suppose I am bloody drunk.' Charlie laughed weakly now.

'Did you or did you not, lad?' Another shake.

'What?' Oh Lord! Lord! his head.

'Ask Nellie here to marry you?'

Charlie turned his hammer-beating head and looked towards Nellie. Her face swam away from her body; it moved round in a circle until it merged into Victoria's. The comedy of the situation became too much for him, and he laughed, a great bellow of a laugh, the way he hadn't laughed for years, perhaps not since the morning of the day when his father had died. Then he heard someone who wasn't at all like himself shouting, 'Yes, yes; is anything wrong in that?'

Hal Chapman allowed a silence of seconds to elapse before enveloping Charlie in his embrace. What did it matter which one of them he had chosen. After all it made no difference did it? The land would be joined and that was all that mattered. He now stepped back from Charlie and slapped him heartily in the chest with the back of his hand, then let out another roar of laughter as the tall figure tumbled once again into the straw. But that over, he turned to where his elder daughter was pulling herself upwards from the hay and, taking her arm, he gripped it and, keeping his eyes averted from her distorted features, led her to the top of the ladder, and there he growled at her, 'Put a face on it. Put a face on it.'

As she wrenched herself from her father's hold, Victoria looked to where Charlie was leaning on his elbows in the straw, his head back and his mouth still emitting laughter; and from him her gaze swept to her sister and their eyes shot hate of each other with the deadliness of bullets.

Hal Chapman, following his daughter down the ladder, shouted the news to the waiting guests below, who were all men, and who, after a moment of surprised silence, cheered and waved their hands up towards the loft where Nellie, now kneeling by Charlie's side, was looking woefully at him and repeating, 'I'm sorry, Charlie, I'm sorry,' while he comforted her by saying, 'It's all right, Nellie. It's all right.'

But what was all right, he wasn't quite sure; he wasn't sure of anything except that he was still tickled to death about something; what he didn't know, because he was so tired he wanted to sleep. Oh, he just wanted to sleep . . . and not wake up again. . . . Was that so . . . not wanting to wake up again? There must be something wrong. He turned on to his side and laid his head on his hand and actually dropped off to sleep again.

## Chapter Three

He was brought up from the depths of sleep to the awareness of an ear-splitting voice calling his name. 'Charlie! Charlie!'

He groaned, went to shake his head, then swiftly put his hands up to it to still the agonizing pain.

'Charlie! Charlie! wake up.'

The light sent arrows of agony through his eyeballs.

'Come on, sit up and drink this.'

Two hands helped to drag him into a sitting position. The cup pressed against his lips burned them, and he jerked his head backwards and the hot liquid spilt over his chin, bringing him fully awake.

'Oh God! God Almighty! where am I?' He squinted into Nellie's face. 'What's up?'

'Drink that coffee. Go on, drink it.'

He gulped at the liquid, and when the cup was emptied and she went to pour another from the pewter jug he stopped her with a quivering, tentative motion of his hand; then shutting his eyes, he lowered his head as he asked quietly, 'What happened?'

'You got drunk. We both got drunk.'

'Both of us?' He squinted at her again.

'Yes; don't you remember?'

He went to shake his head, then hunched his shoulders against the movement as he answered, 'Can't remember a thing. God! I'm cold.'

He looked about him. The winter sun was streaking through the cracks in the barn timbers, watery yet painful to his eyes. He tried to recall what he should remember, but his mind took him no further than the dairy and Polly's face. Polly was going to marry Ginger. Or was she? No, she wasn't; he was going to put a stop to it.

. . . 'We're engaged to be married.'

He consciously stopped his head from jerking around. He did not even turn his face towards her when he said, 'What did you say, Nellie?'

'I said we're engaged to be married.'

Now he did look at her, but slowly, and he repeated, 'We're engaged to be married? Huh!' Even his smile increased the agony in his head. 'What do you mean, Nellie, engaged to be married? Huh!'

'Apparently we plighted our troth.' Her tongue came well past her teeth and lips as she dragged out the last word.

Again he said 'Huh!' but now he laughed. With his two hands holding his head he laughed as he said, 'We must have been stinking.'

'We were.'

'How did we get like that?'

She twisted round on the straw now and picked up the empty brandy bottle and held it out towards him, and when he took it from her and read the label he whistled, then said, 'We went through that, a full bottle?'

'Apparently.' Her voice held a slightly sad note now.

'And the best brandy . . . my! my! that must have cost something.'

'Not as much as you think. It's all smuggled stuff, Father's got friends. I think somehow I told you. Anyway, if he'd had to pay the real price for it I suppose he'd have considered it worth while, as it got us engaged.'

'Your –' He turned on to his knees now and steadied himself by gripping at a bale of straw and his mouth opened twice before he muttered, 'Your . . . your father knows?'

'Yes; they all know.'

'*Aw, Nellie, no! No!*' Now he actually did shake his head, and vigorously.

'Is it so terrible?'

She was kneeling opposite him and he raised his head and stared at her. No . . . no, he supposed, looked at calmly, it wasn't so terrible 'cos she was a very appealing girl was Nellie. But he had no feeling for her, not in that way. Good Lord! no, never in that way, not Nellie. She had just left school, she was still a young girl somehow. If he had thought about marrying into the Chapmans', and he had thought about it, it was Victoria his mind had dwelt on; in fact he could tell himself he had been coached over the years to think of Victoria as a wife. And now her name escaped from him, 'Vicky!' he said.

'Yes, what about Vicky?'

'Nellie . . . well, you know.'

'What do I know?' Her words came clipped, cold.

'Aw, don't be silly, Nellie. What happened last night must have been a prank, we . . . we were drunk. You said yourself.'

She stared hard at him for a number of seconds before rising to her feet and saying in the same tone as before, 'I'd better go and tell them then, her in particular . . . put her out of her misery. Then they'll have to send the bellman round all the villages, telling people they got the name wrong.'

He was standing now, and he repeated, 'All the villages?'

'Yes, all the villages, where the Hodgsons, the Pringles, the Fosters, the Charltons, the Whitakers, and Uncle Tom Cobley an' all live.'

'Oh my God!' He held his brow with his hand, and now his voice low, almost a whisper, he said to her, 'Don't be mad at me, Nellie; it would never have happened if we hadn't got drunk, you know that.'

'No, it wouldn't.' She was thrusting her face up to his now. 'You're right there, Charlie. But I'll tell you this much, there'll come a time when you'll wish you'd stuck to your drunken proposal. I'm no prophet but I know that much.'

'Nellie! Nellie!' He watched her going down the steep ladder, and again he called, 'Nellie! Nellie!'

When she reached the bottom she stopped and looked up at him and when he said, 'I'm sorry, I'm so sorry, Nellie,' she answered back, her voice soft now, 'Yes, I know, Charlie; but it's nothing to what you will be, and I'll be sorry for you then.'

She had reached the open doors when he called again, 'Nellie!'

When she turned to face him he asked, 'My mother and Betty, are they still here?'

'No; the Pringles dropped them off on their way back.' Now the old tart note was in her voice again as she ended, 'Your mother couldn't get away quick enough, Betty an' all. I think they wanted to lock the doors so I wouldn't get in. Whoever you take back there, Charlie, you're going to have a fight on your hands.' She shook her head slowly, then jerked her chin upwards before turning and disappearing into the yard.

God Almighty! He lowered himself down onto the scattered straw. Trust him to make a hash of things. Proposing to Nellie! How in the name of God had that come about? And she had wanted to keep him to it. Yes – he nodded quietly to himself – she had. And now he had Hal Chapman to face. But worse than that, there was Victoria. What must she have felt when she heard the news. Perhaps she, too, was too drunk to take it in; but no, it would take a lot of the hard stuff to deprive Victoria of her senses. More than once he had noticed that she was like her father in that way, she could carry her liquor, it only made her jolly. He must go down, tidy himself up, try to explain away the whole silly affair, and then he must get home and face his mother, and her wrath. Nellie was right in what she had said: whoever he took back to the house he'd have a fight on his hands because his mother was certainly mistress in that house and she intended to go on being so. He had given into her over the years because not having done so would have made his life sheer hell on earth. While he played the master during those first months after his father had died she countermanded every order he gave, and the confusion in the house had been chaotic.

Why did things never go smoothly for him? What was it in his nature that made him the object of ridicule? After three years of managing the farm he still, to put it plainly, had no bloody horse sense. If left to himself he would have bought animals out of pity for their leanness. When in company with other farmers he didn't talk farming; he didn't slosh himself with drink on market days; nor did he inveigle himself with the right people who would drop a case of brandy along with the fodder every now and again. In a way, he knew he was still considered as his father's son, an outsider. That the farm had not gone downhill since his father died wasn't any credit to himself, it was Arnold and Fred who kept the standard high, and kept Sidney Slater up to scratch. Yes, and Arthur too, for Arthur's fear had undermined his promising ability.

And now this latest farce. He'd be a laughing stock; they'd say he'd had to get blind drunk in order to propose marriage to a lass and then when he was sobered up he couldn't go through with it.

What was wrong with him anyway? Was he a weakling?

No, no. He denied this strongly inside himself. He was just a square peg in a round hole, and he had been rammed into it by sympathy for the Bentons.

Polly! There was Polly. He became alert. She couldn't marry Slater; he couldn't let that happen. He must get home and talk to Arthur. Something must be done.

He went down the ladder, but not as steadily as Nellie had done, and when he was on the floor of the barn he dusted himself down, picking the straw from his suit and out of his hair. And he was busy with this when a shadow filled the opening. He turned to see Victoria standing there.

Victoria, looking silently at Charlie, wondered, and not for the first time, what it was she saw in him that attracted her. It wasn't his long, lean thinness, nor his grey passionless eyes, nor his mop of fair hair that he wore over-long. So what was it? Was it his weakness that challenged her strength? Yet it was a strange weakness, for it wasn't gutless. There was a time when she had imagined he was gutless; that was until the day she had glimpsed a fighting light in his eyes when he witnessed Josh flogging his horse for having thrown him and so causing him to lose a race. The winning of the race would have meant little to Josh, for what was a race at a fair but an opportunity to enter everything from a donkey to a stallion, and to have a good laugh at the assortment; but the losing of it on a thoroughbred meant a lot, and this she'd had to point out rather forcibly to Charlie to prevent him from going for Josh.

But did she really want him? Yes, yes, she wanted him; and she was going to have him, for she saw him as her last chance of becoming independent and getting away from this house. No one would believe her if she said that her main aim in life was to depart this place where her mother ruled supreme. And she herself would not believe anyone who told her that she was jealous of her mother, jealous of her looks, of her popularity, of her capabilities, and, most of all, of her power over her husband.

She had always admitted to herself that her home was divided in affection. She had her father's love while Nellie had her mother's; but her mother also had her husband's love and herein lay the core of her jealousy. But she had made herself blind to it. What she wanted she told herself was a home of her own, a place in which she would be called mistress; and it definitely had to be a house with stabling attached, and Moor Burn had the best facilities in that line for miles around. Of course there was Madam MacFell, but she would deal with her when the time came.

Over the past months she had decided that Charlie must be brought up to scratch. It had become imperative that she should have him. Archie Whitaker had dropped from her horizon, he had even got himself engaged, and Josh ... Josh had made it plain he was in no position to marry for years. Being the youngest of four sons was the excuse he put forward. She had been openly careless where Josh Pringle was concerned and had got herself talked about. She knew that her name now was such that she could not hope to find a husband in her own class for miles around. She admitted to herself that she had been foolish, too free, but there was that craving inside her that demanded release. All during her teens her body had burned for this release, so much so that at times it frightened her. Were all women like this, she wondered. Archie Whitaker had told her they weren't, and that she was out of this world. She marvelled now why she hadn't fallen pregnant in those first two months; after that she had made sure she wouldn't.

Now Archie Whitaker was gone, and Josh Pringle was becoming less available. She stilled the voice inside herself which said she had been too much for him. Now there was only Charlie to fall back on, and up till a few minutes ago she thought she had lost this chance too. That little bitch! She shuddered as she thought of her sister and of what she might have done to her last night if her father hadn't pulled her hands away from the plump throat. Afterwards she had managed to control her rage until the last guest had gone, but then she had allowed the storm to break, and by God! it had been a storm. Six ornaments she had smashed, a piece of Worcester, two pieces of Doulton, and her mother's treasured group of Dresden figures; that was before she pounced on Nellie.

And this morning she'd sworn to her father that she'd never rest until she'd done her sister a serious mischief. Then five minutes ago the little bitch had walked jauntily into the dining-room and proclaimed it had all been a joke. They had both been drunk, she said, and she had no more intention of marrying Charlie than she had of marrying Josh Pringle.

She had made a small motion with her head as she mentioned Josh's name, and the motion had indicated the extent of the little bitch's knowledge as much as if she had shouted it aloud.

Well, now things had come to a head, and she must slacken the bit. She must alter her tactics.

She started by walking slowly towards him and putting out her hand and picking a piece of straw from the side of his coat collar.

'They always say you should take more water with it.'

He looked at her in slight amazement for a moment. She wasn't furious, in fact she was looking amused, kindly amused.

He drooped his head and, grinning, said, 'You're right there, Victoria; I'd better get some practice in at holding me drink.'

'Well, don't start on Father's special, a couple of glasses of that would knock a prize-fighter over. . . . That little monkey, she wants her ears boxed.'

He looked at her from under his lids. 'You heard about the result of it, I suppose?' He now gave his head a shake. 'Of course you have.'

'The proposal?' She made herself laugh. 'Oh yes, I heard about the proposal. It's a good job it wasn't one of the Stacey girls you were drinking with.'

Now they both laughed together, for the title 'girls' was a jocular courtesy given to the forty-five year old spinster twins, who were as hefty as their father, the blacksmith. Then their laughter dying away, Victoria turned to the side and, her voice low and flat now, she said, 'I . . . I have to confess though I was a little startled last night when they all came in babbling about it.' She turned her head on her shoulder and looked at him. 'I couldn't believe my ears. I . . . I didn't want to believe my ears.'

'I'm sorry, Victoria.'

'You . . . you don't care for Nellie, do you?'

'Oh no, no' – his words came rapidly now – 'not that way. Why, she's still a little girl. Somehow, I couldn't think of her in that way.'

'You're sure?' She still had her head turned towards him.

'Of course. Well, you should know that.'

'I . . . I thought I did.' She walked away from him now to the distant corner of the barn to where some stacks of grains stood in a row against the timbers, and she kicked against one with the toe of her shoe; her head was down, her hands hanging limply by her sides.

He watched her for a few seconds before moving towards her. Putting his hand lightly on her arm, he turned her towards him and, looking into her face, he said, 'You believe me, don't you?'

She paused a moment, then nodded at him and said, 'Yes; yes, Charlie, I believe you.'

'But it's true, I mean when I said I'd never thought of her in that way.'

Their heads were almost on a level. She stared into his eyes before she asked quietly, 'Have you thought of me in that way, Charlie?'

His lids blinked rapidly, he swallowed, stretched his chin out of his collar, then said, 'Yes . . . yes, I have, Victoria.'

She now lowered her gaze and directed it towards the sacks of grain as she asked, 'Would you have proposed to me if there hadn't been two years between us?'

Dear God! His head was aching, splitting, his mouth tasked like a midden. What must he say? What could he say? He said, 'Yes, yes, I suppose I would, Victoria.'

She turned to him, smiling quietly, and, putting out her hand, she gripped his. 'You'll be twenty in a few months' time and I'll be still twenty-one, at least for a few days; the difference won't seem so much then, will it?'

He smiled back at her, made a small motion with his head and said, 'No; no, it won't, Victoria.'

'Will you ask me then?'

'Yes; I'll ask you then.' As he spoke he had a great desire to laugh, to let forth that bellow that he so rarely gave vent to. Here he was, the quiet, shy, retiring fellow, because that was how he was looked upon by those who thought well of him; anyway, here he was proposing to two sisters within a matter of hours.

'What are you finding so funny?' She was smiling at him.

He bit tightly on his lip, wagged his head from side to side and screwed up his eyes for a moment. When he opened them they were glistening as if with tears and he said, 'I . . . I was just imagining what would happen if I went into the house and said . . . well, if I said I'd proposed to you . . . to two of you in a matter of hours.'

She put her hand over her mouth now as if to still her own laughter, and with the other hand she gripped his as she whispered, 'Well, now that would really cause a sensation, wouldn't it? The gay Lothario would have nothing on you. Charlie –' She checked her laughter, and he checked his, too, as she looked at him and said softly, 'This must be a secret between us for the next few months, eh?'

'Yes, Victoria; just as you say.'

'What about your twentieth birthday?'

'That'll be fine.'

She went to take his arm; then withdrew her hand, saying, 'We . . . we must be careful, mustn't we? Circumspect.' She pushed him playfully now. 'Go into the house and get cleaned up and have something to eat, and look contrite.' She tapped his cheek. 'You're a very bad boy. You know that, Charlie? You got drunk on father's best brandy, you were almost accused of seducing his younger daughter, and you've started a rumour around the countryside that's got to be denied. Go on, do your penance, you're a very bad boy.'

He went from her laughing, but the laughter faded away before he had crossed the yard.

You're a very bad boy, a very bad boy. She had talked to him as if he were ten years younger than her, not two. You're a very bad boy. Would he ever be a man, man enough to manage her?

# Chapter One

## The War 1914

The bloody Kaiser, he was a maniac, him and his little Willie. What had the British ever done to him? Nowt, nowt, said the ordinary man, but be too soft with the buggers, let them live in this country, feed on the fat of the land, make money out of the poor with their fancy pork shops all over the place. We were too soft, that's what we were, live and let live we always said. But we'd show them now. By God! we would. We'd teach them a lesson they'd never forget. Join up we will in our thousands. England must be saved from hooligans like that, maniacs, barbarians. We were a civilized people: couldn't you remain at school beyond the age of thirteen? didn't the old receive a pension when they were no longer able to do their bit at seventy? The Liberals were spending money like water in making things better for the sick and needy, and now that bloody maniac goes and starts a war! Well, the Geordies would soon settle his hash. By God! they would. Just let them get at him; they'd give him some stick for what he was doing to the poor Belgians.

And they did get at him. Those who weren't already in the Territorials or Special Reservists volunteered to go across there and 'wipe the buggers off the map'.

The Northerner is not just patriotic, he is enthusiastic with it, especially when he's got drink in him, and it must be said that a number of volunteers woke up with thick heads and asked themselves what the hell they were doing lying on the floor among this mob, and when a voice bellowed over them they told the owner of it where he could go to, only to be brought to their feet with boots in their backsides. Didn't they know where they was? Well, Corporal Smith, Jones or Robinson was here to tell them where they was, they was in the flaming army, that's where they was. And they could take their choice of the Third, Fourth, Fifth, Sixth, Seventh, Eighth, or Ninth Battalion of the Durham Light Infantry. They could have the pick of any battalion they wanted to join and Colonel Cardiff would be entertaining them all together the night. . . . Move! Move! Get a move on! Look slippy!

Most of the first batch of volunteers from the North-East were pit lads, and they didn't take kindly to orders. As for discipline, there was no need for that kind of thing that they could see; all they wanted to do was to get across the water and fight those bloody Germans.

'You'll meet 'em soon enough, but in the meantime get that bloody shovel in yer hand and dig that trench.'

'What here, in South Shields, Corporal?'
'Yes. Ever heard of coastal defences?'
'An' you? you're for the cookhouse.'
'An' you the latrines.'
'An' you! it's guard for you.'
.... 'Bugger me!'
'I will when I get time. ... Move!'

Arthur Benton was about the only one in his platoon who didn't question an order in those first days. He had been used to taking orders all his life, different kinds of orders, orders that old MacFell had kicked into him, and the polite orders that Charlie had given him; and perhaps he was the only one in his particular section who had been sober when he enlisted.

To Arthur the war had come as a godsend, a means of escape from the farm and that red-headed bastard who had been his brother-in-law now for the past year. At times he would question why their Polly had done it, yet he knew why their Polly had done it, it was to save his neck.

It was some weeks before Arthur, among others, was given a rifle, and it was as well, so scoffed the sergeant at the time, that they would never be called upon to use them. It was a good job Kitchener had sent the Fifth Division of the British Expeditionary Force over to France, because if the winning of the war depended on this lot they'd all give up the ghost.

Arthur didn't mind if he never saw France but the first instant he held the rifle he had a vivid picture of Ginger Slater standing in front of him, and his mind went bang! bang! bang! and he saw Ginger lying with the blood pouring out of him, not only from three places but from his head, his chest, his arms, his legs, his feet. By God! if he ever came across him.

The war became a puzzle to Arthur as it did to many another. Where were all the uniforms? Where were all the big guns? It would appear you only got a uniform if you were going to the front. And the officers, why some of them had been dug up from the Boer War. He wished he had never joined the bloody army. At least, so he wished until the day his unit was sent to Ravensworth Park. From that day Arthur had an aim in life.

## Chapter Two

By the middle of 1915 the war was settled in, in trenches so to speak. It was said in high places that it would have been over by the end of 1914 had it not been for the Germans discovering the value of a trench. It was when the fleeing Germans reached the Aisne and were too weary to run further from the pursuing British Expeditionary Force that they dug trenches, and from then checked the Allied advance. So began trench warfare; bloody, soul-destroying gut-exposing trench warfare.

There was at this time dissension among the generals: Kitchener was going for Sir John French; and General Joffre, the French Commander-in-

Chief, came under Kitchener's instructions to command the British Army. As one general was heard to say, 'You haven't to die before you shed tears of blood.'

There were commanders who didn't speak French and, therefore, had to take their orders through interpreters. There was confusion, there was massacre; but as the propaganda said there was also glory for those who gave their lives for their country.

But as thoughtful people dared to say, who can prove that the dead can enjoy what their passing has evoked?

And the fact now that men dying in their thousands brought forth from English women the hysterical desire that more should join them, was not a phenomenon but merely, in the main, the outpouring of frustration. Why should their man be out there, up to the waist in mud and water and crawling with lice, while even one man went about the streets in a civilian suit?

Charlie had been the target of this frustration more than once as he had passed through Newcastle and Gateshead.

'Somebody drained your liver, lad?'

'Don't tell me you're in a reserved occupation, not a big fellow like you!'

'Flat feet have you? Weak eyes? . . . weak-kneed more bloody like.'

Sometimes he wondered if he was the only one who had been subjected to this, but no, Tom Skelly was suspected of falling accidentally on purpose down a scree hill. The result was a broken leg. No France for him.

Meeting up with khaki-clad men was the worst experience. There were three coming along the street now, walking abreast. He lowered his eyes and went to step into the gutter when he was startled by a hand coming out and grabbing him, and he brought his head up sharply as a voice said, 'Charlie! Why, Charlie!'

'Arthur! My goodness!' They were shaking hands and smiling into each other's face.

'It's good to see you, Charlie.'

'And you, Arthur.'

Arthur now turned to his two companions standing to the side and said, 'Oh, this is Mr MacFell, he's me old boss. Wish he was still.' He jerked his head and laughed. 'Look, I'll see you later on. All right, eh?'

They both smiled and nodded and said, 'Aye, all right. So long.'

'So long,' Arthur said, then turned again to Charlie, asking now, 'Have you got a minute?'

'All the minutes you want, Arthur. Are you on leave?'

'Aye, you could say I was. We think we're for over the water any time now. . . . Come an' have a drink.'

'Better still, you come along to the house with me and have a bite.'

'The house? What house?'

'Oh' – they were walking side by side now – 'you wouldn't know about it but Victoria's aunt died just after the war started and left her and Nellie a house each. Victoria's is in Newcastle here and Nellie's is in Gateshead.'

'You don't say!'

'Yes.'

'And you live here now? What about the farm?'

'Oh, the farm is still going strong, and always will as long as Betty's about. But I'm there most of the time. I pop over here for an occasional week-end.'

'Aye. How things change.'

'Yes, they do, Arthur, they do indeed.'

'Where's your house?'

'In Jesmond.'

'Posh. Oh posh, eh?'

Charlie smiled and said, 'I hope you don't mind, it's a good ten minutes' walk further on.'

'You jokin', Charlie? You're talkin' to the feller with leather feet.'

'How are you finding the army, Arthur?'

'Oh –' The grin slid from Arthur's face and he said soberly, 'So-so.' Then turning his head fully towards Charlie, he said, 'I'm glad I met you, Charlie, I've a lot to tell you. I sometimes thought of takin' a trip out to the farm to have a natter with you, but then I didn't know whether I'd be welcome as there's no one of ours left there now, an' old Arnold and Fred didn't think much of me for goin' off like that, I know. But I just had to get away. You understand?'

'Yes, yes, I understand, Arthur.'

'I knew you would. But you know somethin', Charlie? There's an old saying, if the devil's got you marked out there's no escaping him, and it's true, by God! I've found out it's true. I met up with him again, Charlie ... Slater.'

They both paused in their walking now, and Charlie, shaking his head slowly, said, 'No!'

'Aye. Aye, Charlie. He's a bloody sergeant instructor, would you believe that? That skinny undersized bastard that he was, who could neither read nor write, he's a bloody sergeant, an' by God! didn't he let me know it. Do you know something, Charlie? I nearly added a second notch to me totem pole, I did that. It was the lads, those two I left back there, who saved me skin more than once. Pit lads they are ... or were, sensible, stubborn, good mates. They fought me battle for me, but in a backhand kind of way; they waylaid him one night and they did him up. By God! they did that; he was in hospital for a week. The whole camp was afire with it, but he couldn't lay the blame on me 'cos the bastard had put me on guard duty just afore he went out and I was still on it when they carried him in.'

'Who goes there?' Arthur stopped in the middle of the pavement and took up the pose of holding a rifle at the ready.

'One Sergeant Sidney Slater who's been done up.'

'Pass friends and God be with you.'

Charlie put his head back now and indulged in his rare deep roar of laughter and Arthur, himself shaking with his mirth, flapped his hand against Charlie's chest as he spluttered, 'And the best of it was those two that did it carried him in, found him in the lane they reported.' Again he struck a pose, saluted and said, 'Yes, sir; we, me and Private Blackett, were returnin' to camp, sir. It was Private Blackett, sir, who tripped over his foot in the dark. We thought it was the ... leg ... of ... a couple, sir, who were at it ... pardon me, sir, you know what I mean, sir, but when the foot didn't move, sir, we investigated an' found Sergeant Slater, sir, in a bloody ... in a right mess, sir. Yes, sir. Thank you, sir. .... About turn! Quick march!'

To the amusement of some passers-by, Arthur now did a quick turn a few steps away from Charlie and again they were roaring their heads off, but they hadn't traversed another street before Arthur said solemnly, 'But it was no laughing matter, Charlie, not really, not then. God! he put me through it. And you know what?' He turned his head slowly and met Charlie's gaze. 'We're going to meet up again – it would only be a big injustice if we didn't – an' over there they say a lot of funny things happen. I've heard tell of officers being shot in the back but I won't shoot him in the back, Charlie. No, right atween his two bloody eyes. An' I'll have to be quick, because if he can get me first he will. I know that. Oh, I know he will.'

After a pause while they tramped in step up a broad avenue lined with trees, Charlie said quietly, 'I hope you never meet up, Arthur; and it isn't likely if he's an instructor.'

'Oh.' Arthur's tone was light again. 'Oh, you can never tell with this set-up; they're shakin' you around all the time. In the past year I've been in Durham, Jarrow, Shields, Boldon Colliery, Roker; you're shuffled about like a bloody pack of cards. Them up there, begod! I doubt if any of them know what they're doin'. They've got to make a show to fill up their forms, so they say, you, you and you, pack up your troubles in your old kit-bag and get the hell out of this, and there you land up in some field or some bloody great house. Not that we ever get billeted in the houses; no, that's for the top brass. And some of them officers, nowt but kids with fancy voices, you can't understand a bloody word they say. An' mind' – he now pushed Charlie in the side – 'the poor young buggers look all at sea when the Geordies get crackin'. As one young bloke said, "I can understand German but damned if I can make out a word these fellows say."

'There were these lads from Shields' – Arthur was laughing again – 'they were pit lads into the bargain and when you add the pitmatic to the Geordie twang, well believe me, I can't understand half what they say meself. . . . Oh, we're here then.' Arthur stopped at the gate and looked up the short drive to the detached house. It was built of red brick and the paintwork was black.

'Eeh, by! it's a fine looking place, big an' all. Any stables?' They were walking towards the front door now.

'No, no stables, Arthur, just a coach-house.'

'Miss Victoria won't like that; she'll miss her stables.'

Charlie inserted a key in the front door and opened it, then stood aside, saying to Arthur who was hesitating on the step, 'Come on, come in.'

Slowly Arthur entered the hall. His cap in his hand, he gazed about him. Like the outside, the woodwork in the hall was black and the walls in between white. There was a red carpet in the middle of the polished floor and red carpet also padded the stout looking stairs; the newel post, shining with the dark hue of polished oak, looked as if it had been rooted there.

'Come into the kitchen, there's generally something in the pantry. We have a woman, an old lady, Mrs Crawford, she comes in every morning and sees to the place. But I think her main passion is cooking, and she always finds something to cook with here, we're not short of an egg or two.' He turned and grinned at Arthur, and Arthur added, 'Nor butter, nor cheese, I bet me life.'

'Ah yes, here we are.' Charlie came out of the pantry carrying a pie.

'Ham and egg.' He nodded at Arthur; then putting the plate on the table, he said, 'Coffee or tea? Or something hard?'

'Both if you don't mind, Charlie, I never say no to a cup of tea but I'd like a drop of hard this minute.'

'Well, come on.'

Arthur now followed Charlie back into the hall and through a heavy oak door and into what could only be described as a drawing-room, and the sight of it silenced Arthur for a moment while he stood gaping about him. There was a touch of awe in his tone now as he said, 'By! I've never seen such furniture, lovely. Aren't they lovely pieces! What you call antiques, Charlie?'

'Yes.' Charlie had turned from the cabinet in the corner of the room and he, too, stood for a moment looking about him, and his eyelids were blinking rapidly as he said, 'Yes, Arthur, antiques.'

'Eeh! by! she was lucky.'

'Yes, she was lucky.'

The drinks in their hands, they returned to the kitchen, and presently they sat down at the table which was now spread with pickles, bread, butter, cheese, and the ham and egg pie.

'Help yourself, Arthur.' Charlie nodded across to the khaki-clad figure, and Arthur, grinning widely now, answered, 'I don't need to be told twice, Charlie.'

It wasn't until he had finished a large shive of the pie and was wiping his mouth by the simple procedure of flicking a finger against one corner and then the other that he said, 'Everything goin' all right with you, Charlie?'

Charlie reached out and took a slice of bread, then a piece of cheese from the wooden platter, and finally he cut off a pat of butter and put it on the side of his plate; then he stared down at the food before he said, 'You wouldn't have had to ask that question if you had visited us over the past year or so.'

'Sorry.'

'Oh, don't be sorry for me, Arthur; I got what I asked for. Young fools should be made to pay for their foolishness; the only hope for them is that they don't grow into old fools.'

'What's the trouble? The missis . . . I mean your mother?'

'Yes and no. But even without her there would still have been trouble. We're the trouble, Vicky and I, we're a trouble to each other. It should never have happened. I'm a lazy fellow, Arthur.'

'. . . Lazy? Not you! You can do a day's work with the rest of 'em.'

'Yes, physically I suppose I can, but in my mind . . . well, I never use it, Arthur, I let other people use it for me. I follow where others lead.'

An embarrassed silence enveloped them both now until Arthur, in a high jocular tone, said, 'Did you ever think of joinin' up, Charlie?'

'No, never, Arthur. Can you imagine me with a bayonet.'

'Well, you never can tell. They say snakes are harmless until you stand on 'em. No offence meant, but you know what I mean. And did you see that advert in the paper yesterday?'

'What advert?'

'Why, they're advertising for officers; going round beating the drum didn't do much good, so there's this advert in all the big papers for officers. Why don't you have a shot? You wouldn't have to use a bayonet; by all accounts the top brass stay well behind the lines.'

'Thanks, Arthur, but I'm a good distance behind the lines now and that's where I intend to stay.'

'Aye, well, I suppose you're wise.'

'How's . . . how's Polly? You haven't mentioned her.'

'Well, that's 'cos I know so little about her now. I can't go there an' see her, can I? I only hear of her through me ma; she's up the flue again.'

'Up the . . .?'

'Aw' – Arthur tossed his head to the side – 'gona have another bairn. I don't think of her much, at least I try not to; the very thought of her with him nearly drives me mad. An' she's putting up with it all because of us . . . aw' – he lowered his head and wagged it – 'I mean me.'

'Where is she living?'

'Somewhere in Hebburn, me ma says, she doesn't tell me exactly. Just as well I suppose. Two bairns in two years! She'll have a squad afore she's thirty, an' she'll be old an' worn out by then. You know something?' He again wiped his mouth, but on the back of his hand this time. 'You should have married her, Charlie.'

'That would have been impossible, Arthur. You know it.'

'It might have been then, back on the farm, but not now, this war's turned everybody and everything topsy-turvy. There was a lass in our canteen over at Durham, she's just got herself married to a second-lieutenant.'

Charlie gave a small laugh. 'He might have been a waiter before the war.'

'Aw no, not second-lieutenants, not the officers. No, they're all educated fellows. Some of them now are comin' straight from the universities, all lah-di-dah. . . . You were gone on our Polly, weren't you, Charlie?'

'Yes, I suppose you could say I was, Arthur.' Charlie smiled wanly. 'But we were young then, children really. Things have changed as you said, times have changed.'

And how they had changed. How old was he now? Twenty-three. Was that all he was, twenty-three? And had he been married only two years, not twenty? It was hard to believe that the hysterical scenes, the physical body struggling, and his introduction into the emotions of rage, frenzy and desire had all taken place in less than two years, less than a year, in less than six months.

'What did you say, Arthur?'

'I said I enjoyed that, Charlie, a good home-made pie. But now . . . well, I'm afraid I'll have to be off.'

'Oh yes; your friends will be waiting.'

'Oh, it doesn't matter about them, we'll meet up at the bus, it goes at four. Fancy having to go back to camp on a Saturday night. Any other night in the week I wouldn't mind, but a Saturday! No, the reason for me hurry is I . . . I want to look in on me ma. She's mostly on her own now, she's only got Flo at home. She's sixteen now an' a handful; working in munitions she is; me ma can't get her in at nights. Mick and Peter are in the Navy. Peter gave a wrong age. Isn't it funny how we've all left the land; except you of course.'

'There's still time, Arthur.'

'Aye, by the looks of it, this bloody war could go on for the next ten years. It would be funny, wouldn't it, Charlie, if you an' me met up over there. . . . Colonel Charles MacFell, top brass.' He again struck a pose, of a bullying sergeant this time. 'Spit on those boots! I want them to dazzle me eyes. And Brasso your buttons, 'cos you know who we've got comin' the day? Colonel Charles MacFell.'

This time Charlie wasn't amused, but he patted Arthur on the shoulder, saying quietly, 'After this business is over you must go on the stage; you'd do well, you know.'

'There's truer things been said in a joke, Charlie. They had me in a concert party last Christmas. I did a fresh farm lad milking a cow; I had 'em rollin'.'

'I bet you did.'

They were at the door now. 'Well, good-bye, Charlie.'

'Good-bye, Arthur.'

'Here! there's no call for that.' Arthur opened his palm and exposed the crumpled notes.

'Go on; you'll do more good with them than I will.'

'Thanks, Charlie, thanks. It's good of you; I'll be thinkin' of you.'

'And me of you, Arthur.'

They looked at each other for a moment longer, their hands gripping; then Arthur went hurriedly down the drive. Charlie didn't wait to see him go through the gate but he turned and closed the door abruptly behind him, then stood rigidly still, staring in front of him. He had a longing to be with Arthur, and to be going ... over there, in fact anywhere that would take him away from the owner of this house, and from his mother and sister. ... But it was because of his mother that he was here.

He walked slowly across the hall and up the stairs. The landing was square, with six doors going off from it. He went to the second one on his left and thrust it open. He didn't enter. It was as he always remembered it, the bed unmade, the clothes strewn about the room, the whole seeming in a way to represent his wife. It had her body spread all over it, her mad, thrashing, ravenous body, that was governed by seemingly superhuman urges that were a torment to herself for they could never be satisfied.

He was about to close the door when his eye was attracted to the dressing-table mirror. It lay to the left of him. He paused a moment, then crossed the room and, bending down, peered at the mirror. Three words were written across the bottom corner of it in lipstick. They read 'That's me girl!'

He straightened his back, stared at the writing for a moment longer, then walked out of the room and down the stairs again and into a small room at the end of the hall. This room was lined with bookcases and the only pieces of furniture in it were two easy chairs and a small round table. He sat down and, resting his elbows on the table, lowered his head into his hands.

Well, he knew, didn't he? Why should he feel so surprised, so ashamed, so humiliated? That's me girl! He could see her prancing naked about the room like a demented witch; but the man who wrote 'That's me girl?' wouldn't, as he himself had done, have rushed from the room as if from a witch. No, the one who had written those words would have applauded and said 'That's me girl!'

He had never ceased to be amazed at the fires that burned in Victoria, weird, primeval fires. To live at all, he knew one must wear a façade for there were depths in all human beings that were better not probed, that is if you wanted to live what was termed a normal life; and he also knew that the wedding ceremony was a licence which allowed some of the lava to erupt from the murky depths where the sediment of human nature lay. And he had conformed, he had gone along with it. Natural sex had its place in life, and at its best, he felt, could be a beautiful experience. But what had happened? She had behaved like a stallion at stud, any time of the day or night, the hour didn't seem to matter . . . and without love; yes, that was the worst part of it, without love. He had once said to her, 'You don't act like a woman, you're more like a wild beast,' and she had come back with, 'And you're no man, you're a runt, and you know what they do with runts on the farm!'

He rose from the chair and walked to the window and looked out on the back garden. It was a nice garden; it was a lovely house; in ordinary circumstances they could have been so happy here. He would have gladly left the farm to Betty and his mother and got a job in the town.

And there were books here, hundreds of them. Her aunt had been a cultured woman; if only she had taken after her in some way; and if only her aunt hadn't died and left her this house and enough money to live on, for then she would have had to stay on the farm. But would she? And would life have been any better? No, no; a thousand times worse, for his mother and Betty hated her as much as she hated them.

And now he had come here to ask her to return to the farm, at least for a short while until his mother was on her feet again . . . or died. He must have been mad even to think she would comply. But what was he going to do? Things couldn't go on back there as they were.

As he turned from the window he heard the front door open, and when he entered the hall he saw her standing in front of the mirror about to take her hat off.

She turned towards him, her arms upraised, her face stretched in surprise, but no trace of fear or shame on it, he noted.

'Well! Well! What wind's blown you in?'

She turned to the mirror again and, withdrawing the pins from her hat, she placed them on the hall table; then lifting the hat carefully upwards from her high piled hair, she placed it on top of the pins. Bending towards the mirror, she pursed her lips, then stroked them at each corner with her middle finger. It reminded him of the action a man might make in smoothing his moustache, and it linked with previous thoughts that she was a man under her female skin; yet not enough of a man to want a woman. How much easier things would have been if the balance had swung in that way.

She walked before him now into the drawing-room. She looked big, full-blown was the word to describe her, yet she was handsome, like one of those seventeenth-century Rembrandt women. Her dress was of a blue material and straight, with an overskirt that was parted in the middle. The belt of the dress was loose about her waist, the collar was of a self material – she never wore lace trimmings.

He watched her go to a side table and, opening a silver box, take out a cigarette. When she had lit it and drawn deep on it she looked at him over her shoulder and said, 'Have you lost another of your faculties? Have you gone dumb?'

He closed his eyes for a moment, then said, 'I've come to ask you something.'

'No! No!' She turned with an exaggerated flounce now. 'You're going to beg me to go to bed with you? Oh, Charlie!' When she dropped her head coyly to the side he had the conflicting desire to turn and flee from her while at the same time some part of him sprang across the room and gripped her by the throat.

He walked to the empty fireplace and stared down into the bare iron basket as he said, 'Mother is very ill, young Sarah has left, Arnold has hurt his back and is of no use any more. Betty . . . Betty can't manage on her own.'

'Well! Well!' The words dribbled out of her mouth on a laugh, and she put her head back and drew again on her cigarette before continuing, 'You know, Charlie, you're funny. You are, you're the funniest fellow in the world. You're a weak-kneed gutless sod, but you're still funny because you're so naive, so gullible, so . . .' She tossed her head as she tried to find further words with which to express her opinion of him; then her manner suddenly changing, she stubbed the cigarette out on the first thing that came to her hand, which was an old beautifully painted Worcester plate, and as she ground the ash over the enamel, her voice, having now lost all its jocularity, bawled at him. 'You have the gall to stand there and ask me to go back and look after your mother! You must be flaming mad! Do you remember how we parted? I could have throttled her, the old bitch! As for dear Betty, if I had to come in contact with her again I just might.' She screwed up her eyes and peered at him, then in a lower tone she said, 'You must be barmy, you must, to come all this way to ask me that!'

'My mother is dying. That's putting it plainly. As for Betty, well, you wouldn't have to put up with her much longer, she's engaged to Robin Wetherby, and if they get married she'll go straight over to his place.'

'Really! And so you'll be left on your own. Poor, poor Charlie. Well, say your mother dies and Betty goes, what then? I come back and play the dutiful wife, which would help you no doubt to lift your head up again in the markets; that's if a conchie will ever be able to lift his head up again anywhere. . . . Can you see the picture, Charlie?' She waited a moment while they stared at each other across the room; then she flung her arms wide as she cried, 'If your mother was dying ten times over, and you along with her, you'd never get me back in that house again. I felt tied at home, but it was a home. . . . Your place! What is it but a bloody prison, an uncomfortable, cold, bloody prison. I hadn't even anyone to keep me warm in bed, had I? Eh! Had I?'

'That was your fault.'

'My fault? Aw, don't make me sick. You know what you are, Charlie MacFell; you know what you are, you're a nincompoop, nothing more or less, a nincompoop. You'll never have an experience in your life that's worthwhile, you'll never touch the depths, and you'll never touch the heights; you'll live on that same plane of niceness.' Her lip curled on the last word, and she went on, 'Nice fellow, nice and easy going; nice and polite, *nice, nice, nice*. . . . Get out of me sight!'

He didn't move. 'You had a man here last night.'

Her eyes widened slightly as she pressed her lips together; then she moved her head slowly up and down and said, 'Really! how do you make that out?'

'He left his approbation on the mirror.'

'Oh dear, dear! that was a mistake, wasn't it? I should have rubbed it off. But then I didn't expect to see you today.'

'I can divorce you.'

'You can what!'

'I'll repeat it for you, I can divorce you.'

'Aw no, Charlie, no, don't come that with me. You cannot divorce me, but I can divorce you . . . for non-consummation.'

'That's a lie!' His voice came suddenly loud and sharp, and he repeated, 'That's a damn lie and you know it!'

She took three slow steps towards him; then she stopped and said, 'You try, you try and divorce me, you blacken my name and I'll stand up in the highest court and tell them how I tried every way to make you love me as a man should. And you didn't . . . or couldn't.'

His face was ablaze; he felt the sweat in his oxters. It was he who moved forward now as he growled at her, 'Then I'll contest it. Yes, I'll contest it; with my last breath I'll contest it.'

They glared at each other for a moment. Then lifting her hand she patted her cheek as if in perplexity, saying to herself, 'My! my! Victoria, have you made a mistake and there's a man hidden somewhere in there?'

'Be careful!'

They were glaring at each other again.

'Good-bye, Charlie.'

He looked at her for a moment longer; then swinging round, he went from the room; and she went hastily after him and watched him grab up his coat and hat, but when he opened the door she cried at him, 'Why don't you try Nellie? She might help you out; that's if you can get her sobered up.'

When he opened the gate into the avenue he wanted to run. The anger inside him was acting like a fire stoking an engine; he wanted to use his limbs, to flay his arms, to toss his head. God! was there ever anybody in this world like her? But he had only himself to blame; surely he had known what to expect. Hadn't he gone through it all before? What in the name of God had made him think she would come back to the farm and help him out? Desperation, he supposed.

His walk was on the point of a run when he emerged into the main thoroughfare and there was forced to slow his pace, so that he was near the station when he recalled her words: 'Why don't you try Nellie? That's if you can get her sobered up.' Had she taken to drink that bad?

It was almost a year since he had seen Nellie; he had been to her house in Gateshead when she had first gone to live there. Her place, being in a terrace and three-storey high with a basement, wasn't anything like the one Victoria had, but it was a substantial house nevertheless. The basement and the upper two floors were let off, and Nellie had taken up her abode in the ground floor. The property brought in a small income, and Nellie, who had taken a course in shorthand and typing, had got a job in the office of one of the hospitals. That being so, he now thought, it wasn't likely she would leave it to help him out. Anyway, with the war restrictions, perhaps she wouldn't be allowed.

Should he go and see her? He had only to cross the bridge over the river; he could be there in ten minutes if he took a bus. . . .

The street looked dingy; the tall terraced houses looked like old ladies who had seen better days. He went up the four steps and into the hall that smelt dank and was thick with the aroma of cooking.

Before he knocked on the door he stood listening for a moment to the sound of laughter coming from within, and when the door opened, Nellie stood there, her mouth wide, a glass in her hand, saying, 'Come in. Come

– ' Her voice trailed away and she leaned forward, and then in a whisper said, 'Charlie!'

'Yes, Nellie; it's me.'

He watched her swallow, glance over her shoulder, then smile brightly as she said, 'Well! well! what are we standing here for? Come in. Come . . . on . . . in. Come . . . on . . . in.'

He walked into the room and looked at the two soldiers sitting on the couch, and they looked back at him, while Nellie, going towards them, swung her head from one side to the other, saying, 'This is an old friend of mine, this is Charlie. And this is Andy, and Phil.'

'How-do!' The two soldiers spoke together and their heads bobbed together. And Charlie answered, 'How-do-you-do?'

'Sit down. Sit down.' Nellie was pointing to a chair. 'Let me get you a drink. You're in clover, I can tell you; Andy brought this.' She laughed towards the shorter of the two men sitting on the couch. 'You can't get Scotch for love nor money, but Andy's got ways and means. Haven't you, Andy?'

'Aye, aye, I have that, Nellie; I've got shares in a Newcastle brewery.' His voice was thick with the Tyneside twang.

'Well, you should have, you've bought enough of their beer over the years.' The other man nudged his friend with his shoulder and they both laughed together.

When Nellie handed Charlie a glass with a good measure of whisky in it, he said 'Thanks', then raised it to her and afterwards to the men before he sipped at it.

'It's good stuff.' He nodded to them now, and the man called Andy laughed and said, 'Nowt but the best for the British Tommy.' The silence that followed was broken by Nellie in a loud voice exclaiming, 'What's brought you into town, Charlie?'

'I . . . I had a bit of business.'

'Oh. . . . Everything all right on the farm?'

He paused. 'Well, not quite, Mother's pretty bad and Arnold's off with severe back trouble.'

'Oh, I'm sorry to hear that. You got help?'

'No, that's the problem. Young Sarah . . . you remember young Sarah? Well, she left an' all.'

'Aw goodness me!' Nellie put down her glass and, leaning towards Charlie, said, 'You must be in a pickle then.'

'Yes. Well' – he gave a shaky laugh – 'everybody's in a pickle these days.' Of a sudden he gulped at the whisky and drained the glass, shuddered, then rose to his feet, saying, 'I'll have to be off; I have a train to catch.'

'But you've just got here!' She was standing in front of him, one hand gripping the lapel of his coat. 'Look, stay and have a bite; I'm . . . I'm not at work, I've been off with a cold. Come on, stay and have a bite.'

'I'm sorry Nellie' – he smiled weakly down at her – 'they'll be waiting for me and, as I said, we're short-handed; I'll have to get back.' He turned his head now and looked at the men and said, 'Good-bye.'

One of them answered, 'So long, chum,' while the other said, 'Ta-rah. Ta-rah.'

She went with him into the hall, closing the door after her, and there, gazing up into his face, she said softly, 'You look awful, Charlie. Aren't you well?'

'Yes, yes, I'm all right, Nellie.' But he could have returned the compliment by saying, 'And you look awful too.' How old was she, twenty-one? She looked thirty-one at this moment; her face was puffed, there were bags under her eyes.

'Have you been to see Vick?'

'Yes.'

'Any progress?'

'Just downwards.'

'Well, you're not missing anything there, Charlie.'

'Do . . . do you ever meet?'

'What! her and me? Only when we can't help it. She's doing a stint at present in a canteen. I went in there with the lads one night and there she was. . . . Huh!'

'There she was, what?'

'Oh, nothing.' She shrugged her shoulders, then said harshly, 'What am I covering up? You know how things are as well as I do. Yes, there she was, and aiming to serve in more ways than one.'

'Don't, Nellie.' He turned abruptly from her.

'I can't help it, Charlie.' She was again holding him by the lapels, with both hands now. 'You're a bloody fool.' Her voice was a thin whisper. 'You should never have married her, you know that. She's a maniac. . . . Do you still love her?'

He turned his head sharply from the side and looked at her. 'Love her! love Victoria! Still love her did you say? I can't remember ever having done so in the first place. You said she was a maniac; but no, you are wrong there, Nellie, it was me who was the maniac.'

After a moment of silence she slapped him with the flat of her hand in the middle of his chest and she grinned at him as she said, 'You'd have made a better bargain with me, wouldn't you?'

'Oh, Nellie!' He returned her smile and shook his head, and she went on, 'You would, I know you would.'

He put up his hand and stroked her cheek. There was something endearing about Nellie, and always had been; she was so frank, so open, so adult, yet at the same time so childlike. He leaned forward and put his lips to her cheek. 'Take care of yourself and . . . go easy on the Newcastle brewery, it's bad for the complexion.' He opened the door and went down the steps, and when he turned she was standing just as he had left her, and she did not answer the salute of his hand, nor as he walked away did he hear the door close.

You would have made a better bargain with me, Charlie.

He had no doubt of it, no doubt at all.

Mary MacFell was dying and she was dying hard. She didn't want to go. She was resentful that she was being forced to go; she hadn't got her money's worth out of the place; she hadn't been repaid for what she had suffered at the hands of Edward MacFell, and later from the tongue of her daughter-in-law. And when she was gone who would control the place? Betty? Yes, Betty. That gangling son of hers was no match for his sister.

She gasped at the air as she looked up into the face of her son, the son she had once loved. For sixteen years she had loved that face, but over the past eight years she had come to hate it. Her son was soft; and yet not soft enough to give her control of the farm, not easygoing enough to let her write out cheques. He had stopped her buying furniture and finery. In a way she had suffered as much from his hands as she had from her husband's. . . . But if only she could get her breath.

'Take it easy, Mother. There, there!' He smoothed the pillows; then taking a cup from the side table, he put one hand under her head as he said, 'Try to sip this. Come on, it will ease your throat. Try to sip this.'

She thrust his hand and the cup away from her and the linctus spilled over the bedcover.

He turned from the bed and went to the washhand stand. After dipping a flannel into the basin of water, he went back to the bed and rubbed at the collar of her night-gown and the sheet and the eiderdown; and while he did this she lay gasping, her glazed gaze fixed tight on him. And he was aware of it; as also he was aware of the antipathy emanating from it.

Betty came into the room and, coming to the bed, demanded, 'What happened?'

'I spilt the linctus.'

'Trust you!'

His glance flashed upwards towards her, but she took no notice of it; then as if her mother was past hearing she said, 'Come downstairs a minute, I want a word with you.'

After she had left the room he straightened the bedclothes and said, 'I won't be long.'

When he reached the kitchen Betty was taking a pan of broth from the stove, and after she had placed its sooty bottom on an iron stand on the table she said, 'Robin just called in. He tells me they've got German prisoners working over at Threadgill's place. You want to go and see if we can have some.'

'How can I go and leave her now?'

'She'll last out; Doctor Adams said it could be days or even weeks.'

'I don't agree with him; she's in a pretty low state.'

Betty stopped stirring the broth and, lifting the long steel ladle out of the pot, she banged it down on the table, saying, 'Well, we're all in a low state if you ask me. I'm at the end of me tether. And I'm telling you, Charlie, here and now we've got to talk about things.'

He rested both hands on the end of the table and, bowing his head, said, 'All right, all right, we've got to talk about it. But with me it's the same as before. You may marry Wetherby tomorrow if you like but I'm not having him living in here; if he marries you he's got to make a home for you.'

'Well' – she leant towards him now, her hands flat on the table – 'if I go, who's going to look after the place, inside and out?'

'That wouldn't be your worry. I'd get along somehow.'

'Oh yes, you would. Look' – she moved round the table now until she was within touching distance of him – 'what you hoping for, that when the house is empty she'll come back?'

He lifted his head and stared at her and said, 'No, that isn't my hope, Betty. She'll never come back here; nor do I want her here, but at the same time I don't want Wetherby either.' His voice had risen now.

'What have you got against him?'

'I'll tell you what I've got against him. He's never kept down a job in years. He lives on his old people, and they haven't got much, and if he came here you would find yourself doing the work for both of you.'

Her small body stiffened. 'I couldn't be expected to do more than I do now. I know ... I know' – her head bobbed on her shoulders – 'you don't want me to get married, you're afraid of losing me. I'm worth two men outside and a couple of women inside to you, and what for? What do I get out of it?' Her tone sounded weary now.

'I've told you, marry him tomorrow or any time you like, and when you do I won't let you go empty-handed. But now we'll say no more about it.'

As he turned from her and went up the kitchen again she called after him, 'I will marry him! I will! I'm not going to die in this god-forsaken place looking after you, you with a face like a melancholy owl!'

The green-baized door cut off her voice and he walked across the hall and up the stairs. The whole house seemed silent, empty, as if there was no life in it. A face like a melancholy owl. Yes, he supposed that's how he looked to people, like a melancholy owl. He stopped on the landing. Why didn't he let her bring Wetherby here? If anybody could make him work she could. And anyway, he himself didn't have to live with them, he could go away. He could join up.

What! and stick bayonets into German bellies, blind men, blow off their legs, their arms, disfigure them for life? Join up? Him? Never!

# Chapter Three

It was in March 1916 that conscription for single men came into force, the married men being given two months' respite. Then, on June 5th to be exact, Kitchener went down with the *Hampshire* – the ship struck a mine off Scapa Flow – and so the man whose portrait and pointing finger had admonished every Britisher that his king and country needed him was no more; that he had been a great strategist only to the unknowledgeable, the ordinary man, was an accepted fact by those in high places.

Power is a disease, the only disease that man hugs to himself and bandages with strategy. And so Lloyd George had made himself Secretary for War. Those who, for the last year, had been crying out for conscription waved their banners while their opponents verbally lambasted them as fools, for were there not more than enough men already recruited to fill the gaps in Flanders? And where was the money coming from to equip the new intake? What was wanted was guns and more guns; machine-guns, not merely rifles, machine-guns that went rat-rat-tat-tat, taking a life with every beat.

And what was more, leaders were wanted, young imaginative men, not old dodderers who couldn't see their noses before their faces. This wasn't a war of 'Up men and at 'em!', the Charge of the Light Brigade all over again, but a war that was to be fought out in the ground as it were. Men had to become like moles, looking only to the earth for their habitation, and while being moles they had to develop minds like foxes.

Of course, as it always had been said, all younger generations thought they knew better than the older ones, but in this case a lot of the younger commanders did know better, for they were stressing it was motorized vehicles that were wanted, not horses and waggons. There were twice as many horses in France as there were motor-buses, motor-cycles, and lorries put together, and horses had to be fed, and undoubtedly there would come a time when their straw and chaff would be needed to supplement the bread back home.

It wasn't until July 1st 1916 that the romance went completely out of the war. On that day nineteen thousand men never lived to see another, for the Germans mowed them down as if they had been insects, and, added to the list, fifty thousand crippled in one way or another.

The Somme changed the Britishers' attitude towards the war. The slaughter went on until November, when both sides were brought to a halt. Choked with mud, their senses dulled against death, they dug in for the winter.

Yet poets still wrote poetry – although the tang had become bitter – and officers still behaved like gentlemen. Whenever possible officers' uniforms were immaculate, and to ensure this should be so a batman was as necessary to an officer as was the port in the mess.

There was trouble in Ireland – there was always trouble in Ireland – there was trouble in Russia, there was trouble in Roumania, there was trouble at sea, but Lloyd George still kept giving out his messages of hope to the people. Weren't they pushing the enemy back? Weren't they taking German prisoners? Hadn't they scared off the German Fleet? No mention that the Germans had scared off the British Fleet too.

Such is war. It can be lost on despair, or won on morale.

Charlie stood before a wooden table which was the top one of six in the long, narrow room. He looked down on the head of the soldier who was writing, and like a prisoner up before a judge, he answered the questions thrown at him. Age? Name? Occupation? Eventually a card was handed to him. The arm lifted, the finger pointed: 'Go along the corridor.' But he never saw the speaker's face.

He had no need to ask what he was to do along the corridor. He stood in a queue and eventually he was told to take his clothes off. He was sounded and prodded, his knees were tapped, he was told to put his clothes on again.

'Bloody conscripts!'

'And had to be pulled in.'

'And what a bloody lot! all but the deaf, blind and lame.'

'But you, mate . . . they'll use you for a trench board over there, you're long enough. Go on, get the hell out of it!'

He didn't get angry, it was no use; anyway, he was feeling too numbed to arouse himself and the whole procedure was as he had been led to expect. The ignorant were always bullies; and he told himself he wouldn't find them only in the ranks.

This last assumption was proved when after four hours and twenty minutes of sitting, standing, waiting, he found himself outside being ordered to get into line with another twenty or more men.

'Officer is goin' to inspect you, an' my God! if he doesn't pass out it's 'cos he's got a strong stomach. . . . Get Charlie off yer back, you!'

As the fist hitting him between his shoulders knocked him out of line, Charlie coughed, and when he turned swiftly about and faced the corporal, that individual cocked his chin up in the air, narrowed his eyes and from his jutted lips he said, 'You would like to, wouldn't you, lanky? Well, me advice is, watch it! watch it! If you weren't short on spunk you wouldn't be here now, so you'd better keep the little bit you have till you meet up with Jerry.'

Charlie stood in line again, his shoulders straight now, his face red, his teeth clenched.

He was a fool. Once again he had been a fool. He could have got out of it, he was a farmer, but in a moment of madness he had decided he must get away, away from the farm and Betty and her constant nagging to have Wetherby there. Well, he had potched her on that. Anyway, he had left Fred Ryton in charge and Fred got on well with the German prisoners. Funny that, the German prisoners. He had liked them, and had learned to speak a bit of German from them. One of them had spoken fluent French and he had polished his own French on him. Yes, he had liked the Germans; and now he was going to learn to kill them. But by the time they had taught him to use a rifle the war would likely be over. Pray God it would anyway. If not . . . well a German might get in first and that would solve all his problems.

Divn't let him rile you, mate.' The voice came to him in a whisper.

Charlie didn't move his head but he cast his eyes sideways, then looked to the front again to where the corporal was walking across the square towards a row of buildings on the opposite side.

'He's a nowt!'

'I agree with you there.'

The head was turned slightly towards him, and again Charlie cast his eyes sidewards.

'How did you get here, you're not from these parts?'

'Yes . . . yes, I am.'

'Well' – there came a smothered laugh – 'you divn't sound like it.'

'I come from over near Otterburn.'

'Aw, I'm from Gateshead. Me name's Johnny Tullett.'

'Mine's Charlie MacFell.'

There came the sound of the laugh again. ' "Charlie." And he called you Charlie. "Get Charlie off yer back," he said; that's what made you turn on him likely. Me mother always used to be sayin' that to me when I sat humped up. . . . Look out! Look out! here comes Nancy-Pan.'

The corporal was once more standing in front of the line.

'This 'ere's the new batch, sir.'

'Ye-rs. Ye-rs.'

The young second-lieutenant with a chin that looked as if it had never given birth to a hair walked slowly along the line of men.

'I can see what you mean, Corporal. Ye-rs. Ye-rs.'

At the end of the line he turned and walked slowly back, eyeing each man as if he were viewing something that had been dragged out of a cesspool. Then as if the sight of the men had made him slightly sick and he couldn't bear to address them, he looked at the corporal and nodded to him as he said, 'Carry on, Corporal.'

The corporal carried on. And he carried on, too, in the hut when he never ceased to shout as he instructed them into what they had to do with their bedding and their kit, and what would happen to them if they didn't do what he told them to do with their bedding and their kit. He was in the middle of telling them what life was going to be like for them during the next few weeks when the door of the hut opened and a sergeant came in. The sergeant stood just within the door and the corporal was shouting so loudly that he didn't hear him until the sergeant spoke his name.

'*Corporal!*'

The voice startled every man in the room, even those who were looking at the sergeant, and the corporal sprang round and said, 'Yes, Sergeant. Yes, Sergeant,' and scurried like a scalded cat to his side.

It brought a feeling of pleasure to Charlie when he realized that here was someone who could out-shout the obnoxious individual. He likely could out-bully him too. In any case he evidently had the power to make the fellow jump. He noticed, too, that the sergeant didn't even condescend to look at the corporal as he said, 'Get down to the office, there's another batch there.'

'Yes, Sergeant. Yes, Sergeant.' The corporal almost left the hut at the double, and now all the men watched the sergeant walk slowly into their midst. They watched him turn around slowly and survey one after the other of them; and then, his voice quite normal sounding, he said, 'Been putting you through it, has he?' His tone, Charlie noticed, wasn't unlike that of his talkative companion in the line.

When no one answered the sergeant said, 'Well, you'll get a lot of that in the next few weeks. And you'll have to take it whence it comes; but you and me 'll get along all right so long as you don't pull any tricks, 'cos they won't come off, I'll tell you that for a start. And another thing I'll tell you, I can't abear tricksters. You know the kind? Wife's goin' to have a bairn, poppin' out any minute, browned off with being in the oven.' There was a snigger at this. 'Mother on her death-bed. . . . Likely with the lodger!'

There was actual laughter now, but immediately the sergeant stopped his pirouetting. His face grim and his tone to match, he said, 'Now! now! we'll have no laughin'! No; no laughin'. I'm a funny man, I know that, but I cannot stand being laughed at.'

His features slowly melted and there could have been a twinkle in the back of his eye, but it didn't bring forth a murmur now, and he turned and walked slowly back up between the row of beds, saying as he did so, 'Now we've been introduced, I'll give you one word of advice. Whenever you're told to do anything, jump to it! Believe me, it'll save you a lot of trouble in the end.'

At the door he turned and once again his eyes moved over them all, and then he said in that ordinary tone that was in itself so disarming, 'There's grub over in number three block, an' if you're not there within fifteen minutes you won't eat till the morrow mornin'. And now this is your first lesson in learnin' to jump to it; it'll take you all of fifteen minutes – that's if you go at it – to get your kit put straight, to get your bed made, and this hut left tidy. But of course if you learn to jump to it, well, you might be able to manage it in less.'

He gave three nods of his head then turned and walked out, leaving behind him a blank silence that lasted for about three seconds. Then the silence was exploded by a mad scramble during which Charlie actually laughed one of his rare laughs.

And Charlie's mood remained light for the next week in spite of skinned heels, aching limbs and indigestible food, and ears that were becoming numbed with the shouting, the bawling and the cursing. That was until the shuffle round started. It happened, he learned from one of the old hands, every so often. The numskulls at the top found a lot of empty forms that had to be filled in. But what did they fill them in with? A shuffleabout: postings, here, there and every God damn where.

The postings, of course, didn't concern the new batch of conscripts, it merely concerned one man, their sergeant who everybody conceded was as decent a bloke as you'd ever get in a sergeant. Mind, that wasn't saying much, but still they could have worse.

And they got worse. The rest of the platoon was only affected by the new sergeant being, what they termed, true to bloody-minded form; but in Charlie's case he was an old acquaintance.

The first time Charlie came face to face with the replacement he stared unbelieving at Slater, and when his mind groaned, Christ Almighty! not this an' all, the words carried no trace of blasphemy. It was as if he were addressing the Almighty and asking Him as man to man why He was leading him into these situations.

True, he had walked stubbornly into managing the farm, telling himself that in time experience would sit on his shoulders and make him appear as if he were cut out for the job. Then blindly, weakly like a lamb, no, like an ass to the slaughter, he had allowed himself to be led into marriage.

But this latest situation wasn't of his choosing, either through purpose or weakness; he had been dragged into this. No, that wasn't right; he could have got out of it, he was a farmer. But since finding himself here, strangely, he was beginning to enjoy it; it was the companionship, the rough and tumble among men, ordinary, everyday men like Johnny, raw, blunt, kindly, humorous men. Only yesterday he was regretting not having joined up before conscription; that was until he made himself remember why he was here, merely to learn how to kill. However, that was in the future, at least it had been until this very minute when he looked down the room and saw the new sergeant.

At first Slater didn't recognize him. Using the trick of all sergeants he looked silently round at the men who were standing in different parts of the room waiting for him to speak, but his eyes hadn't traversed the full circle before his gaze stopped its roving and his eyes narrowed, then widened, while his head moved just the slightest bit forward like a bull weighing up the obstacle before it, the human obstacle.

After a moment he allowed his eyes to finish their inspection. Then unlike his predecessor had done on first viewing his new charges, he made no prolonged speech to them, all he said to the assembled men was, 'Well! well! well!' Then marching smartly up the end of the room he stopped before the tall figure, and again he said, 'Well! well! well!' And after a pause he added, 'So they raked you in at last.'

Charlie made no answer, he just stared into the thin face that, unlike the body, hadn't seemed to have grown with the years but still retained the pinched look about it. The only thing that was missing was the look of fear that the eyes had carried until the day he had been given food for blackmail.

'Strange world, isn't it, MacFell?'

Still Charlie didn't answer.

'I was speaking to you.'

There was a short silence before Charlie answered; then in tones that the men might have expected to be used by an officer he said, 'I endorse what you say, it is a strange world.'

Slater's hair was cropped close yet it still showed red, and now the colour seemed to be seeping down into his pale skin and his features went into contortion, his mouth opened wide, his nostrils expanded, his eyes became slits; it was as if he were on the parade ground and about to issue an order, but what he barked was, 'Say sergeant when you speak to me.'

In the heavy silence that followed Charlie pronounced the word sergeant in the same tone he had previously used and it sounded like an insult.

Again there was silence before Slater spoke; and when he did his voice was scarcely audible except to Charlie and those standing quite near to him, for what he said was, 'It's gona be a hard cinder path for you, MacFell. If it lies with me I'll see that there are fresh ashes put on it every day.' On this he turned about and walked smartly from the room, and no eyes were turned to watch him go because they were all directed on the fellow most of them were thinking was barmy to have got the new sergeant's back up like that.

'You know 'im?' They gathered round him now.

'He's got it in for you.'

'What was that he was sayin' about cinders?'

'He'll put you on fatigues. . . . Still it isn't a bad job; keep your hands warm.'

'You must have known him afore.'

'What've you ever done to him?'

'I heard about 'im, he's nicknamed the Red Sod. Take the guts out of a gate-post, they say, he would. I'd go careful, mate, if I was you.'

As yet Charlie had answered none of the questions, but now he looked from one to the other and said simply, 'He worked on my farm.'

'You had a farm?'

Johnny nudged the speaker and said in an aside, 'Aye. Aye, he's a farmer, up Otterburn way.'

'I thought they were exempt?'

'It seems he didn't want to be.'

'He must have been a bugger, ' the voice muttered again. 'He doesn't look like one, anything but, yet you never know. Anyway, the new un's got it in for him for something.'

The voices faded away and Charlie sat on the side of the bed and applied himself meticulously to rolling up his putties, and Johnny Tullett, sitting on the opposite bed, slipped in the button shoe under the top brass button of his tunic and rubbed vigorously at it until it showed a high polish; then holding it from his gaze, he surveyed it, after which he brought it to his mouth, breathed on it hard and began polishing again. And now as he rubbed he said under his breath, 'What did you ever do to him, Charlie, to make him feel like that?'

'Nothing, nothing personally.'

'Funny.'

After a while Johnny spoke again, still under his breath. 'What did he mean by hintin' that your time here was gona be like a long cinder path?'

'He was referring to a cinder path on the farm.'

'Oh. . . . Has it got to do with how he feels?'

'Yes.'

'A cinder path?' The words were like a large question mark, and Charlie looked up and met Johnny's gaze and he said simply, 'My father took pleasure in whipping the lads for any misdemeanour. He did it on the cinder path; it hurt more there when they fell on their hands and knees.'

'Good God!'

'Yes, Johnny, good God!'

They both lowered their heads to their work again until Johnny said, 'I can understand how he feels. Bugger me, aye, I can that, it's enough to colour your resentment for life. Still' – he leant towards Charlie now – 'you didn't do owt like that to him, did you?'

'No.'

'Well, what's he got it in for you for?'

'I'm my father's son.'

'Oh! Oh aye, I see. Has he been long left the farm?'

'Some three years. He left when he was twenty.'

'Is that all he is, twenty-three? God! he looks years older. Is he married do you know?'

'Yes, he left to get married.'

'Did she . . . did his wife work on the farm?'

'Not on ours, the next one.'

Johnny was now staring at Charlie and he asked quietly, 'Do you know her?'

'Oh yes, yes.' Charlie nodded his head emphatically as he said this, and again he said, 'Oh yes, we were all brought up together.'

'Fancy that.' There was speculation in the statement.

'Yes, fancy that.'

Charlie now took his tunic off and started on his buttons, and as he gazed down at the dials of shining brass he saw Polly's face the day she had come to say good-bye to him. She said she had been up to the cottages to have a last look round the old place. There were tears in her eyes, and when he said to her, 'You shouldn't do it, Polly,' she had answered, 'What else is there for me?' and he had turned his head away from her gaze and said, 'Life dictates to us.' Her only answer to this was, 'Aye, I suppose it does.' Then when he had begun to say 'Should you ever need me, Polly . . . ' she had stopped him abruptly, asking, 'Why, should I need you now? Why should I ever need you, I'm gona be married? Oh' – her head had wagged – 'don't worry that he'll ever be tough on me. You needn't worry about that, Charlie, for there's one thing I'm sure of, an' that is he cares for me. He always has, right from the beginnin', and although, well, I don't love him, I like him, and that's not a bad start.' Her tone was aggressive.

'No,' he had agreed with her; 'that's not a bad start.'

When she had offered him her hand he had held it while they gazed at each other, seeing a life that might have been. And then she had turned and was gone from him.

He had stood watching her until she disappeared from view, and when he turned it was to see Slater standing in the middle of the yard.

'Sayin' your good-byes then?' He had ignored the fellow's tone and said,
'Yes, we were saying our good-byes.'

Then Slater's eyes narrowed and his lips squared away from his teeth as
he said, 'You're a loser, you know that. You've wanted her, haven't you? All
these years you've wanted her, but you haven't had the guts to face the
neighbours and take her. Your father offered her to you on a plate, didn't
he? Oh. Oh, she's told me; there had to be a reason why bully-boy Arthur
throttled your old man. An' you know, something I'll tell you that'll surprise
you, in a way I've admired him for doing it, but you, who watched your
father bein' murdered then covered it up, why, I've despised you all these
years. You know, I used to envy you having a mother and father, and as big
an old sod as yours was, I'd have given me sight, aye, I'd have given me
sight just to have been able to call somebody father, to know who he was,
or who she was. But there was you, you watched him being lynched and you
covered it up, but not to save Arthur's neck, oh no, it was because of Polly
you did it, wasn't it? 'Cos you wanted to shine in Polly's eyes, be the big
hero. Now fancy that, you a hero! Well, you've lost again, an' you always
will.'

How had he stood there and taken all that and not struck out? He had
wanted to. In fact, part of him had jumped for the birch stick that was still
hanging behind the door in the harness-room, and he had seen himself
lashing the fellow across the yard and out of the gate; no, not out of the gate,
through the alleyway and on to the cinder path; but all he had done was to
raise his arm and point towards the gate, saying, 'Get out! And now, not
tomorrow, now! You thankless scum.'

'Fancy that!' It was Johnny speaking his amazement aloud again.

## Chapter Four

Had he been in the army only five months? Wasn't it five years, five lifetimes,
five eons?

He was in what they called the new army, the training section of the
reserve battalion. Battalions were shuffled and re-shuffled. The sixteenth
and seventeenth battalions of the Durham Light Infantry became the First
and Second Reserve Battalions. There were young soldier battalions, graduated battalions; a soldier was passed from one to the other, allotted to a
company, and every three months or so the young men were spilled from the
battalion on to a ship, and thus into the mud of France. There was always
mud in France; seasons weren't long enough to dry it off.

It was usually the nineteen-year-olds that filled these drafts, but there
had been a rumour flying round for the last few days that their own lot were
ready for a move, and it wasn't for Durham or Shields, or Seaham Harbour,
or Barnard Castle, or Ravensworth, but France.

Some of the men had the jitters and had to reassure themselves by continually saying they were in a reserved company and were simply a basis for reserve battalions, and that it was just the young 'uns who were drafted to the main battalion; they had been given to understand at the beginning that their unit wouldn't be required to serve abroad.

Who had given them to understand this?

Nobody knew.

Charlie thought he was the only one, at least in his platoon, of thirty men who longed to be one of the chosen to be sent overseas – it must be overseas – because wherever they went here Slater would inevitably go with them.

He had he knew become a different being during the past five months. And the change wasn't due to the army; the army could never have made him hate. He could never have opened his mouth wide enough to let out that piercing scream as he stuck his bayonet into a bag of straw if it hadn't been for Slater. It had been terrifying when it first happened, it had even caused him to vomit. Afterwards he had to get up in the middle of the night and go outside because he couldn't get the picture out of his mind that the bag of straw was Slater. Perhaps if it hadn't been for Johnny he might have tried, but Johnny, the escaped pitman, as he called himself because he had left the pits before the war started, only later to find himself conscripted because he wasn't in a reserved occupation, talked to him like a brother, a comforting older brother. How many times and in how many different ways had he said, 'Hold your hand, lad. Just remember that's what he wants you to do, hit out at him. An' then you'd be for it, the glasshouse. An' likely he's got mates there. What he can do to you now 'll be nothin' to what they'll find to fill your days with. I've heard about some of them bastards. It can't go on for ever. I only know one thing, Charlie, I wouldn't be sayin' this to you if we were out there, 'cos there'd be no more need. I've heard of fellows like him dyin' suddenly, shot in the back while they're facin' the enemy. Hang on, Charlie. Hang on, mate.'

But how much longer he could hang on, he didn't know; the situation was becoming desperate because Slater's latest tactic was to talk at him. Only yesterday, addressing some of the other men in the billet he had said, 'You know some fellows are unfortunate, they never drop into the right occupation, they're put in a position where they have to kill animals, you know, like slittin' a pig's throat, an' God! you should see 'em, yellow they turn, yes, yellow, real nancy-pans! They should have picked a job like servin' in a shop, ladies particularly, camisoles 'n knickers 'n things like that, that's just about what they could handle.'

Some had laughed, being of the opinion that the sergeant was decent enough on the whole; it was how you took him.

Yes, the sergeant was wily enough to be decent enough on the whole. He spoke civilly to others, he gave some small privileges, he joked with others, and so not a few were in sympathy with him.

It was open knowledge now that he had been flogged on the cinder path; in fact some had been given further to understand that the treatment hadn't ceased when he had grown out of boyhood.

Charlie knew that the whole thing had been blown up out of all perspective and it would be no use him trying to alter the picture, even if he felt so inclined, which he didn't.

They had all been given forty-eight hours' leave. Was this the sign? Rumours were flying hither and thither.

'What do you make of it?' Johnny asked.

'It could be. Hope to God it is.'

'Well, I'm not as eager as you, Charlie, but I wouldn't mind gettin' out of this. Anyroad, I'd better go home and see wor lass, and prepare her. She's likely to go mad, she thought I was sittin' cushy for the duration. You wouldn't like to come along of us and meet her, would you, Charlie?'

'I'm sorry, Johnny. If I get another chance I will, but if this is our last leave then I've got a lot of things to do.'

A voice from down the room shouted, 'Can't mean we're goin' across, they give you embarkation leave, an' they tell you you're for it.'

Another answered in a tone deceptively soft at first, 'Who does, the colonel? Does he send for you and tell you to go and enjoy yourself, lad, 'cos this is your last chance?' The tone rose almost to a bellow now. 'Don't be so bloody soft, they keep these things secret. Five minutes after we come back Sunday night we could be skited like diarrhoea into trucks an' off we'll go hell for leather to the bloody south, an' them Southerners will be lining the streets and shoutin' "Here come some bloody Geordie aborigines!' And you know what? They'll get the shock of their lives 'cos they think we still carry spears up here and paint worsels from the eyebrows right down over the waterfall to the toe nails. The Scots, they think they're civilized compared with us 'cos their fellows wear skirts.'

The hut rocked with laughter and Johnny, his mouth wide, looked at Charlie and said, 'Isn't Bill a star turn? I hope he comes along of us wherever we're goin'.' Then his face sober, he said, 'I hope I go along of you, Charlie, wherever you're bound for.'

'I hope you do, Johnny. Oh yes, I hope you do.'

The sincerity in his voice came from his heart, for of all the men he had met in his life he had never known companionship like that which existed now between this rough looking, rough talking man and himself.

'What you goin' to do with yourself?' Johnny asked now.

'First of all, go straight home and leave things in order there as much as I can; then I've one or two visits to make.'

Johnny, now pulling on his greatcoat, muffled his words in his collar as he said, 'You won't do a skip, will you, Charlie?'

'Do a skip? You mean?' He paused before giving a slight laugh and, shaking his head, he said, 'No, no, Johnny; don't worry about that, I won't do a skip.'

'Good. Good.'

He had caught a train to Newcastle, swallowed three mugs of hot, scalding tea and two sandwiches, then made his way to the Otterburn road to see if he could pick up any army transport. Within half an hour he was lucky and got a lift in an army truck which dropped him just before one o'clock near Kirkwhelpington.

He did not immediately walk from the main road and into the lane but stood looking about him. The late November sky was hanging low over the land. It had cut off the tops of the distant hills and its leaden shadow was lying on the fields, which were still stiff from the overnight frost. There was snow in the air; he could smell it. He put his head back and sniffed and listened to the silence. But was this silence? The very air vibrated with different sounds. The old stones gripping each other for foothold on the walls sang; the road under his feet trembled with the distant echo of marching feet; the cattle standing silhouetted in the field below him murmured with the knowledge of instinct, 'We're going to die. We're going to die.'

His lids blinked rapidly, and he hunched the collar of his greatcoat further up round his neck. These were the kind of thoughts he used to think when he stood on the hills alone, wisps of imagination, words linking themselves together in an effort to explain his emotions. Funny, for a moment he had felt a boy again, young, alone, lost, yet one with all this, this aloneness, this wildness, this closeness that gave off the feeling of never ending, eternity past and eternity to come.

He walked from the road now and on to the bridle path, on and on, leaping gates, tramping over fields, going through narrow gaps in stone walls; and then he was in the copse. He never passed through the copse but he remembered the day his father died. Yet today when the thought touched his mind it brought no regret, no feeling of guilt. Those feelings had been washed clean away over the past five months by Sergeant Sidney Slater.

The farmyard looked clean, in fact cleaner than he had ever seen it. As he made his way across it to the kitchen door a voice from the corner of the yard called, '*Bon jour, monsieur*,' and he turned and answered brightly, '*Bon jour*,' then walking towards the man who instinctively stood to attention, he said in English, 'How are you getting on?' and the man replied slowly, 'Oh, very . . . well, sir. Very well.'

'I'm glad.'

'You . . . on leave, sir?'

'Yes; a very short one.'

'Oh.' They smiled at each other and Charlie said, 'I'll see you again before I go. The others all right?'

'Pardon. Pardon.'

Now Charlie answered him in French, saying '*Les autres; sont-ils heureux?*'

'*Oui, monsieur.*'

There was no one in the kitchen when he entered and he went through into the hall, calling, 'Hello! Hello there!' Instantly the sitting-room door opened and he smiled sadly to himself when Betty, disappointment evident on her face and in her voice, said, 'Oh, it's you!'

'Yes, it's me.'

'You cold?' She stood aside and let him into the room where a big fire was blazing in the open hearth.

'Frozen; there'll be snow soon.'

'We had some last week.'

'Yes.'

'What's brought you here today?'

He took off his greatcoat and stood with his back to the fire, his hands on his buttocks, before he replied, 'I've a forty-eight hours' leave. It could be embarkation; I don't know.'

'Overseas!' She stared up into his face. 'I thought you would be in clerical or something like that.'

'Well, they seem to think differently.'

'Are you hungry?'

'Yes, a bit; I haven't had anything since early on.'

'There's only cold stuff, chicken and a bit of lamb.'

'Only!' He laughed down on her now. 'I never realized how lucky we were with regards to food; the eggs they dish up there could never have been laid by hens.'

She smiled up at him, a tight, prim smile; then turning from him, she said, 'You'll have a lot to see to before you go then?'

'Yes, quite a bit.'

She looked at him over her shoulder, saying, 'I'll get you something.'

Left alone, he sat down in a chair to the side of the fireplace and let his gaze wander slowly around the room, the room that had been changed from a comfortable workaday parlour into the imitation of a drawing-room, a French one at that. There was a spidery-legged French Louis suite taking up one corner of the room and next to it and standing underneath a large ornate gold-framed mirror was what his mother always referred to as her *bonheur du jour*, never the writing-desk. Then there was the small nest of tables and the chaise-longue; the only piece left of the old furniture was the suite, and this was covered with a chintz, of which the pattern sported gold garlands and bows. There wasn't a room in the house which hadn't escaped her change, except the kitchen and his bedroom.

When her own money was exhausted she still defiantly went on buying; and the bills had come to him until he was forced to put a notice in the newspaper stating that he would no longer be responsible for her debts. The rows, the recriminations this brought forth rang in his ears even yet. Wasn't it *his* house she was furnishing? He'd bring a wife here some day, wouldn't he?

But not until the day he broke the news that he was in fact bringing a wife to the house did the hurricane of her temper sweep through the place, when she threatened to make a bonfire of every stick in it.

Now she was gone, and he'd soon be gone and he might never come back again. What then? The place would go to Betty; he had made a will to that effect and it was about that he must talk to her. If anything happened to him Victoria would likely put a claim in, as was her right. But under the circumstances she might not. Anyway they could fight that out between them.

She brought him a meal on a tray and while he ate they exchanged hardly a word. He did ask how she was getting on with the men; and her answer was, all right, but she kept them in their place, for after all they were Germans, weren't they, and she was a woman alone here.

After he had finished his meal and she had poured him out a second cup of tea she repeated those words by saying, 'Have you ever considered my situation now that I'm alone here among these prisoners?'

'You'll not be alone as long as Arnold's there. Where is he, by the way? I thought he would have popped over.'

'It's his time off. Anyway he's gone into the town. And what use would he be if any of them attacked me? He can't straighten that back of his.'

'I don't think you need worry about that.'

'Huh!' – she screwed her small tight buttocks down into the couch – 'I'm as attractive as the next; true I'm not like a full blown horse' – he took it that she was referring to Victoria – 'but when it comes down to the needs and seeds, looks won't bother men.'

He closed his eyes for a moment, then turned and looked into the fire before saying heavily, 'I wasn't underrating your looks in any way, you know that, but Heinrich is a gentleman, what he says seems to go with the others. Moreover. . . .'

'Moreover, nothing!' She spat the words at him. 'Will you never grow up, Charlie? He's a gentleman!' She mimicked his voice. 'So is the bull; he's the best of his breed but if he thinks at all there's only one thing on his mind. And it's the same with them, more so 'cos they're frustrated.'

'All right, all right, Betty.' He was shouting now. 'You can have it your own way; Wetherby may come, that's if you get married, but the stipulation still stands that when I return you'll have to find a place of your own. You won't have to do it empty-handed, I can assure you, you've worked hard here, no one harder, so you're entitled to half the profits that are standing when I come back . . . if I come back. If I don't' – he shrugged his shoulders – 'well, then you'll have it all your own way. I've already put that in writing, and also the business of you drawing cheques on the bank while I'm away.'

She stared at him for a moment, then bit on her lip. 'You'll come back,' she said.

He rose from the chair and walked across the room to the window and stood looking out for a moment before he spoke again. 'At the present moment I don't much care, the only thing I want is to be posted, anywhere, Land's End, John o' Groats, overseas.' He swung round and looked down the room towards her. 'Ginger Slater is my sergeant. He's been giving me merry hell.'

'Ginger!'

'Yes, Ginger.'

'Good God! How did he become a sergeant?'

'Because he's smart and he's got a head on his shoulders and he's wily.'

'But why should he want to take it out on you? I knew he didn't like you very much, in fact at times I thought . . . well –' She turned away and put her hand on the mantelshelf and looked down into the fire, and he came towards her now, repeating, 'Well what?' and she turned to him and ended, 'Well, at times the way he used to speak to you and you stood it, well, I thought he had something on you.'

'What could he have on me?' He stared down at her as she bent and lifted a log from the side of the hearth and pressed it into the red glow of the fire, and she was dusting her hands as she said, 'Oh well, it was just a thought.'

'What was?'

'Well, that he had you where he wanted you 'cos you were over pally with Arthur.'

'*What! You mean . . . ?* '

The look on his face told her how wrong she had been, and she repeated, 'Well, it was just a thought.'

'Just a thought. My God?'

He turned from her. She must have been thinking all these years that he and Arthur. . . . No wonder she had treated him like muck. He had the strong desire to tell her the truth, but common sense prevailed for he knew she was her father's daughter and nothing but vengeance would satisfy her.

'Well, what is he getting at you for?'

He turned and faced her. 'He can't forget that he was flogged on the cinder path.'

Her face stretched in amazement. 'You mean he's borne that grudge all this time and now he's holding it against you?'

'What else?'

'You must be mistaken. Father flogged all the lads.'

'He flogged this one too often.'

'It's unbelievable, he must be crackers.'

'No, he's not crackers, he's just got a long memory.'

She was nodding, about to speak again, when the sound of the front door bell clanged through the house and she looked at him slightly surprised, saying, 'The front door, who can that be?'

He watched her hurry from the room; he heard her go across the hall and open the door; he heard the murmur of voices; and then she was coming back into the room, followed by Florence Chapman.

He felt a slight flush creeping over his face. It was almost two years since he had last met his mother-in-law. He had got on well with her. She had done her best to try and smooth the situation that had arisen so soon after his marriage.

He went towards her holding out his hand and she took it, saying, 'Hello, Charlie.'

'Hello, Florence.' It had been her suggestion that he call her by her Christian name. 'Come and sit down.' He led her towards the fire.

'Will you have a drink?' Betty was addressing her now. 'Tea? The kettle's boiling.'

It was evident that Betty was ill at ease yet at the same time curious why this woman who had never set foot in the house since a week after her daughter's wedding should be here now.

'I wouldn't mind a cup of tea, Betty, thank you.'

The request didn't urge Betty to run to the kitchen, but looking directly at Florence she asked, 'Is anything wrong?'

Florence looked from her to Charlie, then back to her, and she said slowly, 'Hal's ill, very ill. The doctor doesn't hold out much hope. I . . . I was going to get word to Victoria and Nellie, I was about to send one of the boys in this afternoon, when Archie said he saw you.' She turned to Charlie. 'He was up on the hill, and he guessed it was you, because as he said, he knew your walk.' She smiled weakly. 'And so I thought, if you wouldn't mind telling them when you get back . . . that's if you're going back tonight?'

He'd had no intention of going back tonight for where would he stay? But he nodded his head now, saying, 'Yes, I was going back. I can go right away; there's nothing to stop me. I'm sorry to hear about Hal. . . . What is it?'

'His kidneys, and he's just been out of hospital a month.'

'Oh!'

He couldn't prevent a sardonical thought crossing his mind. It didn't look as if his father-in-law was going to live long enough to gain any benefit from their joined lands. It had been a bad bargain all round.

She stared at him sadly for a moment, then turned her gaze back to Betty, saying, 'You need never have anything on your conscience, Betty, for you did your duty by your mother, and I think I can say that at times it mustn't have been easy for you, yet here I am with two daughters, who had everything they ever wanted, and what did they do? Under one pretext or another they faded out of our lives.' She now looked at Charlie and, her voice breaking and her eyes filling with tears, she said, 'We haven't seen either of them for six months. In a way I could understand Victoria's attitude but not Nellie's. I . . . I don't know what's come over that girl. I'm afraid for her, Charlie.'

'Oh, Nellie's all right, Florence. It's a long way out here you know, and she's got a job, and nobody's their own boss these days.'

Florence now shook her head and sighed, while Betty, having heard all she needed to know, got up to go out and make the tea.

Florence looked at Charlie where he was sitting opposite her, and she smiled at him as she said, 'You look well, Charlie, very fit.'

'Well, they either make you or break you.'

'Yes, I've . . . I've heard it's pretty tough, especially for the –' She paused in slight embarrassment, and he finished for her on a laugh, 'The conscripts? Yes, they make it tough for the conscripts, Florence. But now my only regret is I didn't join up before.'

'Really!'

'Yes, it's an eye-opener, you think you know people, men. But after all, our circle out here is very small, isn't it, Florence?'

'Yes, I suppose so, Charlie. But . . . but I'm surprised you're liking it.'

'Ah, I wouldn't say I was liking it, Florence, just let's say I'm learning from it.'

Charlie watched her now look down towards her gloved hands, thinking that it wasn't only the men who were different out here, the women, too, seemed to belong to another generation. Florence's coat rested on the toes of her buttoned boots, her felt hat was set straight on the top of her grey hair. How old was she? In her mid-forties yet somehow she looked elderly. Back there in the town the women were wearing skirts up to their calves; he'd actually seen one marching along wearing a coat that came just below her knees. But these, of course, were exceptions. Yet, as Johnny kept prophesying with his rough wisdom, what Newcastle did the day, Shields, Gateshead and likewise towns did the morrow. Hang silk bloomers on the line and there'd come a time when you wouldn't be able to buy a pair of woolly ones for love or money.

'How is Victoria?'

He now looked towards the fire before admitting, 'I . . . I haven't seen her for a while.'

'How long is a while, Charlie?'

'Some months.'

'Oh, Charlie!'

'It's no good saying Oh, Charlie, like that, Florence, you know yourself it should never have happened, we're poles apart. I'm not blaming her, I blame myself, I'm so blooming easily led it's a wonder they don't shear me twice a year.'

'Oh, Charlie!' Florence smiled sadly at him. 'You know what your trouble is, you're too nice. And I'm as much to blame for this mess as anyone. Hal wanted you to marry her. I needn't go into that, you know why, and I wanted everything for Hal that he wanted for himself, but . . . but I also wanted you in the family. I thought somehow you would soften her, change her; I should have known that you can't change people, at least not people like Victoria.' She gave a wry smile now. 'She was christened after the old Queen and it's strange but she has a lot of her traits, she'll have her way or die. . . . Anyway, Charlie, go and tell them how things are with Hal, that he's very, very ill, and that they must come and see him. He'd not asked for

them until last night, and because of that I somehow deluded myself into
thinking that he wasn't as bad as he is, but I know now that his time is
running out. . . . Look' – she got quickly to her feet, her eyes full of tears
– 'I . . . I won't wait for the tea, I'd better be getting back, he misses me.'

'I'm sorry, Florence.' He was holding her hand tightly. 'If there was only
something I could do for you.'

'You can do that for me, Charlie' – her voice was breaking – 'go and see
them both, tell them that they must come. If they don't they'll have it on
their conscience for the rest of their lives.'

They were already in the hall when Betty pushed open the green-baized
door and came through carrying a tea tray, and she stopped and looked at
Florence in surprise and said, 'You're not going?'

'Yes, yes, Betty, I . . . I feel I must get back; Hal worries when I'm not
there. Good-bye.' She didn't wait for Betty to approach her but went out of
the front door, and Charlie followed. He helped her up into the trap, then
he stood aside while she turned the horse around; and he remained standing
on the drive until she disappeared from his view.

Betty was waiting for him in the hall and he said flatly, 'I'd better get a
move on.' He looked at his watch. 'I can't hope to get another lift, I'll have
to get up to Knowesgate Station and catch a train. I expect it'll be quicker
in the end. What time is it?'

As he spoke she turned and looked at the hall clock. 'Three o'clock.'

'I'd better be off then, Betty.' He turned towards a chair and picked up
his greatcoat; then pulling his cap on he stood looking down on her for a
moment, saying, 'I'll just have a look in on the fellows before I go.'

'Yes, all right.'

'Good-bye, Betty.' He bent down to kiss her cheek, and when her arms
came round his neck and she kissed him on the mouth he held her tightly
to him for a moment, then turned from her and went quickly out.

He was lucky and managed to get a ride on a farm cart, which at least
kept him off his feet for about two miles but took longer to cover the journey
to Knowesgate than if he had walked.

He was nearing the station when he saw a car emerging from the quarry
road. When he noticed the direction it was to take he sprinted forward and
flagged down the driver and when the car stopped he bent his length down
and said, 'Pardon me, but may I ask where you're bound for?'

'Aye, you may. Newcastle, if it's anything to you. Want a lift?'

'That's about it.'

'Well, what are you waitin' for?'

It seemed too good to be true.

Sitting beside the driver he expressed his admiration of the car which was
a Daimler, and the driver agreed with him. 'Aye,' he said; 'it's a nice piece
of work.'

Listening to the rough Northern twang and having taken in the equally
rough appearance of the man, Charlie couldn't be blamed for probing by
asking, 'Are you in a firm?'

'Aye, you could say I'm in a firm, lad.'

'Chauffeur?'

The head was turned sharply to him. 'Chauffeur! Do I look like a bloody
chauffeur? Not in uniform, am I?'

'I'm sorry, I just thought.'

'Aye, I know what you thought, lad, you thought a fellow like me shouldn't have a car like this. That's what you thought, isn't it? Like all the rest of the ignorant buggers you'll say I got it through profiteering. But let me tell you, son, this here was got through damned hard work. I was a taggerine man for years, scrap merchants they call us now and I'm one of the fellows that's supplying the wherewithal to see that blokes like you don't get your bloody heads knocked off, afore your number's called that is.'

'Yes, yes, I see.'

'You don't see.'

'I'm sorry if I've offended you.'

'Everybody offends me, but what do I care! You can stand being offended when your belly's full and your arse is sitting soft. What are you, anyway?'

'I'm a private in the . . .'

'I can see that, I'm not blind, lad. What were you afore you were a private?'

'A farmer.'

'A farmhand?'

'No, not a farmhand, I have my own farm.'

'Begod! I thought farmers like pitmen were exempt.'

'I didn't want to be exempt.'

'You must be bloody well barmy!'

'Yes, I think I am.'

The man now turned his head and gave a faint grin. 'Well, it's something when we know what we are, I'll give you that. I'm a successful man an' I mean to go on bein' successful; I can swim through the sneers. It's funny you know' – he cast his glance in Charlie's direction again – 'it's funny you know, you were no exception back there, 'cos everybody takes me for a numskull, for somebody's bloody chauffeur without the uniform. When I open me mouth I can hear them thinkin', Dear, dear! What have we come to, chauffeur talkin' like that! And I can tell you, lad, I mean to go on talkin' like this. I've changed me hoose but I'm not changin' me tongue for the simple reason I couldn't if I tried.' He let out a bellow of a laugh now, and Charlie laughed with him. He was a character and a likeable one at that.

'I was born into a taggerine family and I'll die in the taggerine family, even if they've given us the title of scrap merchants. But I'll tell you something, lad' – he leant sidewards towards Charlie while keeping his eyes to the front – 'it's a comfortin' feelin' to know you're goin' to die in the lap of luxury, and not with your da's working coat over your feet on the bed.'

Again they were laughing.

As they entered Newcastle the man asked, 'Where you billeted, son?'

'Oh, down the river, Shields way, but . . . but I've got some business to do in the city and in Gateshead first.'

'Oh aye, well you wouldn't like to give it a miss an' come along for a bite to our place would you?'

'Thank you very much indeed. And I mean that.' Charlie nodded at the man. 'I would like nothing better, but my father-in-law is seriously ill and one of the things I have to do before I go back to camp is to let my wife know.'

'Your wife? Isn't she back on your farm?'

'No, no; she lives in Newcastle.'

'Oh well, some other time then. Look, here's me card.' He took a hand off the wheel and pushed it into an inner pocket, and when he handed the card to Charlie he said, 'Gosforth. See that, Gosforth. That's where I live. John Cramp's the name. You're welcome any time. Lots of the lads pop in, they're always sure of a bite and a drop of the hard, two or three if they want it, I'm never short. See to number one and let two, three, and four look after themselves. That's the only way you'll get on in this world, lad, and I'm tellin' you from one who knows.'

When he stopped the car he turned fully round to Charlie now and said, 'It's a pity you can't come along, I've got a fancy I'd like havin' a natter with you, not that you've said anything edifyin' like up till now, it's just that I've got a fancy.'

Charlie was laughing again.

'Well, don't look surprised if I take you at your word and drop in on you some night.'

'My pleasure.' The man held out his hand, and Charlie took it and said, 'And thanks for the ride; I don't know when I've enjoyed one more, and I hope it's a long, long time before you find yourself dying in comfort.'

The man seemed reluctant to let go of his hand and what he said now was something that Charlie was to remember later on. 'If I'd had a son like you I would've seen he didn't spend his time in the bloody ranks. I've got all the money in the world, lad, but I've neither chick nor child, it's only the missis an' me an' about three thousand bloody in-laws and relations, all waitin' for me poppin' off.'

They parted on laughter, through which on both sides was streaked a thread of sadness, and while Charlie waited for the bus to take him to the house his thoughts were still with the man. Poor devil; he was rotten with money, the making of which was apparently his only happiness. Life was strange and there were so many unhappy people in it, unhappy people who could still laugh.

He got off the bus and walked up the dark avenue towards the house, thinking as he did so that he would ring. He still had his key but it wasn't his intention to surprise her. He didn't dissect the reasoning for his consideration but he told himself that if she wasn't at home he would use the key and leave her a note. In fact, he hoped she wasn't in for he had no desire to confront her; all their meetings seemed to end in anger.

The house appeared to be in darkness, yet it wasn't completely for there was a slight glow coming through the curtains of the sitting-room. He approached the window and through a small chink in the end curtain he could see the glow was from the fire; and it was a fresh glow implying that she hadn't been long gone from the room.

Perhaps she was in the kitchen. No, she liked plenty of light, she always left lights blazing all over the house.

He inserted his key in the lock and when the door was opened he switched on the hall light, turned down the collar of his coat, looked about him for a moment, then opened the door of the sitting-room and switched on the light there.

As he stared towards the fireplace he imagined that his whole frame was swelling, the long intake of breath was wafting into every part of his body, down to his feet, into his finger ends, and up to the strands of his hair.

Before him, standing behind the couch that bordered a long sheepskin rug which lay before the fire stood his wife and a man. They stood at each side of the fireplace and the flickering rosy light from the glowing fire illuminated them as would flashes of sheet lightning. His wife's nakedness was partly covered by the crumpled dress she was holding to her chest and her hair that was hanging loose about her. She hadn't been as quick as her companion to dress for he had managed to get into his breeches, apparently between the time he had heard the key in the front door and the light of the sitting-room being switched on.

Having fastened the top button the man now stood still. They all stood still, their eyes in a triangle of amazement, anger and embarrassment. It was Charlie who was amazed, and yet at the same time he was asking himself why should he be. It was the man who was showing embarrassment; but Victoria, as usual, was expressing her feelings through anger.

Yet did he detect a trace of fear in his wife's emotion? He watched her drop down behind the couch, then emerge again pulling the dress over her head. The man, his head bowed now, reached to the corner of the couch for his shirt and coat. In silence Charlie watched him. There was something familiar about the man's face; they had met somewhere, but where? As the man pulled on his uniform coat and Charlie recognized the insignia, an exclamation of 'Good God!' almost escaped Charlie's lips. Major . . . Major Smith!

His body was being deflated now, the air was rushing from it and taking its place was heat made up of embarrassment, shame and anger, a fierce anger that was urging him to take a run at this man who had been cohabiting with his wife, to leave the imprint of his fist right between his eyes. No one would blame him, even a court martial would surely find extenuating circumstances in the situation; in any case it would be the end of Major Smith's career.

Victoria was standing in front of him now, hissing through her clenched teeth, 'What do you want?'

He saw her through a red mist. She looked very like a witch, her black hair, her blazing eyes. 'Just a word with *my wife*,' he said.

It sounded silly, theatrical, like lines delivered by a ham actor.

'You've no right here!' Her hair danced as she tossed her head. He could imagine the hair to be snakes and she Medusa, but her look could not turn him to stone, and he proved this for now his voice carried no trace either of the ham actor or of any actor at all, but that of an angry man, for it was so surprisingly near a roar that it startled her, and she stepped back from him as he cried, 'I have every right here! Until I divorce you I have every right here!'

For the first time in their acquaintance he saw that he had frightened her. He saw her glance towards the man who was sitting now, putting on a pair of shining leggings, and he, too, looked towards him as he ended on a yell, 'And divorce it will be!' Then turning to her again, he finished, 'And that's without any stipulations from you. Now I'll tell you why I came here tonight. Your father happens to be dying and would like to see you . . . if you can spare the time.' He watched her open her mouth, then put her fingers across her lips before going towards the door. But there she turned and said, 'I've got to talk to you. Wait, don't go. I'll . . . I'll be down in a minute.' There was almost a plea in her voice.

The man and he were alone now; the man was on his feet straightening his tunic, putting his belt to rights, pulling at the large flap pockets of his tunic, smoothing his hair back, adjusting his tie, anything apparently to keep his hands busy.

Charlie walked up the room until he reached the back of the couch, and now the man's hands became still, hanging stiffly by his sides while they stared at each other.

'I . . . I suppose I should know you, shouldn't I?' The voice was cultured yet had the suggestion of the Northumberland burr in it.

'You happen to be the officer commanding my company.' There was no addition of sir to the statement.

'Oh my God!' The man now turned his head to the side, dragged his lower lip in between his teeth, then said, 'I . . . I fear I owe you an apology.'

'Huh!'

The head was snapped to the front again and for a moment it was the senior officer viewing a private who had dared to speak in his presence without first having been given permission. Then after a tense moment during which their gazes were locked, the slightly greying head was turned to the side again, and now the words coming tight from between his lips, the major said, 'I . . . I understood you were separated, officially.'

'You understood wrong then.'

The major again drew on his lip, so tightly now that the skin of his chin was drained of blood; then once more he was facing Charlie. 'I . . . I understand that she can get a divorce, there are certain circumstances that would provide her . . .'

The major's voice trailed away, and Charlie, his jaw bones working hard against the skin, snapped, 'That's a concoction on her part. I've told her I'll take the matter to court, a high court, if she attempts to make that plea because it's a lie.'

Again they were staring at each other. Then Charlie dared to look his superior from top to toe and back to the top again before saying slowly, 'But this isn't a lie, is it?' and turning abruptly, he marched down the room.

'Wait, please. Wait.'

Charlie turned his head to look over his shoulder and the answer he gave to the major was, 'Tell her she'll be hearing from my solicitor.'

He had closed the front door when he heard her calling his name, and he was out and going through the gate when the front door opened again and she cried, 'Charlie! Charlie! Wait.' But he walked on, taking no heed.

It was strange, he was burning with anger and humiliation yet he was experiencing a sort of elation. For the first time since he had known her, he felt on top. Had she ever run after him before calling him back with a plea in her voice, 'Charlie! Charlie! Wait!'? She was scared, and so was her major. My God! the major. And they said he was a decent bloke an' all, well liked. In a way he could feel sorry for him, but he wasn't going to let pity baulk him in this case; oh no, no, he had a handle, and by God! he was going to use it.

She had been naked, stark naked . . . both of them. She had no shame. But then he must remember she liked being naked. How many men had she sported with before the major, and in the romantic glow of the fire in the sitting-room?

He jumped on a bus that took him over the bridge into Gateshead and as he walked towards Nellie's house he was asking himself who would get the first move in? In a matter of hours, in fact as soon as he returned to camp, he could probably find himself singled out from the platoon and packed off to France, no uncertainty, no hanging about. . . .

Nellie was definitely at home. Her voice came to him as he knocked on the door. She was singing 'If You Were the Only Girl in the World', and as she opened the door she flung one arm wide and, her head back, she sang at him, 'If you were the only boy in the world and I were the only girl'. Her voice trailed away, her chin lowered, and she exclaimed, 'Charlie! Charlie! Oh Charlie!' Putting out her hand, she grabbed his arm and pulled him into the room. 'I . . . I thought you were some friends; I'm expecting some friends. Come and sit down, come and sit down. Where've you been all this time?'

He allowed himself to be pulled towards the fire and for a moment the sight she presented blotted out for him the last hour; Nellie was drunk.

'Sit down, sit down. T . . . take your coat off. Here, s'let me help you.'

Her speech was slurred, and as she reached up to his shoulders and went to tug at his coat he took hold of her hands, and with a slight push caused her to sit down with a plop on the couch. The effect on her was almost the same as if he had douched her face with cold water for she lay back, opened her mouth wide, gasped, and then said, 'I . . . I know what you're thinkin', and you're right, I'm drunk. Well, everybody's got to have something. What did you come for anyway? You never show your face for weeks on end, then you turn up uninvited, yes, uninvited.' She brought herself up from the back of the couch. 'An' I'm expectin' friends.' Suddenly she was yelling at him, 'Don't look at me like that, Charlie MacFell! Keep those looks for your wife; she earns them, I don't. The only thing I do is drink. I know what you think. I know what you think.' She hitched herself to the edge of the couch now.

When he shouted at her, 'Be quiet! Nellie. For God's sake be quiet!' she cried back at him, 'Why should I be quiet? This is my own house an' I can do what I like in it. But . . . but let me tell you something, Charlie MacFell!' She was now wagging her finger up at him. 'I don't do what you think I do in it. No, I don't. I'm not like me sister, I'm no whore.'

'*Nellie!*'

'Oh, you can say *Nellie* like that, but I know I'm speaking the truth, and you know I'm speakin' the truth. An' . . . an' you know something, Charlie?' Her voice dropped now. 'I'm speaking the truth when I tell you I'm . . . I'm not that kind. You know what I mean. You know what I mean. I'm a fool, I'm a bloody fool, Charlie. Pals, I say to them; that's all I want to be, pals. They can come whenever they like, have a drink, somethin' to eat an' a laugh, an' they respect me. Yes, they do. But they think I'm odd. An' . . . an' it's all your fault.' Her body bending now almost double, she began to cry.

God, what a night! What a day! What a life! What a bloody life!

'Nellie! stop it. Sit up and listen to me.' His tone was quiet now.

She sat up and he put his arm around her shoulders, and like a child now she turned to him and lay against his chest, and her body shook with her sobbing and the more he tried to console her the worse it seemed to get.

'Nellie! give over. Come on now, no more.'

When her crying subsided she pulled herself away from him. Her body was still shaking and she was muttering something when there came a ring on the bell, and now she looked over the top of the couch towards the door and groaned, 'Oh no!'

He got to his feet and went to the door, but having opened it kept fast hold of it as he faced the two visitors.

'Miss Chapman isn't well; she's sorry, she'll see you another time.'

'What?'

'I said Miss Chapman isn't well; she'll see you another time.' He addressed the man who had spoken.

'She invited us around for eight.'

'She may have done, but she can't see you tonight.'

'Who the hell are you?'

'I'm . . . I'm her brother.'

'Ger out of me way!' They both advanced on him at once and he was knocked from the door.

'What's your game, anyway, she's got no brother?'

Still eyeing him, they hurried up the room to where Nellie sat on the couch with her face turned from them.

'What's he done to you, lass?'

'Nothing, Roy, nothing.'

'He's not your brother, is he?'

'He's . . . he's my brother-in-law, the one I told you about, the farmer.'

'Well, what's he done to upset you like this?'

The two men were staring hard at Charlie now, and he, staring as hard back at them, said, 'I came to tell her her father is ill, dying, and that if she wants to see him alive she'd better go as soon as possible.'

He turned his gaze down to Nellie. She was staring up at him, her lips apart, her eyes wide.

'Oh, I'm sorry, I'm sorry, Nellie, we didn't know. Only you did ask us round.'

Nellie now looked up into the face of the young fellow who was bending over her and she said, 'Yes, Alec; I . . . I know I did. I'm sorry. Another time.'

'Aye, another time.'

'Sorry, chum' – one after the other they nodded at Charlie – 'our mistake. Be seein' you, Nellie. Ta-rah.'

It wasn't until Charlie closed the door on them that he realized they were both sergeants and the rueful thought crossed his mind that he was certainly combating the higher ranks tonight all right.

When he returned to the fire, Nellie, her hands joined between her knees now and looking like a schoolgirl who had been caught out in some misdemeanour, said, 'Was that true?'

'Yes.'

'How d'you know?'

'I had to go over to the farm today to settle things with Betty because there's a rumour we may be off soon, and your mother got word that I was there and she came across. She was about to send someone in to you but she asked if I would bring the message.'

'Does . . . does Victoria know?'

He wetted his lips and swallowed deeply before answering, 'Yes, yes, she knows.'

'Is . . . is she going straight across?'

He turned from her as he answered, 'I doubt it tonight.'

'Did . . . did you row?'

'I wouldn't say we rowed. Look . . . shall I make you some coffee?'

'Yes. Yes, please.'

He went into the little kitchen and lit the gas and put the kettle on and looked around until he found some coffee. Everything, he noticed, was scrupulously clean and tidy; she might have slipped in some ways, but she still kept her place spotless.

He took some time to make the coffee and when he carried it into the sitting-room she was coming out of the bedroom. He noticed that she had combed her hair and powdered her face.

They sat side by side on the couch silently sipping at the coffee, and it wasn't until she had almost finished the cupful that she spoke. 'If anything happens to Father, Mother 'll crumble away.'

'I shouldn't think so; your mother's strong.'

'Not strong enough to live on her own. She'll want me back there, but I couldn't go, Charlie, I couldn't live there again.'

'You'd be better off there than you are here.'

'How do you make that out? There's nothing there for anybody, except for those who've got a man by their side and . . . and children. And what men are there left there? A woman needs a man. Yes, she does, Charlie, she needs a man, not men, just one man.' Her voice now was throaty and tired sounding.

He turned and glanced at her for a moment before looking back into the fire and saying, 'Very few women, from what I can gather, are satisfied with one man.'

'She's made you bitter.'

He gave her no answer, and again there was silence between them until she asked, 'Is it true what you said about being posted?'

'Yes, as far as rumours go, it's true.'

'Will you let me know where you are?'

'Yes' – he smiled at her now – 'I'll let you know.'

'If the rumours are just rumours, will . . . will you come and see me again, Charlie?'

'Yes, yes, of course, Nellie, yes.'

'Promise?'

'I promise.'

'And . . . and if you're going to be sent over there, is there some way you'll let me know?'

'Yes, yes, of course. I'll drop you a line.' And now he looked at his watch and said, 'I'll have to be off.'

'Must you, Charlie? Couldn't you stay a bit longer?' She was gripping both his hands now, and he found that he had to look at them because he dare not look into her face.

'We've . . . we've got to be in by ten.'

'Yes, yes.' She released his hands quickly and got to her feet. He too rose and got into his coat, and with his cap in his hand he walked slowly towards the door, she by his side.

'Bye-bye, Nellie.'

'I might never see you again, Charlie.'

'Aw, you'll see me again, Nellie, never fear.'

As he bent down to kiss her, her arms came round his neck and her lips were pressed fiercely to his mouth. For an instant he returned the pressure of the kiss and held her tightly to him; then he opened the door and was gone.

In the street once again, he walked rapidly, his mind in a whirl now, but one question that had pushed itself to the forefront he was answering loudly: No, no! that couldn't be, he didn't think of Nellie that way.

But she thought that way of him.

She was still tipsy.

No, she had sobered up; and anyway he had known all along how she felt. But that hadn't mattered as long as he knew how he felt. And now he didn't know how he felt. God! what a situation.

And where was he going to spend the night? He couldn't go back to the camp because they would think he was barmy. . . . The Y.M.C.A. Huh! it was funny. A house in the country, a house in Newcastle, his sister-in-law's place, and he had to go and spend perhaps one of the last nights before he went overseas in the Y.M.C.A.

He could go back and stay with Nellie.

Don't be such a bloody fool! What did he think would happen if he went back there tonight? Wasn't he in enough trouble? In any case, he had already lied to her he was to be in by ten. The best thing he could do was to get settled down somewhere and think over what he meant to do about his wife and her top brass friend.

He got on a bus, walked to a front seat, paid his fare, and was staring out of the window into the dark night when he felt a gentle tap on his shoulder. He turned to look at a young woman who was saying to him, 'It's you, Charlie, isn't it?'

As he twisted further round in his seat and said, 'Why, Polly!' his thoughts gabbled at him. It only needed his mother to rise from the grave and they'd be all here, all the women in his life, not one of whom had brought him pleasure. But to come across Polly of all people tonight! And she wasn't the Polly he remembered. She was so much older, fatter, settled. She looked just like a thousand and one other women that could be encountered on the streets of Gateshead or Newcastle.

'How are you, Charlie?'

'Oh . . . oh not so bad, Polly. And you?'

'Oh, I'm fine. I'm fine.'

As she spoke he repeated to himself, fine, fine. Funny, she could say she was fine and she was Slater's wife. Yet there was no evidence in her face that she was anything other than fine. Her skin was as clear as ever, her eyes were bright, she was still bonny, yet she looked different, ordinary. It was funny, even fantastic, but if he had met her yesterday he would have told himself he was still a little in love with her. But everything had changed since yesterday, and the main thing was, not that he had found his wife with another man, but that he had suddenly felt a deep, exciting warmth seep through him when Nellie had kissed him. But could a moment like that wipe out years of love? And he had loved Polly. Oh yes, he had loved her. But how had he loved her? That was the question.

'Charlie.'

'Yes, Polly?'

'Do . . . do you think we could get off and have a cup of tea?'

He hesitated a moment while he stared at her; then said, 'Of course. Why not?'

They rose together and left the bus at the next stop and they were half-way up Northumberland Street before she said, 'I'll . . . I'll leave you to pick a place. Somewhere quiet, Charlie, but not posh, please.'

'Posh!' He laughed at her now. 'They don't allow privates in posh places, Polly.'

'Well, you know what I mean, it doesn't matter where it is as long as it's quiet. You see it's funny, but I've been sort of prayin' I'd come across you, Charlie, 'cos I wanted to have a talk with you.'

'Oh! anything wrong?' Even although his mind had accepted the burial of his boyhood love, he was hoping to hear that her feelings hadn't altered, that she was unhappy. And who wouldn't be unhappy with a man like Slater? Now if it had been anybody else he would have accepted the fact that she had transferred her affections.

'Will this café do?' She was pointing to a dimly lit window. 'I've been in there before, it's usually quiet.'

'Fine. Fine.'

A few minutes later they were seated at a corner table and, looking across at her, he said, 'Just tea? Anything to eat?'

'No; no thank you, Charlie. It's not long since I had a meal. I've just come from me mother's.'

'How is she?'

'Oh, she's fine, fine.'

He smiled at her before turning and threading his way to the counter.

'Yes, lad?'

'Two teas, please.'

'I was here afore 'im.'

The elderly waitress behind the counter looked at the man in civilian clothes and said, 'And likely you'll be here after 'im an' all, 'cos there's no chance of you being shot, not in those clothes, is there?'

As the young fellow turned his head away muttering 'God!' Charlie wanted to put his hand out and reassure him, saying, 'It's all right, it's all right, I know just how you feel, I've been through it,' but he took the two teas from the smiling waitress and returned to the table.

As he handed Polly a cup she looked around her and said, 'It's packed; I've never seen it as full as this. But then I've never been here at night afore.'

There followed some moments of uneasy silence while they sat drinking their tea. Then in the impulsive way that he remembered she thrust her cup on to the saucer, leant towards him and in a low tone began to talk rapidly. 'I just wanted to say I'm sorry, Charlie, 'cos I know what you've been goin' through these past weeks. He must have led you hell. He . . . he says as much. He's bent on gettin' his own back. In a way I understand him, Charlie. You can't blame him 'cos, you know, your father put him through it, then –' Her eyes fell away from his now. 'And he knows that I was fond of you an' he thought you were likewise. It's all mixed up in his mind. And then there was the business of our Arthur. But as I said to him, why take it all out on you? It worries me, it's the only thing. . . .'

'All right, all right, Polly.' He checked her gabbling and smiled at her as he said, 'It's all right, don't worry. Anyway, I think I'm on embarkation leave so we'll soon be parting, at least I hope so.'

'Yes, I know, I know; but he might go along of you.'

'I sincerely hope not.'

'So do I. Oh so do I, Charlie, for your sake.'

'What about you? How . . . how does he treat you?'

'Oh me! Treat me?' Her eyes widened. 'Oh, I've got nothin' to complain of, Charlie, not there. He's as good as gold to me. I couldn't have a better husband, an' I'd be . . . well –' She turned her face from him as she finished, 'I'd be as happy as Larry if it wasn't that I had you on me mind and how he's treatin' you.'

It was unbelievable that Slater could treat anyone well, the mean little swine that he was, yet here was Polly, his Polly as he used to think of her, almost glowing with affection for him. The longer he lived the more puzzling he was finding people.

'I've got two bairns now, you know.'

'Yes, yes, so I understand, Polly.'

'And I'll have a third come spring.'

She was bragging about his bairns. Could he himself have given her any bairns? He hadn't given Victoria any. But then Victoria was like a species from another planet, a wild Amazon; and she had stated openly that she hadn't wanted children.

'Oh, I'm so glad I met you, Charlie; me mind 'll be at peace now.'

He stared at her. He had always thought she was a bright girl, an intelligent girl. And she was, yes, she was, but as in everything else there were levels. Because she had seen him and talked to him she imagined that he could now accept her husband's treatment as the natural, and even right, outcome of the rejection, frustration and humiliation he had suffered when young. She could never understand that what Slater was doing was taking it out of him not only because he had been flayed on the cinder path, but also because he had been born in the workhouse. It all stemmed from there. He recalled his expressed need for a father and his inability to understand anyone covering up the murder of his own father.

The past was all too complicated, but what was evident here in the present was the fact that Slater could be making a woman happy while at the same time finding new ways each day to torture someone else.

He was surprised when again in her impetuous way she rose to her feet and, looking down at him, said, 'Don't bother to come with me, Charlie, I'd rather you didn't.' She didn't add, 'Just in case we are seen,' but went on, 'There's only one thing. If . . . if you should both go out there together be careful, Charlie, I mean' – she shook her head – 'go carefully with him. Try to understand.'

He was on his feet now shaking her hand. 'Don't worry, Polly, everything will work out. I'm glad you're happy.'

'Thanks, Charlie. But . . . but I must say it, I'm sorry you're not, I am from the bottom of me heart.'

He sat down again and watched her threading her way towards the door. Her back view was broad and dumpy, so ordinary. But what had she said? 'Be careful, Charlie.' That had been a warning. Oh yes, that had been a warning; although she had altered it to 'Be careful with him,' she really had meant, 'Be careful of him, Charlie.'

What a day! Embarkation leave; his sister ravenous for sole control of the farm, for let him face it that's what Betty wanted, sole control; his wife, a brazen whore; his sister-in-law a drunk; and lastly his old sweetheart, for in his mind Polly had always been his sweetheart, telling him in so many words he'd better look out if he wanted to survive.

Well, what better way to end a day like this than to get drunk. . . . But if he did they wouldn't let him into the Y.M.C.A., nor any other place except a common lodging-house.

He had a longing to be with Johnny, to talk to him, to be tickled by his humour and to be soothed by his rough understanding, but most of all to be warmed by his affection.

Women caused nothing but trouble. Wherever there were women there was trouble. The only thing that was worth while in life was the companionship, the comradeship of another man; in that you could rest and be refreshed. . . .

He left the cafe, went to the Y.M.C.A., spent a restless night, and had returned to the camp before twelve the next day.

## Chapter Five

The rumours were still running rife; they were going to France, they were going to Gallipoli; they were going to Aldershot, but one thing was sure, their company was going some place because the officers were on their toes and the N.C.O.s were running round like scalded cats, so said Johnny. He also said he'd go round the bend if he wasn't soon put out of his misery.

It was twenty-three hours now since he had returned to camp and they knew nothing more than they had done before they had been given leave. For the past hour they had been on the square listening to Slater's voice mingling with those of other sergeants bellowing, 'Left! right! left! right! Lift 'em up! At the double! Move! move!'

Although the day was grey and raw each man was sweating when at last they were told to stand easy. Charlie was at the end of the line, his eyes directed straight ahead, his stomach muscles tight as he waited for Slater to walk past him, then round behind him. Sometimes he did it without a word, at others it was with a skin-searing remark. He was coming from the other end of the line but when he was halfway he was stopped by a corporal who had come to his side and was apparently giving him some message. Whatever the message was, Charlie noted that Slater pondered on it before continuing on. And now the dreaded moment had arrived again, he was about to pass. But no, this apparently was going to be one of the mornings when he intended to indulge himself in a frontal attack.

'MacFell!'

'Sergeant.'

'What have you been up to now?'

Charlie made no answer.

'I asked you a question.'

'I don't know to what you are referring, Sergeant.'

There was a long pause before Slater said, 'You are to report to Lieutenant Swaine. Two paces forward, march!'

Charlie marched forward.

'Accompany the corporal. Right turn; quick march!'

He quick marched down the line to the waiting corporal, who turned and fell into step with him. Across the square they went through a passage between two buildings and into another square, this one sporting a lawn which they circled before mounting a set of wide stone steps and going into the building that had once been a college.

The hall was large and men were coming out of and going into different doors; some had either one, two, or three stripes on their arms, others one, two, or three pips.

They crossed the hall now still in step and came to a stop opposite a door marked Four. For the first time the corporal spoke. 'Wait here,' he said, the words coming out of the corner of his mouth. Then he bent stiffly forward, knocked on the door, opened it, and after entering the room he closed the door again.

Two minutes passed, the door was pulled open. The corporal gave a slight jerk of his head. Charlie stepped smartly forward and into the room.

The officer sitting at the desk looked at the corporal and said, 'That will be all,' to which the corporal answered, 'Yes, sir,' came smartly to attention, saluted, turned about and went out.

Also standing stiffly to attention, Charlie looked across the desk and over the head of Lieutenant Swaine.

Lieutenant Swaine was dubbed as a decent bloke amongst the men. He was a Southerner, at least from well south of this area, but compared with some of the others he wasn't bad at all.

'MacFell?' He looked up at Charlie.

'Yes, sir.'

'Stand easy.'

'Well now.' The officer eased himself back in his chair, twisted his body slightly, put his elbow on one arm of the chair and capped the other arm with the flat of his hand as he repeated, 'Well now.' Then went on, 'Let me first ask you a question. Have you ever thought about a commission?'

There was a pause before Charlie said, 'Sir!'

'Don't look so surprised; I said have you ever thought about putting in for a commission?'

'No, sir.'

'Why?'

Charlie considered a moment. 'I suppose it's because I couldn't see myself in command of men, sir.'

'But' – Now Lieutenant Swaine leant forward and gently spread out some papers on his desk and scanned them as he murmured, 'You were a farmer?' He raised his eyes up to Charlie.

'Yes, sir.'

'Then you would have had men under you?'

'Four at most, sir.'

'Nevertheless' – the officer lay back in the chair again – 'you have handled men; you had to give them orders.' He stared at Charlie now before adding, 'I'm surprised you didn't put in for one right away. You went to a good school.'

'Yes, sir; but I had to leave before I was seventeen.'

'Oh well, that's really neither here nor there. Well now, as you know, we're looking for officer material and I've been through your papers and you seem, well –' the face stretched into a smile – 'pretty suitable material.'

Charlie supposed he should have said, 'Thank you, sir,' but he remained silent; he was experiencing a sort of pleasant shock. That was until he was attacked by a thought. Why were they choosing him all of a sudden? This business of recruiting officers had been going on for weeks. Was Major Smith putting him on the spot where he wouldn't be able to do anything about Victoria, at least put him in a position where he would find it very difficult? His jaws were tight, his face straight, his words clipped, as he asked, 'May I enquire, sir, when my name was first put forward?'

'What? . . . Oh! . . . Oh! let me see.' He again thumbed through the papers, then said, 'It isn't here, it's likely in the files.'

The lieutenant stood up, then in a leisurely fashion strolled towards a cabinet in the corner of the room. He pulled open the top drawer, flicked through some files, closed it, opened the second drawer and after some more thumbing picked out a single sheet of paper, glanced at it, then as he replaced it in the drawer he turned and looked at Charlie. 'Ten days ago; but, of course, we have to go into things, you understand?'

'Yes, sir.' The excited feeling was flooding him again and at the moment he could think of only one thing, one person, Slater, and the ecstatic satisfaction of breaking the news to the red-headed swine.

'You . . . you haven't any children?' Again the papers were being flicked through.

'No, sir.'

'Your wife runs the farm?'

'No, sir, my sister; my wife lives in Newcastle.'

'Oh!' The head was back on the shoulders. 'You have a house there?'

'Yes, sir.'

'How nice, how nice; and convenient; nice to slip home at times.'

'Yes, sir.'

'I myself am from Dorset; it's quite a way.'

'Yes, sir, it is quite a way.'

'Well now, you know everything doesn't happen overnight. Well, that is, not quite.' He gave a little laugh here, then said, 'You'll have to do a little training, and so although, as you know, a great many of us here are, well, just on the point of making a move, I'm afraid we'll be going one way and you another. Pity, but that's the way of things. But we may meet up again, who knows. Let me see. Ah yes, you can report within the next hour to Second-Lieutenant Harbridge. I'll get in touch with him and he'll put you wise to everything. Now all I can say is –' He rose to his feet, extended his hand, and ended, 'Welcome.'

'Thank you, sir.'

The grip of Lieutenant Swaine's hand was firm, in contrast to his lazy-sounding voice.

'The best of luck.'

'And to you, sir.'

The movement of the lieutenant's head was a signal that the interview was at an end. Charlie came smartly to attention, saluted, turned about and marched out of the room.

The corporal standing outside stared at him but said no word, but with a narrow-eyed, quizzical look he watched him leave the building and would no doubt have followed his progress from the window had not he been beckoned back into the room by the sound of the lieutenant's voice.

As Charlie went through the gap between the buildings part of him seemed to be afloat. He was going to be an officer, *an officer*!

How would he break the news to Slater? Stick it into him like a bayonet or let it be seemingly slowly dragged out of himself by taunts?

Bayonets. He wouldn't be required now to stick a bayonet into somebody's belly, twist it and pull it out, and all the while screaming at his victim. No, he'd be able to finish him off cleanly with a pistol shot. But then again he might never be called upon to use a pistol.

*He was going to be an officer.*

He was really going to be an officer. He had lied when he said that he didn't think he was officer material. He had often wished to be in that position, if only for twenty-four hours. And now he had been given the chance, not only for twenty-four hours but for as long as the war lasted. No, that was wrong, for just as long as he managed to survive in it. But all he wanted at present was to savour the next half-hour.

As he crossed the main square he saw Slater standing in the far corner talking to an officer, and he hurried towards the hut. It wasn't his intention to break the news to him when he was alone, no, he wanted the same audience around him that Slater had felt he was entitled to.

He found the hut in a bustle of activity.

'It's come! We're moving,' someone called to him.

And another voice cried, 'What did they want you for, Lofty? Did you get it in the neck?'

Before Charlie had time to answer, some joker called out, 'Why, no! man; they're short of generals and they asked him to step in.'

'Stranger things have been known to happen.'

There was a pause in the bustling for a moment as all eyes were turned in his direction; then when he went to his bed and, instead of grabbing at his kit, sat down on the edge of it, some of them gazed steadily towards him.

'Come on! you'd better put a move on.' It was Johnny speaking to him now. 'We're due outside in ten minutes ... Oh this bloody cap!'

'I shan't be coming with you, Johnny.'

'Either me bloody head's swollen or it's shrunk ... What did you say, Charlie?'

'I said I'll not be coming with you.'

'What's he done to you now, put you in clink?'

'No.'

'Well, what, man?' He was bending down to Charlie now, whispering, and Charlie, putting up his hand and gripping his friend's tunic, whispered back, 'Say nothing yet, I want to hit him with it, I'm getting a commission.'

'Bugger me! No!'

'Yes.'

'God Almighty! of all the things I expected to hear. Eeh!, Charlie lad! Charlie!'

When Johnny's two hands came out, Charlie said quietly, 'Not yet; let him come in first.'

'Aye, aye!' Johnny backed from him and flopped down on to his bed and he shook his head slowly now as he said, 'By! I'm glad for you, I am that. And yet what am I talkin' about? That's the finish of us, isn't it? Officers an' men from now on. Aw, I'm sorry about that, yet at the same time, eeh! I can hardly believe it.'

'What can't you believe?'

One of the men hugging a pack up the aisle stopped for a moment and glanced at them, and Johnny, looking towards him, grinned as he said, 'Charlie here's tellin' me his great-granny's gone on the streets, an' he's given me her number. Would you like it?'

'To hell with you!'

'And you an' all, mate.'

'Come on! Come on! Jump to it!'

Slater had entered the hut. He was throwing his orders from left to right as he walked briskly forward; then he came to a dead halt when he saw Charlie sitting on the side of his bed. Johnny, having now got to his feet, was busy gathering his kit together.

'Well! well! what have we here? A sick man no doubt.'

Charlie remained seated. A momentary stillness crept over the room as the men looked towards the tall figure sitting upright on the bed, all their eyes expressing the same thought: Silly bugger! he was asking for it now all right.

'You're goin' to report sick, eh?'

'No, Sergeant.'

'No! Yet here you are reclinin' on your bed. Surely you've been told' – he moved his hand in a slow wide motion to encompass all in the room – 'that we're off for foreign parts!'

'Yes, Sergeant.'

'Well then, you've decided that you don't want to go 'cos . . . well you're more than likely to see a lot of nasty blood an' there'll be bang-bangs?'

This pleasantry was received without the sound of one titter, there was something going on here that the men didn't understand, except that some of them thought that Lofty must have gone mad and had decided to do for the sergeant and stand the consequences. And who could blame him?

'On your feet!'

There was the slightest pause before Charlie unfolded his long length and stood upright, but not too straight, certainly not to attention.

'Now, Mis-ter MacFell, you either get *fell* in' – Slater stressed the pun – 'or I'll assist you with me boot in your arse.'

'Sergeant, I'd advise you to be careful!'

The tone had the effect on the men in the room of an electric shock. Their eyes stretched to their fullest as they listened to the long-suffering and easy-going fellow they knew as Lofty saying, 'As at this moment I am not in a position to put you on a charge but nevertheless I can report you. For your information, Sergeant Slater, I would inform you that I have been recommended for a commission'. Whether the promotion would be starting at this precise hour he didn't know, and neither would Slater or anyone else in the room, but what he did know, and what he was experiencing at this moment, was an amazing feeling of triumph as he watched the effect his words were having on Slater. For the moment the man seemed dumbfounded and there was on his face, not the same look of fear that had been on it, as Charlie remembered when a child, but the look of a defeated man. But it remained only a matter of seconds, and then Slater had turned from him and was bawling at his platoon, 'Out! Out the lot of you! Get goin'!'

He was marching up and down the room now hustling and bustling while Charlie remained standing perfectly still by the side of his bed; that was until Johnny gripped his hand and said, 'Well, so long, lad.'

'So long, Johnny.'

'Think we'll ever see each other again?'

'Yes; yes, I do, Johnny. I'm sure we shall, somewhere some time, and if not now, after the war. I'll never forget how you've helped me over the stickiest patch of my life. I think I would have done murder if it hadn't have been for you.'

They stared at each other for a moment, until Slater's voice, almost screaming now, filled the hut crying, 'Come on! Come on!'

'Bye, lad.'

'Bye, Johnny.'

After bustling the last man out of the hut, Slater didn't follow him, he banged the door closed behind the man, then walked slowly back up the room until he was once again confronting Charlie. But he seemed to find it difficult to speak now; when he did he said, 'So you wangled it somehow, did you? 'cos you couldn't have got it any other way. Oh' – he looked about him – 'as you said yourself you don't know when exactly you're comin' into your glory so to all intents and purposes you're still muck to me, and there's nobody here to hear me say it.'

'No, for once you haven't got an audience, Slater. And it may surprise you that I didn't wangle it, it was offered to me.'

Their eyes were locked in mutual hate; then Slater, his mouth twisting, said, 'There's something fishy here 'cos I've blacklisted you all the way through, I haven't said a good word for you.'

'Well, all I can say to that, Slater, is that the officers are not the fools you take them for, and when they have been summing up my capabilities most likely at the same time they have been summing up the lack of yours; otherwise, surely, if for nothing else but your raucous voice you should have been a sergeant-major by now.'

'Be careful!'

'Oh, as you said, there's no one to hear us.'

Slater swallowed deeply, took one step back, went to move away, then turned and faced Charlie again; and now he said, 'This is a flash in the pan; you're a loser; you were born a loser; you couldn't even keep a wife. I managed that, and I've got two bairns to show for it.'

The quick steps died away, the door banged, he was alone in the hut. Again he sat down on the edge of the bed. Slater's last words were rankling; you couldn't even keep a wife . . . you're a loser; you were born a loser.

For a moment he was overcome by a fear of the future when he'd be entering the company, not of men, but . . . of officers. Would he lose out there an' all?

It would be up to him, wouldn't it?

Yes; yes, it would.

He did not spring from the bed, determined now to start as he meant to go on, definite, full of purpose and patriotic enthusiasm. Instead, he took time gathering up his belongings before walking with them towards the door. But he did not go out on to the square, for it was packed with men, the men of 'A', 'B' and 'C' companies, almost the whole battalion. He watched the R.S.M. strutting about like a stuffed peacock, and the company sergeant-majors following suit, for all the world like dominating cocks shooing their families together. The lance-corporals acting as markers, the corporals and sergeants were outdoing themselves in throat-tearing commands.

. . . And the officers, the second-lieutenants, the lieutenants, the captains, all batmen – spit and polished; and standing apart, yet commanding the whole, was the major.

Charlie's eyes were fixed tight on him. Although he couldn't make out his face from this distance he told himself he didn't look any different in his clothes.

In his clothes!

Would anybody believe him if he were to tell them that that dominating figure was the man who was to be the means of getting him his freedom . . . But wait! what had he let himself in for? Could he do it now?

Orders were ringing out: 'By the right quick march! Left! right. Left! right.' A band was playing, the mass was moving, feet were stamping, arms swinging: rank after rank disappeared, until, just as if a wave had washed over the place, the square was empty.

In the strange silence, he again asked himself the question, Could he do it now? Could he name the major? If he did his promotion would likely be squashed; these things could be fixed. But say he were still allowed to get his commission, life would become unbearable when the story got around. He was wise enough to know you got no medals for disgracing a major, and under such circumstances.

And then there was Slater.

You're a loser; you were born a loser.

No, if it meant being tied to Victoria for life, well, that would have to be. Anything was preferable to being the butt of Slater's maliciousness which, were he to return to the platoon now as a private, would mean one or the other of them ending the conflict.

He straightened his shoulders, picked up his gear, and walked out of the hut, across the square, through the alleyway, around the circle of lawn and up the steps and into the wartime life of an officer.

# Chapter One

## Mud

The second-lieutenant looked extremely smart. He was unusually tall but he was straight with it. When he was saluted in the street he answered the gesture almost as smartly as it was given. But he'd have to get out of that; Radlett had hinted as much.

He liked Radlett, at least he didn't dislike him; but he wasn't at all keen on Lieutenant Calthorpe; very old school, Calthorpe, without the good manners one would expect from that kind of upbringing. He spoke to some of the men as if they were serfs.

The captain was as different again, a very understandable fellow Captain Blackett; but the major, oh, the major, he talked as if he were still in the Boer War. Radlett said openly he was a fumbling old duffer.

It was funny, Charlie thought, how some people were able to voice their opinion of others and get off with it. For instance now if he had called the major a fumbling old duffer ten to one he would have been up on the carpet before his breath had cooled. Radlett acted and talked like an old hand but he was almost as new to the game as he himself was.

As he left the Central Station to board a bus that would take him across the water to Nellie's, the glow that had been with him since early morning began to fade. Another man in his position would be making for home. He had two homes but he was going to neither: the home among the hills was too far away to get there and back comfortably in a forty-eight. Moreover, you had to chance getting transport. And the home where his wife resided was barred to him now for good and all. So there remained only Nellie's; and even about this visit he was feeling a little trepidation, for he hadn't done as he promised and written to her.

It had been understandable in the first two or three weeks because everything had moved so fast. He had been kept at it all waking hours. They called it a crash course in pips, and it was certainly that all right, for as Radlett so grotesquely illustrated in his garrulous way, the only thing they didn't ram into you was how to die with your guts hanging out. Did you yell, 'Carry on, men!' before you pushed them back, or let them drip as you waved your fellows on crying, 'Good luck! chaps.'

Anyway, he had forty-eight hours and he was going to enjoy it. Why not? He would take Nellie out. Knowing Nellie, she'd get quite a kick out of his change in fortune. But then it might not come as a surprise to her after all, because if she had visited home and run into Betty, Betty would surely have told her. Yet again it had been a good three weeks before he had informed Betty of his change in position. Still, he was looking forward to seeing Nellie.

A passenger walking down the aisle happened to catch the end of the cane that lay across Charlie's knees, and when he had retrieved it from the floor and handed it back to him, saying, 'I'm sorry, sir,' Charlie smiled at him and said, 'That's all right,' and the man jerked his chin and smiled back, saying, 'Good-day to you.'

'And to you.'

Amazing the difference a pip made and, of course, the style of the uniform, the leather belt and the rakish cap, not forgetting the trench coat. Oh yes, the trench coat finished the ensemble off.

But let him be honest with himself. He liked the difference it made and the deference it commanded. He had felt a different being since first donning this uniform; it had magical properties, it enabled one to issue orders, although until now he had been mostly on the receiving end. Even so, when he'd had to deal with the men in the platoon to which he had been assigned, he had carried it off all right.

He felt that in a way he had an advantage over the other officer trainees for he was the only one of his bunch who had served in the ranks, so he prided himself that he knew how the men would view him, and above all things at this period he wanted their opinion to be, 'Oh, he's a decent enough bloke, Mister MacFell.'

*Second-Lieutenant.* How long would it be before he was fully fledged? Was it as Radlett said, you only stepped up when the other chap above you fell down dead? Radlett had the uncanny knack of putting his finger on the realities; it was a known fact that there was rapid promotion on the battlefield. Well, he didn't want his promotion that way, so he'd better make up his mind to be satisfied to stay as he was. . . .

The twilight was deepening as he neared Nellie's house and it had begun to drizzle.

Before going up the steps he adjusted his cap, then his collar, and finally tucked his cane under his arm.

On entering the hall he was assailed by the usual smell of stale cooking, and he thought for a moment, Why does she stay here, there's no need? She could let her flat and get a better place.

He rapped smartly on the door! Rat-a-tat-tat! Rat-a-tat-tat! drew himself up to his full height and waited.

Again he knocked, louder this time, and when there was no reply his shoulders took on a slight droop.

He was knocking for the third time when a voice came from the stairway to his right, saying, 'It's no use knocking there.'

He walked to the foot of the stairs and looked upwards. A woman was leaning over the banisters and as he stared up at her she said, 'I'm sick of telling 'em, one after the other, it's no use knocking there. They should put a notice up.'

Slowly he mounted the stairs until his face was directly below that of the woman's, and now he said, 'She's left?'

'Left! I don't know so much about leaving, I'll say this much for her, she tried to. No, she didn't leave, they carried her out.'

'What do you mean, she's not . . .?'

'Well, it isn't her fault. She tried hard enough, and she might be even yet for all I know.'

He now ran up the remainder of the stairs and round on to the landing until he faced the woman and, his tone brisk now, appealed, 'Please explain; she . . . she was a dear friend of mine.'

'She was a dear friend of everybody's if you ask me.'

'She's my sister-in-law.'

'Is she? Oh, well, you got the gist didn't you? She tried to do away with herself, gassed herself. They all use gas, it must be the easiest way . . .'

'When did this happen?'

'Oh, four days ago. And it was someone like you knocking on the door that saved her, one of her pals.' The woman now peered up at Charlie and demanded, 'Why wasn't she taken in hand? A bit of a lass like that on her own. And then them there every night. I tackled her about it once and she invited me in with them. Mind, I didn't go, but she said it was tea and buns and a bit of a sing-song, that was all. Well, I ask you. Anyway, she was off work for a week, cold or something, and it was likely being on her own got her down. One of her pals came up and asked me to look in on her. Well, I did; but I couldn't keep it up for I'm out all day you see, munitions, and I've got two bairns and I've got to pick them up from me mother's every night. Anyway, I came in this night and there were these two sergeants hammering on the door. They were the same ones that asked me to go in and see to her. And then they said they could smell gas. Well, that's about it. They did smell gas. Then there was the divil's fagarties: the doctor, the polis, the ambulance.'

'Where is she now?'

'Still in hospital, I should say.'

'Do you know which one?'

'Not really; it'll be the infirmary likely.'

He turned from her without saying, 'Thank you', but the look that he left with her caused her to lean over the banisters and yell after him. 'Don't take it out on me, mister! Anyway she brought it on herself, drink and men. Can't tell me it was all tea and buns and . . .'

Her voice faded away as he banged the door closed behind him.

Neighbours! Someone lying alone ill in a room and nobody bothering, except the soldiers. Even back on the hills, even as dour as some of them were, they would travel miles in all weathers to give a helping hand to each other in times of trouble; and in the poorer quarters of the town, in the back-to-backs, he'd like to bet no one would have lain for a day without someone coming in.

It was in the third hospital he visited that he found her. He could have found out immediately by going to the police station, but somehow he baulked at this for it would be admitting that she had by her action touched on something criminal.

Yes, a stiff-faced nurse said, they had a Miss Chapman here, but it was long past visiting hours; and moreover, she was under surveillance and rather ill. Was he a relation?

'Yes,' he said; 'I'm her brother-in-law and I'm on a short leave. I'd appreciate it if I could see her for a moment or so.'

He had to pass the staff-nurse, then the night sister before he was admitted to the small side ward, and then he was told briefly, 'Ten minutes at the most.'

The nurse stood aside and allowed him to enter; the door closed behind him; and then he was standing in the small, naked room, where the green-painted walls lent a hue to everything, even to the face on the pillow.

He walked slowly to the bedside. On closer inspection he saw that the face wasn't green, but white, a dull, pasty white, and so much had it altered since he had last seen it that he thought for a moment there had been a mistake and he had been shown the wrong patient. That was until the eyes opened, and then there was Nellie looking up at him. The expression in her eyes remained slightly vacant for a moment or so; then he watched her lids slowly widen and her lips part three times before she whispered, 'Charlie.'

He did not speak for he was finding it impossible at the moment to utter a word, but he bent over her and clasped her hands between his own.

'Charlie.'

He nodded at her now.

'Thought . . . thought you'd gone.' Her voice was like a croak.

He shook his head slowly.

'Forgotten me.'

'No . . . held up . . . one thing and another.'

They continued to stare at each other; then without letting go of one hand he turned and pulled a chair to the side of the bed and sat down, and as he leant towards her she muttered hoarsely, 'Know what I did?'

For answer he said softly, 'Forget about it; you're going to be all right.'

He now took his handkerchief and wiped the gleaming blobs of sweat from her brow, then he tucked the bedclothes closer around her chin, and as he did so he felt the steam from her body on his hand. She was ill, very ill and so changed. Of a sudden he wanted to gather her into his arms and comfort her, soothe her, saying, 'It's all right, Nellie. It's going to be all right, I'll look after you. From now on I'll look after you.'

'What's that, my dear?' He put his head closer to her mouth.

'I . . . I was lonely . . . nothing to live for.'

'Oh Nellie. Nellie.' He now stroked the clammy hand lying limply within his own. 'You've got everything to live for; you're so young, Nellie, and so, so bonny . . . lovely.' He spaced the words and inclined his head downwards with each one, then ended, 'And you have friends who care for you.'

When her head began to move agitatedly on the pillow he said hastily, 'Now, now, Nellie; don't distress yourself, please.'

She became still. Her eyes were closed and now from under the compressed lids there appeared droplets of water that weren't sweat.

'Oh, Nellie, Nellie, don't! Look.' He shook her hand gently and, his tone aiming to be light, he said, 'They'll throw me out; they told me you had to be kept quiet and I hadn't to distress you.'

Her tear-filled eyes opened and she looked at him a moment before she said, 'You always distress me, Charlie.'

'Oh! Nellie.'

'Oh! Charlie.' She smiled faintly now, but even as she did so her face became awash with tears.

He sat gripping her hands now unable to pour out the words speeding from his mind because he was suddenly and vitally aware that their meaning would express emotions that would go far beyond words of comfort, and he couldn't . . . he mustn't allow this complication to come about.

'I'm . . . I'm sorry, Charlie.'

'Oh, Nellie; I'm . . . I'm the one who should be saying that. I . . . I was utterly thoughtless; I should have written.'

'Yes, you should.' In the two admonitory small movements made by her head he glimpsed for a moment the old Nellie and he smiled at her as he said, 'It won't happen again.'

'That a promise?'

'Definitely.'

'Where are you now?'

'Outside Durham.'

'For long?'

He paused before he said, 'I'm not sure; you can be sure of nothing in this war.'

He was about to ask if her mother had been when the door opened and the nurse standing there said simply, 'Please.'

'Oh, not yet . . . oh, Charlie.'

He was standing on his feet now but still holding her hands and he bent over her, whispering, 'I'll be back, Nellie.'

When the look in her eyes told him that she didn't believe him, he bent further forward and placed his lips on hers; then looking into her eyes again, he said, 'I'll be back.'

She said no more and he went from the room.

In the corridor he said to the night nurse, 'She's very ill, isn't she?'

'Oh' – the voice was airy – 'she's not as bad as when they brought her in. She's lucky to be alive. You know she tried suicide, don't you?'

He stared at the nurse. They said some of them were as hard as nails and they were, especially when dealing with their own sex.

'Good-night.'

'Good-night.' The nurse's opinion of him was expressed in her farewell. It was a certainty she wasn't one of those who were impressed by an officer's uniform.

He paused in the corridor. Nellie hadn't noticed that he was no longer a private; but then she was too ill, and anyway Nellie was the kind of person who would lay little stock on rank.

What would he do if she died?

He didn't know except that her going would set the seal on his ineffectiveness, the ineffectiveness that stamped his whole make-up. Not one thing had he done off his own bat. He had allowed himself to be led up to or pushed into every situation in his life. There was that one time he could have taken the initiative by sticking to the gun that Nellie had fired. Had he done so he knew now that his life from then would have been different. But what in effect had he done? walked backwards out of the situation and, as he deserved, fallen into a trap.

He was, he knew, one of those people who are dubbed nice fellows, men who are never strong enough to alter circumstances, men who surfed as it were on the waves of other people's personalities, until finally being dragged into self-oblivion by the undertow.

'Can I help you, sir?'

He looked at the night porter, and after a moment's hesitation, he said, 'Yes; when are the visiting hours?'

'Saturday, sir, is the next one between two and four; and Sunday the same time. But I think they make allowances for uniform.' He smiled.

'Thank you.'

'Thank you, sir. Good-night.'

'Good-night.'

As he went down the hospital steps and walked into the starlit night he thought in normal life men are kinder than women, less hard. He'd had evidence of it with his mother and Betty . . . and Victoria. Yes, and even Polly. But people would call Polly sensible, not hard. And then those nurses back there, tough individuals. He should hate women, yet the only person he hated was Slater.

What about Major Smith?

Yes, what about Major Smith? Truth to tell he didn't know how he felt about the man. He thought he despised him rather than hated him. Strangely, he saw him as a weaker man than Slater. Yet he would have to be a strong type both physically and mentally to hold his own with Victoria.

He had heard nothing from Victoria since that particular night; she was likely waiting for a move from him and sitting on hot bricks wondering what he was going to do about her dear major.

He stood outside the iron gates and looked up into the sky. Somewhere Zeppelins were dropping bombs out of it; somewhere else the stars were being outshone by the flashes of artillery, and all over Flanders' fields men were lying staring sightless up into the heavens. Yet momentarily all this was being obliterated by a flood of personal feeling, an all-consuming feeling.

He walked on, boarded a bus, afterwards walked on again. Then he entered the Officers' Club in the centre of the city for the first time, and he did so without a feeling of embarrassment. He was not merely Second-Lieutenant Charles MacFell, the grouts of the officers' hierarchy, he was Charlie MacFell, who was vitally aware that he was loving someone, really loving someone for the first time in his life, and that because of it he imagined he would never again be ineffectual.

## Chapter Two

'There you are, sir, shining like Friday night's brasses.'

'What was that, Miller?' Charlie turned to his batman who was brushing him down . . . He'd have to make himself get used to this and not take the brush from the man and do the job himself.

'It's what me mother used to say, sir. Everything in wor house was cleaned on a Friday, and we'd lots of brasses on the mantelpiece. They used to shine like silver, and me mother used to say to wor lads, "Now scrub your faces till they shine like Friday night brasses." '

Charlie smiled at the man. He was a nice fellow was Miller, always cheery. He had been assigned to him when he finished training and he felt that he had struck lucky for he had been so helpful. He was a real morale booster was Miller.

'There you are, sir.' The batman took two paces backwards and surveyed his handiwork. 'You know, sir, I think you're the tallest officer in the camp. What is your height, sir?'

'Six foot three and a half.'

'Aw, good. Good.'

'What do you mean, good?'

'Well, sir, Private Thompson is betting on Captain Blackett, and . . . and he said he could top you, sir. But you've done 'im by half an inch.'

Charlie laughed. 'I hope the half-inch proves worth your while.'

'Well, a dollar's not to be sneezed at, is it, sir?'

'No, it isn't.'

As the batman handed Charlie his hat and stick and Charlie responded by saying, 'Thank you', a habit he found he couldn't get out of, there came a knock on the door, and when Miller opened it, a corporal stood there. Stepping smartly into the room, he saluted Charlie, saying, 'Lieutenant Calthorpe's compliments, sir, and would you meet him in number two room?'

Charlie hesitated a moment before saying, 'Yes, thank you. I'll be there.' Then he looked at his watch; the bus went in twenty minutes.

As he crossed the square some of the men in his own platoon were walking towards the gates; their faces bright, they were laughing and joking among themselves. Many of them, he knew, would be making for home, others would have a blow-out in the first pub they came to.

Lieutenant Calthorpe was standing before a mirror adjusting his tie. He didn't turn when Charlie entered the room but, putting his face closer to the mirror, he said, 'Ah, MacFell, I'm sorry an' all that but there's been a change in the time-table. I should've seen you earlier but I was held up. It's just this, I'd like you to change with Radlett; he's coming into town with me. He's got a little business to see to.' He turned round now, straining his neck out of his collar as he ended, 'Rather important. Be a good fellow and take over for him. Make it up to you tomorrow, the whole day off if you like.'

There was a significant pause, then he turned so smartly about that he almost overbalanced Calthorpe's batman.

Standing outside the block, he looked towards the far gate where Radlett was standing beside his car, but before taking a step in his direction he warned himself, Be careful.

Radlett's unblinking round blue eyes looked straight into his as he said, in that drawling twang that was so like Calthorpe's, 'I'm sorry. It's rotten luck, but what could I do? He wanted a lift into town and transport that would get him back . . . well, latish. He said he'd make it up to you tomorrow. Of course I know, old fellow, that leave on a Sunday around here is equal to being drafted into the cemetery.'

Charlie made no reply, and Radlett added, 'You won't hold it against me, old chap, will you?'

'Oh no, certainly not.' The tone was the same as that used by Radlett, and the second-lieutenant stared at him for a moment, then said, 'Good.

Good.' But then he added. 'Of course, if I were in your shoes I'd be flaming mad.'

'Perhaps I am.' He stared pointedly at Radlett before turning abruptly away.

In rank he was the same as Radlett, yet he knew that in the eyes of the lieutenant, the captain, and the major, he was an outsider; not only had he come up from the ranks but he was a conscript. To be placed in only one of these situations would have been enough to stamp him as an outsider, but the double infamy was, he had been given to understand, if albeit silently, an insult to the regiment. Though it was likely this company wouldn't see Flanders, still it was hard lines if it had to be the recipient of the dregs of the army.

Oh, he knew the feeling that his presence created in the mess all right, yet he had played it down till now, but he'd had enough and he'd make this plain, at least with Radlett, when doubtless his attitude would be passed on to the lieutenant.

All morning he had felt in a state of excitement about seeing Nellie again. Three days ago he had written to her and told her he'd be with her some time over the week-end. It was a good job, he thought now, that he hadn't stated an exact time.

He made for his room again and when he opened the door it was to find Miller sitting in his chair with his feet on the camp table and a mug in his hand.

So abruptly did the man get to his feet that the tea splashed in all directions and Charlie stepped quickly back, putting out his hand to ward off the splashes.

'I'm sorry, sir, I . . . I thought you had gone, sir.'

Charlie threw his hat on to the bed, and as he took off his trench coat he said, 'So did I.'

'Something gone wrong, sir?'

Charlie looked at the batman. He was a man old enough to be his father, and he smiled wryly at him as he said, 'The lieutenant wanted the use of a car. I don't happen to possess one.'

'Aw, rotten luck, sir. He changed you over with Lieutenant Radlett then, sir?'

'Yes, Miller, yes, that's what he did. . . . Is any tea going?'

'Yes, sir. Oh yes, sir; I'll brew you up one immediately.' The man went to move away, then stopped and stared at Charlie and moved from one foot to the other before saying, 'Sir, can I speak me mind?'

Charlie's eyes widened slightly before he nodded, saying, 'Yes, yes, of course.'

'Well, sir, it's like this. A man can be too easy-goin', too soft, kind that is, and some folks don't understand. You've . . . you've got to throw your weight about, not too much, you know, sir, but just enough to let them know you can't be sat on. And . . . and I'm not talkin' about the men, sir, the platoon, no, your platoon's all right, they understand and appreciate things, but there's t'others if you get me meanin', sir. I'm sorry if you think I've spoken out of turn, sir.'

Charlie nipped on his lower lip for a moment; then his voice coming from deep in his throat, he said, 'Thank you. Thank you, Miller. I may as well tell you that I've been thinking along similar lines myself, but it's heartening to know that one has a little backing.'

'Good, Good for you, sir. One last thing I'd like you to know, sir. You're . . . you're well liked among the men.'

Charlie smiled broadly now as he said, 'Well, if that's the case it's because I remember, as I gather you all know, that not so long ago I was one of them, and in a way I suppose' – he shook his head – 'I still am. That's the trouble, if trouble it is. . . . Anyway, what about that tea?'

'On the double, sir, on the double.'

As the man went out of the room Charlie sat down on the chair Miller had vacated and he thought, That's the only piece of ordinary conversation I've had with a man for months.

He fingered the pip on his shoulder. Was it worth it? It was questionable. What was he talking about, remember Slater!

He had made use of the first half of his full day's leave by paying a quick visit to the farm. He had not intended to do this but he had heard of a transport lorry having to make a delivery to a camp up on the fells. It only took a little back-hander to the driver to persuade him to pick him up again an hour later.

Betty greeted his unexpected arrival with her usual lack of enthusiasm. Her only comment about his commission was, 'Well, you look tidier in that than you did in the other rig-out.'

Everything on the farm seemed to be working well, except she voiced her usual tirade against the prisoners; they didn't like a woman over them, she said, but she let them know what was what. His reaction had been, poor devils, but, of course, merely as a thought. When he had enquired if she had heard anything about Nellie, she had answered, 'How do you expect me to get news here except what I can gather from out-of-date papers? She doesn't bother to come over here' – meaning Florence Chapman – 'and I can assure you I have no time to trail over there. So what has she done now, the smart Miss Nellie?'

But he didn't inform her what Nellie had done, only to say she was in hospital with pneumonia, and when he had bidden her good-bye and left the farm and was walking through the fields – his fields – he had asked himself which was preferable, to be living alone back there with Betty, or to be in the army? And without hesitation he plumped for the latter. What it would be like after the war he dreaded to think; but then again there mightn't be any after the war for him if he was sent over there. And that was a journey that could quite easily come about in the near future, for although the battalion wouldn't move as a whole, it was being broken up and sections sent hither and thither almost every week.

It was a quarter to three when he arrived at the hospital. He hurried along the corridor, past the wards where every bed had its visitors, to the small side ward. He didn't stop to ask the nurse for permission to enter but went straight in, then came to a stop at the sight of the soldier sitting by the bedside holding Nellie's hand. He noted immediately that Nellie looked much better for she was sitting propped up against the pillows; he also noted that the fellow sitting by her side had a possessive look about him. The soldier was quickly on his feet, he was a sergeant, and although he didn't stand to attention he stood slightly away from the bed.

It was Nellie who spoke first. 'Hello, Charlie,' she said.

'Hello, Nellie.' He moved to the bottom of the bed.

'Don't you remember Alec? You know, he and his pal were together that night you called.'

'Oh yes, yes.' He smiled towards the sergeant now, and the man, relaxing somewhat, smiled back at him, before turning to Nellie and saying, 'I'll wait outside a bit, dear, eh?'

'Yes, Alec.' He went to take her hand, then changed his mind, but he smiled widely down on her before turning to go out of the room.

'Come and sit down, Charlie.'

He took the chair by the bed. 'How are you? You look better.'

'I'm feeling fine now. You did remember him, didn't you?'

'Yes, yes, of course, Nellie, I remembered him.'

She looked at him for a moment in silence. 'He's . . . he's been a very good friend to me, Charlie.'

'Yes, I'm sure he has, Nellie.'

'He . . . he was a bit embarrassed to see you, I mean being an officer.'

'He needn't be.'

'I got your letter.'

'Good.'

'I . . . I couldn't write back, I felt so tired.'

'I didn't expect you to. I'm so glad though to see you looking so much better.'

She nodded at him, then turned her gaze from him and looked down towards her hands as she said, 'Mother'll be here today. She's going to make arrangements to take me home for convalescence' – now she slanted her eyes towards him – 'and to see that I don't try anything funny again.'

'You won't. And I'm glad you're going home.'

'I don't mean to stay there Charlie, I couldn't, but I'll be glad to rest for a time. It isn't that I'm physically tired, it's . . . it's more in my mind.'

'I know.'

'Charlie.'

'Yes, dear?'

'Alec wants to marry me.'

As he stared into her eyes there rushed through his mind a voice as if coming from a deep well, shouting, 'Charlie! Charlie! will you marry me?'

'Do . . . do you care for him?'

'I like him.'

Who else had said that? Polly.

'Enough to marry him?'

'It all depends, Charlie. I'm lost, I'm lonely.'

'But I thought. . . .'

'Don't say you thought I had lots of friends, Charlie, please don't. They were soldiers, young fellows who hadn't a fireside to sit beside, and I wanted to laugh and dance and sing; I wanted all kinds of things, Charlie, to make up for what I lost. You know what I'm saying, Charlie?'

He was silent, lost in the depths of the revelation in her eyes.

When his gaze dropped from hers and he bowed his head and she said, 'I didn't mean to embarrass you, Charlie,' his chin snapped upwards and his voice was loud as he cried, 'You're not embarrassing me.' Then he closed his eyes and covered the lower part of his face with his hand, saying, 'I'm sorry, I'm sorry Nellie.'

She gave a small laugh now as she said, 'Don't apologize, it's nice to hear someone shout; they've been going round here for days whispering as if they were just waiting to lay me out, which I suppose they were, at first anyway.'

'Nellie' – he gripped hold of her hands now – 'I'm married, I'm still married to Victoria and she's your sister, but I've never wished for freedom more than I do at this moment. Now do you understand me?'

He watched the colour spread over her face; then, her voice a whisper, she said, 'That's all I wanted to hear.' But now her head gave an impatient shake and her face twisted for a moment as she said, 'No, it isn't. No, it isn't . . . Charlie –'

'Yes, dear.'

'Will . . . will you put it into plain words?'

Bringing her hands to his breast now, he pressed them tightly there, and he stared at her and gulped in his throat before he said, 'I . . . I love you, Nellie. I think I must have always loved you.'

She lay now looking at him for a full minute before she spoke, and then she said, 'You're not just saying it, Charlie, because I'm down? You see I know you, you'd swear black was white if it meant pleasing somebody. That's true, isn't it?'

'I suppose so.' He nodded at her. 'It could have been once, but not any more; the easy-going, good old Charlie was shot dead some months ago. I'll tell you about it some time.'

'Victoria?'

'Victoria.'

'Will you divorce her, Charlie?'

'Yes, as soon as this business is over.'

'Kiss me, Charlie.'

He kissed her. His arms about her, he lifted her up from the pillow and with her arms around his neck they clung to each other. When he laid her back they laughed into each other's face and, his hands on each side of her head, he pressed it into the pillow, then he kissed her again.

Following this, they were silent for some little time. Their fingers interlocked, they remained looking down at their hands until she said, 'I'd like you to know something, Charlie.' When he waited she went on, 'The lads, the soldiers, I haven't been with one, I mean I haven't let any of them sleep with me.'

He looked away from her for a moment before he said, 'Playing the big fellow, I should say it wouldn't matter to me if you had, but . . . but I'd be lying.'

She stared straight into his face now as she asked, 'We won't be able to be married for some long time, will we, Charlie?'

'No, I suppose not. Some months ago I was about to go to a solicitor, I'd all the proof I needed, but then almost overnight this happened' – he touched his shoulder – 'and . . . and I was in a fix because the proof was in the army, high up. But the minute I'm discharged the proceedings will start. I can assure you of that, dear.'

'But that could be a long time, Charlie, or never.'

'Don't say that, Nellie. Don't say that.'

'But it could, Charlie, so listen to me. Once I am home back . . . back in my own place, I want to come to you.'

He made no response to this for some seconds; then taking her joined hands, he brought them to his lips, and as he held them there the door opened and her mother came in. . . .

Florence Chapman, taking in the situation, stared at them fixedly for a moment; then walking towards the bed, she said, 'Well! Well now!'

Charlie had risen to his feet and was holding the chair for her and as she sat down he said, 'Nice to see you, Florence.'

Her face was straight as she turned it up towards him, saying, 'I don't think I can return the compliment, not at the moment, Charlie.'

'I can understand that, Florence.'

Florence stared at him. It was only a matter of months since she had last seen him, but he didn't appear the same Charlie. The flatness had gone out of both his manner and voice, even his stance was different, but perhaps that could be put down to his uniform. It was hard to believe that this was the same young fellow who had caused havoc in her family. But of course he wasn't really to blame for that, that had been Hal's doing, God rest his soul, Victoria had merely been a tool.

And what a tool her daughter had turned out to be, for she was now man mad. But hadn't she always been man mad. And of all the men she had to marry it had to be poor Charlie MacFell. But why was she thinking poor Charlie? That adjective could no longer be applied to him for here he was chancing his arm again, and of all people with Nellie, while he was still tied to Victoria. Well, she'd put a stop to that. What next? she wondered. She looked now at her daughter and, forcing a smile to her face, she said, 'You're better?'

'Yes, Mother, much better.'

'I've just had a word with the sister. She says if you keep up this progress I can take you home next week.'

'Aw, that'll be good.'

'And it'll be for good, I hope? I was talking to Ratcliffe in Hexham the other day. He could sell your house and. . . .'

'No, Mother.' Nellie had pulled herself up from the pillows as she said again, 'No, Mother, I won't sell the house and . . . and I must tell you now, far better be above-board, Mother, but I mean to return to the flat once I get on my feet. And another thing . . . I can say this, Charlie, can't I?' She looked up at Charlie now and when he nodded to her she went on, 'Charlie and I love each other. It's no news to you that I've always loved him, and . . . and if he hadn't been forced. . . .'

'That's enough, Nellie! Nobody forced him. Nobody forced you, Charlie, did they?' She now turned her heated face up towards Charlie, and he, looking down at her, said quietly, 'No, you're right there, Florence, no one force me. Coerced would have been a better word, quietly coerced.'

'Charlie!' Florence Chapman stared up into the long face. He had changed, changed completely, indeed he had; the old Charlie would never have come out with a thing like that. That's what an officer's uniform did to one, she supposed. Yet she had always known that he wasn't as soft as he made out to be; there was a depth there and a sly depth if she knew anything about it. But he was right, he had been quietly coerced, and she, as much as Hal, had had a hand in it, and when things had gone wrong almost from the start she had known periods of remorse and guilt. But remorse or guilt wasn't going to let her countenance this new situation. And what did they think Victoria's attitude would be when she knew that her sister was aiming to get the better of her in the end? Because that was how she would view it. And although she herself had no use for Charlie, and had made that very, very plain, she would, if she knew anything about her daughter, put every spoke possible in the way of Nellie getting him, even maybe to depriving herself of the freedom she so definitely wanted. . . . But wait. She must remember that that had seemingly been her daughter's intention up to a few months ago. Then of a sudden she had stopped discussing the matter. She again looked up at Charlie, a deep frown between her brows now. There was something fishy going on and she couldn't get to the bottom of it.

She now watched her son-in-law take her daughter's hand and say, 'I'll leave you for a while, dear; I'll be back before the time's up.' And when he did not excuse himself to her she stared at his back as he left the room and when the door had closed on him she looked at Nellie and said, 'We're acting the big fellow these days, aren't we?'

'He's always been a big fellow, Mother, but none of you could see it.'

'Dear, dear!' Florence shook her head. 'What infatuation can do! The old saying that love is blind is surely true. . . .'

'Mother!' Nellie was leaning forward now, her breath coming in short gasps, and she pressed her hand tightly against her breast bone as she said, 'Don't run Charlie down to me. And I'm not blind with love; I began by liking Charlie MacFell when I was a little girl, because you were always laughing at his father, making fun of him. You laughed at the ideas he had for his son, and then you all laughed at Charlie as he grew up because he didn't farm like the rest of you, or drink like the rest of you, or whore like the rest of you. . . .'

'Nellie! that's enough.' Her mother's voice held deep indignation. 'I'll say this, that if he didn't do any whoring, his father made up for it. And who's to know what he did anyway?'

'Mother, you know as well as I do that everybody knew what everybody else did in our community, but I think Charlie was the only one who didn't know that your eldest daughter was at it from when she was fifteen and she never stopped, and now she's almost a licensed prostitute, her name's a byword in some quarters.'

Florence Chapman was standing on her feet now. Her lips were working one over the other as she pulled on her black gloves; then she adjusted the fur collar of her black mourning coat before she said, 'I can see you're well enough to fight again, Nellie, so I'll leave you and hope to find you in a better mood on my next visit.'

'Mother! please.' Nellie put out her hand. 'I'm sorry, I'm sorry; but you know what I say is true. You know it, you do.'

'She's my daughter the same as you are.'

Then face up to the fact that if you can condone the life she leads, then you've got to let me have my way of life, and my way of life from now on is with Charlie and he with me; and I'm telling your something, Mother, and this is true, if I don't have Charlie I'll take no one. The reason why I tried to finish it –' she now drooped her head and paused before going on, 'I didn't think he even thought of me as a friend any longer, because he hadn't shown up, and hadn't written – he could have been dead, there was no word of any kind – and . . . and I knew that without him life would be totally empty. You could say I'm young and I would get over it, but I knew I'd never get over Charlie. I don't know why, I can't explain the feeling, but without him there is nothing. As you know I tried drink, but that didn't do any good.' She lifted her head sharply now as she said, 'But I never tried men, only as pals. I thought of it more than once. Oh yes, yes I did, but I knew I couldn't bring myself to it. Funny' – she slowly shook her head – 'the difference between us, our Vic and me, both from the same parents, same blood, yet we're as opposite as the poles, and you know, Mother, you won't believe me when I say I'm sorry about this because we're irrevocably divided and you need comfort from us both, you need us as a family now more than ever and we'll never be a family again.'

Florence stared at her daughter. How was it that everything, everybody had changed? Was it the war? Would things have been different if there hadn't been a war? No, not with her daughters. It was as Nellie said, they were irrevocably divided. She had always loved Nellie better than Victoria, but in this moment she felt she loved neither of them, they had gone from her, life had taken them as the grave had taken her Hal. Oh, how she missed Hal. What were children after all compared to a husband? Children were mere offshoots of a moment's passion, they were of your body yet they didn't belong to you, whereas a husband who was no kin, no blood tie, a stranger in fact, became your all, your life merged with his and when he left you all that was vital in you went with him. She turned away from the bed and walked out of the room.

In the corridor she looked first one way then the other. A sergeant was standing at one end, and at the other end stood Charlie. They were both looking towards the door behind her. She turned her back on Charlie and walked in the direction of the sergeant and she passed him without apparently seeing him, yet he stared hard at her.

When Florence had gone Charlie and the sergeant looked at each other over the distance and when Charlie made a motion with his head the sergeant grinned, gave a salute, and went hastily into the side ward.

Knowing it wouldn't be long before the sergeant came out again, and not wanting to witness the look on the man's face, he went into the main hall and stood to the side.

He hadn't long to wait, not more than five minutes, then he saw the man marching towards the door. He didn't look to right or left but went straight through the main doors and disappeared from view.

As he hurried back to the ward he felt a spasm of pity for the fellow, who was likely thinking, Bloody officers, they get in because of their uniform.

When he entered the room again, he made no comment on either the sergeant's or Florence's visit; he didn't speak at all, all he did was to gather Nellie tightly into his arms and hold her there.

# Chapter Three

It was a conspiracy. Why him? Why his platoon? Radlett was older than him. As for Lieutenant Calthorpe, he had been in this depot for over a year now ... yes and would likely remain here until the end of the war, if he knew anything about it. In any case, if he had to go why wasn't Radlett going along with him and not the new young fellow who was so raw he still thought it all a merry game?

But why was he asking such damn silly questions?

He wouldn't have minded in the least being sent over there if it wasn't for leaving Nellie. She was still at the farm and he'd seen her only twice since she had come out of hospital, and now with this lightning move there'd be no chance of seeing her again.

If he could only be with her for just five minutes, just five minutes. He'd a damned good mind to walk out and take the consequences. ... And what would be the consequences? Absent without leave. But what could you expect from someone who in the first place had to be dragged into the army. The result would be worse than the white feather, the colour would be yellow.

Things would have been simpler, he thought, if he hadn't discovered how he felt about Nellie; much simpler, yet he wouldn't wish his feelings to be other than they were at this moment.

He had been told to stand by, and he was standing by, but in the hope that all those for embarkation would be given at least twelve hours' leave. Wasn't there a rule about this? But then who considered rules when chits were flying about? You did what you were told, or else.

'I'm glad I'm goin' with you, sir.'

'Thanks, Miller. I'm glad you are too.'

'Where do you think we're bound for, sir?'

'I'm not exactly sure at the moment, Miller.'

'Could it be across the water?'

'It could be.'

'Well, if that's the case I'm afraid I won't be looking forward to it, sir.'

'Only a fool would, Miller.'

'They were breakin' their neck to get across there this time last year, sir, but they've changed their tune now I think. The Somme did that for 'em.'

'Yes, the Somme did that for them.'

'Do you think there's any chance for any of us gettin' a bit of leave, sir?'

'I don't know, Miller; quite candidly I'm as much in the dark as you with regard to that, but I certainly hope we get a few hours.'

'Yes, so do I, sir. There's the missis, she's likely as not to go and raise hell ... I mean play up, sir, if I don't say her ta-rah.'

They smiled at each other; then Miller proffered his usual comforter, 'Will I brew up, sir?'

'No, thanks, Miller; I'm going to the mess and there's a meeting after.' Hastily he looked round the room. 'Everything ready?'

'Yes, sir. An' I did as you said, I just packed two of the books. What's goin' to happen to the rest, sir?'

'Oh.' He glanced towards the bed, then laughed and said, 'My replacement will likely use them to heighten the bed, it's too near the floor.' They exchanged smiles again before he went out.

When the door had closed on his officer, Miller looked towards the small pile of books in the corner of the room and nodded, Aye, that's likely what the next one would do. Poetry books, and books in French, and others that were as understandable as that one written by a fellow called Platt-o. Funny fellow his officer, nice, kind, a decent bloke, but somehow he still didn't seem to fit in. It was a pity. He was glad he was going with him; he felt sort of protective towards him somehow.

# Chapter Four

The dock had the appearance of a madhouse. There were two ships lying alongside, both discharging wounded; ambulance men were running hither and thither with stretchers; nurses were assisting limping men, leading blind ones; Salvation Army lasses were handing out mugs of tea; non-commissioned officers were issuing orders; the only people who seemingly weren't joining in the mad frenzy were the lines of soldiers, who stood at ease, their kit-bags by their sides.

Charlie's platoon was at the end of the jetty. He and his men had been assigned to 1/6th Durham Light Infantry. The 1/6th, 1/8th and 1/9th were battalions that had been made up of remnants from other companies. As Charlie's new lieutenant had laughingly said, 'The stroke apparently indicates we are not all there, but let's get across and we'll show 'em. What do you say?'

Charlie could do nothing but confirm his superior's words for he was still both angry and worried inside by the fact that there had been no embarkation leave. And now here he was in the midst of this madness. Yet it was an ordered madness and strangely in parts a jocular madness for the wounded men were throwing jokes at the waiting platoons. That their cheerfulness was in most part the outcome of hysterical release at being back in Blighty didn't matter, it had a cheering effect on those waiting to take their place in the mud.

For the men knew they were going into mud. It was strange but they didn't talk of killing, or of being killed, but of how to combat mud. One joker had cut out a pair of cardboard snow-shoes, and Charlie's new captain by the name of Lee-Farrow had encouraged the joker and all those with him by saying, 'That's the spirit, boys. That's the spirit.'

It was funny, Charlie thought, the little things that bought loyalty. All the men would now consider the captain a decent bloke, whereas back in camp his platoon had considered Captain Blackett a bloody stinker because he rarely addressed them; and yet he was a very good fellow. His lieutenant came up to him now, saying, 'Everything all right at your end?'

'Yes, sir.'

'Taking their bleeding time to unload.'

'They must have been heavily packed, sir.'

'I'll say . . . God! I wish we were across and settled in.'

A sardonic smile rippled somewhere in Charlie . . . I wish we were across and settled in. It sounded as if they were off on a holiday trip with an hotel at the end of it.

They both moved aside now as a line of stretcher-bearers came towards them. There were five stretchers; on the first two the men were conscious and were looking about them; on the third stretcher a man's whole face was bandaged up except for a slit where the mouth was; on the fourth stretcher the man looked asleep; and on the fifth one the man looked already dead.

Charlie was turning his gaze away when he almost flung himself round again and towards the last stretcher; then addressing the lieutenant, he said, 'Could I be excused for a moment, a friend?'

'Carry on.'

He now hurried after the line of stretchers, and when he reached the end one he looked across at the nurse on the other side and started, 'Is he?'

'No, no.' She shook her head. 'But he's in a bad way.'

When the stretchers were lowered to the ground to await their turn for transport, he bent down and whispered, 'Arthur! Arthur!'

There was a flicker of the eyelids, the head turned just the slightest.

Again he said, 'Arthur! it's me, Charlie.'

The lids were raised slowly, the jaw dropped, the lips moved, they said Charlie but without making a sound.

'Oh, Arthur.'

'Excuse me, sir; we must get him in.' The stretcher was lifted again, the jaw moved, the lips moved, Charlie put his hand out and cupped the ashen face. 'Oh, Arthur.'

'Excuse me.' He was pushed gently aside; the stretcher was lifted up into the ambulance; he turned and looked at the man who was giving some kind of instruction to the nurse. She climbed up into the ambulance, the doors were closed, and it drove away.

The man spoke now. 'You knew him?'

He gulped in his throat; there was an avalanche of tears pouring down inside him.

'He . . . he was a friend.'

'I'm afraid he's in a bad way.'

'What's . . . what's wrong with him?'

'Almost everything I should say; he's lost both legs and an arm.'

God Almighty!

He was closing his eyes against the pictures when a voice acting like an injection in his own arm yelled, 'Fall in! Come on now! Come on now! Look slippy! Fall in!'

Without further words he and the doctor parted.

Now he was at the head of his platoon, looking along them, seeing them all without legs and minus an arm each.

'Quick march!'

The quick march developed into a mark time, then into a scramble up the gangway, and they were aboard.

The quay had seemed crowded and it was a long quay and the boat seemed very small compared with it, yet everyone who had been on that quay seemed to have boarded the boat. They stood packed like up-ended sardines, one against the other, and as the ship left the quay and a cheer went up, he thought, We're mad. Everybody's mad. Life had become so cheap that they were cheering for death.

Poor Arthur. Poor Arthur.

Good-bye, Nellie.

# Chapter Five

He was seasoned; he had been pickled in mud, blood, and slime. The anatomy of man had been laid bare for him to examine in the first week in the trenches when his sergeant's belly was split open. It was in that moment when he had reviewed the squirming mass of intestines that a strange, almost lunatic thought struck him. It was the first time his whirling mind told him that the sergeant's innards had seen daylight. It was in that moment too that he lost his fear. What was death after all? A mere blowing from existence into oblivion, you wouldn't know anything about it. In a way it was better than being maimed, burned, gassed, or blinded. If he had to go, well, that was the way he wanted to go, like his sergeant had gone.

Yet there was another side to this business of dying, the side that was still alive . . . over there, his sergeant's wife and her four children. But one tried not to dwell on this. Such things were docketed in the corner of the mind where Nellie dwelt and from where she was apt to escape and occupy the narrow camp bed with him.

He was sharing this particular dug-out with Lieutenant Bradshaw. He like Bradshaw, he had come to respect him. Beyond his ah-lah fashion of talking he was a nice fellow. Three of his brothers in a Kent battalion had been killed near Arras last year; another had gone on the Somme; an uncle had been killed near Hebuterne early in this year. He seemed to have relatives in all the regiments; a cousin who had died in the 20th Wearsiders and another brother who was severely wounded in the Pioneers.

Bit by bit, Charlie was able to gauge his companion's family history. They were army people on his mother's side but not on his father's. His father was a judge. He, Bradshaw, was one of six brothers, and all four who had been killed had been going in for law. There was only himself and his elder brother left.

He had come close to Bradshaw in the last few months. He was flattered that Bradshaw thought him so well-read, even admitting that he was no reader himself, not of literature at any rate, mathematics was his subject. He felt he would have got a first at Oxford if he'd had time to finish, but he had wanted to get into this business.

The weather had been stinking. It was April but there had been snow; there was mud everywhere, and when going over the top should you slip and fall you swallowed it, and you hadn't to be surprised if as you groped and pulled yourself to your feet there was a hand outstretched to help you.

The first time he had gripped such a hand he had sprung back as if he had been shot, and he had felt he wanted to vomit as he stared down at the stiff wide-spread fingers appealingly held out to him.

There were days when the mud was the sole enemy, when it bogged down horses, guns, lorries and even the new monsters, the tanks, and at times like this the spirits of all those concerned would sink into it, only to be dragged upwards by their lieutenant's voice.

Bradshaw was popular with the men. Charlie himself was popular too, he knew that, but in a different way from Bradshaw. The men would talk to him, ask him questions, try to pump him; they never took that liberty with Lieutenant Bradshaw. Of course Bradshaw was a pip up, that might be the answer; but no, there was a subtle difference between them, it was in the tone of the voice, the tilt of the chin, the look in the eye. Bradshaw always remembered that he was in command, that was the difference.

But at the particular moment spirits were high and they had right to be. They had heard that the 10th had broken through the Hindenburg Line from the West and then within a few days had been relieved by the 6th and 8th, and the 5th and 9th. And as news of further advances by other divisions came through so morale soared, from the still spruce top brass behind the line down to the lice-ridden Tommy in the thick of it.

There was rejoicing too that the casualties had been light compared with other battles for only seven officers and around three hundred and fifty N.C.O.s and men had been killed and wounded – that was all. Cheap payment for the Wancourt line.

At times Charlie likened the whole affair to a game of chess played with the Mad Hatter and Alice; that the divisions, brigades and battalions, even platoons ever got themselves sorted out was a miracle to him. In some cases they overlapped so much, with the result that chaos followed and with chaos unnecessary death. But that was war as played out by the generals.

It was the middle of May and both Charlie and Lieutenant Bradshaw had decided long before this that their Blighty leave was overdue. They had been relieved and had had a few days behind the lines twice within the past months; but what was that? As Bradshaw said, they'd never had a real bath. He would, he said, be quite content to drown in steaming hot water. Of course, he had added with a laugh, it would be an added comfort if he had a companion by his side at the time.

'What are you going to do when you get back, Charlie?' They had come to using Christian names by now.

'The same as you, first go off, although I won't let the water up to my eyebrows, there's no outlet beyond; then I'll have the biggest meal that's ever been cooked, roast lamb, six veg. I'll have the veg on a separate plate because there won't be room for them on the main one, and then I'll have three Yorkshire puddings, two with gravy and one with milk and sugar.'

'Oh my God!' John Bradshaw screwed up his face in disgust.

'Well, what would be your choice?'

'Salmon, a whole salmon, fresh, straight out of the river, lightly boiled and floating in butter and nothing else, nothing . . . no vegetables, just the whole salmon to myself, and wine . . . wine, of course. Then a whole bottle of port, thick, sliding, tongue-coating port. And then I'd be ready to meet the ladies. Of course, you won't want any ladies, you'll have your wife, and by the number of letters you get from her I imagine she'll be as eager to see you as you are to see her.'

'Yes, yes, I hope so.'

Nellie . . . his wife. Well she'd be as good as when he got back.

When he got back? The thought caused him to say, 'Do you think they'll clip us and we'll be in the next push?'

John Bradshaw remained silent for a moment. Then he moved his tongue around the inside of his lower lip before pushing it into his cheek and saying, 'I hope the hell not; but there's something in the wind. The pressure must be off the Germans now on the Russian front, and the French are no more bleeding use, and so it would appear it's solely up to us. One good sign is the stuff they're bringing up looks enough to blow the bleedy world to bits. Anyway, we'll see, Charlie boy; we'll see.'

Second-Lieutenant Charles MacFell and Lieutenant John Bradshaw didn't get their leave, but like thousands of others their senses had become dulled with the continuous bombardment of the past fortnight.

In the early morning of June 7th Charlie, walking along the duck-boards, stopped here and there and, when he could make himself heard, spoke to the men leaning against the parapet, their guns by their side. 'Good luck!' he said, and the answer always came back, 'An' you sir.'

When he stopped near his sergeant he checked his watch, and the sergeant, without speaking, looked at his.

'Three minutes.'

'Yes, sir, three minutes. Good cover, isn't it, sir?'

'Excellent.'

At a curve in the trench John Bradshaw was standing and next to him Captain Lee-Farrow. It was the captain who asked, 'Everything set?'

'Yes, sir.'

'Good cover?'

'Excellent, sir.'

The captain now looked up into the sky, to the stars twinkling between the flashes from the guns. 'Nice night,' he said.

Both John Bradshaw and Charlie, following the captain's gaze, answered together, 'Yes, sir, nice night.' Then in the darkness they smiled at each other without being aware of it.

'Good luck.'

'And you, sir.'

'Better take your positions.'

Charlie and John Bradshaw moved away, and when they parted a few steps further up the trench, Bradshaw said quietly, 'All the best, Charlie,' and Charlie answered, 'And a whole salmon done in butter.'

Another deafening explosion smothered the chuckle, then Charlie was standing in place.

'Thirty seconds.'

'Twenty.'

'Ten.'

'*Over. Over. Over.*' The word ran along the trench like the echo of a song that was cut off here and there by the noise of the band.

How far did he run across the open space before he started to yell? How many of his pistol shots found their target? He didn't know, he heard screams and groans between the deafening blast of the artillery. A shell exploded near him and he was thrown off his feet, but surprisingly as soon as he was down he was up again. He remembered being worried for a flashing second in case his pistol had been blocked with mud. He couldn't remember reloading.

When he fell flat over a body and heard a broad North Country voice, saying, 'Bloody hell!' he shouted 'All right?' and the face close to his bawled, 'Is that you, Mister MacFell?'

'Yes!' He was screaming, and he was answered by a scream. 'Thought it was Jerry. I've copped it in the knee. In the knee, sir.'

'Well, stay put! I'll be back.'

'You will?' There was the slightest trace of fear in the question and he yelled firmly, 'Yes, definitely, I'll be back,' while thinking the man would likely be blown to smithereens in a few minutes, if not by the enemy by his own artillery.

He was going through a maze of blasted barbed wire; it tore at his hands, then he was in a mêlée again, but now he could make out the whirling, prancing figures. 'Thrust it in! Turn. Pull. Thrust it in! Turn. Pull.'

The steel blade was coming at him. He pulled on the trigger of his pistol but nothing happened; the blade within inches of his chest was knocked sidewards, and in the flare of the bursting shells he gave a lightning glance towards the man who had saved his skin. But there was no recognition; as far as he could remember he wasn't one of theirs. But this often happened, companies got mixed up.

It was as they came under a hail of fire from the further German lines that he came across John Bradshaw. In the illumination of a Very light he saw him lying against the side of a trench, his fingers gripping the wooden support that led to a dug-out. He turned him round and saw in the flashes that he was still alive; one arm was hugging his chest and his sleeve was already stained. He grabbed up the pistol that was lying by his side and glanced swiftly around. There were bodies strewn here and there and a few men were still milling about along at the far end of the trench where it turned a corner. As a shell burst overhead he ducked and covered the lieutenant; then shouting at him, 'It's all right! It's all right!' he put his hands underneath his oxters and pulled him into the shelter of the dug-out. Then for the second time in a matter of minutes he yelled, 'I'll be back! I'll be back, John.'

The men at the end of the trench were pinned down now by a barrage of bursting shells.

There was a sudden explosion at the opposite end of the trench and timbers and clay were thrown high in the air.

'We're cornered, sir,' a voice was bawling in his ear, and he nodded at the crouching speaker and, pointing backward, he gesticulated wildly; then waved his arm in a 'Come on!' movement and the huddle of men followed him, stumbling over the bodies strewn on the duck-boards.

Within a few minutes the dug-out was full with fifteen privates, a corporal, a sergeant, and Lieutenant Bradshaw.

It had been an officers' dug-out, as the light of a torch showed, and Charlie saw that it was well equipped, better far than theirs had been, in fact it appeared luxurious. What caught his eye immediately were three towels hanging on a bench near an enamelled bowl filled with water. Gathering up the towels, he went to John Bradshaw and said quickly, 'Let's see the trouble, John?' But he had to force his arm away from his ribs before he could open his jacket. When he ripped down the blood-sodden shirt it was to disclose a bullet wound at the top of his chest.

'I know what to do, sir, I've done first aid.' The voice was to his side and Charlie said, 'Good.'

'We'll tear the towels, sir.'

With the help of other hands the towels were quickly torn into strips, and when the rough bandaging was done, they carried the lieutenant to the bed in the corner of the dug-out and laid him down, and for the first time John Bradshaw spoke. 'Thanks, Charlie,' he said.

'It won't be long before we get you back.'

They looked at each other steadily for a moment; then John Bradshaw merely nodded.

The barrage had lessened somewhat but was still strong, and Charlie issued orders to the sergeant, who relayed them to the corporal to post men at intervals along the trench, and for others to remove the bodies to the far end; but not to go beyond the bend. The trench was long and although there was no sound of fighting activity coming from further along it, it was not known who could be lurking there. They would investigate later. Then he went out, the sergeant going with him.

Cautiously now he raised his head above the parapet. The early morning light showed a sea of barbed wire. What was he to do? He couldn't think of advancing with this handful on his own; but if they stayed here they'd likely all be blown to smithereens.

He turned now and went down the trench and looked over the other parapet in the direction where he imagined lay their own lines, but as far as he could see there was merely barren land pitted with craters, except where two small hills lay to the right. . . . Or were they hills? That was the direction from where the bombardment had been coming, likely they were camouflaged fortifications. He hadn't any idea at the moment where he was. He couldn't remember seeing those two mounds on the map.

What he did see now were two figures slowly emerging from a crater. From this distance he couldn't make out whether they were Germans or his own fellows. He called quietly, 'Sergeant, take a look.'

The sergeant raised his head slowly upwards, then said, 'Blokes crawling this way, sir.'

'Yes; but who are they?'

'Bareheaded, no helmets on.'

'I think there's one of them injured, one's pulling the other. . . . Yes, and they're ours. Come on.'

Without hesitation they both jumped the parapet and, bent double, made for the crawling men. They had just reached them when the barrage of fire was intensified, and it was definitely coming now from the direction of the mounds.

Grabbing one man by the collar, Charlie pulled him unceremoniously forward, and they had almost reached the trench when a shell burst just behind them and the force of the explosion lifted them all and threw them in a bunch back into the trench.

When they had sorted themselves out, they lay panting for a moment and took stock of each other. One of the men Charlie recognized straightaway, it was the man he had stumbled over, one of his own men; and now the man actually laughed at him as he spluttered almost hysterically, 'You said you'd come back an' get me, an' you did.'

The other soldier was covered with wet slush from head to foot, and as he watched the man take his hand round his face, then through his mud-matted hair, his heart actually missed a beat.

No, no! not here; not under these circumstances; not Slater.

But it was Slater, and Slater had recognized him.

As another shell burst near the parapet Charlie yelled at his sergeant, 'Get them into the dug-out.'

No sign of recognition had passed between them but immediately he entered the dug-out he felt an almost desperate urge to speak to Slater, in order to make their stations clear once and for all, yet he had to force the question through his lips.

'What battalion?' he asked. His voice was cool, the words clipped.

Slater stared at him, and his hesitation in answering was put down by those present to shock; fellows did act like that at times, didn't jump to it, they got past it.

'12th . . . sir.'

The sergeant looked sharply at the mud-covered figure, the fellow was acting queer; the way he had said 'sir'; shellshock likely.

Charlie stared into Slater's face for a moment before turning away; then he looked around the dug-out, saying, 'Seemingly they didn't go in for tea, but there's a few bottles of wine there. Open them, Sergeant.'

'Yes, sir.'

'And those tins of beef; you'd better make a meal of it for I think we might be here a little while longer.'

He now went to the corner of the dug-out where John Bradshaw lay, and the lieutenant, looking up at him, said, 'They didn't take all that sector then?'

Charlie shook his head. 'No.'

'They will.'

'Yes, yes, they will. Don't worry.'

'The shelling, where's it coming from?'

'One of the hills on our flank, it's still very much alive.'

'What do you aim to do?' Suddenly Bradshaw bit on his lip and his right arm went across his chest and covered the one that was strapped to his body with the towels.

'Look,' Charlie bent over him; 'don't worry. If our lot don't send rein-forcements over we can hold out till dark. Just lie still.' He nodded down into the pain-twisted face, then went outside again.

The sergeant was standing along near where the last man was posted and where the dead lay conspicuously piled on both sides of the parapet, and he turned to Charlie, saying below his breath as he pointed to the bend in the trench, 'There's movement along there, sir, I went a little way round and I'm sure I spotted a head peering out of a dug-out.'

Charlie remained still for a moment; then drawing John Bradshaw's pistol from his holster and looking first at the sergeant, then at the sentry, he said, 'Come on,' and slowly the three went forward. First pausing before a dug-out, their guns at the ready, they would then jump almost as one man into it. Each was well constructed but not so comfortable, Charlie noticed, as the one they had claimed as their temporary headquarters.

They had almost reached the last dug-out before the trench made yet another sharp bend when Charlie held up his hand and they stood perfectly still.

The minutes ticked away, almost five of them before, signalling to the sergeant to follow him, they both sprang forward and through the opening.

His finger was wavering on the trigger. Instinctively he was about to pull it when 'Kamarad! Kamarad!' The word emerged from three throats at once; two of the men were lying on the floor, the third was leaning on his elbow, one arm thrust high above his head; his trouser knee was soaked red; the second man on the floor hadn't raised his hands because they were holding the side of his head; the first man now stood up, his hands well above his head.

'Come on!' Charlie signalled to the standing man to move forward, then called to the private: 'Stay with them! We'll send someone forward for them.' He went out and followed the sergeant who was now thrusting the German along the trench at the point of his bayonet.

In the passage along the trench Charlie detailed two men to go and bring the wounded Germans down. Back in their own dug-out the man who was acting as orderly exclaimed on sight of the prisoner, 'Blimey! a live one.'

Slater, sitting hunched up in the corner of the dug-out, said nothing, and as Charlie's eyes swept over him, as if unseeing, he noticed, with surprise, for the first time that his sleeve now bore no stripes. Slater had been deprived of the power to bully and blast. Why?

After a moment he said in an aside to his sergeant and with a backward lift of his head in the direction of Slater, 'Put him on guard.'

'I . . . I think he's in shock, sir, shellshock, he won't open his mouth.'

He wanted to say, 'Yes, he's in shock all right, but it isn't shellshock, it's hate that's tying his tongue.'

And as the thought came to him, he swung round to stare into the eyes of Slater. It was as if their steel-hard gaze had willed him to turn, and he experienced a fear that all the guns and the slaughter hadn't so far evoked in him.

'You'd better watch out.' It was as if someone had spoken aloud, for he answered the voice, saying, 'Yes, by God, yes, I'd better watch out.' . . .

It was around midday when he was almost about to give the order to make it back to their own lines that the bombardment from the mounds started in earnest and two men on sentry duty at the farthest end of the trench were killed outright. To add further to the confusion, their own batteries took up the challenge.

He didn't know how far their line had advanced, or if they had advanced at all, but he gauged that as long as there was the crossfire there would be no surprise attack from the German flank to retake this particular section of the line, and so he ordered the remaining men into the dug-out, only almost immediately to feel he had made a mistake and they would all be buried alive, for a shell bursting near up above cracked the timbers in the roof and brought the clay spattering amongst them.

The German prisoners showed little emotion, they sat huddled together staring before them; even the one who wasn't wounded looked dazed.

As the afternoon wore on, the shelling became intermittent from both sides, and then as dusk was about to set in there fell over the whole land a silence. It was a weird silence. Back home Charlie would have thought of it as the silence of evening falling into night; here, he knew, it was the calm before the storm.

John Bradshaw who was doubtless in great pain and who looked pretty sick muttered, 'What are you thinking of doing?' and Charlie replied, 'Once it's dark, make a break for our lines again, go back the way we came. I've been looking at the map. We'll have to move north-west. Battle Wood I think lies to the north, and to tell you the truth I don't know if we've come through two sets of lines or not.'

'I shouldn't think so; our artillery seems too near for that.'

'I hope you're right.'

'I . . . I know they are dead beat but I think you'd be wise to put some of them on guard before it gets too dark, you don't know but what we may be surprised.'

'Yes, I'll do that.'

He turned away now and issued orders to the sergeant to place his men again at intervals along the trench leaving only three men behind. Then beckoning these three men to the opening of the dug-out he said in an undertone, 'You know what to do when I give the signal. Get him on to the stretcher. Don't take any notice of his protests, just get him on to it. Then put the able-bodied prisoner at the front and one of you take the back. When you go out of here turn left.' He pointed. 'The three wounded men' – he jerked his head backwards – 'well, two of you get in between them, you know the drill, and follow the stretcher. We'll be around you. The main thing is to make as little noise as possible. And if they start lighting up, well, drop where you stand. Good luck.'

They made no answer, they merely nodded, and he went out and walked slowly along the trench, first to the right speaking to each man as he came to him, then he retraced his steps and walked to the left.

The last man in the trench was Slater. He was alone in the section where the trench curved slightly. Charlie did not stop but walked past him for some yards to a point where he intended they should climb out and make their way back, or at least join up with another unit, and as he stood peering over the parapet into the dusk he tried to still the churning inside him. The menace of the man had been weighing on him all day and it was never heavier than at this moment. It was with an effort that he made himself turn slowly about and walk back in his direction.

Slater was bending forward against the wall of the trench, his gun at the ready. His eyes were directed towards the top of the parapet and it was to this he seemingly spoke as he said clearly and distinctly, 'I've heard of blokes buyin' commissions in the old days but never one payin' for it with his wife's whoring.'

He was directly behind him, and now Slater turned his head, but not his body, and looked at him.

'What did you say?'

'You heard, you're not deaf. You heard . . . sir.' He put emphasis on the drawn-out sir. 'You didn't think you got it off your own bat, did you, you who hadn't the guts to kill a pig? . . . I wouldn't do that if I was you.'

Unconsciously, but driven by an inner desire to stop this devil's mouth in some way, Charlie's hand had moved towards his holster.

'That would be the finish of you if you did that . . . sir, too many witnesses about. Anyway, you wouldn't have the guts. You never had any guts, had you . . . sir?'

The most terrible thing Charlie was finding about this moment was that Slater's tone was conversational. He was now saying, 'They were all doin' it in their pants in case you named the major, so what was the best thing to do? Well, as Corporal Packer said – he was Lieutenant Swaine's corporal you remember – put you where you couldn't talk. He said he'd never seen such a flap as was on, or a promotion got so bloody quick. . . . Didn't you know that? . . . Oh you must have; you never thought you could get a pip on your own, now did you? As I've always said, you're a born loser, you lost the lass you loved, you married a whore, and now you've even lost yourself and your bloody platoon. A cuckold, that's the name I think the gentry have for a fellow like you, but to me you're just a loser, a pipsqueak loser.' . . .

He was never to fathom out correctly if it was the shell suddenly bursting near or the fact that Slater brought his body swiftly round with his gun at the ready, he was only aware that he was firing his pistol and straight into the man in front of him. The blast of another shell bursting flung him against the opposite parapet and he was lying there, the gun still in his hand, still pointing when the sergeant came running into view. Taking in the truth of the situation straightaway, he shouted, 'What happened, sir? He tried to do for you?'

Another shell burst, and then both he and the sergeant were flung down to the bottom of the trench and his face was hanging over Slater's, staring into the mouth and eyes which were wide as if he had died in a moment of surprise.

'Let's get out of this, sir.' The sergeant had hold of his arm and, bent double, they were running, but before they reached the dug-out another shell burst and the trench caved in behind them.

Then they were inside the dug-out and he was standing upright and shouting orders, yelling them. 'No use waiting any longer. . . . Have to make a break for it. They've got us pin-pointed. Get the lieutenant up. Come on! Look slippy! Look slippy there!'

*He had killed Slater. He had killed Slater.*

What was the matter with him, why was he yelling like this? It was only sergeants who did the yelling.

'You can't go right now, go left outside. Direct the prisoner.'

*He had killed Slater. He had killed Slater.*

'Come on! Come on, move!'

He was outside now hustling them along the trench whilst making his way to the front of them. It was at the point where they had picked up the German prisoners that he ordered them to push the stretcher on to the parapet, and when Bradshaw protested he shouted him down, bawling, 'Shut up!' then 'Get him up and over! All of you, over!'

Amid the scrambling there were curses and so, forgetting now that he himself had been bawling, he ordered, 'Quiet! Quiet! Keep together in two's, follow the stretcher.' He did not issue orders for the two men and the wounded, for they would of necessity trail behind.

Quietly now he called, 'Sergeant!' and when the man came to his side he said, 'I'll go ahead of the stretcher. Keep them together, keep them coming.'

'Yes, sir.'

It was dark now, except for the moments when the sky was illuminated by the flashes of gunfire coming from both the north and the south-west of them; there was no shellfire at the moment from the mound. He couldn't imagine that the hill had been taken; for if that had been so a patrol would surely have investigated the trench.

In the illumination of a Very light he got a momentary impression of their position. He was on the right track, the hill lay behind them to the north, their lines were due west, in fact they couldn't be much more than a few hundred yards away.

Another Very light burst now but almost directly over them, and almost at the same moment the crossfire began.

'Keep going!' he was yelling again, and the sergeant repeated his order, almost on a scream. 'Come on! Keep going!' but before he uttered the last word a shell burst to the right of them and they were all lying flat, hugging the earth.

The sergeant came crawling to his side. His face was near his own and his voice was loud in his ear. 'It's . . . it's our lot, sir; they're aiming at the hill.'

For a moment he didn't answer, the noise about them was deafening. Then there came a slight lull, at least from the artillery to the front of them, and the sergeant's voice came again, saying, 'They're knockin' bloody hell out of the trench, we did it only just in time, sir.'

There were Very lights bursting here and there about them, and now Charlie, twisting round on his elbow, shouted down the straggling line of cowering bodies, 'When the next Very bursts anywhere near, jump to your feet and yell, shout, bawl anything, let them see it's us.'

'We . . . we could be blown to smithereens, sir, the artillery's well behind, they couldn't get in touch in time.'

'That's a chance we'll have to take, Sergeant.'

'As you say, sir.'

Why was it, even in this moment when he was on the border of death, he asked himself, would the sergeant have questioned the lieutenant if he had given that order?

'*Up! Up!*' He had jumped to his feet, the sergeant beside him, but only a few of the men followed suit immediately.

'Wave your arms! Shout! Do you hear? Shout!'

Did he hear someone near bawl, 'What's the bloody good of that? He's up the pole. They'll never hear us in this?'

'*Forward! Forward!*'

Naturally it seemed to the men that they were being ordered to walk directly into the midst of the bursting shells, but they followed. An officer had given an order and it was their duty to carry it out, come hell, high water, or being blown to smithereens; and that was the fate every man thought awaited him.

Yet as they made straight across the tortured land being aided by the flashes of artillery that momentarily pin-pointed the pot-holes, some as big as craters half full of water in which many of them would have drowned, so weary were they, it was as if they were following a known path.

When a shell burst near and they were all spattered with earth the sergeant's voice now almost drowned the echo of it as he yelled, 'Keep going! Keep going!'

Then of a sudden the barrage in front of them stopped, and although the German battery behind them still kept peppering away, it was as if a deep silence had fallen all around them.

Charlie paused, bringing the rest to a halt as there arose from out of the ground in the distance dark shadows, darker than the night. He felt rather than saw them spreading out and he called wildly, 'Hello there! Hello there! I'm Lieutenant MacFell, we are the. . . .'

'Well! what the hell you all playing at standing there! Come on! Come on! Did you ever see the likes of it?'

It was as if they had been bidden to come in out of the rain. They came on, the utterly weary men at a run now, laughing as they dropped over the parapet. The canvas stretcher was eased gently down into the trench, and lastly the two soldiers with the three wounded men between them. . . .

Ten minutes later he was sitting in the very dug-out he had left only that morning, occupied now not only by a new lieutenant and his second, but also at this moment by a captain and a major.

'Have another.' They refilled his glass, and the major for the second time in a few minutes said, 'How you got your fellows through that lot I'll never know, but there's one thing sure, you would have had it by now if you had stayed in that line. Those batteries are cut off but they're going down fighting. They must have had the idea that the whole line was occupied. Well, their number'll be up soon; the cavalry are going over in half an hour. Then we are moving on. . . . Show's going well. You look all in, old chap.'

'It's been a busy day,' he found himself answering in the same vein.

'I'll say. . . . Pity about the lieutenant. But they'll soon dig that out of him back at base. He's lucky, it must have just missed his heart. Well now, we'll have to be about our father's business, won't we?' He turned to his officers and they laughed with him and repeated, 'Yes, sir, about our father's business.'

Turning to Charlie again the major now said, 'I'd have a nap until daylight, then you can go back to base with the wounded and have a wash an' brush up before you return to your unit. Only God knows where they are now.' He shook his head. Then in the same airy tone he ended, 'Very good night's work. Not only did you bring your men back safely and the lieutenant, but three prisoners. They might prove to be helpful, and they don't seem averse to being captured. Strange fellows. . . . Well, good-bye.'

'Good-bye, sir.' Charlie was on his feet. He had managed to salute smartly. The major had reached the opening of the dug-out when he turned and said, 'You'll be mentioned. I think it was a very good effort. Foolhardy, of course, to walk into a battery but nevertheless a very good effort.'

He sat down on the edge of the camp-bed and lowered his head into his hands. God above! Was he dreaming? You'll be mentioned. Good effort.

And for what? For coming backwards instead of going forward. But what else could he have done, he couldn't have left John? Couldn't he? Well, anyway, he seemingly had done the right thing according to the major, whose tone had also implied it was just what would be expected of an English officer and a gentleman.

An officer and a gentleman, not a conscript, and certainly not a man who had been made a cuckold and been paid for it by being given a pip on his shoulder.

God Almighty! He mustn't think about it, he must sleep, sleep. But when he slept he would still think about it, he would never be able to stop thinking about it, not till the day he died. And pray God that would be soon, because he couldn't live with the pictures in his mind.

Against his closed lids he now saw illuminated as if by a battery flash, the office and the lieutenant sitting behind the desk. He heard his own voice, saying, 'May I enquire, sir, when my name was first put forward?' He saw the hand thumbing through pages on the desk; then the man sauntering to the cabinet in the corner of the room; he saw the face turn towards him and the lips mouthing, 'Ten days ago; of course, we go into these things.'

Now the lips were moving again. 'Your wife runs the farm?'

God! how they must have laughed! They had treated him like a country bumpkin, a yokel, a fool. Charlie MacFell the fool. The idiot, and that's what he had been, otherwise he would have pursued the thought that made him enquire as to when his name was first put forward. Hadn't it struck him as being too much of a coincidence that the very day after finding his wife sporting with the major he should have been offered a commission? Hadn't he known in that moment that his hands were being tied? Yes, he had; but he thought he had tied them himself, and all he could really think of was that he had got one over on Slater.

But Slater had had the last word.

'Good effort. You'll be mentioned.'

And would he himself mention that he had shot a private, shot him dead? He'd have to, because there was the sergeant, and men talked, and tales got distorted. But the sergeant could vouch that this particular soldier had acted oddly since first coming into the trench.

Slater could win again; even dead Slater could win. No! No! He mustn't win now, not now, not after that effort, not the effort the major had referred to but the effort it had taken him to draw his revolver and shoot. He must go and report it, report it to the major.

He made to rise from the bed but instead he flopped flat on to it, rolled on to his side, buried his face in the crook of his elbow, and as sleep overtook him he muttered thickly, 'Don't cry. For God's sake, don't cry.'

He was standing to the side of a long white scrubbed table. Sitting behind the table was a colonel, a major, and a lieutenant. He had met this particular lieutenant and major yesterday for the first time, and he'd asked the major for a hearing on a matter that was troubling him; and now he was getting that hearing.

The sergeant was speaking. Standing stiffly before the table he was saying, 'As I said, 'twas pretty rough there, sir. Under crossfire we were, and had been for some time, when this Private Slater came crawling out of a mud-hole with a wounded man. They were both in a pretty bad shape. The man

Slater I think was under shock, sir. He acted funny from the start, aggressive like, jumpy. Later in the day I made him relieve a sentry. It was just on dark, sir. Second-Lieutenant MacFell had told us what he intended to do to get us out of there. The barrage had eased off; I saw him making an inspection, talking to each man as he went along the trench. I . . . I had just given orders about the strappin' up of Lieutenant Bradshaw when I heard the shell burst. It was along towards the end of the trench where the lieutenant had just gone. I ran in that direction and when I rounded the bend I saw the lieutenant lying against one parapet and Private Slater against the other. Private Slater had his rifle in his hands. He had been shot through the chest. I said to the lieutenant, 'Are you all right, sir?' He seemed dazed. He looked down at his pistol and said, 'Yes. Yes, I'm all right.' I said, 'Did he go for you, sir?' and he said, 'Yes; it . . . it must have been the reaction to the blast.' . . .

Had he said that? He couldn't remember. No, no, he hadn't said that.

'He was a man who seemed to resent authority, sir; he had turned on me earlier on when I asked his name and number but I let it pass as I thought he was under shock, sir.'

'No doubt he was. Thank you, Sergeant, You have been very explicit.'

'Sir.' The sergeant saluted smartly, turned about and went out of the room.

Now he was standing in front of the table and the colonel was speaking to him. 'Sorry about this business, MacFell. We all understand how you must feel, and it was very commendable of you to bring it to our notice. Under the circumstances we don't see what else you could have done.' The colonel now cast his glance towards the major and then towards the lieutenant, and they nodded in agreement; then he slowly fingered some papers that were lying in front of him before lifting his eyes upwards again and saying, 'A very good report here from Major Deverell. You got most of your platoon back. Good work. Good work. Well, I think that will be all, gentlemen.'

'Sir.'

'Yes, MacFell?'

'May I ask how Private Slater's dependents will be informed of his death?'

'Oh . . . oh the usual, died in battle . . . bravely, you know. The man was definitely under shock. It happens. Yes, died in battle. One can't do anything else, can one?'

'No, sir. Thank you.'

'Hope to see you at dinner then.' The colonel now got to his feet, smiling as he said, 'You look a little more presentable than you did this time yesterday.'

'I would need to, sir.'

They all smiled at him as if he had come out with some witticism. He stood straight, he looked cool, self-possessed, the kind of officer that men would follow into and out of tight corners. And hadn't he proved he was that type of man? Slater hadn't won. Conscript, cuckold, fool, loser, not any more, not any more. Cover up, lie, play the officer and gentleman, anything to show him, and keep on showing him for he was still alive, in his mind he was still alive.

# Chapter One

## The End of War and
## The Beginning of the Battle

'It's over! It's over! Can you believe it? It's over!' The nurses were running round the ward; they were kissing everybody in sight. Two of them took the crutches from Captain Pollock and, their arms about him, made him hop into a dance. One of the nurses slid along the polished floor, then fell on to her bottom amid roars of laughter.

Six of the ten men in the ward beds were sitting up shouting and joining in the fun, but the other four lay still. Charlie was one of the four, but he laughed when Nurse Bannister, her big moon-face hanging above him, said, 'I'm going to do it, Major, I'm going to do it. There!' She kissed him full on the lips, a long, hard, tight kiss, and when she had finished he laughed at her and said, 'I won't want any sweet today, Nurse.'

'Go on with you. But isn't it wonderful! It's over. Can you believe it? I can't, it'll take time for it to sink in.'

Another nurse came running to the foot of the bed and, amid laughter, she chanted:

'I do love you, Major MacFell,
But why, oh why, I cannot tell;
But this I know, and know full well,
I do love you, Major MacFell.'

Nurse Bannister picked up an apple from a bowl standing on the bedside locker and threw it at her tormentor, who caught it and then threw it to Charlie, but when he caught it he flinched visibly and Nurse Bannister, all laughter disappearing from her face, said, 'That was a damn silly thing to do.'

'Sorry. Sorry, Major.' Nurse Roper was bending above him now, and he grinned at her and said, 'Well, if you're sorry, show it.'

'O.K.' Her eyes lifted to the nurse standing on the other side of the bed before she bent and kissed him on the lips.

'You've got a nice mouth.' She patted his cheek, then hissed, 'Oh Lord! look out, here she comes!' and proceeded to straighten the sheet under Charlie's chin, all the while talking down to him in a quite conversational tone, saying, 'Armistice or no armistice, Major, we must remember who we are, where we are, and with whom we are dealing. Ti-tiddly-aye-ti . . . ti-ti!'

Charlie wanted to laugh, but laughter expanded the chest and that was painful.

As Sister Layton walked up the ward, the hilarity died down somewhat, but the men sitting up in bed called to her in various ways yet all asking much the same question: 'When are we celebrating, Sister? . . . How are we celebrating? . . . Having a dance?'

The last might have been said with bitter irony for most of those in bed had lost at least one leg and the sister, showing that she wasn't without a sense of humour below her stiff ladylike exterior, said, 'Why not! And the first of you to get out of bed within the next week can have the honour of accompanying me.'

There was a pretended scramble which caused the muscles of her face to relax into a prim smile before her usual manner took over, and she was issuing orders to her staff as if this were an ordinary hour in an ordinary day.

When she stopped at Charlie's bed she looked down on him and asked, 'Comfortable, Major?'

'Yes, Sister.'

'Doctor Morgan is very pleased with you.'

'How many did he unearth this time?'

'Oh, quite a few.'

'Did he get the main one?'

She bent over him and smoothed the already smoothed sheet.

'Main one? They are all main ones. Now lie quiet; that's all you're called upon to do for the next few days.'

As she went to move away he asked, 'When will it be possible for me to be moved, Sister?'

'Don't you like it here?' She turned her haughty gaze down on him.

'Yes, yes, I like it, and would be prepared to stay for ever if it was three hundred miles nearer home.'

'We'll have to talk to Doctor Morgan about that.'

He watched her continuing up the ward. You were in their hands, you were helpless. He had already talked countless times to Doctor Morgan who had promised that after the next do he would see about having him moved up North. He wouldn't have minded staying here, not in the least, if it hadn't been for Nellie. It was only a week since her last visit, but it seemed like years; it was a long way for her to come, first to London, then another hour's train journey. It meant her taking three days altogether for a few hours spent sitting by his bed. Yet it was all he seemed to live for, all he wanted to live for. But would he live if they didn't get that last bit of shrapnel out?

How many times had he been down to the theatre? How many pieces had they taken out of him? Peppered they said he was. He didn't remember being brought over from France but the last words he recalled as he awoke in a clean bed in the middle of the night was a nurse wiping his mouth with something wet was a voice saying, 'He'll never make it, he's like a sieve.'

And that is what the doctor had said to him. 'You're very lucky you know, Major; when you came in your were just like a sieve.'

It was odd when he came to think of it, he had gone through battle after battle without a scratch, right up till two months ago; then one day he had walked right into it. It was just after returning from leave, his second leave, one as disappointing as the other. On his first leave shortly after the Messines do, he had found Nellie still at the farm with her mother. She had once again just returned from hospital, after having an appendicitis operation this time, and Florence Chapman had guarded her against him as if he were bent on rape. He experienced the strong feeling that she hoped he would be killed for he knew that she wanted her daughter to herself. She was lonely and prematurely ageing.

He knew before his second leave that Nellie had long since left the farm and gone in for nursing training, and when he returned to the North it was to find that she had been transferred to a hospital in Dorset. Four days of the seven he stayed down there, but spent hardly any time with her; her off-duty hours were limited. Even when they met in his room in the hotel they were strangely both constrained. Although she was warm and loving and he wanted above all things, above all things to love her, there was a barrier between them. The barrier was Victoria. They both knew it, although her name was never mentioned. She loomed up between them as his wife and Nellie's sister.

It was just before they parted that he said to her, 'I've written to my solicitor today, I've asked him to go ahead with divorce proceedings,' and her only answer to this was to put her arms around his neck and press her mouth to his.

Now she was back in the North and he was here, and all he seemed to be living for was to be moved nearer to her, for he knew that once he was on his feet, divorce or no divorce, they would come together.

And there was another thing he didn't like to think about that happened on that leave; he had made it his business to look up Johnny only to be told that Johnny was dead. He had been kicked by a horse while on some kind of a manoeuvre up on the fells. Johnny who didn't want to go to France in case he caught one had died by a kick from a horse. Life was crazy. The whole world was crazy.

'Ah, that's it. Nice to see you sitting up, Major.'

'I'll feel better when I'm standing up, Doctor.'

'All in good time. . . . Well, while I'm here I might as well have a look at my handiwork.'

There was some gentle shuffling, the curtains were drawn round the bed, the bedclothes were drawn back, pads removed, then began the jokes.

'Nearly a complete board for noughts and crosses here. Whose move is it next?'

'Mine I hope.' There was no amusement in Charlie's tone.

'All in good time. All in good time. Healing nicely, Sister, don't you think?'

'Yes, Doctor, beautifully.'

'When can I be moved?'

'That will do for now, Sister. Put the pads on temporarily, leave the dressing, I want a word.'

The nurse now pushed a chair to the side of the bed, then departed.

The doctor sat down, gave a special nod to the sister, and she too departed; then he looked at Charlie, and he said slowly, 'You may go back North once you are on your feet.'

'You mean it?'

'Yes.'

'You got them all out then? I thought. . . .'

'Not quite.'

He pressed himself back against the pillows now and stared at the doctor. 'It's still there then?' he said.

'That's about it.'

'But you said . . .'

'Yes, I know what I said, but when we got in we thought it was a bit tricky. You're a lucky man you know to be alive.'

'. . . And I mayn't be alive much longer?'

'Oh, nonsense! Nonsense! You could go on for years and years until you become a doddery old farmer.'

'That's if it stays put?'

'No, no, of course not; we're hoping it moves. They do you know.'

'But in the right direction.'

'As you say' – the doctor lowered his head now – 'in the right direction.'

'The other direction would be short and swift?' There was a pause before the answer came: 'Yes, short and swift.'

Charlie rubbed one lip over the other before he asked, 'And if it went in the right direction would you try again?'

'Like a shot.' The doctor put his hand over his eyes. 'Sorry, like a surgeon.'

They both smiled now, then the doctor said, 'Of course when I say you may go North it will be into hospital. You know that, don't you?'

'Yes, I suppose so.'

'Well, we can't let you go in the condition you're in at present; it'll be a little time yet. I don't think you realize how badly shattered you were and we've dug into you seven times in the last three months, but if you'd had any flesh on your body you know the shrapnel wouldn't have got so far. You've got to be built up, and it's got to be done before you get back to your farm and pick up everyday responsibilities, you understand?'

Yes, he understood, and also the meaning behind all the doctor's kindly chat. They wanted him in hospital for observation in case the piece of shrapnel inside him decided to move. If it moved in the right direction they could get it out, or given time, he understood it could settle in and make a home for itself where it was at present near his heart.

It was three weeks later when he went North, but before that time he'd had a visitor. It was on the day after he'd had the conversation with the doctor when the nurse, waking him from a doze, said, 'There's someone to see you.' His heart had leapt at the thought that Nellie had made it after all. He'd had a letter from her only that morning to say that the dragon of a sister wouldn't even allow her to put her two weeks' leave together in order to make the journey South, but she had put in for her discharge offering as an excuse her mother needed her to run the farm. And her mother had willingly gone along with her on this, hoping that she would eventually return home.

But when his visitor turned out to be Betty, he was really visibly startled and not a little touched by the thought that she must have some affection for him to have undertaken the journey to this out of the way place.

It was only a matter of nine months since he had last seen her and he was shocked at the change in her. She looked haggard, old, and her expression was even tighter than usual, so much so that it was hard to believe she was only twenty-four years old.

Then in a matter of minutes after the usual greetings had been exchanged he thought he had found the explanation for her visit when, looking him straight in the face, she asked bluntly, 'Is it true what I hear about you and Nellie Chapman?'

He considered her for a moment before replying, 'Well, Betty, if what you have heard is that I intend to marry Nellie once the divorce is through, it's true.'

'You're mad.'

'That's as may be, but that's what I intend to do. And this time I know what I'm about.'

'And what about me?'

'Well, we've been over this a number of times, Betty, haven't we? We agreed that when you left to marry Wetherby I would see that you didn't go to him empty-handed.'

'And what if I don't marry Wetherby?'

'What do you mean, has something happened?'

'I'm not marrying Wetherby.' Her lips scarcely moved as she brought out the words and he stared at her for a moment before putting out his hand and placing it over hers. But it hadn't rested there a second before she jerked her own away from his hold and demanded, 'So where does that leave me now?'

'There'll always be a home for you there, Betty, you know that.' But even as he said the words he was thinking in agitation, Oh no, not this now! Betty's tongue, he knew, could impregnate a house with so much acid that it would turn everything sour. Yet what could he do?

'A home?' she repeated. 'Where? In the corner of the kitchen? I've run that place since my father died, yes, since he died because Mother wasn't any good, and you weren't much better. It would have gone to rack and ruin if it hadn't been for me and now you say I'll always have a home.'

He was feeling very tired and he was becoming increasingly agitated inside. He lay back on his pillows, and a nurse passing up the ward came to his side and said, 'You all right, Major?'

He nodded at her, saying, 'Yes. Yes, I'm all right.' Then the nurse, looking across at his visitor, said, 'Please don't stay long, he's easily tired.'

Although Charlie closed his eyes for a moment he felt rather than saw Betty's impatient shrug and lift of the head.

When he again looked at her she was searching in her handbag for something, and she brought out a sheet of paper, saying, 'Will you sign this? I want to sell some cattle.'

'But you have my authority to sell the cattle; it was all arranged before I left.'

He watched her press her lips together and turn her head to the side, saying, 'Well, I wish you'd tell the authorities that. The laws are changing all the time, men coming round to examine this, that, and the other, and because it's your farm and you're back in England they want your signature.'

She handed him a pen, and he obediently wrote his name on the bottom of the folded sheet of paper.

As she replaced the paper in her bag she brought her short body straight up in the chair and asked, 'When are you likely to be home?'

'Oh' – he shook his head – 'not for some time yet I should think, they're going to transfer me North, but I'll still be in hospital. I don't suppose they'll let me out, for good that is, until I'm fit, but as soon as ever I can I'll take a trip out and see you.'

She was on her feet now – she had pushed the chair back – and she stood looking at him for a moment before she said, 'Good-bye, Charlie.' There was something about the emphasis she laid on the words that made him sit up and lean towards her, saying, 'Now, you're not to worry. Betty. I'll see you're all right, I promise.'

'I'll be all right, never you fear.' She pulled at the belt of her coat, and he noticed that it was one she had worn long before the war. She had never spent money on herself, not like their mother.

'Good-bye, Charlie.' Again it sounded like a definite farewell.

'Good-bye, Betty. Take care of yourself. I'll . . . I'll be with you soon.'

She had walked to the bottom of the bed by now, and she stood there for some seconds and stared at him before she turned and went down the ward, a small, shabby, dowdy figure.

He felt an urge to jump up and run after her and to take her in his arms and comfort her. She must be taking the business of Wetherby very hard. He had always known the fellow was no good, but if Betty had liked . . . loved . . . and was capable of adoring anyone it had been Robin Wetherby. It was odd that this small sister of his who was so accurate in her appraisal of others had not been able to see through Wetherby. Indeed love could be blind. Anyway, he decided he would talk to Nellie about her, and Nellie would agree with him that he must be generous towards her.

He closed his eyes. He had become upset by her visit; he felt very tired, he wanted to sink through the bed and down into the earth, down, down. He'd had this experience a number of times of late. He couldn't understand it. Why hadn't he felt like this during all the battles? But he had, that time on the Menin road just outside Ypres. That was when he had been transferred to the Third. They were making for the Blue Line and were being peppered most of the way by machine-gun fire from the ruined houses, and he had become so tired that he felt his legs were giving out. But it was on that road he realized that in the last extreme officers and men became as one: there were officers who gave their lives for their men and men who gave their lives for their officers. Never again after this did the ah-lah twang of some of his fellow officers irritate him. Whether the breed of officer he had encountered back home was of a different species he didn't know. Perhaps the simple answer was that when a man was confronted with death his spirit rose and faced it. Death had a way of levelling rank.

It was after the Menin road and the battles that followed in October '17 when they fought through rain and gale, mud and slush, when men from colonels downwards died like flies, and when the subaltern often found himself in command, that the pips began to descend on to his own shoulders. . . .

But he was going down again, down, down, he was sinking into the mud. He grabbed at a leg and it came away in his hand. The top was all raw flesh but there was no blood coming from it because it was frozen. Now he was crawling into a hole. It was a big hole, it widened even as he looked at it; there had been water in the bottom which had been soaked up by the bodies heaped there, but those pressed tight against the sides were live. The hole began to spin and he opened his mouth and shouted, yelled, bawled, and all the men scrambled out of the hole, but as they stood up so they toppled back one after the other as an aeroplane came diving towards them, the pilot hanging head down, his face on fire. When he fell among the men he landed on his feet, and he looked young and unscathed and he flung his arms wide and he laughed as he shouted, 'They only gave me days but I've been alive for six weeks and now I've got all eternity!' All eternity. All eternity. All eternity. The heap of men in the middle of the hole got higher, the whirling became faster. A face was pressed close to his; it was the adjutant's. How had he got there? He should have been back at base. He was smiling quietly at him. He liked the adjutant: he had the funniest sense of humour; it was odd though to see him smiling because he never smiled, not when he was being funny. When he came to think of it he had never seen the adjutant smile. But now he was lying on his back smiling.

He was yelling again. His mouth was wide and there was mud pouring into it, it was going down his throat.

'Take it easy. Take it easy.' The curtains were drawn round the bed, the sister was holding him, she had her arms about him, holding him, pressing him to her. He liked that, he liked the feel of her, she was his mother. . . . Oh, not his mother, she was Nellie. . . . *Nellie. Nellie.*

'It's all right, it's all right, let go now. That's it, that's it, relax, relax. You're quite all right.'

Funny, he thought that it was she who had been holding him. He opened his eyes, then gasped, drawing in a great long draft of clean ward air. There was no mud in his mouth, he was in bed.

'I . . . I . . . I'm sor . . . ry.'

'It's all right, it's all right. There now, go to sleep. There now. There now.'

As something sharp went into his arm he muttered again, 'I'm . . . I'm sorry.'

'Bring two hot water bottles, he's cold.'

God! he was going to cry. No! no! he mustn't cry, not that again. Oh no! no! What was making him want to cry now? Was it because she was being so kind to him? She was usually so correct, so stiff and starchy. Camisole Kate they called her because she had a high bust and the nurses said she wore an old-fashioned camisole. How old was she? Forty? Forty-five? She was being very kind to him. What had happened? He was going down again, but there was no mud now. Thank God! there was no mud now. . . . And something else, something else. As a thought struck him he tried to rise and tell her . . . he had been down into the mud again and hadn't seen Slater there. Now that was strange: for the first time he had been in the crater – and Slater hadn't been there.

# Chapter Two

He didn't feel at home in his new surroundings; he was missing Pritchard and Johnson and Thurkel. They had only three legs between them but they had seemed so glad to be alive. The night before he left the three of them had done a form of tap dance in the ward, and even Riley who could only move his head because he had very little else to move, had raised it from the pillow and laughed for the first time since coming into the ward.

And they'd all seemed sorry that he was going. That had given him a nice feeling, a warmth inside. Sister Layton arranged to be the last to say good-bye to him as he entered the ambulance. Putting her head down to him she had said softly, 'Give a thought to Camisole Kate now and again.'

He had looked up into the tight smile and murmured back, 'Oh, Sister! Sister!'

They had been a great bunch, more like a family.

He didn't think he'd ever look upon the crowd here as a family, there were so many of them, both staff and patients.

The hospital was situated in grounds. He hadn't been allowed out in them yet but from what he could see from the window of his cubicle they were full of shambling figures.

His companions on each side of him were captains, one called Fraser, the other Bartlett. They had been in and introduced themselves. Bartlett, besides having lost an arm, was still suffering from the remnants of shellshock; and Fraser, he supposed, was in the same boat, and he never stopped making jokes about his artificial foot. As far as he could gather most of those he had seen were suffering from some kind of war shock. Was that why he had been sent here?

No! no! he hadn't been shellshocked. He felt he had become immune to bursting shells, and until the very last had got the idea in his head that in some odd way he was protected, and he couldn't be blamed for that, he told himself, when men not feet away from him had been blown to smithereens.

The contrast between the patients and the staff was striking. Whereas all the patients seemed to amble, the staff were brisk in step, voice, and manner; another term for it would be hearty. They were mostly nuns and it was likely their usual approach to illness, but it could be wearing. He hankered for the administrations of Bannister, Roper, and Sister Layton.

He was startled when the door was thrust open and a small thickset nun entered.

'Ah! there you are, Major. Waiting patiently for your breakfast, are you? Well now, what about swinging those feet out of bed, putting on your dressing-gown and having it at the window? Look, it's a lovely morning, beautiful. Look at that sun, you can believe that God's in His heaven and all's right with the world. My name's Sister Bernard.'

'. . . Oh my God!'

'What did you say? I heard you, yes I did. Come on.' The sheets were pulled back from him. ' "Oh my God!" you said.'

He didn't move from the bed. Who did she think she was talking to, a child?

'Now come on, come on. You know what the Chinese say: A journey of a thousand miles begins but with one little step. So come on, make it. . . . There you are, that wasn't hard, was it? . . . By! you're a length.' She looked up at him, her peasant-looking face beaming out of the white starched frill encasing it. 'And you know, you get longer lying in bed. Oh yes, you do, it stretches you. I bet they called you Lofty . . . or was it Tich? Some go to other extremes. . . . There you are, sit yourself down. Now that wasn't too bad, was it? And don't look at me like that, Major.' Her face now on a level with his poked towards him. 'We're going to see a lot of each other within the next few weeks and I can prophesy one thing here and now, and that is at the end of it you won't have fallen for me.'

Her head now went back on to her shoulders and she let out a high gurgle that might have come from the throat of a young girl, and at this moment the door opened again and another nun entered, and the first turned towards her and said, 'Oh there you are, Sister Monica. Well, we'll get on with this bed. He insisted on getting up, didn't you, didn't you, Major?' She stuck her finger into his arm and all he could do was to look from one to the other in amazement.

Sister Monica could have been the younger of the two but they were both women in their forties, and he now watched them tackling the bed with such precision and swiftness as he had never seen before.

That done, they both stood before him and Sister Bernard did the talking – the other one hadn't opened her mouth – and now she said, 'When I'm not at you, Sister here will take me place. Don't be deceived by her looks, she's worse than me, we're known as the Toughies. At night you'll have Sister Bridget. But don't think you'll get anywhere with her either, she's worse than us. Well now, your breakfast will be here in a minute, and eat it up, every last crumb.'

Simultaneously, as if they were controlled by one mind, they both nodded at him; then Sister Bernard, bending slightly towards him, poked her face out again and said, 'And don't go complaining to Matron about our manners and treatment because if you do we'll only get worse and give you hell.'

He sat looking towards the closed door for a moment; then his head going back, he laughed, the deep-sounding laughter that on rare occasions in his life released the tension of his body. But he hadn't been indulging in it for more than seconds when the door burst open again and the two black figures rushed in once more.

'Now! now! now!' Sister Bernard had hold of him by the shoulders, and he put up his hands and caught her arm and patted it even while he was still shaking with his laughter, and slowly she released her hold on him. And now as they stood watching him wiping his eyes they began to smile, and then to laugh, and Sister Bernard turned to Sister Monica and said, 'He was just laughing . . . just laughing.'

His face screwed up, his shoulders still shaking, Charlie nodded at them, and Sister Monica, throwing out her arm as if she were about to address a company, exclaimed, 'God's good, we're on our way,' and once again they bounced their heads towards him, then turned and went out while still laughing.

Charlie sat looking out of the window. It had been like a pantomime. How long was it since he laughed like that? Years, years. . . . Those two, the Toughies . . . God's good. . . . He was in His heaven and all was right with the world, their world.

The smile slid from his face, the laughter lines smoothed out from around his eyes. Was His heaven full of the dead? Had He directed them into His many mansions? How did He manage about housing the officers and the men? Surely after dying together they wouldn't be separated up there?

But he felt better for having laughed, his rare explosive laugh; yet he knew it was going to take some time before he settled down in this place, for it wasn't like a hospital at all, more like an asylum, a place not only for broken bodies but for broken minds. . . .

It was the following afternoon. He was sitting in a chair near the window. Captain Bartlett had just gone, and he was feeling exhausted with his constant prattling bonhomie. He understood that Bartlett had been here three months and Fraser four, and while listening to them both he had wondered what they were like when they had first come.

He wasn't like them, was he? Mentally he was all right, except for, well, sort of nightmares; but he only went into those when he felt exhausted.

He'd had a letter from Nellie this morning. She was coming as soon as possible. If only he could see her now, this very minute.

He closed his eyes, then opened them swiftly again and blinked rapidly as Sister Bernard came towards him, saying, 'Let me see, are you tidy and fit to be seen?'

Oh, he wished she wouldn't treat him as a child. He sighed as she tucked the rug around his knees and she came at him quickly, saying, 'Stop your sighing else I won't let her in.'

'Who?' He pulled himself up from the back of the armchair.

'Your visitor.'

'A visitor?'

'Her name's Chapman. She's young, and pretty. And I'm warning you, behave yourself, no hanky-panky.'

He bit on his lip and closed his eyes again and when he opened them Nellie was coming in through the door, and the door had been closed only a second before they put their arms around each other.

'Oh, Nellie! Nellie! Oh, am I glad to see you! Oh, my dearest, my dearest.' He held her away from him for a moment, then pulled her swiftly to him, and when the kiss was ended she laughed and said, 'Look! I've got the cramp bending over like this.'

'Oh! Oh! I'm sorry. Come on, sit down.' He went to rise from the chair, and she stopped him, saying, 'I'm quite able to get a chair for myself, sir.'

Seated close by his side now, she looked into his face as she said, 'You're looking fine, so much better than when I last saw you. Do . . . do you feel better?'

'Oh yes, yes, much better, except' – he gave his head an impatient shake – 'I still get so tired. I can't understand it.'

'Well, you should, you above all people, it's battle fatigue.'

'I suppose so. . . . Oh! Nellie. Oh! it's wonderful to see you.' His arms went out again and pulled her close, and as her head rested against his neck he whispered, 'I dream of this all the time, you and me like this, close, closer, never parting. And . . . and we never will, will we?' Again he pressed her from him and looked into her face, and her lips trembled slightly as she said, 'Never, Charlie. If it lies with me, never. You know that.'

'Oh! Nellie, Nellie, I wish I could put into words how I feel about you. And you know, recently I've thought more and more about the wasted years of our youth, I mean my youth. There you were just a few miles from me and I never realized what I was missing. All I want to do now is to get out of here and back there and start all over again, just you and me . . . and oh, I told you in the letter, didn't I, there'll be Betty. But I'll fix her up in some place of her own soon. In the meantime, you won't mind. . . . What is it? Why are you looking away? I promise you, dear, it won't be a case of Victoria over again, you won't have to put up. . . .'

'It isn't that, Charlie. It isn't that.'

'Then what is it?'

'Oh, nothing, nothing really.'

'It's something about Betty, isn't it?'

He watched her swallow; then she said, 'Well, I . . . I know how she must be feeling, for Wetherby to drop her like that, it must have come as a bombshell.'

'Has he got someone else?'

'Yes, oh yes, and definitely, he went off with Katie Nelson. You remember the Nelsons. They have a farm over Bellingham way. She must be all of ten years older than him. She was the only daughter and her parents are pretty old. You can see the picture, can't you? Apparently Betty didn't know a thing about it until it was all done. Then he wrote to her. It was enough to send any girl round the bend; you can't blame her. . . .'

'Oh my God!' Charlie held his brow with his hand. 'It's my fault really. I should have let her have him there during the war. But I knew once he was in I wouldn't get him out, and I couldn't stand him.' He now looked at Nellie and asked, 'How is she taking it? I mean, she wouldn't do anything silly.'

She smiled gently at him as she said, 'Not Betty, not like me, no, no, Charlie, you needn't worry on that score, she's too practical.'

'Oh, I wish I were home.'

She rose from the chair now and, going to the side of the window and looking out, she said, 'They're lovely grounds here.' Then turning to him again, she added, 'You mustn't rush; you'd be no good at all back on the farm the way you are now, you know that. You've got to get your strength up and get some flesh on your bones, and get . . .' She couldn't finish by adding, 'Get your nerves steadied', for one thing he didn't seem to understand was that it wasn't only his body that had been shattered.

'Get what?'

'Well, I meant get yourself well enough to fork hay.'

'I'll be well enough to fork hay, never you worry. It's odd how I longed to get away from that place and now I long to be back. How's the farm looking?'

She blinked, pressed her lips together for a moment while she swallowed, then said, 'Fine, fine, as usual, and I've brought you evidence of it in there.' She pointed towards a case at the foot of the bed, then added hastily, 'Oh, I forgot. You'll never guess who I saw, and in this very place, today.'

He shook his head and caught at her hand as she sat beside him again.
'Polly.'

'Polly, here?'

'Yes; just as I was going out of the gate. There's a big new wing over there' – she turned her head towards the window – 'at the far side, and Arthur's there.'

He opened his mouth twice before he could say the name 'Arthur? Why! I thought Arthur was gone.'

'No, no, he's still alive, what's left of him.'

'But . . . but when I saw him on the quay, I think I told you, his legs were gone and his arm; they didn't expect him to last.'

'Well, he has.'

'Good Lord!' He shook his head. 'And . . . and I've never given him a thought all this time except to think, Poor Arthur. Well! well!' He smiled. 'I'll have to go and see him.'

'Yes, he'd like that, I'm sure. I told Polly.'

'Was she surprised that I was here?'

'Yes, very surprised. . . . Of course you know Slater's dead, don't you?'

He leant back in the chair. The tiredness was assailing him again. He opened his mouth and gasped for breath; then he said quietly, 'Yes, yes, I heard about it.'

'Polly looked well, quite bonny in fact. But then she was always bonny. You were gone on her at one time, weren't you?' She pushed her face playfully towards him, and he said absent-mindedly, 'Was I?'

She tapped his cheek and brought his gaze on to her as she said, 'You know you were.'

'Yes,' he smiled faintly. 'Yes, I suppose I was. The madness of youth.'

'I was mad in my youth too. I fell in love with a tall, lanky lad, and my madness didn't fade away, it developed into a mania.' She took his face between her hands now and said softly, 'If you and I, Charlie, were to have nothing more than we've got at this moment I'd still thank God that I've loved you. . . . Oh! Charlie, don't cry. Oh my dear, my dearest, please, please don't cry.'

The door opened and Sister Bernard entered carrying a tray laden with tea things and she did not exclaim loudly at the scene before her but, putting the tray down on a side table, she went to the other side of the chair and, lifting Charlie's drooping head, she said briskly, 'Do you the world of good, we don't cry enough. Englishmen are fools, they keep it bottled up.' Now nodding across at Nellie, whose eyes, too, were full of tears, she went on, 'The French and Italians and suchlike, they howl like banshees on the slightest provocation, and they're better for it. Now what you both want is a good cup of tea; I've made it nice and strong.' She indicated the tray with a jerk of her thumb over her shoulder; then looking towards the case at the bottom of the bed, she said, 'I understand he's got a farm, I hope you've brought something worthwhile from it, for in the main it's bread and scrape and so-called jam in here. I suppose we should thank God for that but somehow I can't give praise unless it's due. Well, I'll leave you to pour out the tea.' She nodded her head towards Nellie, and almost without seeming to change its motion she jerked it in Charlie's direction while still speaking to Nellie and said, 'He hates me guts but I don't care, I'm here for his punishment and I'm going to see that he gets it.' Her lips pressed tight together now, a twinkle deep in her eye, she nodded from one to the other, then marched out.

The door closed, their glances held for a moment before they fell about each other trying to smother their tear-mixed laughter.

## Chapter Three

After the first week which had seemed long and endless the days slipped by unnoticed. He woke up one morning to see the window sill banked with snow; it was winter, he hadn't seemed to take it in before. His time was filled with eating and sleeping and sitting by the window.

As Christmas approached the activity in the hospital heightened and an excitement ran through the place. It was the first Christmas of peace, and on Christmas Day he went for the first time from the narrow confines of the ward to the main dining-room and the Christmas tea party, and he found to his surprise that he enjoyed the change and the company. He also discovered that the two toughies were universally beloved clowns, and that in a way he was lucky to be under their care.

He did not see Nellie over the holidays for she was on duty, and when he did see her he was troubled for during her last two visits he had sensed there was something wrong with her. The only comfort he had was the knowledge that it had nothing to do with her feeling for him. He had probed but to no avail; all he could get out of her was that everything was all right and he hadn't to worry, he had just to get well.

He had made himself ask if she had seen Victoria and she had answered no, but she had heard quite a lot about her and did he want to hear it? When he had replied, 'Is it necessary?' her answer had been, 'That all depends on how you feel about her. If you are still bitter you're bound to think that she's the last one who deserves any happiness. I . . . I understand she is going to marry her one-time Major Smith.'

'Really!' He hadn't been able to cover his surprise and added somewhat cynically, 'He's still going then?'

'As far as I understand he's a lieutenant-colonel now and he's never been out of England.'

'No? Well there's greater merit due to him that he has survived with her.'

'Oh Charlie!' she had said; 'it isn't like you to be bitter.' And he had answered and truthfully, 'I'm not the same Charlie you once knew, Nellie.'

But there was something wrong with Nellie, something troubling her. Was it her mother? He doubted it; she had said that Florence seemed willing now to countenance their association; the fact that she would eventually be living only a few miles away seemed to have modified her attitude. . . .

It wasn't until a day towards the end of January that he found out what was troubling Nellie. Then the earth was ripped from under him once again and he felt that Slater's curse was really on him . . . he was a loser, he had been born a loser and he would die a loser.

It was a bright clear morning; there had been snow but it was almost all gone except for that which lay on high ground. Sister Bernard and Sister Monica were busily making the bed when he said, 'I feel like a walk outside today.'

'Good. Good. Now you're talking.' It was Sister Bernard who answered him. When they were together Sister Monica never opened her mouth. It was, he understood, some part of a rule that was enforced upon them that only one should talk.

'Wrap up well, put a scarf on 'cos that sun is deceptive. Don't think if you go and get pneumonia we're going to look after you because we're not; are we, Sister?'

She nodded across the bed, then answered for Sister Monica who simply smiled at her, saying, 'No, we're not.'

He went to the wardrobe and, taking down his greatcoat, he put it on, and as he buttoned it up he looked towards the two black-robed, furiously working figures, and he addressed Sister Bernard, saying, 'Do you know, Sister, you would have made a splendid sergeant-major. The army lost something in you.'

'Sergeant-major indeed!' She pulled herself up to her small height and, bristling now, she said, 'Who you insulting? I passed the sergeant-major stage years ago; I'd have you know me rank is equal to that of a general. I'm surprised that you haven't noticed it!'

He laughed aloud now, saying, 'I'm surprised too. What do you say, Sister?' He was looking at Sister Monica now, and Sister Bernard, leaning across the bed again as if waiting for Sister Monica to repeat something, said, 'Cook-general, she says. Well! when your own let you down what do you expect from others? Have you put that scarf on?'

'Yes, I've got it on. Look.' He turned the collar of his coat back, then asked, 'Do you think it would be possible for me to pay a visit to the annexe?'

'I don't see why not. You know someone there?'

'Yes, someone I knew well at one time.'

'You're never mentioned him before . . . why?'

'I . . . I hadn't thought about it.'

'Well' – she turned from him – 'better late than never. Do you know how to get there?'

'I'll find my way.'

'You needn't go out into the grounds at all, you can keep to the corridors all the way. If you get lost ask a policeman.'

As they both giggled at him, he went out.

They were a pair, they were really as good as a music-hall turn. The stage had lost something in them, especially Sister Bernard.

He had to ask his way several times, and when at last he was walking along what seemed an endless corridor, he could feel the change in the atmosphere. The nurses he passed were young. There were young nurses on his block but they seemed of a different type. There were male nurses here too, but they weren't young, at least they weren't under thirty like many of the male staff back on the block.

He came to the end of the corridor and into a large comfortably furnished hall, with several smaller corridors leading from it. At the far side he saw what he thought to be a notice on the wall, but before he reached half-way across he recognized it was a plaque. On nearing it, he looked at it casually and read: This stone was laid on January 19th, 1914 by John Cramp Esquire whose benevolence has made possible the building of this annexe.

Cramp. Cramp. John Cramp. Yes, the man in the Daimler; the taggerine man, the scrap merchant. Well! Well! And he had done this before he'd made his pile out of the war. Odd that he should have come across the name again. And he remembered the man himself vividly. He was a character.

'Can I help you, sir?' A nurse was smiling up at him.

'I'm . . . I'm wondering if it would be possible to see a Private Benton? . . . I think he's a private.'

'Oh yes, sir, yes, Private Benton. Will you come this way, sir, he's in the day-room.' He was being led along another corridor now. Here wide doorless rooms went off at each side, and he had glimpses of men or what was left of them being lifted from the beds and into wheel-chairs. In one room he saw a patient being laid on a flat trolley face downwards.

Now they were in a large room with a great expanse of polished floor, one wall being made up entirely of huge windows, and everywhere he looked there were men sitting in wheel-chairs; some he saw had legs but no arms, others arms and legs but their bodies remained motionless. There were faces so scarred that he found he had to turn his gaze away quickly from them. And then he was being led in the direction of a small group of men in the corner of the room near the window.

He knew that heads were turning in his direction, and as he neared the group the chairs spread out.

The nurse said, 'Arthur! you've got a visitor.'

'Oh aye?' The last chair was swung round by one hand, and there he was looking at Arthur, what was left of him, a stump of a body and one arm.

'*Charlie!*'

Arthur's voice was a mere whisper at first, and then it exploded into almost a yell as he now shouted, '*Charlie!* Why *Charlie!* Polly said you were here. Aw, man!' The hand was thrust out towards him and he was gripping it; then before he could speak Arthur was addressing the half-dozen men who had made up the group and was crying at them, 'This is Charlie, the fellow I told you about on the farm, he was me boss but we were like mates. . . . Eeh! what am I sayin'?' Arthur now pulled his hand away and flapped it towards Charlie. 'You'll have me court-martialled for talkin' like this, forgettin' meself.' His voice dropped now and he stared up into Charlie's face for a moment in silence before he said, 'Sit down, won't you, Charlie?'

Charlie sat down and, speaking for the first time and with a tremor in his voice, he said, 'It's good to see you, Arthur.'

'And you, Charlie. Eeh! and a major. Who would have believed it!'

'Yes, who would have believed it.'

'Oh, no offence, man. You remember me sayin' to you that day, why didn't you put in for an officer. Did you take me advice?'

'No, I'm afraid I didn't, Arthur; they . . . they just sprung it on me.'

'They knew good stuff when they saw it.'

'Huh!' Charlie turned his head to the side; then casting his eyes about him and noticing that the men were still looking at him, he said, 'Nice ward this . . . the whole annexe.'

'Oh aye. Aye, they do us proud. Well' – Arthur now leant towards him

– 'they owe us somethin', don't they, and they're payin' us in the only way they can.'

'Yes, yes, I suppose so.'

'How are things with you, Charlie? I heard you were badly knocked up, but I see they've left you your limbs, and that's something.'

Yes, it was certainly something. Having been riddled with shrapnel, he thought he had come off badly, but these poor devils in here, God! why did they go on? Yet the atmosphere was cheerful, bright, you could even say happy. But, of course, this was the stiff upper lip attitude, putting a face on things. He wouldn't like to be inside one of their minds at night.

He answered Arthur now saying, 'Oh, I got some shrapnel here and there.'

'Oh aye. . . . Have they got it all out?'

'Well, not quite, so I understand; they've had a few goes but it roams you know.'

'Aye, shrapnel has a habit of doing that. . . . Nurse!' Arthur hailed a young nurse who was passing and as she came towards him he said, 'Bet you didn't know I had a major for a friend?'

'How do you do, Major?' She inclined her head towards him, smiling widely.

He had risen to his feet and he answered, 'How do you do?'

'We were brought up together, would you believe that?'

'I believe everything you tell me, Arthur.'

'Then do you believe I love you?' He had now placed his only hand on his heart and with his face poked towards her and in what he imagined to be dramatic tones he said, 'An' the morrow I go to Sir Humphrey to ask him for your hand.'

'And you'll get mine across your ear-hole if you don't behave.' She had come close to his side now and she caught hold of his hand and, looking across at Charlie, she said, 'He's impossible, this friend of yours, Major; he's a philanderer, no girl is safe where he is.' She now patted Arthur's cheek, and as she made to go away he said, still in a bantering tone, 'Don't leave me, love.'

She was about to make a jocular rejoinder when a strange sound came from the other side of the room and she said quickly, 'Oh dear me! I've got to go. I can see you'll be needed later on, Arthur.' She nodded at him, and he nodded back at her now in an ordinary fashion, and when she had left them he muttered below his breath, 'One of the chaps, he gets depressed like, howls like a banshee. I make him laugh.' He grinned at Charlie now. 'I make 'em all laugh. Funny, isn't it?'

Yes, yes, it was funny. This wasn't the Arthur he remembered. Less than half of him remained, yet in that half he had grown another personality. He remembered the dour, ignorant boy that used to irritate him, he remembered the youth who became a bundle of nerves through fear instilled by Slater. But those people were no more, the war had cut him into bits, yet had left him with a new character, a different character, a strong character. It was a fantastic thought but nevertheless true, he was sure, that Arthur was happier now than he had been in his life before. He had no responsibility, he was being cared for by pretty nurses; he was sure of good food and warmth, and he hadn't to worry about the wherewithal to provide them;

what was more, this Arthur was liked as the other Arthur, the young Arthur, never was.

He was now leaning towards him whispering, 'You heard Slater got it?'

He felt the old desire to open his mouth and gasp for air, but he pressed his lips together tightly before saying, 'Yes, yes, I heard.'

'Died bravely on the field of battle. By God! that wouldn't have happened if I'd come across him. An' I mean that, Charlie, I do. That was one thing I prayed for, to come across him. God! he led me hell. An' you had a taste of him an' all, hadn't you?'

'Yes, yes, I had a taste of him.'

'Couldn't understand our Polly; she was so upset. She got to like him, man, and when he lost his stripes through her she wanted to pin medals on him herself.'

'Lost the stripes through her, how do you mean?'

'Oh well, she was about to have the third bairn and things went a bit wrong and he thought she was a gonner and he wouldn't leave her. He told the doctor he was on leave and he stayed by her for three days, four I think, before they came and took him. I wish I'd been there when they stripped him down. Of course you can't say that to her. She talks about him as if he were a bloody hero.' He paused now, then ended, 'Funny, what the war's done to us lot, isn't it, Charlie?'

'Yes, indeed, Arthur.'

'How's things with you, Charlie, I mean you happy like?'

'Well, you could say yes and no, Arthur. Victoria and I are getting divorced.'

'No! No, man! Is . . . is that why you've sold up the farm?'

'*What!*'

'I said is that why you've sold up the farm and things?'

'Sold the farm? I haven't sold the farm.'

Arthur blinked his eyes, then looked down towards the blanket sagging from his waist, and he said now, 'Well, Polly must have got it wrong. She heard a rumour, likely it was only a rumour, but she heard that you were selling up and likely going to Australia or some such place as that. She thought it was because you were in a bad way and wouldn't be able to manage any more.'

His mouth was open, he was drawing in great draughts of air. *No! No!* He yelled at himself he had to keep steady; there was something afoot that he must see into, and now, right now.

He wasn't aware that he had risen from the chair but he was bending over Arthur now, saying, 'Look, Arthur, I'll be back, but there's something I've got to see to.'

'Have I said something wrong, Charlie, I mean startled you in some way?'

'Yes, I suppose so, Arthur. There's something not right over there. I . . . I have no intention of selling the farm.'

'No!'

'No, none whatever. I'll be back, Arthur. I'll be back.' He squeezed the hand held out to him, then turned and hurried down the ward.

'You're in no fit state to drive a car, Major.'

'Then I can take a taxi.'

Doctor Arlet looked across his desk at the tall, solemn-faced figure before him and he closed his eyes for a moment and shook his head as he said, 'I think you know the position as well as I do, Major, any extra physical activity, over-excitement at least for the present. . . .'

'I am aware of all that, Doctor.'

'Then why take unnecessary risks?'

'Doctor, I am being given to understand that my farm is being sold up, I want to know what it is all about. I left my sister in charge. The farm is my only means of livelihood, that is if I'm given the opportunity to work it.'

'Why don't you get your solicitor, or better still your friend, Miss . . . Miss –' He looked about him as if searching for a name, until Charlie said, 'Chapman.'

'Yes, Miss Chapman. Now she would go out there.' . . .

'She lives out there and I'm now under the impression that she knows more about it than she said, her intention being not to worry me. Now, doctor, whatever way I get out there I'm going, and the frustration of being kept here is going to be more detrimental than my driving a car or sitting in a taxi.'

'I'm . . . I'm not worried about the journey out there, Major.' The doctor's voice was tight now. 'What I am worried about is your reaction to whatever situation you find out there. Doctor Morgan's report said . . .'

Charlie now put his hand to the side of his head as if he were shutting off his hearing and he said, 'I know, doctor, only too well Doctor Morgan's opinion, and I respect it, and also from where I'm standing if this thing inside here moves to the right then I won't need to worry any more about the farm or anything else. But there's a fifty-fifty chance it will give me a break and move to the left, or even north or south, and if that should happen then I'd be pleased to let you all get at it and hoick it out.'

The use of the dialect word brought a twisted smile to Doctor Arlet's mouth, and he said on a sigh, 'Well I won't say I'll wash my hands of you, but I'll say, for your own sake, go careful, both physically and mentally. Now' – he rose from his seat – 'a taxi I think would be the best bet, although it's going to cost you a pretty penny to get out there.'

'I think I'll just about manage it.'

'All right. I suppose you'll have to stay overnight but I'll expect you back tomorrow, mind. Is that a promise?'

'That's a promise.'

He left the taxi on the main road. The driver, looking at him, said, 'Will you be all right, sir?'

'Yes, I'll be all right.'

'Have you far to walk?'

'A couple of miles or so.'

'Do you think you'll manage it?'

'Oh yes, I'll manage it. If I can't walk I'll slide; the sun's forgotten to come round this way.' He indicated the frost-tipped ridges of the fields and the stiff grass.

As he left the road and walked down the bridle path he knew that the taxi driver was still watching and he thought, I must look awful, like death.

It was a few minutes after he heard the taxi start that he stopped and looked about him. The sky was lying low on the hills, the light was grey, yet let the sun appear and the sky would be pushed back and the light would be white and clear. He drew in great draughts of air. If it wasn't for the anxiety within him he'd feel like celebrating his return by leaping over the walls ahead and running across the fields. But would he ever run across the fields again? No mental excitement, no physical exertion, they said. One might as well be dead.

When he came to the copse he was out of breath and not a little fearful. What would be say to Betty? Or what would she say to him? That was more to the point. He hadn't seen her since her visit to the hospital. He'd had two letters from her since, both saying that she was too busy to get away. But that was before Christmas. He hadn't questioned her not visiting him since he had been brought North again. That was Betty, she wasn't given to sentimental sympathy, and so over the weeks her absence hadn't troubled him. Nellie had come and that was all that mattered. Only now was he telling himself that it was strange that Betty hadn't once come to visit him over the past weeks.

The change struck him immediately he left the copse. It was in the silence and the absence of any animals. The cows would be inside but you could always see sheep sprinkled over the hills yonder. The only sound that came to him was from the burn. It was running high. His step slowed as he approached the gap in the stone wall; then he was in the middle of the yard gazing about him. The place was deserted. Was he dreaming? There was no one here, nothing. His mouth opened wide, he gasped at the air, then took his gloved doubled fist and pressed it against his ribs as he warned himself to go steady. He looked first towards the cowsheds, then turned his head and looked towards the house, then again towards the cowsheds.

Now he was in the cowsheds and being unable to believe what his eyes were seeing. The stalls were empty, dry; they had been cleaned out. He turned swiftly about and just stopped himself from running by gripping the stanchion of the door, and as he leant against it for a moment the action pushed his hat on to one side and over one eye, and the detached part of his mind saw himself as a pantomime major, a drunken pantomime major, for now he staggered somewhat as he walked back into the yard.

Straightening his cap, he again looked about him, and as his eyes came to rest on the back door a strange fear assailed him as to what he might find if he opened it, and he turned away from it and went now into the barn. The bottom was swept almost clean, a few implements only lay scattered around. He raised his eyes to the upper platform. That too was bare except for some broken bales of hay.

As if in a nightmare he was walking through the alleyway, and now he was on the cinder path, at least where it had been, for now a rough stone path led down to the cottage and the burn, the work of the German prisoners he supposed. He looked over the hedge to the field where the hen crees stood. The doors were swinging open, there was not a fowl to be seen. To the right lay the pigsties. No echo of a grunt came from them.

He had to have support, so he leant back against the wall of the byres and, his head drooping, he looked down at his feet, and the slab of stone on which he was standing disappeared and he saw his feet were deep in the cinders, and there coming along the path, was a red-headed youth, and when he stopped he grinned at him and said, 'You never thought you'd get a pip on your own, now did you, 'cos as I said you're a born loser. You lost the lass you loved, you married a whore, you even lost yourself and your bloody platoon; and now you've lost your farm. I always said you were a loser, didn't I? You've only got one more thing to lose and when that bit of shrapnel moves . . .'

He was brought from the wall as if he had been shot. His hand flashed from his side where his holster used to lie, and now it was pointing at eye level straight in front of him. He twisted round as if a hand had spun him. His mouth was wide open, he was gasping for air, his eyes were closed.

'*Stop it!*'

'*Pull up!*'

He was leaning against the wall again but bent over now and about to vomit.

He stood like this for some minutes before straightening up, then, after wiping his mouth he went through the alleyway again and into the yard and walked towards the kitchen door. He put his hand on the knob and pushed but it didn't give way. Angrily now, he thrust his body against it but without effect; the door was firmly bolted on the inside. He knew that it had strong bolts but he didn't remember them ever having been used in his time.

He went to the kitchen window and peered in. His hands to each side of his face, he gazed in amazement at the bareness of it. Even the long white wooden table was no longer there.

Like someone indeed drunk, he now made his way to the front of the house, and it was the sitting-room window he first looked through. The room was as bare as it had been when it was first constructed.

He was standing now gripping the knob of the front door. He didn't expect the door to be unlocked and it wasn't. Again he was leaning for support, and now like a child he spoke aloud, one single word 'Why?' Then again, louder this time, '*Why?*'

And where was everybody? This great silence.

As a strange thought entered his mind his head fell back on his shoulders and he looked up into the sky. Was this death? Had he already died? Had his life ceased with the shock of Arthur's words? And was the farm really peopled? Was the farm still alive and it was only he who couldn't see it?

When he tore off his glove and brought his hand down sharp on to one side of the ornamental spikes that supported the foot scraper to the side of the door he knew that he was still alive.

He was walking away from the house now towards the cottages. He didn't hope to find anyone there, yet as he rounded the bend and looked up the hill he stopped in his tracks. There was smoke coming out of one chimney. Again he checked himself from running, saying, 'Take it easy. Take it easy.'

It was some minutes before his knock on the door was answered, and when it was opened there stood Arnold in his bare feet, his linings showing under an old coat. The old man's mouth opened wide, but nothing came forth, until Charlie had stepped into the room and the door was closed, and then he said, 'My God! sir, am . . . am I glad to see you! Oh me God! sir, I am, I am that at this minute.'

It was plain to Charlie that the cowman was suffering from a severe cold and he said to him immediately, 'Get . . . get back into bed, Arnold.' He pointed to the bed that was drawn up to the side of the fire, but Arnold didn't immediately get back into bed, he stared up into Charlie's face, and now, the tears spurting from his eyes, he muttered, 'God! sir, I never thought

I'd live to see the day, but . . . but you're back, you're back. Sit down, sir, sit down.'

'You get back into bed, Arnold, I'll sit down.'

When Arnold had got into bed, Charlie took a seat by the side of the fire and they sat looking at each other for a moment before Charlie said, 'What's happened, Arnold? I . . . I thought the world had stopped going mad when the war finished, but down there' – he motioned towards the door – 'I can't take it in. Where is she?'

'Gone, sir. And . . . and we never expected to see you again, sir, at least' – he lowered his eyes away – 'we didn't at first. We did everything she said, you see, because it was supposed to be authorized by you.'

'The clearance of the farm?'

'Aye, sir, aye; she had a written statement. She had been down to see you in the South and . . . and when she came back she said you were in a very bad state and would never walk again, I mean, not even to manage. She said, well, sir, she sort of gave us the idea that besides you being broken up in body your . . . your mind had gone, shellshock, she said.'

Charlie's head drooped on to his chest for a moment and as a shiver ran through his body he held out his hands towards the blazing fire, and Arnold went on, 'Everybody around was sorry for her, so they helped: Regan took most of the cattle, they didn't go to market, the sheep did; but the pigs and hens and the rest of the livestock, everybody around bought privately.'

'The house?'

'Oh, the house. Every stick was carted away to auction, and we, me and Mary, well, we took everything, sort of as being your wish, until, well, until she didn't talk of selling the farm itself, the land. I asked her about it and she said that would be seen to later. I know now she'd have to have gone to your solicitor, sir, and he would have wanted your word for it and deeds and things. I guessed something was wrong before she left. I smelt a rat, so did Mary, but it was all done so quickly, like lightnin', so to speak. She had got every animal off this farm within a week, and the furniture was out of the house, well, within ten days. When I asked her where she was going she said . . . she said she was going to take you to Australia as soon as you were well enough. But somehow I didn't believe her; neither did Mary. It was the way she went on like as if she wasn't right in the head.'

'Not right in the head?' It was a quiet question, but weighed with disbelief for he could never imagine anyone thinking that his level-headed little sister could do anything that would stamp her as not right in the head.

'Well, sir, one morning as Mary went in she heard a banging, and there was Miss Betty standing kicking the green-baized door, kicking it like mad she was, Mary said, like someone demented. Anyway, as I said, I smelt a rat and I went across to Mrs Chapman, her being your mother-in-law like, although I had heard rumours that you and your missis weren't . . . well, sir, hitting it off and there was a separation. But anyway, she was the only one I could go to for advice, and she said right out it was no use getting in touch with your missis, but what she did do was write to Miss Nellie, and Miss Nellie came out like a shot and she tackled Miss Betty, and there was high jinks in the house. They went at each other like two cats, Mary said. Miss Nellie threatened to bring the police, but Miss Betty said she had your written authority to sell everything, and she waved a paper at her. Also she said that she was entitled to what she had taken.'

Arnold now lifted up a cup from the floor and sipped at it before he went on, 'Miss Nellie came up here after and when I asked her if you were capable of tackling the business she said that was the point, at the moment you mustn't be disturbed. She was in a state; she sat there crying. Anyway, sir, Miss Betty left the next morning an' she put a letter into me hand and said to me that when you came back, that's if you did, I was to give it you. 'Twas then I knew she had done a terrible thing to you, an' quite innocently you had given her the power to do it, but as I said to Mary you've still got the buildings and the land, you can start again.'

There followed a long silence. The room was stuffy; he wanted air, he wanted to open his mouth and draw in great draughts of air; he also wanted to open his mouth and scream as he had heard men scream so often in agony. . . . Start again! He'd never be able to start again. For one thing, he hadn't the money, for if she had cleared the farm she would have cleared the bank at the same time. And even if he had the money where would he get the strength?

It was a great wonder the shrapnel hadn't moved already.

He looked at Arnold now and said, 'May I have the letter?'

'Behind the clock, sir.' Arnold nodded towards the mantelpiece, and Charlie rose to his feet and took the letter from behind the clock; then sitting down again he looked at it. Although it was sealed he knew by the crumpled envelope that it had already been steamed open, but what did that matter. Having taken the double sheet of paper out of the envelope he began to read it. The letter had no heading, it began simply:

If the shock hasn't already killed you, you'll be reading this. What I've taken is only my just right, nobody but you would have expected me to live in that house under another of the Chapmans because the place, both the house and the farm, are virtually mine. My father might have made it but it was I who kept it going, and after working like a black all during the war, to be told by you that I'd be taken care of was just too much. But it wasn't only that, it was the fact that you had the nerve to tell me that you intended to bring another Chapman in there. Well, see how she reacts when she knows she'll have to start and build a home from scratch . . . on nothing!

Most of the furniture in the place was what Mother bought with her own money and it should have come to me; but what happened when she died? The same as when Father died, not a penny not a stick was I left. Well, I feel no compunction in taking what I rightly feel to be mine. You'll likely be advised to take me to court. Well, you can do so if you can find me, but knowing you, you won't take that step, you'll just hide your head in the sand as always.

We never liked each other so I'm not going to end with any fond farewells, yet in a way I feel sorry for you for you were born a loser. It has always amazed me how you ever became commissioned, it was like a fluke. Well, I suppose everybody is allowed one break. That's how I see it and I'm giving it to myself, for nobody else will.

Betty.

The letter was so characteristic of his sister, it was as if she had been sitting opposite him talking at him.

'She's a wicked woman, sir, a hard wicked woman. There's never been a happy moment on the place since you left. What do you think you'll do, sir?'

Charlie leant back in his chair and looked up at the low smoked-dyed ceiling before he said flatly and slowly, 'I haven't the slightest idea, Arnold.'

As he finished speaking there was a sound of footsteps coming along the flags outside the cottages and Arnold said, 'That'll be Mary, she's been over to the Chapmans. Mrs Chapman is taking her on, mornin's like, it helps.'

However, it wasn't Mary who opened the door without knocking but Nellie. She almost burst into the room, then held her breath for a moment as she looked across at Charlie.

Slowly now she closed the door, then came to his side and, taking his hand, said, 'Oh my dear! you had to find out some time, but I've nearly been out of my mind. Doctor Arlet's secretary phoned me. I . . . I seem to have run all the way.' She now turned her face towards Arnold and said, 'You're looking a bit better, Arnold.'

'Yes, miss, yes, I'm feeling much better.'

'Mary will be over presently; I called in home, then rode over.' The last part of her remark was addressed to Charlie and he nodded at her before getting to his feet, and now she took his arm, saying gently, 'Come on,' and looking over her shoulder towards Arnold she added, 'We'll be back. We'll be back, Arnold.'

Arnold merely nodded and watched them go out.

Neither of them spoke until they were entering the yard again and then Nellie said, 'I . . . I was afraid to tell you but I should have; it would have been better than getting a shock like this.'

He stopped and, looking down at her, asked quietly, 'Why should this happen to me, Nellie?' There was no whine in the question, it was more in the nature of a statement explaining that everything that happened to him was negative, everything.

She brought his hand tight into the fold of her arm as she answered, 'These kind of things always happen to nice people, Charlie, easygoing, kind, nice people, they never happen to the smart-Alicks, the rogues, the cheats, or the wily ones, for instance, to your father or mine. But you are different, Charlie, and – ' Her lips trembled and pressed together for a moment before she continued, 'And that's why I love you, because you're so different.'

He made no reply, he just stared at her without speaking, then turned about and walked into the yard where again, looking about him, he asked, 'What am I going to do, Nellie?'

'We'll find a way; I've thought it all out.'

His head came round quickly towards her and although he didn't speak there was a look of resentment on his face. She had thought it all out, he was to be managed again, manoeuvred by another woman.

'Come in the barn and sit down,' she said softly; 'I want to talk to you.'

When they reached the barn she glanced around but there was nothing to sit on, and simultaneously it seemed their eyes lifted to the platform above which were scattered the broken bales of hay, and she now smiled at him as she said, 'Can you risk going up into the loft with me for the second time?'

There was no answering smile on his face but he touched her cheek, then indicated that she should go up the ladder.

When a few minutes later they were sitting side by side on the straw she said quietly, 'I haven't been idle all these weeks. First thing I'd like you to know is I'm . . . I'm finished, my discharge is through.'

'Good. Good.' There was no sound of enthusiasm in his voice but she didn't seem to appear to notice for she went on, 'And I've made arrangements to sell my house. It'll bring a good price, it's got three sitting tenants and an empty flat. And added to that I have a nice little bit Aunty left me, together with what I've saved from my earnings. Now I reckon this will give us a start both outside and inside the house, and then . . . '

'Be quiet! Nellie. Don't be silly. Don't talk rot. You know I couldn't start again on your money.'

'Now! now! Charlie MacFell, don't you come the English gentleman with me.' Here was the old Nellie talking. ' What do you think you're going to do with your life? You've got to have work, some kind of work, everybody has. And you've got more than most to start with; you've got land and a farmhouse and buildings, all you need is stock, and I'm going to buy that stock whether you like it or not. *We're* going to buy the stock because what I have is yours, Charlie.' Her voice lowered now. 'You won't be able to stop me no matter what you say. . . . And don't try, Charlie. Oh, please don't try.'

Slowly he turned and looked at her and, taking her hands within his, he said, 'You remember Slater?'

'Yes . . . Ginger, the one that became a sergeant and put you through it.'

'The same. Well, he told me years ago that I was a loser, and I didn't believe him, and the minute before he died he again told me I was a loser, and still I didn't believe him, but I do today because Betty has proved it.'

'Oh! Charlie. Charlie. You're not, you're not . . . you're just easygoing and quiet and . . . '

'Shut up, Nellie, and listen to me.' He shook the hands within his. 'There's some things you know about me but there's a lot you don't. I'm not easygoing and quiet. I am lazy and weak-willed and vindictive. . . . Nellie, I shot Slater dead. Do you hear? I shot him when he was practically defenceless. He had a gun but he wouldn't have used it on me, he just used his tongue, and I took my revolver and at point-blank range I fired into him.'

When he felt her hands jerk within his, he said, 'Yes, I know how you feel, you're shocked, this isn't what the easygoing, soft Charlie would do, it isn't what any self-respecting officer would do, but I did it, Nellie. *I did it.*'

Her lips were trembling when she said, 'Then there must have been a good reason, Charlie.'

'Yes, I suppose in a way there was, but as I see it now not enough reason to shoot a man dead. I should have left that to the Germans.'

'Then . . . then why did you do it?'

He still held on to her hands, while keeping his face turned away from her, and he looked down on to the floor of the barn and out into the yard, and in his mind's eye he was going through the alleyway and on to the cinder path. He saw himself standing there again watching his father draw blood from the skinny undersized red-headed boy. He saw the thin body bouncing on the cinders. He closed his eyes before turning his head once again towards her and saying, 'It all started out there on the cinder path.'

'The cinder path? You mean the road that runs down to the burn?'

'The same.'

'What has that got to do with it?'

'Everything, everything.'

Now in a quiet resigned tone he went on to tell her about young Polly and Big Polly and the outcome of his father's decision to introduce him into manhood. He took her through the years of blackmail both he and Arthur suffered at the hands of Slater, then the long agony of his term under Slater, and how it was ended by being given a commission.

The only time he stumbled in the telling was when he described why he had been given a commission, and when he came to the scene in the trenches his voice faltered as he ended, 'The humiliation was too great, Nellie. I ... I thought I had achieved something, I was a lieutenant in command of men whom I knew respected me, and then he took the ground from under my feet more surely than any shell could have done when he told me my appointment had been rigged. And what was worse, I knew that every word he said was true was and that I'd known it from the beginning, but the truth was too much for me. ... The most frightening thing in life, Nellie, is to come face to face with yourself, and in that moment I couldn't bear it, and so I fired.'

'Oh! Charlie. Charlie!' Her arms were around him, her lips were covering his face, his brow, his eyes, his cheeks, and when they came direct on his mouth she held him tightly, so tightly that as they had done once before they overbalanced and fell on to the straw, and all the while she was muttering, 'Oh! Charlie. Charlie!'

'Nellie! Nellie!'

Their faces were wet, their tears were mingling.

'Oh! Nellie. Nellie!'

He had been warned, no mental excitement, no real physical exertion, if it moved to the right!

'Oh! Nellie, my love, my love.'

It would be a good way to die. Oh! Nellie, my Nellie.

He was loving a woman, really loving a woman; he was not struggling with a tigress, he was the master, the man, and he was loving a woman, his woman. 'Nellie! *Nellie! Oh Nellie!*'

He had climbed the mountain and the sky was still high above him. He reached up into it and embraced the ecstasy and at the height of heights he was pierced through with pain. It came and went like the prick of a needle, but he experienced it, and he was conscious that he experienced it.

He came down from the mountain bearing her in his arms and together they lay down on the straw.

Still clinging close, they lay in the great silence of peace and fulfilment and stared at each other.

He had killed his enemy, he had loved a woman, really loved a woman for the first time in his life, and death had moved in him but had taken a turn to the left. What more could a man want to begin again?

# CATHERINE COOKSON

# The
# Invisible
# Cord

## Chapter One

### The White Wedding

'Who said I shouldn't wear white?'

'Nobody, Annie, nobody.'

'Don't tell me nobody. You wouldn't have the bare-face to come out with that on your own, Mona Broadbent, so don't tell me that nobody put you up to it.'

'Nobody put me up to it, it was just something that I . . . Aw you, Annie; you're like a ferret.'

'Then there was something said then? Who said it?'

Mona Broadbent sucked in her thin lips, pushed her thin fair hair first over one ear then over the other, and wagged her long melancholy face at Annie Cooper, her best friend, as she would tell you again and again if you had a mind to listen, her only real friend. More like sisters they were, she would say, having started school together at St Peter and Paul's, Tyne Dock, having changed schools together when both their parents shifted to High Shields, and having left school together in 1940 and got their first job together in Culbert's biscuit factory. Then, a year later, again they made a move together; this time into the munitions works, where they got almost twice the money and enjoyed a bit more carry on. They were still in the munition works, but separated for the first time because they had been put on different shifts.

It was three weeks ago now when Mona, as she would have told you, got the shock of her life on Annie informing her, out of the blue, that she was going to be married. And who do you think to? *Georgie McCabe.* Georgie McCabe, that big galoot they had known all their lives . . . well, anyway since they had moved to 114 Weldon Street.

Mona couldn't get over it. Annie and Georgie McCabe! Him a cook in the R.A.F. stationed in some god-forsaken place called Madley. A cook mind you, and he could burn water! Lorry driving was his trade and they'd made him a cook. As her da said, he was Hitler's best friend, a fifth columnist working through the guts. Fry the blokes' eggs in axle grease, that's what he would do. Her ma, too, said Annie must be mad or gone soft in the head, for if anybody in their street could pick and choose it was Annie. Her ma was very fond of Annie; they were all very fond of Annie; because Annie was good-hearted and jolly. You couldn't be dull for long where Annie was. And now she was going to marry the dimmest bloke in the street.

What was up with her? That was the question she had asked Annie three weeks ago. 'What's up with you, Annie Cooper?' she had said. 'There's

Peter Riley, and him first mate. Cock-eyed he's been when he's come home these last two trips squintin' at you. And then there's John McIntyre; he's not to be sneezed at, neither on the parade ground nor off it. He's a sergeant already and they say he won't stay there.'

It was at this point that Annie had turned on her like she had never done before, telling her to shut her mouth, she was marrying Georgie McCabe because she wanted to marry Georgie McCabe, and if she, Mona, didn't like it she knew what she could do. Then she had banged the door in her face.

Now here she was demanding to know why she shouldn't be dressed in white when she knew flaming well why she shouldn't be dressed in white; and she said exactly that to her.

'You know flamin' well, Annie, what Katie Newton was sayin' an' I was just tryin' to break it to you gentle like. But I see you're in one of your moods again so I won't beat about the bush. I heard her sayin' to Florrie Turnbull that it was no use using a white oven cloth to take a burnt loaf out of the oven.'

'Burnt loaf! Just wait till I see her, I'll smack her cheeky face for her. I'll go right up to her, I will, and I'll take my hand right across her . . .'

Annie's voice stopped abruptly, her hand dropped from its demonstrating position, her chin drooped on to her chest; she sat down on the bedroom chair with a plop and there was silence in the room until she raised her head and looked with pleading eyes at Mona and asked, 'Does it show?'

'No, no, Annie, it doesn't at all, you're still as flat as a pancake.' Mona's voice was soft.

Annie screwed up her eyes tight and got abruptly to her feet, then walked towards the window, saying, 'You were never a good liar.'

As she stood looking out of the narrow aperture of the blackout curtains she heard the bed springs creak as Mona sat down. Only once before had she been made conscious that the bed springs creaked, that was the night when Georgie McCabe had eased himself down beside her. She had tried to push him off but not too much; no, she had to be fair, not too much.

They had sneaked away from Hilda Tressell's wedding. Everyone from their part of the street had been to Hilda Tressell's wedding. Her da was paralytic, and her ma had had a drop an' all. It was her da who had made her drink the whisky, and that on top of the sherry had made her go daft. They had cleared the floor and she had done the Highland fling by herself until Georgie had joined her, and then everybody had laughed fit to burst.

Georgie had given her another whisky, and she'd had more sherry, and when she felt a bit sick he took her outside. She couldn't remember why they had made for home or who suggested it. But she could remember them stealing up the street and the creaking of the bed as he lay down beside her.

It was the first time it had happened to her and she had cried, and then she had really been sick. The next morning, even while she felt terrible, she had knelt by the bed and prayed to Our Lady not to let anything happen to her. She had gone to late Mass, and Georgie was there. He had looked a little shamefaced but what he said to her was, 'You'd think I'd get out of bloody church parade on leave, wouldn't you?'

She remembered thinking, him just coming out of Mass and swearing; but then Georgie's swearing was like God bless you! he punctured everything with bloody. His mother and father did too. Yet she wasn't unused to swearing; her da could hold his own at it, at least when he was upset about something. But he never swore like the McCabes, and her mother never swore at all. Her mother was a bit prim, except when she had a drink on her and then she let her hair down. She herself took after her mother in a way, not that she was prim, far from it, but once she had taken drink her hair came down too.

When she had told her mother she was going to marry Georgie she just stared at her, stared and stared at her, but she didn't open her mouth to ask why, yet her eyes had held the question . . . and the answer. It was a full five minutes later when she asked, 'When is it to be?' and she had answered, 'Soon. He's getting a forty-eight.' And that had been that.

Her mother wasn't natural. She should have probed and gone for her. But her father was natural. His probing had gone deep, and when it was finished there had been tears in his eyes. But all he had said to her was, 'My God lass! to wreck your life like that.' Then he had added, 'Well, it's done and can't be undone; and for what part I have in it I'll see it's done properly, you'll have a weddin'.'

Annie looked down on to the street. The houses on the opposite side, not more than thirty feet away, were misted, not only with the November dullness but with the Sunday dullness. Even in wartime Annie thought, Sunday had the power to blot out life; except the service canteens and the churches, the town died on a Sunday. It was fear that filled the churches, her da said. Perhaps he was right there, for she herself was always praying that she wouldn't be hit by a bomb, and if she was, that she would be killed outright and not made blind. She had a fear of going blind because once she'd had her eyes bandaged for a fortnight after getting an infection in them.

Her gaze became focused on three children playing on a doorstep. They were the Ratcliffes. Sunday made no difference to them, they were let out at any time. The two older ones belonged to Betty Ratcliffe, and she was married, but the three-year-old was Jane's. She had him the first year of the war when she was sixteen and she had fought her mother to keep him. Her da had said that it was very commendable of Jane; her ma, as usual when faced with such matters, had just tightened her lips, neither condemning nor sympathizing. But Jane had had to pay for her mistake for her name became mud in the street. They said she'd had two miscarriages since and that she was making a pile out of the army, navy and air force, she wasn't choosey. Well, no matter what they said about her, she seemed to enjoy herself and was always well dressed in spite of clothing coupons. Nevertheless, she always wore a defiant look on her face and never spoke to any of the neighbours.

When she knew she herself had fallen she wondered whether she, too, should brave it out like Jane, but she knew she couldn't, she wouldn't be able to stand the shame of it.

Mona was saying now, 'How you goin' on for coupons?'

She turned and leant her back against the window-sill, saying flatly, 'Me ma and da are givin' me theirs.'

'Are you going to make it yourself?'

'No; I'd only make a hash of it. I'm going to ask Mrs Tyler to run it up.'

There was silence between them now while they looked at each other across the small room; then Mona said, 'Is there any chance of him being sent abroad?'

'What do you mean, chance?' Annie had left the support of the window-sill; her back stiff, she repeated, 'What do you mean, chance? You suggestin' that he should be sent over so that he can be knocked off?'

'No, no, I'm not. You know I'm not.'

There was no conviction in the answer, but Annie's attitude now gave the assumption that she had received an apology – for, her body slumping, she sat down in the wicker chair by the side of the bed . . . Any chance of him being sent overseas? That very question had been in her mind for days, filling her with guilt and remorse. Not that she would want him dead, but she wished he'd be taken out of the way until, as she put it, she could pull herself together.

It wasn't that she disliked Georgie, she didn't, you couldn't dislike him. On the other hand she was only too well aware that he was no cop, and she felt she deserved somebody better than him, somebody with a little more up top. She had always imagined marrying someone better off than herself, and decidedly she had never intended to marry anyone from these parts.

After she left school she had lain in bed at nights and thought how wonderful it would be if she could click a lad who lived in Westoe, or somebody who worked in the town hall. But since the Americans had come her aspirations had grown, even beyond Westoe and the town hall. What if an American officer fell for her? or a sergeant? or even a corporal, because all Americans . . . well most of them, were rich.

But here it was 1943 and she had never spoken to an American, not even a G.I., and she hadn't caught the eye of even one English officer in the army, navy, or air force; nor yet that of a sergeant; what she had caught was a bellyful from a cook in the R.A.F.

Her head moved in slight admonition at the vulgarity of the thought, for such everyday thinking that pervaded her environment had, until recently, been condemned by her as vulgar. She had ideas of bettering herself, if not by marriage, then by getting herself a better job as soon as this war was over. She had in mind to take up shorthand and typing and of becoming a secretary, the kind of secretary that a boss relied on, like you read about in the magazines, and the kind of boss who eventually married his secretary. But now all that nonsense was over and the sooner she faced up to facts the better. She was pregnant, she was going to marry Georgie McCabe, she would have one bairn after another until she finally put a stop to him. She'd live in a three-upstairs or two-downer and eventually consider herself lucky if she had two up and two down like this one. Eventually she'd lose her figure and people would forget that she had ever been bonny, and she herself would forget that she had ever wanted anything better . . .

No by God! I won't. She was standing on her feet, her head wagging at Mona, who moved her position on the bed and, staring up at her, inquired softly, 'You're not goin' to marry him then?'

'Aw you, Mona Broadbent!' Annie was bending forward, her two hands flat in the middle of the bed. 'Some friend you are, sneering about me being married in white, then wanting him dead, and now wishing that I'll not marry him and leave the bairn like Jane Ratcliffe's. Aye, some friend you are. Well, I am going to marry him, and the bairn will have a name, and what's more I'll make something out of him, Georgie, I mean. And I'll not stay in Weldon Street; you can take that from me.'

'All right I'll take it, but don't ram it down me throat.'

'You don't like him, do you?'

'I liked him all right until he ... well, got you into trouble. I used to think he was harmless, all right for a giggle. But he wasn't so harmless, was he?'

'Don't keep on.'

'You started it.'

Annie straightened her back, walked to the box-seat set opposite a chest of drawers on which stood a little swing mirror, and leaning forward, she stretched her top lip downwards and pushed her nose to one side in search of elusive blackheads; then nodding at her friend through the mirror she said, 'I'll surprise you one of these days, you'll see; I'll make something of him if it kills me.'

'It might that an' all.'

Slowly Annie turned on the seat and looked over the bed rail, along which Mona now had her forearms folded with her chin resting on them, and she said, 'You rub it in, don't you?'

Shading her eyes Mona now looked down towards the floor as she answered, 'It's 'cos I'm concerned; and if the truth was told I'm a bit jealous.' She raised her eyelids and grinned at Annie, and Annie asked softly, 'You're not, are you?'

'Aye. Well, it'll be different when you're married.'

'There'll be nothing different; it'll just be the same, we'll always be friends.' She felt better now since Mona had said she was a bit jealous. 'Come on.' She rose and pulled at Mona's arm. 'The tea'll be ready, let's go downstairs.' But as she went to open the door she stopped and, turning and facing Mona, said quietly 'If you hear Katie Newton saying anything more will you deny it for me?'

'Aye, of course.'

'Ta ... and when it comes I can say it was premature.'

'Aye, you could.'

''Cos they do come afore time, don't they?'

'Oh, aye, they do.'

They smiled at each other; then Annie said again, softly, 'Ta, Mona.'

Mona did not ask why she was being thanked again but when Annie opened the door she drooped her head and went out.

As Annie followed her friend down the stairs she thought, Don't let's kid meself. Jealous? She's no more jealous of me than she is of Lottie Collins. And no one in their right mind would be jealous of Lottie Collins, and her the street idiot who had to be taken everywhere by the hand.

# Chapter Two

To say it rained was putting it mildly, bucketing was the expression that was being generally used. It had bucketed from the Friday morning all through the Friday night, and Dennis Cooper had assured his daughter that this was a good thing because there couldn't be much more left up there, and it would dry up first thing. But at eleven o'clock on the Saturday morning he was forced to remark that it was a pity there was no rationing up there. He had seen rain of all kinds in his time, from smut-laden to sleet-laden but this lot he termed spite-laden. He kept up his tirade against the weather for so long that Annie was forced to cry at him, 'Oh, Da, give over! it's not helpin' any you keepin' on. Nobody can stop it, so give over, do.'

Annie knew that her da was going on as he was doing for her sake because he thought the rain would spoil her wedding, her white wedding. Well, although she couldn't stop the rain she could take its effect away by stopping the wedding. She had the power to do that, hadn't she? There were three hours to go yet. She could get into her outdoor things, pack a bag, take the money she had saved, leaving the little Georgie had added in an envelope with a letter to him, then take a single ticket to somewhere. Where? Yes, that was the question, where?

She had asked herself the same question last night as she had lain awake peering into the future, not into the years, but to the coming twenty-four hours when Georgie would be lying beside her in this bed.

It was funny them spending their first night in this house; and funnier still that it was on her mother's suggestion that they were doing it. No use spending money on hotels, she had said, when he was due to get the train at twelve o'clock on the Sunday. She herself had thought there was some slight indecency about the suggestion. Her da, too, might have been of the same mind for he had said neither yes nor nay to it.

Her mother was a puzzle to her, she just couldn't understand her; yet during the past few weeks she had come to realize that her ma didn't want to lose her. 'As long as the war's on,' she had said, 'you can make this your home, 'cos he'll be away most of the time and you'll need someone to see to you.' She hadn't added, 'When the bairn comes.'

At times she wished her mother would put her arms around her and hug her and say, 'There, there, hinny, don't worry; you've got me and your da, we'll see that you're all right.' In a way, she had said the words, but without the actions, and it was the actions, the actions of tenderness that she had needed very badly these past days.

And now, here she was thinking again of taking a single ticket to somewhere. But you had to have somebody waiting for you in that somewhere, and the fact was she hadn't a relative outside the town. Her mother and father were only children, and her mother's parents were dead, while her grandma and granda Cooper lived just a mile away. You couldn't get a single ticket to Laygate.

She turned from her father who was peering out through the lace curtains into the backyard, and she hesitated a moment in the middle of the kitchen while looking towards the scullery, where her mother was wrapping a stack of sandwiches in a dampened tea-towel, and going slowly towards her, she stood in the doorway and looked for a moment at the stubby hands folding over the points of the cloth before she said, 'The table looks lovely, Ma.'

'Well, I've done me best.'

'I know you have.'

'A body can't do more.'

'No . . . Ma.'

It seemed as if it would take an effort for Mary Cooper to raise her hands from the packed sandwiches and look at her daughter, and when she did all she said was, 'Aye.'

Annie gulped on a mouthful of spittle, bit on her lip, then hung her head before she said, 'I just want to say, th . . . thanks for all you've done, Ma.'

She didn't know which way to jump when Mary, flinging out her short arm, pulled the door closed, shutting them in the small well of the scullery, and now, looking into her daughter's face, she said tersely, 'I'm your mother, aren't I, what did you expect from me? To throw you out on the street?'

'No, Ma, no, I didn't. But . . . but you've been kind.'

'Haven't I always been kind to you?'

Annie's eyes flickered to the side for a moment; then she was nodding her head. 'Aye . . . aye, yes, you have; you've brought me up well. I'm not sayin', but . . . but what I mean to say is that, well, under the circumstances you've been –' her head drooped on to her breast and as her voice broke and she said, 'Oh Ma!' her body swayed forward and it seemed a long second before Mary's arms came out and held her, held her tightly, even crushed her. They were both crying now, both muttering, Annie saying, 'Oh Ma! Oh Ma!' and Mary saying, 'Lass, why had you to do it? Why? Why?'

The sound of the front-door knocker being rapped hard and Dennis's voice calling, 'Mary! somebody here,' brought them apart. Their heads turned from each other, their hands rubbing at their faces, and Mary, taking up the corner of her apron, blew her nose then pressed both hands down from the centre parting of her hair which, unlike Annie's, was jet black. Then quickly turning, she pushed at her daughter, saying, 'Get yourself upstairs and get ready.' And on this Annie opened the door and went into the kitchen, to see her father coming in from the passage with Mrs McCabe behind him, and behind her the fourteen-year-old McCabe twins, Archie and Mike, one carrying a large bundle, the other an old kit-bag.

'Hello, hinny.' Mollie McCabe edged her way past the sofa and the table and, her big slack-lipped mouth wide, she laughed towards Annie, saying, 'I've brought some of his toggery along. He's still dead to the world; the bugger was sodden last night but I'll see he doesn't get any till he leaves the church. Don't you worry, lass.' She thrust out her arm, her fist doubled, and punched Annie playfully in the chest as she went on, 'Did you ever see a mornin' like it? Aw well, we'll all be as wet inside as we are out come this time the night. What do you say, Dennis?' She turned now and poked her finger towards Dennis. Then swinging her big flabby body around she exclaimed, 'Where's your mother? Oh, there you are, Mary.' She looked towards the scullery door and Mary, walking slowly into the kitchen, said, 'Hello, Mrs McCabe.'

'Aw!' Mollie shook her head from side to side. 'How many times have I had to ask you not to call me Mrs McCabe. Mollie's me name. Everybody calls me Mollie, even them that hates me guts.' She turned round now and nodded at Dennis. 'Aye, an' there's a few of them I can tell you. Fetch them here, you two.' She now waved at her sons, and they came from the doorway, each humping his bundle forward with one hand and a knee. Then pointing from the kit-bag to the bundle, Mollie cried, 'His odds and sods. I thought I'd bring them along an' you can settle them in afore the dirty deed's done, and at the same time say hello, and ta very much for seein' to things.' She turned now and nodded towards Mary.

She waited for some response, and when none was forthcoming she grabbed the bundle and kit-bag from her sons and, looking at Annie, said, 'Come on, lass, I'll take them up to your room.' And no one saying her nay, she went out into the passage towards the stairs, and Annie, after dividing a startled look between her mother and father, followed her.

In the bedroom, Mollie McCabe dumped her son's belongings into the corner between the chest of drawers and the wall, then she turned and looked at Annie. Her face, now without its wide splitting grin, looked flabby and old, and momentarily Annie contrasted her with her mother. Her mother looked like a young woman compared with her future mother-in-law. But then her mother wasn't all that old, only thirty-six, whereas Mrs McCabe must be all of fifty. Anyway, she looked it.

'Well, it's nearly time, lass.'

Annie blinked, then said, 'Yes, Mrs McCabe.'

'Now, now, lass, you at least'll have to get used to callin' me Mollie, no matter how stiff necked your ma remains. That's if you don't want to call me ma, or mam, or mother, or go the whole hog and call me mater, like they do on the pictures.' Her face went into a grin again, but only for a second; and then she said, 'There's just one thing I want to say, an' it'll be different from what everybody else is sayin', 'cos I know how the yappin's gone. You've let yourself down a mile, they're sayin', takin' up with our Georgie. He's got nothin' up top, they're sayin'; like all the McCabes', they're sayin'. Well, let me say one thing in our Georgie's favour, lass. He's kind; he'd give his shirt-tail away in the winter, he would that. And another thing. You could get a better lad, I won't say you couldn't with the looks of you, but there's somethin' that I don't think you know, 'cos he's short of words like. But it isn't only the day or yesterda' that he started caring for you, he's watched you since you were a bit of a bairn. On his twenty-first birthday when we had a bit of a do he said to me on the side, "I wish that Cooper lass was a bit older, I would have asked her round." An' I remember laughin' me head off and sayin' to him, "What! you'd be brought up for baby snatchin' and learnin' her to drink." But I understood how he felt, 'cos you looked over fourteen. You look much older than seventeen now, lass; you could be taken for twenty and that's no offence, just the opposite. But what I want to get over to you is, he cares for you, and that bein' so you'll be able to handle him like putty. You mightn't think it, me being like I am, likin' me drop an' all that, you mightn't think that I worry about the bairns, but I do, and our Georgie most of all. I've wondered what kind of lass he'd finally end up with. Some dirty slut, I thought, who couldn't keep her spotty-nosed bairns clean. Bad as I am they could never say that about me, that me bairns weren't kept clean, and their bellies full. Well –' she now hitched up her bust with her forearm – 'what I really want to say, lass is, I'm kind of grateful to you for havin' him. Mind –' Her forearm, now depriving her bust of its support, shot out and, pointing her finger at Annie, she said, 'Not that I don't know that you were forced into it. Oh aye; you don't jump over a cliff unless there's a bull behind you. But as I said to his da last night, if anybody can thatch a roof with rotten straw it's that lass. Mind –' her finger was stabbing now – 'I'm not sayin' that there's anything rotten about our Georgie, but you get me meanin', which is, if anybody can make anything of him it'll be you. Well –' she took one step backwards now – 'I've had me say, lass, so I'll get meself downstairs, open me big mouth an' laugh me bloomin' head off, and your ma'll say, polite like, "Good-bye, Mrs McCabe" while thinkin', That woman! common as clarts she is! . . . Ta-rah, lass'.

'Ta-rah . . . Mollie.'

Mollie now gave her a nod and a knowing smile, then went out quietly. But a minute later her high laugh came to Annie where she was standing staring at her reflection in the mirror, her hand over her mouth but her lips moving as she repeated, 'Thatch a roof with rotten straw.'

The reflection moved its head wildly at her. She watched the tears run down the cheeks in the mirror. Thatch a roof with rotten straw. She was only seventeen, it wasn't fair. Through the mirror she saw the white satin wedding dress lying over the foot of the bed . . . Oh God! what a farce. Life was a farce.

The word farce brought back to her a tale that Georgie had told her about the twins. When they were seven years old they were in a class where, on a Friday afternoon, the teacher let the pupils recite or sing a verse of a favourite song, and Archie had put his hand up and said he would like to sing 'All By Yourself In The Moonlight'. Having been granted permission, Archie walked to the front of the class and sang the recognized words, until he came to those in the chorus:

> There ain't no sense
> Sitting on the fence
> All by yourself
> In the moonlight,

for which he substituted:

> Life's a farce
> Sitting on your arse
> All by yourself
> In the moonlight

She had thought it rude, but nevertheless she had laughed, primly at first, then loudly; but that was the night she'd had the sherry followed by the whisky.

But life was a farce, everything about today was a farce. The only good thing, she felt, she would remember about it was that her ma had held her in her arms for the first time in years.

# Chapter Three

It was done.

Two umbrellas had been held over them as they ran from the church doorway across the pavement to the waiting car. There were no sightseers, and for this she was grateful. She had told herself she should be thankful for the rain for she would have died if Katie Newton, and Florrie Turnbull, and the rest of that crowd had been waiting outside the church. And they would have been if it hadn't been the kind of day it was.

Father Carey had married them in a sort of word-gabbling rush; he had seemed in a hurry to get it over. There she had stood in her white dress with her veil held in place by a wreath of Virgin Mary blue forget-me-nots; Mona had made the wreath for her. She had even gone to the trouble of bringing it to the church yesterday and sprinkling it with holy water in a kind of blessing. Mona was nice. She glanced through the rain-filled window of the car before it started and saw Mona standing inside the church door with the best man, Arthur Bailey. He seemed a nice fellow, this Arthur Bailey, superior like. She had met him last night for the first time. Georgie had brought him back from Madley with him. His home was in Hereford; he seemed a different type of fellow from Georgie. She wondered at them being friends; perhaps it was because they both worked in the kitchen.

'Well, love.' She was pulled back on to the seat within the tight circle of Georgie's arm, and now she was looking into his face. It wasn't a bad-looking face, sort of homely; he had his mother's wide slack laughing mouth and his eyes were dark brown, much darker than her own. His eyes were his best feature; the kindliness his mother had talked about was in his eyes. He wasn't very tall, not much taller than her, and she thought that she was still growing. Five-foot eight, she supposed he was, but he appeared taller because of his bulk, he was heavily made.

'Well, it's done.'

It was as if he were repeating her words, and she echoed them, saying, 'Yes, it's done.'

'Happy?'

'I . . . I don't know yet.' Oh dear God! she hadn't meant to say that. She should have just answered a plain yes, it would have satisfied him. Fancy telling a man on his wedding day that she didn't know if she was happy or not. She saw that his face had clouded.

He said soberly, 'Well, I'll have to try to make you know, won't I? It's up to me then, isn't it?'

She didn't answer, she just stared at him. Then they both swung to the side as the car veered round the corner and his arms tightened about her and he looked down into her face, muttering, 'I love you, Annie. I can't put it like I should, I'm not much use with words, the bloody things won't come for me, never would somehow.' His mouth spread into a quick grin, reminiscent of his mother's ever-ready defence, before he went on, 'But one thing I'll tell you. I'll do me best for you. I'll try to go steady, I mean with the drink an' that, and we'll get a home together for the bairn . . . You know what me ma said just afore I came out?'

He was grinning widely now, and she shook her head. 'No.'

'She said she'd break me bloody neck if I didn't do the right thing by you. What do you think about that for a mother-in-law? I asked her whose side she was on. She said Hitler's. That's me ma; she's a case but . . . but she's all right me ma. We would have known some pretty tough times if it hadn't been for her 'cos me da's no bloody good, never has been. Him and work never agreed; he used to get the smit if he went near it, but she wouldn't have it that he was lazy, bawl you down if you said he was . . . Hie! Hie! you're not cryin', are you?'

'No, no. Well, I don't know what I'm doing, laughing or crying . . . You're funny, Georgie.'

'You think I'm funny?'

'Well, not funny that way, amusin'.'

'Aw well, amusin' am I? Well that's one thing I've got in me favour anyroad, an' that's not bad for a start, is it?'

'Georgie.'

'Aye?'

'Promise me something?'

'Anything, anything in the world.'

'Don't . . . don't get drunk the day.'

He stared at her, then smiled, a quiet smile, and bending his head he kissed her on the lips, then said, 'That's a promise.'

As the car came to a stop opposite 114 she asked herself why she had made him promise such a thing, because once he started to drink he'd soon become paralytic, and such being the case she might have warded off a repeat of the incident following Hilda Tressell's wedding.

There were twenty-one at the reception in the front room. Annie and Georgie were wedged in at the top of the table, while five of those seated down the left side and five down the right were also wedged in. The rest had room to move their chairs back. Mary and Mollie McCabe and Mrs Rankin from next door, the only neighbour, together with her husband, who had been invited to the wedding, saw to the filling of teapots and the replenishing of plates.

There had been general acclaim at the sight of the well laden table. How had Mary done it? Cold brisket, a leg of pork, and half a ham, besides salmon sandwiches! Where on earth had she got the salmon! Some of them hadn't seen a tin of salmon for years.

The answers with regard to the food were given by Dennis with nods and winks in the direction of the top of the table, and the guests looked at Georgie and said, 'Ah! ah!' Georgie was a cook, and cooks were no fools.

Annie hadn't looked at Georgie but at her mother who, although she didn't like Georgie, hadn't apparently been above taking the tins of stuff that he had brought on his last few leaves. Then she chided herself. She mustn't think anything against her mother; she must remember what happened in the scullery this morning. Her mother had feelings that she didn't show.

Her da was on his feet, speaking now, her da knew how to do things properly.

Dennis looked up the table towards his daughter and new son-in-law and the action brought a cessation of the gabble and the room became quiet. 'It has fallen to me,' he began, 'to say a few words on this auspicious occasion. For it is an auspicious occasion.' He nodded his head twice. 'My daughter this day has not only changed her name from Cooper to McCabe, she has written that name at the head of a page to a new life.' Again he nodded his head twice. 'It's a clean page and it's up to her what she writes on it.' He turned his gaze now from Annie and brought it to rest on Mary, where she was sitting at the bottom of the table, her hands in her lap, her eyes cast down towards them. And she didn't raise them when, speaking to her pointedly, he said, 'There's her mother. She was only a year older than Annie the day I married her, and from the day Annie was born she has looked after her like a mother should. What credit goes to Annie today is due to her mother.' There was a long pause here while he stared at the bent head. Then turning his eyes once more towards the top of the table, he went on, 'I'm goin' to cut this short, lass, I'm only goin' to say this, that if you look after Georgie as your mother has looked after me and our home, then you won't go far wrong. Now—' his eyes swept the faces all turned towards him, and he commanded, 'Get on your feet, lift up your glasses and drink . . . To Annie and Georgie.'

'*Annie and Georgie. Annie and Georgie. Annie and Georgie.*'

When the company was again seated there followed a babble of voices, everyone talking at once, until the stranger, the best man, rose to his feet; then everyone gave him their attention. Even the twins stopped stuffing food into their mouths and looked at the foreigner, the fellow who talked different. And Arthur Bailey's voice was definitely different from that of anyone in the room. He began to speak with a slow softness, and he kept his eyes on Annie and Georgie as he spoke, saying, 'If there's anyone wishes Georgie and his bride health and happiness it's me. Georgie and I have been pals for the past eighteen months, and I want to state here and now that I'll never find a better. As good fellows go he's one of the best, and I know that Annie will have a happy life ahead of her as long as she has him by her side. Here's wishing you both happiness and contentment.'

The best man's speech was greeted with more applause than Dennis's had received, and Georgie, red in the face, looked at Annie and asked, 'Well now, what do you think of that for a reference, eh?' He leaned over her and punched his pal in the shoulder. Then his attention was drawn towards his mother, whose voice, well above the rest, was exclaiming, 'Now, that's for you. Wasn't that nice? Talk about a pal.'

Nodding in the direction of Arthur Bailey, Mollie now called, 'Thanks lad. Good for you; you'll always be welcome in our house.' Then turning to her husband she shouted at him as if he were at the far end of the street,'Did you get an earful of that?' and when he replied, 'Aye, aye, I heard. Couldn't help but, could I?' she pushed him almost off his seat as she cried, 'Well, let it sink in then, let it sink into your puddle head.' And at this the twins and her married daughter, Daisy, and Daisy's husband, Frank Stewart, and Winnie, her sixteen-year-old daughter, who was but a younger replica of herself, all howled with laughter as if at some great joke, while Mary and Mrs Rankin exchanged looks, then rose from the table, each picking up a teapot, and went into the kitchen.

'That woman!' Mrs Rankin pursed her lips. 'She's as common as muck. It's just as well you'll have Annie here under your wing.'

Mary made no reply to this but she filled her teapot from the spluttering kettle, then placed them both side by side on the hob and, looking to the deepening twilight of the rain-drenched day, she said, 'I think we'd better do the black-outs and put the lights on.' She glanced at the clock as she spoke, and the clock said quarter to four.

The air-raid siren went at a quarter to nine.

The table had been cleared, the two end additions, boards on trestles, had been taken out and stacked at the bottom of the bunks in the air-raid shelter in the yard. Most of the chairs had been brought into the kitchen, but the centre table had been up-ended and placed in front of the little china cabinet. The radiogram had been put in the passageway, allowing for one person only to pass at a time towards the front door, and then this could only be achieved with indrawn breath.

In the front room, interpreting a quick step in their several ways, were Mona and Arthur Bailey, Daisy and Frank Stewart, while Winnie and her mother, shaking with gales of laughter, were trying to get Dennis to do Knees-up-Mother-Brown.

Arrayed around the kitchen were Annie's grandparents and Mona's mother and father, and in between them sat Georgie, talking quite amiably as he was apt to do when nicely warmed, which stage he usually reached with a couple of drops of hard and four pints. This intake in no way suggested that he had broken his promise to Annie, for as he maintained, he always knew where he was until he'd had half a dozen doubles, or failing that, a mixture of anything he could come by from port wine to cider.

He glanced now to where he could see Annie in the scullery drying the glasses that her mother was washing up, and he paused in his talking, until Mrs Broadbent said, 'You're spinnin' them, Georgie, aren't you? Anybody getting bacon and eggs any time they like!'

He turned his attention to the little fat woman again, saying, 'No, no, it's a fact, Mrs Broadbent, true as I'm sittin' here. You get on a bike and go into the country outside Hereford an' stop at one of them cottages or little farms, an' you'll get a feed fit for a king. It's a fact. An' butter and eggs away with you an' all. Lots of our blokes do it, especially the ones living out in Hereford. Cor! you want to see what they bring back. I once refused to give a fellow on guard duty extra butter, 'cos I didn't like his bloody guts, big head he was, and the next week when he was off he comes back and pushes a bloody great slab of country butter under me nose. Even the colour of it made our stuff look like lint. "There, McCabe," he said, "you know what you can do with your butter." ' He now closed his eyes and raised his hand, palm outwards, saying, 'Ladies present, ladies present; better not say what he told me what to do with that butter.'

It was when the laughter was at its highest that the siren went.

For a split second there was a startled calmness in the house as they listened to the wailing sound. Then like a fusillade of bullets they were scattering for the doors, that is all except Georgie, Arthur Bailey and Dennis.

It was Dennis who yelled, 'Don't go mad. Don't go mad,' and the answer he got from all quarters was, 'Fancy it happening the night of all nights.'

'Get in!' Mary was pushing Annie towards the steps of the air-raid shelter in the backyard when Annie suddenly stopped and, turning to her mother, whose hand was still on her arm, said, 'I'm not going in yet, Ma. Anyway it isn't right, we should see them off home . . . everybody.'

'They can see themselves off home, you get in.'

As Mary went to force her down the steps Annie evaded her mother's hands, saying harshly, 'Have a bit sense, Ma; the siren's just gone, they could be ages.'

'They weren't ages last week, were they?'

Before Annie could answer a voice came out of the darkness, saying, 'You get down, Annie. I'm away to see me ma and them inside, I won't be long. Arthur's comin' along of me.'

'Get somebody to see Mona and her ma home, will you, Georgie?'

'Don't be silly girl –' Mary was pulling at her – 'Isn't Mr Broadbent there!'

'Aw, Ma, you know he's got bad sight. He can hardly see in the daylight never mind the dark . . . See to it, Georgie, will you?'

'Aye, aye, I'll see to it. Get yoursel' in, don't worry. But my God, it would happen the night, wouldn't it . . . That bloody man! All this through one bloody man. He's a bastard. . . .'

When Mary reached the bottom of the steps and went into the air-raid shelter she could still hear Georgie's voice coming from the direction of the scullery describing what he would do to that bastard if he only had him within arm's length.

'It's a pity he can't open his mouth without swearing.'

'Who better should he swear at than Hitler, Ma?'

The silence told Annie of her mother's set lips and tight face, and when she had lit the old-fashioned lamp that hung from a nail on the brick wall between the bunks it showed Mary's face as she had visualized it, and she said softly, 'I'm . . . I'm sorry, Ma.'

Mary made no answer, and after a moment Annie said, 'Where's me da got to?'

'Where would he be but at the A.R.P. post.'

'It isn't his night on.'

'No, it isn't, but he's got an urge like other people I could mention to get themselves killed.'

'Oh, Ma!'

They sat on the bunks, one on each side of the shelter, opposite to each other, their knees almost touching, their postures almost identical, heads bent, hands gripped on their laps. After a time Annie said, 'We didn't bring the flask, will I go and get it?'

'No, you'll do no such thing.' Mary's head jerked upwards. 'I've . . . I've got a feeling on me. I don't know why, but I feel it's goin' to be a night of it.'

Annie restrained herself from saying, 'You've had those feelings before, Ma, you have them every time you come down here.

A second later her mother's prophecy brought them hurtling together, their arms about each other. Then they were on the floor, their heads bent towards their knees and making identical sounds as the trembling of the earth passed through them.

When the earth settled they heard the distant pop-popping of the anti-aircraft guns. They didn't speak; their arms still about each other, they waited, and there came the second earth shudder, not so strong this time, further away. Still they waited, not moving. Then came the third, distant this time, just like an echo.

Into the stillness now Mary's voice crept like that of a doddering old woman, saying, 'Hail Mary, full of grace, the Lord is with thee. B . . . blessed art thou amongst women and b . . . blessed is the fruit of thy wo . . . womb Jesus. Holy Mary, Mo . . . Mother of God, pray for us sinners now and at the hour of our death, Amen.'

'Hail . . . hail Mary, full of Grace, the L . . . Lord is with thee. . . .' Again the prayer was repeated. And again . . . and yet again.

When Annie went to straighten up, her fingers caught in the beads dangling from her mother's hand and she interrupted the rosary, saying, 'Ma! Ma! come on get up, it's over.' She had to shake Mary twice before she could get her from her knees.

When they were sitting side by side on the bunk Annie whispered, 'I wonder who got it; I hope they're all inside. I . . . I hope they reached home. I . . . I think I'll just have a look outside. . . .'

'You w . . . won't.' It was as if Mary had just woken up. 'You'll do no such thing, you'll st . . . stay where you are till your da comes.'

'But, Ma! if there are places flat he'll be at it to the middle of the night. Look . . . look, Ma.' She pulled herself away from the clinging hands and stood up. 'They've gone. There's no sound, and the guns have stopped. I'll just go in and look out of the front door. . . .'

'No! No! you'll not. You'll . . .'

'Stop it, Ma; I'm going.' When she slapped at her mother's hands Mary stared up at her and her face quivered in a conflict of fear and anger.

Annie quickly mounted the steps to the yard, then stopped. Fancy slapping at her ma like that. Eeh! they were all in a state. She should have said she was sorry. But her ma wouldn't let her forget it; oh no, she could be sure of that.

Everything was quiet. She looked upwards. The stars were shining, the rain had stopped, it was a clear night.

Who had got it? It had been very near, that first one. She went through the house and opened the front door and, standing on the pavement, she looked up and down the street. There were no fires, no busy to-and-froing of people. Everybody here was all right. But beyond the end of the street, more towards the main road, there was a glow in the sky. When she heard footsteps approaching on the opposite side of the road she called out 'Where is it? Who got it?'

And the voice answered her from the dark, 'Armada Street, Primrose Street, and around there.'

She put her hand to her mouth. Armada Street. That, that was where Georgie lived, Armada Street. Had . . . had they reached home and managed to get into the shelter before it dropped? Her breath stuck in her throat. They could all be dead, all of them. Georgie . . . Georgie could be dead!

The wave of relief that this possibility brought to her also swung her round and caused her to bury her head in the crook of her arm against the stanchion of the door. Oh dear God! how could she? But apparently she could, for her thoughts went on. If he was dead it would solve everything. The child would have a name; she'd still be a married woman and she would get a pension. . . . Oh my God! she was wicked. That's what she was, wicked. She'd have to go to confession, and she wouldn't have to skip it, she'd have to tell Father Carey exactly what she had thought. Fancy . . . fancy wishing Georgie dead.

After a moment she went into the house again, being careful to bolt the front door after her. The whole place looked chaotic. In the scullery she made a fresh pot of tea and put it on a tray with the crockery and carried it down into the shelter.

Her mother was sitting exactly where she had left her. She looked up at her and said, 'Well?'

'Armada Street and Primrose Street and around there.'

'Armada Street?'

The hopeful tone of the voice brought Annie's head down and she felt sick enough to vomit. 'Don't wish him dead, Ma!' She was shouting at the top of her voice.

'Wish him dead? What's the matter with you, girl? Wish who dead?'

'You know, you know . . . Armada Street. You know all right.'

'You're out of your senses, girl. Everything's been too much for you.' Mary sounded now as if she had completely regained her composure.

'Yes, yes, it has.' The tears were spurting from her eyes, her voice was spiralling upwards as if aiming to force its way through the stones and soil above the shelter. 'I know, I know. Happy release it would be, wouldn't it? Happy release.'

'Take a pull at yourself, girl –' Mary was shaking her by the shoulders – 'and stop that screeching. Sit down there.' She pushed her on to the bunk, then busied herself with pouring out the tea. When she handed Annie the cup she said, 'Get that down you. You've had too much to drink, that's your trouble.'

'I haven't, I haven't.' She was shouting again. 'I've only had a port, only one.'

'Drink that tea. And you want to remember, girl, before you indulge yourself in hysterics, that your carry-on is going to affect what you're carrying.'

Her head moving with each sobbing intake of breath, Annie stared up at her mother. It was the first time she had referred to the child. She turned her gaze away, then raised the cup to her lips and slowly began to sip the tea,

It was just as Mary had seated herself on the bunk again that the heavy footsteps sounded on the steps; then the door was slowly pushed open, and Dennis stood there. He looked like a man who had been loading cement, for from the top of his tin helmet to his boots he was covered in a grey dust. His face was all grey, the only spots of colour being the small round dark globes of his eyes and the red gap that appeared and disappeared as he opened his mouth a number of times to speak.

'What is it? Oh my God, look at you! What's happened, man?' Mary was pushing him down on to the bunk.

Staring into her face, he muttered, 'Gi' us a drink of tea . . . Have . . . have you any hard down here?'

'Hard? No, no, we haven't.' The words were jerked out. Mary put her hand back towards the tray and lifted her own cup from it, saying as she did so, 'Tell us what happened, man.'

When he took the cup from her it wobbled in the saucer and she put out her hands to steady it. He brought the cup to his mouth and swallowed the whole of the contents; then he said, 'Billy . . . Billy's dead.'

'Billy? You mean Mr McCabe?'

'Aye, Billy McCabe.' He nodded his head twice. 'Him who was laughing fit to bust an hour or so ago, he'll laugh no more.' He turned his eyes to Annie who was standing close by his side now, her teeth pressed down tight on her fingernails, and he went on, 'They were nearly home, just passing the corner of Primrose Street so they tell me, when the whole side of a house fell flat on him. He was the last one. He said he wasn't goin' to bloody well run for Hitler or nobody else. Georgie and his mother and the bairns were all knocked flat, must have been knocked yards but they weren't scratched, only shaken. But –' he now put his hands up and gripped Annie's arm as he said, 'that's not all, lass. Mona, she got it an' all. An' the young fellow, Arthur. They . . . they had branched off and gone round the bottom of Armada Street, it . . . it caught them both.'

'Oh no, Da, no! no! not . . . not Mona.'

'It's all right, lass, at least it isn't as bad as it could be. They're . . . they're in hospital. But it's the finish for him poor lad as far as the forces go, 'cos one of his legs was crushed to pulp. And . . . and Mona, poor Mona, she got it in the face.'

She thought she was going to faint. She screwed up her face and covered it with both hands. After a moment she brought them to her throat and stood gripping it as she asked, 'Where . . . where are they? Where've they taken them?'

'Ingham. Look, lass.' He put out his hand and grabbed her. 'It's no use you goin' down there, the place is like a shambles. Wait till the morrow. But where you can go, and where you should go now is along to see how Georgie's gettin' on. He had his hands full when I left him.'

'No! No! The all-clear hasn't gone yet.' Mary thrust her hand out to stop Annie turning around, and Dennis's voice, sharp for the first time since he had come into the shelter, snapped, 'One of us has to go along there, and it's her place. Get it into your head, lass, it's her place. . . . Go on.' He pushed Annie and again said, 'Go on!'

She went scurrying up the steps and into the black backyard. In the kitchen she paused for a second and groaned aloud, 'Oh God!' Mr McCabe was dead. She felt as if she had picked up a gun and fired and hit the wrong one. When her stomach heaved and she went to turn towards the sink she checked herself, saying, 'Give over, Pull yourself together.' Then she ran upstairs and dragged on her coat.

There was a lot of movement in the streets, people hurrying backwards and forwards, voices calling. It took her five minutes to reach the McCabes' house. She had only been in it twice before and hadn't been enamoured of what she saw. The furniture was a mixture of dilapidated and modern, with the modern additions more kicked about and knife-scarred then the older pieces.

She knocked on the door. It was opened by Winnie. Winnie was crying; she was still wearing her bridesmaid's dress which had been chosen with an

eye to utility rather than to prettiness. Earlier in the day it had been a dark
blue colour, now it was grey and black in parts.

The door led immediately into the kitchen and there, seated round the
table, were Daisy and her husband and the twins. Mollie was standing by
the open fire pushing a pan from the hob into the glowing coals. She turned
about and looked at Annie, and Annie walked towards her, then stopped as
she almost fell over the end of the oxidized kerb.

'I'm . . . I'm sorry. Ever so sorry.'

'Aye . . . aye, we're all sorry, lass.' Mollie straightened her back. Her
mouth was no longer slack and her face looked as if it had never smiled.
Annie noticed with surprise that she wasn't crying and that her eyes showed
no sign of recent tears; her voice was level when she spoke, and her manner,
in fact everything about her, was quite different from what she had expected.
She watched her turn towards the table and sit down opposite a plastic tray
decorated with cabbage roses, on which stood a brown earthenware teapot
and a tin of condensed milk, and, reaching out to the nearest cup, she ladled
a running spoonful of the milk into it, then filled it with the black steaming
tea and handed it to her.

Annie didn't want any more tea, she felt she never wanted to eat or drink
again. Her throat was so full that nothing would pass down it, but nevertheless, she took the cup from the proffered hand and said, 'Ta. Ta, Mrs
. . . Mollie.'

'Sit down, sit down, lass. . . . Move yourself over, our Archie, along the
form there.'

When Archie had shuffled along the form and pushed against Mike,
Annie sat down in the place he had vacated, and Mollie, looking at her,
said, 'He had his faults but I ask you, and God, who hasn't? But he wasn't
lazy. No, he hadn't a lazy bone in his body. He drank. Aye, more than his
share, but I'm tellin' you this, he sweated his guts out to work for it. But
afore anything else he saw that we were all fed.' She looked around the
table. 'Aye, he did that. An' clothed an' all, for as he used to say, if their
bellies were full they wouldn't need so many clothes on their backs. He was
one for a joke when he could think of it. He was like Georgie.' She now
stared into Annie's face and, as if she were qualifying the statement she had
just made, she added, 'He hadn't much up top either, but there were worse.
Aye by God! there were worse. He never looked at another biddy, I'll say
that for him.'

Annie had been shivering with the cold when she entered the house, now
her body was hot all over. She wished, oh she wished Mollie, in fact
everybody, would stop referring to Georgie as a nitwit. Where was he
anyway? Where was Georgie? She asked the question.

'Where is Georgie now?' she said.

'At the hospital, lass. Aye, I suppose you heard, your da would tell you
about . . . about Arthur. Aye, our Georgie's proper cut up with one thing
and another, an' he feels responsible like for bringin' Arthur all this way.
It's his leg. He said it was in a mess when they got him out. An' your pal,
Mona; hit her in the face it did. My God! this has been a night. Marriage
an' death; only the middle has been missed out, we only wanted a birth,
that's all. . . . Pity –' her head nodded now – 'pity you're not on your time,
lass; you could have completed the sayin' the night; from the church to the

birth, from the birth to the burial, from the burial to hell in the mornin'. You know, it goes to the tune of John Peel.'

Annie was gazing at Mollie with a stupefied stare. She wasn't meaning to be funny, yet there she was sitting, sullen looking, dry-eyed, saying a thing like that, and telling you it went to the tune of John Peel. She felt she wanted to laugh, high screaming laughter. Was she going to go off her head? She looked around at the others. Nobody had spoken, not a word; they all looked half-asleep, dazed. Was she dreaming?

The front door opening abruptly proved to her that she wasn't dreaming. She turned with them all to watch Georgie coming in. He looked at her as he walked to the table, and when he reached her side, he said, 'Hello,' and she was forced to answer, 'Hello.'

'You shouldn't't've come out,' he said.

'I'm all right,' she answered.

'How . . . how did you find them?' asked Mollie, looking up at him.

He turned to her, saying 'Wouldn't let me in; they're not lettin' anybody in.'

'Do you want a cup of tea?' she said.

'No.'

'Have somethin' to eat then?'

'No, no, I want nowt to eat. What time is it, me watch has stopped?' He looked at his wrist-watch, and Mollie turned towards the mantelpiece and, after gazing at the clock for a second, she said, 'That says ten to eleven, but it's either fast or slow, you can never go by it.'

There followed a silence, during which he placed his hand on Annie's shoulder; then after a while, he said, 'Come on, I'll see you back home.'

When Annie had risen to her feet he looked down at his mother and added, 'I'll be back shortly.'

'No need, lad.' She, too, had risen to her feet. 'No need.'

'I'll be back all the same.'

Annie made no farewells but walked towards the door, with Georgie behind her, and Mollie behind him, saying again, 'I tell you, lad, there's no need.' And on this he turned on her, crying, 'Well I'm bloody well comin' back whether you like it or not.'

The three were standing on the step now. Mollie pulled the door behind her to shut out the light and she asked quietly, 'Where did they put your da?'

'The mortuary.'

'Think they'll let me see him?'

There was a pause in the darkness before he said, 'It wouldn't be much good.'

There was another pause before she answered, 'Like that, is it?'

'Like that.'

Annie heard Mollie smacking her lips as if she had just eaten something tasty; then she said, 'Look, lad, I mean this. Frank'n Daisy are stayin' an' there'll be no place for you to sleep. It's like that, you see, so go on with Annie an' sleep where you intended the night. Come round first thing in the mornin' an' we'll talk things over. Perhaps you could ask for a bit of compassionate leave or somethin'.'

'Aye, I'll try for that. . . . But you're sure you'll be all right if I . . . ?'

'I'll be all right, lad. Though it doesn't matter much at the moment one way or t'other.'

There was another silence before Georgie said, 'Ta-rah then, Ma.'

'Ta-rah, lad. Ta-rah, lass. I'm sorry for all this, hinny.'

Annie couldn't speak for a moment; it was as if his mother was blaming herself for the raid, for the upheaval of the wedding, for the spoiling of their first night together. She said softly, 'Ta-rah, Mollie,' then turned away.

They had walked the length of three streets before Georgie spoke, and then he said, 'I'll never forgive meself.'

'What?'

'Arthur catchin' it. Comin' this way just to do me a good turn and then bloody well catching it. He's a nice bloke.' His head was turned towards her and she peered at him through the darkness; she wouldn't have been surprised to know that he was crying for his voice had a cracked sound. 'Best pal I've ever known, never made a pal like him. And he's class. He is, you know, he's class.' His voice had risen. 'Not like us, me, scum. His people've got a fine house in Hereford, ten great rooms and a bloody big garden. Near as big as a park it is, two acres. He's got a sister married to a solicitor, and two brothers. One's an accountant. He's the black sheep himself he says. Hasn't got any brains, he says, but he has more brains than the whole bloody establishment at Madley. But he plays them down. He has a kink that way makin' on he knows nowt. His people are swell. They are, they are, Annie, swell. When he first took me to his place I was like a cat on hot bricks; you never saw such a house. And after what I come from there was all the difference atween Buckingham Palace an' the netty. And another thing, his mother made me as welcome the second time an' the third as she did the first. I was just meself, I'd be hard put to try an' be anything else, an' she nor his dad didn't think, Aw, here's Georgie, the bloody numskull, comin'. ... You know somethin', Annie, you know somethin'?' He was shouting now. 'You're just as good as you make folks think you are. That's somethin' I've learned, you're just as good as folks think you are. Tell them you're a numskull an' you are a numskull. By God! I've learned somethin' since I've been away. I could buy the lot around here at one end of the street an' sell them at t'other. I could that. And you know somethin' else? Arthur stayed as an A.C.1. 'cos he wanted to be along of me, along of me mind. He could've been L.A.C. Bloody fool, I said he was, bloody fool, 'cos there he was, helpin' the other bods with their papers to get through. He's got a kink; I keep tellin' him, he's got a kink. He was nearly a conchie, an' he said he would be if he was moved out of the kitchen. Ask him to kill a bloke he said an' that's what he would be, a conchie. And I believe him. By God, there's not many like him. And to bring him all this bloody way to give him a packet. He was as safe as houses in Hereford. Hereford, they don't know there's a war on there. I've been there eighteen months, an' they've had one bloody raid, one bloody little raid and the bastards thought it was the end of the world. The only ones that get their packets are the poor bloody goons coming down in the Black Mountains. But Arthur ... but Arthur –' his voice had dropped now to a thick murmur – 'without a leg, maybe both. And he loved to walk. Tramp the countryside he would whenever he got the chance. ... God Almighty! I'll never forgive meself to me dyin' day.'

'Don't! don't! Georgie. 'Tisn't your fault'. She gripped his arm. 'Don't look at it like that. Perhaps it was for the best; if . . . if he didn't want to fight. . . .'

She slipped into the gutter as he pulled his arm from her, crying, 'Christ! he wouldn't want to lose his legs to save himself from fightin'. He could have been classed as a conchie and had it easy on some farm or other. Christ! to lose his legs.'

'I'm sorry, Georgie, I didn't mean. . . .'

After a while he said, 'It's all right; I know you didn't mean anythin' like that.' He took her arm again, and his voice almost indistinct now, he said, 'Aw, Annie, the night of all nights, I was goin' to show you what a decent fellow I could be, I wasn't goin' to get drunk. Well, I didn't get drunk, but I was goin' to treat you as I know you would like to be treated 'cos . . . 'cos like Arthur you're different. And I know you're different. I'm bloody lucky. I've thought all day, when I was in the church, an' especially as I was sitting at the table, I thought, Georgie McCabe you're a bloody lucky bloke. You've got a pal like Arthur, an' a wife like Annie. . . . And now, now this. . . . I'm sorry.'

She wanted to say, 'I'm sorry an' all, Georgie,' for she'd come near to loving him at this moment; but they had reached the door of the house and she opened it and as they went in the thought occurred to her that he hadn't once mentioned his father.

Her mother was in the kitchen busily putting things to rights. She stopped what she was doing and looked at them; and then her eyes focused on Georgie. His clothes were begrimed, his face was dirty, but besides being dirty it had a sad heavy look about it and in spite of her feelings towards him she said kindly, 'Sit down, lad. How's your mother taking it?'

'Pretty well, thanks, Mrs Cooper. Pretty well, considerin'.'

'Have you found out how your friend is?'

'Pretty bad, Mrs Cooper, pretty bad. Mona an' all. But we won't know the details until the morrow, things are pretty hectic down there at the hospital.'

'Yes, yes, they would be. Can I get you a drink of anything?'

'I'll . . . I'll have a drop of hard if there's any left, Mrs Cooper. Thank you all the same.'

'Yes, yes, of course, Georgie. What . . . what about you, Annie, do you want anything?'

'No, Ma, nothing. I'll go up and take me coat and things off.'

'Yes, do that, do that.'

As she made to go towards the passage doorway leading to the stairs she was stopped, as also was Mary about to go into the scullery, by Georgie saying, 'You go on to bed, I'll be up later.'

It was as if they had been married for years. She glanced over his head towards her mother before swinging her gaze sharply away; then, with her back turned towards him, she said, 'Yes, I'll do that, I'm tired.' And to this she added, 'Will . . . will you look in, Ma?'

There was a pause before Mary said, 'Yes, yes, I'll be up in a minute.'

In her bedroom under the muted light given off by the green crinkled paper over the pink lampshade, she undressed rapidly, not pausing as she sometimes did to examine her figure through the foot square of mirror, or hold it at an angle as she peered for a blemish on the skin of her shoulders or thighs. She did not even stop to take the powder off her face with a thin layer of Pond's night cream, before adding a thicker layer which promised beauty in the morning. Scrambling, she got into her nightdress, not a new one, but her best one, which she had made herself and adorned with a herring-bone yoke; then bundling her underclothes into a drawer, for there seemed to be something indecent in the casual way she had draped them over the back of a chair, she got into bed.

Her bed wasn't a single bed, nor yet a full-sized bed, it was of the size her mother had once described as, doing at a pinch. It was covered with an artificial pink silk bedspread under which was a matching feather-stuffed eiderdown. Even in her present state she had been careful to turn the bedspread well back – her mother couldn't stand the top being crumpled.

Stretching her length out, not in the middle, as she was wont to do, but towards the edge, she pulled the sheets up under her chin and lay waiting. And within five minutes her mother opened the door.

Mary had always come in and bidden her daughter goodnight. She would walk to the bed, straighten the turned-down bedspread, pulling the corners into points, sometimes even folding it once more to ensure it was not rumpled. At one time she had taken it off altogether, until Annie had complained that the eiderdown slipped off in the night when the bedspread wasn't there to hold it in place. Then she would pat the bed two or three times, saying, 'Well now, settle down; you're all right, aren't you?' and Annie invariably answered, 'Yes, Ma.'

'Very well then,' would be Mary's response; 'goodnight. Don't keep that light on, mind. Goodnight.'

But tonight she did not enter the room, she was beginning a new pattern. The door half-open, she stood with her hand gripping the knob and, looking towards her daughter, she said, 'All right?' and when Annie, after a moment, answered, 'Yes, Ma,' she said, 'Goodnight then.'

'Goodnight, Ma.'

When the door closed Annie bit tight on her lip to stop herself from crying. She could have come in, she could have done what she always did, turn the bedspread, pat the bed, stand near her. She never kissed her, she didn't expect to be kissed, but she could have come in; tonight of all nights she could have come in. After she had held her tightly in the scullery she thought things would be different. Oh, her ma! her ma was a funny 'un.

She heard her da's voice now coming up from the kitchen talking to Georgie. She was glad he was back. Georgie wouldn't feel so bad having him to talk to.

As she lay listening to the deep rumbling of the voices her body relaxed somewhat. Then after some time she heard her mother come upstairs and the door across the little landing open and close, and she knew her da would soon follow.

But her da didn't soon follow. The voices downstairs went on, and on, and on, and their low drawl turned into a lullaby so that in spite of herself she dropped asleep. . . .

She didn't know what had wakened her. It wasn't Georgie entering the room or getting out of his clothes, for when she opened her eyes she saw him sitting in the wicker armchair to the side of the bed dressed in pyjamas. His back was bent, he had his elbows on his knees and his face was buried in his hands. She lay staring at him for some time. He was making a smothered sound and aiming to compress it with his hands.

Slowly she hitched herself over to the other side of the bed and, throwing the clothes back, she brought her feet to the ground. Then tentatively she put out her hand and touched the side of his head, whispering, 'Georgie! Georgie!'

His head jerked and sank lower, and she moved nearer to him and said again, 'Georgie!'

Like a child now he turned towards her. Her arms instinctively went about him, and as his head pressed into her shoulder and she felt his wet face against her warm flesh she stared, slightly open-mouthed, at the wall in front of her.

She had imagined all kinds of things happening on this night but the last thing on God's earth, she told herself she could have imagined, would be holding him while he cried. It was odd but she had never heard a man cry, she had never seen a man cry; women at funerals, yes, howling their eyes out, but men, no. Yet in this moment, Georgie, who was crying like a child, appeared more of a man to her than he had done before.

She did not question her actions when she eased him up from the chair and sat him on the side of the bed; then, having thrust the bedclothes well back, pressed him gently downwards and pulled the covers over him; after which she put out the light.

Getting into the bed from her side, she now drew him towards her, muttering softly, 'There now, Georgie. There now. It's all right.' But instead of her gentleness easing his grief it seemed but to increase it, and she had to pull the bedclothes up over their heads in case the sound of his sobbing should penetrate across the landing.

When his spasm of grief eventually subsided he muttered thickly, 'I'm sorry, Annie, I'm sorry.'

'Nothing to be sorry for, Georgie.'

He lay inert against her, spent; then after a time he said, 'Me da wasn't such a bad bloke, you know.'

'No, Georgie, no, he wasn't.'

'I'll never be able to look Arthur in the face again.'

'That's silly, Georgie; you're not to blame.'

'I am. I begged him to be me best man.'

'He wanted to be.'

'Aye, aye, he said he did, but . . . but he had an awful lot of trouble to get off. He'd had two forty-eight's recently, an' what's more he's been on a charge. He's against church parades.' There was another pause before he said, 'I'll . . . I'll have to stand by me ma, Annie. She'll need help; she's still got three of them to see to; there'll be no pension, him being casual like in the docks.'

'That's all right, Georgie. We'll sort that out after, don't worry about that.'

'There's nobody like you, Annie.'

She was silent.

'Me da said that, he said it only yesterday mornin', and he was solid and sober. He said "You're lucky, chum, she's another like your ma, she'll stand by you." Me da was all right; he was what he was 'cos things made him that way. Bloody governments, Conservative or Labour or National, all alike; no work, no bloody chance for a man with brains, never mind without. It's like Arthur says, you're what your en-environ makes you, Annie.'

'Yes, Georgie.'

'I'm, I'm sorry I'm no good the night, Annie.'

'Oh, Georgie! be quiet, be quiet. Go to sleep.'

'Thanks, Annie. There's nobody like you, Annie. . . .'

He was no good the night. . . . It was funny how your prayers were answered; but what a price to pay for such an answer.

# Chapter One

## Demob

'Ma, don't give him any more taffy; his first teeth won't be in five minutes afore they'll be ruined. You're spoiling him.'

'Spoiling him! Look who's talking. If I'm spoiling him you've already ruined him, lifting him up every time he whimpers. If he's able to walk by the time he's five he'll be lucky. Spoiling him indeed!'

'Will you two stop it!' Dennis's voice was low and tired-sounding. 'If that bairn ever survives it'll be a miracle to me. Torn in two he'll be between you. An' she's right.' He was nodding towards Mary now. 'He won't have any teeth by the time you've finished stuffin' bullets into him.'

'They're less harmful than sips of beer.'

'Sips of beer won't do him any harm, woman.'

'No? Between you and Mollie McCabe he'll be well on the bottle afore he can walk, and then by the way you're going on he'll never walk straight. Next time I see her at it I'll tell her about it, no matter what you say.'

'You'll do no such thing, d'you hear?' Dennis's voice was grim. 'Twice you've seen her give the child a sip, and that's all, and the way you manoeuvre things she doesn't get much chance to get near him. If you had your way you'd put a notice up: No McCabes allowed. Not even the father. So there you have it.'

Dennis had risen to his feet, thrown down his paper, and was stamping out of the kitchen when Mary's 'Well!' checked him, and he turned to her and repeated, 'Aye, well, now you've had it.'

'Perhaps you'll think of moving your lodgings.'

Dennis had reached the passage, but he seemed to spring back to the doorway and, poking his head in, he cried, 'I might at that, you never know,' before disappearing again.

Mary turned and looked at Annie, but Annie had her head bowed over the child. When, however, Annie did look at her mother, the expression on Mary's face made her say, 'Don't take any notice, Ma; you know he's only kiddin'.'

'It's come to something.' Mary's lips were trembling. 'That family, that woman.'

'She means no harm, Ma.'

'That's right, you take her part an' all.'

'Well, she doesn't. What harm has she ever done you? She's got an awful life of it really. Having to go out to work and still see to the others when she gets home, and Winnie being such a handful, and the twins not much better.

That's one thing I'll be glad about anyway when Georgie is demobbed, he'll see to them.'

They now looked at each other. Then, her gaze dropping away, Annie turned about, hitched the child farther up into her arms, and went into the scullery, where she took a wet flannel from a peg by the sink and wiped the child's mouth, saying, 'Keep still now, keep still.'

The child had been named Terence which had quickly been shortened to Rance. He had fair curls, a round face and dark eyes. To match the face the eye sockets too should have been round, but they were oval-shaped and gave to the eyes an oriental quality. He was apt to go into deep sulks; deprived of his own way, he didn't scream or kick as might have been natural but, pressing his lips together, he would hold his breath until he nearly choked, then when thumped on the back and forced to take in air he would assume a grieved silence which in one so young made the adults say, 'Now would you believe it! He knows what he wants that one and means to get it. By! he's a marler.'

In his small world young Rance captivated all adults, with the exception of Dennis, who was wont to say more often as time went on, 'That young fellow wants his backside smacked, an' if I had anything to do with it he would get it afore and after meals.'

When Mary came into the scullery Annie went on wiping the child's face as she said, 'Ma, I . . . I think I'd better tell you, I'm after a house.'

'. . . What!' The word had a startled sound; it gave the impression of utter incredulity. 'What!' she said again, then added, 'After a house? Since when?'

'Oh. Oh, I've been on the lookout for some time.'

'Well, of all the underhand. . . .'

'Now, Ma.' Annie turned round, throwing the flannel into the sink as she did so, then said bitterly, 'Georgie will be out next week, he'll be out for good, and what life do you think we're going to have here? You still can't stand the sight of him; nothing he does is right.'

'Is it right for you? Let me ask you that. Truthfully, answer me truthfully, girl. Is it right for you? The things he does!'

'Not all, Ma, not all. But I'll have a chance to correct them if we're on our own.'

'He can't open his mouth but oaths come out . . . obscenities.'

'Don't dare say that, Ma. You know I wouldn't stand that. He doesn't use bad language, it's just swearing, just ordinary swearing. And you'd think you'd never heard swearing. Believe me, me da can hold his own when he gets going. Bloody and bugger are nothing to it.'

'Don't you foul your mouth, girl. Huh! this is forthcoming events casting their shadows before; you'll be as bad as his mother before you finish up.'

'I won't be as bad as his mother.' Annie's voice was low now. 'And if I was like her I wouldn't be bad. Mollie isn't bad, she's rough, but not bad. She's better than some I could put a name to.'

'How dare you! How dare you, girl! My own daughter saying. . . .'

'I'm not meaning you, Ma.'

'Oh no!'

'Look, Ma. We're fighting, we're fighting now and Georgie isn't here. If Georgie was here he wouldn't sit by and let you get away with it. He mightn't, as you infer every time you can, have much up top, but he's got that much up top he wouldn't stand by an' see you going for me. That's just one of the things I want to avoid, so we'll be moving. Just after Christmas we'll be moving.'

Annie turned away as she saw her mother's face crumple, saying softly now, 'It won't be far, just down below Thornton Avenue.'

'My God! Thornton Avenue, near the Arab quarter. You've taken it? You haven't, have you? You haven't taken it?' Her voice was a thin squeak and Annie answered, still quietly, 'Yes, Ma, I've taken it; and it's not in the Arab quarter.'

'It's the dock quarter. If it's round the dock quarter it's round. . . .'

'Yes it's the dock quarter. It used to be Hanlin's coal depot. The house is in the yard. It's not bad at all, and I'm lucky to get it. It's got two up and two down like this, but it's bigger. I mean the rooms are bigger. And the scullery, why, why I'm tellin' you, Ma, it's nearly as big as the kitchen, it is.' She went on talking as her mother slowly turned from her and walked away. And when the child put its hands on each of her cheeks and pressed her mouth outwards she leant her face towards him and whispered, 'Oh Rance. Rance.'

The atmosphere in the house was not much lighter when at six o'clock that evening Mona came in unexpectedly.

'Why, hello! I didn't think to see you till the week-end. When did you get back? . . . Ma!' Annie turned her head and called upstairs. 'Here's Mona. . . . Sit down. Sit down. By! you're looking fine. Well tell us. Why did you come back so soon?'

Mona, an entirely different Mona from the bridesmaid of that February day in '43, smiled broadly and turned her head fully round to look towards Dennis as she said, 'Tell us, she says, Mr Cooper, and she doesn't let us get a word in, does she?'

'Well, you should know her by now, Mona,' laughed Dennis. 'But as she says, sit yourself down. Have you had any tea?'

'Yes, yes, I went straight home from the train and had a meal.'

'You're looking bonny, Mona.'

The smile did not slide from Mona's face as it sometimes did when any reference was made to her appearance. At first she had found it hard to adjust to a glass eye and a zig-zag scar that started at the lobe of her left ear and traced its way across her neck to disappear between her breast bones. Yet the fight to adjust to the new condition had given her a self-assurance and an animation that hadn't been hers before. Before the raid she had been a plain girl, a dull girl some would have said, mousy. She was still plain but it was a different plainness; her nervous animation had, in a way, released her personality.

She swung round now in her chair and looked to where Mary was entering the room, saying, 'Hello, Mrs Cooper.'

'Oh hello, Mona. You're back soon. I thought you were staying until the week-end?'

'I was, but something happened.'

'I knew it.' Annie nodded at her father. 'I knew something had happened to her. I could tell as soon as she came in.' Annie now pulled her chair up close to Mona, adding, 'Well, come on, don't keep us in agony. And anyway, if you don't open your mouth and tell us, I'll tell you, and I'll only have one guess out of three.'

'Aw you!' Mona pushed at her, and they laughed at each other knowingly. Then whipping off her glove, Mona held out her hand.

'My! My!' Dennis's exclamation was deep and sincere. 'By lass! isn't that lovely. A half-hoop of diamonds. Aye, it's bonny, grand.'

'Oh, it is, Mona. Oh, it's beautiful, lovely.' Annie's response was utterly genuine, without a trace of jealousy in it, but when at last Mary spoke, looking down at the extended hand she said, 'Very nice. Yes, very nice. You're very fortunate. I suppose you know that, Mona, very fortunate.'

'Yes, Mrs Cooper; nobody knows it better than me.'

Annie looked at her mother as she turned away and it was on the tip of her tongue to exclaim, 'You're a bitter pill, Ma. That's what you are, a bitter pill. Yes, she's fortunate, but trust you to rub it in.' She said now, quickly, 'What are they like, his people? I'm sick to death of hearing Georgie on about them. Royalty, that's what he thinks they are, royalty.'

Mona dropped her hands back into her lap. Then with her head on one side and her face straight, she looked directly at Annie as she said, 'They were a surprise, Annie. Perhaps it was me, but somehow I don't see them like Georgie sees them.'

'Snotty?'

'Snotty!' Mona turned and looked at Dennis and, a smile breaking her lips now, she nodded at him, saying, 'Yes, Mr Cooper, that's what I would say, snotty. Nice you know, nice, but snotty. And, and Arthur, well, he doesn't seem to belong among them. He's not a bit like them, except perhaps his sister, Olive. She's just a year older than him. She's nice enough. I like her. We didn't have much to say to each other but ... but I liked her. Though I couldn't say the same for her husband. Oh now –' she again nodded towards Dennis – 'if he lived around here do you know what they'd call him, Mr Cooper?' She gave a little giggle. 'A b ... nowt.'

'Oh, one of them, eh?'

'Yes, Mr Cooper, one of them. But Annie –' she turned fully round again – 'you'll see them all for yourself at Christmas.' She hunched her shoulders up. 'You've been invited, you and Georgie, for the Christmas holidays.'

'What! Us?'

'Aye. .... Eeh! there I go sayin' aye. .... Yes, Mrs McCabe.' She now assumed a high-faluting tone. 'Your husband will be bringing you the invitation come Wednesday week as ever was.' She now burst out laughing, then looked towards the scullery door where Mary was standing. They all looked towards the scullery door, and Mary said, 'What's that I was hearing?'

'I was saying that Annie and Georgie have been invited to go to Hereford for Christmas, Mrs Cooper.'

'That's what I thought you said.'

'Well –' Annie was now on her feet – 'if that's what you thought she said, Ma, you're not looking very pleased about it.'

'Well, should I be, leaving us here on our own, at Christmas an' all?'

'Oh my God! Ma.' Annie put her hand to her head, and Mary said quickly, 'That's it. Start to shout and wake him. .... And mentioning him, what about him?'

'He'll come with us, of course.'

'You're not traipsing the countryside with that child in the depth of winter and bringing him back here with pneumonia. Oh, no. Oh, no, me girl.'

'Ma!' Annie's voice was ominously quiet. 'Let me ask you a question. Whose child does he happen to be?'

'Aye, that's a good question.' Dennis rose from his chair and gave his wife one long look before leaving the kitchen and going into the passage. There was a pause that gave him time to put on his coat and cap, then the front door banged.

Annie now looked towards her mother, and Mary, through tight lips, muttered, 'You're determined to spite me, aren't you, girl? Not only jumping at the chance to spend Christmas with strangers but depriving me of the child at the same time.'

'Ma!' Annie's voice was still quiet. 'It surprises me, an' it has done since he was born, that you should take such an interest in him. Hating the father of him as you do, I wonder you look at him, 'cos don't forget, he's Georgie McCabe's child. And it's Georgie McCabe will let you know that once he's back for good. As for this Christmas business, I'll see what he says, and if he's willin' that I should leave the child with you I will, otherwise he'll come along of us.'

Her face red now, she turned to Mona, saying, 'He'll be asleep but would you like to come up and see him?' and without waiting for an answer she stalked from the room and Mona followed her.

Quietly Annie turned the handle of the bedroom door and they went in, and when they stood by the side of the cot that was placed near the bed Mona whispered, 'He gets bonnier.'

Annie made no comment on this but, staring down at the child, she said, 'Life's hell here, Mona; I'm getting out. I've got a house. It's not in a very good quarter, it's not far from the Mill Dam docks. It used to be Hanlon's coal depot, near Bunton's Corner.' She lifted her eyes and looked at Mona, then nodded and said, 'I know what you'll say, sailors, Arabs, the lot. But to tell you the truth, Mona, I wouldn't mind if there were Arabs upstairs and downstairs and left and right of me, anything will be better than living here when Georgie's back.'

'Yes, I can see that, Annie.' They moved from the cot to the farthest corner of the room, and there Annie asked in a low murmur, 'Do they really want us to go for Christmas?'

'Arthur does.'

'You say Arthur does, what about the rest?'

'Oh, it's a kind of open house, there's always people dropping in, all kinds of people. They're a bit arty-crafty. You know the type. You remember the Miss Burgess that used to teach standards four and five at school, well, they're something of that type, only more so if you know what I mean. During the war I understand they entertained all kinds.'

'That's why they accepted Georgie I suppose.' Annie's voice was flat.

Mona forced herself to say, 'No, no; they like Georgie. And Arthur thinks the world of him, he does really.'

'Oh, I know Arthur likes him, but I think that's just because Georgie likes him so much. Georgie's always been grateful because Arthur took notice of him.'

'I don't think it's like that.'

'Oh, I know what I know, Mona, and we two don't need to cover up things. Anyway –' she turned towards the door – 'they must have liked him for himself in some way else he wouldn't have kept going back. He's not so thick-skinned that he wouldn't have noticed how they felt, I mean if they were just tolerating him for Arthur's sake. Anyway –' she turned her head and looked at Mona and whispered, 'I'll see for meself if I go, won't I? And tell me, how did Arthur come on about the job?'

Mona smiled wryly and jerked her head. 'He got it and turned it down. He said he didn't fancy sitting on an office stool for the rest of his days. You know what he's after now? A little pub out in the wilds. It's sort of two stone houses stuck together, miles from anywhere. And the views are beautiful. But I said to him, "Nobody'll come here for beer", and he said I'd be surprised 'cos in the summer the hills are thick with hikers. It's costing four hundred and fifty pounds, but he says when he's finished with it it'll be worth one thousand four hundred and fifty. I think his father's glad about it, if only that it's a good distance away. Arthur gets in his hair. They're an odd family, a mixture. Anyway, as you say, you'll see for yourself. And we'll get a giggle, if nothing else, eh?'

'Aye, Mona.' Annie nodded at her. 'I could do with a giggle. My God! yes, I could do with a giggle.'

## *Chapter Two*

'So you have left your baby at home?'

Annie stopped herself from exchanging a glance with Mona who was sitting to the side of her; instead, keeping her eyes on the woman opposite, she answered briefly, 'Yes.'

'Nice to get away from babies at times, isn't it?'

'Yes.'

'It was at your wedding that Arthur caught it, wasn't it?'

'. . . Yes.' She knew fine well that Arthur had caught it at her wedding. She was his mother, wasn't she, yet anyone more unlike a mother she had yet to see. She was sixty-five if she was a day but she acted like a skittish lass. Arthur was the youngest and she must have had him late. His brother, Peter, the one sitting on the couch near the fire, looked older than her da, and he was at that. From what she had gathered from Mona he was thirty-nine and the brother, David, sitting near him, was thirty-eight. There was over ten years, Mona said, between those two and Arthur and his sister Olive.

Having bairns late must have knocked her back into her second childhood, Annie thought. Talk about being mutton dressed up as lamb; she jumped about like a spring lamb, she was never still. And if she had remarked on her leaving the child once, since she had come into the house, she must have done it half a dozen times. She didn't seem to pay attention to what anyone was saying to her except when she was talking to the men. Oh, she paid attention then all right.

The house seemed full of men. There was the father, whom everybody called Gerald and who in his way was as skittish as his wife. Then there were the brothers, David and Peter, and the snotty one, Olive's husband, James Partridge they called him. He was standing now in the far corner of the drawing-room talking to another man named Ron. Ron had a tiny moustache and he looked like one of those fellows in that funny book Georgie had brought home, called *Plonk's Party*. It was all about the air force and the types in it. Then there were Arthur and Georgie; they were at the moment in the billiard room knocking the balls about. She hoped they stayed there, at least that Georgie did. The way he had greeted everybody when they came in made her feel embarrassed, he had acted as if he were back home. He had called the mother Gwen, and she had called him Georgie boy.

Mona was right. She had hinted pretty broadly that they would all take some sorting out, and they would that. She had been right about Olive, too. Olive was nice, she was what you would call a natural kind of girl – or woman. She looked thirty-five but she could be only twenty-eight, as she was just a year older than Arthur. And she had a nice child too, cute; he had spoken to her a short while ago. He had taken her hand and said, 'Hello. Do you know what I am going to get from Father Christmas?' He spoke beautifully. She would love Rance to speak like that one day, but there was little chance with Georgie about.

She had replied no, that she had no idea; and then he had made her laugh by saying sadly, 'Nobody seems to know what I am going to get from Father Christmas.'

'David.' The mother was calling across the room while screwing round on the couch and drawing her legs up under her like some loose-limbed carefree girl. 'Let's have a drink before dinner.'

Annie looked towards the son, David, who had his slippered feet well on to the big open hearth, and he yawned before he answered, 'If you have it now, sweetie, there'll be nothing for after. And don't forget it's Christmas Eve in the morning.'

'Christmas will be taken care of, darling. Richie has promised to drop in.'

'Oh! Oh!'

Annie's eyes followed David as he pulled himself up languidly from the second sofa and walked across the room to where a miniature bar had been erected in the corner. It had a counter stretching between the walls, and the shelves arranged against the walls supported bottles, all empty, and hanging from a wrought-iron bracket, that had once graced the front of an inn, was a sign on which was painted in red letters THE NAUGHTY BULL.

Annie turned her head slowly and looked at Mona. They were exchanging glances when the mother let out a high girlish shriek and, unwinding herself from the couch, stood straight with her face clasped between her hands while looking towards her eldest son and exclaiming, 'Oh Peter! you'll never forgive me. I forgot to tell you, Liz phoned when you were out. She wanted you to ring her back. Oh darling, I'm so. . . .'

The man with the balding head almost sprang from the couch now, crying, 'My God, Mother! that's hours ago. And she'll have been waiting all this time. She'll blow her top.'

As he hurried towards the door he looked towards his brother-in-law, James Partridge, and exclaimed, 'She's the limit, I tell you, she's the limit.'

Mrs Bailey now dropped petulantly down on to the couch again and, addressing Annie and Mona in a plaintive voice, she said, 'Well, there's so much to be thought of. And it was just as Olive arrived, and I wanted to see the child. He's sweet, isn't he, I mean Alan. Wonderful for five; so advanced, don't you think? . . . I must go and see about dinner or we'll never eat.'

She again bounced to her feet and turning her attention from the girls to her son, who was standing behind the bar filling glasses, she called to him, 'Bring mine into the kitchen, David, that's a dear boy.'

'Will do.'

Annie leant her head against the back of the couch. It wasn't real; all this wasn't real. Did they live like this all the time? Had the war made them like this? No, no; you could see similar set-ups on the pictures. Yes, that's what it was like, like looking at a film where all the people were larger than life, and funnier than life, and odder than life. Oh aye, odder than life.

But that woman, the mother of three grown men and a daughter, and a grandmother into the bargain, she wasn't real. Yet there was one thing real about her, and she knew what that was all right. She was man-mad; she was the kind of woman that would still be man-mad when she was seventy. That type never gave up. In a way she was like that Miss Swillwell back home, who even went after the young priest. There had been quite a do about that. She used to come to Mass dressed up to the eyes in the most startling colours. Way out she was. They said the gas man wouldn't go to her house alone, he always took a pal with him. . . . But then there was an excuse for her; you could be sorry for her for she had never been married. But this one here was well married. Why hadn't her husband put a stop to her gallop years ago? But he seemed like all the rest, treating her as if she were a young scatter-brained girl.

Of a sudden she had a great desire to be home. Over the distance 114 Weldon Street glowed with comfort and sanity. But they were to be here till the day after Boxing Day, and it wasn't Christmas Eve yet.

To save the last minute rush they had travelled down today, for tomorrow the trains would be crammed full. As it was, they had been bad enough; they'd had to stand for five of the eight hours in the freezing corridors. During the whole journey Georgie had aimed at cheering them up with details of this place and the reception they would get, and what Arthur and his mother and the rest of them would say when they saw him in civvies.

Their arrival was in a way the beginning of the end for her. She hadn't believed her ears when Mrs Bailey had taken Georgie in her arms and hugged him as she cried. 'Oh Georgie boy! you look wonderful,' for in her opinion nobody with two eyes in their head could say that Georgie looked wonderful in civvies. His suit, besides being a workhouse grey, was as ill-fitting as any she had seen on the old fellows who came out on a Sunday from Harton Workhouse. As her da said, it fitted where it touched; and he had said it openly to Georgie, but Georgie's answer was, he didn't care a bloody damn; he'd wear anything, even a shift, as long as it wasn't air force blue.

As she looked down the long drawing-room that was over furnished with couches and chairs, she had the crazy idea of saying she was going for a walk, then phoning Mr Wilson's shop on the corner and asking him to bring her mother to the phone. And when her mother came she would say to her, 'Phone the house and tell them me da's bad and I must come back.'

Eeh! the things that came into her head. She pulled herself up from the couch, saying softly to Mona, 'I'm going upstairs a minute,' and Mona said quickly under her breath, 'I'll come with you,' and they left the room without anyone commenting.

The drawing-room led into a large hall. This, too, was over furnished and had a musty smell. The whole house, Annie thought, had a musty smell, and it could do with a good spring clean, especially their bedroom. She had already remarked on the condition of the house to Georgie, but he had laughed and said, 'They're not like us back home, lass; they don't lay stock by the same kind of things. You'll see, you'll see.' He had appeared very knowledgeable, and she had thought how odd it was that Georgie, of all people, should be mixing with folks such as these, for in spite of their odd ways they were what you would call educated. Oh yes, she granted them that, for their accents hit you.

In the bedroom, she went straight to the wardrobe, took out her coat and, putting it round her, said softly to Mona, 'I'm freezin'; the whole place is like ice.'

'I know, I should have warned you. I've got two vests on under this and some fleecy knickers.' Mona plucked her dress away from herself at different points.

'Mona.'

'Yes.'

They stared at each other. 'I don't like it here.'

There was a pause before Mona answered, 'You'll get used to it; you'll get used to them; but I'll tell you something. I don't take much to it meself, 'cos I know they think Arthur's let himself down a mile in takin' up with me. Yet at the same time I sense it was sort of expected of him. You know what I mean? He's not one of them, he's the odd man out.'

'Good thing too. That's something in his favour. Oh my goodness! Mona, we'll get our death here. Are all the rooms like this?'

'Yes, except Gwen's.' Mona pulled a long face as she added, 'Arthur says that's the only thing his mother concedes to age, the need of a fire in her bedroom. And she has them all choppin' down trees in the wood. When I was here last she said to me, "Ooh! I wouldn't dream about using the co-al; that's needed for everyone's comfort; but a lettle bit of wood now. . . ."'

Mona's imitation of their hostess was so true to life that they had to smother their laughter against each other.

'Put another cardigan on,' said Mona now, 'and let's go down to the billiard room. . . .'

Just before they left the room Annie asked, 'Are there any other women coming, the place seems full of men?'

'David's wife is due tomorrow; the Peter one, he's parted from his.'

'Then who's this Liz who's going to blow her top?'

'Oh, his fancy piece.'

'Coo! they have them here an' all?'

They pushed at each other and again they laughed. . . .

In the billiard room, Georgie hailed them loudly, crying, 'Wondered when you'd turn up. Come and stand by me, love; you always bring me luck. This bugger's going to fleece me.' He nodded and grinned towards Arthur who was chalking his cue. 'Lost five bob to him already; we won't have enough for the groceries when we get back.'

Annie did not go to Georgie's side but stood with her back to the low fire

in the deep grate and, lifting her skirt slightly at the back to catch the
warmth, she said, 'Serve you right for throwing your money about.'

'I'll stand by you, Georgie.' As Mona went round the table Arthur turned
towards Annie and, after looking at her for a moment, said, 'Cold?'

'A little; it's freezing outside.'

'It's freezing in here too. I'm sorry about that.'

'Oh no, it's me, I always feel the cold.'

Arthur now came towards her with his jerky gait, which spoke only
slightly of his artificial leg, and still chalking the cue, he said, 'I want you
to enjoy yourself, Annie.'

'What?'

He now raised his eyes to hers and added softly, 'You must find my people
rather strange, their ways I mean. I do myself at times. And not just at
times, most of the time. But there, we are as God made us.' He stopped
speaking and stared at her, and she knew he wasn't referring to the whole
family but to his mother.

She answered quietly, 'Don't worry about me, Arthur, I'll enjoy meself.
It's Christmas, the war's over, it's marvellous, everybody startin' a new life.'

She glanced towards Georgie, who was standing beside Mona and explaining the game to her, talking of in-offs, off the red, and potting, and in the
seconds she listened to him he used two bloodies. She brought her gaze back
to Arthur's and, her eyes blinking now and her head drooping slightly, she
said, 'Georgie and his swearin', don't they object?'

'Object! . . . To bloody? No, of course not. And it's just like God bless
you! coming from Georgie. Is that what's been worrying you?' His long pale
face widened into a smile. 'Don't be silly, Annie.'

'I can't help it; it isn't everybody that would take it as God bless you! And
he gets a bit much at times.'

'Georgie's all right – nobody better.'

She looked straight into the face before her, and for the countless time she
asked herself what this man saw in Georgie, because in every way they were
as opposite as poles. His face had a tender refined look, and she could only
class his manner as, learned. In this moment she was puzzled too that he
should choose Mona for a wife, because Mona was ordinary. Well, by that
she meant just like herself; and let her face it, they were both like fish out
of water in this house. Georgie alone was unaffected by the atmosphere. If
he was out of the water, he wasn't aware of it.

'Come on –' Arthur took her hand – 'we'll take them on and show them
how to play, eh?'

She was protesting that she didn't know the first thing about it when the
sound of a bell echoed through the house.

'Ah, now we can eat.' Arthur smiled at her, adding, 'We'll show-em after
dinner eh?' Then lifting his arm, he bent it at the elbow and looking across
the table at Mona said, 'Miss Broadbent, allow me,' and Mona, laughing,
put her arm through his. Then Georgie, in an absurd imitation of Arthur's
voice, said, 'Mrs McCabe, aa-low me. Aa-low me.'

As they marched out of the billiard room, across the hall under the gaze
of James Partridge who was descending the stairs, Annie thought, We must
look daft, ridiculous; no wonder he looks down his nose.

The following morning they were forced to rise early in an attempt to get

warm for the room was like an ice-box and the bedclothes were inadequate.
As Georgie exclaimed under his breath while laughing indulgently, it was
bloody well worse than a Nissen hut, for there you did have the old stove
going.

It was only eight o'clock when they went downstairs but Arthur already
had the breakfast going, and in the muddled, none-too-clean kitchen, Annie
sat close to the stove and made her way through two large rashers of bacon,
two sausages and an egg while Georgie disposed of twice as much.

The next to arrive for breakfast was Mona, looking as frozen as she felt.
The two brothers, Peter and David, followed, but they took their meal into
the dining-room. Then Olive brought the child down. 'Isn't it terrible?' she
said. 'How did you sleep?' She looked from Annie to Mona, and they both
said together, 'Oh, very well, thank you.' Then they laughed.

After Olive had given the child his breakfast and was eating her own she
looked at her brother and asked, 'What's the programme for this morning?'

'Well,' Arthur smiled, 'if I can gather anything from the sight of your
faces I think it's warmth we want both inside and out, so if we don't want
to freeze for the next few days I propose we go wood cutting. What do you
say, Georgie?'

'Suits me. And I'll make these two work for their grub.' Georgie nodded
from Annie to Mona.

'Would you take him with you?' Olive made a slight motion with her
head towards the child while looking at her brother. 'He'd love that. I've got
to go into town; there's one or two things I need for the X . . . m . . . a . . . s
tree.'

'Of course, of course.' Arthur rumpled the small dark head of his nephew.
'We couldn't go wood cutting without Alan. Fancy you suggesting such a
thing.' He now bent down to the boy. 'We wouldn't dream about chop-
chopping without you, would we?'

The round, dark, merry eyes looked up into the long face, and the child
said, 'You're funny, Uncle, funny . . . funny . . . funny peck . . . Daddy says
you're funny peck.'

'Get on with breakfast, Alan, and stop chattering.' His mother's voice was
sharp. She turned from putting the finishing touches to a breakfast tray and
pushed her son none too gently on the shoulder, saying now, 'Behave yourself
and stop your chattering.' Then glancing at Arthur with an apologetic look
she said, 'I'll take Mother's up,' and left the kitchen.

As if he were just answering the boy's remark, Arthur now muttered
under his breath, 'There are some of us funny peckculiar and some funny
ha-ha.'

There was deep bitterness in the words and Annie looked sharply from
him to Mona, who was staring at him as was the child; only Georgie wasn't
giving him any attention, he was busy lighting a cigarette. . . .

The frosty air was bracing, and the men were sawing with more energy
than skill, while Mona, endeavouring to keep a small log upright in an
attempt to split it had them all laughing at her efforts.

It was as Annie and the child were gathering frozen chips from a previous
chopping that the boy, suddenly dancing from one foot to the other said, 'I
want to go to the jig.'

'Jig? Oh, I get you.' She laughed out loud. 'Come on then.' She took his
hand and ran him behind some low bushes. But there he continued his dance

and, looking up at her, said, 'I mustn't do it outside; Mummy said I mustn't do it outside.'

'You mustn't? Oh well, then we'll go inside.' She took him by the hand again, and shouted to the others, 'I won't be a minute, just taking him to the . . .' She poked her head forward and in a loud whisper called, 'The jig.'

'The what?' It was Mona's voice following her, but she didn't stop to explain.

The road through the wood was rough in parts and she drew the boy from a run to a walk, saying, 'We'd better go careful or we'll be sliding on to our . . . bottoms, won't we?'

For answer the child said, 'I want to go to the upstairs jig.'

'All right, you'll go to the upstairs jig. . . . Why do you call it the jig?'
''Cos.'

''Cos what?'

'Well, 'cos Mammy calls it the jig, thing-me-jig.'

'Oh.' Her laugh was high. 'Thing-amy-jig.'

'Daddy says water closet, Grandma says parlour, but I say jig. . . . What do you say?'

She was laughing inside as she thought, I'd better not tell him netty. 'Oh, I say jig an' all.'

'You do? How old are you?'

'Oh, very old, nineteen.'

'Nineteen? I'm nearly five. My birthday is on the first day of the year.'
'New Year's Day.'

'Yes; I'll be five on that day.'

'My! My! Here we are then.' They were going through the side door. 'You go upstairs; I'll wait in the sitting . . . drawing-room for you.'

'You won't go away?' He gazed up at her.

'No. Go on –' she pushed him and stopped herself from adding, 'before you do it in your pants.'

She watched him run to the bottom of the stairs, but there he turned to her and, crossing his legs, he did a little dance while he said, 'I like you.'

As she watched him now scampering and laughing up the stairs she thought, And I like you; you're about the only natural thing in this house.

There was no one in the drawing-room. She went towards the fire that had only recently been lit and stood with her back to it and lifted up her dress and exposed her legs to the flame. The communicating doors leading into the dining-room were partly open and after a moment she was aware of someone entering and a voice saying, 'We'd better get this while it's hot.' She recognized the speaker as that Partridge man, Olive's husband, and the voice that answered, 'Where is everybody?' she attached to the man Ron.

'Oh, about. I saw from my window that Arthur has taken the Geordie aborigines down to do some wood cutting. There's a gang, don't you think?'
'Odd types.'

'Odd! that's putting it mildly. Just been dug up, I should say. What do you make of Beauti-bloody-ful McCabe? Did you ever hear anything like it last night? Talk about an ignoramus.'

The answer came on a laugh 'He's a bit much.'

'A bit much! The man makes my hackles rise.'

Annie had left the fireplace. She was standing within a foot of the communicating door. She could see them both sitting at the table, and she wondered that they weren't aware of her presence, or aware of the anger that was oozing from her in sweat now. Geordie aborigines! She wasn't sure what an aborigine was but it was something nasty. . . . Ignoramuses!

'How did Arthur came to take up with him?'

There was a short silence now before James Partridge answered in a quiet tone, ' Well you know, Politics red, and tastes masculine, if you know what I mean.'

'No . . . really!

'Well, I can't see any other explanation, can you? McCabe's impossible, in every sense of the word. Now why should Arthur. Well, I ask you!'

'I see what you mean. But it's a bit of a nerve bringing him home, isn't it?'

'Oh, not when you work it out. He became one of Gwen's suppliers when Arthur got his packet at the fellow's wedding. Her source of bacon, butter, cheese, etc., etc., etc., would have dried up if she hadn't cultivated dear Georgie. Of course the supply had been double when Arthur was there to carry home his share; but the Georgies of this world are very versatile. The swill cart from the camp used to pass the bottom of the road here. Georgie and the driver had an understanding. A special swill can for him if he dropped a swill can off in the corner of the wood. . . . Oh, Mother Gwen's an organizer in more ways than one. Richie, he's good for the drinks; Arthur Tollet, he's the beef, mutton and pork end; then there's Sam Rawley from near Breinton Springs, he supplies the poultry, eggs and cream; the only things she hadn't been able to organize is a coal man. It was stooping a bit too low even for her, yet I think she scraped the barrel when she co-opted dear Georgie. But if dear Georgie only knew, this is his farewell party. She has no more use for him now that he's demobbed; it was only on Arthur's insistence that he was invited. There was a sort of family conference and to say the least, it was embarrassing. . . . I'm no snob, but I considered it a bit much. Apart from everything else there's still the officer and men part of it. You know what I mean?'

'Yes, yes, indeed, I do. It's a pretty awkward situation, especially with Taggart coming this afternoon. He's not the one to suffer fools gladly.'

'I'd thought of that and I'll have to put him in the picture. God, I've met some fellows in my time. There were a mixture in my company, real prize types, but that McCabe beats them all. The fellow gets up my nose like no one else has. . . .'

'*Does he now? Does he? Does he?*'

As the doors were flung back the two men jumped to their feet, their faces turning scarlet as they looked at the infuriated girl facing them

'Well, let me tell you something, Mister Upstart. He might get up your nose, but no matter how far he went he wouldn't be able to stop you smelling your own stink, because you're rotten, putrid, that's what you are. Your mind and everything about you. When I tell my Georgie what you've suggested about him, he'll knock your –' she paused, then she said it; she didn't only say it, she bawled it, 'bloody brains in. That's what he'll do to you. You! Who do you think you are anyway? They tell me your father keeps a draper's shop; well, let me tell you that my grannie kept a draper's shop an' all.' There was no need to explain that her grannie's shop had been in a house window and was run on the shilling club basis. 'So we're both from the same social standard, aren't we?'

They continued to stare at her as she glared at them while some part of her mind was telling her that standard wasn't the word she should have used. But what the hell! she wasn't looking for right words the day. This fellow! She wanted to swear at him, really swear. She wanted to cry at him, 'You snotty nosed bugger-a-hell!' which expression was a favourite one of Mollie's. It was odd, but at this moment she felt like Mollie. And she might have said it had not the far door opened and Gwen Bailey, entering hurriedly, said, 'What's the matter? What's all the shouting about?'

Annie stormed down the room towards her now and, pushing her face close to that of the astonished woman, cried, 'Ask them. And I've got something to tell you, an' all. You won't have to put up with our obnoxious presence over the holidays because we're goin', we're goin' now. You've got no more use for Georgie; he's served his turn. An' let me tell you something. I haven't known you twenty-four hours but it didn't take me a quarter of that time to realize that I've got no use for you.' And on this she stormed past the startled Gwen, across the hall and to where the child was standing at the bottom of the stairs watching her approach, and she spoke to him as if she were speaking to her own child as she said, 'Go into the wood this minute an' tell Georgie to come in at once. I want him. Do you hear?'

Looking up at her, his mouth gaping, the boy said, 'Yes.' Then, 'Yes, I'll tell Georgie,' and at this he ran out of the house, and she ran upstairs.

Once in her room, she almost staggered towards the bed and leaned over the bottom rail gasping. That lot! that rotten, snotty lot! Geordie aborigines are we? And him saying that about Georgie. Georgie'll kill him, if Arthur doesn't. Oh, I'll be glad to get out of here. On this she straightened up, rushed to the wardrobe, pulled out her clothes, then opening her case, she bundled them in, swept the few toilet accessories off the dressing table, grabbed up the two pairs of shoes standing under the side of the bed, and was dragging on her coat when Georgie burst into the room.

'What the hell's up? What's happened? What you say to Gwen? She looked at me daggers, she did. Look! I'm asking you, what the bloody hell's up?'

She snapped his hands away from her coat and stood staring at him. She had meant to blurt out everything that she had heard, but in this mood he might go downstairs and knock that fellow's brains out. She had seen him in a fight once when he was drunk; he had not only used his hands but, like a wild bull, had rammed the fellow with his head. And were she to tell him now what that Partridge had suggested it would likely have a worse effect on him than drink. She gulped in her throat and said, 'They've, they've been using you; we're only here on sufferance. We're . . . we're going home. We're going home this minute.'

'Now look here, you hold your hand.' He took her by the shoulders. 'You just can't walk out like this. Who was it anyway? What was it you heard?'

'That Mr Partridge and his pal, he, he . . .'

'Aw them! Gob skites, bloody gob skites, that's all they are. Aw, I know them. I've got their measure, they don't frighten me. Look. . . .'

'No . . . you look, Georgie.' She pulled herself away from him. 'We're going home, at least I am. You can please yourself, but I'm leavin' this house this minute.'

'You're bloody well not! You're not gona bloody well show me up.'

'I'm leavin' this house, and now.' Her voice was quiet, the tone coldly decisive.

He stared at her. Then grasping his hair, he swung away from her, then back to her again before he said, 'But what they bloody well gona think?'

'They've thought already. In any case let me tell you something. This was the last time you were going to be invited here. She's got no more use for you; you've got no more to carry from Madley. Get it?'

'Yes, I get it, and I'm not such a bloody numskull as you take me for. I know that half me welcome's because I've kept them supplied. I know that. You're not tellin' me anything.'

'And what do you think the other half of your welcome was made up of, eh? Go on, tell me. Not because they liked you.'

'And why not? Why shouldn't they bloody well like me? Look, I haven't got the mange or anything.'

'Oh!' She bowed her head. 'Oh, for God's sake! Georgie, shut up. Are you comin', or are you not?'

'I'm not bloody well gona walk out of the house just like that because you found they haven't fallen on me neck just 'cos of me personality.'

'Georgie!' Her tone was quiet again. 'There's more to it than that, but I'm not telling you the rest of it until we get out of this house . . . until we're home.'

His brows contracted, his cheeks moved upwards, pushing his eyes back deep into their sockets and through narrowed lids he said, 'More to it? What do you mean?'

'I'm saying no more until we're out of here. Now are you coming?'

'Look, I want to know. More to it, you say?'

'You won't get another word out of me until we're out of here. An' I've told you. Look, our things are in the case; you only need to put your hat and coat on. It's up to you.'

'Just give me an inkling of what you mean.'

'I'm doing no such thing, not now, and that's final . . . final.'

His eyes on her, his mouth slowly dropped open while his tongue moved over his lower lip; then turning suddenly, he grabbed up his coat and cap from a chair, grinding out between his teeth, 'Talk about a bloody kettle of fish! Nice state of affairs. An' what you gona tell your mother, eh? What you gona tell her? That we've been thrown out?'

'I'll think of something.'

'You bet your bottom dollar you'll think of something. I'm not having her lookin' down her bloody nose at me and saying "Ah! Ah! Georgie's friends. There's friends for you, turfed them out. . . ."'

'Shut up! an' come on.'

There came a knock on the door and when Annie opened it Mona was standing there, her face white and her one good eye wide and staring. Sidling past Annie and into the room she looked from one to the other and asked in a whisper, 'What's it all about?'

Annie shook her head and looked down as she said, 'I can't go into it now, Mona, I'll just say I overhead enough to realize that we're only here on sufferance, and to them downstairs we're just a lot of . . . Geordie aborigines. That's what they think we are, Geordie aborigines.'

'What!'

She turned and looked at Georgie. 'That's what he said we were. Geordie aborigines!'

'Who the hell said that?'

'Him, Partridge.'

'I'll Geordie aborigine him. By God! let me. . . .'

'You'll do nothing of the sort.' She pushed at him, then turned quickly to Mona, saying, 'I'm sorry, Mona, but it'll make no difference to you. . . . Where's Arthur?'

'He's . . . he's in the dining-room raisin' Cain.'

Annie turned to Georgie now. 'Have you got everything?'

'No, I haven't got everything; I've lost me bloody senses. If I hadn't I'd slap your blasted mouth for you and put you in your place.'

It was with a sense of weariness that she turned from him, saying, 'That'll be the day.'

The trite expression seemed to deflate him and after staring at her for a moment he picked up the case and followed her on to the landing. There, he turned to Mona and said quietly, 'Go and tell Arthur I want a word with him, will you?'

A few minutes later they were standing in the conservatory with their faces turned from each other, looking out through the glass partition on to the overrun garden and weedy drive.

A wave of high voices came to them as a door opened and closed; then Arthur hurried towards them, pulling on his coat. His usual pale complexion was almost scarlet, his eyes were blazing with a temper she would have never thought him capable of. He was looking at Georgie and it was a full minute before he spoke. 'I'm sorry,' he said; and it seemed just as an afterthought that he turned to her and repeated, 'I'm . . . I'm sorry, Annie.'

She did not speak but made a movement with her head and closed her eyes, and when she opened them again he was once more looking at Georgie.

Georgie had his head to the side, looking down towards the floor. He hadn't spoken to Arthur. His silence on the matter appeared odd to her, his manner appeared odd. She stared at him.

It was Arthur who spoke again, saying, 'Olive will drive you to the station; I won't come along, Georgie, I'm packing up.'

Georgie's head jerked upwards to this and he began now, 'There's no need for you to. . . .'

'It was bound to come sooner or later.'

'Where will you go?'

'To the Crawfords.'

'Oh!' Georgie was nodding his head slowly now as he repeated, 'The Crawfords,' but it didn't appear that he was very enamoured of the Crawfords.

'What about Mona?'

Arthur turned his glance towards Annie, saying, 'She'll come with me of course. This will only mean we'll settle into the other place sooner than I thought.' He now pointed through the conservatory window, saying, 'There's Olive going to the garage. I'll keep in touch.' Again he was looking at Georgie, and Georgie said briefly, 'Aye, aye,' then turned away, opened the door and went out on to the drive.

'I'm sorry, Annie.' Arthur was looking into her face now. She didn't answer him but stared back into his eyes. They were nice eyes, kind eyes.

He was a nice fellow, seeming in no way connected with any of them back in the house. He turned hastily from her and, running out, caught up with Georgie. She watched him speaking earnestly for a moment before she moved, and before she reached them they had parted.

Olive was standing by the car. She made no remark, she just looked at them, then opened the door and they got in. Nor did she speak during the three-mile journey to the station; not until they were again standing outside the car did she open her mouth, and then she almost repeated the words that Arthur had said, 'This was bound to come sooner or later, you know. I mean, with Arthur. I'm sorry, I'm very sorry you've been involved in it. It . . . it isn't fair.'

There was a short silence, during which neither Annie nor Georgie made any comment. Then, her eyes cast down, Olive said, 'Further, I . . . I must apologize for my husband, his attitude is unforgivable.'

It was now impossible for either of them to make a comment.

She raised her eyes and held out her hand, and when Annie took it Olive said, 'I wish I could have got to know you better. And . . . and Alan will miss you; he quite took to you.'

There seemed a slight hesitation before Olive held out her hand to Georgie, and to him she merely said, 'Good-bye,' while he replied as briefly, 'Good-bye.' Then they turned from her and went into the station.

Nobody but a fool would travel on a Christmas Eve. If she had heard that once from fellow passengers during the journey she had heard it a hundred times. When they did manage to get a seat they were packed like sardines, but for most of the time she had sat on the case in the corridor, that was when she wasn't standing up to let people pass. The only time Georgie had made any comment on the situation was when they were changing trains at Birmingham. Standing on the platform he had muttered, 'Bloody nice state of affairs . . . Merry Christmas!'

She had made up her mind that what she had to tell must be said before she entered the house, but she didn't know how she was going to put the thing over, because as soon as they got out at High Shields he would most surely start questioning her, and he'd raise the street when he heard what she had to say.

But when they left the station at High Shields and walked down the dismal and almost empty road leading into King Street he didn't open his mouth. His head was down, his shoulders were hunched against the cold and he carried the case as if it were filled with lead. They walked up towards the market and crossed over it; it was no use taking the tram, it was quicker going up the side streets.

When they were almost half-way home and he hadn't spoken she suddenly bawled at him, 'Well! you been struck dumb?'

Still walking on and looking ahead, he answered her, 'Do you want me to start in the street?'

'Well, that would be better than starting when you get indoors.'

'There's no need to start at all.'

'What!' She paused in her walking, astonished at his attitude.

'Well, put the onus on me if you like. Tell her I opened me mouth as usual an' had a row with one of them. Tell her what you bloody well like. We'll soon be out of it, so it makes no matter.'

She was walking one pace behind him now, peering at him through the weak lamp light. Suddenly her hand shot out and, grabbing his arm, she pulled him to a stop and half towards her, and thrusting her face forward she hissed at him, 'Do you know what he was saying about you? Do you? I didn't tell you afore in case you would do something, like murder, but do you know what he was saying?'

'Look, that fellow would swear that Jesus Christ was on the fiddle.'

'It wasn't anything to do with fiddles.'

'Look, there's folks passing, stop your bawling.'

She drew her head back from him, and her eyes narrowed still further. Him checking her for raising her voice in the street! *Him!* There was something odd here. She felt a sickness in the pit of her stomach, and as if the nausea had suddenly erupted and burst from her mouth she spewed at him in a hiss, 'He hinted as much as you . . . you and Arthur . . . were queers . . . pansies.'

His face, which was usually fresh coloured, was tinged blue with the cold, but as she stared at him she watched the hue change into a dark red. She heard him rather than saw him gulping. She was about to endeavour to calm him by saying, 'Now, Georgie. Georgie, look,' when his voice came at her, not bawling, in fact when he spoke he scarcely opened his lips. His wide mouth looked frozen into a thin line, and his words sounded thin and his indignation forced as he said, 'Why, why didn't you tell me this back there?'

It was a second before she answered, 'Because I was afraid of what you might do.'

'If you had told me I would have knocked his bloody head off, the dirty minded bugger. . . . You didn't believe him, did you?'

'Believe him? Believe him? . . . No!'

'By God! if I had him here I know what I would do to him.' He turned from her and walked on, the case seeming to pull his shoulder down more than ever now, and he had gone four full paces before she moved and then with each step she took she protested loudly in her head, 'No, no! you're crazy.'

Anyway, it couldn't be, could it, not with a fellow like Georgie, big, tough, strong? And he had given her a bairn! And he was full of it still, couldn't satisfy him. And Arthur? Well, Arthur wasn't big, or tough, but he was refined, educated, and he was going to marry Mona. . . . Yet there was something, *Something*. She felt it inside of her, and it was making her sick. She wanted to vomit, really vomit.

She had adjusted herself to his swearing, his uncouthness, giving herself compensation by thinking about his generosity and the certain kind of honesty he possessed, but there were some things you couldn't give yourself compensation for.

There was something between him and Arthur Bailey. What was it? It couldn't be that, could it? Just look at him. She looked at him, and the very fact that he was walking on ahead and hadn't turned and said, 'What's up with you? What you doddering behind there for?' increased the sickness in her.

She wished she could explain things to herself. She knew she was very ignorant about most things relating to sex at any rate. She would have said she knew enough to get by. A normal man took you, you became pregnant, you had a baby, and that was that. On the reverse side of the coin there were pansies and queers, yet what the name actually implied she didn't know, only that it was something nasty. With a sudden movement she turned towards the end wall of a house, put her hand out, bent over and vomited.

He was by her side now holding her head, saying, 'God! what's up with you?'

When it was over and he had wiped her mouth on his handkerchief she leant against the wall and, her head down, she muttered, 'I'm sick.' And he gave an answer that made him normal to her again. 'It wouldn't take a bloody blind dog long to sniff that out. Come on,' he said; 'come on and get home.' Picking up the case in one hand, he put the other arm around her shoulders, and thus they returned home.

She was sick on Christmas morning; she was sick the following morning, and the following morning after that. She was pregnant again.

# Chapter One

## The Garage

'Hold that bag up straight, Rance.'

'Oh! Ma, I'm all mucky.'

'You'll be more mucky if you don't do what I tell you. Hold it up straight.'

Annie stooped down, thrust a shovel into a heap of coal and went to scoop it into the bag, but when Rance took one hand away from the top of the canvas sack and half the coal sprayed on to the ground, in one movement she threw down the shovel and thrusting out her other hand boxed his ears.

When she saw the tears spurting from his eyes and his hand holding the side of his face, she had to stop herself from throwing her arms around him and hugging him to her, crying as she sometimes did, 'Aw I'm sorry, I'm sorry. Your ma's sorry.' But tonight she felt worn out and irritated to the point of screaming, besides which she was filthy dirty with coal dust.

As Rance ran across the yard towards the house door Anastasia, whose name had hardly been repeated from the moment the priest had spoken it, came towards her and said solemnly, 'Will I hold it, Ma?'

Annie sighed as she answered, 'All right, Tishy, get a hold of it. But it'll mean you'll have to have a bath afterwards mind.'

'Aye, Ma . . . I don't mind havin' a bath.'

'Hold it steady.'

Annie shovelled up more coal, and because her five-year-old daughter could not be expected to hold the sack as firmly as Rance, she did not throw the coal into the sack but tipped it gently forward, thinking to herself as she did so, I'll get a long way in a long time like this, an' it getting dark an' all. By! I'll have something to say to him when he gets in. Where does he think he is till this time? If he's stopped at The Red Lion again I'll eat him wholesale, I will. By God! I will. She had to stop herself from throwing the next shovelful into the bag, and this irritated her further and she said to the child, 'Leave it down. Go indoors and wash your hands. I tell you what. Put the kettle on, and when it boils give me a shout and I'll come and make a cup of tea. Go on, that's a good lass.'

'All right, Ma.' As the child ran across the yard Annie paused for a moment to look at her. Of her four children Anastasia had the kindest nature. Sometimes she thought, and without vanity, that she was the only one who took after herself; yet at the same time she wished that it wasn't only her nature that she had given to the child, but one or two of her presentable features as well; or that, if she had only inherited Georgie's eyes, which were his one good feature. But Tishy was like nobody on either side of the family.

From the moment she was born she was as plain as a pikestaff. For the first three years of the child's life Annie comforted herself by thinking, They say it's the ugly ducklings who turn into swans; but here she was now, five years old and there was no trace of the swan to be seen; nor did she think there ever would be. The child's hair was a mousy brown and was as straight as a die, not a kink in it. Her brows too were straight, as was her mouth. Her nose was snub, so snub that, as Georgie said, you would think somebody had wiped it along the flags. Then her eyes, although quite large, indeed seemingly too large for her face, appeared colourless at times, while at others they looked merely a light grey.

And so Annie would comfort herself with the thought, Well, there's plenty of time, while telling herself that even time couldn't alter her child's nose or put a bow to her mouth. Her final thought always with regard to her daughter was, that apart from her temper, she had a nice nature, and that was something.

Bill had arrived the year after Anastasia. Bill took after his father in looks, but already at four he seemed much brighter than Georgie, for he could read and count rapidly, and when he once started talking nobody could shut him up until he himself decided he had no more to say. His silences at times were as forceful as his conversations. Bill, Annie thought, was a case. Then her latest acquisition to the family was Kathy. Kathy was two years old, as pretty as a picture and the star in Georgie's sky, as Rance was in hers.

Rance. She felt guilty at times about her feelings for Rance. Perhaps she had poured her love out on him because she found no outlet with Georgie. Perhaps it was because he was her first child, or perhaps it was because he had inherited her own looks. Whatever it was she knew she loved him more than all the others put together; and she knew this wasn't right, because whereas Bill was a case, Rance was a handful, for he was always getting into scrapes, and she had a devil of a job at times to stop Georgie from lathering him.

It wasn't so strange that the boy didn't like his father for from an early age he had felt Georgie's hand across his bare rump. Then again, Georgie never spoke to him but he swore. It was odd, she thought, that Rance hadn't picked up Georgie's swearing, but Bill had. Bill at four often came out with bloody, or bugger, and protested with hands, feet and voice when he was chastised for it. Yes, Bill was a case, but it was Rance, she knew instinctively, who needed her more than the others.

Even Kathy at two had an independence about her that was lacking in Rance, yet the boy was as loud-voiced and bumptious as his father at times. Of course, the bairns he mixed with round about didn't help any, she was well aware of that, and if it rested with her, another year, two at the most, would see them out of it. She had thought at first there was a lot in coal, but the most that was in it, at least for her, was damned hard work. But it was paving the way to better things.

When they had first moved in here in the January of '46 she was living in a sort of dull despair. The Hereford business, as she had come to think of it, was still very much in her mind, yet lessened somewhat by the very fact that Georgie had made her pregnant again. How could a man be like that . . . odd, queer, if he could give you a bairn and want you at all odd times of the night or day? It didn't fit in, did it? She had wished there was someone she could talk to about it. The only person who would know about such things was Mollie, but she was the last one she could go to, being his mother.

When Mona and Arthur were married in the middle of January '47 and they weren't invited, she had been indignant. The excuse that they were being married in a registry office in Hereford didn't satisfy her as it seemed to Georgie. The fact that Georgie rarely spoke of Arthur kept her suspicions alive, yet his answer to her statement, 'You seem to have dropped Arthur, and he you,' seemed logical, for he said, 'Look, it was wartime. You strike up friendships in wartime an' they just last during wartime, the majority of them anyway. Left alone, they die a natural death. Some silly buggers like to keep things goin', so they have these get-togethers each year. Well, I met Arthur an' he met me. We were different types, as has been bloody well pointed out often enough. He was educated an' I was as ignorant as a pig, a come-easy-go-easy-God-send-Sunday type, but all right to have beside you when you had your back to the wall. Well, he had his back to the wall when he first joined up, an' I stood beside him. An' that's what it was all about.'

Georgie's summing up had given her a new aspect of the situation. A refined type like Arthur would undoubtedly have his back to the wall among some of the roughs who were in the forces, and he'd be grateful to have a big bouncer like Georgie for a friend to fend off the enemy so to speak.

So there she had left it, and got on with the business of carrying Anastasia – which name she had taken from a story in a weekly magazine – and furnishing the house, which necessitated travelling around the second-hand shops looking for bargains.

When Georgie had failed to get set-on with his old firm, or with any firm that required lorry drivers, for the town at that time seemed full of ex-lorry drivers, he took the job of helping to unload coal at a yard which supplied a number of coal merchants. It never struck Georgie that he had the facilities at hand to start up a business of his own, and even when she broached the subject he had laughed it to scorn. 'Where am I goin' to get the money for a lorry?' he said. 'Or are you thinkin' of me going round the streets with a bloody cart and horse?' To this she had answered that everybody was hiring things these days. Pentons, behind the station, had lots of second-hand cars and lorries in; she had seen them.

It took her three months to persuade him that there was something in the suggestion. His last stand against it was, he'd be working eighteen hours a day and he couldn't last long at that rate humping coal.

He started with loose coal on a flat lorry, selling it by the bucketful. It took almost eighteen months before they graduated to sacks. The problem here was that he required another hand, but, as he said, if he had to pay a fellow to fill the sacks he might as well give up for they would never be able to save enough to buy a decent lorry and get started properly. And so she became the other fellow.

Each day she filled the sacks ready for the following day, that is when her stomach wasn't too big and prevented her stooping. She also attended to the barrows that came to the yard.

The barrows were usually soap boxes balanced on a pair of bicycle wheels, the shafts rough pieces of wood, and the usual order from a barrow-holder was, 'Bob's worth, Missis.'

Filling a bucket, she would measure out a bob's worth; then, no matter how pressing would be the call from indoors with one or the other screaming, she had to watch the barrows until they were well outside the gate. A couple of nice big 'roundies' whipped up every time a barrow came into the yard could deplete the profit considerably by the end of the week.

Her five years of drudgery in the house and the depot had caused anger to develop in her mother, and pity in Mollie. Mary considered it a disgrace that her daughter should shovel coal like any cinder heap picker, whereas Mollie was emphatic in saying that it was a bloody crying-out shame that a lass like Annie should have to work so and be blacked up to the eyes every day. But there, as she had said at the beginning, if anybody could make a roof out of rotten thatch it was Annie, and by damn! she was doing it.

Annie liked Mollie, more than liked her; she had a deep affection for her such as she had never had for her mother. Moreover Mollie was kind, and those first hard days she had never come to the house empty-handed; even now, she always brought something for the bairns; whereas the only thing her mother brought with her was disdain.

Her da, too, had been kind to her in the early days. When he came on his own he talked all the time, had a good crack, as he put it, but when he came along with her mother he just sat silent.

As the years went on Annie had become more and more sorry for her father, and she warned herself that no matter how Georgie turned out she must never treat him like her ma did her da. And yet the strange thing was she knew that her da loved her ma. She didn't think her mother loved anybody, not even herself; she seemed incapable of affection. . . .

Well, there they were. Annie looked at the sacks, ten of them. They would give him a start tomorrow. Now she was going to have a bath, but oh Lord, she wished she hadn't to heat the water and carry it into the shed. That place was like ice. If they were here for good she'd have had a bath put in before now, but they weren't here for good. No! Oh no!

For some time she'd been chewing on the idea. She hadn't said anything to Georgie about it because he would have bawled her out. 'What!' he would have said. 'Are you mad? Takin' on a bloody garage! What next?' Yet he could take an engine to bits and put it together again and not mislay a screw. He couldn't write a letter to save his life; his own name and address was about as much as he could manage. She had to do all the bills because he couldn't reckon up, but give him a piece of machinery and his mind seemed to work. It was very odd, she thought, but he never seemed to realize his own capabilities, perhaps because he had come to accept the general opinion of himself, he was dim.

She went through the back door and into a large stone-floored scullery, where a gas stove stood next to a shallow brown sink. Fixed in the corner of the wall opposite was a wash-house boiler with a wooden lid on top, and pressed against the front stonework of the boiler, his two hands holding a knife which was inserted in a piece of box wood, was Rance, and she cried at him, 'What you doing, boy! Be careful; you'll cut your hands off.' She grabbed the knife from him, saying, 'What's this?' as she tossed a pile of narrow laths to one side.

'Aw, Mam, give over, I've just cut them. I'm goin' to make a hutch.'

'You're going to make no such thing. Haven't you been told you can't keep a rabbit out there. Now we've had all this out afore. Your da's told

you.' She pushed him to one side. 'Are you stupid, boy?' Even as she said
it she knew that he wasn't stupid, only grimly determined to have his own
way. This was an odd trait in the boy. You could tell him and tell him he
mustn't do a thing, and he would go on doing it as if he had never heard you
speaking.

He stood by the wall now, his hands behind him, staring at her grimly
as he said, 'I want a rabbit.'

'When we move. If we move into a cleaner place where . . . where there's
no coal dust, then you can have a rabbit. And . . . and a dog. I told you, I
told you the other night.'

'I want a rabbit now.'

'Will you be quiet, Rance!'

'Peter Smedley's got a rabbit and he's only four doors down.'

'Well, he's four doors down, he's not in this yard, and we want all the
space we've got. You know we do. We can hardly turn the lorry now, and
the walls are taken up with the sacks.'

'I could keep it in the backyard here,' he jerked his head towards the door.

'You're not keeping it in the backyard here.' She now closed her eyes and
bowed her head and said, 'Rance! Rance! Don't let's start this all over again.
Look, I promise you as soon as we leave here you'll have a rabbit, and
anything else you want.'

'When's that?'

'I . . . I don't know yet but . . . it'll likely be soon.'

'I want it now.'

'Get in there!' She thrust out her arm towards the kitchen door and when
he didn't move she pulled him from the wall and pushed him forward. 'And
let me hear another word about that rabbit from you and I'll tell your da.
Mind, I mean it, I mean it this time. Mention that rabbit again and I'll tell
your da; and then you know what'll happen, and you needn't come to me
to save you.' She thrust him into the kitchen where Kathy, Bill and Tishy
were sitting on the mat before the high-grate open fire and she called to
Tishy, saying, 'You were going to get yourself washed; then get yourself
washed. And get Kathy's clothes off and wash her face and hands, an' Bill's
an' all. Then get yourselves to bed. That goes for you an' all, Rance.'

Having banged the door on them she stood for a moment with her hands
gripping the sink. When Rance went on like that he did something to her,
churned her up inside. Oh, she was tired, dog, dog tired; she must put an
end to this before it put an end to her. She knew she was strong and healthy,
but the coal would break her heart before it broke her body.

When the outer door opened swiftly she turned her head and looked at
Georgie standing there. 'I'm back,' he said.

'I didn't hear the lorry.'

'No, I made it take its boots off an' come in in its stocking feet.'

She laughed wearily. He could be funny at times.

'You all right?'

'No, I'm not.'

'Thought you weren't. See you've got all the bags ready.'

'Me back's telling me that an' all.'

'I'm starvin'.'

'Well, you'll have to wait while I get this grime off me.'

'Oh aye; how long will that be?'

'The water's hot –' she nodded towards the boiler – 'Give me fifteen minutes.'

'Leave it for me if it isn't too much like glar, an' I'll get the thick off me an' all.'

'All right.' She nodded.

After he had closed the door again she remained standing and looking towards it. He had spoken to her for some minutes and he hadn't sworn once, not even a bloody.

She'd gone for him last week about his swearing, that was after Bill had come out with a mouthful in front of him. 'You see,' she had said, 'four years old and swearing like a trooper. Nice state of affairs, isn't it?'

'Aw,' he had laughed. 'You know me. I can't remember a time when I didn't swear.'

'Well you could try to curb it in front of them, couldn't you?'

'It comes out natural, lass,' he had said.

'Then try being unnatural for a change.'

'What! d'you want a bloody miracle?' he had laughed.

She was about to turn towards the boiler when the door was pushed open again and he thrust his head through and said, 'You know somethin'?'

'No, what is it?'

'I opened me mouth and I bloody well didn't swear. Didn't you notice?'

'Aw, Georgie!' She burst out laughing. 'Go on. Go on.' She flapped her hand at him.

'Is that all you're gona say, go on, go on? No praise? Why can't you be kind to me an' say, "Georgie, you're a bloody marvel, that's what you are, Georgie, a bloody marvel"?'

Swiftly she picked up a dish cloth from the bench and threw it at him, and he caught it in his hand and rubbed it round his black laughing face and closed the door again.

It was moments such as these that lightened the load and made living bearable.

# Chapter Two

'It's a crying-out shame. And I would put it stronger than that if these bairns weren't here.' Mollie glanced down to each side of her to where Tishy and Bill were hanging on to her hands. 'By! I would an' all. 'Cos look at you! What do you look like? A docker, that's what you look like, a female docker. Twenty-five you are and the way you look now you could give yourself another ten years. Carry on like this, me lass, an' your bonny looks'll be no more. I'm tellin' you. Just look at your hair. . . . Oh! our Georgie. I could bash his brains in for him, I could that.'

'Oh, be quiet, Mollie. Sit yourself down, and I'll wash me hands and make a cup of tea.'

'You'll do nowt of the sort. If anybody's goin' to sit down it's you. Get out
of me road, you two.' She playfully pushed the children aside; then lifting
the kettle from the hob she thrust it into the heart of the fire, and as quickly
lifted it back on the hob again, saying, 'I'll put it on the gas, it'll be quicker.
And don't say "Aw, but think of the gas." ' She pulled a face at Annie as
she went towards the scullery.

Annie, sitting back in an old leather chair, closed her eyes for a moment.
It was good to have somebody to boss you nicely.

Mollie's voice came to her now, crying at the children, 'Don't do that, else
I'll skelp your backside for you,' and they answering her with a laugh. They
all liked their Grannie McCabe; except Rance. He preferred his Grannie
Cooper, because she had always spoilt him.

After a moment she called out, 'How's things?'

'Oh, fine, lass. I've got a new lodger.'

'What!. . . . Another?'

'Aye, another. Micky was gettin' a bit too hot, even for me. Talked about
marryin'. But you know what?' Her head came round the door and her
voice, although tones lower, was still loud. 'I've got an idea he's got a wife
in Liverpool.' She now took three quick steps into the room and, bending
over Annie, said, 'More than a bloody idea. I found a letter in his pocket,
an' the piece that wrote it wasn't just a very dear friend. God! the things she
said.' She now put her head back and laughed, and as her whole body
wobbled with her emotion she flapped her hand sharply against the mound
of her stomach, crying as she did so, 'Lie down! your father's not workin'.'

At this Annie let out a roar of laughter, and she and Mollie pushed at
each other until the children's voices came from the scullery, yelling, 'Kettle's
boilin', Gran. Kettle's boilin'.'

As Mollie ran into the scullery with the lightness of foot that was
surprising for her bulk, Annie sat back in the chair again. Aw, Mollie was
a tonic. In some way Georgie took after her. 'Lie down! your father's not
workin'.' That was funny that was. Pregnant women were supposed to have
said that during the days of the slump when the child inside them kicked.
It was a favourite saying of Mollie's and never failed to elicit Annie's
laughter.

When Mollie brought the tray of tea into the kitchen Annie said, 'I've got
hopes we may be out of this soon, Mollie.'

'No! What's in your head now, lass?'

'A little garage. A lock-up. We could rent it for five pounds a week. It
isn't very big but it's got pumps an' all that. The snag is he wants a hundred
and fifty for the goodwill. And then he wants to sell the tools an' things.
When we get in what's owing to us, it'll only come to just over a hundred;
but I mean to borrow the rest from somewhere, even if I have to go to a
money-lender.'

'By God! you'll go to no money-lender, lass. That's jumpin' into the jaws
of the wolf all right. No money-lenders.' She came towards Annie now, and
bending over her she wagged her finger in her face as she said slowly, 'Now
promise me, no money-lenders. By! the ruinations I've seen caused by money-
lenders. By God! I have that. Court, that's where the money-lender'll lead
you to, court. Look, tell me what you want an' I'll lend it you. But no
money-lenders, lass.'

'You!' Annie pulled herself up straight in the chair. 'But . . . but how can . . .?'

'Never you mind. . . . I've been workin' behind the bar for years, haven't I? An' when they say, "Have one yourself, Mollie," what d'you think I do? I'd swim out of that bar if I took all that was offered me. What I do is chalk it up to myself. Trust Mollie. And then there's our Winnie and Archie and Mike, they've been workin' for years, an' they pool their bit. Not forgettin' the lodger.' She knocked Annie back into the chair, and again they were laughing, but only for a short time for Annie said, 'But . . . but I might need a hundred pounds, Mollie.'

'Well, you can have a hundred pounds, lass.'

'Aw, Mollie!'

'Now, now, don't take on. I'd give anythin', lass, to see you out of this place for you're killin' yourself. Aw, give over, stop it. What the hell are you cryin' for?'

'Aw, Mollie! Mollie!' Annie had turned her face into the corner of the chair, and when Tishy began to whimper Mollie shouted to her, 'Go on you! don't you start. Look, take Bill outside. . . . Here!' She pushed her hand into her bag and drew out sixpence. Go and get some bullets. Share them mind. Go on.' She pushed them towards the door.

When she came back to Annie she said, quietly now, 'Come on, give over, lass.' And she shook her gently by the shoulders, and Annie, reaching towards the rod that ran underneath the mantelpiece, pulled from it a tea towel and dried her face with it, then, looking at Mollie, muttered, 'What can I say? What can I say, Mollie?'

'Say nowt.'

'You're so good.'

'Me!' Mollie now drew herself up and, giving a good imitation of Mae West, said the famous words, 'Goodness had nothing to do with it, dearie.' Again they were laughing; only, Annie's laughter was still mingled with tears, and suddenly she stood up and, throwing her arms about Mollie, whispered, 'Aw, how I wish you were me mother, Mollie. Time and again, how I've wished that.'

'Well!' Mollie's voice was slightly thick now as she held Annie and patted her back. 'That's the nicest thing that's ever been said to me. An' I wish I was your mother, lass, I wish I was. Now look.' She pushed her away. 'Have this cup of tea, then go an' get yourself washed an' done up a bit. Make yourself as bonny as you really are, then take me along to see this place. . . . But wait, you say it's a lock-up, where are you gona live?'

'We'll have to stay here until I can find some place.'

'Well, the sooner the better. . . . Just a tick now.' She wrinkled her brow and, with her finger pointing, she said, 'Wait; there's a Mr Stanley comes in our place, the best end, saloon. He lives somewhere behind the town hall. He's movin'; going to Harrogate; opening a business there. His house is his own property an' he wants to rent it. I heard him, I heard him tellin' the boss. I don't know what kind of a place it is, but it'll be no hole in the corner if he had it, 'cos he's respectable. Look, I'll ask him the night. He's bound to be around the night.'

'Oh, Mollie. But behind the town hall . . . they're all big houses there.'

'Not all of them. And anyway, why shouldn't you go to a big house if the rent is reasonable. There's six of you, you need a big house. Look, lass, start the way you mean to go on. By God! if I had me time over again you wouldn't find me in Primrose Street. If I was your age and had your head, lass, by! I would go places even if I had to take our Georgie along of me.' She smiled derisively now, then said, 'God forgive me! I shouldn't always be at him; he's me own, and he's not bad, is he?'

'No, Mollie, he's not bad. He couldn't be, he's too like you.'

'Go on with you.' Mollie gave her a push towards the far door, saying, 'Now hurry yourself up and get that muck off you; I'm dying to see this garage. An' I tell you what, we'll go round about the town hall, an' have a look at the houses there. Why not, eh? why not? *Westoe, here we come!*'

## Chapter Three

They had rented the garage, they had rented the house near the town hall, and even bought some of the furniture in it, and were moving in two weeks' time, and today was Rance's seventh birthday and everybody was happy ... except Rance.

'What's the matter with you, boy?' asked Annie.

'Nothin', Mam.'

'Well, stop sulking.'

The boy made no denial against sulking.

'You've had a lot of presents, haven't you?'

'Presents!' When he turned his eyes disdainfully up towards the ceiling she cried at him, 'You should consider yourself lucky, damned lucky. Just look at the other bairns around the doors; some of them don't get a decent meal never mind presents like you've got. A fountain pen, a school bag, a train set, and what else? Money, you've had over a pound in money. Boy, you don't know when you're well off. What do you want?'

She regretted asking the question as soon as it was out, and she expected him to say, 'You know what I want, I want a rabbit,' but he didn't open his mouth, he just turned away and went and sat in the corner of the room near the fireplace. And now she barked at him, 'You keep that face on when your granda and grandma Cooper come and just see what you'll get when they leave. Anyway, there was something I was going to ask you, where've you been all afternoon?'

'Out.'

'I know fine well you've been out 'cos you haven't been in, I haven't seen hilt nor hair of you. Where were you out? I sent Tishy looking for you. Where were you?'

'About.'

'Oh, my goodness boy, one of these days I'll lose my temper with you and knock you from here to Hull. Go on, go and get yourself cleaned up, you look like a muck heap. They should be here any minute. Go on.'

She watched him turn slowly about and with dragging step go into the scullery. She shook her head. That rabbit, it was coming between him and his wits. She had promised him he could have one when they got into the new place – there was a big backyard there – but no, no, he wanted one now for his birthday. Where did he get his stubbornness from? Not from her, and not from Georgie. Yet for all that he remained so lovable. And he was so bonny. Every time she looked at him she wanted to put her arms around him and hug him. . . . She knew what she would do. On Monday she would take him down to the pet shop and let him pick a rabbit. She'd pay for it to be kept there until they moved. Perhaps that would satisfy him.

She was about to call him and tell him what she intended to do when the back door opened and she heard Mollie's voice, saying, 'Who knows but you'll be goin' to work in a bowler and umbrella yet, lad,' and she knew that Georgie was with her.

They both came into the kitchen laughing. Mollie crying at the top of her voice, 'I'm tellin' this'n here, with a garage of his own, an' a house not a kick in the backside from Westoe, he'll be goin' to work rigged out in an umbrella an' bowler.'

'On the bloody dole more like. If you want my opinion, we've bitten off more than we can chew.'

'Georgie!' Annie spoke his name with a heavy flatness, and he replied with equal flatness, 'Aye, Annie.' And Mollie burst in, 'You leave everything to Annie, lad. If anybody's got a head on their shoulders she has. Just you leave the reins in her hands and you can lay your bets on the race.'

'Bets on the race.' Georgie looked towards Annie where she was arranging plates of cakes down the centre of the table, and he laughed as he said, 'I've never taken long shots, always been against betting on bloody outsiders.'

'She's no outsider, she's a favourite, aren't you, lass?' Mollie leant over and gave Annie a whack on the buttocks, and after a startled exclamation Annie, laughing now, turned to them and said, 'Would you like me to do a gallop round the house to show you?'

There came the sound of the back door opening and Mary Cooper's voice, saying, 'Happy Birthday, dear,' and the voice seemed to subdue Mollie's exuberance, for with an unconcealed sigh she sat down to the side of the fireplace. When Mary entered the room it was a moment before Mollie turned her head and looked at her, then they exchanged a cool greeting.

Mary gave no greeting to Georgie, but looking at her daughter, she said, 'You didn't get him a rabbit then?'

Annie nipped at her bottom lip before answering quietly, 'No, Ma. He's had to do without one all the time he's been here, and as we'll be gone in a fortnight I can't see the sense in fixing up a hutch now.'

'The yard's cleared of coal.'

'I'm well aware of that, but as I said. . . . Oh! –' she shook her head – 'for heaven's sake let's forget about that rabbit. He'll get one.' Now her voice was rising. 'He'll get one in the other place. I promised him . . . and I promise you, Ma.'

'There's no need to raise your voice.'

'It would make God raise his voice.'

There followed a short tense silence until Rance and Bill with Kathy toddling behind them came into the room, and Mollie, turning to Rance, said on her usual high note, 'Well now, boy, we only need your granda and Tishy here and then we can start on that tea. Just look at that cake, did you ever see anythin' like it? Seven candles on it an' all! . . . This'll be them now.' She screwed round in her chair and looked towards the scullery, and a minute later Dennis Cooper came into the room holding Tishy by the hand.

Dennis's face was unusually straight; his mouth had a grimness about it that caused Annie to say immediately, 'What's the matter? What's up?' Then she looked down at Tishy, whose face was white, and Dennis said, 'She's been sick.'

'Sick?' Annie went to her daughter and, dropping on to her hunkers, looked into her face and said, 'Been eating something, dear? What did you spend your pocket-money on?'

For answer Tishy put her hand into her coat pocket; then holding out her palm showed her mother the sixpence, and Annie said, 'Well, what's made you sick? You didn't have anything greasy for your dinner.'

'She'll be all right, just let her sit quiet.' Dennis drew the child away from Annie and placed her on a cracket near the fender, saying, 'Sit quiet, hinny; you'll be all right. Sit quiet.'

'And what's the matter with you?' Mary looked keenly at her husband and Dennis replied, 'There's nowt the matter with me, except perhaps I'd like a cup of tea.' His voice was lighter now but there was still no smile on his face.

Annie stared at her father for a moment. There was something wrong here. Her da had taken no notice of the other three, and he never entered the house but he ribbed and joked with one or the other of them. 'Well –' she answered him now – 'the tea's ready; if you'll all sit up I'll get you served. . . . No, don't you sit there, Rance, sit you opposite your cake.'

Smiling, she pulled her son to the chair opposite the cake, and amid chatter and laughter they all seated themselves round the table and she began to pour out the tea. It was as she placed the last cup in front of herself that there came a hammering on the back door.

As the heads turned in the direction of the scullery Georgie said, 'Somebody still thinks we're sellin' coal, an' he seems in a hurry. Perhaps his fire's gone out.' His wide mouth stretched into a laugh as he pushed back his chair. A minute later Annie, straining her ears above the renewed chattering of the children, heard him exclaiming loudly, 'I don't believe a bloody word of it. He wouldn't.'

There was another voice now, angry, high; then Georgie entered the room again, followed by Mr Peter Smedley from four doors down.

Their entry and the looks on their faces silenced all at the table. Georgie looked at his son and Rance stared wide-eyed back at him.

'Where you been this afternoon?'

There was a moment's pause before Rance answered, 'Just out, Da.'

'Out where?' Georgie slowly advanced towards the boy and Rance, his face draining of colour, his voice quivering now, said, 'J-j-just out.'

'You went along the river.'

'No . . . no, Da.'

'You're a bloody little liar.'

Annie was on her feet now staring at Mr Smedley. 'What's he done? What's the matter with you? What's he done?'

'Drowned wor young Peter's rabbit, that's what he's done.'

Annie's hand went to her mouth and pressed her lips tightly for a second;

then she was protesting loudly, 'What! Don't you tell me that, he wouldn't do that. Rance . . . never! He loved that rabbit as well as young Peter did. You never did such a thing, did you, boy?' She was stretching across the table towards him now, and Rance, looking straight into her face, said, 'No, Mam, no.'

'There you are then, there you are.' She had rounded on Mr Smedley, and he, barking back at her now, cried, 'Well! he did.'

'Did you see him?'

'No, I didn't, but Tommy Blake did. He had threatened he would do it, an' \not for the first time. My Peter came back home from the match an' he found the hutch empty. Tommy Blake said he had seen that one there –' the man's arm was thrust out towards Rance now – 'leaving the backyard with something under his coat. He said he was makin' for the river. You drowned her, didn't you? An' her full of young. You drowned her, you cruel young bugger you!'

Annie was staring not at Rance, and not at Peter Smedley, but at Georgie now. Peter Smedley had called his son a cruel young bugger and Georgie was doing nothing about it, only staring down at the boy.

When Georgie's two hands gripped Rance's shoulders and lifted him bodily from the chair she screamed at him. 'Leave him alone! He would never do such a thing, never!'

She thrust her way between the wall and the intervening chairs and went to grab the boy from Georgie's fierce grip; but, taking one hand from Rance's shoulder, Georgie thrust her roughly away, almost overbalancing her, and when she fell against her father Dennis held on to her arm while he shook his head sharply at her, warning her to remain quiet.

'Did you drown that rabbit?' Georgie's voice was unusually quiet, but when the boy gave no answer, just stared at him, he bawled in such a way that everyone in the room started. '*Do you hear me? Did you drown that rabbit?*'

When he began to shake the boy like a dog would a rat Annie shouted, 'Stop it! Stop it,' and Mary, getting to her feet, went towards them crying, 'Leave the child alone! Do you hear me?'

At this, Dennis shouted in turn, 'An' you hear me, woman. Sit yourself down an' mind your own business.' Then looking at Annie, whom he still held firmly, he hissed at her, 'Keep out of it. Leave them alone.'

Annie turned an agonized glance on her father but the look in his eyes stayed her further protests. She could see he was for Georgie. It was as if he believed what they were saying about the child.

'Did you drown that rabbit, yes or no?'

The boy's head was wobbling on his shoulders like a wired jack-in-the-box and at last he gabbled out, 'N . . . no, Da. N . . . no, Da.'

When Georgie released him the child fell to the floor with a thud and Georgie turned and looked at Peter Smedley, and Peter Smedley said, 'He can say no till he's black in the face, but I know he did.'

'He says he didn't.'

Georgie was advancing on Peter Smedley now and there was menace in each step he took. What would have happened next was prevented by Tishy, who during the altercation had left the table and had sat on the cracket, with one side of her pressed tight against the wall. But now she was on her feet, screaming at her father, 'He did! he did, Da. He did! he did! we saw him. Granda an' me, we saw him, an' I was sick. He did. He did.'

Georgie stopped and, turning, looked down at her. Then he moved his body slowly round until he was facing Dennis, and Dennis answered the question he was silently demanding, 'She's right,' he said dully; 'we saw him at it.'

Like a scurrying rabbit himself, Rance now dived under the table screaming hysterically, 'I didn't mean to, Da, I didn't mean to. It was 'cos he was braggin'. It was gona have little 'uns an' he said he'd have more than me. She was going to have little. . . .'

When Georgie hauled him out by the legs Annie dragged herself from Dennis and, rushing to Georgie, tried to pull the boy from him, at the same time screaming at him, 'Leave him be! I'll deal with this, leave him be.'

'You've dealt with him too bloody long.'

She was knocked flying by the flat of Georgie's hand; then with the other he picked the boy up bodily and made for the door.

It took Mollie and Dennis all their time to hold Annie now, and in the melée of her shouting and the children crying, Rance's screams came down to them from above.

Mary, standing with joined hands, gazed up at the ceiling and cried, 'He'll kill him! he'll kill him. He forgets what he's doing when he gets that belt in his hand. I've seen him at it afore,' and Dennis cried at her in turn, 'Well, if he does, you'll have something on your conscience, woman 'cos you've helped to ruin him . . . an' you an' all, lass.' He glared into Annie's face, showing her an anger that was unusual for him. 'You've broken his neck one way and another; between you you've broken his neck. Vied with each other, you have, to give him what he's cried for. Well, listen to him now; he's getting what he's cried for an' rightly this time.'

The screams had faded into a muted sobbing. Mollie, who had shown Mr Smedley the door, now shooed the children out into the yard, and into the comparative silence that had fallen on the house Dennis, turning to Mary, said, 'Get your hat and coat on.'

'I'm not going, I'm not leaving this. . . .'

'Get your hat and coat on, woman, and now. And see if you can mind your own business for once.' As his hand came out to push her she cried at him, 'You! Dennis Cooper, mind who you're talking to.' Nevertheless she put her hat and coat on and under his grim stare went out without a word of good-bye.

A few minutes later, when the sobbing became intermittent, Mollie said with unusual quietness, 'Well, I'll be off an' all. . . . But lass, don't hold it against Georgie for what he's done, 'cos you know, I agree with your da, that bairn's been spoilt as none of the others have. Sometimes it happens with the first one an' sometimes it's the last. With me it was our Winnie, still is; I always made Georgie carry the can for everythin' that the others did. What he's just done is what I should have done to our Winnie many a time, an' she'd be less trouble the day. So don't hold it against him, lass. Ta-rah; I'll be seein' you.'

'Ta-rah, Mollie.' The words came from Annie's mouth as if she hadn't used her lips for a long time.

Alone in the kitchen now, she sat away from the table. The plates were still full of sandwiches and fancy cakes, not a bit had been eaten; she had baked and iced for two solid days. But what did it matter about the food? What did matter was that Rance, her bairn, her beloved son, and he was her beloved son, had taken another lad's rabbit and drowned it, and she was to blame. Oh yes, she was to blame. She should have let him have a rabbit in the yard even if it had been choked to death with coal dust. She hadn't realized what the rabbit meant to him. But she should have, for he had told her often enough; she had become sick to death over the past year listening to his craving for a rabbit.

The door opened and Georgie entered. His face and thick neck were scarlet; the blue of his eyes was pale, like steel. He looked at her across the room and after a moment said, 'Nice thing we've bred, haven't we? Well, I've made sure of one bloody thing, it's the last rabbit he'll drown.'

She gave a gasp as she thought for a moment he had killed the child, but a distant snuffling brought from her a long-drawn-out breath.

She stared at the man opposite her, who in this moment was unrecognizable. Gone was the gauche good-tempered softie; and it looked as if he might never return.

Bringing up the children had lain with her and she hadn't believed in punishment, at least no lathering with a belt; a box across the ears or a hand across the buttocks was the most they ever received. If anyone had told her that Georgie would unmercifully thrash his son she would have laughed and said, 'I'll believe that when I see it.' And now she had to believe it, and although her heart was sore for her son there crept into her lukewarm affection for the burly man standing staring at her a modicum of respect.

# Chapter Four

The street was one of those that went off Erskine Road. It had the distinctive name of Bewlar Terrace. The house was No. 17 and its advantages were many; besides having six rooms, it also had the real luxury of a bathroom. There was a large backyard and an eighteen foot by twelve foot, iron-fringed front garden; moreover, it was within a few minutes' walk from the church and not much further from the Bents Park and recreation ground, and this latter solved the problem of the bairns having somewhere safe to play.

Annie's main joy in the house was the bathroom. For the first week she had taken a bath morning and night and saw to it that the children had at least one bath a day. The only one she couldn't get into the bath every day was Georgie. He'd had enough washing back there in Madley, he'd said, to last him a lifetime. Once a week would do him, twice if he was pushed, and nothing she could say would alter that.

She had warned him about his swearing. Although he had cut it down quite a bit he had only to get excited and his language coloured the air like blue smoke.

Apart from a polite nod, Mrs Tressel, her neighbour on the right, had studiously ignored them. She had an opinion of herself that one, Annie considered, all because she engaged a daily from nine till twelve. But Mrs Brooks on the left of her was all right, kindly she was. She had looked over the wall one day and given the bairns a bag of bullets; it was a kind of introduction. Although she had been nosy and wanted to know all about them she had seemed quite impressed when Annie had informed her that her husband was in the car business and had his own garage. She had ended by saying they had been in the coal contracting business but had given it up as it was much too dirty; she had hoped that Mrs Brooks wasn't acquainted with Burton's Corner and Hanlon's coal depot.

Yet she didn't bother about her neighbours. Let them hang as they grow, she said to herself; you mind your business and they'll mind theirs. She was starting a new life in a respectable district, in a fine house. And a fine rent they had to pay for it an' all, seventeen and six a week. Still, she supposed they were lucky to have got it. And the pieces of furniture she had brought from the owner were, in her estimation, simply wonderful and dirt cheap. A three-piece chesterfield with covers on for seven pounds, and a big sideboard that filled one wall of the dining-room – he had only charged three for that, and it was made of beautiful wood that you could see your face in – furthermore, he had sold her a complete bedroom suite, a carpet and other odds and ends all for ten pounds.

She was set up, they were all set up. The main thing for her to do now was to see that Georgie made a go of that garage, and if hard work could do that he would certainly achieve something in a very short time, for during the past month he had been there from seven in the morning till nine at night.

On this particular afternoon Annie was about to get herself washed and dressed up to take the bairns for a walk to the garage, at the same time taking Georgie his tea. She liked going to the garage. When a customer came in for petrol she willed him to ask for six gallons, not one or two as was the rule, and on a day when there wasn't a car in for repair she felt depressed, even while telling Georgie that they must creep before they walked and it was early days yet, and a slow start augured a fast ending. She wasn't quite sure about the latter saying; she wanted trade to come fast but not to end.

She said to Bill, 'Come and get your face and hands washed, we're going to see your da,' and Bill replied as always with a question, 'Walkin' or on the bus?'

'Walking.'

'Aw.'

'Aw.' She ruffled his hair, and he now said to her, 'When can I go to school?'

She gave a little sigh as she replied, 'I've told you, not until next year when you're five.'

'Tishy goes.'

'Yes, but she's five.'

'I'm as big as Tishy.'

'I know you are but you're not five.'

'Why have I to be five?'

'Oh, Bill, come on.' As she went to grab his hand the door bell rang and, leaving him, she crossed the hall, thinking, 'Who's this now? Somebody else selling things? Honestly, they were worse round here than they were at Burton's Corner . . . Then she opened the door and gasped and exclaimed on a high note, 'Well! Mona!'

'Hello, Annie.'

'Hello, hello. Come in, come in.' She put out her hand and drew Mona over the threshold and led her into the front room, talking all the while. 'When did you come? You should have let me know; another ten minutes and I would have been out. Well! you're a sight for sore eyes. Sit down, sit down. Where's Arthur? My! this is a surprise. Look, don't let's sit here, come into the kitchen and I'll make a cup of tea; come on . . . Oh, it's good to see you.'

All the time she was talking she was warning herself not to lay it on too thick. She hadn't seen Mona more than half a dozen times since that memorable Christmas and the last time was two and a half years ago when she came home for her father's funeral; Arthur hadn't come with her. She had seemed different then but she had looked smart, so smart she had felt a little jealous of her. But now she looked anything but smart, she was as different again. In her perceptive way she knew that something had happened to Mona. It wasn't that she was suffering under the handicap of having only one eye, she had got over that; she had once said it was the price she paid for Arthur and it was cheap. But there was something not right. She looked low, bad.

Abruptly, she stopped her chattering and quietly asked, 'Anything wrong, Mona? You been bad or something?'

'No, no, Annie. No, I haven't been bad. How's the bairns?'

'Oh, look at them.' She pointed to where Bill and Kathy were standing silently gazing at the visitor, and she called to them 'Come and say hello to your Auntie Mona. Come on.' She reached out and pulled them towards Mona, and nudging Bill, she said, 'Say hello, Auntie Mona.'

'Hello.' Bill now cast a sharp glance up at her and Annie knew that his next question would be, 'How is she me Auntie Mona, I haven't seen her afore?' and she put in quickly, 'Lost his tongue. He'll deafen you with his chatter in a minute. This is Kathy. You haven't seen her.'

'No, no, I haven't seen her. Hello, Kathy.' Mona bent towards the child and touched her fair curling hair, then moved her fingers gently around the pink cheeks as she said, 'She's bonny, beautiful.'

'Yes, the only one of them that's got any looks, except Rance isn't bad. But looks don't matter so much with a lad. Tishy though is still as plain as a pikestaff. Poor Tishy, she's going to feel it later on. Still, there's plenty of time, she might change, plain ones often do. . . . Oh, the kettle's boiling. Have you had anything to eat?'

'Yes, we had some lunch at my mother's.'

Annie noticed that Mona said lunch, not dinner. She had changed in more ways than one. After a moment she asked, 'Do you ever see Arthur's folks?'

'Very seldom; his mother's only been to see us once.'

'Only once.'

'Yes, but it suits us. I've seen Olive once or twice since James died. Oh, did you know he had died?'

Annie put the teapot on the tray then turned slowly towards Mona, saying, 'No.' Then, after a pause, she added, 'I suppose I should say I'm sorry, but then I'm not all that much of a hypocrite. How is Olive?'

'To tell you the truth she seems much more alive since she's been a widow. The boy's nice, Alan. He's ten now. Arthur is very fond of him. Olive let him stay with us for a holiday this year.'

'I wasn't wrong about Olive; she seemed nice then.'

'Yes, she's nice.'

When the tea was poured out and she had buttered some scones and placed a sandwich cake on the table she asked, 'How's Arthur getting on?'

It was a moment before Mona said, 'Oh, all right.' Then lowering her head, she gave it an impatient shake, a characteristic gesture that Annie remembered from the early days.

'What is it, Mona? Something is wrong.'

Mona still had her head bent and there was another pause before she said, 'Yes Annie; everything's wrong, everything's wrong.'

'I'm sorry, I thought. . . .'

'Yes, so did I. I thought it was going to be heaven. The little pub out in the wilds, just us two until the family started.' Her head had sunk deeper on to her chest, and Annie asked quietly, 'No sign?'

'No; nor will there be.' Her head came up sharply now and showed the tears dropping slowly from her left eye. Then swallowing deeply, she muttered, 'He doesn't . . . he can't. What I mean is he's . . . he's incompetent.'

As Annie watched Mona's head swing down again thoughts began tearing along the by-roads in her mind, irrelevant facts, such as Mona was talking differently. A few years ago she would have explained Arthur's inadequacy with the term, he's no use. Another by-road was being swept with a remembered sickness, and along another the essence of fear was rising like a thick mist.

'He tries. Oh, he does, and he gets upset. But he's so nice. Oh, he's so nice, Annie. That's the worst part of it. I go through agony because of myself and how I feel, but at the same time I go through agony for him an' all. I don't think we can go on like this. You see he won't discuss it. Now he's talking about moving away from there because it's too lonely for me . . . and it is. Oh, it is lonely. It would be different if . . . if there were bairns about. You know what I mean, Annie. . . .'

Annie nodded slowly.

'But . . . but for most of the year just him and me together. He reads . . . reads and reads, all the time. I say all the time, that's wrong, he's very good about the house, and he keeps the garden lovely. And of course in the height of the holiday season there are people in the bar. But . . . but that only lasts for a few weeks. Other times we can go days and never see anyone, and in the winter. . . . Oh, Annie, the winter. He used to talk to me about books and music, and at first I thought it was marvellous, I was being educated. Now when I see him putting a record on, or sitting down with a book, I want to scream and throw things.'

They stared at each other in deep sorrow filled silence until Annie said quietly, 'Drink that cup of tea.'

Mona sipped at her tea, and Annie, words of comfort failing her because of the significance of Mona's confidence, sat staring down into her tea. . . . That Partridge fellow had been right then; he was right after all. And where did that leave Georgie?

As the sickness reared up in her she attacked it. Georgie's a normal man; if ever there was a normal man he's one. My God! doesn't he prove it enough. . . . But back there in those war years, had he been normal then? Yes, yes, of course he had. Aw, there was something she couldn't understand about this, something fishy.

She started visibly when Mona said, 'Arthur thinks he'd like to work around here; it would be better for us both, me being back among my own people.'

Now her mind was yelling at her, Oh no! not that! She made no comment, and Mona went on, 'But it's funny, I seem to have fallen between two stools, I don't feel a bit at home here now, at me mother's I mean. Her way of life seems different altogether from what I've been used to these last few years. You know what I mean?'

When Annie nodded but still made no reply, Mona looked about her and said, 'It's a lovely kitchen. It's a lovely house altogether. What a change from the depot. I bet you didn't know you were born when you moved in.'

'That's true enough.' Annie smiled weakly. 'We were lucky to get it, and there's nobody knows it better than I do. . . . About Arthur getting work around here. There's, there's nothing for his type. Well, what I mean to say is, he couldn't do labouring and he wouldn't go into a shop or anything like that.'

'He wouldn't mind going into a bookshop; a good class bookshop, he's always fancied running a bookshop.'

Annie got to her feet and went to fill the teapot, saying, 'He'd die a slow death with a bookshop round here. Well, what I mean is, it would have to be something besides books, sweets and cigarettes and a paper round and such. A bookshop . . . well. . . . Of course that's only my opinion; but you know few people buy books except paperbacks, they go to the library for proper ones. By the way, where is Arthur?'

'Oh, he went down to see Georgie. We called in at your mother's as we had to pass the door before going to Burton's Corner and she told us of the change, so Arthur said you go and see Annie and I'll go and have a natter with Georgie.'

A natter with Georgie. A natter with Georgie. What was she getting all wound up about? Her life was secure, nothing but death could alter it. Or could it? Anyway, why was she getting in such a lather? It wasn't as if she had any real feeling for Georgie, was it? She knew that she hadn't been in love in her life, and there was very little chance now that she ever would be. What was she frightened of, apart from the other thing, and that in itself was ridiculous? Was she afraid that he would go off and leave her to fend for herself and the bairns? Now that was daft, because that was the last thing he would do. But even if he did she was quite capable of working and she would bring them up somehow. Other women had had to do it and she wasn't like some who married just to have a pay packet coming in without going out to graft for it. There was still a lot like that about. So what was she afraid of? What she should be doing at this moment was sympathizing with Mona because, my God! she must have had a life of it. You could, she knew from experience, get too much of a good thing, but taking all in all she considered that was the lesser of two evils, for to be married to a man who was 'no use' must be awful. Well, it had certainly told on Mona. It had put years on her. She said now, 'Has Arthur been to a doctor?'

'No.'

'Well, he should; you should tell him to get himself there.'

'Oh, I couldn't, Annie. We . . . we don't talk about it.'

'Don't talk about it! Then you should; it's about time.'

'Mam, are we gona see me da?' Bill was standing in the kitchen doorway.

'In a minute. Go and play. Where's Kathy?'

'Sittin' on the front room couch wettin' her knickers.'

This brief and telling reply brought Annie springing from her chair, apologizing to Mona as she rushed past her into the front room. She brought Kathy back into the kitchen, divesting her of her wet pants the while and chastizing her with, 'You're a naughty girl. You know how to go to the lav now. Oh, I've a good mind to. . . .'

'She did it on purpose.'

'Be quiet! and don't be silly.' She turned on Bill. 'How could she do it on purpose? Now, now! stop that snivellin'.' She shook her small daughter impatiently while Bill insisted, 'She did. She said she was gona an' she did.'

For the first time since coming into the house Mona laughed. She leant her elbow on the kitchen table and, supporting her head with her hand, she laughed while Annie, keeping her face straight, said under her breath, 'I mustn't let on . . . I don't know what he's going to be when he grows up, likely something in Parliament, 'cos he'll have the last word if it kills him.'

Of a sudden Mona rose to her feet, saying, 'I'll be going, Annie; I promised Mam I wouldn't be long. She wants me to go and see Auntie Joyce, and I expect Arthur's back by now. We'll look in tomorrow night. Will that be all right?'

' 'Course. 'Course. Any time.' Annie did not protest at her going, nor did she say, 'Just wait a minute till I change her and get her coat and hat on and we'll walk down with you.' Instead, leaving Kathy and Bill in the kitchen, she accompanied Mona to the front door, and there they looked at each other in awkward silence for a moment before Mona said, 'Well, bye-bye, Annie. See you tomorrow night then.'

'Bye-bye, Mona. We'll be looking forward to it. Don't have too much tea for I'll have a meal ready.'

'Now don't put yourself out,' Mona answered from the front gate, and Annie replied jocularly, 'Would I ever now!' Then she watched Mona walk down the street before she closed the door.

She did not go immediately into the kitchen but went into the sitting-room and straight to the couch and felt the cover to see if it was wet. Yet she wasn't thinking of the cover but planning what she was going to do. She next went into the hall and looked at the clock. Rance and Tishy should be in from school any minute now.

As she entered the kitchen she heard the back gate open and Rance came racing up the yard and burst into the kitchen, crying, 'Mam! Miss Warrington said me drawin' was the best in the class, she said it looked like a real mota car an' I told her it was a real 'un, one of me dad's.'

'Oh, that's fine. I'm glad she was pleased with you.' She smiled down on him. 'Where's Tishy?'

'Comin'.'

'What do you mean comin'? I've told you to see to her from school, haven't I?'

'Aw, you know what she's like, Mam, she won't stay with me. I tried to grab her and she kicked me.'

She shook her head. It was strange but her two eldest children had never got on, not even when they were babies. Rance had resented the arrival of a second baby and his reactions to it had made the elders say, 'Oh, it's natural, he feels his nose has been put out.' And as she grew, Anastasia's reaction to her elder brother was even more aggressive than his, and it had deepened since the business of the rabbit.

'I'm goin' out to play. Can I have a slice, Mam?' Rance was on his way to the pantry when Annie checked him, saying, 'No, hold your hand a minute, I'm going to set your tea. Now listen. I'm . . . I'm going down to the garage to see your dad, an' I want you to look after the house till I come back.'

'Aw, Mam, I want to go out to play.'

'You're going to stay here till I come back; I won't be more than half an hour, and then you can go out to play.'

'Has our Tishy got to stay in an' all?'

'You've all got to stay in.'

'She'll fight me.'

'I'll speak to Tishy.'

'She'll still fight me, an' if she does I'll kick her, I will, I will.'

'Now, Rance, behave yourself. If there's any trouble when I'm out that'll put paid to the puppy. Now mind, I'm warning you, there'll be no puppy for you.'

As she hurriedly laid the table for the four of them, the boy sat sulking. His chin resting on his folded arms on the kitchen window-sill, he stared down the backyard. Rance worried her at times, because the traits of his nature were so opposed. She knew that among boys of his own age he did quite a bit of bullying, yet he was afraid of Tishy, and his fear caused him to retaliate – she never used the word underhanded or sneaky when thinking of his reactions to his sister, but told herself that against the open hostility of Tishy he had to be on the defensive.

When he turned quickly from the window and seated himself at the table she knew Tishy had entered the yard, and when the child came into the kitchen she said to her, 'Hello there.'

'Hallo, Mam. . . . Mam.'

'Yes, dear?'

'Guess what?'

'I don't know. Something nice happened?'

'A-hah. I think I'm gona be picked for the May pocession.'

'Procession, Tishy.'

'That's what I said, Mam, pocession. Miss Willard heard me singing, "O Mary, we crown thee with blossoms today, Queen of the Angels an' Queen of the May"; an' she said I sang good.'

'Oh, that's nice. Wash your hands now quickly an' sit up and get your tea.'

'Am I . . . am I not goin' out to play?'

'Not until I come back. I'm just going to slip down to the garage to see your dad and I want you to be a good girl.'

Tishy went to the sink and washed her hands. This done, the tap still running, she put her hands under it and scooped some water into her mouth and started to rub her tongue with her fingers.

It was her choking that brought Annie's attention to her and she cried, 'What are you up to, child? Are you trying to choke yourself?'

Tishy spat into the sink, wiped her mouth on the roller towel, then walking to the table, took her seat before she said casually, 'Father Ryan says people who swear should have their mouths scrubbed out.'

'But you don't swear . . . do you?'

'No . . . but . . . but I think things, swear things.' The child stared up at Annie, her mouth set in a thin line, her eyes wide and serious.

Suppressing a smile, Annie put out her hand and touched her child's head, saying, 'Get on with your tea.' At times this daughter of hers was so honest she was embarrassing.

She now ran upstairs and put on her coat and hat, and glancing at herself quickly in the mirror she turned her face first to one side and then the other. Was she getting a double chin? . . . Aw, of all the things to ask herself at a time like this when her mind was full of the other business. She was barmy at times, stupid, daft.

In the kitchen again where they were all seated round the table, she addressed herself to Rance, saying, 'Now mind, remember what I told you.'

The boy didn't answer, but Tishy asked, 'What did you tell him, Mam?' and before she could speak Bill supplied the answer, saying, 'He'll not get his puppy if he wallops you.'

Annie sighed, then cried at them, 'Now I'm warning you, all of you. Any trouble an' you're all for it. Now mind . . . and see to Kathy. Do you hear, Rance? See to Kathy.'

'If Grandma Cooper comes she'll see to her, then can I go out?'

'No, Boy, you can't, an' that's final.' She stared at him hard before turning away.

Grandma Cooper! Her mother had not been near them since they moved. She'd made her mouth go about them living at the depot but since they had got some place decent, and better by a mile than what she 'had, she had ignored the fact. Her da had said, 'Leave her be, she'll come round, if it's only out of curiosity.' But she was a long time in coming round. Oh, her mother was a queer creature.

She caught a bus to the bottom of Fowler Street, from there she walked to the garage.

The front of the garage lay back from the main thoroughfare. It had two sets of double doors at the front and two petrol pumps. It also had a back entrance, and it was to this Annie made her way. Having passed through an alley, she came into a broad lane, bordered on both sides by six-foot stone walls. In the middle of the lane a large single door led into the back of the garage. It was partly open and she went through, past the car pit, above which a car was suspended, and round the corner into the main area. At the far end near the front doors was a make-shift erection that served as an office, and she came to a dead stop when she saw, standing in its doorway, Arthur Bailey, and facing him, Georgie.

When neither of them turned towards her she realized they hadn't seen her, and instead of going forward she stepped back into the shelter of the raised car and stood with her fingers against her lips. When she heard their footsteps approaching the middle of the garage she urged herself to move. She didn't want to be caught standing here as if she were listening. But she didn't move for the footsteps had stopped.

'It would be like a new life, Georgie.' That was Arthur Bailey's voice, and now Georgie answered, 'I cannot understand you, man; there's nowt but muck around here.'

'It isn't places that matter, you know that, Georgie, it's people.'

'Aye, aye, you're right there.'

'You could expand. As I said I'll put all I've got into it. I could do the buying and selling, and you could teach me a bit of the mechanics . . . Think about it, Georgie, will you? You've got no idea what it'll mean to me. As I said, it'll be like starting to live again. . . . Think about it, Georgie. . . . Please?'

The last words were a plea and they brought her fingers pressing tighter against her lips.

'I'll . . . I'll have to talk it over with Annie.'

There was a pause before Arthur Bailey's voice came again, saying, 'Yes, yes, of course. And . . . and you could point out to her that she'd have Mona with her again. She would like that, I'm sure, they used to be good friends. It could work out, Georgie, it could.'

'All right, Arthur, all right.'

When she saw them standing close together, Arthur Bailey's two hands gripping Georgie's, her body swayed forward, and she had no power to stop the protest rushing up from the depths of her and spurting from her lips almost in a scream, '*No! No!*'

The men started as if they had both been shot, then stood transfixed for a moment gazing at her before she turned and ran.

When she reached the entrance to the alleyway she heard Georgie's voice calling after her down the back lane, and as she came out of the other end of the alleyway and ran down the street, she could still hear him shouting, 'Annie! Annie! Do you hear me, Annie?'

A passer-by tried to stop her. 'What's up, lass?' he said. Frantically she thrust him off and went on running.

Because she knew she must look mad tearing along the main street she jumped on to a bus that was picking up passengers and she alighted at the next stop, boarded another and within ten minutes was back in the house. . . .

Preparing for what was to follow, she bundled the children out to play; then she waited. She knew he'd either close the garage up or leave it in care of the lad.

He stormed in the front way almost banging the door off its hinges. She heard him go into the kitchen, then the front room, then come up the stairs. She had chosen to wait for him in the bedroom, for here their voices would be less likely to carry to the neighbours on either side, at least they wouldn't be able to make out word for word unless they made a point of coming up into their own bedrooms and putting their ears to the wall.

She was standing with her arms folded looking out of the window when he entered the room.

'What the hell do you mean?'

She turned slowly towards him. Her lips trembling, but her voice low, she said, 'If you don't want the whole street to know what I mean stop your bawling.'

They glared at each other, their angers equal, Annie's depriving her face of all colour, Georgie's flooding his to a purple hue.

She said now, still low, 'You're not taking him on.'

She watched him gulp twice before he replied, 'That's up to me.'

'Oh no, it isn't. Let me tell you somethin', Georgie McCabe.' She took
one step nearer to him and gripped the end of the bed rail. 'You bring him
into the business and I walk out. Now think on what I'm saying. That fellow
comes in, I go out.'

Again they were staring at each other in silence. Then taking his fist, he
beat it against his head, and the sound made her wince. She watched him
go round in a small circle, his body almost bent double, and when he stopped
he was gripping his grease-streaked hair, and he cried at her, 'What the
bloody hell's up with you, woman? Spit it out! Go on, spit it out!'

'All right, all right, I'll spit it out.' Her head was bobbing on her shoulders.
'That . . . that Partridge fellow. I told you what he suggested, I told you,
and when I did you didn't fly off the handle, did you? One would have
expected a fellow like you to go back there and wring his bloody neck but
you didn't, did you? You didn't even put up a show of doing it.'

He was leaning towards her now, his hands flat on the middle of the bed.
His lower jaw worked from one side to the other before he could get his
words out, and then, the saliva spraying from his lips, he said, 'Do you
know what you're saying? You're telling me I'm a bloody queer.'

She stared at him while the tears swelled her throat to bursting point.
Yes, yes, that's what she was telling him, she was telling him he was a
bloody queer, and she knew he wasn't. What was up with her? Was she
mad? No, she wasn't mad because there was something fishy, something not
quite right, and she said so.

'I'm . . . I'm not saying anything of the sort, but what I am saying is
there's something not right with him. You know it yourself, you do, you do.'

She watched him droop his head slowly forward now and she cried at
him, 'I'm right aren't I? I am, I know I am.'

As he twisted his body round and slumped on to the edge of the bed the
sickness within her erupted, but it, too, stuck in her throat. She leant back
against the dressing table, her two hands pressed tight into her breasts as if
to check the heaving inside her.

Leaning forward now, Georgie put his elbows on his knees and dropping
his joined hands between them he began to speak in a tone which seemed
to be derived of all emotion. 'All right, he's queer,' he said, 'but I'm not
. . . not that bloody way anyroad.' He cast an infuriated glance towards her.
'And what's more he's not, not really. He's the odd man out, an oddity if
you like. God help him, he's neither one thing nor the other. I'll tell you
something now.' He turned his head slowly and looked at her. 'I wish he
was queer, real queer, for his own sake, then he'd have something. As it is
he has nowt.'

He now rubbed his hand around his face, and there was a pause before
he went on, 'When we first met in the cookhouse I knew he was different
in more ways than one 'cos we were bloody well poles apart. But you know
somethin'? He was the only one up till then who hadn't treated me as a
bloody numskull. I appeared as somebody real to him, so he said, an' I could
understand what he meant after meetin' his folks. And that's another thing
I'll press home to you, I was never taken in by them. Me brains might be
scarce but what I lack in them I bloody well make up in cuteness. I can
weigh people up. Oh aye, I can that. I'm like me mother there, and the more
they take me for a bloody fool the more I learn about them. Oh, I took his

folks' measure all right. I was good for a laugh, I suited their purpose. But at the same time they suited mine, an' . . . an' I was seein' a different way of life, a kind I'd never seen afore, a different way from our bloody hand-to-mouth kind. If you want to know something –' he turned his head and looked at her – 'I was grateful to him for noticin' me, just noticin' me. Do you understand that?' He thrust his head forward now. 'Not a bloody soul afore had given me credit for havin' a grain of gumption. I was Georgie, the easy-going gullible galoot, on a level with Barney Skillet and John Fowlcroft, the two blokes in our street who couldn't even keep their bloody noses clean. So there you have it. An' as for what you heard that stinking sod Partridge say, well whatever grounds he had for it I don't know, but it didn't apply to me, let me tell you that.'

He turned his head from her now and gazed down at his joined hands and said with unconscious humour, 'If you think I'm queer then I must have bloody well created a new species. Four bairns I've given you an' could do with it six times a day, that's not countin' overtime. An' then you think I'm queer. Bloody God!'

She rushed out of the room and across the landing and into the bathroom, and when she stood heaving over the sink he came and put his arm around her shoulders and held her head. Then he wiped her mouth, as he had done on the only other occasion when this subject had been mentioned between them.

The tears streaming from her eyes, she now gazed into his homely looking face, and there came to her in one great shock of surprise the fact that she loved him. She loved Georgie McCabe, the big loud-mouthed numskull, and that was the reason for her . . . carrying-on, as she had done. Whatever affection or love he had to give she wanted it directed towards her, and her alone.

Intuitively she knew it wasn't love he had for Arthur but compassion, but her intuition had warned her all along that compassion was a dangerous ingredient when combating love, and she was still afraid of it.

She said softly, 'Don't take him on, Georgie; please, please, don't take him on.'

He looked back into her eyes for a full minute before he answered. 'All right, lass. If that's how you feel about it, things'll stay as they are.'

When she fell against him and her crying mounted and her arms, for the first time that he could remember, held him tightly he stared over her shoulder while stroking her hair. A question slowly coming into his mind, he pressed her gently from him and looking into her streaming face, he asked her quietly, 'Tell me, Annie, do . . . do you like me? I mean . . . I mean more than just puttin' up with things . . . with me like?'

When she blinked and nodded her head twice he said, 'Honest?' and she muttered, 'Honest. Honest, Georgie.'

His lids blinked rapidly before he pulled her to him and held her tightly, and what he said thickly, and with a certain wonder, was, 'Bloody strange thing, life.'

# Chapter One

## Alan

Georgie McCabe had got on like a house on fire. Everyone said so; even Mary grudgingly admitted as much, but she never failed to qualify it with, 'Our Annie's been behind it all. If it hadn't been for her he would still be shovelling coal in the yards.'

Mollie, of course, gave Annie full credit for her son's success. She would continually say, 'Well, lass, didn't I say if anyone could make a roof with rotten straw you could?' And she would add, 'But the straw wasn't so bad after all, was it, lass?' to which Annie invariably answered, 'It was you that said it was rotten, not me, Mollie.'

In the thirteen years that had elapsed since they had moved to 17 Bewlar Terrace, everything, from an outsider's view, had seemingly gone McCabe's way; not only had he been able to buy the garage but also to extend it by acquiring two shops to the right of it and a house to the left, the latter having since been converted into an office downstairs and a mechanic's flat above.

The McCabe family itself had also expanded in a truly surprising fashion. Take the daughter, Tishy. At eighteen she was about to leave home and go to a teachers' training college. She was a clever one was Tishy, relations and friends alike said this. They said it to her face; but, as some said behind her back, she had to have something to make up for her looks; it was a shame that she should be so awfully plain and it showed up more so because Kathy was so bonny. It didn't matter about Kathy not having any brains, you didn't need brains when you looked like her. A great future was prophesied for Kathy by both relations and friends. She could win a beauty contest, she could be a model, she could even be picked for a film star.

Then there was Bill. Bill was the brightest of the lot. Bill had passed his 'O' levels with flying colours and even the masters at school prophesied that his 'A' levels were a foregone conclusion. In another year's time, Bill would be heading for the university.

. . . And Rance. Rance was his father's right-hand man in the garage. He was a marvel with cars; that's why he had left school at fifteen. If he liked he could have done as well as Bill. At least this is what Annie persistently said, and in his hearing.

Yes, the McCabes had got on. And now they were thinking seriously of another move, to a bigger house in Westoe. Although Tishy and Bill would soon be at college, Rance showed no sign of leaving home. He had girls in plenty but their acquaintance didn't last long. And then there was Kathy to consider. Annie decided that Kathy would have a better chance of meeting someone nice if they moved into Westoe, and she was anxious that Kathy should meet and marry someone nice, because she knew that Kathy, like Rance, needed to be taken care of.

And with regard to Annie herself; both family and friends all agreed that no one would believe that she was the mother of two strapping young men and two fine girls. Why! they assured her, she didn't look twenty-eight, let alone thirty-eight. But when she looked in the glass Annie knew that such reckoning was fulsome praise. Nevertheless she also saw that she didn't look her age. Surveying her unlined skin, clear eyes and abundant healthy hair, she would sometimes nod at herself and say, 'Thirty-two, Annie, perhaps thirty-three. Long may it last.'

She was standing in front of the mirror now trying on a new dress. Up till three or four years ago she hadn't bothered very much with her own appearance, her time had been taken up with running the house, seeing to the children and trying to control Georgie's increasing intake of liquor, besides keeping the accounts of the garage. But since she had passed the latter business over to Rance she had more time to give to herself and, what was equally important, money to buy decent clothes. She went to Binns now for her things, and her last two outfits had select name-tags attached to them.

She was very pleased with what the mirror showed her at this moment, and then, as she often did, she thought of Tishy, and was attacked by a spasm of guilt. As at other times she saw now imposed on her reflection in the mirror the face of her daughter. How was it, she asked herself yet again, that the others were all so presentable; Kathy beautiful, Rance good-looking even in spite of his sullenness, and Bill, although not promising to be Rance's height, was at seventeen very attractive, his stocky body and blunt features giving him something which, she grudgingly admitted, was lacking in Rance; while Tishy, poor soul, had nothing to recommend her but her voice. It was this, her only asset, that also emphasized the difference between her and her brothers and sister still further, because even from a child she had spoken differently from them; the northern inflexion was less noticeable in her voice than in theirs, and she always pronounced her g's. That was why, Annie supposed, she had come out top in English. It was strange, she thought, that her daughter should speak so well when all her life she had listened to her father reiterating bloody and bugger.

But what, after all, was a good voice when you looked like she did. Her face so thin, her mouth still made up of two straight lines, and her nose still as snubbed as it had been when a baby. . . . And her eyes. Well, her eyes could have been bonny. . . . No, that wasn't the word, not bonny . . . attractive? No, not that either. Compelling? No. No, she could never find a word with which to describe Tishy's eyes. But she remembered once when Tishy first went to the high school her rushing in one night saying her teacher had given her a book of poems to keep because she had read her poetry so well. And there and then she had sat down at the kitchen table and started to read, just like that. She hadn't known she could read aloud; she knew she read a lot but she had never heard her read aloud. And in amazement she had listened to her saying:

Woman much missed, how you call to me, call to me,
Saying that now you are not as you were

When you had changed from the one who was all to me,
But as at first, when our day was fair.

Tishy had looked up at her then and her eyes were full of tears when she
said, 'It's called "The Voice". It's by Hardy, Thomas Hardy.'

It was at that moment that she thought, her eyes are beautiful, but she
had never seen them beautiful since for she had never read aloud again.

And of the four of them, Tishy was the most stubborn. Whatever she
thought was right out it would come, and no arguing would change her
opinion. The things she said at times startled her. None of the others talked
as Tishy did, not even Bill; although she had heard her and Bill discussing
things which were beyond her. Only last week they had been on about
ghettoes and protest marches and the rights of the individual, as if everybody
they knew was in prison. That discussion had nearly ended up in a row for
Rance had turned on them, saying, 'For God's sake! shut your traps, the
both of you, you make me sick.' It was then that Tishy had come out with
one of her irritating wisecracks. 'One day,' she said, 'you'll take ill and
they'll find you've got an abscess on the brain and when they open it up it'll
be so full of ignorance it'll be a record.'

On this particular occasion she had caught hold of Rance's uplifted arm
even while she knew that he wouldn't dare strike Tishy, knowing she would
have turned on him like a wild cat.

Annie had always been puzzled about Tishy's attitude towards her elder
brother. She could have understood it if her frustration had been turned on
Kathy for, since she was a baby, Kathy's looks had emphasized her own
plainness. But she had never been nasty to Kathy, and she had always had
an open affection for Bill.

Over the past weeks Annie's feeling of guilt with regards to Tishy had
increased for she found she was looking forward to the late summer when
Tishy would leave home and go to the training college.

Thinking of her now she said to herself as she tried to get a back view of
her dress in the mirror, 'I must get her well rigged out, smart things, good
cuts; her figure isn't bad, but it could be better.'

At this moment the door opened and she started slightly as Georgie came
into the room.

'I didn't hear you come in.'

He looked at her for a moment, then walked to the bedside chair and,
dropping on to it, stretched his legs out before saying, 'You know I wish I
had a penny for every time you've said that to me over the years. I've got
feet like a corporation horse –' he wagged them from side to side – 'I can
hear them clop-clopping even in me stocking feet. The trouble with you is
your mind's always on some damn thing or other.'

She looked back at him through the mirror and asked, 'Do you like it?'

'I've seen it afore, haven't I?'

'No, you haven't seen it afore.'

'Aye, it's all right.'

'Oo . . . h!' she groaned. Then, her eyes becoming fixed on his through the
mirror, she asked, 'What is it, something up?' And she had turned to him
before he answered, 'Aye, there's something up; it's our Rance.'

'Our Rance?'

'Aye, our Rance.' He brought bitterness into the name. 'Mr Phillips came into the garage this mornin' and after I'd filled him up I just put it to him nicely. "Do you want to settle up your bill?" I said.

' "Bill?" he said. "Why, you're gettin' a bit sticky, Georgie, aren't you? You've never asked for me bill afore. I settled up last month; I never let it run more than two months." Was my bloody face red! I didn't know what to say. I said there must've been a mistake. I'd take a look at the books again, perhaps it hadn't been entered. But that didn't pacify him very much 'cos he left, sayin', "Then you want a new book-keeper, don't you?" And away he went, an' it's my bet he won't be back again.'

'Did he have a receipt?'

'Aye, he says it's home and he's goin' to bring it along. By the tone of his voice he'll push it under me bloody nose. . . . Well, I looked at the books again and there it was, nothing down. Three months owing for petrol and twenty-five quid for repairs.'

'What did our Rance say?' Her voice was quiet.

'I'll tell you what our Rance said.' He got to his feet now. 'Our Rance said he couldn't understand it. Aye, he said, he had given Mr Phillips a receipt and he had put the money in the till. Why he hadn't taken it off the book he just didn't know.'

'Well then he's explained it. Don't you believe him?'

'Look woman, I may not be so bloody hot on figures but if he had put that money in the till wouldn't the balance have been a bit on the heavy side at the end of the week? Two months' petrol and twenty-five quid for repairs would have tilted the weekly check-up wouldn't it?'

'But you don't always check up at the end of the week.'

'No, I don't, I leave it to him most times, but once or twice lately I've had a check up on me own, 'cos now I'm goin' to tell you somethin', Annie. This isn't the first time I've suspected him.'

'What! Our Rance? Don't be silly. Don't be stupid, man. Our Rance! It would be like cutting off his nose to spite his . . .'

'Oh no, it wouldn't; he doesn't happen to own the bloody garage, does he?' His words were slow as were the movements of his head. 'And another thing I'm gona tell you, somethin' that you don't know, somethin' that I should've told you a while back but knowin' how you worry your guts out over one and another of them, him in particular, I kept it to meself. . . . He's at the gamblin' lark.'

'Our Rance!'

'Oh, bloody St Patrick! stop repeatin' our Rance. Aye, our Rance. Get it out of your head, lass. He was never meant for the priesthood or the monastery. He's got faults, and as I see them, bloody big 'un's. Of course, for you the sun shines out of him. You've wiped his backside for years.' He was walking up and down the room now. 'The others could go to hell, me included, as long as . . . our Rance was all right.'

'That's not fair, that's not fair. I've treated them all alike.'

'Like hell you have! I could flay the living daylights out of Bill, but let me lift me hand to Rance and all hell was let loose. Well now, face up to it, your wonderful Rance has been fiddlin' me books, our books, so he could sit in at nights at Connelly's. And what's more he's got in with the right bunch, Pete Cullender and Maurice Boulder an' that lot.'

'Pete Cullender!' Her voice was a mere whisper now. 'You mean the Cullender that was in the papers last week?'

'Aye, the one and the same Cullender who was in the papers last week.'

'He wouldn't, not our Rance.'

'Aw, for God's sake!' He was bawling now, and she hissed at him, 'Stop it! Keep your voice down; do you want the whole street to know?'

His voice lower, he leant towards her, saying, 'It won't be only the street that'll know, it'll be the town if he keeps this up. You'll have to speak to him. He won't listen to me, I'm only his bloody father; but you tell him from me that his bloody father knows what he's up to, an' let me find out one more thing and he's out. Do you hear? I mean that, he's out on his arse. Well now –' he tugged both sides of his coat together, pulled in his lips and ended, 'Having said that I'll have some tea,' and he walked out of the room leaving her standing staring at the door.

Rance. Rance. Rance fiddling the books. She couldn't believe it. Well, if she didn't believe it Georgie must be making it up. But she knew her husband well enough to know that it would be impossible for him to make up something like that against his own son. Yet the relationship between him and Rance had always been strained. Up till Rance was fifteen he had lathered him for his misdemeanours and she had to admit he had been justified. The last lathering he had given him was after the schoolmaster had asked to see them both and told them that Rance was running a small gang of shop-lifters who operated on a Saturday morning between the market and King Street. They hadn't been able to believe their ears, at least she hadn't. Thankfully the matter hadn't got into the court, for which clemency they had to thank the fact that one of Rance's henchmen was the son of a man of some influence in the town. On that occasion she had thought that Georgie would kill him, and perhaps he might have if she hadn't thrust herself between them and taken some of the blows from the leather belt which were meant for the boy.

The idea of Rance going into the garage was not only to provide him with training towards a career but in order that Georgie could keep an eye on him. And apparently he had up till now, for there had been but one incident over the past few years, and this she had never got to the bottom of. She hadn't told Georgie of it, and when she had confronted Rance and demanded why a man called Bilby should come to the door and tell her that if he didn't keep away from his daughter he would do for him, he had answered, 'Aw, my God! would you believe it. It's her he should be doing for, not me; she's still at school an' I can't walk down the street for her.'

'Where does she live?'

'Sunderland Road.'

'But what do you have to do along Sunderland Road, you don't go that way?'

'I met her when I went to meet Alec comin' from the tech. He knew her, he said she was bloke barmy.'

'But why should her father pick on you?'

'Don't ask me. God! the things folk get up to, they would hang you!'

His indignation with regard to this incident had reassured her he wasn't in the wrong, but all the indignation he might show with regard to the present affair wouldn't prove his innocence to her for she had only to think back over the last few months. The fine gold wrist-watch he suddenly sported. Came by it second-hand, dirt cheap, he had said. The new suit that she knew now had never come from Burton's. And then there were the odds and ends in his room: that real leather brief-case, not plastic like Bill's and Tishy's; those two silk shirts that he had supposedly bought at a sale in Newcastle, again dirt cheap.

The old feeling of sickness began to churn in her stomach. She'd have to speak to him; more than speak to him, go for him, and she hated going for him. He had only to look at her in that particular way with that look he kept only for her, that look that always seemed to cry out for her love, and she was undone.

When she had discovered that she had a deeper feeling than mere toleration or affection for Georgie, it hadn't detracted one iota from the feeling she had for her elder son; in fact her feelings towards the boy had seemed to deepen as if to prove to him that her love for his father was in no way derived from that which she had for him.

'Mam.' The door suddenly opened and Kathy put her head round. 'Can I come in?'

'Yes, yes, dear.'

'What's the matter with dad? Somebody's going to get it if I can read the signs. He's got his billy-goat look on. You two been at it?'

'No, we haven't been at it, miss. What do you want?'

'Oh, nothing, nothing.' Kathy shook her pretty head and her pony tail swung from side to side. 'I was just going to give you details of my latest suitor, that's all, that's all.'

In spite of herself and the way she was feeling, Annie laughed and said, 'What! another one?'

'Oh, this one's different. This one will suit the house in Westoe. Oh yes, yes.' She now strutted up and down the bedroom while Annie took a comb from the dressing table and drew it through her hair.

'What's his name?'

'Mr Percy Rinkton.'

'Never-'eard-of-'im.'

'Well, from what I know you certainly will soon; he wants to come and see you . . . or dad.'

Annie swung round and they looked at each other, and Kathy made a deep obeisance with her head. 'Yes, yes, he's that kind of a fellow, everything above board.'

'Well, that's a change.'

'What do you mean, that's a change? All my boys are above board.'

'You want your ears boxed.'

'I want a new dress.'

'You've got some hope; you've had three already this year.'

'I'm a growing girl.'

Looking through the mirror at her daughter's quickly developing bust, Annie nodded and said, 'And how!' And at this they both laughed. Then Annie, her tone serious, asked, 'Well, what about this fellow?'

'Ever heard of Doctor Rinkton?'

'Yes, yes, I've heard of Doctor Rinkton.'

'Well Percy Rinkton is Doctor Rinkton's son. No kiddin'. No kiddin', Mam.'

'We're flying high all of a sudden. How old is he?'

'Twenty-odd. What do you think of that, a man.'

Annie turned fully round now and looked at Kathy and said seriously, 'Yes, a man; and you want to be careful. Have you been seeing him?'

'I've spoken to him –' she pursed up her mouth and screwed up her eyes and counted on her fingers – 'one, two, three, four times. I first saw him at a dance, St Patrick's do. But be prepared to receive the first shock, he's not a Catholic. The second time I met him was when I got off a bus. I lurched into him. The third time was in Phillips's bookshop, you know, at the bottom of Fowler Street. He was buying books; he looks a bit bookie. And the fourth time was this very day. He was waiting for me coming out of school. Stopped me at the corner and very precisely asked when I was going to leave school, and I told him as soon as ever I possibly could 'cos I hated it.'

'Oh, Kathy, you didn't!'

'Honest I did. I did. And anyway, as I've told you before, it's no use keeping me there. I haven't any brains; I'm not like Tishy, I'm all bumf.' She gave a lift to her bust, and again they were laughing, leaning against each other now. But after a moment Annie chastised her, saying, 'You'll get your ears boxed one of these times, me girl, for the things you say. But go on.'

'Well then, he asked how old I was, and I told him knocking sixteen. "When?" he said – he's a stickler for details. "Next month," I said. Then you know what? He said would I ask my parents if he could come round and see them.'

They were standing apart now and Kathy, laughing at the expression on Annie's face, said, 'No kidding, he did. That's what he said, could he come round and see you? And I said, what for? and he said, well, he would like to get everything straightforward.'

'What did he mean, straightforward?'

'That's what I would like to know.'

'What did you say then?'

'I said ours was an open house, people were going in and out all the time, it was like jail, and I was sure you'd make him very welcome.'

'You didn't!'

'I did, Mam.' She pursed her lips again. Then he asked if tomorrow afternoon would be convenient, and I said, yes, tomorrow afternoon would be quite convenient, being Saturday and you having nothing to do and being very bored with life . . .'

Annie's hand came out quickly and slapped the side of her daughter's face, but gently.

'Well, what could I say? You have to meet him, he's a scream. He's . . . he's . . . well, I can't tell you what he's like, he's so, what's the word? aboveboard. Yes, that's the word, aboveboard. Aw my goodness!' She closed her eyes and shook her head widely from side to side now. 'And how aboveboard! He tickles me to death, Mam.'

'I don't know about being tickled to death –' Annie raised her eyebrows – 'it's a new approach, I'll say that. Does . . . does he look very old-fashioned?'

'Old-fashioned! No. He's just precise, like his name, Percy. Awful name isn't it, Percy?'

As Annie was about to speak she heard Georgie's voice shouting from below, and she said, 'We'll talk about this later, there's your dad bawling for his tea.'

'Mam.' Kathy pulled Annie to a halt as they were going out on to the landing and whispered, 'I'll die the day I see me dad and Mr Percy Rinkton together. Aw, that'll be something.'

Annie now pushed her daughter none too gently towards the stairs, saying, 'And you've got something coming to you, you young monkey.' Then she added, I'll deal with Mr Percy Rinkton.'

They were both laughing as they went down the stairs, but before Annie reached the bottom she knew that she would have someone else to deal with before she met her youngest daughter's latest suitor, and in that confrontation there would be no laughter or amusement.

Georgie had gone out for his usual evening drink, and so, apart from Tishy who was upstairs studying, she was alone when Rance came in. Before he had taken off his coat in the hall she tackled him. 'Come on in here a minute,' she said, going towards the sitting-room.

He didn't immediately follow her but, straightening his tie, said, 'What is it? I want me tea, I'm going out.'

'You'll get your tea in a minute; I've got to have a word with you.'

He followed her into the room and closed the door but he didn't look at her as he walked towards the empty fireplace, and there, taking a cigarette packet from his pocket, he extracted a cigarette and lit it.

She let him do this and take the first whiff before she said, 'What's this I'm hearing from your dad?'

'Well, what is it you're hearin' from me dad?' He had his back to her, looking down on the ornamental glass screen that fronted the empty grate.

'Now, Rance, I want no hanky-panky.'

Glancing at her over his shoulder he said, 'Who's giving you hanky-panky? I don't know what you're on about.'

'You know fine well. What's this about Mr Phillips's bill that you forgot to enter up?'

'Well, that's all about it, I forgot to enter it up.'

'Twenty-five pounds for repairs and two months' petrol, that surplus would have stuck out like a sore thumb any week. We don't deal in thousands you know.'

'Look, Mam –' he turned, took a step towards her and held out his hands as if in supplication as he said, 'He checks up the till every night, doesn't he? He goes over the books every Friday . . .'

'You know fine well he makes pretence of going over them, he hasn't got a head for figures; you've always known it.'

'Hasn't a head for figures? By lad! you try doing him out of sixpence and he'll let you know whether he's got a head for figures or not.'

'It's different when it's in writing.'

'Look, Mam –' his voice was soft, appealing – 'are you accusing me of pinching the money?'

She stared into his eyes and as always, like some young lass in love, she felt herself assailed by a weakness which now prompted her to say, 'No, of course I'm not.' But one of the level-headed chambers of her mind opened its door and out of it came the answer to his question. 'You're gambling,' she said.

His voice still quiet, he replied, 'All right, I'm gambling. And I've been winning. I've got proof of it upstairs, the things I've been buying. You've noticed them surely.'

'You said you had got them on the cheap.'

'Well, I had an' all, and that's gambling. Anyway, what's wrong with sittin' at the tables now and again? Our auspicious neighbour three doors down, she's there every bloomin' night.'

'Well, you must be an' all to see her.'

Of a sudden his quiet demeanour vanished and his teeth ground against each other for a moment before he burst out, 'What the hell! Christ Almighty! I'm not a boy any more, Mam, I'm a man. I'm bloody well doing a man's work and more.'

'Stop that swearing and cursing.'

'Oh my God!' The words came out on a rising, mirthless laugh. 'That's the funniest thing I've heard in years, you tellin' me to stop cussing, when you've lived it and breathed it for how many years? Twenty-one. Twenty-one years you've been married, and your husband's got the nickname of "Bloody McCabe" and you chastise me for swearing. God! that's a laugh. Look –' he bent towards her – 'don't you see the funny side of it?'

'Don't change the subject.' He was an expert in this line. She would start on one thing and before she knew where she was he was arguing about something entirely different. 'Stick to the point, Rance . . . for once,' she added; 'and the point isn't swearing, it's . . . it's stealing, thieving, and from your own. And there's your dad. Be he what he may he wouldn't do anybody out of a farthing . . .'

'Aw, Dad! Dad wouldn't do anybody out of a farthing.' He was mimicking her now. 'Dad's a bloody saint and that's swearing to it again. Underneath that rough exterior of his an' his big ignorant mouth he's a bloody saint . . .'

'*Rance!*'

'Never mind Rancing me, Mam, I'm gettin' tired of hearing about Dad's virtues. Hardly a week goes by but it's: "He has his drawbacks, he's rough and ready, but . . . but underneath . . ." Well, let me tell you something. In my opinion you must have been bloody well blind all these years not to see you've been married to a gormless nowt.'

Her hand was raised to come down on him when he barked at her, 'Don't! Don't do it, Mam, because if you do I'll walk out, and that's the last you'll see of me.'

As her hand slowly dropped to her side and she felt the blood draining, not only from her face but seemingly from her whole body, he said, his tone now as different again from what it had been a moment previously, for it was now like that of a young boy, 'I meant it, Mam, I meant it. I would, I would I tell you, I'd leave you . . .'

The more he protested the more she knew that it was an empty threat. Rance would never leave her unless it was for a woman, and the woman would, unknowingly, have to be taking her place.

When her head bowed and the tears ran down her face his arms came about her and he held her, muttering all the while, 'Oh, Mam! Mam, give over. Come on, give over. Look, I swear to you I didn't take that money. Look at me.'

She looked at him through her misted eyes and she muttered, 'You're speaking the truth?'

'Honest. Honest to God.'

She said now, 'What about the lad, young Jimmy, could he have got at the till?'

He turned his head to the side as if thinking; then, looking at her again, said, 'Not that I know of. Look, Mam, as I see it the money was in the till and Dad picked it up on the Friday night. You know what he is, he stuffs everything into his pockets. He's got no method.'

'But . . . but he brings the money straight back home.'

'Not always. Remember that night he didn't get back here till half past ten and then he was paralytic?'

Yes, she remembered that night about a month ago. He had met two fellows he had known at Madley and had taken them to the club, and the three of them had staggered back here at closing time. She drew herself slowly from his arms and as she wiped her face she said to him, 'I'll put up with anything, Rance, as long as I know you don't fiddle, especially your own. You know what I mean?'

He put out his hand and touched her cheek. The touch was a caress such as none of the others ever gave her. Still, she never blamed them for that, because there wasn't the same feeling between them and herself. Although she loved each one of them the feeling she had for her eldest was akin to passion. The colour came flooding back into her face at the thought.

He was smiling at her now. 'Now can I have me tea?'

'It's all ready,' she said quietly turning from him. When she went to walk out of the room he put his arms around her shoulders and when in the hall he looked up and saw Tishy coming down the stairs he deliberately hugged her to him before taking his arm away.

At the sight of her daughter Annie lowered her head and hurried into the kitchen, but Rance didn't follow her; instead, he made for the stairs, saying, 'I'll have me wash first.'

He did not wait for Tishy to descend the last two stairs but pushed past her, and in the passing she said quietly, 'Dear Rance,' and he said in the same ironic tone, 'Dear Tishy,' and the exchange was like blows delivered straight into the other's face.


# Chapter Two


Tea on a Saturday was a haphazard event. It was usually a busy day at the garage and Rance might not get in before six, and Georgie nearer seven. If the school was playing football or cricket at home, depending on the season, Bill would come in demanding a meal any time between six and eight o'clock – the refreshments he'd had at the school tea never counted. When he was playing away she never knew what time to expect him back, but as she remarked, she always knew when he was in because he banged every door he came through.

Tishy usually attended some project or other on a Saturday afternoon. If not, she would take the train to Newcastle and wander around the old quarters, or spend hours in the museum, or the library; and she always took these trips alone.

The procedure for Kathy on a Saturday evening was to take the time between five and seven to get ready for the weekly dance, to which she never went unattended.

But on this particular Saturday the pattern had altered slightly. Kathy had been invited to spend the week-end with her best friend, Van Brignell, and an hour ago she had left the house to make the two-mile journey to Harton village with enough clothes in her case to last her a week. And Tishy, showing the first signs of a summer cold which, from experience, she knew would make her snub nose scarlet and keep her eyes watering for a week if not taken in time, had decided to forgo her Saturday jaunting and to nurse her cold while getting on with a bit more swotting.

So Annie, having the house practically to herself, decided she would wash her hair. She went to the hairdresser's only when she needed a trim for she had what she called good-tempered hair; it had a deep natural wave in it, and fell into place immediately after washing. Once her hair was dry she'd do her face and get into her new dress and be ready if Georgie managed to get home early; then perhaps they would go to the club for an hour. She felt she wanted to be taken out of herself. That scene with Rance last night had upset her, and then, later in bed, she hadn't been able to convince Georgie that Rance hadn't touched a penny of the money. His last words to her before he went to sleep were, 'You know summat; you still take me for a bloody numskull,' and she had been more disturbed than she cared to admit when he had turned his back on her. That had never happened before; she was always the one who did the turning away . . .

She did not wash her hair in the bathroom but in the kitchen sink, because it was larger and if she splashed a bit it didn't matter. She hated to see the bathroom messed up.

She had just wound a towel around her head and was about to switch on her electric hair-drier when the front door bell rang.

'Oh no!' She said the words aloud. Who could this be on a Saturday afternoon? Everybody was accounted for; there was only Tishy in and nobody ever called for Tishy; and it wouldn't be anybody selling on a Saturday afternoon. Strange, but they didn't come round selling on a Saturday afternoon; the morning yes, but never in the afternoon. She had often thought that was strange. It was no use shouting for Tishy to go and answer the door because she hardly showed her face to the family when she had a cold on her. Oh Lord! She glanced in the mirror, doubled the lapels of her blue woollen housecoat further across her chest, tightened the belt, then went out of the kitchen, across the hall and opened the door.

'Oh.' She gaped at the strange man standing before her. He was tall, taller than any of her men, six-foot and more he must be, and he was big made with it. His face was long and his lips full and his eyes a dark brown, a very dark brown. Well! well! Kathy had hit it this time. Mr Percy Rinkton was indeed a man, every inch of him. This fellow was certainly nothing to laugh or joke about; if she didn't do any worse than this she'd be all right; in fact, she couldn't see her doing any better, at least where looks were concerned. His face wasn't exactly handsome but it had something about it that, in her estimation, was better than good looks. He had taken off his hat and he was staring at her, his mouth slowly widening into a smile, when she said, 'You're Mr Rinkton, aren't you? Oh, I am sorry.' She put her hand on to her head and patted the towel. 'Fancy seeing me like this! But they're all out, and I was washing my hair.' Again she patted the towel. 'Kath's gone to stay with a friend; she'll be ever so sorry she missed you . . .' That monkey. She hadn't believed her. Wait till she saw her. And her to go off for the week-end like that knowing this fellow meant what he had said.

'I . . . I think there's been a slight mistake.'

His voice was nice an' all, quite posh, and there wasn't the slightest trace of a northern accent in it. 'What's that you said?'

'I said I think there's been a slight mistake, I am not Mr . . . who did you say, Rinkton?'

'You're not?'

'No, I'm not.' His smile had widened even further. He looked very amused and she became slightly embarrassed. 'You're not Mr Rinkton?'

'No, as I said I'm not Mr Rinkton. But we've met before, you do know me.'

'We've met before?' She screwed up her face at him. 'Never, never.' Now she was shaking her head as she thought, He's a con man; that's what he is.

'But yes, yes. I might have changed somewhat, but you, you haven't at all. I would have known you anywhere in spite of your turban.' He nodded towards her head, and again her hands went up to the towel. Her face was straight as she said, 'Who are you then?'

'My name is Alan Partridge; we last met when I was five years old.'

She had to snap her lower jaw up to prevent it dropping any further, and then her mouth opened wide again before she brought out the name, 'Alan . . . little . . . ?' She closed her eyes and shook her head, then said, 'No longer little. Oh please, please, come in. Come in.' She stood aside and let him enter the hall. 'Well! well! who would believe it. But . . . but you didn't recognize me, you can't.'

'Oh yes I did, and I do.'

'Look. Look.' Her hands were moving at random. Then closing her eyes tight again, she said, 'Oh, give me your hat and coat and let me get this thing off my head and then we can talk. My! my! is this a surprise! I . . . I thought you were the young man I was expecting to come and ask after my daughter, my youngest daughter. He was doing it in the old-fashioned way, he was coming to ask if he could take her out. Look, would you mind coming in here and waiting a moment?'

'Not at all.'

He walked past her into the sitting-room, and she darted to the side of the fireplace and switched on the electric fire; then patting the cushions into place on the couch she said, 'Do . . . do make yourself at home. Give me five minutes, will you, five minutes?'

His smile was wide again. 'Ten if you wish it, fifteen.'

'Look, my eldest daughter's upstairs; I'll bring her down and she can talk to you.'

'No, please, don't bother. Go on, dry your hair; I'll sit here and wait, very, very patiently.'

They looked at each other, then both burst out laughing, and she turned from him and ran into the kitchen and, picking up the hair-drier, she flew up the stairs and plugged it into the bedroom socket.

Her hair was only partly dry when she switched off the machine. Quickly getting into her dress she applied a dab of powder to her nose and a lipstick to her lips. Then as she went to leave the room she stopped, drew in a deep breath and asked herself what all the excitement was about. And she gave herself the answer. He had remembered her. After all these years he had remembered her. As Kathy would say, it was enough to boost anybody's ego. What was your ego anyway? Oh polony! When her mind got going it asked the daftest questions. Get downstairs, she said to herself.

When she passed Tishy's door she paused and, an idea flashing into her mind, she thought, Oh that would be wonderful. But it would be too good to be true. And with that cold on her there wasn't a hope.

Get downstairs, she said to herself again.

When she entered the room he rose to his feet. Wasn't that nice. Nobody had ever done that for her since she had met Arthur Bailey. She had forgotten for a moment that he was connected with Arthur Bailey; he and Mona seemed to have dropped entirely out of existence. She had seen Mona only once since the day she confided in her, and that was when she had come to bury her mother. They had exchanged a few words at the graveside, nothing more, they had been like strangers. She had been very upset about it.

After saying, 'Do sit down . . . would you like a cup of tea?' he answered, 'Yes, but not yet. You come and sit down.'

She sat down on the edge of the settee and asked, 'How's your uncle, your Uncle Arthur?'

'Oh, he was very well the last time I saw him.'

'Have you come this way on holiday, though –' she shook her head and laughed now – 'I don't know why you would pick Durham after Herefordshire.'

'Well, I have picked Durham, at least Northumberland, but not for a holiday. I've . . . I've just been appointed to a post in Newcastle University.'

'No!'

'Yes.' He gave a chuckling laugh. 'I was on the short list and, three parts of the selection committee being out of their tiny minds, they chose me. I still haven't got over it yet.'

She knew that he was talking himself down and she shook her head as she said, 'What's . . . what's your subject?'

'Mathematics.'

'Oh! mathematics. Bill, that's my second son, he has nightmares about maths. He's pretty good at most other things but maths have always bedevilled him. He's going to be a teacher too.'

'He is?'

'And my daughter, Tishy – short for Anastasia – she's going to be one an' all.'

'Oh.'

'She's clever, Tishy is, cleverer than Bill.'

'How many family have you?'

'Four. Rance is the eldest, he's twenty; Tishy eighteen, Bill seventeen and Kathy just on sixteen. That's the one I thought you were after; the fellows are never off the door.' She put her head back and laughed.

'She sounds attractive.'

'Oh, she's that all right, and very well aware of it. But tell me, how did you know where to find us?'

'Oh, Uncle Arthur gave me your address. He said you might still be here. He said if I found you I had to give you his regards and also remember him to your husband.'

A chill passed over her causing her to shiver slightly.

'How's your Aunt Mona these days?' She felt she should have asked this before, but she was still peeved with Mona. She felt she had been snubbed by her, yet in her heart she knew the real reason for Mona's silence. Mona knew it was she who had squashed Arthur's proposal to join Georgie in the garage.

'Oh.' He uncrossed his legs, then recrossed them again before he said, 'I ... I don't know, I haven't seen her these last five years. They ... they separated you know.'

'Separated? ... No, no, I didn't know. Where is she?'

'In London as far as I can gather.'

'I'm ... I'm sorry. And ... and your uncle?'

'Oh, he's still in the same place. It's rather a lonely life for him but he seems to prefer it that way.'

'Yes, yes.' She nodded her head; then on a lighter note, she said, 'And your mother? I remember your mother very well.'

She remarried about a year ago and is now living in America.'

'Really! and you're all on your own?'

'Yes, and I like it that way. I had to practically knock her unconscious before she would go. She still looked upon me as thirteen and not twenty-three.'

'But I suppose you miss her?'

'Oh yes, I miss her. Not so much now; I've had a year to get used to it. My life's very full, and besides I was away from home so much. I was at Oxford for four years.'

'Oxford!' There was a slight note of awe in her voice, then she added, 'Bill hopes that he might get into a university ... it must be wonderful to go to a university.'

'Oh, I don't know. It's just like school, only you have a longer leash on you.'

When a silence fell between them and he sat staring at her, a half-smile bringing one side of his mouth upwards as if he were amused at something, she blinked and said, 'I can't get over it. Fancy you remembering me from all those years ago.'

'Well, I was five, and they tell me a very precocious five.'

'I can't remember anything from I was five, hardly from I was seven.'

'I can remember the conversation we had regarding an unmentionable place.'

'An unmentionable place?' She screwed up her face at him.

'The jig.'

'Aw, yes.' She was nodding and laughing now. 'The jig. Yes, yes, I remember.'

'And so did my mother. She said I repeated that conversation daily until I was nearly eight. She was for murdering me. And then I suddenly stopped and never mentioned it again until I was almost fourteen; then out of the blue it came into my mind and when I said to my mother "Do you remember how I used to go on about the jig?" she put her hands over her ears and said, "Oh, don't start that again." So you see what an impression you made upon me.'

'You mean the jig did.'

'No, you. But, you know, I still call it the jig.'

Again there was silence, and again he was staring at her. And then he burst out, 'You know, it's amazing, I can't get over it, I mean how little you've changed. It's as if I were five last week; you're so like the memory I've retained of you.'

'But . . . but it's such a long time ago, over eighteen years.'

'Yes, it is.' His face unsmiling now, he nodded; then after a moment he said, 'I suppose what helped to imprint you in my mind was that I remember that Christmas as one big holy row. My mother went for my father, my grandmother went for my father, then she went for my Uncle Arthur; if I remember rightly practically no one was speaking to one another on Christmas Day, and they practically threw my presents at me, so the only happy memory that remained of that particular Christmas was of a lady who ran with me through the woods and laughed with me and discussed – jigs. And I must tell you this, a lady who I thought had come from a strange land.'

Annie put her hand over her mouth as she laughed. 'My Geordie accent.'

'No.' He lifted his finger and wagged it at her now. 'I won't say it was your Geordie accent, not after listening to some of the townspeople this past week or so. But seriously –' he shook his head – 'I can't understand a word some of them say.'

She now cocked her chin upwards as she said, 'Well, all I can say is your education has been sadly neglected in one quarter, anyway.' Getting to her feet, she added, 'I'm going to make you a cup of tea whether you want it or not. When did you last eat?'

'Oh, at lunch-time, I had a good meal.'

'And you're not hungry?'

He smiled at her again with his lips closed, and she said, 'That's my answer. Would you like to come into the kitchen? We can talk while I get you something.'

As they went towards the kitchen the door opened and Tishy came out, and they all stopped for a moment and looked at each other.

'Oh, Tishy, there you are. You won't know who this is. Someone I knew a long time ago, Mr Alan Partridge. Alan, this is my eldest daughter, Tishy.' Oh – Annie groaned to herself – didn't she look a sight; her little nose was like a red blob.

Alan smiled at the tall young girl standing before him, holding her handkerchief to her nose. She had an unusual face, he thought, and didn't look a bit like her mother. He held out his hand. 'How are you?'

'It's pretty evident,' she said, 'isn't it?' and Annie thought helplessly, That's Tishy all over, straight to the point.

Alan laughed and said, 'A double whisky, a whole lemon and a spoonful of ginger in boiling water. You'll be a new man – woman in the morning.'

'I'm going to make a cup of tea –' Annie looked at Tishy – 'and something to eat. Come on back and talk; you're bound to have something in common as Alan is going to teach at the university, Newcastle. What do you think of that?'

'Tishy turned a sidewards glance towards the tall man and after a moment she said, 'You are?'

'Yes.' Alan moved his head towards her. 'And I hear you're going in for the same racket.'

'Well –' Tishy was walking back into the kitchen – 'nothing so grand as the university; I'm going to a teachers' training college.'

'They informed me politely at headquarters that I would have been better equipped for the job if I'd had a year's training, too.'

'They did?'

'Yes.'

'Well –' Tishy sat herself down and crossed her legs – 'if I could trade, I know which one I'd take. What's your speciality?'

'Maths.'

'Oh! maths . . .'

'Don't say it like that, Tishy, you are very good at maths.'

Tishy turned and looked at Annie, and in a patient tone she said, 'There are maths, Mam, and maths. What I was very good at was merely maths.'

As Annie watched her smile at Alan, her cold apparently forgotten for the moment, wild ideas again began darting through her mind. She drew in a quick breath and said, 'Well, you two can get on discussing maths – and maths, I have something better to do. Maths comes very low down the list of my subjects, food is my speciality.' She nodded towards Alan, and he, with a broad smile, said, 'Well, I'll attend your classes any day; food, too, is my speciality – the eating of it anyway.'

During the next twenty minutes Annie busied herself about the kitchen, but kept her ears cocked to the conversation which moved from maths to the present student attitude, then on to teachers' salaries, and from there to the writings of Tolkien – she had never heard of him – and from time to time she wanted to stop and look at them, particularly at Tishy. She had never heard Tishy talk like this. Then, of course, she didn't know how Tishy talked outside the house, she had never met any of her friends. Tishy didn't seem to make friends, she was a loner, that was the trouble. Yet here she was talking twenty to the dozen.

Now they were on about old books and the various places you could get them in Newcastle. Tishy was mentioning particular shops by name, and recommending them to him. Well, well! she was a deep one. But then, there was nothing deep about knowing the names of second-hand bookshops. But it wasn't that she was really meaning. For the first time she was seeing her daughter in a new light. She glanced again at her face. It hadn't altered . . . yet it had. Her mouth, when she was talking like this in an animated way, didn't look so thin; and there was a light in her eyes. Nothing could ever take away her plainness, but definitely her daughter had another face if she cared to show it. And now she was showing it as she said excitedly, 'I came across an old book the other day, not in a bookshop, in a junk shop. It was lying among the tuppennies, it's called *Elbert Hubbard's Scrap Book*. It's marvellous, the things it's got in it. Look, I'll get it.'

Annie stopped to watch her rush out of the room, then she looked at Alan. Alan was already looking at her and he said, 'You've got a highly intelligent daughter. How old did you say she is?'

'Eighteen.'

He moved his head to one side, then said, 'Well, if she's a sample of your family I'll have to keep up to the mark with the rest, won't I?'

'Oh, they're not all like Tishy. Well, I mean, Rance – he's the eldest – he had no head for learning, not Tishy's type of learning. Bill has; he's a year younger than Tishy. And Kathy, oh Kathy's like me, all tongue and no brains.'

'Nonsense!' It was like a schoolmaster speaking, and she laughed out aloud, but she immediately turned to her work again as Tishy came into the room holding a faded red-covered book in her hand.

Thrusting the book on the table before Alan, Tishy opened it and, showing the portrait of a dark-haired, intense and rather handsome-looking man, said, 'That's him, Elbert Hubbard. Isn't he nice?'

'Yes, very handsome. And an American I'd say.' Then he added, 'Oh, 'tisn't so old, it was printed in 1923.'

'Well, it's over forty years ago.'

Alan looked at her for a moment and laughed gently, then said, 'Yes, I suppose that's a long time.'

'Look,' she said, 'it's got everything, articles, quotations, the lot. Look at that one: "The religions of the world are the ejaculations of a few imaginative men." Emerson. What do you think of that?'

'Very good. But you must remember that Emerson himself was an imaginative man.'

Again Annie stopped and looked towards her daughter. Tishy was a Catholic, a firm Catholic because she never missed Mass, and there she was talking about the religions of the world as if she believed in them. She watched them turn the pages, then listened to Alan saying, 'Oh now, I'm with Darwin and what he says here: "If I had my life to live over again I would have made a rule to read some poetry and listen to some music at least once a week; for perhaps the parts of my brain now atrophied would thus have been kept active through use. The loss of these tastes is a loss of happiness and may possibly be injurious to the intellect, and more probably to the moral character, by enfeebling the emotional part of our nature." '

'Do you like music?' Alan was looking at Tishy, and she answered after a moment's pause, 'Yes, and no. I don't really know what I like yet, I haven't had time to sort it out. One thing I do know, I don't like heavy classical.'

'No?'

'No. And another thing I do know is I don't like pop. Oh, I loathe pop.'

Tishy now turned and glanced at Annie, and Annie stopped mixing a batter and, pursing her lips while she assumed an indignant pose, looked from Tishy to Alan and said, 'She's getting at me. That's who she's getting at; she's getting at me because I like pop. Well, light stuff you know, like they have on in the mornings.'

'Like they have on in the mornings,' repeated Tishy scornfully. Yet she smiled as she spoke. Then looking at Alan again she made, at least to Annie's knowledge, the first joke in her life for she said, 'You know she's not my mother, she's not the mother of any of us. I mean, how could she be, just look at her!' She thumbed over her shoulder and in sotto voce ended, 'She's gaga, but she might grow out of it when she's turned twenty.'

As Annie compressed her lips and knocked her floured hands against one another as if getting ready to do battle, Alan leant his head towards Tishy and said, 'I know what you mean, she was just like that when I was five years old. And her conversation, oh dear, dear! Do you know what she used to talk about? – jigs.'

As Annie said 'Oh! Alan,' it seemed to her that he had been in that kitchen all his life, at least since he was five, for he already seemed a part of it.

It was at this moment that she heard a key turn in the front door. Wiping her hands quickly on a towel, she went out of the kitchen and saw Rance making for the stairs, and she looked towards him, saying, 'Why, I didn't hear the car. What's the matter, you're all grease? Why didn't you come the back way? Come in the kitchen and get washed, and I want you to meet somebody.'

'Is there any hot water?'

'Plenty.'

'Well, I'm going to have a bath.'

'But you had a bath this morning. Where've you been? I thought you were going to the match. Your dad said Jimmy was staying on this afternoon with him.'

'I . . . did go to the match.' He was partly up the stairs now. 'But I had a job to do after for a friend. I'm going to have a bath.'

She stared at him for a moment before she returned to the kitchen. There, Tishy was saying, 'I like this bit because I know heaps of people like this. Listen: "There are some faults in conversation, which none are so subject to as men of wit, nor even so much as when they are with each other. If they have opened their mouths without endeavouring to say a witty thing, they think it is so many words lost; it is a torment to the hearers, as much as to themselves, to see them upon the rack of invention and in perpetual restraint, with so little success. They must do something extraordinary in order to equip themselves and answer their character else the standers-by may be disappointed and be apt to think them only like the rest of mortals."

'Don't you know people like that? They've got to be clever or bust. I've taken an oath that when I get in front of a class I'll only tell them half of what I know and let them find the other half out for themselves. We've got a teacher at school; my hackles rise every time he opens his mouth . . .'

'Are you forgetting something, Tishy? You're talking to a teacher now.'

'No, I wasn't forgetting anything, Mam.' Tishy turned and looked at Annie. 'What I'm doing in a roundabout way is to inform him that if he knows what's good for him, he'll not spread his brains out on the desk.'

As Annie, aghast, said 'Tishy!' Alan began to laugh. It was a deep rollicking kind of laugh that didn't seem to match his refined-looking exterior. It was a laugh you might have expected from some burly sailor, it was an infectious laugh, and the next minute both she and Tishy were laughing with him. Yet all the while she kept her eyes on her daughter. Never, never, had she seen Tishy like this with anyone else, and with a cold on her an' all. Wouldn't it be marvellous, marvellous, if he and Tishy . . . Oh! wonderful. And why not? Looking at her daughter now she seemed no longer plain. A few moments ago she had thought her animation could do nothing for her looks, but it had.

Annie moved her head slowly as she kept rubbing the tears of laughter from her face and she thought it was funny how life worked out. She had always regretted letting herself be persuaded to go to the Baileys that Christmas, yet if she hadn't gone this man, because he was a man, he wasn't just a youth he was a man, wouldn't be sitting at her kitchen table now laughing into her daughter's face, and she into his, the daughter for whom she'd had no hope. Oh, it was wonderful how things worked out.

Tishy, still laughing, was on the point of saying something when the clatter of a bucket rolling, followed immediately by a spate of cursing, came from the backyard. Putting her hand to her mouth, she looked at Alan and said, 'Now you'll see something I bet you've never seen before, and hear something too. That's Gran McCabe. What a pity Gran Cooper isn't here. Boy, you'd know what entertainment was then. Arsenic and old lace . . .!'

'Tishy, be quiet! That's enough now.' Annie spoke harshly as she pulled open the kitchen door and called, 'You all right, Mollie?'

'All right? Do you leave that bloody bucket and shovel stickin' out there on purpose? The times I've split me shins against it.'

Mollie limped over the threshold. Then, her mouth half-open, she gaped at the man standing at the opposite side of the table, and glancing quickly from him to Annie, she said, 'Oh, I'm sorry, lass; I didn't know you had company.'

'Get yourself in.' Annie pushed her; then closed the door before saying 'This is Arthur's nephew. You remember Arthur?'

''Course I remember Arthur, I'm not in me dotage. Hello lad.' Mollie extended her hand.

'Hello. How are you?'

'Almost bloody well legless if you ask me.' Mollie sat down now and began to rub her shins. 'There hasn't been a time in the last ten years when I've come in that yard but somebody's set a trap for me. An' what you laughing at, miss?'

'At you being legless, Gran.'

Mollie stared at her granddaughter for a moment as if she, too, were noticing some difference in her. But as usual she said what came foremost to her mind, and this was, 'You've got a cold on you again, I see.'

'Yes, Gran.' Tishy's voice was flat now. 'Don't let me forget it.'

'What you cooking at this time of night for?' Mollie now turned to Annie, and Annie replied, 'I'm not cooking, I'm just knocking up something for the supper. Bacon and egg pie and a batter pudding. You going to stay for a bite?'

'Not just for bacon an' egg pie. Is that all you've got?'

'Well, there's cold meat, cold ham, or a leg of raw pork in the fridge, help yourself.'

'Poor meat house.' Mollie leant across the table towards Alan who was staring at her fixedly. 'Mingy on the grub.' She winked as she finished, and he, falling in with her mood, nodded solemnly and replied, 'I thought as much.'

He continued to stare at the old, fat, flamboyantly dressed woman, who he guessed was Georgie's mother. She looked a character. He watched Annie now put a hand on her shoulder and, bending forward, say, 'Well, you'll stay for a cup of tea?' Annie was nice to the old girl, not a bit ashamed of her, as many would have been, for she not only sounded but also looked a type. He had come across some different types in the few days he had spent in this northern and foreign quarter of the country, and not only among the working class, yet he found them all refreshing, it was as if he had come into a new world. On reflexion, he didn't think he could be more interested in, or more amused, or entertained by people if he had gone as far as Australia.

These people were different, a class on their own, although he had already learnt that they were sharply divided into top, middle and bottom, much more so than back home. There was a snobbery here that he hadn't met with before.

'What did you say your name was, lad?'

'Alan.'

'Oh, Alan. Well, Alan, what do you think of the north?'

'Not much.'

'You'd better watch it, miss.' Mollie was wagging her finger at Tishy. 'An' let him speak for himsel'.' She now leant across the table towards Alan, saying, 'Best place on earth, lad. We're one big family in this neck-o'-the-woods. But mind, just like any family, there's good, bad an' indifferent in it, an' if I had me way I'd put half of them in sanitary confinement . . . sanitary confinement.' Her laughter gushed out. 'But you know what I mean?'

They were all laughing as he said, 'Yes, yes, I know what you mean.'

'There's one or two saints, a few sinners, but the majority are buggers. Just like any family. You know some folk think there's only three good people in the world, themsels, the Pope, an' God, an' he's a bit of an also-ran these days; I'm sorry for the poor bugger.'

'Oh, Mollie! Mollie!'

As the laughter filled the house Mollie got to her feet, adding. 'And here's another bugger off home. Good night, lad.' She held out her hand and he, already on his feet, took it and shook it warmly. His mouth was wide and his eyes wet, and when he said, 'I hope we meet again,' Mollie turned to Tishy and, digging her in the shoulder with her finger, said, 'There, what do you think of that? He sounded as if he meant it an' all; I'm not past it yet.' And on this she went to go out of the back door, but Annie taking her by the arm, led her firmly round the table, saying, 'The bucket and shovel's still there and I don't know why on earth you've got to use the back door every time.'

"Cos I'm on me way to our Winnie's and it's a short cut.'

When they stood at the front door Annie said, 'Are you on your way to Winnie's?'

'Aye, I was goin' along there but I thought I'd drop in an' tell you I've just left our Georgie; he was in the bar of the Wheelbarrow shortly after opening time. I had just popped into the snug an' I caught sight of him, an' during the time it took me to down a gin he had knocked back two doubles, and likewise the fellow that was with him an' all, an' there was no standin' of turns, he paid for both lots. I thought if that's the pace he's goin' and early on in the evenin' he'll have to be carried back home the night, so I asked Phil to tip him the wink and tell him I wanted a word with him outside. And you know what?' She laughed now and pushed at Annie with the flat of her hand. 'When he came out he said straightaway, "What the hell do you want? You know, Ma, I left school last week." That's our Georgie. Well I just said I wanted a word with him, I hadn't seen him for the past two weeks or so, an' I asked him who his friend was as I hadn't seen him around either, an' he must have been of some importance to have two doubles stood him. He said it was business; he said he had the fellow interested in a car, a new one, and the bloke was going to trade his in. An' what do you think?' Again she pushed at Annie but, her look aggressive now, she said, 'The bloke had won a packet on the pools only last week, but there was our bloody daft Georgie doin' the payin'. Anyway –' her voice dropped – 'I told him to get himself around home while he could walk, but the answer I got, lass, made me think that you won't see him for some time. An' then you know what to expect when you do. So I just thought I'd drop in and warn you in case you were sittin' waiting to go out. You've had some of that afore.'

'Thanks, Mollie, it was good of you. And you're right, I was expecting to go out; I thought he'd be home early and we'd go to the club.'

Mollie walked carefully down the two steps on to the pathway and there she turned and said, 'As things are in the kitchen I hope he doesn't show up for a bit. An' I'd get rid of that nice young fellow afore he comes in if I was you.' Then, her voice rising, she ended on a laugh, 'I should think he's had enough of nature in the raw when he's seen me. What do you say, lass?'

What Annie said was, 'Oh! Mollie,' and her tone was full of deep affection. 'If he meets no worse than you through life he won't do so bad. By! he won't.'

'I wish everybody thought like you, lass. I shouldn't tell you this but I can't help it. I saw your mother in the market yesterday an' she cut me dead. She looked through me like a pane of glass. Not that it bothered me mind, for if she had spoken to me every word would have been like a pin in me skin. But it made me think of what me own mam used to say. "Always treat women as snakes," she said, "until they open their mouths, and then you can hear if they've had their fangs removed." Good night, lass.' Then her voice quiet, she said, 'Did I ever tell you you were canny?'

When Annie closed the door she said again to herself, 'Oh, Mollie,' then, 'Oh, me mam! If it wasn't that her mother was under the weather these days she'd go along there and tell her something.'

She stood looking down the hall now towards the kitchen door while thinking, She's right, I'd better get rid of him and soon, within the next hour anyway.

A few minutes later she was saying, 'I hope you don't mind eating in the kitchen, it's warmer in here than the dining-room.'

'Aw, Mam –' Tishy made a face at Annie – 'stop putting it on.' Then she turned to Alan. 'Christmas Day, birthdays and funerals, that's when we use the dining-room.'

Annie swung the cloth over the table; then putting her two hands flat on it, she lowered her head and said, 'See what I'm up against.'

'Yes, yes.' Alan nodded, his smile broad. 'Handicapped on all sides; I'm terribly sorry for you.'

'You look it.'

As she set the table she thought it was odd she could banter with this stranger. She glanced at him now where he was sitting side by side with Tishy looking at the old book and laughing over the quotations. He was nice, so nice he could be one of the family. Wouldn't it be wonderful if he took up with Tishy, and at the same time made friends with Rance. Of course Rance was younger, but a man like this would have a steadying influence on him. And Rance hadn't a real friend, not that she knew of. What was that saying, 'God moves in a mysterious way His wonders to perform.' Yes and every word of that was true. God did move in a mysterious way. She must get herself to Mass. She had been sliding of late, and sliding was putting it mildly. Her Easter duties, that's all she had gone to for some years now, but if God took in hand the destiny of her two children about whom she worried most, then there was nothing she wouldn't do for Him. She'd promise Him she'd be at his altar rails every Sunday morning, rain, hail or shine . . .

'There, sit up, and I'm not going to apologize for it because if I do, that one –' she jerked her finger towards Tishy as she addressed herself to Alan – 'she'll say "Why! it's a banquet to what she usually gives us." '

Before sitting down she went into the hall and called up the stairs, 'Rance! are you coming? I've got your tea out,' and his muffled reply came back from the bathroom, 'I can't get down for a minute or so, put it in the oven.'

Ten minutes later when Alan had finished a second helping of the bacon and ham pie and pronounced it simply first-rate, she was saying, 'Our Rance must be giving himself a beauty treatment,' when the sound of a car door being slammed turned her eyes sharply in the direction of the hall and almost at the same time as Tishy exclaimed, 'That must be Dad,' the front door opened and banged with a resounding clash and Georgie's voice rang through the house, crying, 'Where is he? *Where are you, you bloody thieving snipe?*'

'Georgie! Georgie!' Annie had rushed into the hall and, catching at his arm, she gabbled, 'Be quiet! there's . . . there's someone here. Look, listen.'

'Do you know what he's bloody well done, that weak-kneed golden boy of yours? Do you know what he's done? Now you'll have to believe this 'cos it's starin' you in the face, at least it bloody well stared me in the face when I opened the garage door . . . A stolen car and two bloody tykes working on it. The buggers were actually spraying it, new number plate, the lot, a Morris 1100; I tell you, they were in wor garage . . .'

'Georgie! Georgie! listen, be quiet!'

'No! You bloody well listen, for once in your life you listen to me, and not him. I had to choke it out of the buggers, but choke it I did. He's in this racket up to the neck, running it, running it, and underneath me bloody nose. You know what this could mean? The polis, jail.'

As he made for the stairs she held on to him, crying, 'Georgie! listen, listen.'

'I've listened to you long enough where he's concerned. Leave go of me!' When he thrust her from him she staggered back and fell against Tishy, and they both would have fallen if Alan hadn't thrust out his arm and steadied them. But once Annie had regained her balance she ran towards the stairs again. She didn't mount them however, for Georgie had stopped half-way up, and there above him on the landing was Rance. For some seconds they both stood looking at each other. Then Georgie spoke, and what terrified Annie now was the quietness of his tone as he said, 'You had it all planned, hadn't you? The old boy never goes back once he leaves the garage on a Saturday night. Had enough, he's always said, hasn't he? Everythin' would be clear until the Monday mornin'. But tonight I got a customer, bit of a bonus, and I go back to me garage, *my garage*, out of which I've kicked the arse of more than one whose asked me to join in a fiddle. Come to the wrong shop, mate, I've said. Out, at the double, if you know what's good for you. Honest Georgie, that's me.' Now his voice almost rose to a scream as he ended, *'And the fiddle was bein' played under me bloody nose an' by me own son!'*

When he leapt up the remaining stairs Annie screamed and as she went to run after him Alan gripped her firmly, saying, 'No, no, stay where you are.'

'Let me be! Let me be! Let me go!' She was twisting and turning in his hold; and now Tishy was crying, 'Stay out of it, Mam! Stay out of it!'

For a moment she stopped her struggling and gazed upwards, as they all did, towards Rance, whose crouched body had taken on the appearance of a wrestler looking for an opening, and his words came in a growl from his throat as he faced his father. 'Your garage. Your house. Your bloody this, an' your bloody that. Everything's yours, or so you'd make people think. But you own nowt. Do you hear? Nowt, because you haven't got an atom of brain in your thick skull; the only thing you've got is a big mouth. Everything you have right from the beginning you owe to me mam; if it wasn't for her you'd be scavengin'.'

It happened, seemingly, in the blink of an eyelid. One second Georgie was standing on the stairs, the next he was on the landing, his arm drawn back, his fist doubled. But the blow never reached its objective, for Rance's foot came up and caught him in the groin, and like a stick being snapped in two and with the sound of the crack escaping his lips, Georgie's body doubled and fell backwards.

Annie's and Tishy's screams did not die away even when Georgie lay in a twisted heap at the foot of the stairs; not until Annie dropped on her knees beside him and she tried to straighten him out did her yelling fade into a moan.

'Be careful, I wouldn't touch him. You'd best get a doctor.'

She took no heed to the low trembling voice at her side, but continued to tug at Georgie's legs. Yet when she felt herself being lifted from the floor she didn't struggle.

Alan now turned to Tishy, who was staring up at Rance, where he was leaning over the banister, his hands hanging slack and his eyes staring out of a chalk-white face. 'Here,' he said, 'take care of her for a moment.' He had to push Tishy on the shoulder before she turned to her mother; then he knelt on the floor by Georgie's side and slowly he laid his ear against his chest, and kept it there for a full minute.

When he stood up they were both looking at him and he made a small movement with his head, and on this Annie yelled, 'No! no!' and pulling herself from Tishy's hold she dropped to the floor again and, gripping the lapels of Georgie's coat, she looked down on to his still face, and again she cried, 'No! no!' Then 'Aw, Georgie! Georgie! don't go. Aw, don't go . . . Oh my God! My God!' She now turned her head and looked up at Alan. 'He . . . he can't be. Say he can't be.'

'You'd better call the doctor.' Alan now wiped the sweat from around his mouth with his fingers.

'Oh God alive!' She put her hand out and tentatively stroked each side of Georgie's face; then her body jerked at the sound of Tishy's voice crying, 'You've done it! You've done it at last, haven't you? You always wanted to do it. You've murdered him. You dirty rotten, stinking swine you! you've murdered him. When they put you in jail for life I'll cheer. Do you hear? I'll cheer. I'll cheer.'

'Stop it! Stop it, Tishy!' Scrambling to her feet, Annie pulled Tishy from the foot of the stairs, and Tishy, staring at her through tear-blinded eyes, cried, 'You won't be able to save him this time, will you?'

'What are you saying, girl? Don't be silly.' Annie was shaking her.

'Don't, Mam, don't!' Tishy pulled herself away from Annie's grasp. 'I'm saying he murdered me dad, that's what I'm saying, and you can't get him out of that.'

Annie's lower jaw moved twice before she looked up to where Rance was still hanging over the banisters. Then returning her gaze to her daughter she said under her breath, 'It ... it was an accident. You know it was an accident.'

'Accident? Oh no, you won't get him off with that, Mam. He lifted his foot, he kicked dad down.'

'They were fighting; it was ...'

'*No! No!*'

Annie turned to Alan and she moved her head from side to side in bewilderment for a moment before she muttered, 'Look ... look, after her, will you? Take her into the front room.'

'Hadn't you better phone the doctor?'

'Yes, yes.' Annie now put her hand tightly over her mouth. 'I'll ... I'll do it in a minute, but ... but take Tishy away, will you?'

She watched him go towards Tishy and put his arm around her shoulder and forcibly lead her into the front room. Then holding her head in her hands, she stood looking down at Georgie and all her mind kept saying was, Oh my God!

It was a full minute later when she slowly mounted the stairs, and, lifting Rance from the banisters, she supported him as they went towards the room. Having pushed him down into a chair she slapped his cheek sharply with her hand, saying, 'Rance! Rance! look at me. Listen.'

When he brought his gaze to hers and spoke his voice sounded quite ordinary as he asked, 'Is he dead, really dead?'

She moved her head once and they stared at each other, her eyes looking deep into his, and the significance of what he had done getting through to him, his shoulders hunched up round his neck, he covered the sides of his head with his hands and groaned, 'Oh Christ Almighty! Christ Almighty!' After a moment he looked at her again and said, 'I ... I didn't mean it, Mam. You know I didn't mean that.'

She didn't say, 'Yes, yes, I know.' What she said was, 'Listen. Listen, Rance.' She bent close to him now. 'You've got to convince Tishy.' In this moment she didn't think of the the stranger, the man who had witnessed the whole thing, the outsider, she was only concerned with her daughter's reaction. 'Stay quiet now,' she said; 'just stay quiet. I've got to phone the doctor. I'll ... I'll be back. Stay quiet.' She went out and closed the door but didn't go immediately across the landing; instead, she stood with her back to the wall asking herself how this had come about. Half an hour ago she had been in the kitchen laughing and happy, and now Georgie was dead, and Rance would go to prison.

Her mind went completely blank for a moment and when the blankness passed the first question she asked herself was, Why ... why am I not crying? What's the matter with me? The pain in her heart was so great as to be almost unendurable: she had lost Georgie, Georgie who was a good man at heart. In spite of his rough ways and not having much up top, he had been a good man. He had known his limitations, nobody better; his blustering had just been a cover up. And to have his son throw his ignorance in his face, and to die at that moment. Oh, Georgie. Georgie. And Rance. Rance would die an' all. If they put him in prison he'd wither and die. She couldn't bear it, not to be parted from both of them at one stroke.

She went slowly down the stairs her eyes all the while on the still figure at the bottom. But she couldn't believe what she was seeing. Her world had gone mad. She stooped and touched his face again, saying, 'Oh my dear, my dear.' Her body was full of tears but her eyes were dry. Why wasn't she crying? Why couldn't she cry? She looked towards the table where the phone was, and as she went towards it Tishy's voice came from the room, saying brokenly, 'He's no good, he's bad, bad right through and she can't see it.'

She didn't pick up the phone but went into the room and they both turned towards her. She didn't speak until she had sat down on the chair opposite the couch where they were sitting; then looking at Tishy, she said, 'There's not much time; I'm going to ask you something. But first of all I'm going to remind you, lass, that I've given to you all your life.'

Like a flash Tishy's voice came back at her, filled with bitterness, saying, 'Given to me? You've given me nothing, Mam. Nor Bill, nor Kathy. What you've had to give you've given to him, and we all know it.'

'You're wrong, quite wrong, I love you all.'

'You like us all, but you only love him.'

'You're wrong, girl. Anyway, it's going to be up to you whether he goes to prison or not.'

'Me?'

'Yes you ... It was an accident; your dad slipped and fell down-stairs ...'

'With a boot in his stomach.'

Annie closed her eyes tight and bowed her head, and remained like this for some seconds. Then looking at her daughter again, she said, 'You ... you needn't have been there, you ... you could have been in the kitchen with Alan.' She now looked at Alan, and he was staring at her through narrowed lids, a look of utter perplexity on his face, and she said to him, 'You ... you'll stand by us in this, won't you?'

His eyes widened now, his lips parted; then he turned his head to one side and looked towards the floor, and when she put out her hand and caught his and, gripping it, said 'It ... it means nothing to you,' he could make no answer. What could he say? Could he bring up principles, ethics? Could he say he had no intention of condoning a murder, because in a way that is what it had been? When that fellow's foot had come out and caught his father in the groin he himself had winced aloud. But she was repeating, 'It is nothing to you, is it?'

He was saved from making any comment at the moment by crying, 'Involve him. Go on, Mam, involve him. He's a stranger, he hasn't been in the house a couple of hours and you would involve him? I tell you –' she turned and looked at Alan now while she swept the tears from each side of her chin with the back of her hand – 'she would take the blame herself rather than let him suffer. It's always been that way.'

'Stop it, Tishy. Stop it this minute. I'm in trouble, bad, bad trouble.' There were tears in her voice now although her eyes were still dry. 'I've lost your dad, I don't want to lose my son too. I wouldn't mind so much if he had died an' all but if he goes to prison that'll be the finish of me. I couldn't bear it.'

Tishy lay back against the couch and put her forearm across her eyes, and Annie, getting to her feet, said quietly, 'I'll phone the doctor . . .'

From the moment she phoned the doctor her mind began to work in a way that surprised her. In any one else she would have called it cunning. After she had put a blanket over Georgie she went into the back garden and towards the bottom end of the right-hand side, and there, peering over the railings, she looked up at the Tressels' house. It was in darkness, which meant they were out. And there was no light in the house beyond either. Thank God for that. The Brookses on the left; they were all right, they were away for the week-end. There was someone in the Lauries' beyond but they wouldn't have heard anything. And anyway, their youngsters always had the television or a record player blaring.

This done, she crossed the hall again, keeping her head turned from Georgie now, and went upstairs to Rance. He was lying on the bed but still had his shoes on. He sat up when she entered the room and looked towards her with the same look in his eyes that used to be there when, as a child, he would appeal to her for protection against his father's thrashings.

She sat on the bed beside him. She did not take his hands as she would have done when he was in trouble, but she said to him, 'Now listen to me. You were in your room, in here –' she now dug her finger towards the floor – 'changing to go out when . . . when you heard your father shout. You guessed he must have slipped at the top of the stairs, caught . . . caught his foot in that piece of carpet that overlaps. There's . . . there's a nail out, it's been out for some time. I . . . you'll remember –' she nodded her head now – 'I kept on at him to have it tacked. I could have done it meself if I'd only thought, a simple job like that . . . Did you hear me? Did you hear what I said?'

'Aye, Mam. Aw, Mam.' His hands came out and clutched at hers but she made no response to them as she asked, 'That's all you've got to say.'

He gulped before he said, 'Our Tishy, and that fellow?'

'The fellow, he's Arthur Bailey's nephew, Mona's husband you know. He'll . . . he'll be all right. It's our Tishy you've got to worry about. Now I want you to come downstairs and in your own words tell her, tell her you never meant to do it.'

'To our Tishy?'

'Yes, to our Tishy.'

'Aw, I couldn't, Mam.'

'What do you mean you couldn't?' Her voice was harsh now. 'It's either that, or prison.' She spat the word out at him, and when she saw his stomach contract as if he were going to vomit she said, 'Facts are facts.'

'She hates me.'

'Aye, she might, but you've got to convince her that you never meant to do this. And you didn't, did you?'

It was a second before he looked at her and said, 'No, Mam.'

She had not thought that the pain in her breast, the pain that was tearing her body apart, could become worse, but his answer had given it a new depth. There was a bitterness in her voice as she said, 'You'll have to be more convincing than that to her. Come on . . .'

Annie had to help him down the stairs and pull him away from the support of the banister as he stood gazing down at the covered body lying at his feet. When he entered the sitting-room he staggered like someone drunk, then stood some distance from Tishy and stared at her where she was sitting alone on the couch. The man was now standing at the head of it and was staring at him; but he took no notice of him, he kept his gaze fixed on Tishy. He couldn't remember a time in their lives when she hadn't hated him, or he her. He swallowed twice, rubbed his hand up and down his thigh, glanced towards his mother before looking at Tishy again and saying, 'I . . . I didn't mean it, I didn't.'

She glared at him. Her eyes were red and swollen but she was no longer crying and she said slowly, 'You could go on saying that from now until eternity and I wouldn't believe you.'

His teeth clamped together but without force; he had no energy left in him, no feeling of anything but fear, and it was the fear that overcame his pride and propelled him to the couch to sit beside her and mutter in desperation, 'It's true, it's true Tishy. He was going to belt me. I wouldn't have stood a chance against him, I never have. He would have busted my face up, I could see it in his eyes. I . . . I only did what I did in self-defence. But I never meant him to . . . Honest. Honest. Oh my God!' His whole body heaved. He put his hand tight across his mouth, swung himself up from the couch and dashed out of the room. But he didn't reach the kitchen sink; it was with his head against the kitchen door and within sight of the prone figure at the foot of the stairs that he vomited and retched as if he would bring his heart up, while Annie held his head, as Georgie had so often held hers.

Perhaps it was the sound that softened Tishy somewhat, for, looking up at Alan, she said, 'And what will you say? She's taken it for granted you'll go along with her.'

For answer he said, 'She's in great distress, if I can help I will.'

'Distress about whom? Me dad or him?'

'I . . . I wouldn't know.'

'No, you wouldn't know, but I do. Me dad's dead and she hasn't shed a tear; her whole concern is for her darling Rance.'

He stared at her for a full minute before he said, 'I'm not meaning to minimize your emotions at the moment, I'm sure you were very fond of your father, but . . . but I think it's a known fact that when a person cannot cry their inward pain may be very intense, and if this state continues it can be very detrimental to their health. Crying is a safety valve; it's not to say that you feel less emotion, only it's shown in a different way.'

She looked at him for some time before saying, 'You've got nothing to do with all this really, and now you're in the thick of it. Why don't you go before the doctor comes . . . and the police?'

'Well, as I see it the very fact that I'm here may help matters . . . It's very odd –' he looked around the room then shook his head – 'I've been wanting to come for years. I knew I would some day.'

Breaking the silence that followed, she asked, 'Why?'

He looked into her face as he said, 'I wanted to see her again, your . . .'

'Mam?'

'Yes.'

'But you were only a child, a baby, when you last saw her.'

'It doesn't matter. I remembered her vividly, and I knew that sometime I'd have to see her.'

Tishy kept her penetrating gaze tight on him for some time, then slowly she took in a long deep breath and drooped her head on to her chest.

# Chapter Three

'If you insist on doing the books then that means you don't trust me.'

She couldn't say outright that she didn't trust him, what she said was, 'It isn't a case of trust. I'm concerned for the garage; it's my livelihood as much as it is yours.' She did not say, 'It's my garage.'

'Mam, look.' He leant towards her. 'I'll work me fingers to the bone if you'll leave things to me, but if you're going to be trotting around after me every minute . . .'

She rose to her feet as she said, 'Whether you like me trotting around after you every minute or not, Rance, I'm coming to the garage, and I'm going to see to the books.'

He was facing her now. 'It's no place for a woman, it's a man's job, the garage.'

'No!' Her voice rose. 'Neither was Hanlon's coal depot any place for a woman, but I had to run that. And we wouldn't be where we are today if I hadn't.'

'I know, I know, Mam. And that's part of it. I want you to sit back and have it easy; you're getting on, you'll soon be forty.'

'My God! getting on. Soon be forty. But if I was sixty it would be the same . . . And look.' She closed her eyes and sat down with a thud on the chair again. 'I'm tired, Rance; I'm not feeling too well . . .'

'Isn't that what I'm getting at? I know you're not, and I just want to relieve you of . . .'

'You can relieve me of a lot of things, Rance, and worry is one of them. You can relieve me by going along steadily and remembering what we've just experienced.'

He turned away from her, his head hanging as he said, 'Aw God, Mam, don't bring that up again.'

'Don't say it like that –' her voice was low and bitter – 'as if it was everybody's fault but yours.'

He turned his head and looked at her over his shoulder. 'You're turning against me.'

'No, I'm not. I wish I was. Do you hear that? I wish I was. I wish I could; it would only be fair to turn against you. And another thing while I'm on. There's going to be no more gambling.'

'Look, Mam, don't tie me up altogether.' His thin, pale face was twitching. 'What's done's done, I'll never forget it, but you can't tie me up, you can't tie me hand and foot because of it.'

'I say there's no more gambling.'

'Mam, there's worse things than gambling.'

'Yes, there might be, but to me it's quite bad enough when it drives you into the stolen car racket.'

He had been about to speak; now he gaped at her while she stared at him. Then slowly he said, 'You believed that . . .?'

'I'm no fool, Rance. Neither was your dad, although you took him for one. And I'm going to tell you this, and it's taking me a lot to say it, but if I ever find you out in any jiggery-pokery like that again it would be the finish for you, at least with me. I've . . . I've stood by you in all things and my latest stand would be condemned by everybody if it ever came to light.'

'But Mam!' He was appealing to her with both hands. 'I tell you that car was on the level. The blokes were just sort of havin' garage space an' the use of the sprayer. . . .'

'Quiet, Rance!'

As she gazed at him she marvelled that he could protest his innocence so vehemently on this point. As she had said, Georgie was no fool, and if he had been blind drunk and his mind befuddled when he had accused him she would have still believed him. Let her face it: there was a weakness in her son, an underhandedness, a cunning, the awareness of which made her sick when she thought about it, for he was the same now as when a small child, he thought he had only to look her in the face and repeat a thing over and over again to convince her it was true.

Why did she love this son more than the others? Tishy was right, she liked the others but she loved Rance. Only once had she felt any hate for him; that was the moment when she stood by the grave and watched them lowering Georgie down into it. In that moment it was as if Tishy were inside her crying out, 'He's no good. He's no good. No man is any good who could lift his foot and kick his father down the stairs.'

There had been a coroner's inquest and they had brought in the verdict of 'Accidental Death'. There had been no queries; it was well-known that Georgie McCabe drank heavily. The only place there had been any talk was in the Wheelbarrow. Georgie, they said, had had a few doubles, yes, but what was a few doubles compared to what he could carry? He had been all right when he left there. It was a pity Pat Reynolds hadn't gone with him to the garage. He was to come to his house with the car, Reynolds said, but he hadn't turned up and it was just over an hour later when he had fallen downstairs. Funny, wasn't it? He'd be missed, would Georgie. Good sort Georgie; always open-handed, if you were broke you were always sure of a set-in if you met Georgie. Such was the public verdict on Georgie.

Annie rose again from the chair now, saying, 'Why don't you get yourself married and settled down?'

'What! married! Why should I? I don't want to marry, not . . . not yet anyway. And if I married I'd have to leave you. What about that?'

'Don't worry about me.' She shook her head slowly.

He came towards her, stood close to her and looked into her face as he said, 'But I do worry about you, Mam.'

She stared back into his eyes for a moment before turning away. She wished she could believe it, she wished to God she could believe that. She wished she could believe anything that he said.

Tishy was in her room sitting before the mirror. She looked first at one profile, then at the other. If she put colour on it might make her face look plumper, not so scraggy. She tried colour; then rubbed it off again. She'd wear a brownish lipstick, not a red. And what about her hair? Should she take it straight back or part it in the middle? She parted it in the middle. Her face looked softer now. If only her nose weren't so short and her lips were fuller. She pursed her lips and said, 'Prunes. Prunes. Prunes.' Then, with a swift movement turning her head to the side, she muttered aloud, 'Oh, what does it matter! He's seen me as I am, and he likes me as I am.' She looked in the mirror again and her smile softened her face still further, and she nodded at herself saying, 'He does like me; he wouldn't have taken me to Newcastle if he hadn't, would he?'

She thought she would remember last Saturday for the rest of her life. She had felt so proud to be seen with him for he was no boy, or lad, he was a man. He looked like a man, he talked like a man, and he acted like a man, not like the sixth-formers who used to follow them home from school. Well, they hadn't followed her. She wondered now why she had been so silly as to pray that one of them would. But last Saturday she had been out with a man. They had browsed around the bookshops, they had gone through the museum, then they'd had tea. He hadn't suggested taking her to a show, but she felt sure he would have if it hadn't been so soon after her dad's death.

She felt guilty about being happy and it being only a month since the funeral, but she couldn't help it. It was strange, but, in a way, it was because her dad had died that Alan and she had become so close. And they were close, weren't they? She asked the question of herself in the mirror, and it was some time before she answered, saying, 'Yes, because we think alike about so many things, and we get on well together.' He laughed at the things she said. He thought she was very witty, and she could be witty when she was with him. Her mind worked overtime when they were together; he stimulated her. When she was with him she forgot that she was utterly plain for in his company she took on a personality, a vivacity that made her bubble and brought her alive.

She knew that her mother was all for the association. For one thing, if she married Alan it would get her out of the house and away from Rance, and that is what her mother wanted more than anything. The fact that she'd be out of the house for months on end when she went to training college wasn't the same thing; this would still be her home, she'd still come back.

Oh, to be married, to be married to Alan; to have a man of your own, someone who belonged to you, loved you. She had never thought anybody would love her, not the way she looked. Why was it, when her mam was so good looking she should be so plain? plain? . . . Why? And their Kathy beautiful, and Bill good looking an' all. It wasn't natural, to say the least. And what was more, it was unfair. And then there was their Rance, looking like a plaster saint, whereas he was a devil. But Alan didn't care how she looked; he liked her for what she was. Oh she wished he were coming today. He had been two week-ends in the last month. She wondered if her mother would suggest him living here when he came to take up his new post; he could always travel up to Newcastle. She would put it to her.

She went to the wardrobe and took out a dress. Although she wasn't in black all her clothes seemed dark and dingy. She'd like something bright, gay; but it was too early she supposed. Yet why not? Her dad would have said, 'Go ahead and don't be a bloody hypocrite.'

She went downstairs and found Annie lying on the couch in the front room. Going to her, she said, 'You all right, Mam?'

'Yes, yes, Tishy, only I'm so tired. I suppose it's not being able to sleep.'

'Are you taking the pills the doctor gave you?'

'Yes, I'm taking them.'

'What about the sleeping pills?'

'I'm not taking those; they make me feel terrible the next day. I don't want to get used to sleeping pills.'

'Mam.'

'Yes, dear.'

'Would . . . would it seem awful if I went out and bought a new frock?'

'Bought a new frock? No, lass, no. Why should it? Your dad used to say buy something cheery, bright, you remember? But you never did. Get yourself away, lass, and buy something cheery.'

'It . . . it won't seem disrespectful?'

'Who to?' She lifted her hand heavily and touched Tishy's arm; then patting it, she said, 'Go on, make yourself bonny.'

A cynical expression swept over Tishy's face as she said, 'Aw, Mam, don't ask the impossible.'

'Now, now, stop that. You've never looked better than you have these past few weeks. Get something warm looking, with a pink tinge in it, eh? Have you enough cash?'

'Yes, yes; I've never spent anything for months.'

'Go on then.'

'You're sure you'll be all right?'

'Yes, I'm all right, lass.'

They smiled at each other; then Tishy went out, and Annie, letting her head sink back into the cushions, thought, All right? I don't think I'll ever feel all right in my life again.

The feeling that was weighing on her wasn't, she considered, natural. Sorrow was one thing but she felt she was carrying a load that was becoming unbearable, and if it didn't soon drop from her then she would die. She had thought, quite often during the past few weeks, that she could quite easily die. The feeling wasn't only sorrow at Georgie's going, or at the crime her son had committed, it was more of a weakness, the sapping of her strength caused not a little by the stratagems she'd had to use when dealing with the doctor, and the police, and not forgetting Tishy. In the days between that dreadful night and the funeral she had marshalled and manoeuvred people like a general with an army. Looking back, she didn't know how she had accomplished it. The only one to whom she hadn't to lie to convince or coerce had been Alan.

Strange, she thought now, how he had to come into their lives on that particular night. It was, as she had said before, God moves in a mysterious way His wonders to perform, and although Georgie's death hadn't brought him to the house, the circumstances around it had certainly brought him and Tishy close together.

Tishy put her head round the door, saying, 'I'm off then, Mam. Sure you're all right?'

'Yes, lass, I'm all right. Don't forget, a nice colour, something warm looking.'

'All right, Mam. Bye-bye.'

'Bye-bye, dear.'

She had the house to herself. At one time it had been nice to have the house to herself, but now it was as if there were never anyone in it; even when the four of them were sleeping upstairs it was still empty. Although she had come to love Georgie in a peculiar sort of way she hadn't realized just how he had filled her life until he had gone from it. Seeing him off in the morning and waiting for him coming in at night had been but a habit, part of a pattern, but in bed, lying by his side and being loved by him, and being told in his own rough way that she was a wonderful lass and that he'd be nothing without her, that hadn't been a habit, or part of a pattern, that had been something special which made her realize that it was only she who knew the real Georgie, the man beneath the bluster, the man alive to his own inadequacies, the man who knew that his only defence was to bellow and curse. Oh, she missed him. Oh, how she missed him.

Her eyes closed, then opened slowly again as she heard a car draw up outside. It wasn't their car, she knew the sound of their car. Somebody after Kathy she supposed. She waited for the front door bell to ring, but it didn't. She imagined she heard footsteps going up the side path towards the back door. As she heard the back door open she thought it must be Rance. But it hadn't sounded like their car. When the voice from the hall said, – 'Anybody at home?' she pulled herself up on to her elbow, saying, 'Oh, in here, Alan, in here.'

She was lifting her feet slowly from the couch when he entered the room. 'You're not well?'

'Just tired, Alan. I didn't expect you. Tishy's just gone out shopping. Sit yourself down; I'll get you a cup of . . .'

'You'll do nothing of the sort. You were resting, so go on resting.' He bent down swiftly and with one hand lifted her feet on to the couch again while with the other he pressed her back into the cushions.

'I'll make the tea; I can manage that, I think.' He smiled at her.

'Take your things off.'

'I will in a minute.' He pulled up a chair towards the couch and sat down, saying, 'Have you seen the doctor?'

'Yes, yes; I was there on Wednesday. He just said to rest.'

'You don't feel well, do you?'

'No, Alan, I don't feel well, but strangely I couldn't describe just how I feel, it's as if there were a gathering in here, you know –' she patted her breast – 'like an enormous boil coming to a head. But . . . but enough about me. How's things with you?'

'Oh, moving.' His voice sounded flat, and when he stopped and stared at her, she said, 'We didn't expect you.'

'I know, but . . . but I thought I'd better come. . . . There was something. . . .'

'Oh.' She waited, and after a moment he said, 'It's rather difficult. . . . It's been a strange month, hasn't it?'

'Very strange, Alan.'

'I . . . I feel I've known you for years, never stopped knowing you.'

'It's the same with me, Alan; there seems to have been no break.'

'That's it, no break. I . . . I was saying something similar to Uncle Arthur. I went over the other day and told him; he . . . he didn't know about Georgie.'

'No, of course not.'

'He . . . he was very upset.'

'You . . . you didn't tell him the facts?'

'Oh God no. You didn't expect me to, did you?'

'No, no.'

'He . . . he was very fond of Georgie, you know that.'

'Yes.' She lowered her eyes and looked to where her hands were lying limply one on top of the other on her stomach.

'He cried.'

'Arthur?'

'Yes, he cried like a child. It upset me.'

'Yes, yes, I suppose it would.'

'I'm very sorry for Uncle. He's been cast out by some of the family, and to the others he's just a joke.'

'Why?' She wished she hadn't asked that, it was asking the road she knew. She saw him hesitate about giving her the answer; he was looking away from her as he said, 'Perhaps you didn't know, but that's why his marriage failed, he's a homosexual.'

There, that was the word, the word that had been buried for all these years. She was going to be sick. You could say odd, funny, pansy, you could say they wore drag, painted their faces, used scent, and went to bed in nighties, it didn't seem to matter until you put that word to them. . . . And what had he said just a minute ago, that Arthur had cried because he'd heard Georgie had died. He must think that Georgie. . . . She was sitting up straight now, her voice cracking as she cried, 'Georgie wasn't like that. He wasn't, he wasn't.'

'No, I know.'

'Then why did you say Arthur cried; that's inferring that . . .'

'No, no, Annie, no, no. Listen –' he caught hold of her hands – 'listen to me. He was telling me that Georgie was the only real friend he'd had. From what I can gather Georgie became friendly with him before he knew anything about that, but when he found out it made no difference to him. But it made a lot of difference to Uncle because at last he had found someone who didn't treat him as an oddity. He knew from the beginning that Georgie would have no hanky-panky, but as I see it he used Georgie as a sort of alibi, a sane clean alibi, if you know what I mean, to hold up to his folks, and others. If people saw he had a friend like Georgie, well they wouldn't think there was any hanky-panky. That's how I see it.'

The lump was moving from her breast up into her throat and when she tried to get words out it halted them. 'Georgie . . . Georgie, he was . . . he was a . . . good man; there was nothing like that . . . about him.' The lump was choking her, she couldn't bear it. She put her spread hands over her face and when his voice came to her, murmuring softly, 'Oh, Annie, Annie, I'm sorry. Oh, Annie,' and his arms came about her, the lump burst. The tears spurted from her eyes and her nose, the saliva ran out of her mouth as if an explosion had taken place inside her. Her crying rose like wailing notes on a scale, and when they reached a crescendo she thrust her face into his breast and, as if he were talking to a child, he whispered softly, 'There now, there now. It's all right, it's all right. That's it, cry it out. This is what you need. Cry it out.'

When she had cried it out and her sobs were subsiding she raised her head and looked at him. She was still lying on the couch but he was sitting at the head of it and the upper half of her was in his arms. When she felt his fingers stroke her wet hair away from her brow she shivered.

'Feel better now?' he said, his voice still a whisper, and she made a slight movement with her head before saying, 'I'm sorry.'

'Oh my dear, what is there to be sorry for? You should have done this that first night, you would have felt much better by now. You've been storing it up.'

'Yes, I suppose so.' She had a strange feeling, as if her body had been drained of all its blood. She felt weak and empty, but at peace now. He was right, it would have been much better if she could have cried at the beginning. She knew she should get up, she shouldn't lie here, it wasn't right lying like this in this young fellow's arms. What was she thinking about?

She was on the point of putting her hand out to make a move when the door opened and Tishy entered, and as she looked into her daughter's face across the distance she wanted to die, really die.

As she struggled upwards away from Alan's slackening hold, she muttered, 'I ... I collapsed. I've ... I've had a good cry, and Alan ... he came unexpected.'

She was on her feet now. Alan, too, was standing. 'Did you get your dress, lass?'

Tishy didn't speak. She looked from her mother to Alan and waited.

And Alan looked back at her for a moment before stretching his neck up from his collar, 'I ... I know I wasn't expected, but I have something to tell you, to tell you both.' He turned his gaze to Annie for a moment. 'I thought, well I'd put it off long enough, but ... but under the circumstances over these past weeks I didn't think you'd be interested in my business. But ... but I think the time has come when I'd better tell you. You see, I'm ... I'm going to be married.'

Tishy hadn't moved, nor had the expression on her face altered, but Annie sat down in a chair and stared up at him, her face still wet and her mouth agape. She stared at him as he went on in an apologetic tone, 'I ... I would have told you that first evening if it hadn't been, well, for what happened. And then ... well, you were so distressed. Following that I ...'

His voice was cut off by Tishy holding up a paper bag and saying on a high note, 'I got the dress, Mam. It's pink. Get it bright you said, it's all pink.' She wagged the bag at arm's length before her, then turned round and went out.

Annie rose slowly to her feet and looked at Alan, and her voice low and trembling, she said, 'You shouldn't have done this, Alan; it ... it was cruel. You ... you could see how things were going with her.'

'No, no, Annie, I didn't, not really. And she's so young, still at school. ...'

'She's in love with you.'

'Oh no! No. She hasn't had time, it's only a month.'

'Don't be silly. What time does it take for a young lass to fall in love?'

'Not long, I suppose.' His voice was grim now. 'Nor that long to fall out of it again. I tell you it didn't strike me.'

'Oh, Alan.'

They stood staring at each other. His face was red and his Adam's apple jerked violently before he said, under his breath, 'If I were to fall in love with anyone here it certainly wouldn't be with Tishy, Annie. Don't you understand it wouldn't be with Tishy?'

She didn't move but she dropped her head backwards on her shoulders as if to see him better.

'I've been engaged for three years and the longer it goes on the less I want it. But everything's arranged. She's the grand-daughter of Grandma's friend. Friends of the family.' His tone was bitter again. 'Annie.' He leant swiftly forward and gripped her hands. 'It may seem mad to you, but not to me. If you would say the word, tell me that, if I waited a year, any time, then you would . . .'

'Shut up!' She jerked her hands from his and, putting one to her throat, she stroked her finger and thumb down each side of her neck as if to slacken the muscles. Then she muttered under her breath, 'You'd better go, Alan, and now.'

'Annie.'

'Please, that's enough. I'm fourteen years older than you, I'm nearing forty. Even the suggestion is indecent, not forgetting that my husband is hardly cold in his grave yet. Now go on, get yourself out, and I'm . . . I'm sorry to have to say this, Alan, but, but don't come back. . . .'

Not until she heard his car start up did she move. Slowly she sat down on the couch. Her hand outstretched gripping the rounded side of it, she stared before her, not thinking of Tishy upstairs, likely crying her heart out, nor yet of Georgie, whom an hour ago she had been missing so much, but she thought of the young girl she had once been and the dreams she'd had then, and she imagined that if such a man as Alan had come into her life at that time she wouldn't have had to bury her dreams. But they had been buried when she married Georgie and were now in the grave with him.

Alan had been born much too late.

# Chapter One

## Tishy

'Stand still, will you Kathy.'

'Oh, Mam, I told her it was too long; I said I didn't want it covering my toes.'

'It's not covering your toes. Don't forget you had high heels on when she measured you, and also when she fitted you. Why didn't you tell her that you intended to wear flat? But stand still,. it only needs a little tacking up into the ruche, it'll never be noticed.'

'It'll make the hem uneven.'

'Oh, don't be silly, Kathy. It's supposed to be uneven, isn't it, scalloped.'

'Yes, but it'll hang down more on one side than the other.'

Annie got up from her knees and surveyed her daughter standing in her wedding dress. 'Well then,' she said, 'pull it up the other side and you'll create a new fashion.'

'Mam! Mam, don't joke.'

'What do you expect me to do, girl, cry? Aw, come on.' Annie put out her hand and tapped her daughter's cheek. 'You look as if you were preparing for your funeral instead of your wedding.'

Kathy sat down on the side of the bed, then jumped up immediately, saying, 'Oh, help me off with it.' And when the white gown was laid across the foot of the bed, Kathy, shrugging her long shapely body into her dressing gown, turned to her mother and said in a flat voice, 'Mam, I'm beginning to get nervous, sort of frightened.'

'And you'll be worse before you're better.'

'You're some help.'

'Come and sit here.' Annie pulled her down beside her at the head of the bed, and, looking at her with her head on one side, said, 'Everybody goes through this you know; although the things they're frightened of might be different. I'm not going to go into the birds and the bees with you.' She now pushed her daughter in the shoulder while bending forward and laughing as she continued, 'Do you mind the time I tried to give you a bit of advice on that subject? Do you mind what you said?'

Kathy, laughing now, said, 'Buck up and be a rabbit, Mam.'

'Aye, buck up and be a rabbit. I didn't know whether to laugh or box your ears, but I'll tell you something I remember feeling at the time.'

'What?'

'I felt you were much older than me.'

'I still feel I'm much older than you, Mam, because in some ways you haven't got a clue. Tishy says it's because you shut your eyes to things, but I think it's just you.'

'Well, thank you very much, both of you.' Annie turned her head away in mock indignation, and Kathy said, 'Well I like you like that. I always thought you were different from other mothers; Mrs Bates, for instance. When Jane first asked Linda round there to tea, Linda said that Ma Bates looked as if she was fighting off age with a hatchet and it had slipped and caught her in the face.'

As they both pushed at each other and laughed, Annie said, 'That was a cruel thing to say.'

'Well, you know Linda; she has a tongue like a rapier. But she's right, she's right most of the time. The other day in the shop when we had that beauty expert down from Newcastle and she kept yarping on about the indefinable something, charm you know, allure, she said people couldn't put a name to it, or lay a finger on it, and all the while she was putting over to us how much of it she had. Of course, Linda twigged this immediately and she nearly made me choke by whispering, "Poor soul she must have lost her something in the monkey puzzle".'

As Annie looked at her daughter's animated, beautiful face she recalled to mind a vivid picture of the times when she and Mona had sat on the bed talking like this. She herself had been to Mona what Linda was to Kathy, yet at the same time the positions were partly reversed for Kathy had the looks and charm yet idolized Linda whereas Mona had idolized herself; but her daughter's friendship, she felt, would fade away just as her own had with Mona once the marriage got under way.

The marriage! She would never cease to wonder what this beautiful girl saw in Mr Percy Rinkton. She could have had her pick of any fellow in the town; they had swarmed round her like bees for years; yet she was going to marry that stiff-necked, pedantic know-all. What was it about him that attracted her? His persistence? for God knew he had been persistent enough, and so formal about his courtship that at times she had wanted to scream at him.

He had allowed six weeks to elapse after Georgie's death before coming to the house to ask formally for her permission to take Kathy out.

Although Kathy had predicted his visit she had laughed her head off when she knew he had been; she had doubled her legs under her on the couch and rocked herself with her mirth. 'I wouldn't be found dead with him,' she had said. Yet when he called again and saw her personally and asked her to go out she hadn't laughed at him, she had been coy and said she was so very sorry but she had a previous engagement.

The name of Percy Rinkton became a household joke, bringing flashes of humour into the dull atmosphere.

During that year Kathy's suitors came and went, only Percy Rinkton remained faithful inasmuch as periodically he would knock on the door and ask if it was convenient to see Miss McCabe . . . Miss Kathy McCabe.

It was during a slack period of suitors that Kathy first went out with Percy Rinkton and from then on she stopped laughing at him. He was no longer a joke, he was someone to hold up to the family, especially to Bill, as an example of manners and interesting conversation.

But it was Rance who said to her, 'You're not serious about that little runt, are you?' and when she had turned on him they'd had their first quarrel, because whereas Rance hated Tishy with a deep intensity, his liking for Kathy went just as far the other way. From then on Rance made it his business to pick an argument with Kathy's suitor whenever an opportunity afforded; that he repeatedly got the worst of it didn't seem to get through to him. Percy Rinkton's clinical logical reasoning was thrown aside as claptrap by Rance.

Bill, too, laughed at Percy. While conceding that the fellow had plenty up top he nevertheless pointed out at every opportunity in the beginning that the fellow was an inch, if not more, shorter than she was, and she was still growing. 'By the time you're twenty,' he joked, 'he'll need a step-ladder to reach you.'

But the more opposition there was to Percy Rinkton as a suitor the more Kathy became determined to keep him in that category; and now, three years later, she was about to marry him, and Annie still couldn't understand it.

It was, she supposed, a very good match for her youngest daughter. Percy came from one of the best families in the town. His father was a leading doctor, he himself was an accountant, a fully fledged one at that. She had nothing to complain of at his people's reception of them. His mother wasn't uppish at all, she was really a canny body. Mrs Rinkton was forty-six years old, only four years older than herself but she always looked upon her as an elderly woman. Percy himself was twenty-six and that was a nice age for a man to marry. Everything about Percy and his family was correct. Perhaps that was the trouble, it was too correct, it was irritatingly correct; it was all right being good mannered but when somebody popped up from his seat every time you entered the room it got a bit too much.

Last night she had tried to make a breakthrough when he had said to her. 'What am I to call you in future? I can't go on calling you Mrs McCabe,' and to this she had answered, 'You shouldn't have gone on calling me Mrs McCabe all this time, Percy.'

'Then what shall it be? . . . Mother?'

He had been startled when she said, 'Oh good God! no, make it Annie.'

The look of shock on his face had caused her to laugh and when he said, 'Oh, I . . . I really couldn't,' she demanded, 'Why not? Anyway, call me what you like but not Mother.'

Mother to Percy, that would be too much. She smiled inwardly as she now said to Kathy, 'We were supposed to be talking about you, not me,' and, her voice losing all its banter, she added, 'Are you quite sure in your mind, lass, you know what you're up to?'

'You mean with regard to how I feel towards Percy?'

'Just that.' . . .

'Yes, Mam. I love Percy. I know you think that's strange, but you see I . . . I know him like none of you do. When . . . when we're alone together he's not so starchy.'

Annie only just prevented herself from saying, 'Thank God for that.'

'It's . . . it's sort of nerves with him, he's . . . he's got an inferiority complex.'

'*Percy!* with an inferiority complex?'

'All right, Mam, you can say it like that, but that's what it is; he's naturally good mannered and this shyness makes him force it home more.'

Again Annie only just stopped herself from exclaiming, 'Shyness!' Percy Rinkton shy; a fellow who had persisted in knocking on her front door for a full year, knowing that the object of his attraction was likely to turn him down for some other fellow. Percy Rinkton shy? Well, perhaps she hadn't a clue about people, perhaps this daughter had a deeper insight into human nature than herself, for all her experience; but then her daughter was the product of this new generation. The young people of today frightened her with their perception and knowledge; things that were hidden in her young days were now stripped bare and flaunted on posters, papers and books, not only laying bare the body, but the mind. The latter was more frightening still. There were things in the mind that should be kept hidden; everybody had things in their mind that should be kept hidden.

'Mam, do you think our Rance will play up?'

'No, don't you worry about Rance; I'll see to him.'

'Tishy always says when he's quiet he's up to something. He's been quiet for the past week or so.'

Yes, Rance had been quiet for the past week or so. She didn't need that to be brought to her notice. He was up to something all right; only one thing she was sure of, it wasn't connected with the garage. The garage was clean, figure-wise with regard to the books, and materially as to the place itself, for never a working day had passed since Georgie had died but she had visited the garage. This remained the bone of contention between her and Rance but she ignored it.

But Rance, she felt, had other irons in the fire. He wasn't gambling, it wasn't that, he didn't stay out late enough. He'd been at her this past while to move to Westoe. Only last week he had tried to induce her to take a house that had been turned into two large flats. 'Why two flats?' she had asked, and he had answered that he'd like a flat of his own. 'Well, you go and take a flat,' she had said, and he had looked at her a long while before saying, 'You know I couldn't leave you.'

When he spoke like that to her she forgot her fears concerning him; she forgot that there was that cell in her mind in which was stored his real worth; such words blotted out his lifted foot and the kick in the groin. Rance would never leave her because he needed her. It was as if the umbilical cord had never been cut between them. When he spoke to her in that way it caused some part of her stomach to jerk as if he were tugging at the cord, reminding her that they could never be separated.

Sometimes in her anger against him she thought that nature, in siphoning off nearly all her affections into her first-born and leaving little for the rest, had played a dirty trick on her. Tishy was right, Tishy was nearly always right, she liked the others but she loved Rance. Yet of late a strange element had entered into her love and it disturbed her. It couldn't be said it was dislike. Or could it? Or hate, when she thought of his lifted foot? Oh no! No.

'Our Rance is drinking.'

'Rance drinking?'

'Oh, you didn't see it but he came in the other night late and almost staggered up to bed; he was all bright-eyed and sloppy, he even spoke civilly to Percy. Well, I wouldn't mind him getting drunk on my wedding day if it keeps him civil.'

Annie repeated, 'Our Rance drunk? He hardly ever touches the stuff.'

'He's sly, he does it on the sly.'

Annie rose from the bed and went towards the door, thinking, It might not be such a bad thing if he did drink, it would loosen some of the tensions in him, for a time at any rate. The door knob in her hand, she turned and smiled at Kathy, saying, 'Well, I'll get him bottled up on the day, eh?' she had ignored the remark that he was sly.

'Aw, Mam.'

Kathy looked at her and shook her head, and in the action and the words there was an impatience underlying a kindly tolerance, and it made Annie feel for the moment that indeed she was younger than her daughter; or was it that she was just gullible?

# Chapter Two

They were all in the front room, Kathy and Percy, Rance, Tishy, Bill and Annie. There was no talk of the wedding that was to take place in two days' time. Bill was talking about his future as a teacher. When he went back to the university after the Christmas vac it would be for the last time. He wished, he said, he was staying on now and trying for his Ph.D., for by the sound of things they were lining up for teachers' jobs.

To Tishy, who was in her first year as a teacher at the secondary modern, the solution was to move away, get out of the north-east. 'The trouble with us in this corner of the globe,' she said, 'is that we are too insular. Metaphorically speaking, everybody in the north-east has the chummy back lane, back-to-back mentality. People won't move. If they do it has to be within easy reach of the town in which they were born. If they go farther afield they develop symptomatic phobias.'

'I'm with you there,' said Bill.

'Don't talk rot.'

They all looked at Rance, but he didn't lift his eyes from the evening paper.

After a moment Percy Rinkton spoke. 'I should say that the regional feeling remains more marked in the north-east than anywhere else in the country,' he said, stressing as usual the last consonant of each word. 'Yet one cannot but say that things have changed. The two wars in this century have acted as catharses on society. For instance, in the First World War you needed money and education to die as an officer, whereas in the last war any Geordie could get some sort of commission in the army, or the navy for that matter, be he an insurance agent, a lorry driver, a car mechanic or a . . .'

'Or a bloody cheapskate accountant.' Rance had thrown the paper down and was glaring at Percy. 'Car mechanic!' His lip curled. 'Any apprentice car mechanic in this town could buy and sell you, mate. And let me tell you something. You wouldn't be where you are the day if it wasn't for your bloody . . . papa.'

'Rance! stop it!'

Percy's face had drained white in the last few seconds, but looking steadily across at Rance he said, 'You are bent on asking for trouble, aren't you? But I'm not going to argue with you.'

Rance had risen to his feet and was glaring at Percy where he was sitting, his back tight against a straight-backed chair, and he said, 'You know what you can do, mate, you can take a single ticket to hell.' And on this he went out, and Annie, after closing her eyes tight for a moment, followed him.

Tishy was the first to move. She got up, went to the fireplace and, grabbing a piece of coal with the tongs, flung it on the fire, saying, 'He's a pig, an utter pig.' Then turning to Percy she said, 'I'm sorry, Percy. Take no notice.'

'Oh, I don't, I don't.' Percy gave her a weak smile. Then looking at Kathy as she sat with her head bowed and her hands tight under her oxters as if protecting herself against the cold, he said, 'It's all right, dear, don't be worried for me. I . . . I understand Rance. Yes, yes, I understand him. He doesn't understand me but I understand him.'

Bill, leaning his head back in the corner of the couch, now exclaimed, 'Well, if you do, Percy, you're about the only one who does; even Mam can't understand him and she's worked on him long enough.'

'And for him.'

Bill nodded at Tishy as he repeated, 'Yes, and for him, and she'll likely go on doing it until the end of her days. . . .'

In the kitchen Annie was giving the lie to this. 'Look,' she was saying, 'we've had about enough of this, and we've all had about enough of you. You're not merely rude, you're ignorant, raw ignorant.'

'He makes me sick.'

'Because he's different from you.'

'Yes, he's different from me, and thank God for that. Who'd want to be like that pip-squeak? I ask you!'

'That pip-squeak, as you call him, has something, Rance, that you'll never have, and that's brains. And he uses them.'

'Aw, now we know whose side you're on. We know where we stand don't we?'

'I'm on nobody's side, I'm only trying to point out to you that you can't go on like this. You've been like a bear with a sore skull for months.'

'And if you had any sense you would be acting in the same way and putting a stop to our Kathy making a bloody fool of herself letting her marry him. Do you want to get rid of her? With her looks she could have picked and chosen, but you let her take a neuter like him.'

'What do you mean, a neuter?'

'Just what I say. He's not half a man; you've just got to look at him.'

She stared at him grimly before she said, 'That's got to be proved, hasn't it?' Then she went on, 'Now look here, Rance, I'm warning you. You cause any trouble on Saturday and you and I are finished, finally. She's the first one to leave home and she's going to leave it peaceably if I have anything to do with it. You create the slightest bit of trouble and you're out. Do you hear me?' She placed her hands flat on the table and leant over it towards him. 'I've shielded you for years; I've got their backs up 'cos I put you first in everything. . . .' She stopped abruptly as the kitchen door opened suddenly and Tishy came in.

Tishy, the door closing behind her, stood with her back to it and stared at them, and they at her. Tishy at twenty-two looked tall, even taller than her five foot seven because of her extreme thinness. Her face had hardly altered at all in the last four years but she looked much older. This was due mostly to the way she dressed her hair, which was drawn tightly back from her forehead and kept in place by a band on the back of her head. Her thin lips scarcely moved as she said caustically, 'Having a job to get through to him?' She did not immediately take her eyes from her mother when Rance took a step towards her, his teeth gritting audibly, but when she did look at him she held his gaze for some seconds before she said, 'You do anything to upset Saturday, just anything mind, one little thing, and it'll give me great pleasure to go down to the police station and tell them that I've been withholding information, vital information, with regard to a murder.'

She made no movement when she saw Annie's body slump further over the table, but kept her eyes tight on those of Rance and watched them darken to a blackness in which his hate smouldered.

It was the sound of the doorbell ringing that snapped the tension. Turning away she went out of the kitchen, but was back within a minute and, looking to where Annie was now sitting by the side of the table, she said, 'It's ... it's Mr Wilkins from down below, he wants to have a word with you.'

'Mr Wilkins?' Annie rose slowly to her feet.

'I've put him in the dining-room.'

Annie stood for a moment holding the back of the chair, then her head moved just the slightest in Rance's direction, where he was standing with his back to her, both hands gripping the mantelpiece. Young Susan Wilkins had been running after Rance for the last year or so; she made a nuisance of herself. He had taken her out once or twice to a dance, but then, as always, he had grown tired of her. He never kept his girls long but Susan waylaid him at every opportunity. She knew that he often left the car at the bottom of the street and came in the back way in order to avoid her. She was a silly girl was Susan.

She went through the door that Tishy was holding open for her, across the hall and into the dining-room. Mr Wilkins was standing to the side of the fireplace and he turned immediately towards her, and she saw that he was in a very agitated state. 'It's about Susan,' he began; 'she's gone, left home. She left a note. Her mother found it when she came in; she's nearly round the bend.'

'Oh, I'm sorry, Mr Wilkins, I am indeed. Have you no idea where she's gone?'

'No, none at all. We ... we wondered if Rance might give us a lead.'

'Rance?'

'Yes, she thought a lot of your Rance.'

'Yes, I think she did, Mr Wilkins.'

'Well, he might have seen her the day.'

'But ... but Rance has been in the garage all day and ... well, you know he's never taken Susan out for months.'

'I ... I know that, but ...but I thought he might know who she was friendly with; she wouldn't tell us. And ... and there is something else.' The man now bowed his head in shame as he said below his breath, 'She's started smoking.'

'Oh –' Annie gave a little laugh – 'that's no crime, Mr Wilkins; they all do it sooner or later.'

He lifted his sad bulbous eyes and looked at her as he said, 'No ordinary smoking, drugs.'

There was a long pause during which her heart seemed to miss a beat before she said, 'Oh no! Mr Wilkins,' and he replied, 'Aye, I'm afraid it's true. It was one night last week. She came in sort of dazed, and then she started to act daft. We've noticed she's been, well, not herself once or twice before, but it never dawned on us until we searched her room, and then . . . well, her mother nearly went mad. She shook it out of her. It apparently started at the party Rance took her to a few months back; somebody gave her a cigarette.'

'Not . . . not Rance?' Annie could scarcely hear her own voice.

'She didn't say who gave it to her, she just said somebody gave her a cigarette, but she didn't take to it all at once. I think she got miserable when Rance dropped her. She wouldn't face up to the fact that he didn't want her. Her mother told her; she was young and these things happened and she'd get over him, but . . . but she never seemed to, and lately she's been getting worse.' He rubbed his hand across his eyes, then round his chin as he muttered thickly, 'It's the shock. It's the shock, you see; her mother'll never get over it. I'm going to the police, I'll have to report it, but . . . but I thought if Rance could give us a lead.'

He stared at her for some time before she said, 'Yes, yes, all right, Mr Wilkins, I'll get him.'

Rance was no longer in the kitchen, and she had just reached the top of the stairs when she saw him coming out of his room dressed for outdoors. She stood in front of him and said without any preamble, 'Susan Wilkins has run away; her father wonders if you could give them any lead to where she might have gone.'

'What me! I haven't seen her for weeks, well –' he shook his head – 'days; it's over a week since I spoke to her.'

She stared at him as she repeated, 'Mr Wilkins wonders if you can give him a lead as to who her friends were, she's on drugs.' Her eyes looked straight into his, but his lids did not flicker nor did his expression alter as he repeated, 'Drugs?'

'That's what I said.'

'Well, I ask you, what lead could I give him on that? You don't think . . .?'

'I think nothing, I just want you to come down and tell him if you know any of her friends.'

'But I don't. How should I?'

'You took her out, you took her to a party.'

'Yes, but that was years ago.'

'It wasn't years ago.'

'I tell you, Mam –' his voice was low, harsh – 'I don't know who she's been going round with, an' I don't want anything to do with it.'

'Well, come down and tell him so.'

Pushing past her now, he growled, 'All right, if that's what you want I'll tell him so.'

Annie looked at Rance as he faced Mr Wilkins. There was that withdrawn look on his face, his cover-up look, as she termed it to herself. 'I wish I could help you,' he was saying, 'but I don't know who she's been going round with.'

'Can you remember who she met at the party? It was there all this started when this, this fellow gave her a cigarette. . . . Cigarette. My God! I wish I could lay my hands on him just for a minute, that would be enough.'

'The party was packed; there were people there I'd never set eyes on afore or since. Let me think.' He lowered his head. 'There was Arthur Devlin, Ronnie Mason . . . but Ronnie was married last week.'

'Arthur Devlin. That Arthur Devlin's no good. He was in the papers the other week.'

'Was he? I don't know anything about that. What had he done?'

'Robbed somebody, and was up for grievous bodily harm an' all. That's what worries me, her knowing that lot. You should have more care who you introduce young lasses to.'

'Look, Mr Wilkins, she plagued me to take her, I didn't bloody well press her.'

'No, perhaps you didn't.' Mr Wilkins's voice was flat and he sighed deeply.

'Hadn't she any girl friends?' Annie asked now, and he answered, 'Yes, she had one particular one, Connie Blackman, but they had a row.'

'Still, perhaps she'll be able to help you?'

'Aye.' Mr Wilkins now moved slowly towards the door, then added, 'There's only one real place we can go for help and that's the polis. But it's the scandal; it'll kill her mother.' He turned his head towards them and repeated, 'It'll kill her. Respectable we've been all our lives, respectable, and now this.'

Annie followed him into the hall and as she opened the front door for him he said, 'You know, it's funny, but at one time you were always afraid of some fellow taking your daughter down; the thought of a lass coming home and saying she was going to have a bairn hung like a nightmare over people; now if Susan was to walk in the door and say she was pregnant I wouldn't mind a damn. Anything but drugs.'

Annie nodded at him dumbly and he went out. When she closed the door Tishy was standing in the hall looking at her; then coming towards her she whispered, 'Susan on drugs?'

Annie gulped deeply in her throat. 'She's left home,' she said.

Tishy turned now and looked through the open dining-room door where she could see Rance standing at one side of the table. He was straightening his tie as he looked at his reflection in the mirror and Annie, following her gaze, hissed at her, 'No! girl, no, you're wrong this time. No.'

'Just as well then, isn't it?'

As Tishy was going up the stairs Rance came into the hall, shrugging his overcoat on to his shoulders, and he stood looking at Annie for a moment before he said, 'Satisfied?'

'He thought you might be able to help him; you can see he's desperate.'

'And you thought I was mixed up in it, didn't you?' His voice was low. 'What do you take me for?'

'I thought nothing of the sort.'

He pushed past her and went out, banging the door so hard that the house shook.

It was about fifteen minutes later when she excused herself to Kathy, Bill and Percy, saying, 'I'm going to have a bath while the going's good. Tomorrow night everybody will be lining up and there won't be enough hot water.' She smiled at Kathy.

'Are you going straight to bed, Mam?' asked Bill, and she answered, 'Straight to bed? Of course not. Who's going to cut sandwiches for the supper and . . .?'

'You go to bed if you want, Mam –' Kathy nodded towards her – 'we'll fend for ourselves.'

'Thank you, miss!' said Annie with mock humility, aiming to bring a little lightness into the sombre atmosphere.

'You're very welcome, Annie.'

'I'll Annie you if you're not careful.' She pursed her lips at her daughter, then went out smiling. But as she mounted the stairs there was no smile on her face as she said to herself, 'Now stop it. Don't be insane, woman; he can have nothing to do with this.'

In her bedroom, she collected her dressing gown and slippers from the wardrobe, and as she closed the door she stopped and looked towards the wall, then cocked her head to one side. There was somebody in Rance's room. Her hand went to her throat. Had he sneaked back to pick up something? Oh my God! No. No. The only other person upstairs was Tishy, and wild horses wouldn't have dragged Tishy into his room. Should she let it go? What would be his defence if she surprised him now? Couldn't he come back and pick something up without being accused of being in a drug racket? It was as if he were already answering her. He always had an answer.

She found herself rushing out of the room and on to the landing and thrusting his door open. Then she stood with her mouth agape. There, standing on a chair, her hands groping along the top of the high Scotch chest, was Tishy.

'What in the name of God, girl, are you doing?'

Tishy turned an unperturbed face towards her, saying, 'One of two things, Mam: trying either to prove your fears are right or to set your mind at rest, whichever way you like to take it.'

'You've got a bad mind, our Tishy; you'll never rest till you see him behind bars, will you?' She was standing close to the chair now looking up at her daughter. 'Come down out of that.'

'I will in a minute, Mam. It's some time since you cleaned the top of this, it's thick with dust.'

'I'm not a giraffe, I can't get up there every week; it gets done in spring-cleaning.'

'Give me something to force the lid up.' Tishy put her hand down and Annie barked at her, 'I'll do no such thing! That blanket box has never been opened for years.'

'That's all you know, Mam. Parts of it are clear of dust, but it was a piece of fluff hanging over the edge that led me up here in the first place. I've never seen lumps of dusty fluff hanging from anything in this house before.'

'*Z Cars* is missing out not having you in the gang.'

'There might be something in that an' all. Will you hand me that file off the dressing table or will I have to get it myself?'

Annie grabbed the file and thrust it into her daughter's hand. As she watched Tishy trying to prise up the lid of the top of the six-foot tall chest which she had picked up in a second-hand shop years ago, part of her mind was gabbling prayers.

She saw the edge of the lid move upwards. She watched Tishy peering downwards, then slowly turn her face to the side and look at her. And her expression was almost triumphant. Then putting her hand down into the blanket box she drew something out and said, 'Hold these.' And she handed down to her a flat packet of banknotes held together with an elastic band; then another and another and another and another.

When Tishy had stepped off the chair she twisted it round and said to Annie, 'Sit down,' and Annie sat down. Then she looked up at Tishy helplessly, and Tishy said, 'Well?'

'He –' she had to gather spittle into her mouth before she could go on – 'he could have won it gambling.'

'He's not supposed to be gambling, Mam; he was supposed to give it up.'

'How do we know what he does when he's out? Anyway, it could be ordinary gambling, not the tables; he could go to the betting shop any time of the day.'

'Do you think that amount of money came from gambling? Give it here.'

She took the bundles from Annie's unresisting hold and Annie watched her lay it on the bed, take the rubber bands from each bundle in turn and begin counting. Each time she spoke it was as if a knife were going through her. 'There's a hundred single pounds in that lot; and there's sixty five-pound notes in that one; a hundred in that one, and a hundred in that one; six hundred altogether.'

Tishy now sat down on the side of the bed and said quietly, 'He's either been cooking the garage books for a long time or he's in some racket.'

'He can't cook the books.' Annie shook her head slowly. 'I see to them; you know I do.'

'Some pay cash, don't they? You're only there about an hour in the day; he could have a job in and out every day for a week.'

'He wouldn't do that.'

'Well, it's better to think that's how he got this –' she flicked a bundle of notes aside – 'than from some other racket, say the one connected with Susan Wilkins.' Tishy's voice had taken on a harsh note and Annie's was equally harsh and low as she hissed back to her, 'Don't say that! Don't say it. Do you want to kill me, girl?'

Tishy now bowed her head and, putting her hands between her thin knees, she pressed them together before saying, 'There's only one thing I want. I want you to open your eyes and see what's before your nose in order that you won't get hurt; but I know that's an impossibility, for as long as he breathes he'll hurt you.'

'Tishy! Tishy! look at me.' There was a pleading note in Annie's voice, and when Tishy lifted her head, Annie said, 'If I open my eyes, as you put it, and say, all right he's getting this from some racket, am I going to be less hurt than if ... if I thought he had any dealings with ... with drugs? I'd die of shame in either case.'

Tishy got to her feet, saying quietly now, 'It takes a lot of shame to kill people, Mam.' And as Annie gazed at her she felt, as she had done last night while talking to Kathy, younger than either of her daughters. Neither of them closed their eyes to facts that were staring them in the face; but oh God! she could stand anything staring her in the face, except drugs. If this money was from that it meant he wasn't only taking drugs, he was profiting by the degradation he brought on others.

Of all the base creatures in the world the lowest, in her estimation, were those men who sold drugs to the young; slimy, stinking, putrid, were the adjectives she attached to them. She couldn't, she couldn't think that her son, her Rance, could be capable of such vileness. He was weak; oh yes, she admitted that; and he was a liar, he could look you in the face and swear black was white and you believed it in spite of yourself; but he wouldn't put youngsters on the road to hell, would he, just for money.

Tishy was searching through the dressing table drawers, but now she did not protest, she only stared at her, watching the swift movements of her hands, and waited. She watched her go to the wardrobe and take down his suits one by one and go through the pockets. When, out of one pocket, she brought a half burnt cigarette she took it to the light and examined it; then after a moment she put it back where she had found it. She watched her inserting two fingers into the watch pocket in the inside of a jacket. She watched her pull out a crumpled piece of paper, press it straight between her fingers, and read it; then, coming towards her, she held it out, saying quietly, 'This could be it after all.'

When Annie looked at the betting slip that registered a five-pound bet the wave of relief that passed through her made her feel faint. Pressing the slip between her hands as if holding something precious, she looked up at Tishy and said, 'Oh thank God! lass. Thank God! I don't mind about that; I don't mind if he gambles his shirt away.' With a bright eagerness, she now said, 'Put that money back, lass, and remember how it was placed. Leave everything as you found it. Oh, thank God! Thank God! She went towards the bed and herself folded up the betting slip and returned it to the inner pocket of the coat. Then she hung the suit back in the wardrobe.

A few minutes later she watched Tishy step down from the chair and lift it to the side of the bed, and she said to her, 'Come on now. Come on.'

On the landing, she stood looking at her daughter for a moment. Then with tears in her voice, she said, 'I couldn't be happier if I had won the pools.'

Simultaneously they turned away from each other and went into their rooms, Tishy to stand, as she often did, with her back to the door, her head well back on her shoulders looking upwards towards the ceiling. Her mother hadn't upbraided her for trying to expose him; she hadn't waved the ticket in her face and said, 'There! I knew my Rance wouldn't do such a thing as that'; she had just grasped at the flimsy evidence and literally held it to her as if it were an innocent child.

She moved from the door and sat on the dressing table stool and gazed at her reflection in the mirror and asked of it, 'Do I want him to be caught out on this?'

No; not that she didn't think he was capable of any trickery, or fiddle, but there was a special kind of disgrace about drugs that she wouldn't wish on him, not the taking of them so much but the selling of them.

What would have transpired if she had proved he was in this racket? Would it have benefited her in any way? Would her mother have suddenly stopped loving Rance and turned her affection wholly on to herself? No, of course she wouldn't. Her mother would never love her more than she did at this moment, and she knew that this love had for its main ingredients maternal duty threaded with pity.

Why did she hate Rance so? Was it that since she was a child she had been aware that he claimed her mother's whole attention? Or was it that since she was a child she knew that she herself had craved love? Her granda had been the only person who had really loved her. And then again his love had been born of pity; he had been sorry for the poor little lass because she looked so plain, for the ugly duckling that he had prophesied would turn into a swan.

'Why am I not pretty like Kathy, Granda?'

'Because you're a late starter, hinny. Just you wait; come sixteen or seventeen you'll turn into a swan. You've a swan inside you, it just has to come out.'

It didn't come out; the transformation didn't happen; but at odd times she still thought she was a swan inside. She only needed somebody to love her and she would turn into the swan.

Oh God! how she needed somebody to love her. She rested her face between the palms of her hands, her elbows on the dressing table, and moved her head slowly at herself, and her reflection answered the movement. She was chock-a-block with love. If she didn't give vent to it in some way it would choke her. Would she end her days pouring it out on animals, a cat, a dog, a budgerigar, as so many women did?

Perhaps Stanley Stone might ask her to marry him. He was showing an interest, but then he would show an interest in anybody who would listen to him. He never stopped talking. God! fancy having to pass your days with a fellow like Stanley Stone. Why did parents give a child a christian name like Stanley when their surname was Stone? Stanley Stone, Barry Butcher, Clare Clark, May Minton. She knew all these people and the joint christian and surname names gave to them a silliness that seemed to seep into their characters. What about her own name, Tishy? Could you find a sillier name than that? There had been a horse called Tishy; the name now indicated a non-starter. And she was a non-starter, and how!

But she wasn't a non-starter in her mind; that was active enough. She knew she had never met a man as intelligent as herself, except one. When she allowed herself to think of him she didn't know if the pain that assailed her was created by love or by hate, for always when he came on to the screen of her mind she did not see him standing tall and shamefaced saying, 'I am going to be married,' but she saw him sitting on the couch, her mother lying across his knees and he with his arms about her, the look on his face like that of a man filled with deep, desire-filled love. No pain she would ever receive would come anywhere near to that which had rent her in that moment.

She had seen Alan twice in the past three years; the first time was eighteen months ago. She was shopping in Binns in Newcastle when she saw him walking slowly towards her. She had turned quickly about and gone up a side aisle, but while making a purchase she watched him and the young woman who was with him, and it was on her she focused her gaze, thinking the while with renewed bitterness, She's almost as plain as me. She was dowdy into the bargain. He must have picked her for her brains, she concluded. What a pity she hadn't got in first.

The second time she saw him was about three months ago, in Newcastle Central Station. She was making her way to the platform from where she would get the train to Shields when he came through the barrier from where the London train had just drawn in. For a moment she hadn't recognized him and she had stopped and stared. He looked so much older; there was no youth left in his face. Again her thoughts were cynical: he must be finding marriage hard work.

She stared into the mirror now with something of impatient surprise; it was as if she were looking at a different face, for the tears were running down the cheeks of her reflection. As her tongue came out and licked the salt drops she murmured aloud, 'Don't let me make a fool of myself at the wedding. Let me be happy for her.' Then dropping her face on to her crossed arms, she whimpered like a child, 'I wish me granda hadn't died. Me granda loved me, and there'll never be anybody else now, never.'

# Chapter One

## The Cottage

'Well if you don't put your name to it, Mam, I'll get it on me own.'

'A twelve thousand pound house . . . on your own! Things must be looking up.' Annie closed the hamper into which she had packed foodstuff and, pushing it towards Rance, said 'Put it in the boot for me.'

Rance went to lift the wickerwork hamper from the table but stopped in the act and, leaning heavily on it, looked to where Annie was picking up her handbag from the chair, and he said, 'Mam, I mean to have that house, with or without you.'

'Then you'll have it without me. Twelve thousand, huh!'

He lowered his head and looked down at his white knuckles gripping the handles of the hamper, and after a moment of silence he ground out, 'Mam, I'm twenty-seven; I've got to have a life of me own.'

Like lightning she rounded on him, crying now, 'Who's stopping you having a life of your own? I've told you for years to get yourself away. Take a flat. I've even gone and got you a flat. A life of your own! Don't you dare say to me I stopped you having a life of your own. Look, boy.' She leant across the table towards him now, her face only inches from his, and her voice came as a hiss as she went on, 'Get yourself away, do what you like, and leave me my life. I want a life of me own too, but I don't see it sharing a ten-roomed house, me in one part and Benny and you in the other, because he would be there wouldn't he?'

'He's a good pal.' His voice now was like that of an adolescent defending a friend.

'Pal!' Her lip curled.

'He's never done anything to you.'

'No, but I don't like him; he's too smooth, shifty. And his friends in London. Every time you come back from there you'd think you'd been on the razzle for a week. I've asked you this afore, and I'll ask you again, what's his real business? You can't tell me he can run that car of his and live like he does selling panties and girdles; reps don't make all that much. You can't tell me.'

'You've got no idea of what they make, Mam. It's a big business.'

'Big business, is it?' She nodded at him now. 'Well, you must be in it too if you can afford to take on a twelve thousand pound house.'

'I've got a bit put by.'

'A bit!' She stared at him hard.

'Benny will come in with me if you won't.'

'Well, Benny can go in with you because I'm not leaving here to live in half a house that's costing twelve thousand pounds. No, thank you. Now put that in the boot for me, will you?'

'You'll be sorry.'

'Sorry, what for? 'Cos I don't want to uproot my life? This house is good enough for me. It's too big for me as it is. Bill's gone now, that only leaves you and Tishy, and it wouldn't surprise me if she isn't off before the year's out. It won't be Stanley's fault if she isn't, so under ordinary circumstances that would leave the two of us. Surely there would be plenty of room here for you then.'

'You could never make this place into flats.'

Now Annie banged her fist on the table. 'Flats! flats! flats! For God's sake! go and take your house and make it into as many flats as you like, but without me.'

He stood now, his teeth gritted, shaking his head at her; then he muttered, 'Sometimes I could, I could . . .'

'You could what?'

'Mam –' he was a little boy again – 'it's too big to run as a house for the two of us, I mean Benny and me, and . . . and the main point is I want you, I want you about. You know that.'

Yes, she knew that, but it was a long time since the thought had brought her any happiness. Although she couldn't stand Benny Warlister she had wished more than once of late that Rance would go to London with him and stay there, yet at the same time knowing that had Rance made this proposal she would have done all in her power to prevent him because there was something not right, to her mind, about Warlister. As she had said, he was too smooth, too polite. When he buttered her up, telling her that she was a fraud and couldn't possibly be the mother of four grown-ups, she wanted to push him on his back and say, 'Get out of my house and stay out.'

Suddenly she said, 'What about Tishy in your scheme of things? You don't plan for her to come to the new house, do you?'

'No, I don't.' His face and voice hardened. 'I've had enough of her to last me ten lifetimes. She could stay here with her Stanley, that's if she married him, but I'd like to bet she'll never marry anybody.'

'She's like you then, isn't she?'

'I'll marry when I'm ready.'

'Well, so will she. But the trouble with you is you don't like anyone. What about Bill and his girl? You can't stand her either, can you, because she's coloured? And then there's Percy. One of these days that fellow is going to hit you in the mouth.'

'That'll be the day.'

'It will, and it'll come. But the point in question is, I can rely on all of them coming to see me here, but if I go into your house. . . .'

'It won't be my house, it'll be our house.'

'It'll be your house, my flat in your house. Tell me something, are you thinking of putting it in our joint names? It would have to be if I was standing half, wouldn't it?'

'That can be gone into.'

'It's been gone into.' She picked up her light coat and put it round her shoulders, saying, 'Tishy won't be back from abroad till Friday, but I'll be home by then. Bill and Alice, well, you never know with them, it could be any day. I've been round to Kathy's and told her. I think that takes care of everything.'

'And I can take care of meself, is that it?'

She stopped on her way to the door. 'Well, if you're going into flat life it'll be good practice, won't it?'

'Mam!' He had her by the shoulders now, his face crumpled almost as if he were going to cry. 'Look, don't go and leave me like this. When you go off in a tear I'm worked up for days.'

Again and again this side of him attempted to break her down. She wanted to put up her hands and smooth his face straight, but she didn't; she remembered that only yesterday she had looked in the Scotch chest, as she did now from time to time, and found that there had been another three rolls of bank-notes added to the amount she had last seen. Sometimes she found no money in the box at all; then it would gradually grow. Besides the Scotch chest there was also a desk now, but she could never find out what it held. He had bought the desk himself, and it had arrived with a patent lock on it. She had tried to open it with several keys but without success. Her son, she knew, was in some racket; what it actually was she daren't let herself think.

One of the main reasons for her going to the cottage now was to get away from him, for she felt that if she didn't she would come into the open, not to ask questions, but to accuse him outright, accuse him of the thing that was keeping her awake at night.

He was saying now, 'Will . . . will you think about it because . . . because you know how I feel about being separated from you?'

She lowered her eyes and as she turned from him, saying, 'Yes, all right, I'll think about it,' he put his arm around her shoulders and said, 'It'll work out, it'll work out fine.'

A few minutes later, as she drove down the street, she thought, Yes. Yes, I'll think about it, but that'll be as far as it'll go. . . .

It would take her two hours to get to the cottage, so long as she wasn't held up in Newcastle. She had owned the cottage now for over two years, and she had come by it in a very simple way. Taking a cottage in the wilds of the Cheviots she would have said was not her idea of a holiday retreat. Now if it was a chalet on some quiet beach, that would be more like it.

She had been on the forecourt of the garage one day when a Mr Sampson, an old customer, had come up to her and said, 'I'm sorry to tell you, Mrs McCabe, I'll soon be coming for my last fill-up; we're leaving, going down south.'

'Oh, I'm sorry about that,' she had answered; 'you've been with us a long time, Mr Sampson.'

'Yes, ever since your husband started, and that's some time ago now. What is it, over twenty years? But these things happen. You've got to go where you're sent these days, that's if you want to get on. What's more, when you're getting on in years you don't say no, that's if you're wise.'

'You're right there, Mr Sampson,' she had said.

'I would have been off last week if it wasn't for this damn cottage of mine. We've sold the house but I can't get rid of the cottage.'

'A cottage?' she had repeated.

'Aye, it's up in the Cheviot Hills and everybody wants it, until I state the price, and then they say, "What! fifteen hundred for a cottage. You must be mad, man." I paid seven hundred and fifty for that place ten years ago and I've spent over a thousand on it, having it gutted and completely rebuilt inside, that's not counting the week-ends of labour me and the wife put in and the lads an' all when they were younger. But now "Fifteen hundred!" they say. I took a bloke out there at the week-end and you know I got that mad at him I nearly did him in and buried him in a pot hole. He knew what I wanted for it afore we left, and he stood there having the neck to offer me eight hundred, and that was his last word he said because there was no piped water, and why wasn't there? I told him if he wanted piped water he should stay put in the town. But you see the way the brook is placed it would have cost me another mint to get it up to the cottage. Anyway, it's a good job he came in his own car else I'd have made him walk back.'

After they had both stopped laughing she said, 'Is it back of beyond?'

'Truthfully aye, it's back of beyond, and there's not many places left the day that's back of beyond. That, to my mind, was always the beauty of it. We could get away and forget all about everything. Many's the time I've gone up there by meself on a Saturday night feeling dead beat and come down on the Sunday night refreshed and armed for another start. Mind, I can't say I haven't had me money's worth out of it; we've had wonderful summers up there; but it hasn't been used much lately. The wife's got rheumatics you see, an' the lads are married and gone away. But I'm telling you, Mrs McCabe, I'd sooner burn it down, and believe me I mean it, I would, I'd sooner burn it down than take a penny less than I'm askin'.'

'Would you let me see it, Mr Sampson? Mind, I'm not promising anything. I don't know if I'd like the wilds, haven't seen much of them except passing through the country on my way to the Lake District in the car.'

'Be pleased to, Mrs McCabe. What about tomorrow?'

'Tomorrow'll do nicely, Mr Sampson.'

When the morrow had come she saw the cottage. They had left the car in a copse at the end of a narrow track a mile from the main road, and after climbing over a broken stone wall, which took a hundred yards off the journey Mr Sampson informed her, she saw a grey stone house, standing on a rise. It wasn't her idea of a cottage and not pretty at all, and she made up her mind there and then that it wasn't for her. But she hadn't seen inside it then, nor the view from the window, nor had she sat on the top step and drunk a cup of tea while she looked over the wild and beautiful land enclosed by hills.

By the time she had taken the rough road down to the car again she had bought the cottage.

As she was passing through Gateshead she was tempted to stop and call in on Mollie, who had for some years now lived with her daughter Winnie, but she knew that once she got talking to Mollie she might be tempted to unburden herself, and so she went straight through, over a bridge into the maze of traffic, and fifteen minutes later she was passing through Gosforth on the road to Ponteland.

The farther she went the wider the country opened out, and when some thirty miles later she came to Otterburn she didn't stop at the Percy Arms as she usually did when she was alone and treat herself to a good lunch, but drove straight on until she passed Elishaw; then she turned into a road that was little more than a cart track and a few minutes later she drew the car to a halt within the shelter of the copse. Opening the boot she took out the hamper and small case and began the long trudge up to the cottage.

It was fifteen minutes later, after having to make stops to rest, that she arrived at the foot of the steps and looked upwards. She always paused here, as much from weariness as from her delight in seeing the place again, for no matter how often she came upon it after an absence of even a short time it brought to her a sense of peace.

When she unlocked the door she was assailed by a musty smell and she wrinkled her nose against it. Nobody had been here for the past month and it had rained almost incessantly up till a week ago, when the weather had changed, and now the second week in June the weather was giving them a tropical summer.

Before she brought the case and hamper up she went round opening the windows, telling herself as she did so she must make an effort to get out here once a fortnight during the summer, or at least get some of them to come out. It was odd, she thought, that during that first year the place had never been empty except for a couple of days at a time from May until late September. Kathy and Percy had spent weeks up here. Kathy was carrying the baby at the time and she always said it would grow up to be a wild man of the moors because she had roamed the hills so much during the early months of pregnancy. It could well be right too, for young Percy, at two-and-a-half, was a rip, and you needed a lead on him like a dog to know where he was. Now she was carrying her second, the trip together with young Percy was too much for her.

Bill had used the cottage that first year as his headquarters, all through the summer vacation; he and his pals had kipped around in sleeping bags four to a room.

And Tishy, she had spent every week-end up here, and often of an evening when there was no one here she would ask for the loan of the car and set off straight after school and not get back until midnight. She liked to go places on her own. Tishy was still a loner, in spite of having Stanley.

And Rance. Rance was the only one who had never taken to the cottage. He considered she was mad in the first place for paying that price for it, and after his first visit he said the place would drive him starkers. Yet last year he and Benny had spent a week-end up here. She hadn't liked that.

As she unpacked the foodstuff into the cupboard she let out a long relaxing sigh. This, too, was strange but she felt more at home in this kitchen than she did in the one at home. It had neither running water nor electricity, every drop of water having to be carried either from the rain barrel at the back or from the burn three minutes' walk away. The lighting, like the cooking, was supplied by calor gas, and the canisters took some lugging up the hill. She paid nearly as much in tips as she did for the gas.

She made herself a pot of tea and, having set it on a tray, carried it into the main room. It was the sight of this room that had clinched the bargain immediately. The original three small front rooms of the cottages had been made into one, twenty-two feet by eighteen, and the sculleries at the back had been converted into a kitchen, on to the end of which had been built a glass porch to provide more light.

She had bought the place as it stood and she had altered nothing of the furnishing and little in the arrangement. The narrow floorboards were polished a light mahogany colour and the only floor covering was four large

orange and green rugs. The front door opened into the middle of the room.
The windows on each side were not large, but the old-fashioned frames had
been taken out and replaced by modern ones which opened outwards. On
the end wall to the left of the door was an open fireplace with a surround
of natural stone.

The furniture was ordinary and comfortable; a well-worn three-piece
suite which she had had re-covered in chintz, a dining table, the legs of
which showed the imprints of numerous toe-caps and which she had been
unable to erase even with regular polishing; the six chairs were plain and
sturdy and the china cabinet that had once graced a drawing-room had two
small glass panes missing – but still remained a valuable piece, so Percy
said.

The stairs that led steeply up from the right-hand side of the room near
the kitchen door were open and had no balustrade, merely a thick rope.

There were two bedrooms, three at a pinch, the latter being a seven by
six storeroom. All the windows were on floor level, and Annie had not yet
become used to lying in a bed which seemed at times to be floating in the
sky, or resting on top of hills.

She sat now in the easy chair drawn up in front of the open door. She had
taken her shoes and tights off and she was waggling her bare toes with the
joy of a child. In a few minutes she'd change into slacks and get some water
up from the burn, then fetch more wood in, for no matter how hot the day
it always got chilly as soon as the twilight began.

Could she live here on her own? She shook her head uncertainly at the
question. Perhaps; yes, she thought she might be able to.

If she had to pick one of them to live with, who would it be? Tishy?

Yes, Tishy. But why Tishy? Tishy didn't need her in the same way Rance
did; Tishy was sufficient unto herself; she had an inner force, an inner
strength. So why Tishy?

Because she needed Tishy. Was that it? Yes, yes, she supposed so. Anyway,
she needed someone. Of late, she had felt very lonely; well, not so much
lonely as alone. You couldn't be lonely with them all popping in and out
and making demands on you, but you could be alone in the midst of them.

She thought of Georgie. Would he have liked it up here? No; like Rance
he would have said it would have driven him crackers. You had to be a
certain type of person to enjoy more than a passing glimpse of these fells and
moors because they were secret places.

What did she mean by that?

Well, she supposed. . . . Oh she didn't know what she meant, she was
going off all poetic. This is what always happened when she sat here; she
never thought like this at home. This place brought things out of you. If you
just sat quiet something crept into you, stirred your thoughts, made you
think as you had never done before – and made you pleased that you could
think that way. Yes, yes, indeed.

When she awoke with a start she realized she had been dozing. Would
you believe it! dropping off like that. But she had been tired when she
arrived, and disturbed, and that was putting it mildly. She had told Rance
she would think about it. Well, that's what she was going to do, but not in
the way he expected. She had known for some time she wanted to make a
break, get away, do something different with her life before it was too late.
What exactly she didn't know, but what she knew in this relaxed moment

was that before she left here on Friday everything would be clear in her mind.

She brought up two cans of water from the burn; she filled the straw skips at each side of the fireplace with wood; she set the fire all ready for lighting; she fried herself some bacon and eggs and had two cups of coffee; she washed herself down in soft rain water from the barrel, got back into her slacks and was pulling a red sweater over her head when she heard the knock on the door.

It wasn't unusual for someone to knock on the door; hikers often stopped and asked for hot water, some would ask if she had any eggs for sale, only to be informed that she didn't keep hens. There were even those slap-happy bare-faced picnickers who would come with such requests as: would she fry them a pound of bacon and half a dozen eggs? or had she any bread or cake she didn't want? They had gone through their own supply at dinner-time and had nothing left for the second meal. If they were youngsters she would meet their requests if she could, but if they were grown-ups she had learned to deal with them. Sometimes she got only a black look after delivering a homily on being prepared, but on other occasions she got a mouthful of abuse.

When she opened the door a young man stood there, definitely a climber by his clothes. 'Good afternoon,' he said. 'I'm sorry to trouble you but I wonder if you would be kind enough to put a drop of hot water on this tea?' He held out a can. 'Me friend has sprained his ankle and we're getting him down. We thought we might be stranded for the night but the other fellow –' he pointed behind him – 'he's a hiker, kindly offered to make a sling out of his sleeping bag. We've got a car down on the road. How far do you think it is to Horsley?'

'Oh, about two miles, but you want to go straight down now and cut over to the right.'

'Oh aye. Well, I'll tell him. It's only our second trip out.'

'Would you like to bring him up and rest here a while?'

He looked back down the trail where one figure was standing and the other lying on the ground, and he said, 'It's pretty steep and by the time we would get up here we could be well on our way. But thanks all the same.' He smiled apologetically.

'Yes, you're right. I'll be about five minutes.'

'Thanks. I'll be glad of a rest. May I sit down here for a minute?'

'Yes, you're very welcome.' She hurried into the kitchen, and after a moment his voice came to her, saying, 'By! it's a nice place this.'

'Yes,' she answered; 'I like it.'

'A bit lonely.'

'For some, I suppose.'

'You'd never dream there was a habitation here until you come round the hill.'

'No, you wouldn't . . . we're sheltered in a way. Where do you hail from?'

'Wallsend.'

'Oh, Wallsend. I'm from Shields.'

'Get away!'

'Yes, it's a small world.'

'Aye, it is. But it doesn't look small from up here. Eeh! you could lose yourself in these hills and never be found. Robby was getting the wind up; that's why I didn't leave him and go and get help on me own.'

After a few minutes she came back into the room carrying a tray with his steaming can on it; it also held three cups and saucers, a bowl of sugar, a jug of milk and a plate of buttered scones, the whole of which she had expected to last her during her stay, but then, she had told herself, she could always knock up some more.

'Don't bother to bring the tray back, I'll come down and get it.'

'It's very kind of you, missis. I'm very obliged to you.'

'That's all right. I hope you'll do the same for me some day when I break my ankle.'

They both laughed; then he went down the hill and she stood and watched him pouring out the tea and handing the scones round, and when after a while the three raised their hands to her, she walked down the steps, then on down the hill, to pick up the tray.

When she reached the track they were cutting at an angle over the slope below her, and the young man holding the back of the sling turned his head round and called 'Ta-rah! And thanks again.'

At this, the man in front also turned round and looked towards her, and as he did so the small cavalcade came to a jolting stop. The man stared up at her, and she stared down at him. She heard the young fellow at the back say, 'What is it?' She saw the man in front move his head, then walk on.

She stood watching them until they had gone over the hump and were out of sight. Then she stooped and picked up the tray and went slowly up and into the house. She did not take the tray into the kitchen but laid it beside her as she dropped on to the couch.

Him! after all this time. But it was him all right. She hadn't recognized him at first for he was so altered. But he had recognized her, and she had altered too. Oh yes, she knew she had altered in the last six years, and not just in one way, she was older looking, much older looking. .

She must have sat for half an hour before she rose and took the tray of crockery into the kitchen. After she had washed up the cups she went upstairs, and the first thing she did was to look in the wardrobe. She had brought only one dress with her – she lived in slacks most of the time up here.

She took the dress from its hanger and laid it on the bed, then went to the mirror, and there she peered at her face. She hadn't many lines yet, a few under her eyes, one faint one starting at the right-hand side of her upper lip. There were one or two strands of grey in her hair, but they were at the back. She hadn't seen them herself, it was the hairdresser who had told her. She pulled the bedside chair round and sat down before the mirror; then taking a lipstick from the tray, she carefully made up her lips, applied a faint dusting of rouge to her cheeks, and was on the point of applying some eye liner when she banged the pencil down on to the table.

What was she up to? Well, he'd come back and she wanted to look decent.

All right, he'd come back, so what of it? What hadn't happened six years ago wasn't likely to happen now, was it? Be your age. She glared at herself in the mirror.

When he came in how should she greet him?

Well, how should she greet him? Politely, ordinary like, no fuss. She rose and, taking her dress from the bed, she hung it up in the wardrobe again, then went downstairs. The clock said ten to six. If it had taken him half an hour to get down to Horsley it would take him a little more to get back, then add the time for seeing those chaps off and he should be here any time now. She'd kept the door shut. When he knocked it would give her time to compose herself.

Why did she need to compose herself?

Oh, for God's sake shut up, woman!

By half past six he hadn't come. At quarter to seven she said to herself. 'There now, sure, weren't you, absolutely positive he'd come back. What about his wife? He's likely left her at some spot on the hills and is going to pick her up later. ... You, you want your head looking, that's what you want. They say women in their forties go daft, and you're proving it. You must have started the change in your mind if nowhere else.'

For two pins she'd get in the car and go back home. If she started off now she could be home before dark. Well, she'd better make up her mind before she put a match to the fire. She stopped herself from going to the window yet once again by saying, 'Enough of that now. Enough of that. Go or stay. Decide now.'

It was as she stood in the middle of the room pondering that she heard the scraping of rough boots against the stone steps, and when the knock did come on the door she held her hand tight against her waist. She told herself not to rush, to take things easy, then went towards the door and opened it.

It was a full minute before either of them spoke, and then he said, 'I knew it was you; there couldn't be two of you. I . . . I would have been back before now but those two chaps knew as much about cars as they did about climbing and that was very little. We couldn't get the thing to start; just the matter of an empty tank. We . . . we had to go for petrol.'

He was explaining all this to her as if he had left her a short while before and been held up.

'Come in,' she said.

He came in, wiping his feet assiduously on the doormat before stepping on to the bare floorboards. He did not look round the room but at her and asked, 'How are you?'

'Oh, very well. And you?'

'Very well.' He inclined his head towards her, smiling slightly now. The action, and his voice made it sound as if he were amused as he would be at a child who was trying to be over polite. Then, the smile leaving his face, he said, 'I remember saying this to you before, and I have to again, you don't change.'

'Nor you; you still lie gallantly.' She turned from him and moved down the room, saying, 'Won't you sit down? I was just going to put a match to the fire.'

As she struck the match and set the paper alight he said, 'What an extraordinary room! You get no indication from outside. I've passed this place for years. Have you been long here?'

She took the bellows and worked them and the flame licked up between the wood before she said, 'Nearly three years.'

'How is the family?'

'Oh, very well. Kathy's married, has a little family of her own now.'

'How nice. And . . . and the others?'

'Oh, just as they were, although Bill may be marrying soon I think. I lost my mother and father though.'

'Oh, I'm sorry. Your mother-in-law – Mollie, wasn't it? Is she still alive?'

'Oh very much so. They'll have to shoot Mollie, I think.'

She put down the bellows, dusted her hands, then coming towards him, she asked, 'Would you like a cup of tea, it's some time since you had the last one?'

'I would indeed. I haven't had a meal since twelve. . . .'

'I . . . I can make you something.'

'Oh no, please, I didn't mean that. I was going to say I've got some grub in my pack. Would . . . would you mind if I brought my pack in for a moment? I don't suppose anyone would steal it, not around here, but then again I'm not so sure. I was washing my feet in a burn once when somebody went off with my boots. It was only for a lark; I found them hanging on a tree about a mile farther on. And the foxes can get a bit nosy too, and they don't wait for the dark.'

'Yes, bring it in by all means.'

'Oh, not in here.' He looked round the room. 'Is there a shed at the back?'

'No, no,' she said hastily – the only shed at the back was the one that covered the Elsan pan – 'but there's an annexe to the kitchen where we store the deck chairs and things; it'll go in there.'

'Good.'

She watched him go quickly out of the door and down the steps; then she closed her eyes and bit on her lip. She had told herself she must act ordinary, but she could never act so ordinary as he was doing. It was unbelievable. Nobody coming in would believe that he had just dropped in out of the blue. He was so self-assured. That, she supposed, came from teaching, and not just schoolboys, but men. What was he now, thirty? Good gracious! he looked so much older. He had grown gaunt in a way, there was hardly any flesh on him. But that could be the hill climbing; the energy that took left men with only bone and muscle.

She sat down weakly on a chair, saying to herself the while that she couldn't believe it, she couldn't believe it. From the time she told him not to come back she hadn't been able to get him out of her mind for months. At night she would lie thinking about how she had lain in his arms and cried, and she would recapture the feel of his arms about her and hold on to the look in his eyes when he had said, 'If I had fallen in love with anybody it wouldn't have been Tishy.' And then she would think, Oh Georgie, I'm sorry. I'm sorry.

During those months too, the relationship between Tishy and her had been strained. Tishy would go for days, even a week at a time, and not open her mouth. She had wanted to say to her, 'He was only being kind, acting like our Bill or Rance would have done if they had been in.' But Bill or Rance would never have held her like that. She would never have laid across their knees and been cradled in their arms.

She recalled now that Tishy had never mentioned his name again; but she had got over him for she had taken up with Stanley Stone, and gradually her manner had thawed and returned to normal.

'I'm amazed. What a lovely kitchen. The whole place is delightful. How . . . how did you come across it?'

He had come in through the kitchen door, and now she rose and went past him and re-entered the kitchen, and as she put the kettle on the stove she told him briefly how she had come to own the cottage.

'What is it called?'

'Sheepcote Cottage. It was originally a shepherd's cottage; then they added on to it and made three farm cottages. I understand that the original end, where the fireplace is, is over three hundred and fifty years old.'

'I've no doubt about it. These . . . these places were built to last and to stand up against the weather. Do you use it often?'

She hesitated before saying, 'Yes, pretty often, but not so much as we used to. Everyone was newfangled with it the first year and the two hours' journey was nothing. You know, people's enthusiasms change.' She gave him a half smile as she spread a cloth over the formica-topped kitchen table, then said, 'You would prefer hot bacon and eggs to cold sandwiches if I'm not mistaken?' and he answered, 'You're not mistaken.'

As the bacon sizzled in the pan, and the eggs spluttered and he sat behind her at the table, talking all the while, she told herself that it was fantastic that she should be up here cooking him a meal after all this time. Of one thing she knew she was glad, and she emphasized this to herself, she didn't think she liked him now, in fact she was sure she didn't. He talked too much, too easily, too freely. But then, hadn't he always talked easily and freely? Still, he was different, and she was glad he was different. It had knocked all that nonsense on the head; funny, how you nursed a thing for years, blew it up out of all proportion, gave to a little incident a meaning that was ridiculous to say the least. Oh, women were fools. All of them were fools. From their early teens onwards they made fools of themselves in a thousand and one ways. And she could cap them all. First, Georgie and then . . . Oh, she shouldn't think that way about Georgie.

'There.' She put the plate of bacon and eggs on the table before him, and he smiled at her, saying, 'Thanks.' Then, as he picked up the knife and fork to begin eating, he paused and asked, 'Where's yours? Aren't you having any?'

'No, I had something just a little while ago. I'll have a cup of coffee though. I can drink coffee at any time.'

For the life of her she told herself she couldn't sit at that table and eat with him. There was something about him that was disturbing, but in a different way from that which she remembered. Yet he wasn't acting differently from what he had done seven years ago. His actions, his voice, his manner were still that of the young man of twenty-four. That was the point, he was no longer that young man, seven years divided him from that young man, and those years were written on his face. He appeared like an older man acting the boy. He startled her now by repeating her thoughts aloud. His voice grave, he said, 'I've been imagining that I had just come into your kitchen on that night, the second time we met. Do you remember?'

Did she remember! would she ever forget? There were periods when, night following night, Georgie hurled down the stairs towards her, sometimes knocking her over and tumbling with her down a further flight.

He said no more until he had finished eating, by which time she had brewed the coffee and carried it into the sitting-room. She placed a small table near the chair to the side of the fire and on it she put his cup, while she placed her own on a similar table but at the end of the couch farthest away from the chair.

When he asked from the kitchen door, 'Shall I wash up, I'm quite used to it?' she turned to him and said hastily, 'Of course not! Anyway, I've got to heat water. They can wait till the morning.'

As he came down the room she pointed to the coffee, saying, 'Do you take sugar?' She didn't add, I've forgotten, but ended, 'I'm sorry I didn't ask whether you like it black or white? I made it white.'

'That's how I like it, and without sugar, thank you.'

He sat down and when he picked his cup up and it rattled in the saucer she realized with surprise that he was as nervous as she, and it enabled her to speak to him calmly. 'Are you still teaching in Newcastle?' she asked.

'I was up till last term; I've left.'

'Oh!' She raised her eyebrows slightly.

'I may be going to America in August to teach at a university there; in fact, I'm sure I'm going.' He smiled now as he nodded, 'I have a research scholarship.'

'Oh! that's marvellous.'

'Well, that remains to be seen.' He was smiling again. 'I may get my head blown off on the campus.'

'Oh, don't say that. Yet there have been dreadful riots over there, haven't there? But then, why go to America for riots; we've got an assortment of them here, haven't we?'

'Yes, indeed.'

'I suppose your wife is looking forward to it; most women like the idea of going to America.'

He now sipped from his cup, then placed it on the table to his side, but he didn't look at her as he said, 'My wife won't be going with me, we were divorced two years ago.'

... 'Oh! Oh, I'm very sorry.'

'It would be very boorish of me to say I'm not, yet it would be true.'

She remained quiet, until the silence became embarrassing; then she asked as evenly as she could, 'Do you ever see your uncle now?'

'Uncle Arthur? Oh yes. I came from there yesterday. He doesn't live so very far away, just beyond Hawick. It's over the border in Roxburgh. Do you know it?'

'No, I haven't been that far. ... How is he?'

'Very well. Very well indeed. Strange, but he was talking of you the other day.'

'Oh yes?'

He did not go on to say what Arthur Bailey had said but added evenly, 'And who do you think I saw last year?'

'I wouldn't know.'

'Mona.'

'Really!'

'And in Paris of all places.'

'Paris! ... Mona?'

'Paris ... Mona.'

'Was she on holiday?'

'Part that, and part honeymoon; she had just married again.'

'Really! Well, well.'

'And she looked marvellous, radiant.'

Annie moved her head slowly; she could never imagine Mona looking radiant.

'He's an Australian and a very warm Australian by the way he was spending money, and judging from the hotel they were staying in. But he was a nice fellow. I rather liked him, no swilling pints and slapping you on the back which, unfortunately, is the general picture of the Australian; quite an intelligent man.'

'You saw them a lot then?'

'Not a lot. I met them two or three times; we had a few meals together.'

Mona in Paris in a posh hotel with a rich Australian for a husband. Funny how things turned out. A girl with one eye and no looks to speak of could marry for a second time, and a rich man into the bargain. Oh now! down dog, she said to herself; cut out the bitchiness. Surely Mona was entitled to some compensation to make up for those sexless years with Arthur. She'd had her troubles with Georgie, but a starved body hadn't been one of them. Yet over these last few years she had known what it was to have a starved body, and more than once this has caused her to give a thought to Mona. . . . And now she was married again. Well, good luck to her.

She said now, 'How is your mother? She's in America, too, isn't she?'

'No, not now; she's gravitated to Switzerland.'

'Is she still . . .?' She stopped; it would be tactless to ask if she was still married. But he had guessed at the question and he laughed at her now as he said, 'Oh, she's still married, very much so. And very happy, I'm glad to say.'

'That's nice.'

Everybody he knew seemed to be happy. She felt herself receding farther and farther away from him. She wished he would go. She looked towards the window and said, 'The mist has cleared, thank goodness. It's very cold at nights when the mist settles. I should say it will be dark soon to-night; the sun went down early. It's funny how you get to know the weather up here; some nights the twilight seems endless, and at other times it seems to gallop towards the dark.'

He stared at her for a moment before bringing himself to the edge of the chair and rising to his feet, and she felt the colour rushing to her face as she, too, rose from the couch. She had been tactless, she might as well have told him openly to get himself away.

'I'll be off.'

'Are you making for the inn?'

'I'm not quite sure. If it's a fine night and the moon comes up, as it should, I'll go on walking. It's a wonderful feeling walking across the hills in the moonlight.'

'Yes, it must be, I must try it some time.' She laughed ironically, and he said, 'I wonder you haven't done it before, the tracks leading from here are all clear cut. . . . May I go through the kitchen to get my pack?'

'Yes, yes, of course.' She followed him down the room and through the kitchen, and after picking up his pack from the floor he put it outside the door; then standing on the square of flagstone he said, 'You're not afraid to stay here alone?'

'No; it's funny but I'm much more nervous in the town. I bolt and bar every door and window when I'm home.'

'You should lock up here, too. Remember –' he gave her a twisted smile – 'there are people who walk about in the moonlight.'

She ignored his joke and her face was straight as she said, 'I've never had any intruders so far.'

'It's been nice seeing you again, Annie.'

Her answer to this should have been, 'And you too'; but all she said was, 'Thank you.'

He held out his hand and she placed hers in it. He did not squeeze it with undue pressure, or hold it longer than was necessary. And then he was saying, 'Good-bye.'

And she answered, 'Good-bye.'

With a swing he brought the pack across his shoulders, then walked along the side of the house and round the corner and was gone.

She stepped back into the kitchen and slowly drew the bolt in the door. She went into the sitting-room and to the window and, standing to the side of it, she watched him going down the hill, not towards the inn but in the direction of the copse and the road that led to Otterburn. When she could no longer see him she walked towards the fire and, seating herself in the chair on which he had sat a few minutes earlier, she stared into the flames.

She could not in this moment describe how she felt. She had wanted him gone, and now he was gone she felt a loss, greater than that she had experienced seven years ago, oh much greater, because at that time the memory of Georgie was still clinging heavily to her.

There was stillness all around her, she was enveloped in it, and the aloneness that was in her flowed from her and filled the silence. The room was full of it, the house was full of it, all those miles of moors and hills were full of it; and he was walking away untouched by it.

For God's sake! don't cry.

Quickly she pulled herself up from the chair, placed a wire guard around the fire, locked the front door, then went upstairs, thinking as she did so, Thank God for one thing, Tishy isn't here.


# Chapter Two


The twilight hadn't been short, it had been long, and she had lain staring into the sky until there was nothing to see, not even the reflection from the window, for there was no moon, as he had foretold, and it was a starless night.

She didn't remember at what hour she fell asleep but she woke at first light and watched the dawn bring back the hills and clouds. She heard the birds in the copse start their dawn chorus. She heard some moor animal scream and an owl hoot, and she thought, Yesterday I was disturbed but I wasn't really unhappy, today I'm disturbed and I'm unhappy. But the unhappiness had clinched one matter in her mind: she was going to make a break, she was going to get right away, to some place where nobody could get at her; and not just for a week, or a fortnight, but a month, two months, three months.

Tishy could see to herself, Bill would get married, and Rance, well he could have his house, or his flat, but without her. She'd go on one of those cruises. She always despised the widows who went man-hunting on cruises; but she wouldn't be going man-hunting, she'd just be getting away, giving herself time to think, to find out what to do with the remainder of her life.

The sun was well up when she went to the window and looked towards Corby Pike. It was beautiful in the morning.

She walked across the room to the small window set in the side wall, it was the only one that wasn't on floor level, and from here she could see the continuation of the Pike where it met up with Highspoon. The sun was filling the craggy hollows with softness, it was giving a velvet sheen to the greenery that tightly cloaked the hills. It was beautiful. Why couldn't she stay here?

*No! No!* She swung around quickly, pulled her dressing gown from off the rail of the bed and put it on as she went out on to the tiny landing. She descended the stairs, went straight into the kitchen and put the kettle on. She opened the cupboard door and looked in. Should she leave all this tinned stuff here? Some of the others might want to come. Tishy would, most likely.

When the kettle boiled she brewed the tea and, having set the tray, she carried it into the sitting-room and, as she did every morning when it was fine, she went to open the door so that she could take in, as she drank her tea, the wonder of the moors. She had put the tray down on the table and had unlocked the door, but on pulling it open she sprang back, clutching at the front of her dressing gown as she made an unintelligible exclamatory sound.

He was sitting with his back against one stanchion and his feet against the other. He looked up at her and blinked before getting to his feet. His hair looked rumpled, as did his clothes. She looked at his sleeping bag draped for airing over the hand rail of the steps.

'I'm . . . I'm sorry I startled you.' His face was unsmiling, his voice flat, serious sounding, matching the sombreness of his looks.

When she could speak she said, 'You . . . you haven't been there all . . . all night?'

'No . . . no, just since dawn.'

'Where did you sleep?'

He pointed without speaking down towards the copse, then said, 'Your car makes good shelter.'

'You slept out?'

'Of course: yet I had no intention of doing so last night. But . . . but I found I had to.'

He was still standing outside the door, and now as if talking to an unruly child she said, 'Come in, come in; you must be stiff. Here.' She went quickly to the tray and poured him out a cup of tea; then after handing it to him she hurried up the room and, taking the bellows, blew on the fire, and he called to her, 'It's all right, I'm not really cold.'

When she returned to him he was standing just where she had left him, inside the door, and again she spoke to him as if to a boy. 'Go to the fire, I'll get you something to eat.'

He made no reply but obediently he walked up the room and, sitting in the chair, he put out his hands to the licking flame.

When she came back into the room she stood some way from him as she asked 'Do you like hard or soft boiled eggs?'

'Oh, medium, please. Can I help?'

'It doesn't need any assistance to boil an egg.'

Still acting the mother, she turned sharply away and went into the kitchen again, and a few minutes later she called from the doorway, 'Would you like to come and get it?'

When he entered the kitchen he did not sit down but, looking at her across the table, he said softly, 'Annie, I'd like to talk to you.'

She returned his look for a moment before she said, 'There'll . . . there'll be plenty of time to talk later, after . . . after you've eaten.' She pointed to the place that was set for him, with two eggs on the plate, but before he sat down he went to the other side of the small table where one egg reposed in an egg cup and drew the chair out for her.

The three slow steps she took towards her place could have given the impression that she was slightly drunk. She did not look up when he took the seat opposite to her and she did not speak until a smell of burning pervaded the room; then she sprang up, saying, 'Oh my goodness! the toast.'

When she retrieved two black squares from under the grill he smiled at her for the first time and said quietly, 'I'm glad you can make a mistake.'

She cut more bread, made more toast, poured out more tea and finished her egg, and all in silence. It was when she finally looked up and found his eyes on her that she said, 'Why on earth did you sleep out there all night?'

'What would you have said if I had suggested you offer me a bed?'

She moved her head slightly before she answered, 'I would have told you to go down to the inn. I thought that was where you were making for anyway.'

He said now, 'Did you sleep?'

'Of course I did.'

'You were lucky, I didn't.'

When he held her gaze she suddenly got up from the table, and pulling the belt of her dressing gown tightly about her, said, 'I must go and get dressed.'

'Why? You look beautiful as you are.'

She turned from him now and, resting her hands on each corner of the stove, she bowed her head and said, 'That's enough of that, Alan. Don't start something that's going to bring embarrassment on us.'

'I'm not starting anything, Annie, I'm merely continuing something that began years ago. Come here.'

Before she could stop him he had gripped her hand and was pulling her out of the kitchen and through the room to the couch; and now sitting on it, he pulled her down beside him, saying, 'If nothing else I'm going to talk, and you're going to listen. Out there last night I was made to believe there's such a thing as destiny, that each one has it written for him from the day he is born. I could say it's even mapped out before that. Now this is how I see it. Look –' he took her by the shoulders and pressed her back into the couch – 'don't sit there like a ramrod, look at me, Annie, and listen to what I'm going to say. It begins with Uncle Arthur. Why was Uncle Arthur born a homosexual? Don't shrink like that, Annie; you might as well turn away from the mention of male or female; it's a quirk of nature, as we ourselves are. Well, Uncle being what he is, he meets Georgie. . . .'

She tugged her hands away from him, at the same time edging along the couch, and her voice was high and indignant as she cried, 'Georgie was never like that, I told you before.'

'I know he wasn't, I know he wasn't, Annie. Look, don't get upset. It was because Georgie wasn't like that, he was just the opposite and the kind of fellow, from what I gather, who would in the ordinary way make a big joke of it, but he didn't. There was something in Georgie below his roughness that understood Uncle Arthur's predicament. Uncle was going through one hell of a time mentally when he first met Georgie, not having the real guts to be a conscientious objector, knowing himself for what he was, pushed into a camp full of male specimens, their conversation enough to sicken a pig, and let me tell you the male in herds can become sick-making, no matter from what class they come.

'Are you listening to me?' He shook her two hands.

She didn't answer but stared at him now, and he went on, 'Well, now as I understand it, Georgie swore and cursed and was a bit of a rough neck, but there must have been in him a sensitivity that was hidden from most people. So we have the situation where, because he understands Uncle Arthur's plight and is sorry for him, Arthur's gratitude knows no bounds. He takes him home, and it's as if he were yelling, Look, I've got a friend, an ordinary bloke. They were all well aware at home that class forms no barrier in cases like Uncle Arthur's, but from what mother said I think they all believed, that is with the exception of my father, of course, that here was an ordinary friendship. Anyway Uncle Arthur's gratitude, as I said, was boundless, so what must he do? Invite Georgie and his wife for Christmas.' He paused and gazed at her until her eyes dropped away from his, then he went on softly, 'And a little boy of five meets Georgie's wife and recognizes immediately that she is different from anyone else he has ever known, and they talk – of jigs.'

This did not bring a smile to her face, her eyes were still averted, and again he went on, 'I can still hear my father and mother quarrelling. At different times during my childhood I would look at my father and think, You're James Partridge, because on that memorable Christmas I witnessed their first open row. There had been many before that, but discreetly covered, I understand, for my sake; but it was on that day I heard mother say, "You're a swine, James Partridge. That's what you are, a swine, a pushed-up, cheap swine." I used to ponder on what a pushed-up cheap swine meant. Eventually I discovered, in my father's case, that it meant that he came from a very ordinary family, so ordinary that after marrying mother he disclaimed any connection with it.

'I didn't hear anything of Uncle Arthur for some time following that Christmas. Then after Father died I went to stay with them; I only went the once. It wasn't a happy time. Years later, during my first walking tour, I called on him and found him living alone, and from that time I felt for him as Georgie must have felt, a liking and a compassion for his situation. I said to him once, "Do you ever see the woman who came to the house for Christmas, that time there was the big row?' and he looked at me in surprise, saying, "You remember that time all those years ago? You were only five." And I said, "Of course I remember it. I particularly remember the woman, her name was Annie,' and he said, "Yes, her name was Annie and she was a nice girl. Georgie's lucky".'

When she moved uneasily on the couch and went to draw her hands from his he held them firmly, saying quietly, 'I'm not finished yet. Grandmother had a friend, who had a granddaughter called Jane, she was three years younger than me. "Wouldn't it be nice," said the grandmothers, "if our grandchildren married." They got their heads together very early on and they arranged that I was pushed at Jane, and Jane was pushed at me, every holiday. I had other girls; in fact there was one at college on whom I was very keen. I wanted to live with her, not marry her, I decided I wasn't going to marry for years, and this particular girl was quite willing to fall in with the suggestion, but at the last minute I withdrew. I had been home and there was Jane again; there were certain things expected of me, play up and play the game. Jane left school when she was eighteen. She didn't go on to college, it was considered that she wasn't very strong. Everyone protected Jane; I followed where the others led. Jane was sweet, she was good company and intelligent; she had nothing to speak of in the way of looks but she was attractive. Strangely, she was very like Tishy, I mean in that once you got to know her her looks didn't matter, in fact you saw a certain beauty in them. Anyway, Jane and I became engaged. It had to happen, my grandmother had arranged it, and any seed Grandmother planted bore fruit. Perhaps you remember my grandmother. I think of her as the eternal miniskirt.'

Annie was looking at him now, waiting, and he leant his shoulder against the side of the couch for a full minute before he spoke again. 'When I showed no inclination to rush into marriage Grandma became annoyed. Since Mother had married again and gone off to the ends of the world, as she put it, it was her responsibility to see that I acted correctly. I used to think it was this attitude that drove me to take the position in Newcastle, but now I know that Grandma was merely part of the plan that had been mapped out for me, for I wasn't in Newcastle a day before I thought, I must look her up, that woman. Now why after all those years should I have thought that? In the ordinary way I shouldn't even have remembered what she looked like, let alone the conversation we'd had, but I did remember, and very clearly, for your face, Annie, was etched on my mind.'

She looked at him, her eyes unblinking; then she bit tightly on her lip and bowed her head.

'Well, you know what happened the first night I saw you. And the following month appeared to me as long as a year. I couldn't believe that I'd only been in your life four weeks, I felt I knew all about you, everything you thought; I anticipated your very actions, your very words. I would say to myself, Now she's going to do so-and-so; Now she's going to say so-and-so. I seemed to be living inside you. When I came and took Tishy out, it was merely to help you, to get her away from Rance. Also to give her the chance to expand, because she did expand in company, the right company. She was good to be with, and strangely I felt as if I were a psychiatrist effecting some kind of a cure on her, turning the introvert into an extrovert.'

He now let go of her hand and, taking a handkerchief from his pocket, wiped her face with it; but before he had finished he was talking again. 'Towards the end of that month there was a show-down. Jane's father wanted to know what I was up to. Jane's mother wanted to know what I was up to. Her grandmother was indignant, as was mine. Jane was twenty-two, I was twenty-three, what were we waiting for? everything was ready. Well, what was I waiting for? I named the date, told them I was going to look for a house this end and came back to tell you, to tell you and Tishy, for I knew then that it was time I told Tishy. But believe me I never imagined that she would be so hurt; she was young but she was a girl very modern in her outlook; I had done nothing to make her think that I was being other than friendly. . . . Then you cried and I took you in my arms and I knew I had never known happiness before . . . but it froze when she came into the room and I saw her face.'

He now turned from her and bending his body forward, he placed his elbows on his knees, joined his hands tightly between them and moved the pads of his thumbs against each other as he said, 'Two months later I married Jane and entered into a private hell. You know, there's a great deal to be said for promiscuity. I would advocate a trial run to every couple no matter what their morals, in fact I'd make it compulsory.' There was a deep bitterness in his voice now. 'Jane didn't like sex – it was nasty – our so-called honeymoon was a nightmare. At the end of it she wouldn't let me near me except to wipe away her tears, hold her hand or to stroke her hair. Even this she just tolerated. Why hadn't I become aware of this before we married? I soon understood she had put up with my surface love-making then because she wanted to marry me. What she wanted was a combination of father, brother and male nurse. I tried to get her to a doctor, but no. And so, after six months of it, I went to Grandma, and Grandma went to her grandma, and I was told to have patience. Her rejection of me, I was given to understand, was the result of a bad experience she'd had when she was twelve years old; a young uncle had raped her.'

The pads of his thumbs were still rubbing, and she brought her eyes from them to his face as he went on, 'I became very understanding, very gentle; I became her father, brother and male nurse. On the surface Alan and Jane were every so happy. During the second year I realized that this could go on for ever, and I knew I couldn't stand it. Now it was me who wanted a male nurse. I went to my doctor. He said he would see her, but she wouldn't see him. I went to my solicitor. He said divorce would be quite easy. I went to Grandma, and her reactions were pure Victorian. No one would have guessed that she had been sleeping around for years. "Divorce!" she said. "No, you can't possibly. Jane's a nice girl." Yes, Jane was a nice girl; but I didn't want a nice girl, I wanted a wife. Anyway, two years ago I got a divorce, but it was too late to save me having a breakdown.'

'Oh, Alan.' It was the first time she had spoken his name since she had seen him yesterday, and he turned his head slowly towards her, saying, 'I once heard someone say that they wouldn't wish the devil in hell to have a breakdown and I can endorse that.'

'Oh, I'm sorry.'

He smiled now, saying, 'Well, since it's brought the first kind response from you, what I should say now is that I would go through it again just to get the same results, but I cannot be so gallant. What I can say though is that I know now it's all part of the plan. You see if it hadn't been for the breakdown and having to go away for treatment, I would have run from this country like a scalded cat; but during this bad period I seemed to lose all my initiative, all I wanted was to get away from people, to be by myself. I took to walking again. This helped me back to normality. Anyway, this post came up in America and after long debate I took it. And I made up my mind that as soon as term ended I'd get my ticket and fly away. Yet what did I do? I plumped for one last holiday on these hills. I'm not due in the university until early September, so I told myself I'd stay with Uncle for a month and still have plenty of time left to see something of the country in which I was going to live.'

He hitched himself back on to the couch, turned towards her and took her hands again and, looking into her eyes, said, 'Yesterday morning I set off early, saying to Uncle, "Expect me when you see me," and I walked and I walked. Then rounding a butt I come across those two idiots sitting like lost lambs and I devised a way of getting the injured one down to the road, and in the process we are all very dry and hot and longing for a cup of tea, so we stop at a cottage.' He pulled her hands towards him now. 'Do you see what I mean about it all being mapped out? Coming across those fellows yesterday, I would say on reflection, brought me to about the middle of the map; there's still the other half to be worked out. Do you get what I'm driving at, Annie?'

'Oh, Alan, don't, don't.' She went to withdraw from him again, but he held fast to her hands. 'Do you like me?'

She shook her head even as she said, 'Yes, yes, of course, I like you; no . . . no one could help liking you.'

'You're not answering my question: Do you like me?'

'Yes.' Her head was bowed deeply on her chest now.

'I love you, Annie.'

'No, Alan, no.' The movement of her head was wider now. 'You can't; you know nothing about me, except for that one month.'

'I've known you all my life; I was waiting for you when I was five. I recognized you. You know something? I follow no religion. I believe that religions are merely shelters for weak and frightened men, and God was created by man to assuage the inexplicable hunger in him. It is well known that all religions down the years have been but different forms of tyranny, the means of creating gods with which to provide men with power and, in turn, to subordinate nations. As for Christianity, it is but the modernization of heathen rituals. This can all be proved. Yet last night, lying out there, looking up into the blackness, I believed in God, or at least in a mind that can plan, and I couldn't discard yet again an idea that has been in my mind for a long time concerning you. When I first thought of reincarnation I laughed at it, yet last night I was forced to believe in it. How other did I recognize you at five years old? . . . We have met before, Annie.'

Her head had stopped shaking, she was looking at him now in utter bewilderment. She wasn't a very good Catholic but she was a Catholic. She believed in God. She had sometimes questioned the Virgin Birth but then, she had told herself, if God could do anything, then he could set a seed in a woman's womb. Really when you came to think of it there was nothing to the Virgin Birth, He having in the first place created life. She had thought this out in her teens and she hadn't veered from it since. The Church was in a bad way now; there was the question of the pill, and priests were leaving to get married, which she thought was shocking. And this knowledge had made her a bit uncomfortable when going to confession. What if Father Campbell were sitting on the other side of the grille thinking of a woman while she was telling him her sins. These things could become disturbing if you gave your mind to them. But she hadn't given her mind to them, she had only kept praying to God to keep her family straight. And when her mind touched on the word straight, she thought of Rance. Now here was Alan wiping away the foundations of all religions and making reincarnation believable. Could they have met before? It sounded fantastic. Yet, as he had made out, it was strange how they had come together again after all these years. But he was still so young. Yet he didn't look young, he looked nearer forty than thirty-one; and she wasn't sorry for that, for it lessened the years between them.

What was she thinking about? This was madness. Yet deep within her she knew it was a madness that was welcome. She knew, even more than he did at this moment, that it was the beginning of something, a new existence filled with wonder and love, the kind of love she had dreamed of before she had lain on the bed with Georgie.

'Could you love me, Annie?'

Her head was swinging again. In spite of how she felt she couldn't say it. To put it into words would sound indecent somehow.

'You do love me, you must; it would be impossible for me to have felt like this about you for years, to have been waiting for you for years, because that's what I have been doing, and then you to say that you don't love me.'

With a movement that startled her he was holding her face between his hands. Then, his mouth dropping on hers, he pulled her still resisting body towards him and held her fiercely, until, as if a spring had snapped, she leant heavily against him.

Minutes passed and they still clung together. His mouth left her lips and moved over her face, and when she said, 'Oh, Alan! Alan,' he answered, 'Annie. Annie.'

Of one accord they rose from the couch. Their arms about each other, they went towards the stairs.

When she took off her dressing gown and got into bed she kept her face averted from him while he undressed.

When he laying facing her he did not immediately take her into his arms but lay looking at her as if in wonder; then his hand going gently to her breast he said, 'Oh, Annie. Annie, my love, this is the beginning of the other half.'

# Chapter One

## The Breaking of the Cord

Tishy came home to an empty house. Having obtained no answer to her ringing of the front door bell, she went round the back and found the door locked. After searching through her bag she found her front door key and, after letting herself in and bringing her cases from the pathway, she went straight into the kitchen. It had a deserted look, an unlived-in look; there were dirty dishes in the sink. That was unusual; her mother never went out and left dirty dishes in the sink. The solution came to her that Rance was here on his own and that her mother was away, likely at the cottage; she had said that she might go there for a day or two. Anyway, Kathy would know.

She took off her light coat, put the kettle on, because her first need was for a cup of tea, real tea, and she wanted something to steady her nerves. Not that tea would do much for her nerves, the state they were in at the present moment. But ten days of Stanley Stone had almost brought them to breaking point. How had she tolerated him all these years? Likely because she'd experienced him in small doses. But ten days of Stanley Stone putting over Stanley Stone had given her a terrifying insight into what it would be like to be Mrs Stanley Stone; not that she had ever really contemplated it.

She sat down in the chair by the table and ran her hands through her hair as her mind shouted at her, 'Oh, face up to it, you did contemplate it. It was either him or a dog, cat and budgerigar, remember?' She put her head back now and gave a short laugh. There had been quite a scene at the airport, subdued but nevertheless intense. What was it her granda used to sing? 'We parted on the shore, oh we parted on the shore; I said, Good-bye Love, I'm off to Baltimore.'

'Where you off to?' Stanley had said. 'Where do you think?' she had replied flippantly; 'Hong Kong? I'm going home and I don't want any more company.' As he had walked beside her out of the airport he had been speechless for the only time during their ten days together. When she said, 'I'm taking a taxi,' he had said, 'Why? there's the bus.'

'You take the bus, and I'll take the taxi, and I don't want company.' He had stared at her for some seconds before saying, 'I can't quite make you out, Tishy; you're a funny lass.'

'Yes, I know, both funny ha-ha and funny peculiar. Good-bye, Stanley.'

So that was the last of Stanley – until school started.

As she got up and mashed the tea she said to herself, 'What have I lost, anyway? I don't believe he had any intention of ever asking me to marry him, he never even tried to make it with me. I must be the only girl in this decade who has been with a fellow for ten days and remained intact. What if he had tried ... would I?' She stared across the kitchen wanting to hear herself give an answer. What she said was, 'He doesn't want a wife, he wants an audience. I must have been a godsend to him.'

As she drank her tea she thought, I'll go to the cottage next week. There'll just be Mam, I'll like that.

Her tea finished, she was on the point of going into the hall to phone Kathy when she heard the key turning in the front door. A minute later Rance entered the kitchen. He stared at her blankly and she at him. They never spoke to each other unless it was absolutely necessary, but now, looking towards him, she said, 'What's happened?'

'Oh.' He looked down at his bandaged hand and his arm, which was in a sling, and said, 'I tried to slice my thumb off.'

'When did it happen?'

'Around dinner-time.'

'You went to the hospital?'

'Yes, of course. They put eight stitches in it. They say it'll save the pad, it was only hanging by a thread.'

She grimaced and said, 'I've just made some tea. Have you had anything to eat?'

'Not since this morning, I haven't wanted anything. But there's half a chicken in the fridge from yesterday.'

As she set about getting him a meal she asked 'Where's Mam?'

'At the cottage. I expected her back before this.'

'How are you managing with the car?' she asked now.

'I'm not; one of the fellows brought me home.'

There was no more conversation between them, and after she had buttered some bread and cut up the chicken for him she left the kitchen and, picking up her cases, went upstairs. After unpacking she went into the bathroom and felt the tank. There was plenty of hot water so she decided to have a bath.

Twenty minutes later she was leaving the bathroom when Rance opened his bedroom door and said, 'Will you help me change my coat? I can bend the arm but I can't get my hand through the sleeve, one side's all right but I'm stuck with the other.'

Even before she moved towards him she felt the revulsion rise in her, and when she eased his hand into his coat sleeve the feeling inside her was so strong that she admonished herself sternly, saying, 'He's your brother; you're taking animosity too far.'

'Will you knot my tie for me?' In the same breath he added, 'Mam should be back by now. What's keeping her?'

She kept her eyes away from his face and firmly on the tie as she thought, Yes, Mam would have dressed you. You would have liked that. Oh God! why was she so bitter against him?

'Will that do?'

He turned round and looked in the mirror, then said, 'Fine, thanks.'

They both turned now as the front door bell rang, and he smiled and nodded at her, saying, 'That's her; she's forgotten her key.'

Tishy ran down the stairs and opened the door to see Percy standing there.

'Oh, hello, Percy. I thought it was Mam and she had forgotten her key.'

'Hello, Tishy. You had a good time?'

'Oh . . . oh yes, Percy, I suppose I can say I had a good time. But give me England; at least if you get watery cabbage you know it's watery cabbage. But by the same token I hardly spoke to a foreigner, everybody seemed to be English.'

'Well, as I've always maintained, Tishy, if you want to meet people you want to get away from, go abroad.' Percy laughed his thin, piping laugh, and Tishy laughed with him, saying, 'That's Irish, but it's true.'

'It is indeed.'

Tishy now led the way into the front room. To her mind Percy and kitchens didn't seem to go together; he was the kind of person who only relaxed in formality, and as Kathy had confessed, she could get him to do almost anything but sit down to a meal in his shirt sleeves.

He turned to her now, saying, 'Kathy phoned several times this afternoon, she thought Mam would be back. Then she phoned me to say that my mother had called in to take them out to the beach and would I keep phoning in order to make a certain request. Well, I did up till five o'clock, but got no reply.'

'It was just about five when I got in.'

'Well, well.' He smiled widely at her now. 'I should have kept to the maxim of try, try, try and try again, shouldn't I?'

She made no reply to this but answered his smile, then he said, 'If Mam doesn't return in time I wonder – but really I feel it is a bit of an imposition when you haven't been in the house five minutes to ask you to baby sit for us. Mother would do it, but between you and me, Percy junior takes advantage of her and she gives in to him, and I'm afraid she pacifies him with sweeties, and you know –' he nodded at her now – 'how many children's teeth have been ruined by a grandmother's indulgence.'

'Well, we'd like to be off at seven. Oh, I do feel it's an imposition. But the invitation came at short notice, I only received it this morning. It's to do with a very important client. Well, it isn't only the client that's involved, it's his father also, and his father has come up from Cornwall. Oh, it's a very involved story. It's got to do with a trusteeship about which we are acting, and my client said would we like to come to dinner at his hotel in Newcastle this evening at eight. But I do think it's an . . .'

'It's all right, perfectly all right, Percy, I'll just get into some clothes and be round by seven.'

'You're sure you're not too tired?'

'No, not at all.'

'Oh, Kathy will be grateful. You see she expected her mother to be home. And she's had no word from her; you know, she usually phones when she goes down to the road for milk.'

'She hasn't heard at all?'

'No, not at all. But she told Kathy before she left that she would be back today. Well, I must be going, but thank you again, Tishy.'

'That's all right, Percy.'

As Percy made towards the door, Rance entered the room.

There was a feeling of enmity between the two men, but whereas the enmity that existed between Rance and Tishy could lead to open quarrels, Percy refused absolutely to quarrel with his brother-in-law and Rance's hatred against him had grown more deep if anything because of this. Percy's coolness and correctness infuriated him, yet now when he wanted to ask a favour of him he could be civil. 'Are you going back into the town?' he said.

'I wasn't, why? . . . You've hurt your hand?'

'Yes, tried to take my thumb off.'

'It must be painful.'

'It isn't that so much; they numbed it, but it's sticking out like a sore thumb,' he laughed. 'I'll get used to it in a little while but at the moment it's stiff.'

Percy said coolly, 'You want dropping somewhere?'

'Yes, back to the garage if you wouldn't mind; I've got an appointment there at seven.'

Percy looked at his watch. 'I could take you there now if that would be all right? It would mean you'd be early, but I must be in Newcastle by eight.'

'Yes, that'll be fine.'

Tishy, knowing that taking Rance to the garage would take another fifteen minutes of Percy's time, said, 'Why not phone for a taxi?'

'Oh no; if we go now it'll be all right. I myself should hate hiring a taxi if I had a number of cars at my disposal.' With his short quick steps Percy led the way to the front door, saying over his shoulder, 'And thanks for tonight. We should be leaving about quarter past seven, not later.'

'I'll be there, Percy.'

'Oh.' He turned towards her. 'Shall I come and pick you up?'

'No, you won't. I can use my feet. You'll be lucky if you get to Newcastle on time as it is.'

'Just as you say, Tishy. Good-bye.'

'Good-bye, Percy.'

Rance didn't speak, nor did he turn his head in her direction and she closed the door before the car started up.

She was about to mount the stairs again when she heard the hard rapping on the back door. Now who could this be and her in her dressing gown.

She went through the kitchen and opened the door to see Mr Wilkins standing there, a strange dishevelled Mr Wilkins. But then Mr Wilkins had been going strange for a long time now, ever since Susan ran away, and he had got worse this last six months since he had been made redundant, for it had given him more time to go searching for Susan. He almost knocked her on to her back now as he pushed past her into the kitchen, crying, 'Where is he? Where is he?'

'Who, Mr Wilkins? Who do you want?'

'You know who I want. Shielding him you've been, you and your mother. Shielding him, the lot of you.'

Without again asking, 'Who do you mean?' she knew; but she still said, 'Who do you mean, Mr Wilkins?' and he cried at her, 'Your Rance!' He now went marching through into the hall yelling, 'Come down, you bugger you! come down, you bloody swine, out o' that!'

'Mr Wilkins! Mr Wilkins! Listen to me, please.' She caught hold of his arm. 'He isn't in.'

'Isn't in! Don't you tell me he isn't in. The missus said she saw him comin' in.'

'That was some time ago.'

'You can't hoodwink me.' He now swung round and burst into the sitting-room; from there he went to the dining-room, and he was about to go upstairs when she cried at him, 'He isn't in, I tell you, Mr Wilkins; he's gone to the garage.'

'The garage? the garage?' His head was bobbing as if it would come off his shoulders. 'I'll garage him when I get him. By God! I'll garage him.'

'Mr Wilkins, please, please.' She again caught hold of his arm. 'Try to calm down. Tell me, what is it?'

'What is it? Why ask the road you know? You've known all along what it is. It's my Susan. But I've got her back and she's told me everything. It was him that started her on it, an' not her alone. You know what I'm going to do? I'm going to the polis. You know what pushers get. My God Almighty! how many bairns has he ruined . . .'

The truth was out at last. It had been staring them in the face for years. In her heart she had known all along what it was, but her mother had pulled a shield over her eyes with the betting slip.

As he now stormed back into the kitchen and towards the door she cried at him, 'Wait! wait till my mother comes in, Mr Wilkins, please . . . Please!'

'Wait for your mother?' He turned on her. 'No, by God! an' let her shield him again? She'd shield him with her life. Yet when she sees what he's done to my poor Susan I . . . I don't know. A wreck she is, a wreck. But she's home. In Doncaster I found her. Mrs Nesbitt who used to live in 42, they moved there, and she phoned John Pollock down below and told him she knew where Susan was. An' John run me through yesterday. We've just got back, just got back this minute, an' I'll not rest, I've sworn I'll not rest or eat, until that brother of yours gets his deserts.'

'Please! please, Mr Wilkins.' She was running down the yard after him now, but like someone demented he tore away from her.

From the back gate, with her hand pressed tightly against her mouth, she watched him. He did not go into his back yard but ran to where a car was parked at the end of the lane. It wasn't his car; he had sold his when he lost his job; it was Mr Pollock's old red banger.

Oh my God! She was back in the kitchen, her two hands covering her cheeks now. A pusher. Drug takers were victims, but pushers were creatures, vermin who, solely in order to make money, ruined thousands of young lives. They were the most . . . She rocked from side to side and shook her head; she could find no words adequate enough to describe such people, and her brother was one of them.

Her mam. Oh! She dropped down on to a chair. This would break her. It would kill her. It wasn't so much the public disgrace that would affect her but the fact, as Mr Wilkins had said, that her son had ruined the lives of young girls. And how many? Yes, how many? All that money in the top of the Scotch chest; and that had been three years ago.

She got up now and began to pace the room. What should she do? Mr Wilkins would have likely gone straight to the garage. There would be a fight, and by the look of Mr Wilkins there could be murder. The garage was closed. There'd only be Rance in it and whoever he was going to meet. But she wasn't going to worry about Rance, let him take his chance. It was her mother she was worrying about. Mr Wilkins would be as good as his word; he'd go straight to the police and they moved quickly in such cases. If only her mother were here and she could break it to her.

She must get dressed. She ran upstairs and scrambled into her clothes;

then, downstairs again, she stood undecided what to do. Her mother might turn up any minute and if she wasn't here and the police came ... She'd better phone Kathy. No. No, there was no need to tell Kathy or Percy tonight for they had this important dinner on, and if they were to go she must get round there. She looked at the clock. It was quarter to seven. She'd stay till seven. She could phone a taxi for then.

At five to seven Kathy rang. 'Oh hello, Tishy,' she said. 'You're back all right then? Did you have a good time? Is Percy there?'

'No; he was here, but he should be home by now. He was running our Rance to the garage. He's hurt his hand, Rance, I mean.'

'Oh Lord!' Kathy's tone expressed her impatience. 'He's cutting it fine. Is Mam back?'

'No. I'm wondering what's keeping her. I understand she was coming back this afternoon.'

'Yes, so she told me, at least she said some time on Friday. She'll turn up before dark; she hates driving in the dark ... Oh! wait till he comes in, I'll give him the length and breadth of my tongue ... By the way is anything the matter, you sound funny?'

'... No. No. Nothing the matter ... and Kathy, don't go for Percy, it wasn't his fault. Our ... our Rance should have taken a taxi. I said so.'

'The garage closes at six, why did he want to go back there?'

'He had to meet someone, I don't know who, I didn't ask, you know me. By the way, I've ordered a car to bring me around about seven; in fact, it should be here any minute now.'

'All right, Tishy. Thanks for sitting in at such short notice.'

'That's all right. Be seeing you.'

'Be seeing you.'

Tishy stood by the table for a moment and drew in a number of deep breaths before she went into the kitchen and wrote a note to Annie telling her she was baby-sitting at Kathy's, and to ring her up as soon as she came in. She ended by saying, 'It is important that you ring me immediately, Mam. There is something you should know.' She underlined the last words.

The taxi came at seven, and seven minutes later she was entering Kathy's house.

Kathy, dressed in a green velvet semi-evening dress and looking more beautiful than she had done in her single state, came to meet her, saying, 'I can't understand it. It's nearly ten past, and we should be leaving at quarter past.'

'Ring the garage,' said Tishy quietly.

Kathy rang the garage, but there was no reply.

'Ring the office,' said Tishy now. 'He may have gone back for some reason or other.'

Kathy rang the office, and there was no reply.

When a whimpering sound came from upstairs Kathy said, 'No, don't go up, he'll just keep you at it. He'll go off in a little while, he's dog-tired. He was in the water all afternoon.'

They were sitting looking at each other when the clock struck half-past seven, 'Something's happened,' Kathy exclaimed, jumping up, 'I know it has, he would have been back else. This is important; this dinner, it's very important.'

'Look, don't get all het up. But there's one thing certain, you won't get there by eight o'clock. Do you know where you were going?'

'To The Royal Station Hotel.'

'Well, phone them and leave a message. Say your husband's been delayed; he'll ring later as to what time he'll arrive.'

Kathy made the necessary call and she had just replaced the receiver when she said, 'I'm going to phone the police; there . . . there could have been an accident.'

'If there had been an accident you would have heard before now.' Tishy felt sick. If only her mother were here. 'Wait,' she said; 'I'll phone home again.'

When there was no reply to the ringing Kathy said, 'I'm not waiting any longer, Tishy, I'm going to phone the police.'

Kathy spoke to a policeman, who put her through to another policeman. He sounded very calm. No, he said; there hadn't been a report of an accident during the last three hours.

'I'll go to the garage,' said Tishy, 'but I'll have to go home first to get the keys.'

It was ten minutes before a taxi came to take her home. On the journey she prayed that her mother would be in, but the house was as she had left it. She picked up the keys, returned to the taxi, then later dismissed it in King Street. Whatever she was going to find in the garage she didn't want the taxi man in on it.

She was trembling as she opened the main door. She had to switch on the lights because it was dark inside. She walked slowly past the office, then round by the pit. There was a car above the pit, and she glanced underneath. Looking along to the end of the garage she saw that the doors were partly open. When she looked out into the lane, there was no car parked there. She closed the doors and bolted them, then as she returned up the garage she saw, in the far corner, Rance's own car. She went towards it and looked inside. Then she stood gazing about her. She couldn't understand it. Had he persuaded Percy to take him off somewhere? No, Percy wasn't the kind of man to be persuaded. Behind Percy's correct exterior and pedantic manner there was a will as strong as iron; his courtship of Kathy had been but small evidence of it.

She looked at Rance's car again. If she had the key she could drive it. There was no key in the ignition but she knew where the spare one was hidden. It was her mother who had insisted on putting a spare key under her car after she had locked herself out once, and she had suggested that Rance do the same.

She pulled the sticky tape off the key, then opened again the back doors that she had recently bolted. She backed the car into the lane, and left it there while she returned into the garage, rebolted the doors, hurried out through the front gates, locking them after her, then ran into the back lane again. If there had been anyone about, her actions might have been questioned, but she saw no one.

Driving the car out of the lane, she turned it in the opposite direction to that by which she had approached the garage. This way she would avoid the main road. But she hadn't travelled more than fifty feet when she drew the car to an abrupt stop, for there, parked in a line of cars, was Mr Pollock's car, the one she had seen at the end of the lane, the one Mr Wilkins had taken. She couldn't mistake it, it was red and a botched-up affair with dabs of grey rust preventative here and there along the bottom of the doors.

She found that she was trembling. Mr Wilkins had got to the garage then. But where was he? If he had come out he would surely have taken the car back home to Mr Pollock. Their Rance, Percy, and Mr Wilkins, where were they? She put her foot down on the starter and the car leapt forward.

She was outside the house again, but as she stepped from the car she looked to the right of her and saw Mr Pollock standing in the Wilkins's front garden, and Mrs Wilkins was on her doorstep and Mr Pollock's voice was loud and carried to anyone who had a mind to stop and listen, saying, 'It's bloody unfair, Jenny, that's all I can say. I went out of me way to take him there yesterday. I've lost two days, you know that, I've lost two days. And how does he repay me? Goes off with me bloody car, and not a by your leave or can I. I tell you, it's taking advantage, it's taking advantage.'

She heard Mrs Wilkins speak in a tear-filled voice, saying, 'Come in, Larry. Come in, and don't raise the street.'

As Tishy opened the front door Mr Pollock was repeating, 'Don't raise the street? It's enough to make anybody raise hell.'

'Mam!' She was standing with her back to the door. But there was no reply, and she closed her eyes and said, 'Oh dear God; bring her, bring her soon, because I don't want to have to do anything. If I do she'll blame me, she'll hold it against me for the rest of my life. She'll say I'd just been waiting for the chance.'

She went into the kitchen and added to the note: '8.30. Please, please, Mam, phone Kathy as soon as you come in. There is trouble.'

In the street, Mr Pollock was coming out of the Wilkinses' again. Should she go and say to him, 'I saw your car parked near our garage?' No, no, she must do nothing, nothing at all until her mother came on the scene. Yet she was fully aware that in the meantime something dreadful could be happening. Their Rance was vicious, he was bad, innately bad; she had known it since she was a child. He was sly and wily, and clever with it because he was one of those people who could look you in the face while swearing your life away. He had no moral sense. That was his trouble, he was utterly devoid of moral sense.

When she reached Kathy's it was to find her crying bitterly. 'Something's happened, Tishy, I know something's happened, I feel it, and it's to do with our Rance. He's been going round with funny people. That Benny Warlister. Percy saw him the other day and he said he looked like a prosperous gangster of the Al Capone type. Do you think I should phone the police again?'

'No, no; wait.'

'What's happened to Mam? Why isn't she home?'

'That's what I'd like to know. But it's likely the spell of good weather, and she wanted a break, she needed it. I tried to get her to come with me but she wouldn't.'

Jumping up suddenly, Kathy said, 'If I have to sit here and do nothing I'll go mad. There's no way of contacting Mam, is there?'

'You know there isn't, Kathy; the only way is to go there. I could do it but it would take me two hours, and two hours back, and then there's the chance I might pass her on the road.'

'If she's not here shortly she won't be coming. She won't drive in the dark.'

'No, that's certain.'

'What are we going to do?'

'Wait; that's all we can do.'

'Oh, Tishy, Tishy, I'm frightened.'

'Now, now –' Tishy put her arms about her sister – 'there'll be a simple explanation, you'll see' . . . Oh dear God! if there only could be a simple explanation.

At quarter past nine the front door bell rang and they both rushed to the door together, then stared open-mouthed at the policeman and plain-clothes' man.

'Mrs Rinkton?' The plain-clothes man looked from one to the other.

'I'm . . . I'm Mrs Rinkton. Something's . . . something's happened, my husband?'

'May I come in?'

She stood aside, and they came into the hall but moved on further before the man said, 'Your husband's in hospital, Mrs Rinkton.'

'In hospital? So there has been an accident?' Kathy had her hands to her throat.

'I . . . I don't know about an accident, Mrs Rinkton, but –' the man seemed slightly uneasy – 'it is rather a complicated business. A short while ago a phone call was put through to the station to the effect that a car was parked on some waste land and that there were two men in it and one was bleeding. He had been stabbed.'

'Percy!'

'No; your husband was apparently unconscious, the man who was stabbed was a Mr Harry Wilkins. They are both in the General Hospital.'

'It's all right; it's all right. Sit down and put your head between your knees.' It wasn't Kathy to whom the policeman was speaking but Tishy.

'Right down,' said the policeman. 'That's it.'

After a while she muttered, 'I'm all right. I'm all right.'

'I . . . I must go. I can go, can't I, I mean to see my husband?'

'Yes, yes, of course. We'll take you now.'

'I . . . I must change this.' Kathy was patting the front of her dress. 'We . . . we were going to a dinner.'

The two officers looked at her, their glances seeming neutral, without either condemnation or sympathy.

She turned from them and ran up the stairs, and Tishy asked, 'Is . . . is the man badly wounded?'

'I can't rightly say, miss. I . . . I think they are going to operate.'

'What relation are you to –?' The plain-clothes man nodded towards the stairs, and she answered, 'My sister.'

'You knew her husband well?'

'Yes, oh yes.'

'Did you know anything about his personal life?'

'Personal life? What do you mean?'

'His habits or . . . or was he addicted to, say, drugs?'

'Percy?' She gulped deeply. 'No! No, not Percy; he's highly respectable; he's an accountant and Doctor Rinkton's son.'

'That doesn't mean much these days, miss. You could be the Queen's cousin and still fall for drugs.'

'But . . . but what makes you think that Percy, Mr Rinkton? . . .'

'Well, they were found on him and ... and he's under the influence of them.'

Oh God no! She drooped her head on to her chest as she groaned inwardly, 'Oh, our Rance! our Rance!' But he'd not get off with it this time. In any case, when Mr Wilkins came round he would tell them ... if he came round. What if he didn't? Percy would then have to fight his own way out. Oh no, no, she couldn't let that happen. Anyway, there was always Mrs Wilkins and Susan ... Where was her mother! *Where was her mother!*

Kathy came running down the stairs and said, 'You'll stay, won't you, Tishy?' Tishy nodded at her.

On the point of leaving, Kathy turned and said, 'His mother. His mother and father, they should know ... His father, he'll know what to do.'

'You go on, I'll phone them.'

'Tell ... tell Dad to come to the hospital, will you?'

'I'll do that.'

When the door had closed on them Tishy went slowly into the dining-room and to a cabinet in the corner of the room. Taking from it a bottle, she poured out a good measure of brandy and drank it at one gulp, then sat choking and coughing.

Doctor Rinkton brought his wife and Kathy back to the house at half past ten. He had almost to support them through the front door. In the drawing-room, Kathy, looking up at Tishy through her tears, said, 'The world's gone mad. They say that Percy has been taking drugs.'

'My Percy taking drugs.'

Tishy now looked at Mrs Rinkton. She was in great distress. Then she turned her gaze on Doctor Rinkton, who was saying slowly, 'There's something very wrong here, very wrong. My son would no more take to drugs than he would run along the street naked.'

Tishy glanced from one to the other before she asked, 'What did he say? what did Percy say?'

'He hasn't come round yet, he's got concussion.' It was his father speaking. 'But he's also under the influence of drugs. They found two punctures in his arm and a packet in the car. I tell you, there's something very wrong here.'

On a high choked cry now Mrs Rinkton exclaimed, 'My Percy to stab anyone! It's fantastic even to contemplate. Someone's done this. They've done this. I've said to you someone's done this. They intended to kill that man, and Percy too, and make it look ... My Percy wouldn't hurt a fly.'

Doctor Rinkton came and stood directly in front of Tishy now and said quietly, 'Kathy tells me that Percy gave your brother a lift to the garage. Have you seen your brother since?'

She had to force the word out: 'No.'

'Is he likely to be home by now?'

'I ... I could ring.'

'I'll do that.'

She watched him go into the hall and she didn't move until he returned, saying, 'There's no reply,' then added, 'Why did he want a lift, your brother? He drives, doesn't he?'

'He had hurt his thumb.'

'Then he couldn't drive at all?'

'I ... I shouldn't say so.'

The doctor blinked and turned away, and now Kathy looking at Tishy asked pitifully, 'Mam, she's not back yet?'

'No. It doesn't look now as if she'll be back tonight.' Tishy paused a moment, then said, 'I . . . I could go and get her.'

'Would you, Tishy?'

'Yes.'

They stared at each other, then nodded. Tishy, turning away, said, 'I'll call in home first and if . . . if she's there I'll phone you.'

She went out into the hall for her coat; then re-entering the room, she went hastily to the couch and hugged Kathy to her for a moment, saying, 'It'll be all right. Do you hear? it'll be all right.' Then straightening herself, she looked from Doctor Rinkton to his wife and she repeated, 'It will be all right. Believe me, it'll be all right.' Then she ran from the room and the house.

## *Chapter Two*

It had been raining when she left Shields, but by the time she was through Newcastle the thunder was frightening, with the lightning picking out the countryside all around her. Fortunately the traffic on the road was light, except for the heavy night lorries. At one point, when nearing Otterburn, it was as if a thunderbolt had dropped just behind the car for the pressure of it brought her crouching over the wheel. When she turned into the narrow road leading to the copse it was running with water like a mill stream.

Her headlights didn't pick out the Mini until she was nearly upon it, but she managed to bring the car to a sharp skidding stop; then sat back and closed her eyes for a moment, telling herself that she would never forget this night as long as she lived. Reaching over to the back seat she picked up her mac and the battery lantern. She struggled into the coat, pulled the hood over her head, then stepped out of the car and into ice cold water that came over her ankles. She could not hear her own exclamation above the fierceness of the wind. She had to fight her way up the first field, and when she reached the wall she clung to it, then lay against it, her back to the wind, in order to get her breath.

Twice as she went up towards the cottage she was almost lifted off her feet. Before mounting the steps she clung on to the iron post for a moment; then she was at the door knocking and calling, 'Mam! Mam!' She tried the latch, hoping that perhaps Annie had left the door open. She went down the steps again and fought her way to the back door. This, too, she found locked. She did not thump on this door, knowing it would be no use; if her mother hadn't heard her at the front, she wouldn't hear her at the back. But there was a way of getting in. She opened her bag and groped in the side pocket where, she knew, she would find a nail file, and this she inserted in the framework of the glass window in the kitchen annexe. With the first sharp lift the latch gave and the windows of their own accord burst outwards. Putting the lantern through she climbed in, then fell over the deck chairs. When she was on her feet again she forced the windows closed, and, picking up the lantern, went through the kitchen and into the sitting-room. Her mother was here all right, the embers of the fire were still glowing. She dropped her bag on to the couch so that she could take off her mac, which she threw down beside the bag; then, the lantern in her hand, she mounted the stairs.

'Mam! Mam!' She thought she'd better call so as not to frighten her.

When she pushed her bedroom door open and lifted the lantern high she stood staring at the sight before her. A short while before she had said she would never forget this night, but all that had happened so far paled now into insignificance. There in the bed was her mother lying on her back, her shoulders and breasts bare, and on his side, his arm across her, lay Alan Partridge.

'*Mother!*' She screamed the name at the highest pitch of her voice; it tore up out of her throat. Then again, '*Mother!*' Not Ma, but Mother. You couldn't get condemnation into the word Mam, not as you could into that of Mother.

'W . . . what! Who! O-oh God! God!' Annie was sitting up, clutching the bedclothes up around her chin now. 'Who . . . who is it?'

'Who do you think? Her voice was still a scream. She looked down the beam of light and watched Alan pull himself up and blink and shade his eyes against the light. Now he was scrambling out of the bed and he didn't bother to cover himself up. She turned and ran from the room and down the stairs. After crashing the lantern on to the table, she went to the couch and, throwing herself on it, buried her face in a cushion and bit on her lip till the blood ran.

When she heard Annie beside her she didn't move. 'Oh my God! girl, you . . . you shouldn't have come. It . . . it isn't what you think. Look . . . look at me.'

When Tishy felt the hand on her shoulder she sprang away from it. But she looked at Annie, and now, dry-eyed but the tears breaking her voice, she cried, 'You're . . . you're filthy! You're a filthy old woman!'

'I'm not. Don't you dare say that. Oh!' Annie groaned now and turned away, holding her head in her hands. Then as swiftly she turned to Tishy again, saying, 'It's all right, it's aboveboard, we're . . . we're going to be married, I'm going to America. It doesn't matter about age.'

Tishy slowly drew herself up from the couch and, peering at Annie through the diffused light of the lantern, she said with slow bitterness, 'Well, I don't think you'll be going to America just yet. And when you do you might have to take long trips back to visit your son in prison.'

She watched her mother's lips tremble, she watched her fingers tapping her chin in small rapid movements, and it was a full minute before Annie said, 'What do you mean? What's brought you?'

'I'll tell you what's brought me. I've come to tell you that your son's a drug pusher. I tried to tell you three years ago, but you waved the betting slip at me. Well, now Susan Wilkins is back and she's spilled the beans, and her dad went after your dear Rance and Rance stabbed him. But what else did he do, eh? What else did he do? I'll tell you, he's got Percy in the hands of the police under suspicion. Percy gave him a lift to the garage because he had hurt his thumb. What happened after that is not yet clear to anybody, but this I do know, he stabbed Mr Wilkins, knocked Percy out, then he must have injected drugs into him and he left drugs on him. So if you're interested, that's why I am here, that's what I've come to tell you, and if you hadn't been so busy whoring you would have been home now where you're needed.'

'If it wasn't for –' Annie gulped, then went on, 'If I knew you weren't a liar I . . . I would slap your face for you this minute and for more reasons than one.'

'Why don't you?'

Now Annie, her hands again at her head, said, 'I can't . . . I can't believe it.'

Alan walked into the rim of light and to her side. He now had his trousers on, but the rest of him was bare. He put his arm around her shoulders and looking at Tishy, he said, 'I'm . . . I'm sorry, Tishy, it had to be broken to you like this but . . . but it isn't what you think.'

'Oh! Oh!' She turned away, flapping her hand at him. 'I've already heard that. And anyway it's no business of mine, but if you could spare my mother for a few hours there are matters she'll have to see to before she goes to America. And also –' she turned and looked to where they were standing beyond the rim of light close together, and she had to force her vituperation out while she still had a voice left, 'And you'll have to keep it dark, won't you, Mr Partridge? It wouldn't do if it became known in your high scholastic circles that you were stepfather to a murderer, because if Mr Wilkins dies that's what he'll be, that's if he doesn't manage skilfully, as usual, to put the blame on someone else, Percy this time.'

'*Stop it!* Your bitterness will burn you up one of these days, girl . . . I –' Annie now turned to Alan – 'I must go. I must get dressed.' She pulled herself away from him and stumbled across the room towards the stairs, and Alan, looking towards the dark outline of Tishy, said, 'I'm deeply sorry about this trouble with Rance, but I'm more sorry that you have taken this attitude against your mother because of me, she's not to blame in any way. Nothing was planned. I was on a walking tour, I was helping an accident case over the fells, we stopped here for water. That was how it happened, nothing was planned. You mustn't hold anything against her.'

'Oh I don't, not really. I mean, what chance would she have against you. You tried your best seven years ago, didn't you?'

She waited for an answer but he remained silent, and she went on, 'Fourteen years younger than her. No woman could stand against that: flattery alone would get them down.'

'Tishy! Tishy! you're being cruel.'

'Oh my God! don't come that with me. Now let's get this straight, Mr Partridge. Your fine manners, your smooth tongue will never cut any ice with me, and don't, I'm warning you, come the old "we could be very good friends", for when you become my stepfather I'll be sick, nauseated, by the very unnaturalness of it.'

The wind howled around the house, a blast hit the windows, and for a moment the stout walls shuddered. She watched him turn slowly about and walk towards the kitchen.

When she was alone she went to the couch again and hung over the back

of it for support while she told herself she mustn't be sick. She . . . must
. . . not . . . be . . . sick.

As Annie descended the stairs, Alan came from the kitchen with a lighted
lamp, and after placing it on the table he went straight to her and, taking
her hands, said, 'Shall I come with you?'

'No, no.' She shook her head. 'Stay here. I'll . . . I'll write.'

'Write? But I can't just wait for a letter, I'll come on tomorrow.'

'No, no. Please, Alan, please, just stay here, just wait.'

'I'll phone you.'

'Yes, Yes, do that. Sometime tomorrow, in the afternoon.'

'I'd rather you'd let me come with you.'

'No.' She was shaking her head widely. 'I've got to explain to them.' She
turned from him and walked towards the closed door where Tishy was
struggling into her mac again, but before she reached it Alan was by her
side and as if they were entirely alone he pulled her round to him, saying,
'This makes no difference, you understand, about Rance? This makes no
difference? No matter what's happened, promise me it'll make no difference.'

'I promise, Alan.'

'Sure?'

'Yes, yes, I'm sure.'

'Nothing's going to stop you coming away with me?'

'Nothing; I promise you, darling.'

They were in each other's arms.

She couldn't bear it. Her mother was shameless, utterly shameless. She
pulled open the door and a blast of air filled the room. The wind checked
her running down the steps; it drove her sideways towards the iron railings
for a moment. Without waiting to share the light of the lantern she went
tearing down the hill, but from the wavering light she knew that her mother
was close behind, and when she paused at the broken wall Annie caught up
with her. They did not speak but lay against it for a moment panting, before
going on again.

Even when they reached the copse they still didn't speak, and Tishy got
into the car and backed it harshly into a bank of mud, then drove it forward,
sending the spray window high.

She did not wait at the end of the road to see whether the Mini were
behind her; it wasn't until she was on the straight stretch going towards
Otterburn that the headlights came up on her and remained at the same
distance for most of the journey . . .

From the moment they entered the house it was as if the incident in the
cottage had never taken place, at least from the way Annie acted, for, almost
pulling Tishy into the front room, she demanded, 'Now without any heroics
you tell me what's happened right from the beginning.'

'I've . . . I've told you already.' Tishy's teeth were chattering with the
cold.

'Well, tell me again.'

So, slowly and without venom now, more as if she were answering the
inquiries of a stranger, she gave Annie the details, beginning from the time
Rance had come in. When she had finished Annie sat down and stared
straight before her. Why was it that nothing lasted? She had been in heaven
for the past three days, and that was the right description; every minute she
had spent with Alan had been nothing short of heaven. And now she had

been thrust into hell. She believed every word that Tishy had said; Tishy was no liar, she didn't even exaggerate. She also knew that she was right when she had pointed out that she had used the betting slip as a cover up. She recalled the times of late when she had looked at Rance, and looked quickly away again, refusing to believe what her mind was telling her. She had, on these occasions, blinded herself by reasoning that if he were on drugs he would take them every day, wouldn't he? They all did; it got a hold of them. But Rance could go for days without coming with that odd look on his face, and her having to practically drag him out of bed the following morning to get him to work.

Then there was the fact that had kept niggling at her: she had never seen him with his shirt off for years. And again her twisted reasoning had turned on her and said, You know he's always been fastidious about his clothes, and his person. But what about in the garage? He never rolled his sleeves up like other men when doing a job, but always kept them buttoned. Yet it wasn't necessary for a boss to go around with his sleeves rolled up, was it? She had always given herself the answer she wanted to hear.

She looked down at her feet, wet and covered with mud, then at Tishy's, and as if to prove she had left her other self completely back there in the cottage she said to her, 'You'd better get those wet things off.'

As she walked slowly to the door, Tishy said, 'What are you going to do?'

She turned to her. 'I don't know, I'll have to talk to him first. I should say if all you tell me is true, that there's nothing I can do, is there?'

As she entered the kitchen Tishy was behind her, saying, 'But you would if you could, wouldn't you? You would still help him to get out of it.'

Annie had reached the stove. She looked from the kettle to the cup and saucer and teapot that were on the table; then she put her hand on the kettle and turned and gazed at Tishy, and her look said, 'He must be in.' The next minute she was rushing out of the kitchen, across the hall and up the stairs.

She did not tap on her son's bedroom door but thrust it open and switched on the light. He was in bed, his head almost buried under the clothes. She went to him. She did not touch him, but said loudly, 'Rance!' Then again, 'Rance!'

'What . . . what is it? Oh! He turned over and looked at her. 'Hello, you're back? He was blinking the sleep from his eyes.

'Yes, I'm back. And you're back apparently. Get up!'

'What!'

'I said get up! you heard me.'

'Now look! it's the middle of the night.'

'Get up!' It was a bellow and before the sound had faded away she had gripped the bedclothes and pulled them from him, then stood staring down at him where he lay fully dressed, even to his light overcoat. After gazing at him for a moment she backed from him, then went to the wardrobe and pulled the door open. There were no suits hanging on the rails but his suitcase was there. When she lifted it out she found it was heavy.

Looking towards the bed, her eyes lowered to the floor, she saw the outline of his other case. She went slowly towards him again where he was sitting on the edge of the bed now and she asked grimly, 'Going some place?'

He didn't answer, but after staring at her for a moment his head drooped.

She now whipped the chair from the side of the bed and, climbing on it, thrust open the top of the Scotch chest. It was empty. When she stepped down he was staring at her, his eyes wide and his mouth open, and she nodded at him. 'Oh yes, I know about it; and I knew there was some fiddle you were up to, but God in heaven!' Her head now moved in a slow sweep from one shoulder to the other. 'I wouldn't have it that you were making it from drugs.'

'People need them, Mam.'

'What?' She had not made out his muttering, and he said again, 'People need them, it's . . . it's sort of medical . . .'

'Medical! My God! you can sit there and delude yourself that it's, it's . . . sort of medical.' Her voice had been low, but now it rose to a shout. 'Is it medical to stab a man? Is it medical to arrange it so as your brother-in-law takes the blame? Though how, in the name of God! you expected that to pass I'll never know. You must have been hard up for an escape route to pin this on Percy. But the dirtiest trick you've ever done in your life was to pump him full of your filth.' Her lips curled back from her teeth. 'You've always hated him because he was streets above you, not only in class but in every other way, but to . . .'

He thrust his head towards her now and for the first time he showed fight by saying, 'You've never liked him, so what are you on about?'

'No, it's true I never cared much for him, but at this moment I love him, and if it lies with me he'll not bear this suspicion a minute longer.'

He now rose to his feet and stood staring at her while his whole face, his whole body, quivered and he reverted back to the pleading little boy as he said, 'Mam, look; give me a chance. I . . . I could have been away, miles away out of the country but . . . but I wanted to see you again. I waited . . . I waited hours in the rain. I . . . I couldn't come in because –' he dipped his head, shook it, then lifted it again and looked at her where she was standing as if she had died, so colourless, so immobile was she, and, his voice almost a whimper, he said, 'I . . . I couldn't go without seeing you. Then when you didn't come I knew I'd have to because, because I've got to be there –' he stopped, swallowed deeply then ended, 'I've got to be there before five.'

Her voice came stiffly through her pale lips. 'Where?'

'Oh, it . . . it doesn't matter.'

'Where?'

'You . . . you wouldn't know the place, it's outside of Newcastle. Anyway, what does it matter?'

'You're hopping off by plane then? I suppose Benny has arranged it all.'

He was gazing at her with that little-boy-lost look in his eyes, but he made no answer until she said, sharply, 'Take your coat off!'

'Now, Mam, Mam, I don't want to argue.'

She had advanced on him. 'Take your coat off. If you don't I'll tear it off.'

'Look, Mam –' he moved a step back from her, 'Look, I've hurt my hand.' He held out his bandaged hand towards her then added quickly, 'Stop it, you'll get hurt. I'm telling you, you'll get hurt.'

'Don't worry about me. Take your coat off.'

When the back of his legs touched the bed he took his coat off and, flinging it behind him, said, 'There now! Are you satisfied?'

'No. Take the other off.'

'Look, Mam . . .'

Her hand shot out and with a blow to the side of the face she knocked him backwards on to the bed. When he went to right himself she thrust her hand towards the dressing table, and after a second of groping clutched at a metal statue. It was about a foot high and represented a running boy. He had bought it a few years previously, and no matter where she put in his room he would always move it back on to the dressing table. Now she held it above his head as she cried, 'Take that coat off else I'll brain you!' and then, 'I'll take it off for you.'

'Ma-am!' He drew out her name as if he were singing it, and she barked at him, 'Don't mam me any more. Take your coat off!'

And he took his coat off.

'Now your shirt.'

'No, Mam, no . . . Aw no, Mam.'

'Get your shirt off.' Her voice was low and almost toneless now.

'Mam, I'll tell you anything, anything you want to . . .'

'All I want at this moment is for you to take your shirt off. *Now! Now!*' Her voice rose as her free hand shot out and grabbed the front of his shirt. The next minute they were struggling together.

Neither of them was aware that the door had burst open until Tishy cried, 'Mam! Mam! stop it!' With a fierce tug she managed to pull Annie away and with her came the sleeve of Rance's shirt, and the sound of it tearing was like a knife being drawn against glass.

Annie was now leaning back against the dressing table, the top of the sleeve gripped against her waist. The other end of it, still attached to Rance's wrist, was in this moment symbolical of the cord that had ever been between them. As she stared at the pock-marked flesh her lips slowly moved away from her teeth; then as if it were a reptile she threw the shirt sleeve back at him. 'You filthy! filthy –' she swallowed deeply now, gulped at some spittle and began to cough.

'Come away. Come away.' Tishy was leading her from the room as if she were an old woman, and she seemed to have turned into an old woman for she allowed herself to be led. She made no resistance until she had reached the hall, but when Tishy guided her towards the sitting-room door she slowly pushed her aside and walked towards the front door.

'Where you going? They . . . they won't let you in the hospital at this time of night.

'Hospital?' Annie turned slowly and looked at Tishy. 'I'm not going to any hospital, lass, I'm going to do what I should have done years ago.' Even her voice sounded old.

'Mam! Mam!' Tishy's voice was low and agitated. 'Hadn't . . . hadn't you better wait? Don't go out in this state.'

'Huh! it's funny.' Annie was shaking her head now. 'You tell me to wait; you've been pitching the truth at me for years, urging me to do something, and now you're telling me to wait. Well, the time's come, lass; the waiting's past.'

As she picked up her coat casually from the hall chair Tishy muttered, 'Wait. Wait a minute; I'll get mine, I'll come with you.'

'No!' Annie's voice was firm now. 'No, you keep out of this. He's going to have no one to blame but me.'

'But Mam!'

'No, I've said no, girl.' And on that she opened the door and went out.

Tishy stood in the porch watching her fight her way against the wind and rain towards the car. At one point the wind billowed her coat over her head and she turned her back and lifted her hands up in order to pull it down, and the lamplight shone on her face, picking out each white feature and setting it in a cameo to be forever remembered.

Not until the car had moved off did Tishy close the door; then characteristically she stood with her back to it and looked towards the stairs, and all she could say was, 'Dear God! Dear God!' In this moment her own pain was utterly blotted out; she could think only of those two, and she didn't know whom she was most sorry for, her mother or Rance. That she should feel the slightest pity for him amazed her. He was filthy, unclean, he was as good as a murderer, and at bottom he was a snivelling coward; yet a moment ago, when from the doorway she had watched them struggling, she had known that one good blow from him could have knocked her mother flying, and he hadn't lifted his hand. She had seen her mother gripping his bandaged thumb and the pain of that alone must have been excruciating; still he hadn't hit her.

She stumbled into the sitting-room and, her arms folded about her thin body, she began pacing the floor. Soon the police would be here. They would take him; he would go to prison. For life, if Mr Wilkins died. She'd always hated him, she still did, yet in spite of herself there was rising in her a pity for him, and strangely, she knew, it was not because he might have to spend the rest of his life in prison but because he had already lost his mother. If he had ever loved anyone as much as himself he had loved her. All her life she herself had been jealous of the love between them; more so, because she knew that her mother had returned his love twofold; but during the last hour she had seen that love turn into cold hate.

Her teeth began to chatter, her whole body to tremble. She must have something hot to drink. She mustn't land up with one of her colds, not at this time.

She went into the kitchen and put the kettle on the stove. A few minutes later she had mashed the tea, and a few minutes later still she had drunk two cupfuls so scalding that it burned her mouth.

There was no sound in the house except the wind tearing down the chimneys. What was he doing up there? Scheming for some way finally to get round Mam? But surely he would see that was impossible now.

It was about half an hour later when the kitchen door opened and he came in. He was fully dressed again but without a tie. After one glance at him she turned her head away; but he came slowly towards the table, and in a voice that he had never used to her before in his life, he said, 'I'm sorry, Tishy.'

When she looked up at him she felt for a moment that her heart would break, for she was seeing him as her mother had seen him all these years, the vulnerable, weak boy, needing something that no one could give.

'Where is she?' He moved his head back towards the wall, indicating the sitting-room, and she shook her head, she couldn't speak. Hadn't he any idea of where she was? He must know where she was. Yet she herself hadn't known what her mother's intentions were until she had voiced them.

Apparently taking her silence for an affirmative answer, he turned from the table and made towards the door, but there he paused and, looking back at her, he said, 'Good-bye, Tishy. I doubt if we'll ever see each other again. I'm . . . I'm sorry.'

She now spoke his name as she had never spoken it before. 'Rance,' she said softly, 'Mam . . . Mam's gone out.'

He turned fully towards her but stood still. She saw the expression on his face change. She saw fear like a mask drop over it.

'Where? Where's she gone?'

When she didn't answer, he simply stared back at her. Then she saw him change into the Rance that she knew, the one she had been acquainted with all her life. His face going stiff, his jaws locking, his anger set the blood in his head pulsing until his face looked almost purple.

'She wouldn't, she wouldn't do that. She wouldn't!' He was bawling at her now, and, her pity of the previous moment vanishing, she cried at him, 'Well, she has.'

'Aw no! No!'

As she watched the expression on his face changing again, she became afraid and rose from the chair and moved to the end of the table. He looked like someone gone mad and when he screamed at her, 'The polis station! She's gone there?' she thought it better to remain quiet. She saw him dash into the hall: but before she could move he was back, saying, 'How long? how long?' He looked at his watch.

She was going to say, 'Long enough for her to have told them everything,' but what she muttered was, 'Not . . . not long.'

He ran from her now and not until she heard the wind rushing into the hall did she move. The front door was open, his two cases were standing at the bottom of the stairs. As she went slowly forwards to close the door she heard the car being revved up, then on a screech tear down the street.

She closed the door once again, but this time she didn't stand with her back to it but ran into the kitchen and, laying her head on her arms on the table, began to cry. She cried for her mother; she cried for Rance; and then she cried for herself and the deep inner loneliness inside her. She cried for how she looked, how she appeared to other people; she cried for the course her life would take from now on.

Meanwhile Rance was speeding erratically down Fowler Street which was fortunately bare of traffic. He did not turn the car into King Street but took a side road into Keppel Street where the police station was, and his headlights immediately picked out Annie's car parked on the opposite side to the station and about thirty feet along the kerb from the main door.

He drew the car to a screeching halt in the centre of the road as his eyes took in a small group of people outside the station door. There were three officers and a woman. When the group broke up, two of the officers went along the pavement towards a parked car. The third man spoke to the woman and, as she turned away he remained standing watching her crossing the road to her car.

She had her head deep down on her chest when his headlights fell on her, then her head jerking she lifted her arm to shield her eyes, but not before he saw the look in them and it told him what she had done . . . His Mam had given him away. But no, she couldn't. She wouldn't, not her, she loved him. She had always loved him. He'd had her love as her husband never had. In fact he knew he was her husband, her lover, everything to her. All he'd had to do was to touch her and her eyes told him what he needed to know, that she was his. That he had a power over her none of the others knew anything about, and because of it she was the one person who would always stand by him. Even a short while ago when they had struggled together he had known her fury would pass as it always had done. He had even been making plans in his mind to send for her once he got settled abroad, for he'd really be in the money then . . . But here she was, backing away from him, her face full of terror.

He wasn't aware of starting the car, but he was aware of plunging his foot down on the accelerator and of the hard bump as the front wheels mounted the pavement.

She hadn't her arm over her eyes when he hit her, her hands were outstretched towards him. When she fell forward over the bonnet he reversed just the slightest then rammed the gears forward again. She had slipped down now and on the second impact he could not see her.

He was attempting to repeat the operation when they got the door open and dragged him out on to the road.

Tishy hadn't moved until she heard the door bell ring and she didn't get up until it had rung for the second time. Then, like someone dazed, she went through the hall and opened the door, and there stood a policeman and behind him on the pavement near a car was another.

'Miss McCabe?'

'Yes.'

'I've . . . I've some sad news for you.'

She stared at him, then from him to the other officer, then back to him again.

'Your . . . your mother has met with an accident.'

'My . . . my mother?' Her voice was high in her head, then she repeated, 'My mother?'

When she gripped the door with both hands the policeman said, 'Can I come in a moment?' Then he looked back towards his companion before stepping over the threshold.

'Sit down,' he said.

It was the second time a policeman had said that to her within the last few hours, but she didn't sit down. 'Where . . . where's my mother?' she said.

His gaze flicked from her for a moment and he repeated, 'You'd better sit down.'

'My mother, what's happened to her? What's happened to my mother?'

'She . . . she had an accident.'

'You've said that.'

'She . . . she was run down by a car.'

'My mother was run down by a car in the middle of the night? She was going to you, she was going to the police station.'

'She had been to the station, she was coming out. I mean she had come out, she was walking across the road to her car, when this car comes at her . . . full tilt.'

There was something final about the words, full tilt; it was as if he had no need to explain any further. There was a deep blackness coming towards her. It was thick, shrouding the policeman and dimming his voice as he went on, 'It . . . it was your brother's car. I'm very sorry to have to tell you this but . . . but it wasn't really an accident, he . . . he rammed her. There

were witnesses. The Inspector had come to the door with her and . . . and
. . . a . . . patrol . . . car . . . was . . . coming . . . in . . . from . . . the . . . other
. . . end . . . of . . . the . . . street . . . It . . . is . . . a . . . dreadful . . . thing
. . . not . . . really . . . understandable.'

Not really understandable. Not really understandable, *Not really understandable. Not really understandable.*

# Chapter Three

They came into the house one after the other, Tishy first, then Kathy, then
Bill. They walked like people in a dream and they all wore similar
expressions on their faces, it was like a family resemblance. But once the
door was closed on them they began, as it were, to unfreeze. Kathy started
to cry slowly and painfully. Her head buried in her arms and her arms
against the wing of a chair, she gave herself ease. Bill, too, began to cry.
Hiding his tears, he went straight upstairs.

Only Tishy didn't cry now. When she came out of the faint last night –
or was it this morning? Anyway, it was some time long ago – a strange
thought persisted in her mind saying, She cannot be dead that way; she was
going to be married and go to America. She knew that if her mother had
married Alan she would have died to her, but now she had died in a different
way. She had told herself she would have preferred that she had died in the
first way and not like the policeman had said. She hadn't really believed the
policeman until she had entered the mortuary. Even then she couldn't
associate that bandaged face and broken body with her mam. They had said
he hadn't been satisfied with crushing her against the wall, but when she
fell he had backed and did it again before they had overpowered him.

She had moaned, 'Oh Mam! Mam!' while at the same time feeling that
her mother had knowingly brought this terrible end on herself. She should
have known that Rance wouldn't stand for it. Anybody else could have given
him away but not her, not the one who had shielded him since he could
breathe, not the one he had been capable of convincing, hoodwinking, and
bamboozling; not the woman he had loved – the only woman he had loved,
for she hadn't just been a mother to him, she had been everything, if only
in his mind she had been everything, and she must have been aware of this.
She herself had been aware of it, and this had been the cause of her deep
jealousy.

She couldn't analyse her feelings against Rance at this moment, nor
measure the depths of sorrow for her mother, but what was to the forefront
of her mind was a rising feeling of resentment against Alan Partridge. If it
hadn't been for him her mother would have been here on Friday, and
although that wouldn't have stopped Mr Wilkins coming and exposing
Rance, things would never have reached this pass, for her mother would

have done something, managed something – she always had – but instead of being here he'd had her in bed.

She made tea automatically and called Bill downstairs and the three of them sat around the kitchen table drinking it; nobody wanted to eat, individually they felt they never wanted to eat again. They sat in silence for almost five minutes before Kathy said, 'What'll happen to him?'

A space of time passed again before Bill answered, 'He'll likely get life for one or the other, although Mr Wilkins might pull through. But then there's the other thing.' Bill couldn't bring himself to voice the word, drugs. It was too dirty, much viler than murder; murder was often the outcome of passion, but drug-running was something else.

He now ran his hands through his hair and, looking at Tishy, said, 'What's going to happen to the business?'

'The business?' She spoke as if coming out of sleep. 'I . . . I haven't thought.'

'That Jimmy Lake seems a good fellow.'

'Yes, yes.' She nodded. Jimmy Lake was a good fellow. She had thought often that if it wasn't for Jimmy Lake there would have been very little business done in the garage. But what did it matter about the garage, or Jimmy Lake, or anything else? Why was Bill talking about the garage? He had just come back from the mortuary. She looked at his face. It was pale; he looked sick. She looked at Kathy's face. Kathy wasn't the same person she had seen last night in the green velvet dress; the years had mounted on Kathy since last night.

After a while Kathy said, 'I'd better get home,' and when Bill, rising from the table, said, 'I'll run you back,' Kathy looked at Tishy. 'Come back and stay with us,' she said, 'both of you.'

'No, no, thanks all the same. I'd rather stay put.

'We've got to get used to it,' said Bill.

'Just for the time being. Percy's mother seeing to things, she would. . . .'

'We'll be all right.' Bill took her arm. 'Don't worry.'

'Gran McCabe'll have to be told.'

They turned and looked at Tishy and Bill said, 'I'll slip over later. I won't be long. Go and lie down.'

'She didn't answer, but turned her head away and stared at the kitchen cabinet on the wall opposite.

The day passed somehow. There were tentative knocks on the door by a few neighbours offering their sympathy. Mrs Wilkins wasn't among them; she had her own set of visitors. The phone rang innumerable times. After Bill had banged the door in the face of three separate reporters he phoned the police, and shortly a patrol car came to a stop a little way down the road, and stayed there.

Tishy was passing through the hall when the phone rang yet again. Wearily she picked it up. It was someone phoning from a call box. She heard the coins drop, then as the voice spoke she took the phone away from her ear and looked at it as if confronting the speaker.

The voice came again. 'Hello. Who's there?'

Still she didn't answer.

'Hello. Who's there? . . . This is Alan Partridge. I . . . I want to speak with Mrs . . . Mrs McCabe. Hello. Hello.'

Slowly she brought the mouthpiece nearer and, her voice low and harsh, she spoke into it. 'You can't speak to Mrs McCabe. Mrs McCabe is dead.' And with that she banged the receiver down.

She shouldn't have done it, not like that. How other should she have broken it to him then? Gently, easing his hurt? when he was to blame for most of what had happened!

Don't. Don't. She bent her body forward and gripped her head with her hands. Recriminations, blame. Where did they get you? She was gone, dead. Nothing could bring her back. She had been a lovely mother, a lovely woman, young looking, like a girl. But she had called her old, and filthy. Recriminations. She should be heaping them on her own head. She was. She was. She would never forget the things she had said to her mother in the cottage.

After a moment she mounted the stairs and as she reached the top the phone range again, and Bill, coming from the bathroom, said, 'I'll take it.'

A few minutes later he knocked on her door and when she said, 'Come in,' he stood within the opening. 'It was Alan Partridge,' he said; 'he . . . he seemed shocked. He wanted to know if he had heard aright, what you had said. He must have met mother lately. He talked oddly. He seemed very shocked.'

She did not say as she might have, 'He would be, seeing that the last time she slept was with him.' No, that was something only she knew, and it wouldn't go any further, they wouldn't understand, Kathy less than Bill. Yet she understood. Oh yes, she understood how her mother had fallen for him. He was the easiest person in the world to fall for; he had everything going for him, had Mr Alan Partridge.

When she turned her head away Bill went out and closed the door, a vague memory stirring in his mind. He recalled that after his dad had died their Tishy had taken up with Alan Partridge, and then it had come to an abrupt end. He never knew why.

During the evening she went to the hospital with Kathy to visit Percy. Percy was conscious now, but still dazed, not able to take in what had happened to him. She left Kathy with him and his father, and returned home to find Alice, Bill's controversial choice of a future wife, in the house together with her mother and father.

The grizzled-haired, ebony-skinned big Negro, whose colour made that of his daughter appear as merely a deep sunburn showed his sympathy in a most genuine fashion, as did his wife, a faded and much painted blonde about half his size.

It was Tishy's first meeting with Alice's parents, and some part of her was touched that these people should openly show that they were connected in any way with such a family as the McCabes had now become, having in it a man who was not only a drug-pusher but a murderer.

When the visitors were leaving, Bill, taking Tishy aside, whispered, 'Do you mind if I walk Alice home? I won't be half an hour.'

'Go on,' she said. 'I'm all right. Don't worry about me.'

'Nobody will trouble you; there's still somebody on the watch, though the car went a short while ago.'

So she was in the house alone when the doorbell rang, and she paused before she opened the door. Then she heard someone say, 'What is your business?' and when she opened the door the policeman and Alan turned together towards her.

'Do you know this man, miss?'

She looked through the gathering dusk at the white face. Did she know this man? Oh yes, she knew this man. In a way she had been expecting him, but not so soon; she thought he would arrive tomorrow morning.

'Yes, constable, thank you.' She stood back, and Alan went past her into the hall, and she purposely took a long time in closing the door, for she didn't want to look at him again. His face looked bleached, and there was a look in his eyes that as yet she couldn't put a name to. Her head down, she moved past him into the sitting-room, and he followed. As she pointed to a chair she didn't speak, nor did he, not even after he had sat down.

From the apparently small fact that she was standing and he was sitting she gauged the extent of his distress. He had almost been as meticulous about this point of etiquette as Percy, only his manner of doing it was more easy, more relaxed. She put her hand on to the mantelpiece to support herself while she looked at him; and now he said, 'I can't take it in. No matter how often I tell myself, I can't take it in.' He now put his hand into his macintosh pocket and pulled out a newspaper and, unfolding it until it was half its width showing big black headlines, he said, 'Why? Why should he do it when he loved her? She ... she had told me about him, the tie that was between them, how ... how difficult it was going to be to break. It was the only real tie, she said; but she would break it.'

When she slowly lowered her head, he put in on a slightly higher note, 'Oh ... oh, I'm not inferring that she meant it would be easy to leave you, or the others, but she reckoned on your understanding. It was only him she thought might not understand, and he didn't, did he?'

She looked into his eyes now and recognized the look that was deep in them as remorse and guilt. He imagined that in some way he was responsible for this crime.

It would be rough justice to let him stew in his own juice, but she couldn't do that. She said flatly, 'He knew nothing about you.'

He got to his feet now but didn't come towards her, just stared at her, one hand held in front of him opening and closing as if trying to grasp at something that evaded him.

'You mean she ... she hadn't told him?'

'No.'

'Then I in no way contributed to ...?'

'No.' Her voice was high now. 'You can go away with a clear conscience on that point anyway. What he did wasn't because he thought she was leaving him for you. But I'm going to tell you this: if it hadn't been for you she'd have been home on Friday, and in her usual way she would have tackled this business and straightened it out. And she would have been alive now.'

A moment ago she had eased his personal agony, now she had added to it tenfold. When his lips began to tremble and he hunched his shoulders and his head drooped she cried at herself, 'Why had you to say that?' Now he turned from her, one hand covering his face, and he began to cry audibly, like a woman might.

Bill had cried, but it had been a silent crying. She had never heard a man cry like this before. It didn't seem right that a big man like him should give way to grief in such a fashion.

When he continued to cry she stood behind him and said, 'Sit down. I'll get you a cup of tea. I'm ... I'm sorry. I'm sorry I went at you like that, I shouldn't have.'

Obeying her, he groped at the head of the couch. His elbows on his knees, his face buried in his hands, he continued to cry, and it was impossible to bear the sight and not to touch him.

She went into the kitchen, the kettle was already spluttering on the low ring. Hastily she mashed the tea, and when she took the tray into the room a few minutes later he was lying back on the couch, his hands hanging limply at his sides.

He was still crying, but silently now; his eyes were blurred with his tears and his face awash with them.

'Drink this,' she said.

It seemed an effort for him to pull himself forward. He took the cup from her, then put it down on the table again and, taking a handkerchief from his pocket, he wiped his face a number of times before getting abruptly to his feet, turned the collar of his raincoat high up around his ears and without looking at her he walked towards the door.

She felt completely at a loss. She didn't know what to say now. He hadn't spoken since she had thrown the accusation at him. It seemed as if he were going without uttering a word when, at the front door, he asked under his breath, while still not looking at her, 'When ... when is the funeral?'

'Wednesday,' she murmured; 'two o'clock.'

He said no more, but opened the door and went out, his face down, his face half-buried in his coat collar.

She did not wait to see which way he went, or if he had come by car. Quickly she closed the door and leaning her face against it in the crook of her arm she moaned aloud.


# Chapter Four


They stood in a small group in a side street where they had parked their cars some distance from the court-house. The trial was over and they were not talking about it any longer. What Kathy and Percy, Bill and Alice, were all trying to do now was to persuade Tishy to come back to them.

For the third time Bill said, 'But what will you do up there on your own? You'll go mad.'

'Well, if I'm to go mad I'd much rather be on my own. ... I'll be all right, I tell you, I'll be all right.' She looked around them. 'I ... I just want to get away for a time.'

'Don't we all!' Kathy hung her head; then looking at Tishy, she said, 'I didn't mean that nasty, Tishy.'

'I know. I know.'

'I think we should go home and discuss the business, go into it further, now we are all together,' said Bill now.

'What more is there to discuss? I've told you I'd like the cottage as my share, and if it doesn't run to the price that we agreed on, then I'll take out a mortgage.'

'Don't be silly,' said Bill and Kathy almost simultaneously.

'Anyway the garage is carrying on,' said Bill, 'and Jimmy'll make a good job of it. We should talk about what he suggested last week, expanding.'

When Tishy closed her eyes Bill said on an impatient note, 'Well, somebody's got to do the talking. And there's another thing.' He stopped and looked away from them and down the narrow street before he said, 'There's the fourth share. He . . . he may want it some day, you never know. Life doesn't mean life any longer and . . . and he may recover. . . .'

His voice trailed away as Tishy turned towards her car. Unlocking the door she got into the driving seat, then looked at them where they were standing on the pavement now gazing down at her. Kathy, bending forward, said, 'We'll come over on Sunday no matter what the weather.'

'All right.'

'How long do you intend to stay?' asked Bill.

'I don't know.'

'You'll have to send a note to school next Tuesday if you don't turn up.'

'I'll see. I'll see.'

Speaking for the first time, Percy said, 'If you want us, phone me any time at the office, Tishy – any time.'

'I'll do that, Percy. Good-bye.' She looked from one to the other, and they said, 'Good-bye, Tishy.'

She started the car, brought it out of its parking space, then drove off down the hill and out of Durham, and as she left the city behind she said, 'I'll never come here again as long as I live.'

She stopped in Newcastle and bought some food, just the necessities, milk, bread, tea, sugar, butter, some fruit and steak. She was caught up in the five o'clock rush of traffic which put another half an hour on to her journey, but it didn't matter. She wasn't impatient, she had all the time in the world before her; even wedged in between cars, lorries and buses, with their combined noise pressing in on her, made no impression on the void that she was living in and which stretched before her ad infinitum. The concern of her family, the fact that she was but twenty-five, and that even plain women had been known to marry when they were thirty or over, afforded her not the slightest consolation. In fact, she didn't see any compensations for herself. What she saw was a life of teaching and the thousand and one irritations that accompanied the word, which was recognized even by those who considered it a vocation, and she wasn't one of them. She saw the sameness stretching down the years until she retired – retired to the cottage.

Why did she want to return there? Why? It should be the last place she should want to go to. Somewhere at the back of her mind she had the faint idea that she would be nearer her mother there, yet the picture of her mother, as she had last seen her in that room, should be no inducement for her to return, just the opposite if she were using her reason.

But she could find no reason in the urge to return to the cottage, only the fact that it was the only place in which she could be alone with her misery. . . .

The long twilight was beginning when she parked the car in the copse.

From the boot she took out a suitcase and the bag of groceries, and slowly made her way up the field. When she reached the broken wall she rested for a moment and, leaning her arms on the top of it, she looked about her. The strange white light that cloaked the moors on a fine day was being diffused now into grey. There were pink patches on the hills, and inky black hollows, and sloping stretches of green rolling like carpets to the valleys.

She took in a deep breath. This is what she needed, the ever changing picture, the unpeopled picture, the lonely desolate picture. Here she would find some sort of peace, but more important still here she could hide herself and her feelings and no one would say, 'Now you must forget about the past and pull yourself together; we've all got to live.'

Gran McCabe had said that to her yesterday. She had meant well. 'No one will miss Annie more than I will. Lass and woman, I liked her. Salt of the earth was Annie. She could tackle mountains. She tackled my Georgie when she was but a girl, and made a man out of him. God rest his soul, an' hers an' all. She made one mistake in her life an' it was a natural one. It wasn't that she fell with Rance afore she married but that she broke his neck from the day he was born. . . . Well, it's over, lass. God makes the back to bear the burden, that's what I've learned from life, so come on now, your back might be narrow but it's tough. You've got your mother in you, and you've got your dad in you, and perhaps a little bit of me an' all, eh?'

Strange, how people like Gran McCabe could face life. When she had asked her if she should pick her up on the way to the trial, she had answered, 'I'm hard up at this minute, lass, but I wouldn't take a thousand pounds an' look on him again, for God knows what I might be driven to say, or do, meself. No, lass,' she had said; 'do you know what I am going to do the day? I'm goin' to bingo, that's all he's worth to me, I'm goin' to bingo, 'cos I'm goin' to tell you somethin' that I've never mentioned afore, an' it's this, I've always thought there was somethin' fishy about the way my Georgie died. I'd seen him just a while afore in the pub. He'd had a drop, but he wasn't drunk enough to fall downstairs. When he was home along of me, he'd come in paralytic night after night, mortallious, stinking, but he always made those back stairs, an' they were as steep as a cliff. No, lass, from me first sight of Annie I knew there was something there I'd better not probe into. . . . Can you throw any light on it for me, lass?'

And because it would make no difference now she had said, 'He kicked me dad downstairs.'

Mollie had nodded as she said quietly, 'I knew it, I knew it was somethin' like that . . . aye, I'll go to bingo.'

She picked up the bag and case again and walked slowly up the hill. The evening light was shining on the windows of the cottage, softening its hard exterior. As she neared the steps she thought, I've got to make this my home. When she reached the verandah she put down the case and took her key from her handbag, but when she went to insert it in the door she found that it was open. Pushing it forward she tentatively entered the room; then her face stretched and her mouth fell into a gape.

The place was filthy. What had happened? Had tramps been in, or hikers? She looked at the floor, mud stains all over it. There was unwashed crockery on the table to the side of the couch; the couch itself was pushed up close to the fire. Her gape widened; the fire was on. She went slowly up the room and rounded the couch but keeping her distance from it. Then she stared wide-eyed at the figure lying there asleep under huddled-up blankets. If it hadn't been for the colour of his hair she would have taken the man for a stranger. The face was unrecognizable with its ragged beard and a thick growth on the cheeks. The couch was not long enough to take his length and he was lying on his side with his knees bent. He was breathing deeply like a man in drink. She looked round for evidence of bottles, but as far as she could see there weren't any.

The hearth had a pile of ash on it which meant it hadn't been cleared for days. There was burnt pieces of wood lying near the edge, almost touching the rug. The place could have been burned down.

As she went to turn away the soles of her shoes brought a squeak from the floor boards, and he moved. He turned on to his back, and she watched his tongue come out and lick around the thick stubble on his lips. Then he groaned and went to turn on to his other side but stopped and, slowly opening his eyes, peered at her through his flickering lids. Closing them again, he kept them shut for some seconds. When he again looked at her he slowly pulled himself up into a sitting position and was about to speak when he began to cough.

After the spasm had passed he said in a voice, thick and croaking, 'I . . . I can go any time. I . . . I had the key and . . . and looked in a while ago. . . .' He closed his eyes again, and now his body slid down until his head was resting on the arm of the couch.

If he wasn't drunk or getting over a drinking bout then he was ill. She forced herself to say, 'Aren't you well?'

'What?'

'I said, aren't you well?'

'Off colour, that's all. I . . . I can go any time, kit's outside . . . sleeping bag . . . I can go any time.' He said no more but slid further down the couch.

After a moment she went slowly down the room, picked up the bag of groceries and the case from the verandah, then went into the kitchen.

It looked as if he had used every dish in the place. The washing-up bowl was full of plates, cups and saucers. There were three dirty pans on the stove, there was the remains of a loaf on the table and a tin of corned beef with the lid half opened.

She looked in the pans. One held congealed porridge that had shrunk away from the sides of the pan, which meant it had been there some days; another had held milk and was burnt; the third pan had three potatoes stuck to the bottom.

What was she to do? Go back home, leave him? . . . She couldn't just walk out and leave the place like this; nor him for that matter. She picked up the half opened tin of corned beef. He must be ill.

She went to the kitchen door and looked towards the far end of the room. He was still lying down. In ordinary circumstances he would have been up and talking . . . and walking away.

Why had this to happen to her? Why? Talk about turning the screws. The last person on God's earth she wanted to be confronted by at this time was him. She had stood enough, it wasn't fair. Oh! She turned about on an inward groan; then going into the room again, she lifted her case and went upstairs.

On the landing she hesitated and looked at the door through which she had rushed on that far off night. She went to pass it. It would likely be in the same state as down below. With a jerk she thrust it open.

It was just as if her mother had left it at the end of a visit, everything neat and tidy awaiting her return. Even the odd things on the dressing table were arranged carefully, not as her mother might have arranged them, but in a straight line in front of the mirror. Why had he done this, straightened everything up?

Slowly she closed the door. He must have stayed downstairs all this time. But surely he hadn't been here since she had last seen him? She wouldn't know until he told her and by the look of him he wouldn't be able to tell her much for some time. Hurriedly now she went into her room and changed.

Downstairs again, she went to the couch. His eyes were closed as if he was sleeping. She touched his shoulder. 'How . . . how long have you been like this?'

He lifted his lids and blinked at her, then shook his head.

'When did you last eat?'

Again he shook his head, and at this she left him and went into the kitchen.

The first thing she did was to clean a pan and heat some milk. When it was ready she spooned two heaped spoonfuls of glucose into it, then took it to him.

'Sit up,' she said abruptly, 'and drink this.'

Obediently but slowly, he pulled himself upwards; then leaning his shoulder against the back of the couch for support he took the cup from her and drank the milk. When he had finished he handed her the cup back, saying, 'Thanks . . . thanks,' then slid down the couch again.

Standing looking down at him, she said, 'You should see a doctor.'

He shook his head, and after a moment of silence he muttered, 'It's over. I'm better now; I'll be on my feet tomorrow.' Then turning his head and looking at her, he added, 'I'm sorry. I . . . I meant to be away.'

'How long have you been here?'

He made a small movement with his head, then drooped it forward as if thinking. 'Two weeks . . . three. I don't know.'

Her own head was shaking as she went from him. Halfway down the room she stopped and looked about her. 'What a mess!' In the kitchen she repeated the words, then added, 'Well, it won't clean itself, will it? You'd better get on with it.'

She was getting on with it; she was in the act of washing some of the glar from the floor when with a startled exclamation she turned and looked towards the kitchen door, and there he was, like some wild man of the hills, supporting himself with hands outstretched against the stanchions. When he shambled forward and steadied himself by gripping the table she did not say, 'Where do you think you're going?' but watched him making his way through the annexe and out of the back door. The Elsan pan was at the bottom of the garden forty feet away. He had a temperature; he must have had it for days and he'd been going out there.

She went on scrubbing the floor. She didn't even look up when a few minutes later he passed her on his way back into the room; nor did he speak to her. . . .

By ten o'clock she had order restored in the kitchen. Also she had made him a meal of sorts, mashed potatoes and corned beef and boiled rice, but he had hardly touched it. She had brought in wood and made the fire up, then fastened the guard round it. Now she had to force herself to do something else, something distasteful. She went upstairs and into the boxroom and, lifting up the chair commode that Annie had thought it necessary to install to save passages down the garden on wet and stormy nights, she carried it down the stairs by easing it from one tread to the next. Having placed it in the alcove to the side of the fireplace, she found the most difficult part of the proceeding was yet to be accomplished.

She stood at the bottom of the couch. 'I'm . . . I'm going to bed,' she said.

His eyes were closed; he seemed to be in a continuous doze.

'Oh yes.' He moved his head once; then turning on his elbow, he raised himself slightly and said, 'Thanks. Thanks. Tishy.'

She blinked; her face tightened. She turned half from him, saying, 'In the corner there.' She thrust her arm backwards. 'I brought the commode down.'

He made no answer and she went to the table, turned down the lamp to a flicker, hurried into the kitchen and extinguished the lamp there, then back in the room, she glanced towards the glowing fire before mounting the stairs.

When she entered her room she closed the door and, going to the bed, she slowly lowered herself down on to it and, gripping the pillow, asked herself why in the name of God had she to be let in for this an' all.

## Chapter Five

On the Friday afternoon she went down the hill, took the car and drove to a call box. When she spoke, Percy said immediately, 'Oh hello, Tishy. How are you?'

'I'm . . . I'm all right, Percy,' she said; then went on hurriedly, 'Look . . . look, would you mind not coming up on Sunday, Percy?'

'Are you all right?'

'Yes, yes, I'm quite all right, but I would rather you didn't come up on Sunday.'

'Kathy will be worried.'

'Tell her not to worry, I'm perfectly all right.'

'Are you coming down for school on Tuesday?'

She didn't answer for a moment but turned her head and looked down the long bare road. Then her glance swept over the moors before she said, 'I . . . I'm not quite sure yet; very likely I'll be back on Monday night, but I'm not quite sure yet. I'll phone you again Monday morning.'

'Is . . . is anything wrong? I mean are you not feeling . . .? Look, Tishy, Kathy's worried about you. If we could just pop over for . . .'

'No, Percy, no, please. I'm asking you particularly, Percy, not to bring Kathy. There's . . . there's a reason, and I'll explain it later.'

There was a moment of silence before he said, 'Very well, as you wish, Tishy. But . . . but we just thought you'd be lonely.'

'I'm not lonely, Percy.'

'I'm glad of that, Tishy.'

'Good-bye, Percy.'

'Good-bye, Tishy . . . I'll expect you to phone on Monday.'

'I'll do that. Good-bye.'

Once she had replaced the receiver she did not delay, but hurried out to the car, then drove away.

She stopped at the first general shop she came to, and so many were her purchases that the grocer himself carried out the two cardboard boxes and placed them on the back seat of the car. He told her he had been very pleased to meet her and would be equally pleased to serve her at any time. Her cynical thoughts suggested that it mustn't be every day a passing motorist left four pounds seventeen pence with him

She had to make two journeys from the car to the wall, and again two journeys from the wall to the house.

When she entered the room with the first box and dropped it on the table Alan looked at her over the head of the couch but didn't speak, and she in turn gazed at him and only just prevented herself from saying, 'Why! you've had a shave.'

He looked different, but worse than when he had his beard on, for his cheeks were hollow and his eyes deep bedded in their sockets, while his skin had a muddy tinge. Looking at him now it was hard to believe that he was good looking, handsome, or at least that he had been at one time.

When she brought the second box in she said to him, 'The old fellow nearly salaamed, he carried the stuff out for me.'

'It looks heavy.' His voice was thin and flat.

'It's the milk, there's four pints. And there's a frozen chicken; it says roaster, but I bet it's an old boiler. It's so big it must have been the mother of them all; it was the only one he had.'

In the kitchen she did not unpack the groceries straight away but put some milk on to boil; then having made two cups of coffee, she took them into the room, set the tray on the table near him and lifting one of the cups went and sat on the chair near the fire.

'It seems lovely out,' he said.

'Yes, it is.'

'If it's like this tomorrow I'll make a move.'

She made no reply but sipped at her coffee. It was the first time he had made any reference to leaving, and she didn't know if this remark referred to him finding his legs again or going away.

The conversation for the most part over the last three days had been monosyllabic. A few minutes ago she had spoken at more length than she had done since she had first seen him lying there; she surprised herself when she said, tartly, 'You'll get on your feet, but that's as far as you'll get I should imagine, for the next day or so.'

'I've . . . I've been a nuisance.'

She didn't contradict him.

'I . . . I meant to ask you before you left if you would phone my uncle. There's . . . there's a phone box along the road. About a mile I think.'

'Yes, I know it.'

'He . . . he thinks I'm abroad.'

'Abroad?'

'Yes, when I last saw him I said I would likely go abroad.'

'Won't he be wondering at not hearing from you?'

'He's used to not hearing from me, then my turning up suddenly.'

'What would you want me to say to him?'

He took a deep breath before he answered, 'You . . . you could tell him he could bring the car and pick me up. You could direct him how to get here.'

'Yes, I can do that. But you've got to get down to the copse, and you won't make that for a few days unless you're carried. Shall I tell him to bring a stretcher?'

He turned his head and looked fully at her; then after a moment of staring into her face he said, 'I can always tell when you're vexed, Tishy. I only suggested this because I don't want to impose on you any further. It . . . it was different when I was here on my own.'

'I should say it was.'

He turned his gaze from her, his head drooping. 'Yes, yes, the place was in a shambles. I'm sorry about that. Annie . . . Annie kept it so lovely.'

It was the first time he had mentioned her name and her teeth dug into her lip. She lifted up the cup and drank from it as he began again, his voice a little above a mutter now, 'I . . . I meant to come to the funeral but once back here I knew that I couldn't go, because then I would have to admit that she was dead and my mind rebelled against accepting the fact. I . . . I stayed on here until I knew it was over. Then I went to my uncle's, but I couldn't stay there. Then I went to my flat in Newcastle, but . . . but I couldn't rest. I took my kit and came up here again. I slept out a few nights and got wet, and didn't eat, and every day I looked for one of you coming. I don't know why.' He shook his head. 'I don't know why. And then when I knew I was ill I came inside. I thought at first some hot grub would soon put me right; then the old trouble hit me.'

He turned his head slowly and stated simply, 'I had a breakdown. The main ingredient of it was fear, of what I don't know. Well –' he shook his head – 'that's about it. I don't know what would have happened if you hadn't come on the scene. I knew I was near the end of my tether; another few days and you'd likely have found me dead I suppose.'

'Very likely.'

'When do you go back?'

'I don't know, I haven't made up my mind, not fully. I'm due back at school on Tuesday but I'm of two minds whether to go or not.'

'Oh . . . oh you mustn't let me stop you.'

'You won't stop me.' Why did she say it like that? Why had she to spit everything at him? Couldn't she call a truce?

It was as if he were thinking along the same lines for he said now, sadly, 'I know I won't stop you, Tishy. I . . . I was just meaning . . . well, I didn't want to put you to further inconvenience. . . .'

She closed her eyes and bowed her head and said, 'I'm . . . I'm sorry.'

'You know, Tishy,' he said, 'we should talk,' and at this she got up and went hastily down the room.

On Monday she went down to the phone box. She told Percy she wouldn't be coming home that night and would he send a note to the school to say that she wasn't well and that she'd be sending a letter or a doctor's certificate.

Percy's concern touched her. Wasn't she well? Wouldn't she let one of them come over? Bill was very worried about her being there on her own.

'Percy,' she said quietly, 'I am not on my own, I have someone with me, and . . . and I don't want to be disturbed for a few days. Don't let any of them come, Percy. Please, do this for me.'

'Yes, yes, of course, Tishy. As long as you're all right, that's all we need to know.'

'I'm all right, Percy,' she had said; 'perfectly all right.'

But as she walked back to the car she knew that she was far from all right. She could go and get that doctor's certificate and send it to the school because she felt that there was something about to snap inside her. There was a constant feeling of sickness in her chest; her temples felt as if they were being drawn into the middle of her head; there were emotions building up inside her that she was becoming afraid of.

When she arrived back at the cottage and entered the room she walked straight to where he was sitting by the side of the fire, and she looked at him and said, 'I couldn't get through to your uncle; I tried three times.'

'Oh, he's likely away on one of his jaunts. Well, perhaps . . . perhaps tomorrow; or do you think you could run me over? I'd be very obliged if it wouldn't be putting you out too much.'

She turned from him as she said, 'Yes, yes, I could do that. But . . . but if there's no one there, how are you going to manage?'

'Oh, I'll manage. You've got me on my feet, I'll manage.'

She didn't turn to look at his face as he spoke but continued on down the room, saying, 'I'll make a cup of tea.'

As she waited for the kettle to boil she sat down on the edge of the kitchen chair and leant her elbow on the table and dropped her head on to the palm of her hand. She felt tired, utterly exhausted. She had been here six days and she had been on the go from morning till night. It wasn't only looking after him, and the cooking, and getting the place put straight; there was also the water to be brought up from the burn, and the wood to be chopped. That reminded her; they were getting low on wood. She'd have to go down to the copse shortly and bring up a few more branches. . . . But if he was going tomorrow would it matter? There was enough to last till then.

The kettle whistled and she made the tea, then took the tray into the room. And now it was she who sat on the couch.

She made no attempt to open the conversation, nor did he speak until he had finished his first cup of tea. Then, leaning over and putting it on the tray, he said, 'What happened to Rance, you never said? Has the trial come off yet?'

There was a pause before she answered, 'It was last Tuesday. I came straight here from the court.'

'Oh! . . . what did he get?'

'Her Majesty's pleasure.'

'Oh my God!'

'Are you sorry for him?'

'No, no. Yet I don't know. Her Majesty's pleasure. But in some cases it just means a set number of years.'

'In his case I think it will be life.'

'Why?'

'They brought him in insane; he was sent to Broadmoor.'

'Well, that's about the only thing they could do, because he must have been insane. Did it . . . did it come out about your father?'

'No. . . . Well, it couldn't, could it? There was only me . . . and you left who knew about that.'

'Yes, that's true.'

As she poured out more tea she spilled it over the edge of the cup and she shivered as she remembered back to the court-room. A moment before they brought him into the dock she had thought, If they let him off I'll tell them about Dad. She had wanted him to be confined for life because he was bad, evil. He was a danger to anybody he came in contact with, he mustn't be allowed to go free, yet the moment she saw him she knew he would never be free. It wasn't that he'd be aware of being imprisoned in a cell, or within walls, he was already deeply imprisoned within himself. She hardly recognized him. His eyes were fear-filled yet vacant. He had looked towards them where they were all sitting together, but seemingly without recognition, except that his gaze strangely enough lingered on Alice, and she had wondered why he should be looking at her. Perhaps it was because he had always objected to her and now found, in the colour of her skin, something left for him to hate.

When the sentence was passed on him he had shown no emotion whatever. Bill was the only one who saw him in private before he was finally taken away, and the meeting seemed to have unnerved him. It was Alice who asked, 'Did he say anything?' and Bill, after a moment of evident distress, muttered, 'It was awful, awful. All he said was, "It won't be long before I see Mam, will it, Bill?" He spoke like a child.'

Alan said now softly, 'I . . . I would have made her very happy you know, Tishy. It wasn't a matter of years; there was an affinity between us. I . . . I must have recognized it when I was a small child. You know . . . you know I told her that because of this feeling I believed in transubstantiation; I felt we must have been together in some other existence. It may sound silly but . . . but I still firmly believe it. Perhaps in that existence too we were torn apart; in the next one we might be more lucky.'

She was on the point of springing up when he said, 'Don't think badly of me, Tishy. And . . . and you must never think badly of her, for she was full of concern for you.'

He had closed his eyes, and there was silence between them until she forced herself to ask, 'What are you going to do? I mean when you're quite well?'

He lifted his head now and looked at her. 'Oh, I've an appointment at an American university. But this time last week I thought that was that. I had managed to cable them before I went down. I said I might be delayed . . . Delayed!' He gave a small laugh. 'And it if hadn't been for you, Tishy, I would have been . . . finally. I'm sure of that now.'

'When do you intend to go then?' Her tone was abrupt.

'Oh, it's more than three weeks before term starts; I can give myself a fortnight. I'll be pulled round sufficiently by then.'

'Do you want to go?'

He didn't answer her for a moment but turned his head and looked down the room, then towards the stairs, before bringing his eyes back to her. 'Yes, yes, I want to go, Tishy,' he said. 'I'll never be healed if I stay here, either in mind or body. It'll be a new life. You see ... well, you're not to know, but ... but Annie knew all about it. My marriage went wrong; there was a divorce; it was a very bad time.'

It was odd but even when her mother had said to her, 'Everything's aboveboard, we're going to be married and go to America,' she hadn't said in reply, 'What about his wife?' She remembered seeing him with the girl that once, and feeling still more cheated when she realized that he had chosen someone almost as plain as herself.

'It's strange,' he said now, 'but prior to the first time I came to your home that night seven years ago I would have said that my life had been easy going; there had been small frustrations, annoyances, disappointments; but when I look back now it would appear that on that particular night I experienced an earthquake and my world has rocked ever since, and I don't think it will steady until I get away from this country into another atmosphere, another way of life.'

She rose now and picked up the tray, and he said apologetically, 'I'm sorry, I've kept talking.'

'It does one good to talk sometimes.'

He watched her moving down the room. She walked well, straight; she had a good figure in the modern sense. But she was a strange girl, Tishy. She had a strength about her that frightened him. Nothing, he felt, could break through her armour; she was one of those people who were sufficient unto themselves. How had she been born of Annie, Annie who was soft and loving and giving? Oh! Annie ... Annie ... will the pain of you ever leave me? He rose from the chair and, walking to the door, he opened it. Then turning his head in the direction of the kitchen, he called, 'I'll go out and stretch my legs, Tishy, practice for tomorrow.'

She came into the room almost at a run, then stopped abruptly some feet from him, saying, 'Be careful. Don't go far; you haven't got your strength back yet.'

He smiled gently at her. He was touched by her concern, she wasn't all bristles.

She waited until he had gone down the steps, then she moved to the window and watched him and she had to check herself, from running to the door and shouting, 'Don't go down the hill, you'll only have to walk up again.' She watched him until he came to the wall, then go beyond it down towards the copse, and when he was out of sight she sat down on a wooden hall chair standing to the right of the door and leant her head against the wall. ...

When, almost half an hour later, he hadn't returned she was on the point of going down the steps, but she saw him coming from the shelter of the trees, and so she went into the kitchen and put the kettle on, thinking as she did so of the countless times she had put the kettle on and heated milk for coffee during the last week. The making of tea or coffee had in a way become therapeutic for her; when her mind dashed along forbidden channels she would go to the stove and put the kettle on.

She heard him panting as he came in at the door, and when he entered the kitchen she turned her head towards him, saying, 'You're out of puff.'

'Yes, yes I am a bit, but I walked as far as the road. Bit too long, but just as well I did. I saw a taxi passing. He had been taking people to the inn. I . . . I asked him to come back for me around five; I thought it would save you tomorrow, and you can get away early.

'What is it?' He came towards her. 'Don't you feel well?'

She put one hand out quickly towards him as if thrusting him away, the other went to her mouth and she said through her fingers, 'Go on, leave me alone, I'm . . . I'm going to be sick.'

'No. No, why should I? What is it?'

She was leaning over the washing-up dish now, and when she retched he put his hand out and held her brow. As the sweat from it stuck to his fingers he said, 'What's . . . what's upset you like this? The tinned meat?'

She retched again; then turning away from the dish and him, she wiped her face on the roller towel that was hanging on the back of the door, and he watched her helplessly for a moment before saying, 'Come and have a cup of tea.' He lifted the tray and went into the room, and after a moment she followed him. He had put the tray down on the table that was standing on the hearth-rug to the side of the big chair and waited for her to sit down. But she didn't. Instead, she stood at the back of the couch and placing her hands on it she gripped the upholstery while gazing at him in silence.

'What is it, Tishy?'

'Alan.'

He seemed slightly startled by the use of his name; she had never called him Alan during all the days they had been together. 'Yes, Tishy?'

'Don't . . . don't leave me, Alan. Don't go. Please, please, Alan, don't leave me.'

His face became thinner in its stretching. When he brought his mouth closed, he gulped but said nothing, just stared at her, and her next words brought his head bowing to his chest for it was like seeing her ripping her body apart and exposing her innermost depths, 'I've . . . I've got to say it, because it's the only time in my life I'll say it to anybody. . . . I love you. I've always loved you. You're the only one I'll ever love, or can love. Without you there's nothing. From that first night I knew that I would love you and nobody else, and I thought a miracle had happened when you took me out. I thought you loved me, me who had nothing to offer, in looks anyway, because I knew I was irrevocably plain, which no amount of titivating could improve. And . . . and when I found it was the last thing in your mind I wanted to die, doubly, because you wanted Mam.'

'Oh! Tishy. Tishy. Don't, don't.' There was agony in his voice as he lifted his head and looked at her.

The tears were streaming down her face but she went on, 'I hated Mam. For a long time I hated Mam. I'd fought for her love for years, but she gave it to Rance; everything she had she gave to Rance; and then it seemed she had taken you. But, of course, that was wrong. She wasn't to blame there, but . . . but try as I might I couldn't hate you, I never hated you until –' now she lowered her head as she murmured – 'I . . . I saw you in bed with her. But I only thought I hated you, for now I know I didn't. I could never hate you, Alan, I love you too much. Please, please, take me with you. I . . . I know you don't love me, but . . . but I've so much to give you, and . . . and you need looking after. And I promise you I won't be possessive; I . . . I just want to be near you. I'm not asking you to marry me; you can have me on the side, or anyway. . . .'

'Tishy! Tishy!' He was grinding the words out through his teeth. 'Don't! What can I say? Your mother and I were. . . .'

'I know, I know.' She flung her head from side to side. 'And I don't care. Do you hear? I don't care.' She was shouting now. 'I care about nothing only being with you. I thought yesterday I would do anything, try to get my face altered – they can remake noses, look at Cilla Black. I'd scorned such ideas before, but I'll do it now.'

'Tishy! be quiet! Please, please, be quiet.' He had swung away from her and as he walked towards the window she bent her body over the couch. She was gabbling as if talking to herself. 'I've been quiet for too long, for too many years; I've hidden all I've felt; I've built up a cast-iron case around my feelings. Plain people like me are not supposed to have any feelings; feelings are just the attributes of good-looking girls. Any good-looking girl attracts a man's sympathy, but not people like me, no, not people like me. I've been quiet too long. I may never talk like this again; in fact, I know I won't. I'll never beg like this again in my life, but I'm doing it now.' She straightened up and turned to him, the tears spurting from her eyes now. 'I need you, Alan, and no one's ever needed you before, not even Mam. She didn't need you as I do. She'd had a husband and four children; in a way she'd had a full life; I've had nothing to call my own. You know the future I saw for myself? I saw myself here, ending my days in this cottage; that was, after I had spent years teaching other people's children, and for recreation joining literary groups, or poetry circles, or pottery classes or some such bloody nonsense.' She now tossed her head wildly. 'A life in doing voluntary service, a life of good works; and the reward? a dog, a cat and a budgerigar, and, of course –' her head was bouncing up and down now – 'there's always the television.'

She didn't know that he had moved from the window and was by her side. When he spoke her name she started and blinked up at him through her streaming eyes.

Her tears weren't enhancing her, but it was the very look of her that dragged pity from him. Yet pity wasn't enough. He told himself that he could no more take her than he could commit incest. He liked her; strangely, he liked her a lot. He remembered he'd enjoyed those trips to Newcastle with her. She had sparkled then. But as for marrying her; it had never crossed his mind even then. And now Annie lay like an insurmountable obstacle between him and his pity.

He knew that women who looked like Tishy, and of such intelligence, often made a great success of marriage, and also that, as she had said, he needed someone, he needed someone to care for him, more so than he should have to care for them. The balance of love was never equal; there was always one partner who loved, and the other who was willing to be loved, and this, too, seemed to work well. He could do a lot worse than take her at her word, and she needed him. As she had said, no one would ever need him as she needed him. . . . But . . . but let him remember. A few short weeks ago he had spent three blissful days and nights with her mother in this very cottage. The whole thing would be indecent, definitely indecent. It wasn't the fact of what people would say, because unless she had told the family no one except herself knew about his association with her mother, but he knew . . . he knew.

She was drying her eyes now while still looking at him, and after a long moment during which they were both silent she said in a small whisper, 'No?' and he answered, 'I'm ... I'm sorry, Tishy. If it was at all possible I ... I would, but –' he shook his head.

She drew in a long shuddering breath; then turning from him, she went down the room and mounted the stairs; and he took his chin in his fist and gripped it until the pain from his nails digging into his flesh became unbearable.

She remained upstairs a full hour, and he sat staring into the fire and feeling as he had never done, not even in the depths of his matrimonial trouble, for his emotions now were a mixture of shame and regret, and the regret made him apologetic to the memory of Annie, for he knew that if it wasn't for Annie he would, in his present state, have clutched at the straw being offered him. Yet Tishy was no straw, more like a sturdy life raft that one could cling to in order to sustain life.

The feeling of guilt was emphasized further when he asked himself if his association with Annie would prevent him from ever taking another woman. Time was the great healer, it was said. A more appropriate version would be, a blotter-out of events both good and bad. But the question of whether he would ever take another woman wasn't relevant to this situation, for Tishy was just not another woman, she was Annie's daughter. ... Yes, Annie's daughter, who during the last hour had proved herself to be Annie's daughter, for she had stood there pouring out her feelings for him. It was as if Annie had come back.

Yesterday he had wondered why there was no evidence of Annie in Tishy. Now he realized he had been blind, for beneath that hard, cynical veneer Annie was very much alive, honest, vulnerable, loving. But it was the fact of her being part of Annie that was the obstacle. And there was no way round it that he could see. The quicker he got away the better.

When she came downstairs she did not turn left and go into the kitchen as he expected her to do, but she came towards him. She had changed her clothes and was wearing brown slacks and a green sweater. She had washed her face and her hair had been freshly combed and looked damp. She appeared very young.

She said to him, 'I'm ... I'm sorry for embarrassing you'; and when he waved his hand before his face she said, 'Let me speak just this once more. I did embarrass you, I know I did, but what I said had to be said. If I'd let you go without telling you I would have imagined for the rest of my life that things would have been different if only I had spoken out. Well, I ... I don't want you to feel bad about this, I don't want you to go away now and worry and think that I'll do something silly, like ... like committing suicide, or anything like that. I can't stand moral blackmailers, so I'll ask you just ... just to forget the last hour or so if you can.' The muscles of her throat worked, and then she ended, 'I'll ... I'll get you some tea before you go.'

He couldn't speak, not a word. All he could do was to gnaw on his lip and move his head in a despairing fashion. Then he turned and leant his arms on the stone mantelshelf. Don't worry, she had said; I won't commit suicide; I can't stand moral blackmailers. At least once a week for a year Jane had threatened him with just that. 'If you dare mention divorce again I'll commit suicide. If you dare go to your grandmother I'll commit suicide. If you dare go to the solicitor I'll commit suicide. If you leave me, Alan, I swear to you

I'll commit suicide,' until at last he had said, 'Right! do it. Do just that.' But Tishy had said, 'Don't go away and worry that I'll do anything silly, like committing suicide. I'll live with you on the side,' she had said. 'You can live your own life, as long as you let me stay with you; she had said. 'I just want to be with you,' she had said, 'just to be with you. I love you, Alan,' she had said. That was odd, wasn't it? That was odd. She was the only one who had ever said, 'I love you, Alan.' Jane had never said it. 'You're sweet,' she had said; 'You're a dear,' she had said, but never, 'I love you, Alan.' And when he came to think of it, Annie had never actually said, 'I love you, Alan.' She had said beautiful things, beautiful because they were ordinary and simple and meaningful, but she had never said, 'I love you, Alan.'

When he heard her coming into the room he turned about, then went towards her to take the heavy tray from her, but she made a movement with her shoulder and continued to carry it down the room and set it on the table.

After she had poured the tea she handed him a plate of buttered scones, and he shook his head and muttered, 'No'; and the scones remained untouched while they both sat in silence drinking the tea.

When she went to refill his cup he rose abruptly from the chair, saying, 'I'll ... I'll get my pack together,' and she looked up at him and said, 'It's all right; I've brought it into the kitchen. I dried off the things the other day. It's all ready.'

'Tishy.' He screwed up his face as if in agony, then went down the room, his head bent.

He brought his pack from the kitchen and went outside and put it on the verandah; then buttoning his coat he stood in the open doorway looking across the fells. He must have been standing like this for five minutes when he heard the car hooter; three times it hooted before he turned round and looked at her. She had risen from the couch and was standing at the corner of it. Her hands were behind her hiding their trembling. He came quickly towards her.

'Good-bye, Tishy.'

'Good-bye.'

'Thank you. Thank you for all you've done for me, for your care and everything.'

'That's ... that's all right.'

'Good-bye.'

'Good-bye, Alan, don't worry.'

Concern again. Her concern was that he shouldn't worry.

'Oh! Tishy, Tishy, I–' his whole body writhed as if in pain – 'I ... I can't leave you like this, I can't.'

'It's all right, it's all right. Go on, Alan, go on. Please. Look.' Her face was quivering. 'I'm telling you, I'm all right, just go ... now. Do this for me, go *now*.'

'No, Tishy.' The words came quiet and flat; and then he said again, 'No, Tishy; I'm not going now. And ... and I'm not going by myself. I can't; I've ... I've got a feeling Annie wouldn't want me to. But ... but I must tell you, Tishy, there's, there's nothing left in me; I've ... I've got nothing to offer. You deserve something better, I'm, I'm like an empty husk.'

'Look, don't. Don't. I'm sorry I put you on a spot. I am. Look, just ...'

Her hand had gone to her mouth and the tears were spurting once more from her eyes, and when her body swayed he put his arms about her, saying, 'There now. There now. It'll be all right.'

Moments passed, then slowly she raised her head and looking up into his face, she said, 'Yes, yes, it'll be all right. I'll . . . I'll make it all right. Oh, Alan, I promise you I'll make it all right. You'll see, you'll see.'

The hooting of the car horn came stridently at them, and they turned and looked at the open door and he said, 'I . . . I must go down and tell him.'

'No, no, let me, I can run . . . I can run.' She began to dash about, first to the door then back again, saying, 'Money! my purse.'

'Here!' He put his hand in his pocket. 'Give him that.' He pushed a couple of notes at her, and she smiled at him while rubbing her hand over her wet face.

He stood at the door and watched her running like a young gazelle over the field, through the gap in the wall down to the copse, and when she was gone from his sight he closed his eyes tightly as if shutting from his gaze some gigantic obstacle with which he knew he must grapple if he ever hoped to find himself and live.

## TITLES IN THIS SERIES:

**Eric Ambler**
The Mask of Dimitrios
Passage of Arms
The Schirmer Inheritance
Journey into Fear
The Light of Day
Judgment on Deltchev

**John le Carré**
The Spy Who Came in from the Cold
Call for the Dead
A Murder of Quality
The Looking-Glass War
A Small Town in Germany

**Raymond Chandler***
Farewell My Lovely
The Lady in the Lake
Playback
The Long Goodbye
The High Window
The Big Sleep

**Joseph Conrad**
Lord Jim
The Nigger of the 'Narcissus'
Typhoon
Nostromo
The Secret Agent

**Catherine Cookson**
The Round Tower
The Fifteen Streets
Feathers in the Fire
A Grand Man
The Blind Miller

**Catherine Cookson**
The Mallen Streak
The Girl
The Gambling Man
The Cinder Path
The Invisible Cord

**Monica Dickens**
One Pair of Hands
The Happy Prisoner
Mariana
Kate and Emma
One Pair of Feet

**F. Scott Fitzgerald***
The Great Gatsby
Tender is the Night
This Side of Paradise
The Beautiful and Damned
The Last Tycoon

**Ian Fleming**
Dr. No
Thunderball
Goldfinger
On Her Majesty's Secret Service
Moonraker
From Russia, With Love

**C. S. Forester**
The Ship
Mr. Midshipman Hornblower
The Captain from Connecticut
The General
The Earthly Paradise
The African Queen

**E. M. Forster**
Where Angels Fear to Tread
The Longest Journey
A Room with a View
Howards End
A Passage to India

**Fourteen Great Plays***

**John Galsworthy**
The Forsyte Saga:
The Man of Property
In Chancery  To Let
A Modern Comedy:
The White Monkey
The Silver Spoon  Swan Song

**Erle Stanley Gardner**
Perry Mason in the Case of the Gilded Lily
The Daring Decoy
The Fiery Fingers
The Lucky Loser
The Calendar Girl
The Deadly Toy
The Mischievous Doll
The Amorous Aunt

## Richard Gordon
Doctor in the House
Doctor at Sea
Doctor at Large
Doctor in Love
Doctor in Clover
The Facemaker
The Medical Witness

## Graham Greene
The Heart of the Matter
Stamboul Train
A Burnt-out Case
The Third Man
Loser Takes All
The Quiet American
The Power and the Glory

## Ernest Hemingway*
For Whom the Bell Tolls
Fiesta
The Snows of Kilimanjaro
The Short Happy Life of Francis
Macomber
Across the River and into the Trees
The Old Man and the Sea

## Georgette Heyer
These Old Shades
Sprig Muslin
Sylvester
The Corinthian
The Convenient Marriage

## Franz Kafka*
The Trial
America
In the Penal Settlement
Metamorphosis
The Castle
The Great Wall of China
Investigations of a Dog
Letter to His Father
The Diaries 1910-1923

## Rudyard Kipling
The Just So Stories
Stalky and Co.
Puck of Pook's Hill
The Jungle Book
The Second Jungle Book
Kim

## D. H. Lawrence
Sons and Lovers
St. Mawr
The Fox
The White Peacock
Love among the Haystacks
The Virgin and the Gipsy
Lady Chatterley's Lover

## Norah Lofts
Jassy
Bless This House
Scent of Cloves
How Far to Bethlehem?

## Robert Ludlum*
The Scarlatti Inheritance
The Matlock Paper
The Osterman Weekend
The Gemini Contenders

## Thomas Mann*
Death in Venice
Tristan
Tonio Kröger
Doctor Faustus
Mario and the Magician
A Man and His Dog
The Black Swan
Confessions of Felix Krull,
Confidence Man

## W. Somerset Maugham
Cakes and Ale
The Painted Veil
Liza of Lambeth
The Razor's Edge
Theatre
The Moon and Sixpence

## W. Somerset Maugham
Sixty-five Short Stories

## Ed McBain*
Cop Hater
Give the Boys a Great Big Hand
Doll
Eighty Million Eyes
Hail, Hail, the Gang's All Here!
Sadie When She Died
Let's Hear it for the Deaf Man

**James A. Michener***
The Source
The Bridges at Toko-Ri
Caravans
Sayonara

**George Orwell**
Animal Farm
Burmese Days
A Clergyman's Daughter
Coming up for Air
Keep the Aspidistra Flying
Nineteen Eighty-Four

**Jean Plaidy**
St. Thomas's Eve
Royal Road to Fotheringay
The Goldsmith's Wife
Perdita's Prince

**Nevil Shute**
A Town Like Alice
Pied Piper
The Far Country
The Chequer Board
No Highway

**George Simenon**
Ten Maigret Stories

**Wilbur Smith**
When the Lion Feeds
The Diamond Hunters
Eagle in the Sky
Gold Mine
Shout at the Devil

**John Steinbeck***
The Grapes of Wrath
The Moon is Down
Cannery Row
East of Eden
Of Mice and Men

**Mary Stewart**
The Crystal Cave
The Hollow Hills
Wildfire at Midnight
Airs Above the Ground

**Evelyn Waugh**
Decline and Fall
Black Mischief
A Handful of Dust
Scoop
Put Out More Flags
Brideshead Revisited

**H. G. Wells**
The Time Machine
The Island of Dr. Moreau
The Invisible Man
The First Men in the Moon
The Food of the Gods
In the Days of the Comet
The War of the Worlds

**Morris West**
The Shoes of the Fisherman
The Second Victory
Daughter of Silence
The Salamander
The Devil's Advocate

**Dennis Wheatley**
The Devil Rides Out
The Haunting of Toby Jugg
Gateway to Hell
To the Devil – A Daughter

**\* Not currently available in
Canada for copyright reasons**